ONE STEP IN THE CLOUDS

Recall the Epicoun:
Night, welling up so soon,
Mere sank us in soft snow
At the stiff frozen dawn,
When Time had ceased to flow
– the glacier ledge our unmade bed –
I hear you through your yawn:
'Leaping crevasses in the dark,
That's how to live!' you said.
No room in that to hedge:
A razor's edge of a remark.

I. A. Richards (from 'Hope')

ONE STEP IN THE CLOUDS

An omnibus of mountaineering novels and short stories

Compiled by
Audrey Salkeld and Rosie Smith

Diadem Books · London

Sierra Club Books · San Francisco

UK COPYRIGHT INFORMATION

British Library and Cataloguing Data:

One step in the clouds: an omnibus of mountaineering novels and short stories
1. English literature. Special subjects. Mountaineering. Anthologies.
I. Salkeld, Audrey II. Smith, Rosie
820.8035

ISBN 0-906371-92-9

Published in Great Britain in 1990 by Diadem Books, London

All trade enquiries in U.K., Europe and the Commonwealth to Hodder and Stoughton Ltd., Mill Road, Dunton Green, Sevenoaks, Kent TN13 2YA

Photoset by J & L Composition, Filey and Vitaset, Paddock Wood.

Printed and bound in Great Britain by Mackays of Chatham

US COPYRIGHT INFORMATION

The Sierra Club, founded in 1892 by John Muir, has devoted itself to the study and protection of the earth's scenic and ecological resources – mountains, wetlands, woodlands, wild shores and rivers, deserts and plains. The publishing program of the Sierra Club offers books to the public as a nonprofit educational service in the hope that they may enlarge the public's understanding of the Club's basic concerns. The point of view expressed in each book, however, does not necessarily represent that of the Club. The Sierra Club has some sixty chapters coast to coast, in Canada, Hawaii, and Alaska. For information about how you may participate in its programs to preserve wilderness and quality of life, please address inquiries to Sierra Club, 730 Polk Street, San Francisco, CA 94109

First published in Great Britain in 1990 by Diadem Books, London. Published in the United States in 1991 by Sierra Club Books, San Francisco.

Library of Congress Cataloguing in Publication Data:

One step in the clouds: an omnibus of mountaineering novels and short stories / compiled by Audrey Salkeld and Rosie Smith
p. cm.
Includes bibliographical references.
ISBN 0-87156-638-9
1. Mountaineering—Literary collections.
I. Salkeld, Audrey.
II. Smith, Rosie, 1954-
PN6071.M738054 1991
808.83'9355—dc20 90-41260
CIP

Printed and bound in Great Britain.
10 9 8 7 6 5 4 3 2 1

ACKNOWLEDGEMENTS The compilers and publishers wish to thank the many people who have assisted with contributions and help to this book: to Trevor Jones for agreeing to the use of the name of his well-known Tremadog climb for the title, to Edward Salkeld for his text illustrations and cover collage (based on an image from Arnold Fanck's 1929 film *The White Hell of Piz Palü*), and to the late Mrs I.A. Richards for permission to quote from her husband's poem, *Hope*, to introduce the book.

All the contributors are thanked for allowing their work to be used and for their unstinting support for the book's ambitious concept. Most of the contributions had previously appeared in other publications as noted in the Bibliography. In addition we are indebted to various literary agents, publishers and executors: Michael Shaw (Curtis Brown and John Farquharson) for permission to use *One Green Bottle* and *North Wall*, and Vivienne Schuster (of the same agency) for support with *Meltwater*; to Pat Kavanagh (Peters, Fraser and Dunlop), Peter Matson (Sterling Lord Literistic) and North Point Press (Berkeley) for clearing the way for the use of *Solo Faces*; to Michael Kennedy (*Climbing*) for permission to use *Children Like Climbers Often Fall* (the author being untraceable), Rev. Z. Edwards for *Scenery For a Murder*, and Rose Elton for *In Hanging Garden Gully*.

The compilation of the book, and particularly the Bibliography, proved an exhausting and time-consuming exercise which relied on the help of many people. We wish to make a special acknowledgement to Jill Neate for help and scholarship. Much information has been provided by the Librarians or Contracts Depts of many British and American publishers. We also wish to thank the following organisations and individuals: Ernst Sondheimer and Geoffrey Templeman (*The Alpine Journal*), Jack Baines (Anglesey Books), Allen Steck (*Ascent*), Andrew Evans (Book Trust Information Service), Alison Bailey and Mrs Jackson Hill (British Library), George Watkins and Ken Harrison (Fell and Rock Library), Pat Lewis and Bernard Newman (*Mountain*), Katherine Trippet (Octopus Books), Miranda Taylor (*Punch*), Al Alvarez, George Bott, Robin Campbell, Janet Carleton, Lord Chorley, Kevin Fitzgerald, Terry Gifford, Livia Gollancz, the late Sir Tom Hopkinson, Jennifer Luithlin, George MacBeth, Geoff Milburn, Josephine Pullein-Thompson, Showell Styles and Janis Tetlow. Finally the compilers wish to pay tribute to their long-suffering partners, Peter Salkeld and Martin Allen, for their crucial support in bringing this project to completion.

Contents

Short Stories

Novellas, Novels and a Play

Appendix

INTRODUCTION

by Audrey Salkeld and Rosie Smith

The best literature of mountaineering is no more written for mountaineers than was Hemingway's *The Old Man and the Sea* written for fishermen. *William Dowie*

But isn't *all* mountain writing fiction? *Jim Curran*

There is wide subscription to the idea that most climbing fiction has failed. 'You'd have thought that by now writers would have given up trying to turn the climbing experience into a novel,' pronounced *Climber and Hillwalker* magazine recently.* Time and again, when putting this book together, we have bumped against the same well-worn attitude. 'Such a dearth of good mountain fiction!' Almost automatically people say it. Elizabeth Coxhead's *One Green Bottle* (1951) is occasionally cited as the single possible exception, or A. E. W. Mason's *Running Water* (1907) – and all the rest might as well never have been.

It simply is not true! Certainly, until recently, you could assert with confidence that novels and stories which were *strictly* climbing-based were few and far between; and many among those that did exist were bad. Dire, even. But not all. At almost any time over the last hundred years there have been climbing stories to measure highly against whatever literary yardstick you cared to employ. And many of the most celebrated and popular authors of their day introduced mountaineering into at least one of their works: John Buchan, H. G. Wells, Stella Gibbons, Vladimir Nabokov, Mary Renault, Mary Stewart, Alistair Maclean, Arthur Ransome – just a few names pulled at random. Even Salman Rushdie's *Satanic Verses* has as one of its central characters a young woman, Alleluia Cone, who climbs Everest without oxygen and ever afterwards keeps bumping into the tam-o'-shantered shade of Maurice Wilson – until that is, in a final ironic twist, she falls to her death from the Everest Vilas (*sic*) in Bombay.

To the novelist, mountaineering offers no shortage of plots. Tension, drama, triumph, tragedy, romance and intrigue can be permuted in endless variation and set into extravagant landscape. This is something *non*-mountaineering authors have always recognized. Any number of thrillers have been based on the North Wall of the Eiger; manhunts conducted over icy passes; secret missions dispatched to remote Himalayan frontiers. But all too often, entertaining though these may be, such stories ring false to the mountaineer-reader. Some element of first-hand authenticity seems lacking, or the action slips too easily into melodrama. At the other end of the scale, there have been mountaineers eager to try their hand at fiction, but who have lacked the necessary storytelling and characterization skills to quite pull it off. The successful mountaineering story has to be a successful story first, and on

* *Climber and Hillwalker*, November, 1989, page 10.

top of that be totally convincing to mountaineers. If not written by a person who is him- or herself a climber, it has to be by someone in full tune and sympathy with mountaineers, someone who enjoys their uninhibited confidence and who is prepared to undergo total immersion in the subject. Even then, it remains a tricky business and will always run the risk, however well done, of being ultimately rejected by mountaineers simply *because* it has been written by an outsider.

'The trouble with good non-climber writers who turn to climbing is that they see our sport as *too* dramatic,' says David Roberts. 'Just as Hemingway romanticized bullfighting.' Claire Eliane Engel, observing the scene in 1950, remarked that 'novelists seem to be stricken with palsy in mountain air.' *True* stories of great climbs or mountain tragedies, she maintained, were so perfect in all their details that it was difficult to imagine more effective or better-planned episodes. She had unconsciously put her finger on the major source of resistance: climbing is considered by its adherents to be somehow too *sacred* to fictionalize. Its vivid real-life dramas and intense loyalties, its acts of heroism and the all-too-frequent encounters with violent death are too precious, too poignant, too much part of some private lore and myth to become the raw material of fiction. Pillaging such treasure is seen at best as exploitation or trivialization, at worst as desecrating shrines. This ignores, of course, the role of fiction as a tool for sorting and making sense of experience and emotion, of enlightenment – or indeed of entertainment – but then, entrenched positions are not necessarily governed by fact or reason!

Hugh Merrick, after trying his hand at five alpine novels, had every sympathy for writers who failed in this field: he was, he knew, perfectly competent to produce a well-written story in which the situations and details were authentic and free from the howlers of the non-mountaineering novelist, yet the great mountaineering novel of his aspirations eluded him. 'I no longer believe in its possibility,' was his sad conclusion in 1974. George Pokorny, reviewing mountain fiction for *Climbing* magazine a few years later, although unwilling to deny it altogether – as an ideal – felt forced to agree that the really superb mountaineering novel had yet to be written.

In the last ten to fifteen years, however, there has been a tremendous surge in fictional mountain-writing – as we hope this book bears witness. American authors, in particular, have breathed vigorous new life into the climbing short story. This is no quirk of fate or geography: it can be directly attributed to the fact that the prime stimulus to new writing is having an outlet, and American climbing magazines have a far better record than British ones for publishing and reviewing works of fiction. *Climbing, Rock and Ice* and the late-lamented *Mountain Gazette* have all regularly printed short stories, nor should we forget the role played by the Californian journal *Ascent*, which perhaps more than any other has introduced fiction writers to a receptive audience. (No less than six stories were included in the 1989 edition.) Indeed, in the United States the climbing short story has not been limited to the climbing press. Peter Lars Sandberg published many of his pieces first in *Playboy*; Kim Stanley Robinson appears regularly in sci-fi collections; and *The New Yorker* has from time to time printed work by Al Alvarez, Stanislaw Lem and others.

In our innocence, when we first began putting a collection together, we had worried that the most likely climax to any climbing story would be a fall, and that by stringing stories end to end in a single volume all we would be doing would be calling emphasis to this. It hasn't turned out that way at all. We have been astounded at the diversity and ingenuity of most of the stories. And they bridge every recognizable *genre*. Detective thrillers, ghost stories, espionage, romance, farce, psychological drama – practically every style of writing and type of story that exists can perfectly well have the mountains or mountaineering as a major element. Naturally some themes and preoccupations do recur, and for ease of study we will discuss stories under loose groupings, but it should be noted that many do not sit comfortably in these categories and some completely defy categorization.

Aspiring Women

At the turn of the century *The Alpine Journal* reviewed a work which had just been published in Berlin – *Die Alpinisten* by Franz Wiehmann – maintaining that it deserved special mention for being the 'first novel yet published in which the characters are primarily climbers.' Interpretations vary: several books and climbing short stories had been written before this date (as can be seen from the appended Bibliography), but let that stand. The story will offer as convenient a point as any from which to range, forwards and back, across the fictional scene – especially as it demonstrates a popular preoccupation of its period, that of the 'Suffragette' mountaineer. (The term is applied broadly here to describe a strong-willed woman out to prove herself the equal of any man.) There were already a number of women climbers by the time this story was written, but the attitude of the men towards them remained very much that of the choleric who blustered to *The Times* in 1881 that 'ladies and incapables' should be kept off the mountains.

Wiehmann's book has proved elusive and no doubt its German text would confound us, so we are obliged to *The Alpine Journal* reviewer for a summary of the plot: the hero, a poet, considers that no married woman ought to climb since 'she belongs to her husband and not to neck-breaking mountain peaks.' Said hero is, however, obliged to relax this view when, climbing alone one day, he finds himself sharing a stone-swept couloir with a young woman every bit as competent and independently-minded as himself:

> On the top the lady's stocking – for she does not wear puttees – bursts at the ankle, and the poet, seeing her fair skin, must needs kneel and kiss it energetically, despite her question, 'You know, of course, that I am a married woman?'

They make violent love on the icy summit, heedless of an impending thunderstorm, and afterwards compromise the woman's virtue by passing the night alone together in an alpine hut.

The shocking phenomenon of women in mountains was picked up also in English stories: three in particular appeared around this time in the popular magazine, *The Strand*, all fairly frivolous in tone. Frank Savile's *The Suffragette* (1908) describes a headstrong hoyden who, in her bid to establish superiority, attempts an ascent of the notorious 'Eastdale Pinnacle'. She has, of course, to be rescued by the mere man of the tale – to whom she then submits romantically, and lives happily ever under. Miss Cayley, the heroine of Grant Allen's *The Adventure of the Impromptu Mountaineer* (1898) is made of altogether sterner stuff (she has, after all, stroked the Girton boat). This time it is the young man who gets into trouble and has to be rescued: our game heroine descends to him on a rope into which she has had the foresight to tie forty-seven looped footholds! His prompt offer of marriage is turned down (not without heartache, it must be said, and really because, as the named heroine of a series, she is needed for further episodes). *The Conversion of Mr Bertie Vallance* by A. Coralie Stanton (1901) is a similar tale. Again, a very capable female (Olga Braun, far-famed for an ascent of Kunchinjinga which has won her the membership of *every* known Alpine Club!) is called upon to rescue a not-so-capable young man, the Bertie Vallance of the title, a bumptious little prig but one who sees sense in the end!

It is interesting that the threat, to men, of women climbing is still perceived as an issue today: in one form or another it has remained a subject regularly explored by novelists and short-story writers. In 1972 the American writer, Peter Lars Sandberg, produced a tongue-in-cheek piece, *The Old Bull Moose of the Woods* (one of those he sold to *Playboy*) which was immediately condemned as 'outrageously sexist' by a group of Chicago women's libbers. Dermot Somers, in his *Climber and Walker,* looked at the problem, from a woman's point of view, of being a better climber than her (male) partner – his heroine burns off her companion on the Walker Spur, but who will suspect or grant her credit for such prowess unless she brags?

When Elizabeth Coxhead's *One Green Bottle* appeared in 1951, it was immediately hailed as something special. Jack Longland found it 'by far the best novel about climbing' that he had read, and one that succeeded as triumphantly with readers who did not climb as with those who did. Wilfrid Noyce suggested it may have 'started a new direction in mountain writing' – which indeed it did, at the same time reflecting the new direction which climbing itself was adopting as the sport became increasingly accessible to people from all walks of life. The then-Bishop of Chester condemned it for its explicitness. It is the story of Cathy Canning, who came to the Welsh mountains from the impoverished back streets of Birkenhead, and how her character flourished with the discovery of rock-climbing and wider horizons. 'I believe that many other readers will, like myself, be more than half in love with her before they finish,' declared Longland stoutly:

> They will, in seeing her squalor-bred sullenness dissipated, fancy with Michael Derwent, watching her absorbed in the intricacy of a hard climbing pitch, 'that the face she turned to the rock must be tender and charming': and they will feel with almost unbearable poignancy the lonely courage with which Cathy at the end of the book turns her back on the mountains.

The book is still widely held as a classic, although the fate meted out to its heroine by the author has always proved difficult to swallow. After finding real love with a young school-teacher, Cathy turns her back on her new life and tramps back to Birkenhead to 'rescue' the worthless young criminal who lives in the same house as her family. It is not that she likes him particularly, nor is bound to him by any promise, but – we are made to understand – her new-found moral strength has shown her where her 'duty' lies. Whether you find this unbearably poignant, as Longland; 'unsatisfactory artistically' and 'cruelly unnecessary', as Noyce; or downright outrageous, as it seems by modern standards, it is a major stumbling block. (So unsettling, indeed, that Jim Perrin felt compelled to rewrite the book's ending in an imaginary interview conducted with Cathy Powell recently.)*

Against this, the book is well written and remains compulsively readable, even if the unrelentingly dour picture painted of Cathy's working class roots seems stylized and shallow now. No colour or warmth or nobler aspects shine through that would make one accept her going back to it. *One Green Bottle* is a story of class and gender, a simplistic rendering of the social system in England immediately after the war – as perceived, it has to be said, by someone firmly rooted in the privileged middle classes – but (and this should not be forgotten) it predates all the social realism made fashionable by Sillitoe, Osborne and other Angry Young Men. Class divisions were clear: people in those days knew their place – and could recognise the place of everyone else from his or her accent. Coxhead gives her women sexuality and minds of their own – it was the fact that they took precautions against getting pregnant that so shocked the good Bishop – she speaks eloquently against injustice, yet in the end she baulks at bursting the fetters of her time. She is unable to right the wrongs, to allow free traffic between the classes – and cannot escape the conviction that 'illicit' sex has to be 'paid for'. Cathy and her friend Dorothy (the youth hostel warden) are doomed to lives of self-sacrifice, Dorothy's no more acceptable than Cathy's. Women are strong, rang the message, but their strength is for the nurture of men weaker and more feckless than themselves.

The loneliness of the hard climber

It might have been expected, given the open-armed welcome from establishment climbers to *One Green Bottle,* that Lucy Rees' *Take it to the Limit* would have been similarly embraced. If – in 1951 – Cathy Canning could sleep with a salesman in exchange for a pair of climbing boots, and with the man she loves out of wedlock, and cause little affront (except to the bishop), you would have thought that thirty permissive years later no eyebrows would be raised at further tales of North Wales goings-on. You'd have been wrong. *The Alpine Journal* threw its arms in the air. 'Oh dear!' it wailed. 'Another exposé of what things are like at the high sharp end of the climbing scene. . . . The main body of mountaineers is much different from this, easier to accept and more pleasant by far to know. Do they care very much what motivates the lunatic fringe?'

Lucy Rees, boosted by recollections and fantasies of the legendary and now sadly late Al Harris, had recreated the extrovert anarchism of Deiniolen in

* *On the Rock with Cathy Powell,* Climber and Hillwalker, December, 1988.

the late-sixties. But it would be a shame if, believing it to be merely the cavortings of the lunatic fringe, readers were put off from discovering here a well written, moving and essentially moral story. It looks back less with nostalgia or any glorifying of hedonism than with bitterness for lost innocence and thwarted promise. The central figure, Luke, young, restless, is the apex of a tragic love-triangle: he and his older, more stable climbing partner, Bob, are both loved by the same woman, Kate. The action moves swiftly between Wales, Scotland, and the Lakes to reach its climax on a big-wall climb in Yosemite. Scenes are set with vivid economy. Conversations live. There are wistful echoes of Salinger, and the outcome is achingly sad. It is a book of a period, but timeless. And long overdue for reappraisal.

Solo Faces by James Salter (1980) also explores the problems and the ultimate loneliness of the hard climber. It has been criticized for its minimalist style, and for unashamed machismo as well as an intensity-for-its-own-sake. Some climbers were dismissive, too, because they did not see the author as a 'true believer': he climbed for a while with Royal Robbins, largely it seems as research for this novel, then went his way. Those who hoped for a second story were disappointed, although Salter did script the interesting and successful film about an Olympic ski star, *Downhill Racer,* which starred Robert Redford and similarly examined the isolating effects of ambition and élitism.

Polished to a fine lustre, *Solo Faces* is plainly the work of a talented writer and, minimalist or not, packs in a deceptive amount of detail. It has a compelling story line even if it can promise no happy ending. Salter was fascinated by the briefly incandescent career of the American climber Gary Hemming, who took the Alpine world by storm in the middle sixties with his bold climbs and even bolder rescues. Darling of the French press, *Le Beatnik* grabbed the headlines for one last time in 1969 when he plugged a bullet into his skull. Salter's driven central character, Vernon Rand, is clearly a Hemming figure (but without the gun). The story examines the seesaw swoops between elation and despair, between fulfilling climbs and the brutal knocks climbing can deliver, until finally, a slow losing of grip has to be faced as age and alienation take their toll.

As a novel the book did respectably well, satisfying such demanding critics as Al Alvarez, Norman Mailer, Graham Greene – but many climbing reviewers lost sight of the whole by getting hooked up over whether Salter had or had not explained climbing jargon fully – a perennial problem when making climbing stories accessible to a wide public. And that terse style, that they found uncomfortable, too – such a long way from dear Winthrop Young!

Age and the loss of climbing powers

Ageing is a recurring preoccupation among both novelists and short story writers. Old man, young man, climbing together – we see it in Al Alvarez's *Night Out*, which concerns an epic in the Dolomites and drew its inspiration from a climb on Cima Grande which Alvarez made with Mo Anthoine. The theme reappears in Pat Ament's *Moment of Personal Peril,* Les Ellison's *Doubt*, and David Roberts's *Backing off,* where the older man feels obliged to rein in his young companion's impetuosity – and in so doing realizes that their partnership can never again be one of equals.

John Long's *For Everything its Season* is a little more complicated: here again we have the experienced climber and the younger climber, but a mystery as well – for the young man's brother has earlier been killed climbing with this same man, and in circumstances which have never been fully explained. Long is one of the most invigorating of today's story tellers. A larger than life 'adventurer' himself – he has been described as the guy in the Camel advertisement stepped off the page – his tales are gutsy and the prose often as crazed and breakneck as some of his own escapades. His job these days is writing film scripts; climbing stories are a diversion.

All these last-mentioned are short stories, as is *The White Graph* by Irish writer, Dermot Somers. This centres on a climber recovering from the combined effects of the failure of his marriage, financial difficulties and emotional breakdown – a full-blown mid-life crisis. However, he is now climbing again, in the Alps, and drawing wisdom and the strength for survival from the experience. But he can only do this at the expense of other peoples' egos. His young, male partners, therefore, have to be sort of one-climb stands, casual pick-ups in climbing areas.

La Fourche by Anne Sauvy is a chilling Faustian fantasy (one of several we came across), in which her ageing hero buys back youth from the Devil along with climbing skill, the like of which has never been seen before. New routes, popularity, fast cars, good looks, gorgeous women . . . he commands them all . . . and the first winter solo ascent of Everest (without oxygen) to boot. He leads a charmed life but one day the only girl he has ever loved dies when they are climbing the Grandes Jorasses together. For the first time Faustin realizes the worth of a soul . . . and time is running out . . .

Gwen Moffat, who is perhaps best known for her meaty detective stories, was another to choose the ageing theme when she first ventured into 'straight' fiction. The central figure of her novel *Hard Option* is the leader of a mountain rescue team. He finds it increasingly hard to keep up with younger colleagues, but there is no way that he is prepared to relinquish to them any of the responsibility or glory that goes with his position. In the end, it is an adulterous liaison with a cool-headed, young woman climber that brings about his downfall. And what a downfall! With a relish bordering on vindictiveness (one is reminded of Charlotte Bronte's emasculation of Mr. Rochester), Gwen Moffatt sees to it that the poor man is brought very low indeed: he is made to confront all his inadequacies, as a climber and as a lover, and then, when his mental disintegration is almost complete – when he's lost his wife, his best friend, this girl that he loves and every last vestige of human pride – Moffat really puts the boot in: she strikes him down with a paralyzing stroke (yet still manages to make the last line of the book sound hopeful)!

Humour

Many aspects of mountaineering appear absurd to outsiders, as indeed they do even to mountaineers; it is of little wonder then to find that from the very first humour has occupied a healthy place in mountain fiction. Alphonse

Daudet, in his second Tartarin novel, had his inflated hero upholding the honour of Tarascon on the mighty summits of Switzerland: *Tartarin on the Alps* (1885) is an exquisitely written, gently satirical tale that has worn its first century well.

At a time when worthy Victorians were broadening their minds with travel – and overloading library shelves with equally worthy (but tediously wordy) accounts of their adventures – irreverent pieces like Tartarin, or like Jerome K. Jerome's contemporaneous 'Three Men' books, or Mark Twain's *A Tramp Abroad* (1879, which also lampooned the increasingly popular pursuit of alpine-climbing) offered welcome light relief. Later, H. G. Wells's wry *Little Mother up the Mörderberg* (1910) followed the same tradition, as did the evergreen *In Hanging Garden Gully* by C. E. Montague five years after the Great War.

In 1956, W. E. Bowman's *The Ascent of Rum Doodle* took as its target Himalayan expedition climbing of the gritted teeth variety. Its doughty hero, Binder, has been described as Mr. Pooter (*Diary of a Nobody*) with an ice axe, and the book is generally seen as a skit on all that 'New-Elizabethan' ballyhoo drummed up after the first successful climb of Everest. Bowman himself always maintained it was a passage in Tilman's *The Ascent of Nanda Devi* that set him off. (Heresy, after all, is an integral ingredient of satire!) *Rum Doodle* has long been something of a comic cult, though it must be said that readers have always divided sharply between those who fall about, helpless with mirth, and those who can muster only a grudging smile.

The story follows the fortunes of an attempt on the 40,000½ ft. peak of Rum Doodle in Yogistan under Binder's leadership. His ill-sorted companions (Tom Burley, Christopher Wish, Humphrey Jungle, Ridley Prone . . . *et al.*) turn out to be as quarrelsome as they are inept, and Binder's intricately laid plans look set to founder on rocks of monumental bungling and human frailty. That the team finally reaches its lofty objective is really only thanks to its efforts to escape the meals of the expedition cook. A curt review in *The Alpine Journal* dismissed the book as 'laboured':

> There are some neat hits, which all can enjoy, and one remark by O. Totter – 'when you are swinging helplessly at the end of a hundred-foot rope, it is important to know that the man on the other end is a *friend*' is almost worthy of Kai Lung. But there is, generally, too much forced humour and the incessant conversations about the love-lives of the various members of the party are tedious, as is the constant dragging in of the cooking disabilities of the native Pong.

Even 'the quaint Victorian pictures,' the reviewer opined sourly, 'strike one as weak.' Reception on the other side of the Atlantic was far less starchy. 'This is the antidote for the indigestion that follows reading too many mountaineering books,' enthused *The American Alpine Journal*. The book's continued popularity has been ensured by regular reprints – and the adoption of *rum-doodling* into the universal vocabulary of mountaineers.

A more recent little piece in similar vein is Greg Child's *No Gentlemen in the Himalaya,* which has the unlikely scenario of a Catholic priest secretly organizing an expedition to the Himalaya as a cover for something sinister.

He is investigating a new religion which has sprung up in a valley below Nanga Parbat, the main symbolism of which centres on paper aeroplanes and the mysterious catchword 'Bool'.

The quiet wit of G. J. F. Dutton's farcical 'Doctor' stories – all set in the Scottish Highlands – continues to gain a following. His collection *The Ridiculous Mountains* has just been republished, and we are also happy to be able to include here a fresh adventure that has not appeared in print before. Dutton's fellow countryman Robin Campbell has shown ingenuity in bringing a resuscitated Sherlock Holmes and Doctor Watson to the Highlands to investigate mysteries involving real-life mountaineers. (Many believe them better than the originals!) Collie and Raeburn are integral to the action of *The Adventure of the Misplaced Eyeglasses,* and *The Case of the Great Grey Man* (set on Ben Macdhui of course) features Munro (of the Tables fame). Both appeared in recent issues of *The Scottish Mountaineering Club Journal.*

The Gearfreak Caper by 'Rex Slim' (or more properly, by Guy Waterman) is a pastiche of all those American down-at-heel-detective yarns, and Nick Barrett's amusing little *Rescue at Stoney* parodies Damon Runyon's *Guys and Dolls.* Dave Gregory's 'Old Man' stories, on the other hand – one of which is included here – are uniquely his own.

Topical satire is one of the more obvious applications for humorous writing, and broadly speaking this should be regarded as fiction since it depends so heavily on invention. However, because, to be appreciated, it also relies on the reader being *au fait* with events and cliques and private jokes, and because of its often flimsy or ephemeral nature, we have not considered it very seriously when rounding up material for this book, nor when listing pieces in the bibliography. Suffice it to say that in climbing as in other fields of life, there are never enough good humorists, and the premature loss of any one of them is a serious blow. None is more sorely missed than Tom Patey, whose high calibre satirical writing – prose and poetry – universally delighted and was in a class of its own.

Ghostly stories

Ghost stories belong most properly to oral tradition: they need shadows and flickering firelight to be best appreciated. All the same we have included several, though not the one that is perhaps most famous of all: the original tale of the Big Grey Man of Ben Macdhui. The giant spectre that stalked Collie in the mist has been 'sensed' on occasion by other people, too, and Affleck Gray's book recounting these various manifestations is once again in print. Another spooky story that 'got away' is W. H. Murray's *Leighton Johnstone's Resurrection,* which he would frequently relate on Hogmanay at JMCS Meets. There is a version of this to be found in his book *Maelstrom*: it is a Rip Van Winkle tale of a climber who disappeared on Ben Nevis to re-emerge six months later. Invented on the spur of the moment, Murray soon found that people believed the story of deep freeze survival. Later, when he sent it for consideration to a couple of magazine editors, they too swallowed it whole, and took umbrage, refusing to publish it, when he explained he could not produce 'cuttings' from *The Scotsman* to back it up!

Crime

Inventing an amateur sleuth, who can then be used over and again, is common practice in crime fiction. Kevin Fitzgerald's 'Commander Feston' appeared in several fast-moving stories in the late forties and fifties, and Showell Styles (under his pseudonym of Glyn Carr) developed Sir Abercrombie Lewker, a portly Shakespearean actor manager who solved climbing murders around the world in an impressive string of stories between 1946 and 1969.

To an extent, these characters become the *alter egos* of their creators, going where they go, sharing their tastes and personal quirks. Gwen Moffatt's Melinda Pink, a kindly, middle-aged, semi-retired climber and writer, and devoted conservationist, first took shape in 1973 and is still exercising her deductive powers. Moffat's plots are inventive with the ring of authenticity that is the result of dedicated homework: she will sidle up to a parked sports car and measure whether or not a body would fit into its boot; her butcher advises on the grislier intricacies of dismembering corpses. She shows flair, too, in the way bodies are disposed of. (One she had composted with the grass clippings in a hippy commune.) The stories are well paced and sufficiently mind-bending to keep you alert and guessing to the end, but although Gwen Moffat's books retain their links with climbing, it is probably true to say that her readership now is drawn largely from the non-climbing public. Certainly few of her more recent novels have been reviewed in the climbing press.

Peering into the future

Futuristic writing has proved particularly popular with short story writers. Mostly, they are concerned with the way climbing might be conducted in the next century and postulate what form new equipment will take (like heated chalk bags or crack binders), or they worry about the effects the imposition of outside interference or control might have. Often this is covert comment on society's generally doomward-course. Big brothers abound. There have been several 'when-the-bomb-drops' stories: Martyn Berry in *Last Climb* (1964) has two men scaling Cloggy as atomic 'rockets' land all over Britain; Dermot Somers, in his powerful *Nightfall* (1983) places his climbers on the Eigerwand when Armageddon strikes.

Kim Stanley Robinson's *Green Mars* describes an expedition to Olympus Mons, the tallest mountain in the solar system. A convincing alternative 'world' is created for Mars, but it is a world that has been tampered with, greened, by earth-scientists and populated with a bewildering array of mongrel species created by the very best bird and mammal designers. Throughout the expedition, the hero, Roger – who preferred the planet the red-way it was when he first saw it as a young man – cannot shift a weight of depression. Nowhere could he see . . .

> . . . Mars, just Mars, the primal Mars. Clenching a cold, rope-sore fist, Roger thinks, *they forgot*. They forgot what it was like to walk out onto the empty face of old Mars.

And that is the nub of his isolation. Only too well does he remember the endless, windswept desert, the brilliant golden light – and it is this ability to remember back nearly three hundred years that sets him apart from his antique fellows. Less than one percent of the population share the gift (or curse) of powerful, long-term recollection.

The leader of Roger's expedition is a woman he loved way back when he was a young canyon guide and she a city lass on one of his treks. Naturally, she has no memory of this, but there is still some of the old magic there; and it is this warmth of affection, coupled with the fact that on the summit of Olympus Mons beyond reach of the new atmosphere, Roger finds traces of Old Mars, that gives him the strength to face a few more hundred years!

Thinking Man's Futurism is one way perhaps to describe Graham Sutton's strange *Damnation of Mr Zinkler*. It is unashamedly classicist (mythological allusions, Greek quotations, all that), and dated now, too – as one would expect of a book written in the early thirties – both in style and in attitudes expressed. Hitler and Mussolini, for instance, are regarded with amused respect, this being before the implications of their new fascism had penetrated British (upper class) consciousness. (After all, if one is a decent chap oneself, it's hard to imagine the other fellow isn't also.) In other ways, however, the novel is remarkably forward-looking and explicit, and still holds much to concern us today – though you do need to first acclimatize to its quaintly ripping-yarn dialogue ('Oh Kit, I'm rottenly sorry,' she murmured . . . 'It's the most putrid thing that has ever happened to me' . . . 'You blasted wart-hog!' . . .), which rises at times to heights both giddy and inspired:

> You leave your wife and buzz off to Kashmir, and then when you've excelsiored your bellyful, come back and wonder why she isn't meeting your train! It never struck you she'd a life of her own: or that she might want something more from a marriage than a house in Mayfair and a lot of boy-scout gup about comradeship – which you never gave her by the way: or that she might get bored with a cock-virgin in hiking boots . . .

After an accident on Eagle's Nest Arête, Wykehamist Kit ('Rock') Grenfell, a famous climber/explorer (a sort of composite of the 1933 Everesters – a Longland on Greene legs) hovers between life and death in a Keswick hospital. He 'wakes' to find himself in Hades, the brave new underworld, where people 'live' for three hundred years before passing on to another existence. Patched up from whatever caused their 'death' in the first place, they age no further, but cannot again 'die'. Nor can they again be mended, so a cult of Safety-first persists. 'Life' is so ordered by the state that all risk-taking is outlawed. (This is where Sutton is at his most ingenious and prophetic – in the Hades social structure and economy.)

One of the people Kit meets 'Down There' is a recently-demised film magnate, Mr Zinkler, a man with no affection for rules and directives, who is bent on making a climbing film. Kit agrees to play the star, and eventually climbs back to life – real life that is, in the full knowledge that it will almost certainly be one of permanent crippledom – by climbing up the shaft which links Hades to Earth.

Missions and expeditions

While considering the literature of the thirties, it's worth mentioning James Hilton's *Lost Horizon*, not because it is a mountaineering novel – (really, it isn't) – nor for adding *Shangri-La* to our language, but for being the forerunner to a host of Himalayan spy and adventure stories which cash in on monkish mysticism and/or international intrigue. Few of these, however, match up in excitement to the original. Frank Smythe published *Secret Mission* in 1942, the story of an inventor who devises a secret weapon, then flees with his plans to the Himalaya to escape foreign agents – a book including much comment on Nazism. More recent examples of the 'mission' sub-genre include Andrew Garve's *Ascent of D13* (1968, secret weapon lost in aircrash), Robert Hardy's *Face of Jalanath* (1973, sabotaging nuclear installations), John Masters' *The Himalayan Concerto* (1976, intelligence gathering on the Tibetan border), Duff Hart-Davis' *Heights of Rimring* (1981, Nepalese spy thriller), and Bob Langley's *East of Everest* (1984, guerrilla activity against Chinese in Tibet).

Expedition stories provide more than action: they constitute a particularly good vehicle for exploring psychological interplay. This is because (as in the ever-popular desert island or airplane-crash scenarios) the cast list is finite and interdependent: outside influences can all but be ignored, except in the form of 'emotional baggage' that the characters bring with them. Joanna Cannan's intelligent and well-written *Ithuriel's Hour* (also known as *The Hour of the Angel*), is one such story, first published in 1931. Sir Clement Vyse organizes an expedition to Chowo-kangri 'that tall mountain, lifting on red limestone precipices, into sapphire skies, a pyramid of untrodden snow.' He is an old-fashioned leader, autocratic, dogmatic, who very soon falls out with Ullathorne, the man to whom he has entrusted climbing leadership (and whose wife he also covets). Tensions increase, dividing the fidelities of the rest of the team.

> David [Vyse's son, in his tent the night before the final attempt], shocked and miserable, drove the bedraggled shuttlecock of his loyalty backwards and forwards between his father and his friend. But after all, it seemed that the stars were right, for, before midnight, curiosity and misery and even Ullathorne's own heartbreak were blotted out in sleep; and a porter with toothache was the only man who stayed awake till dawn.

Vyse and Ullathorne reach the summit; there is a sudden flaring of temper and a man dies. Murder, was it?

In Wilfrid Noyce's one attempt at fiction, *The Gods are Angry* (1957), expedition leader Jim Catteridge's small band is also riven by the clash of personalities. Several 'expedition' stories have been used to illustrate or comment upon national ideologies – James Ramsay Ullman's ridiculous *The White Tower* – and stage plays too if we think of the verseplay *The Ascent of F6* by W. H. Auden and Christopher Isherwood or its more recent derivative by Chris Judge Smith and J. Maxwell Hutchinson, *The Ascent of Wilberforce III*.

Greg Child's short story *In Another Tongue* is interesting for offering an alternative view. The tragic events which claimed the lives of thirteen expeditioners on K2 in the summer of 1986 are seen from the perspective of the Balti porters who watched and waited below. Barry Collins, in his powerful one-man play *The Ice Chimney*, sought to recreate the last tortured hours of Maurice Wilson on Everest. Mallory and Irvine have crept into a surprising number of stories: Guy Waterman's *The Bronx Plumber,* Jeff Long's *In Gentle Combat with the Cold Wind,* Kim Stanley Robinson's *Mother Goddess of the World* are all to be found in this collection. A French story, which we haven't seen in translation, appeared sometime in the nineteen-twenties. In André Armandy's *Terre de Suspicion* an aeroplane sets off from Paris to fly to Everest. The pilot refrains from dropping a French flag on the summit when he sees there a Union Jack fluttering in the breeze; it can only have been left by Mallory and Irvine!

Expeditions also serve in the 'Awakening-of-Consciousness' department. One that has a reputation for being 'heavy', both philosophically and wordily is Michael Tobias' provocative *Déva.* It starts with a lot of physical masturbation and you wonder after a bit if that isn't self-parody of the intellectual masturbation to follow. But it does have a plot! And that is the quest by alpinist pilgrims after ineffable wisdom. They find it – to a greater or lesser extent – in a remote Himalayan Garden of Eden, peopled by a handful of holy mystics (horny, holy mystics, it must be said).

Reviewers have experienced difficulty in consigning *Déva* to any simply-understood category. 'The temptation with this imperfect, at times pretentious, gem of a story is to vulgarize it, to compare it with, say, *Raiders of the Lost Ark,'* essayed Jeff Long, continuing, 'It lacks the pace of *Raiders,* . . . but in its frantic casting forward after the adventure of knowledge, Tobias has come up with an erotic Himalayan fantasy worthy of Jules Verne, Henry Miller and the *Bhagavad Gita* combined.' That wasn't enough. Later in the same review, having remarked upon its 'zebra skin of imagery', its 'incredible plot', its 'premise as wild as its characters,' its prose, 'often non-grammatical but almost always lyrical,' Long claimed for *Déva* that it was a 'twenty-first century novel about our own times. In the fantasy tradition of Colin Wilson's *The Mind Parasites* and René Daumal's *Mont Analogue.*' Stuart Pregnall threw in a few more names: 'a little like Kerouac, a little like Gilbrahn and a little like the Dr Bronner's soap labels.' For good measure leading American poet William Everson added, 'in the same genre as John Fowles' *The Magus.*'

Such a bewildering multiplicity of echoes to be found or imagined in Tobias' work should not surprise us. He is reputed to see himself as a natural successor to Joyce, Kazantzakis and Beckett, yet his earlier works have aroused outrage, agitation, and derision among climbers – but above all mystification . . . Tobias-the-Obscure. In places, you wonder if Tobias is just waffling deep and meaningful gobbledigook, or if you perhaps are an out-and-out philistine, and in the end you suspect both might be true. Some extracts seem to be mere lists of words – academic and philosophical name dropping:

> Spirit? A combination, of intuition, reptilian ego, slimy, mud-caked volition. All earthbound. I am celebrating a limbo of myself. Rhapsodic with an animal parody so vivid, so alluring . . . Jeffers in Big Sur, Lawrence in Taos, Neruda on

> the beach in Malaysia, Kazantzakis in Murmansk, Shelley on the Mer de Glass [*sic*], Lermontoy in Tiflis, Basho in the far North of Japan, Sappho at the white cliffs of Lefkas (off which she jumped – Katapontismos –), Claude Geléé in the Campagna, Hukosai before Mount Fuji . . . with all my western enumerata, I felt firmly, squeamishly linked to a tradition of the hypnotic, the suggestive . . .

In short, Tobias never uses one metaphor where ten will do, but every so often you detect a hint of self-amusement, as in Chapter Sixteen when he declares, 'My metaphors were failing me?' If you can get past the blocks of sheer wordiness (and there are many of them), *Déva* is highly entertaining, the narrative itself descriptive and amusing, and it certainly does not shrink from poking fun at the people and concepts it promotes. It is worth persevering to gain access to this. (Those who have read Bernard Amy's short story, *The Greatest Climber in the World* would recognise a possible basis for this novel.) The ending is excellent. But who has the last laugh? The reader, the author, the narrator, or *Déva*? And how many climbers have sneaked off afterwards to spend hours staring at lichen and becoming one with the rock?

Another ambitious work is Elizabeth Arthur's *Beyond the Mountain*. Here again, the scene is a Himalayan expedition ... or at least the central character, Artemis, is a member of an all-women's expedition and the mountain is climbed during the passage of the narrative; yet to a large extent the story concerns itself with events that have taken place beforehand . . . (the emotional baggage we spoke about). Artemis reflects upon the tragic deaths of her husband and brother in an avalanche. She remembers many scenes and incidents, and retraces the tortuous paths of her relationships with the two men. She was so close to her brother as to almost cross the acceptable bounds of sibling love, and had a passionate and stormy time with her husband, who she was contemplating leaving when the accident happened. Her experiences during the course of the expedition are cleansing and painful by turn, but she is finally able to work the guilt and pain from her system in a long and vicious storm high on the mountain. Only then can she relate properly to the other women.

In recent years, a new category of literature has crept into publishers' catalogues and bookshops. What is new about *'Women's writing'*, however, is merely the name. Many classic works that before were regarded simply as of general interest now find themselves sucked into this modish catch-all. Doubtless, it flags work by women that other women should be aware of, but it can also be argued that it cuts into these works' overall acceptability. Men can now wash their hands of a whole raft of literature as having nothing to do with them. Climbing fiction, fighting as it is for serious recognition, could well do without this extra division, yet the authorship and content of *Beyond the Mountain* will sadly automatically place it beyond the consideration of many men. And whenever it *is* read and commented upon, by men or by women, you will never be quite sure that the criticism has not been compensated – one way or another. So when Arlene Blum states on the book's cover that *Beyond the Mountain* is the most compelling climbing novel she has ever read, that it is elegantly written and extremely moving, unkind sceptics will remark that surely it was Ms Blum's own Annapurna expedition which provided the inspiration for Elizabeth Arthur's book, as her own person affected the shape of its heroine, Artemis? And equally, when Greg Child asserts amusingly in *Mountain* that he has a soft spot for bad novels and that *Beyond the Mountain* is the latest acquisition to his collection – 'Enid Blyton does *Heart of Darkness*' – can we be *absolutely* sure that his rejection of the fictional 'lusty American nymphs tripping through the verdant foothills of Nepal' does not carry the merest tinge of bias, based on his own views of women on expeditions and what they ought to concern themselves with?

Well – it's a talking point. Most would agree that the novel represents a bold and imaginative step into largely trackless territory; most would also agree that it is, ultimately, flawed. It is only where to draw the line that is at issue.

Recent novels

Some years ago, in deep midwinter, a plane carrying a cargo of smuggled marijuana crashed into a lake in the High Sierras. Climbers were first upon the scene. By the time official agencies caught up, the frozen lake was pock-marked with chainsaw holes and there was little left to find. That year a lot of smart new climbing gear appeared on the rocks around Yosemite Valley . . . Sounds like fiction? Indeed, but true nevertheless. The event did however spark off two quite exceptional novels.

First was Jeff Long's *Angels of Light*. This really is a climber's novel, in that its rough language and drug references, as well as its assumption that no jargon needs describing, will automatically place it beyond the reach of 'mainstream' readers – very much to their loss, let us say. Three reviewers saw the book as a modern-day Western, and it is easy to see why – the Camp 4 bums around whom the story is based are outlaws. There are deep and unquestioned loyalties binding them together; action is fast, and retribution violent. You'll go a long way to find climbing description as vivid as this:

> By the movements of Tucker's head, John could tell the crack was oddly shaped. Freeing one hand from the crack, Tucker rapidly pawed through the clinking hardware, spreading the bunched metal and slings with a small slap to see what there was. That innocuous slap, its impatience, further confirmed what John had guessed: Tucker was too wiped to waste muscle on anything but a sure fit, and the crack wasn't going to allow a sure fit. Tucker powered himself farther on, running the rope out another three feet in search of some crack that would take his protection. He pawed at the rack and fished a piece loose, one of the large tubes. He unclipped it and tried to stuff it into the crack. The movement of his hands was slightly too fast, a bad sign. Nerves. A moment later his right knee twitched, not more than a hint of sewing-machine leg, but still a hint. He was getting scared.
>
> John spared a glance at the belay anchor. Three solid nuts, one slotted to take an upward pull. If – when – Tucker fell, John was going to get yanked up into the wall. The anchor would hold. John saw that he could catch the fall. But Tucker was going to smash against the wall like a watermelon on a cord. John moved tight against the anchor, bracing for the pull. He was spellbound.
>
> Tucker kept trying, all his effort devoted to inserting the tube and covering his ass. When nothing worked, he did something John had never seen in all his days

> as a climber. Instead of clipping the piece back on the rack, he simply tossed the useless tube over his shoulder, just cast it away. The tube dropped through the air. Not once did it skip off the lower wall. The overhang was profound and the metal disappeared without a sound. Tucker thrust his hand into the rack again, unclipped the largest spring cam, tried it once, twice, then tossed it, too, into the void. Forty dollars.
>
> 'No,' wailed Tucker, and he tried to scoot his hands deeper into the crack. He was too tired to rest, and if he rested he'd only get more tired. His hands started slipping. John expelled his air, clamped his hands tight on the ropes. Tucker fell.*

The other story inspired by the airplane crash was *Vortex*, a powerful first novel from the Canadian writer, David Harris. This is published here for the first time.

To develop the smuggling theme, Harris has shifted his main action to the North Cascades on the US/Canadian border: two climbers discover a crashed light aircraft on Mount Redoubt with a contraband cargo and an injured survivor. By rescuing the man, they get sucked into the deadly business of drug-running, and the story is told both from their point of view, and that of the San Fransisco cop who is trying to bust the drugs-ring.

Swift cutting between these two fields of activity, and the containment of the story almost completely within dialogue and action (ie, few descriptive or ruminative passages), makes for very slick, film-like editing – and no doubt it was always in the author's mind that this might eventually transfer to the screen. That is not to suggest that the writing is not skilful – it is – compact and clean. The characters are strong and believable, you want to know what happens to them, and although this is a very long book, the sense of menace is maintained to the very last line.

But the point really to make is that although this story is about climbers, and includes climbing episodes, it is climbing set into a wider context – in the same way that Dick Francis in his thrillers explores all around the racing world without overloading them with actual race descriptions.

Winner of the 1989 Boardman/Tasker Memorial Award for Mountain Literature was a book called *Climbers*. At first reading, this novel of M. John Harrison's is enigmatic indeed. The substance and meaning of it lie just beyond grasp until quite near the end, when barely-visible threads draw the narrative tight.

Most of the chapters would stand as short stories in their own right – and to prove the point, we have included one in this collection – each providing a neat little cameo of a character or two, a mode of life or a certain landscape. What appears to be random relation of events is suddenly focused when the narrator meets Pauline and events start to go forward, taking on more form for the reader. A startling revelation in the penultimate chapter leads to passages that give a feeling of *déjà vu*, and rightly so, for they link back to lines from earlier in the book and it is then that the light dawns and the reader realizes what has been going on.

* Printed by permission of William Morrow Publishers, Inc.

Harrison constantly touches on mundane, everyday existence, feeding teasing fragments of overheard conversations that sound tacky, comical or predictable to the narrator as adult, but bursting with mystery, hidden meaning and indications of established lifestyle to the narrator as child.

His descriptions of landscape, situation, feelings have an unnerving way of hitting the point, capturing essence in a minimum of words: '. . . his neck bent in the attitude of the inmate of a camp.' For anyone who has climbed 'Up North' many passages will be intensely evocative; for those who haven't they give a good insight. The main climbing characters (all males) may also be reminiscent of people you know if you've ever mixed with those who live near and climb in the Peak District, Yorkshire, Lancashire. Some non-fictional climbers wander in, too: Jill Lawrence, Martin Atkinson, Ron Fawcett and the ubiquitous Dirty Derek.

Climbers creeps up on you, works itself into your mind, has you almost smelling the damp, lichenous rock, the dingy city street, the stale odours from the old man's flat downstairs. You get to know it all the while you think you may be missing the point: the ending isn't apocalyptic, but it leaves you with a feeling of understanding and of leaving a group of friends and acquaintances, a way of life. Harrison doesn't 'censor' his characters: they have bad points and unpleasant habits and are every bit as irritating at times as your own climbing mates can be!

This novel has proved controversial, generating unprecedented coverage in the British climbing press – much of it highly vituperative. Several reviewers have taken exception to what they see as the book's bleak portrayal of the climbing scene. The question was raised, too: what *is* fiction? When fragments of realism and autobiography are bonded in a story, where does fact stop, and fiction start? And should we be concerned to categorize items on one side of the line or the other? Does it really matter? Ed Drummond writes short stories, but they are recognizably autobiographical so cannot with equanimity be called fiction: yet they are rounded and polished, characterizations are well drawn – it is a fictional style of writing. Harrison says he suggested including photographs in his novel, but had to abandon the idea since it so threw his publishers. How on earth could fiction possibly be illustrated by 'real' pictures, they wanted to know.

When awarding *Climbers* the coveted Boardman/Tasker prize, the judges expressed one reservation: its contemporary litter of expletives, they found 'tiresome'. It is a little surprising, in this day and age, that this is still seen as a problem; that people still object to reading words they must hear about them all the time. How else could contemporary realism be conveyed without employing contemporary vernacular? How else reflect the obscenity and shock of sudden violence without recourse to violent and shocking language? Wouldn't it be a little odd to demand of climbing's fictional populace a restraint its factual protagonists patently do not observe? Yet we know traditionalists will never be persuaded that any 'literature' worth its salt can be carved from such rude material. 'Bad language' is and will remain a highly sensitive and personal issue: everyone's tolerance threshold is different. When Barry Collins' play *The Ice Chimney* was premiered at the Lyric Studio in Hammersmith, members of a ladies' alpine club, invited as guests of the production company, so forgot good manners as to protest loudly from the front row. They were unable to see beyond the words given by the author to the dying Maurice Wilson to the torment and defeat those words expressed.

There may be those who consider some of the stories in this book similarly over-littered with contemporary expletive. To them, all we can do is apologize in advance – while yet defending their inclusion! A little controversy, we believe, will prove no bad thing for mountaineering fiction. That at least has been proved by Harrison with his *Climbers*: the book cannot be ignored. Everyone is talking about it.

People may be curious to know how we came to make the selection for this book. From so much material, what guidelines did we employ? Very few really. The main thing we insisted on was that we had to have really enjoyed reading the stories that finally went in. Diversity was needed, we felt, rather than a theme. We wanted people to see the range and quality of what has been and – more importantly – is being written. We believe there has never been a better time than now for mountain fiction. Once and for all we hope to have scotched the myth about the dearth of good mountain fiction – whether or not, for you, the 'really superb mountaineering novel' has yet been written.

Inevitably, there will be some stories you like better than others, but we feel confident everyone should find here plenty to enjoy and think about – and when you do, discuss it with your friends. Authors need to be read and talked about, need encouragement . . . it's a lonely life.

This collection by no means exhausts the field. There were many items we were regretful not to have been able to include. No matter! With luck, we or someone else could be putting together another collection before very long.

Meltwater

by Joe Simpson

WHERE TO now, Jimmy? Dead Jimmy, long gone dead Jimmy? What now friend?

No more glory Jimmy, long gone Jimmy. No laughing eyes, blue blue eyes; no power left to you now. Where have your dreams gone, friend?

All gone in a moment; one endless moment. A rigid body, limbs distorted, a greyish blue pallor and your teeth bashed in. Blood trickling from your ears and snow hard packed, obscenely, in mouth and nostrils. A rictus grin – was it pain or fear? Only the merest hint of blue from your eyes as you stare at me from the snows eternally. Already glazing in the high mountain sun. A congealed, dead fish glance, turning to a cataract stare. Long gone now Jim . . . dead Jimmy.

'*Chai*,' said the old man, proffering a chipped glass. I smiled my thanks and took the sweet milky tea. He nodded his head in an abrupt embarrassed way, then turned his attention to the fire.

I looked closely as he cooked. Other than Jimmy, he was the first person I had seen in three weeks.

Of indeterminate age, near toothless, with the mouth set hard among the leathered wrinkles of his face. Two piggy black eyes squinted mischievously from a mass of crows feet. Whitening eyebrows and a salt and pepper close-cropped haircut added dignity to a face of incorrigible naughtiness.

He squatted back on his haunches and fed the fire small slivers of wood and helpings of straw. The flames licked the blackened cooking pot. A mixture of rice, lentils and potatoes bubbled beneath the steam. The aroma filled the small mud and stone hut.

Cow dung and straw layered the floor. The fresh animal smell gradually faded to the cooking and the smoke. There was no chimney and my eyes watered. A corrugated tin door rattled in the wind and snow pattered wetly against it. Small gusts eddied round the gaps in the tin, making the smoke swirl. Tears ran down. I shivered, wet cold from the day's walk.

The old man muttered to himself as he attended to the cooking. A low murmur, like song, or prayer, whispered from his hunched-over figure. I watched his lips move. Then he sighed, a long drawn sign that said everything, and my stomach rolled over with fear as he murmured into song again.

Was he praying, I wondered. Should I?

The meal over, not a word spoken, the old man carefully put down his plate and looked at me. His eyes were serious and sad, incongruous in his laughing face, and he said, 'Jini dead' and sighed.

'Yes,' I said, 'Jimmy's dead,' and the door rattled to a fresh cold gust.

He had said it every night. A three day ritual, and I was starting to welcome it; getting used to the idea.

In the past I'd imagined a time like this. I'd play-acted in my mind how I would react, how it would all feel. I'd almost got it right, but for the loss, and the numbness. All gone, to nothing. Dust to dust, the Christians say. Fuck the Christians. He was gone as if he had never been. I thought of him as It. Glazed over eyes and a bloodless face. It reminded me of the sheep we had slaughtered. Laughing nervously with stained ice axes, unsure where to start with the knife, and the huge golden eyes staring mute from the battered skull. Dead eyes that seconds ago had glowed. It was all gone away now.

The old man wrapped himself within his blanket, turned his back to me, pulled his feet in foetally, and murmured as sleep took him.

In the dark I fingered Alice's letter, unsure if I wanted to read it again. I thought of her, and It. She, swaddled in white antiseptic sheets, blue eyes also, and dark fringed. Her face shading from grey to purest white. Lips a thin grey line, hardening. Smiling wanly, unaware, as the sickness shone through her skin, and she couldn't help but give quick glances at her mother. Anxious looks that asked what was happening and more that mother could never answer. She would smile back at Alice, lean forward and pat her hand. Then, when Alice would turn again to talk to me, I would feel rather than see the sudden tightening of her shoulders, an unconscious hunching in on herself. When I glanced at her I would see the white tooth marks pressed to her lower lip. Alice was dying.

In the morning the old man left me. He walked away from the hut with a soft wave of his hand, without turning, and the wet morning mists wrapped him from sight.

On his leaving the loneliness flooded back. With Abdul gone as well the three day illusion had evaporated.

He left laden with presents, objects I no longer needed or wanted. Cooking pots, a pressure cooker, my old rope, Jimmy's down jacket and walking shoes. They were stuffed haphazardly into an old red rucksac, torn in places, with its straps hanging loose and tattered.

I sat on my rucksac outside the hut. A damp mist gusted around the hills. From below I could hear the steady roar of the rain-swollen river. Boulders rolled heavily in the flood. Deep knocking rumbles could be heard from within the rush. We had crossed it yesterday with the help of the rope. There were no more obstacles to cross. A short morning's walk would see me safe in the village. Then the merry-go-round would begin.

I looked up the valley into the mists. There was no indication of what lay beyond. The cirque of snow peaks crescented around the spit of moraine gravels that had been our camp for so long. Some burnt and half-buried litter, blackened and soggy in the rain, cigarette butts in the gravel, a flattened area where the tents had stood. These signs would soon be washed clean.

How many days was it now? Five since Abdul had found me. Five lost days blurred into vague memory of happenings. Dazed days. Striking camp and walking out. Following Abdul's careful old man's footsteps. Abdul, solicitous to the point of irritation. Three days down. Three days of wet cloud-wrapped walking. Heavy rucksacs and the jarring downward steps. Down, down, away from the spit of moraines. Leaving the brilliant white glacier behind to be swallowed by the mists. Only a faint meandering shadow line in the snow showing where we had been. Occasionally, the sun would catch the deep footprints, marking them out as a clear black line running up the glacier.

Where the mountain jutted down into the glacier bay another line, running horizontal to the bay, cut a continuous undulating wave around the cirque. The bergschrund ran a clear marker between mountain and glacier. The dark footsteps, a continuous line rather than separated steps, weaved up over the hollows and bulges on the glacier and stopped abruptly at the bergschrund. Not far to the side a tumbled scar of fallen snow marked the path of an avalanche. Drag marks led to the open maw of the bergschrund. Above this there were no signs of movement.

At two in the morning Jimmy left. The sky was clear, a three quarters moon glared a white light on to the cirque. Rock walls gleamed a strange silvery leather white in the moonshine. The sky was magnificent. Myriad stars spread out, glinting brightly as only they do at altitude.

'Back in four days,' he said, squeezed my shoulder, and trudged away. His headtorch glimmered a beam of yellow light ahead of him gradually dimming as he walked up the moraines towards the glacier. I heard the familiar jingle of hardware rattling on his harness, then silence. He had gone, and I drifted into sleep.

The morning sun woke me. I was uncomfortably hot in my sleeping bag. The orange sides of the tent flickered shadows across me. From outside I heard the steady gurgle of our stream. It ran, silver sided, through a chaotic maze of black moraine hills. Its source was the glacier, and the water spilled in grey pools close by the tents. Grey water, full of silt. A finely ground mix of mica, mud and water tainting the cooking for so long now we no longer noticed. A dull booming echoed around the tents. Ice cliffs falling to the glacier from Snow Peak.

I shuffled out of my bag, crawled from the bell entrance and stood up. Clear blue sky and the merciless glare of the cirque greeted me. Reaching into the tent I pulled my sleeping bag into the sun, turned it inside out and slung it across the ridgepole to dry.

I walked barefoot across the sharp-edged gravel to a large boulder and peed a long golden rush of last evening's tea. Shielding my eyes with my hand, I squinted up at the mountain as I stood there. Jimmy had made good use of the frozen pre-dawn start. I spotted his tiny figure silhouetted against the morning sun two thousand feet above me on the ridge. There were no signs of his footsteps on the long and menacing snow slopes sweeping down to the glacier. A pang of jealousy and self pity ran through me. Already he was nearing the high point of our last attempt where we had cached a good supply of gas and food in a snowhole. He disappeared for a moment behind a distinct spire of rock jutting like a dorsal fin from the crest of snow. As he reappeared I could see how well he was going. He was stronger now, and fitter after our two previous forays high up the ridge. The week of hot sunny days and clear freezing night skies must have consolidated the snow ridge. Last time it had been a grimly exhausting slog up deep wet snow.

I walked slowly back to the tents feeling sharp twinges in my thigh again. There was no helping it, much as I tried to convince myself otherwise – the hamstring was torn. One fall with a heavy rucksac on the black rocks near the camp had been enough. That tired slip after the long stormy descent had finished my chances on the mountain. But for that, I would be up there now – dammit!

I idled away the day with little jobs that soon bored me. After restrapping my thigh with elastic bandage I tentatively began the short walk to the snowy edge of the glacier, hoping for a better view of the mountain. Soon the twinges became a continuous ache, forcing me to hobble slowly back to camp. In a black mood I fiddled morosely with my camera, changing lenses and filters, still hoping for a spectacular photograph of Jimmy's now tiny black shape on the ridge above our snow hole, but it was no good. I threw the lot into the tent in disgust.

Cooking endless brews of sweet tea at least let me vent my frustration on the temperamental petrol stove. Eventually I retired to the shadow of the tent doorway propped up on ski sticks to shield me from the unbearably hot sunshine. I turned my back on the mountain, listened to Vivaldi on my personal stereo, and read a cheap adventure story about poachers in Africa. When the sun dipped westward behind the crest of the cirque the bitter cold of early evening drove me inside.

At nine o'clock I stepped out into the cold with my headtorch and stared up at the darkened mountain mass looming above. I could dimly make out the steep buttress seamed with ice runnels and snow patches which reared above the ridge in the final wall beneath the summit. Faint vestiges of cloud scudded across the night sky in thin streaked bands, eerily silvered by the first few glimmers of starlight. The wind moaned down from the mountainside. The weather was changing. Suddenly a flash of yellow light blinked at me. Then another. One . . . two . . . three. A long dark pause and I smiled to myself as the tension left me. All was well. Jimmy was safe for the night. I blinked back an acknowledgement.

Safe and high. Far higher than I had expected him to reach that day. Climbing alone he would have moved so much faster than a roped pair.

By noon of the following day I had watched Jimmy make steady progress up the summit buttress towards the easy snow slopes leading to the summit. From the speed he was moving I guessed that he had dispensed with the rope at the snowhole and gone for the summit in a quick dash. Through the four hundred millimetre lens on my camera I could see his careful methodical movements but I couldn't make out whether he had left his rucksac at his previous bivouac site. He needed to move fast. The streamers of cloud of last night had developed into banked cumulus rapidly covering the sky. Snow plumes jetted from the summit and the ridge below the buttress. The wind had increased. At two o'clock he reached the summit and turned almost immediately back down. There was an urgency in his movements now, seeming to increase with my own growing anxiety. At three the clouds enveloped the mountain and I saw no more. At nine it was snowing at base camp and no light flickered down from above.

Next day a few inches of snow lay around the tents. The water in the pans had a skin of ice, and the mountain was hidden from me. For a brief moment in the late afternoon the clouds parted and I thought I saw a small dark movement below the buttress. By the time I had reached for my camera there was nothing more to be seen. If, as I suspected, the movement was Jimmy, then he had put the worst of the descent behind him. He could reach the snow hole tonight and it was well stocked with gas and food; enough for one person to sit out the storm for several days. My glum mood lightened at the thought, but I wondered what the descent and high bivouac in the storm had taken out of him.

Two long days passed. Days of wet snow and blanket cloud. Occasionally the wind howled from above the clouds and I shivered in my sleeping bag. At night the temperature dropped viciously. In the mornings I knocked the hoar frost from the sides of the tents and with cold fingers fumbled at the stove. My thigh was strengthening but it was too late to be of any use. There was nothing to do but wait. Empty hours spent trying to ignore the insidious worries overpowering me. Did he reach the snow hole? If he didn't, could he have dug in and survived this long without food and fuel? Was that him I had seen or a rock flickering in my vision as I'd anxiously searched the mountain?

I tried reading, but my attention kept wandering as gusts of snow rattled the tent walls, making me wonder what was happening two thousand feet higher. Only the tiresome need to feed myself and make hot drinks briefly let me forget. So I lay there, impotent and scared. Come down Jimmy, come down safe, youth. The camp had become a bleak dark place of dismal black gravels, wetly snowed boulders looming through grey wraiths of mists; the loud stream was now silent as its source froze. Booming sounds muffled by the clouds echoed around the tents as avalanches broke free from the high ringed walls of the cirque. And always the sibilant wind sounds rising and fading, mourning at me from the hidden mountains.

As darkness heralded the start of his seventh night on the mountain I glanced anxiously at the sky for signs of a break in the weather. At midnight a lone star glimmered through a rent in the cloud curtain. An hour later more stars and the silver shine of moonlight broke through. The clouds were lifting. It was warmer. The wind had died.

I awoke early. The light was blued in dawn's slow start. I sat outside huddled into my down duvet with the stove hissing busily. Streamers of cloud spewed in plumes from the summit. Isolated clumps of cloud, broken remnants of the storm, drifted apart on a light southerly wind. The sun crept slowly to the horizon, announcing its arrival with the paling blue in the east and the blue black night sky fled. There was no sign of Jimmy. I stared at the snow ridge. A small dark shape sprung a buzz of hope then I realized it was a rock. Familiar features had changed with the dusting of fresh snow. Above the dorsal fin of rock I could see no sign of our snow hole. The tight knot in my stomach began to unwind as I prepared myself to accept the worst. A hollow emptiness replaced the tension.

I turned off the stove and slopped boiling water into my mug. More tea. Always take plenty of hot sweet tea for shock. Doesn't do much for grief, I thought. 'Come on,' I said, 'Come on, show yourself, for God's sake.' Nothing moved. I stood up slowly. My thigh no longer hurt so badly. At the boulder I peed with my back to the mountain. When finished I turned to the tents, head down, eyes averted from the mountain. For an hour I managed to avoid looking up. I ate porridge and chocolate. As I prepared another drink I forgot myself and glanced up without thinking.

A black speck moved slowly down the ridge. Black against the now blinding sunshine.

'J I I I M M M M M E E E E E!!' I yelled exultantly, leaping to my feet and pumping my arms in the air.

The cry echoed around the tents. The small speck stopped moving. Then an arm raised wearily in acknowledgement and he moved painfully on again. I stared at him. Even at this distance I could see the exhaustion in his movements. He seemed smaller. The deep snow was hiding his lower body. He was wading down. Shrugging forward in those familiar wallowing motions of tiredness.

Within minutes I had grabbed my rucksac, fastened the gaiters on my boots, grabbed the ski sticks and set off towards the glacier. I walked as fast as my thigh would allow. The sack was light, laden only with the stove, food, medicines and my camera. For a while the ridge was hidden from view as I moved through the twisted path between the high black moraine hills. I was breathing heavily as I rounded the last spur of muddy black gravel and the fresh snow of the glacier glared blindingly in the morning sun. A faint dull roaring sound echoed for a moment, then died. I climbed over the crest of the first undulation on the glacier and stopped to check Jimmy's progress. There was nothing to be seen.

It was silent within the cave. He roused himself slowly from the torpor of days lying entombed. His watch showed it to be morning. Another day. The eighth. He shuffled his body round towards the entrance and reached for his axe with wooden fingers. For the umpteenth time he poked the shaft of the axe carefully through the snow, anticipating the sudden roar of the storm and the gust of powder against his arm. Silence, and then a beam of bright sunlight streamed through the hole he had made. The storm was over.

He rolled away from the entrance and lay back. Eyes closed, he felt the weight lifting from his body. Thank God, it was over! There was no burst of excitement, no exultation. He was too tired for that. Yet there was relief. A steady calm feeling. He smiled at the roof of the cave as he opened his eyes. The roof gleamed a bluey-white colour from the sunlight outside. The scallop shaped marks of the ice axe adzes were glistening with ice. The steam from the stove and his body heat had melted the roof only for it to freeze again in the night. He dragged his eyes away from the all too familiar sight. He was going down.

When at last he was ready he stood up through the roof of the cave and blinked in the glare of sunlit snow slopes. He swayed, dizzy from days of lying still. There was a strange disembodied feeling in his head. Physically he felt fine. For sure, he was tired, and the tips of his fingers were blackened by frostbite. He had escaped lightly from the terrible descent to the cave in the storm. Often he had wondered what would have been if he'd failed to reach the cave. He'd eaten well, rationing his supply of gas carefully. Yet somehow he felt distanced from events as if he had stepped outside of himself and now watched his wallowing attempts to descend with a dispassionate curiosity. As he struggled against the snow he shook his head sharply from side to side, as if it would clear away the muzziness inside. He felt that he hadn't woken up completely. His head ached as it would with a head cold.

His memories drifted back over the past days of storm. The unnatural silence in the dark cave. A single candle fluttering a weak yellow light across the scalloped walls. The hiss of the gas stove and it's faint glimmering blue light adding to the candle flame shadows. The brushing sounds of nylon against nylon as he swept the insidious powder snow from his sleeping bag – a constant battle to remain dry and a poor remedy for the boredom and solitude.

He cursed his weakness and the deep tiring snow. The sunshine that had been so welcome now seemed a cruel extra burden. Quickly his movements slowed, his mouth dried with his heavy breaths for air, and when he rested, slumping sideways in a careless sitting position, he faced away from the sun, seeking shade behind his rucksac.

Although he could see the two tents nestling amid the moraines there was no sign of movement. It was early yet. He'd always known they would be there, but irrational thoughts in the cave had often frightened him into believing that for some reason they would be gone. Somewhile later as he forged down the ridge he heard a shout and glanced down at the tents. A tiny figure stood between them, arms up high. He smiled and raised his ice axe in acknowledgement.

From where he stood he could see that soon he must leave the ridge and begin to descend the snow face leading to the glacier. For a moment he wandered aimlessly about, unsure. Was it safe? He kicked at the snow wearily, but there was really no choice. He knew that he must get down that day. There was no gas left, and he was worried about the way he felt. His head was not right.

After another fifty yards along the ridge he turned down the slope. Immediately it was easier to move. It was much steeper than the ridge and he used the angle to make sliding steps down through the deep snow. Small waves of snow hissed down beyond his steps. His mood lightened and some of the tiredness went with the thought of reaching the camp. He sensed the danger on the slope but it was from a distance. He had decided to go down; he must go down despite his fears so the danger seemed less personal. It was a gamble and he knew he would win. He had no idea how long the good weather would last but he knew that to be caught in another storm would finish him so he stepped on down the snows. The menace put him on edge, made him tense and alert. Adrenalin strengthened him and much of the tiredness was forgotten.

As the slope became steeper he was forced to turn into the slope and kick steps, using both axes for support. He could see the flurries of sugary snow falling down between his legs to the glacier far below. More snow seemed to fall than he had disturbed.

From far within he felt the first trembling warnings. He was slow to react. Everything was wrong. He knew it, but he couldn't act. The sun had taken its toll, burning away his will to resist; the lethargy had so overwhelmed him that he seemed to be struggling up from deep sleep but failing to wake. He looked at his arms buried deep in the snow and tried squeezing his fists tight on the axe handles. As in the morning on first waking there was no strength in the grip. He shook his head, taking a deep breath as he did so. It was far too dangerous. For a moment the warning was clear in his mind. He must return to the ridge. He must get back to the safety of the ridge, away from these trembling slopes.

He rested his head on to the snow, thinking of the struggle back up to the ridge, and his fear of the slope faded. Perhaps it would be alright. The thought of retracing his steps was too much. He leant into the fifty degree angle, almost lying against the snow, with his legs deeply buried. One hour, just one hour and he could be safely down on the glacier. It was against all his instincts to go down and yet he didn't want to spend another long day alone on the mountain. Never climb on slopes within twenty four hours of heavy snowfall. He knew it needed at least this time for the snow to consolidate. A hot melting day followed by a freezing night would settle the slope. If only he had awoken earlier when it was dark and freezing, but it was too late for that. He must go back to the ridge.

Laboriously he began to climb back up the furrow of his footsteps. Three steps up, two steps down. As soon as he had decided to go up his fears came rushing back. He had at last acknowledged his mistake, and with that he was seized by an almost convulsive panic attack. Like turning his back on a darkened doorway when he was a ghost-fearing child, he now tried to run from the menace he had felt as a distant nagging doubt but which now consumed him. The slope was lethal. He must get off, quickly, quickly.

He had waited too long. The sun had done it's work on the snow, and its heat had sapped his will to act quickly. Too tired to care, too thirsty and craving the comfort of base camp, he had stepped beyond the limits. At first he thought he was sliding further down than usual after a step but a quick glance above him and to the side told him the truth. Standing upright, one arm still buried in the snow, he could see that he was moving downwards. Above, a crest of snow was curling down towards him. It looked deceptively soft and harmless until it hit him. Flipped violently backwards, he slid head down with the gathering rush of snow. Instinctively he tried to swing round and attempt an ice axe brake, but the snow pushed him under and he struggled in panic to get his head above the surface.

Four days of continual storm had deposited over four feet of snow on the mountain slopes. The hard old névé ice beneath held the massive weight of fresh powder in an uncertain bond. Now the sun had finished the inevitable process. Meltwater seeped between the surface of the névé and the new snow. Layers slumped downwards in short slides then held tentatively in balance again. A few more slips spread out across the entire length of the slope. Hundreds, perhaps thousands, of tons of snow hung poised above the glacier. Then Jimmy began his descent. As the first huge block of snow moved, with the helpless figure trapped upright within it, a chain reaction crackled across the slope. From just below the ridgeline the whole slope began to slide down, ponderously and silently at first before it gathered momentum and surged into a deepening roar in its lunge for the glacier bay.

Within the churning mass some sections of slope swept down faster than others as imperceptible differences in the slope accelerated it away. Huge shearing forces developed at the edges of these masses of moving snow. It was no longer soft wet sugary snow. It had become a solid overpowering force. As strong as any river in spate, it rushed down with gathering speed until it began to ride on a cushion of air. At its head it pushed a mass of displaced air creating a blast force that would kill before the following snow even touched its victim. Jimmy had triggered a monster.

It had hung poised waiting for the puny fly-like creature to disturb its quiet slumber. Time seemed stretched as he tumbled within the maelstrom. He knew at once what was happening and though he realised it was hopeless he tried at first to resist. For a moment his head cleared the snow and he gulped, sucking in the powder-laden air and almost immediately beginning to drown. He thrashed his arms from side to side trying desperately to stay on the surface, and for a moment he succeeded. Then his twisting body crossed the shear forces on the edge of his initial sliding mass. His hips were ripped back and up above him as the slower moving snow gripped his lower body. The immense force flipped him head down again but not before his legs snapped above the knee. He felt nothing. His back had snapped in the violent arching twist.

He still waved his arms, or maybe the snow waved them for him, he couldn't tell. He felt numb though he didn't understand why. The powder had melted instantly in his lungs and though he fought for breath there was none to be had. It seemed hours since the start though it was only seconds. He felt no fear now that the initial panic and struggle were over. His chest burned with pressure pains and he sensed rather than saw which way he was moving. As he broke surface again he was blind. Snow had packed his glacier glasses. His mouth, nostrils and ears were plugged solid. He was dying, deprived of all senses, but his mind worked feverishly on. The hard packed snow leeched away the few weak tears as darkness came over him. He could hear from very far away the dull roaring sound; within the avalanche the sounds were muted. Across the glacier bay its thunderous progress echoed around the mountain walls.

A fine rain began to fall. The mists swirled low over the rushing grey water. I stood by the cairn we had built on the way up. My footsteps, and Abdul's, still showed in scuffed dark streaks in the fine silt of the river bank. I glanced back at the hut; there was no-one to be seen. I'd half expected Abdul to have returned. He would have waited, silent and patient, until I returned to my rucksac. Then, wordlessly, he would have nodded to me, tugged my elbow and turned away expecting me to follow; but he too had gone.

I watched the mists playing down the course of the river. It seemed to steam in its rage to descend. The knocking heavy thumps of the boulders echoed up from the roaring waves. We had crossed here on the way up. In crossing it we had felt for the first time the isolation of our adventure. Filled with hopes, dreams of summit days in bright snow-blinding sunlight, we had forged on not once looking back to this dirty Rubicon. The opposite bank was dim and blurred by the mists but the dark steps leading away to the north were still visible.

I sat down, back against a rounded boulder and faced the water. The cold wind sucked down by the icy waters made me shiver and my fingers shook as I re-read Alice's letter. Childish writing of gentle thoughts that wished me well in the mountains and to hurry home. A brave dismissal of her illness, or perhaps she really didn't know. These waters came direct from the glacier. In time he would come past this boulder sweeping past in the same violent chaos that had put an end to him. He would go on down to the village and through to the Indus until he drifted slowly in the river's wide and sluggish delta thousands of miles from here in the brackish salt waters by the sea.

He had never wanted it this way. Never thought it would come to pass, though he had accepted it was possible. At least he'd had the choice. I broke down the old cairn and re-built it taller and more secure by the boulder. I thought to bury the letter at its base but changed my mind. The torn up paper span for a moment in an eddy by the bank and then the current caught the pieces and they swirled from sight. I stared after them oblivious to the cold wind then turned and walked to my rucksac. I shouldered it and followed Abdul's tracks towards the village. That little part of her should join him, I thought, brother and sister together before it ended for good.

B-Tower West Wall

by Peter Lars Sandberg

LET ME confess this to you. They killed Baker as soon as we went in the door. They shot him twice in the chest: two men in business suits; pistols with silencers. Baker was a big man, but the bullets stopped him as if he had walked into a tree. I think he was dead before he hit the floor, but he lay there for a while with his legs thrashing and my son Chip, who had always thought a lot of Baker, pressed his small face against the front of my parka so he wouldn't have to watch.

'*Dad, Dad,*' he pleaded, as if he wanted me to explain what was happening, to make it not true. I couldn't. All I could do was hold him and die with him, if that's what it was going to be. He was twelve, and except for the television news, where it never seems quite real, he had not seen a man get killed before. I had, but never like this.

It was a few minutes after nine p.m. We had spent the weekend in New Hampshire, climbing rock in Huntington Ravine, had just got back to the city. Baker had parked his truck under the building, had come up for a drink. I was a widower, he was divorced. We had served together, Special Forces, Vietnam, back when it had begun. Now he was dead. I looked away.

All the drapes in the apartment were drawn, though I remembered having left them open. Most of the lights were on. I could hear the traffic on Tremont Street, six stories down: sirens and horns.

'Shut the door, McKim,' one of the two men said to the other. They both wore gloves. This one was young, late twenties, medium build. His hair was red and longish and crossed his forehead in bangs. He had wash-blue eyes and a lopsided nose and when he spoke, the tone of his voice was persuasively calm, as if in his view Baker's dying counted for nothing at all.

'Look,' I said, trying to keep my voice steady. 'I don't know what this is. I don't care what you do to me. But let my boy go.'

'There's some clothes in the bedroom,' the redhead said. 'Sports jackets, slacks, street shoes. Put them on, both you and the kid. There's an empty overnight bag in the closet. You put your climbing shit in that bag: pants, boots, parka. The kid won't need his. McKim will go in there with you while you change.'

I nodded. McKim came up next to me. He was a couple of years older than the redhead, dark complected, heavier set. He had the thick neck and wrists of a man who might have been a wrestler once or a catcher in a trapeze act. His suit was expensive, $250, maybe $300. It smelled like cloves.

'You screw off or make noise or give McKim any trouble,' the redhead went on, 'and your kid will wind up as dead as your buddy. You got that?'

I told him I did.

McKim went with us into my bedroom, where we changed clothes the way we'd been told to. My wife's picture was on the dresser. When she had turned thirty, she started having headaches but was misdiagnosed. By the time the doctors got it right, she was a long way toward being dead.

McKim took off his gloves and inspected his nails. They were cut short and filed smooth. He had not closed the bedroom door. I could hear the redhead talking on the living-room phone. 'Yeah, yeah, we've got them,' I heard him say. 'Tell Sights to meet us there in half an hour. Yeah, yeah. No sweat.'

Chip looked up at me. He was in his jacket and slacks now and looked nice, the way he always did whenever I took him out to a good restaurant, except he was pale and his lip was shaking; but he was holding on and I was proud of him for that and scared.

'We'll be OK,' I told him. 'We'll do what they want us to do and when they're through with us, they'll let us go.' I glanced at McKim, hoping he'd back me up on that.

He didn't.

We took the elevator to the garage. They had a limousine waiting, a dark-blue late-model Caddy with a phone antenna in the centre of its trunk. An old man drove. He wore plaid slacks and a white shirt with the sleeves rolled back and he didn't ask anybody where he should go and nobody told him. The redhead sat in front. Chip and I sat in back, along with McKim and my overnight bag. I held Chip's hand. It was early September, cool enough so that the old man had the heater on low. There was an east wind coming in off the harbour; the few women on the street who wore skirts had to hold them down with their hands. We drove west on Commonwealth.

'Dad,' Chip whispered after a while. 'Where are they taking us?'

'I don't know,' I said. 'To the Carlyle, maybe.' That's a new 30-story hotel in the Back Bay. We pulled into the half-circle drive at the main entrance. The redhead turned around and looked at me.

'I'll be behind the kid when we go in,' he said in the calm way he had of saying things. 'You won't try any shit.'

'No,' I said.

Once the four of us were out, the old man drove the Caddy away.

The lobby of the Carlyle was jammed: a pharmacists' convention going on; men with short haircuts and plastic I.D.s pinned to medium-wide lapels. No cops in sight. I wouldn't have called them if there had been. McKim went to the main desk and got a room key, then we took a crowded elevator to the fourth floor, which I knew was the first floor of rooms.

'He's already here,' McKim said as we walked down a long corridor. The carpet was blue and smelled as if one of the conventioneers had tossed his cookies onto it.

'I told him half an hour,' the redhead said.

'Yeah, well, he's here now. He took the other key. I don't like that shit.'

'He's all right.'

'He sucks,' McKim said.

'He does his job; forget it. Open the door.'

We had reached the end of the corridor. McKim let us in to room number 418. Once we were in, he pulled the door shut behind him. The room was smoky, the drapes drawn. A wispy thin kid in black slacks and a blue button-down sat sprawled on one of two queen-size beds. He was smoking a cigarette, watching TV highlights of a programme that had been played earlier that afternoon: Patriots-Bills. Baker and I had bet on it driving back from Huntington Ravine. Baker had won. I had told him to come on up for a drink.

The kid had dark hair with a bald spot the size of a butter plate. He wore the kind of heavy-framed glasses people used to like in the Fifties. The lenses were the thickest I'd ever seen. They magnified his pupils so that when he looked at you it was as if he were seeing you through a couple of stewed prunes.

'Is this the man?' he said without getting up.

'Yeah, right,' the redhead said.

'He looks older than I thought he would. Why did you bring the boy?'

'Never mind the boy, Sights. You just get your shit together. Show him what he's going to do.'

Sights stood up, stretched, yawned. He may have been tired, but I'd have bet right then he was nervous, too. Chip's hand was small and moist in mine. I loved him. I've heard about fathers who don't love their kids, but I've never met one. I guess I've been lucky.

'You've done a considerable amount of direct-aid climbing, is that correct?' Sights said.

'I've done some,' I said. He sounded like a third-string professor at the kind of college I might have made if I'd had time to make one.

'Long's Peak Diamond, El Capitan, The Fisher Towers . . .' He ticked them off.

'They're standard climbs,' I told him. 'I haven't done anything a lot of other people haven't done just as good or better.'

'You were profiled in the *Globe*.'

'Once. Five years ago. I haven't been west of Chicago since.'

'But you still climb, correct?'

'I do when I can. Look, I'd like to know what this is all about.'

'Tell him,' McKim said. There was an ice bucket and bottle of Chivas on the vanity. McKim was pouring himself a drink. The redhead had gone into the can.

'They want you to do a climb for them,' Sights explained.

'What climb?'

He went to the window and opened the drapes. The room we were in had a close view of the Bennington Tower, a floodlit 52-storey high-rise.

'That one,' Sights said. 'They need to get into an office on the forty-second floor.'

The hotel was part of the Bennington Plaza complex, the biggest and newest collection of buildings in Boston. The Bennington Tower was the hub of the plaza wheel. It had over 1,000,000 square feet of office space and restaurant on top where Chip and I had gone a lot. He liked the view and a waitress named Sadie who would always tell him Chip was hip and bring him desserts that weren't on the menu.

'Right now we are less than a hundred feet above the plaza roof,' Sights said. He'd gotten a green Forrest pack from the closet and taken from it what looked like photocopies of building blueprints and a half-dozen original diagrams. He'd spread them out on the bed near the door. McKim sat on one side of him, I sat on the other. Chip and the redhead sat in the chairs. 'The façade lights go off at midnight. That's because of the energy crisis. They used to stay on all night.' He blinked at McKim through his thick glasses, as if he was proud of having that kind of information.

'So what do we do?' McKim wanted to know. 'Just cut the shit.'

'As soon as the façade lights are off, you rappel from here down to the plaza roof. He'll show you how; it's not difficult. Then you walk three hundred feet across the plaza roof to the corner of the west wall of the Tower. That's the one we're looking at.'

'Which corner?' McKim said.

'The left one as you face it. There's less traffic on that side, less reflected light. The facade itself consists of hard aluminum mullions that run symmetrically in rows up the wall, and hard aluminum sills that run symmetrically across it. Where they intersect, they form rectangular boxes. Each box is two and a half feet wide and six and a half feet high. There are over six thousand of these boxes on each of the four walls. They are functional where they frame a window, decorative where they do not, but they are all made of the same material. The mullions and sills are three inches thick and extend seven inches out from the building itself.'

Sights showed us how it looked. His blueprints and diagrams were clear, sharp and detailed; they showed the various elevations of the Tower, the curtain-wall design, the corridors, stair wells, elevators.

'Why the corner?' I asked.

'Because it's the only place where the sills are not flush with the wall. You've got a two-inch gap where you can loop a sling and hang a stirrup.'

'What happens when we get to the forty-second floor?'

'The office they want is in the centre of the wall. You will have to traverse ninety feet, stepping from box to box.'

'Any protection on that?'

'Nothing I could figure,' Sights admitted. 'But with seven-inch platforms to stand on, I don't see why you should have any trouble.'

I studied the drawings he'd made, tried to memorize them, tried to discover a way out for Chip and me.

'All right,' I said finally. 'Suppose we don't have any trouble. We're forty-two storeys up and I'm ninety feet out on the wall. I've got nothing to anchor to and no way to protect him coming across—'

'That was the most difficult problem I had, 'Sights admitted. He looked satisfied as hell. He got up and went to the closet, came back with what looked like a two-and-a-half-foot length of one-inch pipe with a chrome sleeve and rubber cups at each end.

'Have you ever seen one of these?' he asked. I told him I hadn't. McKim told him he had.

'It's a portable chinning bar,' Sights explained. 'It's designed for doors. You turn the sleeve and the ends tighten against the frame. If you use enough torque, a man weighing three hundred pounds could hang from it all day.'

'So what?' McKim said. 'What good is that going to do him?'

'I put that in the box in front of the window you want,' I said.

'Correct,' Sights said. 'That will give McKim a fixed rope on the traverse and something to tie on to while he works on the window.'

'Very beautiful,' the redhead said. I didn't know he'd been listening, but I guess he had, and Sights looked pleased.

'How the fuck do we get down?' McKim wanted to know.

'You traverse back to the corner and make four rappels. Then you walk back across the roof of the plaza. You will have a penlight to signal with. When you do Red will lower a rope and up you come.'

'Have you got ascendeurs?' I asked.

'Jumars,' he said. 'Two pair in the pack. Karabiners, five-step web stirrups, slings, everything you need. There are three hundred-and-fifty-foot ropes in the closet: two for you to take and one to leave here.'

'It sounds like a hell of a lot of trouble,' I said. 'Why not take the elevator and jimmy the office door?'

'The offices shut down at five p.m.,' he told me. 'Seven days a week. The elevators are computer programmed. Once the cleaning crews are out – usually by eleven – the only one that operates is the express to the restaurant. All the office doors have electromagnetic locks. There are infra-red scanners in the halls and emergency stair-wells. Pinkertons patrol the lobby and the plaza outside the building.'

'How thick is the window?' McKim wanted to know.

'They vary, depending on wind load and building height. That high, you should figure half-inch glass in a double-glazed unit.'

'What about alarms?'

'There aren't any. Except for the floodlights and the Pinkertons in the plaza, there is no outside security at all.'

'How come?'

'They think it's impossible for anyone to go up that way.'

'How the fuck do you know what they think?' McKim said.

Sights smiled.

'I asked their security chief,' he said. 'I told him I was doing a term paper.'

I asked McKim if he'd ever climbed before, though I knew he hadn't. He shook his head.

'How high will we be?' I said.

Sights blinked. 'The Tower is eight hundred feet. By the time you get to the forty-second floor, You will be about 600 feet above the plaza roof.'

'That's a long way up for anybody who hasn't climbed,' I said. 'If I'm going to do it, I'd rather do it alone.'

'You don't pick locks, do you?' the redhead put in. He had got up and was pouring himself a drink. He wasn't really asking, but I told him I didn't pick locks. 'Don't worry about McKim,' he said. 'You just get him to the right window and he'll take care of the rest of it.'

They paid Sights off and he left. I couldn't tell how much they gave him. but it was in cash and it looked like a lot.

'Are you going to do it, Dad?' Chip asked me. He'd got up to give me his chair and I'd taken it and pulled him down onto my lap. We'd scrubbed up at noon in a mountain stream in New Hampshire. His hair smelled terrific: like sun and leaves.

'Sure,' I said, trying to sound calm. 'It should be easier than what we were doing in Huntington.'

'Will it take a long time?'

'I don't think so. Couple of hours, maybe.'

'What should I do?'

'Sit tight.'

'Do I have to do what he says?'

'Yes.'

'Can't I—'

'You do what he says. I don't want you to worry about me; I'll be fine. OK?'

'Sure. OK.'

I held him tight. Ever since they'd shot Baker, I'd been trying to figure a way out of this jam we were in, but so far nothing had come up right, everything too risky, too liable to get us both killed. All I could do was wait and hope. McKim had gone into the can to change clothes. When he came out, he was wearing fatigue pants, a black sweat shirt like mine and a pair of Royal Robbins Kletterschuhs. He had a holster suspended from a wide black leather loop on his left shoulder. The holster had been especially made for a modified automatic with a silencer. He stood next to one of the beds, shoving his wallet keys and change into his trouser pockets. I looked at him. I'd been right about his build. He looked strong as hell.

'What time is it?' he asked.

'Ten-thirty,' the redhead said. 'You've got an hour and a half.'

The facade lights went off at 12 and we were on the plaza roof at 12:10 a.m. McKim had taken the bottom half of the window unit out; I'd used the vanity to anchor our rappel. Once we were down, he blinked his penlight and Red hauled up the rope. When I thought about Chip alone in that room with one of the men who had killed Baker, I felt weak, as if someone had drained off half my blood.

It was dark and cold and I could feel the wind coming at me damp and salty as we hurried across the plaza roof. The roof surface was fixed gravel and what noise we made going across was lost in the noise of the late traffic on the city streets. The stream of headlights, the glitter and flare of restaurant signs, movie marquees and arc lamps all seemed a million miles away to me, like a promised land I'd only be able to dream about and never reach. Where I was was dark and cold and deadly with McKim just beside me, sure of himself because he knew I wouldn't do anything to risk my son's life.

'Get started,' he told me when we got to the northwest corner of the Tower. I wondered how sure of himself he really was about this climb we were about to try. And I wondered, too, what they were after in that office on the 42nd floor. Something big. Something worth killing an innocent man for.

I uncoiled one of the ropes we had, tied one end around McKim's solid waist, the other around my own. He would carry the second coiled rope and the Forrest pack, in which he'd put his tools. I showed him how he should follow me after I'd gone up one lead.

'Get started,' he said. And I did.

I went up a rope's length, moving as quickly as I could. Sights had been right. The aluminum sills curved at the corner and gapped from the wall. I'd stand on one, reach half a foot over my head, loop a sling, hang a five-step web stirrup. Then I'd go up the stirrup, gripping the adjacent vertical mullions to steady myself. Once I was standing on the next higher sill, I'd reach down, retrieve the stirrup and repeat the process. It was awkward at first, but I got on to it quickly.

I ran the rope out, anchored myself and gave McKim a snug belay as he came up with his own stirrup and sling. I found it was easiest to stand sideways on the sill with my back to the wind that was blowing hard along the north wall of the Tower. I was already higher than we'd been in the hotel. I could see the lighted window of 418, but Red had drawn the drapes again and I couldn't see in. God help Chip, I thought, if anything goes wrong.

McKim came up. I could hear him grunting and cursing just below me in the dark. There were no stars visible, no moon. The light from the streets below bounced off a lowering overcast of cloud. Though they were just 300 feet away, I had trouble seeing the corners of the hotel, could not see the upper floors at all. If anyone on the street happened to glance up at the Bennington Tower, there was no chance he was going to see us, and just now I was glad of that.

'Far enough,' I told McKim. 'Tie yourself in. I'm going up.'

We made the 42nd floor in five leads. McKim got slower on each one. During the fourth and fifth leads, he lost his grip on the mullions twice and fell back and I had to stop him with the rope. He was winded, silent and, I think, more scared than he'd figured on being. At the end of it, we were 600 feet above the plaza roof, shrouded in fog. The mullions and sills were cold and wet. The big panes of glass on the north wall creaked and popped in the wind.

'*Christ*,' McKim croaked. He stood just below me. I could hear him, but I couldn't see him.

'Tie yourself in,' I said. 'Give me the extra rope and the chinning bar.' When he did, I tied the chinning bar to the back of my waist loop, then made one end of the extra rope fast to the sill just above my head, draping the loose coils over my left shoulder. I told McKim how he should do the traverse. I took the penlight from him and told him I'd signal when I wanted him to start.

He sounded as if he wanted to talk some more, but I didn't and I stepped very slowly and carefully from the corner into the first box on the west wall.

It was bad standing there: too close, too tight. I felt as if someone had put me in a coffin. I wanted to step back to get some breathing room, but all I had to stand on was that seven-inch sill. I kept my left arm high so the coils of the extra rope wouldn't spill off and I moved from the first box to the second. I had to squeegee water off the surface of the mullions before I could get a fair grip on them. My leather gloves were soaked.

According to Sights's diagram, the window of the office they wanted was 30 boxes in from the corner of the 42nd floor. I counted each one as I stepped around, then rested a few seconds, then stepped around to the next. The weight of the chinning bar and the extra rope pulled like a hand behind me. Twice I pressed my face against the cold window glass and rested a full minute. My heart tripped in my chest. Sooner or later, I knew I'd have to make a move, for Chip's sake and my own, but I still couldn't think what it would be. The redhead and McKim weren't going to let us go, I was pretty sure of that. We'd seen them kill Baker and they hadn't told Sights anything about it nor explained to him why they'd brought Chip along. My guess was they'd be needing Sights again and that's why they were keeping his nose clean. I guessed they wouldn't be needing us again.

As I kept moving toward the centre of the west wall, I heard sirens in South Boston, a long way off, and jets taking off and coming in at Logan, in spite of the fog. I wished Chip and I were on one of them, going to Puerto Rico, maybe, someplace in the sun.

When I was able to, I set the chinning bar high up between the mullions that framed the window they wanted. I couldn't see anything inside. I screwed the bar in as tightly as I could, yanked it a couple of times, then slowly let it take my weight until I was hanging from it. I weighed 190 and it held me solidly. I pulled all the slack out of the extra rope, tied it to the bar, stepped one box over and signalled for McKim to come ahead. Somehow he managed to spot that wink of light through the fog; I think he would have spotted it if I'd been three states away. He came quickly, wanting to get it over with, feeling safer with the fixed rope to clip to than I'd felt without it.

'Tie onto the bar,' I told him when he reached it. 'It's safe. You can hang from it, lean back, whatever you want.'

He didn't answer, which was just as well, because at that moment I saw what I was going to do, all laid out like a colour film on a small white screen in my brain.

McKim cut out the lower half of the outside panel of glass and taped it to the upper half. Then he cut out the lower half of the inside panel and dropped it onto the carpeted floor of the office. He did it fast and clean and told me to follow him in.

It was pitch-black inside and smelled of cleaning fluids. I could hear a soft whirring sound, as if the blower in a heating unit had come on. According to Sights's diagram of the suite, there were three rooms: the private office we were in, a larger reception area, and a file room. McKim got a three-battery flash out of the pack and told me to follow him. We were still roped up. I coiled the slack as we went. He headed for the file room. Shadows cast by the beam of his light bobbed and shrank.

The files were colour-coded and numbered. From what I could see, there were a lot of them: They covered three walls of the room from floor to ceiling. McKim moved the flash impatiently; it appeared that he knew exactly what he was looking for but couldn't find it. The cabinets were heavy-gauge steel and locked. The colours were pastel: yellow, orange, buff, green, blue. The numbers seemed to run in series: A/100, A/110, and so on. McKim swore. He was on his hands and knees now, moving slowly, checking the numbers on the bottom row.

'OK, I got it,' he said finally. 'Hold the fucking light.'

I put the beam on the green vinyl pack. He got out an aerosol can of silicone and a small leather packet of lock picks, which he unrolled on the carpeted floor. He blew a jet of silicone into the file lock, chose one of the picks and went to work. I couldn't see my watch, but I don't think it took him a minute and a half to open the drawer. It was blue and the number on it was N/100. It rolled out quietly. McKim reached in. I could see his thick wrists and stubby fingers moving over the legal-sized folders, quickly at first, then slowly as he neared the back.

'OK, got it,' he said, this time more to himself than to me. He pulled out what looked like a pocket-size ledger, and then two more.

'Give me some light,' he said. I did. He sat on the carpet, looking at the ledgers. Each of them was bound in worn red leather with a gold Roman numeral embossed on the centre of the front cover: I, II, III. The ledger sheets themselves were coded and filled with neat columns of figures. McKim grinned. I hadn't seem him do that before. I stood over him, the coils of rope in my left hand, the flash in my right. It was quiet in the room, as if the walls and floor and ceiling were all six feet thick, as if we were inside the main vault of a bank.

'Fucking Nancarrow,' he said, looking up at me.

I nodded as though I didn't know what he was talking about, but I did and he knew I did.

'If you've got what we came for, let's get out of here,' I told him.

'We just blew that son of a bitch away,' he replied.

'OK, swell,' I said. 'My boy's waiting for me. I'd like to get back to him.'

'Fuck you,' McKim said. He started to get up. He was about halfway up when I kicked him. I kept the light on the left side of his face and kicked him just under the chin, the way I would have punted a football. I heard his teeth snap, heard him grunt, saw him bang against the file cabinets, then sag to his knees. I was edgy as hell but mad, too. I came up next to him and swung the flash against the back of his neck. The light winked out. I heard him groan as he went down. In the pitch-darkness of the room, I found him, groped for the pistol in his shoulder holster. I though he had to be damn near out, but suddenly he was boiling up under me, shoving his fist in my gut, locking his hands on my throat. I could hear him snarl, spit blood. I tried to pull his hands away but couldn't. When I began to black out, I found his pistol, with some difficulty pulled it out of the long holster, put the silencer against his heart, pulled the trigger once. It was a Beretta .380. It bucked a little. There was hardly any noise. I felt McKim slide away from me.

I could have picked up one of the office phones then and called the police. I could have told them about Baker and McKim and Sights and Nancarrow and the old man in the parking garage at my place who had probably fingered Baker while we were on our way up. I could have told them where the redhead was and how he was holding Chip as a hostage, could have let them be responsible for trying to get my son out safe, and maybe I should have, but I didn't.

I figured the way things had been going in this country for the past ten years, I'd most likely be the one they'd lock up and the redhead would go free or do short time and Chip would get killed or hurt bad when the cops raided the room. He was all I had, and if anything was going to happen to him, it was going to be my fault and not someone else's.

I found the penlight and untied the rope that still connected me to McKim. I went through his pockets. He was carrying the hotel-room key, a small bottle of glycerin, a thick roll of aluminum-backed tape, the straight-stemmed cutter he'd used on the glass, his wallet and the packet of lock picks. I took everything except the wallet. I put the ledgers in the breast zipper pocket of my parka. I put on the shoulder holster with the pistol in place.

There were a toilet and a closet in the private office where we'd come in. There were some clothes in the closet, including a couple of sports jackets. I took one and tied it around my waist. It was 1:40 a.m. From here on, I knew I was going to have to move fast and be lucky. My heart was beating as if it were coming through my shirt. The office had got cold; I was having trouble catching my breath.

I backed out of the hole McKim had made in the window, reached up for the chinning bar, pulled myself up. I couldn't see anything and because I couldn't, I felt disoriented and I closed my eyes and thought about the Bennington Tower and how Sights had said there were over 6000 boxes on any given wall and how I was now in one on the west wall, 42 floors up, standing on a seven-inch sill that helped form one of those boxes. I thought how I was exactly thirty boxes from the northwest corner and how I had made the traverse safely once without protection and how, if I was careful, I could make it again.

I untied the fixed rope at this end, let it go. I loosened the chinning bar and tied it to my belt. Then I was stepping slowly from box to box again, counting each one as I went. The mullions were cold and slippery; it was all I could do to hang on to them. My hands and forearms ached. I'd stand face in, with my soles flat and heels hanging over the 600 feet of space between me and the plaza roof. Then I'd move around the vertical mullion that separated me from the next box. When I got to the corner, the wind was blowing hard. I could hear the north wall creak and pop as if it were about to let go. I knew skyscrapers swayed with the wind and wondered how much this one was swaying right now.

I put my hand behind the gap in the corner sill and leaned back. The fixed rope lashed at my left. I squinted up. The atmosphere was heavy with the brackish smell of the harbour. A hundred and fifty feet above me, I thought I could see where the restaurant lights brightened the overcast. I checked my watch. The place was due to close in five minutes. I prayed some people had just come in or were taking their time with a late snack, as I knew they often did.

I was going up there. I was going up past the restaurant, up the building cap to the roof. There I was going to find a 100-foot antenna and a maintenance door that led to a storage room off the kitchen. The blueprints Sights had gotten had laid it all out for me, had told me everything except whether or not I could reach the roof edge from the last of the corner sills and, if I could, whether or not the door on the roof would be unlocked.

Using the stirrup, I began to move up. It seemed to take forever. I had to tell myself over and over to take it easy and not make a stupid mistake that would get me killed and probably Chip also. The wind wanted to blow the stirrup away. I could hear it crack like a flag under me when I was standing in the higher steps. My eyes streamed tears. My gloves were soaked and stiff and my fingers were numb. There were no more planes. When I listened for street noises, all I could hear was the racket the curtain wall of the building was making, the same splitting and popping noises the frozen surface of a lake will make in the dead of winter.

Come on, move, I told myself. But I was lead-footed and slow. When I finally got level with the restaurant, I gambled that no one would be looking out because of the fog and mist that wrapped the building like a bandage, and I leaned around one of the mullions and looked in.

The lights were soft. Most, but not all, of the tables were empty. I saw Sadie rolling the beef cart back toward the kitchen. I'd always liked her. She had the same kind of figure my wife had had: lean, small-breasted, graceful. If she hadn't been 15 years younger than I was, I'd have asked her out. Faintly through the double sash I could hear the music they always piped in after the gal at the piano bar quit. I wanted to be in there. I wanted to be one of the people I saw, sitting at a table, eating, drinking. When I thought about it, I felt tired, as if I couldn't go on; and sad as hell, too. I don't know why, but that's the way I felt looking into that place.

I used the penlight to check my watch. It was 2:25.

I continued climbing up the corner until I reached the roof cap. It felt like smooth wet marble under my gloved hand. The sills and mullions ended here. I held on to the last of them. Fifty feet above my head, one of the antenna lights blinked off and on at two-second intervals, giving the overcast a slight red glow. The wind rushing past the north wall tugged at my parka sleeve and pants leg.

I untied the chinning bar from my belt, screwed it out as far as it would go and shoved it up through the gap in the last sill, then tied it off with the same sling I hung the stirrup from. Then I began to go up, using the chinning bar to steady myself the same way I had used the vertical mullions before they'd run out. I balanced up on the balls of my feet, one step at a time. The stirrup wobbled under me. The wind wanted to push me back. I kept my face in the lee of the west wall, my cheek pressed against the roof cap. The chinning bar extended waist high beyond the last sill and I hung on to it and hoped to God it wasn't going to pop out on me or slip back through the gap.

According to Sights's blueprints, the roof was recessed to drain toward its centre. A masonry lip four inches high and four inches thick kept any build-up of rain water from spilling over. When I finally stood gingerly on the last sill, I let go of the bar and reach up arm's length and felt with my finger tips the edge of the masonry lip. I didn't want to commit myself but knew if I was going to, I'd have to do it quickly.

I stepped up on my toes, stretched and reached until I had the lip with both hands, and I began to pull myself up. I kicked the wall with my feet, felt my forearms knot up and cramp, felt the strength begin to go out of them, knew in an instant I'd never make it. I pulled with everything I had left, wondered if the masonry was strong enough or whether it would suddenly break off in my hands and I would fall back and down all the way to the plaza roof. I cursed myself for not having rigged up some kind of protection. I closed my eyes and pulled and kicked, and just before I would have given it up, I found the chinning bar with my right foot, pushed down on it, pulled myself up and over. For a few seconds, as I lay on the roof trying to get my wind, I had the same good feeling I'd always had whenever I'd worked hard to get to the top of something. Then, in the red glow from the antenna lights, I hurried across the roof to the raised steel hood where the maintenance door was set and I tried the door and it was locked.

Everything came down on me then, everything that had happened since McKim and his friend had killed Baker and taken Chip and me away. I wanted to scream. I wanted to smash something flat. I wanted to find the jerk-off who'd put a lock in a door like this and tie a knot in his nuts. When I tried to pick the lock with one of McKim's tools, my hands shook so badly I dropped the tool, and then all I could see was a lot of bright red with the image I had of those two pistols with silencers and Baker falling back and I took the handle of the door in both hands and began to turn it and kept turning until I heard something give and then the door was open.

A short flight of steel steps led to the storage closet. I used the penlight and went down. I could hear people talking in the kitchen. I got out of my parka and into the sports jacket I'd brought. I wouldn't look any too good, but neither did a lot of folks these days. I transferred the ledgers from the parka to my combat trousers. Then I went to the closet door, which was not locked, and I opened it a crack.

I could smell frying grease and some kind of cleanser. It was hot. Three men in white aprons and hats stood along a stainless-steel counter. They weren't looking my way. I stepped into the kitchen and was almost to the restaurant door before one of them called to me.

'Hey, no customers back here,' he said.

'Sorry,' I told him. 'I took the wrong door. I wanted the head.'

He told me where it was, but I already knew. I checked to be sure Sadie wasn't anywhere close by and then walked through the restaurant. At one of the tables I passed, a college kid in levis and a turtleneck sweater was finishing a beef sandwich and a bottle of Bass Ale. Come as you are. That's how it was these days. For once I was glad.

The maître de smiled at me when I walked by his station, but he was busy sorting receipts and didn't recognize me. There were a half-dozen people waiting in the lobby for the high-speed elevator. I waited with them, wondering what they'd say if they knew there was a dead man in an office on the 42nd floor and I was the one who had killed him, or what they'd say if they knew how I'd gotten in here and where I was going now and what I intended to do when I got there. Then I tried not to think about it or about anything else.

The elevator arrived at last. Nobody got off. The seven of us got on. We faced front. It took 30 seconds to go from the 52nd floor to the main lobby.

The place was crawling with Pinkertons. I stayed with the group until I was in the section of the plaza that joined the Bennington Tower with the Carlyle Hotel. Then I broke off and headed for the hotel door. It was a revolving door and I was about to go through it when a Pinkerton stopped me and wanted to know if I were a guest. I told him I was and showed him McKim's key and he waved me on.

The hotel lobby was empty. I went up to the desk clerk and asked him to hold the ledgers for me, not to mention them to anyone else, not to give them to anyone else except the police if I didn't pick them up in an hour. He looked nervous and asked me my name and room number and I took a chance and told him McKim, 418, and he said OK and put the ledgers into his safe.

I took an elevator to the fourth floor and went down the long corridor again. It seemed like I'd gone a mile before I was finally standing just outside the room. My legs were shaking. The corridor was empty and silent, but I could hear the sound of the TV, muffled by the door. I wondered whether Chip was still in the chair where he'd been when I last saw him or whether he'd gotten sleepy and the redhead had let him bag it on the bed. I tried the key. It went halfway into the lock, then hung up on something. I eased it back out, dipped it into McKim's bottle of glycerin, tried it again. This time it went all the way in without a sound.

I wondered if the chain lock were on. McKim hadn't used it, but I didn't know about the redhead. I took the pistol out of the holster, held it in my right hand with the silencer alongside my cheek. Then, with my left hand, I turned the doorknob as slowly as I could and began to open the door. I'd figured the redhead would be watching TV or looking out the window. I hadn't figured he'd be sitting on the vanity, looking at me as I opened the door, but he was. His wash-blue eyes widened until his eyebrows were lost somewhere behind his bangs. I don't know if he was going for his gun when I shot him. I didn't give a damn. I put a bullet in his chest and watched him sit up a little straighter and then pitch toward the floor.

'*Dad!*' Chip shouted. He'd been lying on his back on one of the queen-size beds and he came to me and put his arms around me and he was safe and alive and if anything in my life has ever made me happier than that, I don't know what it was.

'Take it easy,' I said. 'We've got some things to do.'

I picked up the ledgers at the desk and we left the hotel. According to the newspapers I'd read, Joseph Nancarrow had been an accountant for the New England Syndicate for 12 years. A month ago, he'd made a deal with the prosecutors, had bought himself immunity in exchange for the financial records McKim and the redhead had gone to so much trouble to steal. It's that kind of world. No use pretending it isn't. I had the ledgers now and I got in touch with the prosecutors and made a deal of my own: a new life for me and for Chip.

My name used to be Hank Gage. It's not Hank Gage anymore. I used to be a manufacturer's rep. I'm not that anymore, either. No chances. No loose ends. That's the only way to fly. I still climb, though. Today Chip and I are going to drive to the high country and do a 1000-foot headwall. It'll take two days. Tonight we'll be snug in our hammocks, hanging from *pitons* a long way up. The wind will blow clean through the high trees. Before we fall asleep, we'll hear the coyotes bark.

Hey, look, I'm glad I told you about it. Whatever you read in the papers was bull. This is how it happened, just this way. I didn't leave anything out. My son wanted it straight. Oh, yeah. In case you're wondering, he's a little older now. I don't call him Chip anymore.

La Fourche

by Anne Sauvy

translated by Jane Taylor

IN CHAMONIX there's an old saying which goes: 'Every conceivable sign is a sign of bad weather, and the worst of all signs is the absence of signs . . .'

There is something in this. For the habitué, the Chamonix Valley, which enjoys quite unusually heavy rainfall, is a veritable compendium of weather signs all indicative of storm and rain: west wind; red sky in the morning; pale or watery sun in the late afternoon; halo round the sun; stars particularly brilliant; pall of smoke lying flat along the valley; tap-water flowing milky; mountains looking very close; cottonwool clouds or, worse yet, clouds in long trailing reddish fronds; long plume of cloud on Mont Blanc; hat on the Verte . . . True cognoscenti turn to the animal kingdom as well: trouble is on the way if flies are unusually aggressive, if bees hover around the hives, if slugs take to the road or spiders take shelter, if swallows sweep along the ground, or if the cows are lying down (this last, unfortunately, has become more difficult to observe in latter years as more and more holiday flats leave less and less room for cows . . .) At high altitude there are other signs to alarm the alpinist, such as humming ice-axes, hair rising gently on the scalp, or a faint sound of crackling. And absurd as it may seem, some few alpinists (no doubt for uncomfortably Freudian reasons) attach importance to the movements of the barometer and the *obiter dicta* of the weather forecast . . .

The weather-signs are legion then, but there was a time when one sign was universally recognized as infallible: the arrival in the Chamonix Valley of the unfortunate Georges Faustin.

No sooner was his tent up, indeed sometimes no sooner had he set foot in the valley, than the cloudless blue of the sky would turn a livid grey, heavy clouds would mass on the horizon, and rain would begin to drip dispiritedly on the larch trees and chalet roofs. These premonitory signs were followed, invariably, by a prolonged depression which settled over the Alps and whose dampest days were those which Faustin chose to walk up to a hut.

At first it was just a joke. Every year the phenomenon provided some of the best laughs of the season, and indeed one year when Faustin was known to be on his way and when the forecasts, predictably, were growing progressively more gloomy, some climbers paraded on the square with a banner reading: 'Save Our Season! Faustin Out!' But the joke soon wore thin, and there came a time when more prudent climbers would discover the dates of Faustin's holiday before laying their own plans.

Faustin himself was never discouraged. He became a walking catalogue of species of Chamonix rain: Scotch mist, drizzle, driving, freezing, thunderstorm, cloudburst . . . Over thirty years of experience, he built up an impressive Alpine list comprising all varieties of hut-bashes-in-pouring-rain, descents-in-white-out, hurried-retreats-in-blizzard – all adventures which may have had their heroic moments, but which scarcely added up to glory. In all those years, he had achieved only a short list of climbs and the quality of those fell well short of his dreams. In spite of appearances, he was perhaps not so bad a climber; but his career was necessarily a modest one, and it was allied with an unhappy reputation for bringing bad luck.

Everybody knew him. He was always around, hovering on the fringes: every Thursday evening in winter at the Club Alpin headquarters in the Rue la Boétie, and in summer occasionally in a hut, but more often in whatever bar was currently 'in': the Potinière, the Drug-Store, the Choucas. There he would be, with his long, thin nose and mournful doggy brown eyes, battening on other people's stories and other people's jokes; on occasion he would try and get in some anecdote of his own, but no-one listened and he would break off, with an apologetic smile, in favour of some other speaker who was better able to please an audience.

But nothing dimmed his enthusiasm. The mountains were his life, and his life contained precious little else. He lived alone. Very few people remembered that he had, once, almost, got married, and that the engagement had been abruptly broken off when his fiancée unwisely asked him to choose between the mountains and herself. Faustin, unhesitatingly, had chosen the mountains. In professional terms his life was no more successful; when young he had spent his time climbing rather than studying, so that now, over fifty, he held a mediocre post in a rather second-rate laboratory, where he still spent much of his time dreaming of the mountains like an adolescent. Every inch of every wall of his little flat was papered with superb photos of soaring ridges, plunging faces, sparkling snows. He had the complete range of Vallot Guides, Kurz Guides, topo-guides, and spent every winter evening planning every detail of every route for the following summer – the one that would be *the* summer, *his* summer. This time he would be one of a remarkable team doing the most sensational routes – and the following autumn he would come back to Paris the uncrowned king of the Alps. *La Montagne* would phone to ask him for articles: *North Faces Across the Oberland*; *5 × 4,000: A Two-Day Solo Epic*. And that would teach them to call him 'poor old Faustin'. But then, invariably, inexorably, the grey drizzle would set in as his season started.

Surprisingly he seemed reasonably content with his lot and with the very modest place he held in Alpine circles. But as he grew older, the climbers he had known in his youth drifted away, and the younger generation, while perfectly polite, rarely wanted to climb with him. True, he had never found it easy to find partners, but he had scarcely admitted this even to himself. To save face he would refer, sadly, to the death of one of his first climbing friends, Paul, killed many years before on the Meije. When asked with whom he was going to climb the next summer, he would always say:

'You know, since Paul died, I've never really had a regular climbing partner . . .'

In point of fact even with Paul he had never really climbed very much, but this had been his nearest approach to a team.

And then it finally happened. For once the summer was perfect: the weather was totally reliable and all the routes were in condition. There was never the slightest need to send an 'apprentice' staggering sleepily out at two in the morning to check on the weather: always, invariably, it was good. The nights were just cold enough to ensure that there was snow in the couloirs; the days were just warm enough so the rock was always dry. The dream-season.

Faustin was by now older and slower and gloomier, and apt to get breathless, and no-one was interested in climbing with him. Days went past. From down in the valley he gazed up at the dazzling sky, the sunshine flooding over white snow and red granite. He put up a little notice in the Club Alpin, and was contacted by a shaggy, self-confident student. They set off together for the Papillons Ridge: the young man fell off twice, and when things got awkward he had an unfortunate tendency to call out for his mother, but on easy ground he soon outdistanced his companion and stood waiting with ostentatious patience. Their first expedition together was their last.

Another week of perfect weather went past. Faustin hung around the valley, not daring to go off even for a low-level walk in case he missed a possible climb. And every evening he would go down to the Guides' Bureau where everyone met to look at the forecast (it was always the same: 'Continuing good weather. Outlook settled') and to listen to triumphant accounts of other people's routes.

'How about you, old man?'

'Oh well, you know . . .'

He was more and more miserable. He'd planned his season so carefully, praying that *this* time the weather would finally be favourable. Well, the weather was favourable, but . . . And then there came the first glimmering of a possible partner, a young lad called Claude Auxy, not a bad climber. It turned out that neither of them had ever done the Brenva, and as it happened

Claude was stuck in the valley because his usual partner had pulled a tendon.

Georges Faustin was filled with child-like excitement as he went into the supermarket to stock up on food for the route. He chose the items with a sense of almost paternal solicitude: 'A bit of ham – he's young, he'll need proper food – chocolate, yes, young people like that, I'll get some good stuff, Swiss . . .' Claude Auxy, simultaneously and in the same supermarket, was doing his own shopping, not realizing that his future partner was just on the other side of a row of shelves. He met Jean-Pierre and explained his plans.

'You're joking!' exclaimed Jean-Pierre, 'You're never going to climb with that old has-been! He was never up to much at the best of times, but he's completely past it now. And besides, he's real bad luck. No kidding, if you set foot on the Brenva with him today, by tomorrow morning it'll be peeing with rain. Forget it! Otherwise . . .'

Faustin didn't stay to listen to the rest. When Claude Auxy got back to his tent a little later, he found a note to say that Georges had thought better of it – and he was profoundly relieved: now he could forget the web of Machiavellian excuses he'd been dreaming up to get out of it.

Georges Faustin, however, had come to a decision. He would show them he wasn't finished: one last flamboyant gesture if it killed him. Before his inner eye passed the depressing vista of the years: a catalogue of petty failures, minor humiliations, broken dreams. Alone if need be he would take on the South Face of Mont Blanc, the Brenva, even the Sentinelle . . . He would fight to the end and return victorious. And come to that, if he didn't return, would it matter? He felt as if he was floundering in a great sea of bitterness.

He would allow himself two days' respite: one to get fit, one to rest and organize his gear. He was living in a nightmare. He was tortured by the thought of how he must have seemed to everyone all those years, and by the thought of the lonely, friendless old age that lay ahead. And deep within him the fear was growing: the fear of the Brenva solo. And yet he could not give in: he clung to his plan, his last remaining illusion, with an old man's febrile pig-headedness . . . All around him the sun shone; in him was nothing but a flat, leaden sense of despair. From time to time he was shaken by a wish for revenge: if he were killed, Claude, Jean-Pierre and the rest of them would be sorry. They'd see what they'd done . . .!

This welter of feelings and motives was whirling in his mind as he stepped off the téléphérique at the Col du Géant into the vast solitude of the mountains. Somewhere there was still a faint hope that someone would see him and stop him, give him a fatherly lecture on the dangers of solo climbing, beg him to come back. But no-one took the slightest notice of him. He set off, very slowly, down the Vallée Blanche and then up towards the Tour Ronde. Oddly there was not a soul about, and the late afternoon sun flooded over a deserted glacier. He'd made up his mind to spend the night in the old hut at La Fourche; true it would mean an awkward start the following morning, but the way up to the new hut at Le Trident involved crossing a difficult bergschrund. And besides, the other climbers in the hut would be bound to offer him a top-rope in the morning.

Faustin trudged doggedly on, bent under his rucksack. Every time he stopped for a breather, he shivered with cold and apprehension. The curved bowl of the Combe Maudite seemed positively menacing. For the first time he registered the real meaning of the word *maudite*: accursed. And as he climbed, the word *maudite* beat in his mind – and around him crowded the Mont Maudit and the Aiguilles du Diable, the Fourche, the Trident . . . What on earth had possessed them to give mountains names like *Accursed Mountain*, the *Devil's Needles*, the *Pitch-Fork*, the *Trident* . . .? He felt increasingly apprehensive, increasingly threatened.

At last he came to the foot of the couloir leading up to the hut, and as the shadows lengthened he made his way painfully up. He forced himself to concentrate on every step, and visualized his arrival in the hut. It might well be crowded; in fact he might well have to sleep on the floor; but at least he'd be among friends. He'd step through the door: 'Not another lot! Alone? Great! You must be pretty good, I guess, you don't get many solo climbers over this way. Where are you heading? Us too! Fantastic! We're a rope of three. I don't suppose . . . you wouldn't consider joining us, would you?' He savoured the scene and improved on it as he struggled up, aching and breathless.

His disappointment was all the more acute therefore when he found the hut empty. Empty! Unheard-of in good weather at the height of the season! Perhaps everyone who wanted to had already done the Brenva? Perhaps the weather had been so good that all the climbers had given up out of sheer exhaustion? Still, it was not too late – he needn't give up hope. But no-one came. The light faded. The great South Face of Mont Blanc loomed larger in the grey twilight, cold and hostile. He tried not to think about it.

It was a depressing evening. It would have taken very little to make poor old Georges burst into tears. He was terrified: terrified of the ordeal which awaited him the next morning, and which was now unavoidable since he could not bear to go tamely back, defeated, to the valley. The nightmare grew bleaker and more hopeless. The hut was cold and damp and not very clean, and the blankets smelt musty. By the light of a single, flickering candle he ate what might well be his last meal. He picked at his food, with a queazy memory of all the other last meals that must have been eaten here. He went out, huddled his duvet round him and made his way up to the col. It was pitch-dark and the absolute silence was broken only by the occasional clatter of a falling stone, or creak from the settling glacier. Sheet lightning flared suddenly behind the Aiguilles du Diable, and they strode black and menacing across the horizon. Faustin's spirits plummeted. He went back into the hut, took a sleeping-pill, pulled a couple of blankets over his ears, listened fearfully to the whispering wind and then finally, thankfully, receded into sleep.

It was the light which woke him. He was vaguely surprised not to have heard the climbers coming in, and faintly irritated to be woken up. To hell with them, he thought, fancy turning up like this in the middle of the night! And he snuggled down further under his blankets. But then a further thought struck him: how quiet everything was! Was this another lone climber? Or had the other one already gone to bed? Faustin peered out under his lashes. The man was sitting in the corner in the candlelight, and he was stuying a sheet of paper which he must have brought with him. His face was nondescript: not particularly handsome, nor particularly plain, just the sort of face that Faustin liked, friendly and pleasant but with none of the showy good looks of the self-confident natural winner. Faustin was delighted not to be alone; he went on watching. The man looked to be a little above average height, well built. He wore grey wool climbing breeches, climbing boots, a red V-neck sweater. His face was clean-cut and very brown (this couldn't be his first route of the season), and he had thick black curly hair. He was sitting with his chin in one hand, holding the paper with the other, and he was so still, so dramatically lit that Faustin thought at once of Georges de la Tour.

But there was something odd about him, something Faustin couldn't quite pinpoint but which left him faintly uneasy. He stared at him again more closely, and it was then that he noticed, sticking out of the thick black curly hair, two neat little shining horns.

Faustin jerked suddenly and completely awake. Out of his subconscious swam scraps of stories, bits and pieces of legend – how he regretted having dismissed them so lightly! – which led him to suppose that his companion could only be the Evil One.

However sceptical or cynical you are; however often you have disclaimed the supernatural; even if you are so world-weary as to undertake a route way outside your capabilities with no expectation of surviving it, it is nevertheless an appalling experience to find yourself with no warning, at midnight, in a lonely hut, three thousand metres up, and face to face with the Devil. Faustin was duly appalled.

His companion was still motionless. He sat with his chin on his hands, apparently lost in thought. And an idea struck Faustin: did the Devil realize that he was not alone? That there was someone in the hut? And come to think of it, what *were* the Devil's powers? A bit late in the day to think of that! If only, he felt, he'd spent a bit more time on the supernatural, he'd have had some idea of what to do, but as it was he lay absolutely still, trying to stifle his breathing. He even shut his eyes in case they caught the reflection of the candle – then decided it was worse not to see what was going on, and opened them again the merest slit.

A few endless minutes crawled past. And then Satan spoke:

'Well, now, old chap,' he said, his voice pleasant and surprisingly human, 'your life hasn't been up to much, has it?'

And gently but inexorably he set out the failures, the disappointments, the absurdities, which had so far constituted Faustin's life. He relayed a number of telling remarks made about him by acquaintances. He listed the opportunities Faustin had let slip. None of it seemed meant unkindly – indeed he sounded sympathetic – but it was said with ruthless clarity and stripped away all the half-truths which usually enable one to conceal unpleasant memories. Faustin's life was, in short, a wash-out. He had started with certain undeniable advantages, he had achieved nothing, he had contributed nothing. Nothing whatever.

When the Devil drew to a close, Faustin was no longer able to conceal the fat tears which came rolling down his face and splashing damply onto the pillow. How could he have made so little of life? How could he now be declining empty-handed into old age?

'And yet you know,' the Devil went on, 'it's not as though the rest have been like you and missed out on everything. You've had a pretty bad deal. Happiness isn't just a myth, you know. For every woman you've met who's looked happy and fulfilled, there's been a man like you. Everything you've bought has been invented and manufactured by someone like you. Every advance in science has been pioneered by someone like you. Every book you've read has been written by someone like you. Nothing's impossible. And take you, for instance: Hell knows there are enough climbers who've been on expeditions to the Himalaya or South America, even had routes named after them! There's always a few who turn their dreams into reality. You're just about the only one, really, who's never had as much as a taste of what he wanted. And you can take my word for that, too . . .'

Silence fell again. The silence of despair. Never had Faustin seen himself with such awful clarity.

'And yet . . .' said the Evil One, 'and yet . . . It's not too late. You *can* still have everything you ever wanted. Everything . . . You can start all over again. All you've got to do is sign this little sheet of paper, and tomorrow morning you can have it all. That Maserati you used to yearn after, the white one . . . And the girls to go with it . . . Actually you won't even need the Maserati – one glance and they'll fall into your arms. And just think: muscles like iron, absolute fitness, superb sense of balance, perfect eye for a route . . . First ascents everywhere . . . full-scale expeditions . . . lectures in the biggest halls in Paris if that's what you'd like. First winter ascents . . . And if I'm emphasizing the climbing side, it's only because I know that's what you're interested in, but really you could do anything – Nobel Prize for Physics – President of the Republic – the Académie Française . . . Just imagine . . . And look, more than likely you're going to get killed tomorrow, and if you do it's suicide as near as damn it, and then I'll have your soul anyway. So all you're doing really is signing away a soul you've pretty well mortgaged already, and that's it – for the next twenty-four years!'

He was persuasive, and he had picked his moment. He took out a little Opinel pen-knife and a goose-feather quill, and waited. Georges Faustin didn't hesitate; not a murmur came from his conscience. Admittedly the document when he came to look at it seemed a little more sulphurous than was strictly necessary in the twentieth century, but if you treat with the devil you treat with him, and he swallowed the text without a quibble or a qualm.

'Oh great Mephistopheles!' it read, 'Lord and Master, I, Georges René Faustin, recognize you for my God, and renounce Christ and Mary and all the Saints and the Holy, Roman, Catholic and Apostolic Church. You undertake to provide all worldly advantage for me for the next twenty-four years, in return for which at the end of that time you will be sole master of my body, my soul and my life. Written at La Fourche, on the Mont Maudit, in the unseen presence of Satan, Beelzebub, Asmodeus, Moloch, Lucifer, Pan Lord of the Incubae, Lilith Lady of the Succubi, and all other infernal Powers. In witness whereof, I sign with my blood.'

Faustin took the little pen-knife, pressed the point into his left palm, caught the drop of blood on the quill, and then, with never a backward glance, he signed the pact.

Everything had vanished. Faustin was alone in the little hut, vaguely aware that he had been dreaming. The effects of the sleeping-pill had not quite worn off; he yawned and crept further under the blankets.

A few hours later, his alarm-watch woke him. For a moment or two he did not know where he was, and he smiled wryly at the nightmare he'd had. Then he stretched out a hand for his head-torch and pressed the button. He stared, rigid with shock: those long, slender hands! He was breathless. There was no mirror in the hut and of course he hadn't brought one. He was so dumbfounded that he fell back on a sequence of simple mechanical acts: he lit the stove, he set the billy of water on it, he made some tea . . . And then he got his gear and set out – to discover now, with joy and astonishment, that his body was transformed and renewed. His every movement was supple, rhythmic, powerful. He felt no sense of strain as he strode down the steep slope to the Brenva Glacier. In the starlight his sense of sight was preternaturally acute: he could make out every minute hold, judge the quality of every scrap of snow or ice. His legs were firm and muscular, his arms strong and supple. Effort brought not pain but happiness – and when he came to the Col Moore, he turned not right towards the Brenva Spur, but quite deliberately left, towards the Peuterey Ridge.

The climbers sprawled on the terrace of the Potinière on that warm early evening would long remember the advent of Yann Faustin on the Chamonix scene. The first manifestation was the long, low, white Maserati which slipped smoothly into the parking space which fell empty, quite by chance, just as he pulled up. A radiantly smiling young man leapt out, in perfectly faded jeans and a spotless, freshly-laundered, white T-shirt. His tan was impeccable and his tousled fair hair blew becomingly in the breeze. With a carefree laugh he flung himself into a chair.

'Hi, Gros Louis!' he said.

Gros Louis, who was very short-sighted but preferred not to wear his glasses in public, replied with every sign of confidence:

'Hi, old man!'

The newcomer's eye fell on Jules and Gilbert, and he reminded them that he'd been in the Argentière Hut a year ago when they were trying to decide whether to do the Tournier Spur. Within seconds, everyone felt that he must be the only one around who didn't remember this striking young man, and the conversation picked up again. Gilbert, all southern verve, was just describing how that morning he'd been on the Brenva Ridge and seen someone soloing up the North Face of the Blanche, straight up and over the bergschrund.

'And he didn't even hesitate, you know, just straight up over the bergschrund! And you know what an overhang there is there at the moment! And then he went up towards the Peuterey Ridge. Must have been on the summit of Mont Blanc by twelve at the latest!'

'Half past eleven,' said Yann, with a slight laugh.

It took them a moment to realize that he was talking about himself. But the way he told his story, gripping but self-deprecating, held everyone's attention. He'd been on the bergschrund when a great ice-block, the size of a wardrobe, had come thundering down and smashed on the glacier just beside him. He'd been lucky: when it shattered, all the bits had missed him. But his ice-axe had been knocked out of his hand, and he'd only managed to rescue his rucksac with a frantic grab for one strap. He'd had to finish off the route with an ice-dagger and an ice-screw. But still, what an amazing route! He still couldn't get over it! But he was pretty glad to be back, he could tell them! He laughed, and paid for a round of drinks.

It was the beginning of a marvellous life. Even the speed with which his former self was forgotten did nothing to dampen his spirits. He took down his tent early one morning when everyone was asleep – and no-one bothered to ask questions later. He sold his old Renault down at Sallanches, where no-one knew him. He wrote to his employer and his landlady and told them he'd been offered a very promising job abroad and was leaving immediately, and asked the landlady to dispose of his furniture and effects and keep the proceeds to defray expenses. Only one person was likely to ask awkward questions: the tax inspector. Faustin sent off a polite letter and a substantial cheque: conscious of his duties as a citizen, he said, he apologized for not filling in his tax-return, asked the inspector to use the cheque to sort the matter out and to give the residue to the Widows' and Orphans' (Tax Division) Benefit fund. Surprised and touched by this unusually elegant and beneficent act, the inspectorate did, with earnest rectitude, precisely what it had been asked to do.

It took forty-eight hours exactly. By then everything was sorted out, Georges had disappeared for ever, and no-one gave him a thought. Much later he was to know a second's resurrection. A friend asked Yann:

'You're no relation of an old bloke we sometimes see around, are you? He's called Faustin, too – Georges.'

'Never heard of him,' said Yann with a smile.

It was all the obituary that Georges was to get.

There is little need to go into the details of the next few years. Very soon Yann was recognized as the best climber in France, the best in Europe, the best in the world . . . And moreover the best-known. Newspapers snatched at every morsel he told them about his earlier life. He'd been born in Iceland where his father was consul, then brought up all over the world, wherever his parents were posted. His upbringing had left him very cosmopolitan, and with a remarkable knowledge of languages. He'd been orphaned early, but he'd been left an apparently inexhaustible fortune which grew effortlessly under his control. He dreamt up ingenious and profitable climbing-aids; he lent his name to a range of sportswear, then to casual wear in general; he set up his own factories, then devised a distribution network which soon had world-wide coverage. Everything he touched turned to gold.

But fame and fortune did nothing to spoil his charm and good nature. He never sought publicity. In fact he remained natural, unspoilt, hail-fellow-well-met, and was always ready to give due weight to his seconds and his teammates. Everyone liked him. His business career might be highly successful, but he was always quite ready to fly back from New York or Tokyo so as not to miss a planned ski-trip. And once back he was the driving force, never tired, never down-hearted, always good-tempered and cheerful.

For the mountains remained his great love, and no wealth, no fame, no love-affair (and they were many) ever distracted him for long. He did all the great Alpine routes with consummate ease. Weather and conditions were nearly always right for him; he became known as a lucky beggar. He did the aspirant guides' course and the guides' course (a pointless formality really, but one cannot buck the system) and graduated from both in top place, with the highest marks ever awarded. He took part in a number of expeditions, national and international, in the Andes, the Caucasus, and of course the Himalaya. His was the rope that did the first ascent of the North-West Face of Nuptse (until then thought to be unclimbable) and of the Fifth Ridge of Ama Dablam. The whole world gasped when it learned he'd done the first winter ascent of Everest, solo and without oxygen. He took part in a number of dramatic rescues; on one occasion, single-handed, he saved eight of the world's best climbers who had been stranded on the North Face of the Eiger by appalling weather conditions.

Yann never tired of success. He'd spent so many frustrating years in part one of his existence that he could only savour every second of existence number two. And so, carefree and triumphant, the years slipped away . . .

It was Margot's death that seemed to dim Yann Faustin's zest for life. Few Alpine tragedies have ever combined such drama and such romance.

Yann, of course had had countless affairs – a modern Don Juan, his every appearance was greeted by a bevy of frenzied and nubile young women. But not one of his conquests had he ever taken seriously. Margot Buthiers was different. She was neither one of the liberated tom-boys who haunt Alpine circles, nor one of the beautiful animated clothes-horses who hang on the arms of celebrities the world over. Margot was young and lovely and pure. Yann fell deeply in love with her at first sight; he took her climbing, and she turned out to be a natural. Gossip-columns followed every phase of their courtship, every route they did.

It was not long before there was talk of marriage. Yann was getting on for thirty-two, still young enough not to give too much thought to the fate that awaited him. It hung on the horizon, of course, and occasionally flickered across his consciousness – a faint but very distant menace, so distant that Yann could ignore it and think only of his happiness with Margot.

It was then that he decided that Margot should do the North Face of the Jorasses. It was in excellent condition; the Walker was fully pegged up, the weather forecast was good. Margot was very fit and should have no trouble, especially since she would not need to do any depegging. And in any case Yann would be beside her all the way, ready to look after her.

The bad weather came down out of a clear sky just above the Black Slabs. They were already too high for retreat to be possible. Yann knew they would have to go on up, although he would probably have to help his companion on the more awkward pitches. The wind rose and howled round them, hurling flurries of stinging hail. Verglas formed on every hold. The cold became ever more bitter, but the climbing was delicate and they had to climb bare-handed. The wind and the cold sapped the girl's strength surprisingly quickly. At first Yann remained quietly confident and simply redoubled his own efforts. He swarmed up every pitch, belayed himself, then fixed a rope down to Margot and came down to show her the holds and give her moral support. She still had a remnant of will-power, but she was visibly flagging and she whimpered like a child as the storm tugged at her.

Yann was still convinced he could save her, at whatever cost to himself, but he suffered agonies with her. For the first time in twelve years he was at a loss. Should he call on God, or on the Devil? Too late . . .

When night fell they were still well below the summit. They would have to bivouac on a narrow, sloping, snow-covered ledge. To save time Yann was tempted to solo the next few pitches and set up fixed ropes, but Margot could not do without him. He settled her in the least uncomfortable corner of the ledge, belayed her securely, wrapped both duvets and all the spare clothing round her, tucked her into a bivouac sack and spent the whole night melting snow to make cups of hot tea; she sipped them with difficulty. Every so often he abandoned the stove to massage her feet and hands; as the circulation was restored she could not control her moans.

Never had any bivouac seemed so endless! But things were no better the following morning. The face was thick with verglas and every hold was iced up. The wind still whined round them and the cold was still intense. The cloud was all round them: no hope of a rescue helicopter. They could only go on. The summit was a mere three hundred metres away, but in conditions like these, that meant several hours of desperate climbing. And below them, hidden in the cloud, were a thousand metres of impossible descent.

Yann tied Margot's rope for her, got her dressed, conjured a little watery smile from her, gave her a sip of coffee and a bite to eat, and went on. It was even worse than the previous day. He could not climb fast enough to prevent Margot, back on the belay ledge, from being overcome by cold and exhaustion, and every time Yann came sliding back down the abseil rope, he would find her lolling on the peg, her eyes closed. He had to wake her up, shake her, bully her into climbing again.

At two o'clock that afternoon, he realized that Margot's hands in the mittens he'd given her were horribly swollen with frost-bite. They could go no further. He spent the last few hours of daylight rigging up another bivouac. She was weakening rapidly. In the middle of the night she was delirious. Meaningless words and phrases tumbled out, punctuated by whimpers:

'The forest – the field – we won't climb again, will we, Yann? – Shall we get married, Yann? – look at that lovely little chalet . . .'

She died as the first faint light crept across the sky.

A few hours later the weather began to lift. A few scraps of blue appeared through the heavy clouds. No-one ever knew how Yann had managed to haul her lifeless body to the summit of the Jorasses, or how he brought her safe down the snow-covered slopes of the south face. He stumbled into the

Boccalatte Hut as pale as death, his face haunted, with what remained of his intended wife held close against his heart.

He never got over it. Life resumed its course, and the mountains were not forgotten – but the vital eager Yann Faustin was no more. Everyone assumed he knew the reason why; the only puzzling thing was that Yann's grief seemed to grow with the years, rather than diminish.

In point of fact, of course, Yann's preoccupation was two-fold. On the one hand there was his real and heart-felt grief; on the other, a new sense of disquiet, until now masked by his self-confident happiness. His brush with death, its snatching away of the person nearest to him when as usual he had remained invulnerable, had been a terrible blow.

Not a night now passed but he spent it meditating on life and death and afterlife. Others could at least shelter behind doubt or uncertainty. He alone *knew*. No longer could he doubt the existence of his immortal soul, since he had sold it for the aptly named mess of pottage, no longer could he doubt the existence of the Devil and therefore of God. He might have wondered if he'd dreamt that night in the Fourche Hut – but he had proof in his transformation from the grey Georges Faustin into the flamboyant Yann Faustin. In any case it was pointless to rack his brain for rational explanations: it had all been decided, once and for all, on that strange night in La Fourche.

The twentieth century had paid little attention to the Devil; hoping that earlier ages might have been more specific and more helpful, Yann threw himself into avid research. He bought books on philosophy and theology and metaphysics; he haunted libraries and second-hand book shops. His sources agreed on one thing: in any lifetime there came moments of decision, anodyne and innocent on the surface perhaps, but fundamentally irrevocable. None of his readings gave any clue as to how to dodge the consequences of decision.

One day he was in Paris and walked past a church. He made up his mind suddenly; he would act as so far he had hesitated to do, consult a priest and find out what remedy the Church might suggest. He was at the end of his tether; he'd drunk a little too much the previous evening, he'd been unable to sleep, and the only recourse, he felt, was a specialist. Until that moment his contacts with the Church had been infrequent and perfunctory: a few duty funerals or weddings. And since that night at La Fourche, he'd felt a certain reluctance . . . But childhood memories evoked a vision of a priesthood which knew all about heaven and hell. Only to a priest could he admit the true cause of his distress.

In the sacristy he found a little notice telling him to apply to the reception office across the road. He found this faintly annoying: the setting would be out of kilter. An elderly lady sitting behind a desk asked him to wait while she contacted a priest. She didn't, to his chagrin, seem to recognize him . . .

The priest was an anonymous figure, in jacket and slacks; he ushered him into a little modern office. The setting made Yann's predicament seem even more outlandish.

'Father . . .' he began. He stumbled over the unfamiliar words and choked to a halt.

'Well?' said the priest.

'I've got this dreadful problem . . . I . . . well, I . . . I hardly know how to put it. I've . . . sold my soul to the devil.'

The priest stared at him, then started on a long and practiced speech. Man, he said, was always free, and no choice he could make would condemn him utterly; true 'Evil' (the Devil if Yann preferred) was always present in the world and in ourselves, but until the very last moment it was never too late, and in the sight of God, if the sinner truly repented . . .

'But it *is* too late,' cried Yann, 'I've seen the Devil himself, and he'd got horns just like in the stories!'

'Now listen . . .'

'No!' Yann was shouting. 'And to prove it, I've been given another life!'

'Now calm down,' said the priest, visibly flustered, 'you'd better make another appointment and we'll talk about the whole thing when we've got more time. But first . . .'

When Yann came out into the street, he had in his pocket a sheet of paper with the name, address and telephone number of an eminent psychiatrist. He'd promised to ring for an appointment and then come back to the priest. He tore it up and never came back. He'd had such high hopes – might there be some sort of miracle? – and all he'd got was doubts about his sanity. He must bear his burden alone, and every day the burden became heavier.

And yet life went on. Yann continued to make money, effortlessly and mechanically. He led clients on routes, did some high-class climbing of his own, took part in rescues, gave slide-lectures, introduced his own films, signed his own books. But it was all routine, all curiously joyless. He started drinking. The lines etched themselves deeper and deeper into his face. Younger men came eagerly onto the climbing scene and displaced him, but he scarcely cared. Yann no longer looked outwards; his life had narrowed to a long, dark tunnel.

At long last summer came round again: the twenty-fourth summer. And the actual anniversary of the act crept nearer. On the day itself, Yann packed his rucksack and set off for La Fourche. He'd see the Devil, and offer him anything, anything at all, if he would only release him from the pact . . .

When it became known in the valley that Faustin had disappeared, no-one had any clear idea where to look for him. The weather was bad, so there could be no helicopter search. When a mechanic in the téléphérique station said he'd seen Yann setting off alone with his gear, a rescue team was sent up to search the Vallée Blanche and Combe Maudite. Almost by chance they stumbled on his body lying crumpled at the foot of the path up to the Fourche Hut. The rescuers put the remains in a bag; nobody seemed eager to say very much. The official report spoke of 'multiple injuries'. One of the guides who'd been in the rescue team was less discreet. 'The body,' he said, 'looked as if it had been clawed to pieces . . .'

A Storm From The East

By David Roberts

TAKE BACK the hope you gave, – I claim
Only a memory of the same. *Browning*

He cast upstream into the eddying pool under the tussock-heavy bank, pulled the line in, and felt the bite. He cast again and hooked the trout. Not a large one, he judged, as he played it in; but now there's one for each of us for dinner. If she's sick of glop, maybe she'll like trout. He flipped the fish up into the weeds, dropped his pole, found the thing thrashing in the grass, got the hook out (only a shallow lip catch) and broke the fish's neck backwards.

The sun set behind the square-shaped peak – only a number still in Bonney – which he had planned for their last climb tomorrow. He cleaned the fish in the cold water quickly, throwing the guts and eggs into the weeds, running his thumbnail up inside the spine to get the last pockets of blood. His knees hurt from squatting, and he thought suddenly, with regret, about his wife. Aching knees, the nag of an old pulled muscle, familiar pains in places where youth was painless: marriage, his own marriage, ten years old this month. He had often said to her, 'We have to go to the Wind Rivers some time. You'd love it.' But for all those early years in Alaska – those expeditions on which he had dragged her, half-willing; those days when she would sit in base camp and read long novels waiting for him to get back from some 'important' climb – they had never found time to go to the Wind Rivers together. Now he was here with Diane instead.

He strung the two ten-inch trout on a piece of parachute cord and pushed his way through the hip-high grass, still wet from the afternoon thunder-shower, back toward the trail. She hates fighting so, he thought, that we can't even talk about what's wrong. It's not just that she's only nineteen, not just that her beauty has kept her spoiled and sheltered all her life; it's not the little things that she complains about, like her back pains or her period. We're wrong for each other, and I can't let her go. He touched the soaked knees of his breeches. They'll dry out a little in the tent this evening, he thought, then some more on the way up to the climb tomorrow, if it's nice, with the sun behind us. He glanced at an unnaturally clean opening in the trees beside the trail. Better than the old-time horse-packing fishermen's camp sites, with their nailed-up hitching posts, tin cans, over-sized fireplaces, grills and even coffee pots left behind, yes. But you could spot a NOLS* solo site almost as

* National Outdoor Leadership School

easily: the fire-scarred rocks carefully scattered, the paperless deposits of plainly human shit, a certain rearrangement of the pine needles. You ought to be glad, he reflected, still to be able to have a whole cirque to yourself in the Wind Rivers in July. But it was harder fishing now, thanks to NOLS. He remembered Petzoldt, thirteen years ago, an Outward Bound instructor so zealous he helped his boys clean their tents for points toward the patrol competition, bragging coyly about 'some places I know up in Wyoming where you could run a *real* wilderness school.' Himself a nineteen-year-old then, precociously instructing students older than himself, listening in the mess hall whenever the legendary man talked – all the more legendary because of those vanished years not even his best friends knew how he'd spent (or so the older instructors said). Himself asking shyly for stories about the early days in the Tetons, about whether they might have made it on K2. ('Charlie wanted to go down. I didn't,' Petzoldt had said, and that was that.) Now the old man had been kicked out by his own board of directors, the fish were scarcer in the Wind Rivers, and he himself was growing tired of 'real' climbing.

'Diane,' he said as he approached the tent. 'Are you awake? Look.'

Her face appeared at the zippered door. Her hair was down, long and loose and dishevelled the way he liked it best. Her beauty made his chest constrict. He held up the fish; she smiled. 'Good,' she said. 'I was getting hungry.'

'Let's cook inside,' he said. 'It looks like it might rain again.'

'That was great,' she said in the candle-lit tent. 'They're best when they're fresh.'

He kissed her, feeling the reluctance in her unopened lips. 'I hope it's nice tomorrow. I'd like to do that buttress.' This was the only level on which they could talk, and even here the wrongness was leaking through.

'It's not all that important to me,' she said.

'It'll be fun. It doesn't look hard. Maybe 5.4 or so, at the top.'

She crawled further into the double sleeping bag. 'How many days do you think it'll take to hike out?'

'Probably one and a half.' There was a silence. 'Why?'

'No reason.'

He waited, fighting his own urge to nag the thing open. He wished he had something to drink. That itself was alarming; only in the last year or two had he begun to miss booze when he was in the mountains. (And Petzoldt, a teetotaller in 1963, had gotten drunk last year in a bar in Lander and picked a fight . . .) 'What are you going to do after?' He tried to ask the question gently.

'I don't know.' She stretched lazily. His fingers stroked her hair, which sparked in the candle-light. She wouldn't look at his face. 'Take off somewhere. Maybe go see my brother in Utah.'

'Hitch?'

'Whatever. I'm almost broke.'

He resisted the impulse to offer to drive her to Utah. It was no good hanging on like that. If in the fall, she came back . . . 'I love you, Diane.' A single drop of rain fell on the tent fly. She smiled, avoiding the ritualistic answer. 'Do you want to read?' he asked, running his fingers through her hair.

'No. I'm really tired.'

'I'll blow out the candle then.'

She lay in the darkness with her back to him, passively accepting his arm under her head, the other around her waist. He listened to the rain drops, gathering and spattering; a slight wind came up, shaking the fly. The strong acrid scent of the snuffed candle was all through the tent. He put his hand on her left breast, clasped it through the cotton shirt; his fingers moved, admiring its shape. 'Would you like to make love?' he asked, dreading and knowing her answer.

She took a long time with her silence. Was it real conflict, he wondered for the hundredth time, or only her horrid idea of tact, finding the softest way to say no? 'Not really,' she said at last. 'I've still got a headache, and I'm really tired.'

'All right.' His hand lay still on her breast. She'll make someone a perfect hypochondriac wife, he thought bitterly; but because of her looks, he'll take it and keep taking it just as I do.

'I'm sorry,' she said. 'Maybe it's the altitude.'

'It's just–' He cut himself off.

'What?'

'Never mind.'

'No, go ahead and say it.'

'It's just that we haven't much.' His exasperation felt like the near edge of tears. 'I could understand when you were having your period. But we used to so much more. And remember how we talked about this trip, about being together so completely?' She was stiff in his arms. 'I want you all the time, Diane.'

She took a deep breath, the up-tight, scolding kind. 'It wasn't just my period. It's something about this double bag. I always feel the presence of your wife in it.'

'I wish you wouldn't always call her "my wife". She's got a name.'

'Oh, fuck.' The rain came down harder. Perhaps there would be no last climb. Another day in camp, then out? What did it matter? There had to be a last one of everything.

'Look,' he said, trying to steer back toward calmness. 'That shouldn't bother you. We've separated, it's probably over. I don't think there's much chance of us ever getting back together.' He laughed softly, without humour. 'I gave her the typewriter, she gave me the sleeping bag.'

'It's not my fault,' Diane said.

'What?'

'Your separating.'

'No. Nothing's your fault, not when you're nineteen.'

She was silent again, and he could read the anger in her rigidity. He apologized; 'It's not your fault. We would have split anyway.'

'Let's not fight.'

'No, I don't want to either.'

'Let's go to sleep and hope it's nice tomorrow,' she said.

He buried his face in the hair at the nape of her neck. 'Let's do sleep. I love you, Diane.'

In the night he had his usual fishing dream. He was with his father, and then he wandered off from his father, as usual, to find the best spot on the lake. With every cast he caught something: the fish were, as usual, too large, multicoloured monstrous inedible things. The hooks were hard to get out, the fish flipped wildly before he killed them, their necks were too strong, he didn't want them, he had to catch them for his father.

The dream changed, however. He caught a small delicate lovely fish, a soft thing with green and brown shades along its sides. He looked at it, and saw grey human eyes, pleading eyes. His wife's eyes? He put it back in the water, coaxing it to live. The fish shivered, started to swim, reeled on its side, its belly up, the colour of skin.

He awoke abruptly and lay for a long moment in terror. His arms were around Diane still, who slept on. The rain had stopped. He took deep breaths deliberately, making the dream dissolve, and closed his eyes and begged for sleep and for sun in the morning.

'Diane,' he said, shaking her shoulder, 'wake up. It's perfect. Let's eat fast and get started.' The air in the tent was awash with orange.

Diane opened her eyes. He drank in her young face, its boldness unaffected by a smear of charcoal under one eye. 'Oh, no,' she laughed easily, stretching. 'I wanted to sleep late.'

'The sooner we start, the less chance of getting into a storm,' he said. fussing with the stove. 'It'll be a fine climb. It's a natural line.'

'All right, you.' Diane sat up and poked him playfully in the ribs, as she had when things had been best between them, months before. 'Man, did I sleep. I was one tired little girl.' Without self-consciousness, she whisked her cotton pullover over her head, leaving herself naked from the waist up while she rummaged for a clean turtleneck. He gazed at her breasts with a remorseful longing.

Later, as they walked briskly toward the buttress, traversing a meadow fresh with the scent of marsh marigolds, he turned to her and said, 'I had a bad dream last night. About my wife.'

'See. You call her that, too.'

'I was being ironic.' He didn't want to share the dream, after all.

'What happened?'

'It was strange. She was a fish.'

Diane laughed out loud. 'What a beautiful day. Do you have to go so fast, though? Take it easy and enjoy life.'

He slowed his pace, brooding on the dream. Why did his father wander off, always, in the repeated script? But no, it was he who wandered off, to find the best fishing. He knew he felt guilt about the separation, and he had had disturbing dreams before, but none quite so distressful as this one. All those years she had waited for him to come back from climbs, marking time until the phone call from Alaska, performing her superstitious housewifely mantras in aid of his safety. As Diane would never have to do. What a waste of years, of love, of the idealized freedom he had sought from them, his mountains, rather than from her. But it was too late; there had been too many failed reconciliations already, and if he went back and told her that things had fallen through with Diane, it was not enough of a change to bring them back together.

The climb was a little harder than he had expected. Leading each pitch, he became absorbed as of old in the intricacies of protection, and despite his poor shape, found he was enjoying himself. On each belay ledge, as he watched Diane climb skilfully up toward him, he admired her grace and talent, so far beyond the shaky determination his wife had shown early in their marriage when he had hauled her up 5.3's at the Gunks. Yet for all her malaise, those climbs had had magical import for her; for Diane climbing was just a sport, another outdoor game she did well, like skiing or tennis. The very things that had made him fall in love with her – her youth, her skill, her beauty – now irked him. He found himself perversely wishing that a given move would cause her more trouble than it actually did.

At 10:00 a.m., atop the sixth pitch, he noticed suddenly that the valley below, far to the east, was filling with dark clouds. They themselves remained in perfect sunshine, but the clouds were clearly moving west and rising. A deep premonition of danger passed over him: the very worst storms on Longs Peak came from the east, in mid-morning; and once before in the Front Range a storm had chased him from below and from the east, the lightning beneath him, rising and engulfing him as he scrambled upwards to escape it.

When Diane joined him, he said, 'I don't like the looks of those clouds.'

She turned and stared. 'Why? It's just fog, down in the valley.'

'Look how fast it's moving.'

He climbed the next pitch with greater haste than he normally would have, protecting it sloppily. At the top he belayed her, and grew impatient with her deliberate pace. Just as she joined him again, they heard the first rumbles of thunder. The tiny orange rectangle of their tent below had vanished in the clouds.

'Look, Diane, we've got to move faster. It would be best to be off this thing by the time the storm hits.'

For the first time her face showed apprehensiveness. 'Maybe we should go down.'

'No, that's crazy,' he said, irritable because he really wasn't sure. 'I don't like the anchor we'd have to use on the third pitch, and I don't like rappelling in lightning.' Yet he didn't want to be out on the plateau at the top either. 'Let's move.'

But he was out of shape and took a long time figuring out a 5.7-ish move. All at once the clouds whooshed upwards by him, bringing a dank wind and obliterating the sun. Just before he reached a belay ledge the rain began:

heavy, isolated drops like hail. He got in a good three-nut anchor and started belaying Diane. He could tell by her hurried movements that she was scared now, too. Lightning flashed beneath them, and the thunder cracked, less than two seconds behind. The rain suddenly became furious, blinding his glasses and soaking his cotton shirt. He tugged on the rope, playing Diane in toward him. Her feet slipped on the hard move; he hauled her back up to it and past it.

She arrived breathless, just as another flash of lightning struck somewhere beneath them. 'What should we do?' she said, her voice hinting panic.

'Wait it out here. Clip in and get on your sweater and cagoule. Off belay?' He dug the clothes out of the pack, put on his own, helped Diane with hers. 'There's only about a pitch left,' he said. 'Let's hope this just goes by us and off to the west.'

'Are we safe here, do you think?'

'Relatively.' As if in refutation, a bolt struck, simultaneous with its deafening report. 'Fuck,' he muttered, 'that was close.'

'Aren't you scared?' Diane asked. She leaned against him, and he felt her shoulders shaking slightly.

'Yeah. It's exciting, too. Look at it.' He watched the wildly rushing vertical columns of mist, saw as through water the illumination of a distant spear of lightning. But Diane kept her head huddled against his chest. 'In Harlin's article about the Eiger, they see this storm coming that they think means they've had it. He talks about wanting to watch it right to the end, absorb everything that's going on. I understand him.' He put his arm around the rain-slick cagoule on her back.

'What's that?' She sat up suddenly. He heard it too: the faint whining from the metal things they carried. His hair was tingling, and the zipper of his cagoule was scratching his lip with electricity.

'Crouch,' he said, 'so that only your feet are touching.' She moved slightly away from him and obeyed.

'Shouldn't we get rid of the hardware?' she yelled.

'No, that's superstition.' He tried to assess the ledge they were on. The only thing wrong with it was that, like the buttress itself, it protruded eastward into the storm. He gave himself ten feet of slack in his anchor and said, 'I'm going to look around the corner.' He shuffled away from Diane and reached the end of his tie-in. He was just a foot short of being able to see around the corner. He leaned on his right hand and peered.

He never heard the crash. For a second it seemed that he was glued to the rock by the leaning hand. An awful clarity lit the rock face before him, cleaning his brain of all thought. Then it was dark.

He woke instants, centuries, later. Unanchored, Diane was weeping, holding him. 'What happened?'

'It hit us,' she said hysterically. 'The lightning hit us!'

'It couldn't have. We'd be dead.' His right hand hurt. He looked at it and saw the seared whiteness of burned skin all over his palm and fingers. He tried to move the hand, but his whole arm was numb. Yet he felt comparatively calm. 'Are you all right?' he asked Diane.

'Yes. Oh, Jesus, I thought you were dead! Your whole body twitched, and you hand was stuck to the rock. Then I thought you were dead.'

'My hand's burned. It must have struck the rock near me, and I got the ground current.'

'Let's see.' She took his hand, saw the burn, and started crying again. Another flash of lightning came, a bit above them. She whimpered, and he himself felt a new surge of fear. He wondered what was wrong with his arm. In the moment of electrification, it had seemed as though the answer to some important question had been placed suddenly before his eyes, there in the clarified seams of granite. But what had it been?

'You should be anchored,' he said. 'How bad is this burn?'

She stopped crying. 'It looks like it hurts.'

'It doesn't. Not yet. Didn't you get any?'

'I felt the charge, but that was all. Are you hurt anywhere else?'

'My toes are numb.' He looked at his boots. 'And I've got a headache.'

'We were lucky.'

'Yes. It's going by us, I think. Even the rain's letting up.' He squinted upwards. 'I can't use my arm much, though. Can you lead this last pitch, after the rain stops?'

'I'll try.' Her voice was regaining its self-assurance.

They waited. Diane put her arms around him, her cheek against the hooded side of his head. Slowly the numbness of his hand woke into pain. He felt nauseous for a moment, and was afraid he would faint. The rain stopped; gradually the clouds diffused, and all at once the sun broke through.

'Can you?' he asked.

'Give me the hardware.' They stuffed their cagoules back in the pack, he awkwardly; using only his left hand, then setting up the belay for his left hand. 'Just pull the rope' he said. 'I can't feed it very well.'

As she started climbing, he realized how scared she was. Her calves trembled as she stood on small footholds, and she wasted time finding the right piece of protection, fumbling angrily with karabiners. What if she can't do it, he pondered. What if we have to back off this whole goddam thing? But she seemed to gain confidence with each move, and after a while he knew that she was going to finish the pitch. Beyond the plateau, invisible to the west, the storm moved on, retreating with increasingly distant thunder. The raw smell of ozone was all through the air.

Back in the tent in the late afternoon, Diane slept from sheer exhaustion. He stirred a pot of soup idly with his left hand. He had taken a codeine pill for the pain, and he felt a giddy euphoric drowsiness. Most of the feeling had come back to his arm, so that he could move it all right; the burn was the real nuisance. He had taken off his boots and looked at his feet; there were tiny burns on the soles, roughly along the semi-circular lines of the boot nails. Painful for walking tomorrow, but not impossibly so.

As he looked at her lovely sleeping face, his thoughts wandered backwards. In the spring, when things had been going well between them (and so badly with his wife, just before the separation), he had thought that this kind of trip might substitute for the more serious climbing he was starting to turn his back on. That love might give the climbing purpose, as jaded ambition no longer could. Yet, he reflected, it had not been love, but danger, the accident, that had given the day meaning, that had turned an ordinary climb into an act of love.

The soup began to boil; he turned down the stove and scraped the pot bottom with his spoon. His wife would never have been able to lead that last pitch. Yet the one time in his life when he had come closest to fulfilling his romantic ideal had come with her: the three weeks they had spent alone together, eight years ago, paddling a Klepper kayak the lengths of those two huge fiord-like lakes in the remotest corner of southwestern Alaska, neither of them at home on water, himself unable to swim. That was the closest to love . . . love instead of ambition. But he had not known it then. He had only been twenty-three. Because of that ambition he had seen in her fear of bears, her hatred of mosquitoes, her nervous waking in the night, only silly obstacles to further penetration into the coves and corners of the lakes, up towards the nameless mountains to the west.

In the middle of the night Diane woke him. She had taken off all her clothes and was removing his. He struggled to be awake, to make sure it was not a dream. She was crying and kissing him. He helped her pull his breeches and underpants off, and let her touch and kiss him all over. 'Don't hurt your hand,' she whispered, moving inside the cavern of heavy down and nylon. At last she turned and lay on her back; he hovered over her, leaning on his left hand, while she held him and guided him into her. 'Oh, Christ, Diane, I love you so much,' he said. She moved under him, moaning quietly, and he took all the time he could, delaying and waiting and starting again, because he knew this would be the last time.

A couple of miles down the trail the next morning, he turned for a last look at the cirque where they had spent nine days. The calm morning sun shone on the grey granite; automatically, his eyes still sought out routes and lines, and he stared for a while at the 800-foot buttress on which they had probably made the first ascent. Diane paused too, looking back. 'How's your hand?' she asked politely.

'Okay.' He held it up. 'The burn's starting to scab.' His feet were tender, but not in very much pain.

'If you want another codeine, tell me,' she said. 'I've got the medical kit somewhere.'

He looked at her; she glanced away from his gaze. 'Should we name our route?'

'Whatever you think,' she said.

'I'm against names. There are too many already. I like numbers just as well.'

They survive, he thought, all our ways of using them. They stand there, aloof and inhuman, while we stretch our lives across them, and come close to death, perhaps, for the wrong reasons, with the wrong companions. They've withstood all the ways Petzoldt himself came to them, from his first boyish forays when they were as wild as the Arctic, to the last years when he filled them with boys in the name of profit. And they'll survive my own uses, from the time with Michael ten years ago when we had the Cirque of the Towers to ourselves for two weeks and measured our sights against Beckey's routes and Robbins' traverse, to these nine days with Diane, to whatever use I'll find for them twenty years from now. They shine under the sun and stand there, waiting for us to figure ourselves out. He looked at Diane. Already she was turning back to the downward trail, impatient to hike on out.

Midges

by G. J. F. Dutton

MIDGES HAVE been much maligned. They not only protect us, provide an unsleeping Air Umbrella for our precious West Highland scenery: they can also help us to a First Ascent – or to understand what a First Ascent is really about. They are great teachers of ethics. As we discovered to our cost. Although we made that First Ascent – the Best-Seller of its day – with the help of midges, we were ashamed of ourselves, the Apprentice and I; we still are.

Yet, as a Munro is a Munro, so a First Ascent is a First Ascent, and nowadays nobody is perfect; moreover, the germ, so to speak, of this biological weapon emanated from the Doctor, hitherto so upright a man. He was not in the climbing team – the grade was too high – he was Base for the expedition; Base indeed. But he ensured our success; if it can be called a success when the vanquished, however disreputable, trudge off with the moral victory.

Enough of snivelling. To the story. It is a lesson for all climbers. It should be told. For, as the Doctor observed by the Primus that evening, peering into his glass through a penumbra of equally thirsty uncountables: 'Too much competition – *poogh* – tends to obscure the – *poogh* – essential Spirit.'

The Apprentice had to cross to Harris for that first ascent. His fellow-Weasels were Alpineering and rivals were athirst. So I joined him; the crux coming last, I could at worst be hauled over it. The Doctor was there to cook, and watch the fun.

The weather steamed close and cloudy, after weeks of cold rain. We waded over a sopping hill, and the great cliff Sròn a' Mheanbh-Chuileag rose imperturbably before us. Our eyes scurried nervously about it. No one was there. We would be first! Straight up the centre unrolled the only possible line, Leac Mhòr, the Great Slab, that unclimbed new discovery everyone was raving about. It had been attempted only the week before by a couple of teams but, as the Apprentice pointed out, they came from Glasgow. They had, nevertheless, pioneered as far as the crux. *That* appeared impossible – it jerked outwards above us like a vast flight of stone steps seen upside down from underneath.

'Great,' declared the Apprentice, a little hoarsely.

We splashed down to the river gravel for a meal. Our domestic help began to make jammy pieces and set up the tent. The Apprentice and I, adhesive from sweat and apprehension, stripped and plunged into a fine bellowing pool, frothy with spate.

'Don't!' called the Doctor. 'It's dangerous!'

We looked at each other. We had all of us forded and swum (often by accident) much fiercer water than this. The Doctor had now turned not only cook but nursemaid. Nonsense. Perfectly safe.

'The midges!' he shouted. 'They'll get you when you come out.'

So what? We two were going up the Slab, not festering round the tent like him.

As we munched our pieces, vastly refreshed, and insulated by the Doctor's unseen rucksack from infinite bog, we ridiculed his prognosis. Ah, but immersion, he averred, removed the body's protective layer of oils. 'You mean dirt?' suggested the Apprentice, through his crumbs. 'Exactly!' It appeared that the accumulated greases of the skin impeded midgy mandibles. They found it difficult to sook. Washed, we would be a naked lunch to unnumberable multitudes of Chironomidae. This place in this weather would generate the most ravenous midges within the whole lengthy jurisdiction of *An Comhairle nan Eilean*. The Doctor had already identified them as the two worst of the whole bloodsucking bunch, *Culicoides heliophilus* and *Culicoides impunctatus*. So there.

A few of the brutes had already appeared that morning. They bit us even in our then well-enough-larded state. As the old man at the last croft had remarked, 'The midges is no very *good* the day.' So we rubbed in more midge-repellent and hurried across to the climb, the Doctor remaining entrenched behind turned-up collar, pipe smoke and Natural Oils.

I do not want to remember the rest of that day. Instead of climbing out of midges, we climbed into them. The Sròn was the west end of a high boggy tableland, its top and sides dribbled with bog; it stood in a bog. So, from bottom, sides and top midges screamed out at us, radars blaring, rockets firing. Faces, hair, necks, ears, eyes, backs of hands, wrists, crawled with a million engines, tracers incessantly stung and flashed. Torture of infinite needles. Jab, jab, jab. Hell, hell, hell; more hell . . .

I gave up half-way, blind and one-handed. The Apprentice lasted a little longer, banging in a runner at the crux. But he ran out of oaths, and midges swarmed into the vacated territory. We spun down, coiled ropes and vanished. Flies were nothing to this.

At the tent, we dived into bags, head and all. The Doctor, puffing valiantly, made supper. Midge-netting kept most outside, and those within – chastened by St. Bruno – congregated along the ridge-seams and were periodically incinerated by a brandished Primus. Numbers gradually decreased. We uncovered heads, warily.

'Midges no very good the day,' observed our companion genially, poking the pot. He remained unchastised, for cooks are the Sacred Fools of climbing, licensed jesters, dear to the belly. And he had warned us.

That night, sleep was fitful; we were iridescent with bites, and refugees wandered wakefully about our hair. The Apprentice tossed, in a rage of frustration. First ascent . . . first ascent . . . and last chance.

We rose late, to a midgeless morning. But the steamy weather promised another yesterday. However, the Doctor had not been idle. He produced two midge-helmets for us: his spare stockings, with slits for eyes. 'And you can wear your own spare socks as gloves, the ends pierced for fingers.' That, and the remaining midge cream, would see us up to – maybe over – the crux, now the way there was familiar. We blessed him as he stirred the porridge, twinkling grand-maternally.

The Apprentice crawled out, stood up, and gazed happily at the Sròn. Then his eyes popped. He groaned, swore, stamped, slapped thighs and cursed again. We all peered out.

Below the crag stood People. We were forestalled. Who?

'No, no; Oh NO!' wailed the Apprentice. 'It's *them*!'

'Who's Them?' asked the Doctor, beginning to regret his slit stockings.

'Wee Dander,' sobbed the Apprentice, '*and* Greetin Jimmie; *and* The Porpus.' He named three legendary figures. 'And there's Else and Big Ian to look after them . . .'

We were suitably silent. Wee Dander was one of those youthful prodigies who – for a few years – climb apparently everything with unstopping ease and no little scorn. More than that, he would never write up his routes, never bother to record them. He had no use for journals or guidebooks, or other people. He was pure Oral Tradition, pure Hero, sheer Me; free as the wind. Hateful, no doubt; but enviable in many ways. His companions tied themselves always second and third on a rope that was invariably the best you could buy, like the rest of his kit – which he never did buy: the three of them, aided by Else and Big Ian, took whatever they needed from any unoccupied tent or car they came across. Hateful. Dangerously enviable.

They saw us and ambled over as we swallowed our now tasteless porridge. Wee Dander was indeed wee, a laddie, in tatty shirt and shorts, with an open expressionless very pale face and uncannily penetrating blue eyes; any age between twelve and seventeen. He bent over and picked a piece of bacon from the pan the Doctor was frying and nibbled it carefully. Then he picked a couple more pieces and threw them to his companions behind. All three masticated in silence.

We looked them over, refusing to speak first. Greetin Jimmie was a long skeletal youth in grubby denims and greasy shirt; his equally oleaginous hair sprawled to a thin pimply face, dreepy red nose and sparse fringe of unappetizing gingery beard – or he may not have shaved that week (it was indeed difficult to imagine him shaving). A dismal enough streak, from knocky knees to watery eyes. The Porpus – round and polished as the playful

Cetacean – bulged from relatively clean sark and shorts; he grinned even while chewing, small pink nose and ears oscillating independently. He rolled an enormous boulder across and sat on it; it was one the Doctor and I had failed to move when pitching the tent.

Before Wee Dander could appropriate more breakfast the Doctor smartly tossed the rest to us. Our guest was then moved to communicate.

'Saw yer runner. Been up, eh?' A hard, clear, raw-fish accent.

The Apprentice, wrestling with honesty, said he'd had a look and come down early, but would be up the day right enough.

'Like hell.' (Pause) 'But thanks fer the runner; nae use here – 'll dae fine fer the Ben next week, though.' (Pause) 'Well; we'll jist awa up. See ya.'

And he sauntered off back to the cliff. Greetin Jimmie nodded morosely at us and followed his leader. The Porpus, still managing the odd chew, beamed and waved a flipper. He clanked away uphill; they were particularly well-equipped that morning, having passed a Mountain Adventure camp the day before.

They paused at our pool. The Porpus gesticulated. He wished to gambol therein. Wee Dander scowled; and was moving away when the Doctor, to our astonishment, leapt up and shouted.

'Hi! Don't go in! It's dangerous . . .'

What the devil? We looked at him bewildered; then at the three. But the Doctor knew his man. Wee Dander stopped dead. His eyes unslung their Kalashnikovs. *He* was not going to be head-mastered by any what-ho! tweed-brandishing establishmentarian.

He stripped off and dived, right into the considerable whirlie under the waterfall; and stayed down a long while to prove his point. The Porpus rolled and splashed, gleaming epidermally, while Jimmie, even dirtier with his clothes off, waded in slowly, rubbing long thin shanks bitterly and fading gradually to a pale shrimp-pink.

The Apprentice smiled for the first time in twenty-four hours. That, of course, is why we climb with the Doctor. A practical man, so *good* with People.

We took it easy. We watched them rope up; we saw Big Ian and Else unfold some sort of encampment on the bog beneath the cliff. We kitted ourselves out, packing midge-helmets and socks carefully, and used up all the midge cream so we needn't tell a lie later. The Doctor stayed to guard the tent. We strolled across in the gathering fug, regarding emergent midges almost benignly. Of course we were a little dirtier now, more naturally repellent . . .

Wee Dander proved a marvellous climber. He was already entering the crux. He would easily get over, he contemptuously pocketed the Apprentice's sling, he flowed with a lovely movement, elastic as rubber. Greetin Jimmie stalked after him like a vertical pond-skater; multilimbed, and impeccably adept at ropework. The Porpus, whose job was never to peel but to hold the others when they did, scuttled like a crab. It was a great team to watch. We felt ourselves almost wishing them success.

Then they began to jerk, increasingly. Early Warnings had sounded, the defenders were busy. Progress slowed, became intermittent. The rope twitched, agonizingly; coiled, uncoiled, gave forth sobs and cries. It was not so nice to watch. A beautiful animal was being done to death. The leader crouched between moves, slapped bare thighs and neck, his second agitated beneath a cloud, the third man beat bongo-drums about his waist-band, jangling in disarray.

We came up to Else, a plump vaguely belligerent Amazon, and Big Ian, even larger and grinning hugely. 'Bloody midges,' he remarked, rubbing with vigour. What went on above was not of great concern to him. Else swore low and continuously, rummaging in an ample knee-length jersey, well adapted to supermarkets.

A great crash above us, and we all fled. Wee Dander, blinded by midgery, had peeled on the final step. Greetin Jimmie, enmeshed in his web, shot up – still scratching – to a sentry box. The Porpus, smacking his backside, sat down in space and held them all; a large sling of Mountain Adventure cutlery had meanwhile slipped off his tray and nearly brained us.

It was a curious sight; three in tension at various angles, writhing and scratching like St. Vitus. Somehow, Wee Dander fought back up, Jimmie slithered down to his stance, The Porpus swam to the surface. But all magic was gone. The lower pair, fisting eyes, faces and limbs in a frenzy, implored their leader to come down. Wee Dander tried again. And again; wiping his forehead – milling with millions – blindly against the cold Precambrian. Terrifying. At the very profile of the last step we watched him slip, slip, recover; slip, recover.

Then he abseiled down. And, yes; we were sorry.

They stood beside us, two of them rubbing and cursing. Wee Dander, his pale face bloodstained, crawling with tormentors, looked straight at us. His teeth had bitten his lips white.

'Any . . . midge . . . cream . . . ?' It must have cost him.

We had used all ours up, the Apprentice explained. He displayed the flattened tube. He did not look at me; nor I at him. Silence.

'Aye,' said Wee Dander.

Else and Big Ian had packed up the tents. They all moved off, hunched and muffled, pummelling zipped anoraks, Wee Dander leading. He slowed, the others overtook him. He stopped, looked back and spun something towards us.

'Yer runner,' he said.

And went on.

We deserved it.

October Day

by K.V. Crocket

HE COULD still remember – how could he forget? – the dusty flakes of lichen from the black rocks. They darkened his fingernails for days, a constant reminder of his adventure. If asked, he could not explain why the rocks attracted him so. It was not as if they were particularly appealing to a skinny fourteen year old, warm only because he was moving, happy only because he was away, for a few hours, from his dominating family life, classically Victorian; stern father, free and easy only with the beatings; timid mother, kind words too late. His sisters Ruth and Ethel were good to him, but they had their own lives to live, on top of which they helped look after Granny. Now *there* was an auld witch! He hated having to give her a kiss every day, what with her hairy chin that looked as if it should scratch but somehow didn't. And close up she smelled funny.

He had school friends of course, you had to, given that the roughs were apt to pick on you on the way home if you travelled alone. The collar and tie picked you out three tenements away – he was never bold enough to do what Wee Jamie did, removing his tie once out of sight of the Teacher, to replace it in the relative safety of one's lane. Though right enough Jamie *did* get caught once by a nosey neighbour, bluffing his way out of it by pretending a coughing fit.

It looked as if this was his last year at school. Soon he would be joining his father in the family business. He would be glad to leave; the petty rules and discipline he found stifling. At school one had to teeter along the narrow path acceptable to the senior pupils and teachers. To be stupid or too clever was equally damning. Once, in a wild bid for spiritual freedom, he let slip his interest in birds, telling the class about the injured blackbird he had found and nursed. How could he communicate his feelings for the poor animal? Its body surprisingly warm, so that he almost dropped it on first picking it up, with its wee heart tripping so fast it should likely burst. The class laughed and he sat down, red-faced, never to mention it again.

Though skinny, he was possessed of a surprising, wiry strength. Later in life, when appreciative of such a build, he would remember his mother Jessie. She was from the Islands, Harris, with the soft speech, music to his ears, contrasting with the coarser, grating cadence of the Lowlands, the faint nasal whine of Edinburgh rising at the end of each sentence like a gust of wind off the Forth. His mother had worked on the family's croft until the age of twenty, when her father had died of one chesty cold too many, pneumonia taking him away effortlessly, as it did so many. Moving to Edinburgh to serve for an aunt, she met her future husband during a Saturday afternoon's stroll in the park. His mother was never heard to complain, no matter the hours spent washing and cleaning, cooking and cleaning, polishing and dusting. She rested, he sometimes thought, while sewing or knitting in the evening, the gas mantle popping and hissing on the kitchen wall.

Sometimes she would hum a working tune from her youth, while father, ink-stained fingers the give-away sign of an office worker, would rustle his evening newspaper in irritation, the while secretly straining to listen. These were the best times at home. And then there were the bad times, with the same old stupid arguments, mostly about money. Clothing for the children had to be bought, Ruth was being courted, while the young boy's jacket from last year was already too small, his thin wrists poking out beyond the leather-reinforced cuffs like the bony joints from which his mother sometimes made the weekly broth. She seldom raised her voice, arguing her case patiently in between her husband's angry outbursts. From her, he realized later, he drew his secret strength and stamina.

Today he was alone. It was a Saturday, the best day of the whole week, with a whole penny to spend and three whole hours to himself. Saturdays were compressed between the weekly tedium of school, with messages and odd jobs to do after school hours, and Sunday, an agonisingly long day of stiff collars, Church sermons and Bible School. No, Saturday was *the* day of the week. His best friend Angus was away to visit relatives in Glasgow, an annual event, given the expense of rail travel, while Wee Jamie was in bed with the chickenpox, visitors forbidden. The elder sister Ruth was 'walking out' with her young gentleman, while his father, who was struggling to make a success as a private brewer, was not due to finish work until 4:30 p.m., Saturday being an early finishing day. His mother, sensing his bottled energy, shooed him out, first making him promise to be home for four o'clock, for in mid-October darkness would not be far behind.

Elated, he headed for the park, fifteen minutes' run away, even for an undersized adolescent. Two weeks ago, he and Angus had almost reached a bird's nest on the rock, before Angus had become frightened at the height reached, insisting on retreat. The rock had been dry, but their leather boots had been next to useless, slipping hopelessly on the smooth basalt. He had been exalted at the situation, twenty feet up the dirty corner that had beckoned, white streaks and an untidy mass of twigs pointing to a nest on a small ledge above. Angus, at his heels, was unhappy from the start, more at home following a smoking tar cart through Edinburgh's dirty streets, or gawking at the life and bustle of the Saturday market area, well-heeled townies contrasting with muddy gaitered farmers, dogs snapping and weans greetin'. Retreat had been tedious, placing Angus's feet and hands on holds – once he had climbed down past him, that is. But today was different; today he had no impediment, save himself. He liked Angus, but he felt that reaching the ledge and its nest was to be a personal challenge.

The day was dry but cold, the wind off the Firth cutting through his cardigan and tweed jacket. Again, he was too young to appreciate his mother's wisdom, and the fitful parcels from the Islands, with their smoky lengths of tweed that could make a warm jacket for a wee boy. His nose was running as he reached the rocks, panting a little from the trot through the park. There had been a crowd of rowdies at the gate, and for a moment his heart shrank at passing through, but then a family sailed into view, out for an hour of appetizing air. These he used as a flanking convoy might do, in the Great War (still 35 years ahead), slinking past his potential trouble-makers, invisible in the crowd. Animal behaviourists in the far-away scientific future would stumble upon this defense mechanism, call it their own, and write learned papers about the advantages of travelling in flocks, schools and herds, but small boys had known and used this survival trick for centuries.

He loved October above all months of the year; its colours and smells, lengthening nights with smoky fogs, gas lights guttering yellow in the streets, hot chestnuts sold from barrows. In the park he raced through deep drifts of fallen leaves, keeping his boots low so as to extend the sound into a satisfying swish, swish.

The corner was still there, as was the pile of twigs above on the ledge. He could see the dry pile of turfs thrown down on their previous visit, fingernails satisfyingly dirty with the effort of prying the grass out of the corner. If pushed to explain why, he would in all probability claim a destructive urge, the same as pushing rocks off a cliff top, or of filling paper bags with water to throw at girls across the playground. He had quickly learned, however, that vegetation often concealed useful holds, flat ledges for their feet, slim cracks for thin fingers.

The start went easily up a corner with ledges, until blocked by a jutting roof. It was from below this obstacle that he and Angus had retreated on the previous occasion. A few feet up and right of this was the ledge and the nest, but first he had to move left on to a smooth pillar then somehow climb up this a short way before the ledge could be gained. He had had no experience until now of real climbing, unless one counted the time a visiting teacher had given them a Magic Lantern show, showing the Geography class a series of Alpine views. The show had been exciting, as much because of the hot and smoky source of light as by the actual views, potentially interesting panoramas made dull by the pontificating Geography teacher. The only climbing shown then had been on the glacier, long alpenstocks and longer skirts, ladders and coiled ropes. Today he remembered none of these things, excited by the battle ahead.

Below the roof there was a small ledge, an average enough specimen of its type, large enough for a rest, too small for comfort. His smooth-soled leather boots could just rest on the ledge without curling up and off, while a flat handhold above allowed some measure of security. There was no one about as he explored the rock about the roof. The wall on the right leaned over, cutting off access that way. The roof above, had he but known it, was possessed of good holds on top, but moves over such obstacles were as yet alien to him, and he perforce looked to the left for a way up. Stretching away up and left, he could just manage to touch the lip of the ledge he wished to gain, but it was such a delicate manoeuvre that each time he reached out he could feel his boots slipping off the ledge.

Looking down he took in the panorama across a swell of roofs, a nearby factory roof with the white-painted name 'Craigside Works'. Long lines of tenements stretched towards the Firth, fading rapidly in the smoky haze that was Industrial Edinburgh. He had been brought up with the mash smell of the breweries, and if asked by a stranger to comment on it would have expressed surprise at the mention of it.

He was cold now and becoming a little frightened. Instinctively he knew that he would have to move soon, or be defeated. Until then he had been keeping both his feet on the ledge, but now he put most of his weight – the little that was – on his hands, and taking his left foot off the ledge shuffled his right boot to its far end. Carefully reaching up with his left hand, he found he was able to grasp the edge of the big ledge. Satisfied, he reversed the sequence of moves and stood squarely on the ledge under the roof. Far away, the tinny sound of a street musician could be heard for a moment, escaping, much as he was, from the narrow streets below. He turned to the left again, blowing on his fingers in turn to warm them. The move out was made again, left hand clamping on to the ledge. It felt secure, and, encouraged, he took his right hand off the familiar hold and reached up. His foot came off just as his right hand touched the ledge beside his left, his right knee banging painfully on the rock. Heart beating wildly, he pulled up with all his desperate, boyish strength, toes scraping the pillar. A clump of grass came into view, but he knew from his previous attempt not to trust its feeble roots. His left elbow was on the ledge now and with his right hand pushing down on the edge, breath rasping, he levered himself slowly over the rim.

When his feet were firmly up on the ledge, his hands grasping a good flake on the wall ahead, he realized what he had done, and to where he had journeyed. He had been frightened, that was true, but not to the point where he had lost control. For a moment, almost too fleeting to remember later, he had been oblivious of everything but the movement, the position, the rock. Some metaphysical barrier had been lowered or weakened, a doorway had been offered, and he had stepped through, and up.

The ledge had been gained, the nest lay ahead, with an exit above to the cliff-top, following an easy groove. There were no eggs, it was an old, abandoned pile of twigs, but strangely he felt no disappointment, moving happily up the final groove. As he raced the setting sun back down through the park, its huge, red orb without heat, he smelled as if for the first time the subtle, peppery odour of the dead leaves, filling his lungs until they would burst, the cold air catching his throat.

Leaving the park, winding through the cobbled streets in the twilight, he knew he was changed. Something had been gained on the rocks, and something lost. He felt strangely older, old for his years. As he swung into his lane, cooking smells kindling a sudden hunger, he knew, with clarity and growing excitement that he would return, would explore further the pleated crags and hills above his smoky city.

Ulrich the Guide (or The Mountain Inn)

by Guy de Maupassant

translated by Alys Hallard

SIMILAR IN appearance to all the other little wood-built inns scattered throughout the Hautes-Alpes just below glacier level in those bare rocky gorges intersecting the snow-capped mountains, the Schwarenbach Inn serves as a refuge for travellers passing through the Gemmi Pass.

During six months of the year it is inhabited by its owner, Jean Hauser, and his family, but as soon as the snow begins to get deep in the valley, so that the road to Loeche is only just practicable, the father and mother with their daughter and three sons leave their little mountain home in charge of two guides, an old man named Gaspard Hari with one of his companions, and Sam, the huge mountain dog.

The two men with their faithful keeper remain until the following spring in their snowy prison, having no other view than the immense white slope of the Balmhorn, surrounded by pale, glittering mountain peaks, until they are finally shut up, blocked, as it were, buried under the snow, which heaps itself up around them, and then presses close round the little house, bars the door, reaches the windows, and, in fact, wraps the inn round completely in its white mantle, and then falls thickly on the roof.

On the day when Hauser and his family set out on their journey back to Loeche, the winter had set in, and the descent was not without danger. The three sons went on first with the mules laden with luggage; then came Jeanne Hauser and the daughter, Louise, mounted on another mule.

The two guides walked behind with the father, for they were going to escort the little family to the beginning of the descent. They passed by the frozen lake which is between the great rocks near the inn, and then they continued along the valley, which looked like an immense white sheet, on each side of which rose the snowy peaks. A flood of sunshine fell on the white, shining, frozen desert, lighting it up with a cold, blinding flame. There was no sign of life in this ocean of mountains, no movement in this vast, measureless solitude. Not a sound broke the profound silence.

Gradually the young guide, Ulrich Kunsi, a tall, strong-looking Swiss with long legs, got ahead of Hauser and old Gaspard Hari, and overtook the mule on which the two women were riding. The younger of them watched him advancing, and a happy light shone in her eyes. She was a pretty young girl, but her fair hair and her pale cheeks looked as though they had lost their colour through these long sojourns in the mountains surrounded by ice and snow. When Ulrich had overtaken them he slackened his pace and walked alongside of them, his hand resting on the crupper.

The Mère Hauser began at once to go over again all the details she had given him about the precautions necessary for the long winter season in the little inn. It was his first winter up there, while old Gaspard had for the last fourteen years spent his winter months under the snow in the Schwarenbach inn.

Ulrich Kunsi listened, but his eyes were fixed on the young girl, and he did not take in the sense of the words which fell on his ears. Every now and then he nodded his head and answered, 'Yes, Madame Hauser,' but his thoughts were far away, though his tranquil-looking face remained impassable. They arrived at the Daube Lake, the long surface of which, all frozen as it was, stretched out smooth and flat as far as the end of the valley.

On the right the dark rocks of the Daubenhorn rose up perpendicularly by the enormous moraines of the Lämmeren glacier upon which the Wildstrubel looked.

As they approached the Gemmi Pass, which is the beginning of the descent to Loeche, they suddenly came in sight of the immense horizon of the Valais Alps, from which they were separated by the deep, wide valley of the Rhône. It looked, in the distance, like a whole world of white, irregular mountain-tops, some flat and some pointed, and all glittering in the sunshine. There was the Mischabel, with its two horns; the huge mass of the Weisshorn; the heavy-looking Bruneckhorn; the high, formidable pyramid of the Matterhorn, the man-slayer; and that monstrous coquette, the Dent Blanche. Then, down below them in a hole at the bottom of a frightful abyss, they could see Loeche, the houses of which looked like so many grains of sand thrown down into that enormous crevice which the Gemmi Pass closes, and which begins over on the other side on the Rhône. The mule stopped at the beginning of the path which goes winding along, turning back and going on again, fantastic and marvellous the whole length of the mountain on the right until it reaches the almost invisible village at its foot.

The two women dismounted on to the snowy ground and waited until Hauser and Gaspard came up with them.

'Well, good-bye,' said Hauser, shaking hands with the two guides, 'and keep up your courage till we meet next year.'

'Yes, good-bye till next year,' said old Gaspard.

The Mère Hauser then shook hands with the guides, and then it was Louise's turn. Ulrich Kunsi whispered, as he held her hand in his: 'Don't forget us up there under the snow,' and she answered, 'No'; but so quietly that he guessed what she said rather than heard it.

'Good-bye again, then,' said Jean Hauser, 'and take care of yourselves up there, you know,' and shaking hands once more with the guides, he stepped on in front of his wife and daughter to lead the way down to the village. In a short time they were out of sight, hidden by the turn of the winding path.

The two men then retraced their steps and walked slowly back in the direction of the Schwarenbach inn. They went along, side by side, without speaking. They would be alone now – face to face with each other for the next four or five months.

Presently, Gaspard Hari began to tell about his life the previous winter. He had had with him Michel Canol, who was now too old to venture it again, as, of course, there is no knowing what may happen during those long months of solitude. It had not been so monotonous after all, for the chief thing is just to make up one's mind to it from the very first day, and then, too, they had found all kinds of things to do, and had played at various indoor games when they wanted a change.

Ulrich Kunsi listened mechanically to the old man's words, but his thoughts were with the little family on their way down to the village along the winding path of the Gemmi Pass. Soon the two men caught sight of the little inn, which was only just visible like a tiny black speck at the foot of the monstrous wave of snow. When at last they arrived at their destination and opened the door, the large dog with his curly hair began to jump up and frolic round them.

'Now, then, my lad,' said old Gaspard, 'we've got no woman here now to cook our dinner; you set to work and peel the potatoes, and we'll soon have something ready between us.'

The following morning the time seemed to go very slowly; at least, so thought Ulrich Kunsi. Old Gaspard sat by the fire smoking his pipe, while the young man gazed out of the window at the dazzling white mountain opposite the house.

In the afternoon he went out for a walk and amused himself with following the tracks of the mule on which the two women had ridden the day before. When he reached the Gemmi Pass he lay down on the ground at the edge of the abyss, and looked down at Loeche.

The village in its rocky well was not yet hidden by the snow, which, however, had nearly reached it, but was stopped by the pine forests which sheltered the environs. Its low houses, as seen from that height, looked like so many stones in a meadow. Louise Hauser was down there now in one of those grey houses. In which one, though? Ulrich Kunsi could not tell, as he was too far away to be able to distinguish them separately. How he wished he could go down to the village, now, before it was too late.

The sun had by this time disappeared behind the high crest of Wildstrubel, and the young man wended his way once more back to the inn. Gaspard was still smoking, but on seeing his companion he proposed a game of cards. They sat down to the little table facing each other and played for a long time, and then had their supper and went to bed.

The next few days were just like that first one – clear and cold, but no fresh snow. Old Gaspard would spend his afternoons looking out for the eagles and the rare birds which ventured on these icy summits, whilst Ulrich took his favourite walk down to the Gemmi Pass in order to have a glimpse of the village, and then on his return they would play at cards or dominoes, and stake some trifling object in order to add to the interest.

One morning Gaspard, who was up first, called out to his companion. A moving cloud, thick but light, of white foam was falling on them and all round them noiselessly, and was burying them gradually under a heavy, mossy mattress. This continued for four days and four nights, and the two men had, to keep the door and windows clear, to hollow out a passage and cut some steps in order to get up on to this icy powder which, after twelve hours' frost, was harder than the granite of the moraines. They had to live now almost like prisoners, scarcely venturing outside of their dwelling, and each of them accomplished regularly the everyday household tasks which he had from the first undertaken. Ulrich Kunsi did all the cleaning and the washing, and he also cut and carried the wood, whilst Gaspard's share of the work was the cooking and seeing to the fire.

Their regular, monotonous tasks were relieved by their games at cards and dominoes, and both of them being very quiet and placid, they never quarrelled. There were never any impatient or sharp words, and they were never even bad-tempered, for they had both taken in a good stock of resignation in order to be able to endure this winter sojourn on the top of the mountain. Sometimes old Gaspard would take his gun and go out chamois hunting, and whenever he had luck there was great feasting in the little Schwarenbach inn.

One morning he set out on one of these expeditions. The thermometer was eighteen degrees below freezing-point, and as the sun was not yet up the wily huntsman hoped to surprise his prey round about the Wildstrubel.

Ulrich, finding himself alone, did not get up till towards ten o'clock. He was naturally a good sleeper, and would have liked to stay in bed in the morning more often, but was ashamed to give way to his laziness when Gaspard was there, as the old guide was such an early riser and always so energetic. On the morning in question Ulrich took his breakfast in a leisurely way and gave the dog his. Sam, too, spent nearly all his time now, night and day, in front of the fire sleeping.

When the young man got up from the table a strange, sad feeling came over him, a sort of horror of the solitude, and he wished that Gaspard were there to have their customary game of cards. He missed it, as it had become quite a habit now to sit down after breakfast and have their game until it was time to prepare for the next meal.

Later on, as he could not settle down to anything, he set out to go and meet Gaspard, who was to be back home towards four o'clock. The snow had levelled the deep valley, filled up all the crevices, hidden the two lakes entirely from sight, and covered the rocks so that there was nothing to be seen now between the two immense mountains but an enormous smooth white basin, all dazzling and frozen.

For the last three weeks Ulrich had not been down to the edge of the precipice to look at the little village. He wanted to go there before climbing the mountain slopes which led to Wildstrubel. Loeche was now also under the snow, and the houses were scarcely visible at all, buried as they were under this pale mantle. Turning to the right, Ulrich reached the Lämmeren glacier. He went on with his long, mountaineer strides, his iron-tipped staff striking the snow, which was as hard as stone, whilst, with his eagle glance, he looked round in search of a black moving speck in the distance on this measureless sheet of snow.

When he had arrived at the edge of the glacier he stopped suddenly, wondering to himself whether Gaspard had taken this road, and then he walked on along the moraines with a quicker step and a feeling every minute more and more anxious. It began to get dusk, a pink shade came over the snow, and a dry, frosty wind blew in gusts over its crystal surface. Ulrich called out in a shrill voice that vibrated through the air and broke the death-like silence in which the mountains were wrapped. It could be heard for a long distance over the deep, still waves of the frozen foam, just like the cry of a bird over the waves of the sea, and then it died away again and there was no answer. Ulrich walked on and on, and the sun was sinking gradually lower and lower behind the mountain crests, which were still purple from the reflection of the sky; but the deep valley itself was turning a leaden grey.

Suddenly the young man was seized with a strange fear. It seemed to him as though the silence, the cold, the solitude, and the winter death of these mountains were entering his soul, and as though they would stop his blood and freeze it in his veins, as though they would stiffen his limbs and make of him a motionless, frozen being. This idea took possession of him, and he set off running as fast as he could go towards their dwelling. 'Gaspard must have come back by now,' he said to himself; the old man had doubtless taken another road; and he would find him seated before the fire with his dead chamois at his feet.

Presently he came in sight of the inn. There was no smoke from the chimney. Ulrich hurried on faster and faster, but when he opened the door there was only Sam, who jumped up in greeting; Gaspard Hari had not returned. Terrified at the old man's long absence, Ulrich turned round as though he expected to see him hiding in one of the corners. He then busied himself with lighting the fire and making the soup, hoping that by the time the evening meal was ready Gaspard would be back. Every few minutes he would go to the door and look out to see whether he was in sight.

It was night now, a pale, wan sort of night such as one has on the mountains, a livid dusk, lighted up from the edge of the horizon by a clear, yellowish crescent, which was just ready to fall behind the mountain-tops. The young man went back into the house, sat down and warmed his hands and feet at the fire, while he turned over in his mind all the accidents which were possible.

Gaspard might have broken his leg, he might have slipped into a crevasse, or stumbled and sprained an ankle. If so, he would be lying there in the snow, chilled through and through, stiff with the cold; he would be in utter despair, shouting for help, calling out with all the strength he had left, and his voice would fall on the silent air. There would be no one to answer him.

But where? The mountain was so vast, so rugged, and so dangerous to explore, especially at this season of the year, that ten or twenty guides might search in every direction for a whole week before finding a man in that immensity. Ulrich Kunsi, however, decided that if Gaspard Hari were not back by midnight, he would set out with Sam to search for him.

He began to make preparations for his expedition. He put enough food to last for two days in a knapsack, took his steel crampons, and fastened a long, stout cord round and around his body. He examined his iron-tipped staff and his axe, with which he would probably have to cut steps in the ice. Then he sat down and waited. The fire was blazing in the grate and the dog snoring away on the hearth, while the clock beat time regularly within its wooden case like the heart of a human being. Ulrich sat waiting, listening intently for any sound in the distance, shuddering when the wind rustled over the roof and against the walls.

The clock struck midnight, and the first stroke startled him. Unnerved, he put some water on to boil to make himself a cup of strong coffee before setting out. When the clock struck again he roused Sam and then, opening the door, started in the direction of Wildstrubel. For over five hours he continued his ascent, scaling rocks, cutting footholds in the ice, advancing slowly, and sometimes having to haul up the dog after him with his cord.

It was nearly six o'clock when he arrived on the top of one of the peaks where he knew Gaspard was in the habit of coming to hunt the chamois. Ulrich waited now for the daylight. The sky was getting paler over his head, and suddenly a strange light flashed over the immense ocean of pale mountain-tops which stretched for a hundred leagues around him. It was as though this strange, weird light had risen from the snow itself, to fall again into space.

Gradually the highest peaks in the distance changed to a delicate, fleshy-pink, and the red sun appeared behind the heavy giant heights of the Bernese Alps.

Ulrich Kunsi now started on his way once more. He walked along like a huntsman, with his head bent, looking out for tracks, and encouraging the dog every now and then with a 'Search, Sam! Search! Good dog!'

He began to descend the mountain again, now gazing down at every precipice, and now and again calling out; but his voice always died away in the dumb immensity, with no answer on any side. Sometimes he would kneel down, with his ear to the ground to listen, and would imagine he heard a voice, and set off again quickly, calling all the way; but not another sound would he hear, and he would have to sit down to rest, exhausted and despairing.

Towards mid-day he took some refreshment and fed the dog, who was as worn out as his master, and then they started once more on their search. When night came they were still going along, although they must have walked over thirty miles. As they were too far from the little inn to think of getting back, and too tired to be able to continue their way, Ulrich hollowed out a hole in the snow and crouched down in it, with the dog, under a rug that he had brought with him slung over his shoulders.

They lay down together, the young man and the dog, trying to warm themselves by huddling together, both frozen to the very marrow of their bones. Ulrich scarcely slept at all; he was haunted by all kinds of visions and shivering all over in every limb.

The day was just beginning to dawn when he got up. His legs were as stiff as bars of iron, and he was so low-spirited that he could have cried out in anguish, whilst his heart beat so fast that he felt it would stop altogether at the slightest sound he might now hear.

The idea suddenly came to him that he too was going to die of cold in this terrible solitude, and the very horror of such a death roused him to action. He began to descend the mountain, this time in the direction of the inn. Several times, he stumbled and fell and the poor dog lagged behind, limping on three paws. They reached Schwarenbach towards four o'clock in the afternoon, and found the house as empty as they had left it. Ulrich made a fire, and after he and the dog had eaten something, he fell asleep, too worn out to think about anything.

He slept for a long time – a very long time. Suddenly the sound of a voice, of a cry of his own name, 'Ulrich!' roused him, and he got up hastily. Had he been dreaming? Was it one of those strange cries which one hears in dreams when one's mind is ill at ease? No; he heard it again, now distinctly – a cry which vibrated, and entered into his very soul.

Most certainly someone had called, and it was his name he had heard, 'Ulrich!' Someone was near to the house; there was no doubt about it.

He rushed to the door, opened it, and shouted with all his might.

'Gaspard, Gaspard, are you there?'

There was no answer, not a murmur, nothing. It was dark, but the snow could be seen as white as ever.

The wind had risen, that bitter, icy wind which cracks the stones and leaves nothing alive on those deserted heights. It swept along in sudden gusts, more withering and more deadly even than the fiery wind of the desert.

Ulrich cried out again: 'Gaspard! Gaspard! Gaspard!'

Then he waited again, listening. All was dumb on the mountain. A mortal terror took possession of him, and he shook in all his bones. He rushed back into the house, slammed the door and fastened the bolts, and then sank into a chair, shivering all over from head to foot.

He was certain, absolutely certain, that his comrade had just now called him with his dying breath. He knew it just as one knows that one is alive or that one is eating a piece of bread. Gaspard Hari must have been slowly dying during two days and three nights down in some hole, in one of those deep, immaculate-looking ravines, the whiteness of which is more sinister than the dense gloom of any subterranean passage.

He had been dying during those two days and three nights, and now a few minutes ago had drawn his last breath as he thought of his young comrade, and his soul was no sooner free than it had taken its flight towards the inn where Ulrich had been sleeping, and it had called him by virtue of that mysterious and terrible power which the souls of the dead have of haunting the living. It had cried out, this voiceless soul, to the young man as he slept; it had uttered its last farewell, or its reproach, or perhaps its curse, on the man who had not sought long enough on the mountain.

And Ulrich felt as though it was there with him, this soul, near him, behind the wall on the other side of the door which he had just bolted. It was roaming about like a night-bird which rustles against the lighted windows with its feathers, and the young man almost shrieked aloud in his awe and terror. He wanted to get up and rush away, but he dared not open the door; he dared not now, nor ever would dare go out again, for the phantom would be there day and night, hovering round the inn, until the old man's body had been found and placed in consecrated ground.

It began to get light, and Ulrich felt more reassured at the return of the brilliant sunshine. He prepared his meal, fed the dog, and then he sat down again in despair and torture at the thought of the old man lying amongst the snow.

When once more the darkness began to cover the mountain, fresh terrors assailed him. He walked about the dark kitchen, lighted only by one flickering candle. He walked backwards and forwards from one side to the other, taking long strides and listening – listening intently to hear whether the fearful cry of the previous night came across the gloomy stillness of the mountain. And he felt himself alone, the wretched man, more alone than any human being had ever been!

He was alone in the midst of this snowy desert, more than six thousand feet above the world of human beings – alone in this frozen land. A wild idea took possession of him, to get away at all costs – to get away, no matter where, no matter how, to rush down to Loeche, to throw himself down the precipice! But alas! – he could not even open the door, so sure was he that the other, the dead man, would bar the road for him, in order not to be left up here alone.

Towards midnight, tired of pacing and overwhelmed with anguish and terror, he sat down on one of the kitchen chairs, for he dreaded going to bed.

Suddenly, once more, the strident cry of the night before fell upon his ears, and this time so piercing, so shrill, that Ulrich instinctively put up his arms to ward off the spirit, and in doing so lost his balance and fell over.

Sam, the dog, roused by the noise, began to howl and to walk round the dwelling to discover the danger. At the door he bent his head and sniffed along the ground, his ears pricked up and his tail straight out.

Ulrich, wild with terror, had risen from the ground and, holding the chair in his hand as a weapon, he called out, 'Stay there! Do not come in: I will kill you if you come in.' And the dog, more and more excited by his master's threatening tone, barked furiously at the invisible enemy who was daring to defy Ulrich.

Gradually, however, Sam began to calm down, and at last went back to his place on the hearth, but not to sleep. He just lay there looking anxious, his eyes shining, and growling every now and then. Ulrich, too, managed to master his terror, but opening the cupboard took out a bottle of brandy, and drank several glasses one after the other.

His thoughts began to get confused, but his courage came back and a fever began to burn in his veins. The following day he scarcely touched any food; but he drank more brandy; and for several days he went on like this – every time the thought of Gaspard Hari came to him he would go to the brandy-bottle and drink until he dropped intoxicated. There, he would remain, his limbs feeble, his face against the ground, in a drunken stupor.

No sooner, however, had the burning liquor lost its effect than the same terrible cry, 'Ulrich!' roused him like a pistol-shot through his brain, and he would get up and stagger along, calling Sam to help him.

The poor dog seemed to be losing his senses too, like his master, for he would dart to the door, scratch with his paws, and gnaw at it with his long, white teeth, whilst the young man went back to the brandy and drank a draught of it like water, so that it might once more lull him to sleep. At the end of three weeks the stock of brandy had come to an end, and this continual intoxication had only calmed at intervals his terror, which now became more and more exaggerated.

He paced up and down in his dwelling like a wild beast in his cage, putting his ear to the keyhole of the door at times to listen whether the other was still there and defying him in angry tones through the wall. At night, no sooner did he begin to doze, worn out as he was by fatigue, then the sound of the voice would make him spring to his feet.

At last one night, in sheer desperation, he rushed to the door and opened it, so that he might see who was calling him and oblige him to be silent. A gust of icy wind met him and seemed to freeze him through and through, and he banged the door to and bolted it again, without seeing that Sam had bounded out.

Then, shuddering, he threw some wood on the fire and sat down to get warm again. Presently he heard a scratching noise at the wall which made him start, and then there was a sound like a human voice wailing.

'Go away!' he shrieked, and a long, sad moan answered him.

All the reason which he had left gave way now in the face of this new horror.

He kept repeating his loud cry, 'Go away,' and wandered looking for some corner in which to take refuge.

The moaning continued, and the other wandered round and round the house outside, scratching against all the walls. Ulrich threw all his weight against the oak sideboard, full as it was of provisions and of china, and with almost superhuman strength he managed at length to push it against the door as a barricade. Then piling up everything that remained in the way of furniture, to the very mattresses off the beds, he stopped up the window just as though the enemy were besieging the house. Some terrible dismal groans were now heard from outside, and Ulrich answered by groans also.

Some days and nights passed like this: the one outside the house roaming round and round it, scratching at the walls and the door with such force, that it seemed as though the wood-built building would be demolished; and all the time the one inside listened to every movement and answered the terrible, lingering moans with shrieks of terror.

At last one night there was silence again outside the house. Ulrich could hear nothing, and, thoroughly exhausted, lay down on the floor and fell asleep. When he awoke he had no memory of anything: not a thought came to him, it was as though his very brain had been emptied by that overpowering slumber. He was hungry, and he found some food and ate it.

Winter was over and the Gemmi Pass was once more practicable, so the Hauser family set out from the village to go back to their inn on the mountain. When they reached the top of the pass, the two women got on to their mules to continue the ascent, and they began to talk of the two guides who had been shut up on the mountain all the winter. As soon as the inn was in sight they saw that it was still well covered with snow, but there was smoke rising from the chimney, and this reassured Jean Hauser.

As they came nearer, they discovered on the very threshold of the inn the skeleton of an animal which had been torn to pieces by the eagles – a huge skeleton it was, and lying on its side.

They all examined it, and the Mère Hauser exclaimed, 'It must be Sam!'

'Gaspard!' called out the father, and he was answered by a cry from inside the house, but it was a strange, piercing cry, more like the utterance of an animal than that of a human being. The Père Hauser called again: 'Gaspard! Halloa!' and another cry like the first was the only answer.

The father and sons then tried to open the door, but it resisted their efforts. They went into the empty stable and fetched a long piece of wood, which, with all their strength, they managed to push in. The door cracked and finally gave way, the wood breaking in pieces. Then there was a fearful noise, which seemed to shake the house, and there inside, behind the sideboard, which had turned over on to the floor, they saw a man glaring at them – a man with long hair falling to his shoulders and a long, wild-looking beard; his clothes hung in rags on his body.

The others did not recognise him, but Louise Hauser exclaimed. 'Oh, mother, it's Ulrich!' and then the Mère Hauser saw that it was indeed Ulrich, although his hair was snow-white. He let them come up to him; he let them touch him; but he did not answer any of their questions.

They took him down to Loeche, where the doctors pronounced him mad. No-one ever did discover what had become of his companion, the old guide, Gaspard Hari.

Young Louise Hauser nearly died that summer. She went into a long decline, which was attributed to the cold on the mountain.

The Virgins of Imst

by Jeff Long

TEN YEARS before I wandered into the village of Imst for a few months' work in the mill, a Yugoslav had found a lover like the one I did, and the huge mountain to the east had sheltered a dead saint in a cave. Because those Austrian Alps breed such precise echoes, it still seems perfectly natural that the Yugoslav and I were so much alike. Poor, foreign and naïve, we also shared a vulnerability to our similar lovers who lived and dreamed with parallel abandon below the nearby mountain.

Matija was his name. Catholic as a rosary bead, he was nevertheless a strapping twentieth-century heathen, tall and bashful, but unafraid. Among other things he was a climber, though in a village tucked at the back of a Tyrolean valley hugged by steep green meadows and steeper mountain walls, the mere fact of this held no special rank. Most of the local menfolk were, or had been, mountaineers, too.

As alpinists go, the climbers of Imst have always been a mediocre breed, congenitally cautious, saddled with more pride that skill. They climb together, practise rescue missions together, drink, quarrel and yodel, tease each other's wives, and above all obscure their mutual failings as climbers, acting exactly like the neighbours they are. What distinguished Matija that summer was that he was the finest climber Imst had ever seen.

And yet, as the story came to me, you could never have guessed he had an extraordinary skill, he was so ridiculously humble. The moment he was in public his dark eyes locked onto the cobblestones. He had the habit of blushing at his accent, and was mutely diligent at the lumber mill where he held a summer job. I had the same job, I climbed, I kept to myself, and like Matija ate my supper at the cheapest inn in town, the Hofhaus. When a group of local men would arrive for an evening of red wine and tall tales, I'd wolf down my cheese noodles and meat and timidly exit. As I closed the oak door behind me, their pipe smoke would billow in thick, lazy domain. Erika was his love, or came to be towards the end of the summer, coltish and wildly attractive. She was blessed with roan-gold hair, a Swiss model's legs and incongruously Italian breasts. Barely twenty, Erika had already located each and every beauty mark her archangel had hidden on her body, which is to say that her life was an uncomplicated task. She preened herself in an old-fashioned, lusty sort of way and was desired just as simply.

That summer Erika was still a virgin. She didn't act like one with her ribald coquetries and even more suspicious melancholies, but the villagers knew. This daughter was still a pure creature. Having grown up among such a wise alpine bourgeoisie, Erika had not failed to learn the price of certain commodities, the value of certain flowers. She knew just what she wanted out of life and thought she'd figured out how to get them . . . a big white house with an old tile oven, new furniture, a view of the lake, a cat, and maybe later some children. But for all her deliberateness Erika was young and susceptible to less articulate needs. One August night when the moon was ripe and you could practically hear the chamois rustling on the cliffs, Erika lost her plotting innocence.

I should tell this story the way it was told to me, but that's not enough. Matija may not have had humble black eyes, Erika may not have connived with her virginity so deviously, and it may not have been August when she invited him to her window. But it went something like that; a soft knock at the garden window, the starched linen curtains were drawn aside, and there stood Erika, her nightgown a solid white in the silver night. I had such an affair with a girl named Crystal, a midnight adventure that was repeated through the coming two months.

On the first night she opened her window, before she could whisper even a word of greeting or restraint, without the slightest chance of cunning, her gown fell open. Unaddressed but demanding, her two breasts hung in the perfect order of a woman's flesh, dappled by the moonlight. Erika, like Crystal, as virgin as dew, was no doubt frightened by her accidental nakedness, perhaps even angry with Matija for being so enchanted by it. And then she drew him in and closed the window. There seemed to be nothing else to do.

Erika wanted Matija no more than Crystal really wanted me, but we were, the Yugoslav and I, both young and momentary, good for a secret. In that constricted Tyrolean universe where every shadow had a name, the people I called my friends were friendly, the lover was loving, but there was a limit. Unaware of our poetry, Matija and I succumbed, like images in a mirror, to the Austrian midnight and its innocences. From what I remember of the story, Matija was 21, too.

The spring before Matija arrived in Imst two young bucks from Innsbruck, 'rock gymnasts,' as the Imsters secretly disparaged them, attempted to climb the large, rotten wall of rock that sits high above the town to the east. This wall forms the geometrically clean face of a mountain called Sonnenspitze, or Sun Mountain, named for its peak which marks the sun's first appearance and very last shining. At the centre of the wall, Sun Wall, a cave mouth forms a perfect dark O. Nowadays it's known as the Virgin's Hole.

No one in Imst had ever given much thought to what might lay in the cave because the Sun Wall had all the earmarks of the edge of the world. Sharp and chaotic, its rock is more treacherous than rotten coral. I once bouldered near the base of the Sun Wall and found the holds as large as they were worthless, so fragile that a wrong breath, much less a wrong move, would fracture the rock. It was unforgiving, just left unclimbed, and yet when the two boys from Innsbruck showed up there was a sudden embarrassed furore. This was, after all, a local mountain. It was felt that the rock gymnasts should go monkey around on their own walls. The sentiment went unheeded.

The two Innsbruckers came prepared. Expecting difficulties, they laid siege to the wall in American big-wall fashion, spending days and days on the vertical face, sleeping in hammocks at night. Finally after a week of strenuous acrobatics, with the whole village suffering their minute progress hour by hour, the two boys reached the cave.

Storm clouds had been blossoming all morning, so there was some question about whether the young climbers would weather it out or descend. The climbers of Imst began to prepare a full blown rescue of the two boys. Knowing the Imsters as I do, I doubt there was much solemnity as the locals stomped around the town square in their knickers and boots, hefting big packs and draping bandoliers of musical pitons and coils of rope over their shoulders with sweeping flourish. To this day I can't figure out how they were going to rescue the boys. They certainly weren't about to climb up to them, and the wall was so overhung they couldn't have lowered down. For all their strutting around, in the end they were as helpless before the storm as the two boys were. After a fair amount of festive posturing the group set off to wait and see what would happen.

As it turned out, the two Innsbruck climbers had noticed the storm, too, then measured its severity against their dwindling food supply and decided to reverse direction without further ado. Their descent turned into one of those small epic tragedies for which the Alps are notorious.

The storm struck. All through the night the two young men battled their way downwards, blown by the wind and anointed by gentle, soaking snowflakes. Their exhaustion was compounded by the delicacy of the wall which required just as much care as had their gingerly made ascent.

Not long before dawn, one of the climbers lost his grip on the ropes and fell to his death. The other boy continued down, orchestrating the rappel with bleak uncertainty. Hours later, nearly dead, he lowered himself into the very centre of the now sombre Imst rescue team. In spite of his horrible journey back to earth, the boy feverishly insisted on relating a remarkable discovery.

There was, he swore to God, a body up in that impossible cave. Without headlamps, and because of the storm, the boys hadn't investigated any closer, but both of them had seen the unmistakable contours of a woman's body. She was white as pine, nude and impeccably preserved. According to the exhausted young climber, she'd had long black hair, and extending from the cold shadows he'd seen a half open hand, palm up. The boy was utterly convinced that she was beautiful, perhaps due to the beckoning hand and her awesome solitude. Then, the boy sobbed, they had descended.

Father Weissbrod's pulpit had served him as a podium on more than a few occasions in his 48 years as the pastor of Imst. From it he rarely hesitated to scold adulterers and liars, or warn against various political sympathies, once going so far as to compose a sermon on inflation and the Volkswagen. The ageing priest was bored. It has been a quarter of a century since the last war, 27 tedious years of blessing sinners and herds of healthy cattle and leading invocations to the Holy Spirit on behalf of Imster small fry as they departed for regional ski meets. On the first Sunday after the disaster on Sun Wall, Father Weissbrod electrified his parish with some news of his own. He had made a discovery.

'The pure are like God,' I once heard the old priest postulate. 'He draws them to his breast and makes them little gods.' In a more educated church this pagan sentiment, that God makes mini-gods, would have cocked more than a few eyebrows, but there in Imst it was taken as part and parcel of the gospel. Ten years before I sat in church and heard the shaggy-headed priest, he scanned his congregation and, with forgotten drama, revealed something to the effect that papal evidence spoke of a certain immortal woman.

More than 1,000 years ago, the body of Mary Magdalene disappeared from its resting place in the convent at Les Saintes Maries-de-la-Mer in the Camargue, and legend had it that the prostitute-turned-saint had been assumed into Heaven. This was given increasing credence over the centuries as Mary Magdalene visited such locations as Chartres and Le Puy, always manifesting herself in the form of lifelike statues. True or not, several churches owe their existence to her divine appearances, for which an enduring human faith or gullibility may take credit.

Barely three days had passed since the two boys from Innsbruck had descended from the cave on Sonnenspitze, when Father Weissbrod revealed in great detail who the woman in the mountain really was. 'She is, God bless us, the saint.' He expected more scepticism than he got. There were a few slow witted scowls, but aside from these the Imsters immediately embraced the miraculous corpse of Mary Magdalene. Suddenly Imst had a purpose beyond its crops and cattle. Out of the great blue, Imst had a naked saint.

It must have seemed a raw injustice to Erika in that twentieth summer of her life when the young men, all of whom she'd known since childhood, callously fell in love with the saint lodged high within the Sun Wall. There were four or five highly eligible men in Erika's realm, but just as she was familiar with who they were, they were familiar with Erika. They'd been tormented by her hot and cold charms long enough to understand her virginity, and rather than pursue another season of fruitless competition for her attentions, they turned their thoughts to the wall and unfamiliar chastity.

With inch-long beards in the style of a famous South Tyrolean climber, or moustaches fashionably cropped, the young men took to congregating in the town square, there to mull over the geological citadel that had begun to loom in their dreams. Tirelessly they discussed methods of reaching the woman in the stone.

Purity has odd rhythms. The distressing thing about that 'summer of the saint,' as Imsters still refer to it, was that the bachelors, one and all and all at the same time, turned into spiritual bridegrooms of the mysterious female. Against the unreachable beauty which the corpse in the cave represented to those stallions of Imst, Erika didn't stand a chance. When she leaned provocatively across the glass counter top at the bakery she worked for, the young men's eyes celibately scanned the rows of bread, the pastries dusted with sugar, their own hands . . . surveying everything but that langorous cleavage which no one had yet touched.

Unfortunately for Erika, the woman in the cave was untouched, too, with the difference that the saint had become equated with an innocence so vast and grave that every male could aspire to be worthy of it. Ignorant of the fractures in Erika's twentieth year, nonchalant about the lady in the mountain, Matija was noticed one day by a lonely, lovely girl who hungered with a vengeance.

Matija, shy and unadorned, had his small pretensions. I was told, for instance, that he shaved daily with an open razor just before his evening supper, and that he wore white T-shirts more religiously than an American. He preferred black bread over white, a taste I shared with him, even though in Austrian circles black bread is considered pauper's food. Not without a touch of pride, Matija used to wear a wool hat from Plancia, his hometown, whenever he was outdoors, even at the lumber mill where sweat and sawdust eventually discoloured it. Sometimes he would run home from work, a long-legged canter that seemed much too ambitious in the eyes of the Imsters.

'What are you training for?'

And he'd stop, puzzled. 'I'm just running.'

The villagers would grin and continue strolling along, leaving behind a suddenly baffled Yugoslav. My blue jeans came under similar scrutiny, I know, and my dislike for climbing with a helmet. Small idiosyncrasies operated as borders, and where there were borders there was inevitably trespass.

To the locals it was bad enough to have two lads from nearby Innsbruck almost bag the neighbourhood wall, but it was downright spooky to see a Yugoslav make a shambles of the neighbourhood climbs. In the course of three weekends and a national holiday, the transient systematically demolished every existing route on and around Imst, then in the following two months invented previously unthinkable lines up vertical faces and smooth slabs. The only thing that prevented him from making a second attempt on the Sun Wall and its Virgin Hole was that no one was bold enough to accompany him. A full decade later I contemplated the face myself, but it just didn't seem worth the danger.

The face is a massive trap spring-loaded with bands of decayed schist and roofs that are propped to collapse, all of it punctuated by falling rocks that whistle from out of nowhere. For a climber this kind of senseless risk is marginally seductive. So, as horrified as the locals were, they couldn't help but debate ways of unlocking the wall. There had to be a way. They talked all summer.

'See the voyeur?' Matija may have asked Erika late one night, as I once asked Crystal. A small grey mouse, archetypal with pink ears and round beads for eyes, continued staring back at the two naked creatures in its room. With amused solemnity Matija would have kissed Erika just as insistently as I kissed Crystal, and later, after healthily climaxing, we dropped off to sleep, not meaning to, but captured by our own warmth. It was dangerous to fall asleep because I had to be gone well before the morning turned light. But this one night we indulged ourselves. Hours later, just before dawn, there was a loud snap in the darkness.

'Oh,' murmured Crystal, half rearing up with the quilt to her chest. 'The stove is dropping ashes.' But it wasn't the stove, it was her mousetrap. Our voyeur was dead. As if by design his tiny life had been given to wake us. I marked that moment as a magic one, despite the fact that while I dressed, Crystal matter-of-factly emptied the trap with the same hands with which she'd been touching me, and then reset the deadly mechanism for its next victim. If only Matija and I had paid more attention to such inauspicious perceptions.

The summer of the virgin was a breathless one, unusual for the mercy it showed. It wasn't without threats, but as if by virtue of 'their' saint the threats remained distant ones. The weather was unstable, for one thing, and the farmers were nervous about their crops. As it turned out, they pulled in a respectable harvest just days before the massive freeze in late September. One of the big wedging machines at the lumber mill broke down and for a while it looked like several of the workers would be laid off. Somehow a local machinist persuaded the machine to operate until the season was finished. Most threatening of all was the continuing possibility of a police investigation into the cave on Sun Wall.

Dead people have a way of turning up in the mountains. It's not unusual for solitary mountaineers, or German tourists, or sometimes a herder caught by late spring avalanches, to show up months or years after their accidents. But the discovery of the female of Sonnenspitze was different. Her location was sensational, her identity a complete mystery. She might have been an incredible suicide or the victim of a climbing murder, the police allowed, or maybe even the grisly remnants of an espionage operation during the last war. The constable sternly insisted that sooner or later he was going to get around to a full scale investigation, but he never had the opportunity.

Matija probably asked for nothing more than the covert security of Erika's room and her touch, never taking the time to consider the indignities of tiptoeing across strawberry plants in order to crawl through a window. I know I never did. I only had thoughts for the façade Crystal and I covered ourselves with.

With my sleep cut by half it was only a matter of a fortnight or so before delirium took over. What felt like love, totally pervasive, dreamlike and warm, was in good part plain old exhaustion. The nights took on an invincible tone. It seemed that Crystal and I were surrounded in the daytime by fugitives and liars, that the deception wasn't ours but everyone else's.

We talked about running off to Greece and marooning ourselves on the beach of a random island, leaving Imst to stew in its suspicions. But for Crystal such talk was simply one more excitement in the overall adventure. She wasn't about to sail off into never-never land with an American pauper. She'd risked as much as she was going to by having me in her room. I should have guessed, but lying there with her soft body in my arms, I took her at her word. I prepared to make our escape.

Matija's midnight love couldn't have gone much differently. There's a pattern to these things: darkness, whispers, a flurry of bold regrets prefaced by 'if only', and dispassionate masquerades after the sun had risen. You don't need wine to get drunk in a situation like that. Matija must have been just as disorientated as I was, consumed by the night, testing the fabric of each dawn with tired caution. I felt practically transcendent. I'd gone from being the oddball American who ate black bread and wore blue jeans to being a clandestine lover, possessing Crystal like a secret. I had, it seemed, penetrated the village.

Confident of the risks involved, trusting nothing but his nocturnal senses and his lover, Matija continued to visit Erika's bedroom by night and turn trees into planks of lumber during the day. Surely by late September he'd grown used to the prejudices of the village and had begun to understand the pride with which the lovely saint was coveted. Erika probably talked about it herself, and may on occasion have wished out loud that she, too, could have her purity back. With early snows impending, the season was nearly ended. Matija was collecting a final few schillings for his escape with Erika when love showed its true face.

Two months of midnights had passed without incident. Stealing across the stone fence, Matija dodged through the withered strawberry patch and arrived at Erika's window. By habit he stuffed his wool hat into his jacket pocket, so there would be no chance of his forgetting it in Erika's room, then he reached up and tapped at her window. There was no answer.

He tapped a second time. I sometimes had to repeat myself, too, while huddling in the shadows beneath Crystal's window box. The linen curtains parted. I don't have to imagine the nausea he felt when a bearded face, it doesn't matter whose, appeared behind the glass. The most hideous part was that it smiled just before drawing the curtains shut again. We fled.

I've seen Erika. Two children and ten years have marked her beauty with slight laugh lines and a double chin, otherwise it is the same Erika. There's no way of knowing if she regretted betraying Matija's trust. She may never have entertained the possibility of his love in the first place. But I like to think that for part of that morning after, while she picked hot rolls and pretzels from the bins and dropped them in white sacks for the customers, she felt a twinge of sorrow. If Erika cared even that much, the village didn't care at all.

It was by now the end of the summer and most of the labourers had returned to Yugoslavia and Italy. The mill's owner certainly didn't mope over the sudden disappearance of one more of his foreign workers, especially since this one had neglected to pick up his last pay cheque. Such was the stuff of village jokes about foreigners.

It was four days later in the town square, while a politician from Ehrwald stubbornly touted himself with a PA system and boxes of campaign buttons, that Matija turned up once again. More precisely he was located disturbingly high overhead, hovering in the pink alpenglow on the Sun Wall. First a drowsy trombone player in the local band, then a plump frau with late summer marigolds in one hand and a tether to her cow in the other, and then others, all the others . . . looked up toward the cave of their whore-turned-virgin and discerned not one black dot but two, the unfamiliar dot still several inches below their holy cave. No one could believe their eyes until it was plain that everyone was seeing the same thing. A climber was approaching their cave.

Just as stunning, the climber was alone. Soon an educated murmur had bolted through the crowd, identifying the dot as that Yugoslav, Matija. It was a safe deduction, he was the one man capable of soloing the wall. But why was he doing it? The politician continued enunciating his promises to the rapt audience without the slightest idea that, several thousand feet behind and above his makeshift podium, Matija was serenely stealing his thunder.

Those several inches separating Matija from the cave were in fact several hundred feet of treacherous stone, meaning he had a good six to ten hours more of climbing. He wouldn't reach the cave until next day at the earliest, but to the good people of Imst it was just inches or less that separated their saint from desecration. That fear was poisonously immediate, for Matija was, *ad infinitum*, not of the town of Imst. He was unpredictable, an animal possessed by God knows what kind of chaotic reasoning. It's not hard to see how tales of dragons and ogres managed to thrive in the midst of such xenophobia. No one allowed that maybe he was climbing up to see for himself, to confirm what no one else could seem to. Or maybe he was climbing to the cave to genuflect and continue on to the summit. No one granted him the slightest benefit of his character.

Instead, the villagers reacted with doubt and loathing. A Yugoslav, it was whispered, was capable of many things. He might push the body to the ground or ink his signature on her sacred flesh as proof that he'd been there. Alone, the animal could do anything, even foul the vulnerable corpse with his carnal touch or, if he was short of food, try to eat it.

Emergency sessions of every sort were announced; the village mayor discussed with his council and the walking club debated, and the firemen agreed that their saint was in imminent danger. While the people prayed that God would ward Matija away from their cave, Erika kept her rosy mouth shut.

There are still a few believers in Imst who will tell you that the storm which rose up the same night is enduring proof of some miraculous element, be it saint or symbol. As the story goes, nothing from the Innsbruck weather station to old Hanajorg's infallible prostate gland had predicted the swollen ice clouds that engulfed the stars and swallowed the upper two-thirds of the Sun Wall.

Next morning when the villagers looked through roughly melted circles on their frosty windows, they saw every house and street encased in a single, all-encompassing sheet of transparent ice. Everything had turned into a glass replica of itself, not only houses but animals too. Horses died that night, soaked with rain and then frozen solid by the terrible cold. The mountain was hidden from view by clouds, but there wasn't the slightest doubt that it was lacquered with a cold sheet of verglas too. Matija, it was broadly surmised, couldn't possibly have survived.

The villagers were well satisfied with this meteorological retribution, it reinforced the sanctity of their virgin in the well, exposing a great protector who held His hand over the small secrets of the world. Under the guise of a mass held for Matija's dubious survival, the villagers celebrated sweet justice. Father Weissbrod could barely conduct the mass. Instead of delivering the sermon, he gave a wink that everyone understood.

For days the strangely persistent clouds hung over the mountain and its town. The Imsters stayed close to their ovens, only venturing out for precarious walks to the grocery store or to the Hofhaus for gossip. The rescue climbers speculated with lurid detail about what condition Matija's body would be in when they finally recovered it. As to how they would retrieve the Yugoslav's corpse from the face, none could finally decide.

At last the weather unknotted its deathly fist. The clouds thinned, the streets thawed. Exactly five days after the Imsters had first seen Matija nearing the cave, the mountain surfaced. Everyone looked toward the wall and with a gasp saw just one solitary dot, the mouth of the cave. Fresh consternation broke out. The rescue climbers immediately set off for the base of the wall to try and find the mangled Yugoslav, his rope crystallised around his waist. He wasn't there. Immediately four of the fastest men were dispatched to hike up the back way to the summit, where it was hoped Matija may have struggled before expiring. He wasn't there either.

That left one place. But suddenly it seemed all right that he was there. Matija must have reached the cave, he must have died in the presence of the saint. With a spontaneous change of heart the villagers instantly preferred this version of the story, it invested the tale with a rustic integrity. Matija had turned to the eternal virgin in the cave, risked all, and reached her with his last breath. This was adoration. It was a perfectly religious ending. But it wasn't the end.

For a week, then two weeks, the rescue climbers just couldn't get to the cave. They tried to go down on long ropes, but the wall was too overhung, and after a few timid false starts they quit trying to climb up. At last they contacted the national rescue team in Innsbruck, which in turn sent up a helicopter. While the helicopter hovered a few metres away from the wall, a volunteer swung back and forth on the very tip of a rope tied to the struts. After a dozen misses, he finally managed to pendulum right into the cave's mouth. Even before he scrambled to his feet inside the cave, he'd found Matija's wool hat.

All alone in this deathly place, with the irregular thunder of rotor blades reminding him of his lifeline back to safety, the rescue man probed the gloom with his headlamp. Starting at the front of the cave, he explored back into the deepest recess. There was no Yugoslav. But deep in the rear, blanketed with shadows, lay that other body. It was well preserved, and as the Innsbruck boy had said, it was clearly female. With great reverence the man knelt down and turned the woman's body over.

Now, having visited the museum in Vienna, I feel sorry for that rescue climber who expected a mask of unearthly beauty and found instead what is now sealed in airtight glass and labelled the Virgin of Imst. It's still a mystery how she got up there in the first place, and a mystery, too, where Matija disappeared to. Back to Plancia, I guess.

The message of the Virgin doesn't lie in the scars that her people carved into her face as a child, nor in the oddly delicate hand with its fingers curled so. There's real poignancy to those tiny white flowers woven into her black hair despite the huge brow, but the message isn't there, either. It lies for me in that instant Matija turned the virgin saint over and found the face of a Neanderthal girl. I still miss Crystal in a way, but like Matija, I've realized that there's nothing more to say.

The White Graph

by Dermot Somers

IT'S BEEN snowing now for three days, snow to 2,000 metres last night. I'm getting nervous; it's just like the first time twelve years ago. That summer, too, I came from chaos . . . drink, debt, divorce – I didn't care, I was in Chamonix where the sun shone and nothing mattered but sky-high rock, ice, and dreams. Rousie, Tut, Minksy – warlords of the Alps – were on Snell's Field pulling off First British Ascents every day of the week. Seemed you only had to stroll off the campsite to bag a first ascent if you were one of their gang. They hadn't heard of me yet – but I was determined they'd never forget. I came to the mountains of my mind like a thunderbolt, mad with pain and a rage to do great things.

The Blaitière was a buzz-route then, the West Face of the 'Blat', famous for the Fissure Brown. The good weather hadn't ended and we marched uphill the day we arrived. I'd a mate from Salford in tow, so morose he hardly ever spoke. We humped our new Joe Browns all the way to the Plan des Aiguilles full of paraffin, tins of stew, and no stove, broad feet tormented in narrow French boots. We bivvied badly by the Lac Bleu and ate the stew cold, grease and all. The Blat was the biggest crag I'd ever seen, but it looked easy. I couldn't make a figure 4 of that rock-scar though – more like South America after an earthquake.

We left the bivouac before dawn and got to the Fissure Brown at nine. Started in the wrong place and climbed dribbling, gravelly pitches before we found the famous crack. From far below it looked like a secure hand-and-fist job, which meant it must be stinking offwidth. Close up, in the morning mist, it was a broad black cleft in cold granite. A short pillar at the foot, and after that nothing at all but the Fissure itself. The face leaned back a bit but the crack bulged to contradict it. No wedges either. I'd been promised wedges; sometimes, they said, you could climb it like the rungs of a ladder and get on with the real climbing then. It had been stripped by some thieving purist.

I attacked at a run in rucksac and boots, that mad flourish meant to bulldoze an obstacle with a frenzy of confidence. Like a bad fighter. Foreign leather thudded on foreign rock, and rebounded. Fists, arms, shoulders rattled within the crack. I squirmed up a few feet and stuck solid, arm-wrestling the mountain. The right edge of the crack leaned out past my shoulder and the rucksac jammed. That crack had a feel for Joe Brown. The harder I wriggled the more firmly the sac jammed and dragged my hands out of the crack. I had no sense of discretion then, no idea how to retreat gracefully and sneak back streamlined so that the Fissure wouldn't notice me any more than it had to.

Instead I pulled brutally. Trying to pass through a narrowly-opened door with a rucksac on. Something had to give. And it wasn't even a French crack. I didn't have the excuse that it was some kind of Frog-stuff that a Brit wouldn't know how to stoop to. Brown did it first, Joe-bloody-Brown whose routes I was flashing in Wales with the arrogance always typical of the next generation but one.

Something gave. It sounded like muscle or bone, it should have been, but it was only the metal stiffener in the toughest sac ever made. Bending to my fury.

The left edge of the crack is composed of little overlaps, snub shapes as tightly moulded to the rock as paint-runs to a doorframe. Nothing to get the fingers behind, the rock gloss-cold and hostile. Higher up, a peg. Someone had nursed a blade into a fault. I hung on it, swung on it nearly an hour before I got the next moves figured – a hex wedged between crystals, slings to step in, slings to haul on and a sling to lasso, and the huge squashed rucksac still on my back.

My mate said nothing, but the pile of butts grew around his stolid feet. He accepted that this was how it was meant to be, because I said so, and there was no reason to doubt it. Above our heads a thousand feet of grooves and cracks burrowed into the low, grey clouds towards the summit – where we bivouacked exhausted and storm-tossed in the dark after twelve hours' climbing, never thinking not to finish what we'd begun, since life was hard anyway so why would climbing be any different.

So where does this wisdom – this sanity – come from at last? Is it a victory over myself, or just the peace of exhaustion? Hardly. Exhaustion brings dullness, not peace; and there are no victories, just compromise – between reality and desire. Wisdom, I know now, is a kind of dignified cunning. The same goes for sanity. Quote me on that.

What happened in those bitter years? I could describe the breakdown maybe – or the climbing, its occasional success – the lifestyle, relationships like feverish collisions, rebuttal and rebuff . . . but what really happened overall was – hardship. Emotional hardship – as if time was a long journey in bad weather and I could seldom see clearly enough to know if I was getting anywhere at all. But sometimes the clouds parted and there was a flash of intense perspective. Lucid moments when the heart was seen to have failed again. The shape of my life linked those moments together.

A black graph. The white graph is only its shadow. An illusion.

In a cold dawn, less than a week ago, I left the Plan cable-car at a run. My partner this time was young and ambitious, a good rock-climber, if hints were facts. We met in the Bar-Nash. First route of the season for both of us.

He was keen enough to do the Blaitière though I got the feeling he was lowering his sights. He knew a lot about the trendier lines on the face but I was set on the old British route and there was no argument. He knew I'd been on it before – when he was a boy. I think he viewed the idea with as close an approach to indulgence as he could manage.

I tried rapport for a while – 'What d'you do for a crust, Andy?'

'I don't . . .'

Shivering in the dark in Cham while the guides filled the first 'férique – 'You married yet, Andy?'

He jerked his head at the boring idea. They don't scramble to marry in their teens like we did. Not the smart ones anyway.

'You?' He had no interest . . .

'Yeah. Four kids.' He was totally shocked; obviously I'd sold out. No commitment to climbing. He shuddered at the prospect of dribbling snapshots, or worse still – when courage was wanted on the route would I plead fatherhood?

So I didn't tell him I hadn't seen my kids for two years. While I'd been locked away. Or about their various mothers . . .

I set a scorching pace across the moraine, breakneck boulder-hopping to rattle him. I know there's no way to beat these younger lads technically – all you can do is concede their strengths, and maybe gain a little on the rough ground. Andy tried to keep pace with me, once or twice he found quicker detours, until we left the moraine and headed up the glacier below the Brégeault Ridge.

The remote smoothness of the Blaitière had broken into features; the Red Pillar, the slabs, the grey scar, the sceptical wrinkles of the Brown route – all showed the versatility of a face that used to be known for one route only.

Irritated by Andy's grimness I didn't pause for crampons. I counted on the gravel embedded in the ice to get me up the glacier, guessing from his comments that he might be less cocky on ice. Last year his first season finished in a crevasse in the Argentière Basin. Could happen to anyone, sure; those holes are so crowded it can be hard to get in.

'Ice is basically boring,' he'd lectured me, 'same move over and over. Now, Rock makes you Think . . .'

A dead giveaway; never done any mixed!

No, I wasn't putting him down competitively – just storing up space for myself in what I feared could be an unbalanced day at my expense. It worked so well I was almost ashamed when he crawled onto the rock white-faced after resorting to crampons on the lip of a crevasse for the last snowbank. A fall there would have corpsed him. He admitted to feeling shaky but he put it down to a bad stomach, 'Dodgy bottle of wine last night . . .'

Pathetic! Obviously it was altitude, acclimatization, arrogance – but he had to learn all that himself. He was in the right company. Efficiently sorting rock-gear and ropes I offered – without actually pausing – to sit around for a while till he recovered.

'Nah, I'm alright.' Curt, as if to say, Rock? I won't have any problems. It's you I'm worried about, mate!

The grey stubble and the belly can have that effect. But it never fails to disappoint me how fucking military the young alpinists are now, as if – under a veneer of anarchy – survival is a strict Commando-code forbidding any weakness or self-doubt.

Well, if he fancied discipline . . . 'You start,' I gave him his orders. 'There's the Fissure Brown. It's offwidth and it overhangs, but it's not too bad otherwise.'

He looked as shattered as his stiff lip allowed; 'Don't think I feel up to it yet. . . .' Nausea churned audibly in his stomach, like an undigested fry. He looked around for a hole to crawl into. Not broken enough yet to drop his salopettes on the windswept terrace. 'Okay, I'll start,' I offered. Kindly, exultantly, I was prepared for this: one of those victorious moments brought about by willpower and pure need. It was going to be my day after all. 'I'll do the variation-start. No sense repeating myself . . .' To the left of the Fissure Brown – and climbing to the same belay – there is an alternative pitch, a hand-crack! Visually stunning. The first section is littered with easy flakes, and then the clean crack rises, sinuous and soaring, as if it had sloughed all its features without quite extricating its tail from the clutter. And up at the top there is a thin, sharp snake-bite.

Beside this elegant pitch the Fissure Brown is a boa constrictor. How had I missed it a dozen years ago when I needed it most? And Brown? Had they ploughed their muscular furrow by choice, or had the hand-crack been cleaned into view since?

I'd been briefed and I came prepared; two big hexes and two large Friends, not the kind of gear you drag up alpine routes without advice.

I like jamming-cracks. Don't ever go by grade; there are cracks designed to encourage you up a wall, and cracks that try to throw you off – no matter how hard or easy. The two starts to this route are perfect examples of that.

After the flakes the pitch came clean, and then it was perfect handwidth, no holds, and so deep it must go right to the core of the Mont Blanc range. I swear a distant breath of lava warmed my fingertips as I reached inside. I might fail here for want of strength or will but I could not fall off. The grey rock clamped me to it, clenched me hand and foot, owned me. . . .

I was gripped like a fossil, a lichen, a micro-insect whose wildest scuttlings down a hundred generations could not take it off the mountain. This crack absorbed everything. It was no random fault like the Fissure Brown but one of those points where the perfect geometry of rock forces the imperfect nature of the climber to submit, no – not to its difficulty, but to its relentless form and meaning. I'd been thinking a lot about climbing while I was ill, and it was as if I'd created this pitch for my return. But already, on the first move, I was afraid. Afraid of myself. Afraid I would be climbing this ruthless crack forever, jamming on past the belay, past the Fontaine ledges, past the summit, climbing on into personal space, permanently locked away in its cold, burning grip.

I climbed it to preserve my identity, my freedom – flailing forward the way a swimmer among sharks lifts himself whole out of the water; I climbed without a pause for protection, lifting myself whole from the rock with every stroke . . .

Yeah, I know that's complex – schizoid maybe, but I take climbing seriously. I'd a lot of time to work it out. Sometimes, at bare and powerful moments it stood for all the things I've never done or felt. 5a for ninety feet, at the top it squeezed, demanded more, a 5b finger-jam with the toes twisted and chewed, exposed ankles trembling, a ropelength from the terrace, too fast and late for protection now. A huge handhold. . . . Like too much dope too soon, heart and brain ejaculating through the skull. I doubled over on the belay to control the dizziness, the fear of pitching head-first down the crack – and found I was staring down the cold slot of the Fissure Brown, listening as I groaned and cursed towards the light in that tunnel of years.

Andy came up greyfaced, technically perfect, mentally stunned. No aesthetic spark. Looking at the thin mouth and inward eyes I knew he never recognized – never trusted – anything outside himself. And that he was ideal for me; I could do him no harm.

'Mad bastard!' he grunted, and then in case any admiration had shown through, 'didn't have gear in your day, did they?'

'You still sick?' I didn't wait for an answer, 'I'll go ahead for awhile.'

I felt great, perilously liberated from myself and yet complete, as if a thin gap – the width of that crack and no more – had opened up between me and the past. I'd have to cross over again on the way down, but things might be different, or I might have changed by then. You can't change reality, I know, but you can see it differently. For a while.

A groove hung above us, steep, tight, V-shaped, heading into overhangs. I worked it grimly before, a miner in a sullen seam. Now I could bridge, chimney, shimmy, lean out or in, use the groove or refuse it. Clip a peg and skip the next three. I whooped past belays to run out a full rope every time, forcing Andy to climb with me till I reached the stance I fancied.

The overhang on good holds. Strenuous, not hard. Belayed above, I scanned the routes I knew; the North Face of the Plan had lost its simple trick, the séracs a shambles, the ice-corridor gone and no safe way through. Over on the Peigne the North Ridge was deserted too, a grovelling grooveline totally out of vogue. But the routes on the slabs would be alive with dancers dressed for the crag, a cluster of bolts the only summit they sought. I could hear them yodelling on the Blaitière too.

'Wheeeeeeeeeee-Hah!' I responded. Good luck to them!

Andy was on the overhang. He'd solo it at home if he stooped to the standard, barely 5a, but he grappled with gritted teeth, body trembling with the effort of altitude. Yet he unclipped a sling from a peg and looped it neatly around his neck while clinging to the rock with failing fingers; just because I was watching him. Pride! 'Pull on 'em, Andy,' I goaded, 'That's what they're for!'

A ferocious glare, and I tried to think how to say I hadn't pulled on them either – because I hadn't *needed* to. . . .

The route unravelled at a manic pace, grooves, cracks, a delicate slab, all free and sound. Heart and breath raced like rock and roll towards a climax, yet I consumed every move with the greed of the half-starved, the long locked-away. What else is there, apart from good sex, to equal it? Big-game hunting? Bull-fighting? War? Hemingway missed out on the best.

Andy was losing his grip. I had to be impressed with his staying-power, though, he'd a hell of a last gasp in him. He'd suit me alright. Badly dehydrated too, and I'd left the water-bottle at the foot of the route. Yeah, sorry. . . .

We were on target for a three-hour ascent; not bad for a first route. He was too burnt-out to argue, too proud to plead, but his whole manner was a violent complaint against the route.

He wanted to go down – I could feel it in the drag of the rope, hear it in his strangled curses. He couldn't handle the climbing on the day, so he didn't care about the mountain. It was not a thing in itself apart from his capacity for it.

I may come across as a hard bastard here, but I do have standards. I have respect. Even at my worst a dozen years ago I only wanted to match up to the magnificence of the Alps, to find some reflection of them in me. Andy wanted to use them to exhibit his own talent, and when it didn't work out he blamed everything but himself. Especially the mountain.

The last pitches to the Fontaine Ledges were sustained cracks, sweet and cunning as anything on a Yosemite wall. People abseil off there, the best climbing over, the summit irrelevant. I'd been to the top so I felt no need to go again – but I owed Andy a little further education. No, I didn't want to make a better man of him – I wouldn't presume – I was just trying to stop him getting worse.

'We're going to the top, Andy. . . .' He was slumped on the last belay, destination and descent on his face, '. . . it'll take another couple of hours.'

He had breath to spare for a snarl, 'I'm not going to any bloody top! There's just rubbish left. . . .'

'Is that so? You'd better traverse off to the Brégeault Ridge then because I'm going up. I'll nip down the Spencer Couloir on the other side, so I won't be back this way.' That was a bluff; I wouldn't touch the Spencer at dawn never mind midday.

He almost came. The soldier in him struggled to submit to discipline. Then the human being, the failed mountaineer, conquered him for the best. 'I don't want to go any further,' he whimpered, 'I want to go down . . . now!'

'Want to?' I echoed with interest, 'Want to! Why?'

He scraped together the shreds of his ego, and threw them away; 'I'm not able to go on. I'm done for . . . burned out . . .' If there'd been enough liquid in him he would have cried.

'Why didn't you tell me, Andy?!?' Full of shocked sympathy and surprise I fixed an abseil.

Maybe I did rub his nose in it; but believe me he needed it – just as I need the elation, the power, the control that I know – I know – are only an illusion. The fact I can race up a small mountain won't make me any better at the other things I do and don't do. Still, it will calm me if I make it endure; it will dissolve the poison in my blood, the anger that builds up and up till it threatens the heart and must be purged.

If there is any such thing as wisdom for me it means knowing when to cut loose. And choosing a victim, to spare the ones I love.

If I do half a dozen routes with Andy now, get the Walker and the Frêney done, maybe shoot over to Zermatt, I just might . . . pull things into shape this winter. If she's crazy enough to let me try.

Time Reversal

by Anne Sauvy

translated by Jeremy Bernstein

'AH, PAPERS everywhere . . . what *are* these bits of newspapers? You're collecting clippings now? Come on, father, give me all that. There is enough of a mess around you as it is.'

'No, Odette, no! Wait a second! Don't throw away that one especially. And that one also. I am saving it!'

'But it's a date! Do you want to save a date, cut from a newspaper? And afterwards, everyone is astonished that there is a mess here! You're not reasonable! Oh, all right. I'll throw away the rest of the paper and tonight I'll straighten up. But, for God's sake, don't start cutting up newspapers again. I have enough to do without that. And don't look at me like that. I don't need your complaining on top of everything else. I have to go now. I am going to be late for work. Don't try to get out of bed by yourself. Don't try to go to the bathroom by yourself. Wait for the nurse. And don't forget to take your drops.'

My daughter gave me a light kiss on the forehead and disappeared. They say I am the one that talks nonsense. But she's the one who repeats the same things every day. I can hear her close the outside door as she leaves. I was able to save the clipping from the newspaper – and even the date.

I am tired. Outside the window I can see three chestnut trees. I know them well. Their leaves are already beginning to turn even though it is just the beginning of October. I ask myself – how awful – if I will still be here in the spring to see them blossom. It isn't amusing to be old – not amusing at all. It is boring to wait to die. I wait for the nurse to come, and later, my daughter and her husband. I know that behind my back they say I am senile. It isn't true! It is absolutely not true! There are things I remember very well . . . above all, my youth . . . oh, what good times. They have taken away almost all my things – my books, my maps, my photos – but the memories remain . . . fortunately.

What a pity! I was beginning to fall down at home. At first I tried to keep it secret, but one day they found me on the floor, since I was not able to get up by myself. What a pity! I was no longer able to live at home and my daughter . . . fall! I didn't fall when I used to climb. It was out of the question to fall!

All right . . . where was I? What was I thinking about just now? Something nice. Ah yes . . . that little newspaper clipping I saved. Hardly an article. If my daughter had not been late for work she would have thrown it away with the rest. Now, maybe I can hide it in a book. And the date, too. It was a little silly to have clipped the date. I found the clipping in yesterday's newspaper, alongside all the articles about Euromissiles, assassinations, inflation, new taxes, trade deficits, etc. What a nightmare.

But there was that little news note. I put it in front of me and read it and re-read it. I couldn't – or didn't want to – understand. It brought everything back fresh ... as if it happened yesterday. To think back on it is my best distraction. I am alone. I race past days and seasons. I reverse the flow of time ... and above all, there is *that* memory! My God, that was sixty years ago!

It was the last day of September and the weather was superb ... with a light that was both golden and shimmering. The sky was infinitely blue. We were just twenty. The whole of life offered itself as an immense promise. And the present was a thing of joy because we had just succeeded in doing the Charmoz-Grépon traverse.

I was with Charles Maisoncelle and we were climbing without a guide. From the beginning we were very anxious because that very evening we had to catch a train back to Paris. In order to be on time we left the hotel Montenvers in the middle of the night. The fog obscured the night sky. The air was cold. The timid glow from our lanterns barely lit our steps. But the higher we climbed, the more the fog dissipated. And little by little we could see the stars scintillate against a beautiful background of black velvet. Sleep still weighed on us. In the night the mountains we could make out seemed far off and inaccessible. We arrived too early in the morning at the base of the rock, and took advantage of that to stop and eat. The sky gradually whitened and the stars went out one by one. With the growing daylight our confidence returned.

When we began to climb, the neighbouring cliffs appeared to us in full detail. The rock was inviting ... solid. Our muscles responded with strength and elasticity. Ah, such happy climbing! We felt perfectly warm even before the sun rose. We moved both rapidly and safely. We very quickly reached the summit of the Charmoz. Our happiness was tinged with a feeling of anxiety about the climb we were about to do. But at the summit of the Grépon, all that was forgotten.

I will never forget Charles' shout of pure joy. What a panorama – a feast for the eyes! Without a word we shook hands. It was truly an unforgettable moment. We stayed on for a minute, bathed in that special light of early autumn ... palpable, enveloping, moist. But as the wind started to rise we began the descent, and soon we found ourselves back on the glacier. The snow, which had been hard in the morning when we climbed it, was now soft and deep despite the lateness of the season. We leapt down the slope in great bounds, not paying too much attention to our rope, which lay between us on the snow, soaking up water. There would be plenty of time to dry it later.

We were like two young madmen driven crazy by our enthusiasm for life. Before 3 o'clock, we were at the Rochon des Nantillons. Plenty of time to get back to the valley and even visit the climbers' haven, Patisserie des Alpes.

But ... man proposes and God disposes. Just as we reached the rognon we heard the thunderous sound of a terrible rockfall. It was in the direction of the Grands Charmoz. An immense block had detached itself and smashed at the base of the mountain, producing a boiling cloud of grey dust. The earth trembled even where we were. It was a terrifying spectacle. We stood transfixed until the mountain once again became silent and then . . . and then we thought we heard a cry.

We all but ran down the rognon to see if someone had been trapped in that furious rockfall. Soon we saw him, half-seated on a rock, wounded, signalling to us desperately.

His two friends, he told us, had been killed in the avalanche . . . nothing could be done for them. He had been thrown to the ground under a large block – the one on which he was now resting – and it had shielded his body – a miracle. At first, because of his curious clothing and alpine equipment, I took him for a foreigner. But when he began to speak, it was clear he was French. He had many cuts and bruises, but most seriously a broken leg.

Fortunately, my companion, Charles Maisoncelle, was an intern just finishing his medical studies in the Cochin hospital. He was able to put the stranger's leg in a makeshift splint, but when we tried to move him, it caused him such pain, we had to stop. He said that there was no need to stay with him while we went for help, and we promised to get back down to the valley and give the alert as soon as possible.

We helped him to swallow a little brandy and, since he had no heavy sweater, I left him the new Tyrolean loden jacket I had bought at the beginning of the summer. We didn't ask him what he and his friends were doing in the spot where we found him – well off the usual route. I did ask his name – Xavier Berthiand – a courageous young man for whom we felt the greatest sympathy. I promised I would learn what happened to him afterwards.

Despite our fatigue we decided to take the shortcut through the Alpages de Blaitière, which leads directly down to Chamonix. We raced down the snowfields, moraines and finally the trail as quickly as we could and were soon back in Chamonix. My flannel shirt was drenched in sweat when I got to the Bureau des Guides. Still in a state of shock, I told about the avalanche and the accident. The guide promised that he would organize a caravan of eight guides that same evening and go to the Montenvers, and that at dawn they would go to the injured man and also, if possible, bring down the bodies of his friends. I asked the guide to keep me posted and also to recover my loden jacket.

Eight days later I got a letter. It was so strange that I kept it and have it still. It read, 'Monsieur, as I promised, we put together a caravan of guides to look for the young man who was injured. We slept at the Montenvers that night, and the next morning went to the base of the Grands Charmoz. What I am now going to tell you will probably surprise you as much as it did us. We found no-one. We looked everywhere – even in the crevasses near the bottom. If the young man had been able to leave by himself, how could he have carried the bodies of his friends? And who could have helped him, especially this late in the season when the mountains are almost deserted? Living or dead, we saw no one.'

There was a postscript: 'As for the avalanche you spoke of, it did not seem to have been as substantial as you thought. There were a few rocks here and there that probably fell recently from the wall – but that was all. But I simply can't explain what happened to the bodies.'

I have often thought about this since, and just as often wondered about what happened to Xavier Berthiand. Was he rescued? The mountains have their mysteries.

Time passes. A dozen years later, Charles Maisoncelle was killed on the Weisshorn. I am old, but to avoid the moods of my daughter and the ruckus of my grandchildren, I bring back images of our youth in the mountains ... those little climbing huts with smoking stoves ... the sparks that our hob-nailed boots gave off on the rock ... summits swept by the wind ... and sometimes I ask myself about that injured young man, without finding any clue to the puzzle.

And yesterday, that strange item in the newspaper. Strange, that is, only to me. For anyone else it would be a dry – perhaps sad – banality. The newspaper was dated the second of October – the dispatch was sent on the first – and what is described took place on the 30th of September. The article was entitled 'Another Mountaineering Accident'. It said: 'Yesterday at about 2:30 p.m., a giant rockfall took place on the flanks of the Aiguille des Grands Charmoz in the Mont Blanc range. A rope of three climbers, who had just rappelled down the Cordier Pillar, was swept off by the rockfall. Almost by a miracle one of them, Xavier Berthiand, a 24-year-old native of Blois, escaped the catastrophe suffering only some bruises and a broken leg. Some climbers were descending the Nantillons glacier and were able to offer first aid.'

'The two companions of the wounded man, whose names we do not know, died in the avalanche. The wounded man was able to signal the helicopter of the Protection Civile, which was returning from a reconnaissance of the Aiguille de Peigne. It landed immediately. That evening, Mr. Berthiand was evacuated to the Chamonix hospital and the bodies of his comrades were also brought down to the valley. This accident has brought to 39 the number of deaths in the Mont Blanc massif during this summer's climbing season.'

In the days after I found the clipping, I was in a state of constant turmoil. I needed proof. I needed to know that I was not totally mad. I wrote to the hospital in Chamonix giving my name and address, but, of course, not my age.

This morning, someone knocked on the door of my room. Despite all the warnings, I went and opened it. I did very well and did not fall. It was the mail ... a package for me! I went to my chair and opened it. Inside was my Tyrolean loden climbing jacket. In a pocket I found one of the handkerchiefs my sister had embroidered for my twentieth birthday. In the pocket, too, was a drawing of the route the wounded man had taken before the accident. He must have taken it from his pocket to put in mine. A note from the hospital said that after the severe shock of the accident, Xavier Berthiand was now doing well and wanted to send his warmest thanks to my friend and me.

My old climbing jacket! I put it across my knees so that my gnarled fingers could caress the thick waterproof loden of which I was so proud. I can already hear my daughter ... 'Where did you dig out that old rag?' I will laugh silently. For now I know.

In The Crevasse

by Ben Santer

FOUR O'CLOCK in the morning.

I can hear the wind whistling through the cracks in our stone wall. We are lying in a small hollow beneath a boulder the size of a house. There is not more than a foot and a half of clearance between the stone floor and the stone roof. Yesterday, we walled off part of the entrance to our 'Hotel Argentière', using what flat rocks we could find. Now the wind can play tunes on the wall, using the holes and cracks like stops on a flute. Spindrift hisses softly against the nylon of our sleeping bags.

The noises I've made, crawling to the wall and looking out through a hole, have woken Tony. His sleeping bag rustles as he tries to sit up.

'What's it like out there, Ben?' His voice sounds muffled and distant.

'It's snowing.' Fine, driving snow.

'Do you think there's any point in getting up?'

'Not now. Let's have a look later.'

Seven o'clock in the morning.

Tony is shaking my sleeping bag, trying to pull me back from the edge of a bad dream, and I can't seem to hold on to any part of the dream, but I know it's bad, and I know that I'm afraid, and now. . . .

Now it's gone, and Tony is still shaking my sleeping bag.

'Hey Ben! Wake up!'

'Hnnnhhh? Whass wrong?'

'Look outside!'

So I crawl to the wall and look outside. The snow has stopped; the wind has died. Across the Argentière Glacier, the summits of the Droites and Courtes are catching the first light. Pale reds seep down their North Faces, displacing shadows, transforming simple rock and ice into something more, something richer. The sky is a washed-out watercolour blue, and you can almost tell its coldness just by looking at it. The colours have been asleep, just as we have been asleep, and now they need time to awake and develop.

'What d'ye think, Ben?'

'What time is it?'

'Just gone seven.'

'That's a bit late to start, isn't it?'

'Yeah, but the weather's great. And it's been a cold night. Everything'll be frozen dead solid.'

'The Courtes and the Droites caught a little new snow.'

'Doesn't look like it'll be enough to bother us, though.'

'So what do you think we should do?'

'I think we should go for it.'

'If you say so, I'm game.'

'I'm game, he said – so they shot him!'

'I've heard that one before, somewhere.'

'How could you? I just made it up.'

'Crap, Santer.'

'You pack the gear?'

'If you make the tea.'

'A deal.'

We pack and sup, and then prise apart the cold leather of frozen boots. Getting my feet into my boots is like fitting the proverbial square peg in the round hole. This part of the morning ritual has to be performed without gloves. By the time the crampons are strapped on, my fingertips need sucking and rubbing until they start to tingle again. The tingling is almost a pleasant feeling.

We crawl out of the bivouac cave.

'God! If that boulder had shifted during the night, we'd have been flatter than pancakes!'

'More like crêpes, I think.'

'I've never seen a rock as big as that.'

'I guess it's lucky for us that this place isn't noted for earthquakes.'

Behind our Hotel Argentière, the Milieu Glacier rises in a broad sweep, flanked on either side by granite walls topped with serrated ridges. Near the summit, the glacier's angle steepens. The size of the thing is a bit frightening – particularly if, like us, you're still green behind the ears, in your first 'Alpine season', on your first real Alpine climb. It's in Gaston Rebuffat's book – one of the hundred classic climbs in and around Chamonix – and if it's in Rebuffat, it must be good. The Aiguille d'Argentière. Just over 3900 metres of it, give or take a few metres either way (depending on which postcard you buy).

Perhaps I'll be a real 'alpiniste' if I climb this. A real alpiniste, like the tight-faced, tight-fisted men and women in the Chamonix téléphériques and cable cars, the climbers with their rucksacs bristling with North Wall hammers, 12-point crampons and sharp-picked axes. They are initiated in the mystery of what it means to be an alpiniste. The aura of mystery and hidden strengths surrounds them, clings to their speech, their expressions and the way that they move. Perhaps today I'll penetrate the mystery.

A scree slope leads to the darkened snout of the Milieu Glacier. The going is hard. We set out unroped, with Tony in the lead, moving quickly to make up for our late start. My concentration isn't as good as it should be. I can't seem to focus my attention on the ground in front of my feet, or on Tony. I'm not monitoring the performance of my legs and lungs or thinking about the technical difficulties of the route. I'm not altogether 'here'.

I'm in Germany. I'm with my parents and sisters in Rodgau, where I left them eight days ago. My father is dying of cancer, and here I am, on the

Aiguille d'Argentière. I might as well be light years away, for all the good I'm doing him. Why the hell am I here, anyway?

You've been with him for the last six months. You can't help him, you know. There's nothing you can do. It's good for you to be here. You'll be more help when you go home.

But it's wrong, being here. It's wrong, wrong, wrong. What if he dies while I'm here? What will I feel like then? I'll carry that guilt with me for the rest of my life. I didn't do everything that I could have done. I didn't have all the time with him that I could have had. I didn't say all the things I could have said, that I wanted to say. I didn't ask all the questions that I always wanted to ask him. About the war, and about his mother and father (the grandparents I never knew) and his little brother Bernd – what sort of people were they? What was that time like? When I think of all those unasked questions, I wonder why the hell I'm here when I could be back in Germany with my father. What's the fucking point in putting one foot after the other for the next eight or nine hours?

The point is that you delude yourself if you think you're a great help at home, some rock-steady spiritual support for your father and the rest of the family. It's pure delusion – get that straight. You're no tower of emotional strength. Whenever you're home, your frustration at being so totally helpless boils over. You get angry too quickly. You start feeling sorry for yourself. You give in to self-pity. So you might as well stay here for a few weeks. Maybe a little distance is what you need in order to put things into perspective.

Okay, okay But this is it! Fertig! Finito! After today I'm going home. I'll get the first train I can out of Chamonix. I'm sick of climbing. It makes me sick, sick, sick.

You always were a bit melodramatic. Too much of an actor. Grief isn't a part that you play. It's not a role you have to act out. It isn't something that becomes more intense if you say it's name more often. No one's asking you to play the grieving son, and walk around with a face of stone, with all the lines of your suffering etched into it. Grief needs no name or face, and you're always trying to put names to it.

Look – I wasn't prepared for any of this. No one lectured about Death at University. You couldn't take any courses in how to deal with Death. I know I'm making mistakes. Maybe I'm doing more things wrong than I'm doing right. Six months ago, someone pulled the carpet out from under my life, and I'm still lying on the floor with a stupid grin on my face. But I'll get up some day. I swear I'll get up again.

The snow on the surface of the ice crunches beneath my feet. Maybe I'm going crazy, holding conversations with myself. You'd better clear your head, fella. This isn't the place for people who've got their heads screwed on the wrong way. It's not a place very forgiving of mistakes. You'd better watch yourself. Go back home tomorrow, if that's really what you want to do. But today you'd better watch yourself.

Tony is 50 or 60 metres in front of me. Every few minutes he turns around and grins, just to make sure that I'm still there, that the gap between us isn't getting any wider. Neither of us takes any pictures. There is no time for sightseeing, just time for motion. Motion, motion, motion. Success is continuous motion, and stopping is failure.

Now we are on the Milieu Glacier itself. Rocks and pebbles are frozen hard on its surface, cemented with the cold. Occasionally I hear the high-pitched whine of rocks tumbling from the twin ridges, rocks melted loose by the morning sun. I hear the *crrrack!* as rock hits rock, and see the splinters fly like shell fragments. I hear the dull *thump!* of the rock as it impacts on the ice, cratering the surface. The sounds are not comforting. I cringe instinctively when I hear the *wheeee! crrrack! wheeee!*, and try to make myself smaller, more compact, less vulnerable. I'm beginning to understand what it means to be an alpiniste.

This place looks like something straight out of a Dali painting. Ice, ice, and all of it fluid, seeming to change into something else – hugging the contours of the underlying rock, here smooth, and here broken, where it pours over a break of slope. Ice fissured in long crevasses; you look down them, and the ice shimmers green, streaked with dark bands of dust, one band for each year. Summer alternates with winter, thin black bands alternate with thick white bands, until the glacial clock is swallowed in the heart of the darkness. Down there are the traces of summers and winters that this place knew long before I existed. It's a strange thought.

We thread our way through the maze of crevasses like soldiers searching for safe passage through a minefield. We are still unroped. August has been hot, and all the crevasses are *aper* – readily visible. Last night's snow was not heavy enough to cover any of them, and it holds a plain trail of footprints. As long as those ahead of us knew where they were going. . . .

Tony stops at the first major barrier – a crevasse about two metres wide and a hundred metres long. The tracks are not easy to follow at this point. There seem to be several possible crossing places, all of about equal difficulty. Tony waits for me to join him.

I guess all of us have sudden, irrational impulses. Usually we don't act on them. But now some temporary insanity takes control, and tells me that I can easily jump five feet. What the hell is Tony stopping for anyway? There is no safety mechanism to protect me from myself. I start running, without even bothering to take off my rucksac, and then jump like a little boy jumping across a puddle, but the stakes here are bigger than wet feet or scraped shins.

And there's nothing wrong, it's no problem, I've jumped it easily, but the landing is sloping, and the ice is hard, too damn hard, and the crampon points dig in no further than fingernails on a blackboard, and it's going wrong, it's all going wrong, such a stupid bloody mistake. Stupid, stupid, stupid bloody mistake.

Everything happens so quickly. The contact with the ice. The sliding backwards towards the lip of the crevasse. Tony's shout. There is no time for surprise, or fear, or even comprehension. No time to see the film of my life unwind. No pain. Only an unstoppable sliding. I feel like a man caught up in the current of a vast river, unable to reach either shore – a man who hears the roar of an unseen waterfall, and sees a fine drizzle of spray in the distance.

And then the sliding is over, and gravity's rules are no different for me than for the stone I saw ten minutes ago, falling from the ridge. Hands and feet instinctively strike out against the ice walls, but there is nothing that they can do now, nothing to hold on to. Dying must be a loss of control – the sensation that forces too powerful have gained the upper hand, that nothing can be changed, that 'free will' has no meaning, and that waiting is the only thing left.

Then the waiting is over, and something is squeezing my chest and lungs – tight, tighter, tighter – there must be a breaking point. Bone must break, cartilage snap, skin rip. Stop, stop, stop. Stop the falling, stop the air rushing, stop the squeezing, stop the darkness. Stop, stop, stop!

Then the falling is over, and the ice relaxes its grip on my chest. Nothing is moving. I am not moving; the air is not moving. I can hear the blood pounding, *kaTHUMP, kaTHUMP, kaTHUMP* in my ears, and it's hard to believe that the sound is only inside my head, and not something external, not the sound of a giant drum, booming in the blackness beneath me. Strange that I can hear a sound inside of myself. And strange that I'm still alive – for I must be alive if I can hear the blood in my ears, see the ice in front of my face, feel it pressing against my chest, and hear Tony shouting my name. I must be alive if I can see my hands bleeding.

Tony is still shouting. I can't understand the words. He is at the end of a long, dark corridor, always shouting the same words, over and over again. The words are exhausted and have spent their energy long before they reach me. My tongue is thick and heavy. My voice is dead, frozen at the back of my throat.

Now the words make sense.

'Ben! Ben! Are you okay, Ben? Are you okay?'

Tony, I'm okay, I'm alive – I'm all right, I'm okay, really I'm okay, and I'm trying to tell you that, I'm really trying hard, Tony, but my voice won't work any more Tony, and nothing's coming out. Maybe I've lost it for good, and maybe it's just shock, Tony, and it'll all come back if I wait, so don't go – don't think that I'm dead, because I'm not, and I'm trying to tell you that. It's like the time that car hit me, and strangers picked me up out of the road. I couldn't say anything for a full minute at least. It was only shock – that's all it was.

'Are you okay, Ben? Ben, are you okay?'

Don't go Tony, don't go, don't go. It's coming back, it's all coming back, just wait another few seconds. Don't give up on me now.

'Ben! Where are you? Are you okay? Say something if you're okay!'

Please don't go Tony. Don't leave me here.

'Where are you, Ben? Answer me if you can hear me!'

Now it's coming, Tony – I can feel the words take shape at the back of my throat, and all I have to do is move my jaw muscles and lips. It's building up inside like the pressure in a champagne bottle, and it's coming out now, now, NOW. . . .

'Tony! Tony!'

'Thank Christ for that! Oh Jesus, are you okay, Ben?'

I can see him now. I can see the dark pin-point of a head, edging over the lip of the crevasse, outlined against a slit of blue sky. How far away is he? Thirty metres, maybe forty? It's difficult to judge.

'Ben! Are you okay?'

'Yes!'

'Is anything broken?'

'I can't tell!'

'What's your position?'

What is my position? My feet are resting on snow. Is this the bottom? No, it can't be the bottom. The snow has holes in it. Black holes. So this can't be the bottom. It must be a kind of snow bridge. Ice is pressing against my chest and back. I can feel the coldness of it through my clothes. I'm in a kind of bottleneck, almost unable to move. I can feel the dull throbbing of blood in legs, arms and fingertips, almost as if they were pulsating. There is no pain. I can't see or feel any broken bones. . . .

'What's your position?'

'I can't move!'

'Listen Ben! I'll set up a belay and get a rope down to you! Do you understand?'

'Yes!'

'Hold on, ol' son! I'll be as quick as I can!'

The pin-point head pulls back from the crevasse rim. Suddenly I am alone.

You must keep moving. Move your hands and fingers. Move your toes in your boots. Can't you feel the cold trying to get inside of you? Can't you feel it trying to freeze the living, moving parts of you? You know what happens to people who don't move at this kind of temperature. They lose things. Fingers and toes. They fall asleep. It's pleasant. Sleeping means they don't have to fight anymore. They just give in, and relax, and sleep. So move, damn you! Move, move, move! You've made one mistake too many today – don't make any more. Beweg' Dich, beweg' Dich, Bewegung brauchst Du, so move, MOVE!

All right, I'm moving, I'm not giving up.

Your hands are bleeding. You'd better stop the bleeding.

Tell me what I have to do.

The first aid pouch is in the top pocket of your rucksac. Reach around, unzip the pocket, and take out the pouch. Then open it. There are gauze bandages inside it. Wrap them around your fingers and knuckles, and use the tape to keep the bandages in place. Don't make the tape too tight – you'll cut off the blood circulation. Just tight enough to stop the bleeding.

Blood trickles down my fingers as I bandage them. The drops pulse with each heart beat. They haven't given up being a part of me – not even outside the body. They still throb in synchrony with the heart. The drops move to the fingertips and swell, the way a water drop grows when it hangs on the lip of a tap. When they are ripe they fall like red berries, burning holes in the snow at my feet, a random spattering of red on white. They freeze to death.

Grab hold of your thoughts. Keep them fixed on something. Fix them on your parents and sisters. Think what they would feel if you die here. Think what they would have to face.

They wouldn't understand this. It would be so senseless, so stupid, so bloody stupid.

You'd leave them all the suffering you've avoided. The dead are released – the living suffer and shoulder the burdens. They're the ones who have to bring you home and bury you. They're the ones who have to understand, to come to terms with it all. They're the ones with the memories, the memories like scabs that they pick open every day – they look at a picture that you painted, they find a letter that you wrote, a shirt that you wore.

It would be so senseless. It would hurt them so much.

You remember the white mouse, don't you? The white mouse that your little sister had in America? You were in England, and your family was in America. You remember it now, don't you? It's name was Benjie. They all loved Benjie. Benjie the mouse. Your mother loved it, and Jenny and Mitchi loved it, and even your father loved it. Then Benjie died, just like that. Your father came home from work in the evening and opened the door and everyone was crying and he asked what was wrong and Michelle, little Michelle said that Benjie was dead. And she didn't think when she said that, and of course she meant Benjie the mouse. But your father didn't know that. He just saw the three sobbing women and heard that Benjie was dead – and thought that you were dead. Benjie, his own flesh and blood – not Benjie the mouse. And there was one instant, that one instant when no one could say a word, that one second before your mother shouted 'Benjie the mouse!', and in that one second they thought that he was going to have a heart-attack. You remember that, don't you? The 'Benjie the Mouse' story. But what if it weren't Benjie the mouse this time? What if it were the real thing? If that one second continued for ten seconds, or sixty seconds – ten minutes, a week, a year?

I can't hurt them like that. I won't hurt them like that.

So you'd better think about staying alive, huh? think about moving. Think about what you're going to do when Tony gets the rope down here.

Okay I'll think about that.

Think about how you're going to tie prussik knots if you need them. Think about which slings you'll have to use for waist loops and foot loops. Think about getting these things ready. Just in case you need them to get out of here.

'Ben, hey Ben!'

Tony is back.

'Are you all right?'

'Yes! I'm glad you're back! It's kind of lonely down here!'

'Sorry it took awhile! I've got a good belay! Mind your head! I'm throwing the rope down ......
NOW!'

I hear the hiss of rope coils rushing through the air. Loose shards of ice tinkle on the plastic of my helmet.

'I've got it, Tony!'

'Great stuff, our kid! D'ye think you can climb out?'

'I'll try!'

Clumsy, bandaged hands fumble with a figure-of-eight knot. I've tied this hundreds of times before. Now my fingers feel as if they belong to someone else. There isn't much slack left in the rope. Maybe a couple of metres. If Tony used five or ten metres for the belay, then I've fallen at least 30 metres. I clip the knot into the karabiner on my climbing harness and close the screwgate, then bend and twist until I can remove my ice axe and hammer from the securing loops on the rucksac. The waiting is over now. The present is all that matters. Not the immediate past or future – just the here and now.

'Tony! Have you got me?'

'I've got you!'

'I'll try to climb out!'

'Okay!'

But it's hopeless, hopeless. There isn't enough room to swing the axe or hammer. The picks bounce off the ice, only nicking the surface. I try again and again, but it's no use, I'm not getting enough leverage.

Keep cool now. Just keep cool. Don't panic, and don't waste your energy trying to climb out of here like that. You won't get anywhere. You've got plenty of time as long as you keep your head together and do things methodically. You'll have to prussik out of here. You know how to do that. Think of all the times you've practised on the railway bridge.

'Tony! It's no good! I can't climb out! There's not enough room! I'll have to try prussiking out!'

'Just tell me when you're ready!'

Okay, tie the prussik knots. Just like on the railway bridge. Clip the top prussik into your harness with a short sling. Clip a long sling into the bottom prussik, and use that as a foot loop. Remember to slide the knots up the rope alternately. You can only slide them when you take your weight off them. They'll lock once you put weight on them.

'Tony, I'm ready! Start to prussik now!'

'Okay!'

Slide your waist prussik first. Then the foot prussik. Waist prussik. Foot prussik. Waist prussik. . . .

'I'm not moving! I'm not moving!'

Easy, easy now. Of course you're not moving. A kernmantel climbing rope has stretch in it. You should know that. When you load it, it can stretch to a length up to 20% greater than its unloaded length. You're loading it with your body weight – 60 kilograms. Remember that that's going to stretch the rope, and you'll have to take up that stretch before you'll move anywhere. So just keep calm and keep going.

Stretch, that must be it. Got to take up the stretch. . . .

Waist prussik. Foot prussik. Waist prussik. . . .

Soon I begin to move upwards. 'Inch by inch, little by little . . .', as the song goes. The crevasse widens just enough so that the ice isn't pressing against my chest any longer. 'Step by step, move a little closer. . . .' Move a little closer to that strip of blue sky. Move a little closer to sunlight and colours, a little closer to flowers and grass and soil, closer to the sound of falling rock, the sound of water running over ice. Closer to the sound of laughter, to the warmth of an embrace – move a little closer. Move away from the ice and the blood-drops spattering the snow. Cheat the ice, beat it, defeat it! Move up from the darkness, the cold that wants to crawl inside of you, move up from the silence and the frozen stillness. 'Step . . . by . . . step, little by little. . . .' Closer, closer.

I've found the correct sequence of movements now. Rest on the waist prussik. Push the foot prussik up the rope. Stand in the loop of the foot prussik. Push the waist prussik up the rope. Repeat and repeat and repeat, until the sequence of movements becomes automatic, like a kata in karate.

I can hear the blood pounding in my ears, pounding as hard as it did just after the fall, pounding like a fist inside my skull. The pounding becomes a voice, a sequence of words, a needle in an endless groove. I can almost hear the words.

KaTHUMP! KaTHUMP! . . . KaTHUMP! KaTHUMP! . . . You're going TO LIVE! You're going TO LIVE! . . . *KaTHUMP! KaTHUMP! . . .* You're going TO LIVE! You're going TO LIVE! . . . *KaTHUMP! KaTHUMP! . . .*

It's only the blood pounding in your head. There's no voice, no words. And if you don't concentrate now, you're NOT going to live. Forget about words in your head, and concentrate on moving the prussiks instead.

Exhaled breath condenses in tiny clouds. I'm getting the feeling back in my fingers and feet. I can feel them throbbing and tingling. The blood in the snow is receding, losing detail, like a dream that you can't hold on to when you wake up. Sunlight is moving down one wall of the crevasse, forcing the shadow back. Ice crystals glint with a sudden Cinderella brilliance. I'll reach the light soon. I'll reach it and be warm again. The blood is still *KaTHUMPing* in my head, and it's getting louder. Surely even Tony must be able to hear it now. In a minute he'll stick his head over the edge and ask 'What the hell's that pounding noise, Ben? What are you doing?' and I'll tell him not to worry, it's only the blood in my head.

How long have I been here? Hours or minutes? Minutes or seconds? Or perhaps I've been here or in dark, cold places like this for years, and now I'm moving out into the light for the first time, finding the real world, learning how to live.

The thin blue crack is widening. Maybe this is what a diver sees and feels coming up through the slow stages of decompression. Holding on to his lifeline, able to see the surface but not to touch it. Forced to wait by the nitrogen in his blood. Does the blood pound in his head, does he hear words and voices?

There are only five metres left. God, oh please God, I've only once asked you for something really big, about my father, and now I'm asking again, don't let the rope break, don't let it break now, and it's such a small thing to want, and there are only a few metres left now. . . .

Three metres. Ten feet. Now the rope is spinning. First in one direction as it twists, and then in the other as it untwists. The world is losing its focus now, the way it did when I rode the painted ponies on the merry-go-round, but this time the carousel doesn't stop and I can't get off and something must be broken somewhere but if I sit tight and close my eyes it'll be all right, nothing will happen. . . .

Is the rope moving, or am I moving, or is the ice moving? What revolves and what is stationary?

'I'm losing it again. I'm losing control.'

Don't give up now. You're close, very close. Just keep moving. Waist prussik, foot prussik. Keep moving, and you'll get out of this place.

And I'm still moving, my hands are still moving, shifting the knots in a kind of muscular reflex.

One and a half metres. Five feet.

I can see the curling lip of the crevasse now. The rope has gouged a groove in it. The lip is sneering at me, pulled back to expose white teeth, as if to tell me that I was lucky this time, and that maybe next time I won't be so lucky. I can feel its contempt for me. . . .

You're close enough now. Get out your axe and hammer. Hit them in hard to the lip. Kick your front points in. Kick them in hard.

KaTHUMP! KaTHUMP! . . . KaTHUMP! KaTHUMP! . . . You're going TO LIVE! You're going TO LIVE!

Now pull up on the axe and hammer. It's okay – you can trust them. Kick your feet in higher.

KaTHUMP! KaTHUMP!

Push off with your feet! Pull on the handles! NOW!

And I can see Tony now, just a couple of metres away from me, and his face is taut as a mask, there are drops of sweat on his handlebar moustache, and he is pulling in the rope as I am pushing my feet off the wall, and the ice spits me out face first into the snow and bright, bright sunlight, and the blood in my head is going to explode and burst my ear drums but it's all right, really it's all going to be okay, I'm going to live. . . .

And nothing will ever be the same after this.

Summertime

by Al Alvarez

THE SUN was misty, its light diffused and weak, blurring the long folds of the valley, yellowing its greens, and swallowing the distant lake and village in a vague glow. The air was damp and warm and they were tired. It had been a long slog up, shirtless, sweating, rucksacks bumping damply against their backs, boots heavy. When they reached the cliff above the little tarn its two great walls were already festooned with climbers. They trudged heavily along the foot of the East Buttress, changed into lighter boots, sorted their equipment, and stowed their rucksacks neatly under an overhang. Then they stepped delicately out on to the steep West Buttress and climbed across to the wide ledge where their route began. But others were there before them, so they sprawled lazily and in comfort, feeling their sweat dry, grateful for the north face shadow and the cool rock curving above, dropping away below. The party in front was taking its time to cross an abrupt smooth slab, the leader talking, mostly to himself in a light nervous voice, as though to cheer himself up. Occasionally they heard small sounds of other climbers on the two looming buttresses, calling to one another at a distance. Lazy day. Their fatigue was pleasant, lulling. Alan began to doze, wake, doze. John was whistling softly to himself: 'Summertime, and the living is easy . . .' Alan dozed.

Then for no good reason, he was wholly awake. There was a faint noise from the direction of the East Buttress and a slight disturbance at the corner of his eyes. Then silence and the humid midday lull.

'Someone's come off,' said John.

Alan looked to where he was pointing and could see nothing.

'You sure?' he said.

'I think so.'

Nobody moved on the cliff or screes. The disturbance had been no more than a puff of wind: a cool momentary breath and it was gone. Silence. Then someone hurried along the foot of the East. Another man followed him, then another, running awkwardly on the steep path. There were voices calling, a sudden urgency in the air.

'He hasn't moved,' said John, and pointed again.

There was a vague shape on the scree. It was crumpled and still. Two men slithered down towards it, loose stones cascading in front of them. They bent over the motionless figure, then straightened and shouted faintly upwards.

'We'd better get off and see if we can help,' said John.

'What the hell,' said Alan. 'It's just some idiot who's slipped and twisted an ankle.' He felt irritated at having to turn back from a climb; another day lost.

'Even so,' John apologized, 'we'd want someone to do the same for us.' Alan made him feel foolish and pompous, like a dull schoolboy.

Alan grunted resentfully and stood up. Carefully and slowly they traversed off the climb. When they reached the rucksacs Alan flopped down and began to unlace his climbing shoes.

'We'd better change into boots,' he said grudgingly. 'Just in case we have to lug some bloody stretcher miles down the mountain.' Anything to waste time.

Somewhere on the cliff high above them a man was shouting in a self-important voice about a radio: 'Turn it to Emergency. Call Alpine Valley 3. We're Alpine Valley 2. It's in my pack. In my pack. Turn it to Emergency. Even at that distance he sounded as if he liked giving orders.

John and Alan ambled slowly back along the path. By the time they reached the foot of the East Buttress a small group had gathered on the scree and more were waiting uneasily on the path above, as though frightened to go too close. The body had not moved. A climber, caught in the middle of a route and unable or unwilling to go down, hung poised on the vertical wall above, peering down on the scene like a stone gargoyle on a church.

'Where's that bloody radio?' A man clambered hurriedly back on to the path.

Alan touched his arm: 'Who is it?'

'Dave. Dave Evans. He's not conscious.'

'Oh no.' Alan felt his stomach turn over once, heavily. The other man's face was greenish.

'His skull's split wide open.' he said. He was trembling.

Together John and Alan slithered down the scree. Dave was lying on his side, his back towards them. One hand was behind his knee, puffed up and jaggedly cut. The nails were purple and oozed blood. His legs lay at odd angles, like a doll's, and the hair on the back of his head was matted and bloody. Three men bent uncertainly over him. Alan and John sat down on the opposite side of Dave's body.

'How is he?' asked John in a small voice, as though not wanting to disturb a sick man.

'It's very bad.'

They all waited in the sticky air. Alan wanted to go round below the broken body and look at his friend's face. But he hadn't the nerve.

Suddenly, one of the other three said urgently: 'I think his heart's stopped. I can't feel his pulse.'

'Give him artificial respiration,' said another.

They turned Dave on his back. His face was the colour of putty, a dead grey, his head a lumpy, gaping mass of blood.

'He's shaved off his beard since I last saw him,' thought Alan inconsequentially.

'Push on his ribs as hard as you can,' said one of the men. 'Don't worry if you break them. They're probably broken already. Just push with everything you've got. Once a second.'

Obediently a second man straddled Dave's body, leaned with arms stiff against his chest and began to push, reluctantly at first, then with a gathering, desperate energy. The man who had given instructions pinched Dave's nostrils with the fingers of one hand, and, with the other, made a funnel of his lips. He put his mouth to Dave's and blew hard, as if he were inflating a child's balloon. Then he turned his head, sucked in air, and blew again. His lifted mouth was covered with Dave's blood. The third man began counting slowly: 'One-and-*two*-and-*three*-and-*four*-and . . .' At each number, one man shoved on his chest as though he were doing press-ups and the other blew into his mouth. The inert body quivered with their efforts.

'*Thirty-nine*-and-*forty*-and-*forty-one* . . .'

Every so often, the climber giving Dave the kiss of life paused to spit. Once he retched violently and sucked in his breath through clenched teeth like a man screaming. Whenever he lifted his mouth, Dave's lips shuddered with an obscene farting noise.

More people came up. Each couple of minutes the men changed. They came and sat heavily on the scree, their lips smeared with blood.

'I don't think we've a hope,' one said. 'The deep wounds in his head are congealing already.'

But they went on just the same, and the terrible, loose farting noise continued.

'I wish they'd leave him alone,' said Alan.

'He's got two kids, hasn't he?' said John.

'Three,' said Alan.

Another climber came and sat down beside them. He was panting like a long-distance runner. His face was as grey as the dying man's; he had a drooping, melancholy moustache.

'What happened, Paul?' asked John.

'We'd unroped to come down,' Paul gasped it out. 'He took a – short cut – across the – blocks at the top. I think – something – came away. He went quite – slowly – bounced – on a couple of ledges. Very slowly. I thought he'd – stop himself. Then he just – went on – over the edge – of the main – face. Three hundred feet.' He paused, shaking his head. 'I thought he'd stop himself,' he repeated in an accusing voice.

'Maybe the rock knocked him out when it came away,' said John consolingly, as though Paul were somehow to blame.

'He should have been wearing a crash helmet,' said Alan.

'*Twenty-one*-and-*twenty two*-and-*twenty-three*-and . . .' Again the vibrating, farting noise came from the crumpled body.

Then another, busier note began, faintly at first, on the other side of the mountain, but growing swiftly more demanding until the whole amphitheatre of rock seemed to shake with the din. A helicopter sidled out of the misty air over the ridge of the valley. It circled once high up, then swooped down over the tarn at the foot of the scree and dropped a smoke flare.

'Idiots,' said Alan in his aggrieved voice. 'Why are they playing games?'

'That's to see which way the wind is blowing,' said John.

The helicopter circled again and then began to nose in like a feeding insect, vivid yellow, its blades whirring. Everybody struggled back up the scree to the path, leaving Dave on his own in the encircling noise.

Three men crouched in the opening of the machine, dressed like spacemen in silver suits and helmets. Two of them were laughing together, as though one had just told an unexpectedly good joke.

The chopper hovered, whirling up dust. One of the spacemen swung suddenly out on a cable, clutching a bulky stretcher. As he descended, he waved his feet in the air like a baby in a high chair. The helicopter circled again fussily. Then another figure was winched down, holding a neat doctor's bag. He hung at the end of the wire, stiff, formal and unmoving, like a figure on a mediaeval tomb. The chopper whirred off once more towards the ridge while the two spacemen busied themselves with the lonely body on the scree. At last one of them stood and waved, and the great hungry insect sidled in again. The first spaceman rose slowly, hugging Dave's shrouded body to him like an enormous Christmas parcel. Once again, he and his companion on board smiled brightly to each other as they manipulated their unwieldy load into the belly of the machine. Then the doctor ascended as formally as before, and the helicopter buzzed importantly back down the valley.

The climbers sat, stunned by the silence, as the dust settled.

'They got him out in under an hour,' someone said at last.

'Not bad, not bad at all.' The men began to stir and stretch.

'Will you tell his wife?' John said to Paul.

'I suppose I've got to.' Paul was still staring down the valley into the glowing mist where the helicopter had vanished. He seemed abstracted, as though he did not yet believe what had happened concerned him.

Alan got up stiffly. 'I don't want to climb now,' he said. 'My stomach feels like knotted old rope.'

'No,' said John, 'Let's go back down.' He sounded relieved.

They moved slowly back towards their rucksacs, exhausted, empty, uncertain, like two old men.

High on the cliff above, the single climber still poised, transfixed on his tiny ledge, watching. From his waist a rope curved across the face and went out of sight round a corner of rock to his waiting, invisible companion. The summer air was thick and gold with dust.

In Hanging Garden Gully

by C. E. Montague

TO CLIMB up rocks is like all the rest of your life, only simpler and safer. In all the rest of your life, any work you may do, by way of a trade, is a taking of means to some end. That end may be good. We all hope it is. But who can be sure? Misgiving is apt to steal in. Are you a doctor – is it your job to keep all the weak ones alive? Then are you not spoiling the breed for the future? Are you a parson or politician or some sort of public improver, always trying to fight evil down? May you not then be making a muff every day of somebody else who ought to have had his dragon to fight, with his own bow and spear, when you rushed in to rob him and the other little St. Georges of discipline and of victory? Anyhow, all the good ends seem a good long way off, and the ways to them dim. You may be old by the time you are there. The salt may have lost half its savour.

No such dangers or doubts perplex the climber on rocks. He deals, day by day, with the Ultimate Good, no doubt in small nips, but still authentic and not watered down. His senses thrill with delight to find that he is just the sum of his own simple powers. He lives on, from moment to moment, by early man's gleeful achievement of balance on one foot out of four. He hangs safe by a single hand that learnt its good grip in fifty thousand years of precarious dodging among forest boughs, with the hungry snakes looking up from the ground for a catch like the expectant fieldsmen in the slips. The next little ledge, the object of all human hope and desire, is only some twelve feet away – about the length of the last leap of that naked bunch of clenched and quivering muscles, from whom you descend, at the wild horse that he had stalked through the grass. Each time that you get up a hard pitch you have succeeded in life. Besides, no one can say you have hurt him.

Care will come back in the end: the clouds return after the rain; but for those first heavenly minutes of sitting secure and supreme at the top of Moss Ghyll or the Raven Crag Gully you are Columbus when he saw land from the rigging and Gibbon when he laid down his pen in the garden house at Lausanne. It's good for you, too; it makes you more decent. No one, I firmly believe, could be utterly mean on the very tip of the Weisshorn. I could, if I had known the way, have written a lyric about these agreeable truths as I sat by myself in the tiny inn at Llyn Ogwen where Telford's great London-to-Holyhead road climbs over a pass between three-thousand-foot Carnedds and Glyders. I was a convalescent then, condemned still to a month of rest cure for body and mind. But it was June, and fine weather. Rocks had lately become dry and warm.

There are places in Britain where rock-climbing cannot honestly be called a rest cure. I mean, for the body. Look at the Coolin – all the way that a poor invalid must tramp from Sligachan southward before he gets among the rough, trusty, prehensile gabbro, the best of all God's stones. Think of Scawfell Crag, the finest crag in the world, but its base cut off from the inn by all that Sisyphean plod up the heart-breaking lengths of Brown Tongue. From Ogwen you only need walk half an hour, almost on the flat, and then – there you are, at the foot of your climb. The more I considered the matter, the more distinctly could I perceive that my doctor, when saying 'Avoid all violent exercise,' meant that if ever I got such an opening as this for a little 'steady six-furlong work,' as it is called in the training reports, I ought to take care not to miss it.

But I was the only guest at the inn. And to climb alone is counted a sin against the spirit of the sport. All the early fathers of climbing held the practice heretical. Certainly some of them – Whymper, Tyndall, and others – climbed by themselves when they had a mind to. Thus did King David, on distinguished occasions, relax the general tensity of his virtue. But these exceptions could not obscure the general drift of the law and the prophets of mountaineering. Then came another pause-giving reflection. If, as the Greeks so delicately put it, anything incurable happens while you are climbing alone, your clay is exposed, defenceless and dumb, to nasty *obiter dicta* during the inquest. 'Woe unto him,' as Solomon says, 'who is alone when he falleth!' Insensate rustic coroners and juries, well as they may understand that riding to hounds in a stone-wall country is one of the choicer forms of prudence, will prose and grumble over extinct mountaineers. Their favourite vein is the undesirable one of their brother, the First Clown in *Hamlet*, who thought it a shame that Ophelia (she seems to have slipped up while climbing a tree) 'should have countenance in this world to drown or hang herself more than her even Christian.'

No mean impediments these to a sensitive, conscientious nature's design for seeking health and joy among the attractive gullies and slabs that surround Llyn Idwal. Against them I marshalled all that I could remember of St. Paul's slighting observations on the law; also any agility that I had gained in the Oxford Greats school in resolving disagreeable discords into agreeable higher harmonies. Black was certainly not white. Still, as the good Hegelian said, black might, after all, be an aspect of white. In time it was duly clear to my mind that sin lies not in the corporal act, but in the thoughts of the sinner. So long as the heart sincerely conversed with the beauty of the truths on which rested the rule of never climbing alone it mattered little what the mere legs did: your soul was not in your legs. One of casuistry's brightest triumphs had been fairly won, my liberty gained, my intellectual integrity saved, my luncheon sandwiches ordered for eight in the morning – when somebody else arrived at the inn.

He stood confessed a botanist – he had the large green cylindrical can of the tribe, oval in section and hung by a strap from the shoulder, like the traditional *vivandière's* little cask in French art. He was also, I found while we smoked through that evening together, a good fellow. He had, too, a good leg, if one only. The other was stiff and unbendable at the knee. He had broken it last year, he said, and the bones seemed to have set only too hard, or else Nature had gracelessly grudged to the mended knee-joint of her lover a proper supply of whatever substitute she uses for ball bearings.

His name was Darwin. 'No relation, really,' he humbly assured me. His father was only some obscure squire. The son's Christian name had been Charles at the font, but on coming of age the dear fellow had felt it immodest to prey any more than he need upon his eponymous hero's thrice-honoured names. So he had meekly converted the Charles by deed poll into Thomas. This lowly and beautiful gesture convinced me, as you may suppose, that here was the man to go climbing with. He was indeed one of the innocent, one-thoughted kind that wake up happy each day and never turn crusty, and always think you are being too good to them.

One lure alone had drawn him to these outworks of Snowdon. Some eccentric flower grew on these heights, and a blank page in one of his books of squashed specimens ached for it. Was it so lovely? I asked, like a goose. He was too gentle to snub me. But all that fellow's thoughts shone out through his face. Every flower that blew – to this effect did his soul mildly rebuke mine – was beauteous beyond Helen's eyes. All he said was: 'No, not fair, perhaps, to outward view as many roses be; but, just think! – it grows on no patch of ground in the world but these crags!'

'It is not merely better dressed,' said I, 'than Solomon. It is wiser.'

It was about then, I think, that the heart of the man who had gone mad on the green-stuff and that of the man who knew what was what, in the way of a recreation, rushed together like Paolo's and Francesca's. What had already become an *entente cordiale* ripened at tropical speed into alliance. Darwin had found a second, half-invalided perhaps, but still the holder of two unqualified legs, for to-morrow's quest of his own particular Grail. To me it now seemed to be no accident that Darwin had come to the inn: it was ordained, like the more permanent union of marriage, for a remedy against sin, and to avoid climbing alone.

We got down to business at once. A charming gully, I told him, led right up to the big crag over Cwm Idwal. Not Twll Du, the ill-famed Devil's Kitchen. That, I frankly said, was justly *detestata matribus* – wet and rotten and lethal, and quite flowerless too. My gully, though close to that man-eating climb, was quite another affair. Mine was the place for town children to spend a happy day in the country: the very place also for starting the day's search for the object of Darwin's desire. In saying this, too, I was honest. Lots of plants grow in some gullies; ferns, mosses, grasses, all sorts of greens flourish in a damp cleft, like hair in an armpit; why not one kind of waste rabbit-food as well as another? You see, I had not been a casuist merely, before Darwin came. I had used the eyes Heaven gave me, and reconnoitred the gully well from below, and if any flower knew how to tell good from bad, in the way of a scramble, it would be there. I ended upon a good note. The place's name, I said impressively, was Hanging Garden Gully, no doubt because of the rich indigenous flora.

His eyes shone at that, and we went straight to the kitchen to ask Mrs.

Jones for the loan of a rope. I had none with me that journey: the sick are apt to relinquish improvidently these necessaries of a perfect life. Now, in the classics of mountaineering the right thing in such cases of improvised enterprise is that the landlady lends you her second-best clothes-line. Far happier we, Mrs. Jones having by her a 120-foot length of the right Alpine rope, with the red worsted thread in its middle. It had been left in her charge by a famous pillar of the Scottish Mountaineering Club till he should come that way again. 'The gentleman,' Mrs. Jones told us, 'said I was always to let any climbing gentlemen use it.' Heaven was palpably smiling upon our attempt.

The sun smiled benedictively, too, on the halt and the sick as they stood, about nine the next morning, roping up at the foot of their climb. 'A fisherman's bend,' I took care to explain, as I knotted one end of the rope round Darwin's chest.

'The botanical name,' he replied – 'did I tell you? – is Lloydia.' How some men do chatter when they are happy! Can't carry their beans.

We were not likely to need the whole 120 feet of the rope. So I tied myself on at its middle and coiled the odd 60 feet round my shoulder. 'A double overhand knot,' I confessed, as I tightened it round me. 'A bad knot, but for once it may do us no harm.'

'The vernacular name,' said the garrulous fellow, 'is spiderwort.'

'Tut, tut!' I inwardly said.

The lower half of that gully was easier than it had looked: just enough in it to loosen your muscles and make you want more. Higher up, the gully grew shallow and had greater interest. The top part of all, as I remember it now, might be called either a chimney or crack, being both. In horizontal section, it was a large obtuse angle indented into the face of the crag. The crag at this part, and the gully's bed with it, rose at an angle of some 60 degrees. Now, when you climb rock at an angle of 60 degrees the angle seems to be just 90. In early mountaineering records the pioneers often say, 'Our situation was critical. Above us the crag rose vertical,' or, 'To descend was impossible now. But in front the rocky face, for some time perpendicular, had now begun to overhang.' If you take a clinometer to the scenes of some of those liberal estimates you blush for your kind. The slope of the steepest – and easiest – ridge of the three by which the Matterhorn is climbed is only 39 degrees. But this, though not purely digressive, is partly so. All that strictly had to be said was that an upright and very obtuse-angled trough in smooth rock that rises at 60 degrees cannot be climbed.

But in the very bed of our trough there had been eroded, from top to bottom, a deepish irregular crack in the rock. Into this crack, at most parts, you could stick a foot, a knee, or an arm. Also, the sides of the large obtuse angle, when you looked closely, were not utterly smooth. On the right wall, as we looked up, certain small wrinkles, bunions, and other minute but lovable diversities in the face of the stone gave promise of useful points of resistance for any right boot that might scrape about on the wall in the hope of exerting auxiliary lateral pressure, while the left arm and thigh, hard at work in the crack, wriggled you up by a succession of caterpillarish squirms. This delectable passage was 80 feet high, as I measured it with my experienced eye. An inexperienced measuring-tape might have put it at fifty. To any new recruit to the cause – above all, to one with a leg as inflexible as the stoniest stone that it pressed – I felt that the place was likely to offer all that he could wish in the line of baptisms of fire. Still, as the pioneers said, to descend was impossible now: the crack was too sweet to be left. And Darwin, thus far, had come up like a lamplighter, really. I told him so, frankly. Alpine guides are the men at psychology. Do they not get the best out of the rawest new client, in any hard place, by ceasing to hide the high estimate that they have formed of his natural endowment for the sport? '*Vous êtes – je vous dis franchement, monsieur – un chamois! Un véritable chat de montagne!*'

I was leading the party. I was the old hand. Besides, I could bend both my knees. Desiring Darwin to study my movements, so that he presently might – so far as conformity would not cramp his natural talents – copy them closely, I now addressed myself to the crack. When halfway up I heard the voice of a good child enduring, with effort, a painful call upon its patience. 'Any Lloydia yet?' it wistfully said. Between my feet I saw Darwin below. Well, he was certainly paying the rope out all right, as I had enjoined; but he did it 'like them that dream.' His mind was not in it. All the time he was peering hungrily over the slabby containing walls of the gully, and now he just pawed one of them here and there with a tentative foot – you know how a puppy, when first it sees ice, paws the face of the pond. 'These botanists!' I thought. 'These fanatics!' You know how during a happy physical effort – a race or a hunt, a fight or a game – you think, with a sort of internal quiet, about a lot of old things. There came back to my mind the old lines that I had once had to make Latin verse of:

How vainly men themselves amaze
To win the palm, the oak, or bays,
And their incessant labours see
Crowned from some single herb or tree.

Meanwhile I took a precaution. I first unroped myself. Then I passed the rope, from below, through the space behind a stone that was jammed fast in the crack. Then I roped myself on again, just at my old place on the rope. A plague of a job it was, too, with all those 60 feet of spare rope to uncoil and re-coil. But you see how it worked: I had now got the enthusiast moored. Between him and me the rope went through the eye of a needle, so I could go blithely on. I went. In the top of the crack I found a second jammed stone. It was bigger than number one: in fact, it blocked the way and made you clamber round outside it rather interestingly; but it, too, had daylight showing through a hole behind it. Sounds from below were again improving my natural stock of prudence. You can't, I thought, be too safe. Once more I unroped, just under this chockstone, and pushed the rope up through the hole at its back. When the rope fell down to me, outwards over the top of the stone, I tied on again, just as before, and then scrambled up over the outer side of the stone with an ecstatic pull on both arms, and sat on its top in the heaven that big-game hunters know when they lie up against the slain tiger and smoke.

If you have bent up your mind to take in the details, you will now have an imposing vision of the connections of Darwin and me with each other and with the Primary or Palæozoic rocks of Cambria. From Darwin, tied on to its end, the rope ran, as freely as a bootlace runs through the eyelets, behind the jammed stone 30 feet above his head, and then again behind my present throne of glory at the top; then it was tied on to me; and then there were 60 feet, half its length, left over to play with.

Clearly Darwin, not being a thread, or even a rope, could not come up the way that the rope did, through the two needle-eyes. Nor did I care, he being the thing that he was, to bid him untie and then to pull up his end of the rope through the eyes, drop it down to him clear through the air, and tell him to tie on again. He was, as the Irish say of the distraught, 'fit to be tied,' and not at all fit for the opposite. If he were loose he might at any moment espy that Circe of his in some place out of bounds. There seemed to be only one thing to do. I threw down the spare 60 feet of the rope, and told him first to tie himself on to its end, and then, but not before, to untie himself from the other. I could not quite see these orders obeyed. A bulge of rock came between him and my eyes, but I was explicit. 'Remember that fisherman's bend!' I shouted. Perhaps my voice was rather austere; but who would not forgive a wise virgin for saying, a little dryly, to one of the foolish, 'Well, use your spare can'? As soon as he sang out 'All right' I took a good haul on what was now the working half of the rope, to test his knot-making. Yes, he *was* all right. So I bade him come up, and he started. Whenever he looked up I saw that he had a wild, gadding eye; and whenever he stopped to breathe during the struggle he gasped, 'I can't see it yet.'

He came nearly half-way, and then he did see it. He had just reached the worst part. Oh, the Sirens know when to start singing! That flower of evil was far out of his reach, or of what his reach ought to have been. Some twelve feet away on his right it was rooted in some infinitesimal pocket of blown soil, a mere dirty thumb-nailful of clay. For a moment the lover eyed the beloved across one huge slab of steep stone with no real foothold or handhold upon it – only a few efflorescent minutiæ small as the bubukles and whelks and knobs on the nose of some fossil Bardolph. The whole wall of the gully just there was what any man who could climb would have written off as unclimbable. Passion, however, has her own standards, beyond the comprehension of the wise:

> His eye but saw that light of love,
> The only star it hailed above.

My lame Leander gave one whinny of desire. Then he left all and made for his Hero.

You know the way that a man, who has no idea how badly he bats, will sometimes go in and hit an unplayable bowler right out of the ground, simply because the batsman is too green to know that the bowler cannot be played. Perhaps that was the way. Or perhaps your sound climber, having his wits, may leave, at his boldest, a margin of safety, as engineers call it, so wide that a madman may cut quite a lot off its edge without coming surely to grief. Or was it only a joke of the gods among themselves over their wine? Or can it be that the special arrangements known to be made for the safety of sailors, when in their cups, are extended at times to cover the case of collectors overcome by the strong waters of the acquisitive instinct? Goodness knows! Whatever the powers that helped him, this crippled man, who had never tried climbing before, went skating off to his right flank, across that impossible slant, on one foot and one stilt, making a fool of the science of mountaineering.

I vetoed, I imprecated, I grew Athanasian. All utterly useless. As soon could you whistle a dog back to heel when he fleets off on fire with some fresh amour. I could only brace myself, take a good hold of the rope in both hands, and be ready to play the wild salmon below as soon as he slipped and the line ran out tight. While I waited I saw, for the first time, another piquant detail of our case. Darwin, absorbed in his greed, had never untied the other end of the rope. So he was now tied on to both ends. The whole rope made a circle, a vicious circle. Our whole caravan was sewn on to the bony structure of Wales with two bit stitches, one at each jammed stone.

You see how it would work. When Darwin should fall, as he must, and hang in the air from my hands, gravitation would swing him back into the centre of the chimney, straight below me, bashing him hard against the chimney's opposite wall. No doubt he would be stunned. I should never be able to hoist his dead weight through the air to my perch, so I should have to lower him to the foot of the chimney. That would just use up the full 60 feet of rope. It would run the two 60-foot halves of the rope so tight that I should never be able to undo the bad central knot that confined me. Could I but cut it when Darwin was lowered into provisional safety, and then climb down to see to him! No; I had lost my knife two days ago. I should be like a netted lion, with no mouse to bite through his cords: a Prometheus, bound to his rock.

But life spoils half her best crises. That wretch never slipped. He that by this time had no sort of right to his life came back as he went, treading on air, but now with that one bloom of the spiderwort in his mouth. Apologising for slowness, and panting with haste, he writhed up the crack till his head appeared over the chockstone beside me. Then he gave one cry of joy, surged up over the stone, purring with pleasure, and charged the steep slope of slippery grass above the precipice we had scaled. 'You never told me!' he cried; and then for the first time I noticed that up here the whole place was speckled with Lloydia. The next moment Darwin fell suddenly backwards, as if Lloyd himself or some demon gardener of his had planted a very straight one on the chin of the onrushing trespasser in his pleasaunce. You guess? Yes. One of his two tethers, the one coming up from behind the lower jammed stone, had run out; it had pulled him up short as he leapt upon the full fruition of his desire.

He was easy to field as he rolled down the grass. But his tug on the rope had worked it well into some crevice between the lower jammed stone and the wall of the crack. We were anchored now, good and fast, to that stone, more than three fathoms below. What to do now? Climb down and clear the jammed rope? Leave that lame voluptuary rioting upon a precipice's edge?

Scarcely wise – would it have been? Puzzled and angry, I cast away shame. I knew well that as Spartan troops had to come back with their shields or upon them, or else have trouble with their mothers, a climber who leaves his tackle behind in a retreat is likely to be a scorn and a hissing. Still, I cast away shame. Ours was no common case; no common ethics would meet it. I untied us both, and threw both ends of the rope down the chimney; then I let Darwin graze for a minute; then I drove him relentlessly up the steep grass to the top of the crag, and round by the easy walking way down.

As we passed down the valley below, I looked up. The whole length of our chimney was visibly draped with the pendent double length of that honest Scots mountaineer's rope. 'I don't really know how to thank you enough,' Darwin was babbling beside me, 'for giving me such a day!'

But I felt as if I were one of the villains in plays who compromise women of virtue and rank by stealing their fans and leaving them lying about in the rooms of bad bachelors. Much might be said for climbing alone, no matter what the authorities thought. A good time it would be, all to myself, when I came back to salvage that rope.

The Escapist

by David Craig

COLIN BANKS stood on a ledge high up on the south buttress of Green Pike, gripped by knowing that in another fifteen minutes he would have to commit himself and step out onto the sheer wall to his right. Part of him strained back and away from the insane danger of it. The sheep feeding on the grass slope two hundred feet below, the pair of ravens planing over on the easterly breeze and barking to each other – those were the sane species, living in their element, not forcing themselves to stretch into the impossible. But another part of himself craved the climbing, felt tame and trapped among streets or in the lowlands, and only fired fully into life when the high rocks came into sight and his eyes were drawn upwards along the ramps, faces, and pinnacles that linked the valley floor to the skyline.

'What did you do here?' A call from below, from his partner, Lawrence. 'Have you reached the big crack?'

'I'm just below it.'

'Lay away leftwards from it. Gain a few feet, then pull up on a fist jam and make a high step right to a little sharp flake. Right?'

'Okay. I'm climbing.'

Colin leaned back against the rock wall and pulled on the red and yellow ropes which dropped out of his sight below his feet. There was slack to take in – Lawrence was moving slowly up again.

Here on a stance, in the middle of a sheer crag, was now Colin's favourite refuge. He was safe from everything but his own thoughts. Automatically he looked southwards towards Branston, fifty miles away across the dales and the bay. Two cooling towers just showed, pale-grey bodies amongst a haze of diffused sunshine. Eight years before it had filled him with happy warmth to know that his home was there, a mile inland from the power station. Mandy wheeling the twins home from the shops, bending down and widening her eyes to make them laugh, racing the last few yards so that the push-chair rattled and jounced on the uneven pavement and the wee boys went into hysterics and swayed from side to side, exaggerating the movement. Where would she be now? Round at her friend Joanne's, bitterly analysing the deadness of her marriage. And the boys would come home from school to find both their parents out and the house smelling of unwashed dishes and soot from a fireless chimney. But would the boys be any less unhappy if he ended the present purgatory and left home for good?

He pulled on the ropes. There was slack on the red one. He took it in till it was firm between himself and Lawrence struggling down below, then braced himself anew on the ledge. As so often happened in these minutes of perfect privacy, his problems – the situations that screened themselves over and over in his head – flowed in on him unstoppably. The stages of his marriage now seemed marked by rows – searing rows in which too much was said, accusations were stabbed home which then fulminated endlessly, like fires underground. The first row in front of the children still shamed and hurt him the worst, though it had been far less violent than later ones. From that time on, he often thought, the feeling of wellbeing in the family had come to seem a pretence which everyone saw through, which wasn't worth maintaining.

In the middle of a warm May day they had gone out to attack the mini wilderness at the foot of the garden. 'At long last,' said Mandy – Colin had fantasized bold creative improvements in the tangle of nettles, elder scrub, and junk, and this had come to count as a promise he had failed to keep. Today they had got up late – Colin liked to lie naked beside Mandy as the sun shone strongly out of the east and glowed yellow on their bedroom wall. But Mandy was disinclined to make love. Half her mind was on the boys, whose voices were rising shrilly from below. When at last they dressed and went downstairs, the kitchen floor was sprayed with milk and cornflakes.

'Andrew made me,' said Ian, pouting his lower lip and starting to breathe fast and jerkily.

'I didn't! You spilled them first. And then you grabbed my plate.'

'Didn't. I was trying to reach the packet.'

'You grabbed my plate. You're always wanting something of mine.'

'Boys! High time you were out in the sunshine. Col – for godsake take them out and get something organized while I clean this lot up.'

'You come too. It's too fine for housework.'

'How can I? Look at the floor. So long as you keep them happy and stop them fighting . . .'

Colin was glad to step out of the house, with its litter of toys and soiled clothes. As for his guilt at Mandy's taking on her burden of motherhood yet again, he was used to it – it tainted everything, but he could lose himself in the handiwork, in the atmosphere of turned earth, hedges coming into flower, swifts whistling and arcing across the blue.

'Ian – bring the spade. Andrew, can you manage the barrow?' They looked comical, like two of the seven dwarfs, staggering along with full-size garden tools. He took the fork, the shears, and the sickle and led the way behind the shed and into the rank greenery of the wilderness.

'Now – which things have you to look out for?'

'Those ones.' Ian pointed at the nettles.

'That's right. What else, Andrew?'

'Those pricky ones' – pointing at a thicket of wild raspberries.

'That's right. Your wellies would have covered your legs better. Let's get cracking. I'll cut down these long stems. Ian, you cut them into bits, okay? You try and pile them in the barrow, Andy.'

For a good half-hour they worked away amongst the smell of crushed leaves. The sky sparkled between sprays of luminous green. 'It's hard,' said Ian, shaking a stem between the blades of the shears and trying to break its last tough fibres. He put the shears on the ground and wiped his brow, imitating Colin.

Eyeing his brother, Andrew cautiously picked up the shears, and when Ian said, '*I'm* doing that,' Andrew retorted, 'It's my turn now.'

'Fair enough,' said Colin hopefully, and felt balmy relief when Ian said, 'I'll pile these bits in the barrow.' Both boys went busily to work again. For a while Colin crunched into the press of raspberry canes with the sickle. Presently, felled greenery lay scattered everywhere and he took the fork and began lifting the mass aside so that he could see the shape of the ground and what wanted doing next. Pure peace stole through him like soft heat. Then behind him one of the twins screamed, high screams pumping out as though mechanically. Colin turned and crashed through the greenery, which thwarted him like wire. Ian was lying crouched on his side, both hands to his leg. It was streaming blood. Andrew was staring, terrified.

'He took the hook – the hook – and it slipped, and –'

Mandy came running down the path. 'Colin? Ian!' She knelt beside the stricken boy, put her arm round him and held him against her, then firmly lifted one of his hands from his leg. A lip of flesh sagged from the little plump calf and blood welled over it. He screamed again, on a mindless panic note. 'He didn't have the *sickle*?' Mandy's voice was stark with surprise and she looked up at Colin briefly with eyes that burned hostility into his skin. 'Lift him into the house. I'll hold his leg. Andrew – come. Don't cry, love. Come on. We've got to get Dr Dawson!'

They walked in a huddle up the path to the house. Ian was made comfortable on the settee with newspapers under his leg and Mandy held the lips of the wound shut and cuddled him into quietness while Colin negotiated fiercely on the phone until the surgery promised to get hold of the doctor 'as soon as possible'. Andrew was soothed with orange juice and he came through and offered a drink of it to Ian, but Ian only nestled his head deeper into his mother.

Mandy was perfectly calm, expressionless, the skin glossy and tanned on her cheekbones, her blond hair swept behind her ears and gathered in a comb at the back of her head. Colin couldn't get her to exchange signals with him. So it was for the rest of the morning and into the afternoon, while Dr Dawson came and cleaned the leg, put in stitches with a local anaesthetic, and gave Ian a shot against tetanus. The house became utterly quiet. An alien smell of disinfectant tinged the warm air. Ian was asleep, his cheeks flushed and his thumb in his mouth, and Andrew was staring drowsily at the Test Match on television with the sound turned off. Mandy sat with her hands in her lap, in a strangely old-fashioned pose of decorum, looking down the garden. Colin started to mark work he had brought home from school.

'How often is this going to happen?' Colin looked round at his wife. She hadn't moved, or looked at him. Her voice sounded numbly stating rather than asking.

'Mandy! One piece of sheer bad luck – '

'Bad luck? You let them do anything.'

'I do not. I told them to watch out for stings and thorns.'

'Stings and thorns. And you let a four-year-old have a sickle.'

'I did not let him have it. He found it.'

'Don't quibble. He got his hands on it because you let them do anything. You've said so – "let them explore, find out by trial and error". You're a bloody theorist.'

'What do you want for them, Mandy? A tame life – no adventure? Non-people, congealed in some office –'

'Theorist. Bloody theorist. Use your common. Stuff your ideas. Little vulnerable people want looking after, that's all.'

'I do look after them. Not just protecting them. I want them to grow, and get into life for themselves . . .'

Mandy turned and looked at Colin with clear still blue eyes, as though appraising a stranger.

'It's so familiar, the way you are with them. You let them do anything. You do what *you* feel like. You're just pig bloody selfish. That time you climbed up outside the fire escape at your father's hotel. Little Ian was scared – he knew it was dangerous – but he sees you doing crazy things, so he imitates you. He'll follow you to his death one day.'

'You hate my climbing.'

'Keep your voice down. I'm not discussing that again. We'll never agree about that. It's how you are with them. You can't say no. Are you so anxious to be liked?'

'Look – I am *natural* with them.'

'That's right – you do what you feel like. You're like a boy – a greedy boy. A father should be something else. Not just a playmate. And what is all this frenzy down at that end of the garden? Having an eyeful of that new young talent across the road?'

'The what? Mandy – I don't even know who you mean.'

'Oh – you're so innocent. Nobody's that innocent. Oh well – look at her as much as you like. Do what you like. Who believes in monogamy any more? Couples locked together.'

'*You* want to escape.' Colin grabbed her by the wrist and she gave a gasp of pain. 'You're talking about yourself. You're tired of fucking me – '

'Stop shouting, you bully. Stop telling the boys – '

'You're tired of me. I'm too sedentary. And too adventurous. And too self-centred – and too attentive – nothing's right for you. Nobody would please you. Well, I'm not going to try any more. Why try and please a *bitch*?'

The ugly word split the air. His voice was amplified by pent-up anger. Ian woke with a violent start, then let out a yowl of distress. The poison in the grown-ups' hissing and then rising voices had got to Andrew and he suddenly cried heartily, as though he too had had a physical wound. Mandy and Colin wrenched themselves out of their deadlock. The hours till the twins' bedtime passed in cooking, shopping, playing, washing up. Colin was promising himself to love Mandy into peace again when they had the sitting room to themselves. But the row seemed to have left nothing unsullied. His grievance was like a sour cud in this throat. On an impulse he grabbed his jacket and went down the road to the Freeholders' Arms while Mandy was still reading to the twins upstairs. When he came back two hours later, the car was gone; and when Mandy came up to bed around midnight, all she would answer to his resentful questioning was, 'Out. You went out so I went out.'

They should have tried to settle some of the issues there and then, should have agreed at least on how to behave with the children. But the scope for dispute seemed endless. Colin played and replayed her words in his mind but flinched from bringing things up with her and she seemed content to avoid him and keep her thoughts for her friends.

This burst of memories had lasted maybe half a minute but Lawrence had gained height and Colin was ashamed to realize he had failed to take in rope. Looking down past his toes, he saw his friend's helmet bobbing like a solid red balloon among the grey slabs and edges of the crag.

'Take in, Col! Take in! This is a gripping place.'

'You wait till you mantelshelf onto this stance – fly on a wall stuff.'

At that moment Colin came to see, with a pang, that he was using the climbing as a drug – the delicious extremity of it left him no awareness to spare for the wear-and-tear of his struggles with Mandy. He had heard of cancer patients pulling out their own hairs one by one to distract themselves from the bad deep pain. But climbing wasn't agony – even the more desperate moments were shortlived and they released a flood of wellbeing so full it made you feel you could do anything – wing off into mid-air, float up the rock-face immune to gravity. It even felt for some minutes as though you could seize the miseries and *impasses* of your daily life and will them to melt and evaporate. If he could make himself climb beyond his limits, might he not be able to use the same power on the awful intractable grievances that had plagued them for years now? It had come to this: there was nothing that wasn't fated to turn out badly and give them fuel for conflict. That luckless party on Midsummer Eve the year before . . . Steve and Toni had asked them to their famous annual booze-up, which always, if it was fine, spilled out into the garden, into the pockets of turf enclosed by spurs of limestone, or if people got really high, right out onto the Knott beyond. Everyone called it

The Orgy – drink was unlimited, the upstairs bedrooms creaked with excitement. Colin and Mandy were just old enough to take a faintly aloof and amused attitude to these adolescent fevers.

They parked the car beside the pub and walked down the few yards of high street, still warm with heat stored by the stone-walled cottages. *Lucy in the Sky with Diamonds* was singing out from the open windows at Steve and Toni's. They stepped into a cave of shadow, aromatic with Martini, fresh sweat, and cigarette smoke, low-lit by table lamps with crimson shades which made even familiar people look indefinite and strange. Armchairs were full of shapes, mostly couples sprawled together. More people seemed to be heaped on the floor. Colin stepped on an arm, apologized, and felt a hand grip his ankle and then slide up his leg.

'Mandy! Colin!' Toni's face hovered towards them from the back of the room. 'You're late. Kid trouble?'

'Not really. They're sleeping like lambs.'

'Great. Oh! Ouch! I know you, Phil Barnett – keep your hands off. Mandy! Look after this.' She tilted a green bottle towards them as one of the shapes pulled her to the floor. Mandy saved the bottle as it started to spill wine onto the nearest bodies. Taking Colin's hand, she led the way through to the back. It was nearly as crammed. They sat on the floor with their legs fitted between various other legs and bottoms and passed the wine to and fro to each other, drinking rather fast to catch up with the atmosphere around them. Just six feet away from Colin and straight in front of him a small dark girl was sitting with her intense black eyes seemingly fixed on him. She looked like Nana Mouskouri. Music blasted in – a drunken hand must suddenly have turned up *Sergeant Pepper*. As Colin tried to avoid the dark girl's eyes, he heard Mandy whispering fiercely, 'Get drunk then! I want to dance.'

'Yes, let's,' he said at once, but she had already got to her feet and a moment later he saw her stepping over bodies and across the passage to the other half of the house. Everything felt unreal. The dark girl's eyes seemed to press into his, then her head swung loosely leftwards. Amongst the hubbub he picked out what she was saying to the man beside her: 'Drift away . . . Like to drift away 'n' lay 'round in the sun with nothing on . . .'

The bottle was empty. Colin eased himself to his feet, telling himself he was going to search for drink, denying to himself that he was keeping tabs on Mandy. His bladder felt unbearably tight and he climbed upstairs between whispering couples. Water was rushing in the bathroom. He looked in and saw an old friend, Bill Britton, sitting in the bath fully clothed, his legs over the edge. The taps gushed, water was rising round his hips, and a girl in a Spanish blouse was pouring drink from a bottle straight into his mouth. He was half choking, laughing, trying to speak: 'Netta! Bitch! Mercy! Ohhh . . .' Colin smiled sportingly, sketched a carefree wave of greeting, and went up one more floor. A bedroom door was ajar. He felt suddenly sickened to see a woman with Mandy's hair and Mandy's tanned shoulders squatting on a bed with a man underneath her. She was half naked. Her face looked briefly out at Colin from the dressing-table mirror – it wasn't Mandy at all but a girl scarcely twenty. He went back downstairs. Heavy rock had replaced the

Beatles and the dancers were making the floorboards shake. Mandy wasn't among them. Colin recognized nobody – no Steve, no Toni, no familiar faces from the staff room or the cricket club. Suspicion flushed back in. But perhaps she had gone to get some supper? He went through to the kitchen, feeling his head swelling with the wine. Candles were spilling wax onto a long scrubbed table covered with pots of paté, plates of cheese and pineapple, *baguettes* two feet long. A middleaged man with a preposterous gut was standing beside the open fridge and tearing a leg from a cold roast chicken. Colin glared at him as though he were an enemy and the man seemed to sneer. No sign of Mandy. He stormed through into the garden. The air smelt of night-scented stock. To the north, above the rough black skyline of the Knott, a flawless afterglow filled the arch of the sky with electric blue, shading into smoky apricot in the north-west. A yelp of uncontrollable laughter, a woman's laughter, came from the hawthorn bushes beyond the far end of the garden. The party was eddying outwards, propelled by booze and music and the heady air of summer, into the dusky wilderness where mounds of blossom glimmered like icebergs.

Colin turned back to the house and took another bottle of white wine from a fresh crate under the kitchen table. The remaining clear point in his brain was telling him to drink no more, to hold on to his wits, but this clarity seemed to have become a spectator, who watched his idiotic behaviour and let it happen. Time swam in his head like cigarette smoke. Hours later, as a blue morning came glowing through the kitchen windows, he found himself on the floor, leaning against the fridge, with a blonde girl on his knees. She had snuggled her frizzy hair close in to his chest and was saying in a sleepy, ill-used voice, 'Gimme a kiss – go *on* – *gimme* a *kiss* . . .' Colin felt no desire at all, nothing but headache and humiliation.

The back door opened, letting in air cooled with dew, and Mandy was looking at him sardonically. 'Tear yourself away, Colin,' she said. 'We have not been asked to breakfast.'

Colin felt utterly wronged. Was she getting at him to cover her own guilt? They picked their way out between empty bottles and a few people slumped on cushions. The moment they were in the street, he broke out angrily.

'I was looking for you – for hours.'

'Really? Why didn't you enjoy yourself? Isn't that what we came for?'

'Yes. But together.'

'Sitting on the floor getting pissed? With not a word to say to each other?'

'Mandy! Can't we simply be at peace together?'

'We so often are.'

'You're picking this quarrel.'

'What! It's you who're all uptight.'

'And you're perfectly calm?'

'I am. And so is the morning. Everything's calm and blue and lovely.'

'So you feel great. It must have been a wonderful *walk* . . .'

'It was.'

'You're telling me you just went for a walk –'

'I did. We went up through the woods – the bracken's just uncurling, all green coming through the old coppery stuff – and then through the copse where you found the slow-worm –'

'You went to one of our places!'

'Why shouldn't I?'

'We – you said we.'

'Oh – the woods were full of people. You know what it's like at these do's.'

'I know what it's like all right. Fucking in every corner. I felt out of it, I can tell you.'

'Join in, then. You're hopeless at parties. You don't know how to enjoy yourself.'

'I enjoy myself with *you*.'

'Do you? It never seems like it any more. Anyway, you stifle me. We are two people, you know. Not some kind of two-headed monster, or Siamese twins or something.'

'You lead your life and I'll lead mine? That recipe for disaster? Is that what you're saying?'

'Colin, don't be boring. I'm not in the mood for a row. If parties aren't one of the things we can manage, don't let's go, that's all. I can go dancing by myself.'

'You're trying to peel away from me aren't you?'

'You do when you climb. Anyway I simply want to dance.'

'But *we* can dance. We have danced!'

'It doesn't work, though. You can't keep time. Oh – don't make me argue. Let there be one uncomplicated thing . . .'

Colin glanced sideways at her. It was true – she was serene, her face was smooth, her stride springy. She seemed perfectly free and at ease in this blue morning. While he felt sluggish, rasped, his brain heated and tired at the same time. He didn't know what he was feeling. Jealousy, envy, righteous hurt mingled and threatened to choke him, drops of frustrated sexiness were collecting in him like poison. He clutched Mandy by the upper arm, bare in the summer dress. He wanted to caress her and hurt her.

'You're trying to wound me,' he said in a growling, brutal voice. 'You calculate it like a torturer.'

'Wound you?' She was wrenching to free her arm. 'I can't wound you. You don't care enough. You only care for you.'

'Who made me stop caring?' He was driving his fingers into her flesh. 'You've goaded and stung me – needled me about every fucking thing – the children, the neighbours, my friends. You're needling me now. Why?' He had her by both arms now, he was shaking her with all his strength and glaring straight into her eyes. He looked mad and distorted.

'You just – want to know – ' her words were jerked from her by his shaking – 'if I – had a fuck. That's what's – bugging you.'

'You did! I know you did! You fucking slut!'

'Your breath stinks. You were too bloody pissed to even give that little doll what she wanted. You are abject. Ohhh!' She screamed as Colin's furious lunges toppled her backwards. Her head bounced on the flags at the roadside. She rolled onto her side, put her hand into her hair, and stared unbelievingly at the wet blood reddening it. She got up, looked round for her handbag, picked it up, and ran off down the street on a wavering line. He caught her up in the car a few moments later and slanted to a stop, half blocking her way. She leaned on the wing, breathing in gasps, and then got in. They drove back home along the dry emptiness of the early morning road, frozen into their own thoughts. They had not been out together since.

Colin leaned forward on the belay. Lawrence's fingers were trying the small flake holds, fixing onto them like separate little animals inching up the rock. His face came into sight, looking quizzical behind his heavy glasses, and he squinted until his pupils disappeared into his nose, then rolled his eyes. 'Christ, Colin – how much more? This is like Nelson's Column.'

'Just one pitch after this – the best.'

'The worst, you mean. You can lead it. I'm at my limit.'

'That's what it's all about. Don't hang about, Lawrie. Your fingers will wear out.'

As Lawrence pulled up on ever more slender holds and then set his palms on the ledge beside Colin's feet, ready for the mantelshelf, Colin looked again to his right, for a last appraisal of the coming ordeal. The sheer wall pushed into space, it was undercut below, and the one line across it, on a rising diagonal, led off round a corner. Not even the reassurance of a visible goal. The diagonal consisted of a rock lip sometimes one, sometimes two inches wide, a slender gangway, breached in one place where a section had flaked off and dropped to the scree two hundred feet below. The handholds were mere contact points – nothing to grip – the only way to move along that face was by balancing delicately, centre of gravity held close in, feet set sideways, until you reached that gap. Then the stride, bridging across at the full stretch of your legs. It was a step through the air, through the invisible fear barrier and onto a plane of unreal freedom, a place you'd never hoped to reach but which in its turn would gradually settle into reality around you.

As Colin had these thoughts, he knew that a lower level in himself was churning with the nausea of fear. This would die down, the fear barrier would part and vanish, the dizzy moves would become simply the next steps that he had to take, the next ten minutes of life that waited to be lived. Lawrence was crowding up onto the ledge beside him. 'What a way to spend Easter,' he said, holding his arms out sideways and dropping his hands from the wrist. Colin tried to grin and his lips stretched over closed teeth.

'Give us the gear,' was all he said, and while he clipped slings and metal nuts back onto the harness at his waist, Lawrence tied onto the belays. The sun soaked into them, warmth reflected from the pock-marked grey rock near their faces, and a light breeze made their foreheads feel the cool of sweat evaporating.

The wall pitch now reared before Colin like a test. It had come to him that if he could make it, then, by the same token, he could make it out of the impossible situation at home. He could leave, go off and live in his own way. He was not helpless. The way up that wall loomed frighteningly hard but it could be done. By his own nerve and cool-headedness and the leathery strength of his own arms. Lawrence was looking at him quizzically, registering his uncharacteristic quietness.

'Well,' Colin said. 'It'll not get easier by hanging about. And it's closing time at 3.' He turned his head and shouted, 'I'm coming, you bloody rock!' He untied from the belay, turned to face the crag, and stepped away sideways. He grasped a pinnacle which terminated their ledge, felt it solid in the palms of his hands, then let go with his left and pulled sideways on a small rough edge. He set his left foot in a shallow pocket beyond the ledge, put his right foot beside it, gathered himself into balance, and reached with his left foot for the start of the slender gangway. The churning inside him had stilled. His fingers found small roughnesses on the face above head-height and the solidity of the rock passed into him and poised him. The slender gangway rose by a two-foot step onto a flake top and his left leg rose, flexing smoothly at the knee, lifting him in balance, while the abyss behind and below him sucked at him. Now the break in the gangway. The transit through emptiness into the plane where he had never been. He began to feel unable. That gap was surely too broad – stretching would unsteady him and peel him off – there were no cracks for a nut runner to protect the move – he wasn't able. He went on moving. The movement itself would carry him and his qualms and quailings across the void. His left foot squirmed on the far edge of the gangway beyond the break. His left palm curved slightly round a boss of rock, feeling for balance. The fingers of his right hand let go of a tiny edge and hovered helplessly. Now he started to move his weight leftwards across the void and his right leg wavered in mid-air before pulling after his left.

He was standing on the far side. The gangway led off round the corner, still thin, still sharp, and then he was looking up the final chimney crack. His mind was dimming after the concentration of the last few minutes but his body was unscathed. He pulled up off the gangway, reaching high for broken edges on both sides of the chimney, knowing the drop hollowing beneath his feet and feeling strength pour through his shoulders into his arms in a flow nothing could prevent.

As his mind recovered itself, he came to know how fleeting a thing he had done. It was over, almost before he had taken the measure of it. Forty feet above was the mossy, short-bitten pasture of the hilltop – a zone of pure peace. Other mountains rose and fell around them. The road, the village, and the fields were like a large scale map below. Further off, the green lowlands, the bay, the cooling towers. The short sharp thing had been done. Now came the long haul into alien terrain where the dangers were all undefined and might last for years.

Gaz and Sankey

by M. John Harrison

ON AND off through 1984 I went climbing with an awkward, grinning lad called Gaz, who worked at the butcher's in the town. You often saw him at dinner time, a head taller than anyone else in the street, clumping across the zebra crossing by the health food shop in the steel-trimmed work clogs favoured by generations of local slaughtermen, his red hair cut in a kind of savage brush. He was eighteen or twenty. He had transport, a fawn Vauxhall which he sometimes drove like a maniac. When he spoke he made aggressive bobbing movements of his high head and shoulders; this was out of shyness. He was always impatient to get to the crag, and he came out with one or another of us whenever he could take a day off.

At the beginning of May he and I went to Trowbarrow Quarry in Lancashire, where I wanted to try a route called The Coral Sea. Coral Sea is fun not because it is hard but because it's a steep slab covered with tiny delicate fossil imprints, so that you are climbing even more than usual on a kind of frozen time. We found that ICI had closed it and put up trespass warnings. We wandered about anyway to emphasize what we thought of as our clear right to be there, scuffing the wood sorrel and craning our necks in astonishment at the evil zinc-grey face of the old workings.

'It's meant to be limestone, but it never looks like it to me,' said Gaz. 'All the books say it is, but it never looks like it to me.'

Trowbarrow Main Wall, a hundred feet high, totters on a single pediment of rock: as it slips inevitably away to the right, Jean Jeanie, Cracked Actor, Warspite Direct, all the cracklines are widening stealthily . . .

'You just can't settle down in a place when it's banned,' Gaz complained.

He went twenty feet up the oppressive Red Wall in his torn and dusty running shoes; warned himself, 'Oops! Don't look down!', jumped off with a thud and stared sulkily across at the abandoned explosives store with its fringe of rank weeds.

'Looks like bloody *Dr Who*.'

Earth, 1997: everyone lives under the ground and wears identical clothes. Something appalling has been done to their sexuality and they walk round staring directly ahead of themselves. 'Not much different to now.' Every fifteen minutes a voice like the station announcer at Preston says something nobody can understand and they all walk off down a different corridor. Can the doctor help them?

'For fuck's sake shut up,' said Gaz, 'and let's go somewhere we can *climb*.'

Though the climbs were easier we had a much better time at Jack Scout Cove, a narrow defile at the end of a caravan site which opens out on the sudden shocking spaces of Morecambe Bay near Silverdale. As you face the sea the cliff goes up on your left, whitish, dusted with the same lichen you can see on any other limestone crag, say at Giggleswick or Malham: custard yellow, dry and crusty. You get to the top among yew trees bent and shaved by the sea wind.

I had been there once as a boy. I knew that, but you couldn't say I remembered it.

The right bank of the cove is a clinted slab overgrown with whin, short turf and hawthorn bushes. From there the tourists can gaze out to sea or at the weed-covered rocks at the base of the cliff like green chenille cushions in the front room of a fussy old woman. They murmur and laugh, their children shout. When Gaz and I were there the hawthorn wasn't yet in blossom. Sheep moved about on the turf.

'You see those green tags in their ears?' said Gaz. I'll be cutting them out on Monday morning. One quick slit of the knife and out they come!'

'For Christ's sake Gaz.'

'I could get you some eyes to put in people's beer.'

They have given the climbs in this cosy place queer existentialist names, Victim of Life, Unreal City, Lemmingsville.

'What's *your* name Louise?' asked one little girl confidingly of another.

Gaz got out his cheap denim shorts and faded union jack T-shirt and undressed shyly. The women eyed him. They were out from Leeds and Bradford for Whit Week by the sea, with their bare red shoulders and untalkative husbands. Gaz's arms and legs were peculiarly white, as if he spent all week in the cold store. He always looked underfed but full of uncontrollable energy.

'Mummy, those men are in *our cave*!'

We traversed the whole cliff a few feet above the tideline, our shadows bobbing on the rock, dwarfing then stretching themselves, sending out an elongated arm or leg. All morning the water rose steadily, the colour of the water in the Manchester Ship Canal. 'You wouldn't like to fall in that,' said Gaz. And then: 'What are these fucking little shrimps doing up here?' Laying away off a big white flake with his feet tucked negligently up and to one side so that he looked as intelligent as a gibbon, he probed about one-handed in a narrow crack full of things like lice with long springy tails. Suddenly he shrieked and threw himself backwards into the air, landing in the sea with a huge splash. When he came up blowing and laughing the children stared at him in exasperation. He said: 'One of them jumped in my eye! Right in my eye!' He rubbed his face vigorously.

Whenever anybody mentioned Jack Scout Cove after that he would wink at me laboriously and say, 'Those fucking shrimps, eh?'

In the afternoon we lay on the clints in the sun. The tourists accepted us companionably. The tide was on its way out and a transistor radio somewhere down on the damp sand played 'Green Tambourine'.

When you hear an old song again like that, one you have not thought about for years, there is a brief slippage of time, a shiver, as if something had cut down obliquely through your life and displaced each layer by its own depth along the fault line. Without warning I was able to recall being in Silverdale as a child. In the cafe hung a picture by a local water colourist, of two rowing boats apparently moored in a low-lying street: he wanted eleven pounds for it but it was worth more. I sat rigid with delight beneath it, a thick slab of steak and kidney pie cooling on an oval plate in front of me. 'Eat your lunch, eat your lunch.' Great channels of slowly moving water in the mud; strange flat peninsulas with the sheep chewing the tough grass; the empty thin hull of a crab in a pool shaped like a waving boy.

At about four o'clock Gaz sat up and clapped his hand to his face.

'Fucking sun bathing!' he said. 'I'm going to regret this tomorrow.'

He examined gloomily the reddening patches on his thighs.

'Better get going I suppose.'

We drove down to Junction 28 on the M6, where we squatted at the base of a wall in our patched baggy tracksuit trousers and headbands, like the remains of a punitive expedition gone native among the tribes in the killing humidity. 'Junction 28,' runs the advert, 'the best place to eat sleep and be merry.' Everything was closed. Only the take-away was open, and they had no Danish pastries.

'That would be a 'small' in America,' Gaz told me with a kind of sneering nostalgia, remembering the Pepsi-Colas of Pasadena where he had been, it turned out, with the Venture Scouts. He put some chips in his mouth.

'What you've got there would be a 'small'.'

He brightened up.

'You get to the bottom of it there and it's *full of ice*.'

Teenagers, out for an afternoon in the car in their tight clean jeans and striped cotton tops, eyed his burnt arms nervously. Old people walked past, pretending to ignore us but carefully avoiding our feet. 'Closed,' they murmured, staring numbly ahead. 'Closed.' The caravans rolled south along the motorway, full of children and dogs. Little Asian girls with great laughing eyes and white teeth caught sight of our bruised and chalky hands and immediately became thoughtful: the women, in paper-thin lamé trousers, hurried them past.

'Another hole in me shirt,' said Gaz. 'What a fucking sight I look.'

We ate our chips and even threw a few of them at one another in a sort of desultory slow motion, while the teenagers looked on, prim, embarrassed.

Gaz walked off to the car.

'I'm sick of being stared at now,' he said.

So he went, as he put it, arseholing down the M6 with the radio turned up full: AC/DC, Kate Bush, Bowie's 'Station to Station' already a nostalgia number. How many times, coming back after a hard day like that, has there seemed to be something utterly significant in the curve of a cooling tower, or the way a field between two factories, reddened in the evening light, rises to meet the locks on a disused canal? Motorway bridges, smoke, spires, glow in the sun: it is a kind of psychic illumination. The music is immanent in the light, the day immanent in the music: life in the day. It is to do with being alive, but I am never sure how. Ever since Gaz had fallen off into the sea I had felt an overpowering, almost hallucinogenic sense of happiness, which this time lasted as far as Bolton.

Gaz never simply threw a rope down a crag; he 'cobbed it off the top'. He didn't fall: he 'boned off'. If the moves on a climb demanded as well as strength or delicacy that kind of concentration which leaves you brutalised and debilitated when you have done the moves, he called them 'poiky'. 'That was a bit bleeding poiky,' he'd say, hauling himself desperately over the top and trying to control the tremor in his left leg. 'Fuck me.' He soon recovered though. 'A bazzer that. A bloody *bazzing* route!' He had made up some of these words himself. Others, like 'rumpelstiltskin', which he used to mean anyone eccentric or incompetent, he had modified to his own use.

I saw a picture of him when he was a baby.

His parents kept it on the sideboard at home by the clock with the brass pendulum and the long chains. It was in a wine-coloured cardboard frame with gold edging and in it he looked older than his own father.

One Sunday we were sitting in a steep gully at Tissington Spires. It had been sunny all the way down in the car. Now if you looked into Dovedale you could see a feeble light bleaching out the moss and stones. The water was a gelid blue-grey colour in its deepest stretches; above it tumbled bleak slopes of rubble, destabilised by tree-felling and littered with huge raw logs; two or three anxious sheep stood between the river and the rock.

Loose stones trickled down the gully. It was as cold as a bus shelter in the centre of Leeds on a Friday night, and as crowded, with climbers standing or sitting awkwardly wherever roots or dead branches crossed the steep dusty slope. Their quiet voices came back from the rock. When a few specks of rain blew through the ruined trees, a shaven-headed boy looked up and laughed; then down at the purple tape in his hand, his neck bent in the attitude of the inmate of a camp.

There was a woman with one of the teams further down the gully, where a lot of dead wood had made it easier to find somewhere to sit. She had blond hair cut in an exact neat fringe above her eyebrows. Gaz, waiting in the queue for his turn at Yew Tree Wall, stared at her idly, biting the hard skin round his fingernails. She was belaying a climber on the wall. She fed him some rope, took it back in, running it deftly through the Sticht plate. He swapped feet uneasily on a sloping hold and asked himself, 'I wonder if I'm supposed to be able to reach that? Apparently not.' He tried again, slithered back to his original position. 'You bastard.' The minute figures of tourists by the river, catching the clatter of his equipment, shaded their eyes helplessly and tried to see if anything had happened. The girl looked up at him and when he still didn't make the move shivered with a mixture of boredom and cold.

She tried to pull the sleeves of her long sweater down over her wrists; smiled quickly at nothing, as if she was practising the expression. The boy with the shaved head wanted to take a photograph of her but she wouldn't co-operate. 'Come on now. Big grin. Big cheesy grin.' She reminded me of someone but I couldn't remember who. When I told Gaz he nodded, still watching her.

'I've seen her about,' he said. 'I've seen her a few times at the Bradford wall too, on a Tuesday night, climbing in pink tights.' He chuckled. 'Not bad! I wonder if she's married? Eh?' And he ducked his head in her direction with a significance I wasn't sure I'd caught. I laughed.

'Would it make any difference to you?'

He looked away, so I left it.

'It's not a climber she reminds me of,' I said.

On the crux of Yew Tree Wall, a yawning lean to the right from the tips of two fingers hooked into a knife-edged pocket, Gaz lost his balance and had to grab an old aid sling threaded into the rock.

'Well that's fucked that then,' he said viciously. 'Back to stuffing mince into plastic bags tomorrow.'

We abseiled off the tree at the top.

'You drive fifty miles to do a route, wait two hours for a lot of pillocks to clear off it, then you pox it up by pulling on a piece of tat.' All the way back along Dovedale to the car he was in a foul mood; in the pub at Wetton that night he looked round with hatred at the tourists.

'All these dossers,' he said loudly. 'What are they ever going to do with their lives?'

In country pubs like this there is always a plump boy with a brand new French tracksuit-top from the Gratton catalogue sitting opposite you with a packet of vinegar flavoured crisps. At the back of the room bikers plan their outrages: they will have a fire at the camp site, drink tinned beer, tease a dog. A middle-aged man walks stiffly past – under his tweed sports coat he has a striped shirt, a coloured scarf tied like a neck brace.

'They come out here at the weekends . . . If they walk down Dovedale like the fucking Pickerton Ramblers they think they've had a big adventure. "'Excews me,'" he mimicked. '"Could a climber like that *reelly* fall off? I mean reelly *hurt* himself?'"

'Yew Tree Wall won't go away,' I said. 'You can come back to it any time. Next Saturday if you like.'

'How do I know that? I might die. It might fall down. Anything might happen. I might drive me car into a wall and end up in a wheelchair.'

He drank his beer.

'It ruins your whole weekend, something like that. All you've got to look forward to is another week of dirty water, your hands in fucking dirty water till they split. You want to try it, you do.'

He got up and went to the lavatory, his great height and lurching, hunch-shouldered walk making him look even more dejected.

'Been out doing some climbing then?' the fat boy asked me. He offered me a crisp and when I had taken one sat forward companionably.

'Rather you than me,' he said. 'I bet you've seen some accidents at that game.'

In country pubs like this women from nearby towns, dressed to the nines, eat steak sandwiches from a paper napkin, holding their hands delicately in front of them like a praying mantis, gold bangles dangling from thin wrists. It's their night out, and their feet must be killing them. Every so often they lean down and with a furtive but curiously graceful motion adjust a shoe which is nothing more that a few slim red leather straps. After you have been climbing all weekend this gives you a sharp sexual surprise. With their make-up and perfume, their white shoulders displayed suddenly as they turn to someone and laugh, they are like women from another planet. You watch covertly to see if they will betray themselves further; they never do.

On the way home Gaz had the air of someone watching himself clinically to see how late he dared leave his braking. It was a kind of bitter investigation of his own technique. Once he swerved into the opposite carriageway of the A515 and drove along it waiting for me to say something. In the dark car I couldn't make out his expression. He said, 'Who did that girl at Tissington remind you of, if it wasn't a climber?'

'I can't remember.'

At that time of Gaz's life driving and climbing were like two aspects or definitions of the same thing. Cars stood for the wish, climbing for the act.

I think of him showing off on a Saturday morning in the scattered early traffic of the B6106, or flirting with the tight little corners of the Strines Road on the way from Huddersfield to the climbers' cafes at Grindleford and Stoney Middleton:

The brickworks lurch past on one side, on the other white faces peer at us momentarily through the streaming windscreen of a Land Rover. The roads are still plastered with last year's orange leaves. Stone walls, sodden verges, sudden drops assemble themselves out of the mist only so Gaz can annihilate them; junctions and old gates yawn out at us and are snatched away. The Vauxhall rocks and dips as he forces it into bends fringed with dripping oaks and tilted white signposts. Everything is fog and wet, everything is at the wrong angle, after every narrow squeak he gives me a sidelong glance I pretend not to see. At Bole Edge, where the dark, feathery conifers close in over the road, the mist thins without warning: *an old man on a bicycle* is silhouetted at the top of the hill, wobbling along against the bright morning sun!

Something else danced one Saturday among the heat mirages in the middle of the road.

'Did you see that, Gaz? It was a hare! It was a bloody big hare!'

'It were only a bit of newspaper.'

Later the reflection of my watch flickered on the dashboard; the limestone factories swam like casinos and amusement palaces in a golden haze; trapped in the obsessional net of drystone wall on the long sweeping rises by the A623 east of Buxton, groups of beech trees caught fire suddenly in the sunshine. Gaz accelerated. It was like being in a video game.

I sometimes called for him during the week; at the back door of the butcher's, at quarter past twelve, dinner time. All I ever saw in there was a dozen large pork pies neatly stacked in wire delivery trays; someone's racing bike propped against a spotless wall. Gaz liked you to think his job was a bloodbath, but if you asked, 'What do you actually do in there?' he would only wink and – flicking a cube of raw meat, dark red and speckled with sawdust, off his jeans – grumble, 'Bugger all most days. Mind you, I bust one of the machines this morning.'

I wanted to know what the hooks in the ceiling were for. They slid on rails and looked as if they would bear quite heavy loads. He scratched his head.

'Oh, this and that. Generally we hang stuff on them.'

Staring into the pet-shop window at a sort of cxpanding plastic maze he said, 'Me sister's got one of those. I never see what she keeps in it. It's always asleep when I get home. I know she keeps something in it but I've never seen it.' And then, looking slyly at me, 'I wonder if you can *eat* it –?' Whatever he did at the butcher's was only tenable as a nightmare – sheeps's eyes in the beer, plastic tags slit from lamb's ears, quartered hamsters. With an unguarded comment he might show it up, to himself as much as anybody, as boredom and drudgery. 'I've gone right through these clogs. I'll have to get new,' he said as we sat on a bench in the sun. He unwrapped his sandwiches and opened one. 'Fucking hell. Banana again.'

Though he made a considerable impression on me, I didn't actually see as much of Gaz as I would have liked, because he climbed mostly with Sankey.

Sankey was always so cautious and indirect, so ready to defer to your opinion. He wondered casually if you had a couple of days free that week: he knew full well you were on the dole. With him everything was open to negotiation. If, driving to a cliff he had known all his life, you asked, 'Do we turn right here?', he would consider for a moment and then say, 'Yes, yes, you can. Or of course you can go up round Ilkley if you want to. It's sometimes quicker that way.' And when you stared at him: 'Well it probably is further to go. But now you *can* get on to the A650, some people do prefer that way –'

By then you had missed your turning.

This drove Gaz mad, and he wouldn't have Sankey in the front seat of the Vauxhall with him. They got on all right in Sankey's car, a three-wheeler van about which he was very defensive. To improve its fuel consumption even further he had taken the passenger seat out, so that you sat in the back in the dark with the ropes and piles of equipment. They took me to Almscliffe in it one day: it bumped and banged along the Yeadon by-pass, rocking from side to side. 'I'm going to puke up!' shouted Gaz. He gave me a wink. 'I keep thinking, what if we get a puncture in the front wheel? I mean, you've only got the one, haven't you?'

Sankey turned himself round in the driver's seat.

'They're very safe, these,' he said. 'Very safe cars.'

Horns blared at him from the approaching traffic, into whose lane he had wobbled. For a moment all we could see of him was his elbows jerking about in silhouette as he sawed at the steering wheel. Gaz clutched himself among the rucksacs; it was an old joke, you could see, but a good one.

At Almscliffe you can't get out of the wind. It hisses in the greenish cracks and flutings. It blows from all directions at once even on a summer day. The dust gets into your eyes as you pick your way down the cold dark gullies that dissect the main mass of rock, while all around you Lower Wharfedale spreads its legs in the sunshine – farmland, spires, viaducts, hedges and trees. It might be a landscape much further south, much earlier in the year, great swags of blossom at the edge of every field. But up on the horizon the power-stations lie hull-down in ambush among the East Yorkshire coal pits.

Gaz got straight into his harness and on to the rock.

'I'm scared!' he complained after he had jammed about forty feet up into the wind. He was just passing a thing like a melted, dripping end of an old candle. The crack he was climbing arrowed above him into the blue sky. Soon he would get his foot stuck in it.

Being there is like watching an old elephant, dying split-skinned in its own tremendous ammoniacal reek, gazing patiently back at you in a zoo. It hasn't moved for a long time, you judge, but you can still detect the tremor of its breath – or is it your own? Meanwhile the children shout and try to wake it up with buns. At Almscliffe the visitors walk about bemusedly, shading their eyes, wondering perhaps why the zoo-keeper has let them in on such a tragic occasion. They are generally middle-class people, careful not to drop their sandwich papers from the top. The crag bears them up passively, while bits of route description, boasts and obscenities circle round them on the wind.

'No you go left there and then swing round again.'

' . . . Syrett . . . Pasquill . . .'

'Go left from where you are!'

' . . . Black Wall Eliminate in the rain, nowhere to rest, that fucking bog waiting for you underneath . . .'

'Left! You go *left* you maniac. Oh fuck, look at that.'

This has never been a quiet place. It was the first of the great outdoor climbing walls, the model of a local crag. Its enthusiasts – parochial, cliqueish, contemptuous of the performance of outsiders and resentful of their cheery unconcern for precedent – believe that the sport was invented here. Generations of them have brought the rock to a high polish, like the stuff that faces the Halifax Building Society. Every evening local men – Yorkshire men, who hardly ever speak – do the low-level traverses until they learn to allow for the shine of the footholds, the flare and brutality of the cracks. Their arms and shoulders grow strong. Their clothes fray. They develop a slow way of looking at you. Down Wharfedale they have wives and kiddies and bicycles just like anyone else, but all they think about is which one of them will solve the Last Great Problem.

It won't be Gaz, anyway.

In his orange-dyed karate trousers, with his runners jangling and clanging mournfully, he gingerly unlocked his foot. 'What grade is this? Rubbish!' Fucking and blinding he made his careful way up: pulled in a few feet of rope: vanished somewhere among the bottomless clefts and queer boulders of the summit, where picnickers looked at him like owls. After a moment his head popped back over the top. 'Come on! Never mind sitting on your arses down there, get some climbing done!'

As he brought me up he dangled his legs over the top like Pinocchio and stared out over the plain towards York, where the tourists would be making their way from shop to shop in a muzzy, good-tempered dream.

He was in one himself.

'You want to jam that crack mate,' I heard him advise someone on another climb, 'not layback it.'

After a moment he kicked his legs disconnectedly and sang in a maudlin voice, 'I don't know what to do when you disappcar from view . . .'

Soon a great loop of rope hung down in front of me.

'For Christ's sake Gaz pay attention. Take in. Take in! If I fucking fall off –'

'You're not going to. Stay steady. Steady. You're all right. Can you get your hands in the break? Just stay steady and you'll do it,' he said. 'It's easy.'

He took the rope in tight anyway.

'Look,' he said, leaning out at an odd angle against his belays so that he could see down the climb; it made him look as if he had been photographed in the act of throwing himself off. 'See there? Just above that bit of a rib there? . . . No *there*, above you, you wollock! . . . That's it, just there. Can you see a tiny little lay-off?'

I said I could.

'Well don't use that, it's no good.'

The sun came down and scraped into the irregular corners like Gaz's mother scraping an oven. He moved his shoulders uneasily and exchanged his pullover for a T-shirt with a design advertising a northern equipment firm: 'Troll Gets You High.'

We had something to eat. Then, forced into inhuman, expressionistic postures by its grim logic, Sankey strained and contorted up Wall of Horrors, until his impetus ran out just under the crux. He stretched up: nothing. He tried facing left, then right, grinding his cheek into the gritstone. His legs began to tremble. All the lines on the rock moved towards him, in a fixed vortex. When he lurched suddenly on his footholds everyone looked up: he was only sorting through the stuff on his rack for something to protect his next two moves. If he took too long to find and place it he would come off anyway. His last runner was lodged in a crack like a section throught a fall pipe, fifteen or twenty feet below him.

'Can you get something there?'

'Can you get anything in higher up?'

He didn't hear us.

He was fiddling about in a rounded break, his eyes inturned and panicky, his head and upper body squashed up as if he was demonstrating the limits of some box invisible to anyone else. Under the impact of fear, concentration, physical effort, his face went lax and shocked, his age began to show. By 1970 he had climbed all over the world; he had done every major route in Britain; the 'new' climbs were his only hope – violent, kinaesthetic, stripped of all aid. 'Wall of Horrors!' he would say. 'John Hart talked me up that, move by move, first time I led it. Years ago. It overfaced people then. Ha ha.' He was forty five, perhaps fifty. As I watched him I wondered what he was doing it to himself for.

All the time Gaz was watching him too.

He had to predict when Sankey would go. He had to mother him. The runner in the fall pipe was too close to the ground to be much good: if Sankey boned off, could Gaz run sideways far enough quick enough to shorten the rope? I didn't think he could. He fidgeted it backwards and forwards through the Sticht plate, which clicked and rattled nervously.

Up in his invisible box Sankey twisted one arm behind his back to get his hand into his chalk bag. His shadow moved uneasily on the buttress over to his left, the shadow of the rope blowing out behind it. Chalk moved off into the turbulence as he shifted his feet.

The sun went in.

'Okay, kid,' he said. 'Watch the rope.'

Suddenly we saw that he was calm and thoughtful again. He stood up straight and went quickly to the top, reaching, rocking elegantly to one side, stepping up.

Things have moved on now, of course, but Wall of Horrors still meant something then. When he came down several kids were waiting to talk to him. One or two of them – boys of fourteen or fifteen who were on the boulders or at the indoor wall every evening – would solo it one day soon, and later come to think of it as a 'problem' rather than a climb; against that time they were willing to give him uncontrolled admiration. His lead would give their achievement bulk and meaning. They were dressed in white canvas trousers, sweatshirts and pullovers with broad stripes, in imitation of the American and Australian climbers whose pictures they saw in the magazines; in two or three years they would be wearing lycra tights, courting anorexia in search of a high power-weight ratio, exchanging the magic words of the New Climbing: 'redpoint', 'ripped', 'Martin Atkinson'.

One of them said, 'Are you Stevie Smith? I've seen you climb before haven't I?'

Sankey gave his nervous laugh.

'No,' he said.

He sat down tiredly among some boulders and began sorting through his equipment, strewing orange tape slings about in the dust as if looking for something that had let him down. Then he just sat, absentmindedly clicking the gate of a snaplink until Gaz brought him some coffee from a flask. As we walked away from the cliff the backs of my hands smarted in the wind. I saw the shadow of a dove flicker over the rock in the warm, slanting light. These birds live in the high breaks and caves. They ruffle their feathers uncertainly, hunch up, explode without warning over your head; they come back in the evening. Sankey's eyes were losing the empty, exhausted look that had entered them on the wall.

On the way home Gaz said, 'I wouldn't mind being an owl in my next life.' Then he said, 'I'm getting married next month.' He had to shout to make himself heard over the engine of the three-wheeler.

I didn't go to the wedding – something intervened – but I needn't have worried, because a climber called Normal told me about it later.

'You should have been there,' he said, 'All the lads were there. What a send-off! And after they'd gone we went over to Running Hill Pits in Sankey's car and *climbed a route*. In our penguin suits!'

He showed me a photograph he had taken of Sankey nearing the top of a climb called Plum Line, in a hired morning suit and polished black shoes.

From what I could make out Sankey had tied on to the rope with a couple of turns round his waist. His face was a white smear. Runners hung out of his trouser pockets.

'We were pissed out of our minds!'

Normal shook his head reminiscently as I leafed through the rest of the prints. They were all blurred: Gaz, with an appalled grin like an expressionist self-portrait, standing as if he had one leg shorter than the other; Normal himself, holding up a glass of beer and a chalk bag; someone I didn't recognise looking back over his shoulder as he came out of a door marked 'Men'.

'We shook chalk over them instead of rice. We were well pissed!'

'You didn't take any of his wife,' I said. 'I'd like to have seen her.'

'She's very nice,' said Normal sentimentally. 'Very nice. They went to the Isle of Man, she'll enjoy that.'

That night Sankey rang me up.

'I wondered if you were going out climbing in the week?' he said. 'If you were free?'

'Sankey, Margaret Thatcher pays me to be free.'

Margaret Thatcher had paid me for a brand new pair of Fires, too.

'Ha ha,' Sankey said cautiously. 'Only that I thought we could go to Millstone and do Time for Tea Direct Finish. If you felt like it. If you've got nothing else on.'

I lost touch with Gaz, although I had a postcard from him on his honeymoon at Douglas, and another one about six months later from the Verdon Gorge in Provence, which said in deeply-indented block letters: WELL HERE WE ARE IN VERDON, WEATHER IS WICKED KEEPS SNOWING, HARRY AND DAVE GOT BENIGHTED 300FT FROM THE TOP THEY HAD TO SLEEP IN A TREE THE FIRST DAY. THE ROCK IS INCREDIBLE POSTCARD DOESN'T DO IT JUSTICE. SEE YOU GAZ. (I didn't know who Harry and Dave were but the Defile des Cavaliers, with its luxuriant vegetation and slightly pink limestone, looked nice: it might have been Symonds Yat, or Trow Gill in Yorkshire, but I suppose that was an effect of scale.)

I met him again by accident in Lodge's supermarket one Saturday morning about three years after the wedding. He didn't seem to have changed. His wife was with him, a short girl in dungarees, with one breast noticeably larger than the other and long hair which she pushed back continually from her face. She put her arms round his waist from behind and rubbed her cheek against his back. They had a toddler which sat in its pushchair watching them silently.

'Fucking hell,' Gaz said to me. 'I'll always remember you leading that – what was it? – Wall of Horrors! Wall of Horrors, what a name! Poiky stuff!'

'That was Sankey,' I reminded him. For some reason I felt flattered anyway. 'Wall of Horrors is a bit strong for me.'

'You don't want to do yourself down,' Gaz told me. 'You were always a good climber. You just needed that bit of steadiness.'

After they had done their shopping, they said, why didn't we go upstairs where you could have a cup of tea? That was what they usually did. Gaz paid, and his wife insisted we have cakes. They gave the little boy a drink of something bright red, but he couldn't seem to manage the glass well, and he didn't take much interest in it. He seemed bemused. The clatter, the steam, the Saturday-morning laughter made him blink. Gaz looked out of the window at the phone boxes in the square. 'Same old place,' he said with his typical grin. He still worked at the butcher's: I wouldn't have seen him there because he still worked in the back. He winked. 'Still fetching the green tags out!'

When I thanked him for his postcard he said, 'Verdon! Oh it was fucking great. Thousands of feet of limestone, 5b and 5c pitches all the way. Dave was so freaked he couldn't even *second* some of the pitches. Then we found out he didn't know how to prusik! We had to pull him up on the rope like a sack.' He laughed and pushed his cup away. 'Six run-outs of 5c, and no dinner all day, then you have to lead at 6a! Fucking appalling!'

A waitress came over and said to his wife, 'I forgot to give you a spoon for your tart, love.'

Gaz stared uncomprehendingly after her as she walked off. 'Fucking bazzing!' he said less certainly, as if he remembered his enthusiasm but had forgotten what he was talking about. He got up to fetch us all another cup of tea. Over the noise of the woman at the next table his wife said,

'I always tell him I wish he'd go out climbing more. He does love it. But he likes to be with the kiddy at weekends. They do, don't they?'

The child was a sad little thing. Its hair stood on end, much like Gaz's, and it was hard to tell whether it would smile at you or cry. When she saw me trying to attract its attention she said complacently, 'Tired out, the poor little mite.' She chuckled. 'He gave me a fright this morning,' she said, leaning forward and lowering her voice. 'You'll never believe what he did.' She had got up, she told me, at five in the morning, to find that it had stuck elastoplast dressings on the limbs of its soft toys and immured them in the nine-inch gap between the double glazing panes. 'I don't know what he thought he was doing, do you?' She offered the child its drink, and it stared at her.

'Mind you,' she went on, 'don't you find you're so pleased with what you've got that you don't really care how they turn out? I mean, if he's just average that'll suit me. People tell me he should be taking a bit more notice now, but I say you're only a kiddy once, aren't you? Let him be a kiddy for a bit, eh?'

Over her shoulder I could see the phone boxes in the square. Up on the steeply terraced streets above them a man had locked himself out of his house. He walked to and fro outside it for a minute or two, threw himself violently against the front door. Nothing. He knocked on a neighbouring door. Nothing there. He looked round warily then flung himself at his own front door again. He was so far away that everything he did had a kind of jerky, miniaturised savagery and motivelessness. Eventually he walked off rubbing his shoulder. A few spots of rain came down.

'I haven't got any of my own,' I said.

The Case Of The Great Grey Man

Edited by Robin N. Campbell

from the case notes of John H. Watson, M.D.[1]

AUGUST 189– was undoubtedly a low point in the psychic life of my friend Sherlock Holmes. The weather was unremittingly fine, Mrs Hudson was consistently managing to achieve a five minute egg and Holmes' Persian slipper contained a new supply of rare and treasured Turkish tobacco, but despite these amenities breakfast was a scene of misery throughout the month. Following a perfunctory meal Holmes would lie spreadeagled on the ottoman for the remainder of the morning, clutching his brow as if in pain. The cause of this wretched condition was the case of James Phillimore, one of his few failures.[2]

Holmes had been invited by Lestrade of the police to assist at the arrest of Phillimore, a War Office scientist suspected of passing secret information to a foreign power. We had gone one evening in July to Phillimore's house, a large establishment in North London with extensive grounds, to effect the arrest. Under Holmes' supervision the grounds were surrounded by a force of twenty men. It was a perfectly vile evening, black as pitch and with a westerly breeze bringing deluges of warm rain upon the watchers. Holmes and I took positions at the front gate by the carriage. Phillimore was arrested at 2:00 a.m. and an officer waited with him while he dressed. Eventually we saw Phillimore emerge at the door of the house and peer upwards at the rain. He said something to the constable – apparently a request to return to fetch an umbrella – and turned back into the house.

When he did not emerge we immediately searched the house and grounds, but no trace of him could be found. It seemed that he must have contrived to slip past the cordon of police. At first light, Holmes and I examined the grounds to the rear of the house. We could find no sign that Phillimore had

[1] These case-notes were discovered some years ago in the bottom of a box of lantern-slides, thought to have been donated to the Club Collection by J. Norman Collie. The first set of notes formed the basis for an earlier adventure of Holmes and Watson, an account of which appeared in *The Scottish Mountaineering Club Journal* 1979 (Vol. xxxi, p. 360). The writer began work on preparing a version of the present case shortly after that date and offers apologies to impatient readers for the long delay that has ensued. This delay is due entirely to his own dilatoriness and not at all to Dr Watson's notes, which – as usual – are a model of precision and clarity. Readers may be surprised by the accuracy of Dr Watson's Gaelic: in fact, his names are by no means accurate and his notes are punctuated by apologies for his 'poor transcription of these barbarous names.' I have done my best to render them in SMC-Gaelic of the period.

[2] The case of James Phillimore is discussed by Watson in the account of the case of *That Bridge*. In the introductory paragraph to that case Watson observes that 'Somewhere in the vaults of the bank of Cox and Co., at Charing Cross, there (is) a battered tin dispatch-box containing (unpublished case reports). Among these unfinished tales is that of Mr James Phillimore, who, stepping back into his own house to get his umbrella, was never more seen in this world.'

It seems certain that this is the case recounted here. No doubt Watson preferred to pretend that Phillimore was never seen again and that the case was unfinished so that the politically-sensitive material in the case should remain secret until circumstances were favourable to publication.

passed through the gardens, despite the presence of a quantity of soft sand on a path which he must have used if he had escaped that way. Word was sent immediately to the ports and a hue and cry raised in the newspapers accompanied by a description of the missing man. Although Phillimore could hardly be mistaken – he had a large burn scar on his left cheek, the result of some mishap in his laboratory – no further report of him was confirmed. He had simply disappeared into thin air.

By the end of the month I was very much alarmed by my friend's depressed condition, aggravated in no small measure by his resumption of the deplorable habit of cocaine. Police interest in the case had all but ceased. Holmes' own inquiries consisted solely of some unanswered telegrams directed to obscure addresses in the Low Countries and two visits to his brother Mycroft at the Foreign Office. Mycroft had confirmed that Phillimore was indeed a foreign agent, supplying intelligence to anarchist groups in Europe.

'Forget the case, Holmes,' I urged. 'My prescription is sunshine and sea air. Biarritz perhaps. At once.'

'Am I so dilapidated, Watson, that I must wrap myself in rugs and sit on a beach?' he replied. 'No. Phillimore's escape was prepared, not fortuitous. He will act soon and I must be here and ready.'

It was not until mid-September that Holmes showed some recovery of morale. When I joined him at the breakfast table that morning his eye was bright as he held out a letter.

'At last, Watson, something worthy of my powers. Read it and then we'll pack.'

I noted that the letter was from Holmes' cousin Norman[3] and read its contents with growing disbelief.

'A giant spectre? In the Cairngorm Mountains? What superstitious twaddle, Holmes! Surely there can be nothing in it?'

'But Norman has met this spectre on the slopes of Ben Macdhui and as a trained scientist would not fabricate it. Certainly, he panicked and fled down through the wood of Rothiemurchus, but equally certain something caused him to panic. This is no mere figment of the Celtic imagination.'

I read further: the spectre had been 'seen' by some of the ghillies on the Duke of Fife's estate, usually in mist and high on Ben Macdhui, and had even driven one unfortunate Highlander over a precipice. When the dying man was found he had croaked out with his last breath – 'Fear Liath Mór' – the Great Grey Man.

'What tommyrot, Holmes!' I ejaculated, 'This farrago is worthy of your powers? Barely worthy of the Strand Magazine, I should judge.'

But my friend could not be dissuaded. 'Come, Watson, clean air was your own prescription. Pack your bags and be sure to include your service revolver and Alpine boots.'

[3] The reference to 'cousin Norman' here makes absolutely certain the tentative identification with Norman Collie proposed in the notes to the previous case. As is well known, Collie encountered the Grey Man sometime in the 1890s. He did not publicly mention the encounter, however, until many years later at an Annual Dinner of the Cairngorm Club. For details of Collie's and (some) other encounters with the Grey Man, see Affleck Gray's *The Big Grey Man of Ben Macdhui*. Lochar Publishing, 1989. Moffat DG10 9JU

I hastened to my task and by nightfall we were speeding north by train. The following mid-day found us chugging through the pinewoods towards Ballater. Holmes gestured at the passing countryside with enthusiasm, 'Royal Deeside, Watson. The Queen's home and a castle on every hillock. For once my headgear is appropriate enough.'

He was certainly in better spirits. At Castletown of Braemar we took rooms in a hotel and in the evening met the Head Stalker over maps and whisky downstairs.

'So, Mr Scott,' said Holmes, 'because of the mist the apparition has not been clearly seen, but it has the shape of an enormous man and stalks the high plateau.'

'Just so, sir. It has a slow and steady way of walking and makes only about a yard with every step. It's a slow lumbering sort of beast. I've seen its footprints in the snow, you see. But it breathes like a mortal man. I've heard it gasping and wheezing as it came after me.'

'And how long has this been going on?'

'Och, there's a long tradition of it, but it's only in the last month or so that me and my men have been bothered.'

'Poor old Donald,' he gazed morosely into his whisky. 'One of my best men he was and him frightened right over the edge of Coire Sputan Dearg of Macdhui. Creag Fear Liath Mór we call it now, the crag of the Great Grey Man.'

'And have there been any other curious occurrences?' asked Holmes.

'Nothing that I would set much store by,' said Scott, draining his glass, 'but one of the men has a story about seeing an enormous bird, also on Ben Macdhui, and of course there are the usual reports of faeries, ghostly lights flickering on the slopes of Morrone, and so on.'

'My goodness, Holmes!' I put in, 'Not another giant bird[4]! This place is a veritable menagerie of the supernatural. Surely you don't believe this balderdash!'

Holmes refilled our glasses. 'Tut, tut, Watson. Such scepticism ill becomes a doctor of medicine, who cures diseases he does not understand with specifics of unknown compostition. Restrain your doubts.'

Holmes and Scott were occupied with their maps, no doubt identifying the haunted slopes of Morrone, when the door burst open and an exhausted Highlander staggered into the bar.

'Mr Scott,' he cried. 'The Great Grey Man has killed again!'

He collapsed at our table, clutching the bottle firmly as he fell. When order was restored he was questioned by Holmes and Scott. Apparently another corpse had been discovered that day in Coire Sputan Dearg. The body had been identified as Dundee Wullie, a well-known visitor who roamed throughout the range looking for quartz gems. Wullie's remains had been brought down to Derry Lodge at the foot of the mountain.

'Capital, Watson!' whispered my friend. 'Tomorrow we shall examine the body. Perhaps my methods and your medical skills will provide some clues.'

[4] A reference to the previous case described in Note 1.

On the following day at the crack of dawn we took a dog-cart up into the mountains by way of an excellent forest road. Bouldery hills bulked around us as we emerged from the pines at a high meadow beside a grey stone house. A ghillie met us with a pony and loaded up our baggage. He was to take it through the mountains to a place on the north side, over some dreary pass, the 'Lairig Ghru' by name, and would then return with a cart to meet us.

Scott led us over to a grim-looking outbuilding. As my eyes adjusted to the gloomy interior I made out the carcasses of several stags hung around the walls and the corpse of Dundee Wullie laid on a table in the centre of the room. We tied handkerchiefs about our faces – a feeble defence against such an army of odours – and bent to examine the remains, while Scott held up a light.

'Well, Watson, what are your conclusions?' asked Holmes after a time.

'They are obvious,' I replied. 'The man died from multiple injuries received in a fall.'

'Indeed,' said Holmes, 'and what do you make of these marks on his wrists?' He pointed to some faint bruises.

'That is more your province than mine. Perhaps he struck them against the rocks in his death throes.'

'Perhaps. But it seems to me that his hands may have been recently tied.'

Holmes crouched beside the corpse, asking Scott to bring the light closer. With his penknife he scraped something from the fingernails onto a sheet of paper. He bore this outside and proceeded to examine it with his glass.

'Further evidence of foul play, Watson. These are animal fibres.' Holmes gave a curious and unbecoming smirk, folded the paper carefully and put it in a pocket.

We returned to the shed and Holmes set about searching the victim's clothing. A pathetic collection of possessions emerged. A bag of oatmeal, a pipe, tobacco, a flask of whisky, a short-handled pick, a Bible, and a few miserable rock crystals. Finally, with a cry of triumph Holmes rushed from the shed with a crumpled piece of paper.

'Torn from a notebook, I'd say. Perhaps it is a trophy from his murderer.'

'Murderer?' said I. 'You are certain, Holmes?'

'Yes, Watson, there is more to be found up there,' he gestured at the mountain, 'than a Great Grey Man.'

We examined the paper, which I reproduce (*facing*).

'What do you make of it, Holmes?'

'It is a timetable, Watson, but I don't yet know what events it records. Let us go to the mountain now. There is nothing further to be discovered here.'

We took three ponies from the stables and set off up the hillside. At the last trees Scott tethered the ponies and we continued on foot by a pleasantly graded path beside a rushing stream. As we gained height, however, the heath gave way to stones and patches of old snow, and Ben Macdhui, defended by a frieze of decaying black crags, impended ominously on our left. Eventually we toiled up a fierce slope of slippery boulders below the largest of the crags. Scott pointed to a small cairn.

'Donald met his Maker right here, Mr Holmes. I marked the spot for the constable, but it's a very cowardly and superstitious wee policeman we have here. A damned Macdonald from the Isles. He wouldn't come up the hill at all, and Donald a good friend of his forbye.'

We moved over shortly to a further cairn, which Scott identified as the last resting place of Dundee Wullie. Here we took breakfast and recovered our wind. I passed the time by questioning Scott about his employment while Holmes busied himself with his notebook. Apparently today and tomorrow Scott had no particular duties except to keep track of the better stags on his ground. But on the following day it was possible that there would be a stalking party from Balmoral.

'There's a lot of guests there this year, you see. They've taken the shooting here and on Beinn a' Bhuird, as well as on their own ground, of course. I have a man out this morning on Cairngorm of Derry looking for beasts.' Scott

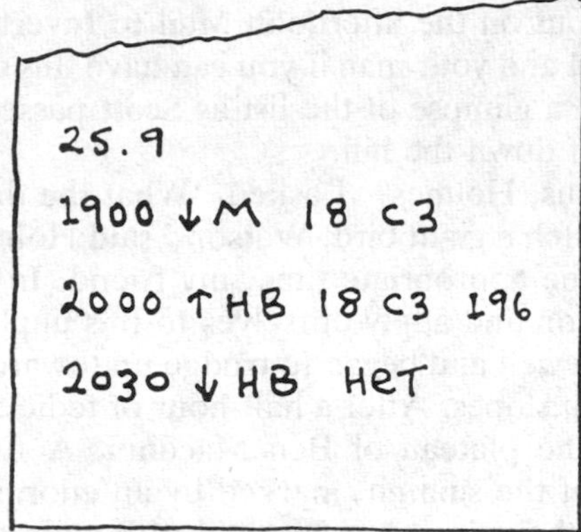

indicated the mountain on the other side of the valley and added slyly, 'The Grey Man's scared them all over to there, or so the men say.'

As he relieved himself of this witticism we heard a rattle of stones and saw Scott's man come bounding down the opposite slope like a bashi-bazouk. He plodded up to us more slowly.

'You'll want to speak to this fellow, Mr Holmes,' said Scott with a sniff. 'He's the one that's seen the giant bird.'

After the new arrival had taken a pull from his flask and made his report to Scott, he addressed us in an almost impenetrable patois, of which I offer a fair rendering.

'It was last week, sir. We were up on Cairn Toul with a shooting party and I was standing by with a pony. It had just gone four o'clock when they shot a beast, right up at the head of the Garracorries. The stalker marked it with a flag for me. So I had to get up there with the pony, clean the beast and load it up. By then it was going dark. It was a long slow way from there round the slopes and down to the bothy at Corrour. I crossed the Dee about six o'clock and stopped for a bite to eat. The pony drank and rested a bit and I took a few drams. It was a fine clear night and very mild. Anyhow I must have dozed off, because it was eight before we started off again. I'd got the pony up and we were just setting off when I saw this huge bird hovering up by the top of Ben

Macdhui. It was like an enormous eagle and it just moved back and forth on the breeze. I watched it for a few minutes hoping that it might get a whiff of the stag and come down for a closer look but it never budged. After we turned the corner of the hill I lost sight of it.'

'How large was the bird, would you say?' asked Holmes.

'Oh, the wing-span would have been about ten or twelve feet, sir.'

'Thank you!' said Holmes. 'Your information has been most valuable. Indeed, it confirms the serious view that I have taken of this case. I must issue certain warnings and make some urgent preparations.'

He bent once more to his notebook, while Scott interrogated his man about the whereabouts of stags. After a few minutes Holmes removed several pages from his notebook and gave them to Scott.

'These telegrams must be sent immediately,' he said. 'The long list is to be telegraphed to Lizars in Edinburgh, Scott. There is no time to be lost if these materials are to be put on the afternoon Mail to Inverness. There will be a guinea apiece for you and your man if you can have this despatched by noon.'

I strained to catch a glimpse of the list as Scott passed it to his man, who immediately sped off down the hill.

'A Branly apparatus, Holmes?' I asked. 'What the devil is that?'

'It is a device to catch a giant bird, Watson,' said Holmes with a smile. 'All will be revealed at the appropriate time, my friend. In the meantime let us desist from speculation and apply ourselves to this unpleasant slope.'

We bade Scott farewell and began to trudge up towards a stone-filled gully leading to the summit slopes. After a half-hour of tedious effort we stumbled over the rim onto the plateau of Ben Macdhui. A further dreary incline brought us in sight of the summit, marked by an enormous sprawling cairn.

Soon we reached the cairn. A great field of boulders stretched out in all directions. We moved out to the north.

'Look for traces, Watson, – for anything unusual,' said Holmes. 'Fire your revolver if you find anything.'

I was instructed to hold close to the western edge of the plateau while Holmes worked further east, moving slowly and stooping occasionally to examine the ground. In truth I saw nothing unusual, just boulder after wretched boulder against which I regularly stumbled and barked my shins. Suddenly I was enveloped in a cloud of thin mist and lost sight of my companion. I made to return to the cairn, but became unsure of my direction. A film of moisture clung to my cape. The breeze revealed occasional glimpses to some distance. I sighted the outline of the cairn and began to plod towards it. Again the mist obscured my view, but I was sure of my line now and moved on steadily amongst the boulders. After a little I stopped for breath and wrung out my moustaches. While thus engaged I was startled by a sound from dead ahead. Suddenly a huge figure lumbered out of the murk! My first impulse was to run, as terror gripped me. The Great Grey Man! But my army training proved its worth. I stood my ground, drew my revolver and fired a round over the creature's head. When it did not stop I fired again at its chest. It stopped abruptly but did not fall. Instead it turned aside and moved rapidly away to my left. What should I do? Holmes would undoubtedly have given chase, so I set off once again through the boulder-field, swearing and stumbling in the effort to catch up. A pistol shot rang out some considerable distance off to my right.

'Over here, Holmes!' I cried in response to his signal.

The beast increased its pace and I hurried on in its wake. After some minutes the ground began to fall away and the boulders to thin out revealing a pavement of smooth and slippery granite. I noticed with some relief the shadowy form of Holmes well over to my right on a converging course. Between us we should be more than a match for the creature if it turned at bay. But just then the mist began to thicken until it became as bad as the worst London fog. As Holmes hurried to join me we lost sight of the monster completely.

'I fear we have lost our quarry,' I remarked.

'You are too pessimistic, Watson,' observed Holmes. 'Look, you can see on that boulder the place where it brushed against it. The creature has left a trace!'

Indeed. So it had. I bent to inspect the scrap of greyish-yellow fur plucked from the beast's limbs by the rough granite. Holmes had by now found the next such trace and we moved forward once again in pursuit. But after a hundred yards more of steady descent Holmes halted.

'The mist is lifting,' he said. 'Let us save our legs.'

I could see that my friend was right as usual. As the fogs dispersed I told him about my set-to with the Grey Man, confident that, wounded as it must be, we should find him soon. But when all was clear we gazed only on empty slopes.

'The beast has gone to ground, Holmes. What sort of creature do you suppose we have to deal with? Presumably you can tell something from the fur?'

'Fur, Watson? Certainly these are animal hairs, like those which I removed from Wullie's fingernails, but they belong to nothing more intimidating than a sheep!'

'A sheep?' I gasped.

'Yes,' said Holmes. 'It is Belgian yarn. Mixed S and Z twist. You may compare it with the descriptions in my monograph 'European Fabrics Identified from Traces'.'[5]

'Good gracious, Holmes! Then it is merely a man.'

'To be precise it is a Carnival Giant from Flanders with a man inside.'

'But how do you know all this, Holmes? You show no surprise!'

'Indeed, Watson. I knew it, or most of it, some time ago. You see, this is Phillimore's work.'

'Phillimore! But how?' I demanded.

[5] From a note in an early Journal (*SMCJ*, VII, p. 114) describing an excursion to Arran in 1900, it seems that Harold Raeburn must have known of this recondite skill of Holmes. Raeburn comments on the Corrie Boulders as follows: 'They rarely permit an admirer to leave without retaining something, may be cuticle, may be garment. Were there a Sherlock Holmes in our Club, I have no doubt he would be able to infer for many days after, what particular member had been on the boulders by the structure and colour of the woolly fragments from his stockings or knickers, or the anthropometrical patterns on the pieces of skin from his fingertips left behind by the climber.'

Holmes' involvement with the early SMC, as recounted here and in the earlier adventure (see note 3) left other marks in the first few journals, e.g. see Dr Inglis Clark's remarks in *SMCJ*, VII, p. 202.

'It is time to explain my reasonings, Watson. Let us begin at the beginning. When Phillimore disappeared from his house there was a westerly breeze and sand in the garden. Surely that suggests a means of escape?'

I racked my brains but could think of nothing.

'You must have heard of gas-filled balloons,' said my friend. 'The sand was ballast discarded to effect a rapid ascent. Mycroft was able to confirm my speculation for me – Phillimore was studying the military application of aerial machines. He kept a balloon carefully hidden in his garden, as insurance against discovery of his treacherous activities.'

'And of course he would land in Belgium!' I interrupted.

'Yes, Watson. He collected the Carnival Giant and other equipment there before coming here, possibly with a southerly wind but like as not by more conventional means.'

'But how on earth did you know that he was here, Holmes?'

'I did not know. I made an assumption. According to Norman's letter, what did Donald say before he died?' he asked.

'Ferrliemore,' I said in an approximation of Scott's pronunciation and clapped a hand to my brow in astonishment.

'Was it "Ferrliemore" or "Phillimore"?' said Holmes. 'I assumed Donald's last words named his assailant as an English traitor rather than a Scottish monster. Phillimore's description was well-known and his burnt face could hardly be mistaken. Besides, we learned this morning that Donald and the constable were friends – he was sure to have known about Phillimore.'

'Astounding, Holmes! Truly astounding! But what on earth is he doing here, terrifying and killing the local men with this bogus monster?'

'Well, we can be sure that the monster is employed to keep curious people away from Ben Macdhui. Dundee Wullie must have disturbed Phillimore at his real work, whatever that is. He was overpowered, his hands bound, and eventually disposed of in the same manner as the unfortunate Donald. Come, Watson, let us see what else we can discover. I fancy the giant is lurking not far from here.'

We had searched around the massive boulders for only a few minutes when I found it, laid out flat in a crevice between two of the largest specimens. I called out to Holmes and he hurried over. The ogre measured about twelve feet and was topped by a gigantic and hideous mask of painted wood with long straggling beards and moustaches. The torso was supported by a wire framework which fitted over the head and shoulders of the carrier, who would be entirely concealed beneath the long grey skirt. The belt around the middle of the robe was punctured with two eye holes. I should have shot the creature in the stomach rather than the chest!

I fingered the frayed edge of the bullet-hole in the centre of the tunic. 'A mortal wound had it been a real giant, wouldn't you say, Holmes?'

'Indeed, Watson, your days in the Army were not wasted.'

Holmes bent to examine the bullet-hole more closely, assumed a thoughtful expression and then turned to me with a decisive look.

'I think we can learn no more here without disturbing Phillimore too greatly. I imagine he has us under observation from a distance and he may have a rifle. Besides I have no wish to apprehend him until we know what he is about. Let us leave now and go in search of our dinner.'

I thought it strange that my friend should abandon the field so abruptly with the scent so hot, but I suspected that he still knew a great deal more about the case, despite his recent spectacular unburdening, so I raised no objection and we set off northwards together. After some time we made a very steep and laborious descent into the pass of the Lairig Ghru, and after a further hour or so of wearisome work through boulders and bogs we were met by the ghillie with two ponies. These brought us down through pinewoods to a better track where we harnessed them to a dogcart and proceeded at a steady pace down through the forests and across the Spey to our hotel, the Lynwilg, which we reached around four o'clock.

After tea and a restorative bath I joined Holmes in the lounge where we took whisky beside a blazing log fire. Holmes pulled out the scrap of paper salvaged from Dundee Wullie's jacket and passed it over to me.

'This paper is evidently a log of messages sent and received,' he said.

'First there is a date, the 25th of September, then a series of times given in the foreign manner. Seven o'clock, eight o'clock and half-past eight. The messages come from 'M' and go to and come from 'HB.' What do you make of it, Watson?'

I thought hard. How could messages be sent to and from the summit of Ben Macdhui? By pigeon? Hardly. Perhaps by lights. By seven o'clock it should be dark enough, after all.

'Morrone?' I ventured. 'Could this be the 'M'?'

'Good, Watson!' said Holmes. 'We are in agreement. And that is one more supernatural occurrence explained. Messages are sent from Morrone, by flashlight, at seven o'clock. Proceed.'

But my inspiration was at an end. 'It must be in code, Holmes,' I complained. 'That word 'het' is Flemish I believe, but it means only 'the'. That can hardly be right.'

Holmes consulted his watch. 'Well, Watson, it is useless to speculate before we have all the facts. We will collect some more shortly with the aid of the contents of the parcel I am about to receive.'

A moment later the landlord entered bearing a large package. 'The boy has collected this from the station, sir, as you asked. You may use the field to the north of the house for your experiments.' He bowed and left.

I stared at Holmes in perplexity. Were we to be distracted from the case by his misplaced enthusiasm for chemistry? He opened the parcel eagerly and withdrew a very odd collection of objects – a Chinese kite, a glass cylinder filled with a grey substance, a large roll of fine copper wire and the earpiece of a telegraph. 'Come, Watson. I will need your help. You need not look so apprehensive. This is not chemistry but its gentler sister physics.' He brandished the cylinder, 'This is the Branly apparatus you were so curious about.'

When we arrived in the field, Holmes assembled the kite and attached it to the fine wire.

'Send it up a good way,' he urged, 'where it will fly steadily.'

Although it was some thirty years since I had flown a kite, I set to with a will and soon it was pulling strongly against the moderate northerly breeze. Meanwhile Holmes was busy with the other equipment. When he had connected the end of the roll of wire to the glass cylinder he beckoned me over and handed me the earpiece.

'Listen!' he said. 'Tell me what you hear.'

I clamped the instrument to my ear. 'A hideous crackling, like burning brushwood,' I replied.

'Indeed, Watson. That is the music of the ether. It comes from a band of electricity that stretches high around the Earth. We have made a wireless telegraph receiver!'

Suddenly it began to make sense to me. Of course. This was the Marconi apparatus – or a relative of it. The Queen had recently installed one on the Royal Yacht, so that she might receive regular reports of the Prince of Wales' conduct, or his 'health' as the Times had put it. And above me flew a giant bird, doubtless of the same unusual species as that seen on Ben Macdhui!

'Good heavens, Holmes! So this is Phillimore's giant bird,' I gestured aloft, 'and he is sending messages to some distant point with its aid!'

'Yes, Watson. By flashlight from Morrone, then by wireless telegraph perhaps out to sea. My information from Mycroft makes it likely that Phillimore is communicating with a foreign anarchist group. Circumstances suggest that their target may be at Balmoral. I took the precaution of recommending that security be doubled there, before we left Scott this morning. We will know more at eight o'clock when we eavesdrop on Phillimore's signal! In the meantime, let us secure the equipment and return for our dinner.'

I brought the kite down and covered the equipment with my cape before joining Holmes in the hotel. There was one other guest, a distinguished-looking individual no doubt, but wearing Highland costume. From his conversation with the landlord, who addressed him in deferential tones as 'Mr Munro', it seemed that he too had crossed the mountains from Braemar today, but during the hours of darkness. He had then spent the day sleeping in the hotel and now proposed to return by a different route this evening! I accounted this behaviour deeply suspicious and whispered as much to Holmes during dessert, but my friend reassured me.

'No, Watson. I have heard of him and of his eccentric nocturnal wanderings. He is a sound man, a harmless mountaineer. Indeed he is a close friend of our guide on the Ben Nevis case, Raeburn.' With that, Holmes rose and introduced himself to the stranger.

'I am Sherlock Holmes, the consulting detective,' he said, 'and this is my associate Dr John Watson. Forgive me, sir, I could not help but overhear your conversation with the landlord. Are you perhaps acquainted with our good friend Harold Raeburn?'

The stranger nodded to Holmes. 'I am,' he replied, 'And I have heard from Raeburn of your exploit on Ben Nevis a few years ago.'

'Dr Watson and I are engaged on a difficult case now,' Holmes continued, 'and would be greatly obliged for your assistance, sir.'

Munro gave a guarded consent and over coffee Holmes explained the extraordinary facts of the case to him. When he produced Dundee Wullie's scrap of paper, Munro became suddenly alert.

'My goodness, this is Russian!' he exclaimed. ''Het' is pronouced 'nyet' and means 'no.' This symbol that looks like 'c3' is a Cyrillic abbreviation for a compass direction, 'severo-zapad,' which means north-west. The number 18 must be a code of some sort. 'HB' is transliterated as 'NV'.'

'Russian?' said Holmes. 'I am sure you are right, of course, but we are not at odds with Russia. What interest would Russians have in mounting an attack on members of our Royal Family?'

Munro pushed his coffee cup aside and leaned forward anxiously. 'Then you have not heard that the Tsar is at Balmoral?' he asked. 'I am a Queen's Messenger, Holmes, and I brought Nicholas there in great secrecy, only last week. He has been stalking with the Prince of Wales. I accompanied them a few days ago, on Beinn a' Bhuird.'

'What day was that?' asked Holmes.

Munro tugged his beard reflectively. 'The 26th,' he said.

At that moment the hall clock struck the quarter-hour.

'Come,' said Holmes, 'we must go out and listen to these Russians. Watson, you will call out the messages. They will be in Morse, of course. I will take them down and you, sir, will fly our kite!'

Munro seemed unperturbed by these strange instructions and joined us instantly in the hall, impressively caped and sporting a silver-mounted stick and a dilapidated and generously-dimensioned Scotch bonnet. Russian in Morse! I knew Morse code from my Army days, of course, and proceeded to go over the alphabet in my mind. But were there not more characters in Russian script than in English? Perhaps they used codes not needed for English. I recalled, too, Munro's explanation – when decoding the wind directions a moment or two ago – that Russian 'c' was equivalent to English 's'. Did that mean that if they wished to send an 's' they would use the code for 'c'? What a nightmare! My head was spinning! What a heavy responsibility! I resolved to call out the English letters and to hope that we could make sense of it afterwards.

We strode out to the field together. It was a fine clear night, but moonless and would soon be damnably dark, I thought. Munro launched the kite with aplomb and – or so it seemed to me – a degree of skill that suggested familiarity. Perhaps he was conversant with the new arrangements on the Royal Yacht! I applied the ear-piece and could soon hear the eerie crackle once more. Holmes lit the lantern, produced his notebook and consulted his watch. 'Almost eight,' he hissed in my unoccupied ear. 'The message will certainly be repeated, so don't despair if you miss something at first.'

These words of reassurance steadied me and when the message arrived I began to call the letters out briskly.

N – V – STOP – N – V – STOP.'

Then came a pause and the same obscure message repeated.

'Merely a call sign, Watson,' murmured Holmes, 'to allow them to tune their equipment.'

After a further repetition and a pause, the message proper arrived.

3 – 2 – STOP – S – STOP – 5 – 3 – STOP,' I called out. This was followed by two repetitions and then silence. After a few minutes we brought down the kite and returned to the hotel.

In the lounge Holmes attempted to unravel the message.

'What we have here, gentleman,' he said, 'is a message from Phillimore to his colleagues. First we have the number 32, then 'S' – the abbreviation for North – and then the number 53. Now, for the numbers I have no theory, but what is to the north is very likely the forecasted wind. Phillimore is an expert on aerial engines and my hypothesis is that the terrorists will make their attack from what is known as an 'airship'. The Brazilian aerialist Santos-Dumont has lately perfected this new engine of war and we must assume that Phillimore has advised these Russians how to build one. They cannot sail against the wind, so knowledge of wind direction is vital.'

'But, Holmes,' I interjected, 'you cannot be sure of this?'

'No, but it fits!' cried Holmes. 'By what other means could Russians penetrate 40 miles inland and why else should Phillimore be involved?'

'And these numbers?' asked Munro. 'What do they signify?'

'That is the great difficulty,' said my friend, 'for they are undoubtedly a code.'

'It couldn't be, could it?' said Munro suddenly. He pursed his lips and frowned, tapping the table nervously. 'D'you know, Holmes, I believe it is! They are using my list of mountaintops as a code! I will fetch a copy of the list from my room.' Munro retuned a few moments later bearing a slim volume. 'Look here,' he said, flipping the pages, 'number 53 is Cairn Etchachan, a dependency of Ben Macdhui, you see. And 32 . . . that is Cairngorm of Derry.'

'He is right, Holmes!' I cried. 'Scott said there might be stalking there tomorrow!'

'Might be, might be,' Holmes muttered irritably. 'Let us see. On the 26th the Royal Party went to Beinn a' Bhuird. What number is that?'

'Eighteen,' said Munro, 'which was the number of Dundee Wullie's message. And 196 . . . let me see . . . that is a small peak nearby.'

'That is conclusive, gentlemen,' said Holmes. 'The system is clear. Phillimore gets word of the next day's plans from Morrone. No doubt some treacherous domestic from Balmoral is responsible, possibly bribed by one of the Tsar's own staff. Phillimore sends that information, the forecasted wind and another location to his colleagues. I fancy the other location is a suggested landing place for the craft. The landing place should be close enought to spare them an arduous march but far enough to allow them some chance of making their escape afterwards.'

Munro passed an anxious hand over his head. 'I never dreamed that my topographical researches should be put to such an evil use!' he complained. 'I have a further thought for you, Holmes. The worst terrorists in Russia, or elsewhere for that matter, were the old People's Will, who blew up Tsar Alexander in his carriage. My information is that this group is broken up and inactive now, but the Russian name for the Will of the People is Narodnaya

Volya. I fear this is our 'NV.' This business is worse, much worse, than I had expected. They are desperate men and have an impressive record of achievement in their hellish work!'

It was time to go out to the field once more and collect the anarchists' reply.

'Pray god it is 'nyet' once again,' implored Munro. After what seemed an interminable delay, the call-sign and message came. I stammered out the letters,

'D – A – STOP – 0 – 4 – 0 – 0 – STOP – 5 – 3 – STOP.'

Back in the hotel we held a rapid council. They were coming to Cairn Etchachan at 4:00 a.m. and would march on Cairngorm of Derry from there, to lay an ambush. Eventually we evolved a plan. Munro and Holmes were to search for Phillimore in the vicinity of Cairn Etchachan, in the hope of locating the landing site and extinguishing whatever landing-lights Phillimore would set.

'They will surely be magnesium or carbide,' said Holmes. 'Waterproof at any rate and damned hard to put out. Once the ship has a good sight of them it will find its way down, even if we do put them out. This will be a chancy business.' I was to lay a diversion. I would be lowered down the face of a convenient (!) precipice and would set a light there. With luck the anarchists would not see the precipice until too late and the airship would founder. We began our preparations.

After some hours we had assembled lights, ropes, a cart and some ponies and set off once again through the gloomy pinewoods. We reached the road end at half-past one. The night, though still moonless, was bright with stars and the dark trench of the Lairig Ghru was outlined clearly to the south. We hung the rope and lamps from our saddles, mounted our ponies and set off. The breeze, slightly fresher now, whistled among the tall pines. After an hour we reached the top of the pass and dismounted. The ponyman would continue through the pass to Derry Lodge. With luck he would forestall the stalking party and inform Scott of our plans.

We then began the ascent, infinitely laborious, of the eastern flank of the Lairig. Munro led the way, a grotesque figure in his voluminous cape and ridiculous hat, while Holmes and I followed in his footsteps as best we could. I must have pitched full-length against the slope fifty times before we gained the rim of the plateau, but suffered no serious injury. The light was better above and we proceeded slowly but less painfully across the flank of Ben Macdhui, passing not far from the place where we had found the giant. Huge boulders lay everywhere like massive slates on a roof, cold and silver-grey in the starlight. We came in time to the edge of a precipice overlooking a deep chasm. I could make out a dark loch a thousand feet or more below.

'Here will do,' said Munro gruffly and began to unwind the rope. I lit one of the carbide lamps, which burned malodorously and shed a sinister greenish light, and fastened the rope to my waist. I shook hands with Munro and clapped Holmes warmly on the shoulder, 'Depend on me, Holmes,' I said. 'I will lure the wretches onto the crag.' Holding the lamp before me, I slipped and slithered down the cliff-face, as Holmes and Munro paid out the rope. The crag was fortunately not too steep and was well provided with ledges.

When I had descended a sufficient distance I found a commodious platform and signalled to Holmes to secure the rope above. He did so, waved briefly and left.

I was alone. I turned the hissing lamp down to conserve fuel, and fashioned a seat of sorts from coils of the rope. If our calculations were correct I had less than a half-hour to wait before the airship would arrive. From my perch I could make out the dark bulk of the mountain Cairngorm itself blotting out the lower stars in the northern sky. Further east, the new moon hung low above some distant hills and struck a glimmer from the eastern shore of the loch far below. Beneath me, the rocks stretched endlessly down into black shadow. As I stoked my pipe I reflected that the sky was too bright for our ruse to succeed. All would depend on Holmes and Munro and their desperate search for Phillimore on the plateau above me. I worried too that my friend's powerful imagination and ruthless style of reasoning may have led him astray. After all, what proof was there that it really was Phillimore who was stationed on Ben Macdhui? A fancied similarity of names seemed a pitiful foundation on which to base the supposition of an airship-borne attack. Perhaps they would come overland from the coast instead and our hectic preparations would be of no avail. We would have done better to attempt to get through to Balmoral by a night drive, I thought. Thus does our faith desert us in the dark and lonely places of the earth!

I surveyed the sky to the north once more. The mountain opposite seemed larger and nearer now. Then it came to me that our luck had changed: it was cloud that I was seeing, not mountain, moving south and speedily too. I held my watch down to the lamp and saw it was now 3:45. Perhaps I would still have a part to play! I checked my revolver, laid it on a handy ledge and sat back to wait and watch.

The cloud mass now stretched above me: the moon had gone from sight and I was confident that the cover was effectively complete. I turned up the lamp, bathing the rocky terrace in sickly green light, and adjusted the reflector so that it pointed to the north. After some minutes, as I peered towards Cairngorm I suddenly saw a bright star. At first I thought the cloud must be breaking, but then it disappeared and came again in a short flash. A signal, surely. 'N' in Morse. I thought furiously. Of course, I must return 'V'. Narodnaya Volya! I hurriedly removed my cap and, lifting the lamp, returned the signal. By now it must be quite close, I felt sure. I gripped my revolver and stood behind the lamp, staring into the blackness. Yes, there it was! I could make out the cabin and the thin shrouds leading up to the gasbag. Just at that moment the moon thrust through the cloudbank to the east. The ship showed clearly now, caught by the moonlight and my own lamp. Silently and swiftly it bore down on me – huge, alien and menacing.

I recalled Holmes' parting words of advice – 'Hold your fire until the ship has passed above you, Watson, or they will surely pick you off.' – so I continued to wait. Over the hissing of the lamp I heard cries of alarm from the ship and could now clearly see bags of ballast being thrown overboard. Plainly they had seen the mighty crag looming in front of them! The ship began to rise slowly. It was soon directly above me and seemed certain to crash into the precipice. To my horror I saw two bodies hurtle from the cabin! The fallen men screamed as they plummeted into the rocks below and bounced off down into the depths. However, the trick was successful: the airship rose steeply into the gloom and now looked certain to clear the edge of the precipice. I fired and fired again at the huge bag, without apparent result. As the great ship passed beyond the bristling edge a single shot rang out in reply, but the round clattered harmlessly into the rocks at my side.

I put my revolver down to cool and took stock. At least I had accounted for the two wretches who had suddenly found themselves drafted as ballast-bags. Perhaps the bag would lose gas, if my shots had found their mark, and other unfortunates would be cast out to share their fate! After this grim encounter, the slope of rocks above me seemed a puny obstacle. I resolved to tackle it at once, rather that wait for rescue. I tied the rope around my waist, leaving a short tail to which I fixed the lamp, and began to work my way upwards from ledge to ledge, hauling on the rope at difficult places. This went well enough – indeed, it might have proved more unpleasant in daylight – and before long I was standing once again on the solid ground of the plateau.

I immediately searched the southern sky for a sign of the ship. At first I thought it must have crashed or – perish the thought! – landed, but then I chanced to look up. To my astonishment I saw the ship thousands of feet above me! Evidently they had discharged far too much ballast: unless they soon released gas from the bag they would surely succumb from cold or asphyxiation. I coiled the rope, slung the lamp from my waist and set off towards the summit of Cairn Etchachan, which lay less than a mile to the south, in the hope of finding Holmes or Munro.

The cloud had now almost gone and in the fitful moonlight I made my way slowly across the bouldery ground. From time to time I looked upwards to follow the progress of the ship. It had passed beyond Cairngorm of Derry, so far as I could judge. Though little more than a faint grey smudge now, it had surely begun to descend. As I approached the final slopes it fell more and more rapidly and finally crashed into a distant hill, bursting instantly into flames! I did not waste time or conscience with remorse for the men on board: they had come to assassinate and deserved no better fate. Nor did I permit myself to exult in their misfortune: there is no pleasure to be got in the death of a fellow being – a lesson I had learned well in the Afghan wars.[6]

[6] Some of the wreckage from this disaster was found many years later and wrongly attributed to the visit of a German airship during the later years of the Great War. The episode is described on p. 99 of Henry Alexander's SMC *Cairngorms* Guide (1928 edition). 'On the slope of Sgor Dubh, opposite Derry Lodge, a flare light was dropped during a night in April, 1917, by a German airship which apparently lost its way over the Cairngorms. The vessel came inland at Arbroath and passed over Cortachy, Glen Clunie Lodge, Inverey and Derry Lodge to Rothiemurchus, where it must have turned due east, for it dropped bombs first in Auchendoir, on Donside and then near Insch, in Central Aberdeenshire, finally passing out to sea near Peterhead, and being subsequently wrecked in Norway. In its course it must have gone over the summit of Ben Macdhui. The metal holder of the light was found some years later on the hillside and formed a curious relic, linking the recesses of the Cairngorms with the Great War.'

What an extraordinary coincidence that these recesses should have been visited by two of these rare birds of the air and that a piece of the carcass of one should be mistaken for the droppings of the other!

If the sceptical reader needs further evidence for the veracity of Dr Watson's tale, he need look no further than the minute-books of the SMC, held in the Manuscript Collection of the National Library of Scotland. In the record of the Committee meeting held in Glasgow on the 23 October 1914, it is noted that Harold Raeburn had written to the Club Secretary as follows:

'(the Club) should circulate the Keepers and Shepherds in remote districts asking them to report on any suspicious circumstances and (should) form a small committee to investigate such reports; all with a view to locating enemy wireless sending stations or aeroplane depots.

Surely Raeburn would not have made this fantastic suggestion unless he had known of the earlier incident, perhaps revealed to him in an unguarded moment by his friend Munro.

As I passed the summit cairn and began to pick my way wearily down the further slope towards Loch Etchachan I was met by Munro who led me to Holmes. My friend was sitting smoking beside a lamp and a forlorn bundle, which I took to be Phillimore.

'Congratulations, Watson!' he said. 'You have never done better.'

'I merely followed your instructions,' I replied. 'The Laws of Gases did the rest, I suspect.'

'Indeed there seems much to be learned about the management of these machines. However, I fear there will be nothing further learned by or from this gentleman,' he said, prodding the inert body at his side and twisting the lamp to show his hideously burned face.

'Poor Phillimore! He took poison when we succeeded in seizing him before he could light his lamps.'

We carried the body as best we could a short distance down the slope until we reached the stalking path from the Loch to Ben Macdhui.

'What shall we do now, Holmes?' I asked.

'*Do*, Watson?' he replied. 'We have done enough. Let us wait for Scott and his men. With luck they will bring ponies. I have a strong desire never to take another step across these dreadful boulders.' With that remark, Holmes laid his pipe aside and fell immediately asleep!

Some weeks later a small parcel arrived at Baker Street, bearing a Scottish postmark. Holmes opened it at the breakfast table and held up two thin octavo volumes bound in green calf.

'A note from Munro, Watson,' he announced. 'Two copies of his list of Scottish mountains over 3,000 feet. 'One for you –' he passed it over ' – and one for me. An excellent souvenir of the case, certainly. However, I judge it best to cast mine into the fire.' With a deft twirl of the wrist he sent Munro's gift spinning into the flames.

'Holmes! How could you!' I cried in indignation. 'The gift was well meant and Munro is surely a friend!'

'Certainly, Watson, but we have so far ascended three mountains on his list. There remain 535. Surely you do not care to spend the rest of your life travelling to Scotland to complete the task.'

'Indeed no,' I protested, 'but I feel no such compulsion.'

'Then why did you take the trouble to visit Cairngorm of Derry a few weeks ago while you thought me asleep? And why do your fingers now itch for a pencil with which to place four ticks against Ben Nevis, Ben Macdhui, Cairn Etchachan and Cairngorm of Derry? No, my friend, be mindful of the trouble I have with my habit of cocaine and let your volume join mine in the embers.'

I admitted the wisdom of these remarks with a sigh and regretfully added my gift to the blaze.

'Lochaber no more!' said Holmes with a smile.

That very afternoon we attended a secret and private ceremony at the Palace, where we were joined by Munro. We were received by Her Majesty and by the Tsar himself, who invested all three of us in the Order of the Golden Cockerel and hung about us with splendid sashes, medallions and swords. I could not help reflecting that a modest pension might have suited me better than membership of an exotic order of Russian chivalry and ornaments that I could never decently wear. Afterwards we took tea at Baker Street and reviewed the case from start to finish, so that I might make sure of my notes.

'For my part, Holmes,' I said at the conclusion of our review, 'the most satisfying element of the case was the way in which each of the apparently supernatural occurrences was seen to be an ordinary event.'

'Just so, Watson. And who was it who discounted these reports as imagination feeding on superstition?'

'Indeed you are right. You have often said that imagination is a rare commodity and that it is best to take witnesses' reports as evidential, until you have grounds to discard them. I was quite wrong to complain, Holmes, and I beg your pardon.'

'I wonder whether that gracious apology is entirely merited,' said my friend. 'Tell me, Watson, do you recollect whether you shot the Grey Man in the chest or in the back?'

'Why, in the chest, certainly. It was advancing towards me and besides I could make out its face.'

'Well, *I* shot the creature too – you must have heard my revolver – but in the back. And surely you noticed that only one bullet-hole was to be found in the giant's costume? Of course, it was clear from a moment's examination that the bullet had entered from the back and *emerged* from the chest.'

'But Holmes!' I cried. 'Whom did I shoot, then?'

'Whom indeed, Watson, or What? Let us say you shot Fear Liath Mór and leave it at that.'

Children Like Climbers Often Fall

by Gordon Thomson

WE CLIMB, the three of us: Steven, Davie and myself, haltingly gaining elevation . . . our bivouac only an hour away if Davie can keep up. Steven stays with him all the way, like a concerned parent who stays up all night with their sick child. They are bound by a short length of rope; not for protection, for we are only ascending the broken talus of a lateral moraine, rather so Davie won't wander off as he frequently does. I can hear Steven encouraging him.

'Come on, David, only a little further.'

come on david, steven said . . . i smell water in the air and hear steven . . . feel his breath by my face . . . the pull makes me come and i'm looking down, staring, everything is white and blue and emptiness spills out all around me, i feel cold and my face is warm and light . . . the pull makes me come, the other one watches, he is far away, steven talks and i make sounds and watch as he grows

Steven emerges over a small rise with Davie in tow, who is small and wiry-looking but still very strong. Steven is tall and broad-shouldered but has never had Davie's strength or endurance. Davie used to be able to climb and climb; heavy pack or miserable weather, it made no difference; Davie would just keep right on going. It was more than once that he saved Steven's life. I guess Steven feels that he's reciprocating.

'How are you guys doing?' I say. 'How you doin', Davie?'

'Don't call him Davie, Alan,' Steve says sharply. 'He's not a kid, he's a grown man.'

Steven turns his back on me and walks over to Davie.

'He is a kid, Steven. Just look at him.'

Davie stands there, staring at Steven; a broad smile comes across his face.

'I'm sorry,' I say. 'I know it's tough. How are you doin'?'

'Ok . . . ok, a little tired, but we're not far.'

'No, we're not,' I say. 'Bivvy's right at the top of this talus slope. I'll see you there.'

I cinch up the shoulder straps of my pack and start up the slope. I feel impatient and uncomfortable around them. The three of us used to be close friends. But Davie's accident has changed a lot of things. I look back; Steven stares after me for a moment and then turns his attention back to Davie. Davie is turning circles, tangling himself in the rope. I continue up; gaining on the slope . . . the broad face of the mountain gradually coming back into view.

steven says, david look what you're doing, you're all tangled up, here, let me help you and steven pulls the rope from between my feet and legs and the other one stares and becomes small

I top out on the ridge half an hour after leaving Steven and Davie. They're making their way slowly. Steven is forced to halt periodically to arouse Davie from his wandering and gazing. I turn and am again confronted by the full relief of the mountain; massive, lumbering and disproportioned . . . the summit ridges ringed by overhanging ice cliffs, the northeast face caked with the ice of a moderately-steel glacier . . . the unclimbed central couloir splitting the steep north face to the right of the glacier like a scimitar. Just like in the photographs. I've climbed in this range for over ten years but have never been closer to this mountain. Propinquity matters, I decide. I find a bivvy spot by a large boulder, remove my pack, and wait for Steven and Davie.

The two of them finally arrive over the ridge. Steven stares blankly past me, his eyes focused on the mountain. I wonder if he is having second thoughts about this, if he knows what he is getting us into. Davie stumbles, coming over the ridge, and falls flat on his face, letting out a loud moan. The accident looks so comical, like something out of a Three Stooges movie, that I almost laugh, but contain myself when I see Steven's face. The change in expression is so dramatic and extreme, from calm to tortured, serene to agonized . . . the love he feels for his friend so clear that I find myself again feeling uncomfortable in their presence; remembering the same closeness that I thought I once had with David . . . deep friendship; partners who relied on one another for their lives . . . now strangers, light-years apart.

Steven runs awkwardly under the weight of his pack over to Davie, and I follow.

'David, are you all right?' Steven says, kneeling next to his friend, his voice tight, almost hysterical. I try to calm him.

Steven glares at me, frustration and anger reflected in his expression. He turns his attention back to Davie.

don't worry i hear the other one say. steven takes my pack off and turns me over. are you ok david? i moan and sob, my hand is sore. see, the other one says, he just scraped up his hands a little, i'll get the first-aid kit. i open my eyes and see the other one walking away upsidedown to the mountain. steven puts his arm under my shoulder and lifts me up so that i'm sitting up and looks at my hand and hugs me, i hear water running, turn my head and see the mountain, covered in ice, it looks the same

Afterwards we eat dinner, sort out the gear for tomorrow's climb, and settle in . . . nightfall comes quickly. The alpine glow slowly fades from the face of the mountain as if being turned down by some great cosmic dimmer switch. One by one, and then increasingly more frequently, stars and planets are revealed until the night sky is flooded by their pinpoints of light . . . embryonic, individual, quintessential, ethereal personalities fighting the entropy of the universe . . . and the faint glow of the half-moon as it gradually ascends from behind the north ridge of the mountain, washing out star and planet-shine like a slow wave.

Steven sits with Davie quietly talking to him.

well except for the fall everything went ok today david. steven smiles at me and helps me into bed. everything is going to work out fine tomorrow david, no one is going to lock you away, we'll make sure of that. i lay back and watch the stars . . . we'll do our climb, you won't have to return, everything will work out . . . i climb into blue-white cold, changing into darkness

Steven comes over and sits by me and pours himself a shot of Drambuie; one of the few luxuries we've always afforded ourselves whenever we climb together. Steven speaks first.

'You didn't have to come on this, you know. I know what you're thinking. You think we're going to get ourselves killed . . . no one forced you to come.'

His voice is calm, but I hear its tenseness and see the tight lines drawn across his face, weathered and stern . . . Steven's too young for such an old face. It's my turn now.

'What do you mean I didn't have to come along? You and Dave are my closest friends. I'm supposed to let you run off and try a first ascent of the most difficult ice route in this range with a three-year-old?'

'Stop it!' Steven says. 'He's not a three-year-old. He's a man and a fine climber.'

'He *was* a fine climber, Steven. But not anymore. You don't sustain the kind of brain damage that he did in that car crash and continue to climb. He's a child, incapable of taking care of himself, and the mountains are no place for children.'

'You're wrong, Alan!' Steven says, his voice rising.

'I've climbed with him since the accident. He can still do it. Put an ice axe in his hands and he still knows what to do.'

'You've climbed with him once since the accident and it was only a walk-up at that.' I'm beginning to feel frustrated since I know that I'm not going to get through Steven's deep-seated feelings for Davie. He seems to think that if Davie can do this climb it will prove that he is capable of taking care of himself and that he won't have to spend the rest of his life institutionalized.

'You weren't there, Alan.' He emphasizes each syllable through gritted teeth and clenched fists. 'When we're roped up and making our way up a glacier it comes back to him. He knows what to do, you should see him. He's alert. No wandering around, and he's as strong as he ever was.'

'Being roped up didn't prevent him from falling today,' I say.

'That's unfair,' says Steven. 'That could have happened to anyone. I've seen you make missteps plenty of times.' He pauses and I gulp down the rest of my Drambuie; then he continues, staring at the black and broken talus. 'You want to see him put away, don't you?'

I look directly at Steven, angry now, trying to control my voice as best I can. 'No, I don't want to see Dave put away. However, I do think that he needs help and his family isn't about to give it because they don't want to take responsibility for the problem and the courts aren't about to give him to you. How do you think I feel, Steven? I love Dave as much as you do. To see him like this makes me sick, but there's not a god-damn thing that you or I or anyone else can do about it.' Steven's face remains taut but his hands have relaxed. I feel myself on the verge of tears. 'I've climbed with Dave for a long time,' I say. 'Nearly ten years. I introduced you to him. Now he doesn't even recognize me. He just stares through me as if I weren't there. He's fine with you, though. You're the only one he seems to recognize.' At this Steven looks up.

'He recognizes you, Alan. He's just shy around most people. I think he feels embarrassed by what's happened to him.'

'You really think that he has any idea what has happened to him, Steve?' I'm obviously incredulous, but Steven sloughs it off like a true believer and nods his head.

I finally give up. 'I'm turning in,' I say. 'We'll need an earlier-than-usual start for tomorrow, especially considering the odds that we're up against. We may as well make sure that we at least have enough daylight for a retreat off of the climb.' Steven nods his head in agreement and I almost feel as if he isn't too far gone. Maybe he really does understand the odds of our ever pulling this off.

I tell Steve that I'll set the alarm for 1:00 a.m. He says 'fine' and seems to fall asleep immediately. I lie awake in my bag, staring at the stars, the moon turning an arc across my field of vision, then turn my head towards Davie . . . why didn't you die, Dave? Why the hell didn't you die?

The moon is still high and bright like a floodlight on the mountain when the alarm goes off. I roll over in my bag and try to forget where I am, but Steven gently nudges me and says its time to get up. Big deal, I think. We're about to die and we can't even wait until dawn. Steve has hot water going for tea and coffee by the time I'm up, and is busy getting Davie ready. It's a sight to see a grown man dressing another grown man. But I figure, what the hell, I may suffer all kinds of revelations today. Good start.

An hour after rising we're on our way down the other side of the ridge on which we've spent the night; headlamps shining three bobbing beams of light down the dark slope to the icefield below, redundant in the bright light of the moon. I turn off my headlamp figuring I should save the batteries for when we really need the light. I suggest the same to Steve, who agrees and turns off both his and Davie's lamps. Both of them are roped together. Davie seems more alert than yesterday but is still given to wandering this way and that. I'm amazed that he doesn't trip and fall down the slope, hauling Steve with him. However, they seem to be doing fine, so I set off on my own, telling Steve that I'll meet him at the bottom of the moraine. At that point all three of us will don our crampons, rope up, and be climbing together for the first time in two years. Steve just nods his head, but I'm already on my way before I know whether he agrees or not.

bluewhite light shines in my eyes, i close them, i hear steven, feel the pull, open my eyes, how are you doin'?, steven asks, only a little further, i stare at him, he looks funny, bright blue and orange and red, metal and rope, i look funny too . . . i'm looking down again, falling, everything white and blue, emptiness spilling out all around me . . . the pull makes me come and i follow steven . . . the other one?

By the time Steven and Davie touch the ice I have my crampons on and the second rope out. 'How's Dave doing?' I ask.

'Fine,' Steven says. 'He's moving a little quicker than yesterday. I think maybe things are becoming more familiar to him.'

I reserve judgment and offer Steven some chocolate which he shares with Davie, and then help him with Davie's crampons.

Davie sits on a small boulder perched at the edge of the ice, feet extended and spread out before us as if he were a king being served a sumptuous meal; staring down at Steven while the both of us strap crampons to his boots.

The three of us ascend the ice-fan of the glacier that leads to the entrance to the couloir. I lead, Davie is in the middle, and Steven takes up the rear. The moonlight casts our shadows across the coarse surface of the ice . . . a tiny centipede exposed against the white glare, making its way toward the dark entrance to the couloir.

I glance back occasionally, keeping watch on Steven and Davie. Davie follows mechanically, his ice axe dangling uselessly from his wrist. Incredibly, he maintains his balance on the firm ice, but I am convinced that he will fall at any moment. I stay alert, waiting for the sharp pull, ready to self-arrest, but the pull never comes. Only the sound of the rhythmic plodding of our steps breaks up the ascent. I halt for a rest 100 feet below the entrance to the couloir. Here, the ice-fan steepens to over 45 degrees and funnels upward into the narrow gully that extends for 2,000 increasingly steep and at times vertical feet to the summit ice cliffs.

As Davie nears he stares past me to the couloir above and continues on by.

I call out his name, telling him to stop, but he keeps on going, just like he used to climb before the accident: methodical and oblivious to everything but the climb. Steven sees what's happening and yells at Davie to stop, while at the same time giving a gentle tug on the rope. Davie halts and waits. I see in his face as he approaches me that Steven is unconcerned by all of this.

'It's a good thing that you're here to stop him,' I say.

'Don't worry about it, David's doing fine,' says Steven.

He smiles and looks up at Davie, nods his head, and waves his hand as if greeting an old friend. Davie smiles but is otherwise motionless. I can't help but laugh at all of this. Steven may as well be smiling and waving at some guy in a body cast who is about to be pushed out of an airplane without a parachute for all the difference it makes. Except that both of us are going along sans chutes, too.

'If Dave is doing so fine,' I say, 'why is it that I haven't seen him use his ice axe yet? I've been ready for a self-arrest since we began up this thing and we're not even into the couloir yet.'

'Good,' Steven says wryly, 'it'll keep you on your toes. Don't worry about David. He'll use his axe when he needs to.'

'Wonderful,' I say as I turn my back to Steven and begin up the final stretch, past Davie, to the real start of our climb.

the other one passes me moving quickly, he can't wait, Steven waits, he moves up into the darkness . . . i watch from my window while Steven moves up and over the icy overhang and is on top, he waves, i finally did it David he says . . . we'll do it David he says, we'll get up this thing and you'll never have to be locked away, the other one disappears

I set up a belay in a corner and bring up Davie, tie him in and then Steven. Here the couloir is very narrow, maybe 20 feet across, and steepens suddenly to over 60 degrees and is vertical at points. The crux, near the top naturally, is over 100 feet of vertical ice that leads to the ice-cliffs, which may or may not have a straightforward way through them. From the little that I can see from our belay, the first section of ice looks hard and brittle. 'Great,' I say to myself sarcastically. 'There's no end to all the little challenges we'll have to deal with on this one.'

'Well, friends,' I say, 'this is it.' It sounds incredibly lame but I can't think of anything else to say.

Steven stares up into the darkness. 'Looks like it'll be a good climb,' he says. 'Don't you think so, David?'

Davie, of course, says nothing. The best that I've come to expect from him is an occasional moan.

I gaze down the ice-fan, tracing our steps to the talus slope. The first glint of dawn hints itself in the barely brightening sky; no longer assisted by the moon, which has set behind one of the far ridges of the mountain. I feel like glissading back down the ice slope to the security of my sleeping bag . . . to warmth and sanity.

Steven puts me on belay. I unclip from the anchor and with my northwall hammer and ice axe in either hand, begin.

the other ones moves into the darkness followed by hard sounds like breaking glass that hit steven and . . . he goes for a long time until he disappears . . . steven, off belay says a voice, you're off says steven to the darkness, i'll put dave on tension as he climbs, the voice says, don't pull him up, let him climb himself, steven says . . . how are you doing david? says steven, you remember our climb last month and the climb we did two years ago, don't you? we did bridalveil then, you were hot then, we flashed right up that and the next week you went back and soloed it, remember, this isn't any harder, just a little longer . . . i feel the shafts in my hands, so light, we move together, steven and i, i climb ahead feeling the fresh air, one and then the other, i'm suspended by sharp point against the cold . . . we pause and then continue . . . i stand on air, frozen light, a curtain of ice hangs above us . . . i'm alone in the same place climbing higher towards a shiny pin . . . they watch from below and wave and laugh when i can climb no more, sitting down at the top, mountains rise above me, all around . . . smile and wave, smile and wave, smile and wave . . . the other one stands on top, smiling and patting my back, he squeezes me to him, you did it, you really did it

I bring Steven up over the last difficult section of ice cliff and after 15 hours of hard climbing the three of us stand together on the broad summit that stretches white to blue in all directions from us. We take off our packs and I give David a long hug. 'You really did it. You were right Steven, he did it.' Steven and David say nothing. They both look tired. Steven looks drained and David is no longer as alert as when he was climbing. Steven looks to me and it's clear that he would like to feel as if he and Dave alone had done the climb. As I make my way to the far side of the summit dome, Davie begins to follow and Steven has to give his rope a tug . . . back to normal. One axe and then the other; in perfect control and balance he climbed. I couldn't believe it. All the while he climbed as if in a dream or a trance.

you made it david, i knew you would, i'll untie you now, you're free to go wherever you want, they won't lock you up now. i know that you can never go back . . . afterwards i gaze over the edge and wave to my friends down below, they yell congratulations and say we'll meet in town for drinks . . . i'm looking down, staring, everything is white and blue and emptiness spills out all around me, everything grows . . .

Nightfall is close and it'll be a few hours before we get back, although the glissade down the northeast face glacier should go quickly . . . time to return to where I left them.

The broad summit area is like a desert in miniature, with blending colours and hard to distinguish horizons. At first I don't see either of them. But as I get closer, my pace increasing, finally running until I see the aimless set of tracks that wander and end at the ice cliff's edge, I see that there is only one. Steven sits alone in the snow, head between his knees, silently weeping.

Scenery for a Murder

by J. Menlove Edwards

I DID start by trying to write an essay, but it was soon clear that it was not an essay I wanted to write but the facts; the plain facts as they happened. What do I mean? You will see what I mean. The fact is, there has been murder done, done under their noses, and the fools can't spot the murderer. So I will set it all out: but I will have to be a little careful, for the murderer is a gentleman and very well connected; one is supposed to talk of him carefully, so to speak, as if he wasn't there, or didn't do anything.

But the story.

This is what happened. I opened the paper one morning at home and saw that an accident had happened; a well-known climber killed in the Alps; one of the most notorious slices of cliff in the world; frozen to death on it; three nights out; now trying to get the body; and it was he, my friend. But that is the barest summary. I can tell you more than that. For I was there when it was done.

The first time I saw him was nothing to do with climbing. It was in the Albert Hall. In fact, strictly, I didn't see him; heard him over the wireless. Eight of them; they walked down the centre of the hall on to the platform, and I didn't notice him, naturally, during that part of the business; but then, what they had come for, they sang, a dozen or so of the folk-songs of their country; and then I couldn't help it, for a really fine voice does not need careful comparison or notice to pick it out: it stands out for itself, and this was a young voice, one in a million, high, sung full out, accurate, but a wild voice. What a voice! The Albert Hall faded out in two seconds: he stood still, head thrown back a little; you could see that, though he stood in line among the others.

And even then you could see it was tragedy.

Of course that was years ago. Then one of those strange things happened. I met him. Got talking with a German boy in Berne: was leaning up against the railings watching the sky over the roof-tops and I saw him, quite suddenly, walking past, and you couldn't miss it, the same look, the same attitude; didn't even have to ask his name: it stood out all over him: power, courage, love, honour, the heroes, fame, God, the Devil; no, I can't phrase it, but you can take it from me that it was not the boy so much as the scenery. I've never seen such wild scenery; it stood out a mile. So I got in tow. He was a tall young fellow, and could obviously climb as well as any man, but, as I say, I was in luck that day, and I got in tow.

Skip a few days, and the two of us, Toni and I, enormous rucksacs on our backs, walked slowly out of an hotel, together, sweating we were, brown, in the heat of the sun, out of the village, past the few last houses, beside the hay plots, and up, leaving the fir trees one by one, along the scorched dry bed of the valley, the hills sloping high on either side, up the track towards the thin far-away line of the mountains. I think I have never known a hut walk go so well. Toni looked around contentedly enough, but he seemed not to notice much: yet he seemed to transform the land, he gave it an atmosphere, a scenery, a hauteur, that made the bare places and the vivid sky seem beautiful. Noticeable with me, for in myself I am dull. Like most people, perhaps, the things that happen to me come, pass over me, then they travel on; but as they go I go also, with them, into the past; and if I walk out, for instance, I am often behind-hand and cannot catch up, cannot produce in time the right attitude with which to appreciate a scenery. So to me the effect on the valley was remarkable. He spoke a fair amount, but that was nothing. It was his atmosphere, in which the features of the country became more beautiful than I had known them.

We got to the hut in good time, had a meal and sat over it, and my mind was still running over the same subject so, as we were well fed and he seemed not to mind my talking, I held forth. Now you are all right, I said, I'm not a fool and I know the genuine article – phrase we have in England – when I see it, but I think there's nothing I've hated so much in my time and so reasonably as the love of the mountains. And as I talked I got enthusiastic. Now follow me, I said: take a chestnut, cover it with sugar. He was a shy fellow and looked quickly round, but I make no difficulty of an incident like that and I carried straight on. No, no, I said, cover it with sugar, more, boil it in sugar, say that you are a bad cook, five, six, then, twenty times its own weight of sugar, boil it for two days, no two years, and you get my meaning, you have a fine piece of sugar left, but not a chestnut; after two years it would be a tragedy to go calling a thing like that a chestnut. And a man's feelings are more tender than that, surely. So when a fellow produces thick syrup whenever he sees a hill, he may protest any fine origin for it that he likes, but most of us consider it simply sickening. We are right? Yes, he said. So I went on talking; for he did not understand: he had less experience of having other people's feelings himself than a child of ten.

We went to bed; at least we didn't go to bed, we lay on the floor that night for the hut was crowded out and the breathing was terrible. But who cares; throw off the cloak, make no pretence to be beautiful, cuddle down a bit, all fully dressed, all close together, and it's pleasant enough. No, I had forgotten; funny how one's mind goes on. He must have such feelings, but not the same I suppose; they'd get a different sort of reception in him; try to find out tomorrow; what a hope. So I lay on my back that night, Spartan. But next morning, early breakfast, it was just the same as the day before, the crowd did not count, we were in the heights again, miles away, and man's desires rose up over the sweat of the earth, and chased madly away, out of sight, in the air, where they dallied.

We went up one side of the mountain that day, down the other, over a fine snow col, and stood at about two o'clock in the afternoon by the front of a small tin cabane, miles away high up on the side of the mountains, difficult to get at, used ten or a dozen times a year perhaps, not more, at the top of the small steep armchair valley beneath our cliff; not a valley, a ledge, a slight relenting of the main sweep, existing for no good reason. I was excited. Toni went to bed and I was alone. I became a little frightened inside me, and I stood at the door of the hut. The sun streamed in at the window, the stones shone white before me; the little cabane dwarfed, crouching away; nothing moved; down on the left there was a faint sound of running water, but none visible; then the slope dropped steeply over into cliffs, then beyond that, far below, the valley, a little river in it, with trees and a few pastures, and beyond that the hills, the trees rose steeply up their sides in dark patches, and then more hills, grey-green hills. But up here there was not much green. And the boy still slept. And I couldn't get it out of my mind. Then after a time I got some water in the bucket and made some tea for him. Woke him up. He was quiet now; enjoyed the drink, and he even accepted my attention. Then there was nothing else to do, and we stood at the door of the hut again. The valley shimmered still in the warm sun of the late afternoon, but up here the shadow of the great ridge opposite was coming over us, and there was a slight cold breeze. And, up on the right, dominating the whole, part white in the sun, part black, hard and scintillating, stood the shape of the mountain. He gazed at it carefully, so did I. Then we went in, and went to bed early in preparation for the morrow. Toni looked a little tired. Well, we were here now, and I didn't like it.

Why we got up at that hour of the night I don't know. To miss the avalanches perhaps, the stone falls, but so far as I could see we couldn't miss them anyhow on this route, so what was the use? I expect Toni liked getting up. It was alright for him, he could take it. And as I laced up my boots in the early morning I cursed, and as I ate I was angry, and all the while under the warm shirt my muscles shivered slightly in the cold, and the shiver flitted on and over my mind, so that my heart beat quicker than it should before a climb. Then Toni got up, ready: I am always in a bit of a scramble with my things on an early start, and I went out after him. God, it was black. I am a rabbit at heart, I said. He said nothing. We set off along a tiny track. Panting and unhappy, I said, I yet shall do it. I shall follow this boy until I drop, nor will I ask for sympathy; though with his massive limbs he has no pity for me, me small, following after. Here, where a slight temporary difficulty on this patch of rock makes it impossible for me to keep to his heels, I will make a clatter with my ice-axe, rather louder than the ordinary, and attract his attention so that he will notice the labour of my breathing and go a little slower. No. Now I shall have to run a few paces to catch up with him. No. He has a heart of stone, this boy, he cannot respond. All my kindness, my special treatment is to no purpose. Panting and unhappy. And we picked our way along the head of the valley, crawled up a small rock slope, stumbled over the stones across the tongue of a short moraine; ach; then we stepped off on the snow of the glacier. Ah, now my friend, let me not be angry. In the cold morning air I can forget. Well? You take no notice? You do not understand?

My hatred and my forgiveness have nowhere to go? You have come here welded, set into something, I believe, and your weldedness, your one object, is to climb, apparently, this mountain. But aloud I said do you think we might rest a minute? And he assented.

So we turned and stood, looking outward over the valley, and we were high up and it was dark, and in the cold I shivered and was excited again, and Toni took off his hat, loosened his hair with his hands, and looked out over the dark beneath, over to the north far horizon, with me for a minute, then we went on; and the cliff rose before us, as we turned, bare and dark, standing like a ghost over the glacier. We went steadily up, not difficult, over the grey snow, crisp to tread upon, bending slightly, winding in and out, making our way. We were playing the part now and no mistake. An hour passed and another hour, the glacier steepened, we trod carefully in on the edge of our boots, now and then kicking slightly; the snow was perfect; if all would go like this – then the glacier stopped and the bergschrund lay before us, eight to ten feet wide, uniform, curving, the far side steep, so we stopped too, sat down in a dip on the top of the glacier and ate a little. It was lighter now. Then we unhooked our sacks, drew up our legs, strapped on the crampons and drew them tight round the instep; and then we stood up again and felt strong like conquerors; but there was this damned bergschrund yet. Would it go? So I made myself firm while Toni scouted, and he walked along the edge of the bergschrund to the right a little and said I will try here, and he got on to a little bridge, looked at the wall above split by a vertical crack, thin, the right size, jammed his ice-axe at chest height into it, put a foot high up and lay back on it, then he pulled in a bit, slipped his right arm into the crack up to the elbow, held on so, and with his left hand, a twist, got the ice-axe out and jammed it in higher and so proceeded. Ten feet or more; then the angle eased slightly and the crack was not so good and the ice gave way to brittle snow, but the crack widened also with a thinner crack at the back, and he stood up, jammed himself, cut a wide foothold out on the right, and at last, about a quarter of hour I should say, got on to it. And the snow sloped steeply up before him towards the rocks, but could we stand there? And he rested a minute, and then cut big steps hand- and foothold upwards in good hard snow. It was over 80 feet before he took me up and I needed aid. There was no doubt he could climb. But the cliff looked steep up ahead. A groove and rib structure, the groove going up wide, open and parallel and about 50 yards between. From a distance it looked as if, when you got fed up with one groove, you would climb into the next on either side, but now you could see it better, this was none of your Chamonix stuff, and the rock had no holds on it: nasty. The grooves were backed with a runnel of snow or ice mostly and the ribs with verglas. If you came off you wouldn't hit up against anything outstanding by the look of it either, but shooting the bergschrund you would skate for miles; the odds are, I think, you would not stop on the glacier going at that speed, but would follow it to the mouth of the little valley, tip up over the end of the cliff edge and die.

The dawn had risen unnoticed away on the left, but it was still cold here. Toni was off again and it looked bad. Our groove was rather bare at first, but he kept his crampons on and as there didn't seem to be much in the way of holds, he was using a pressure technique, pressing against the little grooves sideways to keep the snow up, and with hands pressing sideways also to keep himself up, and the method was slow, and produced much scraping sometimes, and now and then it took convulsions for a moment or two when a position became untenable. I can watch a climber and tell what he is doing exactly. Poor old Toni, he didn't like it any more than I did; but luckily in those days he didn't know how much he didn't like it. Then at last, it seemed hours, at 100 feet he got a stance for his feet, stuck in a piton and took me up. Then it looked as if it might get better, but it got worse instead. And so it went on; some patches of ice were more good than bad, though needing hacked hand-holds all the way, and it took a time. I led one or two bits of that, but was not safe on the rest. At midday we had done 600 feet or so; several times he stood on my shoulders; then it got worse and we were getting tired, and towards evening we were not much above 1,200 feet from the foot of the rocks still, but there was the best ledge we had met; carefully roping we might both lie down; so we ate a good meal and felt better, and decided to stay there for the night. Stones had been dropping a bit all day, but it was cold and you hardly noticed them, and what could you do, anyhow? And now the sun appeared on the right, and at last unexpectedly we were warmed, and he sat and watched it set, and I began to think again of what we were doing for the first time that day. Why should he be noticing the sunset? But he was noticing it, watching about the weather maybe, the chances for the night; no, he wasn't looking like that; it was those other things, he could drag those same thoughts out of me still. What a sky it was! Restless, slowly spread her arms out towards us while the sun went down. Look at her. Ha! Red. Light. Straight. A vision. For the faithful a sign. Truth, naked, looking over the mountain. Toni, come down again, come down. But I said nothing. Toni. It was all he knew. It was so he had been taught. And when he was young, early, he had looked out of the window. How do I know that? How? I know it. I was there, I tell you, I was there at the time. The ascension to heaven. I couldn't get it out of my mind. And I knew perfectly well what was going to happen. We were going to go straight up into the clouds, he and I, then we might or might not get down again.

We had arranged ourselves on the ledge and, close together, we would be able to sleep. We were well off, but I did not compose myself at once. His chances of survival for the next two years I thought, are about fifty-fifty: as for me, I have fitted in nobly, have played my part, fool, and have even applauded. I couldn't get it out of my mind. I couldn't get the Alps out either. Then I dozed off.

We slept fitfully through the whole night, waited for the dawn, a lot of cloud about, then we set out. There was little snow on the next bit. I wanted to get on. All this is by the way. I think we both braced ourselves up; we were cold, and there was more cloud drifting around than we liked. The next bit was not too bad either. Three hundred to four hundred feet, quite quickly, three pitons and they only for safety; perhaps we were over the worst; then a tiny ledge and the groove went on under snow, and we stood on the ledge leaning back against the last two rocks to put on our crampons; and that heartened us; I think it would hearten a cow, that particular manoeuvre. Not? You think? With your back against the rock, bent slightly, putting on crampons? Oh, but you know it would! It increases a man's virility, any man's, tenfold. But it did not last. It never does. The next 80 feet took hours, and then it didn't look too good up above. You know what it is when a cliff is too steep to start with and then the whole structure gets steeper, a little bulge. The steepest part was 120 feet or so above us, and a big drop now below; the ice gave out in little runnels 40 feet up, couldn't hold on any longer, north face though it was. He got up 40 feet, 60 feet, 70 feet, in about half an hour, scraped for a quarter of an hour and at last, thank God, managed to get down again, found a crack to stick a piton in at 40 feet, and had a rest. I was shivering hard all that time, watching, and I too was tied to a piton. What to do now? But his blood was up, a light in his eyes, no talk of surrender, he got down ten feet, traversed out right, quite quickly, on next to nothing, got a piton in I don't know how, let himself down on a long loop and swung out for the edge of the groove, got the rib by the nails of his fingers, more gymnastics, stuck in another piton, and rested. The other side sounded harder; I couldn't see; it took a long time; I didn't go that way myself either, there was a sureness about hanging on to a rope and swinging, even a long swing, that was preferable in my mind to the long drawn agony of trying to climb a traverse that you couldn't. I don't know why I'm going into all this, it's not the point, but it sticks in my memory, all this detail. I landed up bump in the next groove, jammed, breathless, into a shallow, square, little overhanging crack, quite a rarity, that crack; and I was surprised; I doubt if there's another crack good enough to jam in on this side of the mountain, and I struggled a bit, I can do that on the rope, got a sort of hold near the top, something stuck, but I gave a grunt of joy, pulled like hell (I am a man with great reserves of strength, though I seldom if ever get the chance to use them) and something snapped and up I went. I was exultant, I felt a lighter man, and it must have been a full second before it dawned on me; my rucksac; the sound of falling; my poor benighted rucksac. Yes, it was making tracks for home. In the wigwam of her fathers she would repose. Now she must be nearing the glacier. There she would burst and her contents would fly from her; separate, they would make their way each to their resting place. The food; birds might have it. A pair of kletterschuhe; by luck a man might find them, sometime. The camera; there would be no use for that now, not in this world. The sleeping things. Oh, the devil. What have I done, Toni? And as I came up towards him I almost began to speak to him of my feelings; but I stopped halfway, he was thinking already more of the cliff again than of me, and that was as it should be; for this groove we were in looked difficult and we were short of time, short of everything now.

We got up a bit, and another bit, or rather he did, then the mists came. Like the words of the prophet they stole over, among the ribs of the cliff, and covered us. Then the snow came. What a mess. We put on all that was wearable in Toni's sac, ate, tied on a piton – we had pitons anyhow – and we scraped in the snow and went on. That did not mean much but we did what we could. So at the end of the second day we were getting tired and we had got nowhere. We got a scrap of a ledge and anchored ourselves, up against each other, ropes crossed. There was a wind getting up now, and the snow swirled round us, coming in gusts, eddying very beautifully, but appallingly cold. What sort of a joy was this? Is there any way out of it? Hell. I for one would be frozen in two hours at this rate. No, I said, slow up; don't let your thoughts run away, silly. Do you know, I've just got it. I have been wondering why I was here. My function is that I am the barometer of this party; I go up and down. Oh no, I had forgotten. As regards pressure that boy doesn't oscillate; if you put him in space he wouldn't alter to speak of; he doesn't know how. Screwed up to a certain pitch throughout his conscious existence, for the last ten years or so, he has had no experience of any variation. If he had a barometer it would not move, unless it had burst perhaps, or unless, protesting, it had begun to vary like me on its own account. My going up and down, then, serves no purpose. My being here is no good. Toni . . . Then I looked at him more closely. One thing was certain. The boy was about done. There was nothing more one could say.

The wind was cold but not very strong. We had a tiny bit of food. I had arranged his ropes very carefully, and mine, and we put our feet in the sac and settled down. We had two balaclavas, four good gloves. The snow coated them and froze. We rubbed each other at intervals. I did not think at all that night. It was too cold. That's all I remember about it. Our hands and our feet froze; later on it became difficult to move arms and legs, and the cold went right through our bodies. But we did it, we lasted the night, and the next morning we took our feet out of the sac, pulled ourselves up into a standing position, creaking, leaning on the stiff cold rope, and trod about as best we could, painful and cold, to get moving. It must have been nearly two hours before we felt fit to go on, and the groove looked hopeless; but you never know on a cliff, and as we went up foot by foot, using plenty of pitons, leading alternately, clearing masses of snow, it seemed not impossible. We kept to very short pitches, he did the harder bits. Once, close above me, he was swept clean off by a small snowslide. I fielded him. He gasped, got a footing, and held on. Are you hurt? he said. Me, no me? Not me, no, I said. He said nothing. His face was rigid and he did not look quite full at me. We went on again. The wind hardened and set round more to the north, blowing right into the groove, colder than ever. Climbing at this rate we didn't get on much, we didn't even keep warm. But we went on steadily, rather desperate. The details of it will not come to my mind now; I doubt if they were ever taken into it. At about five o'clock it looked as if things were getting easier, but the weather was worse than ever, blowing really hard now. We hadn't a chance, though we must be getting near the summit. I looked at Toni and suggested a rest. The storm increased in violence. It might blow itself out any time, but meanwhile it was not possible. Toni was not breathing properly, damn it. I supported his head. He looked at me but could not speak. Toni, Toni, I thought; Toni, why did you listen always to the sounds of the mountains and to those things; and if you had listened sometime to me also, and to my voice. Then his eyes went wild a litle, they were a little wild always, and then he cried, sobbed out aloud on my shoulder. Not long after that he died.

But murder, you say. There was no one else present, you say, no murderer. So? Nobody else? Have you forgotten the singing, have you forgotten the scenery, the wild scenery? And how are you here to tell the tale, you ask? How! Do you not understand?

But the boy himself, Toni, my friend? Did he die? Was he killed? Or I, or was I alone? Well, those are quite different matters, and really I must confess I don't know. But take it which way you like, that does not alter the facts; and make no mistake about it; that does not justify that very wild scenery; nor does it justify murder.

Cannibals

by Jeff Long

NOVEMBER 24, 1972.

KATHMANDU, Nepal – One month after an international expedition of climbers was reported lost on 27,800-foot Makalu in the Nepalese Himalaya, a sole survivor has been found. Daniel Bogle of Eldorado Springs, Colorado, was recently led to civilisation by a Tibetan yak herder.

Bogle claims avalanches trapped him and climbing companion Cameron Corder of Butte, Arkansas, high on the mountain for nearly ten days. The partially eaten remains of an unidentified man were found at the base of the mountain. Bogle denies accusations of cannibalism.

Yes, I survived but not because I ate Corder. For one thing, raw meat doesn't digest at those altitudes. I'd have killed myself with constipation. Besides, there was food up there, though the amount varies each time I tell the story. Sometimes I detail the scene with a cornucopia of food. At other times the tent is bare of morsels, only bones. Over these past ten years, sometimes I've told the truth; other times I've taken liberties. This time, the truth. It's not really my story, anyway. Corder was largely responsible.

I remember him in bits and pieces, not chronologically but in order of biological impact. He had massive hands, suitably enormous for his six and a half feet of muscle and thick bone. His face was furrowed by premature wrinkles. When his eyes chanced upon you, you reacted. Their deep blackness set the tone for the rest of his face, the dark simian brow, the beard and blacker mane of hair. Instinctively you felt that Corder was a creature of melancholy, a naked conscience.

I knew all about Cameron J. Corder, of course, there being no other climbers near his size and power who spoke with an Arkansas drawl. But I'd never actually met him before our introduction in Kathmandu, where the international expedition of British, Italians, French and Americans was mustering rank. Corder and I were the American pair. When Corder first appeared on the brown cobblestones of an alley that reeked of curry and goat blood, my impression was one of a gigantic human animal built for labour and physical, not intellectual, ascent. He was dressed in gym shorts, sandals, and a white T-shirt, clothing that did not hide his numerous scars. Both his legs were scarred with slight pale lines and with deeper, wider purple stripes. His right arm was marked with a shiny dent where a bullet has passed through the triceps.

We shook hands and immediately found a tea shop that served cold Indian beer. Pulling out our photos of Makalu, we smeared our fingerprints up and down the routes, possible and impossible, on the west face of the mountain.

During the remainder of that week, Corder and I explored Kathmandu's charming decadence. Dodging bicycles in alley-ways where old women were laden with twisted firewood or rice. we ferreted out beer stalls and found black marketeers from whom, for the sheer gall of it, we bought Nepalese rupees and Afghan hash.

I was still young then. Twenty-two years old with not a worry. I owned $80 climbing boots, a bellyband of three-inch sling, and $60 worth of metal – enough chocks, pins, and biners to ring like a Swiss cow when I walked with my rack on. No stereo, no car, not even a bed. My prized possession was 165 feet of prime European rope, a blue perlon line freckled with clean white diamonds. I lived to climb. With a bachelor's in philosophy, what else, I took spot jobs as a stonemason, a waiter, even a paperboy. If I went to the movies with a woman, she paid for herself. You see, ascent was everything. And I was so innocent, with so little past.

I can't say when Vietnam took hold again of Corder's mind. Not once in the city had he mentioned that he was a vet. I had heard back in the States that he'd been on a helicopter during the war and that he'd endured some mysterious ordeals. But he didn't talk about them, not until long after we'd passed through the jungle and had reached the mountain. By that time he was possessed.

The longer I think about it, the more it seems Corder could have managed more sanctuary from his memories than he did at Makalu. The acid whiteness of the bleached mountain, its angles and lifelessness, couldn't possibly have been more alien to his memories of Vietnam; and yet he was stricken. I think he may have been reminded initially by that jungle we had to pass through in getting to the mountain. Down there among the rotted Hindi shrines, among the ghostly herds of monkeys, Corder must have begun remembering. The jungle, like other jungles, was lukewarm. Every 15 minutes it had us genuflecting with knives to scrape away the monsoon leeches. Down there, I'm quite sure, Corder's Vietnam loomed up, though he kept it to himself like an embarrassing souvenir until those final ten days of avalanches.

Through September and early October, the climb progressed with talented vigour. All of us in the expedition were proud of ourselves for being so gentlemanly and industrious. Rope stitched the route together, an 8000-foot thread of polypropylene that snaked toward the summit. On October 23

Corder and I occupied the highest camp, Camp VI at 26,500 feet, and were prepared to force the line another 500 feet higher so the British pair could leapfrog and go on to the top. Early the next morning, on October 24, a blizzard set in.

That afternoon the first avalanche struck, taking with it the two Italians at Camp II. The avalanching effectively marooned two French climbers, an Englishman, a Scot, Corder and me on the upper regions of Makalu's west face, all of us at camps above 23,000 feet. The crackle of walkie-talkies was fierce and prolonged that evening as each pair of us debated our alternatives. There were only two really, though it seemed the universe depended on our choice: we could go down or we could stay put. The high altitude had us stunned and delirious, so our decision that night was a poor one. We chose to stay put – the two French in Camp III, the two British in Camp V, and we two Americans in Camp VI.

Tipped at a forbidding 70-degree angle, the face was composed of very hard, blue ice. Our tents were pitched precariously on platforms carved from the snow or stolen from brief ledges of rock. Just above Corder and me, dangling with erotic menace, hung a wide bosom poised to avalanche. We talked about it, willed it to either freeze solid or fall to the north, and hoped that by waiting a few more days we could outwit it. But on October 25 a second slide hurtled past Camp III, knocking the French and their tents into the abyss. We knew we were doomed, too. In medieval times travellers swore that avalanches were giant snowballs, triggered by the flapping of a solitary swallow's wings. Our avalanches were inspired by something even quieter than that – Corder. Or, to be more precise, Corder's sin. So Corder thought.

'Yes . . . yes,' he murmured as we lay in our sleeping bags, hesitating as much to breathe the thin air as to sort his thoughts. With our crampons and axes, our jumars, helmets, and ropes, all our tools for both ascent and descent useless in the tent with us, Corder began to talk about Vietnam.

I'd never heard of soldiers hunting animals in Vietnam, though more than a few American soldiers were killed by wild animals in the surreal jungles of Indochina. As Corder said at the start of his rhapsody, 'Grunts ate monkeys, tigers ate grunts.'

'King Bees,' Corder drawled softly. 'They done it most. Fire up a tiger, go down, gut it, and sell the hide and teeth back in the cities.' Gradually, almost somnolently, I learned Corder's slang. King Bees were CH-34 helicopters that had been manufactured in Korea and were flown by Vietnamese pilots. The term King Bee applied collectively to the craft and its crew. 'They were 90 pounds of person and 500 pounds of balls. They weren't always lucky, but they were always right there, you know. I remember one King Bee, a gunner, he took off into the jungle to fetch the carcass and never came out again. The cat must have got him.'

When the blizzard paused, and when Corder slowed down with his storytelling, I could hear the ropes outside fluttering in the rarefied wind. Individual snowflakes clattered dryly against the nylon tent wall. I half expected the sullen hiss of an avalanche to sweep our tent and us away at any moment. But Corder had started; he kept right on going. At first I was sure he was talking to suppress the avalanche; then, slowly, I realised he was trying to come up with a reason for our predicament.

'American crews couldn't go hunting any old time like King Bees.' He startled me. Hours had passed since his last words. 'We had a whole lot of laws on us. There was trouble for firing things up. But we done it anyway.' Spindrift, driven by the wind, formed a silent dune by a rip in the far corner. The fibreglass tent poles bowed overhead like the ribs of a whale.

'But sometimes it was legitimate, like once . . .' He drew at the thin air. 'Viet Cong used to use elephants for transport, and this one time we spotted a big grey all rigged out with .51 calibre machine guns, one on each side for anti-aircraft. We only had five rockets left, but we went down on it anyway and missed with everything except a white phosphorus. You can believe we burned that beast. It took off like hell, knocking trees down every which way, and it's sure they never got their guns back.'

I was paralyzed by the avalanches that were still to come, stock still and afraid; but somehow Corder's little sketches of Vietnam seemed vitally relevant. He was building to something, and that progression was more dynamic than my own concerns. Already Corder had begun to take possession of our tent. There were two of us listening to the walkie-talkie morning and night at seven o'clock, two of us drinking tea, two of us gasping for air 24 hours a day; but more and more there was only one real presence in that tent, and it was Corder's.

'I was gunner on a Huey,' he took up again. 'There was Huey slicks and there was Huey guns. Slicks carried troops, and guns rode shotgun for the slicks. There was all kinds of guns. Cobras and Bravo models. And then there was November models – the best.' I felt he was comparing himself to me. 'They had every killing thing. Twin miniguns, 20-millimetre Vulcan cannons, chunkers. And fast, man. 160 knots. When we came along with those November guns, we had the power.' His story was not meant for me, though once or twice he remembered me with a glance. He was addressing an image, and in speaking aloud he drew it nearer.

'Roger, Roger, you know. Like, keep your heads down; we're coming in with spook,' he explained. 'Then they'd go "Roger, Roger" and duck their asses down for the fireworks. Those guns was so goddam fast they didn't go bang-bang or rat-a-tat. Just this low grunt for ten or 20 seconds, and that's all she wrote. Even the grass was mowed.' Corder touched the tip of his tongue to each wide split in his weathered lips. Suddenly he looked at me. 'Don't worry,' he winked. 'I'm not crazy, brother.'

A day passed, nearly as cold and dark as night. The wind and snow continued to rattle against the bellowing tent wall. At seven the British called, their voices pinched by the radio's static, their fear, and, no doubt, bronchitis. Our position was the same: wait out the storm. It would let up in a day or two. So we hoped, but it didn't.

I've been asked if I felt despair in that violent region so far above the earth. It wasn't that I trusted Corder's sanity or our decision to wait, nor that I believed the weather would suddenly spare us. There was just so little sense of urgency, how could there be despair?

On the morning of October 28, for no particular reason, Corder and I shared a nearly empty yellow bottle of oxygen. Five minutes for him, five for me. In those five-minute gulps of pure air, the world turned richer, fuller, and focused into smells, sights, and sounds. We had a painful sense of what we had missed. I watched Corder's face suddenly fatten with some vast, oxygenated memory and, with it, distress. Then it was my turn again, and while I stared at him and inhaled the thick air, Corder's exhaustion lines and sunburn and dandruff overwhelmed me.

'You're dying, Corder.' I whispered through the mask, and he nodded back in terror. 'We're . . .'

The oxygen ran out. The mask's rubber bladder collapsed, and we were again stupefied.

Corder's face returned to its side of the tent; his eyes clouded over. The urgency evaporated. I lay back with the cold snow outside and the tired desire to sleep and escape the tedious dream of wind and nylon that surrounded me.

We weren't without certain tasks. Snow had to be knocked from the sagging walls. The walkie-talkie, though it was becoming silent, had to be kept warm with body heat. Water had to be melted for drinking. I made a habit of reaching through the north door to fill cook pots with snow, a special ritual that Corder fouled when he emptied his piss-bottle all over the drinking-water snow.

'Damn it, Corder,' I snapped. He'd violated one of my only taboos, making my presence in the tent even more transparent and unreal. 'Drop Vietnam. Take a look where you are.'

The giant pushed one big bare hand out of the top of his sleeping bag and wiped his eyes. 'I can't,' he insisted in a soft voice. 'It's eating at me.' I didn't retort, though I wanted to. Restraint was all-important; I couldn't afford to have Corder annoyed at me. 'Believe me,' he pleaded, second-guessing my silence. 'It's on me. I got to.'

Afterward Corder was quiet for half a day before resuming his tales. At last, five days into his imagery of Vietnam, Corder began to actually weave a *bona fide* story, not just piecemeal anecdotes.

Not often, but now and then, Corder's November gun would stray on its return from missions in order to hunt tigers and elephants. They always hunted from the air. From up there, Corder told me, the tigers were fluid orange and red lights that glowed through the overgrowth. Elephants were black shadows. Once driven from the trees by rocket fire, the orange lights and black shadows turned into miniature animals. As Corder snaked his miniguns down, the pilot tipped the craft to broaden the field. Excitement mounted. Everyone wanted to reach out to touch the animals and, like magicians, to drop them in their tracks. While I listened for the hiss of incipient avalanches, Corder told me how slow roses of blood would blossom when the rockets hit an elephant's rib cage. He gestured with his hand to show how the tigers would hatefully dodge the November's quick shadow.

To pass the time while Corder unwound his story, I kept a veiled eye on our food. It wasn't promising. There was a small, freeze-dried slab of beef; four fresh tea bags; two packets of Quaker Oats; a cube of cheese, and three marbled Hershey bars. I rationed the food, apportioning equal shares until the fifth night, when I decided Corder had gone crazy. His gentle, twangy voice had begun to accelerate the tale, and he'd even let his tea freeze in its cup while he rambled.

The food was scarce, but I wasn't worried. I believed that, like me, Corder had brought provisions. We'd make it.

'Let me have the food.' I thought I said it aloud. Perhaps I didn't really say anything. When Corder didn't move, I watched myself reach across and pull the man's pack onto my legs. Although it felt light, there was some weight to it, some food anyway. I watched myself upend the pack.

A book landed on my sleeping bag. Nothing more. Corder had brought a Bible.

The afternoon was a vacuum, not a sound except for snowflakes on nylon and Corder breathing.

'We're out of food,' I told him when he awoke. 'Here . . . tea,' and I handed him a cup, then half a candy bar. 'That's it.'

'Where's my gear?' Corder demanded.

I didn't answer. I watched myself not answer. Corder knew I knew.

'Where's my Bible?'

I handed it to him. 'You screwed up,' I said, but without an ominous tone. Corder might have suspected.

He grabbed at the book. It should have been two pounds of food – bread and fish, so to speak – not paper. I lay down, thinking there was a chance Corder had killed both of us. But it was a sure thing that Corder had killed himself. He wouldn't last long at that altitude. Over the next two days sleep and imagination were the antagonists. Every time I closed my eyes, I could see the future: murder, then food.

So, I had made my choice. I started hiding bits of food for myself. If the storm continued, I knew we'd both be dead inside of three days anyway; on the other hand, if there was only one of us, the survivor might last as long as nine or ten days. I wanted to live, and all Corder could seem to think about was death and hunting wild animals.

One incident among the many animals slaughtered and people killed had affected Corder deeply, and that was the death of a white tiger. I think, after piecing together Corder's accounts, that I can understand some of his feeling of guilt. Up in their helicopter, from their vantage point of height and omnipotent fire power, the crew members had lost patience with the common and ordinary. The earth had become a topography for them, small and insipid. Animals and men were now nothing but targets, more to test the crew's indifference than its weaponry. One day, near the border of Cambodia, Corder's crew spied a watery white shape surging through the dark trees below. It was an albino tiger. The gunship dropped lower, hovering like an insect as the young soldiers fed their curiosity about the extraordinary animal. For such a long, long time they had seen nothing beautiful, uncommon.

Beneath the thunder of the rotor blades, the pilot suggested the tiger be spared, and over the headphones the co-pilot agreed. They would show mercy. But just as the gunship started to lift away, the act was spoiled. Corder shot the tiger with his miniguns. I suspect he did it out of fascination, or maybe because of a desire to be completely free of that impoverished landscape or to commit a crime where there was no law. The reason doesn't matter; it didn't matter as the gunship throbbed above the white carcass, and it didn't matter as Corder and I lay half-conscious at Camp VI. The tiger was dead.

On the morning of October 29, our sixth straight day of storm and solitude, we lost radio contact with the British at Camp V, 800 feet below us. We waited until seven o'clock that night, assuring each other that their batteries must have frozen or their antenna broken, but they were gone. An avalanche took them, of course, though to Corder and me they'd been bluntly erased. I accepted their nonexistence without a second thought. The world had become a very plain and simple finger painting for me. Sunset, had we been able to see it, would have been a few broad stripes of colour. The ice would have been purple. The summit would have been an inky triangle. The deaths of six fellow climbers fit quite naturally into this matter-of-fact tableau.

Far from mourning the loss of the climbers at Camp V, Corder accepted it as unsophisticated destiny, part and parcel of his sin. I finally understood – his sin was the murder of that white tiger. But guilt no longer interested me; I was too hungry and exhausted to share Corder's moods.

'It's happened like this before.' He was glaring through me again, a glare I was learning to equate with further confession.

'Hey,' I said soothingly, 'it's okay.'

Corder blinked and emitted a shy, repentant grin: white teeth in a black beard, black and white like a Dürer etching. Death's-head. He lay back, quiet for a few minutes, then launched into his tale again.

After Corder 'fired up' the white tiger, the gunship had hung above the jungle for a moment or two, then arched away from the isolated clearing. The pilot and co-pilot were disappointed in Corder, but no one ever mentioned the tiger again. A week later the gunship was shot down, killing everyone but Corder. Corder put one huge hand on my shoulder as I lay in my filthy sleeping bag and swore to God that, just before he died, the co-pilot had looked him straight in the eye and coldly whispered, 'Don't blame yourself.' At that point, and with enduring guilt, Corder had realized he alone was responsible for the deaths of his friends. It had been he, after all, who had tampered with a pattern of mercy.

Within five minutes a second and third gunship had tracked the distress signal from Corder's ship and had come snapping over the jungle's edge, laying down heavy veils of gunfire all around the craft. Two minutes later Corder was safely plucked from his burning gunship. But for seven minutes he was alone, surrounded by flames, gunfire, and his dead friends, one of whom had accused him with his last breath. For seven minutes Corder was tormented by the belief that an animistic force had pursued and destroyed everyone but him – because he was the guilty one.

After the crash of his gunship and the death of his crew, the giant gunner had encased himself in guilt and horror. He had a prostitute for a girlfriend who habitually dressed in white; she disappeared the same day Corder's Huey was shot down. Even more ominous, he confided to me, every now and then one of his dead crew members would quiver into view on the streets of Ban Me Thuot.

'They wouldn't say nothing, just sort of look at me like I done . . . well the tiger.'

He was reassigned to another gunship, and it was shot down the next morning. Corder survived this catastrophe, too, only to be haunted by the ghosts of two gunship crews.

'So now you know.' He paused. 'What do you think? Crazy, huh?' I knew what I thought, but didn't know what to say. It was a strange story, I cautiously admitted. A terrible story. I was afraid to say any more. He was huge, and I was more than a little convinced that Corder was out of his mind. Eight thousand vertical feet from the foot of the mountain, I was trapped in a tent with a madman.

There were a few edible odds and ends tucked deep inside my sleeping bag, but I felt justified in withholding them for myself. It had come down to that kind of deceit. We were dying. Lives had ceased to be but, as I said, the mountain made us all seem so insignificant.

'You aren't going to eat me, are you?' Corder joked, cocking a wasted grin at me. I looked long and hard at his face, at his black beard and his ragged mane of hair, at his nose scabbed with old sunburn. I thought he could survive on the flesh of his memories. Corder glanced at me. His eyes hungered for forgiveness. Utterly convinced of his sin, he was, in confessing to me, inviting death.

On October 31, my suspicions that Corder was deranged were confirmed when he began to repeat his stories of the white tiger, his helicopter crashes, and his young whore in immaculate clothing. I was lying beside him, my back pressed up against the great wall of his rib cage to absorb every possible bit of warmth.

For the eighth straight day he was talking when I woke from my nauseous doze. The blue and orange tent fabric was coated with our breath, which had turned to hoarfrost. His deep, gentle voice was repeating the story. At first I was groggy, ill from the long frozen night, and I was irritated that Corder was echoing himself. Then I noticed that his tale was more severe and cogent this second time around; it made a little more sense. As Corder droned on, I envisioned the floating gunship that had laced the humid skies. I could feel the miniguns shudder as the tiger leaped high and dropped. I understood the graceful white curve of his young whore's hip.

Throughout the day I lay against Corder's back, delirious from the high altitude, starvation, and his tale. I ached because the snow was hard and cold, and I couldn't move except to face Corder. The tent wall was sucked in and out as the storm respirated. Near dusk I stealthily chewed a piece of cheese, savouring the strength it would give. As quietly as possible, I sipped from a bottle of water I'd kept thawed inside my sleeping bag. Corder rambled on, crazy as a loon.

I had two hopes. One was that Corder would weaken enough so that, even if his madness turned physical, he couldn't hurt me. I was praying that his arms were already too heavy to move. With very little effort Corder could have pushed me through the side of the tent. The drop was a mile and half. My other hope, so primal one might call it a drive, was that by nibbling at my hoarded food I could outlive the storm and descend to safety. Of course, if Corder had discovered my deception he probably would have killed me outright.

The end came as suddenly and innocently as the first avalanche ten days earlier. The tent wall turned dark blue at sunset. In tides the wind relaxed, then slapped at the mountain, then relaxed. Dropping off to sleep, I wondered again when the storm would stop, when Corder would be quiet. He had begun for the fourth time to retell his story of the white tiger. It was all like a dream: the storms and deaths, Corder's immaterial story, my deception with the food. That thought was still with me when I woke up in pitch darkness, unconsciously groaning to protest an absence, a blank spot.

The storm had stopped. There was silence.

'Corder,' I rasped, my voice unfamiliar. 'Corder, you can shut up now.' But he kept talking even after I'd turned on my flashlight and clambered over his rib cage. His eyes were as motionless as his jaw. His powerful features were locked and blue, hollowed by the cold. Corder was dead.

In prying the giant's body from the tent floor that night, I realised I was going to have enough strength to descend. When I unzipped the door, I saw the stars were glittering. The storm had truly broken. There was a long, chilling moment as I hesitated, unsure whether the corpse in my hands was dead or just pretending to be while it continued talking about the white tiger and eternal guilt. Then, with one decisive shove, Corder was gone and I was left alone inside that bony, sagging tent.

I can still feel his heart in my ears, beating, his voice like mine. You should believe me when I say I am not the Cannibal. But Corder is inside me.

No Gentlemen in the Himalaya

by Greg Child

FROM THE very first, I knew that my association with Father McGee would be an unusual one, my suspicion beginning as I stood in front of his address – a Catholic church. It was 1955. I was pursuing an advertisement in the London *Times*, soliciting applicants for an expedition to an unclimbed Himalayan peak.

The church appeared empty. My footsteps echoed in tomb-like silence. As I passed the confessional, a voice, unmistakably Irish, challenged me.

'Have you come about the ad?' it asked.

I said that I had and was instructed to enter the booth. I sat on the tiny stool inside.

'Draw the curtain.'

I did so. I could not see the speaker, for he was cloistered behind a blind.

'Father Flann McGee at your service,' began the voice. A pause, then, in a fiery tone, 'What does the word *Bool* mean to you son?' Bool? It meant nothing. I said as much.

'Well, we'll have a greater understanding of it before the year is out,' he said cryptically. 'But forgive me – I'm jumping ahead of myself. Introduce yourself.'

His tone was now cordial, as one would expect the bedside manner of a priest to be, smacking of a chatty formality given to sipping tea with old matrons on Sundays. I told him I was Andrew Mason, elaborated modestly on my career as a mountaineer and Arctic explorer, and produced a resumé. The blind lifted an inch, devoured the sheet and slammed shut. A minute passed as the priest digested it.

'Highly satisfactory. Now, to explain . . . as you've noticed, I am a man of the cloth, not a mountaineer. However, I have a scientific interest in a certain remote region of the Himalaya, an isolated valley in Nepal. That valley is of great interest to the church, because something rare and exceptional is taking place there. You are bound to secrecy in what I tell you, but the thing of which I speak is nothing less than the birth of a new religion!' His accent hung dramatically in the musty air. Creaking sounds within his cubicle indicated that he was leaning closer, as if to disclose even greater revelations. I leaned with my ear almost touching the blind between us, to better hear him, then recoiled as the blind rattled up, placing us face to face. His bulbous, reddened nose was practically in my ear. A white collar clamped his throat tightly. Folds of crimped neck flesh overhung its side the way a frothy head of foam overhangs the rim of a pint of ale. His few surviving strands of hair were carefully combed across the dome of his skull, which smelt of scented hair oil. Were he not a priest I would have taken his complexion for that of a man who frequently partakes of hard spirits and dismissed the coming talk as the ravings of a crackpot. Instead I composed myself and listened.

'An earth-shaking discovery! A religion in the formative stage, taking its first steps into the consciousness of man. You see the significance this has for the church, do ye not?'

'Indeed, but how do you know of this?'

'Reports from a Jesuit missionary travelling in the region were intercepted by the Vatican.' His voice belied no small amount of smugness. I recalled the age old rivalry between the two orders.

'How do mountaineers fit into this, Father?'

'The report explains the approach in detail. Not only must we trek for days through jungle, teeming with leeches, snakes and the whole dreadful business, but we must cross a desert plateau and overcome a high pass before descending into the city of Yabo La. I need men like you to lead me through these perils so that I may conduct my studies. What's in it for you? The chance to climb the mighty peak of Yabo Parbat! And I might add that the church has given me a blank cheque to get the job done. Are you with us?'

It was tempting. I had heard of Yabo Parbat, a virgin summit nearly 8,000 metres high. Yet there was something unnerving in the notion of wandering through verdant foothills with a priest who conducts his interviews from within a confession booth.

Uncertain though I was, I joined the expedition, tempted by the fruits of adventure and curiosity, and soon found myself aboard the liner *Janzoon*, bound for Bombay.

We were a motley crew to say the least. In the weeks ahead, as we steamed into the tropics, it became apparent that all the competent alpinists of the day had avoided the expedition as if it were ridden with plague. I shall describe a few of our members:

There is a maxim that expedition doctors are either good climbers and bad doctors, or good doctors and bad climbers. Doctor Julius Spring was an exception to this rule, for he was neither. All but drummed out of the profession for his habit of leaving instruments inside patients during surgery, he had joined us to escape a malpractice suit. No living climber had ever seen Spring lay a hand to rock. In fact he had never been seen any closer to a mountain than the nearest bar.

During the cruise Spring became fast friends with Boleskine, a caustic fellow whose habits of leisure fairly approximated those of the doctor's. They also shared a common interest in medicine, and could frequently be found lounging on deck chairs with lap robes drawn over their knees and a cylinder of bottled gas between them, inhaling the contents through face masks. 'Testing the oxygen apparatus,' Spring would babble. At such times Boleskine would break into uncontrolled laughter and for hours find hilarity in any small thing.

Boleskine was the closest thing to a climber on board the *Janzoon* having a list of odd but impressive ascents under his belt, in particular an ascent of the abominably loose White Cliffs of Dover. We all winced at his description of scraping fingers into soft chalk walls, an act akin, he said, to running ones fingernails up and down a five hundred foot tall blackboard. Though the Father had invited him along due to their common Irishness, a rift developed between them, arising from an incident one morning at breakfast.

We all lamented the dearth of good food on board. Boleskine in particular argued that we should be preparing ourselves for the arduous life at altitude by eating like horses while we could. The diet prescribed by the priest was monastic in its meagreness, to say the least. Driven by hunger, Boleskine crept into the hold one night and crowbarred open a crate of what he thought were rations. He placed the small biscuits he found on the table at breakfast intending them to supplement the unpopular porridge that set like lead in our stomachs. The biscuits were small and tasteless and dissolved the moment they hit the tongue. Everyone shook their heads at the worthlessness of them. After all, an army marches on its stomach.

'If this is what we've got to look forward to for snap, then we'll starve.' Boleskine decreed, adding that there were crates full of them below.

The Father looked up to hear Boleskine bitching and flicking crackers off the edge of the table in dismay. One hit the Father in the forehead and dropped into his porridge.The priest adjusted his pince-nez to stare intently at the wafer. A look of outrage permeated his face. He stood open-mouthed at the ill-gotten crackers. 'Are you aware of what you are eating?' he intoned.

'Lousy grub, I'd call it,' hissed Boleskine.

'This is the host, you heathen, the eucharistic bread, to be used only in the holy mass. Not bloody crackers!' The Father stormed away in disgust, while Boleskine shot him in the back with a wafer.

'And he promised me he was a Catholic,' moaned the priest.

In contrast to these layabouts was Dunstable, who ran laps around the ship and did endless chin-ups from the railings. So rigorous was his training that his body came to resemble that of a primate. In his endless search for carbohydrates to fuel muscle tissue, he alone gobbled down the plate of wafers, doubling the priest's horror.

No less disturbing were the Father's equipment designs: eccentric in the least, laughable in the extreme. For instance, there was the bushel of large paper bags he intended the porters to sleep in. They served the dual role of providing shelter and, if necessary, could be burned for additional warmth. Also, there was his peculiar wheeled tent, and thousands of feet of flexible hose, to be laid along the route up the mountain. Little taps were to be fitted to this, into which oxygen masks could be plugged. This would enable the climbers to inhale the richer air of basecamp. To 'pump' it up the pipe a punkawallah would stand below, fanning air into the entrance of the apparatus.

'I may not be a mountaineer, but above all I am a practical man,' he said, patting me on the back, as if he had done us a great service in furnishing us with all these useless flubdubs.

I doubt that such a sight had affronted the eyes of a simple people since the conquistadors pillaged their way through the jungles of Peru, clad in strange armour and with wild malarial eyes hallucinating the fabled cities of gold behind every leaf and fern. The sight of our caravan was an embarrassment. I wished I had followed my initial instincts and fled the confession booth when I had the chance.

Nothing I could say would induce the Father to take his tent off the wheeled platform and go on foot like the rest of us. Even when the trail became impassable to the buffalo pulling it, he unhitched the contraption and had the porters carry him in it like some potentate. Rollicking around the edges of steep gorges, the porters struggled with it while the mad black-frocked priest pointed here and there with his cane, yelling orders in the best tradition of the Raj. Villagers ran from it, as it it were a deity from hell, or stood about laughing and slapping their knees at the sight.

During the march we noticed a strange gastronomic custom of the porters. On seeing a particular species of spider spreadeagled in its web, they would dump their loads, grapple over each other to get at it first, then throttle the ugly beast and eat it whole. The man who forced the furry thing down his gullet walked away looking very satisfied, while the rest scoured the area for more.

We asked Bundok, our Sirdar, what method lay behind this madness. From his pidgin reply we deduced that there were two reasons. Since Bundok lacked a word for any of the English synonyms for coitus, he walked around, thrusting his pelvis about saying, 'Velly good for this, Sahib,' leaving us with the notion that it was an aphrodisiac. Secondly, he explained the spiders contained something that aided the process of acclimatization. Since we would be crossing the high pass into Yabo La in a matter of days, it explained the porters' enthusiasm for the unpleasant arachnids. The ever practical priest sent the men out to gather as many spiders as possible, and at dinner a plate of the revolting hors d'oeuvres was presented to us. The things lay on their backs, with their legs curled up. It was apparent that the Father meant us to eat them.

No one made a move but Dunstable, who saw this as a test of will. He picked one up and popped it down the hatch. The porters cheered and danced about in a pelvic ballet, crying 'velly good.' Dunstable sat silently, allowing us to observe him. Just as it seemed that his stomach would triumph and the thing would not crawl back out of him, his face took on a deathly pallor. His lips began to quiver and the sounds from his gut grew loud and explosive. Suddenly he was given to a fit of vomiting, and thereafter retired for the night. The rest of us sat around the plate silently, till Boleskine suggested we put a wager on it.

'Oi'll give five quid to the man who can hold one of those beasties down. I'm game to try it. Now you're a gamblin' man, Father, how about it?'

True, the Father was fond of a bet. He had spent most of the voyage playing bingo and sipping pink gins with the old ladies on board. The wager made his eye gleam.

'A fiver then is it? You're on!'

Both made short work of the spiders. Their expressions bore testimony to the unpalatability of the creatures, but when money is at stake, Irishmen will do extraordinary things. Locked in inner conflict they stared at each other. Rumblings soon began.

'Give me strength, O Lord,' prayed the priest, but to no avail. A booming cry of 'Ralph' and a thunderous eruption issued from every orifice of his body and echoed about the gorge. Birds and monkeys shrieked in fear as his stomach purged itself of the unwelcome visitor. It was a spent man, besmirched and belittled, who crawled about in the mire at our feet, searching for his pince-nez, sweating like a pig and breathing hard.

'That's five you owe me,' quivered Boleskine, looking the worse for wear. He kept the spider down all right, but the subsequent gases it caused him to emit that night made it quite impossible to come near his tent.

Next, we were beset by heat on the desert plain. The earth was parched and barren. Nothing grew that was not possessed of thorns. All the streams were full of silt and chocolate brown. Regardless, we were driven to drink them dry. In a moment of Christian passion the Father broke open a crate of whisky and bottled soda and shared a good stiff drink with us while vultures hovered hopefully overhead.

That day we reached a village. The name of this place was unpronounceable, but its literal translation meant 'the village of the rotting men.' The people emerged from their burrows to greet us, a rancid and malformed bunch, but jolly nonetheless.

Here the Father held a mass to give thanks and revealed his most innovative invention yet: a collapsible crucifix made of lightweight alloy. After snapping it together he placed a titanium Jesus on it, affixing Him by means of screws threaded through palms and feet. On completion he stood back and admired the cross, exclaiming proudly, 'Vatican technology!' Such was his pride in the erection that one wonders whether he had fallen to some form of idolatory, worshipping the false god of technology. A curious point, but alas, one we shall never solve.

While he preached to the kneeling crowd who understood not a single word, the villagers moved among us, divesting us most gently of all items of value. This we discovered later when Dunstable reached into his back pocket to pay for some trinket and found not a wallet but a human finger. You can imagine his consternation and our mirth when you consider that this occurred minutes after Bundok informed us that the place was a leper colony.

The crossing of the pass was a trying ordeal, and we suffered on all accounts. A recent snowstorm had covered many crevasses and under the weight of the 'holy barge' as Boleskine snidely called the Father's wheeled tent, a snowbridge collapsed, sending four of our best porters to their doom. The barge came to rest with either end catching chasm walls. Empty bottles clanked and rolled about as the inebriated priest yelled 'On noble steed,' oblivious to the tragedy under his nose and unaware that his transport had been ruptured and would have to be scuttled. The physical act of walking sobered the man, who leapt from one delusional frying pan into the fire of another. At every crevasse he would moan, 'If you have any messages for God, give them to me now, for today I shall surely die.'

Despite the diet of spiders we all suffered headaches and confusion from altitude. The only one exempt from this was Boleskine, who had stayed drunk throughout the trek. He reasoned that the dulling of his mental faculties with alcohol helped him adjust to the disorientation of altitude. Indeed, he was our most boisterous asset on the pass.

Those of us who expected to leave the purgatorial desert behind and find paradise in the valley of Yabo La were sadly disappointed. Boleskine sat on a rock, balanced a cigarette on his lower lip and scornfully christened the desolate vale 'Shangri L'arsehole.' But at last we could see the city of Yabo La and our mountain.

As we entered Yabo La we were met by a delegation of scrawny chickens and snot-nosed children. An open sewer ran through the town, along which gondola-like vessels were paddled. A maze of streets led us in circles, past mud-brick houses in various stages of decay, until we found a temple. Chants of 'Bool, Bool, Bool,' came from within. What we found there baffled us completely and unanimously.

Sticks by the hundred were dug into soft mud brick walls. From them dangled pieces of paper. Thousands of them swayed and twisted in the breeze, suspended on bits of string. And each piece was folded into the unmistakable shape of a paper plane.

While we busied ourselves with the mountain the plot thickened. Father McGee remained in Yabo La to investigate the mystery of this faith based on flight. During his absence, while poking around in the Father's trunk, Boleskine found an odd assortment of objects.

'Aha, look at this! The old pervert!' he jested, uncovering the priest's collection of merkins and codpieces.

'Merkins?'

'Pubic wigs. The old boy is a collector of fetishes.'

Beneath these was an intriguing set of documents that put his mission in a very different light. One document concerned the Jesuit who had reported Bool. It painted a picture of a renegade missionary fallen from his faith who had cast off his cassock to go native and become a lowly white porter. Somehow he had been instrumental in the creation of a cult. Another document revealed the Father to be a member of a secret society within the church, a clan of self appointed defenders of the faith, and he was under orders to terminate the sponsor of this paganism. At the bottom of the trunk we found the method by which he would carry out his assignment: a revolver. We replaced everything as we found it and awaited his return.

When he reappeared he looked vexed and troubled. He sat on a crate and knocked back a shot of whisky. 'Madness,' he muttered. 'Madness in the city below.' Luckily he failed to notice that we had converted his confession booth into an outhouse, or I feel that he may have suffered a stroke on the spot.

He explained that Bool had been spawned a few months before, and had spread through the hearts and minds of the people below like wildfire. The Father had talked his way into the temple and made contact with some monks who were folding and testing paper planes, discussing aeronautical properties. With Bundok interpreting, the story he got was this: One day the holy men of the city were praying for rain to break a terrible drought. Suddenly, from out the sky, a vision appeared. A paper plane, flying and hovering, landed at their feet. They picked up this offering from heaven and found a strange inscription written on it in a foreign language. Minutes later a fair skinned stranger entered the temple. Feeling this was a further sign from heaven, they presented him with the inscription and he read it aloud.'Bool,' he said. That night it rained. They were convinced they had met a god.

'Madness,' repeated the priest, taking another belt from the jar.

'This stranger – is he the Jesuit?' I asked.

'Unquestionably! He's in the middle of this, somewhere down there. I demanded to see him, but was told he was meditating upon the meaning of the new faith. He's become a god to these people. It's heresy!'

But the whole bizarre thing had a certain traditionality to it, not unlike the roots of Christianity. An ignorant people, morally bankrupt; an inexplicable vision and a sacred object; the timely arrival of a stranger full of wisdom . . . was it so strange after all?

Boleskine buttoned his trousers after a visit to the Throne Room of the

Mountain Gods, as he called the new latrine. He placed a hand on the Father's shoulder to comfort him. 'It's a topsy-turvy world down there all right. Do you know what happened when I tried to buy a goat with our rupees? They looked at the notes as if they were worthless and folded them into little paper planes, as if that's what I'd given them to them for. Then they showed me their currency. You know what it is? Dried rat claws. In Yabo La, the rat is a unit of currency.'

A week later Dunstable and Boleskine were poised for the summit when tragedy struck. Dunstable had hooked into a fresh cylinder of what he thought was oxygen. One breath and he fell into hysteria, then unconsciousness. He had taken a mighty whiff of nitrous oxide, or laughing gas, a result of careless labelling of the cylinders by the quack doctor.

A great chaos then set in. The doctor refused to climb up to assist Dunstable, due, so he claimed, to a relapse of rinderpest, a disease he had contracted while on the African veldt. Everyone else in the camp was stricken with bad guts. This left it to the priest, who took off with ice axe, bible (should Dunstable need the last rites) and a caged canary. This, he thought, would alert him to dangerously thin mixtures of air, an idea he had got from a coal miner. Holding the cage in front of him like a lantern, he bravely climbed slopes heavy with the prospect of avalanche. The mail runner arrived soon after and was dispatched to assist Father McGee. In the high camp the radio remained switched on, and what we heard transpire was this:

The priest arrived as storm set in. Dunstable was sleeping soundly and Boleskine was in a state of advanced drunkeness. It should be explained that Boleskine had been displaying signs of aberrant behaviour for some time, possibly related to his choice of reading material, namely books on the subject of satanism. Seeing the canary frozen to its perch, he grabbed it and ripped open its belly, in order to read its entrails, which believers in voodoo say have the power to foretell the future. Determined to find a partner for the summit, he pulled the priest's own revolver on him and ordered him to get ready to make history, for their fortunes, as predicted by the bird's gizzard, were rosy.

'Put that gun away. You'll never get away with this,' said the priest.

'Don't be too sure about that Fadder. My daddy found guns very persuasive in dealing with uncooperative partners on mountains.'

'What drivel is this?'

'Oh, Oi've been meanin' to tell yer. Boleskine is a pseudonym. Crowley is the real name – you know, the Great Beast, 666 and all that. Well I'm his bastard son.'

The priest began to babble something, in evident recognition of the infamous satanist and mountaineer. I recalled how Crowley, in 1902 during an attempt on K2, had pulled a gun on an unwilling partner. Suddenly the mail runner arrived. Seeing the gun, he pleaded with the Sahib for he was only bringing the mail. The lad dumped the mailbag, then fled. In it was a letter from the Vatican.

'Read yer mail, Fadder,' Boleskine slurred. The Father opened the letter, read a few lines, then fell to blubbering. Boleskine seized the letter.

'From the Vatican eh? Dear Fadder ... It has been brought to our attention ... serious allegation against you ... secret society within the church ... dubious research ... misappropriation of church funds ... forthwith you are suspended from all duties ... report to your Archbishop immediately ... signed, His Holiness of the Roman Catlick Church himself! Ha ha! You old swindler. Who's a bigger beast then, you or I?'

'Ruination!'

'Not entirely, Fadder. We're about to take a short stroll into history. If only Dad could see me now! Ha! Move!'

This was the last we heard of the Irishmen. As we rescued Dunstable, monsoon clouds enveloped the mountain. No trace of the others was ever found.

So the conundrum of Yabo Parbat lingers: did the illegitimate son of Aleister Crowley prod a defrocked Catholic priest to its summit, at gunpoint?

There is a final chapter to this parable of faith and ambition gone awry. As we left Yabo La snow was falling, soaking and crumpling the paper planes, dragging them into the mushy streets. On the monastery steps I saw a man squatting with a blanket drawn about him: the Jesuit. He offered his condolences over the tragedy. I thanked him, then asked him to explain, once and for all, the truth of this faith predicated on a paper plane.

'The truth? When I arrived the people of Yabo La were isolated, inbred, losing touch with their native Buddhism ... moral turpitude threatened their survival. Then a freak oddity occurred – the priest will have told you – and I seized the moment to guide them back to a spiritual path. Before they believed in nothing. Now they have a direction, a nucleus of hope in their souls.'

'But a paper plane?'

He led me to an altar on which one lay.

'Behold, the birth of faith,' he said cynically. I unfolded it. Written in faded pencil were these words: Buhl – Nanga Parbat – 7:00 p.m. – 3 July – 1953. Suddenly I knew what it all meant.

'And so the word was Bool. That's all I said. Had anyone ever known such power?' said the Jesuit.

A woman, old before her time, as is the way in this land, entered the room with a pot of yak-butter tea. Goitres the size of golf balls adorned her neck like jewels. A toothless grin slashed her leathery face in a cretinous expression of unfathomable idiocy.

'My wife. I took her out of penance for my sins. Marriage to her is a living flagellation.'

'For a man to take a wife of such dire calibre, you must have sinned greatly. That, or you are very brave,' I replied earnestly, while the vacuous hag giggled in the corner.

'Does the inscription mean anything to you? I can make nothing of it?' he asked urgently.

'Oh, its nothing important,' I answered, refolding the piece of paper. A picture grew in my mind. I could see the great mountaineer Herman Buhl standing atop Nanga Parbat, gasping thin air after his great solo climb. I could see him grinning through his frosty beard with hypoxic whimsy as he autographed this piece of paper, fashioned it into a plane and launched it into the sky. It had sailed through the atmosphere, riding across the Karakoram into Nepal, to finally touch down in this wretched place. If only the visionary Austrian were alive to hear of the outrageous folly he had drawn us into. But alas, he was quiet beneath the snows of Chogolisa, perhaps chuckling softly to himself, knowing that great adventures are made up of more than simply the sum of their parts.

In Another Tongue

by Greg Child

THE BALTI porters had returned to the basecamps at the foot of the mountain that foreigners call K2. For the climbers the season of 1987 was over. Winter was in the air. The last expedition was packing up to trek back down the Baltoro Glacier.

Young Karim, and his uncle, Hussein, stood on the glacier, beneath the big pile of stones, crosses, and inscribed plates where foreigners remembered their dead. Both porters came from the village of Ste Ste. This was Karim's first season portering on the Baltoro. It was Hussein's twelfth, and, he promised, his last. K2 stood upvalley. An intolerable wind blew a stream of cloud westwards from its summit. Hussein was telling Karim about the many tragedies on K2 the summer before.

'Success, then death; success, then death. That was the way it was last year. They would reach the summit but never get back down. Some of them are buried here,' Hussein said, indicating the stone memorial.

'And the others?' asked Karim.

Hussein pointed to K2.

'There,' he said.

'They must become very rich and famous to risk their lives like that, *cha cha*,' Karim said, addressing his uncle with the affectionate title given to elders.

'They will tell you otherwise. They will tell you they are poor men, every one of them.'

'But look at all they have! Look at what they leave behind. Enough food to feed a village! Enough boxes to build a village!' exclaimed Karim.

Karim and Hussein looked toward the narrow strip of moraine where the expedition was camped. Tents were coming down, boxes were being packed, bonfires of unwanted things were melting black pits in the ice. Porters and poroks, the fat ravens that roost around the expeditions, stood on the edge of the camp, waiting for things to be tossed to them.

'If they do not become rich by climbing K2, and they are not already rich when they come here, why do they do it, *cha cha*?'

'They answer that question in many ways. But I'll tell you that the truth is one of three things: Either they are liars and all of them are rich, or they tell the truth and all of them are mad, or they have good hearts and are hunters.'

'Hunters?' Karim was confused.

'Yes. They stalk the summit the way we stalk ibex, the way your grandfather once stalked snow leopard and bear. Perhaps for them, each of these mountains is a different animal. Some are easy to hunt. Others, like K2, are very dangerous.'

Karim considered his uncle's analogy while looking from the mountain to the memorial.

'I think the mountain is the one that is stalking the sahibs,' he concluded.

'Yes. But that is all part of the hunt,' said Hussein.

Hussein did not know his age, but he knew that he was too old to carry many more heavy loads into the mountains. He would not have left Ste Ste that year except for the pledge he had made to Karim's father – Hussein's older brother – to look after the boy on his first carry up the Baltoro.

Karim's father, Muhammet, had died the year before when rebuilding a rope bridge that spanned the turbulent Braldu River. Hussein had been with Muhammet, the bridge maker, securing strands of twined willow twigs. 'Hussein, I must ask you to look after the boy if he works as a porter next year. He is of age and the family needs the money. I'd go, but you know that the aqueducts to the upper pastures must be rebuilt and the village can't spare me.'

But Hussein wanted to stop portering, complaining that his knees and ankles crackled from too many carries up and down the Baltoro. He had saved enough money now to make his pilgrimage to Mecca, and he was hoping to go next year.

'We'll discuss it later. I must go to the other side of the bridge and finish some things there,' Muhammet had said. But when he was in the middle of the swaying rope bridge an errant gust of wind had rushed down the valley. The bridge vibrated and bounced like a piece of string. The violent jolt took Muhammet by surprise. He lost his footing, fell into the surging river, and was never seen again. So, like a blood debt, Hussein had accompanied Karim into the mountains, to teach him all he knew about finding the way in and out of that frozen wasteland and to educate him in the strange ways of the foreigners.

'If it's money you want, then it's money I'll teach you about. To get rich, you don't just carry for one expedition, you carry in and out for them all,' Hussein had told the boy. So together, they had gone with Spanish, Japanese, French, and Americans, in and out, to and from the Gasherbrum Peaks, Chogolisa, and K2. Karim watched his pockets swell with rupees. In one summer he earned as much money as his family's land could produce in a whole year.

Karim was only about 20, yet already he had a wife and child, and now, with his father gone, the responsibility of supporting his mother and grandparents and younger brothers and sisters fell onto him. Being a young Balti, he looked beyond the boundaries of his village for a dream of the future. He did not want to be a landlocked farmer all his life. In Karim's short lifetime much had changed in the Braldu Valley. Foreigners were pouring in to climb and trek. The border war with India had brought the army with its helicopters. If you could work as a porter for the army the pay was double. But you were paid to be shot at as well. The border strife was also pushing the road from Dassu toward Askole. It would only be a matter of time before a jeep could drive up the valley in a day, whereas now, the foot journey from Dassu to Askole took three days.

It was to the road that Karim looked for his future. He had been to Skardu where the streets teemed with jeeps and tourists. He'd seen how rich the jeep drivers and jeep owners could become by transporting expeditions and trekkers up the road to the start of the foot trail. To some day own a jeep and take the wealthy foreigners up the Braldu Gorge was Karim's dream.

Old Hussein's dreams were less ambitious. Experience had taught him that all he could count on from life was hard work, and more hard work. With the money earned from the season of portering he would buy another yak and a few sacks of flour to tide the family over the winter. Like last year, spring had been late again, promising a lean wheat harvest. When the snows came in winter, and travel along the valley became impossible, neither dreams of roads or jeeps, nor fat piles of rupees, would feed hungry bellies. These things Hussein knew.

With his dreams of the future, Karim absorbed all the knowledge he could from his uncle, until by summer's end he could sniff his way along the glacier like an ant following a scented trail, sensing the best path through the stones and fissures in the ice. It was as if those instincts of mountain travel had always been with him, and he'd only needed Hussein's coaching to draw them out.

Hussein had been along the glacier so many times that he recognized almost every rock and rise. He showed the boy how to secure a load to his back without rubbing his shoulders raw, the best places to sleep in every camp, the hiding spots in which to store rations, the paths along the river in high water and low water, and what wild plants could be eaten along the way. He taught him which village men to trust and which ones to be wary of, and introduced him to the cliques of his old friends so that Karim would always know someone on the trail and be able to spend a night singing around a fire in a cave or in a stone circle with good people. He taught Karim the peculiarities of the peculiar, like the porter Ibrahim, who often woke up at night screaming of approaching mountain demons, and who could only be sobered with a bash on the head. He showed Karim how to move through snow and probe for crevasses, where there was danger on the glacier and where there was not, the pace at which to move with a heavy load, and how to use a wooden stave for balance on slick ice.

Karim learned these things quickly and learned other things, too. He saw that a sirdar earned a better wage than a porter, didn't carry a load, and gave orders to everyone. He saw that a guide hired by trekkers earned more again, and was provided with fine clothes and good shoes. As was an expedition cook, who earned more than them all. There was money here, and in time he would do these things.

Karim poked at something protruding from a snow patch. He had chanced across the rubbish pit of a past expedition. Hussein bent down and extracted an unopened packet of foreign food. The two Balti opened the packet, sniffed it, but could make nothing of the contents.

'What do you suppose it is, *cha cha*?'

'Who knows? It is a mystery to me how these people eat such things. You know, boy, I've seen them eat pig! Pig!'

The foreigners are strange, thought Karim. They look, live, act, and talk differently. When they come to the mountains they bring a homeful of belongings with them, but they bring so much that they leave half of it behind. And not content with their own things, they buy up the wares from the villages. Old hats, old shoes, bowls, rocks, anything. Karim remembered that when he was a boy his father had taught him to catch grasshoppers and sell them for a rupee to the expeditions. Sometimes the sahibs, usually the ones from Japan, would buy the insect, then release it. Karim's father and his friends always collapsed in laughter when the sahibs bought a grasshopper.

'See? They'll buy anything!' his father used to scream laughing.

The sirdar of the expedition that Karim and Hussein were carrying for called that it was time to gather up the loads and depart for Concordia. Old Hussein looked at K2 one last time. If all went as he hoped, he would never see K2 again.

'*Cha cha*, is it true that no sahibs climbed to the top this year?' Karim asked, suddenly aware that all the labour of the foreigners had come to nothing.

'Yes. The weather has been very bad. Just as I prayed for it to be.'

'What do you mean?'

'After I learned that so many of the sahibs for whom I carried last year had died after climbing K2, I prayed to Allah for storms to rage all summer, so that none of them would try to climb to the top. That way they would live a little longer. And see? Allah does answer a just prayer.'

'Do you really think that Allah has answered your prayers, uncle?' Karim asked with a sceptical grin.

'Of course, boy! You heard the sahibs say it yourself. The weather has been bad all summer, and no one has reached the summit.'

'But one sahib died.'

'True, Karim. That just means I'll have to pray harder next year.'

Rites Of Passage

by Elaine Brook

THE STORM had been lashing them for three hours. A bitter wind flung stinging particles at men and rock alike. The route was indistinct, no more than an easing of the uncompromising rock and ice that reared above them, a breathless scramble over boulders whitening in the increasing blizzard. Ngawang was uneasy. They should have reached the pass hours ago – or perhaps his memory of time was uncertain. It was several years since he had come this way – maybe he had lost the route altogether in the storm. His leather boots had been wet for hours so that he could no longer feel his feet, and despite constant chafing his fingers were frozen.

Ahead of him the others had stopped in the shelter of an overhanging boulder. He crawled in beside them, brushing the snow from the folds of his heavy sheepskin coat.

'Only a few minutes' rest. If we stay here we'll freeze to death.'

The others made no answer. They had all been thin and weak before they started out and now it was only will-power that was keeping them going. Only Lobsang the monk showed any traces of vitality, but even his good humour had been dampened by the storm. He sat quietly now, an oily sheepskin wrapped over his ragged maroon robes.

Ngawang wanted to move. The comparative respite of the cave gave him space to think and the aching loss of Tsultrim was still too much to bear. He wanted to get back out into the storm, to battle with its fury, let it tear and push at him, blotting out all thought except survival. He turned towards the entrance, but Lobsang put a restraining hand on his shoulder.

'Wait. Give them another few minutes. They're exhausted. I'll take a look at your hands.'

Ngawang let out a long breath and leaned back against the rock wall resignedly holding out his white frozen fingers to be warmed. He watched the concentration with which Lobsang worked on his hands, as if so sure they would get over this pass in spite of the storm, to a place where functional hands might one day be useful.

'Doesn't it occur to you that we're probably going to die out there? Aren't you afraid of it or do you just not think about it?'

The monk shrugged bony shoulders and grinned. 'Why? I've spent half a lifetime practising the meditations of the stages of death and rebirth – why be afraid of meeting the real thing?'

Ngawang shook his head and laughed softly. 'You monks. So that's what you spend your days doing, while we chase yaks across the desert. What kept you so fit?'

Lobsang laughed, giving an impish look to his thin, lined face with its shadow of cropped hair. 'Hauling water and running errands for the more wealthy of my scholarly companions. No wealthy family to keep the likes of me in comfort! It pays off, sometimes. Look at me now – I get to run away to Nepal while the fat ones have to stay behind . . .'

Ngawang's face darkened. 'I should never have tried to bring Tsultrim with the baby coming. She'd still be alive if we'd stayed.'

'No. It wouldn't have made any difference. You were already being named as counter-revolutionaries. You would have been arrested within the month. This way, you at least may get out.'

Ngawang did not reply. Life in a foreign country, without Tsultrim, without work or money . . . He hauled himself to his feet and scrambled out of the cave. The wind hit him, throwing him off balance. He strained his eyes against the dull glare of the shifting grey-white snow and cloud, trying to pick out any familiar shape of rock or landmark, but it was hopeless. He plodded upwards, hoping that some instinct born of a lifetime in the desert and mountains would see him through; hoping that the others would have the strength to follow. Behind him, Lobsang pushed the other two out of the cave.

The snow and rock became a blur encapsulated in time; a monotony of ice and wind as rock gave way to interminable moraines and time itself became meaningless. A strangely familiar shape loomed in front of him and he stopped. The cairn of rocks with its ragged prayer flags whipping in the wind was what he had been looking and hoping for, yet now he was afraid it was his own illusion created from his own desperate need to see it. Lobsang ran past him with a triumphant yell and began scrabbling at the snow, looking for a rock to add to the pile.

'We made it! Let's get down!' He pushed the two stragglers into the lee of the pass and the four of them increased their pace, slipping and stumbling in their haste for tamer ground.

Dawa Tenzing found them slumped in the corner of his woodshed when he went out to fetch fuel. He took them in and warmed their frozen limbs while his wife boiled water for tea and porridge. Over the next weeks Ngawang watched dispassionately as his hard white fingers blackened and swelled, then dried, and by some miracle eventually healed although they were deeply scarred and the nails misshapen.

Lobsang found work as a porter carrying butter to the market in Nauche, and eventually Ngawang joined him. It wasn't harder than they had been used to but it was dull and there were already too many refugees crowding the small community. Ngawang was restless. He wanted to try his luck in one of the big cities – Kathmandu maybe, or Delhi. All he needed was some capital to make a start.

Lobsang shook his head. 'Contentment is in your mind, not what you're doing. You'll be chasing dreams till the end of your life.'

'Anything's better than this. Rain, wind, overcrowded huts, fleas and leeches – and precious little to live on at the end of it. Dawa's going on another climbing expedition and he thinks he can get me in, even without papers. It's a good chance – I'm going to take it.'

'Be careful, my friend. It's dangerous work.'

Ngawang laughed. 'You can light butter lamps and chant your prayers for me if I don't come back.'

The Base Camp was a scattering of blue and red tents across the pocked grey-white surface of the glacier. The new equipment was brightly-coloured too; each high altitude porter had been issued with jacket, pants, gaiters, boots, crampons. If we'd had this when we came from Tibet, thought Ngawang, maybe more of us would have made it . . . he pushed the thoughts and images aside. Tsultrim was still too close, perhaps she would always be. Dawa had given him one of the ice axes he had saved from a previous expedition. 'Italian axe,' he had said, as if this carried particular significance. Ngawang had no idea what Italian axe meant, but he memorized the name, feeling it was something he would need to know when he mastered the use of the thing. He handled it carefully, noticing the shine of the steel head, testing the balance of it in his hand.

There were fifteen of the Members, tall angular men with pink faces and light-coloured wispy hair. They joked with the Sherpa porters in loud voices, but even Dawa could translate little of what they said. Everyone laughed at the jokes anyway. The Leader joked the least, spending most of his time giving orders and worrying about money.

Each morning Ngawang and Dawa collected their loads and followed the line of high-altitude porters into the Icefall. It took most of them just over seven hours to deliver the load to Camp 1, and then return through the Icefall to Base Camp. The Leader gave an extra day's pay for each load delivered. Easy money, once you got used to the rhythm of it. The blue-white seracs flanked their route, row on row, like the tall houses in Lhasa but not so solidly rooted in the earth.

Ngawang carried through the Icefall for seven days, and still he felt strong. They paid double to carry to the upper camps; if he kept going like this he'd make enough for his plans in just one expedition. Still, Dawa was going on another one next spring – maybe he should wait. Another expedition would mean more capital, and a better start. They were almost at Camp 1, and instinctively he quickened his pace. He could hear Dawa yelling from above him, and looked up. The rumbling and the darkening of the sky seemed meaningless at first, but even as the realization sank in that this was an avalanche, he still remained rooted to the spot, unable to move. There was nowhere to run, no direction that seemed safer than any other, and then the weight of snow and ice blocks engulfed him, tearing him from his stance and carrying him with it. Crushing darkness swallowed him, ice dust forcing its way down his throat; his whole body filled with a deep roaring of ice which continued even after all movement had ceased.

He struggled upwards through the engulfing snow, knowing there was air and light somewhere above him. The long dark tunnel was suffocating him, yet at the same time it almost seemed that it was drawing him upwards as he fought for air. At last light filtered into his consciousness and he could make out Dawa bending over him, anxiously tugging on the rope that linked them together. As he scrambled to his feet, Dawa turned and without a word headed up towards the camp. Ngawang followed, stumbling at first, but soon falling back in to the rhythm that had become second nature. They would be at the camp soon, he thought. They worked well together, kept the same pace, knew intuitively when the other needed to rest. Together they could do anything.

His eyes were watering in the glare of the sun. He must have lost his sunglasses in the avalanche. He shook his head to clear his vision, but still it was blurred, and the scene rippled around him like a desert mirage. He could see the shape of Dawa moving ahead of him, keeping the same pace as if they were shadows of each other, but he moved through shimmering waves, as if the solid rocks and snow were dissolving into water.

There was someone walking beside him; he sensed it and caught a glimpse of Tsultrim's face, but when he turned there was nothing but space below him with the water ripples evaporating in a mist which rose up around them like wisps of smoke. He must have been more shaken by the avalanche than he thought. He increased his pace, swinging into an easy stride to convince himself nothing was really wrong, feeling a surge of confidence as the figure in front speeded up and kept pace. They moved on together through a vast silence.

Dawa had stopped and was waiting for him. He caught up and opened his mouth to speak, but no words came. Dawa understood and answered the unspoken question.

'We've already passed the camp. We don't need it – we can go to the summit today – we can do the whole thing now, easily . . .' There was a calm confidence in his voice – or was it Lobsang's voice? Ngawang screwed up his eyes, expecting to see Lobsang's lined elfin face, but at that instant his friend turned and set off again, leaning on his axe now that the slope steepened. Ngawang followed, concentrating on the light reflecting from his guide's axe, following it like a candle flame in the mist that seemed to engulf them. It never occurred to him to question the decision: it just seemed quite natural to keep moving upwards through these mists to the summit that must float somewhere above them.

The ice was steeper now – steeper and smoother than anything he had encountered. Dawa began to swing his axe above his head, pulling himself up, using his feet to brace. Ngawang followed his example, hefting the Italian axe and feeling a surge of pride at its beauty and balance. He swung it at the ice above him and a million ice splinters glittered into the cold air. He shuddered as the ice cloud enveloped him and he became part of its coldness as he swung the axe again, moving upwards through the cloud of iridescent fragments like fire sparks against the blue ice wall.

He did not notice when the angle eased, but gradually became aware that he was at the summit, snow and air blazing with an incandescent white light, blinding him. He had forgotten Dawa, forgotten everything except that he had arrived. The very home of the mountain gods, he thought. I'm here. In the silence the light faded and shifted from white to red as the sun sank and night fell. Ngawang slipped into the silky blackness of oblivion.

Later, much later, the clear cold light of the autumn dawn filtered into his consciousness, mixing and dissolving with it, reaching out into an infinity of light and space.

Shovels scraped in the snow, following the yellow rope through the tumbled disarray of the Icefall to its source deep in the ice. The blade caught on a different texture and mittened hands scraped snow from the outline of the body and the broken shards of the Italian axe, glinting in the watery sunlight.

'Poor bastard. Didn't stand a chance.' The Leader stepped back, easing his hands from the shovel, twitching with irritation as his companion retched into the bloodstained snow.

'For God's sake get a grip on yourself,' he snapped, then paused, holding on to his anger, nurturing it, needing it. 'We've got to keep together if we're going to get someone on the top of this damn mountain.'

In a filthy hut on the trail to Nauche, Lobsang dreamed he saw his friend wearing new clothes, smiling at him. He rose before dawn, and without a word to his companions, went to light butter lamps in the temple above the village.

The Way of the White Serpent

by John Daniel

I HAVE always looked to the mountain. I have watched it loom against the stars, darker than night, or gleaming faintly with moonlight. I have watched the soft glowing colours of the new sun emerge on its flanks and die in the blaze of day. I have seen the mountain summon the clouds to its heights and casually dismiss them, a proud and powerful man. I have seen it lift and lower its snows with the turning of the seasons, a beautiful woman changing her robes. Often, fishing in the stillness of the very new light, I have touched the water of the river and wondered how long ago it was the mountain's snow, and where beyond our valley the mountain was sending it, and if it carried back the spirits of our young ones who have gone to the mountain and not returned. All my seventeen turnings of seasons, since my eyes first perceived forms in the world, I have looked to the mountain, wondering and hoping.

It is the ancient teaching that the mountain was created by the Chooser at the time of the Dawn, numberless seasons ago, when the world was filled with the light of ten thousand suns. The Chooser drove the first of our people to the valley and imposed the curse, making the mountain for His own dwelling. There He sends down the river that gives us life, and watches, for our own well-being, that we do not wander from the valley; and there we send our young ones under the stern scrutiny of His wisdom. When the time comes that we are fit, He will remove the curse and depart, His dwelling will crumble into nothing, and the people will be free to go forth into the world.

But Eran, my teacher, says there is no Chooser, only the mountain itself. It was here long before the Dawn of our people, he says, and long before the deer and hawks and fish were here, before the forests and meadows, before even the valley itself. Eran says the mountain has been here since the time the very substance of the world was drawn together. Only the wind came before it, and only the wind will remain when it is gone.

For many seasons, ever since it shrugged him from its side during a Choosing long ago, Eran has journeyed to the mountain. He speaks of his visits only to me, for it is strictly forbidden to approach the mountain unless one is called to a Choosing. Transgressors are given the Darkness. The people are fearful of offending the Chooser: fearful that in anger He will harden the curse, stripping our seed of women altogether; fearful that He will never restore us to the time of legend, when it is said that a woman was born for every man.

Eran is an Old One, a member of the Council. He is well familiar with the teachings, but still he has gone to the mountain. The teachings are illusion, he says, the mountain truth. He speaks of it with love and reverence, as one might speak of a woman and a great teacher in one. He speaks, and I listen: for the mountain has shown him a secret, and he has shared it with me.

It was only five seasons past, though the path from then seems much longer, that the girl called Natahla came to womanhood, passing the sacred blood. Great excitement stirred the people like wind in the trees, for it was said no girl of her beauty had ever before walked in the valley. Like the other young ones, I knew her only from stolen glimpses. None but her mother are allowed near a ripening girl: the guardians, the men who are not men, ever surround her with their spears. But I would wait high in a tree while the sun traversed the entire sky, on the hope she would pass beneath. I saw the hair that flows even below her waist, the colour of the last deep light of the old sun – I saw it flash as it shifted across her back with her walking. I saw the lightness of her step, the proud tilt of her head, the trembling of her breasts as she moved. And more than once the sound of her laughter would rise to my hiding place, the song of her joy piercing me with the pain of longing.

The day the Council of Old Ones assembled to select the six for the Choosing, the young ones ran games in the meadow. We laughed, we made play, but in each of us the fires of hope and fear blazed fiercely. The Darkness claims most who are called for a Choosing, but the Darkness is preferable to the unhappiness of never knowing woman. For those who are not called, and those who are rejected by Chooser and Darkness both, the paths are few and sunless. Many live out their seasons in the ways of youth, fishing and hunting, running games and drinking the aged berry juice, squandering their seed in fruitless couplings with other men. Others, that the torment might be relieved, have the pouch of seed removed and take the rigorous training to become guardians, pledging their lives to the protection of our ripening girls and paired couples. There are some, the renegades, who forsake valley and people, going to live as animals in the hills; they are taken by the madness of loneliness, howling in the night of strange objects and other peoples in distant places. A very few strong ones, such as Eran, are able to hold their seed and turn their longing within, eating the mushroom and exploring the hidden pathways of the spirit. These are the ones of widsom, the teachers; but to a young one burning for woman, their path is as empty as the others.

Two things gave me hope that I would be called; that my father, before he was given the Darkness by the renegades who carried off my mother, had spawned a girl, showing our line to carry the female seed; and that my name as a fisherman was known to all the people. The Council selects for a Choosing only those who have proven their power, and while others were great hunters or trappers, and still others danced more skillfully or ran games with greater strength, I exceeded all in my way with the fish. So I hoped. But doubt still possessed me, and when my name was called among the six it came like a cool water to a punishing thirst. We were led into the great stonelodge of the Council to listen, standing in a row before the fire, as the Speaker pronounced the ancient words:

'The Chooser calls six to His dwelling. Upon one He bestows His grace. The Chosen One will be paired with woman, to make a home with her and care for her. He will give her his seed, that she might bring forth the new ones. He will be blessed among the people of the valley. The Chooser, in His wisdom, for the good of the people, will decide. So it has been since the Dawn. Now look upon the one to be paired.'

On the far side of the fire Natahla was brought forth, fair skin aglow, hair and proud eyes glinting, and with a trembling warmth spreading through me I vowed I would have her or not live.

For a full turning of the moon, under Eran's instruction, I ran by the river and climbed tall trees to build my strength and wind. With his help I sewed pelts into wrappings for my hands and feet and a great robe to keep my warmth in the mountain night. From deerhide I made garments to preserve my skin from the abrasion of rock and ice, and a carrying bundle to strap on my back. I fashioned a stout sapling into a staff, lashing a spear point to the lower end for piercing the crusted snow, boring a hole in the upper end and tying through a loop of hide to wear around my wrist. From long spear points I made handclaws for biting into ice. I dried fish, baked flat cakes of grain, made a water pouch of skin sealed with pitch . . . By day I watched the mountain, at night I could see only Natahla.

Eran shared with me his knowledge of the mountain. He counselled me to beware, on the ice rivers, the great fissures that were often concealed by a treacherous covering of snow or spanned by snow bridges ready to collapse . . . to climb the high chutes while the sun was very young, before the mountain loosed its rain of rocks . . . on the heights, to move slowly, with rhythm . . . to hold the eyes half-closed against the blinding glare of sun . . . to refuse the embrace of sleep, which in the cold of the mountain night promised warmth but delivered one to the Darkness.

'Your eagerness will destroy you if you do not restrain it,' he warned. 'One error can mean your ruin, for the mountain's paths are unforgiving. It is a strange world, a frightening world. Foolish paths will appear sensible. Unreal visions may come to your eyes. Do not be deceived. Remember the things I have told you, and look for guidance to the stillness within.'

'Is it not the Chooser,' I asked, 'who hurls down the stones and collapses the bridges and sends untrue visions?'

'The mountain is a living spirit, like the streams and winds, a spirit of great power and many moods. But it bears neither friendship nor malice toward our people. The stones it sends down are not cast in anger; they are only gestures of its endless dance of power. The mountain knows nothing of our curse. It cares nothing for who succeeds and who fails.'

'I will master it,' I said fiercely. 'I will be first of the six to the highest place.'

'So also did I vow,' Eran smiled. 'But your heart is great, fisherman. It will take you far, whatever your path.'

By the new light of the appointed day, the six of us left the valley with our watchers to assume the starting places of the Six Ways. A casting of stones in the Council determines the assignment of the Ways. Each is different, but none is gentle. The mountain's flanks are mild in only one place, on the side facing the old sun, where one can walk from a camp in the forest to the highest place and return in the light of one day. Even as we set out for the mountain, the delegation of the Council were ascending this mild side with the carven wood idol of woman: on the bed of stones at the highest place they would leave it, beseeching the Chooser to grant it to that young one who would spawn girls. And the Chosen One, bearing the idol that proved his success, that meant the greatest happiness for him and the greatest despair for any others who survived, would descend this side to the camp where the delegation waited to escort him back to the valley, to Natahla.

We journeyed that day and the greater part of the next, at first following the river and then leaving it to climb gentle slopes, the mountain screened from our eyes by the forest. On the second day our group diminished by twos as watchers split off with their charges. It is the duty of the watcher to deliver his young one to the beginning of his Way, seeing that he does not steal an early start and that no one assists him. My own watcher led me far around the mountain, through silent forests of great trees, across narrow rushing streams of the coldest water, finally turning directly up the steepening slope as the trees became small and twisted, unlike any I had seen. A cold wind began to sing. Glimpses of a great whiteness came to me, until at last the trees were mere bushes scattered among rocks and the mountain rose clear before my eyes. The ridge on which we stood formed one bank of a vast ice river that flowed steeply, greatly cracked and shattered in places, from a source high in a darkness of rock. And above, a thin white streak wound upward through rock. And through stone towers into the sky.

'The snow path is my Way?' I asked.

The Watcher nodded. 'The Way of the White Serpent.'

'And where the Serpent ends is the highest place?'

'The highest place is beyond sight, up further snows and rocks, but the upper reaches are mild. The Serpent is deadly. It is said that the ice river snarls, the Serpent attacks.'

'The mountain does not frighten me.'

'The Chooser is the teacher of fear,' the watcher replied coldly. 'All who visit Him learn. You begin at the new light.

We waited the night in the shelter of a small growth of trees, sleep hovering near me but never touching, forever dancing away on the wind. Natahla's face and the mountain were a single fire within me, fiercely burning but empty of warmth. At the first trace of light, staff in hand and bundle on back, I descended to the ice river and turned my steps upward, grateful to be underway at last, alone with the journey. The wind had lulled, leaving the gentle crushing sounds of my footsteps alone in a vast stillness. The mountain, alive with the colours of dying coals, did not seem so immense: I dared to think the highest place would be mine in one light. My spirit surged and my legs lifted eagerly.

But the mountain grew as the sun travelled its path. The upper reaches, the Serpent, seemed to recede even as I approached them. The bank of rock disappeared and the ice river swallowed me into its shattered flow. Great crevices barred my way, some without bottom, and from the depths of blue ice and darkness I thought I felt a cold sucking breath. *A living spirit* ... Delicately, scarcely breathing, I stepped across sunken spans of snow, balancing with the staff, gently digging in my toes, frigid emptiness pulling on either side. My progress crawled, as even the crevices themselves lost individual form in a monstrous chaos. Where the river made its steep cascades, blocks and great towers of ice reared wildly, sprawling against and upon one another. I was no longer walking but clawing my way, a wingless hawk, using the staff with one hand and an ice-claw with the other, gouging out steps for my feet. My path became a thread worked by a madman. There was no mountain, only the bluffs and gorges of this fractured vastness of ice, only my clumsy insect strugglings, only my fear ... but too, in this world strange beyond a dream, a faint pull of recognition, as if I had been here before, or perhaps always been here.

The sun, a fire too large, blazed upon my back even as the ice stung my hands and feet through the furs. The river was speaking now: long groaning rumbles from deep in its bowels ... sharp cracks, like trees snapping in the wind ... the giant footfalls of snow bridges collapsing into the depths. *The ice river snarls* ... As I clawed up a steep block, a huge tower to one side groaned and shuddered like a beast in agony, then collapsed with the splitting sound of thunder. The block shook; I clung, waiting to be thrown into the abyss and crushed, but the quaking subsided from the ice, remaining only in me. I listened to my breathing for a time, seeking the strength of the inner stillness, and bit higher with my claws.

The sun was turning old as I mounted the ice river's highest slope and looked into the chasm formed where it split away from a wall of black rock. Wet and broken, the wall rose almost straight up to the height of two tall trees: and there, bulging out through a gap in the stone, dripping a trickle of water as if in cold mockery of my hopes, hung the icy lip of the White Serpent. I sat to rest, rubbing my burning feet, my heart struggling. The wall towered darkly, no clear paths up its fractured surface. There would be places to grip and step, but one slip . . . *Fear is a trapped beast,* Eran's words echoed. *It will suck the strength from your blood for its nourishment, then strangle you in its frenzy. Do not feed it. Do not confine it. Let it escape through your breathing* . . . I ate a piece of fish and drank deeply from the water pouch, then lashed the skins tightly around my feet and looped an ice-claw to each wrist. The staff would stay: it had done its work, and would only hinder me on the rock and the steepness of the Serpent.

There was a place where the chasm appeared to narrow sufficiently that I could stretch across to the rock after lowering myself down a distance. A bottomless depth of darkness I entered, a home of frigid vapours and faint voices, never lit by sun. I stabbed the ice, lowering my weight from claw to claw, feet finding no grip . . . until at last, the strain tearing at my arms, I could span the gap. A foot, a hand, and I was clinging to the seeping wall, stiff and shuddering in the cavern's icy breath. Then, one movement at a time, one small fearful reach after another, I was climbing. My limbs began to loosen, my trembling slackened, and as I rose out of the chasm into sunlight the spirit flowed back into me. One hand, one foot . . . lightly I climbed now, reassured by the sun's warm hand on the back of my neck, lifted by the brilliance of sky. A piece of rock tore loose as I stepped, but my hands held fast, and the sound of the hurtling stone only brought laughter to my throat. Pausing to look behind, I made out a small white form shimmering in haze where earth met sky – another mountain, at the far shore of the world.

One hand, one foot . . . the lip of the Serpent was not far above, only a few reaches and steps. But now the rock bulged outward, pushing me away, forcing me to grip fiercely. No milder way opened itself on either side. My legs tremored violently as the void tried to swing them away from the rock. Breath surged in my throat, without rhythm. *It will strangle you* . . . One hand lunged for a higher crack, almost loosening me with the loss of its support. My fingers scratched, gouged, finally caught, but even as they did I felt the mountain's trap falling like a deadweight: I was frozen. To move a hand was to fall. My head turned from side to side, the frantic seeking of an animal at bay, fear coiling within me like a snake . . . a roar filled my ears, feet groping blindly for the stance not there, strength leaching from my rigid, useless arms. Something seemed to be pulling my awareness out of my body: I visioned myself falling, slowly as in a dream, down the sunlit rock into the black maw of the chasm. The roar was thunderous now, a waterfall, and there came over my eyes a dim veil that I knew to be the shadow of the Darkness.

A fierce and helpless cry tore free from my depths and suddenly I was watching my still-clinging form from a distance behind, watching with the brilliant clarity of a hawk's vision. On silent wings I hovered, poised for a lifelong moment between return and release, knowing for the first time that the flesh was only my lodge, that I was something else, something the old ones call the *spirit that soars like wind.* In a lightning rush I was in my body again, stepping up on a tiny knob my toes had touched but feared before, reaching a hand higher, every slight detail of rock standing out with perfect clearness, each necessary movement unfolding itself in sequence, until I was over the bulge to milder rock and a dripping hollow beneath the snow of the Serpent.

I sprawled for a time, spent and trembling, but calm within. I had heard the old ones speak of the hawk spirit flying from the body when the Darkness was near. The body, if it felt its path was not done, could sometimes call the spirit back – and if it returned it brought a marvellous power from the place beyond knowing, lifting for a moment the body's limitations, which exist only because we believe in them. I had succeeded where I might have fallen, because my heart had cried out; but I knew also that the fall was truly as real as the triumph. Eran's words came back to me: *Every moment is a branching of paths. The body walks one only, but the spirit walks all at once.*

Crawling to my left, I reached a place where the Serpent's lip receded, opening a way upward. I dug in my claws and climbed on, mounting the snow stream into its winding, steeply tilted canyon. Rock of many colours towered on both sides: where it was broken I used it to climb, half on rock and half on snow; where it was smooth I kept to the snow, carving steps for my feet. Bits of ice and stone rained down with whirring insect sounds, stinging my face; at times a larger rock would fall, a diving bird, and I would press myself flat until it passed. But after the unforgiving wall, the Serpent was a friend: its snows cradled my hands and feet securely, its steepness was as nothing. Within me flowed the certainty that the Chooser or spirit of the mountain or whatever life dwelled here had assaulted, grappled, and given – and now its heights were open.

But the sun was turning under. Perhaps I could climb through the dark, by the light of the stars . . . *Foolish paths will appear sensible.* With eyes that felt full of sand I searched the walls for a place to await the new light. Then a sudden rumbling above, thunder before the storm. Down the Serpent, hurtling from wall to wall and high out into the air, a torrent of stones was rushing toward me, each as large as a man's head. I heard in their growing din the deadly laughter of the mountain. I lunged to the nearest wall and flattened myself under an outcrop, knowing it was not protection enough, the laughter deafening now, then a pain like fire in my leg and a scraping blow across my back and I was falling, arms clawing wildly . . . then hanging on a sharp spine of rock, the rumbling fading away beneath me and the air filled with the smell of struck flint. *The Serpent attacks* . . .

I pulled myself to a small standing place. The leg burned and bled, but took weight: the wound was not deep. One claw had been ripped away and the bundle was gone, stripped from my back. I sagged against the rock, hands sticky with blood. Already a cold wind was groaning up the Serpent, sounding the mountain's claim of conquest through the last grey light. The dark was coming and I had nothing to keep away the cold, no water, no food, no place to wait. I cursed the mountain and its whimsical moods, its warm yielding and furious rock-hurling, its delight in lifting the spirit to the sky and dropping it like a dry leaf from a branch . . . and in a flare of energy I was moving again, up to the place where the stones had assaulted me and higher, climbing with the recklessness of hatred.

All light had long departed when I felt an opening in the wall on my right. A narrow gully, filled with a mire of loose stones that shifted with each movement, led to firmer rock and then to a mildy sloping ledge, broad enough for many. I crawled in against the steep rock at the rear and lay still, soaking from my refuge the warmth it had hoarded from the sun. Sleep, an enormous current, drew me down.

My shaking awoke me to cold moonlight. I was not alone. Stumbling to my feet to warm myself, I saw his huddled figure in an alcove at the far end of the ledge. For a moment we beheld each other without a word or movement. Then I understood. I went to him, kneeling to gaze at thc hollows that had been his eyes and the pale skin shrunken tightly over the curvings of skull. The hawk-spirit stirred its wings inside me: we were no different, this one who would climb no higher and I who still breathed, two forms of the same being, two futures of the same path . . . '*You came far, brother*,' I whispered, tracing my fingers slowly across his forehead. His water pouch was empty, food gone, but he made me gift enough. I slipped from his withered shoulders the robe that no longer warmed him and laid him gently on his side, finally to rest.

Dancing, I held the cold at bay . . . too weary to dance, I sat and sang my river songs . . . too weary to sing, I watched the moon and stars. Sleep is a woman; she steals up softly, gently stroking one's eyelids, murmuring warmly, asking why one resists her . . . *She lies!* Eran shouts from a far valley of my mind. *The cold sings a song of warmth* . . . and I lurch to my feet, singing and dancing, welcoming the goading pain of my hurt leg. My will was dried, cracked, but still of a piece, still urging. Yet it was changed: the day's path had wound long, leaving the past in the distance of dream. Five others, if still they breathed, were clinging to the mountain's cruel shoulders, keeping vigil through the same dark, watching the same stars. Each could ruin me, but I could not wish them ill. I would climb to outrace them, climb for Natahla, but I would also climb now for the mountain itself: for my hatred of it, but too for something I can speak of only as love . . . for a reason hidden deep beneath my knowing, the reason the winds blow. It is a thing difficult to express to those who have not been on the mountain.

As the very first light opened the dark I was moving up the Serpent. The mountain held back its deadly rain, held its very breath. There was only the biting of my claw and the huge surging of my wind. I was aware of no progress beyond the awkward lifting of my body from one carved-out track to another. My injured leg was stiff, a wooden thing, but moving. Thirst had driven away all other feeling: piece after piece of ice it consumed, flaring up savagely after each, demanding more. The sun grew, the blazing snows seared my eyes, clouding them darkly. Resting, I held them closed, and visions swam in my mind: the valley, impossibly green, the full-flowing river . . . I lifted myself on. The mountain waited, holding still. There was no passage of time. There was only movement.

A gentler slope, softer snow. I could thrust in my hands, kick my feet. For each step gained I sucked chestfuls of empty air that gave no strength. I saw a fish of many colours gasping on the moss of the river bank, the deep clear water curling below, just out of reach . . . The rocks were gone and I was wading a blinding field, sinking far in with each step, fighting a slow current that wanted to pull me down – the field rising to meet me, offering rest, the current ceasing. Always an echo of words lifted me on: *Your exhaustion and pain are your life. Do not trade them for deceitful promises. Think only this: climb until there is no higher place.*

Eddies of wind whistled around me, mocking the weight of my legs, the toil of my breathing. The snowfield extended endlessly into the blue-blackness of sky. A plunging step, the rushing of my angry wind, a step . . . Within me the green-bordered river flowed, and I could not tell its moving from mine, its rolling murmur from my own breath. A voice shouted, faint with distance. Now the river was dissolving my ponderous weight: I gave myself to the warm weave of its current, seeing all colours, approaching understanding of all questions, but something was holding me back . . . The murmur became a laughter, light and resonant . . . *hers*, at last my struggles finished . . . my fingers stroked her breasts, trailed down the gentle swell of her belly, drew us together in a cloak of soft-pressing warmth, the first, forgotten warmth. But a familiar voice shot across a vast distance to pierce me like the cry of a hawk – *no higher place* – the voice becoming a pain of light, spreading from a single point into a blinding radiance, ten thousand suns, the Dawn. . . . I was on my back, facing the blaze of sky. Memory swept off its mask: I had rested on the flat rock for only a moment . . .

The bog of snow gave way to the firmness of stone. My steps had new life: still a caterpillar's pace but in rhythm with my breathing now, one leg following the other of its own will. Entranced, my burning eyes held fast to the lift and fall of my feet. Wind and rock, an open-ness on each shoulder, the broad ridge rising mildly . . . then openness ahead, only a shadowed mass of sloping sides and level top, *no higher place*, wanting to run but legs turned to water, stumbling and scraping against the rocks, caring only that there was no higher place, the bed of stones was before me – I clambered wildly, groping, turning in circles, joy suspended on a strand of web . . . *rocks*. I hurled myself at them, ripping the bed apart, then stopped at a sound from below, straining troubled eyes. Far down the snows of the mountain's gentle side, a figure was moving. Even as I saw him I recognized the sound as the hunter's song of success, and I knew what he carried in his hands. The drift of his song wound slowly through my mind, circled slowly like a hungry vulture, and descended in a rush of darkness.

Someone was rubbing my feet. A bitter wind raged. I lay among rocks, covered with a strange robe. My eyes were on fire . . . all was grey and dark. The rubbing stopped, a shape moved, a water pouch was at my lips. I sucked like a new one until the pouch was pulled away.

'More . . .'

'Later, fisherman. You must not have too much at once.'

'Eran.'

His hand touched my forehead. 'I rejoice that you live, young one.'

Memory flooded back with his words. I struggled to rise and collapsed in his arms, despair pouring shamelessly from my eyes.

'Fisherman, you were chosen to live,' Eran said softly. 'That is much, even without woman.'

'The mountain betrayed me,' I sobbed bitterly. 'It gave the idol to another.'

'His way was not as severe – none is as difficult as the White Serpent. Drink now.'

The wind screamed its vicious laughter. I closed my eyes, drifting downward like a pebble in water . . . then Eran was shaking me.

'The sun is gone and the wind brings a storm, young one. We must start down. If others still breathe, they will not see the next light.'

'There is nothing to go down for,' I whispered.

He gripped my shoulders and lifted my face close to his. 'Only a little one grieves for himself,' he said harshly. 'Your path came close to success, turning away at the last – so it is. But the gift of life cannot be rejected. There are things in this world beyond anything you know, powerful things, things that make us small. If you have the heart to walk the path that is opened to you, you will learn them. Now we go down.'

He bandaged my eyes and put strange coverings on my feet, stiff and heavy; others, soft and warm like furs, he placed on my hands and over my head. The robe bundled around me, smooth and light almost as the air, held off the bite of the wind. Eran tied a length of heavy line between us, and we started: myself first, staggering in blindness over rock and snow, him following, calling out instructions against the wind and holding me on the line when I lost my feet. With each fall I wanted only to lie still forever, but Eran coaxed me on. At times I imagined I was still climbing, driven by the memory of his words. It was a dream, happening to another. I recall only the falling and the struggling up, the wind and at times an icy rain; then the protection of the forest, no longer snow but firm earth underfoot, and finally the arrival at some kind of shelter. Eran made fire and I slept.

The shelter was our home for many days as we waited the return of my strength and vision, passing the time in talk. Eran had built it many seasons past, soon after his own trial on the mountain. It was here his secret journeys from the valley had taken him, to be alone, to reflect, to learn. He had spent the lengths of many suns wandering over snowfield and ridge, absorbing the ways and moods of the being that so deeply stirred his spirit. When the mountain drove him from its flanks in the Choosing of long ago, he too had been crushed and bitter, he told me. But he had also been implanted with a seed that grew like the love of a man for a woman, the mountain finally opening itself and yielding the secret long buried in its snows, the secret he promised to soon share with me.

The day the other young ones and I had reached the starting places, Eran had come to the shelter, with a hope the mountain might spare me. Concealed by night from the delegation of the Council, he had ascended the mild side even as I was dancing off the cold in the canyon of the Serpent. He had hidden himself in the rocks, watching as the other came first and carried off the idol, watching as I stumbled up the final ridge, not revealing himself until I had reached the highest place and my struggle with the mountain was finished.

One day after the light had returned to my eyes, he brought out the robe and coverings that had given me warmth in our descent, looking on as I marvelled at them. All but the foot coverings, which were mostly of hide, were made of substances I did not know: smooth to the touch and almost without weight, coloured with the brightness of the turned-under sun or the open sky. There were other things, too: the long and supple line, a back bundle, claws for the feet of a substance harder and smoother than stone.

Eran smiled at my questions, saying only that the things were gifts of the mountain and that I would learn more when I was stronger, leaving mystery to swim darkly through the reaches of my mind.

My flesh regained life from the greens Eran collected and the dried meat he had cached in the shelter, but my spirit would take no nourishment. I had litle interest in the path ahead, little wish to return to the valley. Even now, I knew, the celebration of the Pairing was in progress: feasting and dancing by light of sun and fire, the traditional casting of grain, the solemn incantations to make the new pair fertile with woman. And in the warm haven of the Chosen One's lodge, the caress and fevered embrace, the little cries of passion, penetration ... *If you meant to deprive me why did you open your heights to me?* my writhing spirit cried out. *Why did you give me life with nothing to live for, an empty vessel, no home for my seed?* In answer came only the wind: the voice of a thousand moods, the voice that had raged and gloated on the mountain now offered from the trees a song of peace, easing my angry pain as the river smoothes a sharp-edged stone.

When almost a full turning of the moon had passed, Eran prepared a bundle one night by the light of the fire; and by the light of the new sun I was following him through the forests of the lower slopes of the mountain, around the mild side and further, ascending eventually to an ice river vaster by far than the one below the Serpent. Eran gave me a strange mask that shaded my eyes from the glare of sun and led me up the gently-sloped river, moving carefully around the crevices that lay in our path. The sun was nearing its highest place when he stopped. A great fissure yawned before us. Removing from the bundle a robe for each of us, Eran lowered himself into one end of the chasm and cautiously descended a steep pathway of steps carved into the ice. I followed. Far down inside, the left-hand wall opened into a small cavern. Eran stopped, motioning with his arm. At first I saw nothing in the dim blue light, then shapes ... two bodies, chipped free of the ice.

'Young ones,' I whispered.

'No.'

I moved closer. A current of trembling swept through me – the feet were bare, one wore a bright robe.

'The things came from them?'

Eran nodded.

'But *who* ... two men ...'

'Only one, fisherman. Look closely.' He gestured at the one still robed. I leaned over the body. Without willing it my hand reached to the smooth skin of the face, the long, stiff, sun-coloured hair.

'She is beautiful,' I murmured.

Eran took my arm. 'Let us return to the light.'

I was still shaking as we sat among the warm rocks and he spoke of the ones below. 'I found them eight seasons past, while studying the fissures. They loomed in the ice, terrifying – I fled, but when my fear slackened I returned and carved them free. I took the foot coverings, the linc that connected them, the back bundles, all the things you have seen. I studied and used them, telling no one.'

'But who *are* they?'

'The ice river slows the current of time to a creep. They must have been lost countless seasons ago, high in the snows of the river's upper reaches.'

'But why was a woman on the mountain?'

'I have thought much of that,' said Eran, gazing out over the ice river. 'Their people walked different paths, their things were different from ours. Their seed was also different, I believe. I can understand it no other way. In their time men did not climb the mountain to be chosen for woman. There were women for all.'

'The time of legend, before the Dawn . . . but why would they climb, if not for a Choosing?'

'A mystery, young one. They may have climbed for a reason we cannot know. It is possible they climbed for no other reason than the mountain itself. What has drawn me to the mountain, again and again? And you, what drive gave you the heart to master the White Serpent, beyond the drive for woman alone? You told me yourself there was something more.'

We sat in silence for a time, listening to the breath of wind as if for an answer. My thoughts turned and twisted, straining to open themselves to vast distances. Finally a feeling shaped itself into words.

'Their appearance is much like ours . . . are we *of* them?'

Eran nodded.

'But their woman, their things . . ?'

'I have no explanation. Here my thoughts lose form and scatter in the winds. But the image of the Dawn haunts me . . .'

'The light of ten thousand suns, the beginning –'

'We call it the beginning, but what do we truly know of it? For these others, if indeed they lived before it, perhaps the Dawn was not a beginning but a death, or a change – a change even in their seed, that female new ones became rare, the number of their people declined, scattered . . .'

'If they lived here and climbed the mountain we would find signs, their *things*.'

They may have journeyed great distances to climb the mountain. We know little of what lies beyond our valley, young one. The renegades babble of strange ruins, other peoples.'

'We are of them. We would remember.'

Eran was silent a moment, his eyes wandering over the ice river, over the heights and blazing snows of the mountain. 'These two have passed seasons beyond count in the embrace of the ice,' he said at last. 'The mountain remembers, and speaks through them, but our power is not as great. The teachings have taken root in our minds, fisherman, and recollection has dwindled under their shadow. The path of time is long and full of turnings. Even as it advances, meadow and forest are overgrowing it. One who turns to trace it back soon becomes lost in the silence of wilderness.'

Eran is old. He feels the shadow of the Darkness upon the path of his body and stays apart from the others, preparing himself for the last flight of his spirit. He knows this to be proper, like the turning of the seasons, and he looks ahead with peace. I too look ahead, but I am still young. I fish and dance and run games as I used to: at times I laugh and at other times, lying awake in the dark, my loneliness rises and I cry. Often, pretending to be fishing at some distant place in the valley, I go to the shelter on the mountain. Using the things of the ones in the ice, I climb and wander, looking and learning.

When the wind carries the clatter of falling rocks, I remember; but no longer do I feel a malevolent spirit in the mountain. When my heart is struggling, when my sorrow engulfs me, I lift my eyes to the heights. The same mountain that deprived me, rising above the world like a figure of dream, like the silent expression of all possibilities, fills me with the breath of courage. Soon I will travel further, to other valleys and other mountains, seeking the pathways of those who lived before . . . and those who perhaps still live. The fisherman will become a tracker. There will be signs.

At night I lie in the shelter listening to the wind, the voice that murmurs of all things and tells nothing. A part of me, beneath the lodge of words and thought, understands the language it speaks. I feel it flowing across vast distances of time, out of seasons and seasons past – through all the generations of my people, through the Dawn and the day of the ones in the ice, from a time before hawks soared the open-ness and fish plied the streams, before the hillsides were robed with forest, before the valley and the mountain and the world itself were even born, from somewhere deep in the endless black pool of sky . . . I lie in the dark and listen.

2084

by Anne Sauvy

translated by Jane Taylor

IT WAS a bright, cold day in April. Boris and Michel reached the last pitch and could feel on their faces the touch of the west wind from which they had been sheltered while on the climb; it would be blustery on the summit. Supposing Frédéric had managed, as they'd arranged, to bring up a picnic, it would be much healthier, in all senses of the word, to be up there in the keen wind.

Boris reached the last stance and brought up Michel who soon joined him, climbing as smoothly and as competently as he had done on the rest of the route. Together they emerged onto the summit platform, where the wind was enough to make them reel slightly. And by a stroke of good luck, there indeed was Frédéric, with a broad smile under his shock of white hair. All of them realized that they were doing something dangerous, but this was a choice they'd made, and come what may Boris and Michel were determined to find out about climbing in the old days: Frédéric must be the only person alive who still remembered anything, except, of course, for the Higher Authorities – and it was no use expecting any information from them.

And what Frédéric had to say was more amazing than anything they could ever have imagined. Back in the pre-industrial age of climbing there had been some two hundred years of nothing but green valleys, meadows and pine forests, wooden chalets and rushing streams – and wild and empty mountains, which were at first thought to be accursed and were soon to be explored and conquered by rugged individualists: no forward planning, no organization, just imagination and enthusiasm. Nobody, even Frédéric, knew very much about this period: it was lost in the dawn of time.

It had been around the end of the nineteen-sixties that some of the more far-sighted authorities had begun imposing much-needed order on anarchy and egotism: the first climbing contests were organized in the Crimea and Georgia, on prescribed routes with points allocated for speed and style. Gradually the whole of Europe adopted this pleasingly uniform system; the Anglo-Americans held out longer than most, in the interests of what they insisted on calling *purism*, but after a while, overtaken by events, they had no alternative but to bow to the new Alpine code of conduct.

It was the French government that first had the brilliant idea of climbing permits, so sophisticated technically that they were twenty years ahead of their time. They took the form of plastic cards each imprinted with the chromosome print of its bearer: the release at the bottom of each route could be activated only by feeding in the card itself and a drop of the bearer's blood. The permit classified climbs into twenty-two different categories, each subdivided according to the precise technique required. The qualifying tests were rigorous, and where on bank holidays, for instance, certain routes had formerly been overcrowded, now they were almost deserted. Very few climbers attempted to break the regulations: the police helicopters had orders to shoot anyone contravening the system, and they took their orders seriously. When eventually international climbing permits were introduced, things seemed set fair for the future.

Unfortunately this happy state of affairs was complicated by a new factor: genetic selection. Governments screened their populations for particularly apt recruits, and then compelled them to develop their aptitudes to the maximum. Very soon the routes were overcrowded again, and commissions of enquiry were set up to look for a way forward.

It was at about this time that selective breeding programmes became the vogue. Like the Dog-Breeders' Association, the Climber-Breeders' Association sought out blood-lines, dams and sires who seemed likely to produce the optimum climbing specimens. There was just one problem: any tangible results would only show themselves long-term, and several generations at least would be needed before the success or failure of the scheme could be assessed.

While waiting for the golden age, climbing had gone on much as before. Some of the variations over this period were worth recalling, even if they were sometimes short-lived and only footnotes, as it were, to the history of climbing as a whole. There was, for instance, the First Ascents Affair.

So frustrated had climbers become by the lack of potential new routes that, unlikely as it might seem, they had got permission to dynamite some of the classic routes so as to create new lines. Public opinion was at first indulgent and became alarmed only when it looked as though these new methods were shrinking the peaks at a startling rate . . . But results had been most satisfactory: no fewer than twenty-nine first ascents of the South Face of the Dibona were recorded, each totally acceptable even for the most exigent purist, and it had been most unfortunate that, just as the charges were being primed for the thirtieth first ascent, the whole Aiguille should have crumpled and collapsed.

This incident had, however, inspired a quite different activity: the Last Ascents Affair. This had had all the hall-marks of true originality, and it demanded the greatest technical competence of all the participants. The rock was pre-charged with dynamite, and the point of the exercise was to see who could set off last, do the 'Last Ascent' and get off the route before it went up in smoke. It was an amusing initiative for anyone looking for excitement, and it was extremely successful with the younger generation of climbers. But there were heavy losses in terms of human lives and of available rock, and in the final resort both First Ascents and Last Ascents had to be banned.

The Robot-Guides Affair had also characterized a considerable period. The Federation of Alpine Guides, realizing that the majority of its members spent their days doing a limited repertoire of routes virtually on automatic pilot, decided to invest heavily in the new cybernetic technologies. A Robot-Guide had been produced, looking more or less like a normal guide, with two arms, two legs and a head, all in stainless steel and specially reinforced to withstand stone-fall. The Federation's insignia was enamelled in jewel-colours on its chest, and round about where its navel would have been was an extensible rope, which let itself out and reeled itself in as necessary. A Robot-Guide was naturally not available for every possible route: even to programme it for a limited repertoire had required feeding in a series of highly complex moves in sequence. Normally speaking, any Alpine centre would have Robot-Guides for only four or five routes, and it took some time, for instance, before the Federation of Guides in Zermatt acquired a programme for the 1200 metres of the Hörnli Ridge on the Matterhorn; for many years, indeed, this represented the summit of programming achievement. In Chamonix, Charlets 1, 2, 3, 4 and 5, the Balmats and the Payots (all similarly numbered) were generally programmed for the N.N.E. Ridge of the M, the Couzy Route, the Papillons Ridge, the Rébuffat Route on the Aiguille du Midi, the Arête des Cosmiques and the Pyramide du Tacul. On each belay-ledge, the Robot-Guide would stand firmly planted on his steel feet in his thick rubber boots and take in the rope as required. The remarkable degree of mechanical sophistication typical of Chamonix even produced Robot-Guides able to lend colour with a few choice phrases at suitable moments. These ranged from general remarks about the weather:

'Chilly this morning. Better get a move on . . .' or (in a force 7 gale): 'I don't know what you're complaining about. Just think of all this good mountain air!' to helpful suggestions in the climbing line: 'Rock's a bit rotten here, watch out.' 'Climb when you're ready! I could hold an elephant on this peg!' 'Don't you worry. Just climb . . .' 'Come on, time you learned to climb a bit faster than that!' 'For goodness' sake, we'll be here all night at this rate!' 'Come *on*, for God's sake!' crowned on the summit by: 'There you are now, you made it . . . I told you it would be all right!'

The Robot-Guides were extremely popular, but two constitutional faults brought about their demise. The first was indirect: a surprisingly large number of their lady clients fell desperately in love with them, finding their conversation unusually polite and patient compared with that of the flesh-and-blood guides with whom they normally came in contact. Unfortunately the Robot-Guides had never been programmed for emotional response, and things became very complicated: a sizeable proportion of the clients went so far as to abandon all thought of climbing in the Mont Blanc Massif.

The other weakness was inbuilt and decisive. Ravanel 14, having been programmed that day for the Rébuffat Route on the Aiguille du Midi suddenly switched over halfway to the Papillons Ridge. In the ensuing accident, three Robot-Guides and five clients were seriously hurt. When the Minister for Alpine Affairs heard the news, he had simply issued a decree forbidding all such mechanical aids – with all the more satisfaction in that a lady had recently left him for a Robot . . .

Next came the Ecological Period, short-lived but draconian while it lasted, which followed on the election of a 'Green' member to the European Parliament. A law was immediately promulgated, forbidding skiing unless the skier dragged a 'track-eliminator' behind him, so that each skier could achieve his birthright, skiing in untouched powder. The apparatus was expensive and heavy, so much so that within a very short time skiing became impossible except on artificial slopes . . . In climbing terms, the dynamite period was left far behind. Ecological ingenuity was carried to extremes. Only rigorously natural methods were permitted. No pegs, no nuts: the emphasis was on the Joe Brown system, which allowed at most jamming small pebbles into cracks. Progressively, more and more modern sophistication was eliminated: no ropes, then no crampons or ice-axes, then no boots or socks . . . There was no knowing how far things might have gone, had the Green Member not been carried off prematurely by a smoking-related disease . . .

No sooner had this lamentable event occurred than a quite new venture developed, the fruit of years of arduous and patient research. For many years it seemed the ultimate in organizational climbing. The material investment required was on an astonishing scale, but the results made the outlay worthwhile. Two thousand routes were selected in each massif, and at mathematically calculated intervals each route was fitted with heat-sensitive sensors, linked to a central computer and able to detect changing weather-conditions or, more importantly, every passing climber. Each climber was then given head-phones and an individual wave-band, and would next be instructed in detail as to the course he was to follow: 'Rope 13, route 1619: slow down, rope 12 is on a loose ice-field. Wait until they are off it. Proceed to the ledge seven metres left, I repeat seven metres left, and rest . . .' 'Rope 12, move faster, you are holding up ropes 13 through 18. No slacking, you are only 374 metres from the summit which you are scheduled to reach at precisely 11.43 . . .' 'Rope 13, do not, repeat *do not*, leave the ledge. Note that this has not been designated a convenience area . . .' 'Rope 5, you are embarking on the narrow cracks – still some danger of verglas. You are two minutes ahead of the specified pitch-timetable, congratulations.' 'Rope 13, you have five minutes to prepare for departure, by the dièdre on your right, I repeat right . . .' 'Attention all ropes: temperature on the face dropping, risk of snow at about 13:30. I repeat . . .'

The system worked superbly. Every day, with no route-finding problems, no waiting at the crux, no hanging about, no tension, and accompanied every step of the way by that reassuring human voice, thousands of ropes advanced in total safety, knowing that they would be made aware of any coming change in the weather, any potential danger, any mistake they might have made – later it even became possible to install sound-sensitive sensors which would give advance warning of stone-falls. On the best-equipped and most popular routes even greater refinements were introduced: a coin fed into a slot on certain ledges would produce a cup of tea, a sanitary towel, a roll of film – or even better, a half-hour's use of a belay peg. Alpine life was transformed.

The worst disaster in Alpine history occurred on 3 August 2052, however. The computer broke down. This was a theoretical impossibility, but even so elaborate a system could not absorb the series of problems which, by coincidence, all happened at the same moment. The main computer link-up had no fewer than two back-up systems, all as reliable as technology could make them. But by a most unfortunate combination of circumstances, just as the main system had been powered down for maintenance, the second noted unusual temperature swings on sensor 122674 (something to do with unmentionable activities by jackdaws on the north face . . .). The second back-up system was still searching its memory banks to account for this unforeseen circumstance, so that the third system was in effect operating alone, when a young climber started up a pitch *feet first* – some sort of ridiculous bet. Such a possibility had never been envisaged at the system design stage, and caused a software error. This, in turn, was detected by the over-ride, which made a vain attempt to transfer control from system 3 to system 2, but again, this had not been allowed for in the specification, and there was an immediate shut-down, destroying several megabytes of memory. Everything, in short, blew . . .

When frenzied efforts restored function, it was found that there had been 829 deaths and an incalculable number of injured. Lost, helpless, groping in a wilderness of silence and danger, thousands of climbers deprived of their support-system had had no idea how to take responsibility for themselves.

It was this accident that led the Higher Authorities (by then in charge of world affairs) to forbid mountaineering: on the one hand it was difficult to provide controlled conditions, and on the other it encouraged the development of an individual spirit of initiative which could be dangerous. (After all, more than half of those marooned by the systems' failure had, surprisingly, managed to make their way safely to the top and down.) And to prevent non-conforming and possibly rebellious tendencies, it was decided to conceal any mountainous terrain behind translucent barriers, whose hazy blue suggested a sea-scape.

Some substitute was, however, essential: there were the Olympic Games to think of. Fortunately, climbing-walls had reached a degree of sophistication which offered enormous possibilities. For many years they had been used only for training for certain specific problems: the Knubel Crack, the Fissure Brown on the Blaitière, the diagonal abseil on the American Direct, the upper pitch on the 40-metre wall on the Cap, and so on. But now a stage of technical development had been reached where a climb could well be reproduced in its entirety. Micro-processors were used to co-ordinate a continuous loop of flexible plastic, which could be set to move more or less quickly according to the capacities of the climber, and which moulded itself as it moved into the shapes of the holds and moves on every pitch of a climb. Climbers were thus able to enjoy all the pleasures of solo climbing without any of the risks, and could even choose what weather to have. They had only to sign up a few days in advance for a Walker-Spur-in-storm-conditions, or a Mustagh-Tower-in-June, or a Fitzroy-with-no-wind . . .

Only the general economic decline spoiled things, otherwise climbers would doubtless have been perfectly happy for ever with the new system. But the Higher Authorities felt that in current economic circumstances, all this complex machinery had become too expensive to maintain and to run . . .

'And now you know why, in 2084, you're reduced to climbing on buildings,' said Frédéric. 'They've been building tower-blocks at such a rate over the last century that at least we're not short of *them*. When I saw you on the North-East Face of Original Building 114, it brought back all my own youth. And there's only one thing that I really regret: this Memory-Pooling Scheme that the Higher Authorities have introduced so that all individual possessions, even memory, can be eliminated. I don't know how I've managed to avoid getting caught so long myself . . . They must have mislaid my identity file somewhere, so that when I get into the Memory-Pooling Chamber, I just have to pretend I've forgotten . . . If I'd told them about the error, I'd have been suspect anyway . . . So far I've managed to avoid all the random checks, or I'd have been found out. And that's how I've managed to hang on to my memories. Then I decided to trust you lads, and I was pretty sure that on an old route like this one there wouldn't be any Subversive Memory Recorders, and when we got formal permission to come here, I thought I'd pass on all I knew about Alpine history. A year from now, of course, it'll all be fed back out of your memories into the Central Memory Pool, along with all the rest . . .'

'But look,' Michel interrupted, 'am I right in thinking that on the other side of that blue screen behind the tower-blocks there are *real* hills?'

'Real hills?' Frédéric sighed, 'Lad, you're looking at what used to be the Chamonix Valley!'

Boris was lost in thought.

'If we could only get through the screens! There'd be real live mountains! Just for us . . . no Higher Authorities!'

Frédéric shook his head, looking dubious.

'I wouldn't risk it myself,' he said, 'I'm much too old now. And it's only a matter of luck that they haven't had my memory drained. But you lads . . . who knows? Still, come on, we'd better get on down. It'll look suspicious if we spend too long perched on this ledge.'

He put the picnic box back in the rucksack, and dislodged the water-bottle in the process. It bounced on the plastic coating over the concrete, and a little black disk slipped out of its mouth, rolled to the edge of the platform and down.

The three men fell silent. Oddly enough, when they came to look at it, the water-bottle seemed quite whole and undamaged.

'Suppose it was a bug?' whispered Boris, voicing what they all feared.

'Come on, let's get out of here!' said Michel.

The lift was slow in coming. It clanked and groaned up to them, filthy, scratched, scrawled with illegible graffiti. It was quite empty. There was a long, anxious descent, in a silence broken only by the clattering of the old lift. They reached the ground floor: the door opened; a serried rank of brown uniforms was waiting.

'The Memory Police!' groaned Frédéric.

Bright Fire, Bright Ice

by Charles Hood

I AM a rich man. When I desire something, I get it. I mean this not only on an immediate level, a date with a famous actress or a matched set of titanium ice tools, but on an overall performance level as well. In my case this means being a very good climber. Not the very best perhaps, though God knows I've tried. But genetics can only be beaten by so much. I do, however, mean very, very good. The best equipment, the best training, the best conditions . . . not only do I have the resources available to utilize the entire globe as my *klettergarten*, but I have the necessary drive to make full use of this opportunity. Starting an approach slog wiped out by jet lag is just as difficult as trying to moan away a hangover at the base of Sentinel. I work as hard at my climbing as any climbing bum around. Besides the usual climbing lore, I am well versed in visa regulations, village medicine, global weather patterns, and international banking loopholes. I am not a dilettante.

Most people I meet or travel with express an envy of my lifestyle, and for many years I agreed with them. Skiing on Baffin, an ice route in Alaska, kayaking the coast of Sri Lanka, and home via a photographic session in the Galapagos would not be an unusual itinerary for a fortnight or four weeks. Then maybe the remainder of the spring in the Sahara, cataloguing and climbing every hill, hump, scarp, crag, plug, tower, slag heap, and tor to be found.

For someone passionately interested in outdoor pursuits, as I am, it is an ideal situation. Besides having become an expert on almost every major or minor range, my list of first ascents has an impressive number of unrepeated routes on it. The stimulation I receive from being in constant contact with the élite climbers in each area keeps me honed and performing at a peak level.

I have also been able to take expeditioning to its extremes. Probably my most publicized trip has been the Antarctica ski traverse. It resulted in two full-length movies and a handsome coffee table picture book, and took two full seasons to complete. Many times on that trip I grew weary of skiing, though I did not think that my taste for being in the wild had been dulled. Yet it turned out to be a more pivotal trip than I first realized.

After Antarctica (which had been my sixth and seventh visits, respectively), I found it increasingly difficult to maintain a steady pace. In the middle of a climb I would lose all interest and vaguely wish only to descend. My trips became more and more infrequent, their intensities more and more diluted.

In simple terms, I was bored. I had become listless, purposeless, exhausted with the limits of snow, rock, water. For almost a year I did nothing. Slept, ate, but both without deriving pleasure from them. I had no sex drive. Nor did I climb. What my body could do was finite. What the Earth could offer . . . Yosemite, the Calanques, Ruth Gorge, The Karakoram, the Mariana Trench . . . was known, boundaried, map-able. I took what Eliot said, 'And place is always and only place,' in the most negative sense possible. After the top of a 5.12 pitch, what then? A trail, a view, another 5.12 pitch? Nihilism may not be logical, but it is a self-supporting institution. Since there is no value, it is valueless to seek value. Since, after all, all you can discover is that there is no value, since obviously, there *is* no value. Et cetera.

People during this period were very kind. I received offers, advice, support from all over the world. Many of the calls I could not bear to take, the mail sat in stacks, too much trouble to read. Yet one day I opened one note at random. It was magic. I still have it memorized. 'You like to climb abroad? So climb *abroad*.' It had a photograph of Europa, one of Jupiter's larger moons, and a phone number of someone to contact at America's NASA. It was unsigned.

I don't know why, but the idea struck my fancy immediately. It was like turning on the burner of a gas range; a turn of the wrist, *poof*, instant flames. I was on my way to the States within 24 hours.

Houston, MIT, Washington, D.C., JPL in California . . . the project started growing in a dozen labs and centres. It was a slow time in the space business and they were delighted to have a new brain child to play with, provided I had the funds, which I did. It took all my resources and then some, but that was not particularly important. I have no dependents, I do not revel in the money for its own sake. Like an ice axe, it is a tool. In this case, a tool to take me to the penultimate in spectacular remoteness.

Europa is about the size of our moon, one out of 14 moons of Jupiter, and discovered in 1610 by Galileo. In mythology Europa was a mistress of Zeus, who sent Talus, the bronze giant, to watch over her. Modern astronomers have called this world 'an icy cue ball', a description as apt as any. Layered over the rocky core is a veneer of water ice 100 kilometres thick, making a total of 10 billion cubic kilometres of ice.

While Europa lacks the gigantic features of something like Mars' Olympus Mons, it does have a varied topography. Internal heating during Europa's infancy covered it with a slushy sea, which eventually froze. The ice has since fractured and splintered. Further eruptions of liquid water have frozen into sharp ridges. From a spy's-eye view in space these features look like a fanned array of tan scratches. My weight on Europa would be the Earth equivalent of only 22 U.S. pounds. Europa has no atmosphere.

The plan was simple. Frozen into a dreamless stasis I would be launched from Earth in a small ship, a voyage that would last many months. Aiming for a shallow valley near the equator, the ship would crash land: hopefully after having approached at an oblique-enough trajectory to skitter along for many kilometres while slowing down, rather than smashing up immediately. Climbers do love race car approaches! Then the computers cry wakey-wakey and out I crawl.

Once on Europa, I should have an oxygen and food supply large enough for six months, though the solar batteries in my suit would keep it operating much longer. The government had not been interested in underwriting me for the billions it would have taken to develop a returnable system, and I was not interested in waiting the years that would have taken. Mentally, I was prepared for the necessary suicide of a one-way trip.

The preparations for lift-off went smoothly. At last it was time to suit up, crawl into my cocoon, and drift into a mechanized hypothermia . . .

The ship slid a long way before stopping. I know that because later from a point on the canyon's walls I could see its track, stretching towards the horizon. Unfortunately for the folks back home many of the instruments – including the cameras – had been damaged in the landing. The original touch-down much have been more severe than intended, judging by the massive dents. But my first concern was not for Kodak's hardware, but with the view. It was . . . *awesome*. The scene flooded into my vision like a swollen torrent: I stared blinking, my jaw slack.

I was standing in a valley or broad canyon, with far-off cliffs on all parts of the horizon. Fracturing the centre of the valley was a pressure ridge that stood out like a freight train of dirty seracs. The sky was completely dark despite the sun (reduced four-fifths) being a hand above the horizon. Looking away from the sun I could see more stars than is ever possible from Earth. Light, slanting off the ice, occasionally pulsed and winked.

The most unearthly sight was Jupiter, which hung out of the sky like an immense orange Zeppelin, about to settle down on my head. I could see its cloud strata very clearly, and was amazed by its *presence*. Seeing it so close was almost like being directly watched over by a brooding and not necessarily benevolent God. Two other moons were in sight, remarkable in themselves but shot pellets compared to Jupiter. All my astronomy prepping flew out the figurative window as I stood there gaping. I felt the way John Muir must have felt when he first saw Yosemite Valley. After a while, hours probably, I finally started working around the ship, transmitting what data I could to Earth and setting up base camp.

The next several days were spent getting a feel for Europan climbing. The ice was both dirty and very hard, similar to Earth's black ice or portions of glacier ice. In many places the constant micrometeorite bombardment had peppered the surface with a thin, crunchy powder of ground ice particles, interspaced with black rock granules.

Some craters had this 'dust' blown away and the impact impression gleamed like a freshly scoured porcelain bowl. Due to the strength of the ice and the low gravity, I had to nick in my hand tools and front-points with the balance and held-breath delicacy that micro-hold face climbing requires.

The walls were rarely more than a few hundred metres high, but that was plenty. On a world where *everything* is for climbing, sheer verticality is not as important. The ice was very stable, at least as far as I encountered. My climbing took two forms usually; climbing-exploring, in which I tried to visit as much new terrain as possible, and climbing-bouldering – working on pure technique, for example long traverses on steep or overhung walls. Of the former, I enjoyed descents particularly.

Bounding five metres at a time I would leap down the cliffs and crater sides in exhilaration, setting new talus running records daily. I felt the definitions of my body changing and expanding with every wall. Of course I took several falls, but the insulation in my suit must have helped provide protection, and I never was hurt to the point of incapacitation, nor did I ever puncture my suit with the axe. The luck of fools?

I was never bored. Sometimes I held imaginary contests. I tried to see if I could throw an ice chip into orbit (not much luck on that), or I practiced lassoing seracs with my rappel rope, jumping high in the air with each toss. I had deliberately chosen to land on the side of Europa that always faces Jupiter. Day and night it put on an unending display. Crescent, half phase, fully illuminated . . . each moment brought a different characteristic into play.

For a portion of the day Jupiter eclipsed the sun, and when the sun first peeped out through the atmospheric 'edge' of Jupiter, the ice was bathed in blood red light. The night side of Jupiter was attractive as well; lightning storms the size of nuclear explosions raged visible in the clouds, while over the poles were faint auroras.

Like most accidents, mine happened as suddenly as a slap. Five days from my ship, where two major ice fractures came together, a type of icefall poured sharply over a large crater rim. Top to bottom was about 500 metres. Unweathered, the ice blocks were strangely twisted in sharp angles and weird fluting.

Absorbed in the maze of forms, I must have been concentrating less, for, near the top, I tried to jump across something too wide for me. Missing the other side, I fell straight down, like stepping into a hole in the dark. I swung out with my arms wildly as I went; my hand hit ice, and I banged deep inside the walls of a crevasse, falling down, down, down, scrabbling, trying to catch onto something.

Had the fall happened on Earth, I am positive that it would have been fatal. Europa was somewhat more lenient, and I ended up wedged head down in a dark chimney of ice. 'Um . . . up rope,' I joked weakly. I was completely stuck. No arm movement, no head movement, nothing. I listened to my own hoarse breathing for a moment, then tried to wriggle backwards. No luck. I tried again. No. Then again.

This time I managed to move a foot, scraping backwards with the frontpoints. This, of course, pushed me in the wrong direction. Twisting my knee I got the foot free and swept again, inching myself back to my original position. Pulling again, I was able to use both feet.

I moved up farther, able to work my hand under my chest and lever with that. After much grunting, I got turned around right side up. But without an axe, I was not sure of my ability to climb out once the chasm widened past chimney width. Still trembling from the fall, I started working my way upward.

I moved slowly, bridled by a new-felt caution. Even if I *had* chosen to die on Europa, I was in no way interested in dying before I had to. About 20 metres up I came to a faintly lit crawlway branching off from the main fissure. Thinking the light came from a shortcut out of the icefall, I wormed into it. It led me into a cavern filled with the most remarkable sight I have ever witnessed.

I was faced with a glowing ball of light. Spherical, orange, as big as me, it dominated the room the way Jupiter did the horizon, somewhere above. My first thought, after pure fear and surprise, was that it was a gas . . . methane . . . sulphur . . . *something*. But that just didn't seem right. I found I could not alter it . . . cause it to rise, settle, dissipate . . . make it react in any way.

There seemed to be the slightest surface tension when I put my arm (cautiously) into it, but I was not sure. It was completely astounding. I studied it from every angle, but had no clue to what it was, why it was there, what purpose it served, or if there were any other pockets of gas like it around the area. It gave off a soft, steady light, but apparently little or no heat, since the ice in the room was as firm as anywhere else on Europa. At last, puzzled but getting nowhere, my thoughts turned back towards the lengthy climb and long walk still ahead of me and I realized I would have to leave.

For one last experiment, I pushed myself as completely into the bubble as I could, so only my feet were outside. Then I gave a hop. It held! My heart was pounding like I was on the spookiest A5 around, but the gas sphere held my weight! I could recline inside of it, and not touch the ice cave floor.

After half an hour of fooling about, the thrill of this began to wear off. I had discovered right away that to get out all I had to do was jump down hard, my immediate concern as soon as I was in. Despite many contortions, I still could not make it react. Nice as the mysterious ball was to lie in, I still had to leave, and my thoughts turned again to the ship.

The sphere began to move. I immediately tried to jump out, but couldn't, even though I had done so many times during the past half hour. I ordered it to stop. It didn't. Squeezing itself out the entrance way, it moved into the crevasse and began rushing up, gaining momentum at an incredible rate.

In just a minute we were out of the icefall, and other than black above and greys below, everything went by in a blur. The sphere came to a joltless halt directly on top of the wreckage of my ship. When the motion stopped, I found I could again step down.

What to give the climber who has everything: a self-navigating flying carpet gas sphere. Experimenting over the next few days, I found I could go anywhere on the planet I'd already been to, including the crevasse, simply by visualizing the destination. I also could visit new areas, through complicated wish projections, or such hop-and-skip methods as picturing the entire moon, being put into orbit, then selectively narrowing my field of vision until we touched down where I wanted to explore.

All this would take only a few minutes. I was very careful not to think of anything deviant while in the sphere, of things such as nuclear explosions or sun spots or hideous science fiction monsters, or anything or place I did not want to visit. I was sure the bubble could turn into a real double-edged sword, and I was not, for once, anxious to test its limits.

I often wondered whose sphere it was to begin with and how it got to our solar system, whether it was natural or created, and whether or not it had any motion of its own. I tried visualizing other spheres, but went nowhere. Was it the wreckage of an interplanetary castaway? The lifeboat of a galactic Titanic? Who or what caused it to be inside the cave? Was it put there for safe keeping, or, like an abused slave, had it run away and hidden itself? I never have found out.

The time came when dwindling supplies forced me to lay plans for abandoning my new home, accustomed as I had grown to it. I had never taken the bubble beyond a very tight orbit of Europa, but felt confident somehow that it would be able to cross longer distances. I mulled over the possibilities. Around Jupiter alone were two more large, icy moons, Callisto and Ganymede.

Throughout the solar system were dozens of spots – from Mercury to Charon – I would like to explore. I thought, too, of the neighbouring stars . . . what marvels could I expect to find in the planetary systems of Centauri, Sirius, Wolf 359? More distantly, what of other galaxies . . . other universes?

I thought also of Earth. Rustling laurel leaves, the voice of a friend, butter pecan ice cream, the smell of wet meadows, the greenness of moss under a damp rock. Sentimental things, but things I had a hunger for in a way that I had never felt before Europa had provided a scenery which almost overwhelmed my capacity for appreciation and supplied also an ideal environment in which to explore extreme physical movement.

Even so, I felt deprived . . . lacking. I had been on Europa seven months. Supplies were very low. I was unsure if I could connect the ship's stasis units up inside of the magic sphere. Contrasting with that homesickness, over and over a second voice cried out, insisting itself into my consciousness. It wanted more climbing, wider horizons, stronger flavours, that final, ultimate wall. It made me stare up at the vast fields of stars, and rub my fingers across my helmeted chin, wondering . . .

I landed first on an uninhabited atoll I knew of near the Cooks, spending a week there stuffing myself with fresh fish and coconuts, swimming every day in warm, caressing water, holding shells to my ear, and getting a delightful sunburn. I visited a number of places after that, spending the past eight months enjoying more things than I ever had appreciated before, including some low level climbing, for shape's sake. Money for provisions was easily found. Who can arrest an orange ball of gas?

It hovers now behind a thick wall of jungle foliage, filled to the brim with star charts, supplies, and the accoutrements of an expedition. How I'll find room for both myself and Terry, my girlfriend, I'm not sure. Tonight I'll finish typing this and we'll have that much more room, anyway.

We leave tomorrow at sunrise.

Night Out

by Al Alvarez

IT WAS unthinkable that it should snow. After all, it was mid-August, and the sharp, yellow Dolomite peaks were baked hard and dry, like biscuit. When the sky darkened and the first sloppy flakes began to fall, the older man thought he was seeing things – it's a delusion, for God's sake; this is August. He huddled back against the rock for comfort and stared out at the darkening air.

Above him, the younger man began to climb faster, moving up the garish overhanging wall from piton to piton anxiously, with a certain tension, as though something were snapping at his heels. 'Christ.' He clipped his rope into the next piton. 'Christ.' He clipped in his étrier. 'Christ.' He swung himself up onto the bottom rung. 'Christ, Christ, Christ,' he muttered in time with each movement. Finally, he reached a small ledge, clipping himself in so that the ropes held him like a cradle. He was half on, half off the ledge, his feet dangling in space. The flakes thickened around him. 'Come on!' he shouted into the void.

There was a long, irritating pause while the older man unclipped himself from the nest of pitons and fiddled awkwardly with the ropes and slings around him. 'Come onnnn' – the voice from above was faint but urgent. 'Okay, okay,' muttered the older man and shouted loudly, 'Cliiimbiiing!' His ledge under its overhang was spacious and comfortable, as those ledges go. He stood up carefully, reluctantly, hooked a finger through a piton beside him, and stretched up and out. On tiptoe, he could just reach a piton in the jutting lip of the overhang. When he clipped an étrier into it, the thing hung a couple of feet out from the rock. He kicked his foot into the bottom rung and heaved, lurching into space. He clipped on a second étrier for his other foot and then hung at the edge of the overhang, peering over it inquisitively, as though over a garden fence. The sticky snow was already picking out the nicks and flat places on the great wall above. It loomed over him enormous, its pale yellow and orange glinting through the snow. The air was crowded with flakes.

There was a tug on the rope at his waist. He glanced up angrily, but could see nothing except the rope leading away into the next tier of overhangs where the younger man was hidden. 'Just you wait,' he said to the rock in front of his nose. He began to climb carefully toward the first piton, thirty feet above. The wall was almost vertical and the holds were small. Fingertips, tips of the toes, he picked his way upward delicately, in a trance of concentration, body away from the rock, balance ready to be shifted at the first faint tremor of a mistake. His mind was blank, all his awareness gone into the poise and counterpoise between hands and feet, fingertips, tips of the toes. He paused occasionally to clear the snow from the tiny incut holds he was moving on, but the weather no longer impinged on him, off in his world elsewhere. Toward the top of the free section, nearing the safety of the piton, he stretched wide with his right foot to a little snow-covered hold one inch long, half an inch wide. His toe, probing it, suddenly skidded on the snow, his balance swung violently off true, and his whole weight came on his fingers. 'Jesus Christ.' His heart lurched like his body. He moved quickly, desperately upward and grabbed the karbiner dangling from the piton. Struggling, he got an étrier into place, stood in it, and hung there panting, frightened. The wall soared away from him on each side, a quarter of a mile wide; between him and the scree slopes six hundred feet below there was only the swirling snow. His legs were trembling; his hands felt weak. It was minutes before the shaking stopped. Then he began to move mechanically up the artificial section from piton to piton: clip, step, stretch, clip, bend, unclip, step, stretch, clip, bend, unclip . . .

Arms aching, he reached the younger man on the ledge. 'What are we going to do about this, then?' He gestured at the darkening air.

'Damn all. We can't go down, so we'll have to go up.'

'How much more is there, do you think?' He tried not to sound anxious.

'I dunno. Maybe a couple of pitches of overhangs – not much more than two hundred feet. After that, it's straightforward.' The younger man paused. When his companion said nothing, he added, 'I wonder what the time is.'

'About three, maybe. I wish we'd brought a watch.'

'Well, that gives us four, four and a half hours of light. Don't worry. I think we've cracked it.'

'There's another thousand feet after the overhangs,' the older man said doubtfully.

'Yes, but easy, easy VS – nothing to worry about.' The younger man had sorted his ropes out by this time and moved away from the ledge into the next set of overhangs. 'It looks all right,' he called reassuringly. 'Quite straightforward. Piece of cake.'

The older man sucked at his pipe and paid the rope out carefully so that it should not drag at his companion's waist. The snow shut him in on his ledge among the overhangs, yet he was dimly aware of the wall stretching endlessly away from him on each side and of the great poised mass above, waiting to be climbed. 'You've done it now,' he said aloud. The sound of his own voice startled him; it seemed impertinent. The rope moved out, round his waist and between his hands, steadily but with terrible slowness. He glanced down once into the void below and felt his senses swim, almost with pleasure. After that he stared at the moving snow in front and didn't look down again. Occasionally, he could hear the faint ringing of a piton being hammered in somewhere above him. A dislodged stone sighed past, a few feet out in space.

There was a long wait until the rope above him was pulled tight. He stood up gingerly, resigned. Then the heaving and struggling began again as he moved cannily, with increasing weariness, toward the next ledge. His arms ached from the tips of his fingers to the base of his shoulder blades. The cold of the rock and the cold of the metal equipment were numbing. But his fingers were still good; they opened and shut on order, could grip, pull, fiddle with ropes and étriers and karabiners. I'm not that old yet, he thought. A voice in his head said, 'Keep your cool. It's fear that makes you weak, not fatigue. Open the valve and the pressure drops. Think about that. Fear makes you weak, not fatigue.' He paused, listening to the idiot mumble. His own voice. 'I'm losing my grip,' he said.

He was through the big overhangs now and standing at the foot of a slightly oververtical wall. The aluminium rungs of the étriers felt reassuring against his insteps. His toes were against the rock. He hooked his waist loop into a karabiner, lowered his arms, shook his hands briskly like a dog shaking himself after a swim, and craned up at the wall. A line of pitons led up a diagonal crack to where the younger man was perched. No problem. He moved up carefully, measuring out his effort like medicine.

When he reached the younger man, they stood side by side, backs against the rock, the toes of their boots protruding into space.

'Comfy?' The younger man smiled.

'You've got snow on your eyebrows.'

'And you've got snow on your beard. You look like Father bloody Christmas.'

They fiddled with the ropes, arranging the belay.

'Not far now,' said the younger man.

'Please God.'

'One more pitch and we've cracked it.'

'Please God. It's getting late. I wish the snow would ease up. I hate the filthy stuff.'

The younger man stood up, jammed his fingers in a crack, and heaved himself off the ledge. 'Don't wait up,' he said, and began to move cautiously toward the first piton twenty feet above. The snow was thicker now and was gaining a purchase on the rock, despite the steepness. It made the footholds seem uncertain and inadequate, as though they had been shrunk and greased by the weather. His fingers were very cold. He paused when he reached the piton and looked down. He could see the older man's bearded face peering anxiously up at him through the snow. He was glad to feel the protecting rope through the piton at waist level.

'No trouble so far,' he called cheerfully.

'What's it like above?' came back his companion's querulous voice.

I wish he'd stop nagging, the younger man thought. He looked up. The wall above was steep and blank; nothing doing. But off to the right was a line of small holds, powdered with snow, a piton at the end of them. The problem was how to reach them. 'Fine!' he shouted into space. There was a sudden flurry of snow, which made him sway slightly where he perched. He muttered, 'Why won't it leave off?' and tentatively stretched up his right hand. The tips of two fingers found a nick; the foothold was a rugosity the size of the knuckle of his thumb. He moved up, holding his breath. To the right was another nick, another rugosity. He slid one left fingertip beside his right, steadied himself, slid a second left fingertip into the nick, and stretched his right hand toward the next hold. It was small and cold and wet. He steadied himself again, gave a little hop, and got his left toes where his right had been. Despite the cold, he was sweating. Warm and dry, this kind of climbing was pure pleasure; now it was agony. He paused, gathering himself for the next sequence. 'Is he going to crack?' he muttured, uncertain if he meant the other man or himself.

On his ledge, the older man stared out at the snow. It swirled round him, blotting out the scree far below. The air seemed darker; he wondered idly what time it was. The rope leading to his companion seemed hardly to move; idly, he wished the younger man would climb a little faster. 'It must be hard if he's moving so slowly,' he said to himself. But he slid away from this thought, letting his mind go blank. There was nothing to be done.

It was another hour before the younger man pulled onto the great ledge that split the cliff at half height. He could feel it was late and knew they were climbing too slowly. Still, it was a pleasure to have room to move freely. He arranged a belay, pulled in the slack rope, and stretched himself out luxuriously while his companion climbed. But he was careful to keep the rope between them continually tight; he didn't want the old fool to come off.

The rope came in surprisingly fast. There was one ominous pause when the older man reached the hard section. The younger man braced himself, expecting the worst. then the rope came in steadily again. Good on you, he thought, and said aloud, 'Thank Christ.'

Finally, the older man heaved himself painfully onto the ledge.'God, that was hard,' he said.

'You shot up it. Bloody good.'

'I wouldn't have led it,' the older man replied. The strain had made them polite to each other, like strangers. 'I'm creased,' he added.

The younger man looked at him anxiously. The older man's face was drawn and grey, his thin beard streaky with melting snow. 'Shove you on a cross and you'd make a grand Christ.'

'Don't joke. I'm on it already.' He sat down heavily, with a little grunting noise. 'Where do we go from here?'

The younger man was still sitting, looking out into the snow. He jerked his head back and up, as though he didn't want to look.

A funnel of loose scree ran up from the ledge to the foot of a great corner where two walls opened like a monstrous book of stone. Though vertical, they were reassuringly seamed with cracks and broken at intervals with ledges. High above they disappeared into the clouds, and from out of the clouds, through the swirling snow, a waterfall fell sheer from ledge to ledge. It was the snow melting on the warmer rocks of the summit, which earlier had been touched by the sun. The older man craned up at the looming rock and the icy grey water they would have to climb through; it seemed disproportionate to their strength. 'I'm tired,' he said.

'We've got to get motoring,' said the younger man, getting glumly to his feet. 'It must be gone five o'clock already.'

'We're not going to get off tonight,' the older man said.

'Let's get motoring,' the younger man repeated, and he scrambled up the scree toward the foot of the corner. The older man stood up and resettled the rucksac on his shoulders. He remembered how that morning they had taken out all their bivouac gear and dumped it in the tent. 'We'll climb faster with a light sack,' the younger man had said, and he had agreed. The dawn had been bright, cloudless, and unusually warm. Why lumber oneself with a lot of extra stuff for emergencies that never happen? 'If we climb light, we'll knock the bastard off in eight hours and be back at the hut by six, swilling minestrone,' the younger man had said confidently. Of course. Of course. Maybe the dawn had been a bit too warm, but who would ever have dreamed it would snow?

I'm going to die, the older man thought. He received the idea flatly and without any emotion, as though it were a piece of information he had known for a long time, like his name or his address or the make of his car. We are both going to freeze to death. Nothing to be done about it. He held this piece of knowledge like a stone, heavy, obdurate, and gradually bruising. What a bleeding silly way to go. He had a momentary glimpse of the face of his child, vivid but a long way off, as though peering down a narrow shaft at him from the light. 'Idiot,' he muttered. 'You've really done it now.'

There was a tug from the rope at his waist. 'Come on!' the younger man shouted from above.

The older man felt old and heavy; there seemed no end to the rock or the unforgiving steepness. Though he climbed as fast as he could, he knew he should be going faster. And all the time the icy water streamed down on him. It ran down his sleeves whenever he raised his arms to reach for a hold; when he looked up, it got in under the hood of his anorak, soaking his neck and oozing down his back; it ran down his legs and squelched in his boots. The stone bumped again in the pit of his stomach. 'What a bleeding stupid way to die,' he said out loud.

They climbed on dully. Occasionally, the older man would complain of his exhaustion and the other would say, 'I know. Me too. But we've got to keep motoring.' At the end of every pitch, both men would crane up hopefully, thinking that the top was near.

Gradually, the snow stopped and the gunmetal clouds cleared away. It was evening. The light was cold blue, the rocks around them blue with water, the ground far below bluish and misty, the peaks in the distance blue.

The older man pulled heavily onto a ledge where the younger was sitting. 'This is it,' the younger man said. 'We'd better bivouac. I can hardly see the holds anymore.'

The older man grunted. The ledge was about two and a half feet long, and less than two feet wide. 'Isn't there anything better above?' he asked.

'I don't want to risk it. It's too dark. There may be nothing.'

The older man grunted again.

'If we get organized a bit, we'll be right cosy,' the younger man said. 'The Lavaredo Hilton. Bang a couple of pegs into the crack behind you for a nice strong belay. Coil the ropes and sit on them. It'll be fine.' He sounded unconvinced.

'Of course it will,' the older man said reassuringly. Now they had stopped climbing, their roles had subtly shifted; it was his turn to be cheerful. He twisted round on the narrow ledge and started to hammer in a piton. For a while, they worked away in silence, coiling the ropes and stringing a spider's web of slings from their waists to the pitons bristling around them. The rest of their equipment – the pitons, karabiners, and slings that festooned them, and the spares that filled the sack – they clipped neatly into the same pitons until the walls round their ledge were as crowded as an old-fashioned ironmonger's. Then they took off their boots, tied them together, and hung them also from the pitons. Carefully, they peeled off their waterlogged socks, wrung them out, and put them back on their feet. Then they took off their shirts and twisted them cumbersomely until the water streamed out. The younger man wore only a shirt and a sweater, the older a string vest, a shirt, and an anorak. Everything was drenched, but at least they were protected from the waterfall by an overhang above.

It was almost night now and a few stars glinted in the cold. The older man towelled himself vigorously with his shirt. 'Fair warms you up,' he said. 'Let's see what else there is in the sack.' He rummaged around and pulled out a pair of old mittens, which they shared – the older man took the right mitten, since his right hand was on the outside; the younger man took the left. There was also a tube of nylon fabric designed to clip onto the top of the rucksac; with one's feet in the canvas bottom, the nylon extension could be pulled up to one's chin and sealed off with a drawstring. The sack and the extension together would have meant a warm night for one person. The men looked at them enviously and with regret.

'You stick your feet in the sack,' said the younger man. 'I'll wrap mine up in the extension.'

'Sure?'

'Sure. It's all the same, anyway.'

Finally, the older man pulled from a bottom corner of the rucksac a crumpled paper bag with six sweets in it and two old lumps of cheese. 'Thank God,' he said. 'I could eat the skin off a skunk's back. We'd better hang on to one bit of cheese and a couple of sweets for the morning.'

'Right,' said the younger man, as if he, too, believed that the morning would be their concern.

They settled into position, chewing gratefully on the food. The sac reached over the older man's knees; the younger wrapped his feet in the flimsly nylon tube as carefully as he might have wrapped a Christmas present.

We have prepared our own graves, the older man thought. And he accepted this idea, in its turn, as factually as if it were the date of his birthday.

'The important thing is not to sleep,' the younger man said. 'It lowers the body temperature.'

'Okay,' said his companion. And within seconds exhaustion had taken them both; they were fast asleep.

It seemed as though they had nodded off for less than a minute. Yet when they woke the air was colder, darker, and the stars were thick in the sky. The moon, rising behind their mountain, lit up the far peaks and made great pools of blackness in the valley below. There was no wind. From a long way off, a cowbell clanked in the darkness.

The older man pounded his hands together. 'Christ, I'm cold.'

'Tell you what,' the younger man said. 'Brace yourself a moment.' He twisted round and pummelled the other man's chest and shoulders with his fists. 'Now you me ... There. That's better. It gets the circulation going.'

The older man fumbled with his pipe, the flame of his lighter making a little pool of warmth in the blue dark. 'You should smoke,' he said. 'It warms you up.'

They huddled close and were silent. The older man pounded his hands together again. 'How about a song?' he said and began immediately, '"My old man said follow the van . . ."'

'"And don't dillydally on the way,"' the younger man joined in.

'"Off went the van with my home packed in it . . ."'

The noise of their singing insulated them from the icy blue silence of the mountain. But when they stopped the night seemed larger and more profound.

'How long have you been divorced?' the younger man said at last.

'Three years.'

'What's it like?'

'Painful and expensive. Why?'

'I've just left my wife.'

'I'm sorry.'

'I'm not.'

'Any children?'

'You must be joking. She kept her pills on the kitchen table. In the cruet where the vinegar should have been. We weren't taking any chances. It was never good enough for that.'

'When did you leave?'

'A couple of weeks ago. Just before I came out here.'

'It's a nasty business.'

'Not as nasty as that marriage. I'm glad to be out.'

'Sure.'

The older man lit his pipe again. There was a long silence. Little by little, the younger man's head nodded onto his companion's shoulder. The older man put his arm round him protectively. Poor bastard, he thought. Let him sleep a bit. Then he, too, nodded off.

He had a moment of pure terror, vivid as an electric shock. A boulder was leaning out on him, pushing him off the ledge, while someone shone a torch in his eyes. When he jerked awake, one buttock was completely off the ledge and the ropes tying him to the rock were taut. The younger man was slumped heavily across him, and when the older man's sudden movement woke him he grabbed at his arm in panic and drew in his breath sharply, as though in pain. 'I was dreaming,' he said apologetically.

The moon had swung round the shoulder of the mountain. It surveyed the two men dispassionately, its cold light glinting on the walls of rock.

'I'm freezing,' the older man said, and meant it. His fingers were numb and stiff.

Again they went through the ritual pounding and pummelling. This time it was much longer before their blood moved less sluggishly and they were comfortable.

'We've got to stay awake,' the younger man said.

'I know,' said the other. 'Do you know the one about the Young Lady of

Barking Creek?' Deliberately and without much pleasure, they swapped limericks and stories while the moon moved slowly out of sight; it had lost interest in them. As the darkness returned, each new story became a physical effort, like another pitch of the climb, and sleep weighed in on them.

Again they sang songs, but now their voices sounded frail and intrusive in the cold, enclosing stillness. Slowly, somewhere out of sight, the moon went down. As the night grew blacker and more icy, their silences became longer, their wits slowed, and the world froze to a halt. One more song, then one more song, and then another song. They seemed to be listening to their own voices from a long way off, small and eerie and distorted, like a record running down. Their bodies felt dull and heavy, as though the blood itself were freezing in their veins.

At last they nodded off again, and when they awoke the air was cold as a knife. The feeling had gone again in the older man's fingers and the right sleeve of his soaked anorak was stiff with frost. The younger man's feet were numb. Now they pounded away at each other and themselves with despair, swearing dully all the time, until at last they huddled together exhausted. There was nothing to do but sit and wait. The older man stared blankly out at the black desert of vertical rock. Then he squinted and rubbed his swollen fingers across his eyes.

'Look!' He pointed. 'The sky's changing. It must be almost dawn.'

The younger man peered out unconvinced. The wall of rock to his left was faintly edged with grey. 'I think we're going to make it,' he said tentatively, as though scared of the idea. It was the first time that either had mentioned that they might not.

The older man breathed on his swollen fingers. It seemed to him curious that his breath should be so warm while he was so cold. He peered out again at the barely perceptible edge of grey. Maybe it was just a cloud on the night sky. The stars were still as sharp as needles.

'I've got to be in Chamonix the day after tomorrow,' the younger man said brightly, since the future now seemed possible again.

The older man laughed. 'Well, you're going to have to get motoring, as you would say.'

The younger man pounded his feet vigorously. 'What about you?'

'I dunno. I think this is enough for one season. Maybe I'll go back to London. As well there as here.'

'What about your kid?' the younger man asked gently.

'Oh, he's off with his mother somewhere. Greece, I think. God knows.' His swollen fingers made him awkward with his pipe and lighter. 'It's a miracle the wind dropped,' he said.

'We'd have been in trouble if it hadn't,' said the younger man.

'Dead trouble.'

Slowly, as though they were reluctant to leave, the stars grew faint and the grey spread. The men stayed huddled together, for it was still too cold to move.

At last the older man took out the little piece of cheese and cut it carefully in half. 'We'd better eat,' he said without relish. The stuff tasted like putty – heavy, damp, cold. They chewed it dully as a duty, then sucked slowly on the boiled sweets, making them last.

The sky lightened gradually, its dirty grey shading into a faint whitish blue. They heaved themselves reluctantly to their feet and began to sort out the equipment. The metal was so cold it hurt their hands, and their boots were hard as stone.

'Hit the buggers with your piton hammer,' the younger man said. 'That'll knock some softness into them.' So they beat vindictively at the frozen leather, as though the boots were to blame for their troubles.

'Maybe I should do the same to my feet,' said the younger man, 'to get some feeling back into them.'

'Allow me,' said his companion.

'How are your fingers?'

'Like your feet – swollen and stupid. Will you tie my laces for me? I can't. Sorry.'

Elsewhere, the sun began to rise, but though the sky grew steadily lighter, the north face they were on stayed cold and dark. They fumbled with the equipment, checking and rechecking, putting off the moment when they would have to move. At last, the younger man stepped out onto the wall and pulled himself up into the overhang. He stayed there a long time, his feet dangling, his top half out of sight. The older man could hear the chink-chink of his hammer on the rock. There was a brief, convulsive struggle, and his feet disappeared over the overhang. Then a pause.

'For God's sake watch it. There's ice all over the holds.' His voice was like a young boy's, light and strained. He was panting.

It was half an hour before the rope went tight at the older man's waist. He stood up, untied his belay, and leaned out over the wall. It was then he realized he was exhausted. His arms and legs were like wood – heavy and stiff and useless. When he slotted his swollen fingers into a hold, he could feel nothing. He pulled experimentally and nothing happened. 'Oh God,' he said. He put his fingers to his mouth and blew on them; he rubbed them violently together. Still nothing. With a spurt of blind anger and frustration, like a child with a broken toy, he started banging them against the rock face until blood came and they began to ache dully. 'Take a grip on yourself,' he said sharply. He leaned out onto the wall again, reached up until his fingers curled over the lip of the overhang, concentrated his will in a kind of knot of hatred, as though this were the last enemy, and pulled. His body tightened, faltered, lurched. He got his other swollen hand jammed in a crack above the overhang, pulled again, and was over the lip. He lay with his face against the cold rock, panting heavily as a dog. 'Maybe we died last night. How could we tell?' He giggled, faltered, and was quiet. Gently, he pushed himself upright, so that he was standing in balance again, and looked up. The rock stretched up vertically and without relief – up and up into the pale morning sky. Above him were shields of thin ice, jaggedly scarred where the younger man had hammered clear the holds.

He stood for a moment, studying the next moves. His heart bumped steadily and he felt warmer, suppler. They were going to live. He moved again up the rock, tentatively, with infinite caution, as though on tiptoe. He had the weird, illogical conviction that the ice had made the rock face itself as fragile as his balance – one false move and the whole mass would slide away beneath him like a pack of cards. He climbed on, scarcely daring to breathe. When he reached the younger man on his ledge, the two of them spoke in whispers. Obscurely, they both sensed that this was the crisis; the mountain was making its play, and their continued existence, for the moment, was an impertinence.

They rested for a while, glad of each other's company. When the younger man finally stood up, the older man whispered, 'Good luck.' The younger man nodded silently, and they smiled at each other.

The older man puffed at his pipe and stared at the far peaks, lit now by the sun. The rope went out slowly, very slowly, and the day grew warmer. Finally, he heard a faint, cheerful shout from above and the rope was taken in. He stood up, put his pipe in his pocket, and flexed his swollen fingers. The air was quiet. For a brief moment, he saw his child again, but this time quite close; he seemed to be shouting something. Then his mind emptied as quickly and utterly as an upturned glass. He began to climb.

The Old Man's Pigeon Loft

by Dave Gregory

HE'S A devious bugger, the old man, Devious. And he makes himself out to be such a straightforward man of steel. 'I'm a man of simple tastes,' he keeps saying. 'I'll try anything once' is another of his favourite dictums. Not that you hear him in conversation all that often. He spends most of his time in his pigeon loft swopping coos with them – or on it. There can't be a piece of roofing felt which comes loose within a mile radius of us but it finishes up nailed to the roof of his loft. I keep telling him it's about time he built himself a new one but he's always got some good reason for keeping with the present one.

I give him a hand occasionally, holding one side up while he nails a spar to the other to delay its disintegration by a few weeks. He never gives up trying to get me interested in the pigeons but once bitten, twice shy. You only need one experience of pigeons clawing on your shirt-front, picking hairs off your chest, to realize that seeing them in a pie is close enough. But the Old Man's pigeons never get into pies. Most pass on by just not getting back from a race. Those that actually keel over on their perch get a little corner of our back garden to themselves.

He never asks me to help on a Wednesday night because he knows we go either to the wall or to a crag if the nights are light. But any other night I can't get away from being pestered to hold this or paint that. That particular Thursday I was going round to Jim's to settle where we were going at the weekend but he got me to promise to be back early to help him rehang the loft door. I was back early enough, as it happened: Jim was in bed, sent there by his mother. One leg in a pot up to the crutch and his shoulder immobilised by strapping. Apparently someone had dropped a piece of scrap steel which lodged in one of the holes in the slotted steel steps on the stairway up to the top level of the shop. Jim, rushing as usual, had tripped on the piece of scrap and done well not to finish up head first in an ingot mould. I had a face as long as a fiddle when I got back. 'What's up lad, had he remembered tha owed him a fiver?' I hadn't the heart to think up a suitably cutting reply and he took pity on me. He talked. 'Why so glum? Tha's not brokken thy leg.' I carefully explained about it needing two to climb as well as tango but he was well ahead of me. 'What about thi other mates?' They would already be organized for this weekend, I told him, and wouldn't want to climb as a three. 'Well lad, Ah'll cum wi'thi.' I didn't laugh. He likes to be taken seriously. I started to explain about his lack of expertise and his advancing age and so on and he heard me out. It appeared that he didn't actually go to sleep when he was slumped in front of the telly. He knew all about having to have a second man and sliding down the rope after to get the 'bit's o' metal' out. 'Tha can do 'em and slide down to get the bits out and if tha teks an old pair o' thi little booits Ah'll have a do at an easy un. After all,' he began, but I beat him to it: 'Ah'll try anything once.' The bargain wasn't finished yet. Saturday he'd 'tek thi climbin' and Sunday morning we'd do a repair or two to the loft. I knew why it had to be Sunday morning. If the job spread a bit, or the loft fell down I wouldn't be hard-hearted enough to refuse to help him in the afternoon. I made one last feeble effort: 'I'd a thought tha'd a'wanted to go to Church Sunday morning.' I said. 'Try anything once?'

'Ah've tried it once,' he said, 'and that were fifty-fifty good and bad.' 'How come?' I said, falling right in.

'Well, Ah got thi mam, that were fifty per cent good and then Ah got thee and that ruined it.' And he looked straight at me and smiled and I felt fond of the old sod and could see the charm that had captivated my mother. And I knew he'd 'tek mi climbing' even if I didn't help with the loft.

We went to Stanage, he with his ex-army respirator case and his snap-in-two overlapping ex-army mess tins and his tea in a thermos with a cork, a cork for God's sake, and all the paint worn off. He was as good as his word. I did a couple and abseiled down for the gear and he did an 'easy un' – all arms and panting – but he got up. I was halfway up the next when Mick and Tom rolled up. 'Wheer's Jim?' they shouted up, and 'Who's your new second man?' I didn't need to explain. He told the tale and finished with 'an Ah think Ah sall stop him if it come to.' And they looked at him standing there in his Bedford cords with braces and a belt and his striped flannel shirt, collarless but with a stud, and his white pinny and they wondered. But although he's only five foot six he's built like a brick shit-house is the Old Man and they didn't laugh, and they looked at the rope going through his gnarly, battered hands and thought that perhaps he would, if it came to. In fact there'd have to be a sight more than nine stone of me on the end before the length of eleven mil he'd got hold of got to moving more than a touch. The Old Man seemed to get on well with the other two but I was very surprised by what developed when we packed up for the day. They asked me along next Wednesday but I said I'd spend an hour on the cutting wall and then go round to Jim's with a six-pack. Tom was on afternoons and that left Mick on his own. To my amazement the Old Man offered to hold his rope. Mick must have thought of those capable-looking hands and said, 'You're on.'

We spent a fair old time on the loft. The Old Man put his foot through the roof at an especially rotten patch and we found a great section of rotten floor. I hadn't the heart to pull his leg and he nodded a bit grey-faced when I said it wanted mending with a new one and that it might cost a few bob or two. We finished on the loft about two o'clock. 'A bodge-up, lad,' he said gravely and spent the best part of the rest of the day in gloomy thought. It took him a couple of days to throw off his blues and forget about the doom to come. He came out with me a few times while Jim was off and we usually finished in the same area as Mick and Tom and their mates. He talked with them a fair bit but for the most part he was very preoccupied. He spent two evenings at the Working Men's Club, 'talking to Alf Bown's lad,' and a couple more talking to the pigeon club secretary. I asked my mother what he was up to. 'It'll be to do with the loft, lad.' 'I can see that, but who's Alf Bown's lad – a pigeon fancier?' Apparently not, he worked in the drawing office at Brown's. He probably orders roofing felt for the steel combine – a good contact he'd be.

He got quite thick with Jim, who kept on hopping round on his pot leg. One Saturday Mick got some overtime, unheard-of of late, and Tom and I went out for the day. When we got back the house was abuzz. Mam and my auntie Beth were laying a table to the ceiling with snap. Dad and Uncle Fred were whirling round a three-quarter finished, brand-new loft, brandishing hammers with a mouthful of nails apiece. A diminishing stack of brand-new timber was piled up against the house back-wall. Alf Bown's lad was sitting on a chair with a drawing board and a blueprint and a cutting list, directing operations. Jim was propped against a 'Workmate' waving a panel saw. His girlfriend, rather attractively dressed for the part in a pair of dungarees, was ferrying timber lengths from the saw-bench to the hammer men.

'Where's the pigeon club secretary?' I said to Mam. 'He's got enough to do,' she said, pushing me on one side on her way to the table, 'without getting under my feet.' 'He's tekken yer Dad's pigeons to that empty loft at number 23 and he'll be feeding 'em now. Go and get washed and shout that lot in.'

They went about ten o'clock and when they'd gone the Old Man said: 'Shall you help us to finish it off tomorrow then, lad?'

'Ay, I will you crafty old sod. You've oppen'd your wallet then? I thought I saw a cloud of moths when I came in.'

He allowed himself a smile. 'Tha knows nowt,' he said. 'That Joe, a mate of thi mate Mick, that Ah've tekken climbing, he's a joiner. He's working on that new housing estate at Wincobank, and he's got a van. Nah ter bed, we've a fair bit ter do tomorra.'

'Tha't devious,' I said, as I opened the door to the stairs. 'Devious.' But he got the last word in.

'Eh up,' he said, as I started up. 'Shall yer see that Louie on Wednesday?'

'I might.'

'Well gi' him a message. I'm ready for the paint anytime he likes. Friday ud do, then tha can gi me a hand at t'weekend.' But I had escaped upstairs. 'Good for thi arm strength, painting is,' came faintly through the bedroom door.

For Everything Its Season

by John Long

IT'S BEEN seven years since Steve Alexander broke this story down at a Mexican restaurant in the mountain hamlet of Idyllwild, after a day's climbing at Tahquitz Rock. The Cochran brothers were there, big strapping twins who the next winter were swept off Peak 60 in the Pamirs by an avalanche. And Art DeSaussure was there too. That was before he became an international star, before Nuptse and K2. He was 20 or 21 then and was overwhelming for all his energy and questions but we put up with him because he reminded us of ourselves at that age, so anxious to make a name for himself and ready to try any climb, anywhere. Four years later, Art died trying to repeat the very climb which he hounded Steve Alexander into telling us about: the landmark first ascent of the Citadel in Sequoia National Park, California.

Art put the question right to him. What about the Citadel? Steve had made the first ascent with Russ Owens, another legendary climber who had vanished after the Citadel climb. Some say Russ simply quit climbing and went to Spain where his mother was born or was a beachcomber in the Solomon Islands, for he was a known loner; but no one ever saw him again. Twelve years had passed since the Citadel climb and no one had repeated it, though many tried. And twelve years had never gotten Steve to say one word about it. But that Art got right in Alexander's face – the kid had to know – and we all thought Alexander was going to go off on him because Alexander was like that. Maybe it was the beer, or the fact that Steve's climbing career was virtually over that made him freeze the kid with a stare and, palms up, say: 'You got to know, do you?!' Art nodded slowly. Alexander looked toward the ceiling, cackled, and yelled out for another beer. He glowered at us all in turn, then laughed in our faces.

'Yea, I'll tell you bastards all right, because I don't care what comes of it anymore.' Alexander didn't care about anything – we all knew that – so I was surprised that he once cared about something, whatever it was. He turned his palms over, glared at us all again, and after the beers came, started his story.

'Everyone knows who Russ Owens was and what he did but there's hardly anyone around now who remembers what he was like. I'm not sure I remember, or ever really knew, because I only did the one climb with him. But I'll tell you right now, these young hotshots today aren't the shit on his boots. None of them. All the pink jumpsuits and diamond earrings and funk diets and Olympian workouts. And just look what they're doing wanking around these scrappy little cliffs, where every toehold's chalked and all the gamble's been engineered away. And they call it 'worldclass'. She-it. . . Now Russ, he couldn't be bothered with anything but the biggest, wildest stuff, stuff you'd look up at and want to dig yourself a hole and crawl inside just to hide from it. Stuff like the Citadel.

'Anyhow, climbers back then were all broke and they all drove junkers. I remember starting for the Citadel in Russ's old Volkswagen van and how it backfired all the way up the Grapevine Pass. He threw it into neutral and we started the long coast into the Bakersfield basin and man, it had to be 100 degrees in that van. He hadn't said one word since we'd left Los Angeles, two hours back. He never talked much. I guess that's why people thought he was arrogant.

'I was 22 then and his invitation to join him on the Citadel caught me totally off-guard. I knew that the Citadel had twice defeated Russ and my brother Vic. You'll remember that the previous winter, Russ and Vic had gone to the Karakoram to climb Nameless Tower. They did all their climbing together, though they never hung out off the cliffside. Some say theirs was the best alpine partnership of all time, but who knows. Well, Vic got killed on Nameless Tower. Russ claimed Vic had slipped off an easy shelf near the summit, and fell to his death. Now my brother was one of the best alpinists in the world – he and Russ had done the most outrageous stuff anyway – so I never could buy that business about slipping off easy ground. Whatever. After Vic fell Russ went ahead and climbed the last ice field and bagged the summit. It was probably this climb, the first ascent of the peak, and the North face at that, which made Russ Owens so legendary. He descended in a whiteout, or so he said, and he never found Vic's body. But I wonder if he ever even looked. I thought that was really cold for Russ to just leave my brother like that so he could make the climb. The climbing community didn't know what to make of it, but a few besides myself wondered about the whole affair. But you can't prove anything, so in a few months the whole thing was just another alpine tragedy, a statistic.

'So there I was, heading to attempt the Citadel; and I didn't give a damn about it. I came to find out about Vic. The truth had to come out over the next few days. I'd feel things out and force the issue if I had to. Who could say what was going through Russ's head, or why he'd invited me? It was plenty awkward just sitting there – no music or nothing. Every few minutes I'd glance over at him but his eyes never left the road and he never said a word.

'We finally got to Sequoia National Park around midnight and Russ parked behind the annexe because he knew someone there. Right off he dragged the packs out of the van and asked, "You ready?" Ready? Ready for what? Here the van was still dieseling and this guy's set to thrash the four miles into the Citadel! I couldn't reckon what was driving him. I shouldered my pack and we hit the trail and the guy takes off like a deer. The sixty-pound packs and his wicked pace were so gruelling I thought he was trying to hike me to death. But so be it, I wouldn't eat this guy's dust so I stayed right on his heels. In half an hour we were both sweat-soaked and steaming, stumbling through a dark pine forest, tripping over roots and stones and my heart was aflame in my chest. Then the trail left the trees and we were fairly jogging out in the open.

'The sky was a high dome of thin clouds, and burning through it was a three-quarter moon with a big red ring around it. The left side of the valley was all steep ramps and towers and minarets. The polished granite shone silver but the hollows and chimneys of the escarpment were jet black and the whole place resembled a weird moonscape. The right side of the valley was a void of dark ramparts but a mile or so beyond, my eyes were yanked straight to the gleaming Citadel. And, man, I couldn't tear my eyes away no matter how hard I tried and I really wanted to because the thing looked so damn awesome. There's a 1,000 foot slab leading right to the base, then it rears vertical for 2,000 feet. We dashed through a wet meadow to a stream below the slab to fill our water bottles. And now there was no escaping it. I could stare straight up and tremble, or gaze into the stream and see its reflection. I closed my eyes and started the ceremony we all go through before a frightening climb, assuring myself that I'd done big climbs before, hard ones, impossible ones, some certainly harder than what lay overhead, which didn't look so bad after all. All the way up the long slab I kept telling myself there was no place on earth I'd rather be. But when we got to the base and I stared up I knew I'd been talking lies.

'The thing stabbed the sky like a giant sabre and I felt sick knowing I had to climb it. "The climb starts in that corner," was all Russ said. Then he dumped his pack and sat down. I looked into the shadows and before I could spot the corner, Russ was laid out and snoring. I was so amped I couldn't think of knocking off, so I slumped back and studied the rock and several times took an elbow just to look at Russ sleeping. The guy spooked me. When again I looked up I knew some part of me was desperate to find out about Vic because only desperation could have gotten me on that bloody cliff. Otherwise I'd have been sprinting away as fast as my legs could take me. I guess I went out but I started dreaming about not being able to sleep and when Russ woke me at dawn I didn't know if I'd slept or not and felt like I hadn't. He handed me a cup of coffee. He still had his headlamp on and in the first light he'd already packed the haul bag and gotten all the gear together because there it was – the ropes all flaked out and the pitons racked. "I'm ready whenever you are," he told me, and turned off the stove.'

Steve paused here. His face was blank and he drained the rest of his beer in one draw and ordered another, again barking at the waitress. Art didn't care about the business with Russ and Vic, he only wanted to hear about the Citadel; but for all his fidgeting, Steve's scowl told him what it told me and the silent Cochran brothers. If you interrupted him, that might be all you'd hear. More beers came, and Steve carried on.

'While I wrestled into boots and harness Russ just gazed across the valley real tranquil like. But once he started climbing there was no stopping him and I knew we were going to scale that bastard or die trying. The first two ropelengths followed a vertical crack in a huge, white corner. I got the second lead, a vicious, leaning thin crack I could barely get my fingers into. But I made it okay and felt pretty good about it. But just above, a huge ceiling shot out overhead and a shallow crack marked the way. This roof had twice defeated Russ and my brother, and a few pitons part way out marked their highpoint. Now Russ led this pitch like it was nothing, dangling in his stirrups and casually banging in pitons that didn't sound so good and, of course, he never said a word. Only after he had turned the roof and I started following the lead, cleaning all the pegs, did I realize they were all so wretched that had he fallen no piton could have checked his fall and he'd 've crashed into the lower wall and died as sure as I'm sitting here. I wondered if my anchor would have held such a fall, so maybe he would have yanked me off as well. If the dupe wanted to risk his life, fine. But we were in this thing together and I didn't fancy him risking my ass as well. I was going to let him hear about it, but after I turned the roof I went dumb.

'There wasn't a ledge above the roof, so we were just hanging there, lashed to a cluster of suspect pitons just over the lip, the ropes looped down and dangling in free space below us. Russ was Buddha-calm and just surveyed the steep wall above. A vertical, wafer thin flake curved up to a big ledge about six hundred feet above us. I don't know what was holding that flake to the wall. We were committed now. Irreversibly. We couldn't get down because if we tried, the end of the ropes would just be hanging in space below the overhang, four hundred feet off the deck. And since we still had about 1,600 feet to go and it hardly looked easy, I wondered if we'd ever get off that wall. I'd started out dead serious but just then I found it all the funniest thing. I didn't care. I laughed. I laughed so hard it echoed across the valley. I figured if we got stranded, it'd give me that much more time to find out about Vic. But my mind wasn't working quite right. I laughed again. It was better to lose it that way than to freeze up, I guess.

'We climbed the rest of that day and I was never in better form. I was climbing unconscious. But as invincible as I felt I saw just how much better Russ was. You know how the best guys stay alive. They know just where their limit is, and they might go right to it but they never cross the line. Not Russ. He'd cross the line every time. He'd get irreversibly committed and he'd just rise to it because he didn't have a limit. It was madness of course, and it was terrifying duty to climb with him because you knew one day he would take a fall that no man could hold, a fall that would take you with him. But I didn't care just then. I must have been scared though I don't remember.

'Anyway, about four that first day, Russ led a really wild pitch up the flake which was creaking and flexing as he jammed behind it. The few pitons he got in were bunk. He reached a point not far below that ledge, less than a rope's length we reckoned. When I gained Russ's stance I saw right off that we were dead-ended. The flake, pinched down so thin you could only get fingertips behind it, was too brittle for pitons, and everything else just rattled around inside, though Russ was trying to slot some wire nuts behind it. When I realized we were stuck my mind cleared and I got really angry – crazy, I guess. Russ still looked calm, and for a moment I thought the clown didn't realize he had finally overreached himself. There was no way up and no way down. So Russ starts rubbing chalk into his hands, taking deep breaths, like he's psyching to actually lead this impossible flake. He was insane; anyone could see that by the way he climbed. Then he unclips from the anchor and hands me the belay rope, like he's set to cast off. "Whenever you're ready," he says to me. I lost it. "We're stuck you fool," I yelled, "don't you see that?!" Nobody could climb that bloody flake. I was sure of it. But Russ is going to try anyway so I've got to go along, right? What else can I do? The only way off is up. But before he kills us both I come right out and ask, "What happened with you and Vic?" "We'll talk about it on the ledge." "The ledge?! We're never going to make that ledge," I screamed. But he just keeps looking straight up, rubbing chalk into his hands. "Whenever you're ready," he tells me again. And he justs keeps staring up, waiting. . . .'

Steve paused again here. His face was flushed and wringing wet and he swilled down two half-filled glasses of water left on the table. You could have heard a candle flicker just then. Steve was so lost in the telling he seemed to have rolled back sixteen years and was hanging on the Citadel. A silent minute passed. None of us moved.

'An army couldn't have held him back, so Russ takes off up the flake and like I said you could only get your fingertips behind it, so even Russ was straightaway desperate, his feet skedaddling all over the polished wall and his arms quaking from the strain. And there's no way to get a piton or anything in the flake – it's just too thin and brittle. He couldn't have let go with one hand anyway and there's not a single foothold, but the maniac just keeps going, laybacking up this flake, his feet pasted right up by his fingertips now. And damn if he's not fifty, sixty, seventy feet above me, and looking to pitch off every move. Soon he's a hundred feet out and I'm thinking: when he falls, he'll rip out my anchor and we'll both plunge 1,000 feet into the talus. At least he's lost in the function but I'm just watching him, and then I just can't look any longer. I glance down and imagine us both plummeting like ragdolls, the talus racing up and then the impact, and I screamed out loud. "I don't want to die," I yelled. I'm so scared I can hardly breathe and I'll do anything to live. And hell if Russ isn't just below that ledge and I'm screaming that he's got to make it or I'll kill him and babbling all kind of nonsense' cause I'm so terrified I pissed my pants. That's right, and I'm not afraid to admit it.

'Then the rope came tight. I hadn't been paying attention to the rope and he's got none left and he's only a few feet below the ledge, hanging on for both our lives. I let go of the belay and he gets another few feet. He claws up a couple more moves and the rope comes tight against the anchor pitons. I untie from the anchor and this gives him enough slack to get his hands on the ledge; but he can't get on it and he's running out of gas and gasping and his feet are bicycling and I see his hands slowly buttering off. So I clip a sling into the anchor and stand in it and this gives Russ just enough slack to claw onto the ledge. I looked down between my legs, got dizzy, and puked. When he finally shouts down that I'm anchored off I'm still shaking pretty bad and can't move for ten minutes.

'When I finally crawled onto that ledge – a big one – I went to the wall, slammed home another four pitons, tied myself in with zero slack and just death-gripped the sling. I hated Owens for dragging me onto that wall, and would have sold my soul to get off it. I couldn't have climbed another inch, I was that fried. We'd get off all right. A single crack shot straight to the summit. No doubt we could climb it. It looked a lot easier than what we'd just done.

'We were finished for the day. The sun was sinking over the jagged ridge across the valley. We were both trashed so we bivouacked on the ledge. I tried to relax but I still hated being convict to both Russ and the Citadel. I stared at him as he emptied the haul bag. He needed a partner to climb this bastard, but there was more to me being there than that; and knowing we could get off made me that much more anxious to find out what the thing was all about. But I was too gassed to press things. Russ got some food out and I ate a few sardines.

'"You're a better rock climber than your brother was," he told me, citing the thin crack I'd led lower down on the wall. What a load of crap. I'd come around in the last year because I wanted to be a player like they were. A big player. But I couldn't have carried Vic's pack. I knew that. Then he says he wants me to be his new partner, that we could do things wilder than even the Citadel, and I started shaking again because I didn't want any part of the Citadel, even less of something harder. Then I thought about Vic and I just went off thinking how brazen Russ was. So I jumped up and started yelling:

'"I'm just going to take over where Vic left off, am I?" And I grabbed him and kept yelling at him and he never resisted, never said anything. I let him loose and went across the ledge and laid down.

'Then Russ unties from the rope, wanders over toward the edge and starts staring straight down. I remember these big white clouds had crept in and carpeted the whole valley. He takes a step forward to where his toes are curled over the very brink.

'"You could drop a piton here and it wouldn't even hit the wall," he said in that calm, measured voice. "It'd free-fall all the way to the base – 1,300 feet." I could breathe on him and he'd fall off. "It's easy to believe something when you want to, or when you need to," he continued. I leapt up. "No matter how outrageous it is," he added. I stood there, staring at his back. He didn't move an inch and never looked back. The truth was outrageous. Russ had pushed Vic off, and now his conscious was begging me to return the favour. I'd known it all along, ever since I'd first heard that lie about Vic slipping on easy ground, and I'd hidden it in my heart like a bullet in a healed wound; and like Vic's death, I was too scared to carve it out and examine it for what it was. No more.

'"But when something's utterly meaningless – even a cold fact – it's almost impossible to believe." His voice was sad but it didn't matter. I took a step toward him, but suddenly froze up.

'"Shut up!", I started. "Shut up or I'll push you off, just like you pushed Vic!!" Suddenly Russ spun around and we were eye to eye, his heels now hanging off the ledge.

'"No you won't Steve, you won't because you're not a killer, and neither am I." I shook horribly, not so sure of either count. "Your brother fell, Steve, slipped right off an easy ledge. God knows how, but that's what happened."

And looking into his eyes, I knew it was so. Russ had brought me along, had risked both our lives a dozen times, just to prove it.

'If I'd been right about Russ it would have taken some of the edge off Vic's death. There would have been some sense to it, and some comfort in seeing Russ pay. Instead, Vic has simply slipped off an easy ledge, and died. Nothing could have seemed more absurd. I sank down and put my head on my knees. The moment just hung there.

'I slept like a dead man and arose okay, but my nerves were shot so Russ did all the leading. The wall actually got steeper. The crack was hard, but good, and the few times it petered out Russ pendulumed over to another crack. Toward the top the exposure was really there because the whole wall just dropped away, 2,000 feet straight to the talus.

'Late that afternoon we finally got to a ledge just below the summit. An easy chimney led 40 feet to the top and I could climb off without a rope. I sat back and started laughing again though I didn't know why. Russ coiled up the ropes and stuffed all the hardware into the daypack. He shouldered the pack and the ropes, then looked up at the last bit to the top.

'"You take it, partner", he told me. He was going to let me scramble off, so I'd be the first on top. A nice gesture, but I wasn't ready. Russ walked back out the ledge and started gazing at the clouds billowing below. He said we had climbed one of the world's great routes, and in only two days. We were partners now and his career was finally back on track. Without the right partner, the last months had hardly been worth living, he said. He had me, we were partners now, and I'd have to climb a lot of others worse than the Citadel, and I couldn't fathom that. Russ, he keeps talking about this new partnership, what it will mean to both of us and it slowly dawned on me that what he was really describing, what he needed and now thought he had, was that magic he once had going with my brother. They really had something, something I couldn't bring back to life any more than I could resurrect Vic. So I'm thinking: the guy doesn't realize that they'd had their season, Russ and Vic, and it had passed.'

'Then it all came together for me. I wasn't his man and I didn't want to be his man. He deserved more. He deserved Vic, and I knew, I tell you I knew he'd never be happy so long as that partnership was denied him. And as Russ kept talking calmly about all that awaited us, as he gazed across the valley breathing in the clear air, I stepped over to the brink and pushed him off. And you know the wall was better than vertical so he probably free-fell the whole way down. And he never even screamed – not a peep – because he knew I'd done him proud. Him and Vic, together forever.

'Forty feet of easy ground and I was on the summit. I went back to the base and found the body, or what was left of it, and buried it on the flanks, in a patch of soot. Then I spread gravel over it and dragged some boulders on top. You'll never find it, but you can look if you want.'

This last detail was said matter-of-factly, not as a challenge, for Steve's voice and face and everything behind it was clearly played out. He simply got up and left.

Leviathan

by Geof Childs

KATHMANDU WAS COOL AND LUSH and muddy from the monsoon. The rail-thin Newar officials at the customs bench passed my bags along with an air of persecuted indifference and returned rapidly to their cold, white tile offices where they huddled in tight crowds around huge pots of tea on kerosene stoves. The odours of East and West mingled with the crowd in the airport lobby: leek and wool, deodorant and leather. The wind gathered from the fields the oxymoronic scents of jet exhaust and ox dung. I hired a stern, hawk-nosed beggar standing near the gate to help me with my belongings and signalled for a taxi.

The city was crowded and surging, much the way I remembered Saigon. Instead of soldiers, though, there were Gurkha policemen wearing crisp, khaki shorts, holding long, peeled switches, and sharing street corners with sniffling Dutch junkies. Instead of Montagnards, Tibetan refugees trotted to market in their red and black rags beneath enormous bundles of willow and alder twigs. Japanese taxis splashed the ooze and crap of the open sewers onto sidewalks and sacred cattle. Dogs lay dead and bloated in the streets. And I, Ishmael O'Brien (you can call me Izzy), found in the back pages of the *American Alpine Journal* by an English eccentric, was once more a pilgrim in someone else's cause. In the thirteen years since my last visit to the Orient, the only thing I'd learned was climbing.

I took a room in the older section of the city at a hotel named the Kathmandu Guest House. There was an enclosed cobblestone parking area out front with a small restaurant off to one side. A yard in the back was furnished with white, metal chairs and graced with parallel rows of neat Sussex gardening. The room had four beds and a large balcony overlooking the main entrance. The manager assured me that the beds were clean and that the water in the showers was always hot. A very attractive woman stood beside me speaking to one of the clerks in fluent Nepali as I paid a week's advance on the room. She wore a black leotard top with puffy, black silk trousers and Tibetan slippers. I thought her to be in her late twenties, possibly European, maybe American. We turned together toward the door.

'It's up there, just left,' she told me in a strong Australian accent as we approached the stairs. Then she smiled. 'And good luck with the showers.'

She walked quickly away from any possibility of a conversation, and I hiked my three leaden rucksacks up the steps. I dumped out everything onto the floor of the room and spent an hour separating my own things from the expedition equipment I'd brought with me. The sun came out and the cement steamed. The humidity sat in my lungs like water. I put on a T-shirt and nylon running shorts and stood at the window for a time looking out on the haze of the Himalaya with my mind full of autumnal Colorado.

After a short nap I ate a light supper in the restaurant outside the hotel and walked through the city to Freak Street in the European Bazaar. The evening light was golden and coruscant. A small, wrinkled Hindu in dirty cotton pyjamas stopped me as I passed under an enormous lattice of bamboo scaffolds leaning against the side of an ancient temple. He took my arm and pressed a small plug of black hashish into my hand.

'If you like,' he grinned, as harmless and beatific as Timothy Leary, 'you come back.'

I walked through the booths and stalls until dark, then climbed stairs to a second-floor coffee and yogurt shop. The owner was a Frenchwoman with vermilion hair and eyes that hung in her head like broken bulbs. She brought me a bowl of sherbet with a mint leaf. With my spoon I crushed the hashish into powder against the table top and sprinkled it on the sherbet. All around me names and phrases were carved into the wood in a babel of tongues. When I went back outside, my head was dancing like a trout on April water. I shuffled brainless and awed down side streets where naked twenty-five-watt bulbs backlit alley scenes as if Vermeer had passed this way on Quaaludes. I walked aimlessly along labyrinthine passages that smelled of urine and dry rot, buzzing in pot-head amazement at everything. I followed some poor, pumpkin-faced child who seemed to me to be rich with omen, but I lost him in a web of side streets. Passing ghostly ruins and a huge, ornately carved stupa, I came to a wide, bustling courtyard filled with night hawkers and costermongers. Along the fence stood God's occasional mishaps, laughing and gossiping and swinging deformed arms or legs swollen with elephantiasis to calls of 'Baksheesh, Sahb? Baksheesh?' One particularly capitalistic dwarf stepped directly in front of me, poking out his hand and forcing a perpendicular grin. His head was tilted sharply against his shoulder and the whole of his face and thorax – from skyward ear to his waist – was a single mass of featureless skin. No clavicle, no breast, no separated arm: just melted, homogenous flesh. An unfinished man; an act of staggering cosmic felicity and umbrage. I studied him for some time, then shook the outstretched hand, thinking to myself that, no, this was indeed not Boulder. I had come a long way on the strength of a voice over the phone and a ticket in the mail.

Two days later, on the eleventh of October, two of the others arrived. I met them at the airport and helped them pass through customs. They had met for the first time in Delhi but weren't able to sit together on the crowded flight to Kathmandu. I had no difficulty, however, in picking them out from among the other passengers.

Hamish Frazier was robust and heavy-set, with a great, ginger-coloured beard that flew loose at his temples and thinned to premature baldness atop his rosy, weathered head. His woollen shirt, tucked carelessly into baggy trousers, barely restrained his huge chest and shoulders. For a climber he had a surprisingly large paunch; for a Scots mountaineer he looked absolutely right. I liked him immediately.

Metilkja Martincz was a different sort altogether. A European hard man, he was taller, very dark and sombre. He seemed broodish: tender, angry and contemplative. His hair hung in a tousled mop; his shoulders were enormously broad, and his hands were almost comically outsized. My hand seemed to disappear in his grasp when we met. Yet his clothes matched, and he was the only one of the three of us I would have called handsome.

Frazier and I loaded most of the gear and ourselves into two taxis while Metilkja went off to the Yugoslavian Embassy to straighten out his visa and visit some old acquaintances.

'Fookin' pigsty, this place, eh, Jimmy?' Hamish enthused as we sped toward town. 'Third time I've been here and I'll be boogered if it smells any better. It's the fookin' cows, ye know, lad? Aye, ye can't have 'em muckin' about the fookin' kitchen without expectin' 'em ta draw flies now, can ye?' Then, turning back to me, 'Where ye got us puttin' up ta doss, lad? The Kathmandu?'

I nodded, somewhat disappointed.

'Right as fookin' rain, then, Jimmy! I imagine there's the usual clutch of Aussie quim standin' by, right? It's a long good-bye on that, these voyages, in't it, laddie?' He laughed ironically for a moment and then turned to watch Kathmandu arrive. After a time he looked back at me, suddenly more serious. 'When's the Major sneakin' inta town?' he asked, as we careened around a corner, scattering shoppers. 'I'll bet a pint he dinna tell ye, now, did he? He's a bit queer for surprises, that one.'

He paused, seeming to think that over, then started in again. 'Fook, I'm hoongry. That wee spot next door still there? Bit dear, I thought, but the woggies cook a potato right. What sort of name did you say Ishmael O'Brien was, anyway, lad?' On and on like that, episodic monologues, almost all of them rhetorical, and less than half, I suspected, meant to be heard.

We hauled the gear upstairs and spent the rest of the afternoon dividing it into two dozen separate piles. 'I've a wee taste, O'Brien,' Hamish finally concluded. He looked tired from the long flight and the heat. We put on clean shirts and went downstairs to the Star Restaurant. The Nepali owner showed us to a table in the corner beside the woman I had met a few days earlier. ''Ello, Sheila,' Hamish muttered in a shammed Australian accent as we took our seats. She never lifted an eye, just kept to her book and tea. Frazier rolled his eyes and ordered six beers.

I had expected him to be more aggressive, louder as a drinker, but mostly we sat in silence. We both drank our first two bottles before he even spoke. He asked if I'd ever met the Major. I said, no; in fact, I knew very little about the man. Hamish looked at me doubtfully, almost angrily, for an instant, then switched his gaze to the room.

'Well, don't you be believin' everything you hear, O'Brien. He's all right. A bit odd, maybe, boot who isn't comin' on these fookin' crusades, eh? Aye, you get caught up in somethin' like this, spendin' your money, dear as it is, to take a whack at killin' yerself for ten minutes o' standin' in the wind on some nameless mountain-top. Vicar's tits, mon, it'll make ye a bit funny, then won't it?'

He was silent again for a moment, searching for the right words.

'You rich, O'Brien?'

I told him no.

'Major's rich as fookin' Croesus, I reckon,' he said. 'Probably crazier than a fookin' Cumbrian goose, too, for all I know about behavin' in public. But I kin tell ye this. He's a right hard man to have with you on a piss-up, strong and steady as any I've ever seen touch axe to snow. Aye, game as they come and a straight man with ye, too. The type that'll see ye through a shitstorm without a word.'

We sat quietly for a while. We each ordered another bottle of beer and Hamish got a sandwich. I asked him if he knew much about the mountain or the route. He said no, only that the Major had taken a close look at it the year before during his solo attempt. Some people, he added, were saying the usual thing about its being the hardest thing attempted at that altitude. The Major had spent two-and-a-half weeks on it by himself, he explained. No food at the end, bad weather, and, for a time, not much hope of getting down alive.

'Lost his mind up there, I suppose,' Frazier said without emphasis or lifting his eyes from the remains of his sandwich. 'Reckon he thinks he can find it again up on top. We'll bloody well find out about that when we get there, I guess.'

He got up, winked, and threw a few rupee notes on the table. I watched him walk out and ordered some tea and a slice of pie. The food came after a while, and I picked at it, trying to sort through my thoughts. I hardly heard her voice.

'You going with them, then, Yank? Is that it?'

It took a moment before it occurred to me that she had spoken. The atmosphere around her had been so hard I didn't imagine it could be talked through. When I turned, she was facing me, smoking a small cigarette wrapped in brown paper. She was impossibly beautiful. I was stunned and a little drunk and desperately in love.

'Yeah,' I stammered, trying to sound urbane and casual. 'We're a mountaineering exped—'

'Right,' she cut in, 'the Kahli Gurkha bunch. I know. The southwest face, I believe?' I nodded and she went on. 'The Leviathan – or something like that. Isn't that what you're calling it? Much better name than the Nepali one, I'm sure. Probably bloody hard to go about raising money to climb a mountain with a name the bankers in London can't pronounce. "The last great problem,"' she mused cynically. 'Get you laid back home, mate?'

I was shocked dumb. Titillated and overwhelmed.

'Look,' she semi-apologized, 'I work for the Sherpa Cooperative. I get all this shit across my desk, season after season. Every year it's someone off to tame the hardest mountain, the worst route, the steepest face. Christ, our records are like obituaries of who's-been-who in the Himalaya for the last twenty years. The young and the starry-eyed off to get themselves killed for the greater glory of European alpinism and usually taking a few Sherpas with them. Hoo-fucking-rah, mate. I haven't seen a bloody Yank over here with his head on right yet, and you're just the same as the rest of them.'

'Thanks,' I grinned. I think I grinned. I tried to grin.

'Oh, look . . . I've offended you; I'm sorry.' She smiled and seemed to slow down for a moment. 'Listen, I'm a bit off, I guess. I don't mean to come down like your bloody Mum or anything. It's just that I've seen this same act repeated so many times since I've been here I get the feeling that somebody ought to step in and say something, whether it changes anything or not!' She caught her rising frustration this time and sat back with it against the bench. She shook her head and smiled. I wondered if she could hear my heart beating.

'"One climbs to know oneself,"' she recited, '"and in so doing at last comes to know nothing. The being has been no more than the doing."' She lit another cigarette, cupping her hand over the flame and letting the significance settle. 'Does that mean anything to you at all?'

'Sure,' I shrugged. 'I guess it does.'

'I knew it wouldn't,' she replied after a pause. She smiled again and exhaled smoke. Westerners seem to glow with spiritual one-upmanship when they have mastered the recitation of some enigmatic Zen parable.

'Do you know what a *chod* is?' she asked next. I shook my head. 'It's a tantric rite whereby the true believer commits himself to encountering his worst fears. A monk, for example, who finds he is frightened of the spirits he believes to inhabit a graveyard, will spend a night meditating in the graveyard. Defeating fear: meeting the dragon and finding out that it is only air, the creation of his own imagination.' I nodded my head, anticipating the lesson. 'That is why you climb. Because you are afraid to. It is your *chod*.'

'My mother will be crushed,' I told her. 'Quitting college was one thing, but if I turn into a monk, it's going to kill her.' I smiled and she did not.

'The monk cleanses himself,' she continued. 'He goes expecting nothing and thus is prepared to accept everything. He empties himself of ambition. You, on the other hand, are not going to the mountain – you are going to the summit. Even if you succeed, you fail, because you never left New York or Iowa or wherever you're from. You just brought it all with you. You transpose instead of travel. There will be no understanding because there will be no humility. You do not come to find your God; you come to challenge Him. You long to stand upon the summit, not to be near God, but to slap His face. The mountain is just your method, your tool, and therefore it holds no revelation for you. There will be no truth of success, no conquest for you. The only God you will see will be Masta, the mountain god of horror.' She stubbed out her smoke and leaned closer.

'Look, don't be daft, will you. Your Major – I've heard the Sherpas talk about him. None of them will work for him. You know that, don't you? They call him a *sennin*, a bloody mountain lunatic! That's why he's had to go ahead to Khandbari to find people. No one in Kathmandu will—'

'Look, lady,' I cut her off. 'I appreciate the introduction to Zen 101. I'm sure everything you say is absolutely true.' She started to speak, but I held up my hand. 'Honest to Buddha, I don't know what the hell you're talking about. You've got the wrong guy. I'm just good old, time-flogging Izzy O'Brien, and all I'm doing over here is going to climb a mountain. No spiritual mission, no ghosts or anything; just see the sights and do a little climbing. You can read whatever you want into that, I guess, but where I'm concerned, that's all there is to it.'

She started to speak again.

'That's it,' I almost shouted. 'I'm sorry; I'm just not that complex. Christ, I thought *chod* was a frigging fish or something.' She laughed over that one. She let her head fall back, and her wonderful breasts vibrated beneath her leotard. I grinned, feeling stupid again.

'Look, mate,' she said finally, 'I'm awfully sorry. Your pie is getting cold.' We both laughed until the mood seemed better. 'My name is Lucy she added, sticking out her hand for me to shake. 'Tell me, O'Brien, do you abuse drugs?'

We said goodnight on the steps below her door. She put her hand on the side of my face, but I made no effort to kiss her. I was beyond arousal, drug-sodden, bewildered, strangely mordant. I listened to her door close and went out onto the balcony. It was 3:00 a.m. and the city sighed. Its potpourri scent and amber lights lolled on breezes that rustled the palm fronds in the garden. Fred Astaire would have danced. I just weaved awkwardly towards our room and slipped quietly through the door, threading mounds of gear.

Hamish was in the far bed, snoring and gagging in perfect tranquility. I took off my shirt and trousers, Lucy still cartwheeling through my brain and slipped under the sheets of my bunk. There was a grunt – distinct, sleepy, and very near – and an unexpected contact with skin. I dived out of bed yelping 'Jesus!' and rolled sideways along the floor. Behind me the entire surface of the bed seemed to rise. I collided heavily with a rucksack and struggled wildly to get the ice axe off it.

'That'd be Metilkja, lad,' Hamish explained sleepily. 'Bonnie great booger he is. Aye.' Then he drifted back into sleep. The Yugoslavian sat smiling as I circled warily to the next bunk, ice axe in hand, trying very hard to seem collected and poised.

'Goot day,' he said pleasantly.

'Good day,' I told him.

In the morning we went to work on the gear heaped on the porch, dividing, listing, and crating the food, tents, clothing, climbing equipment and personal belongings into eighty-pound loads. We packed the loads into plastic garbage cans and covered them with burlap sacks. For two dollars a day a porter would carry one of the loads plus his own food and shelter. Lousy union, but they were still known to strike on occasion; so we were giving away sunglasses, tennis shoes, socks, and mittens. We also had cheap windshirts, with 'Leviathan' emblazoned on the back, packed away for extra commercial leverage later on, should it become necessary. We worked steadily and without much conversation. The sky was clear, and the cement floor reflected the tropical heat at us. It was the first hard work of the trip. Our T-shirts darkened with sweat, Metilkja played depressing Croatian symphonies on his tape recorder. We dragooned a number of gleeful children into fetching pot after pot of tea for us. Hamish referred to the process as the British colonial touch.

By mid-afternoon we had tied off the last package. Twenty-six plastic garbage cans stood in a row, each with 'International Kahli Gurkha Expedition' stencilled on the side in red letters. 'Don't seem like much when you think about it,' Hamish observed, as he clipped an inch off the mainspring of the scale we would carry to weigh out the loads.

'We must be fast on mountain,' Metilkja explained, sounding like a Swiss guide with a mouth full of marbles. 'Odervise . . .' He grinned and patted his stomach, 'Get very thin.'

'Right, well, I reckon starvin' is probably goin' ta be our last fookin' worry on this whale hunt,' Hamish laughed. 'Puttin' up the route is goin' ta be the hard part.'

'Alpine met-tod,' Metilkja concluded. 'Goot weather, we climb fast.' That seemed to me to be about the beginning and the end of it. Get and go; what else could you say? Not enough food or rope to stick it out for long, anyway. 'If you want to last, you got to go fast,' was the expression we had used in Yosemite. No pain, no gain.

We all took cold showers – the hot water was mythical – got into our best clothes, and went out on the town for supper. The three of us and all our gear were scheduled to be flown out in the morning, and the atmosphere of celebration was dampened only by the question marks surrounding the Major's absence. Behind the laughter was the lingering sense that he was already on the expedition and we were holding him back, slowing him down. I think we all had the feeling of wanting to show him we were as committed and hungry as he was, which was probably just the way he wanted us to feel.

We walked back through the city in the last light. Kerosene stoves burned in the small shops and market stalls; rice and lentils and black tea boiled in tin pots. People were bustling past us on foot and pedalling bicyles. A water buffalo lay on its side in the street, legs bucking spasmodically as its freshly decapitated head was raised through a haze of flies to a butcher's bench. Rich, crimson blood pumped into the gutter. The same dull lights threw yellow halos around every act of love and antipathy. Turning to take the unpaved alley that led down to the guest house, we passed a beggar lurking in the shadows behind the wreck of a Datsun taxi. He crept out into the dirt behind us, crouched over slightly to one side, thin and tattered, a crude bamboo crutch held under his right arm. He was wearing the emaciated remains of what had once been a down parka. We had never seen a beggar so close to the guest house, and his appearance caught us by surprise. Hamish took a threatening step toward him, and the beggar cringed back pathetically.

'No, Sahb! Please no, Sahbs,' he pleaded, bending even lower to emphasize his terrible harmlessness. 'Sahbs go Kahli Gurkha, please?' he asked.

We looked at each other. Hamish answered, 'Aye.'

'No go, Sahbs. Very bad, you go. Not good mountain. Masta go Kahli Gurkha. Avalokita Ishvara not go that mountain. Cannot see Sahbs. Masta live mountain. Sahbs go back America, please!' His voice broke with a sob. He paused and caught his breath. When he began again, his voice seemed to have changed, to have risen an octave. 'Baksheesh, Sahbs? Baksheesh?' His shrivelled, cupped hand stuck out at us from his rags.

'G'won, git, ye wee fookin' chough!' Hamish scowled and turned to join us. The beggar dodged off into the darkness and the three of us walked back to the guest house in a profound and insulated silence.

We flew east. The valleys dropped away below us to isolate small hamlets on hogback ridges. No roads marred the landscape. I had been told in Kathmandu that atavistic Hindu sects still conducted human sacrifices in villages not forty miles from where commercial jets disgorged loads of camera-toting tourists on high-adventure tours of the world's most remote region. To the north, the Himalaya lay in the translucent shrouds of the monsoon season.

We landed on a grass runway with a miniature stucco terminal topped by an unattended bamboo control tower. A complement of police, militiamen, traders, and the curious stood watching. Our porters were waiting – thirty of them – under the direction of a rakish, good-looking sirdar named Ang Phu. We shook hands and left him to straighten out the load-carrying while we hiked the six miles into Khandbari, where, we had lately learned, the Major was awaiting our arrival.

The path was six feet wide, gentle, and well used. At the end of each uphill pitch, benches curled in the shade of walnut or plane trees. Everywhere, small Buddhist prayer walls and tiny stupas were decorated with brightly painted mandalas and symbols. It began to rain after we had walked an hour or so. We unfolded our umbrellas and stopped by a rickety tea shop for *chai* and cookies. A Nepali child watched us drink. Her mother brought us bananas, for which Metilkja arose and thanked her with a deep bow, sending her giggling uncontrollably back into a corner. Her husband, a withered and tough-skinned old man, bought out his faded ledger. It showed that he had carried for several expeditions going into the Makalu area. We nodded, he smiled and came to attention, saluting. 'Ed-mund Hil-lary,' he pronounced carefully.

We arrived at the guest house in Khandbari around five. Ang Phu had caught up with us and showed us to a room with five or six straw pallets where we dropped our light trail sacks and went downstairs to join Major Abrams. He had arranged a side room for dinner and met us at the door.

A tall, lean, dark-haired man in his late forties or early fifties, the Major had sunken cheeks beneath a heavy beard, surprisingly narrow shoulders and an awkward, almost feminine dimension to his posture. Much to my surprise, he walked with a marked limp, one leg being noticeably shorter than the other, though he was obviously not crippled. His squinted eyes threw out deeply weathered crows' feet around the most intense glare I have ever seen. His presence was commanding, whole and authoritative; there was a cool, almost military ferocity about him that made calling him Major far easier than using his Christian name.

He shook hands with all of us. A solid, reassuring grip. 'Ah, Mr O'Brien! The American,' he grinned. 'Good, you've got long hair. Something to pluck you out of the crevasses by!' We laughed. As we took our seats around the table, I thanked him for his help and for the photos he had sent me.

'I'm afraid I really haven't been much help at all,' he apologized, 'but you're welcome, and thank you for the compliment. As you all know, things have been very difficult trying to put this trip together at short notice. Lost paperwork, troubles with permission, the usual Nepal muck-up. Didn't give me much time to help you lads at your end, I regret to say.'

We all assured him that things had run very smoothly for us, largely owing to his efforts, and that we all were keen for the climb. He asked pointed, knowledgeable questions of each of us as we ate. Occasionally he would jot down a note or pause with his head back, studying a response. He seemed warmer and more accessible than I had dared imagine. I thought of Lucy's ersatz-Buddhist hyperbole and nearly laughed out loud.

After we were done eating and everyone but me had produced a pipe, the Major ordered *chang*. It was served hot, in tall bamboo gourds. It smelled richly alcoholic and was the colour of milk. Seeds and rice and bits of leaves floated in it innocently. 'To Kahli Gurkha,' the Major smiled, raising his gourd, 'To the Leviathan. To us!'

We raised our *chang* after him. 'To the Leviathan.'

In the days that followed we hiked along the single spine of a long, fertile plateau. The Arun River lay to our left, grey and floury with the silt of unseen glaciers. On our right the terraced fields were black and ripe. We bought potatoes, carrots, and radishes along with an occasional chicken to supplement our trekking diet of rice and *tsampa*. The Nepalis we met on the trail were tolerant and friendly, although at night when we set up camp near their villages, the aggressive mobs of curious onlookers made us feel tense and militant.

Ang Phu had hired an assistant, a bull-shouldered comedian named Bahm, and two cooks, whom we called Sears and Roebuck. Ang Phu explained that he and Bahm owned a trading business and a small hostel together in the Khumbu-Everest area. Both of them had wives and children and were as glad as we were to be away on an expedition. They were intelligent, articulate, sophisticated men out to do a little work and have a little fun. Mornings, we could hear them laughing; always, as the first sun touched the tents, a cup of tea and a warm *chapati* came through the front flap at the end of a square, brown hand.

None of the rest of us were particularly gregarious men; perhaps the Major and I the least. Hamish could be loud and obscene, and he and Metilkja would walk together from time to time; but by and large we travelled alone on the trail. We carried simple lunches and candy and biscuits in our pockets. Sometime around midday I would stop at a tea shop, sit at one of the tables, and shout '*Namaste!*' to the porters as they came by under their huge loads.

The whole experience for me was an ongoing vision of incredible poignancy and beauty, intensified by my solitude. Images of magnificent and seemingly untellable pulchritude were framed by even greater scenes of almost hallucinatory splendour. I stood in awe of every hut, every rhododendron, every detail. It was a walk like a dream, a fantastic trot. I watched huge leeches wavering at peristaltic attention from the ends of trailside leaves, with tropical wildflowers setting off their grotesque dance in a dazzling profusion of colours and shapes. The sun rose out of the high jungle about Darjeeling and set in the forbidding aridity of the Kampa Mustang. I took my time and exposed roll after roll of film. I crouched underneath my umbrella during the afternoon showers and wrote long, jovial letters to Lucy and to my family. I wrote about the mountain as if it were the Panama Canal: a place one sailed through, not one where people worked and died. I was very brave in print, of course, incapable of even alluding to the possibility of death. There, in the jungle, far away from the wind and snow, I was immortal.

We dropped down from the last Nepali villages, crossed the Arun on a primitive hemp-and-cable bridge, then hiked uphill for a day to the village of Sedua. For the Khumbu Sherpas it was like a voyage backward through time to what Namche Bazaar must have been like before it was 'civilized.' We called it Dodge City, guarded our baggage carefully, and moved on as soon as we could.

The days grew colder and clearer. We climbed steadily. At Shipton Col, I caught up with the Major; he was standing alone, above and to the right of the trail, his piercing eyes fixed on the northern horizon. We were at 14,000 feet and it was cloudless, pefect. Makalu, the fifth-highest mountain in the world, stood out spectacularly. Just to its east I saw Kahli Gurkha. It seemed small by comparison, but even at this great distance its awesome southwest face – the Leviathan – stood out in startling relief. Illuminated by the southern, postmonsoon light, it shone bronze- and sepia-coloured with a blue-white fin of ice along its spiral summit ridge. As Abrams stepped down, his lips were moving wordlessly and his fists clenched so tight the knuckles seemed ready to burst his skin. He strode away from the crest and off toward the Leviathan in brusque, electric silence.

Supper was quiet that night. For the seventh consecutive night we shoved rice and *tsampa* around our plates without much enthusiasm and went to our tents early. Sometime after midnight I got up to urinate and stood for a long time in the moonlight looking down into the Arun Gorge. It was dark down there, as opaque as dirt. I could hear things bumping around: mysterious objects as basic as mud shoving each other about, shifting to the downbeat of eternity. The river, a black scratch on a torpid moonscape, gusted its Pleistocene melodies, life's earliest sonata. Sighs from the centre of the earth hissed their valley song and stirred our nylon houses. I listened for a long time. Walking back in the metallic light, I heard the counterpoint: a dreamer in his guttural, midnight torment. I heard the lost soul of mankind, the private horror of such fragile limitation in such a hard and unlimited universe that it knew of no words. I knew, of course, that the dreamer was Abrams, and that his photos had told us far less about the mountain than his nightmares did now.

Early in the afternoon, two days later, we stood in a gentle snowfall outside the sturdy yak-herders' hut at Kahli La that was to be our base camp. After weighing out their loads, Ang Phu paid off our porters and sent them away with their socks, shoes, and Leviathan windshirts. Bahm and the two cooks built a kitchen out of field stones and our huge canvas tarpaulin. We sorted through the loads and heated water for tea. The mountain was veiled in dense clouds and we neither spoke of it nor looked in its direction. It was there; that was enough to know.

We broke into our best food and had a superb dinner of beef stew with potatoes and barley. The Major produced a can of pears and a large gourd of a Nepali liquor called *rakshi*. For the first time in several days the conversation that night was animated and crude. The Europeans smoked their pipes and talked about climbing in the Alps. I went outside and dug into the small travelling stash Lucy had given me. I stood beside the river taking long draws and feeling the snow wet on my face.

The snow fell steadily for a week. Avalanches sloughed off the peaks around us and roared unseen above the low-hanging clouds in the valley. We sat inside and waited. We killed time reading, writing letters, and playing with our equipment. I hung one of the single-anchor bivouac platforms in the branches of a poplar and watched the Europeans struggle with the notion of sleeping suspended in it. They, in turn, grinned at my lame enthusiasm for the cans of bacon and kippers they included in our climbing rations. We packed it all into our rucksacks along with rockclimbing gear, ice screws, pots and stoves, then for a week we lifted, weighed, divided, and revised our loads. Hamish built a sauna out of willow wands and our tent flies. We would sit in it until the sweat exuded from the soles of our feet, then run and jump naked into the frigid Arun. The Sherpas loved it. They would always gather to watch the spectacle and laugh hysterically.

During the sixth day the snow came down heavily. By noon we were sitting in the hut, idle as monks, and listening to the almost constant rumble of the avalanches above us. We warmed our hands on teacups. The Major sat in a corner smoking his pipe and writing in his journal. An unusually loud, baritone roar drew all eyes to the ceiling. 'That ought to clean the face,' Hamish mumbled. The noise grew nearer and deeper. The ground shimmied. Our eyes came down to meet one another's. Outside we could hear Ang Phu's excited voice and the other Sherpas shouting. Pots and pans began falling.

'Ja-sus fookin' Christ!' Hamish suddenly bellowed. 'It's comin' right fer home!'

We leaped simultaneously to our feet and pushed each other through the door, bounding miraculously through the kitchen without knocking over steaming pots, hitting the clearing on the run, and splitting in three separate directions. The ground quaked, and the shock wave blew snow horizontally at our backs, though by the time I had reached the trees at the riverbank the slide had lost its momentum in the talus breaks above the hut. I stood against a tree to catch my breath, watching the air clear. The main tongue of the avalanche had reached to within a hundred feet of the shack. A few small boulders were still rolling on the debris-strewn lower surface of the slide as Hamish approached.

'Christ's eyes, eh, laddie?' he laughed, wiping mud off his sweater. We walked back together. Metilkja and the Sherpas approached from the opposite direction. Metilkja explained with surprising seriousness that he took this to be a sign, that someday one of these was going to catch up with him. For all the noise a few moments earlier, there was an incredible stillness. Effort and release.

The Sherpas set to reconstructing the kitchen and the three of us ducked back into the hut. The low door on the side of the building facing the mountain was open. Abrams was standing outside, some distance away, smoking his pipe, hands in his pockets, and staring up at the Leviathan as it appeared in glimpses caught through the swirling clouds. Snow powdered the ground between where he stood and the hut, but I saw no trace of footprints. He had been there when the snow came. He had walked toward the avalanche, not away from it. It had stopped at his very feet.

The next morning dawned spectacularly clear – cloudless and sharp. We rapidly put the final touches to our gear and slipped into our windsuits. Ang Phu and Bahm served us a special breakfast of Sherpa horseradish on buffalo sausage with oatmeal and fried potatoes covered with sweet syrup. Hamish honed his crampons and ice axe with a hand file. Metilkja painted his nose and cheeks with zinc oxide. It was going-up day. Abrams wrote a few notes, closed his journal, and placed it in a small plastic satchel hanging near the door. He tapped out his pipe and stuck it in his shirt. His face was set and hard. This was it, the point of it all, and I couldn't imagine any human being with whom I would rather have gone up on the mountain. Abrams had the power. You could feel it in everything he did that morning. His obsession was like a magnet, a beacon. I was amazed at my own fanaticism. The pointlessness, the triviality and expense, the whole dramatic absurdity that underlay our climb struck me at that moment as the most important purpose my life could ever have.

The Major stood and stretched. 'Well, lads,' he said, his quiet voice suggesting neither a question nor command. The three of us rose and he nodded.

'Major-Sahb!' Ang Phu called from the kitchen. 'Mens coming Makalu. Four, maybe five, down valley very near now, Sahb!'

We followed Abrams through the door and saw the men emerging from the trailhead at the willow thicket. They looked grim, bent on a mission of importance and solemnity. The snow sparkled in the sunlight and crunched beneath their huge boots. The Leviathan, cut from the cobalt sky, stood massively indifferent to our meeting. Waiting.

We all shook hands. Their leader explained that they were Dutch, part of a team attempting the south face of Makalu. Tears welled suddenly in his eyes. One of their members, he said, his son, the expedition physician, was missing. He had gone out of one of the tents at high camp two nights earlier and simply disappeared. They wanted our help to search for him. It was two days' travel to their base camp; the search would last no more than a few days, then they would give up. We could be back in a week at the most.

Abrams never blinked. He never paused to search for words. 'You are welcome to food and tea here,' he said. 'You may take our Sherpas to help you if they are willing to go with you. Ang Phu, there, is a fine mountaineer, as competent as any European, I assure you. But we did not travel this far to lose hold of our goal because you have lost yours, sir. I shouldn't ask that of you, gentlemen. I'm sorry. That's final. I hope it all comes out well for you. I wish you good luck and Godspeed. Good morning, gentlemen.'

He turned and walked to his pack, brought it up onto his shoulders, and started toward the glacier. Less forcefully, the three of us fell in behind him.

'It is you I feel sorry for!' the leader of the Dutch party screamed after us. 'I pray that you will find the same charity on your mountain that you have shown us, Abrams!'

The Major did not recoil or turn around upon hearing his name. It was hard to tell if he was even aware of its having been said.

We climbed steadily throughout the day. The going was not technically difficult, and we found the heat to be more of a problem than the crevasses or icefalls. At noon we stopped and took out the ropes. As the angle increased, the snow became wet and heavy. We sank in to our knees and ran short of breath beneath our monstrous loads. We dug a platform into the side of a crevasse and spent a comfortable night. The incline and mire increased all the next day. We reached the bergschrund where the lower glacier fractured at the base of an 1,800-foot ice face and carved out another small platform. We melted snow for tea and tried to make sense of what rose above us. The scale was out of proportion with anything I had ever experienced. The ice face led to a rock headwall, and that to the long, fin-shaped Whale's Tail. Then more snow and the summit. I stacked ropes and whistled with the stoves in joyful ignorance.

The following morning we set off at 3:00 a.m. to take advantage of the cold. We climbed by headlamps, pushing hard to reach the headwall before the sun touched the face and loosened the afternoon stone barrage. Two teams of two – slow-moving dots on a sixty-degree ocean of ice, lost and purposeful as gulls. Metilkja and Hamish, on separate ropes, took the leads. The Yugoslav seemed almost to float, one foot flat and the other front-pointing. He was economical and precise, making it all appear effortless. Hamish, on the other hand, brutalized the ice, kicking and hammering his way up, never pausing, never running down. He wore no cap in the dark, sub-zero cold. The Major and I came along pragmatically at the long ends of our ropes.

By one in the afternoon we stood at the base of the headwall. The mottled and broken skin of the Leviathan reached above us in a turbulent and darkening sky. Hamish and Metilkja dug a cave in the deep powder at the base of the wall while Abrams and I removed the rock gear from our packs.

The Major pointed me to a long, pencil-thin crack that cleaved a narrow buttress and seemed to widen to hand size after a hundred feet. I was the Yosemite wizard, the rock jock; that crack was the reason I was there. I reached high, placed a piton, and hammered it home.

Four hours later I was sitting on my foam pad talking about the wall with Hamish. Our cave glowed with the sparkling light of two stoves and a candle. Abrams and Metilkja cooked. The steam from our teacups hung in the warm, moist air, mixing with the smoke from Hamish's pipe. Life was as sweet and masculine as an after-shave ad. We talked about women and home the way sailors do. We ate cookies with yak butter and jam. Metilkja passed around a flask of Croatian *eau de vie*. Three hundred feet of rope was strung out on the rock above. My first contact with the Leviathan had left me ecstatic. It was more spectacular than I could have imagined: El Capitan at altitude, wide and weathered and old as infinity. Under a muted afternoon sun I had filled its cracks with my hands and feet, twisting and panting, moving quickly, charged by my own elation and energy. The clouds moved in time-lapse speed and snow began to fall – stellar, soft, collated flakes. My cheeks and hands were moist and hot. I drove a piton when the rope ran out and raised the haul sack before descending, breathless, back down to the cave, whispering 'In the morning' to myself.

The snow fell finer and harder the next day. The crack turned incipient and rotten, then disappeared altogether, leaving me swinging from sky hooks with the sweat stinging my eyes. I lost hours drilling holes for lousy bolts. Pitons I had hammered barely past their tips creaked and moved under my weight. I begged Jesus/Buddha, please, just ten more feet. My scrotum shrank in tingling cowardice. Scared to death of where I was and too frightened to go back down, I held my breath and swung on a rotten flake lassoed from thirty feet away to reach for a huge, fragmented block. Around more corners the angle of the face dropped to less than vertical and the cracks were filled with ice. I climbed to a large ledge and secured the ropes. Less than 300 feet for the day. Abrams prusiked the fixed line to join me and we hauled the sacks. His face was contorted with impatience. He knew he couldn't have done it any faster, but he hated to depend on others, on me, to wait on the expertise and judgements of fools. It dawned on me that he did not climb out of love for the climbing. That had passed long ago. It was out of hate for the mountain, for its superiority, its naked power. And strangely, I admired that in him, wished that I could have his ruthlessness. I was his vehicle, I knew, and he could drive me faster. I would give him his snow ridge.

Early the next morning, our fourth on the mountain, we climbed the ropes to the ledges we were now calling the Hilton, and pulled up our umbilical line. To get down now would mean getting up. It seemed like a significant moment; yet it passed without anyone giving it notice. The inclination of the rock continued to ease. I climbed quickly now, rope length after rope length, one boot on rock, one on snow, my mittened hands jammed between dank shelves of granite and rivulets of ice. The snow fell quietly, windlessly. Occasional breaks in the clouds let the sun through, and the rock steamed. We moved steadily up. When I leaned out to study the route, I could see the long, white tongue of snow above us: the Whale's Tail.

The day ended with the four of us suspended from a few shaky pegs without anything approximating a ledge in sight. We erected the bivouac plaforms and crawled into them head to foot, the Major and Metilkja in one, Frazier and I sharing the other. The wind picked up during the night and dipped us gently. In the morning we all were eager to fold the platforms and get back to the solidity of climbing. We moved diagonally, gaining less than 200 feet of altitude in fifteen hours of work. The rock was not steep enough to hang our nylon platforms; so we chipped out whatever small grooves we could from the ice and spent the night there, suspended, with our feet stuffed into our rucksacs. We shivered silently in our individual tribulations, too far apart to pass food or drink. We popped Valium and stared into the storm-basted ribbon of sky that tacked the western horizon.

My feet were cold all night. They ached all day. I led up and left into a system of snow-clogged chimneys that left me, after several hundred feet of climbing, studying a conundrum. Above, the main chimney narrowed to a slot three feet wide and was blocked by an enormous chockstone. Both sides of the passage were coated with thick rime ice, white and warted as the Elephant Man's keister. I dumped my pack and bridged out tenuously. My mind wandered intractably, taking me back to Boulder . . . the corner of Broadway and Pearl, to be exact. Hmmm. Bookstores and French bread, co-eds and foreign cars, and – ah, yes – the 'wall' at Macky crawling with punks carrying chalk bags, so close to the centre of it all, dude, you could touch it. I though of being warm again, and about dying. I looked down and saw myself tumbling tip over tail forever, the rope streaming like a purple and blue contrail, no longer flirting with space but flying at last, oh yeah.

For lack of anything else to do, I nudged up, shoulders and knees, to beneath the stone at the very back of the depression and thrust my axe up into the snow gathered behind it. Pressure, rest; effort, release. An hour later I was standing above the hole I'd chopped, fixing the ropes to a cluster of ice screws and runners. I shouted down to the others to come up. I thought I heard a voice, two shouts, perhaps more, then silence again. After a while the rope went taut with the weight of a climber. I touched the grey ice and wondered: how long? We were on the Whale's Tail, riding the very back of the beast.

The night was horrid and everlasting. I was utterly spent and passed the evening lapsing in and out of groggy soliloquies about how I had to rest, man, curl up in bed somewhere warm, turn on a tap and get water, rest these weary, cold, cold, arms. We sat huddled in our separate miseries and dreamed our lonely panaceas, hardly speaking, dressed in wool and nylon and feathers. My fingers pulsed, and each throb brought excruciating pains behind fingernails as white and hard as porcelain. We leaned off the edge of our sérac and shat hanging from a rope, our turds dropping soundlessly into the impossible abyss.

In the morning it was still snowing. Gentle waves of spindrift hissed down the face in filmy avalanches; so we stayed put and arranged the bivouac platforms. They lacked the gaiety of the cave – they were not so warm or nearly so bright – but they were an improvement on sitting out in the wind and cold with that dark space below and the distance above eating out our eyes.

We dined on freeze-dried shrimp creole and drank lukewarm, urine-coloured tea that tasted like shrimp creole. Food and drink came, and I took it like Communion. Abrams shared my platform, maintaining his complex, pontific silence. I heard Metilkja and Hamish talking quietly from time to time, but their words lacked animation or joy.

We were in deep. Very, very deep.

The snow continued and grew heavier. The spindrift slides came episodically, great waves of rigid surf breaking over us and surging into the void, where, a day earlier, and we might have joined it, hello below, tumbling and spinning earthward like paper. We packed without comment in the morning. We left behind the rockclimbing gear, a stove, the platforms, and some of the food. The hell with it: there was no going back down that way now, anyhow.

We divided into two teams again: Hamish and the Major, Metilkja and me. Hamish and the Major led off, and soon we were into the old stride, the pace of a thousand different climbs: tool, tool . . . step, step . . . rest and gasp for air, then more of the same, the brain as blank as oxygen. The scenery neve varied from grey on white. The air temperature was warm, and occasionally, as the day wore on, we would hear the baseball *whoosh* of a stone. We would never see it and no one ever got hit. We were too tired to imagine any course of action other than what we were doing. Simply plod and hope. Storm-shrouded silhouettes, we climbed in egocentric removal from one another, companions in nothing more than the movement of the rope. We were shadows caught in random highlight against the whited-out sky. There was no sense of progress, no feeling of getting anywhere. Just the unabating impulse to go on.

In the murk of sunset we gathered on a small, uneven ledge and crouched leg-to-leg as Metilkja passed around sausage and cookies. We dug into our packs after headlamps and sweets. Without shelter it seemed pointless to try to bivouac in the open at such an altitude. So in our inependent pools of light, we continued our long crawl, waiting and climbing, waiting and climbing.

The storm, of course, got worse. We were climbing upward into the nastiness of it. The wind came in violent gusts. The temperature dropped. The snow stung our cheeks and walrus snot-cicles hung from our moustaches. I went into long lapses of memory wherein I could not recall if I had been climbing or standing still. I huddled deeper within myself seeking warmth and coherence and would increasingly return to reality uncertain of what mountain I was on, or with whom.

I began to hear Abrams.

At first I thought nothing of the voice. I have no idea how long I listened to it before it broke upon me that I was hearing an external sound. It was more the sporadic wail of the storm itself than of a man yelling. It was, I thought, some shrieking in my own mind. And then, clearly, I would hear it again. A shout, a sentence. I could never make out the words, but I became convinced that it *was* a voice. And in time it occurred to me that the voice was the Major's.

That it did not stop.

That he was crazy. Mad as the moon. A *sennin*.

And that I was on this mountain with him, being led by him, happy about it. Shit, I was laughing. It got so every time I heard that lunatic howl I'd grin as wide as a cat on crampons. The chaos of the storm reduced the revelation of our insanity to scale: who'd have been there but crazy people, anyway? Why go on peg-footing and stiff-lipping as if it all made sense in the first place? I loved it! I, too felt like howling, but I couldn't find the air the Major could.

At the base of a sixty-foot runnel of water ice, the angle increased to near-vertical. I caught up with Metilkja standing roped in to a gathering of ice screws. Above us, Abrams was wailing and shouting, angry and laughing. Two hundred twenty volts of illuminated madness in that wind-bitten gloom. The stoic and dour Croat was grinning, too. We stood there smiling at each other until the screaming stopped and it was Metilkja's turn to climb. I flicked off my headlamp to save batteries and thought of Lucy. She was right, goddammit. The Buddhists were right, too, and hell, so was the beggar in the alley for that matter. Only madmen and tantric Mansons up here, embracing their flaky *chods*, ice-men *sennins* and their mountain Masta. It was just the right place for them.

We reached the bottom of the summit ice flutings sometime after midnight. Maybe later. I remember finding Hamish hanging from all kinds of webbing and icegear and plastered with rime.

'Major's gone up, laddies,' he said slowly. ''Fraid me hands 'ave aboot had it. Lost me fookin' mitts down there when we poot on the torches.' He was trying to grin. He looked spent and sheepish, letting the rope run through hands jelled into rubbery spoons. He had his parka hood up now, but all the hours without a hat seemed to have had their effect. Metilkja took off his pack and dug into it for some spare socks to cover Hamish's hands. I took over the belay, watching Hamish as I let out the line. He seemed calm, happy, a little guilty, perhaps, but warm and unconcerned. Yet there was a blankness coming into his eyes and expression that carried the look of wistful martyrdom. When the line pulled tight to his waist, we unclipped him from the anchors and moulded his hands around his ice axes. He started singing 'The Hair of Her Dicky-Di-Do' and slammed in his tools.

The air seemed suddenly alive with voices, I could hear Abrams and Hamish, and soon Metilkja shouted and started climbing. We moved faster for a time. The snow stopped and the wind released us. I pulled hard, hand over hand, up the rope and turned a great, pillow-shaped cornice to reach the others clustered on the southwest ridge. The clouds below carpeted the valleys in every direction. The still-dark sky behind us shared its diamond stars with the pallid yellow blot of dawn. The Major stood in the saddle, ice axe in his hands, a serpentine black-and-beige rope hanging loose from his rucksac like the severed head of Hydra. His voice was as cracked and scratched as an old recording.

'This is it, boys!' he shouted. 'Here you go! She's up there, not 500 feet, by God, and we're as good as there! Fancy foot you, O'Brien, eh? It's ours, all right, and no wind, no snow to stop us now! Not when we've come halfway around the world to put our footprints up there, I tell you. The hardest wall in the world?' He laughed, pointing the spike of his axe at the heavens. 'Don't let me hear that talk again. Not in front of boys like these! Come along then, Frazier! Another few hundred feet and you can spit in the face of the God that froze your hands man, scuff your boots on His horrible face, if you've a mind to eh?'

His wild hair sprang horizontally as a gust of wind carried off his woollen balaclava. The vapours danced up the wall like steam to reach for the mother-of-pearl clouds obscuring the sullen sky. The Major roared with laughter at the enormous, cosmic illusion of futility in which the mountain wished us to believe. Frazier was enraptured, his eyes glazed. Metilkja was harder to read: he went about his business neither awed nor annoyed. Myself, I grinned like a Mousketeer for Abrams. His madness had fuelled our upward determination, but getting down was going to take a different frame of mind, and I knew my best chance was with the Yugoslav. Frazier was weakening; Abrams was a whirlwind, vague as a chimera. Only Metilkja had the feel of substance.

Metilkja and I lifted Frazier to his feet and the four of us set out. The angle was easier, and we used our axes like canes. We hiked heads down into a burgeoning gale and rested on our knees. Again I fell behind the others and had only the comfort of their footprints and the Major's occasional shout until the mists parted and I saw them standing together twenty feet in front of me.

On the summit.

Abrams was hatless and howling. Frazier crouched with his frozen hands cupped in front of him as if he were holding snowballs. Metilkja stood beside him, looking away to the east. We danced staccato footsteps, buffeted by the suddenly ferocious wind. After only a few moments Metilkja looked over to me and shouted, 'Down! Now!' He gestured with his ice axe in the opposite direction from which we'd come. He spoke as if we were the only ones there. Neither Frazier nor the Major paid him the least notice.

'There is no harder wall, no harder ice, no higher point upon this mountain, lads! Tea in hell, I tell you!' the Major shouted.

'Down! *Now!*' Metilkja screamed and began to stagger off into the full blast of the wind. I gave a sharp tug on the rope connecting us.

'What about them?' I yelled, pointing at Frazier and the Major. Frazier was staring straight up into heaven as the Major babbled his crazy sermon on the mount. Babes in Toyland.

Metilkja looked at me, his haggard, black eyes as hard as glass. His glance shifted for a moment to our team-mates and then came back to mine. The message was clear and I understood. He turned and worked his way down, and I waited for the rope to run out before following him. I looked at the Major and Frazier as if they were apparitions. I felt nothing for them at all. In fact, I felt nothing about anything until the rope pulled tight and I took my first step down; then all I wanted to do was live. It was all lost now. Nothing was important. The climb, the summit, the entire expedition was without meaning to me. I just wanted down and Metilkja was headed that way. He did not need to pull me.

Descending into the storm was worse than climbing up to it. We had fought hard to get up, and now the mountain seemed to want to hold us there. The gale inflated our windsuits and pressed its hands against our chests. The cold was piercing and terrible. My face burned. Inside a thousand dollars worth of high-tech nylon, plastic, leather and rubber, I felt the cold carve through me. I did not turn and look back for the others. I closed them out of my thoughts and concentrated instead on my own wooden steps. There were no voices now: the storm shrieked louder than Abrams's feeble hoots. It gave us back the proportion of our real achievement. We hadn't 'conquered' the mountain any more than a rat conquers the ocean by hiding in a ship's bilge. We'd skittered across the summit and now crept wretchedly away from any protracted confrontation with the Himalaya's true adolescent savagery. We were running away on frozen feet, less victors than survivors.

The hours were fused with snow. We reached a sérac and stood in its lee to rest. My knees ached and my legs felt cold to the bone. I kept my mind off my feet. I had no idea whatsoever of where we were or where we were headed. We stood panting, our eyes interlocked. Metilkja looked withered and gaunt, awful. He motioned with his head to something behind me. Abrams came out of the storm, still hatless and striding confidently, crisp as a Yorkshire birder, Frazier staggering along after him.

'We'll be done with this in an hour, lads,' the old man cheered. 'We head down this ridge till we find the upper valley glacier. I looked this over last year. One man, by God! Happy me, boys, happy me! She'll not hold us off now, will she, eh? We're too close to it now!' he barked, clenching one fist and holding it up to the sky. 'By Judas, don't anyone talk to me about blasphemy! Why, I'd piss up the wind if I had a mind to. This mountain is *mine*, I tell you! Send down her storm and snow; I'll shove it up spout and stand this ice while I will!' Then, lowering his arm, his eyes on fire, he seemed to speak directly to me. 'Heaven and hell by the short hairs! You'll tell them that for me, won't you? Tell them she was *mine!*'

Metilkja closed his eyes and for an instant dropped his head. When he looked back up, his face was full of the old sobriety and purposefulness. He raised his compass and studied it. I touched Hamish's arm and he looked at me. His cheeks were white, his eyes sunken back a thousand synapses from the horrible truths of the tactile world. I wanted to cry. Instead, I smiled and patted his shoulder.

'See you down there,' I shouted, and he nodded his head. I walked away, knowing I would never see him again.

The rope drew me down into a well of storm. I thought about dying once more, about falling, about sitting down. I thought about heat and hallucinated a room full of stuffed chairs and couches with a stone fireplace and brandy glasses on a long table spread with a linen cloth and the dirty dishes of a sumptuous meal. Metilkja was standing in the corner of the room in his wretched, wind-torn, and rime-sheeted climbing suit. He was wiping away the ice from the headlamp he had been wearing since the night before. I turned on my own light and followed him down through the gloomy penumbra beyond the banquet and into the shelter of a crevasse wall. Just beyond, the ice fell away into an abysmal pit of hurricane updrafts and utter blackness.

Metilkja dropped his pack and pulled out a bandolier of ice screws. Nine in all. I had another six. I groped to fathom our behaviour. The madman had said the ridge would bring us to the glacier and the glacier to the valley. But here? And how far down? And into this storm?

Metilkja suffered none of my neurotic ambivalence. He understood function much better than I. He knew that the doing was the important part and that the outcome would either reward or penalize our boldness. One acted out of strength without hesitation or consorting with hope. One suffered the consequences to the extent he was capable of influencing them. Everything else was either magic or religion. Metilkja threaded the rope through a karabiner and prepared to back off. The ends of the rope waved above us like tentacles, blown straight up into the night by the surging wind and illuminated by our headlamps. And again, for an instant, our eyes met. Then he was gone.

After several moments I felt the line go slack and then ran it through my braking device. I tilted backward and slipped down into the maw of the awful night.

Rappel followed rappel. The cold devoured us, and the wind snapped our sleeves and leggings so hard the material parted. My feet were lost, I knew that. I could feel nothing below my boot tops. I waited out my turns in an aura of torpor. No thought or feeling aroused me except to clip into the rope and slide down to where Metilkja would be waiting, his eyes always searching. During those silent, piercing, sombre, shattering, wind-buffeted meetings, our faces were lit by the dim light of each other's headlamps like Welsh miners, and our silence was the only alternative to the storm.

I knew I was barely hanging on, slowing Metilkja down. I tried to meet his glances with my own strong gaze, but I knew he must be aware of my growing incapacity to think or move. I held tight to the ropes after he was down to keep him from pulling them through the anchor, stranding me.

And rappel followed rappel.

After so many that I had lost count, I found myself clipped to a set of ice screws, watching the flickering yellow light of Metilkja's headlamp disappear into the murk, when an enormous block of ice grazed the névé just above me and plunged on into the darkness, down the line of ropes. I was so frightened, so dazed, that I simply swung from my runner, cringing, my eyes closed for what seemed like fifteen minutes. The ropes were free when I lifted them; the stance below was empty when I arrived. Metilkja was not there. No screw protruded from the wall. No Croatian eyes. Just the night and the storm, the roaring black. I hung onto the ropes waiting for him. I poked around in the snow at my feet to see if I had missed a ledge. I swung left and right in small pendulums and called for him.

There was nothing but some crampon marks scraped in the ice.

I screamed his name, but my pathetic yap barely reached my own ears.

Perhaps he had begun downclimbing, I thought. Yes! That had to be it! The climbing was easy for him. We were going too slow by rappelling; so he had abandoned me and simply begun downclimbing. He had seen the same shadows in my eyes as I had seen in Frazier's: the confusion, the dependence I had on him.

I screamed until I couldn't breathe. I collapsed against the ropes, gasping and hyperventilating. Live, I told myself, live, you stupid fucker! You will *do* this thing. He's either dead or left you. They're all dead, but I will not die here, hanging on this wall, running away from this mountain. I slapped my arms to make the blood circulate and took an ice screw off my harness. I will do this thing and I will live. 'I will live,' I shouted, and pulled down on the ropes.

With two screws left I touched the glacier. I huddled in the protection of a small bergschrund and took off my pack. I crawled into my bivouac sack and sleeping bag. Among other things in my pack I found some sausage and two candy bars, along with an extra pair of mittens. My headlamp faded to dull orange. In its last light I found Metilkja's compass lying in the snow beside me.

I awoke at first light. It was overcast and snowing lightly, but the wind had stilled. I felt rested, weak but alert. I packed just the sleeping bag and a few odds and ends, then cut the rope in two and coiled half of it around my shoulders. Everything else I left to the haunting and oppressive silence.

I lost all concept of time. I followed the compass easterly with no notion of how far I'd come, how many crevasses I'd jumped or circled, no idea of how far I had to go. I found no footprints or discarded gear to suggest that Metilkja was ahead of me. The storm had consumed him as I was now being consumed. Everything was astonishingly white and featureless. I felt like Jonah, floating at peace in the saline bowels of the monster. My mind wandered out in front of me. I watched myself and laughed. I hallucinated fire and food. My body split into Metilkja's half and my half; his side was strong and elegant where mine stumbled pathetically, incompetently. I heard voices – singing, whispers, sighs – but saw nothing. No one. Just the enormous, hopeless white. I was exhausted by midmorning, travelling on slowly-evolving sets of rules: walk two hundred paces and rest, two hundred paces and rest again. I lost count and rested. I lied and rested. I quit counting and rested. I came to a huge pressure ridge. Traversing around its south side, I found what looked like the trough a person might make in fresh snow. It was too blown over with spindrift to find bootprints, but I followed its vague, undulating course, squinting to pick out the subtle gradations of white.

I saw the Major from fifty feet away. I felt a remarkable absence of surprise. The colour of his clothing against the blank canvas of snow and sky was sensational. He was sitting up against his pack. His skin was translucent. His eyes were open and his hands were tucked underneath the armpits of his open parka as if he had just stopped to warm himself. He was still hatless, his hair moving slightly in the ground-level breeze. The black-and-beige rope was crisscrossed over his chest and shoulders in a guide's coil. One end had been cut. I stopped in front of him. I knew he was dead; yet it would not have surprised me if his eyes had moved and his face had turned up. Death had not taken him; he had simply exhausted life, worn it out.

Snow clung to the hairs of his face, and his trousers clapped in the wind. He continued staring back at the mountain, beckoning me to turn around, but there was nothing back there for me. Not anymore. There was nothing to say. I lifted Metilkja's compass and continued on my azimuth.

When it became dark, I used the adze of my axe to dig out a niche between two ice boulders. I emptied what little remained inside my pack onto the snow, crawled into my sleeping bag again, and pulled the pack over my feet and up to my waist. In a small stuff sack I found a tube of Chapstick; I tried to eat it and immediately threw it back up, speckling the snow with bright blood. After a time I dozed. During the night the snow changed to rain.

The air was warm and sodden when I awoke. My sleeping bag was drenched, but the rain had also washed away the snow around me, and for the first time I realized that I was no longer on the glacier. I was sitting between stones, not blocks of ice. I was on the moraine. Dirt and earth were below me. I left everything and started walking.

My feet were horrible. I began falling over everything, lying for a long time before I could rise. And then, finally, I simply couldn't get any higher than my knees. That was okay. I was prepared for that. It did not come as a shock or even a disappointment, just new rules for the game. I crawled for a while, the toes of my boots dragging in the gravel and leaving twin ruts behind me like those of a tiny ox cart. I struggled through a shallow stream of fast-moving meltwater and reached a large boulder on the opposite side, where I lay back and rested. I tore off bits of my windsuit and used the strips to tie my mittens to my knees.

The rain was lighter, a fine Seattle mist. Through breaks in the clouds I could look up to splashes of green on the south-facing slopes of the valley. I noted this arrangement without elation or impatience. I was anticipating nothing. I felt no excitement.

I knew that I was off the mountain and that I would live – that, if necessary, I could crawl to the trail between Kahli La and the Dutch camp and from there crawl down to the yak-herders' hut. If the Sherpas had given up on us and left, then I knew, too, that I could keep crawling . . . over Shipton Col, past Sedua, to Khandbari, to Kathmandu, and all the way back to Boulder. It was no folly; I knew I could succeed in this *chod*.

So I progressed, staggering a few steps on dead feet and then collapsing to basic elbows and knees, shreds of my blue windsuit clinging to the ends of willow twigs. I left blood on the first grass that I reached. I sat for long periods waiting for the energy to move, clinging always to my talisman, Metilkja's compass. I dragged myself on my stomach through thickets of willow and alder, occasionally stopping to listen for the sound of voices or feet.

It was raining slightly when I arrived at the trail. I crawled down into the rut of it – soggy with black mud and as empty as my memory – and lay there a long time, breathing slowly, letting the rain wash my face, and gazing up at the mountain through elliptical gaps in the clouds. It seemed as pristine and aloof to me as it had in Abrams' photographs.

Untouched. Unmoved. Unknowable.

Tears ran down my cheeks. I laughed. I laughed and I cried at the same time, gasping and falling over on my side, helium-headed and sick. Just me . . . of all the heartbeats and dreams, of all the struggle and obsession, I alone remained, more an abstraction than an alpinist, dumb as the last, great, silent *thump* at the end of the universe. I was all that was left. I cried and I laughed and I knew nothing. Only the mud and brush and pebbles.

And it was there that the Dutch expedition, returning with our Sherpas from the futile search for their lost son, found me, another soul orphaned by dreams.

The Bronx Plumber

by Guy Waterman

STRICTLY AN armchair mountain-climber, that's me. You'd never catch me up there dangling from a clothesline. I have one cardinal principle about all forms of exercise: I feel the urge to get up and do something physical, I go lie down quietly until that urge leaves me completely.

I do enjoy reading about mountaineering, though. Especially the old Everest sagas. What great romances those struggles were, back in the Twenties and Thirties, when Tibet was unknown and Nepal forbidden. What great heroes those old-time climbers . . . Mallory and Irvine . . . Colonel Norton . . . Shipton and Tilman. Frank Smythe at Camp Six . . . Odell alone at 25,000 feet straining through the mists for one more sight of his friends above . . . General Bruce. Those were the days when men were men.

If I hadn't been familiar with this literature of early Everest, I might never have stumbled onto a most amazing discovery. That's what my story is about. The reader will not want to believe it really happened; I have trouble believing it myself.

You see, I've never had the slightest interest in spiritualism or all that bunk about contacting spirits from another world. When a man dies, he's over with, I've always believed. Your body goes a-mouldering in the grave and when the worms are through with you, that's it. The old Hindoo notion about transmigration of souls from one body to another – that's a lot of hooey. Right? Right! – only you read my story and then tell me how you explain what I *know* happened to me right here in Twentieth Century New York state.

I'm an ex-newspaperman, worked for one of the Big City's dailies that went under during the Sixties. When I found myself pounding the pavement, I decided to freelance it for awhile. Through the death of an otherwise-not-very-wealthy relative, it was my good fortune to inherit some country property up the Hudson River aways, and the little vila that went with it proved a great place to get away from New York contracts and do my writing. So that's where I used to spend three days a week pounding the typewriter, trying to write something that someone somewhere would buy.

This country place is where the strange event occurred. It was a pleasant old seven-room house, with atmosphere all over it of Nineteenth Century fine living. But decadent! A frightful expense, with wiring that must have been put in by Edison's father and plumbing that leaked like a fishnet out of water. I paid the bills because it sure was a great retreat, not only for my writing, but for some great weekend parties, as well, where me and my friends could play at Gatsby on a modest scale.

The view from the back lawn of this old place was stunning – and turned out to have a considerable role in the events of my narrative. It looked out over the broad Hudson at exactly that point where the big river leaves the flat upstate farmland and abruptly cuts its way through the Hudson Highlands, with Storm King rising 1300 feet right out of the water on the west and an even more spectacular cliff called Breakneck Ridge directly across the river. This Breakneck cliff starts right out with a beetling black precipice of 600 feet or so, overhanging most of the way, and then merges into a wild broken ridge that rises in a series of what I think you call 'false summits' until it is eventually higher than mighty Storm King across the river.

I've seen rock climbers on Breakneck Ridge. With a glass you can usually make them out from my back lawn, except that the glass in my hands and those of my friends isn't usually the kind that aids vision, but rather blurs it. Don't get me wrong now: the events that I'm going to describe happened when I was cold sober, or mostly so at any rate.

As I mentioned, the old house that looks out on this great mountain scenery – maybe unparalleled in the East – was a maintenance man's nightmare, its antediluvian plumbing the immediate cause of the events I am about to describe.

There was just one bathroom in the place, but it was the sort of room that Sir Thomas Crapper probably envisioned as the proper setting for his invention. Not one of your modern little two-by-four johns, but a full-sized room, high-ceilinged, probably a bedroom in the days when the outhouse served for those needs, with a couple of tall windows and a long walk from commode to sink, and lots of room for exercise.

I mention this particular room in such lavish detail, not because of any Freudian hang-ups, but because it played a mischievous role in the unusual events of my tale.

It all started with a Harvard-Yale football weekend. As a loyal son of Eli, I had graciously extended an invitation to two misguided disciples of John Harvard, plus another Yalie, plus wives/girlfriends of the four of us, to begin with a Friday night social at my country place, drive over for the Big Game at New Haven on Saturday, back to my place for a Big Night on Saturday night, with rest and recuperation on Sunday. After this rabelasian programme had run its course, during which much wine had flowed and other high spirits, I discovered on Monday morning that my Paleolithic john had water all over the floor (fortunately mostly water). The worthy apparatus was clogged and any effort to flush it merely added another few gallons to the rising water level on the floor.

I had not, until this occasion, need for the services of a plumber in the small town where my villa was located, but had discovered before that locating other tradesmen was not always easy. I was not too surprised, therefore, that the one local plumber was on vacation. Time-consuming efforts on the telephone eventually established the name and number of another artist of the waterpipes in the neighbouring town, but he proved to have entered the hospital on the evening before for a stay of undefined duration. I repaired back upstairs to my little lake and made what efforts I could to poke around at the insides of the source of the problem. These efforts availed me nothing but dirty hands, wet shoes, and a sour disposition.

It was this extremity which caused me to dial all the way back to the Bronx, where in many long years of a work-a-day existence I had lived and still maintained a small apartment and some reliable contacts for services such as plumbing. Even here, the regular man was on vacation, but I did manage to be referred to a certain Giovanni Malvolio, a master of the pipes whom I was assured was reliable and available. And expensive. Especially when he had to be induced to drive all the way out from the Bronx for this one job. But I was rather desperate for the use of my john.

These were the humble events that were the proximate cause of Mr. Malvolio coming into my life and our story. When he drove his old muddy Dodge truck into my driveway, I was certainly glad to anticipate the solution of my leaky toilet, but had no idea what other astounding developments were to grow out of this seemingly routine visit.

Mr. Giovanni Malvolio showed nothing unusual in his physical presence: he was a Bronx plumber. That about says it. On the short side, olive-skinned, balding, slightly overweight and sloppy about the waist, an effect heightened by the tendency of his shirt and undershirt to come loose from the trousers they had once been tucked into. His face showed all the boredom and absence of excitement that one might expect in the life of a Bronx plumber. I should guess his age in the region of fifty years.

This Machiavelli of the pipes dedicated his worthy efforts to wielding the Stilson wrench for a couple of hours, while I took advantage of a spectacularly clear day to work out on my patio on a card table and typewriter. The views of the Hudson and the precipitous highland cliffs on either side of it were exceptionally clear and compelling, though more of a distraction than an inspiration to my literary efforts of the morning.

At length, the dumpy olive figure of Malvolio presented itself to report the reasons of the problems. In fact, he bore in his grimy hand the villain of the piece, the limp crumpled form of a once-proud Yale football pennant. Evidently, one of my Harvard friends, at an advanced hour of our Saturday night revels, his humour somewhat warped by what others of us had regarded as an altogether satisfactory outcome of events that afternoon (i.e. Yale won), had chosen to vent his frustration by symbolically flushing a Yale banner down the john. It had only succeeded in negotiating the rapids as far as the first turn of the pipes, when it had come around and formed a barrier reef past which, after a flush or two, nothing penetrated. The Army Corps of Engineers never reduced a free-flowing stream to still waters more convincingly. I'm sure you're wondering if it is absolutely necessary for me to give you this complete picture of the fate of my unfortunate plumbing. It isn't of course. What is of interest is Mr. Malvolio's strange conduct after the first minute or two of reporting what the trouble was and how he had successfully restored the waters to their normal, happy, free-flowing navigability.

At first, with all the sensitivity one would expect of a Bronx plumber, he had taken no notice of the sweeping beauty of natural landscape before him. When our business was mostly done, however, his eyes wandered to the river and the cliffs and ridges beyond. Then a strange thing happened. His conversation drifted off and his gaze fixed unblinkingly on the arching silhouette of the rising mountain ridge, with the steep drop-off below. He was not excited or tense, but rather almost sleepy and in a dream state.

My first reaction was to take this as the edifying effect of such a lovely landscape on the repressed soul of a city dweller, and I commented pleasantly: 'Isn't that a delightful view?'

His answer puzzled me, though I first thought nothing much of it. He said: 'After that second step, I knew it would all be easy going to the top, I told Norton.'

Now these words obviously didn't make much sense coming from a dumpy balding Bronx plumber, who had apparently never seen a mountain ridge before, and who was standing on my patio with a Stilson wrench in one grimy fist and a limp Yale banner in the other. They didn't make any sense to me certainly and I blurted out: 'How's that again?'

The trance-like gaze on the mountain horizon seemed to be broken by the intrusion of my simple question. Malvolio jerked as one waking from a doze and looked at me blankly for a second, then his eyes blinked and his pudgy face took on again the dull spiritless look of the Bronx, and he repeated, as if in answer to my question, something about the fate of the upstairs pipes. At this time, the import of his unusual behaviour and words of the moment before had not fully penetrated me, so I failed to press the point and our business was soon concluded. Mr. Malvolio and his truck left; it was, presumably the last time I should see this gentleman with whom I had so little in common.

However, when I tried to resume my writing, I found myself thinking about the odd behaviour of my Bronx pipemaster. After a couple of false starts on the work I had been doing, I took a fresh sheet of paper and tried to recall the words which had so incongruously come from that dumpy form. I think I got them down correctly: 'After the second step, I knew it would all be easy going to the top. I told Norton.'

As a mountain climber, you'll attach these words to the Everest legend more quickly than I did at that time. At first, I was completely mystified, but as I sat staring at the typed words, it did come back to me from my readings on the old twenties expeditions. The problem high on the Northeast Ridge which confronted the early Everesters was regularly referred to as the 'second step'. It was this rock band which had turned aside the attempt of Colonel Norton, forcing him out on the north face itself where eventually he worked his way to what stood as an altitude record for nearly thirty years, about 28,000 feet, before a difficult couloir turned him back. It was also this second step which Mallory and his partner Irvine intended to climb directly so as to reach what appeared to be easier ground on the ridge itself and perhaps be able to go to the summit with no further technical difficulties. It was presumed to be on the rock of the second step that N. E. Odell caught the last glimpse of Mallory and Irvine before the mists closed in and the now legendary pair were never seen again.

When my mind recalled all this, I rather jumped with surprise. But also with considerable confusion. What on earth was a city-bound Bronx plumber doing mumbling nonsense about a second step and Norton? Was he secretly a fan of mountain climbing? Had he got hold of the Everest literature and somehow got to thinking about it during our conversation? All explanations seemed contrived, but I was inclined to let the matter go, with a smile at the unorthodoxy of an unlettered plumber, whom one might have suspected of reading only comic books, working his way through the exotic adventures of British gentlemen in far-off Tibet half a century ago.

I mostly dismissed the whole business from my mind and might never have pursued it to its bizarre conclusion, had my archaic second-floor john continued to function as Malvolio assured me it would. However, fate (and nineteenth century pipes) intervened. Less than a month later, the waters backed up again. Again my own efforts proved singularly ineffective.

Disgusted, I started to look up the number of the local plumber when I recalled the amusing little figure of my Bronx friend and the strange words he had uttered, and I was just curious enough to decide to pay the extra cost of getting him out for the job again. It cost me not only more money but more delay, as he was reluctant to come at all and only agreed to work me in three days hence when he could schedule the long drive out to my country escape. But he did come, and this time even stranger events unfolded.

While he was working on the pipes and sprawled out with his wrench behind and under the antiquated geometry, I recalled the words he had spoken on the earlier trip and, somewhat casually, asked him if he were interested in Everest. He repeated the word blankly once, then said: 'You mean, Everett? I do some work for Harold Everett over on Grand Avenue. You know him?'

No, no, I remonstrated, I meant the mountain Everest. I gathered he was a fan of the old books about climbing Mount Everest. This time I really drew nothing. There was a long silence while he wrenched away at a pipe, then he slid out and wiped his hands slowly and seemed to have forgotten my question. Before he plunged back in with a new piece of equipment, I tried again. 'You like to read about the early attempts to climb Mount Everest?'

He looked at me as if I was not only interrupting his concentration at the job at hand, but was mighty strange at that. No, he didn't know anything about that. Apparently he hadn't even heard of Everest, or at least didn't recall that there was such a place. He didn't know anything about mountains and he didn't have time to read.

I tried just once more. 'Then who's Norton?' 'Norton?' he repeated blankly. 'Morton operates a bakery on Grand just one block up from Everett. Do you mean him?' Obviously the world of Mr. Malvolio was constrained within limits that did not include the wind-swept heights of the Northeast Ridge. Defeated, I repaired to my typewriter out on the patio and tried to resume work.

This time when Mr. Malvolio found me to report his successful repair work, I may have been a bit curt in my manner; I suppose I was covering my embarrassment at asking apparently silly questions. In any case, my Bronx friend responded to my shortness with surliness on his part, but while being careful to avoid doing me the courtesy of looking at me during what would have been an extremely brief exchange, his eyes once again lit on the rocky ramparts so foreign to his usual urban vistas. Once again his whole manner altered. His voiced trailed off, his eyes half shut, though still remaining riveted to the far off serrated ridge. Instantly recognizing this trance-like state as that which he had exhibited on his former visit, I ceased speech and almost held my breath for fully a minute. It was Malvolio who broke the silence, murmuring in barely audible tones: 'I wonder if we really could have turned that step on the way down.'

I was enthralled. Was I really hearing these words from this most unlikely apparition, which had just now exhibited a total ignorance of and disinterest in mountaineering of a bygone age? I risked breaking the spell, by quietly asking him what he meant. My venture worked – and his answer nearly made the flesh on the back of my neck crawl.

'Well, I say, we might have tried going out on the snow of the east face. We might have negotiated a way around and got back on to the ridge a couple of hundred feet lower.'

I was aghast. The English mode of speech, on top of the thrust of what he was saying had me utterly spellbound and an indefinable apprehension came over me. Who was – or what was – I in the presence of? As calmly as I could control my stammering voice, I again ventured a question: 'What *did* you do then?'

I was, I confess, almost relieved to note that this new interruption produced quite a different effect. Malvolio's head jerked around, his eyes torn from the distant ridge, his now-unclouded vision focused full on me, and he sullenly grunted: 'What?'

'What did you do?' I repeated.

'I told you, I cleared the pipes, mister. If you're more careful about what goes down the toilet, you won't have these troubles. And it'd save me a long drive. I got to charge you for the time.'

I waved him away, frustrated in my inquiries again. I was unable to think of any pretext for detaining him with any hope of reintroducing that trance-like effect which had produced such astounding words from such a pedestrian source.

But he was scarcely gone before my mind reeled with the enormity of this accidental and highly fortuitous discovery. I resolved to read up on mysticism, transcendentalism, reincarnation, and every form of the occult that I could lay my hands on. In scouring libraries over the next two weeks, I read more foolishness, charlatanism, and quackery than you could imagine and managed to uncover nothing remotely believable on the subject. A number of librarians gave me amused looks along with their assistance and I soon began to feel quite foolish myself.

But here was the evidence of my own eyes and ears before me. A Bronx plumber with no interest in or knowledge of mountaineering was somehow transformed at the sight of a rock ridge into something – I knew not what. Some hidden, buried secrets swam up through his consciousness and surfaced without his willingness or even awareness. What weird irrational explanation could account for this phenomenon?

I don't recall at what point it suddenly occurred to me that the initials of Giovanni Malvolio were precisely those of George Mallory. Indeed, the first three letters of the last names were the same. I scarcely dared notice that Mr. Malvolio's apparent age could well put his birthdate somewhere around 1924 – the year (perhaps the day?) of Mallory's disappearance and evident demise far away on the storm-swept upper slopes of Mount Everest.

With chilling determination, I knew I had to entice that strange dumpy figure back out here. This time I would plan carefully how best to draw him out further, to try to maintain the trance-like state, to penetrate deeper into this inscrutable mystery.

A considerable portion of the next two days was spent in futile efforts to secure the cooperation of my bathroom pipes. Before the waters finally stopped, I had lost a couple of old Harvard banners, one T-shirt, and a purple-striped pyjama top sent to me several Christmases ago by an obscure aunt. Where once those antebellum drains had been all too eager to clog up, they now swept all before them. Finally, though, that aunt's pyjama top (well, not her pyjama top, but you know what I mean) did the trick, and I was soon happily sloshing through water on the john floor towards the telephone to summon my hero of the sewers.

When the next day dawned, on which he had grumpily agreed to come for repairs, I was at first dismayed. A thick overcast of drizzly clouds totally obscured the view from my patio towards the cliffs and rock ridge which had touched off Mr. Malvolio's previous trance-like states and which was the key to my present strategy. To my great relief, however, as the morning wore on, the weather improved just enough for visibility to extend to the cliff line; in fact, I nurtured the hope that the wild misty atmosphere which enshrouded the rocky heights might still further enhance the spirit in which those final days high on Everest might be recalled.

To the plumber's mind, my insistence on working out on the patio on such a cold, damp morning may have confirmed his suspicion of my complete lunacy. However, he did get the pipes flowing again as before; and he *did* come to find me out on the patio as before.

For some reason, on this day his gaze did not come to rest on the distant cliffs as promptly as before. In fact, we went through a considerable exchange of forced dialogue, with me trying awkwardly to sustain the conversation while moving around in an effort to manoeuvre his line of vision to take the cliffs. I was beginning to feel quite foolish about the whole business again, and would have let it drop in another minute. But then . . .

As before, Malvolio's eyes finally lit on the mountain horizon; his lids half closed; his voice trailed off, his jaw hanging slack in mid-phrase; he stood motionless, limp, transfixed.

With my nerves on end, I froze and waited an eternity for him to speak the first words. To my surprise and apprehension, something like a half-smile slowly emerged on the plumber's normally inexpressive features. Then he said: 'Exhilarating rock moves! Especially at that altitude. And then . . . clear sailing to the top!'

He paused. With a monumental effort to control my pounding heart, I spoke as quietly and calmly as I could: 'Then you *did* make it to the summit?'

'Right to the top! No trouble at all on the upper snow slopes, except for being so deucedly exhausted from the thin air. 'Twas much easier coming down, that's certain.'

I found myself numb and breathless. What had I stumbled onto? With infinite deliberation, I ventured the words: 'Then, why did you fall?'

His reply came back in a stammer: 'I . . . I thought . . . I thought I could find the route better, if I went first. It didn't seem like difficult rock.'

His eyes still riveted on the distant ridge, my companion answered, his voice even and calm: 'It was Andy's problems downclimbing the rock. Of course, he'd have had no great difficulty if we'd been fresh. I assumed he could do the move; have no trouble with it.'

As he spoke these words, I found myself drawn by the intensity of his gaze to look myself at the far-off ridge of rock above the precipitous cliff, with the wisps of old rain-clouds still drifting around. As I looked out at this scene and heard the words spoken by Malvolio – or Mallory, or whoever or whatever was uttering these strange far-off words – I suddenly felt as if an unseen force racked my tense frame with one pervasive shock. Then I felt myself lapsing into a dream-like state, my own eyes riveted on the distant rocks. The other voice came to me as through high, misty clouds:

'As he got to the hard move, I saw he was going to come off. I tried to get myself set to catch the fall when the rope came tight.'

He paused. As if from afar, I heard my own voice say: 'But if you had let me go down first, you might have held my fall from above. I knew I was going to fall in time to give you warning. You could have braced yourself, given me tension . . . We wouldn't both have fallen. You could have held us from above, instead of getting pulled off too. But you were in a hurry and insisted on going first.'

'I knew it would be a bit tricky.'

'Not to you,' I heard myself say. 'You didn't even put away your ice axe. Yet you knew I wasn't in your class as a rockclimber. Particularly coming down . . . I'd never done much. . .'

My voice stopped as I felt the weight of his hand on my shoulder. 'Andrew,' he said, 'what point recriminations now? We fell – but we did not fail. We climbed it, didn't we? What could life have held for us after such a triumph? Where could we have gone on to from there?'

He may have said more, but my memory blanks out there. Apparently I blacked out, fell heavily on a wrought iron bench, cutting my forehead, and stretched senseless on the patio. When I was next conscious, my neighbour was washing off the forehead cut, having somehow got me inside and placed me on a comfortable couch. When he saw that I was coming to, he asked how I was and, as I did not instantly reply, suggested that I might wish to get into drier clothes but otherwise take it easy till I felt better.

I half started up. 'But where's Mallory?' I demanded.

'Who?' My neighbour looked somewhat puzzled, alarmed.

'Mal . . . Malvolio,' I stammered. 'The plumber.'

'Oh yes, the fellow who called me over to look after you. He left fifteen minutes ago. Said the pipes ran fine now. Said he'd send you the bill.'

My first instinct was to rush for my car, set off in wild pursuit. But a chilling fear overcame my curiosity. I would go after him later perhaps. Just at that moment I could recall little of our last words together, but the force of what we had discovered, groping together as we both gazed at the mist-shrouded rocky heights, gripped my thoughts.

At my neighbour's insistence I remained quiet; and, indeed, found myself so physically and emotionally drained that I soon drifted into a profound sleep that carried me through the night.

When I awoke the next morning and was stumbling around trying to get myself breakfast, my neighbour reappeared, cheerfully inquiring how I felt this morning. I assured him I was okay, anxious not to remain subject to his protective scrutiny any longer than neighbourly manners required. I was determined to set off to find Mr. Malvolio, wherever he was, whoever he was, to confront him with the enormity of our discovery.

'Say, did you see that awful thing in this morning's paper? Little item in the second section? That plumber of yours, I think it was him. Malvolio – that was his name, wasn't it? His truck struck a bridge rampart on the Interstate yesterday afternoon. On his way back from here, I suppose. He was killed instantly.'

In Gentle Combat with the Cold Wind

by Jeff Long

IT WAS bitter that Halloween midnight, near Nevada. Across the entire desert there was only one movement not at the mercy of the north wind: a small and battered Volkswagen was feeling its way through the night, its passage marked by the wavering beam of its headlights. Even the stars had succumbed to the approaching blizzard, having vanished in cloud.

Peter Guerre, the car's sole occupant, ignored the building storm. Preoccupied with his thoughts, he drove on toward Lee Vining. He was glad, now, that he hadn't told the tale of his solo on Washington's Column. The Column hadn't been difficult, he decided: one long reach above that bolt on the fifth, that was it really, and he'd been faster than ever. Peter Guerre, better known as P.G., the Kingsbury Magician, fast, flashy, taciturn. Globe-trotting from Baffin Island to Patagonia, from Australia to Chamonix, he'd seen some of the best rock on the planet. Youngest climber on the Dhaulagiri expedition in '73, and one of the two lads topping out Lhotse on a Dutch invitation two years later, he'd gone on to cap it all with a staggering two-week solo of Pumori, for which he was still being lionized. At the age of twenty-four, his name was known, his legend inseminated. Ambitious and physically powerful, P.G. was renowned as a master craftsman who tamed stone and ice to his own devices. And, though the accolades left their mark, P.G. had discovered that he could afford modesty, that in fact it enhanced his reputation and gave him an air of intelligent gravity.

He recalled a large film-showing in Aspen last spring. Without a word as to his identity, he had politely introduced the film by title before addressing a softly spoken 'please' to the projectionist who waited to engineer the lights. The room had hushed black, then lit up with stormy, antipodal sunshine. On a whim, P.G. had slipped from the room and left, his silhouette marring the screen momentarily then vanishing. After the film had run for several minutes, a common murmur amongst the audience showed that they had recognized one particular celluloid figure – a young man garbed in a wind-blown, rock-torn clothing, sporting a livid scar down one cheek and brandishing his ice-axe like an educated demon. It was only then that they connected this bellicose Kingsbury Magician with their tall, gentle master of ceremonies. An hour later, when the Himalayan sun sank like a red diamond into the night and the auditorium lights flashed on again, everyone looked around eagerly for the paradoxical Magician. But the hero was gone, the podium empty. The audience, he learned later, had groaned. In his quiet way, P.G. found that very gratifying – existing as a silhouette faster than reality. The mountaineering itself was automatically satisfying, but it took on a double sweetness when he considered that each new climb was also one further appendage to his reputation. He had no idea where the wheel of fame would deposit him; he didn't think about it. It was a hobby as much as a lifestyle. Some people collect butterflies, some collect knives, P.G. collected mountains, though more precisely he collected anecdotes about himself climbing mountains. Often his climbs yielded nothing in the way of kudos. His solo on the Column had been a complete bust in that sense, upstaged by Byrd's solo on the Shield and by some unknown gymnast's ascent of a 5.11 +. But, as had become habit by now, P.G. had said nothing when, earlier that evening, he'd strode into camp, dumped his gear and gone over to stand by a camp-fire. For an hour he listened to the other stories: how Byrd was muttering to himself when friends found him on the summit edge; how the gymnast had overcome the final knob, stood up, and speechlessly dropped his hand in retrospective surrender. P.G. hadn't bothered to mention his own bold sortie of the past few days, because by comparison it wasn't so bold. The tale would come out some other time. And by then he would have vanished again.

A snowflake drifted down into his headlights, then flashed overhead. Two more hours to Kingsbury Grade, P.G. estimated: to home, a bath, food and sleep. He accelerated slightly. If it was snowing here in Lee Vining, it would be coming down heavily upon Kingsbury Grade. Snow on Halloween: a cold night for souls. Veering gently, he swept down off Tioga Pass, then slowed to enter Lee Vining. The town was dead, the Coffee Shoppe closed, the lights at the gas station off. A tenuous outcrop of brick and wood in the daytime, Lee Vining now looked like the end of the world – dark, empty and wordless. P.G. might even have failed to register the town in its brevity and silence, had not a second snowflake lanced his tired stare. Shaking his head sharply, he broke from his trance. As he crossed the outer fringes of midnight and the ghost town, his headlights picked out a third snowflake, a steady, white point. P.G. fixed his faraway highway stare on it. The snowflake didn't drift or dance, it remained stationary. As he drove closer, it assumed proportion, then swelled into an object. At last P.G. saw that his snowflake was the figure of a man, and closer still, that of an old man.

The man was just beyond the town's edge, stock-still and waiting, neither patiently nor impatiently to judge by his posture, just waiting. He stood at the side of the road like a tattered mannequin, hands stiffly lowered, head up. P.G. slowed down. He examined the figure with grim, half-bemused curiosity. The man was dressed in bizarre and ancient clothing: a greasy, torn cagoule, a mouldering balaclava, both calves wrapped in cloth strips. In the chill desert on Highway 395, it was these last that struck P.G. more than the rest – puttees taping the frail legs of an alcoholic. He slowed even more, expecting the hobo to extend his thumb or wave him down. He was obviously in search of a ride, for why else would he be standing here on the side of the road at midnight? The Volkswagen edged closer. Despite the decrepit costume, there was something about the old man's stance that gave him a look of fragility and sad dignity. The man didn't raise his hand. 'Okay,' murmured P.G., and he would have driven on, leaving the man to his obstinacy and cheap wine, but in the glare of the headlights the old man continued to stare with unflinching nonchalance. Ferocity or liquor? P.G. examined the old face more carefully and suddenly jerked his head in shock. Within the wizened crowsfeet lacing of the old man's eyes, the sockets were collapsed, sunken with disuse: the old man was blind.

P.G. stopped with a hiss, cursing the night. He must belong somewhere, thought P.G. – crouched in some empty garage or covered in newspapers beside a garbage can, but at least out of the snow. The old man waited by the car, his cagoule punched and bitten by the Nevada wind. P.G. leaned over and rolled down the window. He had to call twice before the old man's face, sun blackened and with eyes squeezed shut, appeared at the window.

'So,' rasped the old man, 'a ride north.' The proclamation twisted off with the night wind. P.G. shrugged. The old spook could go as far north as he was going, then find another ride. He wiggled the stick out of gear and stepped out. It was bitterly cold, dry and sharp. A little like Lhotse's cold, he decided. His breath trailed him as he walked round through the two spears of light to his passenger.

'North,' mumbled the old man. P.G. opened the car door and guided him by one thin arm towards the seat. The old man limped heavily, scraping the asphalt. P.G. looked down at the cracked boots. Hobnails bordered their soles. Hobnails and puttees – antiquity itself.

'I'm Andrew,' the old man announced from inside the car. P.G. closed the door and walked back round to his own side. 'Andrew,' the old man repeated as P.G. got in. His voice was bare like a worn bone. The manner and tone in which he announced his name located him far outside P.G.'s company, a passive dereliction. P.G. didn't offer his own name. It would have been wasted breath to such an afflicted spirit. The old man, wrapped in his ancient cagoule, seemed anyway oblivious. Whipped by the accumulating storm, the Volkswagen shot away.

'I'm cold,' came a whisper.

'Heat's on,' P.G. answered. It was already hot in the car, and he could smell the vents scorching a handful of junk perlon he'd tossed on to the back floor. Nevertheless the old man was shivering, perhaps as a result of his wait by the roadside. For a time the old man and boy rode in silence, enveloped in the hollow can of a mutual environment, the wind outside pounding at the car. P.G. tried to plug back into his thoughts of the Column climb, but the heat and monotonous darkness seduced him. He had to break violently out of sleep a second time. He reached for the radio to dispel the journey's weight, but just as he pinched the volume knob the old manrapped him with another whisper.

'We climbed,' he muttered. 'We climbed high.'

P.G. snapped a glance at his passenger, but saw only the cowl of his hat and a shock of renegade white hair. Climbing? P.G. interpreted the old man's remark as an ingratiating prelude to a conversation in general. But how could he have known that P.G. was a climber? The ropes and gear on the back seat? The smell of scorched perlon? Then the old man's ragged costume echoed its intimation. The garb was half-a-century out of time, but clearly alpinist in mode. Was the masquerade more deliberate than coincidental? A single moment passed as P.G. explored the possibility that this old man had been waiting for him, Peter Guerre, on the side of the midnight road; an ancient climber lying in wait for a young one. How ominous, P.G. chided himself, a cold blind Halloween vampire.

Since there was no tail to the old man's opening statement, P.G. asked him with sceptical hesitation where he'd climbed. The old man raised a hand, orchestrating thoughts. P.G. watched the hand drop back on to the old man's thigh. Finally the old man spoke, coherent but absurd.

'Everest,' he said. A smile ribbed his face. 'I do remember that, that I climbed Everest.' There was neither modesty nor boasting in the coarse, empty voice. P.G. gave a little snort and turned his head to mock the blind man with a grin. He was amused. By his rigid credo a person who couldn't fire a warthog into 85° ice, or figure out an easy 5.10, was a scrambler, or worse a liar. The old man was a liar.

'Cracker?' P.G. held up a half-rifled box of wheat thins. For several minutes he attempted a dialogue, hoping to recover the talk about the climb. But it was a wispy, halting exchange, acid with the boy's doubt and lamed by the wino's senility. It serviced neither of them. The old, striated face had locked shut. Suddenly, unprompted, the old man rustled.

'Yes,' he declared. 'I climbed Everest.' The statement was vigorous this time, even proud. By the balls, you liar, P.G. grinned to himself. He'd been to Everest himself, climbed Lhotse, been through the Khumbu Icefall, descended by the South Col. He would let the old man build his fiction into a mountain, then, as at other times with other liars, expose the lie with the real mountain. Maybe not though, he demurred. In fact . . . why? This lie and these clothes were probably Andrew's only possessions. P.G. found himself wondering how such creatures come to wander apart from the rest of their race, becoming alley and road animals without an anchor in the world. That's just the way it is, though, P.G. conceded. Every town on earth has drifters like this one: men who appear, utter and then disappear. Their fictions atrophy, and they die.

Just then the snowstorm erupted, flinging itself in erratic, ballooning swirls at the windshield. By the time they'd passed Mono Lake there was a soft white mantle adhering to the scrub brush and coating the highway. P.G. started to chastise himself for having picked up the old man. Now he'd have to drop the spook off somewhere but with all this snow it couldn't be just anywhere. Momentarily, P.G. considered his own home, then tallied the samaritan complications and rejected the idea. Besides, there was a home for such spirits as this in Reno, fifty miles north, hours distant . . . but after all, P.G. sighed, it was merely an inconvenience, an extra couple of dollars for gas, an extra few hours. He found it a little touching that one climber should be giving a hand to another, even if it was to a liar dressed in rags. It suggested the traces of a climbing community, the young tending their elders. And trying to feed them crackers, scoffed P.G., and put up with their bullshit. Everest!

He broke the thought and aligned a new one, slowly rebuilding the Column. Last night at this time . . . two twisted trees, a bolt painted yellow, a thin wafer of rock to sit on . . . and cold. But had tonight's snow appeared last night while he was cadging sleep, P.G. thought, he would have really suffered. The snow had waited though; he wasn't called the Magician for nothing. He always managed to recover from the nights, their loneliness and raw chill. He always had control, slender sometimes, but sufficient.

The old man muttered something loud but incoherent then, disrupting P.G.'s reverie. Giving powerful nods of his woolcapped head, the old man seemed bent on confirming his illusions. P.G. turned his attention back to the road. It was becoming thickly coated with fat snowflakes, stretching on and on.

'Cold?' the old man suddenly barked. There was a rattling deep in his throat. 'Cold?' he asked again, more gently.

P.G. glanced over. His cagoule tucked beneath his chin, the old man sat very straight, his tweeded thighs pointing stiffly forward like old men keep their legs, simply and firmly planted. By the greenish light radiating from the dashboard, P.G. picked out the stained wraps of the puttees, even discovering a petal of rust on the small buckle clasping the knicker cuffs.

'Andrew,' P.G. said.

'Andrew?' answered Andrew. The face smiled at him, but again not at him. The old man was looking far away, somewhere else, dark and alone. P.G. examined the old face and its intense sunburn. For the first time he noticed the perimeters of its stain, two eyelets above the blistered, peeling nose and cheeks. P.G. had seen such faces before; goggles and sun, the mark of alpine climbing. It mildly surprised him. A pair of big sunglasses and a bender in the desert, P.G. guessed. How else such an odd sunburn?

'You still cold?' he asked the old man.

'I was asked to go down,' replied the old man quietly. 'Give me your air, go down. It was very high you see, and I hurt and wanted to go down.' Caught in his mountains, P.G. realized. Old Andrew's stuck on Everest. He respected the old man for that. Impoverished as he was, Andrew still had the integrity to embody his lie.

'So I hadn't any air,' continued Andrew. 'Then I remembered the length of shadows in the afternoon and followed them back down.' P.G. listened, cynical, though not unsympathetic.

'Who were they?' he finally asked. 'Who sent you down?'

'No.' The old man apologized tangentially. 'Names slip by me.'

Sure thing, thought P.G. As much as he liked the old man's bizarre façade, the gall and fatuity, he still resented the actual lie that had been created. Long ago he'd decided that mountains belong to the climbers who touch them, not to flatland men with cheap words and bravado. Ambivalently, still curious though irritated, P.G. rejoined the conversation.

'You can't remember any names at all?'

'There was . . . Tibet of course. We crossed south.' The old man's hand brushed at the air as if to clear away the obvious. A little gold star for geography, P.G. sniffed to himself. 'But the mountain parts I have trouble with,' finished the old man. 'It's been so long.'

'How about the South Col?' prodded P.G. 'You probably remember that, don't you?' A vision of bleakness and wind swept through him eidetically. He saw the area again, shingled rocks and hard scabs of snow, and a single piece of cardboard poking from its grave.

'No,' said Andrew. 'I don't know about the South Col.' He didn't seem intimidated or embarassed by his ignorance, though, and there was no righteousness to his statement. He acted as plainly as when he'd first said his name was Andrew. It confused P.G. He'd expected a pouting, rheumy defense to his attack on the unreal mountain. But the loose smile remained, and this ingenuous amnesia continued.

Pretend, thought P.G., pretend he did climb Everest. Treat the mountain like a mirror: the Nepali half reflects the Tibetan half, the South Col weighs against the North Col, the Khumbu Glacier against the Rongbuk Glacier. P.G. looked at the old man. Let him climb the mirror. Help him climb. The game suddenly intrigued him, this piecing fact with fraud, with fiction.

'Well,' asked P.G. 'did you go through the icefall?' He calculated the mountain, carefully omitting the name of the icefall.

'The icefall?' questioned the old man.

'The Khumbu ice?' offered P.G. It's blue seracs surfaced in his mind again, the moon illuminating sharp holes, tiny orange and blue tents lit up like paper lanterns among the rubble below, and the listless red marker flags on bamboo wands that tilted lower each day, the icefall ingesting them. P.G. caught his breath at the vivid memory, that solitary night in the icefall which he could never share because it was so embedded and complex. He shook his head at the memory.

'I don't think I've been there, that area,' the old man decided after a moment. 'Maybe we went a different way, my colleagues and I.' Okay, thought P.G. Don't hang yourself yet old man. Let's play the game as far as it goes. He didn't ask about the Rongbuk Glacier which lay in Tibet, he wasn't sure about it, nor did he want to know about it for the time being. Khumbu Icefall and South Col went together with the Nepali Everest, and the old man had denied them all. P.G. applauded the old man's consistency. It translated into an attempt from the Tibetan side, illogically but possibly as the old man had claimed. It dated the lie, marking it a lie of the 'twenties or 'thirties. But how Tibetan can Andrew keep his fiction, P.G. asked himself. One wrong answer from the old man and the mountain would vanish into its lie. It would have turned into naïve malice and P.G. would drop it altogether. But the two of them were still ascending Everest, still composing its lines, conceding its unrealities. By building as many blanks as possible, P.G. knew, they could escape pure fact. He shifted into third gear. Snow was accumulating on the highway.

'I was twenty-two years old,' the old man offered. 'I was young. Then I was told, give me your air. Go down.' The old man waved his hand and slapped it softly on his leg, a gesture of fatigue.

'It wasn't Hillary who told you to go down, was it?' P.G. felt certain that Hillary had never sent anyone back down the mountain. There was no reply. The old man was beginning to sink back into his mute images. Don't slip away, old man. P.G. thought.

'Was it Noyce or Odell or Mallory?' P.G. had to dredge their names from nearly forgotten history. The game was complicating itself inwards. He wasn't sure how much longer he could feed the old man blanks.

Andrew mumbled again about the cold and lengthening shadows. And P.G. remembered how shadows stretched long and low on the mountain. It would grow cold while the summit was gradually devoured from below by the darkness, the body of the mountain swallowed bit by bit until at last the very crown faded. Then all the humans would get in their tents.

'Then what did you do? Where did you go down to?' P.G. tried to make his question unobtrusive to the old man's reverie. Beneath the blind sockets the parched, cracking lips moved rapidly. There was a long pause. The old man raised and dropped his hand.

'I can't remember.' It was final. Old Andrew couldn't remember.

'You can't say how high you got?' P.G. persisted, trying to reconstruct the flow of the story, the geometry of the mountain.

'It was very painful,' said the old man. 'It was very cold.'

P.G. remembered that too, how very cold it could be. Everything would freeze. The only way really to thaw out would be to climb, up or down, it didn't matter much, but stasis was fatal. Even illusions were better than simple frozen sleep. P.G. remembered sharing a tent with two other men. Throughout the cold night he had heard them shifting and muttering, talking within themselves. Then in the morning they had all emerged from their unreal worlds, put on their boots and climbed.

The old man sank back into his algid mutters. In the headlights everything was covered now with snow; the flat white world stretched on and on. It was very cold there. P.G. drove on with the blind man pressing on through the black morning. He tried to talk about their mountain some more, but the old man had gone to sleep.

MOTHER GODDESS OF THE WORLD

a novella by
Kim Stanley Robinson

CHAPTER ONE

MY LIFE started to get weird again the night I ran into Freds Fredericks, near Chimoa, in the gorge of the Dudh Kosi. I was guiding a trek at the time, and was very happy to see Freds. He was travelling with another climber, a Tibetan by the name of Kunga Norbu, who appeared to speak little English except for 'Good morning,' which he said to me as Freds introduced us, even though it was just after sunset. My trekking group was settled into their tents for the night, so Freds and Kunga and I headed for the cluster of teahouses tucked into the forest by the trail. We looked in them; two had been cleaned up for trekkers, and the third was a teahouse in the old style, frequented only by porters. We ducked into that one.

It was a single low room; we had to stoop not only under the beams that held up the slate roof, but also under the smoke layer. Old style country buildings in Nepal do not have chimneys, and the smoke from their wood stoves just goes up to the roof and collects there in a very thick layer, which lowers until it begins to seep out under the eaves. Why the Nepalis don't use chimneys, which I would have thought a fairly basic invention, is a question no one can answer; it is yet another Great Mystery of Nepal.

Five wooden tables were occupied by Rawang and Sherpa porters, sprawled on the benches. At one end of the room the stove was crackling away. Flames from the stove and a hissing Coleman lantern provided the light. We said Namaste to all the staring Nepalis, and ducked under the smoke to sit at the table nearest the stove, which was empty.

We let Kunga Norbu take care of the ordering, as he had more Nepali than Freds or me. When he was done the Rawang stove keepers giggled and went to the stove, and came back with three huge cups of Tibetan tea.

I complained to Freds about this in no uncertain terms. 'Damn it, I thought he was ordering chang!'

Tibetan tea, you see, is not your ordinary Lipton's. To make it they start with a black liquid that is not made from tea leaves at all but from some kind of root, and it is so bitter you could use it for suturing. They pour a lot of salt into this brew, and stir it up, and then they dose it liberally with rancid yak butter, which melts and floats to the top.

Actually it tastes worse than it sounds. I have developed a strategy for dealing with the stuff whenever I am offered a cup; I look out the nearest window, and water the plants with it. As long as I don't do it too fast and get poured a second cup, I'm fine. But here I couldn't do that, because twenty-odd pairs of laughing eyes were staring at us.

Kunga Norbu was hunched over the table, slurping from his cup and going 'ooh,' and 'ahh,' and saying complimentary things to the stove keepers. They nodded and looked closely at Freds and me, big grins on their faces.

Freds grabbed his cup and took a big gulp of the tea. He smacked his lips like a wine taster. 'Right on,' he said, and drained the cup down. He held it up to our host. 'More?' he said, pointing into the cup.

The porters howled. Our host refilled Freds's cup and he slurped it down again, smacking his lips after every swallow. I held my nose to get down a sip, and they thought that was funny too.

So we were in tight with the teahouse crowd, and when I asked for chang they brought over a whole bucket of it. We poured it into the little chipped teahouse glasses and went to work on it.

'So what are you and Kunga Norbu up to?' I asked Freds.

'Well,' he said, and a funny expression crossed his face. 'That's kind of a long story, actually.'

'So tell it to me.'

He looked uncertain. 'It's too long to tell tonight.'

'What's this? A story too long for Freds Fredericks to tell? Impossible, man, why I once heard you summarize the Bible to Laure, and it only took you a minute.'

Freds shook his head. 'It's longer than that.'

'I see.' I let it go, and the three of us kept on drinking the chang, which is a white beer made from rice or barley. We drank a lot of it, which is a dangerous proposition on several counts, but we didn't care. As we drank we kept slumping lower over the table to try and get under the smoke layer, and besides we just naturally felt like slumping at that point. Eventually we were laid out like mud in a puddle.

Freds kept conferring with Kunga Norbu in Tibetan, and I got curious. 'Freds, you hardly speak a word of Nepali, how is it you know so much Tibetan?'

'I spent a couple of years in Tibet, a long time ago. I was studying in one of the Buddhist lamaseries there.'

'*You* studied in a Buddhist lamasery in Tibet?'

'Yeah sure! Can't you tell?'

'Well . . .' I waved a hand. 'I guess that might explain it.'

'That was where I met Kunga Norbu, in fact. He was my teacher.'

'I thought he was a climbing buddy.'

'Oh he is! He's a climbing lama. Actually there's quite a number of them. See, when the Chinese invaded Tibet they closed down all the lamaseries, destroyed most of them in fact. The monks had to go to work, and the lamas either slipped over to Nepal, or moved up into mountain caves. Then later the Chinese wanted to start climbing mountains as propaganda efforts, to show the rightness of the thoughts of Chairman Mao. The altitude in the Himalayas was a little bit much for them, though, so they mostly used Tibetans, and called them Chinese. And the Tibetans with the most actual mountain experience turned out to be Buddhist lamas, who had spent a lot of time in really high, isolated retreats. Eight of the nine so-called Chinese to reach the top of Everest in 1975 were actually Tibetans.'

'Was Kunga Norbu one of them?'

'No. Although he wishes he was, let me tell you. But he did go pretty high on the North Ridge in the Chinese expedition of 1980. He's a really strong climber. And a great guru too, a really holy guy.'

Kunga Norbu looked across the table at me, aware that we were talking about him. He was short and skinny, very tough looking, with long black hair. Like a lot of Tibetans, he looked almost exactly like a Navaho or Apache Indian. When he looked at me I got a funny feeling; it was as if he was staring right through me to infinity. Or somewhere equally distant. No doubt lamas cultivate that look.

'So what are you doing up here?' I asked, a bit uncomfortable.

'We're going to join my Brit buddies, and climb Lingtren. Should be great. And then Kunga and I might try a little something on our own.'

We found we had finished off the bucket of chang, and we ordered another. More of that and we became even lower than mud in a puddle.

Suddenly Kunga Norbu spoke to Freds, gesturing at me. 'Really?' Freds said, and they talked some more. Finally Freds turned to me. 'Well, this is a pretty big honour, George. Kunga wants me to tell you who he really is.'

'Very nice of him,' I said. I found that with my chin on the table I had to move my whole head to speak.

Freds lowered his voice, which seemed to me unnecessary as we were the only two people in the room who spoke English. 'Do you know what a *tulku* is, George?'

'I think so,' I said. 'Some of the Buddhist lamas up here are supposed to be reincarnated from earlier lamas, and they're called tulkus, right? The abbot at Tengboche is supposed to be one.'

Freds nodded. 'That's right.' He patted Kunga Norbu on the shoulder. 'Well, Kunga here is also a tulku.'

'I see.' I considered the etiquette of such a situation, but couldn't really figure it, so finally I just scraped my chin off the table and stuck my hand across it. Kunga Norbu took it and shook, with a brief, modest smile.

'I'm serious,' Freds said.

'Hey!' I said. 'Did I say you weren't serious?'

'No. But you don't believe it, do you.'

'I believe that you believe it, Freds.'

'He really is a tulku! I mean I've seen proof of it, I really have. His *Ku kongma*, which means his first incarnation, was as Naropa, a very important Tibetan lama born in 1555. The monastery at Kum-Bum is located on the site of his birth.'

I nodded, at a loss for words. Finally I filled up our little cups, and we toasted Kunga Norbu's age. He could definitely put down the chang like he had had lifetimes of practice. 'So,' I said, calculating. 'He's about four hundred and thirty-one.'

'That's right. And he's had a hard time of it, I'll tell you. The Chinese tore down Kum-Bum as soon as they took over, and unless the monastery there is functioning again, Naropa can never escape being a disciple. See, even though he is a major tulku –'

'A major tulku,' I repeated, liking the sound of it.

'Yeah, even though he's a major tulku, he's still always been the disciple of an even bigger one, named Tilopa. Tilopa Lama is about as important as they come – only the Dalai Lama tops him – and Tilopa is one hard, hard guru.'

I noticed that the mention of Tilopa's name made Kunga Norbu scowl, and refill his glass.

'Tilopa is so tough that the only disciple who has ever stuck with him has been Kunga here. Tilopa – when you want to become his student and you go ask him, he beats you with a stick. He'll do that for a couple of years to make sure you really want him as a teacher. And then he really puts you through the wringer. Apparently he uses the methods of the Ts'an sect in China, which are tough. To teach you the Short Path to Enlightenment he pounds you in the head with his shoe.'

'Now that you mention it, he does look a little like a guy who has been pounded in the head with a shoe.'

'How can he help it? He's been a disciple of Tilopa's for four hundred years, and it's always the same thing. So he asked Tilopa when he would be a guru in his own right, and Tilopa said it couldn't happen until the monastery built on Kunga's birth site was rebuilt. And he said *that* would never happen until Kunga managed to accomplish – well, a certain task. I can't tell you exactly what the task is yet, but believe me it's tough. And Kunga used to be *my* guru, see, so he's come to ask me for some help. So that's what I'm here to do.'

'I thought you said you were going to climb Lingtren with your British friends?'

'That too.'

I wasn't sure if it was the chang or the smoke, but I was getting a little confused. 'Well, whatever. It sounds like a real adventure.'

'You're not kidding.'

Freds spoke in Tibetan to Kunga Norbu, explaining what he had said to me, I assumed. Finally Kunga replied, at length.

Freds said to me, 'Kunga says you can help him too.'

'I think I'll pass,' I said. 'I've got my trekking group and all, you know.'

'Oh I know, I know. Besides, it's going to be tough. But Kunga likes you – he says you have the spirit of Milarepa.'

Kunga nodded vigorously when he heard the name Milarepa, staring through me with that spacy look of his.

'I'm glad to hear it,' I said. 'But I still think I'll pass.'

'We'll see what happens,' Freds said, looking thoughtful.

CHAPTER TWO

MANY GLASSES of chang later we staggered out into the night. Freds and Kunga Norbu slipped on their down jackets, and with a 'Good night' and a 'Good morning' they wandered off to their tent. I made my way back to my group. It felt really late, and was maybe 8:30.

As I stood looking at our tent village, I saw a light bouncing down the trail from Lukla. The man carrying the flashlight approached – it was Laure, the sirdhar for my group. He was just getting back from escorting clients back to Lukla. 'Laure!' I called softly.

'Hello George,' he said. 'Why late now?'

'I've been drinking.'

'Ah.' With his flashlight pointed at the ground I could easily make out his big smile. 'Good idea.'

'Yeah, you should go have some chang yourself. You've had a long day.'

'Not long.'

'Sure.' He had been escorting disgruntled clients back to Lukla all day, so he must have hiked five times as far as the rest of us. And here he was coming in by flashlight. Still, I suppose for Laure Tenzing Sherpa that did not represent a particularly tough day. As guide and yakboy he had been walking in these mountains all his life, and his calves were as big around as my thighs. Once, for a lark, he and three friends had set a record by hiking from Everest Base Camp to Kathmandu in four days; that's about two hundred miles, across the grain of some seriously uneven countryside. Compared to that, today's work had been like a walk to the mailbox, I guess.

The worst part had no doubt been the clients. I asked him about them and he frowned. 'People go co-op hotel, not happy. Very, very not happy. They fly back Kathmandu.'

'Good riddance,' I said. 'Why don't you go get some chang.'

He smiled and disappeared into the dark.

I looked over the tents holding my sleeping clients and sighed.

So far it had been a typical videotrek. We had flown in to Lukla from Kathmandu, and my clients, enticed to Nepal by glossy ads promising them video Ansel Adamshood, had gone wild in the plane, rushing about banging zoom lenses together in an attempt to film everything. They were rrepressible until they saw the Lukla strip, which from the air looks like a toy model of a ski jump. Pretty quickly they were strapped in and looking like they were reconsidering their wills – all except for one tubby little guy named Arnold, who continued to roll up and down the aisle like a bowling ball, finally inserting himself into the cockpit so he could shoot over the pilots' shoulders. 'We are landing at Lukla,' he announced to his camera's mike in a deep fakey voice, like the narrator of a bad travelogue. 'Looks impossible, but our pilots are calm.'

Despite him we landed safely. Unfortunately one of our group then tried to film his own descent from the plane, and fell heavily down the steps. As I ascertained the damage – a sprained ankle – there was Arnold again, leaning over to immortalize the victim's every writhe and howl.

A second plane brought in the rest of our group, led by Laure and my assistant Heather. We started down the trail, and for a couple of hours everything went well – the trail serves as the Interstate Five of the region, and is as easy as they come. And the view is awesome – the Dudh Kosi valley is like a forested Grand Canyon, only bigger. Our group was impressed, and several of them filmed a real-time record of the day.

Then the trail descended to the banks of the Dudh Kosi river, and we got a surprise. Apparently in the last monsoon a glacial lake upstream had burst its ice dam, and rushed down in a devastating flood, tearing out the bridges, trail, trees, everything. Thus our fine interstate ended abruptly in a cliff overhanging the torn-to-shreds riverbed, and what came next was the seat-of-the-pants invention of the local porters, for whom the trail was a daily necessity. They had been clever indeed, but there really was no good alternative to the old route; so the new trail wound over strewn white boulders, traversed unstable new sand cliffs, and veered wildly up and down muddy slides that had been hacked out of dense forested walls. It was radical stuff, and even experienced trekkers were having trouble.

Our group was appalled. The ads had not mentioned this.

The porters ran ahead barefoot to reach the next tea break, and the clients began to bog down. People slipped and fell. People sat down and cried. Altitude sickness was mentioned more than once, though as a matter of fact we were not much higher than Denver. Heather and I ran around encouraging the weary. I found myself carrying three videocameras. Laure was carrying nine.

It was looking like the retreat from Moscow when we came to the first of the new bridges. These are pretty neat pieces of backwoods engineering; there aren't any logs in the area long enough to span the river, so they take four logs and stick them out over the river, and weigh them down with a huge pile of round stones. Then four more logs are pushed out from the other side, until their ends rest on the ends of the first four. Instant bridge. They work, but they are not confidence builders.

Our group stared at the first one apprehensively. Arnold appeared behind us and chomped an unlit cigar as he filmed the scene. 'The *Death Bridge*,' he announced into his camera's mike.

'Arnold, please,' I said. 'Mellow out.'

He walked down to the glacial grey rush of the river. 'Hey, George, do you think I could take a step in to get a better shot of the crossing?'

'NO!' I stood up fast. 'One step in and you'd drown, I mean look at it!'

'Well, okay.'

Now the rest of the group were staring at me in horror, as if it weren't clear at first glance that to fall into the Dudh Kosi would be a very fatal error indeed. A good number of them ended up crawling across the bridge on hands and knees. Arnold got them all for posterity, and filmed his own crossing by walking in circles that made me cringe. Silently I cursed him; I was pretty sure he had known perfectly well how dangerous the river was, and only wanted to make sure everyone else did too. And very soon after that – at the next bridge, in fact – people began to demand to be taken back to Lukla. To Kathmandu. To San Francisco.

I sighed, remembering it. And remembering it was only the beginning. Just your typical Want to Take You Higher Ltd. videotrek. Plus Arnold.

CHAPTER THREE

I GOT ANOTHER BIT of Arnold in action early the next morning when I was in the rough outhouse behind the trekkers' teahouses, very hung over, crouched over the unhealthily damp hole in the floor. I had just completed my business in there when I looked up to see the big glass eye of a zoom lens, staring over the top of the wooden door at me.

'No, Arnold!' I cried, struggling to put my hand over the lens while I pulled up my pants.

'Hey, just getting some local colour,' Arnold said, backing away. 'You know, people like to see what it's really like, the details and all, and these outhouses are really something else. Exotic.'

I growled at him. 'You should have trekked in from Jiri, then. The lowland villages don't have outhouses at all.'

His eyes got round, and he shifted an unlit cigar to the other side of his mouth. 'What do you do, then?'

'Well, you just go outside and have a look round. Pick a spot. They usually have a shitting field down by the river. Real exotic.'

He laughed. 'You mean, turds everywhere?'

'Well, something like that.'

'That sounds great! Maybe I'd better walk back out instead of flying.'

I stared at him, wrinkling my nose. 'Serious filmmaker, eh Arnold?'

'Oh, yeah. Haven't you heard of me? Arnold McConnell? I make adventure films for PBS. And sometimes for the ski resort circuit, video rentals, that kind of thing. Skiing, hang gliding, kayaking, parachuting, climbing, skateboarding – I've done them all. Didn't you ever see *The Man Who Swam Down the Zambesi?* No? Ah, that's a bit of a classic, now. One of my best.'

So he had known how dangerous the Dudh Kosi was. I stared at him reproachfully. It was hard to believe he made adventure films; he looked more like the kind of Hollywood producer you'd tell couch jokes about. 'So you're making a real film of this trip?' I asked.

'Yeah, sure. Always working, never stop working. Workaholic.'

'Don't you need a bigger crew?'

'Well sure, usually, but this is a different kind of thing, one of my 'personal diary' films I call them. I've sold a couple to PBS. Do all the work myself. It's kind of like my version of solo climbing.'

'Fine. But cut the part about me taking a crap, okay?'

'Sure, sure, don't worry about it. Just got to get everything I can, you know, so I've got good tape to choose from later on. All grist for the mill. That's why I got this lens. All the latest in equipment for me. I got stuff you wouldn't believe.'

'I believe.'

He chomped his cigar. 'Just call me Mr. Adventure.'

'I will.'

CHAPTER FOUR

I DIDN'T RUN into Freds and Kunga Norbu in Namche Bazaar, the Sherpas' dramatically placed little capital town, and I figured they had left already with Freds' British friends. Then I kept my group there a couple of days to acclimatize, and enjoy the town, and I figured that if I caught up with them at all, it'd be up at their base camp.

So I was quite surprised to run across the whole group in Pheriche, one of the Sherpas' high mountain villages.

Most of these villages are occupied only in the summer, to grow potatoes and pasture yaks. Pheriche, however, lies on the trekking route to Everest, so it's occupied almost year-round, and a couple of lodges have been built, along with the Himalayan Rescue Association's only aid station. It still looks like a summer pasturage: low rock walls separate potato fields, and a few slate-roofed stone huts, plus the lodges and the tin-roofed aid station. All of it is clustered at the end of a flat-bottomed glacial valley, against the side of a lateral moraine five hundred feet high. A stream meanders by and the ground is carpeted with grasses and the bright autumn red of berberis bushes. On all sides tower the fantastic white spikes of some of the world's most dramatic peaks – Ama Dablam, Taboche, Tamserku, Kang Taiga – and all in all, it's quite a place. My clients were making themselves dizzy trying to film it.

We set up our tent village in an unused potato field, and after dinner Laure and I slipped off to the Himalaya Hotel to have some chang. I entered the lodge's little kitchen and heard Freds cry, 'Hey George!' He was sitting with Kunga Norbu and four Westerners; we joined them, crowding in around a little table. 'These are the friends we're climbing with.'

He introduced them, and we all shook hands. Trevor was a tall slender guy, with round glasses and a somewhat crazed grin. 'Mad Tom,' as Freds called him, was short and curly-headed, and didn't look mad at all, although something in his mild manner made me believe that he could be. John was short and compact, with a salt-and-pepper beard, and a crusher handshake.

And Marion was a tall, and rather attractive woman – though I suspected she might have blushed or punched you if you said so – she was attractive in a tough, wild way, with a stark strong face, and thick brown hair pulled back and braided. They were British, with the accents to prove it. Marion and Trevor quite posh and public school, and John and Mad Tom very broad North country.

We started drinking chang, and they told me about their climb. Lingtren, a sharp peak between Pumori and Everest's West Shoulder, is serious work from any approach, and they were clearly excited about it, in their own way: 'Bit of a slog, to tell the truth,' Trevor said cheerfully.

When British climbers talk about climbing, you have to learn to translate it into English. 'Bit of a slog' means don't go there.

'I think we ought to get lost and climb Pumori instead,' said Marion. 'Lingtren is a perfect *hill*.'

'Marion, really.'

'Can't beat Lingtren's price, anyway,' said John.

He was referring to the fee that the Nepali government makes climbers pay for the right to climb its peaks. These fees are determined by the height of the peak to be climbed – the really big peaks are super expensive. They charge you over five thousand dollars to climb Everest, for instance, and still competition to get on its long waiting list is fierce. But some of the toughest climbs in Nepal aren't very high, relative to the biggies, and they come pretty cheap. Apparently Lingtren was one of these.

We watched the Sherpani who runs the lodge cook dinner for fifty, under the fixed gazes of the diners, who sat staring hungrily at her every move. To accomplish this she had at her command a small woodburning stove (with chimney, thank God), a pile of potatoes, noodles, rice, some eggs and cabbage, and several chang-happy porter assistants, who alternated washing dishes with breaking up chunks of yak dung for the fire. A difficult situation on the face of it, but the Sherpani was cool: she cooked the whole list of orders by memory, slicing and tossing potatoes into one pan, stuffing wood in the fire, flipping twenty pounds of noodles in mid-air like they were a single hotcake – all with the sureness and panache of an expert juggler. It was a kind of genius.

Two hours later those who had ordered the meals that came last in her strict sequence got their cabbage omelettes on French fries, and the kitchen emptied out as many people went to bed. The rest of us settled down to more chang and chatter.

Then a trekker came back into the kitchen, so he could listen to his shortwave radio without bothering sleepers in the Lodge's single dorm room. He said he wanted to catch the news. We all stared at him in disbelief. 'I need to find out how the dollar's doing,' he explained. 'Did you know it dropped *eight percent* last week?'

You meet all kinds in Nepal.

Actually it's interesting to hear what you get on shortwave in the Himal, because depending on how the ionosphere is acting, almost anything will bounce in. That night we listened to the People's Voice of Syria, for instance, and some female pop singer from Bombay, which perked up the porters. Then the operator ran across the BBC world news, which was not unusual – it could have been coming from Hong Kong, Singapore, Cairo, even London itself.

Through the hissing of the static the refined voice of the reporter could barely be made out '... British Everest Expedition of 1987 is now on the Rongbuk Glacier in Tibet, and over the next two months they expect to repeat the historic route of the attempts made in the twenties and thirties. Our correspondent to the expedition reports ...' and then the voice changed to one even more staccato and drowned in static: '... the expedition's principal goal of recovering the bodies of George Mallory and Andrew Irvine, who were last seen near the summit in 1924, *crackle, buzz* ... chances considerably improved by conversations with a partner of the Chinese climber who reported seeing a body on the North Face in 1980 *bzzzzkrkrk!* – description of the site of the finding *sssssssss* ... snow levels very low this year, and all concerned feel chances for success are *ssskrksss*.' The voice faded away in a roar of static.

Trevor looked around at us, eyebrows lifted. 'Did I understand them to say that they are going to search for Mallory and Irvine's *bodies*?'

A look of deep horror creased Mad Tom's face. Marion wrinkled her nose as if her chang had turned to Tibetan tea. 'I can't believe it.'

I didn't know it at the time, but this was an unexpected opportunity for Freds to put his plan into action ahead of schedule. He said, 'Haven't you heard about that? Why Kunga Norbu here is precisely the climber they're talking about, the one who spotted a body on the North Face in 1980.'

'He *is*?' we all said.

'Yeah, you bet. Kunga was part of the Chinese expedition to the North Ridge in 1980, and he was up there doing reconnaissance for a direct route on the North Face when he saw a body.' Freds spoke to Kunga Norbu in Tibetan, and Kunga nodded and replied at some length. Freds translated for him: 'He says it was a Westerner, wearing old-fashioned clothing, and it had clearly been there a long time. Here, he says he can mark it on a photo ...' Freds got out his wallet and pulled a wad of paper from it. Unfolded, it revealed itself as a battered black-and-white photo of Everest as seen from the Tibetan side. Kunga Norbu studied it for a long time, talked it over with Freds, and then took a pencil from Freds and carefully made a circle on the photo.

'Why he's circled half the North Face,' John pointed out. 'It's fooking useless.'

'Nah,' Freds said. 'Look, it's a little circle.'

'It's a little photo, innit.'

'Well, he can describe the spot exactly – it's up there on top of the Black Band. Anyway, someone has managed to get together an expedition to go looking for the bodies, or the body, whatever. Now Kunga slipped over to

Nepal last year, so this expedition is going on second-hand information from his climbing buds. But that might be enough.'

'And if they find the bodies?'

'Well, I think they're planning to take them down and ship them to London and bury them in Winchester Cathedral.'

The Brits stared at him. 'You mean Westminster Abbey?' Trevor ventured.

'Oh that's right, I always get those two mixed up. Anyway that's what they're going to do, and they're going to make a movie out of it.'

I groaned at the thought. More video.

The four Brits groaned louder than I did. 'That is rilly dis-gusting,' Marion said.

'Sickening,' John and Mad Tom agreed.

'It is a travesty, isn't it?' Trevor said. 'I mean those chaps belong up there if anybody does. It's nothing less than grave robbing!'

And his three companions nodded. On one level they were joking, making a pretense of their outrage; but underneath that, they were dead serious. They meant it.

CHAPTER FIVE

TO UNDERSTAND WHY they would care so much, you have to understand what the story of Mallory and Irvine means to the British soul. Climbing has always been more important there than in America – you could say that the British invented the sport in Victorian times, and they've continued to excel in it since then, even after World War Two when much else there fell apart. You could say that climbing is the Rolls Royce of British sport. From Whymper to the brilliant crowd that climbed with Bonington in the seventies: they're all national heroes.

But none more so than Mallory and Irvine. Back in the twenties and thirties, you see, the British had a lock on Everest, because Nepal was closed to foreigners, and Tibet was closed to all but the British, who had barged in on them with Younghusband's campaign back in 1904. So the mountain was their private playground, and during those years they made four or five attempts, all of them failures, which is understandable: they were equipped like Boy Scouts, they had to learn high altitude technique on the spot and they had terrible luck with weather.

The try that came closest was in 1924. Mallory was its lead climber, already famous from two previous attempts. As you may know, he was the guy who replied 'Because it's there' when asked why anyone would want to climb the thing. This is either a very deep or a very stupid answer, depending on what you think of Mallory. You can take your pick of interpretations; the guy has been psychoanalysed into the ground. Anyway, he and his partner Irvine were last glimpsed, by another expedition member, just eight hundred feet below and less than a quarter of a mile from the summit – and at 1:00 p.m., on a day that had good weather except for a brief storm, and mist that obscured the peak from the observers below. So they either made it or they didn't; but something went wrong somewhere along the line, and they were never seen again.

A glorious defeat, a deep mystery: this is the kind of story that the English just love, as don't we all. All the public school virtues wrapped into one heroic tale – you couldn't write it better. To this day the story commands tremendous interest in England, and this is doubly true among people in the climbing community, who grew up on the story, and who still indulge in a lot of speculation about the two men's fate, in journal articles and pub debates and the like. They love that story.

Thus to go up there, and find the bodies, and end the mystery, and cart the bodies off to England . . . You can see why it struck my drinking buddies that night as a kind of sacrilege. It was yet another modern PR stunt – a money-grubbing plan made by some publicity hound – a Profaning of the Mystery. It was, in fact, a bit like video-trekking. Only worse. So I could sympathize, in a way.

CHAPTER SIX

I TRIED to think of a change of subject, to distract the Brits. But Freds seemed determined to fire up their distress. He poked his finger onto the folded wreck of a photo. 'You know what y'all oughta do,' he told them in a low voice. 'You mentioned getting lost and climbing Pumori? Well shit, what you oughta do instead is get lost in the other direction, and beat that expedition to the spot, and hide old Mallory. I mean here you've got the actual eyewitness right here to lead you to him! Incredible! You could bury Mallory in rocks and snow and then sneak back down. If you did that, they'd never find him!'

All the Brits stared at Freds, eyes wide. Then they looked at each other, and their heads kind of lowered together over the table. Their voices got soft. 'He's a genius,' Trevor breathed.

'Uh, no,' I warned them. 'He's not a genius.' Laure was shaking his head. Even Kunga Norbu was looking doubtful.

Freds looked over the Brits at me and waggled his eyebrows vigorously, as if to say: this is a great idea! Don't foul it up!

'What about the Lho La?' John asked. 'Won't we have to climb that?'

'Piece of cake,' Freds said promptly.

'No,' Laure protested. 'Not piece cake! Pass! Very steep pass!'

'Piece of cake,' Freds insisted. 'I climbed it with those West Ridge direct guys a couple years ago. And once you top it you just slog onto the West Shoulder and there you are with the whole North Face, sitting right off to your left.'

'Freds,' I said, trying to indicate that he shouldn't incite his companions to such a dangerous, not to mention illegal, climb. 'You'd need a lot more support for high camps than you've got. That circle there is pretty damn high on the mountain.'

'True,' Freds said immediately. 'It's pretty high. Pretty damn high. You can't get much higher.'

Of course to some climbers this was only another incitement, as I should have known.

'You'd have to do it like Woody Sayre did back in '62,' Freds went on. 'They got Sherpas to help them up the Nup La over by Cho Oyu, then bolted to Everest when they were supposed to be climbing Gyachung Kang. They moved a single camp with them all the way to Everest, and got back the same way. Just four of them, and they almost climbed it. And the Nup La is twenty miles further away from Everest than the Lho La. The Lho La's right there under it.

Mad Tom knocked his glasses up his nose, pulled out a pencil and began to do calculations on the table. Marion was nodding. Trevor was refilling all our glasses with chang. John was looking over Mad Tom's shoulder and muttering to him; apparently they were in charge of supplies.

Trevor raised his glass. 'Right then,' he said. 'Are we for it?'

They all raised their glasses. 'We're for it.'

They were toasting the plan, and I was staring at them in dismay, when I heard the door creak and saw who was leaving the kitchen. 'Hey!'

I reached out and dragged Arnold McConnell back into the room. 'What're you doing here?'

Arnold shifted something behind his back. 'Nothing really. Just my nightly glass of milk tea, you know . . .'

'It's him!' Marion exclaimed. She reached behind Arnold and snatched his camera from behind his back; he tried to hold onto it, but Marion was too strong for him. 'Spying on me again, were you? Filming us from some dark corner?'

'No no,' Arnold said. 'Can't film in the dark, you know.'

'Film in tent,' Laure said promptly. 'Night.'

Arnold glared at him.

'Listen, Arnold,' I said. 'We were just shooting the bull here you know, a little private conversation over the chang. Nothing serious.'

'Oh I know,' Arnold assured me. 'I know.'

Marion stood and stared down at Arnold. They made a funny pair – her so long and rangy, him so short and tubby. Marion pushed buttons on the camera until the video cassette popped out, never taking her eye from him. She could really glare. 'I suppose this is the same film you used this morning, when you filmed me taking my shower, is that right?' She looked at us. 'I was in the little shower box they've got across the way, and the tin with the hot water in it got plugged at the bottom somehow. I had the door open a bit so I could stretch up and fiddle with it, when suddenly I noticed this pervert filming me!' She laughed angrily. 'I bet you were quite pleased with that footage, weren't you, you peeping Tom!'

'I was just leaving to shoot yaks,' Arnold explained rapidly, staring up at Marion with an admiring gaze. 'Then there you were, and what was I supposed to do? I'm a filmmaker, I film beautiful things. I could make you a star in the States,' he told her earnestly. 'You're probably the most beautiful climber in the world.'

'And all that competition,' Mad Tom put in.

I was right about Marion's reaction to a compliment of that sort – she blushed to the roots, and considered punching him too – she might have, if they'd been alone.

'. . . adventure films back in the States, for PBS and the ski resort circuit,' Arnold was going on, chewing his cigar and rolling his eyes as Marion took the cartridge over toward the stove.

The Sherpani waved her off. 'Smell,' she said.

Marion nodded and took the video cassette in her hands. Her forearms tensed, and suddenly you could see every muscle. And there were a lot of them, too, looking like thin bunched wires under the skin. We all stared, and instinctively Arnold raised his camera to his shoulder before remembering it was empty. That fact made him whimper, and he was fumbling at his jacket pocket for a spare when the cassette snapped diagonally and the videotape spilled out. Marion handed it all to the Sherpani, who dumped it in a box of potato peels, grinning.

We all looked at Arnold. He chomped his cigar, shrugged. 'Can't make you a star that way,' he said, and gave Marion a soulful leer. 'Really, you oughta give me a chance, you'd be great. Such *presence*.'

'I would appreciate it if you would now leave,' Marion told him, and pointed at the door.

Arnold left.

'That guy could be trouble,' Freds said.

CHAPTER SEVEN

FREDS WAS right about that.

But Arnold was not the only source of trouble. Freds himself was acting a bit peculiar, I judged. Still, when I thought of the various oddities in his recent behaviour – his announcement that his friend Kunga Norbu was a tulku, and now this sudden advocacy of a Save Mallory's Body campaign – I couldn't put it all together. Why did he just happen to have a photo of the North Face of Everest in his wallet, for instance? It didn't make sense.

So when Freds' party and my trekking group took off upvalley from Pheriche on the same morning, I walked with Freds for a while. I wanted to ask him some questions. But there were a lot of people on the trail, and it was hard to get a moment to ourselves.

As an opener I said, 'So, you've got a woman on your team.'

'Yeah, Marion's great. She's probably the best climber of us all. And incredibly strong. You know those indoor walls they have in England, for practising?'

'No.'

'Well, the weather is so bad there, and the climbers are such fanatics, that they've built these thirty and forty foot walls inside gyms, and covered them with concrete and made little handholds.' He laughed. 'It looks dismal – scuzzy old gym with bad light and no heating, and all these guys stretched out on a concrete wall like some new kinda torture . . . Anyway I visited one of these, and they set me up in a race with Marion, up the two hardest pitches. Maybe 5.13 in places, impossible stuff. And there was a leak too. Everyone started betting on us, and the rule was someone had to top out for anyone to collect on the bets. I did my best, but I was hurrying and I came off about halfway up. So she won, but to collect the bets she had to top out. With the leak it really was impossible, but everyone who had bet on her was yelling at her to do it, so she just grit her teeth and started making these *moves*, man—' Freds illustrated in the air between us as we hiked – 'And she was doing them in slow motion so she wouldn't come off. Just hanging there by her fingertips and toes, and I swear to God she hung on that wall for must've been *three hours*. Everyone else stopped climbing to watch. Guys were going home – guys were begging her to come off – guys had tears in their eyes. Finally she topped out and crawled over to the ladder and came down, and they mobbed her. They were ready to make her queen. In fact she pretty much is queen, as far as English climbers are concerned – you could bring the real one in, and if Marion were there they wouldn't even notice.'

Then Arnold slipped between us, looking conspiratorial. 'I think this Save Mallory scheme is a great idea,' he whispered through clenched teeth. 'I'm totally behind you, and it'll make a *great movie*.'

'You miss the point,' I said to him.

'We ain't doing nothing but climb Lingtren,' Freds said to him.

Arnold frowned, tucked his chin onto his chest, chewed his cigar. Frowning, Freds left to catch up with his group, and they soon disappeared ahead. So I lost my chance to talk to him.

We came to the upper end of Pheriche's valley, turned right and climbed to get into an even higher one. This was the valley of the Khumbu glacier, a massive road of ice covered with a chaos of grey rubble and milky blue melt ponds. We skirted the glacier and followed a trail up its lateral moraine to Lobuche, which consists of three teahouses and a tenting ground. The next day we hiked on upvalley to Gorak Shep.

Now Gorak Shep ('Dead Crow') is not the kind of place you see on posters in travel agencies. It's just above 17,000 feet, and up there the plant life has about given up. It's just two ragged little teahouses under a monstrous rubble hill, next to a grey glacial pond, and all in all it looks like the tailings of a very big gravel mine.

But what Gorak Shep does have is mountains. Big snowy mountains, on all sides. How big? Well, the wall of Nuptse, for instance, stands a full seven thousand feet over Gorak Shep. An avalanche we saw, sliding down a fraction of this wall and sounding like thunder, covered about two World Trade Centres' worth of height, and still looked tiny. And Nuptse is not as big as some of the peaks around it. So you get the idea.

Cameras can never capture this kind of scale, but you can't help trying, and my crowd tried for all they were worth in the days we were camped there. The ones handling the altitude well slogged up to the top of Kala Pattar ('Black Hill'), a local walkers' peak which has a fine view of the Southwest Face of Everest. The day after that, Heather and Laure led most of the same people up the glacier to Everest Base Camp, while the rest of us relaxed. Everest Base Camp, set by the Indian Army this season, was basically a tent village like ours, but there are some fine seracs and ice towers to be seen along the way, and when they returned the clients seemed satisfied.

So I was satisfied too. No one had gotten any bad altitude sickness, and we would be starting back the next morning. I was feeling fine, sitting up on the hill above our tents in the late afternoon, doing nothing.

But then Laure came zipping down the trail from Base Camp, and when he saw me he came right over. 'George George,' he called out as he approached.

I stood as he reached me. 'What's up? '

'I stay talk friends porter Indian Army base camp, Freds find me Freds say his base camp come please you. Climb Lho La find man camera come hire Sherpas finish with Freds, very bad follow Freds.'

Now Laure's English is not very good, as you may have noticed. But after all we were in his country speaking my language – and for him English came after Sherpa, Nepali, and some Japanese and German, and how many languages do you speak?

Besides, I find I always get the gist of what Laure says, which is not something you can always say of all our fellow native speakers. So I cried out, 'No! Arnold is *following* them?'

'Yes,' Laure said. 'Very bad. Freds say come please get.'

'Arnold hired their Sherpas?'

Laure nodded. 'Sherpas finish porter, Arnold hire.'

'Damn him! We'll have to climb up there and get him!'

'Yes. Very bad.'

'Will you come with me?'

'Whatever you like.'

I hustled to our tents to get together my climbing gear and tell Heather what had happened. 'How did he get up there?' she asked. 'I thought he was with you all day!'

'He told me he was going with you! He probably followed you guys all the way up, and kept on going. Don't worry about it, it's not your fault. Take the group back to Namche starting tomorrow, and we'll catch up with you.' She nodded, looking worried.

Laure and I took off. Even going at Laure's pace we didn't reach Freds' base camp until the moon had risen.

Their camp was now only a single tent in a bunch of trampled snow, just under the steep headwall of the Khumbu Valley – the ridge that divides Nepal from Tibet. We zipped open the tent and woke Freds and Kunga Norbu.

'All right!' Freds said. 'I'm glad you're here! Real glad!'

'Give me the story,' I said.

'Well, that Arnold snuck up here, apparently.'

'That's right.'

'And our Sherpas were done and we had paid them, and I guess he hired them on the spot. They have a bunch of climbing gear, and we left fixed ropes up to the Lho La, so up they came. I tell you I was pretty blown away when they showed up in the pass! The Brits got furious and told Arnold to back down, but he refused and, well, how do you make someone do something they don't want to up there? If you punch him out he's likely to have trouble getting down! So Kunga and I came back to get you and found Laure at Base Camp, and he said he'd get you while we held the fort.'

'Arnold climbed the Lho La?' I said, amazed.

'Well, he's a pretty tough guy, I reckon. Didn't you ever see that movie he made of the kayak run down the Baltoro? Radical film, man, really it's up there with *The Man Who Skied Down Everest* for radicalness. And he's done some other crazy things too, like flying a hang glider off the Grand Teton, filming all the way. He's tougher than he looks. I think he just does the Hollywood sleaze routine so he can get away with things. Anyway those are some excellent climbing Sherpas he's got, and with them and the fixed ropes he just had to gut it out. And I guess he acclimatizes well, because he was walking around up there like he was at the beach.'

I sighed. 'That is one determined filmmaker.'

Freds shook his head. 'The guy is a leech. He's gonna drive the Brits bats if we don't haul his ass back down here.'

CHAPTER EIGHT

SO THE NEXT DAY the four of us started the ascent of the Lho La, and were quickly engaged in some of the most dangerous climbing I've ever done. Not the most technically difficult – the Brits had left fixed rope in the toughest section, so our progress was considerably aided. But it was still dangerous, because we were climbing an icefall, which is to say a glacier on a serious tilt.

Now a glacier as you know is a river of ice, and like its liquid counterparts it is always flowing downstream. Its rate of flow is much slower than a river's, but it isn't negligible, especially when you're standing on it. Then you often hear creaks, groans, sudden cracks and booms, and you feel like you're on the back of a living creature.

Put that glacier on a hillside and everything is accelerated; the living creature becomes a dragon. The ice of the glacier breaks up into immense blocks and shards, and these shift regularly, then balance on a point or edge, then fall and smash to fragments, or crack open to reveal deep fissures. As we threaded our way up through the maze of the Lho La's icefall, we were constantly moving underneath blocks of ice that looked eternal but were actually precarious – they were certain to fall sometime in the next month or two. I'm not expert at probability theory, but I still didn't like it.

'Freds,' I complained. 'You said this was a piece of cake.'

'It is,' he said. 'Check how fast we're going.'

'That's because we're scared to death.'

'Are we? Hey, it must be only 45 degrees or so.'

This is as steep as an icefall can get before the ice all falls downhill at once. Even the famous Khumbu Icefall, of which we now had a fantastic view over to our right, fell at only about 30 degrees. The Khumbu Icefall is an unavoidable part of the standard route on Everest, and it is by far the most feared section; more people have died there than anywhere else on the mountain. And the Lho La is worse than the Khumbu!

So I had some choice words for our situation as we climbed very quickly indeed, and most of them left Laure mystified. 'Great, Freds,' I shouted at him. 'Real piece of cake all right!'

'Lot of icing, anyway,' he said, and giggled. This under a wall that would flatten him like Wile E. Coyote if it fell. I shook my head.

'What do you think?' I said to Laure.

'Very bad,' Laure said. 'Very bad, very dangerous.'

'What do you think we should do?'

'Whatever you like.'

We hurried.

Now I like climbing as much as anybody, almost, but I am not going to try to claim to you that it is an exceptionally sane activity. That day in particular I would not have been inclined to argue the point. The thing is, there is danger and there is danger. In fact climbers make a distinction, between objective danger and subjective danger. Objective dangers are things like avalanches and rockfall and storms, that you can't do anything about. Subjective dangers are those incurred by human error – putting in a bad piece of protection, forgetting to fasten a harness, that sort of thing. See, if you are perfectly careful, then you can eliminate all the subjective dangers. And when you've eliminated the subjective dangers, you have only the objective dangers to face. So you can see it's very rational.

On this day, however, we were in the midst of a whole wall of objective danger, and it made me nervous. We pursued the usual course in such a case, which is to go like hell. The four of us were practically running up the Lho La. Freds, Kunga, and Laure were extremely fast and strong, and I am in reasonable shape myself; plus I get the benefits of more adrenalin than less imaginative types. So we were hauling buns.

Then it happened. Freds was next to me, on a rope with Kunga Norbu, and Kunga was the full rope length ahead of us – about twenty yards – leading the way around a traverse that went under a giant serac, which is what they call the fangs of blue ice that protrude out of an icefall, often in clusters. Kunga was right underneath this serac when without the slightest warning it sheered off and collapsed, shattering into a thousand pieces.

I had reflexively sucked in a gasp and was about to scream when Kunga Norbu jostled my elbow, nearly knocking me down. He was wedged in between Freds and me, and the rope tying them together was flapping between our legs.

Trying to revise my scream I choked, gasped for breath, choked again. Freds slapped me on the back to help. Kunga was definitely there, standing before us, solid and corporeal. And yet he had been under the serac! The broken pieces of the ice block were scattered before us, fresh and gleaming in the afternoon sun. The block had sheered off and collapsed without the slightest quiver or warning – there simply hadn't been time to get out from under it!

Freds saw the look on my face, and he grinned feebly. 'Old Kunga Norbu is pretty fast when he has to be.'

But that wasn't going to do. 'Gah . . .' I said – and then Freds and Kunga were holding me up. Laure hurried to join us, round-eyed with apprehension.

'Very bad,' he said.

'Gah,' I attempted again, and couldn't go on.

'All right, all right,' Freds said, soothing me with his gloved hands. 'Hey, George. Relax.'

'He,' I got out, and pointed at the remains of the serac, then at Kunga.

'I know,' Freds said, frowning. He exchanged a glance with Kunga, who was watching me impassively. They spoke to each other in Tibetan. 'Listen,' Freds said to me. 'Let's top the pass and then I'll explain it to you. It'll take a while, and we don't have that much day left. Plus we've got to find a way around these ice cubes so we can stick to the fixed ropes. Come on buddy.' He slapped my arm. 'Concentrate. Let's do it.'

So we started up again, Kunga leading as fast as before. I was still in shock, however, and I kept seeing the collapse of the serac, with Kunga under it. He just couldn't have escaped it! And yet there he was up above us, jumaring up the fixed ropes like a monkey scurrying up a palm.

It was a miracle. And I had seen it. I had a hell of a time concentrating on the rest of that day's climb.

CHAPTER NINE

IN THE LATE AFTERNOON we topped the Lho La, and set our tent on the pass's flat expanse of deep hard snow. It was one of the spacier campsites I had ever occupied: on the crest of the Himalaya, in a broad saddle between the tallest mountain on earth, and the very spiky and beautiful Lingtren. Below us to one side was the Khumbu Glacier; on the other was the Rongbuk

Glacier in Tibet. We were at about 20,000 feet, and so Freds and his friends had a long way to go before reaching old Mallory. But nothing above would be quite as arbitrarily dangerous as the icefall. As long as the weather held, that is. So far they had been lucky; it was turning out to be the driest October in years.

There was no sign of either the British team or Arnold's crew, except for tracks in the snow leading up the side of the West Shoulder and disappearing. So they were on their way up. 'Damn!' I said. 'Why didn't they wait?' Now we had more climbing to do, to catch Arnold.

I sat on my groundpad on the snow outside the tent. I was tired. I was also very troubled. Laure was getting the stove to start. Kunga Norbu was off by himself, sitting in the snow, apparently meditating on the sight of Tibet. Freds was walking around singing 'Wooden Ships,' clearly in heaven. 'I mean, is this a great campsite or *what*,' he cried to me. 'Look at the view! It's too much, too much. I wish we'd brought some chang with us. I do have some hash, though. George, time to break out the pipe, hey?'

'Not yet, Freds. You get over here and tell me what the hell happened down there with your buddy Kunga Norbu. You promised you would.'

Freds stood looking at me. We were in shadow – it was cold, but windless – the sky above was clear, and a very deep dark blue. The airy roar of the stove starting was the only sound.

Freds sighed, and his expression got as serious as it ever got: one eye squinted shut entirely, forehead furrowed, and lips squeezed tightly together. He looked over at Kunga, and saw he was watching us. 'Well,' he said after a while. 'You remember a couple of weeks ago when we were down at Chimoa getting drunk?'

'Yeah?'

'And I told you Kunga Norbu was a tulku.'

I gulped. 'Freds, don't give me that again.'

'Well,' he said. 'It's either that or tell you some kind of lie. And I ain't so good at lying, my face gives me away or something.'

'Freds, get serious!' But looking over at Kunga Norbu, sitting in the snow with that blank expression, and those weird black eyes, I couldn't help but wonder.

Freds said, 'I'm sorry, man, I really am. I don't mean to blow your mind like this. But I did try to tell you before, you have to admit. And it's the simple truth. He's an honest-to-God tulku. First incarnation the famous Naropa, born in 1555. And he's been around ever since.'

'So he met George Washington and like that?'

'Well, Washington didn't go to Tibet, so far as I know.'

I stared at him. He shuffled about uncomfortably. 'I know it's hard to take, George. Believe me. I had trouble with it myself, at first. But when you study under Kunga Norbu for a while, you see him do so many miraculous things, you can't help but believe.'

I stared at him some more, speechless.

'I know,' Freds said. 'The first time he pulls one of his moves on you, it's a shock. I remember my first time real well. I was hiking with him from the hidden Rongbuk to Namche, we went right over Lho La like we did today only in the opposite direction, and right around Everest Base Camp we came across this Indian trekker who was turning blue. He was clearly set to die of altitude sickness, so Kunga and I carried him down between us to Pheriche, which was already a long day's work as you know. We took him to the Rescue Station and I figured they'd put him in the pressure tank they've got there, have you seen it? They've got a tank like a miniature submarine in their back room, and the idea is you stick a guy with altitude sickness in it and pressurize it down to sea level pressure, and he gets better. It's a neat idea, but it turns out that this tank was donated to the station by a hospital in Tokyo, and all the instructions for it are in Japanese, and no one at the station reads Japanese. Besides, as far as anyone there knows, it's an experimental technique only, no one is quite sure if it will work or not, and nobody there is inclined to do any experimenting on sick trekkers. So we're back to square one and this guy was sicker than ever, so Kunga and I started down towards Namche, but I was getting exhausted and it was really slow going, and all of a sudden Kunga Norbu picked him up and slung him across his shoulders, which was already quite a feat of strength as this Indian was kind of pear-shaped, a heavy guy – and then Kunga just took off running down the trail with him! I hollered at him and ran after him trying to keep up, and I tell you I was *zooming* down that trail, and still Kunga ran right out of sight! Big long steps like he was about to fly! I couldn't believe it!'

Freds shook his head. 'That was the first time I saw Kunga Norbu going into *lung-gom* mode. Means magic long-distance running, and it was real popular in Tibet at one time. An adept like Kunga is called a *lung-gom-pa*, and when you get it down you can run really far really fast. Even levitate a little. You saw him today – that was a *lung-gom* move he laid on that iceblock.'

'I see,' I said, in a kind of daze. I called out to Laure, still at the stove: 'Hey Laure! Freds says Kunga Norbu is a tulku!'

Laure smiled, nodded. 'Yes, Kunga Norbu Lama very fine tulku!'

I took a deep breath. Over in the snow Kunga Norbu sat cross-legged, looking out at his country. Or somewhere. 'I think I'm ready for that hash pipe,' I told Freds.

CHAPTER TEN

IT TOOK US two days to catch up to Arnold and the Brits, two days of miserable slogging up the West Shoulder of Everest. Nothing complicated here: the slope was a regular expanse of hard snow, and we just put on the crampons and ground on up it. It was murderous work. Not that I could tell with Freds and Laure and Kunga Norbu. There may be advantages to climbing on Everest with a tulku, a Sherpa long-distance champion, and an American space cadet, but longer rest stops are not among them. Those three marked uphill as if paced by Sousa marches, and I trailed behind huffing and puffing, damning Arnold with every step.

Late on the second day I struggled onto the top of the West Shoulder, a long snowy divide under the West Ridge proper. By the time I got there Freds and Laure already had the tent up, and they were securing it to the snow with a network of climbing rope, while Kunga Norbu sat to one side doing his meditation.

Further down the Shoulder were the two camps of the other teams, placed fairly close together as there wasn't a whole lot of extra flat ground up there to choose from. After I had rested and drunk several cups of hot lemon drink, I said, 'Let's go find out how things stand.' Freds walked over with me.

As it turned out, things were not standing so well. The Brits were in their tent, waist deep in their sleeping bags and drinking tea. And they were not amused. 'The man is utterly daft,' Marion said. She had a mild case of high-altitude throat, and any syllable she tried to emphasize disappeared entirely. 'We've *oyd* outrunning him, but the Sherpas are good, and he *oyy* be strong.'

'A fooking leech he is,' John said.

Trevor grinned ferociously. His lower face was pretty sunburned, and his lips were beginning to break up. 'We're counting on you to get him back down, George.'

'I'll see what I can do.'

Marion shook her head. 'God knows we've tried, but it does no good whatever, he won't listen, he just rattles on about making me a *stee*, I don't know how to *dee* with that.' She turned red. 'And none of these brave chaps will agree that we should just go over there and seize his bloody camera and throw it into Ti*bee*!'

The guys shook their heads. 'We'd have to deal with the Sherpas,' Mad Tom said to Marion patiently. 'What are we going to do, fight with them? I can't even imagine it.'

'And if Mad Tom can't imagine it . . .' Trevor said.

Marion just growled.

'I'll go talk to him,' I said.

But I didn't have to go anywhere, because Arnold had come over to greet us. 'Hello!' he called out cheerily. 'George, what a surprise! What brings you up here?'

I got out of the tent. Arnold stood before me, looking sunburned but otherwise all right. 'You know what brings me up here, Arnold. Here, let's move away a bit, I'm sure these folks don't want to talk to you.'

'Oh, no, I've been talking to them every day! We've been having lots of good talks. And today I've got some real news.' He spoke into the tent. 'I was looking through my zoom over at the North Col, and I see they've set up a camp over there! Do you suppose it's that expedition looking for Mallory's body?'

Curses came from the tent.

'I know!' Arnold exclaimed. 'Kind of puts the pressure on to get going, don't you think? Not much time to spare.'

'Bugger off!'

Arnold shrugged. 'Well, I've got it on tape if you want to see. Looked like they were wearing Helly-Hansen jackets, if that tells you anything.'

'Don't tell me you can read labels from this distance,' I said.

Arnold grinned. 'It's a hell of a zoom lens. I could read their lips if I wanted to.'

I studied him curiously. He really seemed to be doing fine, even after four days of intense climbing. He looked a touch thinner, and his voice had an altitude rasp to it, and he was pretty badly sunburned under the stubble of his beard – but he was still chewing a whitened cigar between zinc-oxided lips, and he still had the same wide-eyed look of wonder that his filming should bother anybody. I was impressed; he was definitely a lot tougher than I had expected. He reminded me of Dick Bass, the American millionaire who took a notion to climb the highest mountain on each continent. Like Bass, Arnold was a middle-aged guy paying pros to take him up; and like Bass, he acclimatized well, and had a hell of a nerve.

So there he was, and he wasn't falling apart. I had to try something else. 'Arnold, come over here a little with me, let's leave these people in peace.'

'Good *reee*!' Marion shouted from inside the tent.

'That Marion,' Arnold said admiringly when we were out of ear-shot. 'She's really beautiful, I mean I really, really, really like her.' He struck his chest to show how smitten he was.

I glared at him. 'Arnold, it doesn't matter if you're falling for her or *what*, because they *definitely* do not want you along for this climb. Filming them destroys the whole point of what they're trying to do up there.'

Arnold seized my arm. 'No it doesn't. I keep trying to explain that to them. I can edit the film so that no one will know where Mallory's body is. They'll just know it's up here safe, because four young English climbers took incredible risks to keep it free from the publicity hounds threatening to tear it away to London. It's great, George. I'm a filmmaker, and I know when something will make a great movie, and this will make a great movie.'

I frowned. 'Maybe it would, but the problem is this climb is illegal, and if you make the film, then the illegal part becomes known and these folk will be banned by the Nepali authorities. They'll never be let into Nepal again.'

'So? Aren't they willing to make that sacrifice for Mallory?'

I frowned. 'For your movie, you mean. Without that they could do it and no one would be the wiser.'

'Well, okay, but I can leave their names off it or something. Give them stage names. Marion Davies, how about that?'

'I think that one's been used before.' I thought. 'Listen, Arnold, you'd be in the same kind of trouble, you know. They might not ever let you back, either.'

He waved a hand. 'I can get around that kind of thing. Get a lawyer. Or baksheesh, a lot of baksheesh.'

'These guys don't have that kind of money, though. Really, you'd better watch it. If you press them too hard they might do something drastic. At the least they'll stop you, higher up. When they find the body a couple of them will come back and stop you, and the other two bury the body, and you won't get any footage at all.'

He shook his head. 'I got lenses, haven't I been telling you? Why I've been shooting what these four eat for breakfast every morning. I've got hours of Marion on film for instance,' he sighed, 'and my God could I make her a star. Anyway I could film the burial from here if I had to, so I'll take my chances. Don't you worry about me.'

'I am *not* worrying about you,' I said. 'Take my word for it. But I do wish you'd come back down with me. They don't want you up here, and I don't want you up here. It's dangerous, especially if we lose this weather. Besides, you're breaking your contract with our agency, which said you'd follow my instructions on the trek.'

'Sue me.'

I took a deep breath.

Arnold put a friendly hand to my arm. 'Don't worry so much, George. They'll love me when they're stars.' He saw the look on my face and stepped away. 'And don't you try anything funny with me, or I'll slap some kind of kidnapping charge on you, and you'll never guide a trek again.'

'Don't tempt me like that,' I told him, and stalked back to the Brits' camp.

I dropped into their tent. Laure and Kunga Norbu had joined them, and we were jammed in there. 'No luck,' I said. They weren't surprised.

'Superleech,' Freds commented cheerfully.

We sat around and stared at the blue flames of the stove.

Then, as usually happens in these predicaments, I said, 'I've got a plan.'

It was relatively simple, as we didn't have many options. We would all descend back to the Lho La, and maybe even down to Base Camp, giving Arnold the idea we had given up. Once down there the Brits and Freds and Kunga Norbu could restock at the Gorak Shep teahouses, and Laure and I would undertake to stop Arnold, by stealing his boots for instance. Then they could go back up the fixed ropes and try again.

Trevor looked dubious. 'It's difficult getting up here, and we don't have much time, if that other expedition is already on the North Col.'

'I've got a better plan,' Freds announced. 'Looky here, Arnold's following you Brits, but not us. If we four pretended to go down, while you four took the West Ridge direct, then Arnold would follow you. Then we four could sneak off into the Diagonal Ditch, and pass you by going up the Hornbein Couloir, which is actually faster than the West Ridge direct. You wouldn't see us and we'd be up there where the body is, lickety-split.'

Well, no one was overjoyed at this plan. The Brits would have liked to find Mallory themselves, I could see. And I didn't have any inclination to go any higher than we already had. In fact I was dead set against it.

But by now the Brits were absolutely locked onto the idea of saving Mallory from TV and Westminster Abbey. 'It would do the job,' Marion conceded.

'And we might lose the leech on the ridge,' Mad Tom added. 'It's a right piece of work, or so I'm told.'

'That's right!' Freds said happily. 'Laure, are you up for it?'

'Whatever you like,' Laure said, and grinned. He thought it was a fine idea. Freds then asked Kunga Norbu, in Tibetan, and reported to us that Kunga gave the plan his mystic blessing.

'George?'

'Oh, man, no. I'd rather just get him down some other way.'

'Ah come on!' Freds cried. 'We don't have another way, and you don't want to let down the side, do you? Sticky wicket and all that?'

'He's your fooking client,' John pointed out.

'Geez. Oh, man . . . Well . . . All right.'

I walked back to our tent feeling that things were really getting out of control. In fact I was running around in the grip of other people's plans, plans I by no means approved of, made by people whose mental balance I doubted. And all this on the side of a mountain that had killed over fifty people. It was a bummer.

CHAPTER ELEVEN

BUT I WENT ALONG with the plan. Next morning we broke camp and made as if to go back down. The Brits started up the West Ridge, snarling dire threats at Arnold as they passed him. Arnold and his Sherpas were already packed, and after giving the Brits a short lead they took off after them. Arnold was roped up to their leader Ang Rita, raring to go, his camera in a chest pack. I had to hand it to him – he was one tenacious peeping Tom.

We waved goodbye and stayed on the shoulder until they were above us, and momentarily out of sight. Then we hustled after them, and took a left into the so-called Diagonal Ditch, which led out onto the North Face.

We were now following the route first taken by Tom Hornbein and Willi Unsoeld, in 1963. A real mountaineering classic, actually, which goes up what is now called the Hornbein Couloir. Get out any good photo of the North Face of Everest and you'll see it – a big vertical crack on the right side. It's a steep gully, but quite a bit faster than the West Ridge.

So we climbed. It was hard climbing, but not as scary as the Lho La. My main problem on this day was paranoia about the weather. Weather is no common concern on the side of Everest. You don't say, 'Why, snow would really ruin the day.' Quite a number of people have been caught by storms on Everest and killed by them, including the guys we were going to look for. So whenever I saw wisps of cloud streaming out from the peak, I tended to freak. And the wind whips a banner of cloud from the peak of Everest almost continuously. I kept looking up and seeing that banner, and groaning. Freds heard me.

'Gee, George, you sound like you're really hurting on this pitch.'

'Hurry up, will you?'

'You want to go faster? Well, okay, but I gotta tell you I'm going about as fast as I can. I don't think I want to tell Kunga to hurry more, because he might do it.'

I believed that. Kunga Norbu was using ice axe and crampons to fire up the packed snow in the middle of the couloir, and Freds was right behind him; they looked like roofers on a ladder. I did my best to follow, and Laure brought up the rear. Both Freds and Kunga had grins so wide and fixed that you'd have thought they were on acid. Their teeth were going to get sunburned they were loving it so much. Meanwhile I was gasping for air, and worrying about that summit banner . . . it was one of the greatest climbing days of my life.

How's that, you ask? Well . . . it's hard to explain. But it's something like this: when you get on a mountain wall with a few thousand feet of empty air below you, it catches your attention. Of course part of you says oh my God, it's all over. Why ever did I do this? But another part sees that in order not to die you must pretend you are quite calm, and engaged in a semi-theoretical gymnastics exercise intended to move you higher. You *pay attention* to the exercise like no one has ever paid attention before. Eventually you find yourself on a flat spot of some sort – three feet by five feet will do. You look around and realize that you did not die, that you are still alive. And at this point this fact becomes really exhilarating. You really *appreciate* being alive. It's a sort of power, or a privilege granted you, in any case it feels quite special, like a flash of higher consciousness. Just to be alive! And in retrospect, that *paying attention* when you were climbing – you remember that as a higher consciousness too.

You can get hooked on feelings like those; they are the ultimate altered state. Drugs can't touch them. I'm not saying this is real healthy behaviour, you understand. I'm just saying it happens.

For instance, at the end of this particular intense day in the Hornbein Couloir, the four of us emerged at its top, having completed an Alpine-style blitz of it due in large part to Kunga Norbu's inspired leads. We made camp on top of a small flat knob just big enough for our tent. And looking around – what a feeling! It really was something. There were only four or five mountains in the world taller than we were in that campsite, and you could tell. We could see all the way across Tibet, it seemed. Now Tibet, as Galen Rowell once said, tends mostly to look like a freeze-dried Nevada – from our height it was range after range of snowy peaks, white on black forever, all tinted sepia by the afternoon sun. It seemed the world was nothing but mountains.

Freds plopped down beside me, idiot grin still fixed on his face.

He had a steaming cup of lemon drink in one hand, his hash pipe in the other and he was singing 'Truckin'. He took a hit from the pipe and handed it to me.

'Are you sure we should be smoking up here?'

'Sure, it helps you breathe.'

'Come on.'

'No really. The nerve centre that controls your involuntary breathing shuts down in the absence of carbon dioxide, and there's hardly any of that up here, so the smoke provides it.'

I decided that on medical grounds I'd better join him. We passed the pipe back and forth. Behind us Laure was in the tent, humming to himself and getting his sleeping bag out. Kunga Norbu sat in the lotus position on the other side of the tent, intent on realms of his own. The world, all mountains, turned under the sun.

Freds exhaled happily. 'This must be the greatest place on earth, don't you think?'

That's the feeling I'm talking about.

CHAPTER TWELVE

WE HAD a long and restless night of it, because it's harder than hell to sleep at that altitude. But the next day dawned clear and windless once again, and after breakfasting we headed along the top of the Black Band.

Our route was unusual, perhaps unique. The Black Band, harder than the layers of rock above and below it, sticks out from the generally smooth slope of the face in a crumbly rampart. So in effect we had a sort of road to walk on. Although it was uneven and busted up, it was still twenty feet wide in places, and an easier place for a traverse couldn't be imagined. There were potential campsites all over it.

Of course usually when people are at 28,000 feet on Everest, they're interested in getting either higher or lower pretty quick. Since this rampway was level and didn't facilitate any route whatsoever, it wasn't much travelled. We might have been the first on it, since Freds said that Kunga Norbu had only looked down on it from above.

So we walked this high road, and made our search. Freds knocked a rock off the edge, and we watched it bounce down toward the Rongbuk Glacier until it became invisible, though we could still hear it. After that we trod a little more carefully. Still, it wasn't long before we had traversed the face and were looking down the huge clean chute of the Great Couloir. Here the rampart ended, and to continue the traverse to the fabled North Ridge, where Mallory and Irvine were last seen, would have been ugly work. Besides, that wasn't where Kunga Norbu had seen the body.

'We must have missed it,' Freds said. 'Let's spread out side to side, and check every little nook and cranny on the way back.' So we did, taking it very slowly, and ranging out to the edge of the rampart as far as we dared.

We were about halfway back to the Hornbein Couloir when Laure found it. He called out, and we approached.

'Well dog my cats,' Freds said, looking astonished.

The body was wedged in a crack, chest deep in a hard pack of snow. He was on his side, and curled over so that he was level with the rock on each side of the crack. His clothing was frayed, and rotting away on him; it looked like knit wool. The kind of thing you'd wear golfing in Scotland. His eyes were closed, and under a fraying hood his skin looked papery. Sixty years out in sun and storm, but always in below-freezing air, had preserved him strangely. I had the odd feeling that he was only sleeping, and might wake and stand.

Freds knelt beside him and dug in the snow a bit. 'Look here – he's roped up, but the rope broke.'

He held up an inch or two of unravelled rope – natural fibres, horribly thin – it made me shudder to see it. 'Such primitive gear!' I cried.

Freds nodded briefly. 'They were nuts. I don't think he's got an oxygen pack on either. They had it available, but he didn't like to use it.' He shook his head. 'They probably fell together. Stepped through a cornice maybe. Then fell down to here, and this one jammed in the crack while the other one went over the edge, and the rope broke.

'So the other one is down in the glacier,' I said.

Freds nodded slowly. 'And look—' he pointed above. 'We're almost directly under the summit. So they must have made the top. Or fallen when damned close to it.' He shook his head. 'And wearing nothing but a jacket like that! Amazing.'

'So they made it,' I breathed.

'Well, maybe. Looks like it, anyway. So . . . which one is this?'

I shook my head. 'I can't tell. Early twenties, or mid-thirties?'

Uneasily we looked at the mummified features.

'Thirties,' Laure said. 'Not young.'

Freds nodded. 'I agree.'

'So it's Mallory,' I said.

'Hmph.' Freds stood and stepped back. 'Well, that's that. The mystery solved.' He looked at us, spoke briefly with Kunga Norbu. 'He must be under snow most years. But let's hide him under rock, for the Brits.'

This was easier said than done. All we needed were stones to lay over him, as he was tucked down in the crack. But we quickly found that loose stones of any size were not plentiful; they had been blown off. So we had to work in pairs, and pick up big flat plates that were heavy enough to hold against the winds.

We were still collecting these when Freds suddenly jerked back and sat behind an outcropping of the rampart, 'Hey, the Brits are over there on the West Ridge! They're almost level with us!'

'Arnold can't be far behind,' I said.

'We've still got an hour's work here,' Freds exclaimed. 'Here – Laure, listen – go back to our campsite and pack our stuff, will you? Then go meet the Brits and tell them to slow down. Got that?'

'Slow down,' Laure repeated.

'Exactly. Explain we found Mallory and they should avoid this area. Give us time. You stay with them, go back down with them. George and Kunga and I will follow you guys down, and we'll meet you at Gorak Shep.'

Gorak Shep? That seemed farther down than necessary.

Laure nodded. 'Slow down, go back, we meet you Gorak Shep.'

'You got it, buddy. See you down there.'

Laure nodded and was off.

'Okay,' Freds said. 'Let's get this guy covered.'

We built a low wall around him, and then used the biggest plate of all as a keystone to cover his face. It took all three of us to pick it up, and we staggered around to get it into position without disturbing him; it really knocked the wind out of us.

When we were done the body was covered, and most of the time snow would cover our burial cairn, and it would be just one lump among thousands. So he was hidden. 'Shouldn't we say something?' Freds asked. 'You know, an epitaph or whatever?'

'Hey, Kunga's the holy man,' I said. 'Tell him to do it.'

Freds spoke to Kunga. In his snow goggles I could see little images of Kunga, looking like a Martian in his dirty red down jacket, hood and goggles. Quite a change in gear since old Mallory!

Kunga Norbu stood at the end of our cairn and stuck out his mittened hands; he spoke in Tibetan for a while.

Afterwards Freds translated for me: 'Spirit of Chomolungma, Mother Goddess of the World, we're here to bury the body of George Leigh Mallory, the first person to climb your sacred slopes. He was a climber with a lot of heart and he always went for it, and we love him for that – he showed very purely something that we all treasure in ourselves. I'd like to add that it's clear from his clothing and gear that he was a total loon to be up here at all, and I in particular would like to salute that quality as well. So here we are, four disciples of your holy spirit, and we take this moment to honour that spirit here and in us, and everywhere in the world.' Kunga bowed his head, and Freds and I followed suit, and we were silent; and all we heard was the wind, whistling over the Mother Goddess into Tibet.

CHAPTER THIRTEEN

FINE. OUR MISSION was accomplished, Mallory was safely hidden on Everest for all time, we had given him what I found a surprisingly moving burial ceremony, and I for one was pretty pleased. But back at our campsite, Freds and Kunga started acting oddly. Laure had packed up the tent and our packs and left them for us, and now Freds and Kunga were hurrying around repacking them.

I said something to the effect that you couldn't beat the view from Mallory's final resting place, and Freds looked up at me, and said, 'Well, you could beat it by a *little*.' And he continued repacking feverishly. 'In fact I've been meaning to talk to you about that,' he said as he worked. 'I mean, here we are, right? I mean here we are.'

'Yes,' I said. 'We are here.'

'I mean to say, here we are at almost twenty-eight thou, on Mount Everest. And it's only noon, and it's a perfect day. I mean *a perfect* day. Couldn't ask for a nicer day.'

I began to see what he was driving at. 'No way, Freds.'

'Ah come on! Don't be hasty about this, George! We're above all the hard parts, it's just a walk from here to the top!'

'No,' I said firmly. 'We don't have time. And we don't have much food. And we can't trust the weather. It's too dangerous.'

'Too dangerous! All climbing is too dangerous, George, but I don't notice that that ever stopped you before. Think about it, man! This ain't just some ordinary mountain, this ain't no Rainier or Denali, this is *Everest*. Sagarmatha! Chomo*lung*ma! The BIG E! Hasn't it always been your secret fantasy to climb Everest?'

'Well, no. It hasn't.'

'I don't believe you! It sure is mine, I'll tell you that. It's gotta be yours too.'

All the time we argued Kunga Norbu was ignoring us, while he rooted through his pack tossing out various inessential items.

Freds sat down beside me and began to show me the contents of his pack. 'I got our butt pads, the stove, a pot, some soup and lemon mix, a good supply of food, and here's my snow shovel so we can bivvy somewhere. Everything we need.'

'No.'

'Looky here, George.' Freds pulled off his goggles and stared me in the eye. 'It was nice to bury Mallory and all, but I have to tell you that Kunga Norbu Lama and I have had what you'd call an *ulterior motive* all along here. We joined the Brits on the Lingtren climb because I had heard about this Mallory expedition from the north side, and I was planning all along to tell them about it, and show them our photo, and tell them that Kunga was the guy who saw Mallory's body back in 1980, and suggest that they go hide him.'

'You mean Kunga *wasn't* the one who saw Mallory's body?' I said.

'No, he wasn't. I made that up. The Chinese climber who saw a body up here was killed a couple years later. So I just had Kunga circle the general area where I heard the Chinese saw him. That's why I was so surprised when we actually ran across the guy! Although it stands to reason when you look at the North Face – there isn't any where else but the Black Band that would have stopped him.

'Anyway I lied about that, and I also suggested we slip up the Hornbein Couloir and find the body when Arnold started tailing the Brits – and all of that was because I was just hoping we'd get into this situation, where we got the time and the weather to shoot for the top, we were both just *hoping* for it man and where we are. We got everything planned, Kunga and I have worked it all out – we've got all the stuff we need, and if we have to bivvy on the South Summit after we bag the peak, then we can descend by way of the Southeast

Ridge and meet the Indian Army team in the South Col, and get escorted back to Base Camp, that's the yak route and won't be any problem.'

He took a few deep breaths. 'Plus, well, listen. Kunga Lama has got *mystic reasons* for wanting to go up there, having to do with his longtime guru Tilopa Lama. Remember I told you back in Chimoa how Tilopa had set a task for Kunga Norbu, that Kunga had to accomplish before the monastery at Kum-Bum would be rebuilt, and Kunga set free to be his own lama at last? Well – the task was to *climb Chomolungma*! That old son of a gun said to Kunga, you just climb Chomolungma and everything'll be fine! Figuring that meant that he would have a disciple for just as many re-incarnations as he would ever go through this side of nirvana. But he didn't count on Kunga Norbu teaming up with his old student Freds Fredericks, and his buddy George Fergusson!'

'Wait a minute,' I said. 'I can see you feel very deeply about this, Freds, and I respect that, but I'm not going.'

'We need you along, George! Besides, we're going to do it, and we can't really leave you to go back down the West Ridge by yourself – that'd be more dangerous than coming along with us! And we're going to the peak, so you have to come along, it's that simple!'

Freds had been talking so fast and hard that he was completely out of breath; he waved a hand at Kunga Norbu. 'You talk to him,' he said to Kunga, then switched to Tibetan, no doubt to repeat the message.

Kunga Norbu pulled up his snow goggles, and very serenely he looked at me. He looked just a little sad; it was the sort of expression you might get if you refused to give to the United Way. His black eyes looked right through me just as they always did, and in that high-altitude glare his pupils kind of pulsed in and out, in and out, in and out. And damned if that old bastard didn't hypnotize me. I think.

But I struggled against it. I found myself putting on my pack, and checking my crampons to make sure they were really, really, really tight, and at the same time I was shouting at Freds. 'Freds, be reasonable! No one climbs Everest unsupported like this! It's too dangerous!'

'Hey, Messner did it. Messner climbed it in two days from the North Col by himself, all he had was his girlfriend waiting down at base camp.'

'You can't use Reinhold Messner as an example,' I cried. 'Messner is cuckoo.'

'Nah. He's just tough and fast. And so are we. It won't be a problem.'

'Freds, climbing Everest is generally considered a problem.' But Kunga Norbu had put on his pack and was starting up the slope above our campsite, and Freds was following him, and I was following Freds. 'For one big problem,' I yelled, 'we don't have any oxygen!'

'People climb it without oxygen all the time now.'

'Yeah, but you pay the price. You don't get enough oxygen up there, and it kills brain cells like you can't believe! If we go up there we're certain to lose *millions* of brain cells.'

'So?' He couldn't see the basis of the objection.

I groaned. We continued up the slope.

CHAPTER FOURTEEN

AND THAT is how I found myself climbing Mount Everest with a Tibetan tulku and the wild man of Arkansas. It was not a position that a reasonable person could defend to himself, and indeed as I trudged after Freds and Kunga I could scarcely believe it was happening. But every laboured breath told me it was. And since it was, I decided I had better psych myself into the proper frame of mind for it, or else it would only be that much more dangerous. 'Always wanted to do this,' I said, banishing the powerful impression that I had been hypnotized into the whole deal. 'We're climbing Everest, and I really want to.'

'That's the attitude,' Freds said.

I ignored him and kept thinking the phrase 'I want to do this,' once for every two steps. After a few hundred steps, I had to admit that I had myself somewhat convinced. I mean, Everest! Think about it! I suppose that like anyone else, I had the fantasy in there somewhere.

I won't bother you with the details of our route; if you want them you can consult my anonymous article in the *American Alpine Journal*, 1986 issue. Actually it was fairly straightforward; we contoured up from the Hornbein Couloir to the upper West Ridge, and continued from there.

I did this in bursts of ten steps at a time; the altitude was finally beginning to hammer me. I acclimatize as well as anyone I know, but nobody acclimatizes over 26,000 feet. It's just a matter of how fast you wind down.

'Try to go as slow as you need to, and avoid rests,' Freds advised.

'I'm going as slow as I can already.'

'No you're not. Try to just flow uphill. Really put it into first gear. You fall into a certain rhythm.'

'All right. I'll try.'

We were seated at this point to take off our crampons, which were unnecessary. Freds had been right about the ease of the climb up here. The ridge was wide, it wasn't very steep, and it was all broken up, so that irregular rock staircases were everywhere on it. If it were at sea level you could run up it, literally. It was so easy that I could try Freds's suggestion, and I followed him and Kunga up the ridge in slow-motion. At that rate I could go about five or ten minutes between rests – it's hard to be sure how long, as each interval seemed like an afternoon on its own.

But with each stop we were a little higher. There was no denying the West Ridge had a first-class view: to our right all the mountains of Nepal, to our left all the mountains of Tibet, and you could throw in Sikkim and Bhutan for change. Mountains everywhere: and all of them below us. The only thing still above us was the pyramid of Everest's final summit, standing brilliant white against a black blue sky.

At each rest stop I found Kunga Norbu was humming a strange Buddhist chant; he was looking happier and happier in a subtle sort of way, while Freds' grin got wider and wider. 'Can you believe how perfect the day is? Beautiful, huh?'

'Uh huh.' It was nice, all right. But I was too tired to enjoy it. Some of their energy poured into me at each stop, and that was a good thing, because they were really going strong, and I needed the help.

Finally the ridge became snow-covered again, and we had to sit down and put our crampons back on. I found this usually simple process almost more than I could handle. My hands left pink after-images in the air, and I hissed and grunted at each pull on the straps. When I finished and stood, I almost keeled over. The rocks swam, and even with my goggles on the snow was painfully white.

'Last bit,' Freds said as we looked up the slope. We crunched into it, and our crampons spiked down into firm snow. Kunga took off at an unbelievable pace. Freds and I marched up side by side, sharing a pace to take some of the mental effort out of it.

Freds wanted to talk, even though he had no breath to spare. 'Old Tilopa Lama. Going to be. Mighty surprised. When they start re-building Kum-Bum. Ha!'

I nodded as if I believed in the whole story. This was an exaggeration, but it didn't matter. Nothing mattered but to put one foot in front of the other, in blazing white snow.

I have read that Everest stands just at the edge of the possible, as far as climbing it without oxygen goes. The scientific team that concluded this, after a climb in which air and breath samples were taken, actually decided that theoretically it wasn't possible at all. Sort of a bumblebee's flight situation. One scientist speculated that if Everest were just a couple hundred feet taller, then it really couldn't be done.

I believe that. Certainly the last few steps up that snow pyramid were the toughest I ever took. My breath heaved in and out of me in useless gasps, and I could hear the brain cells popping off by the thousands, *snap crackle pop*. We were nearing the peak, a triangular dome of pure snow; but I had to slow down.

Kunga forged on ahead of us, picking up speed in the last approach. Looking down at the snow, I lost sight of him. Then his boots came into my field of vision, and I realized we were there, just a couple of steps below the top.

The actual summit was a ridged mound of snow about eight feet long and four feet wide. It wasn't a pinnacle, but it wasn't a broad hilltop either; you wouldn't have wanted to dance on it.

'Well,' I said. 'Here we are.' I couldn't get excited about it. 'Too bad I didn't bring a camera.' The truth was, I didn't feel a thing.

Beside me Freds stirred. He tapped my arm, gestured up at Kunga Norbu. We were still below him, with our heads at about the level of his boots. He was humming, and had his arms extended up and out, as if conducting a symphony out to the east. I looked in that direction. By this time it was late afternoon, and Everest's shadow extended to the horizon, even above. There must have been ice particles in the air to the east, because all of a sudden above the darkness of Everest's shadow I saw a big icebow. It was almost a complete circle of colour, much more diaphanous than a rainbow, cut off at the bottom by the mountain's triangular shadow.

Inside this round bow of faint colour, on the top of the dark air of the shadow peak, there was a cross of light-haloed shadow. It was a Spectre of the Brocken phenomenon, caused when low sunlight throws the shadows of peaks and climbers onto moisture-filled air, creating a glory of light around the shadows. I had seen one before.

Then Kunga Norbu flicked his hands to the sides, and the whole vision disappeared, instantly.

'Whoah,' I said.

'Right on,' Freds murmured, and led me the last painful steps onto the peak itself, so that we stood beside Kunga Norbu. His head was thrown back, and on his face was a smile of pure, child-like bliss.

Now, I don't know what really happened up there. Maybe I went faint and saw colours for a moment, thought it was an icebow, and then blinked things clear. But I know that at that moment, looking at Kunga Norbu's transfigured face, I was quite sure that I had seen him gain his freedom, and paint it out there in the sky. The task was fulfilled, the arms thrown wide with joy . . . I believed all of it. I swallowed, a sudden lump in my throat.

Now I felt it too; I felt where we were. We had climbed Chomolungma. We were standing on the peak of the world.

Freds heaved his breath in and out a few times. 'Well!' he said, and shook mittened hands with Kunga and me. 'We did it!' And then we pounded each other on the back until we almost knocked ourselves off the mountain.

CHAPTER FIFTEEN

WE HADN'T been up there long when I began to consider the problem of getting down. There wasn't much left of the day, and we were a long way from anywhere homey. 'What now?'

'I think we'd better go down to the South Summit and dig a snow cave for the night. That's the closest place we can do it, and that's what Haston and Scott did in '75. It worked for them, and a couple other groups too.'

'Fine,' I said. 'Let's do it.'

Freds said something to Kunga, and we started down. Immediately I found that the Southeast Ridge was not as broad or as gradual as the West Ridge. In fact we were descending a kind of snow-covered knife edge, with ugly grey rocks sticking out of it. So this was the yak route! It was a tough hour's work to get down to the South Summit, and the only thing that made it possible was the fact that we were going downhill all the way.

The South Summit is a big jog in the Southeast Ridge, which makes for a lump of a subsidiary peak, and a flat area. Here we had a broad sloping expanse of very deep, packed snow – perfect conditions for a snow cave.

Freds got his little aluminium shovel out of his pack and went to it, digging like a dog after a bone. I was content to sit and consult. Kunga Norbu stood staring around at the infinite expanse of peaks, looking a little dazed. Once or twice I summoned up the energy to spell Freds. After a body-sized entryway, we only wanted a cave big enough for the three of us to fit in. It looked a bit like a coffin for triplets.

The sun set, stars came out, the twilight turned midnight blue; then it was night. And seriously, seriously cold. Freds declared the cave ready and I crawled in after him and Kunga, feeling granules of snow crunch under me. We banged heads and got arranged on our butt pads so that we were sitting in a little circle, on a rough shelf above our entrance tunnel, in a roughly spherical chamber. By slouching I got an inch's clearance above. 'All right,' Freds said wearily. 'Let's party.' He took the stove from his pack, held it in his mittens for a while to warm the gas inside, then set it on the snow in the middle of the three of us, and lit it with his lighter. The blue glare was blinding, the roar deafening. We took off our mitts and cupped our hands so there was no gap between flame and flesh. Our cave began to warm up a little.

You may think it odd that a snow cave can warm up at all, but remember we are speaking relatively here. Outside it was dropping to about 10 below zero, Fahrenheit. Add any kind of wind and at that altitude, where oxygen is so scarce, you'll die. Inside the cave, however, there was no wind. Snow itself is not that cold, and it's a great insulator; it will warm up, even begin to get slick on its surface, and that water also holds heat very well. Add a stove raging away, and three bodies struggling to pump out their 98.6, and even with a hole connecting you to outside air, you can get the temperature well up into the thirties. That's colder than a refrigerator, but compared to 10 below it's beach weather.

So we were happy in our little cave, at first. Freds scraped some of the wall into his pot and cooked some hot lemon drink. He offered me some almonds, but I had no appetite whatsoever; eating an almond was the same as eating a coffee table to me. We were all dying for drink, though, and we drank the lemon mix when it was boiling, which at this elevation was just about bath temperature. It tasted like heaven.

We kept melting snow and drinking it until the stove sputtered and ran out of fuel. Only a couple of hours had passed, at most. I sat there in the pitch dark, feeling the temperature drop. My spirits dropped with it.

But Freds was by no means done with the party. His lighter scraped and by its light I saw him punch a hole in the wall and set a candle in it. He lit the candle, and its light reflected off the slick white sides of our home. He had a brief discussion with Kunga Norbu.

'Okay,' he said to me at the end of it, breath cascading whitely into the air. 'Kunga is going to do some *tumo* now.'

'Tumo?'

'Means, the art of warming oneself without fire up in the snows.'

That caught my interest. 'Another lama talent?'

'You bet. It comes in handy for naked hermits in the winter.'

'I can see that. Tell him to lay it on us.'

With some crashing about Kunga got in the lotus position, an impressive feat with his big snow boots still on.

He took his mitts off, and we did the same. then he began breathing in a regular, deep rhythm, staring at nothing. This went on for almost half an hour, and I was beginning to think we would all freeze before he warmed up, when he held his hands out toward Freds and me. We took them in our own.

They were as hot as if he had a terrible fever. Fearfully I reached up to touch his face – it was warm, but nothing like his hands. 'My Lord,' I said.

'We can help him now,' Freds said softly. 'You have to concentrate, harness the energy that's always inside you. Every breath out you push away pride, anger, hatred, envy, sloth, stupidity. Every breath in, you take in Buddha's spirit, the five wisdoms, everything good. When you've gotten clear and calm, imagine a golden lotus in your belly button . . . Okay? In that lotus you imagine the syllable *ram*, which means fire. Then you have to see a little seed of flame, the size of a goat dropping, appearing in the *ram*. Every breath after that is like a bellows, fanning that flame, which travels through the *tsas* in the body, the mystic nerves. Imagine this process in five stages. First the *uma tsa* is seen as a hair of fire, up your spine more or less . . . Two, the nerve is as big around as your little finger . . . Three, it's the size of an arm . . . Four, the body becomes the *tsa* itself and is perceived as a tube of fire . . . Five, the *tsa* engulfs the world, and you're just one flame in a sea of fire.'

'My Lord.'

We sat there holding Kunga Norbu's fiery hands, and I imagined myself a tube of fire: and the warmth poured into me – up my arms, through my torso – it even thawed my frozen butt, and my feet. I stared at Kunga Norbu, and he stared right through the wall of our cave to eternity, or wherever, his eyes glowing faintly in the candlelight. It was weird.

I don't know how long this went on – it seemed endless, although I suppose it was no more than an hour or so. But then it broke off – Kunga's hand cooled, and so did the rest of us. He blinked several times and shook his head. He spoke to Freds.

'Well,' Freds said. 'That's about as long as he can hold it, these days.'

'What?'

'Well . . .' He clucked his tongue regretfully. 'It's like this. Tulkus tend to lose their powers, over the course of several incarnations. It's like they lose something in the process, every time, like when you keep making a tape from copies or whatever. There's a name for it.

'Transmission error,' I said.

'Right. Well, it gets them too. In fact you run into a lot of tulkus in Tibet who are complete morons. Kunga is better than that, but he is a bit like Paul Revere. A little light in the belfry, you know. A great lama, and a super guy, but not tremendously powerful at any of the mystic disciplines any more.'

'Too bad.'

'I know.'

I recalled Kunga's fiery hands, their heat pronging into me. 'So . . . he really is a tulku, isn't he.'

'Oh yeah! Of course! And now he's free of old Tilopa, too – a lama in his own right, and nobody's disciple. It must be a great feeling.'

'I bet. So how does it work again, exactly?'

'Becoming a tulku?'

'Yeah.'

'Well, it's a matter of concentrating your mental powers. Tibetans believe that none of this is supernatural, but just a focusing of natural powers that we all have. Tulkus have gotten their psychic energies incredibly focused, and when you're at that stage, you can leave your body whenever you want. Why if Kunga wanted to, he could die in about ten seconds.'

'Useful.'

'Yeah. So when they decide to go, they hop off into the Bardo. The Bardo is the other world, the world of spirit, and it's a confusing place – talk about hallucinations! First a light like God's camera flash goes off in your face. Then it's just a bunch of coloured paths, apparitions, everything. When Kunga describes it it's really scary. Now if you're just an ordinary spirit, then you can get disoriented, and be reborn as a slug or a game show host or *anything*. But if you stay focused, you're reborn in the body you choose, and you go on from there.'

I nodded dully. I was tired, and cold, and the lack of oxygen was making me stupid and spacy; I couldn't make sense of Freds's explanations, although it may be that that would have happened anywhere.

We sat there. Kunga hummed to himself. It got colder.

The candle guttered, then went out.

It was dark. It continued to get colder.

After a while there was nothing but the darkness, our breathing, and the cold. I couldn't feel my butt or my legs below the knee. I knew I was waiting for something, but I had forgotten what it was. Freds stirred, started speaking Tibetan with Kunga. They seemed a long way away. They spoke to people I couldn't see. For a while Freds jostled about, punching the sides of the cave. Kunga shouted out hoarsely, things like 'Hak!' and 'Phut!'

'What are you doing?' I roused myself to say.

'We're fighting off demons,' Freds explained.

I was ready to conclude, by watching my companions, that lack of oxygen drove one nuts; but what was my basis for comparison? My sample was skewed.

Some indeterminate time later Freds started shovelling snow out of the tunnel. 'Casting out demons?' I inquired.

'No, trying to get warm. Want to try it?'

I didn't have the energy to move.

Then he shook me from side to side, switched to English, told me stories. Story after story, in a dry, hoarse, frog's voice. I didn't understand any of them. I had to concentrate on fighting the cold. On breathing. Freds became agitated, he told me a story of Kunga's, something about running across Tibet with a friend, a *lung-gom-pa* test of some kind, and the friend was wearing chains to keep from floating away entirely. Then something about running into a young husband at night, dropping the chains in a campfire . . . 'The porters knew about *lung-gom*, and the next morning they must have tried to explain it to the British. Can you imagine it? Porters trying to explain these chains come out of nowhere . . . explaining they were used by people running across Tibet, to keep from going orbital? Man, those Brits must've thought they were invading Oz. Don't you think so? Hey, George? George? . . . George?'

CHAPTER SIXTEEN

BUT FINALLY the night passed, and I was still there.

We crawled out of our cave in the pre-dawn light, and stamped our feet until some sensation came back into them, feeling pretty pleased with ourselves. 'Good morning!' Kunga Norbu said to me politely. He was right about that. There were high cirrus clouds going pink above us, and an ocean of blue cloud far below in Nepal, with all the higher white peaks poking out of it like islands, and slowly turning pink themselves. I've never seen a more otherwordly sight; it was as if we had climbed out of our cave onto the side of another planet.

Maybe we should just shoot down to the South Col and join those Indian Army guys,' Freds croaked. 'I don't much feel like going back up to the peak to get to the West Ridge.'

'You aren't kidding,' I said.

So down the Southeast Ridge we went.

Now Peter Habeler, Messner's partner on the first oxygenless ascent of Everest in 1979, plunged down this ridge from the summit to the South Col in *one hour*. He was worried about brain damage; my feeling is that the speed of his descent is evidence it had already occurred. We went as fast as we could, which was pretty alarmingly fast, and it still took us almost three hours. One step after another, down a steep snowy ridge. I refused to look at the severe drops to right and left. The clouds below were swelling up like the tide in the Bay of Fundy; our good weather was about to end.

I felt completely disconnected from my body, I just watched it do its thing. Below Freds kept singing 'Close to the Edge'. We came to a big snow-filled gully and glissaded down it carelessly, sliding twenty or thirty feet with each dreamy step. All three of us were staggering by this point. Cloud poured up the Western Cwm, and mist magically appeared all around us, but we were just above the South Col by this time, and it didn't matter.

I saw there was a camp in the col, and breathed a sigh of relief. We would have been goners without it.

The Indians were still securing their tents as we walked up. A week's perfect weather, and they had just gotten into the South Col. Very slow, I thought as we approached. Siege-style assault, logistical pyramid, play it safe – slow as building the other kind of pyramid.

As we crossed the col and closed on the tents, navigating between piles of junk from previous expeditions, I began to worry. You see, the Indian Army has had incredible bad luck on Everest. They have tried to climb it several times, and so far as I know, they've never succeeded. Mostly this is because of storms, but people tend to ignore that, and the Indians have come in for a bit of criticism from the climbing community in Nepal. In fact they've been called terrible climbers. So they are a little touchy about this, and it was occurring to me, very slowly, that they might not be too amused to be greeted on the South
Col by three individuals who had just bagged the peak on an overnighter from the north side.

Then one of them saw us. He dropped the mallet in his hand.

'Hi there!' Freds croaked.

A group of them quickly gathered around us. The wind was beginning to blow hard, and we all stood at an angle to it. The oldest Indian there, probably a major, shouted gruffly, 'Who are you?'

We're lost,' Freds said. 'We need help.'

Ah, good, I thought. Freds has also thought of this problem. He won't tell them where we've been. Freds is still thinking. He will take care of this situation for us.

'Where did you come from?' the major boomed.

Freds gestured down the Western Cwm. Good, I thought. 'Our Sherpas told us to keep turning right. So ever since Jomosom we have been.'

'Where did you say?'

'Jomosom!'

The major drew himself up. 'Jomosom,' he said sharply, 'is in *western* Nepal.'

'Oh.' Freds said.

And we all stood there. Apparently that was it for Freds's explanation.

I elbowed him aside. 'The truth is, we thought it would be fun to help you. We didn't know what we were getting into.'

'Yeah!' Freds said, accepting this new tack thankfully. 'Can we carry a load down for you, maybe?'

'We are still climbing the mountain!' the major barked. 'We don't need loads carried down!' He gestured at the ridge behind us, which was disappearing in mist. 'This is Everest!'

Freds squinted at him. 'You're kidding.'

I elbowed him. 'We need help,' I said.

The major looked at us closely. 'Get in the tent,' he said at last.

CHAPTER SEVENTEEN

WELL, EVENTUALLY I concocted a semi-consistent story about us idealistically wanting to porter loads for an Everest expedition, although who would be so stupid as to want to do that I don't know. Freds was no help at all – he kept forgetting and going back to his first story, saying things like, 'We must have gotten on the wrong plane.' And neither of us could fit Kunga Norbu into our story very well; I claimed he was our guide, but we didn't understand his language. He very wisely stayed mute.

Despite all that, the Indian team fed us and gave us water to slake our raging thirst, and they escorted us back down their fixed ropes to the camps below, to make sure they got us out of there. Over the next couple of days they led us all the way down the Western Cwm and the Khumbu Icefall to Base Camp. I wish I could give you a blow-by-blow account of the fabled Khumbu Icefall, but the truth is I barely remember it. It was big and white and scary; I was tired. That's all I know. And then we were in their base camp, and I knew it was over. First illegal ascent of Everest.

CHAPTER EIGHTEEN

WELL, AFTER what we had been through, Gorak Shep looked like Ireland, and Pheriche looked like Hawaii. And the air was oxygen soup.

We kept asking after the Brits and Arnold and Laure, and kept hearing that they were a day or so below us. From the sound of it the Brits were chasing Arnold, who was managing by extreme efforts to stay ahead of them. So we hurried after them.

On our way down, however, we stopped at the Pengboche Monastery, a dark brooding old place in a little nest of black pine trees, supposed to be the chin whiskers of the first abbot. There we left Kunga Norbu, who was looking pretty beat. The monks at the monastery made a big to-do over him. He and Freds had an emotional parting, and he gave me a big grin as he bored me through one last time with that spacy black gaze. 'Good morning!' he said, and we were off.

So Freds and I tromped down to Namche, which reminded me strongly of Manhattan, and found our friends had just left for Lukla, still chasing Arnold. Below Namche we really hustled to catch up with them, but we didn't succeed until we reached Lukla itself. And then we only caught the Brits – because they were standing there by the Lukla airstrip, watching the last plane of the day hum down the tilted grass and ski jump out over the deep gorge of the Dudh Kosi – while Arnold McConnell, we quickly found out, was on that plane, having paid a legitimate passenger a fat stack of rupees to replace him.

Arnold's Sherpa companions were lining the strip and waving good-bye to him; they had all earned about a year's wages on this one climb, it turned out, and they were pretty fond of old Arnold.

The Brits were not. In fact they were fuming.

'Where have you been?' Trevor demanded.

'Well . . .' we said.

'We went to the top,' Freds said apologetically. 'Kunga had to for religious reasons.'

'Well,' Trevor said huffily. 'We considered it ourselves, but *we* had to chase *your* client back down the mountain to try and get his film. The film that will get us all kicked out of Nepal for good if it's ever shown.'

'Better get used to it,' Mad Tom said gloomily. 'He's off to Kathmandu, and we're not. We'll never catch him now.'

Now the view from Lukla is nothing extraordinary, compared to what you can see higher up; but there are the giant green walls of the gorge, and to the north you can see a single scrap of the tall white peaks beyond; and to look at all that, and think you might never be allowed to see it again . . .

I pointed to the south. 'Maybe we just got lucky.'

'What?'

Freds laughed. 'Choppers! Incoming! Some trekking outfit has hired helicopters to bring its group in.'

It was true. This is fairly common practice, I've done it myself many times. RNAC's daily flights to Lukla can't fulfil the need during the peak trekking season, so the Nepali Air Force kindly rents out its helicopters, at exorbitant fees. Naturally they prefer not to go back empty, and they'll take whoever will pay. Often, as on this day, there is a whole crowd clamouring to pay to go back, and the competition is fierce, although I for one am unable to understand what people are so anxious to get back to.

Anyway, this day was like most of them, and there was a whole crowd of trekkers sitting around on the unloading field by the airstrip, negotiating with the various Sherpa and Sherpani power brokers who run the airport and get people onto flights. The hierarchy among these half-dozen power brokers is completely obscure even to them, and on this day as always each of them had a list of people who had paid up to a hundred dollars for a lift out; and until the brokers discussed it with the helicopter crew, no one knew who was going to be the privileged broker given the go-ahead to march his clients on board. The crowd found this protocol ambiguous at best, and they were milling about and shouting ugly things at their brokers as the helicopters were sighted.

So this was not a good situation for us, because although we were desperate, everyone else wanting a lift claimed to be desperate also, and no one was going to volunteer to give up their places. Just before the two Puma choppers made their loud and windy landing, however, I saw Heather on the unloading field, and I ran over and discovered that she had gotten our expedition booked in with Pemba Sherpa, one of the most powerful brokers there. 'Good work, Heather!' I cried. Quickly I explained to her some aspects of the situation, and looking wide-eyed at us – we were considerably filthier and more sunburnt than when we last saw her – she nodded her understanding.

And sure enough, in the chaos of trekkers milling about the choppers, in all that moaning and groaning and screaming and shouting to be let on board, it was Pemba who prevailed over the other brokers. And Want To Take You Higher Ltd.'s 'Video Expedition to Everest Base Camp' – with the addition of four British climbers and an American – climbed on board the two vehicles, cheering all the way. With a *thukka thukka thukka* we were off.

'Now how will we find him in Kathmandu?' Marion said over the noise.

'He won't be expecting you,' I said. 'He thinks he's on the last flight of the day. So I'd start at the Kathmandu Guest House, where we were staying, and see if you can find him there.'

The Brits nodded, looking grim as commandos. Arnold was in trouble.

CHAPTER NINETEEN

WE LANDED at the Kathmandu airport an hour later, and the Brits zipped out and hired a taxi immediately. Freds and I hired another one and tried to keep up, but the Brits must have been paying their driver triple, because that little Toyota took off over the dirt roads between the airport and the city like it was in a motorcross race. So we fell behind, and by the time we were let off in the courtyard of the Kathmandu Guest House, their taxi was already gone. We paid our driver and walked in and asked one of the snooty clerks for Arnold's room number, and when he gave it to us we hustled on up to the room, on the third floor overlooking the back garden.

We got there in the middle of the action. John and Mad Tom and Trevor had Arnold trapped on a bed in the corner, and they were standing over him not letting him go anywhere. Marion was on the other side of the room doing the actual demolition, taking up video cassettes one at a time and stomping them under her boot. There was a lot of yelling going on, mostly from Marion and Arnold. '*That's* the one of me taking my bath,' Marion said. And *that's* the one of me changing my shirt in my tent. And *that's* the one of me taking a pee at eight thousand meters!' and so on, while Arnold was shouting 'No, no!' and, 'Not that one, my God!' and, 'I'll sue you in every court in Nepal!'

'Foreign nationals can't sue each other in Nepal,' Mad Tom told him.

But Arnold continued to shout and threaten and moan, his sun-torched face going incandescent, his much-reduced body bouncing up and down on the bed, his big round eyes popping out till I was afraid they would burst, or fall down on springs. He picked up the fresh cigar that had fallen from his mouth and threw it between Trevor and John, hitting Marion in the chest.

'Molester,' she said, dusting her hands with satisfaction. 'That's all of them, then.' She began to stuff the wreckage of plastic and videotape into a daypack. 'And we'll take this along, too, thank you very much.'

'Thief,' Arnold croaked.

The three guys moved away from him. Arnold sat there on the bed, frozen, staring at Marion with a stricken, bug-eyed expression. He looked like a balloon with a pinprick in it.

'Sorry, Arnold,' Trevor said. 'But you brought this on yourself, as you must admit. We told you all along we didn't want to be filmed.'

Arnold stared at them speechlessly.

'Well, then,' Trevor said. 'That's that.' And they left.

Freds and I watched Arnold sit there. Slowly his eyes receded back to their usual pop-eyed position, but he still looked disconsolate.

'Them Brits are tough,' Freds offered. 'They're not real sentimental people.'

'Come on, Arnold,' I said. Now that he was no longer my responsibility, now that we were back, and I'd never have to see him again – now that it was certain his videotape, which could have had Freds and me in as much hot water as the Brits, was destroyed – I felt a little bit sorry for him. Just a little bit. It was clear from his appearance that he had really gone through a lot to get that tape. Besides, I was starving. 'Come on, let's all get showered and shaved and cleaned up, and then I'll take you out to dinner.'

'Me too,' said Freds.

Arnold nodded mutely.

CHAPTER TWENTY

KATHMANDU is a funny city. When you first arrive there from the West, it seems like the most ramshackle and unsanitary place imaginable: the buildings are poorly constructed of old brick, and there are weed patches growing out of the roofs; the hotel rooms are bare pits; all the food you can find tastes like cardboard, and often makes you sick; and there are sewage heaps here and there in the mud streets, where dogs and cows are scavenging. It really seems primitive.

Then you go out for a month or two in the mountains, or a trek or a climb. And when you return to Kathmandu, the place is utterly transformed. The only likely explanation is that while you were gone they took the city away and replaced it with one that looks the same on the outside, but is completely different in substance. The accommodations are luxurious beyond belief; the food is superb; the people look prosperous, and their city seems a marvel of architectural sophistication. Kathmandu! What a metropolis!

So it seemed to Freds and me, as we checked into my home away from home, the Hotel Star. As I sat on the floor under the waist-high tap of steaming hot water that emerged from my shower, I found myself giggling in mindless rapture, and from the next room I could hear Freds bellowing the old fifties rocker, 'Going to Kathmandu.'

An hour later, hair wet, faces chopped up, skin all prune-shrivelled, we met Arnold out in the street and walked through the Thamel evening. 'We look like coat-racks!' Freds observed. Our city clothes were hanging on us. Freds and I had each lost about twenty pounds, Arnold about thirty. And it wasn't just fat, either. Everything wastes away at altitude. 'We'd better get to the Old Vienna and put some of it back on.'

I started salivating at the very thought of it.

So we went to the Old Vienna Inn, and relaxed in the warm steamy atmosphere of the Austro-Hungarian Empire. After big servings of goulash, schnitzel Parisienne, and apple strudel with whipped cream, we sat back sated. Sensory overload. Even Arnold was looking up a little. He had been quiet through the meal, but then again we all had, being busy.

We ordered a bottle of rakshi, which is a potent local beverage of indeterminate origin. When it came we began drinking.

Freds said, 'Hey, Arnold, you're looking better.'

'Yeah, I don't feel so bad.' He wiped his mouth with a napkin streaked all red; we had all split our sun-destroyed lips more than once, trying to shovel the food in too fast. He got set to start the slow process of eating another cigar, unwrapping one very slowly. 'Not so bad at all.' And then he grinned; he couldn't help himself, he grinned so wide that he had to grab the napkin and staunch the flow from his lips again.

'Well, it's a shame those guys stomped your movie,' Freds said.

'Yeah, well.' Arnold waved an arm expansively. 'That's life.'

I was amazed. 'Arnold, I can't believe this is you talking. Here those guys took your videotape of all that *suffering* you just put us through, and they *stomp* it, and you say, 'That's life?'

He took a long hit of the rakshi. 'Well,' he said, waggling his eyebrows up and down fiendishly. He leaned over the table toward us. 'They got one copy of it anyway.'

Freds and I looked at each other.

'Couple hundred dollars of tape there that they crunched. I suppose I ought to bill them for it. But I'm a generous guy; I let it pass.'

'One copy?' I said.

'Yeah.' He tipped his head. 'Did you see that box, kind of like a suitcase, there in the corner of my room at the Guest House?

We shook our heads.

'Neither did the Brits. Not that they would have recognized it. It's a video splicer, mainly. But a copier too. You stick a cassette in there and push a button and it copies the cassette for storage, and then you can do all your splicing off the master. You make your final tape that way. Great machine. Most freelance video people have them now, and these portable babies are really the latest. Saved my ass, in this case.'

'Arnold,' I said. 'You're going to get those guys in trouble! And us too!'

'Hey,' he warned, 'I've got the splicer under lock and key, so don't get any ideas.'

'Well you're going to get us banned from Nepal for good!'

'Nah. I'll give you all stage names. You got any preferences along those lines?'

'Arnold!' I protested.

'Hey, listen,' he said, and drank more rakshi. 'Most of that climb was in Tibet, right? Chinese aren't going to be worrying about it. Besides, you know the Nepali Ministry of Tourism – can you really tell me they'll ever get it together to even see my film, much less take names from it and track those folks down when they next apply for a visa? Get serious!'

'Hmm,' I said consulting with my rakshi.

'So what'd you get?' Freds asked.

'*Everything*. I got some good long-distance work of you guys finding the body up there – ha! – you thought I didn't get that, right? I tell you I was filming your *thoughts* up there! I got that, and then the Brits climbing on the ridge – everything. I'm gonna make stars of you all.'

Freds and I exchanged a relieved glance. 'Remember about the stage names,' I said.

'Sure. And after I edit it you won't be able to tell where on the mountain the body was, and with the names and all, I really think Marion and the rest will love it. Don't you? They were just being shy. Old fashioned! I'm going to send them all prints of the final product, and they're gonna love it. Marion in particular. She's gonna look beautiful.' He waved the cigar and a look of cowlike yearning disfigured his face. 'In fact, tell you a little secret, I'm gonna accompany that particular print in person, and make it part of my proposal to her. I think she's kind of fond of me, and I bet you anything she'll agree to marry me when whe sees it, don't you think?'

'Sure,' Freds said. 'Why not?' He considered it. 'Or if not in this life, then in the next.'

Arnold gave him an odd look. 'I'm going to ask her along on my next trip which looks like it'll be China and Tibet. You know how the Chinese have been easing up on the Tibetan religions lately? Well, the clerk at the Guest House gave me a telegram on my way out – my agent tells me that the authorities in Lhasa have decided they're going to rebuild a whole bunch of Buddhist monasteries that they tore down during the Cultural Revolution, and it looks like I'll be allowed to film some of it. That should make for a real heart-string basher, and I bet Marion would love to see it, don't you?'

Freds and I grinned at each other. '*I'd* love to see it,' Freds declared. 'Here's to the monasteries, and a free Tibet!'

We toasted the idea, and ordered another bottle.

Arnold waved his cigar. 'Meanwhile, this Mallory stuff is dynamite. It's gonna make a hell of a movie.'

CHAPTER TWENTY-ONE

WHICH IS WHY I can tell you about this one – the need for secrecy is going to be blown right out the window as soon as they air Arnold's film, *Nine Against Everest: Seven Men, One Woman, and a Corpse*. I hear both PBS and the BBC have gone for it, and it should be on any day now. Check local listings for times in your area.

THE ICE CHIMNEY

THE ICE CHIMNEY

a play for one actor by
Barry Collins

THE ICE CHIMNEY was first presented by the Lyric Studio Theatre at the Traverse Theatre Club, Edinburgh on 19 August 1980, where it won the Festival's Fringe First Award. It was later presented at the Lyric Studio Theatre, Hammersmith from 13 November 1980 with the same cast:

MAURICE WILSON Christopher Ettridge

Subsequently it was broadcast on BBC Radio 3 (1982) and on the BBC's World Service. This is its first appearance in print.

THE ICE CHIMNEY

Scene: The North Face of Mount Everest – at the foot of an ice cliff. The cliff itself is broken by a deep chimney and, perhaps, some kind of gully. Sound of the wind is heard, rising to a howl – the wind of a great snow mountain. These sound effects punctuate the play, sometimes behind the monologue, sometimes only in the pauses – the noise changing pitch and strength, giving the mountain a powerful and varied presence.

Coming through the wind, the breathless, piercing cries of the single character, Maurice Wilson – an Englishman, in his mid-thirties, quite tall, well-built, heavily-bearded, wearing a lightweight climbing suit, gloves, felt-lined boots and under his hood, a balaclava helmet and goggles.

With a last cry, Wilson "enters", plunging down the ice chimney into the snow below. . . . Immediately, the booming of a vast avalanche, heard close-up. Wilson lies, expecting to die – his body frozen, yet quivering, arm over his head, gabbling to himself with fear. Beside him, his rucksac and ice axe.

WILSON: (*As the booming fades*) Hold your collar, be a scholar – hold your collar, be a scholar – hold your collar, be a scholar, never go in an ambulance. Hold your collar, be a scholar . . . Gone.

(*He stops – lying full length in the snow, head cocked. Silence*)

WILSON: Missed me . . . Yah, yah you missed me . . . My name is Maurice Wilson! (*His shouted name echoes back at him – 'Wilson – Wilson . . .'*)

WILSON: Talk to me now, will you – when you've darned near killed me – you bitch, you big white bitch . . . (*lowering his goggles*) Can't see – can hardly see . . . Arm's dead. Throat's burning. S'like swallowing the sun . . . Stop blubbering, Wilson! On your feet! I haven't got any feet! Let's see you crawl, then. It's not a bleeding picnic. Too true, too flaming true . . . (*He laughs*) Half way up Mount Everest with a gammy arm and a few figs . . . Still, wouldn't swap places with the hermits. Think of the lice. Great little climbers. Follow you everywhere; long hairs, short hairs . . . Every man skin his own skunk, say I . . . Blimey, it's cold. Brass monkey weather. Hope I haven't got frostbite . . . Get up – keep moving . . .

(*Struggling to raise himself, he topples over again into the snow.*)

WILSON: Oh God, why have you forsaken me? Why do you fix me like a fly to this wall of ice? Am I not called? Was I not chosen? . . . Almighty father, take me, bury me deep in this mountain's deepest crevasse: let me slip through the steepest mines of the oldest rocks, down into the groin of the earth, where no river runs, where no light shines . . . Or else, Lord, I beg you: let me climb this great mountain, let me stand, alone at the highest height, where no man has stood before, on the roofpeak of the world. And let me then go down unto all the nations of mankind and sing hosannas to the everlasting God, whose disciples can achieve such miracles in the strength of their faith . . .

(*With one arm, Wilson drags the rucksac closer, manages to open it.*)

WILSON: (*Continued*) Eat! Must eat . . . (*He searches the rucksac*) Chocolate, where's the bloody chocolate?

(*Once, twice, he freezes, swings round, peering across the stage, then a third time, arms open.*)

WILSON: Rinzi! I knew you'd come . . . (*laughing*) Can't climb the ice chimney. Best chance for days – sunshine, no snow – and I'm stuck at the flaming ice chimney . . . (*dropping his arms*) Rinzi? . . . Where are you?

(*No reply. Puzzled, frightened, Wilson looks about him.*)

WILSON: I'm not mad . . . Don't let me be mad . . . (*suddenly, a different voice*) 67952 Wilson! Sah! Unauthorized assault on Mount Everest. Sah! Are you aware Mount Everest belongs to the Maharajah of Nepal? Permission to speak, Sah! Who gave it to him? Queen Victoria. Hence the native name, Chomolungma – goddess mother of the world. Now, come on, Wilson, what's a lad like you doing halfway up the goddess mother of the world? . . . Beats 'King Kong'.

(*Again, Wilson turns his head, alarmed now.*)

WILSON: Who's there? . . . Thought it was one of my sherpas. They're still at camp three. Won't budge another inch. Gutless little bastards! I'll never make it on my own. Give in, then – go back. Bollocks! All right, die – just don't expect them to die with you. Paid them, didn't I? Paid them to die? Who's going to die? You can't climb: you don't know how to climb. So what? Did Simon Peter know how to walk on water? Only it's not the Sea of Galilee; it's a forest of ice and the monsoons are coming, and I've still a mile to go – a mile – straight up the sky – and I'm freezing to death while those crafty beggars squat round a fire, stuffing themselves to the gills and counting my money . . . Christ, who could blame them? They're Buddhists . . . Besides, I'm nearly blind . . .

(*Again he looks across the stage, turns away, looks back.*)

WILSON: (*Continued*) Corbett? . . . Corbett, you lovely, lovely man. Haven't seen you since – since . . . the war, since – France . . . If you hadn't pissed on the barrel – that's what I've always said – if old Corbett hadn't pissed on the machine gun barrel, I'd've been a gonner . . . Past saving this time, Corbie, love . . . (*sitting down*) Right codger's trick, that – pissing on the barrel. Red hot, wasn't it? Fair set to jam. And you knelt up to piss on it – and caught one smack in the eye. Fell back on the sandbags, blood everywhere. And I thought – you won't believe this, Corbie – typical ruddy Methodist – I thought, 'Looks bad, that!' So I leaned over to button you up and the Boche chucked me a lead necklace – straight for my throat – only I was down in the hole, on top of you, with your poor cock still in my hand and your blood in my mouth . . . (*pause, as Wilson blinks, rubbing his eyes*) Sit still, Corbie, there's a love: You're all crinkly round the edges . . . Know what; I reckon you're an angel God sent down to look after me. Blessed if I've seen a khaki angel before . . . Did it hurt to die? . . . Put a word in for me, will you – upstairs? . . . Not about the sherpas, though. I'm not supposed to have any sherpas . . . Hear that, God? I've been cheating . . . And Peter said, 'Lord bid me come unto thee, on the water.' And Jesus said, 'Come.' The wind blew up, Peter got scared and started to sink, and yelled 'Lord, save me!' And Jesus stretched out his hand and caught him - and saved him . . . So, if it's not too presumptuous, God, where the dickens were you – when *I* was sinking – in the blizzard – on my first attempt – when I was alone – like I promised – alone – for seven days – trying to climb this mountain – and the snow blocked me, and I called to you, God – where were you – when I *was* afraid, in the storm, and I turned and fled, screaming, down this mountain, as if the devil himself and all his foul fiends were behind me . . .? Don't feel obliged, God: I'm only human . . . Look, I brought my sherpas this time – to show me the way – round the snow troughs, up the glacier, as far as Camp Three . . . Is that why you sent the blizzards back? Is that why you fastened us down, for five days, at Camp Three? Because I cheated . . .? Right, well my sherpas got the message. When the snow stopped, they wouldn't budge. I've left them behind . . . So we're all square, God, you and me. And I'm stuck at the ice chimney, under this cliff of ice – on my own again – like I promised . . . Apart from Corbie . . . Thanks for sending me Corbie – but he's hardly going to get me up the ice chimney, is he? . . . Sorry, God, to be such a nuisance. I mean, what did I expect – that you'd dangle your long white beard for me to climb? (*singing*) 'God moves in a mysterious way, his wonders to perform' . . . Too darned right he does . . . I'm not scared, Corbie. Beats a dugout any day . . . (*shivering*) Listen to that wind. Trying to kill me . . . No. Doesn't know how – doesn't even know how to die . . . Stop screeching! You can't get top 'C' on a tuba . . . (*wind falls*) Hear that, Corbie? Ice-trees, cracking – lower down – great mainmasts of ice, with all their top-rigging – great cathedrals of ice . . . (*taking a small notebook from his pocket*) S'all in my diary . . . For the folks at home . . . 'Wish you were here. Tibet's not a patch on Blackpool. Love Maurice' . . . My head's a balloon, it's ticking. Oh sure, balloons can tick. S'the ultra-violet, coming through my balaclava . . . (*wind rises*) And this wind – scouring me . . . Ey, Corbie, I'd give owt for a bath – stretched out, steaming, with yer toes up the taps . . . Fall asleep, most likely. Daren't sleep. Haven't slept for ages . . . Drop off here and you're dead . . . Got to get up . . . S'all in the diary . . . (*rousing himself*) Wanted to make the summit for my birthday . . . April 21st . . . Long past now. Time's run out . . . (*Tries to write then haltingly reads what he has written*) 'May 28th, 1934. Can't reach camp four. Ice chimney impossible' . . . Should've kept

WILSON: the crampons ... (*Putting away the diary he searches the rucksac*) Crampons. Found a set lower down. Threw them away. Thought I could walk straight up and plant the Union Jack on top. Silly bugger, aren't I? ... (*he turns, holding a camera and a furled flag*) Say 'cheese' ... Need a camera, see, for proof. Delayed exposure. Set the switch. Stand up front. And how's your father ... Immortality! (*Letting the Union Jack unfurl, he strikes a pose of triumph*) Shall I take your picture Corbie? For old time's sake ... (*he looks at the flag, throws it down*) Flaming flags! Nobody's wrapping me in a flag! ... Once took Sarah's picture ... You won't know Sarah ... She was hiding from me, weren't you Sarah? I'll teach you to hide from me ... (*Still kneeling, trying to focus the camera*) Stand still. No, not like that. You were leaning against a tree – no, against the balustrade, with the trees behind you – your hair was blowing in the wind, that's it, and your hand touched your hair – you touch your hair with your hand – and I'm saying – I'm saying: 'Why?' Aren't I? And you say: 'Because I don't love you.' No, no, you say: 'I do love you, but not like that.' As if it were something dirty. And every night I could hear you, you and him, through the wall – Sarah, I could hear you, yelping and moaning, through the wall, with him on you, and you, doing it with him night after night, until I had to move the bed over by the window, so I couldn't hear ... That's why I moved the bed by the window ... And you, all clean and pressed the next morning, with your seams all perfect and your lipstick on the cups and your dainty little yawns behind your dainty little hands, and saying 'Mmmm, it's Saturday – what about a day at the races?' (*Imitating a woman's voice*) Tea, Private Corbett? ... (*And in his own voice*) Cheeky blighter: You always said you could stand a spoon up in my tea ... Perhaps it's as well. Wouldn't mash. Takes an hour just to melt the snow ... Nothing else, I'm afraid. Figs. Biscuits. Chocolate. Fasting, see. Faith, fasting and figs. The whole world knows: 'Solo attempt on Everest ... War hero, Maurice Wilson, a Yorkshireman with eyes like fire, blah, blah, blah ...' They must think I'm dead by now ... I won't go back down ... There's no way back down. Not at night. In the dark with the light out! Please, mam, don't let him turn out the light ... Funny that. When I think of my father, I see myself ... My mother's the only woman I ever loved. No one else. Not real love – love you'd die for. And no one else loved me. Not like that ... Like that, Sarah? Like when you came to me, Sarah – came to my room – then you made me, Sarah – made me do it with you – because you were sorry for me ... Weren't you, Sarah? Sorry for me? Say you were sorry. Say it. Go on. Say you're sorry! ... (*to himself*) I can hear them talking – through the wall. I can hear him – persuading her. As if I'm an animal. And what did he hear? It's like plywood, that wall. He must have heard everything ... Sarah, he's listening. He's got his ear to the wall. Oh God, he must be listening! ... And you

WILSON: begging for it. Like the rest. What makes you so special? I've had dozens of women. Classy women, hanging on for dear life while I take 'em over Beecher's Brook ... (*taking out a ring of keys, jingling them*) House keys, car keys, flats, brothels, hotels – they always give me their keys ... I've kept all their keys ... Next morning, when you stayed upstairs, he came down, for breakfast – and I was in the kitchen. I got up to face him and he cried – and when he came home from work, he brought some beer: we played cards: you danced – you and him – and then he said: 'Do you mind old chap?' And you went to bed – both of you – you with your head lowered, not looking at me ... 'Do you mind old chap?' ... He left me some cigarettes on the table ... That night I coughed blood – downstairs in the dark ... I'm not scared of the dark. Not any more. Not up here. In the dark, there's just that plume of snow streaming from the summit. And down below, nothing – no ice, no rock, no world – only my life, stretching through some kind of funnel, with mirrors for walls, where I can see everything I've ever done, every place I've ever been – and I'm climbing up, out of the funnel, as if I were climbing out of someone's eye, my mother's eye – and my dear, sweet, warm mother is killing me, with her cold wind and her glass cliffs ... Perhaps at dawn – perhaps I could go back down at dawn, when I can see the way. At night, I can only hold on, curled across the funnel, and rock myself, and rock, and rock until morning ... when all the screaming of the night has died and the smiling mountain whispers to me, in all her beauty: 'Try again' – and I crawl out of my tent and look at her, whom I adore, and say 'Yes', or 'Yes alright, we'll try again' ... 'We can always try again' ... Remember that, Sarah? (*he tries to pull himself upright, rolls over, coughing, clutching his chest*) Coughing better anyway ... (*getting back to his knees*) No blood, Sarah! Told you I was cured. Didn't I? (*Swinging round, as if to Corbie.*) She didn't believe me, Corbie. Said I'd been to a clinic ... (*Back again to Sarah.*) How many more times? It was a faith healer! ... (*Shouting.*) Who cares what you think? I fasted. And I prayed. And I was cured ... Go on, laugh! ... (*Now he sings again at the top of his voice.*) 'When I survey the wondrous cross, on which the prince of glory died, my richest gain I count but loss, and pour contempt on all my pride ...' Look at her Corbie! I can see through her nightdress ... Go away! I don't want to – I don't want to touch you – I don't want you – I don't want you anymore, I can't bear to want you, yes, you, you, you, you ... I was so ill, Corbie. Losing weight. Coughing. And nearly out of my mind – with her – and him ... He's the best friend I ever had ... They were killing me. I left a note: 'If you don't see me again, you'll know I'm dead'. Like something out of a book ... I'd heard of a faith healer – in Mayfair. People said he could work miracles. All I had to do was to fast – for thirty five days – taking only water, little drinks of water. Then,

WILSON: when I was purged, and close to death, I was to pray to God, that I might be born again, 'of water and of the Spirit'. And God heard me: God heard my prayer, and I was cured . . . It's alright, Corbie. Everyone smiles. But it happened, the summer before last. And in the war, too, the doctors said I couldn't survive and I spent ten days at death's door . . . I lived Corbie! I lived! And when that happens, you start wondering why. You start to get ideas. About being chosen. And you wonder what you've been chosen to do. And once you've found it, there's no stopping you . . . It was like a vision . . . I'm in a little cafe, in the Black Forest, in Germany – after my fast – and there's an old newspaper cutting – about Everest – Mallory and Irvine disappearing into a cloud, a few hundred feet from the top . . . Straight away, I know: I'm going to climb Mount Everest. Not with hundreds of porters and ponies: not with guides, and yaks, and a three mile baggage train. I'm going to do it alone. Just me, God and the mountain. Conquering Everest by faith . . . I want to tell the world how God cured me. And who will listen? Unless I do something extraordinary, something quite impossible without God's help. And if God can help me climb Mount Everest, what might he do for other people – if they have faith . . . Corbie, I felt I could save the world. I was so sure, so strong – as if nothing could stop me . . . Sarah burst into tears when I told her. 'Who do you think you are? You can't test God!' I'm not testing God. I'm testing myself. 'But you can't climb.' I can learn. 'With one arm?' Yes – tied behind my back. 'All right, all right.' – that's David, tapping out his pipe. It's two in the morning, we're all a bit drunk celebrating my cure . . . 'All right, how are you planning to get there?' Parachute . . . No, really. I'll need a short cut to beat the next pukka expedition. Some beastly aristocrat is flying over the summit soon, taking pictures. If I hitched a lift, I could float down the lower slopes, then walk back up. 'Float? From thirty thousand feet?' Mmmm . . . In that case, I'll do a crash land. 'In someone else's aeroplane?' I'll buy my own. 'You can't fly'. I can learn . . . (*Struggling to his feet, preparing for another attempt of the ice chimney.*) Oh Sarah, I'm tired of seeing people starved and twisted by our stupid, empty lives. I want to show them what they can do – to break out – all of them – if only they believe – if only they believe in themselves. Is that so absurd? 'No, darling – it's wonderful, truly wonderful. We'll help you, won't we, David? I know you can do it. I just know.' And she kisses me. And we hold each other, the three of us. And I can feel the strength flowing out of me – as if I have been touched by the Holy Spirit and I have only to touch them, in turn, and they will be reborn, made new, shorn of all their fears and miseries, set free to walk upon the world like the children of God . . . Are you listening up there? (*Entering the chimney.*) I've done my bit . . . Learned to fly. Made the 5,000 miles to India in an open cockpit in less than a fortnight. And all the way they were

WILSON: trying to stop me, the monocle-men, the desk men. But I beat them – I did it, despite them, when nobody believed I could, because I was a lousy flier, because I couldn't even take off properly, because I took off with the wind behind me and nearly crashed . . . And the pukka expedition – Ruttledge's expedition, – the weather stopped them and they turned back and Everest was still safe, waiting for me . . . I found three sherpas and legged it three hundred miles across the roof of the world in ten days. Tell me, who else has done that? I must have been the fittest man alive. Dammit, I lived through an earthquake in Darjeeling. God – you're not going to stop me now, when I've come half way round the earth – and there's only a mile to go? Holy Moses, I'm not asking for a miracle. I just need a good shove. God, help me. Quit whining. I can't do it on my own. You're not meant to. You never meant to. I did, I do. I want to – I want to – I want to reach out, God – I'm reaching out to you – touch me, take my hands, draw me up, let me come to you, dear God, dear mother of God, release me, save me, hold me, hold me, hold me . . .

(*Wilson almost falls, then pushes himself back into sitting position.*)

WILSON: (*Continued*) 'Maurice, come down out of that chimney.' Aw, mam, it's fun. 'I don't care: it's dirty.' Mam, is all fun dirty? Mam, don't you like having fun? Mam, why does your bum go numb when you shit in a snowstorm? . . . Sorry, mam – but you'd never believe the fun it's been, coming up here. At least I'm getting a kick out of life. At least I've done something unique – well nearly. And I've done it myself . . . What else was there? Swan dive off the Eiffel Tower? Old hat . . . Typically English, what – climbing Mount Everest to prove you exist? And typically English, that every pukka bloody Englishman should try to stop me – stop Tommy Atkins getting big ideas – stop him now, before it's too late, before he cracks open your bank vaults and dismantles your guns and puts the poor in your palaces and the rich men from their gates . . . England all over! There's no hope in England! . . . Telegram, Just as I was taking off? (*Blimpish voice.*) 'Everest flight forbidden. Repeat forbidden. Yours faithfully, the Air Ministry' . . . Oh yes, the lords and ladies can fly over Everest, taking pictures. And the lah-di-dahs like Ruttledge can climb it, with their anchovy paste and their King George chocolates. But Tommy Atkins, from Bradford, with his fingers like putty lumps, who never drinks with the chaps at the aerodrome and tries to handle his Gypsy Moth in hobnailed boots? Can't have him following in the footsteps of Mallory and Irvine . . . 'Right,' I said, 'That's it.' Remember, Sarah? To all those news-paperman. 'Let's see if they can stop me,' I said. 'Who?' they said. 'The Imperial Civil Service,' I said. Always one step ahead of me, so I couldn't refuel – blocking my permits, having me arrested. Yes! At Bizerta. Three armed men, in a car, belting over the runway as I taxied in. Got me down in the back seat, with a gun up my

WILSON: nose. 'Vamoose! Savvy?' I vamoosed. To Tunis. 'Anglais?'. Oui. 'Gasolene?' Oui. 'Please helpa yourself' — and he's pointing to some rusty old drums. Ah, mille fois merci . . .
Crossing into Libya, over the desert, the plane starts shaking itself to bits. Just reach the next airfield when the engine splutters out. Water in the petrol . . . Then Cairo. Yes, I'm in Cairo. Need a permit to fly across Persia. 'Dreadfully sorry, old boy,' – The British Consul's under secretary's deputy assistant stamp-licker – 'Still nothing doing.' So I make it to the Persian border, Baghdad to Bahrain. Like flying through a blast furnace. 'Sorry, no fuel.' Why? 'Consul's orders.' Look, what the hell's happening? Don't shout at me, young man.' Real top-drawer now: Consul's batman – white suit, sweaty armpits, needed a shave . . . 'Am I supposed to stay in Bahrain for ever?' 'Not at all. Go home whenever you like.' I'm going to Mount Everest. 'Quite – but not across Persia – without a permit.' I've applied five times for a permit. 'The mills of God, young man.' Forget it. I'll fly round Persia. 'Charming idea. Unless you turn back, there is no landing strip within range – except in Persia . . . Checkmate, I believe . . . Of course, you could always ask the Persians themselves for a permit . . . Cup of tea?' Cup of tea! He knew darned well the Persians would pinch my plane and stick me in gaol the second I touched down. Never trust the buggers, see – specially when they bring out the tea! 'Right, monkey,' I thought, 'Two can play your little game.' I told him I'd try Teheran, but while he was signing the fuel chit, I took a peek at his wall-map and jotted a few figures down on my shirt cuff. There was a new airstrip at Gwadar, over the Gulf, over the Indian Ocean. I bribed the mechanics to give me a spare drum of fuel and took off, heading north, for Persia – then swung back towards Everest, right over old white suit's head as he stood there, shaking his fist up at me . . . With the extra fuel, I could just make it I reckoned, steering almost due East, course 095 degrees. Only I hadn't any maps. Nine hours. Hardly a landmark. Fraction off line and I was dead . . . Zzzzzzzz . . . zzzzzzz . . .

(Wilson makes the sound of an aeroplane engine, miming his own flight.)

WILSON: (*Continued*) Zzzzzzzz . . . Face like mahogany – yet it seams and cracks in the heat . . . Zzzzz . . . Few boats below – stock still, sea of glass . . . Coastline? Mirages . . . Zzzzzz . . . Cramp! Aaahg! Every time I stretch, I press the rudder, start to veer . . . Zzzzz Sleep. (*His eyes close.*) Sleepy. Mustn't sleep . . . (*He jerks awake, mimes pulling back on the joystick, making the 'plane' climb.*) Christ – nearly in the drink! . . . Zzzzzz . . . Not gonna make it – gonna die . . . Land! Oh thank God, thank God. I've done it! . . . Zzzzzzz (*The engine noise trails away.*) Sure I did it – on the last few drops of petrol, ten minutes before dark . . . Nobody ever flew like I did that day – nobody ever will again. Perfection! Wilson

WILSON: conquers the British Empire! I thought they'd never stop me . . . But they did. Passes, permits! 'Sorry – no can do'. 'Sorry – the Maharajah says 'Piss off''. Week after week. Till the monsoons come. Till I have to sell the plane to see me through to the next climbing season . . . Got my own back in the papers. *Daily Express. Daily Mail.* Loved it – all the fuss and palaver – 'cos it was sending the monocle-men barmy . . . Maybe they were trying to stop me killing myself. All I know is there were police following me everywhere. Up into the Himalayas. Onto Darjeeling. If ever I left town, they were behind me – and raiding my room while I was gone. Cat and mouse stuff. Sooner or later I'd make a run for it, they reckoned that – but I foxed them all with a disguise . . . Picture me, Sarah. Fur-lined cap, with huge ear flaps, and dark glasses, to hide my eyes. Brocaded waistcoat, gold, with brass buttons. Cotton trousers. Vast woollen mantle, down over my boots, hidden pockets sewn into the folds. And the whole lot held up by a twelve-foot sash, in red silk, plumb round my middle . . . Get it? Your actual Tibetan holy man! . . . We slipped out of Darjeeling by night: Rinzi and Tsering up ahead, with most of the gear, stowed in wheatsacks: Tewang and me, an hour behind – me on the donkey, under a rice-paper umbrella, tinkling my bells, and Tewang playing my servant, telling everyone I was deaf and dumb and too dotty to give a blessing, my Tibetan being so wonky and all . . . First sign of a policeman and oops, into the ditch. Then I got cocky, rode straight past 'em twirling my umbrella, tinkling my bells, crooning away to myself – till we were stopped, head-on by a patrol, carrying my photgraph . . . 'English. Blue eyes, Big nose. So tall . . .' (*Wilson demonstrates.*) There's Tewang, face like an angel, passing me the photo, and me tinkling and twirling and shaking my head and honking through my beard and nearly wetting myself trying not to laugh . . . Laugh? I could had died! (*Bursting with laughter, Wilson slides back down the gully – and realises he is alone.*) Sarah? Corbie? Don't leave me! God, don't leave me alone! I can't stand anymore. What are you doing to me? What else do you want?

(*Now he rushes over to the edge of the tent yelling – his voice echoing.*)

WILSON: Rinzi! Rinzi! (*He turns back, with a long wail.*) Rinzi . . .

(*Wilson cries, hugging himself, against the cold, the fear, the loneliness.*)

WILSON: God – my sherpas . . . they're only a few hundred feet away – at Camp Three . . . Won't you let them hear me? . . . If the wind stopped, they could hear me, they'd come to me – I wouldn't be alone . . . It's the wind: Listen to it. I can't get back down in this wind. I'd die before I reached them. And they're only just below me . . . I left them at Camp Three. I cut my own steps from there to the crevasse – and at the crevasse I found the snow bridge . . . Would it hold? . . . and it held, and I walked across and climbed the

WILSON: slope to the great ice cliff and discovered the chimney – the only way up the cliff, the chimney of ice – and I couldn't climb it – for days I've been trying to climb it . . . God, if I can't climb the chimney, why did the snow bridge hold? Why didn't I fall into the crevasse, down the blue walls, pale blue, deep blue, indigo – bottomless indigo . . . ?

(Wilson catches at a blue ribbon fastened to his wrist.)

WILSON: Sarah's ribbon. She tied it to the wing of my plane before I took off . . . For luck . . . It wasn't just luck, God, was it? You brought me to this place, in sight of that plume of snow: you kept me safe in the valley of the shadow of death, you were always by my side . . . Weren't you? . . . Like in France at Meteren. When I was scything down the Boche. You were there – anointing my head with oil . . . Were you blazes! Corbie was, though. Corbie was there – lying down in the green pastures. And the Boche. They were there: all the way down the hill, to the stream to the still waters, which were clogged with blood, the blood of the slaughtered lambs and the salt tears of women who mourned, crying: 'The Lord is my shepherd, I shall not want . . .' And where were you, Lord? . . . Were you really at Darjeeling, when I lived through the earthquake – when the mountains trembled and their sinews cracked, and the poor quarter was buried in a landslide? Were you there when I was digging in the rubble with my bare hands, and all the relatives of the lost ones were digging beside me, in their rags and tatters, and finding only the dead in their broken houses and their gaping street . . . These people – the wretched of the earth: They are my people . . . Where were the monocle–men and the so-and-so's and the don'tcher-knows when we were digging in the ruins at Darjeeling? If I had a child . . . All right, God: Where were you when I tried to get a child? . . . (*Chanting.*) 'Who shall ascend into the hill of the Lord or stand in his holy place? He that hath clean hands and a pure heart; who hath not lifted up his soul unto vanity . . .' Guess what, God: It's muck or nettles now. You'll have to take me as I am.

(*Wilson picks up his ice axe and scratches his initials in the snow.*)

WILSON: . . . M . . . W . . . Maurice Wilson! Oh yes, I'm still Maurice Wilson. Who was I kidding? Fasting's like winter: you grow again – from the same root. You can't spew out your whole past life and have done with it. Unless you're a Catholic . . . Or a brimstone Wesleyan . . . See that line, sinners: That chalk line on the floor of God's house – step over that line, sinners, and be saved! Hallelujah, brother! Amen, sister! Oh, be warned, the rest of you sinners. It's hellfire and damnation, till the end of time, unless you cross that line, that chalk line. Which side are you on, sinners? Are you on the Lord's side? For the end of the world is nigh. And woe betide him who has clung to the rags of this life when he might have been clad in the wings of angels . . . (*Singing.*) 'Give me the old style religion . . .' When I was a kid, I used to pray till my legs were

WILSON: numb from the kneeling. I knew I'd done wrong, but I didn't know how – or how to find forgiveness – except to sit in the family pew, every Sunday, with my body buttoned up tight so the preacher couldn't spy any sins of the flesh . . . Mam, did you ever see dad undressed? No, you just did your duty in the dark. And did you ever dance, did you ever sing, did anyone ever laugh out loud in my father's house, did we ever open the curtains on our hearts . . .? (*Mimicking.*) 'Now then, our Maurice, don't forget to wear your vest if you're going up Mount Everest' . . . Look, God's come all over the Himalayas – and is he blind? Doesn't he still see every sparrow that falls? Well, I'm fallen, Lord. But I crossed the chalk line. I'm on your side, Lord. I'm here. You know I'm here. Right under your nose. So will you stop trying to blow me off this bloody mountain? (*Suddenly Wilson turns, arms thrown wide in greeting.*)

WILSON: Rinzi . . . Am I glad to see you! No – no more salaams . . . Will you give up bowing you daft beggar! . . . S'driving me barmy – on my own. Keep thinking there's someone else with me . . . I know it's the air . . . Yes, I know I need oxygen. Plenty, plenty liquids . . . Yes – and the heat loss. For Christ's sake, you're like an old hen. And you look like one, in that sweater. Notice you never gave it me back. S'big enough for the both of us. Keep us both warm . . . No – I was joking . . . Put it back on, idiot . . . Anyway, I like hens. Used to hypnotize them, when I was a kid . . . Hypnotize! . . . (*He puts the fluence on 'Rinzi'.*) Savvy? . . . Daft creatures, hens. Eggs apart . . . I'd love an egg . . . Brought any chocolate? . . . He hasn't! What, the whole lot? (*Yelling, through cupped hands.*) Tewang – greedy pig! I hope you're sick! Look, for the last time, I'm not coming down . . . Try it! You'll have to kill me first . . . If the weather clears, we can do it in three days, there and back. Trust me. You were with Ruttledge, you've done 27,000 feet, you're the best climber in Nepal . . . From now on, you lead, I'll follow. Scout's honour. Just help me up the ice chimney, then it's a doddle to the North Col, and a kid could cross the North Col, it's only like a long white saddle – then we're almost home . . . I know about the last two thousand feet! Let's get there first . . . I know I'm tired. Who wouldn't be? I've been up and down this flaming mountain for six weeks on and off . . . All I'm asking is three days . . . Jesus, if I'd just had three straight days! Sun one morning, blizzards the next – and the next – and the next – freezing the spirit out of you, till you want to lie down and die, like a dog . . . a whipped dog – that's how I feel – like a cur, at somebody's heel – God's heel – and every time I move, there's another whipping . . . Heel, dog, heel! Down on your belly, where you belong. Stop whining! I'll teach you who's master. You stay till I call, or I'll flog the hide off you . . . Rinzi, what if he never calls? Does he have to break me first? Do I have to die before he calls? . . . God's training me, Rinzi, breaking my spirit, testing my faith. I know what he's doing, the bastard! I hate

WILSON: him! (*Yelling.*) Do you want me to give in? . . . I'm damned if I'll give in – to the feller with the whip . . . But you'll have to help me, Rinzi. I can't do it on my own. Rinzi – I need you. Savvy? I need you . . . No wonder I hear voices . . . Hold me, Rinzi! Hold me! . . .

(*He reaches out, moves forward a step then drops his arms.*)

WILSON: Talk to me, then. Be with me. That's all. Just talk. Like we used to . . . Anything. Tell me anything. Only keep me awake – in case he calls. I want to be ready when he calls, when the wind stops whipping.

(*Feeling ahead of himself, finds the sack, fishes out his diary, searches for the right page, begins to read, tracing the words with a finger.*)

WILSON: What's wrong, God? Haven't you whipped me enough? On the first climb? (*Reading*) April 17th. Hell of a day. Floundering about on the glacier. Kept feeling sick . . . April 18th. Doubt if I'll be on top for my birthday . . . April 19th. . . . April 20th. More snow. April 21st. Wished myself many happy returns . . . (*Singing.*) Thirty six today, thirty six today, I've got the key of the door . . . (*Back to the diary.*) Still 8,500 feet to go . . . April 22nd. Eyes terrible. Throat sore. Getting scared . . . April 23rd. Going back. Weather's beaten me. Damned bad luck . . . (*He hurls the diary away.*) Bad luck, my arse! . . . (*A courtroom voice.*) Sherpa Rinzing, I believe you were present at the unveiling of Mr. Wilson's withers, after he had descended Mount Everest. Now, will you tell the almighty their condition. Were they not a thing of shreds and patches, barely resembling the human buttock at all? . . . Take courage, Rinzing, the Christian deity may or may not have an arse, nonetheless he devised one for his creatures, regardless of creed, class or colour, and can thus be expected to recognise a backside from a bucket any day of the week, even a backside as bruised and disfigured as Mr. Wilson's, when he slid down Mount Everest upon it, at a speed of two hundred and fifty feet per hour, for thirty hours, totalling some seven thousand feet – the fastest descent in the history of Himalayan mountaineering, and proof positive of the stoic proposition, wherever you turn, your arse is always behind you . . . Rinzi, I didn't climb down this mountain – I slid down it, rolled down it, head over heels, down, down to the monastery, half blind, half dead, but half alive, and elated to be alive, and babbling like a lunatic. Almost two days I slept. And nearly a month to recover my strength – fasting, training, walking twenty miles a day. And all the while, planning to come back, to try again . . . 'O thou of little faith, wherefore didst thou doubt?' . . . Dear God, I never doubted! Not for a second. Hour after hour I sat, gazing up at the mountain, through the clouds – checking the maps, rehearsing the route. And I was more sure than ever. As if I had survived an initiation, and was fit, at last, to find the Holy Grail . . . Once I'd left the sherpas, I climbed and climbed, till my chest was bursting, heading for the ice

WILSON: cliff, praying to reach it by nightfall, and reaching it, and camping here at 23,000 feet, finding the ice chimney, my Sea of Galilee . . . And next morning, I tried to walk upon the water, and tried again, and again, day after day and each time I sank, I tried again, and sank again, and again and again . . . until today . . . four hours I've spent in the ice chimney today – cutting hand holds, foot holds, trying to drag myself up the sheet ice then jamming myself across the gap and edging upwards, with my shoulders and knees until at last I reached the overhang – about half way up – maybe thirty feet – where the chimney bends, like an elbow – and at last stretched around the overhang, but lost my grip, clutching at the ice, crying on the Lord to save me – and falling again, thinking I had failed – failed my God . . . Oh God, who failed? How could it be me? I taught myself to fly. If I'd taught myself to climb, I could clear this chimney in an hour. But I never learned. Could Saint Peter swim? See how I trusted you. That was my faith. That's why I threw away the crampons! Because I wouldn't need them – I wouldn't need ropes and hammers and pitons and porters and ponies, because if I had faith, you would show me the way, God – you would be my guide . . . But you didn't, God – did you? Don't you ever want me to climb this mountain . . .? 'And Peter said: "Lord bid me to come to thee upon the water." And Jesus said: "Come"' But you won't let me come will you God? – You're trapping me in the ice chimney so I can't come – so I can never come. I curse you God, for betraying me – for betraying your waiting world . . . I swear to fight God . . . (*He falls to his knees.*) To the death, God! . . . I swear it. Whip away master! Whip away! And for all your whipping, I'll never come to heel. (*Laughing.*) You're no gentleman, God. Me neither. I'll climb this chimney, no sweat – and the next chimney – and all the chimneys, and all the cliffs, till the last cone of rock, and I'll wait there, till the wind drives forth that plume of snow, yes, God, till your white robe trails upon the roof peak of the world, and as it trails I'll catch it and tear it, tear it apart, your white robe, and behold the God who hath denied me – yes, God, I shall see you, and if you have hands, helping hands, I shall bite them, and if you have eyes, I shall spit in them . . . (*He spits on the ground.*) God, I spit in your eye! . . .

(*Once more, Wilson realizes he is alone.*)

WILSON (*continued*): Rinzi! Rinzi! . . . For Christ's sake, Rinzi . . . No-o-o-o you can't leave me, I'm too weak. Coward, thief! murderer! . . . I hope the snow bridge breaks! I hope you die . . . (*Turning aside.*) I don't want to die . . . Rinzi, wait for me! I'm coming with you! (*Another voice, stopping him.*) 67952 Wilson! Sah! Where do you think you're going? Back to dear old blighty – sah. Not in the dark, we're not, sunshine. Unless we're going to get ourselves killed. Are we going to get ourselves killed, 67952 Wilson? No sah. Because that's what England expects, sunshine.

WILSON: Sah! England expects us to get ourselves killed because England thinks we're a right pillock trying to climb Mount Everest on our own, dontcherknow. Yes, sah. On the other hand, England expects a chap to bring home the bacon. And dare we go home without the bacon? No sah. No, sah, we dare not – because we'd get the white feather and the cowardy custard, doncherknow. Yes, sah. So what's it to be, lad? Once more unto the breach, dear friends? Back up the ice chimney? Cannons to the left of us, cannons to the right of us, and in some corner of a foreign field, cry God for Harry, England and St. George? Yes, sah. No, sah. Three bags full, sah. Spoken like a true Englishman . . . And what's all this God-palaver anyway? Was God in the Persian Gulf, when your engine conked, and you took a dive and levelled out with your wheels on the sea and, lo and behold, chug, chug, chug, India here we come? . . . Was that God? Or did you just remember the bleeding manual – emergency re-start instructions, pilots, for the use of? . . . 67952 Wilson! Sah! Say after me: There is no God. There is no God – sah! In your own words, man – as if you meant it . . . Well, we're waiting . . . (*Quietly.*) There is no God . . . Louder! . . . There is no God . . . Louder! . . . There is no God . . . (*Suddenly yelling.*) There is no God! There never was a God. There never will be a God. I don't believe in God!

(*Wilson tears open his climbing suit, rips at his clothes, trying to bare his chest.*)

WILSON: Strike me, damn you! Where's your sword – your terrible swift sword? Kill me! Only do something – say something – show yourself! . . . Why hasn't this mountain split asunder? . . . Why should it? He's not there. How could he be there? If he was, how could he allow it – any of it – the sinning and the sorrow, the suffering . . . How could he allow the world its filthy ways? How could he? How could you? . . . Stop snivelling, Wilson: make up your bleeding mind. Shut up! If there's no God . . . Go on . . . If there's no God . . . Spit it out, man . . . If there's no God – there's no reason for anything – for doing anything – for not doing anything – 'cos anything goes – to the victor the spoils, Deutschland über alles! Who cares? Why should I care? Why should anyone care? It's the weakest to the wall and strip Jack naked. No, you don't, not this Jack – this Jack says you can stuff your world, 'cos I've had a bellyful, and I'm sick of it. I resign . . . And where will cock robin go then, poor thing? He'll hide his head under his wing, poor thing . . . I'll go back to the monastery below the mountain . . . I could be happy there . . . Everybody's happy there . . . (*Chanting.*) 'Om mani padme hum' – 'Hail, the jewel in the lotus'. It's how you say hello to the Head Lama. I got it wrong. He laughed and tapped me on the cheek with his wand . . . Everybody laughs there. Even in chapel . . . Well, temple, really. And all these little flat-roofed houses, painted inside like flowers. And the

WILSON: people, with painted souls. And the services – full of singing, coloured costumes, beating drums . . . No chalk lines . . . And no baths. They never seem to wash. 'Cos it's too cold. Anyway, why wash your body when you've a flower in your soul? . . . Everything's so gentle there, so peaceful. They believe in themselves . . . And they respect me. They know how I've tried. They know what it took – coming up here, on my own. They'll take me in, let me rest . . . I think I could be happy there . . . I'm not dying for nothing, Corbie! Chuck us a fag, love . . . (*Feels in his pockets.*) Gobstoppers! . . . (*Sure enough, he brings out a pack of sweets, sucks one, takes it out of his mouth, licks it, puts it back.*)

WILSON: Found 'em in the gear Ruttledge left. Plums too – Carlsbad plums and gorgonzola. Made me ill. Made me cry. Made me think of home, when I was a kid – climbing gaslamps, floating matchsticks in the gutter, scared of the passage to the outside lavvy, in the dark, and don't put your bum on the seat for fear o' catchin' summat – from all the other folk who shared the lavvy and never put their bums on the seat either, and anyway, there's snakes round the bend, in the lavvy pan. (*He takes out the sweet again.*) Changing colour – yellow, now, red next . . . everything's changing . . . (*Sucks the sweet again.*) Made me think of you, mam. When I get home, I'll show you the sights, take you to London. You can meet Sarah and David . . . We'll sit by the fire, till its late and I'll catch your crochet-work, so it doesn't fall in the hearth when you drop off to sleep . . . Promises, promises . . . I'm not coming home, mam . . . (*Putting the sweet back in the bag.*) Try to understand . . . Sarah, you'll understand. How could I come home? How could I live? What could I do? After all this? I'm sorry . . . I feel so ashamed. I must have been mad . . . I've failed you all . . . (*A loud cry, to everyone and everything.*) Forgive me!

(*Pause. Wilson totters, cold, despairing, sleep again creeping over him.*)

WILSON: Best get some sleep . . . Ready for tomorrow.

(*He hugs himself, shakes his head clear – then pulls down his goggles, wraps the blanket round himself and crawls into the sleeping bag.*)

WILSON: Matthew, Mark, Luke and John, bless the bed that I lie on, through the dangers of the night keep me safe to morning light, Amen. Listen to that bloody wind.

(*The lights fade. The wind rises to a howl – then fades. The lights snap on again – Bright.*)

WILSON: Sunshine. (*He raises his goggles.*) Wind's gone. (*Lifting ribbon at his wrist.*) Sarah, my luck's changed. S'now or never, our Maurice. Two o'clock. Nearly tea time. Trust me to sleep in. I'd be late for Judgement Day.

(*Wilson starts to lower his tent. Looks round at the peak of the mountain.*)

WILSON: Chomolungma! Just look at you. All white against the blue, that shape against the blue, just like you've always been. Waiting for me . . . I feel as if the world were just beginning. It's a sin to move, to make a footprint, leave a mark. I could stay here for ever, looking at you – nothing between us, not another living thing, anywhere – only you and me . . . I could die looking at you . . . If you sing, I'll scream . . . Who else has heard you sing? Not many. And the rest wouldn't believe it if I told them – told them how your whole body shivers with sound, sometimes, when the wind drops, and the sun shines – a kind of humming – like a lama, with his prayer-wheel . . . (*He hums, in the Tibetan way of prayer.*) Mmmmmmm mmmmmm mmmmmmmmm . . . Not that you'd notice, being a goddess, being so beautiful . . . Couldn't you wear snakes in your hair? . . . How can I touch you when you're so beautiful – so perfect? Show me your teeth. Stick out your tongue. Smile . . . Call that a smile? (*Yelling.*) Smile, darn you, smile!

(*Wilson's voice echoes and re-echoes round the stage. Then behind it, growing into a roar, comes the sound of an avalanche, rising, booming, receding – and Wilson turning to watch it go*).

WILSON: (*Laughing.*) That's more like it! . . . Go on, go on – let your bloody face slip . . . Yes. Ye-e-e-es! I'm over here . . . hit me! That's what you want, isn't it, you bitch? . . . (*As the noise dies.*) Oh, you bitch, I'm coming to get you now. And this time I'm coming all the way – hear that? All the fucking way.

(*Wilson starts to take down his tent.*)

WILSON: (*Singing.*) 'I don't want to join the army, I don't want to join the war, I'd rather hang around Piccadilly Underground . . .' (*He stops, coughing at the exertion.*) Christ, if I'm Adam, pity Eve. Do my ribs ache. I ache all over. Even my cock aches. Least I can feel it now – least it's alive. Not crowing, mind . . . S'like an icicle . . . The diary! . . . (*Takes out the diary, and pencil, sits on the rucksac, lifting his goggles and writing slowly.*) 'May 29th 1934. Marvellous day! Off again!' (*Kissing the diary.*) Sarah, the diary's for you – whatever happens. Always the golden-rod, weren't you, Sarah? . . . Listen to me. (*Smiling.*) And stop yawning: anybody'd think you never got any sleep . . . I can see you – both of you – right now – having breakfast . . . Whoever heard of a dog drinking tea. Aw Putzi, Putzi, it's that nasty Uncle Maurice again . . . David's reading the paper – racing page. Put your shirt on me, David. Beats selling insurance. I feel like Lawrence of Arabia, coming up on the blind-side at Akaba. And you could have got a million to one against Lawrence of Arabia taking Akaba . . . Listen . . . (*Faint sound of birds.*) Meteren . . . Nineteen years since I first went into the Line – nineteen years . . . (*Again the bird sound.*) How can you forget? . . . All morning I'd been there. Through the gas and the artillery barrage. Now the mortars. The line had broken. Boche everywhere. Ours the only post left firing. And me the only one

WILSON: alive to fire. I was shitting myself. I was screaming. 'It's me next! Where's mine?' I knew I was going to die. And I couldn't wait. I didn't want to be left. I stood up for them. S'true so help me. I stood up for them . . .

(*Now he seems to be re-living the incident, standing, bent forward slightly, panic-stricken, head swinging, left to right, an imaginary gun swinging loosely, wildly in front of him, left to right, right to left.*)

WILSON: I'm yelling 'Hit me! Hit me! Why can't you hit me?' And the Boche are still coming, fanning across the hill, and I'm raking them, one side to the other, raking them, and they're going down just going down, dropping, like sacks, and more are coming, they're within ten yards of me, and I'm cutting them down as if I had a scythe, cutting them down, and shitting myself, and yelling, 'For fuck's sake hit me! Hit me please – hit me! Hit me . . .' And then it stopped. Everything stopped. The bullets stopped flying. I stopped firing. I stood there, leaning on the gun. We hadn't another man alive in the whole line. Only me. And me. Looking up into the sun, stock still, blind in the sun, until I smelled my hands burning on the barrel – my skin was stuck to the barrel, and I couldn't feel anything, no pain, only the smell of my hands burning, until I pulled them away and clutched them under my arms and fell back against the side of the hole, crying with the pain, and laughing, and crying – and when I blinked my eyes, from the sun, it all began to appear in front of me, a hundred, two hundred men, dead, in front of me, dead or wounded – and moaning – in front of me, and nothing moving, in the gun-pits, along the hillside, nothing moving, except a lark, high above me, directly above me, singing – I could hear it – singing – I could hear it above the moaning – I couldn't listen to the moaning – I listened to the lark – and I cried, until my legs gave way beneath me and I fainted . . . Should've had them treated – my hands. There didn't seem any point. Two yards of bandage and I'm back in the trench, volunteering like mad – every attack, every patrol. Till I caught one too: spurt across the chest. With a wound like that, I should have died, the doctors said. But I lived. Deep down I must have wanted to live . . . Maybe that's why I'm here. I want to live, even if it kills me . . . Wonder where I might have been now . . . Homes for bleeding heroes? – Bollocks! I'd've been down the mill. Like my dad. Working my ticket. End up a boss. With a gold watch for my pains. 'Well done, thou good and faithful servant' . . . Just sat there, my dad, looking at his watch, when he retired – till he dropped dead in his garden. Oh aye, we had a garden by then, didn't we dad? Only he never heard it ticking, his gold watch, 'cos the looms had made him deaf . . . 'Sithee, our Maurice.' What, dad? 'Animals we are, but we needn't live like animals.' No, dad. 'You can better yourself, lad – long as you remember where you came from.' Yes, dad. 'And where you could still end up.' Yes, dad. 'And that's in't pig trough.' Aye, dad! 'Aye, dad! Now you hear this, a right man'll better 'imself

WILSON: and be beholden to no one; but 'e'll tread no one down, either. 'cos them as tread folk down are swine all the same, just fatter swine, with bigger troughs . . .' Sorry I missed your funeral, dad. I never mourned. Never dared. I forgot you. As if I could forget you . . . It's like burying someone in a crevasse. The mountain shifts. And here you are again – not dead to me, still trying to tell me . . . You listen to me, dad. You knew I'd lied, didn't you – about my age – to get to France to do my bit? What for? To win the war, that's what for. Is it? Is it really? Well, let me tell you something, dad: We lost the war. And the monocle-men and the don'tcher-knows, they just won the peace. And when there's another war, to pay for their peace, who'll fight it for them? Fritz and me, with the bayonets in each other's bellies, we'll fight it. Will we hell! We'll say no! Will we hell. We'll walk up the hill, fanning out across the hill, watching the men in front fall over, like sleepwalkers, in the mist, thinking, 'We're next,' and whispering to ourselves, 'Please, God, when I get mine, don't let me be a eunuch . . .' Dad, I wish I'd said, 'No.' Most lads from the mill got marched straight onto the train. Me – officer material, with a crease on my pants and my mother clucking like a hen and handing me a tray of apples – I ask you! – and a Bible . . . Don't need a Bible up here . . . know it backwards. And the hymns – chapel – regular little pillar of the community . . . Not half! I was a snot-nosed kid from the slums of Bradford, whose father was working up from a weaver to a mill manager, and passing on his long johns to them as weren't so jammy . . . Blimey, dad, don't cry! We'll show 'em . . . And I did. Didn't I dad? I showed 'em. I can prove it. I've got a medal . . .

(*Wilson opens his suit at the collar, pulls out a medal, rips it from its chain.*)

WILSON: Captain Maurice Wilson, M.C. . . . Arise, Sir Maurice, go forth, now, and seek the Holy Grail . . .

(*Wilson dashes to the edge of the tent and hurls the medal out into the snow.*)

WILSON: (*Yelling.*) You keep it! Bitch! For all the men you've killed. You'll get nothing else out of me. I'm setting up house here. I'll build a mill. Well, what else would a silly bugger from Bradford build? . . . (*Coming back to centre-stage.*) I'll set traps for the Abominable Snowman and weave his hair into coats for the hermits. Must be cold in those caves. All they wear is their beards . . . It's alright, dad. I know you're not there. Never mind. It's the air. And I'm so tired. I think I got it wrong about the food – the energy loss – it's not like lying on a bed of nails . . . Would you like the next dance, Sarah?

(*Wilson hums a waltz tune and starts to dance, slowly, round the stage, as if he had a woman in his arms – then stops.*)

WILSON: Yes, it is cold, isn't it? Shall I bring your shawl? Funny how your throat always swells in the cold . . . No. Best stay at home, Sarah.

Paint your toenails . . . I'll settle for you, Corbie, Love . . . Chuck us a fag . . . You tight sod! No skylarks on Everest! Choughs though – a colony of choughs near Camp Three. Like little black aeroplanes. Crow family, I reckon – red legs, yellow bills, nest in the crevices, fly higher than any other bird . . . Story is, they follow mountaineers – always a few hundred feet behind, where you can't hear them, clacking, like jackdaws . . . They're following me – waiting – to mob me. Come on you little black bastards! Half a chance and they'll have my eyes . . . Funny – one of the hermits blessed me, promised to pray for me – if I didn't harm any birds at Chamalung . . . Never said anything about them harming me . . . Chamalung – sanctuary of the birds . . . It's a sacred valley. Oh, about 16,000 feet – out beyond the monastery. Monks really, not hermits – nuns, as well, in a little nunnery, right under the mountain . . . Rum business. They believe in reincarnation, so they sit in their cells, year in, year out, meditating – storing up merit, in the eyes of God – by suffering – so that, when they die, they won't be reborn, in any shape or form, if they've suffered enough, their souls will be released into nothingness, free of the torture wheel, gathered into the sleep, of eternity . . . That hermit's been shut in the dark, in a rock-hole, for nineteen years . . . Ever since I went to war . . . Each day, another monk brings him a cup of water and some barley meal. I saw his hand sneak out for the food. Even the hand was muffled, to stop the light touching the skin . . . Touching . . . It's not easy – when your fingers are ribbed and the skin's shrivelled . . . Know what I mean? When you touch something soft, something smooth and round . . . Someone else's skin, I mean – and it should feel like silk . . . Does it feel like silk? . . . With my fingers – my fingertips – I can't really feel anyone else at all . . . How long did you lie there, under me, Sarah? Before you crawled out and went back to him – your husband – behind the wall – the poor man, damn him, the poor, poor man, who couldn't give you a child . . . Or was it you, Sarah? Were you barren for him? . . . No, he blamed himself. And he sent you to me. Because you wanted a child. Both of you. And we were so close, in that house. We might have been brothers – and you, our sister. Except he knew I wanted you. He knew it was driving me mad – in that house, with you, both of you. And he knew that I'd never – that I'd never been . . . And you came to me, in the dark, in your white nightdress, standing by my bed and saying; 'It's alright – David says – it's alright' – only it was wrong – we knew it was wrong – coming to me like that – and me, letting you . . . Wasn't it? Is that why I couldn't? . . . Why couldn't I? Sarah, there's something sick – inside me. I'm not normal . . . Bitch! You make me sick! Making a man feel dirty, making me an animal, to start a child in you, like an animal. That's all you wanted. That's all you ever wanted. That's why you carry that wretched dog around in your arms. Putzi! Aw Putzi, Putzi,

WILSON: who's mamma's little baby then? . . . (*Crying out.*) No! It was for me, too, wasn't it? You gave yourself to me. And I couldn't, I couldn't give myself . . . If only I could have loved you, Sarah. Could I ever love you, Sarah? Could I love anyone? . . . She laid there, Corbie, turning and turning . . . You laid there – didn't you, Sarah? – your hair twisted, your face stained with tears, the sheets twisted round us. And me, twisted round myself, the great knot of myself, my back to you . . . to her, Corbie . . . Sarah! My back to you, Sarah, and you trying to tease the knot free – do you remember? – with your hands, your teasing hands – and your lips, your tongue, your hot breath – trying to loose the seed, melt the seed, frozen within me . . . Until you wept, and said 'Forget me, forget my body – me, in my body,' you said 'Take me', you said, 'Use me, soil me, destroy me, don't be afraid, you won't kill me, I won't die, I won't be cross, I'll still be your lover, your woman, your mother,' you said – until I hit you, I hit you until you cried, until you cringed from my hands, until I took you, until I forced you, until I plunged into you, again and again, until you screamed, and screamed that I was killing you, oh and I would have killed you, if it had meant I could only – could only – could only, if I could only have —

(*With a cry, Wilson suddenly rushes towards the edge of the stage and sets himself, as in a machine-gun pit – feet apart, knees bent, body tensed, trunk leaning slightly backwards, hands at the trigger of the imaginary gun, which springs, as it were, from his stomach. His voice suggests the murderous rattle of machine-gun fire; his hands swivel the 'gun' around upon the audience, raking the audience, along and back, along and back.*)

WILSON: Egegchegegchegegch . . . egegchegegch . . .

(*The noise grows louder, the raking fiercer, the eyes wilder, murderous – until, finally, Wilson slumps to his knees, from exhaustion, then forwards on to his elbows and over on to his back, his body twitching, the twitching becoming a spasm, shaking him, from head to toe, as he lies there. In a panic, he hammers the palm of his hand on the floor beside him, repeatedly, trying to calm himself.*)

WILSON: No! (*Hammering on the floor.*) No! It wasn't like that!

(*Still he shakes, still he hammers the ground, fighting with himself.*)

WILSON: I didn't mean it. Liar! Not the killing . . . the killing . . . I didn't want to. Liar! You loved it! I didn't. Liar! I had to. Liar! Liar! I should know. I was there. It wasn't like that . . . Was it? Oh God, if it had been now – if I'd been there now – at Meteren – and the Boche were coming – up the hill – fanning across the hill . . . Did you see me, Corbie? Just then? I wanted to kill every living thing in the world. I wanted to. I felt it. Welling up in me. Black blood. Like having lice in your mind . . . It was the war, dad . . . After the war . . . Afterwards, the war was a great scab around me, and I daren't touch it, daren't let anyone else touch it, for fear I'd start to

WILSON: bleed again, and bleed, until I was nothing – only numb clay . . . I wasn't always like that, was I? Before the war I could still cry . . . Maybe that's why I wandered so much – America, Australia – always into the sun – trying to dry out the scab around my life . . . Until I came home – until I found Sarah, and Sarah licked away the dry crust as if it had never been there, and showed me the new skin underneath, and touched my new skin, stroked it with her hair, her hands, the tips of her breasts, until my skin seemed stretched so tight that I'd split if she didn't stop touching me, as if her breasts were cutting me, as if her eyelashes were barbed wire, scouring me, until I screamed, and would have died, with the hurt of loving her, if I had not found God – yes, God – if I had not wrapped myself in God, swathed myself in God, layer after layer of God and God and God, giving God your voice, the voice of my own father, crying: 'Who is this King of Glory? The Lord of Hosts, he is the King of Glory' . . . And all the rest is madness. Madness, Sarah! I went mad with God. (*Finger to his lips.*) Shhh! Don't be frightened. Listen. I know you can hear me. Perhaps you can see me. I can see you. Both of you. In the kitchen. With the lace curtains and the paper doyleys, and the flamingo over the fireplace . . . Now, think of me, as I am thinking of you. Feel me – feel the power in me . . . People so close can reach each other from the corners of the universe. I believe that now. I've learned so many things up here. I want you to know – just in case – how happy I feel, how calm – like St. Paul, writing to the Ephesians . . . Dearly beloved, I have tasted the grapes of wrath and found them sweet. Who should I fight, except myself? Who could hurt me anymore – except myself? The war is over. I am forgiven. I have forgiven myself. I have lifted the stone from my heart and found nothing beneath – no trails of ooze and slime – only my heart, my own poor heart, aching with the weight of things done, which cannot be undone, or even understood, until you finally look into yourself, without fear, and see your own face, through your tears, and do not turn aside, as if your face were evil, but look gently at it, as you might look at another man's face, who had suffered like you, and say to yourself, as you would say to him: it is enough – say: don't be afraid – you, who have always been afraid, afraid of being alive, you, who have cowered from happiness for fear of grief – and the voice I hear is my own voice, the voice of my true self, the voice of tenderness, welling up from the real Godhead in me, from the root, the source that links my life to all living things, now and forever, saying; I have found what I came for, I have found myself . . . Saying look at me, look at me thoroughly, and, for all you have seen, am I not still a man? . . . Find the Godhead in yourself, Sarah. And you, David. Find the Godhead in each other . . . Gently now. Whisper it. You don't even need the words. Listen to yourselves, speaking to yourselves . . . What do you hear? Can you hear that I love you – both of you –

WILSON: whatever happens? And I know you love me. I know I am loved . . . Why is it so hard to let yourself be loved, really loved? Why is it so hard to be happy? . . .

(*Starts to get ready to climb the ice chimney.*)

WILSON: I'm going to try the ice chimney again today. If I can't climb it, I shall die trying. That's how I want it, I still have a choice. Right now, I could face the world again. Or I could sit in the snow and freeze to death with one arm pointing upwards like a signpost: 'This way to the top.' Except the Abominable Snowman might find me and put me on his shelf, like a Toby Jug . . . Not yet, though. Because there's still a chance . . . I can see the sky, the blue sky at the top of the chimney – by the last rock pyramid, near the summit. Once I'm round this bulge and out under the sky, I've got some hope again. I'm not beaten, I shan't give in . . . And if I die here, It seems right somehow. Neither up nor down. Never could make up my blinking mind. Die? That's what they all thought – back home. The Englishman's *hara-kiri*: guaranteed stiff upper lip. Sod 'em! I've never felt more alive. No more bleeding hearts and crowns of thorns. I'd rather have Jesus kicking the moneylenders out of the temple. And no more destiny. I've spent fifteen years hunting my destiny, looking for some meaning. Sorry I let you down, dad! My brothers did you proud though – good jobs, nice families. Pulling 'emselves up by their bootstraps, eh? Hard work never hurt anyone, eh? Work for what, dad? Sound a bit Bolshy, do I? Christ, I wish I'd not been an officer. Bootstraps again, see? Still, why bellyache? Wrong, dad! They were using you – like they used me. They're liars – all of them. Ask Corbie how they lied about the war. Was I coming home to run their factories for them – after Meteren, after Wipers? Was I hell! No more orders for me, no giving orders, no taking orders. Tommy Atkins is the bloke on the next loom, dad. He should be running the show – and you and me with him. That's why I scarpered. 'Cos the war had changed everything and England was still the same. 'Cos England stank. I wanted something different. And I looked everywhere for it. I was a farmer, dad – sheep farmer. Sold patent medicines. Built roads. (*Grinning.*) Guess where I ended up? Wellington, New Zealand. Running a ladies' dress shop . . . Sure! Invested all my savings, high quality stock. And I loved it – being around women, seeing them smile, making them feel beautiful, just being near them, never touching – not really touching – never seeing, except when they came out from behind the curtains and turned and turned before the mirrors, like little goddesses, in their skirts and blouses and their silk ballgowns, and their stockings, and the seams . . . Peeping Tom! . . . 'Don't be silly dears, we're safe with Monsieur Maurice, N'est-ce pas, Monsieur Maurice?' Er, oui, madame, oui, oui, oui. Until this little pig sold up shop and went wee, wee, wee, wee, all the way home – and loafed around London until you fell over me in

WILSON: the gutter, David – remember? In the Earls Court Road; brought me a drink; called a taxi; gave me the back bedroom; treated me like a long lost brother . . . Sarah! You're crying! No my darling. Don't blame yourself . . . Look, it was my idea, my damned theory! And I still think it's possible – for one man – even on my diet – if he could climb . . . That was the flaw. Too much faith . . . Knowing me, there had to be a flaw, hadn't there? I am the ice chimney! Stuck in myself. Poor forked Tom – no angel, no demon – just a bit of each . . . Christ a bit of each . . . Do you see now, Sarah? . . . Here endeth the epistle to the Ephesians . . . P.S. every man has his reasons . . . Does that rhyme? . . . The sky, Sarah – I've seen the sky . . . Don't look at me like that. Listen to me, dad, I was wrong, too . . . Should have stayed, should have fought 'em down the mill where I belonged. Dad, I didn't know where I belonged . . . Dad I – need somebody . . . Sarah! Please! (*Crying out.*) I'm your champion!

(*Wilson takes a scarf out of his climbing suit – a silk scarf with blue polka dots.*)

WILSON: You gave me your scarf! . . . Bit greasy. 'Fraid I used it to wipe the butter knife . . . (*Reading a message on the scarf.*) 'Always together. Sarah.' I'll wear it today. (*He fastens the scarf round his throat.*) . . . I'll wear all your scarves today . . . (*From the rucksac he pulls out half a dozen silk scarves, in different colours – all knotted together at the corners.*) Want all the luck I can get today . . . Could deck out a steamer with this lot. . . . Remember that day on the steamer? . . . Funny how the cold always makes your throat swell.

(*Wilson has been tying the string of scarves to his body – around his waist, over his shoulder, across his chest . . . Now he stands, swaying slightly, tears welling up in him, face twitching, breath coming in snorts.*)

WILSON: Sarah!

(*He begins to cry . . . After a moment, he bends to the sack and slowly draws out a full length white nightdress. First he holds it away from himself, looking at it, then clasps it to his breast, between crossed arms, rocking a little, backwards and forwards, lowering his face to the gown, pressing the gown to his cheek, rubbing his cheek against it.*)

WILSON: I can feel you – under your nightdress . . . I'm holding it – against my face – so soft, so soft . . . I stole it. Forgive me, I was mad, wasn't I?

(*wilson takes out of the rucksac a shoe, a brassiere, some knickers . . . and sits down with them.*)

WILSON: Took this as well. From your bedroom. It was under the bed. Did you know if was me? . . . You didn't say anything – when I came back . . . I couldn't tell you. Kept them in a deposit box, at the station . . . I'm glad I can tell you at last – and David . . . Say you'll forgive me . . . Such a pretty nightdress . . . Suits you – with your

WILSON: long waist – and your toes, peeping out . . . Remember how you scorched it, with the iron, and I stitched in a new piece – here, under the shoulder? . . . My mother taught me to sew – all the hours watching her crochet. In my shop, I did all the alterations. And the false pockets in my Tibetan gear . . . (*He picks up the shoe, kisses it.*) Pretty feet . . . I imagine I'm undressing you. I can make it last for hours . . . You like it to take a long time – when I undress you . . . We never – we never do anything else. It stops, somehow – when you're . . . naked – somehow – I'm not there – it's just you, then – and I'm watching you – walking about the room, lying on the bed. You know I'm there, but you pretend not to notice – not even when I whisper to you . . . except when you're wearing the nightdress . . . then it's dark – I can hold you – and we're both shuddering – whimpering – whispering things – before you take it off . . . You never take it off . . . It stops – it keeps stopping . . . that way it never ends.

(*Wilson lays the clothing aside.*)

WILSON: I don't wear it. I swear . . . Too small. Anyway, I'd feel daft up Everest in a nightie . . . It's only to remind me, Sarah – so I can have you with me – when I'm alone, in my tent – not with the sherpas – there's nothing wrong between me and the sherpas . . . Looks bad, I suppose – if I die, and they find my body, if there's anything left of it after the birds . . . Sarah, I don't care – about myself – what they think – only about you . . . Please, let me tell you Sarah! (*Again he cries – wipes his eyes on his sleeve.*) I want to tell you . . . There's another diary.

(*Reaching inside his suit, he takes out a black notebook.*)

WILSON: They'd find this, too . . . Don't believe them, Sarah! Whatever they say! I invented it all. Not about you. I wouldn't write about you – not like this. (*Opening the notebook.*) Other women . . . What I did with other women – in my mind . . . I'm going to read it to you . . . (*Leafing through the pages.*) 'Bonfire night. Fame at last. Lady M challenged me to shoot spunk – fifty pounds a foot – with a straight thousand for hitting an ashtray at five feet. I overshot, in a great arc, and spattered the fireplace. "Ah," she said, "C'est magnifique – mais ce n'est pas la guerre" . . . Armistice Day. Fucked Field Marshal Haig's god-daughter. Whenever she cried out, I pinned a poppy in her hair – once for Wipers, twice for Vimy Ridge, three times for Passchendaele. By midnight, her cunt was like a wreath round a cannon barrel. What larks!' . . . (*Closing book.*) Sarah won't be shocked, will she? Not Sarah . . . Anyway, it was before I met you . . . Fresh in from the Pacific, spending money like water. Togged myself out for Ascot – top hat, tails and a one-armed chauffeur. Anyone for tennis? Dear Sir, may I join you at the pig trough? Not unless you're a pukka pig. With my accent? They looked right through me, as if I were cheap glass . . . And another glass – then another, till I'd drunk my money away. Down the

WILSON: hatch! Daimler to dosshouse. Soup kitchens. Under the viaducts. And the gravy trains rolling overhead. And me, dreaming of Potiphar's wife and her silken daughters, and them lapping my milk through the eye of a needle and whining, fuck me, fuck me everywhere, do whatever you like, do it at the going down of the sun and in the morning and I'll remember you in my husband's will. I'll cut you into our diamond mines, I'll anoint you with oil, I'll give you gold, frankincense and myrrh – as long as you don't kill me – oh, you're killing me – can you kill me again tomorrow? – I'll be in the conservatory, wetting my begonias, signed, your ever-loving Fanny, who'll never get to heaven if you don't slow down, and if you don't slow down I'll take back my rubber plantations – ah, there you are Potiphar, this is Mr. Wilson, dear, he thinks he's a machine gun and he's filling me full of lead, the beast, the absolute beast – isn't he, Potty darling? – the bottom's fallen right out of lead . . . I hid the diary in my mattress. And the key ring. That's what made the bed jingle . . . (*Getting up, Wilson takes a large ring of keys from the rucksac, each bearing a luggage label.*) I've never been with another woman, Sarah . . . They're just keys from all the houses I've lived in . . . And I pretended my women gave me them – my pretend women – with pretend messages . . . (*'Telling' the keys, like a penitent, with beads.*) 'Come up and see me some time' . . . (*And another.*) 'You might have told me you'd pissed in the champagne bucket' . . . Nancy Cunard, Marlene Dietrich, Lady Astor – take your pick – I had them all – especially the aristocrats, the socialites. I took their names from the society columns and had them in my dirty dreams, made them beg at my feet, with their arses in the air and had them, like a dog has a bitch, while their men knelt at the keyholes and fingered themselves into stirrup cups and the chambermaids whipped them with bootstraps . . . It's all in the mind: Now you've heard everything . . . Do you still love me? Can you understand? I wanted to hurt myself, too. (*Picking up the nightdress again.*) Here's your nightdress, Sarah, your white nightdress – take it back love.

(*Wilson lays the nightdress on the ground and, kneeling, puts the other clothing, the shoe, the key ring and the diary upon it, wraps them into a bundle and covers the bundle with snow.*)

WILSON: When I was a child, I spake as a child, I thought as a child – when I became a man, I put away childish things . . . I could love you now, Sarah. I could love a woman now. I could be gentle with her. I could give you your child now, Sarah – our child, David's child. I am like a stream in spring, when the ice cracks upon the mountain – this mountain – which I shall climb, after all. I know I shall climb it . . . (*Rising, looking up into the sun.*) I am magnificent! . . . My whole life has led me to the ice chimney. My purpose is to climb around the last bulge of ice and reach up to the sky, to the sun. Maybe I came here to learn how to die at peace. Like Corbett, eh!

WILSON: Corbie, you old blighter. Can't say I haven't tried. Look at me, all of you, look. The darkness is not worthy of me. Am I not the spirit of rebellion against all that corrupts the life of a man? Dearly beloved, which of you have seen the peasants of this earth, pulling their carts with straps from the shafts around their shoulders – pulling their carts to a new watering place, a canyon in the mountains where the soldiers cannot ride . . . ? That is how we live our lives even when we are safe – like peasants in the soul, drawing our past behind us on the carts of guilt and sorrow, till our spirits bleed with the pulling, like the peasant's shoulders . . . Let me help draw your cart, Ulele . . . What are my cares beside his cares? I owe nothing except to the life bursting within me. On this mountain top, I shall gather in my hand the reins of the horses of life and shall charge them with such lightning that their eyes shall flare, and their tails fly and their manes stand on end. Bareback, I shall ride my horses unto the sons and daughters of men. And my message shall not be hell fire and damnation; it will be redemption. Together, on the good earth, where we find ourselves born, where we live and where we die, immortal only as long as we feed the flame of life within us. Today, I shall forge my own cleft nature into a mighty stallion and shall ride back upon the waiting world. Electrifying every man and woman I touch with the knowledge of their own undying soul. And the downtrodden of this earth shall stand straight and cast off their yokes: and they shall pass on life and the increase of life, to their children, and their children's children, unto everlasting!

(*Wilson bends to his rucksac, fastens it and, with a great effort, swings it up onto his shoulders.*)

WILSON: I am ready. Chomolungma, goddess mother of the earth, I am coming. At last, I am coming . . . (*Stopping to adjust the rucksac, he notices his boots are undone.*) Once I've fastend my bloody boots . . . (*He throws off the rucksac.*) Typical!

(*Wilson sits in the snow, beside his gear and leans forward to fasten his boots. Suddenly, his body is shaken by a terrible tremor. He cries out, clutching at his chest, and falls over on to his side, moaning.*)

WILSON: Aaaaaagh! . . . Ooooooo . . . uhhhh . . . (*Again he grabs his chest.*) Aaaaaagh!

(*Slowly on his side he drags himself across to the snow mound, pulls the nightdress out and clutches it, curling round it.*

WILSON: (*Another terrible cry.*) SARAH!

(*He dies . . . Slowly, the stage light fades to darkness and the noise of the wind fades to nothing. Silence.*)

THE END.

ONE GREEN BOTTLE

ONE GREEN BOTTLE

a novel by
Elizabeth Coxhead

CHAPTER ONE

LIFE BEGAN for Cathy Canning on the day when Bill Powell, who was not her boy, was put away for two years.

It was then that, goaded by an intolerable sense of injustice and by something deeper, something like the panic of the creature in the trap, she closed with the partly jocular suggestion of the young man on the ferry that she should should go with him into Wales for the week-end.

The young man's name was Leonard Head, and he was an insurance salesman, with a new Morris and a petrol allowance from his firm. This suited him fine, for he was also a great mountaineer, a cunning hand at combining business with pleasure, able in a trice to change the navy suit and patter of the business man for corduroys and coils of rope, and to disappear vertically upwards into the mist. So much Cathy knew because anyone who came even momentarily into contact with Leonard Head knew all about him. He was a big mouth. He picked up strangers, girls for choice but any strangers, and told them the story of his life. He picked up Cathy on the Woodside ferry which they both used to come home, he to his parents' villa in Prenton, and she to the ground floor of No. 5 Tooley Street, behind the Birkenhead docks, which none of the Canning family ever looked like leaving, because though it had been condemned twenty years before, a house is a house, and if one has a roof over one's head one goes to the bottom of every waiting-list.

She had not desired his notice. She disliked his big pale face and ginger moustache, and the obvious fact that he was going cheap. She held out for weeks against his cheery good-evenings. It was this talk of Wales that finally caught her. 'We were evacuated there,' she told him.

'That so? I bet you didn't like it. Scuttled back to the nice cosy city as quick as you could, ha-ha.'

'Ay,' agreed Cathy briefly. 'Just in time for the land-mines.' She stared unseeing at the rapidly advancing Woodside stage, while a picture formed itself in her mind of a grey-purple hill outline and a noisy brown stream, and suddenly added, though it had been no part of her purpose to encourage him: 'But it was me mother didn't like it. I did.'

'Did you? Good show!' exclaimed the young man in hearty surprise. 'You'd only be a nipper, wouldn't you? Most of 'em were scared stiff.'

'I liked it all right,' repeated Cathy obstinately. It had been, though she could not explain it to him, like the cracking of a shell, the light pouring through. Though most of the details she could remember were in fact sordid –

her mother's endless altercations with their Welsh hostess, the dirty little bedroom with the sealed window, rain perpetually, a dead sheep in the stream.

'Well, I call that splendid,' said Leonard Head. 'You must have a real feeling for the hills. I can always tell when people have got what it takes. You're a nice build for a climber, too.' He ran his eye over her, lingering on just those points that were appraised by men who were not climbers. 'Tell you what, why not come down with me one week-end? I go every month or so. I could show you a lot of sport.'

'Bet you could,' said Cathy. 'Well, here we are, ta-ta.' She slipped away from him and was down the gangway.

But after that, whenever they met – they only rarely caught the same boat, but when they did there was no avoiding him – he brought the subject up. 'Made up your mind yet? Or are you scared I'll drop you down a cliff?'

''Tain't that scares me,' she would answer, and because it was the reply he expected, he would laugh and feel a dog. She liked him less than ever, but he seemed to imagine he was making progress.

Nor would she ever have given him a second thought, had it not been for Bill's disaster, which cracked her world in two.

It cracked his also, of course, but he only got what he had been asking for. It was she – she who had done nothing – who was so monstrously deceived and betrayed. They all turned against her, her mother and her sister and the street; even her father, her champion whenever he remembered her existence, had the wrong reasons for being on her side. Well, she thought, let them have it their own way. Let them call her bad and heartless; she who had tried to keep her self-respect would try no longer. Leonard Head had a car, and more money than the other men who had wished to seduce her, and instead of a back room in a Southport boarding-house he could offer Wales. Next time she met him, which was on the day Bill was sentenced, she said: ''Course you don't really mean what you're always on about. It's just your line with all the girls.'

'I'll take you up on that,' he cried with a fine show of indignation. 'I've never offered to take a girl climbing in my life before. Except my sister, of course.'

'Uh-huh, your sister,' said Cathy.

'This weekend as ever is,' he insisted. 'Look, I'll phone through tonight to the place in Llandudno where I always stay. It's October now and I don't suppose they're full. Weather looks like holding, too. Are you really game?'

His genuine delight both shamed and embarrassed Cathy. She said in her rudest way:

'No strings?'

'No of course not. What do you take me for? It'll be a pleasure and a privilege to show you my favourite spot of country and my pet sport. As I look at it, other people were good enough to start me off and I ought to do as much in my turn. I mean, for someone like yourself, who's really got the urge.'

Having encouraged him so far, she was obliged to submit when he put his hand under her elbow and guided her down the gangway and into the stage café, where over tea he made his plans. He would meet her by the stage on Saturday at two. He would bring his sister's climbing-boots – lovely little boots they were, hand-made Lawries, but his sister hadn't taken to it, somehow, and, anyway, she was now married down in the south. And what about breeches? Flannel bags would do. Cathy nodded; flannel bags had been an indispensable part of Tooley Street girls' wardrobes in the last years of the war. Something spontaneous and boyish in his enthusiasm reassured her; he really wasn't such a bad sort. And, anyway, he was somebody from outside, somebody who knew nothing of Bill or the Street. No, and he never should.

He wrung her hand in a hearty, comrades-in-sport manner and ran off to catch his bus, and she walked home to Tooley Street, its shadow gradually closing over her, her sharp little white face setting again into lines of sulky defiance as she pondered what explanation she should deign to give about her first week-end from home. Probably none, because they thought her low, and she was low – for if, as Leonard Head had promised, there were no strings to it, then she would simply be taking something for nothing from a chap she didn't really like. Bill was gone, and Ma Powell all broken up, and her mother hated her, and the neighbours when they saw her fell silent, and there was no comfort anywhere, except, far at the back of her mind, faint and flickering like some old, half-forgotten film, that picture of the Welsh hills.

ii

There are deprivations so fundamental that under them the human personality becomes stunted. The inhabitants of Tooley Street lived in the half-dark, like snails at the bottom of an area grating. They saw no green, and the sky was obscured for them by the smoke from the dockyards and the steamers on the river, and the fumes from the gasworks penetrated their lungs and kept their curtains permanently grey. The year wheeled through its glittering pageant and left them totally unaware. The poets had not sung for them, nor were the great stories told or the great music sounded, only the braying of the perpetual wireless, and the glutinous repetitions of the neighbourhood cinema. And always they carried in their hearts the dread of the bad days; not the days of the bombing, that was nothing, that had its excitements, but the long years before, when they had existed, to a man and to a woman, on the dole.

In this harsh existence certain qualities flourished. They were almost all generous in material things and ready to share what they had. They were vital and determined; few illnesses could kill them and few misfortunes get them down. They hated hypocrisy and were quick to unmask any sort of pose. But they were without imagination, rigid, unvarying, all of a piece. The outstanding characteristic of each had become exaggerated, like a starved plant that puts forth one great flower. Some drank; others released themselves in noise, in great bursts of laughter, long volleys of shrieking. Mrs. Canning, Cathy's mother, had become a slattern, perpetually on the whine. Mr. Canning, a left-handed riveter and for years aware of precious skill rusting, knew now that the return of prosperity could bring him neither a better house nor a better wife, and he was consumed by the perpetual smouldering anger of the intelligent man who has not been given words to express and resolve his grievances. The two girls, Cathy and Norma, found their outlet in a precocious sexual awareness. It was the general opinion that both would go to the bad.

Of Norma it was probably true. She was only twelve – a merciful fate rather than any precautions had prevented Mrs. Canning from breeding the string of children to which so many families ran on the dole – but already, with her pretty weak face and mental slowness, she seemed to have the makings of a street-walker. But Cathy at eighteen was virgin still. Along with her father's red hair she had inherited his brains and a smattering of his self-respect, and these, so far, had stopped her on the brink.

She had been many times near it. At school she had learnt nothing, sitting well back with the boys, giggling and flipping notes. She had proved an unremittingly thankless subject for kindly teachers convinced that she could do better if she tried. Since then she had spent her working life in the overall factory across the river, and the rest of her time with boys, in the cinema if they could afford to take her there, or else in the alleys and on the bomb-sites. She was known to be game for a cuddle any night; she had been kissed by every lad in Tooley Street. She was equally skilful at egging them on and at leaving them flat. That she had brought home no baby was not held particularly to her credit. It was generally felt among the mothers that Cathy Canning knew a thing or two and was as hard as they came.

Bill Powell lived with his widowed mother in the top two rooms of the Cannings' house, and though it was true enough, Tooley Street conceded, that Cathy had never stuck to one chap, still he had had a longer run than the others, and it was downright meanness now to make out that he was not her boy. Just what you would have expected: mean, and hard.

And certainly he had been the first of her admirers to make her the honest offer of his hand. 'See here, Cath,' he had muttered at the end of a blissful half-hour against a brick wall, 'how about you and me getting wed?'

'What was that?' whispered back Cathy, sent by kisses into a trance that left her brain numb. He repeated it.

At that her natural quickness returned in a rush. She sprang away from him and stood like a little wasp, shooting her barb into his great lumbering frame. 'Wed!' she cried. 'Don't be so soft. Get yourself a bit of brass and then you can start talking about getting wed.' She left him seared by her contempt.

But he changed his job, finding himself one in a garage on the New Chester Road where, he assured her humbly, there would be tips. And, sure enough, he presently began to make money. He gave his mother a new wireless, one capable of making twice as much noise; and he offered Cathy a fur coat, which she – the street had to admit it, but put it down to her being in the know – refused. He worked queer hours at the garage, often far into the night. Sometimes he did not come home at all, and sometimes Cathy, who slept with Norma in the front room downstairs, would open the door to him in the small hours. She did it for the last time one night at the end of September, when he stumbled in and leant against the door gasping, clutching a bloody rag round his hand. 'You got to help me,' he whispered.

It seemed to her at once that she knew the worst. She took him into the kitchen and lit the gas under the kettle. 'Cops after you?'

'That's right.'

The hand was not only cut but horribly swollen. 'You'll have to take it to the doctor.'

'I can't. They'd know it was me hit the watchman.'

'Oh gosh. Where was it?'

'Warehouse back of Huskisson. They got Jim and Sid.'

'*Them*?' She could not believe it. 'You been going with *them*? Oh Lord, you bloody fool. So that's what it's been all this time. The fur coat and all. You bloody fool.'

'Cathy!' The pain in his hand, the police, his terror, were suddenly nothing to this. 'You got no right to talk to me like that. You know why it all was. I done it for you.'

There was a long moment while it fully came to her what he meant. Then she said flatly: 'Dunno how you have the nerve to say such a thing.'

'But it's God's truth! It was for what you said – don't you remember? How you'd marry me if I had the brass?'

'I never.'

'Yes you did – that's what you said. And how was I to get it? If I'd gone in the yard we'd have had all those years to wait, and then maybe no job at the end. There ain't no good jobs going here, you know that, and if I was to go away you'd take up with some other chap. 'Course I was going to stop it before we were wed. There'll be more pickings at the garage then. It was just to have a bit put by. You wouldn't hold that against me? You wouldn't, now?'

He looked so desperate, so white and sick, that to disabuse him of his great error there and then was not possible. Almost, at that moment, she loved him, and yet she was shaken by fury at a folly so immense.

'Look, we can't talk about it now. You'd best get to bed and get some sleep. Perhaps they won't come after you.'

'Ay, might be. If Jim and Sid don't talk.'

But of course they'll talk, Cathy thought, Jim's white rat-face coming vividly before her eyes. She put her arm under Bill's elbow and helped him up the steep stairs, for he could hardly stand. His stumbles brought his mother out on to the tiny landing. 'What's up?' she asked, and then she saw his hand and his face, and her mouth fell open.

But Bill, oblivious of her presence, of the fact that he was giving Cathy away, of everything but his desperate need for reassurance, was muttering again with increased urgency: 'You'll stick by me, won't you, Cath? You know I done it for you.'

Well, that was that; for next day the police came and took Bill away, and the wireless, too, giving Mrs. Powell to understand that a very serious view would be taken, since the other two under questioning had admitted to more than thirty warehouse raids; and the night watchman was in hospital. And naturally Mrs. Powell told the whole street that her son had done it for Cathy Canning's sake, and that if she threw him over now it would be the meanest thing going. Cathy did not blame her; it was right that she should stick by her child. But that Mrs. Canning should take the same view staggered her. She had known for years that she disliked her mother; nevertheless there was something appalling in the discovery that the dislike was so fully returned.

Only her father took, as always and usually disastrously, her part; and this time his championship hurt rather than helped because it was on the wrong grounds. 'Leave the lass alone,' he said. 'She done right. I don't want no jailbirds in my family.'

'But it's not like that, Dad!' Cathy cried. 'If I was struck on him I wouldn't care what he'd done. He could go to prison twenty times. But I'm not and I never have been. He thought I promised to wed him, but I never – you know how soft Bill is, half the time he don't listen to what you say—' But it was hopeless. If her father, who loved her, could not be made to realize that she had not turned against Bill when his luck was out, then nobody would.

Bill got a Borstal sentence of two years, which Mrs. Powell spoke of as if it were Dartmoor. The street lamented with her; only Cathy, who in the interval had been reading up Borstals in the free library, was robustly unconcerned. 'It's just like a school,' she informed them. 'Football, and workshops, and I dunno what. I daresay he'll have a softer time than any of us.' And, on top of that, announced that she was off for the week-end to North Wales – mountaineering, she called it – with some fancy chap picked up on the ferry, a posh type who owned a car.

Tooley Street was outraged. As far as was practicable in so crowded and vocal a community, she was treated as an outlaw. She might know enough to keep herself out of trouble, but still she was a bad lot, was Cathy Canning; mean and hard and without a heart.

iii

Impossible for her, as the car climbed the gentle spine of the Wirral and the first hills of Wales appeared as a blue frieze across the shining Dee, not to feel her spirits lift. Impossible not to feel warmly towards Leonard Head, who had greeted her so heartily at the ferry – for naturally she would not let him pick her up in Tooley Street – and commented on her canary-yellow coat with the air of a man who knew what girls expected. Now he was boasting, but this Cathy had foreseen. If he could brag in chance encounters on the ferry, his scope would be limitless on a whole week-end, and listening to it amiably was the price she had set herself to pay. Besides, even while boasting, he had for her the freshness of the one person in her world who knew nothing of Bill Powell. He let her into a life without a care.

All the way across Queensferry he boasted, all the way up the pass between the Clwyd hills. About his line of sales talk, the esteem in which the company held him, the car, the allowance it made him on account of the car, the further means by which he diddled it when sending in his petrol account – you might have thought he would keep quiet about that, except that it was evident he never did keep quiet about anything. At intervals he would point out features of the landscape as though he had just created them. 'At the top here,' he told her, 'we see Snowdon and the whole of the main range.' They reached the top, and for once he was silenced.

Where the view should have been were ominous banks of purple cloud. The radiant afternoon was behind them; in front was storm.

'Well, that's a blow,' said Leonard frankly. 'That's the worst of Snowdon, it attracts dirty weather. Damned if I'm taking you climbing in the wet on your first day. Enough to put you right off.'

'I don't mind getting wet,' said Cathy, but she shivered; the wildness of the scene before her brought back the Wales that she remembered.

'I think we'll make for the coast. I've booked for us at Llandudno in any case; spot I know there is a sight more comfortable than these mountain hotels. Then if it clears after tea we can try out Madeline's boots on the Orme. That do?'

To Cathy the word Llandudno suggested strings. Girls in Tooley Street who were lucky enough to sell their virtue dear usually did it in Southport, and other large coastal resorts were doubtless just as bad. But he had seemed, so far, infinitely more interested in himself than in her, and the half-hidden mountains struck her with fear. 'All right,' she agreed. 'But let's have a stab at it tomorrow.'

'Wet or fine,' promised Leonard, smiling. 'I wish Madeline had had half your spirit. It does me good to see you so keen.'

They descended to the Conway valley, hit now by vicious squalls of rain blowing in from the west, and in an astonishingly short time seemed to be away from the menace of the great hills. There were villages, flowery and smiling, then red-brick suburbs; it was safe again, and familiar, and Cathy was aware of a curious disappointment. But soon, to console her, there was the tang of the sea.

The spot known to Leonard Head was called the Myrtle Bank. It stood on the front, with a great many red gables and white wooden balconies, and, though not one of the big hotels, was by a long way the grandest house Cathy had ever entered. She was awed by the swing door, the red-and-yellow scroll carpets, the reception desk with its chilly young lady who accorded Mr. Head none of the recognition he had angled for and calmly looked up his bookings. But not too awed to miss his grin when the young lady handed them the keys of two single rooms. There, said the grin, mightn't you have trusted me, you silly little thing? She was relieved, and yet she reddened and felt young and a fool.

The rooms were on opposite sides of a corridor, and hers had the sea view. 'Bit on the small side, I'm afraid,' said Leonard, 'but then all single rooms are. The doubles are a lot better. Ah well, we can't have everything in this life, I suppose.' To Cathy her room seemed enormous. She could scarcely credit that so much spacious elegance was for herself alone.

Five minutes later he was back with his sister's boots and socks, and stood over her in the kindest way while she painfully fitted them on. Extraordinary excrescences they were on her feet, so heavy, and with all those queer little iron ridges. 'My feet don't feel like they belong to me,' she commented, loping in front of him along the corridor, to his amusement.

'In a real climbing place they don't let you come upstairs in nailed boots,' he told her, and indeed it seemed a sin to press the ridges into the red-and-yellow scroll carpet, which flowed like lava up the stairs and into every bedroom. 'But here they don't know any better, bless their hearts.'

After a wonderfully refined tea, on a tray, with napkins and sandwiches, he put her into the car again and made for the foot of the great green headland which thrust its hog's back out into the sea. And once on its rough grass the boots ceased to feel strange, and instead carried her to the top as though they had a life of their own. On top the wind met her again, salt and tangy, and whipped the blood into her face as she battled along beside him, high above the sea. 'Whew, it certainly isn't the day for high exposure,' pronounced Leonard. 'Now down there, to get the feel of your nails.'

'Oh, I couldn't –' began Cathy, peering over what looked to her like a vertical wall of grass. But he had shot ahead, jumping and lolloping, his boot-nails gripping the slippery grass; and when she forced herself to follow the same thing happened, and she found herself floating down with an extraordinary sense of power and speed. Her feet, which had scarcely known any ground but pavements, were on this rough stuff gloriously at home. 'Eh, that was grand!' she cried as she joined him at the bottom, and for the first time, though he might not be aware of it, there was real friendliness in her voice.

'Oh, bosh,' he said. 'This is only the public park, more or less. Wait till I get you on a real hill in the morning.'

For an hour they ran like children, up and down the slopes. Then the autumn dusk closed in on them, and they turned home. Back in the car, Cathy's uneasiness returned. She knew she was in luck, to be staying in a swank hotel and a fine place like Llandudno. But she could not shake off the sense of being there under false pretences and of costing him more than she was worth.

The dinner increased her melancholy. It was very grand, and not the sort of food she was used to. The hotel was half-empty, the season being over, and the other guests seemed silent and old. Of course it was wonderful being in Llandudno, but Tooley Street was a lot noisier on a Saturday night. Leonard, however, now talked about climbing, and that was an improvement, even though his stories all reflected credit on himself.

'Now what?' he asked her when the meal was over. 'Shall we look for somewhere to dance? Or would you rather just sit?'

'I'd like a flick,' replied Cathy firmly. He couldn't, she calculated, talk through that.

But although it was a highly pathetic film, and a new one, too, newer than any in Birkenhead, the instant the lights went down she seemed face to face with Bill. Perhaps it was because Leonard put his arm around her, which she took as a matter of course; chaps always sat so with girls in the cinema. But for the last six months the chap had been Bill, who was now put away, cut off from them all, having a grand time, no doubt, playing football and getting fancy lessons, and would finally come out with the shame of it upon him, fathers saying they didn't want no jail-birds in their families. . . . As the lights came up, she was crying. Leonard Head was touched and pleased.

'Well, I'm damned,' he said, expertly producing his handkerchief. 'And me putting you down as hard-boiled.'

'So I am,' said Cathy, furious. 'I must of got a cold on the Orme.'

'Have it your own way.' He guided her solicitously out into the windy night. 'But I believe that under that frozen face there's a real soft little heart.' Idiot, thought Cathy. Fat lot you know. 'Now home to bed, I think. You have a stiff day in front of you.'

Nothing, really, could have been kinder, and it must be costing him a mint. She kissed her boys when they brought her home from the pictures; to have refused as much to Leonard Head would have been churlish. At her bedroom door she lifted her face to his. He took advantage, at some length; and he certainly knew the way to do it. Poor Bill's kisses seemed slightly muffed by comparison.

'That all right?' he asked, releasing her. She tried to look stony, being startled herself to find how very all right it was. 'Well then' – his voice sank to a caressing murmur – 'how about changing your mind?'

'There. I knew there'd be strings to it.'

'Now that's quite unfair. It was only the merest suggestion; just to be friendly. And I believe I know what's on your mind. But I can promise you there'd be nothing to feel nervous of. I know my way about. It'd be perfectly safe.' The silence while she thought this over emboldened him. 'Of course I'll shut up if you'd really rather not. Only it seems rather a waste, when we could give each other such a lot of fun.'

'No!' said Cathy on a sudden note of hysteria.

'Righto, no hard feelings. Good night, and bless you.' He marched off to his own room, the friendliest creature in the world.

Cathy, having bolted her door, felt more than ever a fool. How near she had been to yielding he couldn't guess – or perhaps he did. It was such a chance to learn the thing she most needed to know; comfortable, secret, and, as he had promised, safe. It would be honest, too; it was the obvious way to repay. Silly, really, to refuse.

But there were reasons. Not only Bill; not only finding Leonard a bore; not just romantic reasons like in the film. She was desperately afraid, for one thing, of being thought dirty. She came from a dirty home; when every drop of water has to be carried in from a tap in the yard, and then thrown out again, it is not easy for homes to be otherwise. Since she had worked in the overall factory, where most of the girls were better class, she had gone to the public baths once a week, but it wasn't quite the same thing. And she owned only the one set of underclothes, never having had money to spare for what would not show.

The splendour of the washing arrangements at the Myrtle Bank enchanted her. First she washed her hair. Then she washed out her clothes and hung them on the radiator. Then, being reasonably satisfied that Leonard Head would emerge no more, she crept out to the noble bathroom at the end of the corridor. When at last she got into bed she was clean, clean in every inch, clean as any duchess who could have stayed there before.

That'll show them, she thought. But who was to be shown, or what, she had no very clear idea.

iv

The departure of Cathy and her escort next morning from the Myrtle Bank was an impressive sight for such of the guests as chanced to look up from their knitting. She in her cut-down mackintosh and old flannel trousers tucked into the beautiful boots looked near enough to a climber to deceive the inexperienced eye; he was magnificent in corduroys and wreathed with rope. But as the car climbed once more out of the valleys and the mist was still seen to cloak the tops, his confidence seemed to ebb. 'Gives me the pip, this weather,' he told her. 'How about it?'

'Reckon I'd like to get up summat,' said Cathy remorselessly, mindful of her ecstasy on the Orme.

'All right, anything you say.' The car nosed up towards the shrouded hills, and passed a straggling village: some stone and slate cottages, three white hotels. 'This is Llanllugwy, where most of the climbing crowd stay.'

'Llan what when it's at home?'

'Yes, regular tongue-twister, isn't it? There's hardly a Sassenach can manage Welsh place-names. I don't know how it is, but I never seem to have any difficulty—' He was happy again.

The road mounted once more, this time into a high, unrelievedly bleak valley over which one could feel the brooding presence of the hidden hills, which the mist still cut off as with a rule. Presently it skirted a long, steely lake. Beyond this came a right-angled corner, and another valley dipped down to a remote glimpse of sun-touched sea. Right at the top of the pass, commanding the turn, stood a gaunt, square house fronted with slates, scarcely less forbidding than the wall of crags at its back.

'Cae Capel,' Leonard said. 'We leave the car here and walk. Not exactly a jolly spot, is it? House used to be a climbing centre, but now it's been taken for one of those youth hostels. Pity. Some of the hostellers climb, I believe; in fact they're always making fools of themselves and having accidents. Just what you'd expect. I daresay half of them haven't the proper equipment and go out in sandals.

Cathy got out with a growing dread. The place was certainly the least welcoming she had ever seen, and the house was as silent and shuttered as death, though somewhere a waterfall splashed below them. Leonard's rope seemed to take on a menacing air, and she wished they were cosily back at Llandudno in the sunshine. But she had brought it on herself; she had willed to come. She followed him through an iron gate and up a stony path which led them to a higher lake, walled in by yet blacker and more forbidding precipices. One of these slanted down almost to the water's edge; and this, Leonard explained while they were yet at some distance, was the face he had proposed to climb. 'Though I don't at all like the look of it under these conditions. But, anyway, we'll go and rub our noses on it, shall we?' Cathy trudged after him, longing to be home.

The rock was like a whole hillside frozen into stone. The nail-marks of a thousand boots made yellow pathways up it. 'As I thought, wct,' said Leonard. 'To be quite honest with you, I'd planned to lead in rubbers. Seeing that my second's a beginner, and to be quite on the safe side. But I think it may dry – look, there's sun over Anglesey. I propose we hang around a bit and eat a sandwich.' Cathy had no idea what rubbers were, but she felt thankful that for the moment it was not necessary to do anything with that alarming rope.

They sat for half an hour, watching the mist shift a little higher, and a chill wind took the rest of her courage away. Then two more rope-wreathed figures could be seen making toward them along the track.

'Looks like chaps I know,' Leonard said. 'By Jove, I think it is. Jake – I say, Jake!' He rushed to meet the leading climber, who returned his recognition, without, however, looking greatly pleased. They stood in talk for a minute; then he returned to her, wearing a vaguely apologetic smile.

'Look here, I think the sun'll be out in half an hour. The rock'll soon dry then, and you'll enjoy it ten times more. Meanwhile, shall you mind if I tie on after my friends for a bit, just to get the feel of my nails?' Cathy looked blank, not fully understanding what he meant. 'That's all right then. Good girl – just make yourself comfortable. Have another sandwich.'

The leading climber approached one of the yellow lines of scratches, uncoiled his rope and fastened an end purposefully round his waist. Then he began to mount. Cathy watched fascinated; the little yellow steps seemed to take the tips of his toes so neatly, and his nails made a curious and yet delightful sound. He moved as though there were no hurry, but in a few moments he was almost invisible on the lip of a ledge which blocked the first sheet of rock. His voice floated gently down to them: 'Right!'

The second climber picked up the end of the rope and tied it on. Then he took Leonard's rope and tied that on also, obviously glumly. Leonard said: 'It's really no end decent of you, old boy,' and even to the inexperienced Cathy it was plain that he was making himself a nuisance. The second climber disappeared as casually and expeditiously as the first.

It was now Leonard's turn. As he mounted the yellow steps they seemed smaller and less secure, and his nails made twice the amount of noise. At one point he glanced down over his shoulder and remarked to Cathy: 'As I feared. I'm hopelessly out of form.' Then he, too, vanished.

One by one the party came in sight again as they climbed out on to the second leaf of rock, but they were now so high above her that her neck ached with craning up at them. After the third halt they were lost completely in the great rock-face, though for quite a time the sound of their boots and voices could be fitfully heard. Then she was alone.

Never in her life before had she been quite alone.

'Well!' said Cathy aloud after a time, not caring for the utter silence. 'Funny way to take a girl out, I will say.' She sat, forsaken, on his rucksac.

The sun over Anglesey remained over Anglesey. The breeze grew chillier. The steely waters of the lake reflected the low sky and the half-circle of lead-coloured precipice. One could not imagine a lonelier spot.

Half an hour, he had said. She did not own a watch and had no means of knowing the time, but ages seemed to pass, an hour at least. Gradually her resignation gave place to fury. She had been planted. It was the kind of thing that made her snigger when it happened to other girls at the dance-hall; that it should happen to her, and right in the middle of God knew where –! Served her right for picking up soft types and letting them think she would be grateful for anything. She marched up and down till anger and exercise had made her warm again, and then tried, for the fun of it, the first four of the yellow steps. The fifth looked harder, and she was alarmed to find how high she was off the ground. She turned round and slid back to it with a bump.

That was that; but strolling a few yards back along the path, she came on an obviously easier way, a deep groove in the rock, slanting up as far as eye could see. The scratches in it were a positive staircase.

She tried the groove; its walls were comforting, and she felt pleasantly enclosed. Up she went, and it was easy. The spiked boot-nails bit into the rock, just as they had bitten into the grass on the Orme. There were knobs to hold on to and pull. Kicking, scratching, delighted with her cleverness, she made her way up.

She lost all sense of time. She forgot Leonard and her anger, Bill and her grief. In every fibre of her body she lived.

Suddenly, the groove sprouted humps of rock. She could no longer get right inside it; it would take only a toe, and a big arm-pull was needed to progress. She did this twice and then the whole cliff steepened, the groove petering away, but the yellow scratches relentlessly continuing, delicate and rounded. 'Oh gosh,' she whispered. 'Reckon I can't do that.'

Then, and then only, did she think to look behind her. There was space, horrible, appalling space. Down and down the eye plunged, and there was his tiny rucksac, where she had left it, on the grass.

The full horror of dizziness seized her. It seemed that she must let go and end it all.

After a moment the horror passed. She was shaking still, but she knew herself perfectly capable of holding on. It was not enough, however, just to hold on. She could not get up, but it ought to be possible, provided she did not look at the rucksac, to get down again.

But it was no use. Pulling up had been simple, but to lower a toe into those steps that one couldn't properly see and then let go – no, it could not be done. She would have to stay where she was 'till they came back.

But suppose they didn't come back? A bloody fool like Leonard Head was capable of anything. Perhaps if she shouted they would hear her. She tried, and her voice was a frail, pitiful little pipe against the great crags. It was hopeless. She began to cry.

And that was the last straw – to learn that she, the tough Cathy Canning, was really a coward and a sniveller, too. Her tears made her so angry that they were dried up in shame.

More hours seemed to pass. She was acutely uncomfortable, for she had to hold on with both hands, and her legs slowly got cramp. Then it began to rain. Soon a waterfall streamed down the gully. She was wet to the skin in a moment, and found herself uncontrollably shivering. At last she was completely afraid.

And then the miracle of rescue happened. Through the horror of solitude and silence came voices, and somewhere far above her the musical sound of nails. Leonard and his party were returning after all.

She shouted; possessed by a sudden panic dread lest she could not hold on much longer, she shrieked again and again. At last she made them hear her, and there came an answering shout.

They were trying to ask her some question, but the rock above cut off their voices and she could not make out a word. She yelled back her predicament. 'I'm proper stuck!'

The scratching began again, this time immediately above her head. The blessed spectacle of a climber came swinging down the rock-hill, draped in oiled silk and shining like a wet seal. 'Steady,' he called over his shoulder to silence her yelling. 'With you in a tick.' She realised it was a stranger, not Leonard or his friends.

A moment more and he was down beside her, and she was clutching him, sobbing and gasping with relief.

'Steady,' repeated the young man, disengaging himself. 'You'll be all right now. Poor lass, aren't you cold? Just hold on one minute more – on to the rock, not me – while I get you tied on.' He took the rope from his own waist and fastened it round hers. 'Now up you go.'

'Eh, I just couldn't!' she brought out between her chattering teeth.

'Nonsense,' said the young man in the kindest way. 'My friend is just above you and he weighs twelve stone. He can haul you up like a sack of coals if you prefer, but it'll hurt rather. Just have a try. I'll come right behind and shove. Only fifteen feet up, and a perfectly easy walk-off at the top.

'I couldn't,' said Cathy, and the dreadful crying started again.

'Reckon you're from Merseyside,' said the young man, dropping suddenly into the flattest local drawl.

'Ay,' said Cathy, checked in her crying by surprise.

'Then play up Everton!' he shouted; and up she went.

'That's it – that's grand. Not much feeling in your fingers, is there? No, no, don't hold the rope. Never that. Anything but that. Hold yourself out from the rock if you can – splendid – you've got the idea. Once more – just give us a bit of a pull, Stan – up she comes – attagirl – ha, Christians, saved!'

She was landed like a fish on the broad grass terrace at the top of the precipice, laughing and sobbing by turns; and her other rescuer, an enormous creature similarly swathed in oilskins, took the rope off her, slapped her back, rubbed her hands, and got some blessedly hot sweet tea down her throat. At last she was able to sit up and thank them. 'I'd have been for it if you hadn't come. I guess you saved my life.'

'Don't give it a thought,' said the small one. 'Somebody else would have been along in a minute. There's always hosts of people on the Slabs.' Cathy had not observed them, but she took it that he was sparing her feelings. 'Now if you feel you can walk . . . ? Stan will take your other arm.'

And he was quite right; it was nothing more than a scramble. Up, round a grassy corner into a gully, and down over broken rocks and stones, easily, blessedly, till she found herself back on the path and beside the rucksac that she had never thought to see again.

'Now then,' said the small climber as his friend paused to re-coil the rope, 'I don't want to kick a girl when she's down, but you realize that was a damn silly thing to do?'

'Ay, that I do,' agreed Cathy, utterly humbled. She looked at him, and the hint of a smile on his sharp fox-terrier face impelled her to confide. 'I'll tell you how it was. I came with a chap that was going to take me climbing – that's his rucksac – and when we got here he met two other chaps and they all went off together and left me sitting. It just got my goat.'

'I see. Very understandable. But not, of course, a real excuse.'

'Lay off her, Harry,' interposed Stan, looking up briefly from his coil. 'Reckon she didn't do so badly getting where she was.'

'She did very foolishly,' said Harry sternly. 'Look here, we're at the hostel. You better come back with us and get dried out. The warden's a pal of ours. I'll leave a line telling the boy-friend where to look.' And he produced, with characteristic efficiency, pen and pad from under the oilskins.

'Don't fash,' Cathy said. 'I wouldn't care if I never saw him again.'

'You must never leave a party without warning in the hills,' answered Harry, still stern. 'Now we run for it.'

They splashed down the path, now become a stream. The horrible crags, the steely lake fell behind them. The hard line of the road appeared below, and Leonard's car, and the gaunt house. Harry and Stan made for the back door and thumped. 'Hi, Dorothy!' they shouted. 'Rescue!'

The door was immediately opened by a pretty young woman with an anxious expression. 'Here's the body,' Harry said, thrusting Cathy forward, and the young woman's face cleared.

'Thank heaven it can walk – the last one couldn't. You must be soaked, though. Come in.'

Cathy found herself in a big, light kitchen, with a fire blazing in a high hob grate, a gay rag rug on the hearth, and a rocking-chair into which she was pushed. The contrast was so delicious that she nearly cried again.

'Stuck on the hard bit of the easy way on the Slabs,' Harry explained, and outlined the misadventure. 'You needn't tick her off. We've done it pretty thoroughly.' Stan had, in fact, taken no part in the scolding, but seemed content, as before, that his friend should speak for both.

'You mean she got up there by herself?' asked the young woman, pouring out tea. 'And never done any climbing before? Well, I think it's wonderful. I'd never dare. They call it the easy way, but it's quite hard enough even on a rope. She must have a natural gift.'

'Now then, Dorothy,' Harry expostulated. 'That's the amateur attitude that lands you with corpses.'

'Oh, never mind,' said the kind young woman. 'Go and change your wet breeches while I lend her a rug.' When they came back five minutes later Cathy was swathed in a tartan blanket, while the young woman, in whom she had divined an ally, was in possession of all the facts regarding the conduct of Leonard Head. 'Did you ever hear of anything so monstrous?' she indignantly exclaimed.

'The boy-friend certainly sounds a bit of a heel,' conceded Harry. 'But she better not be too hard on him. The plain fact is, he was scared of the Slabs in the wet, and he won't thank her for rubbing it in.'

'Fat lot I care,' said Cathy. 'He isn't my boy-friend. He just offered to take me climbing. I don't ever want to see him again.'

'Oh, it's that way, is it?' He studied her shrewdly. 'Is that nice Morris outside his? You better let him get you safely home. And next time you'll know not to believe every chap who calls himself a climber.'

'But, Harry, how could she tell? It's terribly hard to make a start with climbing when you don't know anyone.' The warden's eyes seemed to send him a message over which he brooded.

'Yes, well,' he said at length, 'how about introducing ourselves? I'm Harry Rimmer and my friend's Stan Bryce; we're from Merseyside like you; draughtsmen with one of the shipping firms. This is Miss Dorothy Elliott, warden of Cae Capel, a figure famed throughout the civilized climbing world. Now you.'

'My name's Cathy Canning.' And as it seemed expected that she should give her occupation, she added: 'I work in an overall factory.'

'Oh? Is it interesting?'

'I dunno – I reckon it's all right,' said Cathy, who had never considered the point. 'I put on pockets.'

'What, all day long? Must be enough to drive you nuts.'

'Really, Harry,' Miss Elliott protested. 'You're far too ready to assume that nobody's job is interesting but yours.'

'Any road, his is dullish between whiles,' the silent Stan unexpectedly interposed.

'I daresay it takes all sorts—' conceded Harry vaguely. He relapsed into cogitation, and Cathy, over her teacup, was able to steal a careful look at her new friends.

Divested of their oilskins, the two young men were an odd contrast. Harry was small, sharp and dapper; he wore a bright blue tweed jacket and evidently considered his appearance. Stan was huge, with an upright bristle of hair and the plainest face it was possible to imagine; just like a small piece of putty thrown on to a large one, thought Cathy, considering his nose. Miss Elliott was a slender girl with a delicate pink-and-white skin, slightly prominent blue eyes, and thin pale-gold hair turning into ringlets on her long neck. She had an air of extreme natural refinement which would have violently prejudiced Cathy against her had they met under other circumstances. She sat now cross-legged on her Welsh rag-rug, with her eyes on Harry, and a gentle, slightly maternal smile curving her pretty mouth, as of an indulgent parent who knew that her little boy was going to do the right thing.

'All right, Cathy Canning,' said Harry at length. 'If you're serious about wanting to climb, Stan and I are willing to teach you. Mind, I said serious. There's a sight too many lasses hanging about this hostel waiting for a chap to come and haul them up something. What we want is a few more girls with guts and technique, who can do their own leading and not be carted round like rucksacs. Got that clear?'

Cathy, although aware for the last few minutes that something must be up, was nevertheless astounded. 'Go on, you don't mean it,' she said when she could find voice. She looked at Stan, declared to be willing too, though how Harry knew it without consulting him was mysterious. Stan, however, gave her his rocky grin and mumbled reassuringly: 'That's right.'

'Now isn't that splendid?' said the warden, beaming. 'You couldn't find a better instructor than Harry. He's even brought me on a bit, and I'm an utter duffer. Now here's what you'll have to do—' She entered into technical detail. '– and it's quite cheap; the charge is one and six for a bed, and the same for a meal. Or you can be a self-cooker; I mean, you can bring your own food and cook it in the pantry at the back. People often do if cash is a bit short.'

'A hellish fag after a day's climbing, though,' said Harry, 'and, anyway, Dorothy's cooking is something you look forward to all day.'

'It's ever so kind of you all, really,' muttered Cathy, swamped in information and gratitude.

'I don't suppose you'll think so when first we start on you,' Harry grinned. 'Next week-end, then. You can come up on the back of my bike on Friday night.'

'I got to work Saturday mornings.'

'Oh?' He frowned. 'Well, better change your job. There's plenty now work a five-day week.'

'Really, Harry,' said Miss Elliott again. 'Her work is probably just as skilled as yours.'

'Well, it's time she had a change from pockets. But in that case you'll have to make your own way here Saturday afternoon. If you get a bus as far as Queensferry you can probably flag a lift – that's what most of the girls do. Your equipment seems passable. Those are nice boots.'

Boots – a disquieting chord struck in the back of her mind. At the same moment a knock sounded on the outer door. 'That'll be the gallant leader,' observed Harry, and went across to open it.

Leonard Head, dripping wet, strode into the kitchen and launched like a naughty schoolboy on the attack which is the best form of defence. 'A nice turn you gave me—' he began, glaring at Cathy across the room, and then became aware of three other pairs of eyes, fixed upon him with knowledgeable amusement. Cathy, secure in the glorious possession of allies, saw with exquisite malice that he turned slowly red.

'Do come in,' said Miss Elliott in her gentle, light voice. 'I'm sorry if you were worried about your friend. But as you see, she is quite safe.'

'Oh – er, it's terribly good of you.' Meeting thus with a real lady completed, it was plain, his discomfiture. 'Fact is, it's such a filthy day – I felt it wasn't fit for her – and then I didn't mean to be so long, but our leader stuck a bit—'

'These things will happen,' agreed Miss Elliott, smiling.

Cathy perceived regretfully that it was her cue to put him out of his misery. 'Reckon we'd best be getting along,' she said.

'Have you a rug in your car?' Miss Elliott asked Leonard. 'then if you'd fetch it – Cathy's trousers are still, I think, too damp to put on.' He vanished, and she added quickly to Cathy: 'Goodbye, my dear, and I hope we'll see you frequently from now.'

'Oh, *yes*,' said Cathy fervently, shook a hand of each of her rescuers, wrapped herself in the new rug and waddled out into the rain, determined that Leonard Head should hear nothing of the prospect opening out before her.

Thus she left Cae Capel for the first time.

V

Benevolent and boastful, Leonard had been dreary enough, but aggrieved and sulky he was even worse. She stared out bleakly at the rain lashing the forests below Llanllugwy. Had it been merely a question of feeling, his sulks would not have signified. But there were the boots.

She could ask him for the loan of them, of course, but that would be just as bad, and she might as well have them for keeps. She was going to have them, anyway.

'A hot bath would be a bit of all right,' she murmured tentatively as they swung into the main valley.

'You've said it. I shall wallow. You just can't think how bloody cold it was up there. You were a damn sight better off—' She had made the first move, thus assuaging his pride, and he could boast again. Five minutes later, describing to her step by step the climb (the sheer nerve of it!), he had talked himself happy. He was naught but a great baby. Impossible to keep up anger against anyone so soft. A sort of compunction mingled with her contempt.

The bath was wonderful, and so was the dinner, with which Leonard ordered a bottle of wine. 'You do know how to treat a girl,' she told him, hating herself for it nearly as much as she disliked the wine; but it did the trick. His talk took a new line: women, how to handle them, what they expected. After dinner they sat on a sofa in the lounge, and he slid his arm along its back behind her.

'Nice and cosy here, isn't it? Nothing like a hard day's climbing to make you appreciate the creature comforts.' Apparently the fact that she, as far as he knew, had not had any climbing had now completely slipped his mind. 'Seems a pity to have to go home tonight. What time must you be at work?'

'Oh, any old time,' said Cathy, and knew the step was taken. For, emboldened by this palpable lie, he said:

'I ought to look in around nine-thirty, but if we leave here at half-past seven the old bus'll do it. You won't mind an early start. I'll just tell them at the desk.'

The sooner the better, Cathy thought, half-stupefied by food and wine and exercise, and therefore almost dulled to revulsion and fear. When he came back she proposed that they should go upstairs, and when they paused outside her door and he said wistfully: 'Same old drill, I suppose?' she heard her own voice say flatly, as if in a dream:

'Reckon you can come in if you like.'

'You're a proper sport. You're a gem. A girl in a thousand. You'll never regret it, I can tell you that.'

'Give us ten minutes,' Cathy said, perceiving for the second time that day a precipice beneath her feet. The fierce modesty of her class all but overcame her. Nothing should induce her to let a chap see her take off her clothes.

vi

Breakfast was so early that they ate it half asleep; but on the drive home she had leisure to consider her feelings, for Leonard was silent at last. He had got what he wanted, and looked as pleased as Punch.

I did it for the boots, she told herself over and over. I did it for the boots. And from somewhere there came an urgent echo: *Cathy! I done it for you.*

He had had what poor Bill ought to have had. No wonder he looked like the cat after cream.

He turned his head, met her eyes and grinned. 'Was it okay?'

'I reckon it was.' And she knew, with shocked certainty, that she spoke the truth. It had been okay.

Her body now knew what for years it had been hungry to learn. She had no standards to judge by but Tooley Street gossip and the films. The first drew such a lurid picture of the bridal night that you wondered any girl dared to get wed; and in the second, scarcely even the villainess would sink so low as to sleep with a chap she didn't like. But both, Cathy was somehow aware, were controlled by a censorship which made them inaccurate guides to life.

'I thought you'd enjoy it,' Leonard said, and one could almost fancy he smacked his lips. 'First time, wasn't it? You had a spot of luck, girlie, falling in with someone who knew the right way to do it, even though I say so myself. We must repeat the experiment – when we've both got time.'

I must be the kind of girl who'd go with any chap, Cathy thought. I must be real bad. Maybe now I've begun I shan't be able to stop. No, it can't be that. I did it for the boots.

He dropped her at Woodside, by her own request. They shook hands and she turned away, clutching her shabby canvas holdall. 'Hi,' he called, 'there's something you've forgotten. Madeline's boots.'

'I'll be keeping those,' said Cathy briefly; and then, as his jaw dropped, added with an open sarcasm which further astounded him: 'You didn't surely think, did you, that you were getting it for nowt?'

'But look here, I say! I mean, I'm most frightfully grateful and all that. Anything else, within reason. I'll write you a cheque, and then you can buy yourself some new ones. But my sister had those made to measure, and she might want—'

'Then,' said Cathy, falling back on Tooley Street's tersest idiom, 'wanting's her share.'

CHAPTER TWO

SHE WAS late at the factory, and forestalled a row by asking for her cards. In the evening she went to the labour exchange, which suggested a laundry. 'What about the Stonyhey, in Tranmere?' said the officer, impressed by her record of three years in one job; most girls of eighteen had had half a dozen. 'It's run by a lady, Miss Hignett. Everyone I've sent there has liked it.' She arranged an interview for lunch-time next day.

Cathy came home to Tooley Street. As she opened the front door she learnt something new about her home: it smelt. Presumably it had smelt the same always, for Mrs. Canning never opened windows because of the dirt from the gasworks. But now for the first time she was able to compare it with places that had only the cold smell of the rain and the hills, and she stood wrinkling her nose in irrepressible disgust.

'Had a good time?' asked Mrs. Canning sharply. She'd have looked like that whatever I'd done, thought Cathy, defiant. She can't possibly know. But it occurred to her to wonder, with a cold fear, whether Leonard Head's precautions were any more competent than his climbing.

'Oh, all right,' she answered offhandedly. 'Reckon I'm going on my own next week-end, though. I can stay in one of those youth hostels.'

'Dunno when I had a holiday,' Mrs. Canning remarked.

'What funny boots,' commented Norma, watching the unpacking. 'You must look a proper sight.'

After the overall factory, the Stonyhey Laundry in a Tranmere back lane seemed a homely little affair. But Miss Hignett inspired confidence, indeed awe. She was short, plump and a woman of few words, and her eyes behind her spectacles were shrewd. 'What made you think you'd like laundry work?'

Cathy's bias at the moment was all towards cleanliness, but something in the glance behind the spectacles compelled the full truth out of her. 'I want my Saturdays.'

'I see. What for?'

Sick mothers and other suggestions occurred to her, but she found herself saying: 'I want to go climbing in Wales.'

'Well, that's quite a new reason,' said Miss Hignett, appearing pleased. 'Wales, did you say? A brother of mine used to be keen. Had you any particular job here in mind?'

'I don't know nothing about it,' Cathy said, but, suddenly remembering Harry Rimmer, added, 'though if it's all the same to you I'd like to move about a bit. I don't want to get stuck again.'

'You can start on Monday in the calendering,' said Miss Hignett. Cathy had no idea what calendering was, but supposed she would learn.

Breaking the change to her mother was, as she had foreseen, unpleasant.

'What's the matter with where you are now?' demanding Mrs. Canning. 'You earn good money and get treated right. All you think about is having a good time.'

'I'll earn as much at the laundry when I'm used to it. Till then I can't give you more than thirty bob a week.'

'A nice thing!' cried Mrs. Canning. 'And after all your dad and I done for you.' She had made this remark so often that she was genuinely convinced of its truth.

'Well, Dad's bringing you home ten quid. You ought to manage.'

'You know as well as I do your dad may be paid off any time.'

'If he is, I'll make it forty bob. But I've a right to my own life, and I must look decent—' Mrs. Canning in her mind completed the sentence: *for my new friends*. She stared at the table, flushed and angry, not so much at the drop in income as at the notion that her daughter was despising her home. She had no words to express this, however. She said on her old whining note:

'Girls like you haven't a notion what a little way money goes.'

'Thirty bob is all I can manage,' replied Cathy in harsh exasperation. 'It's about enough too, considering the sort of home we got.'

As soon as the words were out she was sorry. Loyalty to Mum was an unwritten tenet of Tooley Street. You could curse the Government, your job, your house and the landlord responsible for it, but you always ended with the qualification that our Mum was a wonder the way she made the best of things. Mrs. Canning was, for once, shocked and wounded into complete silence. 'Mum—' began Cathy, trying to unsay it, but her mother turned and walked out of the room.

Oh God, I'm a bad girl! Cathy thought, really knowing guilt. First I go with Leonard and then I say that to Mum. If I start a baby I won't have a friend in the world.

When, two days later, the efficacy of Mr. Head's precautions were confirmed, her spirits bounded up again. Cae Capel and a new job lay ahead; life was opening out at last; nobody need ever know. She could find no change whatever in herself except that, now she knew what it was all leading up to, she had quite lost her longing to be taken to the pictures.

ii

She flagged a lorry on the Holyhead Road, taught by experience that lorry-drivers had kinder hearts than private motorists and less inclination to funny business. The lorry-driver informed her gravely that his firm didn't let him give lifts and he ran the risk of losing his job. Then he opened his cabin door.

It was a day of bright, windy sunshine, more like spring than early October; and as they reached Llanllugwy Cathy saw the great Welsh tops at last. The road forked and another valley opened out, with four great blue mountains grouped at its farther end.

'Would that be Snowdon?' she asked the driver.

'Blest if I know,' he replied. He had come that way twice a week for a year, and it all looked alike to him.

They swung right, and the four peaks were lost; they climbed again to the long lake, so steely a week ago, and now it was blue and rippling and a man was fishing from a boat in the middle. On every side were great mountains; a peak with three startling rock heads dominated the scene. And right at the top of the pass came the house of Cae Capel, shuttered and silent as ever. 'You stopping here?' said the lorry-driver. 'Well, no accounting for tastes.'

Cathy had confidently expected her friends to be waiting on the doorstep, but its only occupant was a plump young woman who greeted her with enthusiasm.

'They don't open till five. I meant to take a walk, but, whew, I got so hot pushing the bike up the pass.' She waved a hand in the direction of Anglesey.

'I was meeting a couple of chaps,' said Cathy, very flat.

'Well, you could hardly expect them to stay in on a day like this?' said the young woman reasonably. 'Anyway you've got me to talk to. I like talking. That's the worst of going off hiking on your own, you sometimes don't open your mouth all day. But my hubby and I can't ever go together because one of us has to look after the kids.'

'You married?' Cathy asked, surprised that anyone who had achieved that settled state should still hanker after the outdoor life.

'Mother of two, that's me. My hubby and I each take a week-end off a month. Well, what I said to him was, we only got the one life, and the kids'll be all the better for having a mum and dad that's seen the world a bit. Anyway, we've got different tastes. I like mountains, and he likes crowds. He's a scream, is my hubby. His idea of fun is rubbing shoulders with folks all day long in Blackpool or Douglas and not speaking to a soul.'

'I daresay that's his story,' said Cathy pertly, and regretted it, for her new acquaintance turned on her a look not without dignity and answered: 'I can trust him, don't you worry. I'm one of the lucky ones. I like to go dancing with the boys myself, but there's no one in the world for me but him.'

'You certainly got it all taped.'

'Yes, I've seen most of the Welsh hostels since we moved up to Warrington three years ago. I was at Lanloogy last time. Aren't these Welsh names the limit? You'd think I was a Welshy by my name, Gwen Evans, but I'm a proper Cockney. I never saw a mountain till we came north, but then I just knew it was the life for me. Lanloogy's a big hostel compared to this, but it's not so homey, and Miss Elliott's tops. I'd come here oftener, but you can't get in in the summer unless you book weeks ahead. Place gets full up with these climbers.'

'I'm going climbing,' Cathy proudly said.

'What, with a rope? My, you have a nerve.'

'It's a sight more dangerous without one,' said Cathy, mindful of the Slabs; and at that moment a motor cycle skidded to a stop in front of them, bearing Harry and Stan. They had not forgotten her, after all. More, they had, as Harry saw no harm in pointing out, come down off Tryfan at a run in order to give her two hours' coaching on the boulders before supper. 'You come too, and have a shot,' he said to Gwen, being evidently in the mood for well-doing on a large scale.

'Try anything once, that's my motto,' agreed Gwen cheerfully, and followed him round to the back of the house.

The so-called boulders were, in fact, the little precipice in the hollow of which the house had been set. They were nowhere more than twenty feet high, but extremely steep, and scratched to marble by innumerable hostellers' nails. Stan put on the rope and shinned up them in a moment. Harry remained below to give instruction and advice.

'First of all, here's how you make a bowline. Twiddle. Rope round you. End through the twiddle, under the whole doings, round and back through the twiddle. Now you do it.'

Cathy could do it at the third try. Gwen seemed unable to grasp it at all. 'Just you tie me tight, chum,' she said at length. Harry smiled at her indulgently. With Cathy he seemed to have an altogether different standard.

'Now up you go, and remember what I told you last time. Hold well out from the rock and feel before you make a move.'

Stan's route was not quite so hard as it looked. Cathy joined him triumphantly, and was rewarded by a fore-shortened view of Gwen, flapping like a large flounder on the end of a line.

She perceived now what Miss Elliott had meant by aptitude. Evidently she had a little, and poor Gwen had none. She was a tough young woman who could ride a bicycle up the savage hill from Bangor, but she was totally lacking in the spring and sense of balance needed to get her vertically into the air. It would have been heartless to laugh at her had she not found it so humorous herself. 'My,' she gasped between flounderings, 'aren't I awful? Aren't I a scream? Aren't I a yell?'

'I'm coming up,' called Harry when eventually she was landed, 'and Cathy will belay me.' Stan explained the principle; you tied yourself to a knobble of rock and took in the rope round your body. If the second fell, his weight came on you without pulling you off.

'Now you climb down,' ordered Harry, arriving. That, of course, was much worse. You couldn't see the holds, it took nerve to lean out from the rock, and you constantly left your hands behind. Gwen was allowed to walk off round the back.

They worked their way through what was evidently a graded routine, each climb being a little harder and giving practice for the next. To Gwen the young men were infinitely charming, dismissing her fears that she was holding the party back. 'We wouldn't have missed you for worlds,' said Harry. No one praised Cathy, who thereby divined that she was doing all right.

The house was by now open, and hostellers arriving, and a dress-circle of spectators gradually formed. Presently they were joined by a real girl climber, carrying a rope. She had hair set in hard, neat waves, and a plain face which was yet extremely self-confident. 'That's right,' she said to Harry. 'Doing your good deed for the day.'

'This is Doreen Lord, the queen of Cae Capel,' introduced Harry, who happened to be on the ground at the moment. 'When you climb as well as she does I'll be satisfied.'

Doreen Lord gave Cathy a patronising smile. 'I hear you got stuck on the Slabs,' she said, and Cathy was disposed of. 'I say, Harry, have you heard that

Johnny was on Clogwyn d'ur Arddu today? Says he's done Longland's. Though of course you can't always believe what he says.'

'Pity he didn't take you with him to check up,' answered Harry, sounding cross.

'Oh, I know my limits. I believe he wants someone to second him up the north wall tomorrow. You'll be tied up, of course. Are you trying to kid that poor girl she'll ever climb?'

'No,' said Harry shortly, 'she just happened along. Johnny Hollinger's crag-happy, if you ask me. These RAF types are apt to be not quite right in the head. Now then, Cathy, you do the route to the right. It has a tricky move near the top.'

Cathy approached the rock with a hot face. She had not followed all the finer points of Miss Lord's conversation, but she understood that Harry was being pitied for having landed himself with two beginners and missed some splendid opportunity, and that Miss Lord was an enemy and would like to see her fall off. She also wished heartily that Miss Lord were not staying to see.

A hush fell on the gallery, and the concentrated interest from behind seemed to brace her. Up she went, confidently, to the tricky move. A sloping foothold should be compensated by a nice nicky handhold; she knew that now. But she could find nothing to hold on to except the flat ledge at the top.

She thought for a long time, the silence growing tense below her; then launched out, and came off. Ping! – went the rope as it took her weight, and worked up, cruelly, under her armpits. Stan lowered her gently to the stance.

'Just have another try,' came Harry's voice, comforting, from below.

Sheer rage lent her wings. It wasn't a question of anything, really, except throwing yourself at it, and showing that bitch – Perhaps Stan helped just a little. Anyway, there she was, and the gallery cheered.

'Well done, ducks,' murmured Gwen. 'Mud in her eye.' And Stan opened his sealed lips to whisper the perfect consolation. 'I've seen her come off that,' he said.

'Not so bad for a start,' said Harry, coiling the rope at the bottom, for it was now supper-time. Doreen Lord had walked away.

Within doors, Miss Elliott gave Cathy her sweet smile of recognition; but she was much preoccupied, and wore the strained air of the naturally unassertive person compelled to exercise authority. 'Doreen and Molly will show you where you sleep,' she said.

They followed Doreen and Molly reluctantly, though in fact Molly seemed a meek and amiable girl, understandably overawed by her commanding friend. The women's dormitory had a big window looking down the pass. Two-tier iron bunks were ranged round the walls. Gwen took the bottom bunk. 'I've climbed enough to last, thanks,' she explained.

The common-room was immediately below, and had the same noble view. It was shabby and inviting, with many battered armshairs, a piano, and a newly lit fire crackling into life.

The hostel was liberally hung with notices, all lettered in the same beautiful hand, so that one did not immediately realize that not all of them were equally official. One over the serving-hatch in the dining room said: 'Our motto – courteous and efficient self-service.' One in the entrance hall said: 'Do not go upstairs in climbing-boots.' One in the dormitory said: 'Do not get into bed wearing climbing-boots.' One in the common-room read: 'Climbers on the summit of Tryfan jumping from Adam to Eve are requested not to take the leap in the reverse direction as this gives the stretcher party ninety feet further to go.' This last was illustrated.

'Somebody's got a queer idea of a joke,' commented Cathy after she had studied it for a while.

'That's Johnny Hollinger,' said Harry, adding self-consciously: 'I'm afraid the lettering and drawing are mine. It was one wet Sunday, when we hadn't anything better to do.'

The famous Johnny Hollinger strolled in late and sat opposite them at supper. He was a little dark monkey, with uncommonly long arms and bright eyes. He was flanked by admirers, and might perhaps be considered the king of Cae Capel, though it seemed possible that Harry Rimmer would dispute the title. At all events, Harry was plainly an honorary sub-warden. It was he who, after supper, set the men to work. '*The warden is not here to wait on hostellers*,' he quoted loudly from the official handbook. 'Where's that cad Johnny got to? I don't care if he has led Longland's. It's damn well his turn to chop the wood.'

Gwen and Cathy, under Miss Elliott's direction, washed up in the pantry at a sink marvellously hedged with drying-racks. Alongside was the stove where the self-cookers made their unsavoury brews. The beautiful kitchen where Cathy had known such hospitality was, it seemed, out of bounds. Another of Harry's notices, saying harshly: 'Warden. Private. Keep out,' barred the door.

But the common-room, with all tasks done and the fire blazing, was a sufficiently delightful place. Talk buzzed; more, it raged. Doreen Lord talked climbing to a large circle. The few present who did not climb, and therefore tended to be meek, heard all about the virtues and talents of Gwen's children. Harry was arguing with Johnny Hollinger: the problem of juvenile delinquency on Merseyside, causes and cures.

'Lawks, Harry, what a crusted Tory you are,' Johnny said.

'Merely a realist,' Harry corrected. 'I admit I am fortunately placed. You with your roots in the peerage never dare be tough about the working classes, any more than Dorothy, who's for ever having to apologise for being a lady. But I come from a working-class home myself, and I say all this talk of insufficient opportunity is bosh. Unless your Borstals are in some degree punitive—'

Unused to following an abstract argument, Cathy was jerked awake by that word. It was Bill they were talking about. His bowed, desperate figure loomed through their illustrations and examples. It seemed to tower over these bright young folks, free as air. Fat lot you know about it, her heart cried bitterly to Harry. Fat lot you know.

A little elderly man who could talk of nothing but his bicycle moved to the piano and struck a few chords.

'I've heard of you,' said Harry instantly. 'You're the chap who can play whatever you're asked.'

'Eh, well, within reason,' said the little man.

'Fetch Dorothy, somebody – we'll make her sing.' The warden was dragged from her kitchen, protesting that she could only stay ten minutes. Her pretty soprano led them in the old country love-songs – all but Cathy, to whom they were quite unknown, and to whom therefore the sweet note of true passion came quite freshly, unbearably ironic and unkind.

Fat lot you know, cried her heart again, and this time it was Leonard Head who with his fatuous presence haunted the room. It isn't like that at all. It's just getting into bed with any chap that happens along. . . .

She found herself, to her horror, crying. She sniffed back the tears and hoped no one had noticed. But looking furtively round, she found two pairs of eyes on her – Johnny Hollinger's, amused and speculative, Stan Bryce's deep-set in his absurd putty-coloured face, and full of shy concern.

iii

'I hear they're taking you on Tryfan?' said Doreen Lord, patting her corrugated waves into place. Cathy knew the anger that seemed to possess her whenever this person opened her mouth, for Harry had not thought fit to communicate his plans. She lifted her shoulders sulkily, which perhaps provoked Miss Lord into continuing: 'I don't suppose you can realize what a piece of luck it is for you, having two climbers of their standard give up their time to taking you about.'

'What makes you think I don't realize it?' Cathy demanded.

'Oh well,' said Doreen lightly, 'I thought probably no one could who hadn't much experience of the climbing crowd. Harry and Stan are quite exceptional. I'm afraid most of us are a pretty selfish lot.' She went down, whistling, to her breakfast.

Johnny Hollinger likewise seemed to know all about their programme. 'Tryfan, isn't it?' he asked.

'Yes,' said Harry shortly. 'I hear you're going to the Amphitheatre.'

'Well, I don't know. It's a hell of a walk. We might wander round to Tryfan too.'

'I thought you'd outgrown it long ago.'

'Come now, does one ever outgrow the Terrace Wall?'

'Well, you won't see anything from there,' said Harry unwisely.

'Oh, won't we? You'll be on the South Buttress, then? In that case we might have a look at the Münich.' Baiting Harry was, one surmised, one of Johnny Hollinger's favourite indoor sports.

After the meal Cathy sought out Stan, who was peeling potatoes. 'You don't want to fash yourselves with me – why should you? I was soft not to see it. You tell Harry I've gone off on my own.'

'Now why on earth—' Stan put down his knife, and answered his own question. 'Eh, it's that Doreen.'

'Well, she should know.'

'I shouldn't mind her,' observed Stan, picking up the knife again. 'Reckon she was sweet on Harry.'

But of course. The obvious explanation, the one that would have stuck out a mile in Tooley Street – Cathy could have kicked herself. Something in the atmosphere of Cae Capel seemed to bemuse her wits. She laughed aloud and went off to find her boots.

It was no use being sweet on Harry, she had known that from the first; though how she could know it was strange, for never before had a young man shown an interest in anything but her sex. But Harry wasn't interested in girls at all. When he had reached a suitable position, he would no doubt marry as a matter of principle; meanwhile, he would regard Leonard Head's obsession with the utmost contempt. Cathy did not phrase it thus explicitly to herself, but it was what she meant when she applied to him Gwen's favourite description. He was a yell.

The divine weather held still. From the terrace high on the face of the great three-headed mountain one could watch white clouds moving with a startling speed across the rock-towers, and their shadows racing away across the moors towards England. Endless climbs seemed to start from here; it was a marvel how Harry knew which one to choose. But once on it, there was no mistaking the way. A rock rib, cut off by vertical drops on either side, led them delicately up into the heart of the crag.

Then, round a corner and under a huge natural roof, the character of the route changed. There were grim little chimneys, where you wedged an arm and a leg, and on aching thighbones forced a way up. There were places that looked simple and weren't. 'A little off balance here,' Harry called consolingly from above. There were places that looked horrific, and when you were actually on them were furnished with just the right holds. Through it all was the fascination of unending variety; you never made the same move twice; you never knew what next. You saw nothing, thought of nothing, but the step ahead.

Only at the belays, taking in the rope for Stan, was it possible to stare around. Then the marvel of the rock scenery, grey ribs, noses and pinnacles supported on nothing and heeling over to the Holyhead Road two thousand feet below, fairly left one astounded. That such places could exist in the same world as Tooley Street was beyond belief. Cathy, never one prone to voice enthusiasm, had it shaken out of her. 'Fancy me,' she exclaimed, 'getting here!'

'It certainly doesn't seem only a week,' Harry conceded, 'since we had to tell you not to haul on the rope.'

'Eh, I'd forgotten that. You won't ever tell on me, will you? I'm not that bad, am I?'

'You show a certain promise, and you'll show more when you can remember to think before you move.'

'Am I better than that D'reen was when she begun?'

'What on earth has that to do with it?' demanded Harry, suddenly cross. 'That's just like a woman – no abstract appreciation, everything personal and competitive. Unless you've done better than some Doreen, you don't think you've done anything. The whole superb adventure of life is reduced to a series of petty crushes and dislikes.'

Cathy, to whom these generalizations were quite novel, considered them conscientiously as she swung her legs over space and peered down to where the sound of rhythmic scratching announced the advent of Stan. 'But everybody,' she said at length. 'Not just women. 'Course I don't think about that bitch when I'm climbing. But it would be grand all the same to show her where she got off. It's only like you are with Johnny Hollinger.'

'There is no sort of parallel,' said Harry, still cross. 'It's true that I'm sufficient of a realist to see Johnny's faults. He's a liar, and a shirker, and I'm not even sure that he's quite honest. But he's always good for a laugh, and the prettiest performer on rock that I'm ever likely to see, and it doesn't worry me in the least that I shall never be in his class. On the contrary, just to think of the way he climbs does me good. So shucks to you.' Stan's face, grinning broadly, appeared under their boot-nails.

Hours passed, or it might be minutes; one lost all sense of time; the mountain seemed infinitely and delectably high. Stan, invited into the lead, vanished up a thin and arrow-straight chimney. She followed; it was delightful. A thin leaf of rock down the middle of the chimney turned it into a ladder, and one swarmed up with a foot on either side. And then, suddenly, one put one's head out into the sunshine and sat on the top of everything, to find Stan, and beside him Johnny and his climbing partner and Gwen and the two girl hikers from the hostel who had all been sitting silently round waiting for the rabbit to pop out of the hole. A wild round of cheering greeted her, and an echo from the central peak – for they were on the south one – flung their voices back. Cathy added her shrieks to theirs, in uncontrollable exaltation – the din was tremendous. Two middle-aged climbers swinging down from the summit glanced at them stonily. One observed to the other, in that cultivated southern voice that carries so far:

'My fault, old man, for dragging you up Tryfan on a Sunday afternoon.' Harry emerged from the hole just in time to hear it.

'Lord, did you see who that was?' he said, his grin fading. 'One of them was Sharland, the Everester – I've heard him lecture. Seems to think he owns the place; I suppose they get that way when they've gone high enough. All the same, it's a pity you had to pick that moment to behave like a bank holiday outing.'

'Oh, be damned to him!' said Johnny. 'We're the real heroes. We brought some beer up the Terrace Wall for you to celebrate in.' And certainly nothing had ever tasted half so good.

'Is there any of Dorothy's fruit-cake left?' Harry peered into the sack. 'What a cook that woman is. To think of it all going in the end to fatten a professor of economics.'

'Has she got a boy, then?' Gwen asked.

'Yes, indeed. Very much so. He isn't quite a professor yet. She's just slumming till he becomes one.'

'Grow out of this inverted snobbery, Mr. Rimmer,' Johnny earnestly advised. 'I wonder what it'd be like to be in bed with Dorothy? Nice, I should think; cool and sweet. Rather like one of those pink satin suckies that fizz in the middle.'

'Keep your foul mouth off Dorothy. And in front of the lasses, too.'

'Oh, I wouldn't want to hurt anyone's feelings. I'm sure it would be equally nice to be in bed with Cathy. Rather like—'

Stan put an enormous paw over Johnny's monkey-mouth. Cathy shrieked anew with laughter. She did not in the least mind smut, and in any case put down all this talk of beds as bravado. None of them knew a thing, really; and she almost began to feel herself a partaker in their noisy innocence.

They moved on to the high central summit, crowned by the two great monoliths of Adam and Eve. Getting up on to each was quite hard enough; the leap from one to the other could not be contemplated. Johnny, however, performed it with ease; Harry a trifle less easily, so that one caught one's breath. Stan devoted himself to hoisting up Gwen, who as usual stuck gamely and declared herself a yell, and the two girls, who were more agile but less game and did not conceal their trepidation.

There had been talk of another climb, but it died away like the breeze, and they all lay supine in the yellow autumn sun. Then suddenly it seemed to be late and there was panic – had they forgotten it was Sunday evening? – hurry, hurry, run. The four boys shot down the tourist track home, and Cathy, already more of a mountaineer than the others, was left to shepherd them on the white-scratched path, watching them slither in their nail-less shoes, urging them to walk and not sit, and in the places where it was necessary to sit, encouraging them with push and pull to make any progress at all. The last stretch, along the road by the lake, seemed footsore and wearisome, and Gwen, who had dropped behind, exclaimed: 'Gosh, if you could see your seat!'

Cathy put a hand behind her and could feel the slit. The flimsy texture of the cheap flannel had disintegrated. The girls giggled, and she made herself laugh, but it was not so funny. Her appearance at the hostel caused gales of mirth and again she forced a grin, but there were tears behind her eyes. All very well for them; they could just go into a shop and buy some more; fat lot they knew. . . .

'Let me see the damage,' said the warden after supper, having set the scoffers to wash up. And so at last Cathy found herself back in that enchanting kitchen, more than ever magical now that the mountain night was closing in against its deep-set windows.

'You could put on a false seat. Everybody does, it's the sign of a serious climber. But there's no wear in this stuff. Oh, but I know, I have the very thing. Land Army corduroys—' she rummaged in a drawer of the Welsh dresser. 'Here we are – I bought them cheap for climbing, but they were too small. They should just fit you.'

'Eh, but I couldn't—' Cathy began.

'If you don't take them I shall only cut them up for dusters.' There was no thanking her; no need to feel overwhelmed, either; for the first time in her life Cathy knew affection for another woman. 'Do sit down, the boys won't be ready for another half hour. I haven't had a chance to talk to you. D'you like it here?'

'Eh, but it's the finest place I was ever in,' Cathy said. To be sitting in the sacred kitchen, wearing the new corduroys, with the delicious stiffness of unaccustomed exercise settling on her, was to know utter contentment.

'They're nice, aren't they, Stan and Harry? They always make me laugh, somehow. I don't know what I'd do without them. Thcy come practically every weekend, and they get me in enough fuel to last till mid-week. Harry says you came up Gashed Crag like a bird.'

'Well, he didn't say so to me.' She knew an added glow. 'Reckon I was pretty awful really. You ought to have seen me stuck in that bottom chimney. Enough to make a cat laugh. But it was fun getting to the top – we all screamed like mad. Two chaps looked at us as if we were dirt. Harry said one of them had been up Everest – Sharland, is it?'

'How disgusting!' said the warden warmly. 'Yes, I know James Sharland. He often stays at the club-hut down the road. It's monstrous the way these people will behave as if they owned the earth. Heaven knows they make enough noise themselves when a few of them get together.'

'But maybe,' said Cathy tentatively, 'we didn't ought to have shouted?'

'Nonsense, why shouldn't you? It's a perfectly legitimate way of letting off steam.'

'Do you shout when you get to the top?'

'Well, yes, I'm sure I must do, often.' Something in that earnest enquiry made her add, rather shyly: 'The only reason for keeping quiet is that sometimes you imagine – well – that you can sort of hear the mountain. But of course that's just being fanciful.'

'Ay,' said Cathy, 'I daresay.' Her gaze, travelling lovingly round the room, came to rest on a coloured picture of a swarthy young man. 'Harry says you got a boyfriend. Is that him?'

'Oh dear no, that's Van Gogh's postman's son. But I'll tell Michael. He ought to feel flattered.'

'He'll see you got some pretty ignorant friends, then,' said Cathy, relapsing into surliness; and saw from Miss Elliott's stricken expression that surliness was not called for. To make amends she added sheepishly: 'I hope for all our sakes you're not thinking of getting wed just yet?'

'Oh, not for another year, anyway. It all hangs on Michael's getting a professorship, and he's young for that yet. We can afford to wait.' But she sighed. What does she want to change for? Cathy thought. It's perfect here; nothing else would be half as good, if she only knew . . . For a moment they were both melancholy; then the warden resumed her bright, professional manner.

'What you say is nice and flattering, but of course there would always be somebody glad to take on a job like this. We're none of us really missed.'

'Everything oke, Dorothy,' announced Harry, who was privileged to enter at any time. 'We'd best be getting along. You ready, Cathy? – because you can sit on behind Stan, he's got the better pillion. What about next weekend?'

'I can some up with you on Friday night – that is, if you really mean it. I changed my job, like you said. I start in a laundry tomorrow.'

Harry was much amused. 'Can it be that I have at last met a woman capable of taking my advice? If so, the prospect before you is bright.'

'Just let him run your life,' murmured Stan over Harry's shoulder. Miss Elliott laughed, and came out on to the steps to watch them go.

It was now night, and the exodus was very nearly general. A group on bicycles, Gwen among them, slipped away down the pass to catch a train at Bangor, their rear lights bobbing red long after their voices had faded. Walkers piled into a friendly lorry. Cathy, perched on top of Stan's rope and rucksac, turned for a last look at the house and the slender figure in the lighted doorway. Then the bend hit it, and they were enfolded in the darkness of the long road home.

But it was not utterly dark. The road shone like a steel ribbon under the light of stars that were enormous in the clear mountain air. The triple peak of Tryfan stood out like black fretwork against them. Llanllugwy was a line of bigger stars; then came a stretch where the river roared close beside the road, and they descended steeply into deeper darkness. All the journey back was magical; even Queensferry, even the dreary outskirts of Birkenhead were transformed into lines and loops of light.

They set her down by the bus-stop, and were off again almost before she had roused herself to thank them. Indeed, it was the well-doing Harry himself who voiced the general satisfaction. 'Ay, lass,' he called back over his shoulder, dropping into the native idiom which with him was a sign of profound contentment, 'but it were a champion weekend.'

CHAPTER THREE

From that time on, her living was the Stonyhey Laundry in Lower Tranmere, and Cae Capel was her life.

It was a long time before the laundry became as profitable as the factory had been, owing to her determination not to remain in a groove; but it was decidely more satisfying. Miss Hignett was an employer who liked initiative. She moved continually round the works, taking the right amount of notice of everyone. Pigeon-holed in her orderly mind were their names, backgrounds, families, and tastes or hobbies where these occurred. She kept her information up to date by the simple method of frequent inquiry. Old Nosey, the girls called her, and affected to find her interest comical; but they were quick to feel slighted if it seemed to flag. They would even sometimes show a mild jealousy of her favour, which Cathy, her own small capacity for hero-worship absorbed elsewhere, regarded with sardonic amusement.

Every Friday she took her rucksac to work, and at a quarter-past six precisely Stan and Harry would pick her up at the street corner. By nine they were at Cae Capel, eating the meal kept hot for them by the devoted warden; but indeed most of the weekend contingent, who came from jobs of one sort or another, arrived late on Friday nights. By ten next day, wet or fine, they were on the crags.

To Cathy the glorious violence of the transition never paled. All week she lived for it; it glowed inside her with a secret pleasure, and often as she watched the sheets coming smooth out of the great rollers a spasm of fierce joy would transform her face. 'Penny for your thoughts,' said her opposite number jocularly the first time it happened; and she was able to reply with perfect truth, though she did not endear herself by so doing: 'I couldn't begin to make you understand.'

It was going at one bound from the bottom to the top; from the sordid noise of Tooley Street and the cheerful noise of the laundry to the great gaunt silence of the rain-swept precipice; from the dull plod of shoes on pavements to the delicate dancer's touch of a tiptoe nail on a tiny hold; from apathetic safety to danger and life. And it all happened so suddenly, in that brief blank of space and time when one clung on to Stan's belt and pushed, head downwards into the Welsh rain.

For after that first weekend it was usually wet. It made no difference; they would have scorned to let any but the worst weather hold them back. Cathy, like the boys, bought an oilskin cape and sat in it as in a tent; nothing of her showed but her little sallow face, and that would presently be whipped pink by the wind. All her spare money went on climbing equipment; she had ceased to care what she looked like at home. Nothing mattered now except the feel of the crag, and the scent of the wet rope on it, and the gradual, splendid confidence of a body learning what it needed to know.

The other lesson it had needed to know was almost forgotten. Leonard Head's very face had faded; all she knew of him was that he had been a bore. Even poor Bill, who had been her true friend, paled as the weeks went by. So much was happening to her that he could have no share in; maybe the same was true of him. Only his monthly letters to his mother, ill-spelt and pitiful (for he had left school almost illiterate and had been taught to write in the Army), brought him momentarily back to sting her with their unspoken reproaches. 'It is not so bad here,' he wrote; but who was to be sure that wasn't what they made him say? And always the same ending: 'All the best Mum and give my love to Cathy,' framed in a child's line of crosses.

Mrs. Powell spared Cathy nothing. That was fair enough; it was her business to stick by her son, though she had been by no means so welcoming to a possible daughter-in-law while he still had an untarnished name. Like Cathy's mother and the rest of the street, she was resentful and suspicious of these mysterious week-ends. There must be a chap in it somewhere, and as for this hostel, it sounded like a tale. Then some young woman walked out of it and lost herself for three days on the hills, with climbers and quarrymen and finally an aeroplane looking for her. Cae Capel had its picture in the papers, and so did Miss Dorothy Elliott, the warden, who was directing the search-parties. Cathy was in a fever of excitement, buying every edition of the evening papers, and continually lamenting that she was not there to help. The street was obliged to concede that that was where she went.

The next time she brought home some climbing snapshots of herself, which

Mrs. Canning, unwillingly impressed, stuck up over the mantelpiece. 'Fancy our Cath!' she said, not without pride. 'Break her neck one of these days, I reckon.' The street stared and gaped and felt shivers up its spine. It was Cathy, sure enough, hanging like a fly on the wall, and stretching away out of the picture was the rope up which presumably she was about to climb. The lass must have a screw loose, which, come to think of it, was what the street had always suspected.

Stan Bryce, it will be realized, had a gift for mountain photography; and the elimination of telltale foregrounds was a study to which he had devoted years of care.

ii

Cathy had been six times to Cae Capel before ever she went to the summit of a mountain, other than that of Tryfan, on which the climbs finished. This essential step in her education she finally owed to her enemy, Doreen Lord.

Not that Harry was without conscience in the matter. He constantly deplored the view of nature as a gymnasium and of mountains as greased poles. So did all the climbers at the hostel; they regularly condemned mere athleticism; all, that is, except Johnny Hollinger, who seemed incapable of any decent pretence. His attitude to the view from the top was summed up in the words of his favourite author: *Let us face it, beauty is a bit of a bore*.

Cathy paid lip-service to the general opinion merely in order to keep Harry quiet, but naturally she heeded his practice rather than his professions. He and Stan never went to summits, and nor did she. When they had finished a climb they went down it again, or scrambled off by an easy way, and went up another. Summits were for walkers, dear souls like Gwen, who had to reach them in order to have anything to talk about. She was at some pains to avoid displaying Doreen's contemptuous attitude to the walker, but she knew herself dedicated to finer things.

That she should have an enemy at Cae Capel did not worry her. She had always had a good sprinkling of enemies, and would have thought herself of small account without one. The only mortifying circumstance was that the creature scarcely seemed to know how much she was detested. One evening she flung across the table:

'Care to tie on behind Molly and me for a change?'

Cathy could scarcely believe it. The foe was delivered into her hands. To respond magnanimously did not occur to her.

'Behind you?' she said. 'You're nuts.'

Doreen stared in purest astonishment; then she slowly reddened. 'I take it that's the local way of saying No thank you. That's the thanks one gets for trying to do the Christian thing and take a bit of the weight off a pal. I suppose you'll go on clinging round Harry's neck for the rest of your life.' She marched off to find Harry and, as it turned out, give him her version first.

Harry was really angry, the first time Cathy had ever known him so. His sense of fitness was outraged by this feminine squabbling among the hills.

'You know she meant it kindly,' he said. 'A climb behind another woman is just what you need next. You go and make it up.'

Her face went stony. 'I'll never,' she answered. 'Never, never. She's been a bloody bitch to me, and I wouldn't go with her, not if I never climbed again.'

'Well, if you're going to take that attitude every time someone says a few hard words to you, you soon won't go out with anybody. And that holds for Stan and me. You can enjoy your own superior company from now on.'

Sheer rage bore her up in the face of the unexpected and dreadful blow. She stormed out of the house to avoid the humiliation of watching all the roped parties start, and was half-way up the Glyders almost before she realized where she was going.

The upper half was, as usual, clothed in mist. The top of the slope was a long bank of scree, and, surmounting this, she found herself on stony flatness. She peered through the white mist and saw something higher – surely the top. But when she reached it, it was merely a clump of rickety boulders, eerily magnified. From it she could make out another, huge as a castle. She hurried to that, and the same thing happened. There were summits everywhere, dozens of summits, and by the time she had made the round of them her sense of direction was gone. She was, in fact, completely lost.

It was a most effective way of cooling down. At first she grinned, her anger switching to her own stupidity; then, obscurely, she began to be frightened. And that was absurd, for of course she was perfectly safe. It was merely a question of getting down somewhere. But it was a queer place, all these stone castles, all so very untenanted. A gust of wind came suddenly screeching through the battlements of the one she was sitting on. She remembered Dorothy saying: 'If you keep quiet you can hear the mountain.' The mountain was certainly doing the talking now.

She had never been alone on a mountain, except for that first day on the Slabs. It dawned on her that she really knew nothing about mountains except how to follow Stan and Harry up a scratched route. She scarcely even knew the names of the different hills, never having listened when she was told. She had never so much as looked at a map.

That girl who had walked out of Cae Capel and been lost for three days – who had had the whole countryside looking for her – who had proved an utter fool, going off alone into the mist – that girl had done, in fact, exactly what she was doing now. She was no cleverer or better equipped, except that she was wearing stolen climbing-boots – and they only seemed to mock her. Suppose she were to be lost for three days? Suppose parties came to look for her, headed by a kind Harry and a triumphant Doreen? Better, far, be dead.

But that, of course, was nonsense. Somewhere below her lay the valley and the lake. Equally, there lay below her the line of the great climbs, and the tracks made by climbers coming off them might quite easily lure her to destruction. She started off again, and found nothing, not track nor precipice nor cairn, and never for a second a rift in the choking, claustrophobic mist.

And then at last the ground fell away. In thankfulness she followed the slope, gently, steadily down. The scree ended, and there was brown grass, and boulders which moved on her approach and turned out to be sheep. She came out of the mist with a gasp, as one who rises out of dark waters. It was raining, but that scarcely mattered. She was off the nightmare hill at length.

Not, however, to anything familiar. No road appeared, no lake; only a sea of brown moor bounded by a stone wall. She crossed this and descended again. Then came a valley floor, and a line of telegraph poles marked a road. The slate roofs of a farmhouse shone coldly blue through the rain. She ploughed her way down to it, trying to fit it in to the dimly remembered landmarks of the Holyhead Road.

It was a big, sprawling place, the house whitewashed and dignified, perched on what seemed to be the summit of a pass. A notice said: 'Apartments: Teas.' She knocked, and a thin, bright-eyed Welshwoman opened the door.

'Sorry to trouble you,' said Cathy, feeling every inch a fool, 'but could you tell me where I am?'

'This is Bryn Glas,' the woman said.

'But that's – oh, lord, I've come right over on the Snowdon side. I must be hours away from Cae Capel. Well – thanks a lot.'

'You are never going back to Cae Capel? And all wet like you are! Come in then; you will be wanting a cup of tea.'

'I'm afraid I haven't any money on me,' said Cathy, turning red. 'Thanks, though. If you could just put me on the right road—'

'Is it barbarians we are then?' exclaimed the Welshwoman indignantly. 'Oh, never you mind that notice. That's for the motorists in the summer. Come into the kitchen. We are just having tea ourselves.' She shooed Cathy into a low room that looked darkly out on to the mountainside. 'This is my brother, Mr. Williams. Evan, the young lady has come over the tops from Cae Capel. Lost, she is, and see how wet!'

Mr. Williams nodded stiffly and indicated a chair.

'And how is Miss Dorothy Elliott?' asked Miss Williams, pouring tea from a wonderful pot all over moulded roses.

'Eh, you know the warden?'

'Yes indeed, she is a good friend of ours, Miss Elliott. A pity the mountain is so high, we don't see her often. But Mr. Williams was out helping her look for the other lost young lady three weeks ago.'

'It is a nuisance they are, these young ladies, yes,' Mr. Williams pronounced.

Cathy hung her head.

'They will be going out into the mist and not knowing the hills. Then they waste our time with searching. Yes, and on a Sunday, too. No chapel for them; just walking off and getting lost.'

'Now, Evan,' protested Miss Williams kindly. 'If they live in the town and don't go out on a Sunday, when are they to see the hills?'

'Yes, it's all very well for you, Mr. Williams,' said Cathy, reviving. 'You try living where I do, behind the docks in Birkenhead, and working all week in a laundry.'

'Shocking,' said Miss Williams. 'It's sorry for you I am. What a dreadful life. There will be a lot going on, though. Always plenty of company.' She sighed. 'And a laundry too, that will be interesting. Here we don't get a lot of company, not in the winter. A fair treat it is to see anyone. I wish there were more getting lost, if they would all find their way down here.'

Cathy thus became aware that gossip was the best return she could make for her tea. She told Miss Williams all about the laundry and the hostel, and aired her view of Miss Elliott's young man, she and Miss Williams being of one mind that he ought to come and visit Miss Elliott, and must be a proper stuck-up Oxford type, too grand for hostels and simple Welsh ways.

In return she was given a second-hand but gruesome description of the state the lost young lady was in when found, and of bodies recovered by Mr. Williams, some alive, some dead. Miss Williams knew just how each one had looked, though she herself never went up the hill and scarcely stirred out of the house, being, like so many of her countrywomen, terrified of the wild. Mr. Williams contented himself with expressions of godly disapproval, and each time Cathy cocked an eye at him and grinned, for she had almost at once divined that he was no more to be dreaded than his voluble and charming sister. The good food and tea, coming after hours of cold and panic, had on her almost the effect of alcohol, and presently she became quite cheeky, and began poking fun at the Welsh place-names.

'It is a very simple principle,' said Mr. Williams, allowing himself to be drawn. 'We have a phonetic spelling that any fool can understand, except the English, of course. But you seem not so stupid as the most of the English, so I will teach it to you. Listen you now.' At the end of the lesson she could get her tongue round Llanllugwy and remember Cymru am byth, and the brother and sister appeared immensely gratified.

A darkening of the little windows brought her to her feet in dismay. It was five, and she was hours from home. 'I do not like to drive my motor on a Sunday,' said Mr. Williams, and rose majestically to fetch it from its shed.

She sat beside him in the rattling old farmer's car, watching the Llanllugwy road unroll in the rain, and her afternoon seemed to her delightful, with the same sense of belonging that she always felt in Dorothy's kitchen. 'They're nice Welshies,' she thought with surprise, for Welshies counted as foreigners in Tooley Street and as such were disliked. But as they reached the familiar fork and turned up towards Cae Capel, her heart grew cold again. The liking of elderly Welshmen could hardly compensate for that of one's climbing friends. A motor-cyclist shot downhill towards them, and pulled up with a grinding of brakes. It was Harry.

'Hello, Mr. Williams, I was just coming for her. We reckoned she'd be round at your place. Miss Williams keeping well? – that's grand. Next fine day we get we'll be dropping in to tea. So long.' Cathy, by this time transferred to his pillion, watched her benefactor vanish, waving, into the rain.

'But how could you tell?' she meekly asked.

'Lord bless you, the top of the Glyders is notorious. Sooner or later everyone comes down on the Snowdon side. Not that that's any excuse, of course,' he added severely. 'I'll give you a compass for Christmas.'

Cathy dug her chin affectionately into the wet oilskin of his shoulder. She had him back, and presently began to surmise why. Doreen – she heard it with a jealous pang – had been invited to join their rope. 'She did all right,' said Harry coldly, and nothing more. But it was evident that Doreen, unable to let well alone, had somehow returned to the attack. I belong here, too, thought Cathy joyously; and knew that she was sufficiently his creation never to be quite cast away.

But if he had forgiven her, she had not utterly forgiven him. Perhaps she was incapable of complete forgiveness. A kind act might be forgotten, but a slight was stored up in her heart for ever. Under her affection there lurked, without her being able to help it, the ghost of a grudge. Not to be beholden – that was the thing to aim at. Not to be ordered about by any chap, or blackmailed with dreadful threats into what others considered right behaviour. 'I'll show them,' she thought, even as her fingers caressed his shoulder. 'Soon I'll show them.' And this time it was not her enemies who were to be shown, but her allies, her benefactors, her own dear friends.

iii

It sometimes seemed to Dorothy Elliott that people were forever thanking her. In fact, she had one of those rare natures to whom it is a pleasure to be grateful. But she never received the thanks without a sense of guilt. It was no credit to her to be of service. It was her happiness, her way of expressing herself. Denied any creative ability, she lived by fostering the abilities of others. It was nothing more, she had often unhappily thought, than a form of battening.

Michael Derwent, her young man, had quickly understood her craving and done his best to satisfy it. He demanded insatiably, and never worried her with gratitude. They had met at Oxford, where both were reading Modern Greats, he with the intention of becoming an economist and she of devoting her life to social service. But it soon began to seem a great deal easier to devote her life to Michael. His tennis sweaters had hung to dry on half the radiators in Somerville.

Their engagement had caused her to revise her ideas; that, and the fiasco of her degree. She had taken a third. Young women were not sent to Oxford – occupying sought-after places which others might have filled more worthily – in order to take thirds. The disgrace had crushed her, and she would not take the easy excuse and put the blame on falling in love. That should no more have distracted her than others were distracted by rowing or dramatics. She simply had no brains.

Michael, fresh from his own triumph, was charming about it. It was his degree they would ultimately live on, he pointed out, not hers. The engagement was to be a long one, and the urge to serve her fellows still burned within her, but she could face no more examinations. She abandoned further studies in social science, and, having always been domestically capable – 'Dorothy is a real home-maker,' her mother had frequently boasted, thereby helping to drive her into the academic maw – she had for three years run canteens in the East End. Then she was offered the wardenship of Cae Capel. It sounded perfect, and it had proved so. Her eighteen months in the mountains had been the happiest of her life.

She had done well, and knew it. Theoretical economics were beyond her, but the practical economics needed to run a continually changing household in a spot eight miles from a market town were magnificently within her grasp. With no help more skilled than that of Margiad, the daughter of the farm down the pass, she had turned it into the best-loved small hostel in North Wales. She had given herself to it with joy, adoring the spaciousness of the winter weeks when few walkers came, and she had time to wander on the hills or read Dorothy Wordsworth by the fire; adoring the week-ends, when the noisy crowds poured in from Merseyside and Manchester, and it was her pride to welcome them out of the urban darkness. Her splendid food and fires made amends to them for having so little, when she seemed to herself to have so much.

She had been, perhaps, just a trifle disappointed to find that most of them were not precisely under-privileged. There was an element of truth in Harry Rimmer's jibe that she had gone slumming. But visitors from the slums were rare. Most of the hostellers were students, only temporarily penniless, or office workers quite as well paid as herself. Johnny Hollinger, whose father was an earl, had proved much closer to the type than Cathy Canning from the Birkenhead docks.

Hence it was that Cathy, from the first, had been to her an object of uncommon interest. Girls from the working class were not unknown at Cae Capel, but most of them were cyclists; the rock-climbers came higher in the social scale. The spirit which was impelling this little pavement flower to seek out not only wild nature, but nature apprehended through the most dangerous of sports filled Dorothy with delighted admiration. The figure of Cathy Canning symbolized for her an achievement which made her job worth while.

For Cae Capel was moulding Cathy; it was absorbing to watch the changes in her as the week-ends flashed by. She was not now invariably on the defensive. She still had her bouts of savage noise, but she was capable of listening to a rational argument, even, occasionally, of joining in. She provided Harry, Dorothy surmised, with a stimulating contrast to the silent acquiescence of Stan. Physically the improvement was as striking. When she first came she had had nothing of beauty but her great mane of red hair. But now she was losing that water-rat look; her face was filling out and taking on a faint colour, and her eyes, without that challenging stare, were the blue-grey of moonstones. She still looked hard-bitten, but then she was; no girl could have kept up, uncomplaining with two young men at the height of their muscular powers without an excessive amount of will and guts. She would never be really beautiful, because her features were too sharp. But she did not need beauty. She had a more than common share of the quality the French call *chien*.

At this point in her meditation upon her little favourite, Dorothy would sigh. She was not without her own admirers; there were, in fact, several diffident young men who would have liked to marry her if they could have detached her from Michael Derwent; but they loved her for her virtues, and she felt herself deficient in the quality the French call *chien*. I'm the sort, she would reflect with a wry smile, that people settle down with in the end.

But Cathy – before Cathy, now, there was surely some future of high excitement. She might do great things, lead a strike of laundry-girls, perhaps, or go completely to the bad; or she might marry a drunkard and have fourteen children and bring them up respectable by the skin of her teeth. One could not imagine her life being quiet, or even perhaps happy, but she ought to be helped to make it outsize. If she'd had a fraction of my opportunities, thought Dorothy Elliott, and sighed again.

She stood now hopefully in the kitchen doorway, still glowing from encounters with Lliwedd and, subsequently with her new friend, Mr. Williams Bryn Glas, whose esteem she had been able to show off to Harry and Stan. 'Quite the little pet, aren't you?' had commented Harry rather crossly, for he himself had known Mr. Williams well, and helped to carry the bodies about for the last two years. Dorothy half-listened, preoccupied with her dishing up, and then perceived there was more to come.

'Harry says I can lead the Amphitheatre Buttress next week.'

'Does he? Oh, my dear, how exciting. I am glad. Your first lead; what fun.'

'I call it soft.'

'Oh, surely not. It's a fine climb.'

'I don't mean the climb. I mean leading them. What's the use of me leading them? They'll only be doing it to please the baby.'

'Nonsense. It'll be the crown of their achievement.'

'I dunno about that. Look here, Dorothy. There's only eight of us in. If I helped you – I'd do all the vegs – and we left everything ready and Margiad put on the spuds, you wouldn't come with me up it tomorrow?'

Dorothy straightened up from the oven. 'But Cathy – the weekend's my busy time.'

'It's the only time I'll ever have. Of course you could manage it if you wanted.'

'I do want. I'd adore. But what about Harry? Wouldn't it be rather hard on him?'

'He'll get over it. Anyway, it was he said I ought to go with another woman; you remember, that day I wouldn't go with Doreen. If you won't, I'll make Gwen. She's always game. But I reckon she'll stick.'

The urgent appeal behind the uneloquent words touched Dorothy. She appreciated, quite as well as Doreen could, Cathy's good fortune, but she was able to guess that it must be galling to feel oneself perpetually under an obligation, when one also felt oneself to be socially inferior and without any possibility of making a return. She said thoughtfully:

'At a pinch, I suppose I could give them stew.'

The joy that transformed the sallow little face was comical. 'You won't let on to anyone, will you?' muttered Cathy, and vanished.

They slunk out of the house like truant schoolgirls next day, though the rest had been gone half an hour before. Even Cathy was subdued, the genuine concern of Harry and Stan over her headache – for they had never known her ail before – lying on her conscience. They left Dorothy's car at the farm under Pen Helyg, and plodded up its great green slopes and down the other side in silence.

The walk to the crag was a long one, and therefore seldom taken with so many other precipices close at hand. In this lonely cwm, with no habitation, no track, scarcely even a view, one felt cut off from friendship and succour; it resembled a Highland glen in its desolation. The great black crag hemmed in its head, and the route took no finding. It followed, relentlessly, a rib bordering one side of the great cleft that carved the precipice in two. Cathy, tight-lipped, put on the rope and ran her fingers, like a pianist warming up, over the lowest holds. 'Oke, here goes,' she said, and disappeared aloft.

Dorothy was a nice climber, graceful and neat, but she lacked the nerve to lead. It was, she shamefacedly felt, a part of her general uncreativeness. When she reached the belay she found her leader using it with classic accuracy. 'That wasn't so easy, pet,' she commented, aware of a second's duty. Cathy grinned back. The tight-lipped look was gone and a delighted confidence was taking its place.

The rib bore them upward, perpetually varied, never alarming; now parallel cracks, now a groove, now a letterbox ('Mind your head!' Cathy called, with a proper leader's care for the second), now a right-angled corner directly above the Amphitheatre, where the exposure was tremendous and one would certainly have been killed if one had let go. 'Oh, pretty,' Dorothy said, and Cathy, as they paused to eat above this, the crux, was in sheer bliss. 'You can't think how grand it is, feeling the rope run out behind you. It's like flying. Go on, Dorothy, you lead the next bit. It's not fair, me having it all.'

'No fear, I haven't the guts. Did nobody tell you what a coward I am?'

'You're a grand second. With you behind me I could climb anything. Gosh, it's wonderful being able to talk as much as I like. If I open my mouth on a climb Harry calls it woman's chatter. Though he talks enough himself about their mucky old stones.'

'Stones?'

'Yeah – ammonites and trilobites – I can't remember half the words.'

'Oh, I see, they've got to geology now. What a one Harry is for self-improvement. It was alpine flora last summer.'

'He takes home sackfuls of stones. He says they tell him what the earth was like before there were men on it. I can't see that it matters if there wasn't anyone about, can you?'

'No, I honestly can't,' Dorothy agreed. 'But of course we'd catch it for saying so.' They exchanged a smile over the whole absurd male sex, with its fossils and its specimens, its pockets full of clutter and its head of ragbag enthusiams, getting it nowhere.

The climb above the crux was even more delightful; a knife-edge which one rode on the seat of one's breeches, then a stone policeman barring the way. The great opposite wall of the Amphitheatre had opened up, a screen of crag on which Johnny Hollinger and his peers held flirtations with death; and away to the east they could look out over the green walls of the cwm to a faint line of hills.

'You see that one with the dot on it?' said Dorothy. 'That's Moel Fammau. The dot is the big cairn on top.'

'What, Moel Fammau that we see from the Wirral?'

'The same, the other way round.'

'It's like looking at home. Gosh, if they could see me now!'

'They'd be proud of you, Cathy, I'm sure.'

'Not they. They think I'm bats. Nobody understands, not even Dad.' She shook off the cloud that hung momentarily over her happiness. 'Come on, we must be nearly at the top.'

Two more rope-lengths took them out on to the great green whale-back of the Carnedds. 'We'll shout,' said Cathy. 'Everesters be damned.' Dorothy did her best, but her very shouts were ladylike, and their voices were carried away by the wind that blew over the second summit of Wales, warm with the threat of rain.

They sauntered home, flopping easily into gossip as frogs into a pond. 'Now you're a leader,' said Dorothy slyly; 'you can afford to forgive Doreen.'

'I don't see why. She got no call to be mean to me. You know what she says about me? "Cathy Canning is common as dirt".'

'Oh dear, how stupid and unoriginal. But you ought to make allowances. The poor girl had hopes of Harry, I believe. It would have been a good match for him, too. Her people have money. And she really wouldn't make at all a bad little wife; lots of push and go, and her husband's interests would be her own.'

'He don't like her,' said Cathy briefly, and Dorothy for a moment sympathized with Doreen, in whom ordinarily she sensed a faint contempt. But they were alike in this: no *chien*.

'What about your boy?' Cathy asked. 'Isn't he ever going to come here?'

'Oh, I hope so, in the summer. That would be a better time to get him interested in mountains. But it's a problem to know where to put him – I shouldn't feel happy to let him take one of the hostel beds. I suppose he could go to Mrs. Evans Parc, but she doesn't reckon to take visitors, not with Margiad out all day working for me, and it'd be a bit primitive.' Too grand for the likes of us, Cathy mentally registered, adding a notch to the tally of dislike she had been building up against Dorothy's boy.

'There's a chap wants to marry me,' she presently brought out.

'I'm sure there is,' said Dorothy smiling. 'In fact, I think I can put a name to him.'

'Reckon you can't. He's doing two years Borstal.' Her friend turned on her a startled blue gaze. And so it all came out.

The relief of telling it was astonishing. She had scarcely realized herself how Bill had ached inside her, how he had been festering, how infinitely far he was from being forgotten. Now he was displayed before a wise and detached observer, not an angry and irrational Tooley Street partisan. Now at last somebody would tell her what was the right thing to do.

Dorothy sat down on a convenient boulder stool overlooking their own valley. Below them lay the car; another half-hour would comfortably see them home. As her anxious, candid eyes surveyed the problem, she realized that she had always known there was something wrong with Cathy Canning; something more than mere social inferiority to account for her prickly defiance. Poor, plucky little creature; heaven grant that one would not fail her now.

'Poor Cathy,' she said at length, 'poor kid.' Cathy met her eyes with a look of joy; she had almost expected to be blamed and reviled again. 'You must have been through hell. But do you love him? That's what it boils down to in the end. Oh, I know it's a stupid question,' she added, watching the bright look fade and knowing that she had lost her hold, 'but I have to ask it. It's something only you can know.'

'Reckon I'm not much of a hand at loving,' said Cathy at length.

'Oh, that's nonsense.' Dorothy was vehement; to say of anyone that they were not much of a hand at loving was to her the worst insult. 'It merely means that you haven't and you don't. To marry him out of pity, or because the neighbours had blackmailed you into it, would be a dreadful mistake. No, not on any account.'

Well, there it was, good, plain, positive advice. The diffident Dorothy suddenly appeared to have the secret of life and conduct in her hand. She continued:

'Look at it this way. If it had been you and not the police who found out what he was up to, would you have married him?'

'I guess not.'

'Well, doesn't that prove that you're only sorry for him because he's been punished?'

Cathy muttered, almost angrily:

'He said he done it for me.'

'He had no right to say such a thing. Knowing you as long and well as he did, he must have known you'd disapprove. His saying it, and trying to hold you with it, shows how weak he is. To my mind it was a cowardly thing to say – worse even than the robbery. And, Cathy, marriage involves more than ourselves. You wouldn't want your children to have a weak father, and perhaps a bad strain in their turn.'

Cathy kicked a stone neatly with the big tricouni in the toe of her boot, and finally observed, her eye following it down the hillside:

'I reckon somebody's got to look after the weak ones.'

Dorothy was pulled up short. She had never meant to go so far and declare a philosophy so patently ungenerous. For of course it was true that somebody must look after the weak ones, and the only real answer she could give was: *but not you*. Not you, because you'll get somebody better; not you, because a life more satisfying and prosperous opens out before you, and you can leave your slum associates behind. That was precisely what she meant, but to say it would be to drive a girl of spirit and courage straight into the young convict's arms.

She resumed with unwonted guile:

'Of course I put it too strongly. I don't mean that you mustn't consider marrying him, only that you mustn't feel yourself bound. Wait for a year after he comes out; several years, perhaps. See if he really has it in him to stick at a steady job. And keep an open mind about the other boys you meet. Look how young you are – no need for you to be tying yourself to anybody for ages yet. I'm six years older than you, and I know my own mind, and yet I'm willing to wait.'

'Yes,' said Cathy unwarily, 'but it's all right for you. You don't really like men.'

She knew instantly that she ought not to have said this, though she had meant no harm by it, but rather to pay tribute to her friend's refinement. But she had dealt a blow.

Out of the mouth of this babe, Dorothy's hidden dread confronted her: that she would be physically inadequate for Michael, that she would disappoint him, and find herself relegated to cook and mother rather than wife. She had even offered to live with him – yes, that would astonish the cocksure little creature before her – and it was he who had declined. 'Sweet,' he had told her, 'you were born to come a blushing virgin to the bridal bed. I wouldn't anticipate that moment for the world.' She had done her best to laugh.

Cathy was plunging on:

'I mean, course you like your own boy, but you don't like being messed around by chaps, and I do. You're good and I'm bad, really, that's what I'm trying to say.' Almost Leonard Head was produced for inspection. He hovered in the wings. If in the end it proved not to be his cue, that was from no sense of shame, but simply because he had become irrelevant. He had ceased to count.

Dorothy roused herself.

'Don't worry, I understand. It's just that you've more of that sort of temperament, and I've less. I don't see that either of us need apologise. People are always setting up standards for young women, as though we weren't quite human and hadn't the right to vary.'

'Gosh, that's true,' agreed Cathy with feeling. They had reached common ground at last.

'But in point of fact, have you wanted to mess about with chaps since you started coming here? Doesn't climbing do instead?'

'I dunno. It might.'

'Well then, just keep it up. It'll take you two years at least to climb as well as Johnny Hollinger, and you'll still have a good forty left to be a wife and mother in. Why hurry to grow old and set?'

'Talking of hurry—' Cathy grinned.

'Lord, yes.' Twilight was upon them; they hurried down to the car. Margiad had opened up the hostel, and Stan came out for firewood as they approached. 'Where have you two been?' he asked.

'Amphitheatre Buttress,' said Cathy briefly. 'Will Harry be mad?' It did not occur to her to ask Stan if he were mad, nor to himself to be so.

'A bit disappointed, I guess.' He was not reproaching her; he was merely facing, with that instinctive wisdom one divined in him, the intrinsically sad and disillusioning nature of life.

Cathy followed Dorothy into the kitchen and tried to drown her guilt in the bustle of preparation for dinner. Presently she felt eyes upon her. Harry was leaning against the door.

'I hear you led the A.B.?'

'Oh, Harry!' Dorothy cried. 'You have to forgive her. She wanted a rabbit for her first lead, d'you see – to make it the real thing.'

'That's okay, seeing she didn't come off.'

'She climbs like an angel. She's exquisite, so light and sure. I had a feeling of utter confidence. Taking her on was the best day's work you ever did.'

Cathy put down her chopping-knife and went over to him. She stood twisting her hands and trying to find words. 'It was grand. Finding the belays, and feeling the rope run out, and all. It was that grand—' For the first time she was grateful to him, really and completely grateful. She thirsted to show him. If it had been a question of marrying him, or of waiting for him to come out of prison, or of sleeping with him at a seaside hotel, she would have done it gladly. But he required none of these services. To her disgust she found herself in tears.

And crying in front of Harry, who was outraged by any sort of fuss!

But this time, oddly enough, he seemed prepared to make allowances. He smote her affectionately across the shoulders and offered her his handkerchief. 'Eh-ba-goom,' he remarked in his thickest music-hall Lancashire, 'tha'rt a loopy lass and no mistake.'

iv

There was only one social distinction at Cae Capel: between those who led rock-climbs and those who did not. Cathy, having moved up into the first category, now had standing and a soubriquet. She became the Merseyside Menace, or alternatively, the Birkenhead Bombshell. Her opinion was asked for; her view of a route had weight.

'Ah yes, the Amphitheatre Buttress,' commented Doreen Lord. 'An easy Difficult, isn't it?'

She was, of course, correct. She herself led Very Difficults, and occasionally, in rubbers on dry rock, an easy Severe. Cathy still had far to go.

She went back into tutelage, except for the rare Sundays when Dorothy could snatch an hour, or the hilarious ones spent generalling Gwen up the most caddish variants on the easiest possible climbs. But for the most part she enjoyed the moral support of the ever-generous Harry and Stan. It was only moral, as Harry was fond of reminding her. Nothing, he was always saying, could save a falling leader; and with eighty feet of rope out behind her on the Slabs, and the weight of it palpable in the small of her back, she knew he spoke truth. Yet she almost never now had the sensation of fear. Her body seemed to know its way up the rock, from easy Difficult to difficult Difficult, and on beyond. Sometimes a pitch was hard, and then the rock became an enemy, a challenge, and she set her teeth. At such moments Harry's pride in her was great. He seldom commended her to her face, but he would talk of her achievements at the hostel afterwards, not thereby increasing her popularity with Miss Lord.

His devotion and Stan's were all the more meritorious because, as Cathy found with a certain artless surprise, climbing behind her made them both nervous. They were ashamed of it, but there was no mistaking it in Harry; he would grow irritable and edgy. She did not divine it in Stan till the day she led her first Very Difficult, which was Avalanche on Lliwedd. Round the tremendous corner of the first traverse, with fine footholds but nothing for the hand except a pressure on thin leaves of rock, she knew the ecstasy of dancing above thin air; there seemed nothing between her and the waters of Llydaw five hundred feet below. She was laughing when Harry joined her, saying snappishly: 'What's so funny?' But Stan's putty-coloured face when he in turn arrived was two shades greyer than usual, and he gripped the belay and panted for breath.

'Here, what the hell's up?' Harry demanded.

'Feeling queer?' inquired Cathy anxiously.

'I'm all right,' muttered Stan. 'Bit of a drop, wasn't it?'

They stared at him. 'But you don't mind exposure,' Cathy said.

'You must be off colour,' diagnosed Harry. 'Anaemic or something. I've heard it takes folks that way.'

'Oh, shut your bloody trap!' said Stan. It was the first time he had ever been known to speak rudely to Harry, or indeed to anyone. Light began to break on Cathy. And when, insisting on reversing the order of the rope, he proceeded to lead them up Red Wall, a far more difficult route than Avalanche, without turning a hair, at last she fully understood. He thinks I'll come off, she told herself, and her instant reaction was one of contempt. What a softy; poor old Stan.

V

'Guess what I've got in Parc coppice,' Dorothy said.

None of them could, of course, though they tried everything from a pet lamb to a pixie. After supper they all four walked down the pass with torches to see.

The road down the pass to Bangor contoured the hillside, but the farms lay on the valley floor and were joined to it by long stony tracks. Parc, the highest and loneliest, was invisible from the road, and all that marked the way to it was the gate and a thicket of gaunt wind-blown larches, the only sizeable clump of trees for miles. Dorothy, gleeful and secretive as a child, opened the gate and threaded her way through the trees, and on the far side, screened from sight of the road and the mountain, stood a caravan.

'I hope you aren't thinking of flitting,' said Harry, 'for you won't get very far in that.'

'Oh, I know, I know. That's the only reason I could afford it, because its too old and heavy for a trailer. I had to have a man with a mechanical horse to bring it from Rhyl. But Mr. Evans Parc says I can keep it here, so now, you see, I have my spare room,'

'Gosh, it's lovely,' said Cathy, entranced. 'Is it for your boy?'

'That's about it,' admitted Dorothy, smiling. 'For my boy.'

'It'll need a lot doing before his lordship can sleep watertight,' pronounced Harry, investigating by torchlight. 'Looks to me like the roof leaks, for a start.'

'Oh yes, it does. I bought some new felt.'

'And it could do with a coat of paint inside and out. Did you buy some paint, too?'

'Now you come to mention it, I did.'

'I perceive your drift. If it should be wet tomorrow—'

'—wet or fine—' put in Stan.

'—we'll do you a spot of home decoration.'

'There's the common-room, too,' Stan added. 'You been saying you'd do something about it for the last six months. This'd be as good a time as any, with so few of us in.'

'But it seems a shame,' protested Dorothy insincerely, 'giving up a precious weekend—'

'It is a shame,' Harry agreed. 'Just you bear that in mind, warden, when the summer crowds start and people try to tell you you shouldn't have favourites.'

'Well, no more I should. It's my job to see that all who want to stay here get the chance. But naturally I can do whatever I like with my spare room.'

The next day, sure enough, was fine, but Harry, with characteristic ruthlessness, mustered his forces. Doreen with her henchwoman Molly, and Johnny with the Liverpool architectural student who was his present climbing partner, were set to distemper the common-room. Stan repaired the caravan roof, Cathy gave the interior a coat of shining white paint, and Harry himself dealt with the exterior green. By daylight the caravan, though admittedly ramshackle, was more beguiling than ever. The situation, too, was perfect, beside a stream in the grassy tree-screened dell; there was room, commented Harry thoughtfully, for half a dozen tents also. In front the ground dropped to the hidden farm, and nothing stopped the eye from travelling away down the great pass, and on out to the remote, sunlit flats of Anglesey.

They all met for lunch in a glow of welldoing and technical achievement. Even Cathy and Doreen managed to preserve a show of civility. By evening the caravan was finished.

'Of course,' said Harry at Sunday-morning breakfast, 'to make any sort of a decent job of it the common-room must have two coats.'

Johnny was looking out of the window. 'I say, it's begun to snow; what fun. D'you know, Harry old man, I believe I've had enough of good deeds for a while.'

'I can well believe it,' said Harry dryly. 'All right, you and Steve go off and make snowballs. The rest of us will finish.'

Forming one of a large distempering party, one which, moreover, included Doreen, was nothing like so exhilarating as working by oneself in the caravan. Harry and Doreen did a wall together, and argued about the raising of the school-leaving age. It seemed to Cathy a profitless subject, and she felt left out and discontented. Molly whistled in an irritating manner through her teeth, and Stan did the ceiling in his usual silence. The room was done by lunch-time.

'There's still time for the Slabs,' said Doreen after lunch. 'They'll be sporting in this breeze. Anybody else?'

'You and Cathy go,' said Harry to Stan. 'I want to put a finishing touch.'

It was the coldest Welsh day Cathy had yet known. A gusty wind blew from the north-east, bringing flurries of snow. In the intervals the sun was dazzling, and the high tops showed white where the snow was already lying. But on lower ground the wind whisked it away like powder, and the great face of the Slabs was clear.

Doreen chose one of the classic routes. Cathy immediately made for a slightly harder one.

'What about it being my turn to lead?' said Stan.

She said nothing, but her angry face as she knotted her bowline answered him. *Don't you see, fool? I'm showing her.*

Stan was never one to make a scene. He followed, but it seemed to her that he followed abominably slowly. She was chilled through, waiting at the belays. The actual climbing went all right, except that sensation every now and then left her fingers and she had to pause and rub, and on the harder moves wait, head into the rock, for a lull in the roaring wind. Doreen and Molly on their parallel route had started first and drew steadily ahead, and as she pulled up from the last pitch she could see them scrambling on round a corner to the right.

'They've gone to the Upper Buttress,' she called down to Stan.

'Reckon I'm off home,' he replied.

When he joined her she was furious. 'There's two hours' daylight yet. You just can't.'

'I can, though. It's not fit, climbing in this wind. I've had enough.'

Cathy glared at his grey, plain face, detesting it. The word coward hovered between them. She knew perfectly well that he was not a coward, and that had he been with Harry he would have gone on, but the fact only increased her wrath. They returned home through the gale, he silent from habit, she from anger. But something of her bad temper abated when she found herself cosily at home, glowing from the swift descent and out of the cruel wind. Harry emerged from the common-room. 'Come and see my touch.'

Above the mantelpiece, on the cream distemper, he had sketched a frieze. The girdle traverse of a rock-face, with climbers strung out across it. Johnny was the leader; cruelly simian; himself, all nose and chin; Stan like a mud-pie, Doreen like a spider, Cathy with scarlet hair and eyes like carbuncles, Gwen at the tail end in the act of falling off. The caricature was ruthless. One squirmed, but one had to laugh.

'It's brilliant, Harry,' said Dorothy, giggling. 'Now, though it breaks my heart to say so, you'll have to paint it out. There are already quite enough complaints that only climbers are welcome here. I daren't play into their hands like that.'

'Oh, Dorothy! Have a heart. Let Johnny see it, and Steve and a few of the chaps.'

'Well, just one weekend then. But it mustn't be here at Easter.'

They sat round the kitchen fire having tea. It was like the first weekend, thought Cathy contentedly; just the four of them, only then she had not belonged, and now she did. 'Sorry I was bitchy,' she took occasion to murmur to Stan, who looked blank; probably he hadn't even noticed.

The howl of the wind outside drowned Molly's entrance. Suddenly she stood in the doorway, holding her hands out queerly in front of her. There were great weals across the palms turning dark red where the blood had clotted.

'Molly!' Dorothy cried. 'Where's Doreen?' She took the girl by the arm and pushed her into the fireside chair.

'I don't think she's dead,' said Molly. 'I don't really. She moved after. She couldn't be dead, could she?'

'No – no, surely not. But did she fall far? Did you remember to tie her on?'

'Yes,' whispered Molly. 'she can't roll any further.' She sat like a child while Dorothy sponged and dressed her hands, giving orders the while with an efficiency which reminded one that she was used, after all, to just such dreadful scenes.

'Harry, will you ring Dr. Gwynne-Williams; you'll find the number by the phone. Tell him the ambulance. Then ring the Llanllugwy Hotel and ask if there are any climbers there. Stan, get on your bike and go down to the club-hut – they aren't on the phone. Heaven grant there's people at both. It takes at least eight to carry the stretcher and we've only four. Then somebody must go up to her—'

'Me!' Cathy cried.

'Well, I don't know – yes, perhaps. It's better for the stretcher-party to keep together, and the equipment weighs a bit even empty. But look here, Cathy, sure you'll be all right? Two bodies and we're done.'

'Of couse I shall. I've been up there a dozen times. It's only a scramble round the top of the Slabs. You know yourself.'

'All right then. Get my flask out and fill it from the pot – lots of sugar. And my big torch. Two rugs in the drawer. The great thing is to keep her warm. Now, Molly.' She got some tea down the girl's throat, and held with her calm, urgent gaze, eyes already glazing from shock. 'Tell us, dear, where Doreen is.'

'You were doing the Central on the upper cliff, weren't you?' Cathy urged, cramming the rugs into her sack.

'And then she fell,' finished Dorothy. 'How far? How far up had you got?'

'We'd done—' Molly put her bandaged hands to her head in a pitiful gesture, 'we'd done – two pitches. That's right – two. I'd done one and she fell off the next. She must have been about sixty feet above me. I thought I could have held her, but the rope burned my hands.'

'People do think that till it happens,' said Dorothy grimly.

'I couldn't see where she fell, but she must have rolled a bit, I think. It took me ages getting down to her – well it seemed ages. She was sort of crumpled. I thought she was dead, but then she moved and groaned. The rope wasn't broken. I put it round a boulder. There wasn't anything else I could have done, was there?' She stared round at them piteously.

'No, you were fine. Now don't talk any more. We'll get her down.' The warden followed Cathy out on to the steps. 'I hate letting you go up alone. I'd come with you, only someone must be at base.'

'You know I'll be all right.'

'And, Cathy, don't touch anything. Cover her up, and if she's conscious try to make her drink, but don't touch anything. The doctor always impresses that on me. Good luck.'

Cathy trudged off up the hill. She was at first aware of little feeling except a vague excitement. There was a crisis; there was activity; she had her share. Only gradually, as she battled her way against the wind, did a picture form itself. This same wind had torn Doreen from her holds. A bright blue jacket would be lying crumpled. Perhaps dead.

In fifteen minutes she was under the Slabs, and, crossing beneath them, found the long scree gully already whitened with snow. It gleamed like a pathway through the fading light. There was no depth to the snow, and her boots bit through it to the unstable stuff underneath. The ascent was long and toilsome, but warming. On a level with the start of the upper cliff there was a scramble round a rocky corner, and along broken ledges. Scratches on the wall above her marked the start of a climb.

But which one? She had only been once on the central, and the start had been hard to find. Everywhere were more ledges, more rocks, more scree. She made out what looked like a body and rushed towards it. It was a boulder.

The light was almost gone now, and panic seized her. She shouted, and the wind swept her voice away; in any case, what hope was there that Doreen could reply? She was useless, she would give the stretcher party no guidance. She forced herself to stop her frantic wanderings, get back to the wall, and work her way steadily along underneath it, examining the ground inch by inch with her torch. Then came a cairn, another line of scratches, and in a pattern that was familiar. This was it! – and then she saw the rope round the boulder, yellow in the light of the torch. She crept forward, suddenly terrified of what she might see.

Doreen lay on her side as if asleep, except that one leg was out at a queer angle. Her mouth was open and a fleck of blood showed on it. Cathy touched a hand and its coldness made her shudder. She's dead, she thought, desperately struggling to get the rugs out of the sack. How do I know if she's dead? What do I do? Then a queer sound came from the livid mouth, something between a cough and a groan.

'Doreen!' Cathy shouted. 'It's me, Cathy – the others will be here soon – Doreen—' It did not seem to matter that Doreen was beyond hearing. She lived, there was hope, some reassurance might perhaps get through.

She rolled the rugs quickly over the poor battered little body – Doreen was such a small creature really, why had one thought of her as tall? – and tried to get some of the tea into the open mouth. Then she crept under the rug and put her face against Doreen's, breathing on it, trying to communicate her own warmth. She had a live body in her arms, not a dead one, and the dread had left her. She seemed to feel something of the punishment it had taken. She knew its suffering in her own blood and bone. For the first time she faced the ultimate reality of pain.

It was inky dark now, and the wind was dropping. The intervals between gusts grew longer, and through them Doreen's breathing could be heard, irregular and loud.

'They won't be long now,' whispered Cathy, fighting to reach the brain behind the closed eyes; and herself started to look for lights. But there was nothing; nothing but darkness and wind. It might be hours yet. The doctor must come from the foot of the pass, and he might not be in when the message reached his house. Climbers had to come from Llanllugwy, five miles. Time passed and was as nothing, could be counted only in twitchings and spasms of pain. Around them was black annihilation, and they two, two poor little bodies fighting to live, were the only warm things in an infinity of cold, indifferent stones.

If you keep quiet you can hear the mountain. Slowly to Cathy, as she lay there in the darkness, the mountain became real. First it had been scenery; then a playground, stood up in the air for her amusement, neatly divided into pitches, crowned with a cairn at the top. And now at last it had its own life, independent of her pleasure, terrible, remote; its own laws, which her friends had been trying all these weeks to teach her, and to which she had carelessly, impatiently conformed. At any moment she might have forgotten them, and it only needed a moment, a second of forgetfulness for the mountain to take its revenge. A jaunty figure in a blue jacket swung up out of sight round a corner, and a few hours later was lying like a crumpled eggshell on the mountain's breast.

She was showing me, thought Cathy. And if it hadn't been for Stan, I was going to show her. This was the answer the mountain gave to those who used it as a stage. This was something more real than cheek and cockiness and hurt feelings. This was the shock of the living body crushed on impersonal stone.

Doreen gave a sudden strangled cry, the shriek of a soul in nightmare. Cathy switched on the torch and peered into her face. Her eyes were open, trying to focus.

'It's all right. I've got you. The stretcher's coming.'

'I fell,' Doreen said.

'That's right. Just a bit of a fall.'

Doreen looked puzzled. Then she said in a loud, distinct voice: 'But I am always so careful—' and instantly lost consciousness again.

Now she's dead, Cathy thought. They often speak like that just before. Oh God, must it be much longer? She struggled up, crept round the first corner, and could see into the lower part of the gully. And there, advancing up it, were lights.

The relief, after hours of peering through blackness, brought tears. She waved the torch; they were a long way off yet, but they must be scanning the hillside. Then she returned to Doreen. The queer snoring breathing had begun again, but at any rate the matter was no longer in doubt. She lived, and would be saved.

Twenty minutes later they were rounding the ledges, guided by Cathy's light. 'Is she alive?' the leader called – a gentlemanly voice, crisp and somehow familiar. 'Yes!' she yelled back. Then the bobbing lights were upon her, and Harry had her by the arm. 'Well done,' he muttered. 'Good old Doreen.'

A dumpy little figure, who must be the doctor, bent over the pile of rugs. 'All your lights, please,' he said. The rugs were lifted, and Doreen lay, livid, in the patch of glow-worm light. The doctor ran his hands over her. Cathy, suddenly unable to endure it, turned her head and stared into the darkness.

'Fractured pelvis,' said the little doctor at length. 'A lot of minor abrasions. Head seems all right. Two of you get that thing assembled.' Thankfully Cathy left his horrid manipulations and lent her torch to light Harry and Johnny as they slotted tubular aluminium into canvas. 'How many are you?' she whispered.

'Nine – no, ten, with the doctor. The organising chap is Sharland. He was at the hut with two pals. The others are from Llanllugwy, that's why we didn't start sooner. Did it seem long?'

'Like hell it did.'

'Poor old Cath. You must be frozen. Did she drink the tea? – well then, you finish it. Was she conscious at all?'

'Ay, for a minute. She said she'd always been so careful. It made me feel bad, hearing her say that.'

'I suppose it's what we all think,' Harry muttered.

'Sharland – isn't that the Everest chap who snorted at us for yelling on Tryfan?'

'What a memory,' said Johnny, even in this grisly moment not altogether subdued. 'Heaven keep me out of your bad books.'

'It's a damn lucky thing for Doreen he was on hand,' said Harry. 'I've been on one or two of these picnics myself, but he has real experience. With ten we should just about manage it. All right, sir – stretcher forward.'

Doreen had ceased to look human; she was a splinted mummy, silent after a morphia injection. She was laid on the stretcher, and ropes were bound with what seemed a cruel tightness over her broken body. It was hard to believe she was still alive.

'All set, doctor?' asked Sharland. 'Right, then.' There was a shuffling in the darkness as the first eight hooked the stretcher straps over their shoulders; they all seemed, without words, to know what to do. Only Cathy stood vacantly. 'You there with the big torch – go ahead and light us.' She scrambled to the front. The stretcher came up on to the men's shoulders, and one of them stumbled a little under the unexpected weight. Then they groped forward.

Cathy found herself agonizingly stiff and incapable of speed; but it did not matter, for the stretcher seemed to advance by inches. The ledges which a solitary scrambler had scarcely noticed required the utmost exertion of eight heavily burdened men working two abreast, and the night turned every six-inch drop into a chasm. The real chasm of the gully was hard to find. She guided them too low and they had to retrace ten hardly won steps. 'God blast and damn you,' said Sharland, gasping for breath. His curses seemed as natural and impersonal as the howling of the wind.

At last they rounded the edge and came out above the gully. There was a drop into it of perhaps twenty feet, down a wall so broken with ledges that one could slither it by day. 'We'll lower her,' Sharland said.

The stretcher was set down, and ropes tied to its four handles. Two men scrambled down into the gully, taking the front ropes with them. The rest propelled the stretcher over the wall, and inch by inch it was lowered till the queer little mummy-like figure with the dreadfully still boots was upright against the rock-face. Cathy seemed to feel the jar through her own body, and put her hand into her mouth to stifle a scream. But from Doreen there was not a sound.

The two below reached up till their hands caught the stretcher handles, and it was guided to the gully floor. 'Right,' said Sharland, 'here we can let her run.'

The stretcher was furnished with wooden runners like a sledge, and on these it slid over the scree of the gully floor, two men guiding it at each side, the others sitting back on their heels and paying out the ropes from behind. They lost height rapidly, and in half an hour were down on to the blessed grass at the foot of the Slabs. From there it was a long carry home.

The stretcher-bearers were wearying now. Even with two reliefs – for the little doctor insisted on taking his turn, saying: 'Lord bless you, man, I've done it twenty times before' – they were needing more and more frequent halts.

'May I try?' Cathy humbly asked Sharland at one such pause.

'No!' he snapped back at her; and then: 'Well, if you like.' He relinquished his strap.

The stretcher came up on to their shoulders again, and it was all she could do not to stagger. A mere one-eighth of Doreen's little weight seemed crushing, appalling. She forced herself forward with the others, gritting her teeth. Tons of lead seemed to be pressing through her thin shoulder-blades. In body and spirit she was mortified. This was what it meant being a girl; you thought yourself as good as any of them, and when it come to a spot of trouble you couldn't do your share.

'Breather,' Sharland said. He took Cathy's strap from her, and she fancied she heard a chuckle in the darkness. 'You ought to try it sometime with a fifteen-stone man.'

But now the nightmare was almost over. They were through the iron gate at the end of the upper lake; they were down the boggy stretch of path, and then down the stony stretch; the hostel lights showed blessedly welcome below them. A great glare of headlights marked the ambulance waiting on the road. Doreen was put straight into it. 'How bad, doctor?' asked Dorothy's anxious voice.

'Can't tell till the X-ray, but I think she'll do. She's young.' He got into his car and followed the ambulance down the pass to Bangor.

The rest of them crowded into the kitchen, where Margiad was ladling out hot lemon and whisky and wonderful soup. They sat in silence, each feeling warmth and life come tingling into his veins.

Cathy looked slowly round the circle of faces, four of them strange to her, but she hardly saw them. Instead she was back again on the ledge, clasping the shattered body, hearing the queer breath. It was all right for them; they had done their part now and could go to comfortable beds; but what further agonies lay before Doreen?

'Are you all right?' asked Dorothy, seeing on her friend's face the same glazed look Molly's had worn hours before. Cathy nodded, banishing the vision, gulping down her soup.

'You won't let it put you off, will you?' Harry suddenly said.

She looked at him, astonished that he should even envisage it. 'I reckon not,' she said, and the jut of her underlip gave him double reassurance. 'It won't make no difference. Except that from now on I'll always be a bit scared.'

A grin went round the circle, breaking the tension. 'That'll do you no harm,' Harry pronounced.

'I daresay the lesson won't be lost on any of us,' agreed Sharland. 'Well, we'd better be getting to our beds. Good night, Miss Elliott.'

'I can't thank you enough,' said Dorothy.

'Oh, nonsense. Climber's duty – pleasure in this case, too, though perhaps that's not quite the word. But they've plenty of guts, your young people.' His hard eyes flickered over them and came to rest for a moment on Cathy. 'And that goes for the lady likewise,' he finished, and summoning his partners, swung out into the night and the wind.

CHAPTER FOUR

DOREEN LORD made a good recovery, but her climbing days were over. Her nerve was broken. She never came again to Cae Capel, and Cathy Canning reigned in her stead.

Her reign lasted two weeks, and then met an interruption as brutal as it was unexpected. The decision of an Argentinian magnate to cancel an order for a new tanker threw her life into chaos. Mr. Canning was laid off at the yard.

Cathy, having worked her way through the calendering and the packing and sorting, had just made another fresh start on the ironing. Each time she dropped back from four pounds a week to the beginner's wage of three, but she did not waver in her resolution never again to become an unthinking machine. There was a particular fascination about hand-ironing, for only the most delicate garments were so treated, and each one required thought and skill. But she would be slow for some weeks yet, and the fall in earnings could not have come at a less opportune time.

Mrs. Canning's housekeeping money was quartered. Naturally she could not manage. She could do better, though, Cathy argued, and knew in her heart how unfair that was. Her father had no less need of food, drink and tobacco because, through no fault of his own, he was on the scrap-heap again. Every penny was wanted in the home. And even if it had not been so, how could she have the nerve to go off into the hills when her father, wearing that sullen look on his face that made it so like hers, sat hour after hour in a corner of the kitchen with the paper on his knee, an angry man, stricken in his power and skill, and forever without the release of words.

Not that she was much comfort to anyone else in the home. She was always, complained her mother, finding fault. She came on a cabbage rotting in the shopping-bag – well, anyone might forget a cabbage, and it had only cost sixpence. But she carried on for half an hour as though all their troubles were due to it. Mrs. Canning heard her in silence, for Cathy was the wage-earner now and could not be answered back. Suddenly aware herself of her immunity, she turned scarlet, tried to apologize, and went out to walk bitterly about the streets.

She would not take up again with any of her old associates. She could not console herself for Cae Capel with the love of the boys in Tooley Street. From the ghost of Bill, however, she found it less easy to escape. Mrs. Powell seemed to be perpetually pursuing her with his letters. Give my love to Cathy. Is it okay with Cathy? Tell Cathy I'll never forget her. And always rows of pitiful little crosses, like the graveyard of love.

'He hasn't got enough to take his mind off me in that place, that's what it is,' said Cathy to Mrs. Powell, for whom she was genuinely sorry. 'You wait till he's out. Then he'll get another girl and forget me in a week.'

'That he never will,' asserted Mrs. Powell with vigour. Bill's fidelity, perhaps at first unwelcome, was now a matter of family pride. 'Come on, Cathy love. It wouldn't hurt you to send him a nice message, for once in a way.'

'Tell him I'm fed up because I can't go climbing,' said Cathy. Mrs. Powell went back upstairs with angry tears in her eyes. How could a lass who was on top of the world be so unkind to a lad who was down?

After three weeks of divorce from Cae Capel, Cathy had a visitor. Stan Bryce, looking hangdog and unlike himself in a neat dark suit and with his hair plastered down, stood one evening in their narrow doorway. Her heart leapt up at the sight of him; then shame for her home blotted all better feelings out. 'Hello,' she said in her rudest way. 'What brings you slumming?'

'Harry and me wondered how you were getting on.'

'Oh, all right. But I can't come back while my Dad's out of work. I wrote it all to Harry. Didn't he get my card?'

'Ay. But we just wondered.'

Norma came peering over her shoulder, and he had to be asked in. The kitchen looked even muckier than usual. But he greeted her mother with shy civility, accepted a cracked cup of tea, and, sitting down beside her father, exerted himself as she could not have believed possible. He knew all about the yard and the cancelled tanker; he and Harry, as one was apt not to remember, were, in their superior way, in shipbuilding, too. Mr. Canning's tongue was mercifully loosened, and he sloughed off the worst of his anger. But Cathy's only increased.

Why had Stan come? She had always made it clear that Tooley Street was out of bounds. Harry, a truly considerate friend, understood perfectly that there was nothing at present to be done for her. Then why had Stan come?

He was there because he was sweet on her. It stuck out a mile now. All those fits of nerves when she was leading, and now this. For the second time in her life she found a man's love an embarrassment and a curse. For of course it was impossible to love him back. One did not necessarily want a film star, but there were limits; and it was absurd that Stan should expect a girl to enjoy kissing his shapeless grey face. But if Harry were to realize – and this visit by itself was enough to make him realize – he would most likely be wild. He would put all the blame on her, for spoiling their beloved sport with sentiment, and for leading his best friend a dance. No one, for one moment, would think of blaming Stan.

As soon as a pause in her father's damnation of the Argentine gave her the chance, she got to her feet. 'I'll see you as far as the bus-stop,' she said.

Her parents exchanged a gratified smile. But Stan, as they walked in silence through the mean streets, knew well enough that her gesture was not one of encouragement.

'Well, give my love to Harry,' she said in a hard, bright voice as they waited for the bus. 'Tell him how it is. Tell him I'll be back just as soon as Dad's in work again. Don't let him take up with anyone else.' By sending all these messages to Harry, she trusted to make it plain, even to Stan's thick intelligence, that he hadn't a chance, that he was to give no trouble, that he was to take himself out of the road.

'Okay, I will,' said Stan, and seemed to screw himself to the real purpose of his visit. 'But look here, Cath, couldn't we – me and Harry, I mean—'

'No!' She turned on him with such ferocity that he flinched. 'No, you couldn't. Nobody could.' And suddenly she was aware that all this violence was unnecessary. Because Stan knew. He knew.

'Goodbye, Stan, and thanks for dropping in,' she said, ashamed of herself and almost fond of him. And she walked away and left him to wait alone for the bus.

'Is that your new boy?' Norma asked. 'No oil-painting, is he?'

'I daresay he didn't think much of you, come to that,' answered Cathy, staring at her sister's dirty painted face. No one was going to criticize Stan in her hearing. But he had, it seemed, another supporter in the family.

'That's what I call a real nice chap,' said Mr. Canning. 'Got his head screwed on, too. Don't you heed yon silly kid, Cathy. Looks ain't everything.'

Ah, but they're something, Cathy thought; and the expression on her face told her father that the plans he had been making for his favourite child would come to naught. Her regret was nearly as keen as his own. The repulsive shell that masked Stan Bryce was a part of the malignant irony which seemed to dog all her affairs of the heart. For she knew that her father had been right, and that she would probably never meet a nicer chap her whole life long.

ii

Thus discouraged, Stan Bryce naturally did not return, and Cathy's banishment seemed complete. She knew she was not quite forgotten, for Dorothy, snatching a month's leave before the start of the summer season, had sent her two affectionate postcards. But presently she began to feel that there would never be any going back, and that her slowly acquired climbing skill would utterly rust away.

'You and your dad! You give me the willies,' complained Mrs. Canning, who held that feelings should be relieved, as her own were, by a bit of a grumble, and was oppressed and disconcerted by this silent, stony rebellion against fate.

Nothing would stir Mr. Canning from the house. Other men had hobbies, but not he. He cared nothing for the Tranmere Rovers; he had too completely lost contact with the soil to take any pleasure in a distant allotment. But Cathy took to wandering off on Sundays with a sandwich in her pocket, and always alone. She went up on to the Wirral heights, to which it was easy to flag a lift, so that she saved even the cost of the bus-fare and from the heathery humps of Thrustaston Common or Caldy Hill she would stare for hours across the shining mudflats of the Dee to Wales.

She was still almost without conscious appreciation of beauty. She gazed into Wales because it helped her to imagine herself back at Cae Capel. The blue cone of Moel Fammau was dear to her merely because she had seen the other side of it from a climb. But sometimes on a fine spring day the shining panorama of the Dee, the dramatic walls of hills on the further side, the curve of the Wirral coast round to Hilbre island, the gold and mauve and slaty glint of sunshine on the channelled sands, pierced with a gentle message her anger and her discontent, so that she returned home a little comforted.

On her homeward road after one of these excursions, a motorist pulled up without her having signalled him, and it was Leonard Head.

'Hello,' he said. 'How's the boots?'

By this time anyone who reminded her, however faintly, of Wales would have had a welcome. She knew she ought to crush his impudence; instead she played up to it. 'Been getting a lot of wear,' she told him; and all the way back to Woodside it was her turn to boast.

Leonard seemed impressed, but characteristically contrived to take the credit to himself. 'My, my,' he said, 'sounds as if I started something. What about the other thing I started? Been making any progress there?'

'If you haven't got a nerve.'

'No hard feelings, I hope and trust? That's right. You know, since I stopped seeing you on the ferry I thought you'd been avoiding me.'

As if he would be worth avoiding! 'I changed my job. I work in Tranmere now.'

'Ah, so that was it. Well, what about a return trip? You might lead me up something, for a change.'

This time she faced the plain and dreadful fact: sleeping with him cost her no pain at all. His way of taking her arm awakened memories, and they were not unpleasant ones. As long as she had Cae Capel she could, as Dorothy had suggested, do without all that. But deprived, she seemed to need an outlet for what must be just natural badness. This time, however, she was not relying on any soft chap's precautions, but took them herself, marching brazenly into a Liverpool chemist's, and leaving again, although the chemist had taken no particular notice, with a burning face.

She laid her plans with care. She was not going near Cae Capel, or risking being seen with Leonard Head by anyone whose opinion she valued. They stayed, as before, at the Myrtle Bank, and climbed on an obscure crag right off the ordnance map, down near the coast among the derelict quarrying villages, a place no one visited unless to escape a bank holiday crowd. After the first pitch she knew, exultantly, that she had lost no form. The sight of Leonard floundering on the end of her rope filled her with malicious pleasure.

'You look such a little bit of a thing to hold a chap,' he remarked at the belay. 'I wonder if you could?'

'Well, no one's come off on me yet,' she answered cruelly. 'I'll tell when you have.'

At night, the warmth of her welcome surprised and at first delighted him. She was hot stuff, he thought; he could swear she'd been having a bit of practice. But he somehow did not care for the speculative look in those queer-coloured eyes that met his over the breakfast table.

'Well,' she said, 'you got it for nothing this time.'

There was a quality in her which made him almost afraid. He was not a fanciful man, but it suddenly seemed to him that he had been made use of, and that he knew now how the professional tarts must feel. He began to take a very great dislike to her, and resolved never to see her again.

iii

The violence that Cathy had done to herself by going for the second time with Leonard Head showed very plainly on her face. Tooley Street, though it had no positive evidence, was quick to observe the change, and she lost the caste which her strange but admired activities at Cae Capel had been gaining for her. She took once more to eyeing boys, and no longer refused every invitation. She stood for a moment poised over the abyss.

But the gate of heaven opened just in time. The Argentine magnate knew a change of heart, or perhaps a reward for his efforts to secure a lower tender. A prosperous summer was ensured for the little streets behind the docks. Simultaneously her increasing dexterity with the iron brought her back again to the four-pound level. Cae Capel was hers for months ahead.

She rode triumphantly back on Harry's pillion to a great welcome; and to great change.

CHAPTER FIVE

FOR NOW it was summer.

Not that the Welsh weather was any less uncertain. The rain could still come down in a slanting wall, or the mists sit in judgment on the tops, parting only for a maddening ten seconds, as one pulled up the Terminal Arete of Lliwedd, to show the sun gleaming on the sands of Portmadoc far away to the west. But the country had ceased, it seemed, overnight to belong to a handful of climbers from Birmingham and Merseyside. It had thrown itself open to the crowd.

Traffic, on what was after all the highway between two capitals, roared unceasingly through the pass. Queues formed under the classic routes on the Slabs. The summits were festooned with walkers, carrying sticks, or even umbrellas to ward off the thunderstorms; and had Mr. Sharland scowled at everyone who shouted the scowl would never have been off his face.

The hostel, by its smallness and position one of the most desirable in the whole circuit, was booked solid as far ahead as regulations allowed. Dorothy, torn between her partiality for the faithful and her resolve that its primary purpose should not be that of a club-hut, forced herself to apply a rationing system. For three weekends out of the four Cathy was to use the caravan whenever she herself had no visitors, and the rest could pitch their tents round it in the glade. The caravan in its furnished state, with cretonne in the windows, seemed to Cathy heaven. For the first time she knew a housewifely pride.

Down at the club-hut Everesters were two a penny, and you could take your choice of conquerors of the Brenva, the Grandes Jorasses or the Dru. This they knew because Doreen's disaster had forged a bond between hostel and hut. After such grim evidence that the hostellers were of the same flesh and blood as himself, Sharland no longer stood aloof. He had, moreover, taken a fancy to Dorothy, her coffee and her kitchen, and she made him pay for his comfort there by keeping her young things entertained. They learnt to know the lethargy and despair of fighting across sloping slabs at twenty-eight thousand feet; they pictured, with far greater longing, the ecstasy of the great ice ridges on the roof of the Alps, or of walls of red granite hung straight above the cross of the Chamonix lights. Touched by their enthusiasm, Sharland invited anyone who would to join the club party at the Montenvers in August. Harry, Stan and Johnny Hollinger were planning to go.

Travelling cheaply, camping, employing no guide, it was to cost them only thirty pounds.

Her joy at getting back again dashed with unworthy pangs of jealousy, Cathy marvelled at the ease with which they seemed able to lay hands on thirty pounds. To the end of her days she would never have half that sum.

Harry might boast of being working class, but what nonsense it was; he had never had to go without. Any talk of foreign travel became, in consequence, sour grapes to her. Even the suggestion of moving north to the Lake District – where, after all, there were also hostels, and to which the fare would not have been great – savoured to her of treachery.

Llanllugwy, that gaunt and shuttered place, had shared in the genial transformation. Striped canvas awnings gave frivolity to slate porches; outside the hotel burgeoned red umbrellas; somebody opened a milk bar. Buses spewed forth tourists at the cross-roads, and anyone who should pass wearing a rope was invariably beseeched to pose for snapshots. And round at Bryn Glas, on the other side of the mountain, it was the same story. Tourists started from there to climb Snowdon; the tougher tourists, those who were not content to be carried up by the Llanberis railway. After their feat they all required tea. Miss Williams, tray in hand, never stopped running, and her niece imported for the summer from Carnarvon washed up forever. Yet there was always a welcome for Cathy, Harry and Stan when they looked in from Lliwedd. Flashing in and out from the dining-room, Miss Williams flung them smiles and tea, and steadfastly declined to take a penny in return.

'But it's coining money I am,' she would say. 'Shocking. A poor thing if I was to charge my friends.'

'Anyway, you got plenty of company now without us,' Cathy would point out.

'Yes, and there's tantalizing! Plenty of company and no time for a word, and all those months in the winter with nobody coming but you and then only when you was lost. Now about Miss Elliott—' She darted away with another *thé complet* and, returning, took up exactly where she had left off. 'What's this I hear about her young man coming? Believe it when I see it, I shall.'

'Oh, he's coming all right. Two weeks end of June. I know because I'm having to clear out of the caravan. But Dorothy's letting me have a bed those two weekends. I think she hopes we'll take him climbing.'

'Well, and we'll be glad to,' said Harry sternly. Cathy tossed her head. She was not to be deflected from her resentment of Dorothy's young man.

'Don't you forget then that I am wanting to see him. You bring him over here – that's a promise. That's one I don't envy,' Miss Williams added shrewdly. 'All you sharp ones sitting round waiting to say that he isn't good enough. The poor boy.'

'He isn't a poor boy. He's a professor or a lecturer or some such, and sure to be no end of a swank.'

'There you are. Hard on him already. Not for a lot I wouldn't be in his shoes.'

ii

But Michael Derwent did not seem to stand in need of sympathy. From the moment of his arrival he had an immense success.

'Go on in and introduce yourselves,' said Dorothy as she gave them their belated Friday-night supper. 'I'll join you when I'm through.'

In the common-room Mr. Derwent was the centre of a rapt circle. He was criticising the Keynesian economics of scarcity, and Cae Capel realised its luck in getting what amounted to a free lecture from a leader of the younger Oxford school. It was no moment for introductions, but Harry had soon joined himself to the argument in his eager fox-terrier way. Cathy contented herself with a furtive scrutiny of Dorothy's young man. He was long, thin and horn-rimmed, with a noble forehead and not quite enough chin; but though one could not call him handsome, his air of confidence and the slightly sardonic twist of his mouth compelled notice. He had, it soon appeared, the professional lecturer's trick of keeping everybody interested by pouncing unexpectedly on the inattentive.

'You now,' he said, suddenly fixing Cathy with a bright stare through the horn-rims, 'what's your line?'

'I work in a laundry,' she muttered, abashed.

'Ah yes. An excellent example of fluctuating demand. Though I wonder if you've consciously envisaged yourself as a pawn in the chaos of economic circumstance?'

'Pardon?' said Cathy, momentarily bewildered; whereas Mr. Derwent, amused by a new sociological discovery, replied: 'Oh – er, granted,' and moved on to somebody less dim-witted.

She sat crimsoning. Of course she could see perfectly well what he was getting at, if he had given her a moment to think and not confused her with long words. Instead he had made her look silly, and in front of a lot of giggling little students incapable of leading a Moderate between them. And Harry, far from leaping to her defence, was now thanking him warmly for his explanation and noting down a reading-list. 'It's the duty of every intelligent citizen to get a grounding,' he declared.

'Yes, my parlour-tricks are much in demand,' said Mr. Derwent with frank self-satisfaction. 'I sometimes think we economists are going to be the little tin gods of this generation, as the scientists were of the last, and the doctors before that, and the clergymen before them.' Dorothy had entered, and he did not rise to greet her, but stretched out a long arm and pulled her on to the arm of his chair with an easy possessiveness which made one wild to see. Dorothy was perhaps a trifle shy, but she put a brave face on it. 'Don't forget, darling,' she said, 'that people turn sooner or later on the little tin gods. You've got it coming.'

The sooner the better, thought Cathy venomously, endeavouring to smile while Dorothy explained to her lover that her three great friends were to take him climbing tomorrow; and as soon as she decently could she escaped to the porch; where Johnny Hollinger, who did not give a damn for economics or the duty of the intelligent citizen, was coiling his new nylon rope.

'What d'you think of the learned boy-friend?' he inquired.

'Not much. I wish Harry wasn't taking him tomorrow.'

'Well, come with me on Cloggy instead.'

She looked at him sharply. 'Mean it?' Her anger against Michael Derwent was forgotten in one moment of elation. She had arrived. She was under no illusions about Johnny's heart. He had always been charming to her, but he had never stretched out a rope to help her in the days when she had everything to learn. Now he thought her good enough to make him an amusing second, and fill in the blank space while his crony Stephen sat for a degree. She broke the news triumphantly to Harry and Stan at bedtime. And they were triumphant, too, though of course they would not show it. They knew that their pupil was entering now on her finishing stages.

Harry repeated his assertion that Johnny Hollinger was crag-happy. 'Just do your best to see that he uses the belays. And for God's sake don't let him move till you've got a good one yourself.'

'Eh, Harry,' Stan said, 'Johnny won't come off.'

'There's a sight too much of this Johnny-won't-come-off attitude about,' said Harry crossly. 'I've just got the lass out of that way of thinking, and you go and start her off again. Anyway, good luck, Cath, and do us credit. You've got to the higher reaches now. I'm only sorry you won't be there to cheer the professor along.'

'Reckon I don't like him much.'

'Now why on earth not? He seems a decent chap to me. Interesting, too.'

Cathy could not give voice to her first grievance, so she stated her second. 'I don't like the way he lets Dorothy wait on him. And why must he call her Dotty? Makes her sound a fool.'

'Well, after all, she is his girl,' said Harry indulgently. 'You mustn't give way to these fits of lesbian jealousy. One day you might grow up and get a boy of your own.'

The walk to Clogwyn Du'r Arddu was a long one, practically to the top of Snowdon and a good way down the other side. They left the hostel early on what was going to be a hot morning, Johnny displaying his usual gift for getting out of housework, and Cathy for once not disposed to be over-conscientious. To while away the hours of trudging, she led him on to talk of his family. It was not done at Cae Capel to appear at all impressed by rank, and Johnny's background was usually hushed up as something discreditable. But to a girl from the Birkenhead slums, earls' sons were, after all, something new.

Johnny did not share the prevailing inhibition. He told her all she wanted to know, and a great deal more which, in spite of her amusement, she considered he ought to have kept to himself. The family fortunes had declined, and the countess was driven to shifts which had their comic side. 'You be thankful your home's not your castle,' Johnny said. 'At least you don't have hordes of tourists dropping cigarette ends all over it on Wednesday and Saturday afternoons.'

Opening the Castle occasionally for charity had been fun, but it became a grimly competitive business when charity began at home. The ducal estate on the other side of the county was a dangerous rival. To counterbalance its superior architectural charms, the countess had her tourists taken round by members of the family in person. But when she caught Johnny telling an enraptured party the exact nature of the services for which his ancestor had been ennobled by James the First, his career as cicerone was brought to an abrupt end.

'You are a scream,' Cathy said, and it occurred to her that Johnny would find Tooley Street terribly funny, too. She made a mental note never to be lured into confidences in return.

But as they dropped over the high pass and down to the great black crag bulking above the grimmest little lake she had ever seen, not even Johnny's stories could keep her from feeling as terrified as though she had never been on rock before. It looked appalling. Where it was not vertical it overhung. Suppose she came off? The disgrace would crush her, and there wasn't even half a chance that Johnny would hush it up.

They changed into rubbers, and queasily she watched him tie two hundred-foot ropes together. 'So long,' he said; an apt farewell, for he proceeded to run out a hundred and eighty feet. She cricked her neck staring up at him, petrified, entranced.

It was true, as Harry had said, that his movements on the rock were beauty. Had she ever seen a ballet she might have compared his to a dancer's grace. He floated; on the hardest moves he seemed to fly. He could adhere to the face with one hand or one foot, could transfer his whole weight in a flash, yet he never jerked or hurried, but preserved an equable flow. The performance opened up for her new worlds, forever, most probably, beyond her reach.

He disappeared altogether, and his voice from some ultimate stance was almost inaudible. She started in a horrible solitude, a loneliness more complete than any she had known as leader. At first she was fumbling, indefinite, cowed by the relentness steepness of the crag, Then, as the fascination of the problem gripped her, she lost consciousness of everything except the immediate conquest of each new move. She arrived beside him, ages later, almost with a shock of surprise. 'Gosh,' she said, exultant, and Johnny grinned. 'Makes you think, does it, love?' He casually took flight again.

At each belay her position scared her. It came to her that on a climb of this difficulty the second ran nearly as much risk as the leader. Johnny would not come off; but suppose he did, and suppose he were to fall twice a hundred and eighty feet, the rope would cut through her shoulder to the bone. There was nothing between them and the grisly little lake; nothing but heat-haze. Then it was her turn to move, and once again she knew the absorption of a body used to the uttermost. She lived as never before.

'You're a wonder,' she broke out in irrepressible admiration when at last they lay above the conquered crag. 'Fancy me thinking I could climb!'

'Oh, you're not so bad,' said Johnny carelessly. He had, in fact, taken little notice of her performance. Unlike Harry, he had given her no word of criticism or advice. It was all one to him whether she improved or not. In him, genius did not take any didactic or missionary form. He just happened to be able to climb.

And now it was over, he relaxed like an animal; he stretched out like a lizard in the sun. Cathy, beside him, felt her toes and fingertips still glowing from the climb, and caught something of his sensuous languor. 'If it could be like this always!' she murmured, half asleep.

'Well,' Johnny murmured back, 'why not?'

She smiled into the heat-haze banked over the Portmadoc sands. 'Well, there's other things in life, I suppose, besides climbing.'

'There needn't be. Of course, if you must tie yourself up and add more brats to the quantities already crawling about that's your look-out.'

'But Johnny!' She sat up, now quite awake. 'Is coming up here all you care about? Aren't you interested in your job, or – or falling in love, or anything?'

'Job, no. Love, yes, by all means, as long as there aren't any boring consequences.' He opened his lazy eyes at last and gave her his impudent monkey look; just such a speculative look, no doubt, as the ancestor had turned on James the First. She said coldly, with Puritan disapproval:

'That's cheating.'

'Oh well, yes, if you like,' agreed Johnny, preparing to go to sleep again.

She was forced to recollect her visit to the Liverpool chemist in search of precautions. Who was she to read Johnny a lecture? Yet it seemed such a pity, somehow. She saw him forty years hence, a little shrivelled nut, a mountain bachelor, with nothing to show for all the skill and courage, all the grace and beauty that had been his. She said slowly:

'I wonder would you think the same if you'd been born the eldest son? The one that's to be the next earl?'

Johnny looked amused. 'Oh, quite possibly. I can't imagine anything making a worthy character out of me. But I must admit that brother Ludovic runs around simply dripping public spirit and noblesse oblige.'

'Well,' said Cathy with sudden magnificence, 'in my family I'm the eldest.'

Johnny found this funnier still. 'Have it your own way, sweetheart,' he said with the utmost amiability. 'But I've noticed that for a lot of people, and particularly women, that means trying to have it both ways. In which case, don't say I didn't warn you. I've thought the matter out, and I know that the life of pleasure is a full-time job. Now let's get back to Bryn Glas and make dear Olwen give us tea.' Olwen was Miss Williams, and it was most unlikely that she had ever given Johnny permission to call her by her Christian name.

It was late when they got back to the hostel, and Harry, elaborately casual, was scanning the road. 'How did she do?' he asked.

'Oh, she came up like a bird,' answered Johnny, and went indoors to stow his ropes.

'I didn't come off, any road,' Cathy said. She could not tell him what she had experienced, yet she was confident that he knew. Impulsively she burst out: 'You'd be just as good as he is if it was all you lived for.'

Harry was pleased with this artless compliment, but a sense of fact impelled him to refute it. 'If I was as good as he is, it probably would be all I lived for. But I'll never be more than a dependable second-rater. I just haven't got the something it takes for these high flights.'

'Well, that's as maybe. How did the professor do?'

'Not too bad at all. We started him off on Pinnacle Two and he made it nicely, all but the Slab. At any rate he never tried to climb the rope.' Cathy giggled; such ancient history no longer held the faintest sting. 'By the way, Dorothy's making you take him out tomorrow.'

'Lor', whyever? Won't you?'

'Willingly, but she's set her heart on it. Seems to think it's the one thing needed to make you buddies.'

'I daresay she means it kindly—' Cathy began, and suddenly inspiration flooded in on her. ''Course I wouldn't hurt her feelings. I'll take him. I'll love to.'

Oh boy, he's asked for it, she thought. And, oh boy, he's got it coming.

iii

Michael Derwent had greatly enjoyed his first day on rock. He was told he shaped well, and he believed it. Fresh from a sedentary academic life, he had held his own with these tough, adenoidal young northerners, and Harry Rimmer's intelligent admiration was greatly to his taste. He failed to see why a change of leader was required.

'But Cathy's my particular pet, darling,' Dorothy explained, 'and a beautiful little climber, too. I know she'd feel it if she wasn't given the chance.'

'One would think, poppet, you could work these maternal urges off on me. You have an expanding-suitcase heart. All right, then; I'm in your hands. But don't be disappointed if I fail to register with your protégée. I don't pretend to have your gift for coming to grips with the untutored mind.'

'Oh well, I suppose I must find her interesting as a type,' said Dorothy with an awkward little laugh. In her heart she had suddenly cried: *You, my dearest, are a snob*. She was not so completely the saint as never to have an uncharitable thought; but she was temperamentally incapable of speaking it aloud.

On the uphill walk next day he cast a cursory glance or two at the little thing beside him; but what his beloved found in her beyond a lot of red hair and a set of very proletarian features, he was damned if he could see. She seemed devoid of conversation. Remembering with an effort that she came from a slum and worked in a laundry, he asked her a few questions about both, receiving monosyllabic answers which confirmed his impression of her dim-wittedness. And certainly that flat Merseyside voice was better kept quiet. They made the rest of the journey to the Upper Cliff in what was, for him at any rate, a vastly preferable silence.

Not till she began to climb did he really look at her again; and then, he noticed with surprise, her whole appearance seemed to change. She lost that plebeian look as she moved purposefully, delicately up the sheet of slabs, her hair like a flaming flower, and he had the curious fancy that the face she turned to the rock must be tender and charming. The slabs were harder than anything he had done the day before, and he was glad of the reach which enabled him to ignore half the sloping holds she walked on. Yet he was not dissatisfied. There was something precise and intellectual, he found, about the sport.

At the top of the slabs there was a terrace where, at her suggestion, they ate their sandwiches. This, with his companions of yesterday, would have been the moment for amusing talk. As it was, he beheld the scenery; the lake far below them, the tourist-loaded charabancs on the rippling white ribbon which was the Holyhead Road. It did not take him long to assimilate a given piece of scenery, and he was soon ready to make a move.

They were now at the foot of the Upper Cliff proper, and to him it looked very steep indeed. From its first pitch the slabs they had just climbed, hard enough in all conscience, were positively flattened out. The holds were good, but the effort needed to hoist oneself up them was great. She seemed to make no sort of effort, and now, an illusion perhaps of growing fatigue, it seemed that the ghost of beauty was walking somewhere above him. He found himself craning up, fascinated, at the chrysanthemum aureole of hair, while over one shoulder he carefully, as instructed yesterday by Harry, paid out her rope. There was something uncanny about the little creature; then he mentally shook himself, for he had rationalized that sort of emotion long ago. Then came her call from above, and it was, once again, his exhausting turn.

And the climb grew progressively harder. Each pitch made new demands on unaccustomed muscles, and the suspicion came to him that this was not at all what his Dorothy, her every thought for his comfort and enjoyment, could have planned.

But the difficulties which so taxed him did not, apparently, exist for the red-headed sprite. She stood now at the foot of a vertical crack, perhaps five inches wide. Into this she inserted one leg and thigh. ''Tain't easy, this, not for a girl,' she remarked dispassionately, the first comment on the climbing she had vouchsafed. Then, with a movement part squeeze, part wriggle, she gradually propelled herself upwards. Ten feet above, the crack ran out on to more broken stuff, and she disappeared.

In his turn he inserted his leg and thigh, and felt about for a handhold to pull up on. But there was nothing. The rock on either side of the crack was perfectly smooth.

Plainly, one had to do it by jamming. He pushed his knee further in, and levered his weight up on it. At once the rock seemed to close upon him like a pair of pincers. He was trapped.

He kicked around with the free leg, and found nothing but air. There was still not the vestige of a handhold. 'Give me some slack,' he shouted. 'I'm going down.'

The rope eased off, and with some trouble he pulled his knee out and slithered back to the start.

'What do I do if I can't make it?' he yelled up, and her answer floated down serenely: 'Just go on trying.'

How he was going to make it he had no notion, but other elements in the situation became abundantly clear. Rage possessed him. He set his teeth and went on trying.

Carefully he fitted in again the already sore knee. He wasted no more energy looking for handholds, but thrust upon it all his weight. Shoving, squeezing, struggling, he hoisted himself by inches. Now the hateful crack was squeezing his shoulders, too. He felt as though half his chest were being ground to powder. The agony was excruciating, and the free half of him was, by contrast, so horribly unenclosed, so suspended over the void. And then, suddenly, his hand could reach the blessedly sharp top of the crack. He could haul on something; he could gradually, with an exquisite sensation of relief, pull the imprisoned leg free. It came up bleeding, and with a great rent in the knee of its miserably ineffective protection, thin flannel trousers.

The broken stuff above was nothing; in ten bounds he was up beside her, fast enough to catch the fiendish glee on her face.

'You bloody little bitch—' he began, and stopped for breath and to think of an expletive vile enough.

'You been quick, any road,' she grinned. 'I reckoned you'd be an hour at least.'

And all at once laughter overwhelmed him. He clutched the rock and yelled. Doubtless it was hysteria, in which case she must have been hysterical too, for she made nearly as much noise.

When at last they were quiet, he said:

'So I did better than you expected, hey? It was sheer fury got me up, I can tell you. I was damned if I was going to be beaten by such a filthy trick. Got it all worked out, hadn't you? What would you have done if I'd stuck permanently? Never thought of that, I suppose?'

She gave him her infernally impudent grin, and he marvelled that he could ever have thought her plain. 'I reckoned you wouldn't.'

'And on what grounds?'

'Eh, well, folk don't. You didn't see any bodies lying around, did you? And besides—'

'Well?'

'There's an easy way round to the left.'

'Well, I absolutely will be damned!' This time he almost laid hands on her. 'And to think it never occurred to me to have a look. There's nothing bad enough for you. You're a public menace. Is every greenhorn the victim of your sense of fun, or was it an honour reserved for me?'

'Nobody ever got my goat like you did.'

'I have no recollection of getting your goat. In fact I don't remember noticing your existence.'

'That was just about it. Sitting in our common-room like you owned it and jawing about economics and making me look a fool.'

'Well, I happen to know a good deal about economics, and it is a subject in which more intelligent persons than yourself find interest. That gives me the right to jaw, as you so elegantly put it. Not my fault if it makes you look a fool.'

'All right then. I happen to be able to climb. That gives me the right to lead you up the Vertical Vice. Not my fault if it makes you look a fool.'

'I suppose there is some sort of parallel, to the uneducated mind.' But he knew now that it didn't matter what he said about her mind. She had triumphed; and he in his turn had not come altogether discreditably out of her baiting. 'What will your dear Dorothy say when she hears?'

'I reckon she won't hear.' She looked at him brazenly. 'And she's your dear Dorothy.'

'Oh – er, yes.' He suddenly regretted having mentioned Dorothy, who plainly had nothing to do with this purely personal duel.

'That reminds me,' she said. 'Have you any money?'

'I suppose so.' He felt in his trouser pocket and produced two half-crowns, with a faint surpise at finding them unflattened by their passage through the crack.

'Then let's get on and finish the climb. There's a farm down the other side of the mountain. You can take me there for tea.'

Mercifully the rest was easier, and soon they were pounding down grassy slopes to the tea he desired more than anything on earth. It affected him like alcohol; his head spun deliciously. She on the other hand, he saw with amusement, became extremely ladylike, and froze the Welsh female who waited on them with her glance. Not till he had paid for the tea did she revert to her normal off-handedness, and, marching him to the door of some back premises, call: 'Hey, Miss Williams, here's Dorothy's boy.'

'What, Mr. Derwent?' the Welsh female exclaimed. 'Whyever were you not telling me before? I wouldn't have charged him. He would have been welcome in here, like you.'

'Eh, well, he's got the brass. And I wanted to know what it feels like being a lady.'

It'll cost more than half a crown to make you that, thought Michael Derwent, and found himself being effusively greeted by the Welsh female, who was, it appeared, an intimate friend of Dorothy's, and wanted to know why he had been so long in coming to Cae Capel, and when he intended to get married. He explained, with what he hoped was adequate politeness, the impossibility of getting married on a lecturer's salary; but he was annoyed. Dorothy herself was always careful not to hawk him about as her possession, and he did not relish having another woman do it for her. Besides, he was by no means quits with the little Canning girl, and all this harping on his engagement was, he obscurely felt, a part of her plan to cramp his style.

'Talking of Dorothy, hadn't we better be getting home?' he said at last with frank impatience. They took their leave, and Miss Williams went thoughtfully back to her oven.

Five miles of road separated them from Llanllugwy, and another five led back to Cae Capel. But she was, he found, as much at home on the road as she had been on the mountain. She knew instinctively which cars to flag, and how to keep their drivers happy while they served her turn. He sat in the back on each occasion, and was disregarded. His friends of yesterday were waiting at the hostel to welcome him, and concerned when they saw his rent and now slightly swollen knee.

'Where on earth did you take him?' Harry Rimmer demanded, and, on getting a straight answer, covered her with angry reproaches.

'Oh, but I enjoyed it,' Michael protested. 'Really I did. I got up, and that's the main thing. I'll go again with her to-morrow if she'll have me.'

'I'll be ironing shirts tomorrow,' she answered. Under the reproaches all her sullenness had returned.

'Oh lord, I'd forgotten you're only here at the weekend. Next Saturday, then.'

'Well, I call that very forgiving of you,' said the redundant Rimmer, on whom it apparently had not dawned that he might be unwanted. 'It's a lot more than she deserves. Now if I'd thought it funny to play her such a trick when she was starting, six months ago—'

And so he lost her. She was able to slip away upstairs, leaving him buttonholed. 'Ta-ta, professor,' she called over her shoulder. 'Have a nice time.' He stared after her in exasperation, for until he had got even with her any sort of time he might have could only be intolerably dull.

iv

Cathy returned much chastened to Tooley Street. It was no good telling herself that she did not mind Harry's disapproval, for she did; he and Dorothy were the two people whose opinions mattered. Furthermore, when he told her she had behaved like an irresponsible child, he spoke, she was beginning to realize, more truly than he knew. As a means of squashing Michael Derwent her scheme now looked remarkably unwise. He had not been squashed; or, if squashed in one direction, he was thrusting up again in another and far more troublesome one. She remembered with horrid clearness the look on his face as he stared after her, and it was a look she had seen before.

She had the sexually successful woman's dread of seeming to fancy herself irresistible; that was soft, an old maid's trick. On the other hand, she was not going to be taken unawares. It was true she had once gone cheap, but Michael Derwent was not to know it. And if he thought he could amuse himself with her just because she was no class. . . .

So, guiding the iron in and out of frills on the season's summer blouses, she endeavoured to work herself into indignation in order to blot out sensations more disquietening. For behind possible insults to her virtue lay the infinitely worse consequence that Dorothy might be made to look silly.

Vividly she remembered the walk home from the Amphitheatre, and Dorothy's earnest advice to her on waiting. At the time it had seemed as if those who were class must be of a different mould from common sorts. And so, indeed, Dorothy was; dear Dorothy, so fresh and cool and ladylike, Dorothy who didn't really like men. It was not hard to see how she managed the wait. But her young man, although so superior and learned, appeared only too like other people, and probably managed the wait by not, in fact, waiting at all. Carries on behind her back, I shouldn't wonder, thought Cathy, putting in more creases than she took out. Oh well, as long as she don't know. But in her heart she felt that her friend was humiliated by the very fact of not knowing; was humiliated by the fatal weakness of being the one who loved most. That was an error into which she felt confident of never falling. Young as she was, she knew men too well. Not the most desirable of them should ever turn her into that utterly vulnerable creature, the one who loved most.

Perhaps it would be better if next week-end she stayed away.

But to be driven out of Cae Capel, her true home and heaven, by Michael Derwent was too much. At such a possibility she revolted. The situation was one of her own imagining. Michael Derwent was a slimy type, no doubt, but he wasn't such a fool as to do his carrying on under his beloved's nose.

Probably he had never given her a thought since. In any case, he had had a whole week to cool down.

By Friday night she had recovered her bounce, and as it was one of Harry's many virtues that he never carried any sort of disagreement over from one week-end to the next, they made the journey in their usual tearing spirits. 'You and Stan take the professor on next,' she did, however, suggest to Harry, who replied, with perhaps a shade of reserve: 'Of course, if he wants us to. But it's up to him.'

Dorothy's bright face in the kitchen seemed a further guarantee; plainly, she had had a happy week with her wayward love. But her words were less reassuring. 'Hello, pets. Somebody go and tell Michael Cathy's here. He's been talking of nothing but your iniquitous conduct all week. That thing you lured him up made a deep impression, and he's thirsting for more. That's Michael all over. He can't resist any sort of challenge, and whatever he does he must do well.'

Michael, thus summoned, came and sat with them while they ate their supper. Harry, who had hoped for another lecture, and was in fact ready furnished with questions on the recommended textbooks he had been studying in the week, was disappointed. All Mr. Derwent now wished to talk about, it seemed, was climbing. The prevalent passion of Cae Capel had got hold of him like any other neophyte. He had lost his Oxford pallor and looked bronzed and wiry, and to Cathy's eye truculent. He had been out three times in the week with climbers staying at the hostel, Dorothy on one occasion snatching an hour to come too, and he told them of his progress, pitch by pitch.

'You seem to be getting on grand,' said Harry politely, feeling that comment was expected, and finding that Cathy, though the conversation was directly addressed to her, concentrated on her pudding.

'I don't know about that, but I'm not quite as green as I was last weekend,' conceded Mr. Derwent with complacency. 'At least I know what a severe pitch looks like from the bottom. As you will find, madam, if you try any more of your girlish games. Where were we going tomorrow, by the way?'

'Harry—' Cathy began, and saw it was no use. Harry was quite put off, and no wonder. Michael Derwent, however, seemed unaware of currents of feeling, and pursued without waiting for an answer:

'I'd thought of Lliwedd. I'd like to have a look at the Snowdon side before I go. We'll take the car.'

Like bloody hell we will, Cathy thought. Snowdon and what else? And it isn't the car; it's Dorothy's car, and you aren't married to her yet and can stop talking as though what's hers is yours. Aloud she said in her flattest voice:

'Reckon I don't feel up to Lliwedd. I'll take you on the Slabs and the Upper Buttress.' It was the shortest walk and the most public setting that could be contrived.

'Oh, well, we'll discuss it in the morning,' said Mr. Derwent airily, as though there were anything to discuss; as though beginners and mere seconds had any right to make their voices heard. Really, beside him, Leonard Head seemed almost modest. But at any rate she went to bed with the satisfaction of knowing that he was no longer a first favourite with her friends.

Next day, of course, he yielded, but with an air of pandering to female whims which she found intensely irritating. And he dismissed contemptuously her last-ditch suggestion that Dorothy should come too. 'What, and hang about half the morning waiting for her to finish her chores? I never heard anything so unreasonable. She's not on holiday, and I am. She can do this kind of thing all through the year, and I'm only here for a fortnight.' Cathy perceived that to insist on Dorothy's claims would not be doing a service to her friend.

They walked up to the Slabs in a silence as profound as on their first expedition, but its quality was different. Then, he had not noticed her; now, he glanced at her sideways with a sly amusement. She did not relish being regarded as a joke, but if that was all it was going to amount to it would certainly be a relief.

But the day and the rock were warm, the Slabs were covered with voluble parties, and the air was musical with every kind of humming, whistling and yodelling from Bach to Irving Berlin. With the caress of granite on one's fingers it was impossible to remain in bad humour. Moreover, she saw at once that his claims were just; he had made astonishing progress. He climbed with his brain; one could see him pause before a hard move and think it out. As they ate their lunch beneath the Upper Buttress, honesty compelled her to give him the praise he asked.

'Well then, what about letting me try a lead?'

Remembering the months it had taken her to reach this ambition, she humbly marvelled at masculine audacity. But she was firm. 'You're not ready for it yet – not till you use your feet more and your arms less. And not with me, any road. I couldn't hold a falling leader. You'd best get Harry to second you if you want that.'

'Ah yes, the obliging Rimmer. A nice little chap, but I confess I amuse myself better with you. When I'm on holiday I do like a rest from the undergraduate mind.'

Cathy was not quite sure of his meaning, but if he imagined he would please her by sneers at Harry, he could think again.

He got up and examined the start of the climb, trying the first holds, and suddenly she saw him as childish in his refusal to take no for an answer. 'I must say this bottom pitch looks easy.'

'Ay, it is, but it's exposed when you get up a bit. I've seen somebody that fell eighty feet off it.'

'Good lord. Was he dead?'

'It was a lass. She wasn't killed, but she gave up climbing.' It came to her that they must be sitting almost where Doreen fell. Strange to think of that grim vigil, mist, wind, soul-chilling solitude; and now it was a happy summer's day, with thyme and harebells in the grass. She had been on the verge of learning something immensely important then; and somehow, she had forgotten it since. . . . Partly in an effort at recapture, she told him the story of the accident. Anyway, it was a lesson that would do him no harm.

'And you stuck with her all those hours? What a damnably creepy experience. I wonder you didn't go out of your mind.'

It had been far from Cathy's intenton to claim any credit for the episode, and she was disconcerted. 'Oh, that was nothing. It was Dorothy had all the worry of getting the search-party together – yes, and she's done it for lots of others, too – it's a terrible strain for her.' But he seemed quite unable to visualize the strain on Dorothy. 'And a fat lot of use I was when the chaps came. They wouldn't let me do any of the carrying, except for one spell on the level.'

'I should think not. A little bit of a thing like you.'

'Oh well,' Cathy muttered, 'when you have the fun you ought to take the raps.' She got up to start the climb, her disquiet returning. She did not wish to be praised, or called a little bit of a thing; she did not wish to have her appearance commented on in any way. That was comic, just like life; when you didn't want a chap to do it, no amount of rudeness would choke him off.

At any rate, the climb kept him quiet. They balanced delightedly up the arete, over the pinnacles, round the corner, along the bastard hand-traverse ('Use your feet,' shouted Cathy indignantly, 'not your knee, not your knee!'). They ended, laughing, almost at the top of the big Glyder, and to the north and west spread the hazy blue rim of the sea. They lay relaxed after effort, feeling the sun bake into them. And then, blest if he didn't start it again.

He sat up, took a long look at her half-averted face, and observed:

'Curious that though you're not beautiful and don't begin to be pretty one should wish to sleep with you just the same.'

'You keep a civil tongue in your head,' said Cathy angrily; and knew at once that she had made a mistake.

She should have laughed; she should have cheeked him back. Now, of course, he thought that he had frightened her, and naturally he would follow up so tempting an advantage.

'Don't be alarmed,' he said. 'Just my naughty manner of speaking, nothing personal. If I've outraged your modesty I apologise. But I didn't somehow put you down as one of those little working-class prudes.'

'Bet you don't know the first thing about the working class,' she said, reddening.

'No, but I'm most anxious to learn.'

'Well, you can learn from somebody else.'

'Dear, dear, I've really upset you. And yet I only told you the truth, and I'm not the first, am I? Come, don't be so illogical. Why must women find it necessary to go through this elaborate pretence?'

Cathy had the unpleasant sensation of being out of her depth. She could handle sauce from her own kind, but his kind had unfair advantages, and every time she opened her mouth she seemed to make it worse. She was resolved that he should not get another word from her, but she had to endure a good deal more banter while she coiled the rope. When it was finished she flung him the coil, said 'Oh, don't talk so daft,' and shot away home down the big scree gully. She could outdistance any beginner on a rough scramble, be his legs never so long, and she was down at the hostel ten minutes before him and safely engaged in useful tasks for Dorothy in the kitchen.

But she could not, of course, stay there for ever, and at dinner it was obvious that Michael Derwent was not going to let the matter drop. He sat opposite her and baited her continuously in a manner more worthy of a silly schoolboy than of an Oxford don. Indeed, the spectacle of Miss Elliott's young man trying to get a rise out of Cathy Canning was sufficiently curious to rouse the interest of Johnny and one or two more alert souls. And the whole evening still stretched before them, when Dorothy would come into the common-room and, unless he had managed to pull himself together, must surely notice. . . .

But it was Dorothy who released her, drawing her away from the washing-up and saying:

'I'm terribly sorry to have to ask you, pet, but I clean forgot to do the caravan after you left this morning, and I've such a pile of office work—'

'Of course!' cried Cathy. 'I meant to do it anyway; you oughtn't to have had to tell me.' Infinitely thankful, she tore off down the road.

The caravan was in a state. Bed unmade, shaving water not thrown out, and his clothes everywhere but in the lockers. This dear place which seemed her own, and which she took such pleasure in keeping immaculate, was profaned by the habits of a spoilt baby. Fat lot of comfort he'll be in the home, thought Cathy indignantly. By the familiar acts of sweeping and dusting she asserted her possession again and drove him out. She became rapt, absorbed, and did not hear footsteps coming through the little wood. As he tumbled up the steps and flung open the door, she spun round.

'Well, what about it?' he said.

'What about what?' She pushed his clothes anyhow into the locker and banged it shut. 'Look, I've almost finished. I'll be out of here in a jiff.'

'Oh no.' He shut the door and leant against it. In the dim light he seemed, with his bright eyes and heavy breathing like someone drunk. But there was no strong drink within five miles of Cae Capel.

'You know perfectly well what I want. All this running away is just silly, isn't it? Because you want it, too. And we'll never have a better moment than this.' And his eye went past her to the big double bunk, neatly made up for the night.

'Get on, you're crazy,' she said.

'And please drop those little-girl airs. They don't deceive either of us. I'm not the first you've led a dance. Perhaps I'm the first that's caught you, but even that doesn't seem likely, somehow. Come on, you're not really the squeamish kind. It'll give me extraordinary satisfaction, and it won't do you the slightest harm.'

'If you think that because I work in a laundry—'

'No, of course I don't. I promise you that the girls I've had who didn't work in laundries made infinitely less fuss. But don't you think you've made enough for honour to be satisfied?' He left the door and came towards her, so that both were conscious of the tiny space enclosing them. She backed away, and he sat down on the bunk, adopting a tone less directly menacing. 'Look, you don't really grudge me five minutes' kindness? Just let me kiss you, anyway. Then we'll know better about the rest.'

It was no use trying to spare Dorothy any longer. She let the name fly at him like a stone.

'Dorothy?' He looked genuinely startled. 'She has nothing to do with it. What Dorothy doesn't know won't hurt her. But if the ethics of the thing is worrying you, it needn't. She and I have an understanding. Till we're married each of us is free.' He seemed quite unaware of the enormous pity to which he had exposed his future wife. 'Why, you know her almost as well as I do. You know she's not the jealous kind.'

'Not at all,' agreed Cathy dryly. 'So you can sleep around, and she can sleep around. And does she?'

'See here,' he said, suddenly angry, 'suppose we leave Dorothy out of it.'

'Ay, that would just suit you,' shouted Cathy, suddenly still angrier. 'Leave Dorothy out of it, because she's too good to be mentioned in the same breath with your grubby goings-on. But don't lay off them on that account; go ahead just the same, under her nose and with somebody who's supposed to be her friend. How dare you talk to me about leaving her out? I wish she'd get herself another boy and give you the chuck.'

'Thank you. You can spare me the rest of your plans for my future. You've refused; let it go at that. I wonder why a woman who's saying no always has to do it so ungraciously? I certainly thought I'd had what amounted to an invitation. However, I see my mistake.'

It sounded like dismissal. Thankfully, in spite of her rage, she edged towards the door.

'But don't kid yourself. Taking that high moral tone has given you no end of a kick, but all it really means is that you find me repulsive. I've seen the sort of look you give other men. That lad who sat next to me at supper – if I'd happened to have golden hair and a beautiful face you wouldn't have let Dorothy's claims stand in your way for half a minute.'

'What lad?' Cathy asked. 'I didn't look at any lad.' And it was quite true; she had been too preoccupied by his rudeness and her own embarrassment to know who sat next to him.

He stared at her, and, as he perceived that her bewilderment was genuine, seemed to crumple. 'Oh, God!' he said. 'What a fool I've made of myself. What a bloody fool.'

She saw that she had him cornered. And then, because she was Cathy Canning, who liked men, because she understood their hungry need to believe in their own attractions, because she had already committed against two of them the crime of undermining that most essential confidence, compunction seized her. She had ticked Michael Derwent off; she had shown him; she had brought him low. And now before she left she ought to do something, say some right word, to help him get up again.

'Look here, it's not true what you said, about me finding you repulsive,' she began in quite a different voice from any he had heard her use, a coaxing voice, almost maternal. 'I like you really. You've plenty of guts, and I'm not saying that if things hadn't been different you mightn't have had a chance.

But I'd only be a bit of fun to you, and Dorothy's the real thing, isn't she? You think the world of her, under all this fool talk. Carrying on behind her back can't be right, no matter what you think you've arranged. You know very well you'd ought to be ashamed.'

'Oh, all right, I suppose so,' he answered listlessly, kicking the strip of drugget on the floor. Then he roused himself. 'Damn it all, no. I've often been ashamed of the way I treat Dorothy, the way I use her and batten on her and get off scot free. But this extraordinary feeling for you is at least disinterested. I stand to gain absolutely nothing by it – I risk losing a hell of a lot. But I'd have risked it all to get you. I'd have gone through fire.'

She was silent, shaken in spite of herself by the real note of passion in his voice.

'What a way to talk! Despicable, isn't it, for a person supposedly educated? No wonder you think me cracked. But I'll tell you something crazier still. I've wanted you because of this incredible place, because of these hills. If I'd met you anywhere else I'd never have looked at you. But when I watched you climbing, you seemed a part of them. I felt that by having you I'd be a part of them, too. You are the mountain. I can't hope that you'll ever understand.'

But she did understand. It was a wonderful thing he had said to her. Looking up at her at last, he could see it for himself.

'Oh, Cathy,' he said, stumbling towards her, 'Cathy, darling—'

For a terrible moment it seemed as though she were compelled to surrender. Then she had jerked herself free of her madness, and had got the door open, and was down the step, and through the grove, and running frenziedly away from him, up the steep mountain road.

V

Now she was really frightened. Nobody, she knew now, could frighten her except herself, and of herself she was terrified. It seemed that there was nothing, no meanness or treachery, too vile for her to be driven to by this fire in the blood. If only I hadn't gone with Leonard, she thought endlessly. That started it off. And yet the poison seemed to come from further back, from Bill, from the furtive back-alley cuddling and the sniggering schoolboys. She had thought that at Cae Capel she would be free from it, but all the time it was working underneath her will and thought, and a chap had only to look at her in that way, to use that tone of voice. . . .

Nothing had happened. That was the truth, but what a half-truth! If Dorothy could have seen and heard them, would she not have been almost more hurt than by the thing itself? As it was, how meet Dorothy, what possible manner put on to deceive her? She ought never to have been good to me, Cathy thought, her throat dry, her eyes stinging; and then the hostel lights came round the corner and it was necessary to have ready an immediate façade.

From the common-room came gusts of laughter. In the hall stood a solitary figure, a tall, fair boy, rather folornly studying the notice-board. This, she realized, must be the lad who had so baselessly roused Michael Derwent's jealousy. There was something uncanny in finding him become flesh and blood. But he looked to be at a loose end, and might be her solution to the problem of tomorrow.

'Hello,' she said.

He turned and politely answered her greeting. He was nice-looking, certainly, with that rather long, grave face, but nothing to notice.

'You on your own?'

'Ay.'

'Like to come climbing with me tomorrow?'

'Well – I haven't done much.' Obviously lonely though he was, he was in no hurry to rush into the arms of strangers. She liked him the better for it.

'That don't matter,' she said. 'We'll go up something easy. Fact is, it'd be doing me a favour. There's a chap I don't want to have to go with, and if I'm fixed up with somebody else—'

'I see.' His youth and shyness did not altogether eclipse amusement. 'In that case I'd be glad to.'

'What's your name?'

'Christopher Thwaites.'

She did not tell him her name. She assumed, and rightly, that anyone who had been more than a night at Cae Capel must know who she was.

'Get the warden to give you a job tonight, then, so that we can make an early start tomorrow. Tell her I told you. Well, so long.'

Looking back on that moment many, many times afterwards, it seemed to her fantastic, incredible that thus carelessly, as a convenience, a mere catspaw, she should have picked up Christopher.

CHAPTER SIX

'THAT'S A funny name,' said Cathy, 'Thwaites.'

They were lying at the foot of the Amphitheatre Buttress, eating bilberries, which here grew large as grapes and aromatically sweet. She had fairly run him out of the hostel in her anxiety to be gone before Michael Derwent could come up the road; and they had done the long walk over the intervening mountain in silence, for he seemed not to feel the need of chatter, and she was unhappy and preoccupied. 'Are you abandoning Michael, then?' Dorothy had asked, and she had answered coolly: 'I promised that lad that's here on his own.' And Dorothy had given her a hurt look, changing – yes, possibly – to a worried one. Well, it's about time she worried, thought Cathy angrily, and yet knew that this sweet unsuspiciousness was just what one loved.

Rightly interpreting her remark to mean nothing uncivil, but merely that she had never heard the name before, Christopher Thwaites told her that it was common enough where he came from.

'And where's that?'

'Wharswick.' The name meant nothing to her. 'It's a mill-town in Lancashire. My father and my mother are mill-hands. But we're almost in the country. We got the moors round us on three sides.'

And, indeed, one could hear the moors in his voice, which she found delightful, without knowing quite why. She merely thought that it sounded homely after Michael Derwent's, and that he spoke bad like herself. Her ear was not qualified to detect the difference between her Merseyside whine and the age-old, beautiful voice of the Pennines.

'And do you work in the mill, too?'

'No, I've a job in Bootle. I'm a teacher.'

She sat up. 'How funny.'

'Why is it funny?' But he grinned, and his long-drawn vowel, 'fooney', made it funnier still. 'I reckon someone's got to.'

'Oh, course. I didn't mean that. It must be grand to be a teacher. You must be ever so brainy. Only I think of them as old and sort of stringy, like what I had.'

'You got to start sometime. I'm twenty-one.'

'But you can't have been at it long?' Only since autumn, he was forced to admit.

'But you don't need brains for my kind of teaching. You can't hardly call it teaching. Fifty in my class – fifty ten-year olds. You just need to be a sort of steam-roller; drive, drive, drive. It's a miracle they ever learn to read and write. It's not our teaching does it. They suddenly seem to teach themselves. All but two or three half-wits, but you got to have them because there aren't enough special schools to put them in.'

'D'you not like teaching, then?'

'Oh, ay, I like it. It's what I've always wanted to do. But every now and then I get a bit fed up.'

'Do the kids lead you a dance?'

'Now and then. The girls are the worst. You aren't supposed to smack them, but sometimes I do. It's the only thing they understand.'

'Sounds just like me,' said Cathy delighted. 'I was a proper terror at school. Sat in the back row with the boys and never learnt a thing.'

'Well, it's nothing to be proud of.'

'Not but what, if I'd had a teacher that looked like you—' And, unmindful of immediately past experience, she gave him her most impudent stare, and was enchanted to find that he could take it without blushing, and merely pulled a cheeky grimace at her in return. I'm not the first that's made eyes at him, she decided with satisfaction, callowness not being among the qualities she admired.

He lived, she found, with a married teacher at Bootle. It wasn't bad, but he liked to get away at week-ends. Once a month he went home, and for the rest he had been working through the North Wales hostels, which were unfamiliar to him, though the Lakes he knew well. Her staying always at Cae Capel he found odd.

'Well, it's the best for climbing.'

'I suppose so. Reckon I like fell-walking better.'

You'll like climbing better when I've done with you, Cathy resolved. 'Is there others besides you at home?'

'No, I'm the only one. Me mother likes kids, and she'd ought to have had half a dozen, but something went wrong when I was born.'

'I daresay she thinks all the more of you.'

'That's so,' agreed Christopher. 'Waited on hand and foot, I've been. Eh, proper spoiled.' But he did not seem spoiled. 'What about you?' he politely inquired.

'Oh, I got a sister, but she's no use.' At the thought of Norma she felt suddenly angry, and, turning, saw three figures descending the opposite hillside. 'Here, if we're going to climb this bloody Buttress, we'd best start.'

She had chosen it because it was easy and distant, and because Johnny Hollinger, impartially distributing his favours, was this morning leading Harry and Stan up the appalling wall on the opposite side of the Amphi-theatre, which was his present speciality. They would have a dress-circle view.

Christopher was not, she found, a complete beginner. He understood rope management, climbing slowly but confidently, and enjoyed himself. On the ledge above the exposed pitch they rested and ate some amazing black parkin which was a secret recipe of his mother's. 'Presently you'll see some real climbing,' Cathy said. The wall confronting them across the chasm seemed to consist principally of overhangs. 'Are you telling me,' said Christopher, 'that chaps get up there?'

'Some chaps.' She was suddenly proud of good-for-nothing Johnny. 'The leader's the best we've got at the hostel. He's supposed to be as good as anybody climbing now. Eh, there he is.' Johnny came into view under one of the overhangs, unexpectedly tiny; with this fly-like figure on it one was better able to appreciate the immense scale of the precipice.

Johnny moved upwards like a spider. Sometimes he would seem to meditate and gain inspiration, for he scarcely ever groped or patted the rock. He established himself by what was, one hoped, a belay, for now Harry appeared. Harry was a nice climber, but his movements, besides Johnny's, were tentative, and one could see him test his rubbers thoughtfully on what were evidently not footholds at all, merely shallow scoops in the rock.

'Whew,' Christopher said at last. 'Shall you ever do that?'

'No, I don't expect so.' She was watching Johnny with the narrow, expert concentration of one performer for another. 'It looks out of my class. Though I suppose I was on something pretty near as hard when I went with him on the other side of Snowdon. But I was scared. Well, let's get on with ours. Then we can walk round and watch them from above as they finish.' They addressed themselves again to their rib, which looked almost level after the horrors across the way.

A climb of that standard, and with three on it, took time. Cathy and Christopher had been lying for half an hour on their stomachs, peering over into the void, before Johnny's foreshortened figure came up over the bottom horizon. They could watch his face as he climbed; it was rapt, self-forgetful, quite unlike the face he presented to the world. He reached a last resting-place some twenty feet below them, and tied on; then Cathy whistled, and instantly saw the monkey-face she knew.

'So that's who you're with, sweetie. We've been worrying something dreadful. We thought it was the professor, but we couldn't make out.' One might feel surprise that three people who had been engaged on a life-and-death struggle on the worst precipice in Wales should have had time for gossip; but not if one knew Johnny. 'What have you done with him? Did he get fresh?'

'Oh, shut up,' Cathy said.

Ultimately the other two joined him, and unroping – for the last twenty feet, a climb by normal standards, did not count in this class – they arrived simultaneously on the grassy top. 'Bit of all right, I'll say,' remarked Harry, who looked strained and tired. 'About the hardest thing I ever expect to do. You should take Cathy sometime. She'd be the first woman on it.'

'Eh, Harry, it's not fit for a lass,' protested Stan. Cathy was reasonably satisfied that she no longer caused him much heartache, but from that to not caring if she broke her neck was a step he was unable, apparently to take.

'This is Christopher Thwaites.'

'We saw you on the Buttress,' said Harry kindly. 'Nice climb, isn't it? One of my favourites.'

'Oh, and mine,' said Johnny. I often dream I'm on the Amphitheatre Buttress, and wake up screaming to find myself on Longland's.'

'He's a teacher,' said Cathy, continuing her introduction. 'Isn't that a scream?' His profession roused in them the keenest interest. At last Harry had found someone capable of appreciating his views on the raising of the school-leaving age.

'What do you teach?' Johnny asked.

'The three r's,' answered Christopher a trifle dryly. 'We still haven't got beyond that in the primary schools, you know.'

'I suppose you were sent to Eton, Johnny?' Harry said.

'As a matter of fact, no. We are a family of Etonians, but the cash was running low and they did me on the cheap. I went to a minor public school in the Midlands, just like the real thing though, filthy initiation rites and slave-system and all. You grammar-school types don't know half your luck. No one thinks your characters will be stiffened by a foretaste of the concentration camp. I understand our friend here wouldn't be allowed to lay a finger on his little thugs.'

'He smacks the girls, though,' Cathy giggled. 'It's the only thing they understand.'

'Oh, naturally,' said Harry. 'Women adore force from their earliest years. You're wrong, though, Johnny, if you think we didn't get put through the mill. School was moderately civilized, but it was all saved up for the first week in the workshops. It's understood that all the old hands give the beginners hell. All sorts of tricks, like being sent to fetch non-existent tools – sounds silly, but it worries you sick when you're new to the job and wondering if you can hold it down. And some places even have the initiation ceremonies – I won't go into details in front of Cathy, but they're not pretty.'

'Ugh, what a vile lot mankind is,' said Johnny fretfully. 'I was never left in peace to enjoy myself till I got into the RAF. We were counted as heroes there, and so they let us alone. I suppose that's why rock-climbers are fairly decent to each other. When we're doing something quite blatantly dangerous the conscience of the bully is satisfied.' And for the moment one saw the ghost of a vulnerable Johnny, one who had known feeling. But it was only a ghost. He had long ago grown himself a second skin.

'Anyway, you've all had better chances than me,' said Cathy, not seeing why she should be left out of this orgy of self-pity. 'I'm one of Christopher's dead-end kids. Fifty of us to a class, and a wonder we ever learnt anything. I'm not going to be ashamed of my ignorance any more. I think I've not done so bad, considering.'

'I've not noticed you making much use of present opportunities to improve your mind,' said Harry.

'Think of all the economics you might have learnt these last two week-ends,' murmured Johnny.

'That'll be all from you.' She got to her feet.

But it was not all from him. He stuck to her like a leech, and presently she gave in and let him detach her from the others.

'Now come clean, darling. Tell me what happened. You know I'll never give you any peace till you do.'

'Look, Johnny, there must be something in you to get hold of. They call you the Honourable. Couldn't you be it for once in a way?'

'Well, perhaps I haven't a very high moral character, but you mustn't underrate my intelligence. I know which side of the bread Dorothy's sandwiches are buttered on.'

'Then you promise to keep mum?'

'I promise.'

'All right – he wanted to sleep with me last night in the caravan. And if Dorothy ever finds out I think I'll die. She looked at me a bit old-fashioned this morning, when I said I wasn't taking him again. Oh, gosh!' And picturing the misery that might lie ahead of her, she felt the tears come.

'Poor little Catherine,' said Johnny, making a genuine effort to hide his amusement. 'I shouldn't worry, though. His time here is nearly up, and Dorothy's too busy in the summer to go in for brooding in a big way. I daresay they'll both have forgotten your existence when they meet again. Horrid for you while it lasted, though. What did you do?'

'Ran.'

'He didn't—'

'He didn't rape me, if that's what you mean.'

'Probably a pity,' said Johnny, who had bottled down the amusement long enough. 'Well, well, fancy your turning out such a siren. It's your misleading looks – that hair, and those eyes. I feel almost sorry for the professor. He must have worked himself up no end. If only he'd consulted me, I could have told him it was no use making you dishonourable proposals. I'm sure he's never tried to seduce anything less than a B.A. before. You ought to feel flattered.'

'All right, laugh.' But she was beginning to laugh herself.

'You know, if you go on looking so seductive and being so unapproachable, you'll probably end by making a really brilliant marriage. It's a pity Ludovic's hitched up. You'd have had a *succès fou* as the Climbing Countess, and made us pots of money with your face on the cold-cream advertisements.'

'Ass,' said Cathy, laughing outright. There was no denying it, Johnny did cheer one up.

'And the new boy-friend was just brought along to get you out of a jam?'

'That's about it.'

'He's rather beautiful, though, isn't he?' He looked with dispassionate admiration at Christopher's figure towering above Harry, and even dwarfing Stan, who seemed more than ever ungainly in comparison. 'Perhaps this time you'll be the one to suffer.'

'He's only a kid, and you're not to rag him. When my turn comes I'll need one my own age.'

'Always this pitiful longing to be mastered. But don't forget,' ended Johnny encouragingly, 'he sometimes slaps the girls.'

When they caught up with the three in front she found that Harry was urging on Christopher to cancel the rest of his hostel bookings and join the camping party in the glade. It was just what she had wished to propose herself, but it sounded much better coming from the boys.

Christopher was obviously taken with the notion, though his north-country reticence prevented him from jumping at it. 'It's right kind of you, and I'll think it over,' was as much as he would promise. 'I might get me mother to send me tent. Can't be next weekend, any road. I've something else to do.'

At the hostel, where there was no sign of Michael Derwent, he drew Cathy aside.

'I reckon it's my turn to ask you a favour.' She was surprised; she had given him a grand day, and the entry into the most desirable of Cae Capel circles, and did not feel herself under any obligation. 'Next Saturday I'm bringing up six of our kids. Just for the day, you know; I thought I'd take them up Snowdon by the PigTrack. But if you'd come with us, we could get them over Crib Goch.'

And miss a day's climbing! – said Cathy's expression unmistakably.

'It was you saying you were once a kid like them that put it into my mind to ask you. They've none of them ever been off the streets before. It'd be something they'd remember all their lives.'

He had done; he was not going to plead with her; take it or leave it.

'Oh, all right, I suppose it won't hurt me for once.'

'That's grand. The education committee are letting me have a car, and we plan to be at Bryn Glas by eleven. See you then. So long.'

Smacks the girls, does he? thought Cathy, grinning as she packed her rucksac. She wondered what the others would say when they found the queen of Cae Capel roped into a Sunday-school treat. At the same time, she experienced a quite curious happiness. It was, no doubt, the gratifying consequence of having agreed to do something unselfish and truly kind.

ii

By the next Friday night this exaltation had worn off. Christopher's face was dim, and every detail of the hateful little scene in the caravan stood out nightmarish, and, since Johnny had laughed at it, with the added twist of farce. And Dorothy took on the aspect of an injured parent, whom one was afraid to face.

There was no putting off the meeting, however, for on the Friday nights when they camped Dorothy insisted on giving them supper in the kitchen, so that they should not have to cook a meal when they arrived tired from the day's work.

'Michael got home safe?' asked Cathy off-handedly. She had decided that not to mention him would look even more suspicious.

'I can only suppose so. I'm afraid he wasn't brought up to write bread-and-butter letters.'

That would be it. He would take it out of Dorothy by not writing; he would make her wretched by going into a sulk. The sheer injustice of it quite deprived Cathy of her appetite. She pushed the good food about on her plate.

'But I do think he enjoyed it, don't you?' Dorothy was continuing with a pitiful anxiety. 'He seemed to be getting really keen. I wanted him to promise me another week in the autumn, before term starts, but he's such a slippery devil to pin down.'

'Well, we did our best to give him a good time,' said Harry stiffly. He was ill at ease; they all were; impossible to prevent her seeing it.

'Indeed you did. I'm terribly grateful. I know he was, too.'

'I'm sorry about last Sunday,' said Cathy. 'But that lad looked so left out of it—'

'Oh, of course. I'm sure Michael understood.'

Damn and blast! Would they ever be back on their old easy footing again?

'Hello, the troops,' said Gwen, putting her head round the door.

'Oh, goody,' Cathy cried. 'I'd forgotten it was your weekend. You can help me with the school-treat tomorrow.'

'The what?'

'Chap I was out with last Sunday is a teacher. He's taking six kids over Crib Goch. Made me promise to help. It wouldn't be quite such a bind with you.'

'But I come here to get away from kids,' protested Gwen.

'Now, now,' Harry grinned. 'Not, surely, from your little wonders?'

'Oh, well. Provided you'll do as much for them when they're old enough. And you'll have to take me up something nice on Sunday.' By sheer persistence Gwen had so far overcome her ineptitude that she could now follow Cathy up an easy Difficult, though Harry always insisted on knowing which crag they would be on in order to avoid the noise.

'Was that boy a schoolmaster?' asked Dorothy, interested. 'And you say he's bringing some of his children? I do call that a nice idea. You'd better take something extra for their tea. I'll knock up a cake; it won't take me ten minutes.' She got out the mixing bowl. She had the house full and looked thoroughly tired, but it was useless to dissuade her; she was as obstinate as she was kind.

'Come on, we ought to get them tents up,' said Stan. Harry reluctantly rose.

'I'll do your washing up,' said Gwen, fetching a tray. Cathy rose to join her.

'Just a minute, Cathy,' Dorothy said.

Oh God, Cathy thought. She knows. She's going to say something. Oh, God help me, what shall I do?

'Is that woman going to give you a holiday?'

Slowly Cathy's wits came back to her. It was nothing to do with Michael. It was about Miss Hignett, whom for some reason, without ever having set eyes on her, Dorothy tended to dislike. Merciful heavens, it was all right.

'Well – I dunno. I suppose it's not due to me. I haven't been there a year. And we're short, with so many leaving when the weather got warm.'

'All the more reason why you need it. It'll be monstrous if she doesn't. Anyway, you know you can have the caravan.'

'You're an angel,' said Cathy fervently. 'but what about your friends?'

'They can come some other time. Anyway, I really can't cope with visitors who need looking after. Cathy, whatever's the matter? You look as white as a sheet. Are you ill?'

'It's nothing,' muttered Cathy. 'Just that it was hot at work today.' Well, that was true.

'Stick your feet up. I'll make tea as soon as this is in the oven. Of course that woman must give you a holiday. I've half a mind to write to her.'

'You might get me the sack,' said Cathy, grinning. 'But I'll ask her on Monday.' Oh boy, it was all right.

An hour later she was in bed in the caravan. It felt queer for a few moments, lying where he had lain last, wanting her. She heard again his urgent voice and saw his white, desperate face. Then she triumphed; her personality ousted his. The place belonged once more to her.

iii

'We'll ride it,' Gwen said firmly. 'We've oceans of time if we don't have to be at Bryn Glas till eleven. And then you can tell me all about Dorothy's boy.' Cathy, who already had the rock-climber's detestation of walking and hated cycling only slightly less, went off with a sigh to borrow Dorothy's bicycle.

She had not meant to confide in Gwen; but of course it all came out on the long, delicious free-wheel down to Llanllugwy, the very ease and speed of the movement inducing an unburdening of the heart. And Gwen was no unfeeling cynic; she was a staunch friend, and a married woman, too, who knew her way about.

Her championship left nothing to be desired. 'Of all the low tricks!' she cried. 'He sounds a bright lad and no mistake. Don't I wish I'd been there? I'd have learnt him some economics he wouldn't forget in a hurry. Poor little Cath.'

'That's all very well,' said Cathy, nettled at the implication that she could not handle importunate lovers. 'I reckon I can cope in the ordinary way. But don't you see, if I'd made a row, Dorothy was bound to find out?'

'Yes, he had you there,' Gwen admitted. 'That's why it was so mean. And that's the chap our Dorothy's going to tie herself up to. Makes my blood boil.'

'Mine too,' Cathy said, and brought out the question that had been tormenting her all week. 'Do you think she ought to marry him? She'll make such a grand wife – why can't she have someone that deserves her? She ought to do a lot better than that.'

'Ah, well, now you're going a bit far.' They had left the crossroads, and were pushing the bicycles up the first steep rise on the Snowdon road. 'I know any chap'd be lucky to get Dorothy, but, all the same, it don't seem so easy for her kind to marry as it is for us. I suppose it's because a lot of their men go to colonies and places, and, anyway, they expect to set up house in a bigger way. I daresay he's earning now more than Bert and I got married on, yet you see they don't consider it for a minute, and won't till he's got his thousand a year or whatever it is they pay professors. Course it's all this hanging about that does the mischief. Ten to one he'll make her a good hubby once they're hitched up. Waiting's the mistake. Just you remember that when your turn comes.'

'There won't be no turn for me,' said Cathy crossly.

'Don't talk soft,' said Gwen. Cathy acknowledged the justice of her reproof by a grin. It was all right for college girls and Johnny Hollingers to think themselves above getting married, but for her, with nothing but a life of manual labour as the alternative, of course it must be the goal.

'I'll have no carrying-on behind my back, any road,' she said.

'Maybe not. But you've got to pay for everything one way or another, that's my experience. You can't expect a fellow to be perfect all through, any more than he can expect you.' And it suddenly seemed likely to Cathy that Gwen's Bert, that paragon of marital virtue, might be a dull little man as well; unquestionably faithful, and willing to take charge of his children every fourth weekend, but otherwise not a patch on his energetic, lively mate.

They were early at Bryn Glas, and looked in on Miss Williams, for if Cathy passed through without acquainting her with the day's plans she invariably found out and was pained.

'Well I never,' she commented. 'A teacher and a lot of kids. He must be an awful good-looking teacher. Is he your new boy?'

'He's awful good-looking and he isn't my boy. I haven't got a boy. Next time I meet one of those machines I'm going to make a record of it, to save me answering daft questions. I can't think why folks are always trying to get me off.'

'Sorry, I'm sure,' said Miss Williams mildly. 'You take this bag of sweeties now for the poor kids.'

As they sat on the wall outside the farm Cathy tried to remember what, in effect, Christopher did look like; after all, he was a stranger, and his image was still pale. But when the battered station brake drew up and she saw his smiling face, with the six little urchin faces peering over his shoulders, his good looks burst on her with a shock of happy recognition. The small boys tumbled out on to the road, and while Christopher backed the brake into the car-park they stood and gaped at Gwen and Cathy, who were each wearing hundred-foot coils of rope and presented what was evidently an awe-inspiring sight.

Christopher came up beaming with pleasure. 'It's right kind of you. I wasn't sure you'd come. We were trying not to count on it, in case.'

'Promised, didn't I?' said Cathy gruffly. 'Brought my friend Mrs. Evans along. She knows more about kids than I do. Got two of her own.'

'It's right kind of you,' said Christopher to Gwen. 'Don't suppose you'll remember any of them apart, but this is Ern, this is Tom, this is Lance, this is Alec, and those two are both Jimmies. Now then, you. These kind ladies are going to take you up the mountain, and you do just what they say. Got it?'

The little boys looked oppressed. Cathy had known them immediately; they were pure Tooley Street, even to the smell, though they were all touchingly clean and their mothers had put them into what were evidently their best flannel shorts. She earnestly hoped there would be no catching on rocks. Individually they were indistinguishable, except for Alec, who was smaller and paler than the others and looked younger, though they were all of an age.

'Are we going right up there?' asked Ern, looking at Crib Goch.

'Ay, and higher,' said Cathy briskly. 'Think you can make it?' Silence.

'What's them ropes for?' Lance whispered.

'She pulls us up with them,' Ern opined.

'Oh no, I don't. We tie ourselves together so that no one gets lost, that's all. If there's any pulling, you pull me.'

Gwen and Christopher were soon discussing Lakeland miles and Pennine records. At first the children kept to heel, looking about them with the vacant faces which in the poor mean bewilderment and dread. But presently the little rocky path, with its steep corners and baby precipices, took their fancy, and they began to gambol. They were far ahead when they reached the first stream. Shouts went up. 'Please, teacher, can we have a drink?'

'Half a mo. You go a bit upstream, Ern, and make sure there isn't a dead sheep.' The prospect was entrancing; they all had to go and look for the dead sheep. They found instead a small, sticky flower, which of course they had to pick.

'That's sundew,' Gwen told them. 'It eats flies.'

'Does it really miss? Can we find some flies and see?'

'It doesn't eat anything now you've picked it,' said Christopher sternly. 'That'll learn you not to pick things.'

Snowdon on a fine July Saturday was anything but a solitude. Cathy, used to climbers' steep and secret little paths, was astonished to find herself moving in a sort of queue. Family parties, men with sticks, girls in sandals, there was no end to the riff-raff. They shook off some of it when they turned aside to climb Crib Goch, but even so had to wait five minutes while a fat pink man and his thin white daughter negotiated the rock-step in the path. This was a broken rise at an easy angle, but the drop was considerable below it, and while the fat man went up it with confidence, the daughter was greatly dismayed. The little boys watched her struggles apprehensively.

'I'll let the rope down to each of them,' Cathy said to Christopher. 'You tie them on.' She advanced upon the daughter and propelled her upwards with discreet shoves on the behind.

The little boys fairly flew up. The rope round their waists gave them enormous self-importance.

'This is a real climb, ain't it, miss?' Ern wanted to know.

'Go on,' said Jimmy One, 'I done harder things than this on the bomb-sites back home.'

Above the rock-step it was a long pull up scree. Cathy watched the climbing face of Lliwedd coming into view across Llydaw, and trusted that Johnny was not on it with field-glasses. 'Gosh, I wouldn't have thought anyone could get up it, miss,' said Ern. 'What'd happen if you fell off?'

'I don't fall off.'

'But you'd be a deader, wouldn't you?'

'Ay, I suppose so.'

'You ever seen a deader what had fallen off?'

'No indeed. What an idea.'

'My dad seen a deader, one what a wall had fallen on. That was in the bombing. He said he was all blue.'

'My dad seen lots of deaders.'

They were well away on a discussion of corpses, as merry as you please, all except little Alec, who looked scared again.

The scree ended at last in a sharp summit, and there was the famous knife-edged ridge of Crib Goch, running almost level to a further summit, with what evidently appeared to the fat man and the daughter to be sheer drops on either side. To a climber's eye they were mere scree-slopes down which one could have run.

'Maybe you'd like to go first?' the fat man suggested.

Cathy agreed with alacrity. Each child was tied on with a middleman's noose, Alec was placed next to Gwen, Christopher brought up the rear.

'Now it's easy really,' pronounced Cathy, surveying her battle-line. 'Plenty to hold on to, and we've got you tied. But no larking, mind. Each of you hold the rope and don't let it get caught or pull the one in front, and you're to hold to the rock with your hands all the time. Right.'

They moved forward, gingerly at first; but the exultation of tight-rope walking on top of the world soon gripped the little boys. They sent their yells ringing across Llydaw. 'Ain't this smashing, miss?' cried Ern. 'We'd all be deaders, wouldn't we, if one of us was to fall?'

'That's it, Alec – easy does it – I've got you,' came Gwen's comforting voice from the middle, by which it was possible to guess that little Alec was afraid.

'Give me your hand – there – I've got you,' said Christopher. Who's scared now? wondered Cathy, and, looking back, saw that it was, of course, the daughter. The two Jimmies were bounding along; but Christopher, as well as overseeing them, was obliged to pull the daughter by one hand while her father pushed her by the other. Lord, thought Cathy, if Johnny Hollinger could see me now.

A shriek went up; Ern, tiring of the slow progress of Alec next to him, had climbed out on to the dizzy crest of the ridge. 'You come down off that at once,' said Cathy. 'It's the one thing never forgiven you, jerking on anybody else's rope.' But her heart went out to Ern. He had what it took.

The thin part in the middle was passed by the daughter *à cheval*, with an occasional stomach-traverse. All the little boys, even Alec, did it upright, and their pride increased.

'We're a lot better than what she is, ain't we, miss?' Ern demanded.

'Shut up,' said Tom, who now revealed himself as the best-bred member, 'she might hear.'

Posing them on the pinnacle which marked the end of the ridge, the fat man took their photograph. The daughter sank gasping on to the first flat spot she had met for hours and ruefully massaged her ankles.

'Going up the next ridge?' the fat man asked.

'I reckon so – they've come so well. And you?'

'I think Nellie's had about enough. We'll drop off here and join the Pig Track. I must say your little chaps are real mountaineers.' He was obviously puzzled by their relationship.

'Let me introduce you to the famous Bootle Quins,' said Gwen. 'And this one' – she indicated Alec – 'is my youngest.'

'Give over, Gwen,' said Cathy; the fat man knew a joke when he met one, but the children were looking alarmed. She explained the composition of the party.

'Well, I call it real public-spirited,' said the fat man. 'We ought to give the kids back home a treat like this one day, eh, Nellie?' Nellie's expression implied that she had enough to do to look after herself. 'Bye-bye for the moment, then; we may meet you on the summit.'

Christopher unpacked his sack. The mothers had sent what they could – mostly fishpaste sandwiches and brightly pink shop tarts now disintegrating into an unappetising trifle. There was Dorothy's cake to fill in gaps, and Miss Williams's sweeties to assuage thirst.

'Now then,' said Christopher, 'if the ladies will kindly look at Lliwedd, we'll go down a few yards on t'other side and get behind a rock.' And he dealt firmly with deviationist tendencies.

'Bless the lad,' murmured Gwen. 'What a nice father he'll make one day.'

'Eh, you must have got to the age that likes them dewy,' Cathy jeered. But her friend was not deceived into thinking that it gave her no pleasure to hear Christopher praised.

The way over Crib y Ddysgyl was easier, but complicated by the need to see that Ern and Lance did not rush up adventurous variants, and it was very long. They all grew ragingly thirsty, and bore up only with the promise of drink on the summit. At the gap between this peak and Snowdon, however, appeared a phenomenon which quite revived their spirits – the tracks of the railway.

'Oo, shall we see the train?'

'Why don't it fall off?'

'I seen about it in the paper,' Ern said. 'See that jagged rail in the middle – well there's a cog on the engine, sort of ratchet like, hooks on to it, see?' It was with difficulty that Christopher, who visualized an engine charging round each rocky bend, could get them to walk on the path at the side.

'This is where we cross the ridge to Cloggy,' said Cathy, astonished that the first step in a climbing day should bring her to the same point she now seemed to have attained by a week's labour. 'From now on it's new to me.'

'What,' exclaimed Christopher, 'you never been up Snowdon before?'

'No, why should I? There's no climbing on it.'

Gwen and Christopher exchanged a look. 'Pathetic, isn't it?' Gwen said. 'They're all like that at Cae Capel.'

'Well, we'll teach her,' Christopher smiled. They teach her! As though anyone could teach her a thing about mountains! She trudged on whistling.

They were now back on the main tourist route, and part of a motley stream beside which the Crib Goch trippers appeared positively heroic. The small boys, fully aware of the distinction, swaggered visibly, and the two whose turn it was to wear the coils of rope drew all eyes. 'We've been over Crib Goch,' Ern informed a total stranger. 'We'd have been deaders if we'd let go.'

The rails ended in a neat station, just like anywhere, and beside it a station buffet, also just like anywhere, except that miles of blue air were visible through its plate-glass windows. Cathy and Gwen assuaged the cruellest thirst of their lives with cup after cup of costly tea, while the children, perfectly contented after one lemonade, spent the expedition's remaining funds on postcards of the train, which were dispatched, bearing the summit postmark, to their families. Ern alone, more conscious of his surroundings, reserved his sixpence for a folded paper *Panorama from Snowdon*, which showed Crib Goch, impressively knife-edged, in the left-hand corner.

In the midst of these transactions the train itself arrived. In a flash they were out on the platform. The tearoom filled rapidly, for the ascent by rail induced, it seemed, a thirst quite as deep as the ascent on foot. Cathy stared, fascinated, at the throng. Some announced their intention of climbing to the actual summit in a moment, but many, like the hair-netted lady at the next table, felt their day's work was done. 'I'm not stirring a step out of here,' she told the children. 'I can see all the views I want through that window.' Even kept in its proper place, behind plate-glass, the void was full of menace in her eyes.

And a mile away on one side was the precipice of Lliwedd; a mile on the other was the savage buttress of Clogwyn Du'r Arddu, where one felt for footholds, inch by inch. . . . This was something from another world.

'Reckon I'd ought to see what those kids are up to,' said Christopher, shouldered his way out, and did not return. When they investigated at length, they found him and the children equally absorbed in and on and around the engine, while the kindly driver explained to them how it worked.

'Is that what we come up a mountain for?' Cathy demanded indignantly. 'Isn't anybody interested in getting to the top?'

'No more than what you were,' replied Christopher, looking up with a grin.

'Eh well, that was different. Anyway Gwen and I are going. So long.'

A two minutes' scramble took them on to the gigantic castle that was the cairn. Among the humanity with which it seethed were Nellie and her father, who obligingly pointed out the landmarks. Although Cathy had now been climbing for nearly a year in North Wales, she could scarcely name any but the Cae Capel summits. Climbing had seemed to stand, as this mass of noisy, community-singing, snapshot-taking people now stood, between her and the vast shimmering landscape, with its message that never quite got through.

Presently they were joined by Christopher and his charges. 'The train was due to leave,' he explained in answer to their sardonic congratulations. The immensity of earth and air spread out below them baffled the children, and their faces took on the glazed expressions of the start. Then Ern spied Crib Goch and his jauntiness revived. 'Look, that's where we been!' – and, unfolding *Panorama from Snowdon*, he was able to see it triumphantly confirmed in print. They crowded round him, the train forgotten. They owned at any rate a little slice of the immensity. They would never again be utterly disorientated in the wild.

'A right sporting lot of kids,' the fat man told Christopher. 'I suppose they're your prize pupils?'

'Well, not exactly,' said Christopher, smiling. 'I picked those that don't get much chance at home. Alec's quite bright, as far as that goes, and so is Lance. Tom and the Jimmies are bird-witted, and Ern's been under the probation officer for the past year.'

'What's that?' Cathy exclaimed.

'Ay – pinching fruit off barrows. Ought I to have told you? Maybe you wouldn't have taken them if you'd known.'

'Eh, don't talk so soft.' She was within an inch of telling him why he had startled her, but this was hardly the spot for confidences. Yet Bill, to whom she had scarcely given a thought for many weeks, rose up and sat on the cairn beside her. If he'd had a Chris, she thought almost angrily; if he'd had someone to show him more interesting things to do than filling up the pools and watching Tranmere Rovers. . . . But that, perhaps, had been poor Bill's trouble. He had always been a looker-on, never done anything on his own account, until, like the bloody fool he was, he started doing a sight too much.

Christopher's voice, reminding her that he had to get the lot of them to their homes by supper-time, recalled her to the descent.

She led them back along the railway, down the zigzags of the Pig Track, and down again to the broad miners' track which was the easiest and flattest way home. But it was perhaps a mistake. The easy going bored the little boys; the slaty surface gave them blisters, and they began to know that they were very tired. They stuck it out, only quarrelling a little among themselves, and expecting at each of the endless bends in the path to see the road. Alec set up a whimpering which was plainly beyond his control, and was carried pickaback for a stretch by Christopher, after which his courage returned and he trotted along with the best.

At last the white walls of Bryn Glas showed ahead of them, and nobody had stolen their car. Miss Williams, although barely at the end of her Saturday rush, was on the look-out. Her bright eyes summed up Christopher, and there were more sweeties all round.

'I'm right grateful—' Christopher began.

'It was a pleasure,' said Gwen sincerely.

'I got my tent.' He looked at Cathy. 'D'you think Harry really meant it?'

'Course. He'd be no end put out if you didn't come when he'd asked you. Next weekend then. See you Friday night.'

'Now then, what d'you say to the ladies for giving you this grand day?'

Oh, schoolie! thought Cathy impatiently. She knew that he was right and that kids shouldn't take kindness for granted, but she resented the sheepish look that came over their tired and dirty little faces, and the chorus of thank-you-misses turned on from a tap. She stood equally glum and sheepish while he marshalled them into the brake and backed it out on to the road.

Suddenly Ern leant out of the window. 'Here, miss, this is for you. So's you'll remember us and take us again soon.' And he thrust *Panorama from Snowdon* into her hands.

The brake swung away down the pass, and until it was lost at the turn in the road half a mile below they all hung out of it, waving, and sending their love and gratitude to Gwen and Cathy and the hills.

'Proper comic, kids are,' observed Cathy, turning to seek a few minutes' repose in Bryn Glas kitchen. 'You can't help liking them.'

'You don't say,' rejoined Gwen, amiably sardonic. 'Seems to take you a month of Sundays to learn what everybody else has always known.'

iv

It was a fact that with the coming of the warmer weather, the Stonyhey Laundry faced staff trouble. It was an annually recurring fact, which Miss Hignett took in her stride. She did now, however, when making new appointments, look for a certain doggedness which would not be easily tempted away by the lure of milk-bars and ice-cream stalls. She thought she had detected it in Cathy Canning, and she was right.

Cathy was actuated by no conscious feeling of loyalty to Miss Hignett. That would have been odious and savoured of sucking-up. Miss Hignett was a boss, and on the other side, and must look out for herself. But there was something soft about giving up a skilled job, at which you could earn good money, simply for a breath of warm air. Any fool could put ice-cream into cornets. She stuck grimly to her iron, busier than ever now that customers sent frilly cottons to the wash. She did not mind how much overtime she worked, as long as it was not on Fridays. She put the money into her climbing equipment, which was now as elegant as any rich girl's; into a second pair of hand-made boots, and shorts tailored to measure, and a nylon rope. Miss Hignett, observing her industry and her faint air of aloofness, saw in her a forewoman of the not very distant future.

'How is the climbing going, Cathy?' she inquired.

'Oh, all right, thanks.' Cathy produced from her overall pocket a snapshot of herself on Holly Tree Wall, brought with just this opening in mind. It had already terrified Tooley Street, but Miss Hignett contemplated it without blenching.

'H'm , well, I hope you take every precaution. Let me see, you haven't been with us quite a year yet, have you?'

'I came in October.'

'Then you are not entitled to a holiday yet.' Miss Hignett was a neat-minded woman, who liked to have the true positon stated. 'But I think you had better take one. Say the last two weeks of next month. Many customers will be away then and we shouldn't be so busy.'

'Oh – thanks a lot, Miss Hignett,' said Cathy, startled in spite of herself into an expression of faint gratitude; and instantly added to herself, as she met Miss Hignett's benevolent gaze: it's the least you could do.

The last two weeks of August were when Harry, Stan and Johnny were going to Chamonix with Mr. Sharland. It would be strange at Cae Capel without them. On the other hand, it would be amusing to know what went on there in the week, to see more of Dorothy, perhaps to make a few new friends.

Her thoughts drifted to Christopher. Teachers got long holidays. He really ought to see it as his duty to protect her, all alone as she would be in the grove.

v

'So you are the schoolmaster?' Dorothy said. The dignified word, so much more attractive than the ugly 'teacher', gave him pleasure, as Cathy was quick to notice. 'What a lovely idea that was, taking the little boys up Snowdon. I daresay a turning-point in their lives.'

Christopher, finishing work at four, had been already encamped an hour in the grove when they arrived and was starting his preparations for supper. But they bore him off to Dorothy's kitchen, assuring him that she would not notice one more mouth. They were determined to include him in every privilege. He had made the grade.

'I'm sure I hope so,' he answered smiling. 'Anyway, they've talked of naught else since. What's more, it was a turning-point for Cathy. Did you know it was her first time up Snowdon?'

'No! Cathy, can that be true?' Cathy hung her head. 'Harry, d'you mean to say—?'

'I was waiting for a snowfall,' said Harry defensively. 'You must admit we had bad luck last winter, nothing but lousy rain.'

'What point is there in going up Snowdon under normal conditions?' Johnny demanded.

'There's more things in life than climbing,' said Christopher.

'The frivolity of the younger generation—'

'But of course he's right,' Harry pronounced. 'They say we never think of anything else here. That's because of a few idiots like you, who haven't two ideas in your heads. It gives a far from just picture of the rest of us. Stan and I can, I think, honestly say that we've tried to broaden our interests. I admit that perhaps lately, with all this talk of Alps – but anyway, we'll soon have worked that out of our systems. When we get back I'm going to take up ornithology seriously. I know you laugh at my dabbling, but this time I mean it.'

'I'm all for dabbling,' said Christopher. 'All I mean is that most folks here don't dabble enough.'

'And then I shall look into this Ogam business. I can't credit what that archaeologist chap was saying t'other night, that there's only one Ogam stone in North Wales. It's probably just that the ground hasn't been fully surveyed.'

'What's Ogam?' asked Christopher, interested.

'Oh,' said Johnny, 'for heaven's sake don't start him off again.'

'Ogam,' explained Harry, unruffled, 'is an early Celtic alphabet, found in inscriptions on stones. It's perfectly simple. You draw a horizontal line, and then you make notches, above or below or right across it. One upright notch is *a*, two are *e*, three are *i*, and so on. The consonants go right through, at different angles.'

'A sort of prehistoric Pitman's?'

'Well, I daresay it was easier to cut in stone than ordinary writing. Or maybe the Celtic Christians used it as a secret code when they were being persecuted – they're bound to have been persecuted, Christians always were. If so, this is just the place where you'd expect to find some. After all, Cae Capel means the field of the church. And the Irish monks, when they came over converting, must have used the pass – there's no other way through the hills.'

'If it comes to that,' said Dorothy, 'a lot of queer things must have happened up and down the Holyhead Road. It sometimes gives me a turn to realize that the hills must have looked the same when the Romans were here. Once or twice on winter nights I've thought I heard footsteps – silly, of course, but I never look round.'

'Eh, give over, Dorothy,' said Cathy. 'You'll make me scared to walk back to bed.'

'It'd take more than a bit of bogus history to make my flesh creep,' Johnny scoffed. 'Now I'll tell you what is queer, and that's to think of the rocks hanging there for hundreds of years, and not a soul on them. Not a scratch. Just moss and loose stones, like we have to garden off bits of the Amphitheatre. They tell me the Needle was green with moss when the first chap got up it. Think of all that potential pleasure going to waste. Can you wonder our lot want to make up for lost time? If anyone's going to haunt these hills after death it won't be a Roman centurion or a Celtic rock-scribbler. It'll be me.'

And one could see him, too, with his light monkey body and his grinning face, floating up just ahead of an exhausted leader on a Very Severe. 'Throw us down a rope, won't you?' Cathy said, but she could hardly feel that Johnny's ghost would be the sort to stretch out a helping hand.

'If you'll excuse us, Dorothy,' said Stan rising, 'we ought to look in at the hut. Mr. Sharland was to see if he could borrow us axes.'

'Come too, Cathy?' Harry asked.

'Not me. What do I care about your axes? And they don't like girls down at the hut.' She was suddenly jealous and discontented.

After the Alpine party had roared away on its motor cycles silence fell in the kitchen.

'I wish you could have gone to Chamonix, too, Cathy,' Dorothy said at last.

'Whoever heard of laundry girls going to Chamonix? That sort of thing is for millionaires.' Then she was ashamed. 'Look, Dorothy, you know I didn't mean it. It'll be grand here. It's just that for a minute I felt I could have shown those French girls where they got off.'

'Well, cheer up,' said Christopher. 'You're not the only one that's not a millionaire. You'd be surprisd how little they pay us teachers. I'd earn twice as much in a factory.'

'What'll you do with yourself in the holidays?'

'Reckon I'll just about afford to go home.'

'Well, you better stay and camp with me.'

'Yes, do, Christopher,' said Dorothy, perceiving that her friend's offhand manner concealed an ardent wish. 'I don't like the thought of Cathy alone down there in the caravan. After all, she's right out of earshot. You could keep an eye on her, and I daresay she'd do a bit of cooking for you. It wouldn't cost you more than just your food.'

'Well, it's real nice of you,' said Christopher, as usual in no hurry to jump at a favour. 'I'd have to go home for a bit, any road—'

'You can go for the first half of August. Cathy's only got the second.'

'And I did sort of promise a chap at home to do a week in the Lakes—'

'Oh, please yourself,' Cathy snapped. 'Course I'm not scared of sleeping alone, nor of ghosts neither. And I'll find plenty of folks glad to second me up anything I like.'

'That's another thing,' pursued Christopher, tilting back his chair, very much at ease. 'I wouldn't want to do nowt but climbing. If I climbed to please you you'd have to walk a few ridges and do a few bike-rides to please me. I want to look at this country proper. You can't get any sort of impression, just shinning up a cliff at week-ends.'

'Thanks, but it's bike-ride enough getting here.'

'Eh, I don't mean a motor-bike. Push-bike. That's the way to see a countryside.'

'Push-bike – I ask you!' Cathy turned indignantly to Dorothy. 'I'll do all right by myself down there. You can see we'd fight like hell.'

'Oh, I wouldn't mind that,' said Christopher gently. 'I rather like fights. That is, with someone my own size. Makes a change.' And he grinned at her with undisguised impudence. Everyone else at Cae Capel might be slightly in awe of its queen, but not he. He was not going to be patronized by the great climbers, nor by anyone else alive.

'Well, I think you'd suit admirably,' said Dorothy, laughing. 'You'll do each other a world of good. That's settled, then. Your home's not far from the Lakes, is it, Christopher? You can go there some other time.' Thus did she arrange her friends' affairs in the way most likely to give them pleasure. Invaluable Dorothy! – would that she could similarly have arranged her own.

'Heard from Michael?' asked Cathy, lingering; his name, she felt, might be brought out in comfort now that she had shown herself so plainly preoccupied elsewhere.

'Not yet,' answered Dorothy calmly, the shutter coming down over her candid face.

Cathy made a mental note: not to ask that question any more.

CHAPTER SEVEN

SHE GOT out of the train at Bangor with the bicycle, Bill's bicycle, that bloody bicycle, which she was bringing solely on Christopher's orders, so that they could waste good climbing days, and which had forced her to arrive by this ridiculous, roundabout route instead of cadging a lorry-lift from Queensferry. The first half of August had been cold as winter, and now, overnight, had set in the first real heat she had ever known in the hills. Miles of heat-softened road stretched before her, the tar melting under the relentless sun. She mounted, and after a mile or two of parkland entered the unknown country that lay beyond the pass, staring about her with heavy distaste.

Except that much of it ran up the mountain, it was just like Tooley Street. Row upon row of wizened cottages were crammed together, without gardens, scarcely with yards, and the grey quarry-dust pervaded all. Strung along the road were the same dour chapels, even the same multiple-stores, that lined the streets at home. And presently the cause of it all appeared, the mighty quarry, a wound laying bare the mountain's bones. An artist might have seen beauty in its purple rectangles, but to her eye it was horrible, a man-made parody of her belove crags. She seemed to feel her boots and fingers skidding off the slate.

So this was what lay at the foot of the pass: this pinched, poverty-stricken country; this slum. Strange that above her in the sky, only a few miles further on, should hang Cae Capel in its austere cleanliness and peace. Or relative peace, for the road was seething. Cars, coaches, stinking fumes, noise. And in this heat! She had at last left the quarry town behind her and was in the pass proper, but her temper scarcely improved.

The Chamonix party had left the night before, after a farewell supper in a Church Street café which Harry had insisted she should attend. 'But you'll come to Lime Street to see us off, surely?' he had said. 'After all, you'll be at Cae Capel twenty-four hours before we're at Chamonix.' He seemed absurdly unwilling to part from her, and grumbled all through the meal that she was not coming too. In the end she grew embarrassed, for Stan was able to part from her very well (and all things considered, one couldn't blame him); Sharland, though invariably gallant, was already enough of a mountain bachelor to prefer any woman's room to her company; and Johnny was beginning to cock an eye. As usual, pointlessly; for it wasn't love that gnawed at Harry, it was merely frustrated pride. He yearned to show his creation to the Alps. 'She'd have done as well as any of us,' he continually lamented.

And when they reached Lime Street, nervous and promising as big stations are late at night, and she saw the ice-axes protruding from the bulging sacks, the feeling of being unfairly excluded all but overcame her. She could scarcely keep a decent grin on her face till the train had jerked itself away. Even today the sense of ill-usage persisted.

The road steepened, and she got off to walk the last sweltering mile. Her nails squashed into the tar. Then, between lorries, she made out a solitary figure coming to meet her. She waved briefly, without a smile. Yet her heart had turned over. He looked so tall.

He looked cool, too, in his shorts and sandshoes; while she was wet to the skin in her thick climbing things, and her face burned from the light beating up off the road. She flung him the bicycle. 'Here, take the bloody thing.'

'You're fair done up, aren't you?' he said. 'I oughtn't to have made you bring it. I'm that sorry.' His concern made her ashamed.

'I'll be all right when I've had a nice sit-down.'

'I've opened up the caravan,' he told her; 'Miss Elliott gave me the key. I made your bed and got in the water. I hope that's right.' She preserved her grumpy face, but her heart was singing. She scarcely heeded the sweltering road.

The blessed clump of trees grew gradually nearer; they turned off through the farm gate, and in a few strides were hidden from the motor coaches, and safe in their green glade. Never had it looked so secret, cool, inviting; just the caravan and the one tent, the little stream purling down to join the river on the valley floor, the lawn of fine sheep-nibbled turf. Anybody could have Chamonix.

In two minutes she was out of her hot clothes and into a new ribbon swimming-suit. 'You won't mind me looking like this?' she asked him.

'I should say not,' he answered, gazing at her with a frank and innocent admiration. 'You look just like those girls on the station posters.'

He had the kettle boiling on his Primus, and a cloth spread on the grass. A handy lad; well-trained; useful. 'I will say for you,' she conceded, 'you been nicely brought up.'

He grinned. 'You've forgiven me about the bike?'

'Long as I don't have to ride it any more, not while this heat lasts. Gosh, it's almost too hot for climbing. We'll just have to bathe and lie about.'

'Suits me. I've got a new game, anyway.'

'What's that?'

'Show you when you've had your tea.'

She followed him down the course of the stream, enjoying the cushiony softness of the thyme-scented grass under her bare feet. Fifty yards down, boulders were jumbled in a miniature gorge. One stood upright, a little apart from the rest, and its face was scarred with a creamy newly-made groove. Christopher picked up a chisel and resumed work.

'What on earth—?'

'I'm making Harry an Ogam.'

'Like what he was jawing about the other weekend?'

'That's right.'

'Well, of all the nerve! What's it going to say?'

He produced a slip of paper on which the pattern of the Ogam and its key were already drawn: HARRY IS AN ASS.

'Help,' said Cathy, 'what a yell! His face when he finds out what it means!' She shrieked with laughter. It seemed to her quite the wittiest piece of cozenage ever devised.

'It won't have to look new like this, of course,' said Christopher, chiselling. 'We'll have to rub it with moss and muck when it's finished. Even then it'll be hard to get a real weathered effect. He just mustn't find it too soon.'

'Oh, you know what Harry is. He'll come back from the Alps with about three new stunts. Most likely he'll have forgotten all about it. You'd be sold if he never found it at all.'

'We'll lay a trail to it,' said Christopher. 'There'll be ways and means.'

Cathy propped her back against a thyme hillock and lay watching him, her idleness the more delicious beside his industry. She had never been able to scrutinize him so closely before. His skin was wonderful. She had joked about his bloom, but it was literally true. You felt that if you were to rub a finger down his cheek a fine golden dust, as from a flower, might come off on your hand.

'There – I wonder if that's long enough?' He took a pencil and patterned out the Ogam as it would bisect the groove.

'How did you learn how to write it?'

'Went and looked it up in the encyclopaedia at the Free Library. It's got all about it, and the whole alphabet.'

'I'd never have thought of that.'

'But you can find anything in a free library.'

'I suppose so. I was only in ours once.' She remembered, with sudden discomfort, the subject she had studied then.

'What a lot I've got to teach you!' said Christopher, smiling.

'Schoolie.'

'Well, of course I'm a schoolie. What else could you expect?'

'It's holidays now, any road. How did you get on at home?'

'Nicely, thank you. I always do. Weather was a bit mucky.'

'What do you do with yourself at home?'

'Oh, walk, fish, carpenter a bit with my dad. There's always jobs. And my mother took a week off from the mill. We did some grand bike-rides. She's a much better cyclist than you.'

Cathy tried to imagine her own mother doing long cycle-rides, and failed. 'She does sound grand, your mother,' she observed a trifle wistfully. 'Reckon she'd just suit me.'

Everything she had heard about Mrs. Thwaites betokened a person altogether admirable. 'A born interferer, that's what she is,' said her son. 'She'll get herself into real trouble one of these days. I'm always telling her.'

But he only spoke to be contradicted, and hear the praise of the parent he adored. She was in all ways the champion of the oppressed: the teller-off of husbands who drank the housekeeping money, the mollifier of incensed fathers, the thorn in the flesh of unjust foremen, the bearder of relieving officers and housing authorities in their dens. And her campaigns seemed to be aimed at getting her friends what they wanted, not what she thought they ought to want. She accorded them the most valuable of all privileges – her respect.

Most wonderful of all in Cathy's eyes, she seemed able to accord it to her child. From his earliest years Christopher had had respect. He had been treated as a separate person, with a right to a mind of his own. He had been allowed his own views, and as a consequence, no doubt, they were almost exactly her views – a fine, rational Socialism, springing not, like Mr. Canning's, from frustration and anger, but from a cheerful belief in the materialistic heaven just round the corner, and a resolve to sweep all their weaker neighbours into it with them. They didn't, said Christopher, hold with religion; but, being luckier and better off than some, they thought it only common sense to use their advantages for the general good.

To Cathy there was enchantment in this picture of family unity. Life could be like that: sensible, tolerant, prosperous, kind. And look, she reflected, still considering the way his long golden lashes lay on his cheeks as he cut at his Ogam, look at the delightful result. Harry might talk about having corners knocked off and going through the mill; fat lot he knew. All it did for you was to make you mean and grasping, as she so often thought herself. But Christopher was generous and unafraid, because he had never been oppressed. Not even by military service, for by the time he was old enough the war was over, and they had put him into Army education, where classes of great hulking illiterates were far more grateful for his zeal and patience than the little girls he now found it necessary to slap. The sun had always shone on Christopher, and thus it was that he had sunshine to spare.

'But haven't you ever had bad times?' she asked. 'Wasn't your dad ever out of work?'

'Ay, for a spell, when all the town was. But I was only a little chap and I don't remember much about it. Except that we went to live at my uncle's farm on the moors for a bit, and that was the only time I ever saw anything get my mother down.'

'Sounds all right, a farm on the moors.'

'Ay, but you don't know my uncle. He's got religion.' In Christopher's view it was evidently a deplorable disease. 'Never speaks a word all week, and chapel three times on Sundays. My auntie and my cousins are scared to open their mouths. My mother tried to make things a bit better for them, and she's been trying on and off ever since, but she don't get nowhere.'

'Does he really not speak?'

'Never a word, except for the farm jobs, and they know most of those without needing to be told. It's a family farm, you see; they work it themselves. All right if it's a good family, but about the worst sort of slavery going if it's not.'

'Well, fancy that sort of thing going on to-day. I wouldn't have believed it.'

'You don't know those lonely places, then.'

'Well, Bryn Glas is lonely enough, and Miss Williams has a grand time.'

'Bryn Glas lonely!' said Christopher, laughing. 'It always looks like Blackpool beach to me.'

'You've not seen it in the winter.' But she was obliged to admit that even in the winter Bryn Glas knew a lot of cheerful dropping-in.

'Now my uncle's farm is on the road to nowhere. Track doesn't go beyond it, and there's no hikers to speak of come on our Lancashire moors. They often don't see a new face for months on end. My cousin Ruth's rising eighteen, but any of the kids in my school know more about the world than what she does. Ay, it's Wuthering Heights all right.'

'It's what?'

'Oh – sorry. That's just a book.'

'You got to get it into your head,' said Cathy grumpily, 'that I never read no books.'

'Well, I'll lend you that one. You might like it, too – there's a couple of Cathys in it, for one thing. Well, I must say, if this Ogam was meant to be a shorthand, it's about the longest-winded one they could have thought up. Daresay I'll leave the second *r* out of Harry and save five strokes. Anyway, that'll be enough for today.'

'I ought to go up and say hello to Dorothy,' said Cathy, regretfully rising.

'Righto, I'll see to supper.'

'But you got tea.'

'Oh, there won't be no cooking. Mother sent a pie.' Admirable Mrs. Thwaites; she had everything.

The shadows were lengthening, but it was not yet cool. In the hostel kitchen Dorothy looked pale with fatigue. 'Hello, pet,' she said, 'settled in?'

'Ay. Bit of all right, too. That lad does all the work.'

'And mind you let him. He's been enjoying himself for a fortnight already, while you were toiling in that laundry. There's some eggs and a lettuce for you – now vanish. I didn't ask you here to do unpaid warden.'

'Stuff,' said Cathy, getting out the chopping-board. 'It's you need the break. Must you really give them a hot dinner on a night like this?'

'You know they expect it. If I gave them the same food raw with a salad they'd all feel convinced they were going to bed starving.' Cathy knew enough of hostellers to be aware that this was true.

She stayed for the dishing-up, and then strolled back down the road with her lettuce. The traffic was thinning now; a little breeze played round her legs; it was evening. After the hot kitchen the glade was more than ever delicious. The mountain skyline down the pass glinted with the last yellow light, and Anglesey dissolved into haze. Christopher had somehow procured beer. Wellbeing was complete.

'It's the best time of the day, this,' she murmured. 'Pity we can't do our climbing at night.'

'Tell you what,' said Christopher, sitting up suddenly. 'We'll go up Snowdon.'

'What – now?'

'Well, say about midnight. There'll be a moon. We'd just get to the top to see the sun rise.'

'Sounds daft. I dunno, though. Harry was saying they start at night in the Alps. Crib Goch might be sporting in the dark. All right then, but mind, this counts as pleasing you. Tomorrow we please me.'

'Tomorrow we'll need our sleep,' said Christopher. 'Anyway, get some now. I'll call you when it's time.'

She had just dropped off when he came banging on the caravan door. She pulled on her boots by moth-infested candlelight, and climbed on to his pillion, still half asleep. The road, the valley, shuttered Llanllugwy had suddenly gone back to the silent emptiness of winter; it was like recapturing the beauty of a face long disfigured by powder and paint. At Bryn Glas all was ghostly; impossible to realize that the tea-hunting hordes had swarmed all over it six hours ago. They started up the familiar track.

Its much-scratched stones shone white in the starlight, leading them safely across rivers of darkness. As they reached the col the full moon came up, and what had seemed easy now looked full of peril; every tiny hollow was turned by that treacherous green light into a fathomless crevasse. The rock-step had to be climbed by feel; a lovely sensation, the distilled essence of ascent. The scree-slope above it seemed unending, for the stored-up heat still breathed out of the stones. Then they were on the edge.

It was a thing of wonder. It rode through the moonlight like a frozen wave. They sailed along it like two little ships, in a gay and confident silence. To speak would be unthinkable. You could not tell what might be listening.

The pinnacles were fantastic, thousands of feet high. And they seemed to move – surely one of them did move?

'You know there's supposed to be a ghost on Snowdon?' whispered Christopher wickedly.

'Oh, shut up,' shuddered Cathy, 'shut up.'

Crib y Ddysgl was more confusing in the uncertain light. The chasm of profound darkness on the left gave it an exciting sense of danger. Into Glaslyn the moonlight could not penetrate. The little lake was too deep in Snowdon's lap.

They stumbled on to the railway lines; breasted the final slope. Nobody, silence; it might have been a virgin peak. Night had mercifully blotted out the waste-paper and the beer-bottles. They pulled themselves up on to the cairn, and were nearly thrust from it by a tearing gale.

Yet everywhere else the night was windless. Only here, on the roof of Wales, did a fierce wind blow. Snowdon's own wind. The spirit, unconquerable, inhuman, of a great mountain that no railway tracks could tame.

Gripping the stones, they stared around. The scene was fantastic, toad-coloured; ink-blues, slate greys, livid green. The ridges stood out skeletal; stripped of its daylight trappings, the mountain showed its naked bones. Beyond, the lesser hills were smudges of dark grey against the milkily luminous sky. Only water showed bright, a filigree of silver where the moonlight caught it. Tarns and llyns, there seemed to be hundreds upon hundreds of them; the gleaming shallows of the Traeth Mawr lay patterned like a necklace on the bosom of darkness; and beyond that again, a winking red line of lightships marked the boundaries of the sea.

An immense exaltation possessed her, as in moments of danger; but here there was no danger, only the sheer power which emanated from the mountain, from these upheaved masses of earth and stone. They were free of their human clutter at last, and she seemed to look through to the very core of the world. This, this was what it meant. *You are the mountain*, a man had said. A strange saying, not true; but one day it might be true. And then, no need any more to grasp and scheme and plan. She clung for warmth to Christopher, but for a long moment she was not aware of him. The mountain alone was real.

'Let's get out of the wind,' he muttered at last, shivering. They left the cairn, and made their way down on hands and knees to the shuttered concrete building of the hotel, transmuted by night into just another cliff. On its terrace there was a little shelter, and there they crouched, huddled in the thin jerseys that were all they had thought to put into the sacks. 'It don't seem possible,' said Cathy, 'that we were half dead with heat this morning.'

'Yesterday morning.'

'Ay, I suppose so. How long till dawn?'

'An hour, I reckon. D'you want to wait?'

'Of course.'

It did not matter how long, how cold. Presently her spirit drifted away again, but she was not asleep. She was leaping out into the great spaces, towards the red lights winking on the sea, towards the silver sands.

They felt the dawn before they could see it; some of the mystery went out of the grey-green night, leaving it flat and dull. They climbed back to the cairn, and, sure enough, the east was streaked with orange. The sky lightened, hours seemed to pass, but still no sun. Then it came up all in a hurry, several inches above the true horizon, masked now with level pencils of mist. And to the west, behind them, it flung a great blue cone of shadow, the shadow of Snowdon, stretching fifteen miles across the land and thrusting its apex into the sea.

Five minutes later the shadow had gone. The mystery was ended. It was full day.

'Let's run,' said Cathy, her teeth chattering. They plunged down from the cairn, down by the railway, down the shifting scree of the track. On the path terraced high above Llydaw they were gasping for breath. At the first stream they flung themselves down on short sweet turf and drank.

'Reckon I could just drop off,' Christopher said.

'Why not?' agreed Cathy; her head was spinning. She rolled over with her back to the sun, which poured through her, baking the cold vigil out of her bones. Almost at once she was asleep.

It was a light, excited sleep, in which she seemed to be delicately balanced, first above a precipice, and then above a great cliff, with the sea below, waiting for her to roll. She woke with a little cry, clutching the turf, and was amazed to find herself on relative flatness. Christopher lay five yards away, and she looked full into his sleeping face.

In the darkness he had been just anyone, a good comrade, a friend. Now she seemed to see him for the first time. She devoured his face hungrily, dragging herself back from the icy spaces. That was all nonsense, about belonging to the mountain. It was nothing after all but a great heap of stones.

She called his name and his eyes opened instantly, for his sleep, like hers, had been light. His bewilderment, his smile as he recognized and welcomed her, made her heart leap up. Why can't we just kiss now and have done with it? she thought. And then he coloured, and embarrassment came between them, as though he read her thought.

'You ought to have waked me sooner,' he said awkwardly. 'I never meant to be so long. Look at the sun – and you know how early they get up on farms.'

In fact breakfast in Bryn Glas kitchen was over. But Miss Williams put the kettle on instantly, and cut bread and butter of an exquisite fineness, as for a tea-party. 'My, but you're off early,' she remarked.

'Finishing late,' amended Cathy. 'We've been on Snowdon all night.'

'Whatever next. As though the days weren't long enough for you to be on the hills.'

'We saw the shadow at sunrise,' said Christopher. 'Is it often like that?'

'Only a few days in the year, so I'm told, though I never was up there to see. You were lucky, then. Maybe your reward from heaven for taking up those little boys. Only you two come?'

'The others have gone to the Alps,' explained Cathy. 'Dorothy's let me have the caravan for my holiday, and Chris is camping.'

'Isn't that nice, now?' Miss Williams's eyes took them fully in, their sleepiness, their exaltation, the way they avoided each other's gaze. 'Silly, to go off to the Alps for what you can get just as well at home. Have you had that record made yet?'

'Now, Olwen,' said Cathy, 'now.'

'What did she mean, about a record?' asked Christopher on the way home.

'Oh, just one of her dotty jokes. You know what those Welshies are. It don't take much to make them laugh.'

ii

Perhaps he thought it curious that she should have changed, all in a minute, from the rapt little comrade of their night on the bare mountain into a sulky shrew. Certainly he looked unhappy and apologetic, fearing that he had tired her, and urging her to get more sleep. She flung herself on to her bunk in the caravan and did sleep, this time long and heavily, and woke with an aching head and a worse temper still. Once again Christopher worked on the Ogam, and she lolled on the turf by the streamside, but now there seemed nothing to say. His family, his fine, fighting mother, suddenly did not bear thinking of. A great many things suddenly did not bear thinking of. But they kept churning round in her brain.

He was so young. Nesh. A mother's boy. They had always got on her nerves, mother's boys; look at poor Bill. She liked them older, with the dew off. Like Michael Derwent, in fact? Like Leonard? Nonsense. Well, anyway, able to say boo to a goose. But Christopher could say boo to any number of geese. He had never let Harry patronize him – or herself.

If he didn't want it – but he was too young, too set in the ways of his nice upbringing, to understand what he wanted. She knew that she had troubled him, that moment after he woke.

It wasn't for a girl to ask. But it was also cheek when a boy asked. If he were to ask her now, this minute, which he never would, it would be almost enough to make her say no.

And then Dorothy. Dorothy who, so trusting, prepared the whole arrangement, lent the caravan. Was that a way to repay her? If anything came out, it might lose her her job. But it wasn't as though this were the hostel. Nobody was planning any funny business at the hostel. (A hard little voice remarked inside her head: *They wouldn't get the chance*.)

But surely Dorothy must have foreseen? She wouldn't expect them to live cheek by jowl like two stuffed dummies and nothing happen? Well, of course she would. She had never been told about Leonard. She thought she had to do with somebody respectable, like herself.

But it wouldn't come out. *What Dorothy doesn't know can't harm her*. She had despised him, she remembered, for saying that. Ah, but that was different. What he had proposed would have harmed Dorothy, whether she had known or not.

But I didn't do it, Dorothy. I wouldn't let him. I stood up for you. I was a good friend to you. You owe me a lot. *(Ah, but do you? He hasn't written to you once)*.

If I'd never let Leonard take me, I wouldn't know anything about it, and then I wouldn't have this awful wanting. Well, not so bad, anyway, not so that I couldn't keep it bottled up. And if I'd never met that Michael, I wouldn't have thought of the caravan as being all laid out convenient. And if Chris had looked like any of the others, I'd treat him as I treat them, just cheeky and safe. That's what I meant to do. That's what I'd planned. *(And now you're lying. You came prepared.)*

I'm not a bad lot really. I've just had bad luck. And I can rise above it – I'll show you. We'll be good children. We won't put a foot wrong. But my God, what shall we do with ourselves? What can we talk about for a fortnight? We'll be bored silly. No, in that case, I'd rather he went away. I'd rather be on my own and pick up strangers at the hostel to climb with. I'd ought to make some new friends.

Well, look, then, I risk nothing. I'll ask him, and if he won't, he can clear out and I'll be no worse off. I'll feel a bit squashed, I dare say, but you got to risk something.

Oh, but not that, Chris, not to hear you do me such an unkindness! I couldn't bear it. I couldn't indeed.

'Do we lie about here all day?' she suddenly burst out in a voice of intense irritation.

'Eh, I'm sorry,' he said, anxious, humble. 'I'd clean forgot it was your turn to choose. Whatever you say.'

She took him up one of the horrid, gutsy little Cribin climbs. It was far too hot for climbing, and the walk there, although short, exhausted them. But some of the devils in her were exorcised as she kicked and fought her way – for she was quite out of form – doggedly up. Christopher did, for him, badly, and came home spiritless and depressed. 'Reckon I'll never make a climber,' he said.

They got themselves a high tea, and, after Cathy had done her evening hour of service at the hostel, went swimming in the lake. A measure of serenity returned to them. The water had icy patches and then hot ones, a strangely exhilarating sensation, and they broke the mirrored image of Tryfan as they swam. They lay on the boulders by the lakeside and dried themselves in the last sun.

'What nice legs you got,' observed Christopher suddenly.

She looked at them, surprised; since she had climbed so much, her calf muscles had developed beyond the delicate spindles that Tooley Street admired. But in truth they were beautiful little legs, finely proportioned, and browned by a summer of climbing in shorts. She said dryly:

'Glad there's something about me you like.'

He did not reply till they were back in the glade; then he asked:

'Didn't I ought to have said that about your legs? I didn't mean to sound fresh. I never feel I talk right to girls. I suppose it's not having had a sister.'

'You fresh? – gosh, no,' Cathy said. 'Quite the other way about. I mean, you never want to kiss a girl or anything, do you?' So had she led on a dozen boys in her time; but never, as now, with a thumping heart.

'Would you really let me?'

'If you asked nicely, I daresay.'

He put a shy arm round her, and forcing herself to seem casual, she turned up her face. His kiss was a boy's kiss, gentle, tentative. It was like having a fresh, sweet-smelling child in one's arms. But when he gained her lips for the second time he grew bolder. He has a lot to learn, she thought. but he'll learn fast.

She drew her face away, and laid her head on his shoulder. Very slowly, very gradually, the current of confidence was beginning to flow back between them. Now was the moment – now, while they were both brave. She said, looking straight at the paling sky:

'Tell you what. You can move in with me tonight if you like.'

He sat up and fixed on her startled eyes, like a young animal baited. 'Cathy! What do you mean?'

'Just what you think I mean. I suppose I oughtn't to be the one to say it. But you've been brought up so nice, you never would. Please yourself, of course.'

'But, Cathy,' he said, 'it wouldn't be right, would it? I mean, suppose it was to get you into trouble, or anything?'

'You needn't worry. I can take care of that.'

Their eyes locked in a long stare, and she saw the double comprehension dawn in his: *You came prepared then, you've done this before.*

'Ay,' she said, at her surliest, 'I let another chap do it with me, and he showed me what was what.' Rage overcame her. There he sat, like a goop – innocent, dewy – well he might be, with his wonderful luck, everything handed to him on a plate. 'All right, you can see for yourself. I'm a tart, or pretty near. Nice company you got into. That's what you get for speaking to strangers.' And she burst into a torrent of tears.

They were tears of hysterical fury; she would have died rather than play for a man's pity by crying. But how was he to know the difference. 'Cathy darling! Cathy love, don't!' he muttered. 'I don't think anything like that. You know I wouldn't. Eh, give over, darling, do.' He had her in his arms, he was quietening her struggles; she suddenly found an infinite comfort in the knowledge that his body was stronger than hers. Her sobbing died away and she lay exhausted, while he rocked her gently and caressed her hair.

'I'm not bad really,' she whispered at last. 'I didn't want to do it with that chap. I've never wanted it till now, with you.'

'Well then, I want it. I want it, too.'

'You'll come, then? But you don't have to come. You mustn't come just so as not to hurt my feelings. It wouldn't work.'

'You can see I want to. It's only that – I'm scared I'll be clumsy. I might hurt you. I never done it before.'

It was her turn to reassure him. 'I know, Chris,' she murmured, and now she could run her hands over his face as much as she liked, for he was hers. 'Don't you worry. I'll make it all right.'

She was lying naked on the bunk when he came to her; her arms and legs, browned by the sun, were almost invisible, but the rest of her body showed startlingly white in the last pale light that filtered through the trees. She heard the catch of his breath as he took her beauty in; then he slipped off the drab raincoat and she saw a body as milky as her own. She opened her arms and gathered him in, on a great surge of laughter and longing, and almost unbearable sweetness.

iii

For the second time she watched him wake. She was up and had the kettle boiling, and still he lay sprawled in that abandoned, childish sleep. There was no waking him with a kiss, either. She had to shake.

But this time, the joy that came with his recognition left no room for any doubts, any guilty misgivings. She was so completely reassured that she could even tease him. 'Well, Mr. Thwaites,' she said, 'you're a bad lot yourself now. How does it feel?'

'Eh, Cathy, love,' he murmured, still heavy with happy sleep, 'it was a good do, wasn't it? I'd never have believed it could be like that. Cathy love, how do I thank you?'

Nothing was too good for the wonderful creature who had brought him this ecstasy. He must do all the work, fetch the water and make the place straight, and clean her boots for her, stopping every few minutes to stare at her in adoring disbelief; till at last it was her turn to mutter, 'Oh, give over, do,' and colour up to the roots of her hair.

'Tell me when you first thought of it.'

'Oh, I dunno.' She cast around for an answer which should not make him too cocky. 'I suppose it was that day we took the kids up Snowdon.'

'But why then?'

'I dunno. Seeing you be nice with them, maybe. And something Gwen said.'

'What did she say?'

'I shan't tell you that.' She had said that he would make a good father.

'But there was nothing so special about my taking them. All us teachers take our kids out now and then.'

'I daresay. There's nothing special about you. Just my luck, falling for one of the ordinary ones.'

'Do you love me, Cathy?'

'What a thing to ask!' she cried in a mock rage that was almost real. 'How dare you try and make me say it? And you not giving away a thing yourself.'

'Oh, Cathy, how can you say that? It's just that I haven't the words to tell you. I don't see how anybody could ever tell you, not what I'm feeling.' And he dropped all the pots and pans and flung himself at her feet, burying his face in her arms.

'Look out, Chris,' she muttered, while tenderness welled up in her. 'It's morning now. Anybody might come.'

'I don't care. Are you ashamed of me?'

'Oh, Chris, love.'

After a while she pulled herself away from him. They really couldn't go on like that all the time. It wouldn't do.

'If you're really set on doing the chores here,' she announced in her most sensible voice, 'I'll go up and give Dorothy a hand.'

'Oh no, Cathy. Don't go away, please. It'll be so hot up there. Oh, all right then.' He relinquished her shamefacedly. 'I dunno what's come over me. I can't seem to bear you out of my sight. I feel you might never come back.'

'Splendid,' said Cathy. 'That's how I like a chap to feel. Do you a world of good.' She marched off triumphant.

Strange to find everything the same at the hostel; it ought to have been transfigured overnight. 'Enjoying yourself?' said Dorothy. 'I must say it's nice to see you here on a Monday morning.' Over coffee they calmly discussed the camp grocery list, which Dorothy was kindly including with her own. Yet surely, thought Cathy, she must see what's happened to me? Surely it shows in my face?

She got back to find the camp immaculate, and Christopher sitting by the stream, abstracted and grave.

'I been thinking, Cathy.'

'Well?'

'Didn't we – ought to get married?'

She knew anger, and then something more painful than anger. He would never realize how he had hurt her with that 'ought'. It would not have hurt if she had been as he was – for she was beginning to understand that Christopher had a chastity, of mind and spirit as well as body, which she had lost long before that first night at the Myrtle Bank.

'Eh, well, Chris,' she said at last, trying to make her voice easy, 'we'll think about that later on. You don't want to be getting hitched up just yet. It'd only be a millstone round your neck. Wait till you've got on in the world a bit.' That had not been Gwen's advice. But Gwen had been thinking of another kind of man.

'You don't take me seriously. To you I'm still just a kid.'

'Maybe.'

'I'm a year older than you. Perhaps you want a chap with lots of brass.'

'That must be it.'

'Now you're making fun of me,' he cried, turning on her almost fiercely. 'You wouldn't care how poor you were, not if you really loved me. You're not that kind.'

'Don't you believe it, lad. All girls are that kind.'

'I'd just about like to strangle you.'

'Our first quarrel.' She looked so complacent that she forced him to laugh.

'No, but Cathy. Just be a dear and listen now. You really won't marry me?'

'Let me ask you a question,' she said. 'Would it ever have come into your head to ask me to marry you yesterday?'

He replied simply: 'I'd never have had the nerve.'

'It's a good thing for a young chap not to have too much nerve. Put it that way. That's why we'll wait.'

'But if I do wait, will you promise?'

'No.' And to his entreaties she would only answer: 'I'm not getting tied up yet.'

'Those – those gadgets,' he said hesitantly. 'I've heard they don't always work.'

'Well, if anything's slipped this time, you shall make an honest woman of me.'

'I damn well hope something has,' he cried with a vehemence that started her laughing again.

They lay in entwined and blissful silence, looking into the running water; then he said:

'There's a question I got to ask you. It'll make you angry.'

'No – ask what you like.'

'That other chap. Was he one of these three?'

For a moment she was, in fact, angry. 'But they're my friends!' she cried. 'What do you take me for?' He looked stricken; poor lamb, how was he to tell? She hastened to make him the amends of complete confidence. 'Look, I'll tell you about it. I never told a soul before, but I'll tell you. It wasn't anyone that comes here. He did bring me up here, that's how I met Harry and Stan and started climbing. But we stopped down in Llandudno. He wasn't a bit of use, not at climbing or anything else. It was low of me letting him, I know. But you see, I had a pair of his sister's boots what I'd borrowed, and I needed them to go on climbing with. And I hadn't any money, so what else could I do?'

'Oh, Cathy!' He was torn between laughter and an agony of pity. 'You are a one. Fancy thinking you had to do it for that. It's you that's the kid. You need someone to look after you, that's what. But what a filthy, rotten swine, to take such a mean advantage—'

Poor Leonard. He was not really such a swine, and she had not gone with anything like the loathing envisaged by Christopher to his arms. Complete confidence was not, after all, on the cards. But who was Leonard, that for his sake she should blacken herself yet further in her love's eyes? So much easier just to let it go, just to let him see her as a little green innocent in need of his protection. And if he believed it, perhaps she could make it true. Was she not making it true at this moment, by not clutching at him when she had the chance?

'Were they those boots I've been cleaning?'

'Ay. They're my old ones. My new ones I paid for myself.'

'I'm going to chuck them in the lake.'

'You'll do no such thing. There's a season's wear in them yet. Here, you're getting above yourself. Run away and play. Finish your old Ogam.'

'That!' He rolled over on to his side and stared downstream in the direction of the Ogam with infinite contempt. 'What a silly kid's trick it seems. Beats me how I could ever have thought it funny.'

'Oh dear,' said Cathy ruefully, 'how you've grown up all of a sudden.'

'Ay. I must have aged years overnight.'

'Don't – you make me feel awful.'

'I shouldn't worry,' he reassured her. 'I'm supposed to be a schoolmaster, aren't I? I'm supposed to be able to teach folks things, not to be finding them out myself. I reckon it was high time.'

iv

They did scarcely any climbing. It was too hot, and they were getting, as Cathy shamelessly observed, plenty of other sorts of exercise. Every morning she did an hour's work at the hostel; Dorothy protested, but it was impossible to keep her out, and if the door had been locked she was fully able to climb in through a window. After that they lay in their grove, separated only by a belt of trees and fifty yards of track from the seething summer traffic of the Holyhead Road, but as secret and remote as though they had been alone in the world.

Sometimes a craving for the sea would take them, and they would get out the bicycles and free-wheel joyously down to the coast. The return was hot and wearisome, but they walked all the big hills; indeed, in a country so small as North Wales, the cyclist who hurried would find himself riding out of it altogether. Up the small hills she was towed with a climbing-rope. To the real girl cyclists, who would never have accepted assistance from their boys, she knew herself to be an object of contempt. This did not ruffle her. Nice sights they would have looked, given the lead on Holly Tree Wall.

Now at last she was coming to know the country; the derelict quarry villages that littered the back of Snowdon, the long lonely lakes where no one went, the strange landscape of isolated hillocks, tiny stone-walled fields and grim little farms softened by climbing roses that lay between the mountains and the sea. She knew the sudden, violent contrast of that swoop into Nant Gwynant from the windy heights of Snowdon; a rich green vale rushing up to meet them, so flowery and well-liking that Lliwedd, towering three thousand feet above it, seemed to belong to another existence. Staring back at the hills from the wide golden estuary beyond Portmadoc, she saw them even lovelier, even more remote. Can I really have been up there? – she would wonder; and it seemed quite a feat to have attained those blue summits, not a mere stroll at the end of a climbing day or in the middle of a summer night.

The countryside teemed with sunburned young people, trekking back and forth between youth hostels, careering in clumps and batches on bicycles, or debouching, if of the more prosperous sort, from racing cars into hotels. Nevertheless they attracted some notice, for they were a conspicuous couple: Christopher so tall and fair, with his slow northern voice and his unexpected smile; Cathy so small and vivid, with her irrepressible swagger and her flaming hair. Few spoke to them, for, though not unfriendly, they were plainly self-sufficient. But a bunch of hostellers down beyond Criccieth, hearing them talk of Cae Capel, wanted to know how one ever got in there. You had to book months ahead, didn't you? remarked one of the boys.

'We're camping, as a matter of fact,' said Cathy. 'But I stop there every week-end in the winter.'

'Are you a rock-climber, then?'

'Ay.'

'It's a grand situation,' said a girl, 'but it wouldn't be much use to us. You've got to be a climber at Cae Capel, so I've always heard. Everyone's dotty about it there. You'd feel right out of things if you weren't.'

Cathy hung her head; just such a reputation had Dorothy striven to avoid, and if she had not succeeded was it not partly the fault of Harry and Johnny and herself? It was Christopher who defended Cae Capel, assuring their questioners that, though only a moderately enthusiastic climber, he had found there a welcome, and friends.

But whether cycling or climbing, floating lazily in the patchy waters of the lake or lying, not quite touching but deliciously aware of each other's bodies, on their thymy turf, they talked. They talked endlessly, never finding time for more than a fraction of what needed to be said. 'If I could, I would give you gold and diamonds,' had said Christopher. 'As it is, you'll just have to make do with the treasures of my mind.' She asked nothing better. She knew herself ignorant, and he could explain anything, with such sweet patience, such clarity, never, like Harry, getting suddenly bored or cross. And, anyway, it wouldn't have mattered what he talked about. She loved to hear the sound of his voice.

But best of all she loved to hear about his home. The saga of Mrs. Thwaites and her campaigning had endless fascinating ramifications, taking one right into the heart of the small, cliquey, clannish community that was the family and the mill. It was one of the delightful results of their relationship, that

Mrs. Thwaites as a subject of conversation was no longer out of bounds. And that was strange, reflected Cathy, for if she had been ashamed to think of his mother on the night when she seduced him she ought to feel ashamed still. But all she felt was a proud sense of kinship. It pleased her to fancy that under their surface differences they were two women who might be alike in more ways than one.

Ever in the forefront of Mrs. Thwaites's projects was that grim farm on the moors, and the need to free her nephews and nieces from its thrall. It was ever-present in Cathy's imagination also. 'I can't get over it, somehow,' she told Christopher. 'It don't fit in with the way folks live nowadays. It's ridiculous. Can't something be done?'

'He's not breaking the law.'

'What can have made him go so queer?'

'I daresay it started with my grandmother always liking my dad best,' opined Christopher, who as a good schoolmaster was not without the necessary smatterings.

'Well, why don't your cousins just clear out?'

'They're only kids. Where would they go? If they came to us the police'd fetch them back.'

'This lass – what's her name—?'

'Ruth.'

'Well, she's not a kid, is she? Didn't you say she was nearly eighteen?'

'Yes, but you'd never think it. She's a bit like one of those whippets that's been ill-treated – sort of shies away when you go near. She was friends with me when we were kids and I lived there, but not now. Few times I've seen her lately she looks at me as if I'd bite.'

'She must be a bit soft in the head.'

'No, she's not that. She can do anything on the farm. And she's not scared of the animals – she set a dog's leg once when it was mad with pain and no one else would go near it. But she's been frightened half-silly by him.'

'Why don't she run away?'

'It's easy to say that. But if you were in her place, not trained to any other trade, and not having a penny you could call your own—'

'If I were in her place,' said Cathy, 'fifty fathers with religion wouldn't make me stop where I didn't like it.'

'No, I daresay that's true. It'd take a lot more even than my uncle to get you down.'

He smiled at her, adoring her spirit and her courage, and she smiled back, revelling in his admiration. But somewhere, right at the back of her head, there rang a little warning bell.

'Mother's got her plans laid, though,' Christopher was pursuing. 'We don't see why Ruth shouldn't be a nurse. You can start at eighteen, and if she went as a probationer into our hospital we'd keep an eye on her and she could spend her free time with us. He'll fight like hell, of course, to prevent her leaving. She's far too useful on the farm. But Mother knows people on the education committee, and everyone's always mad keen to get more nurses. I'll back Mother to find a way.

Cathy was prepared to back her too. The emancipation of the downtrodden Ruth from tyranny took on the flavour of a real sporting event.

'Now tell us a bit about your family,' he suggested. The ingredients of his excellent upbringing had included the principle that conversations should not be one-sided.

But her face turned, in a moment, as sullen as when he had seen it first. 'Nowt to tell,' she said shortly. 'We're just the undeserving poor.'

'I wish you would tell me,' he said. 'How can I really know you, if I don't know where you come from? And if I don't know you I can't feel sure of you, and then it's hell.'

'You wouldn't know me if you saw me at home, anyway. You wouldn't like me, either. I'm horrible there. I don't come alive till I get to this place.'

'Can I come and see it, all the same?'

'No.'

'But, Cathy—'

'I've told you, no. I don't let anybody come. Not Harry, or anyone.'

'But am I not a bit different from Harry?'

'Ay. You matter a sight more. That's why you must come least of all.'

He was silent and unhappy, feeling himself excluded from the hard side of her life, where his love and his longing to be of service might have found their justification. She tried rather desperately to explain herself.

'The person that's really me belongs here. It's coming here that's made me worth your knowing. Harry and Dorothy have done it between them – and now you. But Dorothy, I think, most of all. If you really knew her, and how good she is, you'd understand a lot more about me than you would from seeing my mother and my sister, that I don't give a damn for.'

'Well, I'll go up and see her oftener.' He grinned wryly, defeated. 'But I do like her. I like her a lot, except that I'm sort of not noticing any woman but you at the moment. Why does she look so unhappy? Has she always been like that?'

'Not she. She's ever so chirpy really, a bit like you. But that snooty boy-friend of hers is no good. She gave him a grand time here six weeks ago, and he's never even written to thank her. I think he's not faithful, either' – no need to go into details – 'and now she's beginning to find it out.'

'He seemed to spend most of his time staring at you.'

'How did you – gosh, I'd forgotten you were there. That was your first weekend.' Impossible that it should have dated from that. And Michael Derwent had pointed the way to him – how queer. 'Well, since you saw,' she said. 'Of course, it wasn't anything serious with me. He was just after a bit of fun, and he thought I looked a cheap piece. And so I am.'

'Will you stop calling yourself names?'

'Well, you're the one to know. Look at what I did to you.'

'Yes, and you should have seen your own face when you were asking me. White as a sheet, you were. I thought you were going to faint.'

She was amazed, both that it should have been so – for she had seemed to herself utterly brazen – and that he should have observed it, at a moment when any other boy would have only observed his own feelings. But that was like Christopher; always a little more perceptive than one had any right to expect.

'Was that why you gave in?' she murmured.

But he was not going to let her hark back to that evening any more. 'It don't need any explaining why I gave in,' he said firmly. 'There'd only be explanations needed if I'd held out.'

'I wish there was something I could do for Dorothy. It seems so mean, she slaving away in that hot kitchen and not hearing from her beastly boy, and us down here enjoying ourselves—' She reddened under his grin, but held her ground.

'Let's ask her to tea.'

'Oh – well.' Cathy considered. There were points about the situation that obviously hadn't occurred to him, and so much the better. He was under no obligation to Dorothy. He had just happened to pitch a tent near her caravan. And, after all, there was nothing to betray them to Dorothy, nothing to show. He kept his belongings in his tent. They were always scrupulous to leave no trace. 'I don't see why not. It might do her good.'

Freeing Dorothy from the preparations for her dinner, even for an hour and with Margiad to put things in the oven, was an operation requiring the assistance of all hands. But two days later it was accomplished, and for very nearly the first time since Michael Derwent's departure Dorothy found herself back in her own property.

'I'd forgotten how delicious it is down here. If only we had a bit of grass at the hostel, and some trees. I shall come and sleep here when the house is empty, if it ever is. Haven't you got everything exquisite! This cake tastes home-made – surely you didn't—'

'You haven't provided us with an oven,' said Cathy, 'or we'd have had a try. Olwen Bryn Glas made it for us. We took her the stuff.'

'Friends everywhere, haven't you? You're far better known now in the countryside than I am. I feel almost jealous. I shall start a round of visiting in the winter.'

Christopher was charming to her, shyly calling her Dorothy at her request; and beneath a perfectly respectful manner he was cheeky, too. Each time she aked him kind questions about his life as a schoolmaster he gave her a brief reply and countered with kind questions about her life as a hostel warden. Neither being willing to yield an inch, it became a kind of parlour-game. Cathy gazed delightedly at the two dearest people in her world, both so tall and fair and good and beautiful – a pity Christopher wasn't ten years older, then they might have married, and what lovely, refined children they would have had. . . . Turning to her simultaneously for her opinion, they were surprised to see her start and colour. Dorothy's eyebrows rose in amusement. 'Have we caught you napping, Catherine?'

Anyway, thought Cathy complacently, except for that one unguarded moment, there had been nothing to give the game away. All their attention had been for Dorothy. They had scarcely looked at each other.

Whew! thought Dorothy, dishing up in her kitchen. Whew! So that's it. I feel as if I'd bathed in love. Of course I guessed. I could see by her face when she came here; but I had no idea it had hit her so hard. I suppose it was like that at first with me. Funny how one can't remember. But I know I sat on the lawn once at Somerville in an agony, almost fainting, because I thought he wouldn't come, and when I saw him coming through that red-brick arch it was a different sort of pain. So long ago it seems, but it's only four years really; we've made them long.

I wish it had been somebody older. But he seems a nice creature, and to know his luck. They'll have to wait ages – there I go again! Why should they? I hope they don't. Look at Michael and me, we're no advertisement for caution. Bottling all the feeling down, and then finding, when we take out the cork, that there's no feeling left after all, that it's somehow escaped through a crack in the bottom. . . .

When the meal and the preparations for breakfast were over, and in the brief hour she had to herself before crawling into bed, she sat down and wrote to Michael. It was her first letter since their parting, for she had been waiting for his. He had been on holiday in Italy, a country whence he had not found it possible to send her so much as a postcard. Now at last she took the course which, surely, she ought to have taken long ago, suggesting – not insisting, for she would never condemn anybody unheard – that the engagement should be over.

She sat on in the half-light after it was written, trying to see her life without him. After all, she could make herself useful, she knew herself fortunate in that; so many women had to devote themselves to a man or they went sour. But she had the capacity and temperament to spread over many what would evidently have been a burden of devotion to one. She was already doing it here at Cae Capel, and might some day do it on a more important scale. Arid arguments, perhaps; but though she went to bed still melancholy, her anxiety was curiously resolved.

It took two days for a letter to reach him, and his answer came by wire. 'Don't be a bloody fool writing Michael.' A nice juicy morsel for the post office down the pass, but of course he wouldn't think of that.

She knew exactly what would be in the letter; anger and impatient reproaches, as though she were the one at fault. Michael had always believed attack to be the best form of defence.

She was happy, she supposed, that she had not lost her lover; happy that he needed her, and that she could remain the prisoner of his need. But she knew now that the other life would have been quite tolerable, that the arid arguments had had in them the germ of truth. He had set something free in her by his unkindness. She would never be completely his creature again.

V

Individually the days had seemed enormous, each one so flooded with sunlight and laughter, so crammed with exquisite discoveries. Yet fourteen of them were gone in a flash. Here they were on the last Saturday, facing the last night. 'Cathy,' said Christopher.

He had so many ways of saying her name; cajoling, or caressing, or mocking, or purely impudent. All of them she loved except this one, this anxious, lost-sounding one, which always presaged something bad. And of course she knew before he said it what it was.

'Cathy, have you thought what we're going to do next?'

'I've tried to stop myself from thinking.'

'Well, but we must.'

But of course she had thought; such thinking couldn't be by-passed. And she had her answer ready, but saying it was so hard.

'I don't see,' she said at last, 'why we should try to hide from anyone that we're keen on each other.' She still could not bring herself to use the grand words *in love*.

'Reckon I couldn't, any road. Harry won't like it, will he?'

Curious that he should say that. For who should mind less than Harry, that declared enemy of personal feeling, that lifelong critic of interference? She said defiantly:

'Well, he's got no call to object. He never wanted me that way himself.'

'I hope you're right,' said Christopher. 'I'd hate to upset him. He's a nice chap.'

'But for the other thing—'

She could not bring herself to look at him. She knew that every nerve in his body was taut.

'I don't think we can, Chris. It's awful to – to have to chuck it like that. But it'd be too big a risk.'

Eventually he found voice to answer her. He muttered: 'Anything you say.'

'It's not me saying it. I wouldn't care one damn who knew. Only, you see, there's Dorothy.'

'Why, what's she—?'

'Well, she's responsible for what goes on at the hostel. I know this isn't the hostel, but the caravan's hers, and some might say – well, they might say she lent it to me knowing. And that might cost her her job.'

'I never thought of that. I have been dumb.'

'And with three other lads camping here – four, if Johnny's Stephen comes back – someone would be bound to find out. I don't say they'd mean to give us away if they did, at least I don't think so, but Johnny's an awful gossip. He'll say anything for a laugh, and it might pop out before he knew.'

'Yes,' he said, 'you're right, of course. It'd be a crazy risk. And I'd get you a bad name, wouldn't I? Oh, Cath, love, it's been so wonderful. I ought to think of nothing except how lucky I've been to have it. That ought to be enough.'

'I know it's hard,' she said, and suddenly she felt herself infinitely the older, like some unkind parent taking away a child's happiness. 'We'll just have to plan for next summer—'

'Next summer!' At twenty-one, to lose one's love, through months and months of icy blackness. . . . For the first time his voice was bitter. 'Eh well, I daresay the first two years are the worst.'

'We could—' She hesitated. 'We could find a hotel or something, sometimes. We're not so poor as all that.'

He dug his fingers into the turf. 'No,' he said finally, 'we'll start saving money. And if I wait till next summer, you'll marry me then, won't you? She can lend us the caravan for a honeymoon, and it'll be respectable. No more sneaking about and feeling ashamed. Promise.'

But if I promise then you've promised, don't you see? That's just what I mustn't let happen. 'I'll think about it, Chris,' she said. 'But I'd like it left so that either of us can change our minds.'

'I'll never change,' he muttered, pressing his mouth against the turf. 'I'll never, never change.'

Little Welsh Margiad, Dorothy's assistant, trotting past the glade on her way home as she did every night about this time, made them start as though they had been guiltily surprised. She waved to them and called: 'Miss Elliott says to tell you that singing gentleman is back again tonight.'

'Oh, I remember,' Cathy said. 'He came once before. I think it was my first week-end.' She had hated his songs then; how had Dorothy guessed she would be glad to hear them now? 'He sings all those old-fashioned things,' she explained to Christopher. 'D'you want to go?'

'I don't mind – whatever you like.' He got listlessly to his feet, and they walked up to the hostel in a desolate silence.

The common-room was crowded, mainly with strangers, though of course there were one or two Cathy knew. The circle was tightly packed round the piano, but Dorothy had kept a chair at the back. Cathy slipped into it almost unnoticed, and Christopher sat on the arm, not looking about or answering anyone's smile.

The little brown elderly singer was one of those time does not touch. He looked the same as before, homely and poker-faced, all his expression in his voice and his fingers.

He had been singing to please the party from London; now he broke into a northern tune. A rippling, lilting, splendid tune; the tune that the golden lads and lasses come pouring out to. They sang with him, they rollicked; at the end Cathy turned to Christopher with shining eyes, and even he was smiling. 'If that isn't grand!' she cried. 'Why,' he said, 'did you never hear the Blaydon Races before?' And of course she never had; she had never heard anything.

The singer gave them a couple of grim Border ballads, and then he moved north again, and into the love-songs. This was the music that had saddened and angered her when love had seemed a foreign country. Now it eased and comforted. In her life so poor of words, so devoid of any poetry, it said for her what she could not say. Had we never loved so kindly, till all the seas grow dry my dear, ghost nor bogle shalt thou fear, I can die but canna part – there it all was, the love that she could never speak. His arm slipped round her. He had understood that the message was for him.

'I liked that one about calling the ewes best,' she said as they walked home, and tried to hum the tune; such a simple-sounding tune, but tricky in its melancholy intervals.

'No, you got it wrong,' He whistled it for her. All the tunes were familiar to him. The little man had sung nothing original or out of the way.

'That's it. Is it what you call a folk-song?'

'Well, no, not exactly. I think it's by Burns.'

'Oh, him.' Even she had heard of Burns. 'They all write about dying and parting don't they? I suppose there'd be nowt to make songs of if folk just kept together and were happy.'

'We must try and look at it that way,' he gravely agreed. Even when, as now, he loved her utterly, there was an imp of irony in him which saw her comic side.

That night he seemed more than ever precious, and at last she had words to tell him. She found herself murmuring as he came to her: 'My bonny dearie . . .'

CHAPTER EIGHT

IT WAS coming down to earth again and no mistake. First there was home, smelling worse than ever in the heat, and needing a good scrub right through – but what was the use, asked Mrs. Canning, with smuts all over everything five minutes after? And she had had no holiday, lain in no cool glade. That it was her own fault – that if she had managed her husband's earnings less fecklessly she could have paid for a holiday – that she would in any case have been bored to tears in a glade – none of that altered the fact that her daughter had endless incentives to do better, and she had almost none.

Then there was the return to work. That at least was efficient and clean, but it was now enormously dull. She had to hear about the other girls' holidays, some to Southport, some to the Isle of Man. One had crossed England, fancy, and attained Skegness. And then there were the snapshots; that's my boy, nice-looking, isn't he? – but he never was, not beside Christopher.

And finally there was Mrs. Powell on the rampage once more.

She was to go and visit Bill. 'Cathy, be a dear,' she said. 'You come with me.'

'But I'm in a job.'

'That nice lady of yours would give you the day off, for certain, if you was to tell her why.'

'Any road, I couldn't, Mrs. Powell, It'd be raising his hopes, wouldn't it? I know you think it's unkind of me, but that'd be much worse.'

'I dunno how I'll manage,' said Mrs. Powell, beginning to cry. 'I never been so far from home before.' It was a terrible journey, right down to some place in the Midlands, where the Borstal was.

'I'd go with you for the journey, Mrs. Powell, really I would, if I didn't have to see him.'

'What'd be the use of that? It's you he wants. Every letter, he keeps asking me—'

'Yes, I know.'

A fat, slatternly woman, Mrs. Powell; a weak, indulgent mother, whose folly had partly brought her son to this pass; but ever since the trouble there had been something in her which it was impossible not to respect. Adversity brought out the best in her, as it brought out the worst in Mrs. Canning. Having few ideas in her head, she clung the more tenaciously to those that entered it, and foremost among them was now the conviction that Cathy Canning, hard, unfeeling piece though she was, was yet necessary to her Bill's salvation. She never relaxed, or flagged, or grew disheartened. She had no subtlety, no cunning, no gift for putting herself in another person's place, no weapons but a perpetual lying in wait, a continual harping. She was, on that account, the more formidable, because one could not help feeling sorry for her; almost, in a hypnotized way, on her side.

'Mrs. Powell,' said Cathy desperately, 'I got something to tell you, and you must tell Bill. He's got to give over thinking of me. For I've got a boy now' – she had only just stopped herself from saying 'another boy' – 'of my own.'

'You couldn't do that to him, Cathy. You couldn't. It'd be the death of him. And after what you promised—'

Useless to go into that again; Mrs. Powell did not listen to refutation or argument; she merely repeated what she believed. For the last time Cathy searched her heart and her memory; for it was important to go with clean hands to Christopher, and it seemed to her that breaking a pledge to an old friend in distress would be a far worse disgrace than two casual nights spent with Leonard Head. For the last time she felt assured that there had been no pledge. She had said no more to Bill than any girl in Tooley Street might say to the half-dozen lads who took her, in the course of a year, to the pictures. If he had misunderstood, that was his fault.

She began again patiently, when Mrs. Powell paused for breath:

'You'll be sure to tell him that, won't you, now? That I got a boy, that it's serious, that very likely this time next year I'll be married. That'll give him time to get over it, and as soon as he comes out he can start looking for somebody else. I know it's bad to have to tell him, but it'll be kindest in the long run. I'm sure you can see.'

'He'd never believe me. Thinks all the world of you, he does. He'd never believe you could let him down.'

'Tell him it's a teacher, over in Bootle—' Hateful to have to bring Christopher into it, but if these concrete details would help to fix the matter in her poor mind. . . .

After a long time, it seemed that something might have stuck. 'Well, I don't know how I'm to break it, I'm sure,' moaned Mrs. Powell, dabbing her eyes. 'And he's so looking forward to both of us coming—'

Evidently she had guaranteed that Cathy would appear. 'All the way I'll be thinking of it. I shan't have a minute's peace.'

Cathy, in point of fact, did not have a minute's peace either. All day her spirit travelled with Mrs. Powell, bewildered, badgered, not knowing where to change, and the bearer of evil tidings, down to Bill. She should have left things alone in the evening, have avoided Mrs. Powell, have demonstrated thereby the irrevocable ruthlessness of her decision. She could not bring herself to be so firm as that. Mrs. Powell, getting back very late and very tired, found her rooms set in order, the kettle boiling, and Cathy opcning a tin that she had bought on her way home from work.

And the news of Bill was good, was splendid; she had had a long talk with the Governor; he was very pleased indeed with the way Bill stuck at it, doing so well in the workshops; fine workshops they were, too; he was getting special training that would help him to a better job in the garage when he came out.

'Then he's happy?'

'Oh, well now, Cathy, you couldn't expect that. After all, it's a prison, for all they're so kind. You couldn't expect him to be happy.'

'Anyway, it's not a bad place?'

Poor Mrs. Powell, how could she describe the sort of place it was? In any case, between her desire to paint Bill's prospects brightly and her need to rouse all possible sympathy for his present plight, she was rendered almost speechless. All she could repeat was that Bill was doing lovely, and was counting the days till he got home, and that it was all Cathy this and Cathy that till you'd think there wasn't another lass breathing.

'But my message, Mrs. Powell?' Cathy urged. 'You gave it him?'

'Well, love, I did try. But he just wouldn't listen. It wasn't a bit of use—'

Perhaps she had tried. More probably, when it came to the point, she was only capable of telling him what he wanted to hear. Anyway, impossible to reproach her, tired as she was, and her feet swelling. Useless to tell her yet again that it was making things worse for him in the end.

'I tell you what, love,' said Mrs. Powell, suddenly breaking off her rambling excuses and looking her visitor straight in the eyes, 'I don't think our Bill will ever give up hoping. Not if he was to see you wed to that other fellow, he wouldn't. It's like as if you'd got into his bones.'

There certainly was something hypnotic about her faith and Bill's. It would be almost enough to shake one, if it were not so absurd. And it came over Cathy, for a bad moment, that the glorious world of Cae Capel with its passion and splendour and self-reliance was a dream world, and that this was reality, this sticky world of nightmare, peopled with Powells, even in their weakness tenacious and strangling.

By Friday night the holiday seemed as if it had never been. But the sight of Stan and Harry waiting by the laundry gates took her back, comfortingly, to much earlier days. They were brick red, and had lost most of the skin off their noses. Chamonix had been terrific, beyond anything you could imagine. All the way to Cae Capel Harry had to turn his head and shout out more details, while the motor-cycle swerved alarmingly on the road.

Christopher and Johnny were there already, and had a meal going, for it was too fine a night to feed indoors. The glade seemed full of tents and cheerful noise. Meeting Christopher's eyes, thus surrounded, was terrifying. She was quite incapable of the loverlike greeting which should have shown the others how matters were supposed to stand. She could scarcely bear to speak to him at all. 'Hello,' she said casually, rudely, and devoted all her time to loud inquiries about the Alps. Christopher, his eyes downcast, toiled away at the cooking-stove. He seemed infinitely remote.

'Dear little Snowdon,' Harry gazed complacently around. 'It all stands up better to the contrast than you'd think, doesn't it? I may say we never did anything technically as hard as our best climbs here, and we usually had to sweat up thousands of feet to get at the worthwhile stuff. But that's the whole point of the Alps, of course. It's the tremendous scale. Such masses of everything. There must be endless more new routes waiting to be worked out.'

'There ought to be more *télés*,' said Johnny.

'Shame on you. Those are the cable railways,' Harry explained for her benefit. 'They muck up the scenery disgustingly as it is. But Johnny was always disgracing us by yowling about having to walk.'

'Miles,' said Johnny. 'Usually vertically on ice in the middle of the night, and on a breakfast of stale bread and milkless tea. I ask you.'

'How should I have done?' Cathy asked.

'Eh, you'd have been a smash hit, I mean, by their standards. I believe there are some first-class French women climbers, but we didn't meet them. It was all bonny lasses being carted about by the boy-friend, and screaming every other minute *"Tu m'assures?"* – that means, "You got me?" Or *"Au secours!"* – that means, "Help!" We died laughing.'

'Harry kept on telling them about you. Wherever we went he used to say: *"Il y a oon fille chez noo qui grimpe meeoo que ça."* ' Johnny produced an accurate parody of Harry's French accent. 'Don't you ever go near Chamonix. Your name there is mud.'

'Much chance I have of ever going,' said Cathy bitterly. For a moment she had seen herself leading on the great red granite ridges, poised over three-thousand-foot vertical drops above the glacier, swinging down on the long abseils. To be capable of it and not have the chance, while the silly French girls were led round screaming by their boy-friends – wasn't it monstrously unfair?

'You'd have led the Grépon ordinary,' Harry was assuring her. 'Well inside your standard – you'd waltz up that Mummery Crack. Mer de Glace face, now – that was a bit different. I admit at several points it gave me the willies. That was Johnny's best lead, wouldn't you say, Stan?'

'Struck those Frenchies all of a heap,' acknowledged Stan.

'Ay, I'll say that for our Johnny, no one could care less about the honour of British climbing, but he struck a blow for it that day.'

'Shucks,' said Johnny. 'I was just passing the time the way I happened to like.'

'Now you got to visualize, Cathy—' Step by step, with sketch and gesture and an occasional out-of-focus snapshot, he took her up the Mer de Glace face.

Suddenly she knew that Christopher was watching her. Covertly returning his gaze, she surprised a look of utter desolation. This is what she missed, it said. It was only to make up for this that she came to me.

Do him no harm to think it. Nothing like a little competiton. Oh, but

Christopher, love, you know it isn't true. Nobody, not all the Alps under heaven, could be to me what you were. And before she could stop herself, she had sent him a look that brought the blood up into his face. The look was intercepted by Johnny as neatly as though it had been a football.

Johnny was the hero of this epic now in course of relation, but he was almost without vanity: it was one of his inhuman and dangerous traits. It gave him far more pleasure now to spy out someone else's secret than to hear his own praises sung. 'That's enough about me, chum,' he remarked, cutting Harry off in the middle of the Knubel Crack. 'How did absent friends make out?'

'Oh, we just mucked about,' said Cathy vaguely. 'It was too hot for climbing.'

'Too hot?' Harry stared. 'I'd have thought it was just about perfect. It was with us.'

'But you were all those thousands of feet up,' said Christopher, doing his best. 'And we did go up Snowdon by moonlight.'

'That's right – we thought it'd be like your Alps.'

'Not in the least, I imagine,' said Harry, still much dissatisfied.

'But it's really been sweltering here. Bathing was about all it was fit for. We biked to the coast several times.'

'Ah well,' commented Johnny, 'as Christopher once pointed out, there's more things in life than climbing.'

Harry broke the dangerous little silence by getting to his feet. 'I'll wash up tomorrow,' he told them. 'Tonight I want to have a word with Dorothy.'

He found her putting her feet up at the day's end, and answered her kind inquiries about Chamonix almost absentmindedly.

'Cathy been falling for our little schoolmaster?' he abruptly inquired.

'Why yes, I think so,' said Dorothy. 'Not that they've said anything to me. But it was to be expected, wasn't it? And really, on the whole, a very good thing.' She gave him an anxiously encouraging smile.

'I'm not denying he's a decent enough kid—' said Harry unwillingly at length.

'But too young, you feel.'

'It looks like baby-snatching to me.'

'No, there I'm sure you're mistaken. I admit I've always pictured someone older for Cathy – someone more like yourself.' Not without amusement she saw him wince; really, he mustn't expect to have it all ways at once. 'But Christopher is thoughtful and responsible for his age, and I feel pretty confident that he knows his own mind.'

'Then you think it's serious?'

'Well, why not? Perhaps their prospects aren't of the brightest, but if Cathy carried on with her job—'

'Oh well, if you say so. I'd have thought, somehow, that they weren't quite right—' He brooded, puzzled himself by his misgivings. 'Anyway, who am I to judge? I only hope, though, that she's not going to chuck climbing. I'll have been nicely led up the garden if she does.'

'I'm sure there's not the slightest risk of that.'

'Love and climbing don't mix,' said Harry morosely. 'I've said it before and I'll say it again. And she's just got to the pitch where she ought to concentrate. She's made amazing progress in these last three months – suddenly seemed to shoot ahead. Johnny tells me it was just the same with him. Sign of a great climber – it's the middling ones like me that get just so far and then stick. If I can only keep Johnny up to it – and that's the very devil, having to rely on a selfish little wart like him – we might have her leading on Cloggy by next summer.'

'Oh, Harry, no. Isn't that going a bit far? I mean, only about six women ever have.'

'Yes, and all upper-class types with oodles of holidays. Never a lass from here.'

It was possible that even the upper-class types got no more practice than Cathy Canning, coming every week-end. But Dorothy left this point aside.

'I love you for being so ambitious for her, and I know it'd be a triumph for Cae Capel and do us all credit. But I can't get it out of my head how Doreen Lord looked when she was brought down. Of course one oughtn't to talk to a climber in that jittery way.'

'Doreen was an appalling climber. She never even had the rudiments. Oh, I know she got up a lot of things, but it was chiefly grab and guts. She was heavy as lead, and bound to have a smash if conditions went against her – you remember she fell off something dead easy in the end. Now Cathy's climbing gives one complete confidence. You feel she never makes a move she can't retrieve. And she's every advantage – she's not much smaller than I am and must weigh a couple of stone less. There'll always be certain things she can't do, laybacks for instance, but apart from them I've always thought women ought to make the best climbers. They make the best ballet-dancers, and that's the nearest parallel.'

'All right then, as long as you don't insist on single-minded devotion. It really isn't necessary. Several of the upper-class types you were mentioning are now married women with children, I understand. Our sex is a lot more versatile than you one-track men will ever believe.' And with this warning she sent him home in a more sanguine frame of mind.

Setting up camp always fully occupied their Friday evenings. For Cathy it was, tonight, a fortunate circumstance; she did not have to endure much more of Johnny's pregnant silence, the painful effort made by Christopher to ask Stan questions about Chamonix, and Stan's even more painful effort to reply. By ten, when Harry returned, she was able to plead a perfectly accurate fatigue – she felt, indeed, beyond words, tired and dispirited – and shut herself into the caravan. For half an hour more she heard the boys' voices as they rummaged in sacks and adjusted tent-pegs. Then there was silence. The world slept.

But not she. She knew the weariness that is beyond sleep, the weariness that sets hammers going in the brain. This time last week – so close and yet such miles away – better if we'd never had it at all – better for him, anyway, he didn't know what he was mising – what have I done to him? – what have I done to myself? – on and on the hammers went. She wondered whether, between these four wooden walls that had held her happiness, she was ever to know sleep again. Panic suspicions assailed her that she had stirred up something she could not control.

After an eternity of tossing she opened the top half of the caravan door and leant out on her elbows, drinking in the cool darkness. It smelt of pine and thyme and waterfall, and though there was no moon it was not opaque, for the faintest possible shimmer seemed to come from the Milky Way sprawling across the sky. As her eyes grew used to it she could just make out something white beneath the trees; a face. She gave a tiny call, scarcely more than an intake of breath, and he came towards her. He had been standing there, quite still, quite silent, perhaps for hours.

'I didn't wake you?'

'No. I couldn't sleep, anyway.' She opened the lower half of the door and he stumbled in, out of breath as though he had been running, and muffled his long shuddering sighs in her hair.

'I haven't seen to the doings,' she whispered, but she drew him hungrily closer.

'Shall you mind risking it?'

'Not if you don't.'

'I never did.'

Five minutes after he had taken her he was asleep in her arms.

ii

She woke him at first light, having scarcely, in her anxiety, slept herself all night. She hated seeing the look of apprehension replace the first lazy contentment; hated seeing him creep furtively down the steps and across the dewy grass. And it was not from an enemy that he crept, but from the sight of his own friends; she had brought him to this pass. Still, they had been infinitely careful. No one could have seen.

'Like to look at the Back of the Milestone, Cathy?' Johnny asked at breakfast. 'It ought to be bone dry after all these weeks.'

That was a piece of luck, being asked by him so soon. Perhaps he had got bored with the others at Chamonix. Perhaps, on the other hand – She followed him in two minds.

On the Front of the Milestone played and yelled, hauled and grabbed and scrabbled the vulgar herd, for this was where everyone began, and on a fine September Saturday parties queued up under its start. Round the corner was the Back, reserved for the exclusive use of the handful of climbers in Johnny's class, and not surprisingly they had it to themselves. The courses were short grooves, almost vertical and almost holdless. If the leader fell he fell ninety feet, and was just as dead as if he had toppled off the Mer de Glace face.

How does anyone get up here? debated Cathy, working it out at the rope's end. Of course I shall come off. I wonder what Johnny's like when one comes off. He's so scatterbrained – I hope it occurs to him to hold. Inch by inch, in what seemed to her a quite extraordinary series of balance and pressure movements, she made height. By a miracle she did not come off. It was the hardest thing she had ever done, and she acknowledged that the nerve to lead it would never quite be hers. It was salutary thus to know the ultimate limitations. Nevertheless she reached the top exultant, toes and fingers tingling, and spirits drunk with the heady fever of this king of sports. She embraced Johnny and made him laugh. Then they roped down and went up another one.

He let her enjoy the false sense of security till they had eaten lunch on a heather ledge at the top of the crag. Then he said in his most affable tones:

'Well now, ducky, how about coming clean?'

'Meaning?' said Cathy, the pit of her stomach going cold.

'You and our little schoolmaster. Sleeping together, aren't you?'

She put on a magnificent show of indignation. She abused every corner of his dirty mind. But she knew that there was steel beneath his unconcern.

'If you cast your mind back, my girl, you'll remember that I was a moderately good friend to you as long as nothing was kept from me. But try to string me along and I warn you, you're fair game.'

She knew it was true. Her wry grin admitted it, and at the same time tried to conceal her alarm.

'That's better,' said Johnny encouragingly. 'Your doing, of course?'

'Well, what do you think? And I'm not ashamed of it, either.' She added bitterly: 'I only have to pretend to be.'

'I really don't see any need.'

'Well, for one thing, if Dorothy ever finds out, it'll be the end of me, climbing and all. I couldn't come here again.'

'It'd be awkward for her, I do see,' said Johnny. 'Well, I shan't split on you. But you're afraid Harry will cut up rough.'

He was shrewd, right enough. 'I suppose I must be, and yet I'm damned if I know why. It's got nothing to do with him.'

'Well, in a way, you're his invention. And he's always taken this absurd sex-rears-its-ugly-head attitude, as though one had to be a eunuch to get up a bit of rock. You know, if you'd kept yourself pure and good, and stuck at it till you could lead Very Severes, and perhaps got to be head girl at your laundry, I daresay old Harry would have married you in the end.'

She stared. 'Why on earth should you think that? He don't care a bit about me in that way.'

'No, I know, but some people don't marry for love. The best people, in fact. I'm certain my ancestors never dreamt of doing anything so vulgar, and it wasn't till we let sentiment ooze in and took to marrying pretty faces instead of fortunes that we began to decline. He will marry rationally, and there's a lot to be said for it. You've cooked your goose now, though. He'd never take anything second-hand.'

'You're talking daft. All the same, I admit I'm scared. We hadn't meant to – to go on, once you all came back. Last night we tried not to, but it wasn't any use.' Confidence, even to a Johnny, was horribly easy once one had begun. 'That's one of the things that scares me, feeling I'm turning him into a bad lot like me.'

'Oh, shucks,' Johnny said. 'I'm all for experiencing the passions, and from what I've seen of Christopher I should think he is, too; and furthermore, any chap worth his salt would be, if you want my unvarnished opinion.' Well, nobody would set Johnny up as a worthy character or a judge of morals, and yet, in default of anyone else's, his approval was comforting. 'The point is, how do we keep it from Harry's chaste ears? You better tip Christopher the wink to pitch his tent close to you next week-end – I'll shove ours a bit lower down, and Stan shall put theirs beyond that again, and with its mouth to the view no matter where the wind is.'

'Does Stan know, then?'

'Lord, yes, he did all along. At least, he expressed no surprise when I passed him the result of my dawn patrol. Bit psychic where you're concerned, isn't he? You know, when you're through with Christopher, you really ought to give old Stan a break. He may not be a beauty, but you wouldn't notice that in the dark.'

When you're through with Christopher . . . Her gratitude to Johnny, her reliance on his discretion, were wiped out by that dreadful phrase. What he thought was evident; she was just a step in the education of Christopher, who was destined for better things. Yes, and Johnny, with his wicked monkey face, had a way of being right. She said blankly, all the illusion of comradeship gone:

'It's not like that, Johnny. I know I must seem no better than a tart, but, honestly, I'm crazy about him. I don't believe I'll ever be through with him. It's he, more like—' and shameful tears stopped her.

'There, there, ducks, don't take on so,' said Johnny, patting her soothingly on the back. 'You must have it good and proper. *Vénus toute entière* – no, that's French, you wouldn't understand, and not the sort we learnt at Chamonix, either. But take heart. Look what a little siren you are – no one can resist you. Have your bit of fun with him, wait a bit in case that satisfies you, and marry him in the end if you must. Only get your serious climbing done first, and try and remember what I told you – you can't have it both ways.'

iii

Three weekends more they had of happiness, but the honeymoon was over. Love was inescapably illicit now, and carried with it corresponding hardship. For one thing, any sort of affectionate behaviour in public seemed impossible, and even when they climbed together the tingle of anxiety kept Cathy offhand and constrained, Christopher meek and silent, as though his personality had been blotted out. By nightfall they would both be near panic, and he as he crept through the glade, aware that only canvas walls stood between him and discovery, would feel himself a pawn in some monstrous game, a hide-and-seek gone sour. Often he would be shivering as he fell into her arms.

So little did they seem like lovers that Gwen, bouncing back from her holiday in Arran, at first hardly noticed it. Arran had suited all tastes in the Evans family, Bert finding crowds to mingle with, the children beaches to bathe from, and Gwen roped to strangers to whom she shamelessly attached herself, and who bore her, screaming, over the A'Chir ridge. 'It's tops,' she told Cathy. 'Real climbing, not like Crib Goch. Of course you'd have rioted over it if you'd been there.'

'I daresay,' said Cathy crossly. 'Like I would at Chamonix. I'm getting fed up with all you millionaires telling me what I've missed. Good old North Wales'll have to go on doing for me.'

'Your nice teacher lad is still around, I see. How did you get on with him?'

'Oh, all right.'

Something up, thought Gwen, and consulted Dorothy, who enlightened her. 'But they seem to be at the shy stage. They haven't said anything; at least, not to me. A pity, because I'm aching for the chance of telling them not to wait.' Her smile was rueful.

'Come to that,' said Gwen, 'she knows my views. Bert and I were their age when we married, and we hadn't a brass farthing—' Cathy did indeed know, and was shortly obliged, in the course of an apparently impersonal conversation, to hear it all over again.

That was on the second weekend. On the third, in spite of Johnny's obliging connivance, Harry found out. Of course it was inevitable. Campers sleep for the most part lightly. The wonder was that the secret could have been kept so long.

He said nothing to Christopher. No one, at any time, ever did think of saying anything to Christopher. But after breakfast on the Sunday morning he cornered Cathy at her housework in the caravan.

'So that's what you're up to?' he began.

She did not, as with Johnny, burst into denials. She was not going to lie to him. She merely put down her duster and waited.

His eyes were very bright, and his sharp little fox-terrier face wore the unnatural calm of one who is presently going to explode. Just as I thought, she told herself with a sinking heart; and not all the sense of his monstrous unfairness could buttress her against his anger and hurt.

'You couldn't hardly wait till our backs were turned, could you? It must have been a blow when we came back to spoil the fun. Now I come to think of it, you didn't look too pleased. I suppose, from the moment you set eyes on him, you had it all worked out. The poor lad wouldn't stand a chance.'

'That's true enough,' she agreed, and she could not keep a sardonic inflection out of her voice. 'It's hard to see how he could escape me, short of packing up and going home.'

'Well, of course, it's nothing to me what you do—'

'No, it isn't, Harry,' she cried, and the sardonic note had gone; her cry was pure appeal. 'It don't interfere with you and me at all, not if you'll see it the right way. You've been a grand friend to me. You've never wanted anything else. Can't we just go on?'

'—but your abuse of Dorothy's confidence,' continued Harry, just as though she had not spoken, 'is about the lowest thing I've ever met. You wouldn't care, of course. Hopping quick into bed would be all you'd think of. It wouldn't occur to you for a moment—' and out came all the arguments she had rehearsed so endlessly that first evening in the glade.

She heard him out, her face growing steadily more sullen, and at the end she said:

'Where else could we go? The poor haven't anywhere to make love. I've heard you use that often enough as one of your old economic examples. Of course I had to keep it from Dorothy, but she wouldn't have grudged it me if she'd known?'

'What possible right have you to assume that?'

'Well, I know her. Yes, and I reckon I love her a sight more than you ever will.'

'A nice way you have of showing it.'

'I've had – other ways of showing it.'

'You mean,' he said, digesting this, and it was plain that anger was driving him nearly hysterical, 'because you laid off her young man. You – did, I suppose? There wasn't any funny business here that night?'

'Harry, shut up.'

'Well, in that case, it certainly was kind of you. Never struck me then. I just took it for granted that you'd chuck him out on his ear. But now I realize you were doing something noble for our poor Dorothy. Since you don't mind who you get into bed with, one more or less wouldn't have made much odds.'

'You know you don't mean that.'

'Oh yes, but I do. And I take it just a wee bit hard, that I was never, apparently, in the running. I mean to say, if we'd known you were going cheap, there's several of us, and perhaps with older claims than Christopher, who'd have been glad to join the queue.'

He waited for an answer, and, none coming, marched out white-faced into the glade.

Cathy sat quite still on her bunk. Her very bones seemed to ache. Insult and injustice had always stirred her up to fight, but there was no fighting Harry. She owed him too much. She must take, and try to take without visibly flinching, everything he chose to say. But that he should choose. . . . And the cynic in her that knew about men answered bitterly: *they're all alike.*

Harry stormed up Pen yr Oleu Wen with Stan, too upset to climb, too upset for anything but pounding uphill at an excessive pace and kicking stones about. When they got to the top he had worked off the worst of it and begun to feel a reaction of shame.

'All the same, I'm damned if I can understand it,' he burst out. 'Honest, now, can you?'

Stan, to whom any discussion of Cathy was still almost insuperably painful, made a heroic effort and replied:

'You got to make allowances.'

'For what? Why? She's been given a grand time here. She's had all a girl can want without – without that. Why in God's name should we make a different standard of conduct for her?'

Stan swallowed hard and said:

'Well – I seen her home.'

'Oh,' said Harry shortly, who had not. He pondered for a while, then seemed to shake himself free. 'Let's drop down on to Black Ladders,' he proposed. For him the crisis was over.

On their return he sought her out. She had done a climb with Christopher in the interval, yet he had the impression that she could scarcely have moved from where he had left her sitting, silent and crushed. 'I'm right sorry, Cath,' he said.

She looked at him in a dazed way. 'You mean you forgive me?'

'I mean I'm asking you to forgive me. I hadn't any call to open my mouth, let alone say what I did. Course I didn't mean a word of it. You understand that.'

'Oh yes, Harry. Eh, it's good to have you back.' She took his hard little arm in a convulsive clutch. 'I didn't know I'd miss you so bad.'

'Just can't think what came over me.'

'Oh, that's all right.'

'Fact is,' said Harry, staring out at the fading skyline, 'there's things in a chap's make-up that he don't fully budget for. Things that sort of take him by surprise.'

'Look, forget it.'

'Bad things. Deep things. Terribly – old things.'

She perceived that she need protest no longer. Once his apology made, his thoughts had drifted from her. They were utterly concentrated now on this unhappy contemplation of his own soul.

CHAPTER NINE

OF COURSE it would have been unthinkable to go on once Harry knew. It would have meant subjecting him to a cruel divison of loyalties. Nevertheless she might have done it, for she was beginning to understand that there are no depths to which one will not descend when love drives. But the heavens themselves settled the matter for her. They opened and washed the wonderful summer away.

Gale after gale swept across Snowdon, tore the slates from the roof of Cae Capel, stripped the trees and made it autumn in a trice. 'Caravan roof leaking,' wrote Dorothy to Cathy on a postcard, 'lots of cancellations, can put you all up in the house, let the boys know.' In any case her bookings regularly thinned out from October. The hostel was ready now to welcome back the faithful. It was the end of the camp in the glade.

The first three weeks, they agreed, comparing experiences later (in Cathy's case unwillingly, but Christopher seemed to find in it comfort), the first three weeks of deprivation were the worst. After that things grew, there was no denying it, easier. One began to be able to bear the wait.

In those three weeks they did not meet. Cathy went to Cae Capel as usual, for it seemed to her that she had nowhere else to go. But Christopher spent his first week-end taking his little boys on a blameless excursion to the Ainsdale sand-dunes, and for his second he went home.

He wrote to her from Wharswick; his first letter, and very nearly the first that she had ever received. When she saw the envelope, addressed in his beautifully neat, spidery handwriting, her heart turned over. She could not bear to open it under Norma's prying eyes, but walked to work reading it, bumping into passers-by.

'My darling . . .' it began; just that; no Cathy, as though nobody else existed. It was a wonderful letter. It told her how he missed her; how beginning to save a little money was the only thing that kept him hopeful and sane. And she partly guessed what an effort it had been for him, brought up like herself to northern reticence, thus to put his love and longing into written words.

And then at last they saw each other again, in the North Wales that Cathy had first known, a place of dark and windy rain. They met almost comfortably, the worst of the fever gone, and with it the sense of guilt that had made their manner to each other so unsatisfactory. She found him lounging on the hostel steps when she dismounted from Harry's pillion. 'If you don't want her for climbing tomorrow,' he said to Harry with a return of his old, slow-spoken impudence, 'I'll take her for a walk.'

She put on a show of disgust. 'Whatever for?'

'Because,' answered Christopher, 'it's my turn to choose.'

It was certainly not attractive weather for climbing, nor, one might have thought, for walking either, with the mist solid all over the top thousand feet. But once up on the great Glyder plateau, guiding themselves by the compass, they enjoyed the sense of eerie solitude in a country which a month ago had teemed with picnic parties, jollity and noise. They were again alone as they had been that night on Snowdon, and closer to the mountain than if all its beauties had been spread before their eyes.

'You got my letter?' Christopher asked as they trudged along from cairn to cairn. She nodded. 'Did you like it?' She nodded again. 'I don't believe you did, though.' She felt in the pocket of her climbing jacket and showed him a corner of the envelope, already grubby and worn. It had never left her. 'Then why didn't you answer it?' he demanded. 'I looked for an answer every day.'

At length she muttered: 'Because I don't write good enough.'

'Oh, Cathy! Was it only that? As if I'd have cared!'

'You might, though. You wouldn't half get a shock if you saw how bad I write and spell. I daresay worse than some of your kids.'

'What does that matter? After all, spelling's not your job like it is mine.'

'I ought to write you,' she said. 'and you ought to send me back my letters with corrections. I'd learn a lot that way.' She gave him a sidelong grin. 'But I'll see you in hell first.'

'Well, I don't write and get no answer. Fair does.'

'You must, Chris.' She stood still in her earnestness. 'If you aren't coming up every weekend—'

'I want to save money.'

'Then you got to write to me. If you knew what I felt when I saw your letter on our kitchen table! I nearly went off my head with joy.'

'Oh, Cathy,' he said again, and lifting her face in his hands, kissed her mouth wet with the mist.

'You ought to have felt me thinking of you,' she observed as they set out once more.

'Well, maybe I did. Your face has a funny way of jumping out at me, and sometimes I could swear I hear you calling. Even at home it happened – as if the person I was really talking to wasn't there. They none of them seemed to matter any more. Except Mother; nothing could wipe her out. Anyhow, I reckon you're a bit alike.'

'Are we?' She was immensely delighted; she knew he could pay her no higher compliment. 'Chris, did you – did you tell her about us?'

'Well, yes; I hope you don't mind. She'd have found out, any road. Course, I didn't tell her—'

'No, course.'

'I told her I'd asked you to marry me,' said Christopher loudly, to take that sudden hurt look away. 'and I told her you wouldn't promise.'

'And what did she say?'

'She said—' his grin reluctantly appeared, 'she said you showed a lot of sense.'

Well, that was fine. That was really almost reward enough. Perhaps the miracle might one day happen; Mrs Thwaites might welcome her as a daughter-in-law at last.

'Did I tell you my cousin Ruth's come?' he presently asked.

'No – so your Ma won after all?'

'Ay, but it was a rare fight.' He gave her the gory details; the wicked uncle had run true to form. Ruth had been turned out of the farm without a penny, without even a decent set of clothes – and that after years of unpaid drudgery. Mrs Thwaites had had to provide everything, except for her hospital uniform, in which, admitted Christopher, she already looked a proper little nurse.

'And does she still think you'll bite?'

'Eh, poor kid, she's so scared of them all at the hospital that she hasn't any time left to be scared of Mother and me. We're about the only things she's got to hold on to. If the sister isn't going for her, then it's the other nurses, or the doctor, or the matron. Course it's bound to be hard till she gets used to it. About the only ones she don't seem terrified of are the patients.'

'After all,' said Cathy, 'she's got them down.'

'Now that's unkind.' But he could not help grinning. A bigger cairn reared out of the mist and all but hit them in the face. Presumably it was the top of the Little Glyder; and, taking shelter on its leeward side, they sat down back to back, each propping the other's shoulders, and undid their lunches.

'Funny, no rope to sit on,' Cathy said, wriggling on the hard stone.

'I suppose you'd ever so much rather be climbing.'

'Fathead. No.'

'Well, I like climbing. I've missed it more than I expected. Tomorrow, what's more, I'm starting to lead.'

'Not with me, you don't,' she said instantly. He screwed his head round to peer at her, amused.

'Whyever not, love?'

'Because—' She reddened. 'Oh, lawks, Chris, what a give-away. I suppose it's because I'm sweet on you and I'd be nervous of you falling.'

'But I shan't fall. I'll start on something easy. You know how cautious I always am.'

'Yes, and I want you to lead. It's a grand feeling, there's nothing like it. But not in front of me.'

'Well, well.' He meditated. 'That makes me no end of a heel. I let you go up the most fearful things without turning a hair.'

'That's different. I was leading when you first knew me. You took it for granted, like I did with Harry. But when I was beginning, and there was someone a bit sweet on me, he didn't like seconding me, either.'

'Stan Bryce,' said Christopher calmly.

She stared. 'How did you know? Oh, Johnny, I suppose. Never could keep his silly mouth shut. Anyway, it's over and forgotten long ago.'

Christopher turned and propped himself on his elbow, so that he could see her face.

'He's a lovely chap, is Stan,' he observed, and there was a note of sadness in his voice. 'Nice as they come, and earning a good screw and all. He could have married you right off. I wouldn't want to think that – that I'd kept you from anything better.'

'You needn't worry. I showed him it was no good long before you came. I like the sound of my own voice as well as the next lass, but I'd have got a bit fed up hearing nothing else for the rest of my life.'

'Is that why you like me, because I jabber?'

'That and other things.'

'What things?'

'Give over fishing. You're getting a proper swelled head.'

'How you do hate being forced to say anything nice to me,' Christopher chuckled. 'Can you wonder I won't give you any peace till you do?' He gazed at her, exulting in his power to bring the colour to her face, and in a flash poor Stan was forgotten. 'Why,' he said, 'you're all white.'

'But so are you.'

The mist had laid a pearly rime on their jerseys and their hair.

'You look like a snow-queen or a ghost or something. You look like you belonged to the mountain.' Suddenly he flung his arms round her, all his teasing gone. 'Oh Cathy, Cathy, tell me you love me. You look like something I'll never get.'

ii

Dorothy Elliott drew the winter about her, lovingly, cosily, like a mist-furred cloak. She resumed possession of her house and her life. She was able once more to perceive the beauty by which she was continually surrounded, to watch the curtains of rain shaken over the valley by the north-west wind, to wake in the clouds, pressing like cotton wool against her window, and glimpse through rifts, as the day wore on, first the Holyhead road, and then the far green fields below the pass, and at last the distant sea.

In the week there were few now staying in the house, sometimes no one, and she could lock it after breakfast and take out her car, over to Bryn Glas for a gossip with Olwen, on to Carnarvon to lay in winter supplies at her friend the bookseller's, and round to the sands below Portmadoc, where she would walk for hours, staring back at Snowdon or across to the small enchanted hills of Lleyn. And then there were the delicious evenings spent with Dorothy Wordsworth by the fire, reviving through that most exquisite observation, that perfect sensibility, what had grown stale and perfunctory in her own.

She savoured her existence the more completely because it now had a term. She was to be married at the end of the summer, whether Michael had his chair or not. The decision was his, taken with a violence and an obstinacy which amused and dismayed her. She, it now appeared, was to blame for all their misunderstandings; she had forced him to wait, and thus exposed him to unfair temptation; a couple of furnished rooms in North Oxford were all he had ever asked.

How easily, she would sometimes think, letting Dorothy Wordsworth fall into her lap, how easily I could have been an old maid. How happily I could have gone on like this, enjoying my solitude, my moments of gentle melancholy, freed from all anxious dependence on another person's moods. This marriage will be as profound a disturbance for me as Wordsworth's was for her. But, like her, I have willed it; I have brought it about. Both of us have longed for the pattern of our lives to stand still, and both of us have shattered it ourselves.

The week-end shook her from her musings, as her band came trooping back. No longer was it necessary to banish them to draughty tents and leaking caravans. She gathered them in under her eye again, saw that they had proper meals and that their socks were dry, and noted how they were getting on. She observed that Stan Bryce, for example, was taking the shyest and most tentative notice of a little Welsh student from Bangor University, who was a new face among the regulars, and that Cathy, by discouraging any form of teasing liable to put him off, was doing what she could to further the affair. She understood that Harry Rimmer took no interest in the young lady, whose climbing abilities were mediocre, but concentrated the more indefatigably on Cathy, seconding her with endless patience up routes rendered at least one standard harder by the wind and the rain.

But of course her closest interest centred on Cathy, the child of Cae Capel, who owed it so much, and looked like owing it the ultimate blessing of a happy marriage. Here she ceased to heed inner warnings against interference, and told herself with a matchmaker's frankness: 'I'd like to see Cathy settled before I go.'

There were still no confidences, and they were by no means perpetually together. Christopher only came up every other week-end, and now preferred to do his own leading, at which he was making strides. Usually he led one of the other boys, but sometimes another girl, and on these occasions one could sense a wariness in Cathy, though she never expressed the slightest jealousy. Nor, in fact, did she seem to have cause, for in the evenings he would return contentedly to her side. They were never publicly affectionate, but they behaved, discovered Dorothy, exactly as though they were married. They presented one front to the world. But they were not married, and she would have been glad to know that definite plans were in Cathy's mind.

'Did you know I was getting myself some more education?' Cathy one evening remarked. They were storing for the winter the bedding from the now dismantled caravan.

'No – who from? Christopher?'

'Not likely. He's cocky enough as it is.' No word of praise for Christopher ever escaped Cathy's lips, but no one was thereby deceived. 'No, I'm going to evening classes, to try and write and spell a bit better. Junior English Literature and Composition, it's called, but that's just to spare our feelings. Actually it's all duds or bloody fools like me, that wasted our time at school. But don't tell – anyone.'

'I won't tell – anyone,' promised Dorothy, with a neat mimicry of the inflexion which brought a grin to her friend's face. 'Are you expecting to write many letters, then?'

'Well, I like getting them. It's something to show.'

'I hope, pet, you'll eventually have more than that to show,' said Dorothy, growing grave.

Cathy shook out a blanket; perhaps there was going to be confidence at last. But no. 'I reckon it's a mistake to let yourself count on things,' she said shortly.

'But look here, Cathy—'

'Any road, you feel a fool if you can't write decent letters. If there's trouble, or you're separated, or anything, you might as well be dead. Look at poor old Bill.'

'Bill?' For a moment Dorothy could not remember who he was. 'Oh – the one in Borstal.'

'That's right. He can send a letter a month – that's to his mum, of course, but he knows she'll show it to me.'

'And does she?'

'Ay. Never lets me off. But his letters don't tell us anything, not about what it's like or what he's feeling, not really. And it's not just the bad spelling. He don't know how to put it into words.'

A good thing too, thought Dorothy, much alarmed. 'I admit I hoped that all that had blown over,' she said with a tentative smile.

'It'll jolly well have to. If I've told his mum once I've told her a hundred times. But she hasn't got the guts to tell him. I suppose you can't blame her, in a way.'

'Er – how much longer is it? About a year?'

'Ten months.'

'Oh. I hope he's doing well.'

'Ay, he is, we know that. They've got workshops there, and when they found the garage was willing to take him back they gave him special training. He ought to be all right when he comes out, unless there's another slump by then.'

'I'm so glad. Then you can feel he's really off your chest. In any case you're bound to have grown apart from each other, so much having happened to you both in the two years. I expect he'll realize it as clearly as you do when you actually meet.'

Cathy gave her a curious look, not exactly grateful, not exactly reassured. Enigmatic little thing; one was so fond of her, and yet one could never be sure what went on inside her head.

More than ever Miss Elliott felt it desirable that, no matter how slender their prospects, Christopher and Cathy should reach the autumn man and wife.

iii

When they met in Liverpool, as they did after he had spent a week-end at home, she never failed to see him without a shock of delicious surprise. He looked so out of place among the trams and shipping offices, this tall, radiantly fair boy from the moors, in a city where almost everyone was undersized like herself. He seemed, like a figure in a painting, to carry his own background with him. She was opening her mouth to tell him so when he said: 'Whenever I catch sight of you I seem to see Cae Capel.' The coincidence filled them with delight.

But it was dark when she crossed the Mersey after work on a December evening, because he was to take her to the play. He was waiting on the landing-stage, and perhaps it was only the hard glare of the lights that made him look more like other people, harassed and tired.

'Here's your book,' she said, when they were settled in the coffee-scented Church Street teashop of his choice.

'Did you like it?'

'Like – I dunno. I sat up half the night with it, anyway. I never did that with a book before. Norma was wild.'

'Sounds as if it got you all right,' he said smiling. 'I've always thought the first Cathy is a bit like you.'

'Thank you for nothing. What a bitch. If you come to work it out, away from the grand writing, she just dies of bad temper.'

'You don't think that's possible?'

'I could imagine it,' she said, considering. 'I could see myself doing it if I was done out of something I wanted bad enough. But she didn't know what she wanted. She could have had Heathcliff from the start.'

'And you always know what you want?'

'Always.' She gave him that straight look that made him redden while he laughed. But there had been irony in his question, and once again, this time quite clearly, she heard the warning bell.

'How were things at home?' she asked, and the harassed look returned to his face.

'Oh, Mother and Father are fine. But I'm worried about Ruth. I don't think she's going to make the grade.'

'But I thought she was such a grand little nurse.'

'So she is – the patients love her. But she can't seem to get on top of the book work. I'd no idea there was so much book work in nursing. A lot of it memory stuff, too, and that's just what she isn't used to. I was trying to help her with her anatomy, and it took me all my time. She has her first exam in the spring, and they're chucked out if they don't pass.'

'How daft, if she's good at the job.'

'Oh well, I suppose they've got to keep up their standards,' said Christopher, torn between his professional bias and his anxiety for his cousin. 'She's not stupid, I'm sure of that, but with all the scaring she's had from my uncle a bit of her brain has gone to sleep. I've known it happen with kids from bad homes, but it's easier to help them when they're little. Course I could do more for her if I was home oftener. I feel it's our responsibility, see. We took her away from the farm, and he'd never have her back.'

'If you don't look out she'll fall for you,' Cathy said.

Of all the fool things to say! – and when she had made it a rule never to flatter any man by expressions of jealousy! But she had had a sudden vision of Christopher's head and Ruth's, close together above the anatomy book, and the words had burst from her unawares.

He looked startled, and then, understandably, cross. 'That's nonsense,' he answered hotly. 'Why, I'm just like one of her brothers.'

And did she run away from her brothers? Did she ever treat them as though they'd bite? But never let him guess at such surmises. 'I'm sorry, Chris,' she said with a meekness so unusual that his face cleared at once. 'You're the best judge, of course. I daresay it's just that I like to think I'm the only dim-witted lass on your mind.'

'I wish it was you. You'd be on top of the old anatomy in two ticks. There's nothing you couldn't learn if you wanted.'

'Dunno why you should think that,' she muttered, though in fact her rapid progress in the English Literature and Composition class inclined her to believe that it was true. 'Look how bad I did at school. And I still don't know anything. You'll find me out when we get to this play. I don't expect I'll understand a word.'

'Would you like me to tell you what it's about?'

'No. I've never had a rope let down to me yet.'

'Your head's full of nowt but climbing,' said Christopher, laughing. 'Is it really true you've never seen a play before?'

'Well, I wasn't brought up a millionaire.'

'Don't talk to me about millionaires. You had money enough to go twice a week to the pictures.'

'It wasn't me paid,' said Cathy with a grin. 'The rest of my boys weren't educated like you are. But I will say this: you miss more through being ignorant than through being poor. That's why I'm not going to stay ignorant much longer.'

But after the alarming five minutes needed to get used to Shakespearean verse, her fears proved groundless. She was transported; to new worlds of experience and beauty she seemed suddenly to have been given the key. When the lights went up her face wore the expression he remembered from that night on Snowdon, intent and rapt. 'The black man's going to murder her, isn't he?' she asked, and then quickly: 'No, don't tell me, I can't bear to know how it's going to end.' Christopher, brought up on *Lamb's Tales*, found himself reflecting that ignorance had its enviable side.

She was crying as they came out into Williamson Square. 'Let's walk,' she muttered. 'I'd feel such a fool blubbering in a tram.' They sauntered slowly through the empty streets, which at night-time, stripped of their traffic and bustle, were unmistakably the streets of a seaport and smelt of the river.

'Are you crying for Desdemona?'

'No – just because it was so grand. But it couldn't really have happened, could it? That Iago was too bad to be true?'

'I read some chap's theory that Shakespeare meant him to stand for what time would have done in the long run. Because of Othello being black, I suppose – there was bound to be a flaw in their love although they were both so fine. But of course what Shakespeare meant is anybody's guess.'

'It's likely, though,' Cathy said. 'There's often a flaw, something folks can't help. You can't play for safety in love, not if you want the real thing. You remember where the other woman says she wishes Desdemona had never met him, and Desdemona answers: 'So would not I!' That was wonderful. She knew it had been worth it.'

He looked down at her, vaguely disquieted. 'That's all very well in a play,' he said. 'You'd want a bit more of a run for your money in real life.'

'Ay, no doubt I would,' she said, coming back to him from far distances. 'I'm a great wanter, aren't I, Chris? Always grab, grab, grab. But it won't hurt me to be reminded now and then that there's more to life than that.'

'Just you grab me,' he told her firmly. 'That'd hurt you least of all.'

From the top deck of the ferry the river was a black satin highway barred with wavering lights. Hundreds of times in her life she had crossed it, and never seen till now that it was beautiful. She had been astonished to hear Christopher declare that he thought Liverpool a fine romantic town and could watch the Mersey for ever. Now it was like the lifting of a Cae Capel mist; beauty burst on her, assertive and unheralded. She felt that henceforward she would always see it so. They can't take that from me, she thought, and with such vehemence that she found she had said it out loud.

'Take what from you, love?' asked Christopher, and tightened his hold round her waist. 'Who's taking?'

'Oh, I dunno – I'm daft. It's just that some things seem too good to last. Look, you'd best go back on this boat.'

'No.'

'It's late and you're a long way from home.'

'Never mind.'

They landed and stood on the Woodside stage, watching the ferry cast off again and recede into the darkness. She knew what was coming. To forestall it she said:

'Well, good night, Chris. Sorry I did so much crying.'

'Eh, I didn't mind that. Shows you're not such a tough nut as you make out.'

'Well, you knew that before.'

'Cathy, let me see you home.' Against his side he felt her stiffen. 'Just this once. Just to the end of the street if you like. I won't ask to come in. Please.'

Never had she let him. The entire south bank was very nearly out of bounds.

Well, why not? she thought in a long moment of terrible temptation. When he sees how low it is, and how filthy, he'll be sorrier for me even than he is for her. And she knew that she could not do it. She had taken advantage of him once; once was enough.

'No, love,' she said gently, 'no.'

'Well, I'm coming, anyway.' He was suddenly rigid. 'I shall follow you. You can't stop me – it's a free country.'

'Don't you dare.' She flared into anger to match his. 'If you do, I'll never—' But what was the use of threats, when he knew she would not carry them out? She ended in exasperation: 'Haven't you enough to do worrying over that Ruth without starting in on me?'

'Then there is something to worry over?'

'I never said so. You take me up wrong. It's not fair, going on at me like this, and after what you promised.'

'I ought never to have promised.' And behind his anger there was something frantic. It was almost as though he were the one to threaten her. Why did he suddenly want to come so badly? Why, unless that already – unless that even now. . . .

She stared at him, her heart growing cold, and saw his resolution waver and break. 'Oh, all right,' he muttered flatly. 'Whatever you say. Good night.'

She turned away and left him, and looking back, saw him still standing there, a very young boy, ill-used by his love. Flesh and blood could not bear it. In a second she was across the stage, gripping his arm, and peering up into his averted, stony face. 'Not like that, Chris. Not like that.'

At last he looked down at her; the passion in her voice melted him, and she knew that he was very tired. He put his hands behind her shoulders and lifted her till she could reach his mouth. And for a long time she hung there, kissing him for ever, loving him with all her heart.

CHAPTER TEN

CHRISTMAS STOOD ahead, a landmark equally for those with well-loved homes, and those so fortunately detached that they could make alternative plans. Christopher, of course, was going home and would stay there a fortnight; Harry Rimmer, a good son according to his lights, for he took his mother to the cinema weekly and often gave his father a game of golf on summer evenings, considered himself perfectly at liberty to spend Christmas at Cae Capel in the hope of snow. Stan Bryce, whose inclinations would undoubtedly have been domestic, had been an orphan for some years now and made his home with Harry's family, and Harry's programme was therefore automatically his.

Cathy was sorely tempted to go with them. Her mother and Norma and the street would make an outcry, for which she cared nothing. Her father would make no outcry; indeed, he now scarcely spoke at all; but she knew that her going would leave his Christmas desolate. He saw little enough of her as it was. In the evenings they sat on each side of the fire, he scowling over his paper and she with one of Christopher's books, while Mrs. Canning and Norma giggled with the neighbours or went to the pictures; and they derived a curious comfort from each other's presence. But any real communication with him, any exchange of thought or experience, was now almost impossible. I'll try and cheer him up, she vowed. I'll make him come walking on Christmas Day in the Wirral. But she knew it was no use; the years in the street were slowly turning him into stone.

She had told Christopher there were to be no presents; it would cause talk. She prepared one for him, nevertheless. It was her first letter, over which she toiled for a week. Her persistence in the class for English Literature and Composition, her ruthless monopolising of the instructors, her dogged copying of the exercises, had brought their reward, and she was tolerably confident that her writing and spelling, though they would never be elegant like Dorothy's, gave no cause for shame. To know what to write was the difficulty; no night-school could teach you that. It suited him to be open and loving, but it was not a girl's proper policy, nor her place. She tried to get down on to paper the cheeky way of talking that made him laugh, and was disconcerted to find how hard it was, and that a sort of flat pertness was all she could achieve. But at length she was satisfied, copied it on to pale grey paper with a surface like frozen snow and wonderfully deckled edges, and posted it on Christmas Eve. It might not say in so many words how much she loved him, but he would have to be very dense not to know.

She was herself to receive two unexpected gifts. The first was a piece of news.

'Bill's getting out end of March,' said Norma, meeting her as she returned from work.

'What?'

'Ay. Ma Powell just heard.' There was a shrewd malice in the little creature's grin.

Cathy tore upstairs, and it was true. Mrs. Powell, flabby, wheezing with a bronchial cold, utterly radiant, held out the Governor's letter. Having regard to his good record, his excellent progress in the workshops and the fact that there was a job for him with his former employers, it had been decided to remit six months of his sentence. He would, of course, be on probation. 'They do it sometimes, you know,' Mrs. Powell exulted. 'Not often with a Borstal, but sometimes. Course I wasn't letting myself hope for it. They must think a lot of him, you can see—'

'Eh, I'm so glad,' Cathy kept saying. 'It's wonderful. I'm so glad.' She was laughing and crying, and Mrs. Powell thought her battle won. That they were tears of hysteria she could hardly be expected to understand.

Somehow Cathy got herself away and out of reach of her sister's eye. She was shivering with panic and self-disgust. Could it really be that she didn't want her old friend home, that she wanted him kept in that dreary place, out of her way? Surely no one born had ever fallen so low as that before. But it was true, and how could she deny it? She had hoped to be safely married to Christopher before Bill came back into her life. And now the fact was almost on top of her – three months – a mere nothing. She felt herself without protection or plan.

She found that she could scarcely remember his face. So much, everything, had happened since they took him away. She could see him as he sagged against the door that night, with his crushed and bleeding hand, but that was a hunted animal, not the real Bill at all; and the girl who had confronted him was not herself, but the dreary little chrysalis of herself that had existed before Cae Capel, before climbing. The real Bill was a well-set-up boy, the best looking in the street, and the nicest, too; that she had never denied. He was tallish, and fairish, and not so unlike Christopher if you came to think of it; but then you never would come to think of it, because he so completely lacked the variety of expression that gave Christopher's face its charm.

He was easiest on the eye wearing his garage overalls, or doing something with his hands. But for much of the time his pleasant face would be vacant. He had a maddening capacity for letting other people do the thinking. He would be content to watch the Tranmere Rovers every blessed Saturday afternoon, or to sit twice through a dud film because he had nothing better to do. His passive willingness to be a spectator had always, she knew now, exasperated her, even before she found self-release in a sport of her own.

And now he was upon her. She must see things straight. Straight as Dorothy did; making perhaps a few more allowances; but getting to the same conclusion in the end.

She was so closely haunted by Bill all night that it gave her a shock to see Christopher's writing on an envelope on Christmas morning. He had chosen a lovely Italian painting, of the Virgin and Child with another baby and an angel, sitting in a grotto which they could only, as he noted on the back, have reached by means of a Very Severe. 'I don't call that a Christmas card,' Norma said. 'Your new boy must be nuts.' And indeed it looked curiously out of place on the Canning mantlepiece, among the stage-coaches and robins they had received from their neighbours; though it had Harry's woodcut of the Devil's Kitchen on one side, and on the other a card illustrating Johnny's ancestral castle, for which the general public paid one and sixpence, the profits going to the castle's upkeep.

And immediately after breakfast she was summoned by Mrs. Powell, who held out a parcel, saying: 'He sent me this for you.'

It was a handbag, an amazing handbag, heavily thonged, and embossed with a pattern of roses and thistles and vine-leaves twined round a great central C.

'And never a thing for his poor – old – ma—' ended Mrs. Powell, suddenly bursting into tears.

Cathy stood miserably patting her shoulder, hating and admiring the handbag, overcome by the love and longing and hours of patient labour that it represented. Of course it should have been for his mother. Wasn't that just like Bill, she thought furiously, not to see what was the right thing to do? Wasn't it of a piece with his general softness? Didn't he prove that he still needed someone to tell him, every time?

'Eh, well, I ought not to grumble,' said Mrs. Powell, bravely endeavouring to get the better of her sobs. 'That's the way of life, I suppose. The young ones got to come first. You can't blame him. But this I will say, Cathy – if ever a boy deserved a girl better than what he does you—'

There was nothing to be done but take the bag. With her initial on it there could be no giving it back. The whole street knew by dinner-time.

She could not bring herself to use it, but the thought of it, the sight of it, when she took it out and fingered it at night, clutched at her, yet another of the octopus tentacles with which the Powells were seeking to draw her back. She longed to confide, and almost determined that in her next letter she would tell Christopher the whole story. He was always clamouring to hear her troubles, and, after all, he now very nearly had the right to know. But she could not write again till he answered, and she looked for his answer with passionate impatience. A week passed, and nothing came.

She spent another Welsh weekend, and found, when she got home, a postcard. 'Thanks for yours,' it said, 'grand weather, wish you were here, C.' That was all, absolutely all; all the reply he made to her inky sweat and strain, her hours of thought, her teasing and her fun. She turned the card over, and the picture was not of Wharswick, but of the Napes Needle in the Lakes.

He had said nothing about going to the Lakes.

Well, it was natural enough. His mother and his father were both at work. It would be dull for him at home. It had been his constant habit to go off to the Lakes from Wharswick, as she went off to Snowdon from Birkenhead. All the same, it was strange his not saying. And not sending her a proper answer to her first letter was more than strange – it was mean. Her anger rose.

She had not expected him to be at Cae Capel the first week-end of term, which was always a busy one. But when three weeks had passed without a letter, she hardly expected to see him there the next week-end either. The sight of his tall figure on the steps turned her almost sick with relief, and then her anger returned hotly. He did not look like someone who had been on holiday. He looked tired and spiritless, and she was suddenly reminded of the first days after the return from Chamonix, when he had seemed to switch his personality off and scarcely be there at all.

She greeted him coolly; but taking care to avoid all appearance of reproach. She gave him no chance to be alone with her, but spent what was left of the evening talking to Harry. She observed him covertly, however, and was shocked in spite of herself by his white, unhappy look. It occurred to her to wonder if he were delicate – one assumed all lads were tough, but it might not be so at all. Useless to ask him, but she resolved to ask Mrs. Thwaites the first time they met.

'Are you coming out with me tomorrow?' he said, catching her on her way to bed.

Her first impulse was to refuse, but her longing for him was terrible. 'Okay,' she said.

'I thought we might do a climb.'

Why a climb? Why not one of the long, argumentative walks he loved? Well, obviously, so that they need not talk.

'Oh, all right,' she agreed, showing nothing of her dismay. 'We'll lead through, if you like.' She had done that once in her early days of leading with Harry, and on the climb he had chosen the one who started in the lead got the easier pitches. They would go to the same climb, and Christopher should start.

They walked a part of the way to the climb in silence. The natural thing would have been for her to ask him for news of Wharswick, but how could she, when he ought to have written and had not? She had sworn a dozen times to say nothing about it, and suddenly the words seemed torn from her in the teeth of every vow:

'So you stop writing when I begin?'

He looked down at her, thankful to have the tension broken, even if it were by upbraiding.

'I know, Cath. I'm proper ashamed, I really am. But you know how it is on holiday. You never seem able to fit it in.'

'Oh.'

'Any road,' he said, trying to rally her, 'look at all the letters you owe me. Making out you couldn't write good enough, and when you do write there's not a thing wrong with it. It's me that should be cross.'

So that was what he assumed – that she could all along. Now was the time to tell him of the mighty effort she had made for his sake. Damned if I will! she thought, furious. And he still hasn't said a thing about what was in the letter. I wish I'd made it a lot less friendly. Oh God, I wish I'd never written at all.

'Nice card, anyway,' she said, trying to sound casual. 'It looks something, that Needle. But they tell me it isn't hard.'

'No – only the top move.'

'You never said anything about going to the Lakes.'

'Well, I didn't mean to. I meant to stop at home and save money. But when it turned mild and sunny like that, our moors seemed a bit dull. So I treated myself to a few days' hostelling.'

'All on your own?'

'Why not?' he answered lightly. And it was true that he had often enjoyed his own company in the hills; he had been alone the day she picked him up. This sunny aloofness was one of the traits in him she most admired.

'You must take me to these old Lakes one day.'

'That'd be grand.'

'I've always had a funny feeling about them – as if they were enemy country, somehow, sort of rivals to our Snowdon, I suppose. As if they'd bring me bad luck.'

He stared at her, first startled, and then, inexplicably, angry. 'Well! You do have some daft notions,' he said. Never had he taken that tone to her before. Always her oddities had filled him with amused delight. She felt herself crimsoning. Anybody else would have been ticked off good and hard. But what could she do to Christopher except thrust him back again into this dreary aching silence? He can hurt me all right, she discovered in a moment of icy fear. Why did I ever give any lad such power as that? I ought to be the one to do the hurting. I knew in my heart that they were all alike.

She had reason to be thankful that they had chosen to climb. That was one of the supreme merits of climbing: that while you were doing it it was impossible to think of anything else. Hate receded equally with love, and the only worry you had time for was the worry of the next move. Leading through, they made a rapid pace, and exhilaration gradually gripped them both. The horrible conflicting resentments seemed to be pulled out of them in that grand upward surge. They reached the top very nearly friends, and, plunging down a scree gully, started on another route.

'Look, love,' he said in just his old way, reaching for her hand as they walked home, 'I'm sorry. I dunno what came over me.'

'Never mind,' she answered. The letter, the postcard should be forgotten, or, if that was not possible, at last pushed for ever out of sight. 'You don't look too grand, come to that,' she added, unable altogether to repress her tenderness now that she had regained his. 'Are you sure you're all right?'

''Course. It's just that I'm worried – well, you know.' And his look said: Help me. Ask me about her. Let me confide.

'I reckon we all got our worries, Chris,' she answered gently, and the matter was closed.

She would not help him. She would not hinder him, either; she would refrain from telling him about Bill, and thus reproaching him with his self-absorption. But she was not going to listen to any more lamentations over Ruth.

He must fight his own battle: as she fought hers.

ii

In the middle of February Harry had his wish. The snow fell for three days, turning in the warm damp air of Merseyside to slush and making the streets horrible. but when, with chains on the cycles, they fought their way through to Cae Capel, they found a world transformed.

The hills stood glittering in Alpine scale and splendour; the crags threw shadows of azure. Snowdon and its three outliers floated on a frost-haze, like peaks from a Japanese print. The Holyhead road was rutted inches deep. The great stone walls had disappeared beneath the drifts, and somewhere, buried under their treacherous shelter, were the unfortunate sheep.

Harry, Stan and Cathy spent Saturday morning helping Margiad's father to dig out his flock. After lunch they ploughed over to Bryn Glas – the route itself was sporting – and did as much for Mr. Williams. Their consciences thus salved and their shoulder-blades aching, they felt themselves at liberty to do the Snowdon Horseshoe on the Sunday. Out came the famous Chamonix ice-axes; steps were cut up the Crib Goch rock-pitch and cornices swept from the ridge. 'If this were the Alps it'd avalanche,' said Harry, throwing a stone in a dissatisfied way down the speckless snow-slopes which plunged two thousand feet towards Llanberis. A day of blinding sun and air ended for Cathy with a long sitting glissade, scorched cheeks, and something of the old exultation. It was not Christopher's week-end, and it was now, as even Harry was beginning to notice, plain that she looked happier when he was not there.

But he comes just as regularly, thought Dorothy, anxiously turning over the problem. He seems to have eyes for no one else when he does come. What can be wrong?

What was wrong was that he did not write.

If he'd only told me, wept Cathy in her heart. If I'd only had the guts to ask him straight out. Then at least I wouldn't have made myself sick every morning, looking and hoping and being disappointed. Perhaps he thought he had told me, that day when I reproached him. Perhaps it was understood then that we weren't to write any more. But why? She took out the little bundle of her letters, the letters that had given her such joy, and it was as if the bloom had been taken off them, too; as if they had been written by another, a vanished person. So that when they met, it was impossible for her to keep the hurt and anger out of her voice, and then she drove him further away into nervous silence and apologies half-said.

By the next week-end the snow had gone from the valleys, and everyone was able to tell Christopher what an experience he had missed. But there was plenty of it still on the top thousand feet, and the Tryfan gullies, up which they trooped in a body, were Alpine. On the summit Johnny must needs start a snowfight. Not since the day of Sharland's snub had Cathy so thoroughly reverted to guttersnipe manners on the hills. But now she discovered anew the sheer nervous pleasure of shrieking herself hoarse. Christopher stared at her in astonishment. Do him good, she thought contemptuously. We can't all be so damn refined.

That evening she lay curled up by the fire like a little mindless animal, while Harry held forth on the necessity of snowcraft to the all-round mountaineer. But even half-asleep, she could always catch the tones of Christopher's quiet drawl. He was politely answering questions of Stan's about the Lakes.

'If only this would hold another week,' Harry was saying, 'we could give you some step-cutting practice.'

'I hope it don't. It's only kids' fun, snow.'

'That's all you know. Wait till you get to the Alps.'

'Much chance I have. I want it to turn warm and dry and then I'll lead on Cloggy. There's better stuff there than in all your Alps. Johnny says so himself.'

'You're nothing but a little rock-gymnast,' said Harry disgustedly. 'When I think of all the trouble I've taken—'

She rubbed a bare toe affectionately against the stockinged foot he was drying by the fire. 'Aw, shucks. I do you credit and you know it.'

They grinned at each other; and Christopher's soft voice came hesitantly through the little silence.

'—I'm afraid we funked Broad Stand. I hadn't brought a rope, and she'd never done any climbing—' And then he bit his lip suddenly, and the colour flooded into his face.

Cathy heard her own voice saying:

'Gosh, but it's hot in here.'

And then came Harry's, sharply, from some far distance:

'Look out, Cath – put your head down. You're going to faint.'

iii

It was easily understood next day that she would do no climbing. Her white face at breakfast had shocked her friends. 'Chris will take me for one of his nice walks,' she said in answer to their anxious inquiries.

'Looks to me as if Chris is for it,' murmured Johnny to Harry as they pulled on their climbing-boots. 'Very fatiguing, these indomitable northern women, yes?'

'Oh, shut your bloody trap,' said Harry suddenly flaring. Clever Johnny; but not so clever that he always avoided chirruping out of tune.

She came downstairs quickly, and Christopher marched her off. Their one longing was to get out of sight and sound of the hostel, of their friends, of all possible interruption. They fairly tore uphill. Many climbers' tracks splayed out of Cae Capel, and they could not feel themselves alone till they were high in the cwm and almost on the heels of the retreating snow. Then they turned and faced each other, breathless.

'I'm the lass,' Cathy brought out, 'I've the right to say it first. What we planned – for the summer – that's all off.'

'You – you never mean that you won't marry me?'

'It's not a question of marrying. I mean I won't sleep with you any more.'

The brutality of the phrase hit him like a physical blow. Whatever he had expected, it plainly was not that. And as she saw him flush and then whiten, the anger went out of her. She knew so well that he was only a victim, and that neither girl could have overcome him if he had not had a pitying heart. When, timidly pulling her sleeve, he drew her down beside him on the heather, she came almost with gentleness.

'Now look here, Cath. I'm sorry I lied to you about the Lakes. I'm sorrier than I've ever been for anything. I can't understand what made me – unless it was you being so edgy just after Christmas. But I never really meant to keep anything back from you. There isn't anything to keep. You didn't think that, did you? You didn't think there was anything wrong?'

'Oh no,' she said with profound bitterness. 'I knew there wouldn't be. She's a good girl.'

'I never meant that, either,' he cried hotly. 'You're just putting awful words into my mouth. I took her with me because I was sorry for her – because she had a few days' leave, and because she was getting that wooden look back on her face, like she had at the farm, and like I've seen some of the kids have when they've been bullied half out of their lives. You can't think what a difference it made to her. She looked quite different after the first two days – as if she'd come back to life. Mother hadn't been able to help her at all, and then I did it, easy. How could I not? You'd have done the same in my place.'

'She wouldn't have come back to life for me,' said Cathy grimly. 'She does it for you because you've made her fall in love.'

'I don't see why you think that. You can't know.'

'Yes, I can. I'm a girl and I've loved you, too.'

There was a little silence; then he said defensively:

'Well, she knows it's no go. She knows about us.'

'Did you talk to her about us in the Lakes?'

'Well, perhaps not then. But long before. She knew about you from the time she came to us.'

'And it hasn't kept her from going sweet on you, so what's the odds?'

Again he stared at the heather in silence, with that miserable, defeated look that was so unlike him; then he said:

'Perhaps you're right in a way – because of her being so lonely, and not having anyone of her own age that takes much interest in her but me. But she'll understand, in time. I'll make it clear – I will, honest, Cathy. Only not quite yet. I can't say anything unkind to her while she's in all this trouble at the hospital. I must wait till she's taken the exam.'

'And if she don't pass? And what about the next exam, and the one after that? She has a whole string of them, hasn't she? At what point do you decide you've had enough of the poor lass?' He looked up at her slowly, despairingly, and she ended with infinite sadness: 'You see, Chris, you haven't really thought it out at all.'

'But, Cathy, what's to do?' he said at last. 'You wouldn't want me – just – to shake her off?'

'No,' she said gently, 'no. It'd do something terrible to you, wouldn't it? You've a kind heart. I've always been proud of you for that – and for being so straight. It made you a better sort of person than I am. But you can't keep on with both of us, not without telling more lies – and it did you enough harm telling the first one. That was why you stopped writing to me, wasn't it? – because you couldn't bring yourself to write down lies. It hurt me a bit, not hearing, but I'm glad now that you didn't. For if I had to see you turning into someone mean and shifty, I think I'd die. That's why we must break now. Then we'll have nothing to remember but what was good.'

'But I can't give you up,' he cried. 'I'll never lie to you again, I promise. I'll tell you everything, and I'll have it out with Ruth as soon as – as soon as it's possible. I know you wouldn't want me to hurt her more than I can help. You must stick by me. You mustn't push me away. It'll come all right if you'll only be patient. Can't you wait just a little longer?'

'No, Chris, I can't do that.'

'And why not, for God's sake?'

'Because I'm going to marry someone else.'

Often had she longed to tell him that, and to see him stabbed with jealousy in his turn. But now, when she did see it, the violent shattering of his confidence turned her sick.

'Who is it?' he said at last, flatly. 'Harry?'

'Harry? – course not. It's none of the lads here. A chap at home – you wouldn't know.'

'I don't believe it. Why have I never heard a word about him? Where's he been all this time?'

'In prison.'

'Prison?' he repeated on a gasp.

It was such a dreary little story, Bill's; so quickly told.

'So you see,' she ended, 'I lied to you, too. By not saying anything, when I pretty well knew I'd have to go back to him in the end.'

'But if it's true,' he said slowly, 'that you never promised—'

'It's true, all right. But I reckon that when folks get into terrible trouble they've a claim on you, whether you promised or not.'

'Ay,' he muttered, 'that's just about it.'

Their eyes met in a sudden, cruel clarity of understanding; then, seeming to shake himself, he burst out:

'But that's daft. We've our rights.'

'Have we?'

'Well, you thought so, too. You said you'd marry me. Look, would you be going back to this other chap if there hadn't been any Ruth?'

'I dunno, Chris. I'll never know that now, because you decided it for me. But I think it's likely enough. If he looks – like I think he'll look when I see him, then I don't see how I could stand out.'

'But it's not fair to say I decided. You haven't let me decide anything. You're doing it all. You're going back to him to punish me.'

'Oh no, love, it isn't like that at all. All I meant was, seeing you torn in pieces over her made me understand how I hadn't really forgotten him. I've just shoved him out of my mind – because he can't speak up for himself like she does to you. But that doesn't mean he needs me any less. Do you really think we could be happy, Chris, both of us knowing we'd shoved other folks out of the way? Folk that aren't as strong as we are – that we'd let depend on us?'

'But if we love each other, Cathy?'

'Do we?'

'Well, I do. That's what I think you don't believe, because of all this Ruth business. But I'll never want anyone like I've wanted you.'

'Yes, Chris,' she said at length, 'I do believe it, because it's true for me, too. That's why I've no regrets. I know I ought to be ashamed of the way I let you take me, but I'm not. I reckon lots of folk never have what we've had. That far, anyway, I'm like Desdemona. I know my luck. And I know that kind of luck can't last for ever. It couldn't, even if we'd married. It'll be a comfort to me always, thinking about it. No one can take it from me. But I could lose it myself by trying to hold on to it at somebody else's expense.'

'They must manage.'

'No, love, they can't manage. You understand. You were the one that saw it first. Remember what you said a minute ago. You wouldn't have us shake them off.'

After a long time he got to his feet, but she made no move. 'Well,' he said. 'I don't take no for an answer. Not till you've wed that other chap.'

'You won't have long to wait. I shall marry him as soon as he comes out. And, Chris, I'd rather not see you again till after. Of course I can't stop you coming here, but it would be kind of you not to. It's the last thing I'll ask you, ever.' She managed to smile at him. 'After all, you've got the Lakes.'

'As if I would. You know I only come here for you.'

'Well, that's a pity. It's a grand country. And I shan't be using it myself after next month.'

He brushed that aside unheedingly. 'I'll write to you.'

'If you like.'

'And you write to me. When you've had time to think things over you'll think different. Write to me and tell me you've changed your mind.'

'I shan't do that.'

'You've got my address.'

'That's right, I've got your address. Now goodbye.' She turned from him, and buried her face in the heather. 'I don't want to see you go.'

For a time there was no movement. Then she heard the soft, familiar crunch of boot-nails of the scree. The sound died away toward the valley. When she looked up she was alone.

Her solitude came home to her with a cold horror, as though it were not something she had caused or willed. She could not conceive how she had been so mad. She felt that if she could only run after him down the hill – but there was no strength left in her legs – then she would get him back. She told herself that the whole dreadful thing was her doing – had he not protested, indignantly refused? And yet she knew in her inmost heart that it was not so, that nothing would ever detach him from the little cousin, though it would not have needed much, for all her fine words, to have detached her from Bill. There would be no letter. It was not she but Christopher who would think things over and change his mind. He was gone, gone for ever, escaped back into his own world. And all the memory of the early love-days, the sweet stolen days to which she had no right, overwhelmed her in a terrible wave of longing and loss. She laid her face again on the heather and the bitter tears came.

When she had exhausted herself with crying, she lay mindless, almost asleep. And first she began to hear the mountain – the rustle of the wind through the dry heather, a chough's cry, a stone falling somewhere under the snow. Then she began to feel it, to feel the solid strength of rock under the soft covering of heather, penetrating her own flesh to her bones, to her core. She could feel the movement, the wheeling of the earth through the heavens. *You are the mountain*, someone had said long ago. Now it was almost true, and in that was comfort. She would carry a part of the mountain with her always. That was another thing that nobody would take away.

The little wind grew colder and the day greyer, and, getting at last to her feet, she flung herself uphill, kicking steps through the snow to the top of the ridge, the brutal exercise bringing back courage and warmth. For hours she wandered about the stony summits, scarcely seeing them, scarcely thinking or feeling, merely waiting till it would be time to go home without facing questions; and yet all the time receiving this strange comfort, this reassurance, as of something solid and brave.

She ran back for the familiar scurry, the packing of rucksacs, the settling of accounts. This was Dorothy's most occupied moment, with all the week-enders leaving and the week's first newcomers to be received. But she looked up from her desk to murmur quickly: 'Why did Chris go off early? Is anything wrong?'

'We've split,' Cathy answered. 'I'll tell you everything – next week-end, or very soon.'

She carried with her on the first lap of the road the memory of Dorothy's startled blue gaze. But presently Dorothy, Harry himself whose belt she clutched, everything vanished but her loss. Along this same road had fled Christopher, only a few hours ago. And it seemed to her, light-headed from her sleepless night and her great misery, that she was chasing him, endlessly, on and on between the stone walls and over the great ridges. But no matter how fast she went he would go faster, bearing for ever out of her reach his love and his brightness.

iv

Summer followed, as Harry had predicted, on the heels of snow. A fortnight later it was hot as August, except that no August day could have had such a tang, such a heady, exhilarating sense of the earth set free.

'Well, do you second me, or do I get someone else?' demanded Cathy at breakfast, as she had been demanding all through the journey up the night before.

He looked rueful. 'It'd be a bit hard on me if you got someone else.'

'That's what I think.'

'But why the hurry? You've got all summer. Why not get in a bit of easier rubbers practice first?'

'You know as well as I do that this most likely is the summer. We can't expect last year's luck again. And I always go best when I put on rubbers for the first time.'

'What's up?' asked Gwen across the table. 'Is she hankering after that fearsome thing on the back of Snowdon?'

'Splendid,' said Johnny. 'We'll all go.'

'But you can lead a second rope,' said Cathy quickly. 'I don't want anyone above.'

'You're getting delusions of grandeur,' Harry snapped. 'Fat lot he cares if you break your neck.'

'Indeed you wrong me,' Johnny protested. 'She weighs a lot less than most, but I'd hate to have to carry her all that way home. I wouldn't propose myself in the party if I thought there was the slightest risk. But she's been going nicely ever since Christmas.'

'Climbing on her nerves.'

'I always think that's a peculiarly silly phrase. The first thing we're taught is that we musn't climb on muscle, and I ask you, what else is left?'

Harry continued to mutter, but his own ambitions conspired to defeat him. For this was his long-desired climax: to see her one of the first half-dozen, to know that her skill, at last greater than his, had its foundations in his own patient care. But he was as nervous as a trainer on the day of the great race.

They set out up the Snowdon path in what seemed to him another Sunday-school treat, for Johnny and Stephen were to climb on the second rope, Stan and his Welsh student and Gwen were to watch the first pitch from the littlc lake and then scramble round to greet the victors on top. 'They might bring the stretcher, too, if it'd make you happier?' suggested Johnny, once more chirruping out of tune.

The others beguiled the walk with cheerful argument; the star performers trudged in silence. For Cathy the start was a moment of unspeakable desolation. For it should have been Christopher's week-end; he should have been there to see her in her glory; everyone must know. Yet no one mentioned him; there was a conspiracy among her friends to treat him as though he had never been. It was better so, and yet how could anything be better in such agony? Perhaps I'll fall, she thought. No Powells, nothing more to worry over – perhaps it'd be the best way. Perhaps I'll just let go. And instantly she knew that that would be unthinkable. Death, yes, perhaps, but never like that. Eighteen months of toil and training had been devoted to this one end: not to fall. It was a lesson one could never unlearn.

She set her teeth and her heart against Christopher, and wiped out of her mind everything but the climb. For the last two weeks she had brooded on it with a fierce concentration which blotted out equally the future and the past. It was the immediate incentive for staying alive. She pictured the half-dozen others, slick, smug, superior, with loud southern accents; never having met any of them she was ready to believe the worst. I'll show them, she thought. A laundry girl with a whining voice out of a Birkenhead slum was going to do as well.

No crag was at first sight more daunting. It looked almost ugly above its grim lake, with none of the Amphitheatre's dramatic splendour – just a menacing black bulk. She knew a clammy instant of nervous weakness, a momentary envy of Gwen, going off gaily to a point of vantage on the farther side of the lake. The sight of Harry fastening the two ropes together gave her heart a jump.

'You remember where the belay is? Nothing's scratched up there, you know.'

'Ay, I'm pretty sure I do.'

'Don't hurry – we've lots of time.'

'Ay.'

'But don't stop and think, either,' said Johnny, and for the first time she fancied a grim note under his fun. All right, Johnny, you go first, you do it instead of me – *no!*

'Sure you're all right, Cath?' asked Harry. He was white with nerves.

'Yes, thanks. Ta-ta, all.' She rubbed her feet in the dry scree with a ballet-dancer's gesture and set off.

Night after night she had pictured the climb, but never quite made allowances for its extraordinary steepness. The rock itself seemed inimical; gravity oppressed her. But the first few moves, springy with the delicious lightness of rubber-shod feet after months of heavy boots, brought her confidence back. She dimly heard a little cheer from below as she surmounted the overhang that ended the first lap of the pitch. Then she was out of their sight, alone on the crag, nothing existing in the world except herself and rock.

Now came the crack; she knew well enough what Johnny meant about not stopping to think. One had to flow up it or one would never get up at all. Nothing to haul on – it all had to be done by wedging, and the minimum of wedging consistent with safety, so that one wasted no energy in pulling oneself clear again. The trick was there, learnt on a hundred easier cracks. Up she went.

A little, unkind hand was pulling in the small of her back. These were the two lightest ropes in Harry's repertoire. But the weight of the tremendous run-out was making itself felt. On climbs of this delicacy the smallest check was alarming, and this was an alarm the second could not know. She was somewhere near the point of fear, when suddenly the remembered, blessed belay appeared.

She shouted; Harry could not hear; the overhang cut off voice equally with sight. Stan and Gwen, now visible again across the lake, acted as interpreters. Slowly she took in the rope, marvelling at the amount of it. Harry was a long time, especially on the crack, and she heard his heavy breathing. She thought: then it's quite true that I'm better now than he is. She was astonished to find herself filled, not with triumph, but with sadness. Now they would not need each other again.

His face appeared, pink and beaming. All his nervousness had gone. 'Strenuous, isn't it?' he commented. 'Nice work.' Another shout from Gwen informed them that Johnny was making his start.

She began the next pitch, and the crack was forgotten. This splendid ferocity of endeavour obliterated all thought but the thought of the next move. Time vanished; the day stood still.

She met Harry at the belays, and sometimes she could see Johnny's head, grotesquely foreshortened, far below; but for the most part, owing to the extreme verticality of the cliff, she was alone. Now, if ever, she could say: *I am the mountain*. Fighting it, surmounting it, she felt it pouring into her its comfort and its strength.

After a while she noticed from a belay wait that the lakeside party were no longer there. They must be making their way to the top, and it could not, therefore, be much further off. Then the lid shut down on her again, and when it lifted there was Stan, perched over the edge of nothing – but she had come up that nothing – and holding out a hand. He had the last belay under observation, and he took in Harry's rope for her, for she was suddenly tired. She was ragingly thirsty, too, and chiefly interested in the bottles that Gwen was producing from the rucksac.

Harry arrived presently, on top of the world. 'The perfect second, that's me,' he informed them. 'Congratulate me, all.'

'We do,' said Cathy. 'Me most of all. Give us a back.' She fitted her shoulder-blades against his, and they lay in their favourite summit attitude, propping each other up, while between them flowed a satisfaction too deep for words.

The words he found at last were fatuous. 'Not bad for the lass that got stuck on the easy way up the Slabs,' he observed. 'Not bad for dear old Birkenhead. That'll show them.'

'Oh, Harry!' Cathy cried. 'You talk just like you tick me off for doing. Who cares for showing anybody?' And the half-dozen miasmic young ladies vanished into the prejudice and jealousy that had given them birth. Anyone was her comrade who could lead up that.

Johnny, handing his rope over to the patient Stan, flopped beside them in his turn. 'How does it feel, ducks?'

'Grand.'

'I suppose you think you'll be a worthier girl from now on. But don't kid yourself. There's no moral merit in getting up rocks. Remember me.'

'I will, Johnny,' Cathy promised. 'I'll remember you always.'

'Isn't it a shame, the way I let the party down? But I don't want to crab old Harry's moment. I believe it's the happiest of his life.'

'Miserable idiot,' said Harry, but he did not specifically deny it. 'I don't want her head turned, though. Anyone competent can lead a climb that's been led before. When I see something new called after her, then I'll be satisfied. A pity all the reasonable stuff has been worked out here. If we could get her to the north of Scotland, or perhaps even the Alps. . . . We will, too. All these councils and societies – one should be able to wangle a grant somewhere. And if we can't, I'll pay for it myself.'

'What did I tell you?' whispered Johnny wickedly to Cathy round the corner of a beer-bottle. 'Looks as though you've still got a chance.'

It was six by the time they reached Bryn Glas, and almost dark, but while the boys were backing Dorothy's car from the barn, Cathy put her head round the kitchen door. 'Yes, I heard all about it,' said Miss Williams, who invariably had. 'And now are you satisfied?'

'Ay, that's just about it. I'm satisfied. I really looked in to say goodbye.'

'You're getting married,' said Miss Williams instantly.

'What a one you are – only one idea in your head.'

'Then it's true.'

'Yes, but it's not Chris.'

'I can see that, too,' said Miss Williams, looking fixedly at her friend.

'You remember how he used to say there was other things in life besides climbing? Well, there's other things besides love – did you learn that by your old Welsh grapevine? So long then – be good. One of these days I'll be bringing you in my son.'

V

On this last morning it did not much matter where she went. Anything would be anticlimax, and this the hostel understood. She disposed of Gwen and Harry by commending them to each other. 'Take her up Grooved Arete,' she told him. 'She deserves something special for having lugged about all those beer-bottles.'

'Oke,' said Harry gloomily. 'She'll come off at the long step, and she weighs half a ton.' He, too, was aware that such a triumph as he had tasted needed its expiation.

To Dorothy she murmured, propping the kitchen door: 'Would the warden stand me tea today?' 'Yes,' said Dorothy, with a quick look.

She scrambled round beneath the Devil's Kitchen, and on to the ridge above it, finding the first moss-campion. She drew back her hand from the urge to pull the little emerald cushion starred with pink; it would not live on a backyard wall in Tooley Street. She peered like any tourist down the chasm, and smiled to see the strips of the two lakes caught between its vertical walls. She climbed higher, and the two great valleys opened out, the bend in the road, the house of Cae Capel, the tiny grove of trees that looked so frail a barrier to have hidden passion and delight. She looked over the country and her life there, as over a map, and seemed to understand it all. A snatch from one of the little brown man's songs came into her mind:

And we will all the pleasure prove
That all the craggy mountains yield ...

That was about it. She had had them, all the pleasures. She could look round her and see peak after peak, miles of them, and not one that had not yielded up its pleasures, not one that she did not possess forever in her memory and her heart. First climbing had sharpened her perception, and then love had sharpened it, and now she held the mountain utterly and nothing could take it away. For an hour she lay there, crushing the thyme between her fingers, steeping herself in the great sunny silence and watching the cloud shadows race over the hills and away to England.

The face she presented to Dorothy was rosy and glowing, the face of the heroine, the Cae Capel ornament, the young lady in the first half-dozen. She had packed her rucksac, and set it down on the steps. 'Going home early?' Dorothy asked.

'Ay. I thought I'd flag a lift.'

They ate their meal cheerfully; then Dorothy set the teapot down and braced herself. 'I'm always asking you to do me favours,' Cathy said.

'Well, I don't mind. It's what I'm for.'

'You'll mind this time. It's to tell Harry – and Stan and the others – that I won't be coming again. I'll be writing to Harry, too, but it'd come easier if you tell them first.'

'You don't really mean that. Not – ever?'

'Well, not for a long time, anyway. Not until after your day, I expect. Bill's out next month. I'm going to marry him as soon as I can.'

'I knew it!' Dorothy cried bitterly. 'I knew you always meant to, all along. You never listen to any advice except the advice you don't want to hear. I knew you wouldn't be content till you'd sacrificed your life to that boy.'

'Sacrificed?' said Cathy, and her smile was ironical. 'You mean you think I gave up Chris for Bill?'

'Well, and didn't you? You only had to lift a finger and he'd have stayed.'

'Doesn't that sound grand? It makes me out so noble. But I'm not, you know – I don't suppose I could ever have sent him away just for Bill. I lost him. That little cousin means more to him than me – the one who's not going to be a nurse. He was writing to me every week up to Christmas, proper love-letters they were, and then he took her for a week to the Lakes and was so happy with her he didn't know how to tell me, and after that he could never write to me again. When we had it out he felt terribly about it, poor lad. He couldn't understand himself what had happened. But of course I could see it. He belonged to her.'

'And you – you of all people – to give up like that without a fight! He belonged to you first.'

'That's what you think, because you don't know. I'll tell you everything now. I stole him.'

'Stole?'

'I'm a proper bad lot, Dorothy. I did tell you before, only you wouldn't believe me. I'd had a chap before ever I came here – that soft one who first brought me up – you wouldn't remember. He showed me all the ropes. And then, when you lent me the caravan, I used it to make Chris sleep with me. We were doing it all that fortnight, right under your nose. You see the sort of friend I've been to you. It wasn't his fault at all – I made him. I cried when he wouldn't. Think of that – I cried! He really only did it because he was sorry for me, like he is for her. I know I deserve anything you can say to me. I wish you would.'

'But I haven't anything to say, pet!' Dorothy cried. 'You couldn't tell me at the time, I grant—'

'No.'

'But if you were happy – I mean, it's ridiculous to talk about yourself as if you were a depraved woman. If it was only those two—'

For a long moment the ghost of the suspicion hovered between them. But that, at any rate, she could scotch for Dorothy. She answered, looking carefully at the fire:

'That's right. Only those two.'

'Well then, the very most I'll say is that perhaps it wasn't wise.'

'But you mustn't say that. That's something I can't bear you to say. What you mean is, because I let Chris take me for nothing, then he didn't want to pay. But you can't think that Dorothy. Not if you remember the smallest bit what he was like.'

'Are any of them so different?' muttered Dorothy, almost sullen.

'Some are. He was. Look, I'll tell you what would have happened if I hadn't forced him to it. I'd never have had him at all. Not because he didn't like me – he did – but because he hadn't woken up. He was just a kid still, a kid that had been brought up nice and not known trouble, and he might have stayed one for years. And in that case,' said Cathy with sudden bitter illumination, 'I daresay he'd have escaped Ruth, too. She'd have fallen for him just the same, of course – anyone would – but he'd probably never have noticed it, and a girl like that would never have had the nerve to make it clear. But, anyway, when his time came, it would always have been a Ruth, someone he could pity and look after, not a tough one like me.'

'But you need looking after.'

'No, I don't. Not really. That's what you've always thought because I come from a poor home. He tried to think it, too. He was longing to think it. He was always pestering me to take him home. But I wouldn't, and it's the one decent thing I did. Because it doesn't really matter where you come from or what chances you've had. It's what you're like inside that counts. And inside I'm strong. I don't mean it for boasting. It's how I was born.'

'You'd have made him such a grand little wife—'

'Well, and so will she. Anybody could be a grand wife to Chris. I'll try and be a grand wife to poor Bill, and that'll take more doing. You got to go where you're needed most. I don't have to tell you that.'

'But I – love Michael,' said Dorothy, startled.

'Yes. About the same way I love Bill.'

There was a little silence in which each one looked at her life; then Dorothy roused herself for fresh protest.

'But, Cathy, it's not got to be Bill. Not yet, anyway; not while you're still bleeding inside from the other one. It seems to me terrible – wrong.'

'But it's a job. That's how I look at it. A job that needs doing now. He thinks I've been faithful to him. It's what he's counting on.'

'I know you think I'm worldly and snobbish, but I did want something better for you. Something – well – moderately prosperous. I don't see how he can give you any sort of a decent home.'

'Well, we'll live upstairs with his ma, for a start. Then I can keep an eye on my dad, too. I'm all he cares about.'

'But you'd hate living with his mother.'

'Not half as much as I hate living with mine. I can manage Mrs. Powell. Come to that, I'm almost fond of her. I like the way she stuck by him – and after a fashion she stuck by me, too. I know I can make something out of both those Powells. Look, it's them you ought to be feeling sorry for.'

'But why the break? It'll kill you. You've lived for coming here. Why can't you bring him?'

'No. We'll need every penny, and besides, he wouldn't fit in. It'll be bad enough for him fitting back into Tooley Street, without having to face a lot of my friends, people like Harry who'd be bound to think him – well, you can guess. Johnny said a sensible thing to me once. He said always to remember you can't have it both ways.'

'Who cares what Johnny says? He's just a callous little imp.'

'You may think that, but really it's just that he's decided to have it the other way. I could have, and I didn't think it good enough. I've had a wonderful time since I came here. There's not a girl in England could have had a better time, not if she'd been one of those millionaires.'

'You earned it by your own pluck.'

'That's right kind of you. But the truth is, I got it by the luck of having you and Harry pick me up at the right moment. Well, it's about time I did something for somebody. And it's no use my pretending I can do good all round, like you do. I need a man and kids of my own.'

'You're still only twenty. You can afford to wait.'

'No,' said Cathy, facing it squarely. 'I reckon I need to be settled. You'll never know, Dorothy, just how easy I could go to the bad. That's something you'll never understand. I could have waited, years maybe, for Chris – but I can't wait for Bill. It's now or never. Just give me plenty to do and no time to think, and I'll be all right.'

'You mean you'll be a battered little drudge.'

'Not me. My mother's like that, but I'm going to make a better job of it than what she's done. Poor Mother – I've been a bitch to her always. But I'm better off than she ever was. I've got things inside me to keep me from moping and going under. I got all these hills, for one thing. They're like a part of me now. Even at home I can feel the hills under the streets, and I can see the great valley where the river is. Sounds daft, but I can't explain.'

'Yes, you belong here,' Dorothy said slowly. 'You're taking away more than I shall. You'll haunt me here – I shall never be able to believe you aren't somewhere about the house. I've come to count on you. Stay, for my sake.'

'You count on me?' said Cathy, amazed. 'I'd have said it was quite the other way about.'

'Then you'd just be dense. I need you – I have for months now.'

'You'll be gone yourself in a minute,' said Cathy, smiling and shaking her head. 'But I don't mind admitting it'll make a world of difference to me if we can stay friends. Shall I write to you?'

'Yes, often. And we'll meet.'

'We'll meet.'

They came out on to the steps, and Cathy shouldered her sac. They had never kissed; nor did they now, but shook hands gravely, like allies on the eve of battle.

'Thank you for everything.'

'There's no need. I owe you more than I've given. Shall I come with you till you get a lift?'

'No. I'd like to look back and see you standing there.'

She nodded briefly and marched off down the road.

Twice did she look back and wave, and then, squaring her shoulders, seemed to have put Cae Capel behind her. Dorothy turned and ran upstairs to a window which commanded the road for the mile it ran beside the lake. She knelt with her elbows on the sill, watching, and the little jaunty figure with the hillman's roll grew smaller and smaller, the bright hair dwindled to a russet dot; but it was unmistakably Cathy to the last.

When she had gone, the slate-grey ribbon of the road stretched absolutely empty, and the house itself felt as though no one would ever come there again. For a long time Dorothy knelt on, her eyes shut over tears, and voices called inside her head, as they called a hundred times up and down the echoing stairs: *Cathy, Cathy Canning, Cathy, Cathy, Cathy* . . .

Soon she would be gone herself, and Harry, and all of them. The house would not remember them, nor the hills. They would have left no mark.

But Cathy, surely . . . None had ever lived so fully here. The place was made for happiness, and no one had ever got so much from it. And now it was all over for her, all taken away in a flash.

But why am I always harping on happiness? Dorothy asked herself, groping for her courage in the dark. Happiness is not what matters. It's fulfilling your purpose, finding your treasure, passing it on.

Opening her eyes at last, she saw that the road was no longer empty. Four young things on bicycles were covering the last lap of their journey towards shelter. They were new faces, and when they arrived they did not knock or clamour, but sat in patient politeness on the steps.

She looked at her watch and saw that it was after five. She went to let them in.

NORTH WALL

NORTH WALL

a novel by
Roger Hubank

'In this narrative we do more than record our adventures, we bear witness: events that seem to make no sense may sometimes have a deep significance of their own. There is no other justification for an *acte gratuit*.' M. HERZOG *Annapurna* 1950

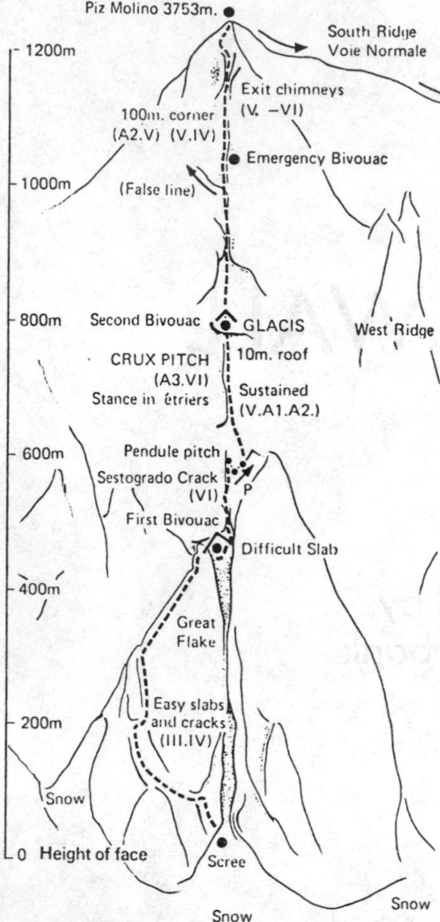

Piz Molino: 3,753 metres

North-East Face Schiavi, Morra, T. Rinuccini, P. Rinuccini; August 1954, in three days.

Technical note: A great postwar climb done by a well-established team. At the time of writing it awaits a second ascent. The face is high (almost 1,200 metres) and, facing north, doesn't come into condition until late in the season. In some years the upper section (above the second bivouac) may never clear of ice. *There is some danger of stonefall.*

The line of ascent is always obvious. The pendule pitch marks a hiatus, as the main feature of the climb (the dièdre) closes for some 70 metres and the link with the upper dièdre is achieved by an airy swing across to a parallel flake crack. Once committed to the upper section, it is probably wiser to press for the top rather than retreat down the face.

The bivouac at the top of the great flake is comfortable (ice patch for water). The second bivouac of the first ascensionists (in a cave at the back of the glacis, immediately above the 10-metre roof) is safe and adequate but devoid of water.

Not all the pitons were left in place. Carry a good selection, especially of thin pitons, for the sestogrado crack (where the line closes). An ice axe and one pair of crampons may be useful. The rock is good.

Descent via S ridge (P.D.: 2½ hours to Masino hut: cairns).

START: 100 metres to right (N) of snow gully descending from E ridge, marked by characteristic tower on R below huge roof in centre of face. From scree gully follow obvious depression trending R to L for 3 rope lengths. Gain crest of arête and follow to brèche overlooking smooth slab and immediately below great flake at L of roof (III and IV: 3–4 hours); first bivouac.

Traverse R along ledge for 10 metres (exposed). Climb slab below R edge of roof (VI: 2 pitons) to diagonal groove and traverse easily upward (R) to corner (good stance in dièdre). Climb chimneys above to gain access to central face. Follow dièdre to point where crack narrows. Stance below crack (étriers: 2 pitons). Climb with difficulty (VI: poor protection) the sestogrado crack to high piton, from which arrange rope and descend 15 metres to make swing R and so gain footing on flake on R wall (piton in place: sling). Traverse up and L for 70 metres to re-enter dièdre (V+: 2 pitons). Climb straight to 10-metre roof, which closes groove. From stance (in étriers) surmount roof (hard: A3 and VI: danger of stonefall at lip) to small glacis. Second bivouac in cave below chimney.

Climb chimney (IV). Follow dièdre (3 rope lengths: IV and V: pitons) to overhangs. A chimney splits the roof above. Climb it (at 20-metre stance: pitons). Climb chimney above (40 metres) to gain upper face (stance in étriers: 2 pitons). A groove bisects the steep slab. Climb it (hard: VI: pitons) to point where vague ramp leads L. *Do not follow this ramp* (piton left by Schiavi after false line taken). Continue straight up to reach clean-cut 100-metre corner. Climb corner on pitons and by free climbing (strenuous) to reach exit chimneys (V– and IV), which widen out to summit ridge, and thus (easily) to top. The LH branch was taken on first ascent, since RH chimney held some large, loose blocks.

PART ONE

CHAPTER ONE

BY NOON they'd climbed more than a thousand metres. At the head of the valley they turned to look back, but Molino was lost far below in the haze, where the river flashed briefly between the rocks.

Though they had travelled far from the village now, the most formidable part of the day's march still lay ahead. And when, at length, they plodded out of the forest and on to the stony rubbish of the terminal moraine, the small man recognized that landscape to which he never came, time after time, without a certain dread. Now he picked his way over the debris to where his companion sat, hunched and motionless, on a flat-topped rock beside the stream.

They were content to linger here by the stream. In the stillness of the amphitheatre the immensity of their undertaking seemed to loom menacingly above their heads. Later it would become a technical problem – something they would work upon together, like craftsmen working upon stone. But now, because they were tired, because they still had far to go, because the moment had not yet come, the north face thrust itself between them with a presence almost as tangible and as cold as the great buttresses which flanked its face.

For almost an hour they sat quietly by the stream. They had little to say to each other. The small man produced some lengths of stringy cabanos, and a hunk of cheese wrapped in grease-stained paper from the side-pocket of his sack. They ate in silence. Occasionally his big, fair-haired companion got up and wandered among the boulders, staring up to where the final summit of the Piz Molino gleamed above the black granite cliffs of the amphitheatre.

'Not unlike the Cima Su Alto,' he said at length.

The small man was groping with a greasy hand among the pebbles at the edge of the stream. The back of his hand was pitted and scarred. Its fingernails worn down. Grained with dirt.

'Didn't know you'd done it,' he said.

He took aim at a target on the far side of the stream.

'What?'

The pebble shot off a small red rock and bounced away.

'The Su Alto.'

'Winter ascent. With Belmonte.'

The big man sat down again on the flat rock, lay back and closed his eyes. He liked the sun.

'Yes,' he said. 'Six years ago on Christmas Eve. We bivouacked on the Gabriel-Livanos ledge.'

The other's arm paused in the act of throwing. The flaky, pale pink weal of a recent burn stood out against the brown edge of his hand. 'Christmas Eve!' His voice sounded incredulous.

'Jean-Louis had a few days off. And the conditions were right.'

The small man's pebble bounced again on the small red rock. His name was Daniel.

Christ! he thought. It wasn't a thing he'd have done himself – not on Christmas Eve – though it was typical of Belmonte.

'What was it like?' he asked curiously.

'Bloody cold,' said his companion and sat up sharply. Though the rock was warm he couldn't rest for long.

'We'd better get on with it,' he said.

They packed the remnants of their meal, hoisted the heavy sacks and made their way slowly, sweating already under the weight and heat, towards the ridge.

It was early when they had arrived that morning in Molino, the square silent. Empty. The sun was just getting up. They climbed down from the lorry, hoisting the big sacks with the slow engine rumble throbbing in their ears, shouting their thanks in bad German, and they saw no one. Only a young boy at the Albergo Montebello looked out of a bedroom window and saw them standing there in the first sunlight outside the Post, next to the poster that he liked. (Daniel had noticed it: two white horses and a girl perched like a bird – CIRCUS ALBERTI, it said, in big curving letters, 13 AGOSTO 1965 – a year ago, exactly to the day.)

Daniel was writing a postcard.

Dear Michel,
We are going to climb the big mountain in this picture. Then we shall come home. Look after Maman.
Love from
Papa

The great north face rose grandly above a pretty meadow filled with flowers. Daniel glanced at it briefly and dropped it in the box. The other card he looked at for a moment (addressed, stamped with a Swiss stamp, it bore no message), considered, and put it back into his sack. Then he saw the small face up at the window, above a box of red geraniums. He waved. The face vanished.

But the boy asked about them later. He asked the old man at the Post.

'There is only one reason why such men come to Molino,' the old man said, unfastening the shutter, nodding in the direction of the Val d'Averta – but the boy saw only the pleasant path past the dairy that led into the pine forest. Later that morning he set off along the path. Between the oaks and chestnut trees. Past the green banks of rhododendron, where the air was heavy with the scent of flowers and crushed grass and the piney smell of the forest. He did not get far. If he'd struggled on through the pine forest, he might have got up to the amphitheatre. But no further.

Even for the climbers it was strenuous. For three hours they struggled upward, stumbling over boulders, slipping on the steep wet banks of gullies, pushing through tangles of branches that struck back to lacerate their arms and faces. At one point the path steepened into a line of footholds traversing upward across an almost vertical wall, which they crossed swaying against the pull of the sacks. As the afternoon wore on the big man again drew further and further ahead. He bored on through gullies and streams, climbing higher and higher along the flanks of the ridge until he vanished from sight.

Daniel was glad to be alone. He was soaked with sweat. He felt sick. His breathing was beginning to hurt. The pack grew heavier. Eventually he could manage only a few yards at a time, staggering forward to whatever support might offer a few seconds' rest as he leant, arm rigid against tree or boulder, bent double under the pack. Gradually the tightness in his chest relaxed. He straightened again and plodded on.

He climbed slowly but steadily up between thinning clusters of pines, from darkness through shadow, and out at last into the sunlight. For a moment he stood motionless. Then he thrust the pack from his shoulders and ran forward through the grass until his boot caught against a stone and he fell heavily. He sprawled there in the warm grass and gazed and gazed: on and on for a thousand metres, up to the snowline and beyond it where the bare rock began, its buttresses, walls and pinnacles streaked by the snowfields and the hanging glaciers and the white, spidery fingers of the couloirs, all a far-off grey and deep shadowy blue, silent, empty of movement, under an empty sky. Far to the right in a deep cleft the snow glimmered between vast granite walls. Beneath it the glacier reared and twisted on its passage down to the valley. And beyond the glacier, flanked on either side by towering buttresses, loomed the enormous bulk of the north-east face. Of its features he could see nothing except the great Gothic arch of the summit soaring above the shadows of the north ridge. The rest was hidden in the gloom. But directly beneath the summit a thin, dark shade slanted down the grey expanse of the face. It was the hundred metre corner, the last barrier, over a thousand metres above the glacier.

In the spring that year, as he walked to mass one Sunday with the boy, he'd tried to pace out the configurations of that gigantic wall. At the end of the lane would be the first bivouac, with the roof above it, at four hundred metres. Halfway across the field, the pendule – the rope-swing across the face. A hundred metres beyond it – where the footpath ran along the river bank – the great roof. Then the second bivouac, then the corner, then the final chimneys. He didn't know about the summit. He wasn't sure he walked that far. For a black and white bird flew out of the hedge in front of them and then he was back in the familiar lane again, with the child tugging at his sleeve.

Now he looked up at the wall. He tried to think of his own countryside stretched out there. But they were not compatible. The imaginative effort was too much. Even with his eyes screwed tight it didn't work. Nothing would stay in place. The bridge collapsed. The river slid down over the field. Everything crumbled into a heap at the bottom of the face.

But it was time to move on. He got up from the grass and hoisted the heavy sack for the last time. Behind him the sun was sinking. The air seemed cooler. A few streaks of wispy cloud hung above the mountains. Cirrus, he thought it was called. He couldn't remember what it meant. Perhaps nothing. Above the deepening shadows on the wall the highest pinnacles of the north-east face were glowing a faint red. A great stillness brooded over the mountains; a silence broken only by the river roaring faintly in the valley a long way below. In this silence and stillness Daniel perceived the interminable cycles which had shaped this landscape. Suddenly he realized that they were never wholly still or silent. That they moved now, imperceptibly. That they would move for aeons after his death. That perhaps there was no final end to their task, no ultimate creation to which they aspired, for whatever they levelled in a million years, they might throw up again. And level again. He recognized that he, too, was as much their creature as the great wall which he had come to climb. For a moment he felt frightened and alone. The sun still shone on the green, empty meadow, on the jagged wall of rock that swept from end to end of the horizon. But he shivered a little. It was getting cold. Then, a little way below the hillock on which he stood, he saw the bright walls of a mountain tent pitched firmly within a ring of boulders. He saw its walls ripple slightly. The main guy quivered in the breeze. Through the entrance, in the dark orange gloom, he glimpsed the blue cover of a duvet. There was the big sack, its contents spilled out upon the grass: tins, bread, fresh fruit. And the stove was perched ready on a large flat stone. A moment later, the tall figure of his friend came up beyond the boulders, coming back with water from the stream.

CHAPTER TWO

NEXT MORNING Daniel woke to the low clank of a sheepbell just beside his ear. The tent wall bulged dangerously. He scrambled out of his sleeping bag, unzipped the door and scuttled out, gesticulating.... The sheep skipped nervously away. Then turned, still chewing, to stare mistrustfully.

It was still early morning. A heavy dew had fallen. The wet grass curled around his feet, between his toes. It swept away in one unbroken, shimmering descent to the valley. He reached under the flysheet, and fished out the rest of the bread – it was stale anyway – and tossed it to the sheep. Then he went to make the coffee. In the ring of boulders about the tent there was a large granite table hollowed at its base and blackened by the fire they had made there the previous night. He placed the stove under the hollow, set the pan upon it and lit the gas.

I ought to write, he thought. Yet he remained squatting there by the stove, staring at the flame.

To leave like that, he thought. Coldly, with just a few curt words.

Within an hour of leaving he'd regretted it. Even as he got off the bus in Chamonix, stepping into the bright exciting world he loved, he felt ashamed.

I should write to her, he told himself.

He feared and hated quarrels. It was like the loss of grace to him. At first, whenever they parted on bad terms (in the early morning, perhaps, as he went to work), he would come back again the first chance he had. He did so in response to promptings, whether of guilt or pity, that seemed external to, and greater than, himself. He got up now and went back to the tent to get the biscuit tin in which he kept his pen and notebook. For three weeks he'd been trying to write; three weeks trying different phrases, different ways of saying things, striving for the right words to say what had to be said. Mostly not knowing what to say. In three weeks, moving from place to place (trying to write the letter), he'd sent over a dozen postcards. Each with a cheerful message, informing them that he was still safe and well, telling of little things he'd bought for the child. The squirrel badge from Cortina. The little doll on skis. And the carved wooden chamois which he held now, in his hand, as he searched in the big sack for the biscuit tin. He found it. Raymond was still asleep.

He crawled out of the tent again and crossed to the granite slab. He opened the tin and took out his passport, his wallet, some postcards, the badge he'd bought for the child and his pen and notebook. There, at the bottom, lay the envelope, clean and white, addressed already and stamped with a Swiss stamp. He wished he'd gone back again. But it would have done no good. She'd have said he'd come back so that he could go again and climb with an easy conscience. Perhaps that was true. Guilt made him mistrust himself.

He opened the notebook. The blank, white page confronted him. It was like a wall that kept out what had to be said, that turned his words back upon themselves. And he shrank back into silence – was kept there, unable to break out. Sometimes he was so defeated by the impossibility of saying anything that he was forced to retreat deep within his own borders, refusing to fight, holding himself back, striving not to feel, until this shrinking in upon himself contended with such resentment that he felt himself driven helplessly back towards resistance. And then he yearned to make a liberating gesture. Something decisive. A break-out that would be irrevocable. A scream of rage: a violent blow. Walking out altogether and never coming back.

He sat now on the granite slab, staring blankly at the notebook. The sun glared back at him from the empty page.

That wouldn't really change anything, he thought. It would be an evasion, a refusal to face the facts. Like a child storming away from the game he couldn't win, the pieces still there on the board. Still waiting a resolution. It would be like suicide. So he stayed, wishing it might be worth it.

In books or sermons, he thought, it's always worth it. And times of anger and isolation were like the hard moves that make a climb worthwhile, so that afterwards the bad moments seem a necessary part of it. Real life, he thought, is different. One stays because one has to.

The sheepbell clanked softly as the animal moved nearer the tent, cropping the short turf. Daniel stirred. He saw that he had written nothing.

But now the water was boiling fiercely. He climbed down from the slab and made the coffee. He put a great deal of sugar into one of the mugs, stirred it thoroughly, and carried it carefully over to the tent. Raymond was awake. He sat up, his knees hunched in the soft folds of his sleeping bag, and drank slowly, holding the mug with both hands close to his face.

After breakfast they sat outside the tent and sorted through the pile of equipment. The sun was rising higher in the sky. The circle of rocks around them shimmered with the first real heat of the day. Far off on the horizon the snowfields sparkled, and across the meadow, beyond the Zoccone spur, perhaps two kilometres away, the Piz Molino towered formidably above the glacier, its snow cone glittering in the pale blue sky.

The face was nearly twelve hundred metres high. It was cold, dark and cheerless. And hidden for much of the day in the shadows of the ridges that flanked it on either side. Only in the early morning was it exposed to the sun. As the day wore on so the shadows crept back across the face. Even as they sat on the grass preparing their equipment the lower half of the face gradually dissolved in darkness once more. All around it, beneath the glacier and beyond the ridges, the sun glared from snow and ice and rock so that it was impossible for the eye to penetrate the dense blackness that draped the wall from ridge to ridge.

But the top of the face was clearly visible. Straight down the middle of it ran a thin line of shadow. It appeared shortly beneath the summit and vanished into the darkness five hundred metres below. The north-east face was split by a huge dièdre – a corner shaped like an opened book which swept for almost a kilometre down the enormous wall. On either side of it the rock bulged forward, until the fault disappeared in a barrier of overhangs and projecting buttresses three hundred metres or more above the glacier. From a small cave at the top of one of these buttresses, where the granite pillar joined the great face immediately below the dièdre, began the first pitch proper of the line the two men knew as the direttissima – the route they had come to climb.

Daniel had seen it first pictured in the pages of *La Montagne*. A huge, truncated pyramid of rock with the same dark shadow slanting down the face. A white dotted line had been superimposed upon the photograph. Underneath it, a caption.

LA VOIE DIRECTE AU GRAND DIÈDRE
DE LA FACE NORD–EST DU PIC MOLINO

Now, confronted for the first time by the face itself, he suddenly felt frightened. Not by the wall. Something else. He didn't know what it was.

But he was conscious, suddenly, of something that had happened long ago.

He remembered the dark alcove under the stairs that led to the dormitory, the two rows of beds – each with scarlet blanket and wooden locker; the dim, red glow of a single bulb; the shrouded cubicle; a sudden scrape of a curtain and (remembered for the first time in years but with the same clutching spasm) Brother Jerome. Every night he stood at the foot of his bed, holding himself very still, as Brother Jerome passed silently along the row of boys. Some of them kept a pair of clean underpants specially crumpled for his inspection. They never wore them. And Brother Jerome had never known. But he clutched his own soiled garment with fingers that trembled as the dark figure, its brass crucifix bumping softly against the black soutane, drew nearer. He must have been eight years old then.

And then, as he sat there sorting through the pitons and hollow steel wedges, it all came back in a flash: the refectory in Lent, the furtive, subdued clatter of plates and cutlery, and the great staircase where the light burned always before the statue of St Joseph. He'd never climbed it. No one had. God lived there, he used to think. And God was like Brother Superior. At Corpus Christi he used to walk gravely before the Blessed Sacrament, scattering petals on the gravelled paths. The white procession pacing slowly past lawns and tall banks of purple rhododendron. While the choir sang 'Lauda Sion Salvatorem'.

As he sat, a little dazed, absorbed in these fragments of his childhood, his fingers sorting mechanically through the pegs, he came back, again and again, to the image of Brother Jerome. Silent and black. Always black. Save for that cold edge of brass gleaming upon his breast.

All the delight Daniel felt in the bright air now left him. He felt flat and a little frightened, without knowing why. He looked out across the sunlight at the shadow beyond the glacier and shivered.

Christ knows what I'm doing here, he thought.

CHAPTER THREE

SCHIAVI . . . Giuseppe Morra . . . the two Rinuccinis.

They would have crossed this meadow twelve years earlier on their way to this face. Ahead of them, three days on the wall. Three days to force the *sestogrado* crack, discover the pendule, find a route up roof and corner until Schiavi led them out on to the summit, exhausted, into a blizzard. As they started down the voie normale Piero Rinuccini collapsed and died. The blizzard thickened. The broad slope dissolved in front of them. The landscape blotted out. They sank up to their thighs. Schiavi drove on relentlessly far into the third night with the younger Rinuccini stumbling on in blind obedience. Until he, too, crumpled into the snow. He died less than three hundred metres from the hut.

As he plodded towards the glacier Raymond's mind turned inevitably to the four Italians. He would have liked a few days' rest at the tent. They were tired – of climbing, of travelling, of carrying heavy sacks. But the weather never settled for long. The face attracted many storms. Stonefall and storms. They could not afford to wait. So he plodded on, stepping skilfully between the broken boulders, with his companion following doggedly behind.

In the remote pasture where the two men walked there was scarcely a sound. No noise of the river. Only grass swishing under foot. The muffled chink of steel. All around them the grass shimmered in the still air. Sometimes a faint tinkling of bells drifted upwards from the pine trees, where the sheep stirred spasmodically, cropping the turf at the edge of the forest. And Raymond plodded on, thinking of the Italians. Without alarm. But taking stock of all the possibilities. It was his custom to do so. The mountain was remote. Inaccessible. The face rarely in condition – except in a dry season. Parts of it were always verglassed. Always difficult. And the consequences of being caught by a storm on the upper section could be extremely serious. He would not court danger for its own sake. There were such men, but he was not one of them. He climbed mountains to earn his living, not to lose it (as some of his friends had lost theirs). He was a professional. Yet there were times when that profession was not enough, when he needed to go beyond the safer limits of the strictly necessary. Even then he refused to risk life wantonly and was contemptuous of those who did.

Courage and determination were not for him merely romantic ideals. They were necessary, like fear. If ever he was frightened it was because he felt himself no longer in control. And the solution was always the same. Either he restored control or he retreated. Stonefall, avalanche, bad weather, he could not control. So he feared them always and avoided them if he could. But the hard move he never feared. Some shrewd instinct, born of a long experience of difficulty, told him whether it would go or not. And if he thought a move would go, performing it was for him merely a technical problem. If it wouldn't go he left it alone. But there was always a possibility that chance might deprive him of his mastery of things. And that he feared. And since such a possibility was both a condition of his calling and a circumstance beyond his control he endured it stoically. On this occasion chance counted for more than he cared normally to accept. But he was well equipped. His ability beyond question. And Daniel a competent second. Raymond had a cautious faith in his power to survive all but the worst misfortune. Yet he kept a sharp eye on the weather.

He never climbed without protection. A few seasons earlier he'd had an object lesson in what happened to people who climbed without protection. A new route on the Triolet, with Sepp Böhlen, from Munich. Sharing the lead, pitch after pitch, for two hundred metres. Then the greasy, overhanging corner. Böhlen embarked confidently, disappeared above the bulge while he remained below, wedged in the tiny stance, paying out the rope, waiting uneasily, waiting for the bang of a hammer.

It was an intimidating place. A bad place to hold a fall. But there was no sound of a hammer. Madman, he thought. The rope crept steadily upward. A few pebbles scattered down the corner.

Then, quite suddenly, a loud screech, the German dropping like a stone clear of the rock, the rope flying out, himself pulling it in desperately to check the fall, the flying coils tightening around Böhlen's thigh, poor Sepp screaming as the bone snapped. He'd stopped the fall. But he'd not forgotten. His hands took nearly a month to heal.

Now, at the height of his powers, his great strength directed by shrewd judgement, Raymond was very good (better, perhaps, than Schiavi at his prime). And he knew it. And sometimes, upon the great faces, the knowledge weighed heavily. He was a profoundly responsible man. After his brother's death on the Aiguille du Plan he'd wandered for weeks alone through the low woods and valleys of his home. Or forced himself up familiar routes, with perplexed clients wondering at the guide who scarcely spoke but took such care for their protection.

Gradually he came to accept that death as he had accepted the deaths of others. Bitterly, and without consent. He never considered abandoning his profession. He never questioned the validity of his work. Nor did he care to answer those who did. Though once, a long time ago in Chamonix, he'd spoken to a journalist.

'You write,' he said hesitantly, 'of our *conquering* mountains – as if we were the heroes of some preposterous war. It's not like that. What you call "victory", or "defeat", is meaningless. That we have survived again is the only victory. It is significant to us alone. There is nothing else.'

They came at last to a steep bank littered with boulders where the grass grew sparsely between heaps of rubble. They had reached the moraine. Below it the Vadrecc del Zoccone rolled past them like a grimy bandage. In summer the snow melted on the lower glacier. The ice was stained with puddles and scarred by the cracks of small crevasses. Patches of gravel and loose stones were scattered haphazardly, and a thin watery film covered the surface. Six hundred metres away a long spur from the Piz Zoccone curved down like a root into the medial moraine separating the main glacier from its tributary, the Vadrecc del Molino. Both were in retreat. The moraine was scattered for many yards on either side of the spur, and the deep ravine of the bergschrund below the rock had filled with rubbish. They descended cautiously through the debris and stepped out across the slippery ice, threading their way between the crevasses towards the ridge.

Even a dry, harmless glacier such as this was a strange place to be. Once it had filled the valley. Now, in its decline, it was retreating towards the snowfields, high in the mountains, which had been its source for nearly a million years. As they crossed the Zoccone glacier Daniel recognized that they had come to a place where time, as he understood it, was negligible. All the years of his entire life could count for scarcely more than a hundred feet in the imperceptible frozen journey that creaked and whispered all around him as the glacier shifted in its rocky bed. Such recognitions frightened him.

They came at last to the spur and climbed slowly over the easy slabs to the crest, twenty or thirty metres above the moraine. They paused for a few moments and looked down for the first time at the Molino glacier. Steep. Narrow. Heavily crevassed. The sun scarcely penetrated its enclosing walls. So the snow never melted here. It softened a little in the early morning, but towards midday, as the shadows lengthened over the glacier, it began to freeze again. They descended to a small shelf, just above the ice, where a bank of snow curled over the deep ravine of the bergschrund, within two or three metres of the rock. Here they took off the sacks, uncoiled the climbing rope and tied on to double lengths, half red, half white. Daniel waited while the leader secured the belay. These preparations always unsettled him.

'Okay,' said Raymond.

Daniel took the ice axe in his right hand and a few coils of the doubled rope in his left, and leapt out, well clear of the bergschrund, on to the hard snow. He drove the ice axe deeply into the snow, well back from the lip, tied back his own rope in a figure-of-eight knot, clipped it to the axe head, and then collected the sacks as they came swaying down from the shelf above his head.

His companion leaped the gap with practised ease.

Then they began a weary trudge up between the Zoccone spur and the long, north ridge of the Piz Molino. Daniel carried coils of the doubled rope in his left hand. He plodded on between crevasses which he couldn't see, following securely in the steps of his companion who read glaciers as other men read books. The shattered séracs stacked insecurely in the icefall, each depression in the snow – he strove to miss nothing. They climbed steadily for nearly a thousand metres until the glacier swung in a wide curve past the north-east face and swept up to its source in the great north-west couloir of the Piz Zoccone.

They halted at the very edge of the ice. They had come almost to the head of the glacier. The high ridge of the Molino–Zoccone traverse in front of them and the spur to the left reared abruptly for hundreds of metres above their heads. Behind them they saw their own steps fading down the steep slope to the valley. Across the bergschrund the twin buttresses of the north wall towered like gigantic pillars before the doors of a dark cathedral. Between these columns a narrow tongue of debris twisted upwards into the shadows of a huge cave. There was no sound. The air was silent and cold. They stood motionless in the snow. And they were silent too, as men stand silently in a solemn place or in the presence of death, except that the strange presence that confronted them was not death. Nor was it life, at least not as they knew life, but rather an indestructible persistence of mighty shapes, forms which stood, or moved with the years, or changed, but were not dissolved: a presence from which, although it did not live as they lived, they yet drew life.

They crossed the bergschrund on a bridge of hard snow and started slowly up the steep scree which choked the gully between the buttresses. As they penetrated further into the mountain the rock closed in on either side, and they passed from the cold light of the glacier into a gloom where the air was thick with the dank, earthy taste of boulder clay. The stones slipped and shifted continually under their feet. The noise clattered between the vast walls, a clatter of harsh reverberations which flowed into each other until the narrow way was filled with clashing sound. Gradually, as their eyes accustomed to the gloom, the outline of the great cave emerged as a thicker concentration of the general darkness, while high above their heads the jutting overhangs of the lower face took shape vaguely in the upper shadows.

At the back of the gully a long diagonal groove curved upwards across the left wall in a great loop towards the main face. At its base the groove opened out into a steep triangular slab streaked with water and split by a number of thin horizontal cracks. The two men halted by the slab. Raymond unclipped the karabiners (the two steel snaplinks by which the doubled rope was fastened to his waistloop) and lit a cigarette, while Daniel re-coiled the rope, dropping it on the scree in doubled loops of red and white until the free ends lay on top. He packed the demountable ice axe in the big sack and laid out the slings, the piton carrier, the two helmets and the big hammer. The leader stubbed his cigarette against the buttress. He picked up both ends of the rope, re-tied each to a separate karabiner and clipped them to his waistloop. He hung the nylon slings and the oval piton carrier across his shoulder, pushed the hammer securely through the tab behind his hip pocket, fastened his helmet and turned to the slab. It was five o'clock in the afternoon.

He moved steadily upward, pausing only to force a steep bulge at the mouth of the groove. Behind him the red and white lines of the doubled rope flashed across the dark granite. Daniel stood in silence, his eyes fixed upon the groove. His hands moved rhythmically, plucking the coils and flipping them upwards, the rope sliding over his shoulder, across his back and out from under his left arm. He could hear somewhere the faint drip of water. His feet were cold. A few pebbles trickled down from the buttress as the rope stirred against the rock. The tips of his fingers were growing numb, but he watched the red and white ropes moving up the groove long after his friend had disappeared. And when the ropes stopped moving and a muffled shout came ringing down between the walls he hoisted the heavy sack on to his shoulders, kicked his boots against the rock and set off to join his companion.

The climbing wasn't hard. After a hundred metres or so the groove ran out below an overhanging wall and the two men traversed a thin line over steep slabs towards the front of the buttress. The landscape shrank steadily beneath them. The rock steepened. As the difficulty increased Daniel began to doubt whether they were on the right line. Schiavi's account of the buttress indicated no climbing harder than the fourth grade. The big sack dragged on the harder moves. Daniel grew flustered. Jumpy. He began to mutter under his breath.

'Hard for four,' he grumbled. 'Bloody hard for four.'

Raymond ignored him.

A long series of walls and corners brought them at last to a dead end under another overhang. They consulted together under the roof. The leader was in no mood to face an ignominious descent to the groove. A thin intermittent fracture in the right wall offered a possible alternative (to Daniel it looked appallingly exposed). Raymond inspected it, his fingers exploring every wrinkle in the granite. Cautiously, he stepped along the crack.

'It's all right,' he shouted, at the end of the traverse. 'It'll go.'

Yet he paused, reluctant to leave the wall. Secure on the tiny holds he could have stayed for ever. Poised, the immensity of air beneath him. But the doubled rope tugged at his back, as if to remind him. And he had not forgotten. He stepped up into the groove.

Daniel settled himself beneath the roof and prepared for a long, uncomfortable delay. He fed the doubled rope out across the wall. It hung motionless for minutes at a time. He heard the bang of the big hammer and the high-pitched wincing of pitons driven deep into the rock. He remembered their first climb together on the east face of the Grand Capucin.

'Never use one peg where six will do,' his friend had shouted down from the first of the big overhangs, then lay back against the pull of the ropes, body arched, legs straddled, thrusting the old-fashioned ladder-like aluminium étriers in opposite directions, and swung the big kilo hammer crashing into the roof. The steel pegs rang like bells over the Tacul glacier.

Daniel looked at his watch. The mistake had cost them nearly an hour. When the shout came he clipped the sack to a knot in the white rope and sent it swaying across the wall.

The traverse was hard and very exposed. Like traversing the very edge of space. But the white rope circled his body. He heard his friend's deep voice singing somewhere in the gloom overhead. He leant backwards happily to hammer out the pegs. It took him a long time to retrieve them, and at eight o'clock, when they climbed out upon a broad platform over three hundred metres above the glacier, they were still some distance from the top of the buttress.

They stopped to rest for a few minutes. Raymond lit a cigarette and sat down wearily on the big sack. The sun was setting. The western flanks of the higher peaks glowed with a golden light that spread slowly over the grey rock. They could see the valley and the village beyond it and even the road winding through the Oberhalbstein and all of it reduced somehow, shrunken, like the surface of a pricked balloon.

'You get a different view of the world up here,' said Daniel suddenly.

The leader nodded. He could still hear the faint sound of sheepbells from the pasture near the forest. Somewhere in the valley, or on the slopes of the meadow, a dog barked. In the village the women were lighting lamps. A bus droned heavily up the hill from the Italian border. Everywhere men were returning home. He sat motionless on the sack, the cigarette smouldering in his hand, gazing down towards Molino, at the life he sensed flowing beyond the village, beyond the dark line of distant hills. But he said nothing. At last he stood up, crushing the cigarette beneath his boot.

'We'd better get on with it,' he said.

Just before nine o'clock they reached the top of the great flake which formed the summit of the buttress. It was almost dark. They could see nothing clearly. A flimsy haze hung like wood smoke in the valley. Above it, on either side, black ridges loomed. The river and the glacier below them gleamed faintly through the dusk, and beyond the horizon the last traces of colour were draining fast from the sky. They came down from the flake easily on to a broad platform protected by the huge overhang of the first roof. A few metres away to the right began the first pitch of the direttissima. The ledge was littered with small stones and there were several large patches of ice. It was a good bivouac. Raymond cleared away the stones while his companion unpacked the big sack. They fixed the tent-sack to the wall with pitons.

Daniel lit the stove. They ate their supper slowly and when it was finished sat on the coiled ropes with their backs against the face and drank the good hot coffee.

They sat for a long time, smoking, staring out across the glacier. It was completely dark now, and very cold. Overhead the stars glittered. There was one in particular, hanging low in the sky, just above the dark, curving line of the horizon. Daniel gazed at it for several minutes. It fascinated him.

'How did it all start?' he asked. 'The stars and everything.'

The leader made no reply.

'You must have thought about it sometimes.'

Raymond shook his head.

'But you must have asked yourself how it all started,' Daniel insisted. 'Do you think it's always been there?'

Raymond considered.

'No,' he said eventually. 'If it was always there ... if there was always *something* there ... then it must have come from somewhere. Nothing can exist of its own accord.'

'Perhaps there was a tremendous explosion,' said Daniel. 'That's one theory. There was this tremendous explosion and all the stars and planets were thrown out into space.'

Raymond considered this, too, in silence.

'No,' he said. 'To say there was nothing, and then BANG – there's something, is absurd. Nothing can come from nothing.'

Daniel grinned.

'Perhaps God created it, after all,' he said.

He would have a lot to answer for, thought Raymond, if he did. But he said nothing, sitting impassively on his coil of rope, the cigarette smouldering in his hand. In the village the lights were going out. Only a handful remained, burning steadily through the darkness.

For a long time after his companion had gone to sleep, Daniel sat alone on the ledge. He's different, he thought. Quite different from me.

At first he heard the sound of the river quite plainly but after a while it seemed to disappear. A few lights glimmered faintly from the village. All around him the mountain was frozen and silent. Profound stillness. For a long time he looked up at the stars. He watched the pinpricks of light that had travelled across unimaginable distances. From stars, worlds (whatever they were) that had been cold and dark for thousands upon millions of years. He thought of the light travelling past him beyond the farthest limit of his galaxy, out into the uncreated future to illumine worlds that had still to be. Once, there was nothing. Not just emptiness, or space, nothing! Then ... BANG ... there's something! Or, say there was always something. Not just something for a very long time, but *always* something. Always! Impossible to think of. He remembered lying in the darkness of the long dormitory, dark but for the glow of the red bulb, a child, trying to think ... to push out the barriers around his childish perception. But now, as then, the effort to hold on faltered and collapsed.

For a long time he sat huddled on the ledge, staring into the darkness. He felt tired. Intensely cold. He began to shiver. Sometimes he dozed but irregular, violent fits of shivering shook his body, and he woke uncertain of where he was, or of what he'd come to do. The cold advanced steadily. He realized, vaguely, that he must get into the tent. But once there, huddled in his duvet and short *pied d'éléphant* close to the body of his companion, he shivered for a long time before slipping at length into a cold uneasy sleep. He dreamt. In his dream he looked down at two hooded figures lodged precariously beneath the crumbling buttresses of a great north face. One paced aimlessly up and down the ledge. The other crouched over a small stove and tried to shield it with his body against the driving rain. He poked at the contents of a blackened saucepan. Water trickled incessantly through the crevices of the overhanging rock above their heads. The wind beat at them. At intervals they argued bitterly, their arms flapping in angry gestures.

Then he woke, sweating with panic, staring into the darkness. And realized he was trapped. Held here between earth and heaven, with no way of escape.

After that, fear kept him awake. At one o'clock he closed his eyes and made a last effort to ward off the nightmare re-forming silently in the darkness all around him. He cast his mind out desperately towards secure, familiar objects: his companion, the outline of the tent, anything. And it came to rest, thankfully, in the image of his own child, sleeping quietly, across the frontier in another country.

CHAPTER FOUR

THAT YEAR the child's birthday came on Easter Monday. He wore the blue coat Aunt Catherine had given him. He wore his shiny rubber boots because of the mud. At first he held his mother's hand, but at the first sound of the fair he tore loose and ran across the field. His boots made a little drumming sound in the grass. When she called his name he ran back towards her, almost tripping at her feet. Then off again, running with immense effort. Head thrown back, short arms thrusting like shuttles. When he saw the white horses under the coloured lights he cried, 'Dada! Dada!' and ran on to see them rising and falling, rising and falling, on the slowly turning roundabout. He couldn't reach the stirrups, but clung to the pole, face glowing, both legs pressed tight against the carved white sides. He called to them. She smiled back and waved her hand. Then the music started. He and the horse rose slowly as the roundabout began to turn. And she prepared to wave. The music blared, the horses flew around and all the children shrieked and waved.

But he spun by, clinging in terror to the leaping pole.

She waved and shouted. Uselessly.

The panic-stricken face flashed past again. If it screamed no one noticed.

The blurred face whirled round with the blue coat and the poles and horses. At last the fairground man stepped to the centre of the roundabout and switched off the motor. Then stepped back again and held the child tightly until the spinning stopped. He was very upset.

It wasn't his fault, Daniel told him. It was no one's fault. He lifted the little boy from the wooden horse (how those arms had clung to him convulsively) and folded his arms around the small, shuddering body.

It was then he heard the voices.

At first he paid no attention. Then it occurred to him that voices had no business to be heard on the north face. He scrambled out and up to the lip of the flake and strained to listen. Nothing – except the noise of the wind. Then he heard it again. Two voices. A long way off. Calling to one another. He wondered if it might be workers at the forestry site in the valley. Sounds carry a long way in the mountains. Then the sharp CRACK CRACK of a hammer. He heard it again, the repeated CRACK CRACK CRACK of a hammer flowing out over the wall. That settled it. He slid down from the flake and rushed back to the tent.

'There's someone on the face,' he said.

Raymond stared at him in disbelief.

'I've just heard their hammer.'

Raymond scrambled out of the tent.

'Might be on one of the ridge routes –' he began.

'No! They're on the face. I told you, I heard their hammer. They're somewhere below the flake.'

'Christ! That's just about all we need. That'll screw everything up.'

But Daniel had climbed back to the top of the flake. He leant in against the easy-angled slab and peered over the edge.

'Two of them,' he said. 'They're below the big ledge. It'll take them a good hour to get here.'

'Right!' said Raymond. 'Let's get on with it.'

He hated chance encounters of this kind. Usually it meant delay. Either they held you up or you held them up. Either way it was bad for the nerves. If anything went wrong you had to help them (and the more people on a hard route the greater the chance of something going wrong). It might even mean competition. Racing to stay in front. He shook his head in disgust.

'Look,' he said, 'You get something to eat. I'll pack the gear.'

He wanted to be on the difficult slab before they arrived. He began to clear the tent while Daniel busied himself with bread, butter, biscuits and a large tube of honey. They worked quickly. All the time the banging and shouting grew louder. The climbers were evidently in high spirits and they moved fast, much faster than Daniel had anticipated. Before they'd finished their breakfast there was a loud, triumphant shout at the very edge of the flake. Raymond shrugged disgustedly. But Daniel went forward to greet the stranger.

He was a very big man, and he wore a faded blue duvet that was too small for him. The padded jacket, stretched tightly across the chest, made him look enormous. He had a broad, red face with immensely thick eyebrows almost joined together, and a scarlet woollen hat pulled down over his forehead. He stood for a moment at the very edge of the flake, staring in surprise. Then he turned, shouted excitedly at his unseen companion, gathered the rope with his left hand and leaped down the slab. He spoke briefly and stretched out his arm with a broad smile. Daniel shook his hand. The stranger spoke again, enquiringly, in the same deep, unintelligible tongue. Then, when Daniel smiled and shook his head, the stranger prodded himself in the chest with an emphatic finger.

'Tomas!' he said.

He spoke very deliberately, extending the syllables as if he were addressing a small child.

'Tomas!' he repeated. Then, waving an arm vaguely over the glacier, 'Jaro!'

'Jaro!' repeated Daniel.

He was glad they'd come. Their voices ringing up and down the rock dispelled the silence that hung about the face. Now everything was restored to life again. Although the sun had gone from the wall, it shone on the lower peaks across the glacier, and the bright light spread like a tide over the meadow. By the forest the sheep were stirring again. He heard the faint sound of their bells – then a fierce voice, shouting, just below the flake. An armful of loose coils swung over the top of the rock.

'Jaro?' asked Daniel, smiling.

'Jaro!' agreed the giant.

The newcomer was a squat, powerful man with a dark beard. He wore a scruffy red cagoule tied at the waist with cord, and a fine white cap of a kind popular with the guides of the Oberland. He shuffled down from the flake and stood beside his friend, peering suspiciously from under the wide brim of his cap.

Silence.

The two strangers stood uncertainly, one anxious and smiling, the other defiant, doubtful of the outcome of this encounter, like men who might have welcomed a gesture of friendship but didn't expect it.

'Coffee?' asked Daniel.

They understood that. The giant beamed and Jaro expressed his thanks in one sombre syllable.

Daniel led them down to the bivouac.

'I'm going to make some more coffee,' he said.

Raymond said nothing. But Daniel knew very well what he was thinking, as he sat impassively on the coiled rope, sorting through the equipment. The big sack was almost full and only the cooking gear and a few scraps of food remained to be packed.

'I'm going to make some more coffee,' he repeated.

Raymond looked up. He stared for a moment at the strangers but he didn't speak to them. He picked up the torn packet of Celtique from the ledge, took out a cigarette, and replaced the packet carefully in his breast pocket.

Hurriedly the giant fumbled for something. He found it, bent down, and offered a shiny new Feudor to Raymond who reached up to take it. He flicked it. It didn't work. He flicked it again several times, pausing fractionally between each attempt. Eventually a tiny flame jumped and hovered precariously above the nozzle. He lit his cigarette, handed back the lighter and nodded his thanks. Then bent down again to his work.

Daniel wanted to explain that his friend was a good man and a fine climber. But he didn't know the words. And the coffee wasn't ready. He picked up the tattered packet of biscuits and held it out to the strangers.

'Biscotto,' he tried. Then, in German, '*Keks?*'

He took the tube of honey and offered that as well. They stared at him blankly.

'Honey,' he said.

Since he couldn't remember 'honey' in any other language but his own he buzzed at them like a bee, bobbing his head and flapping his arms ridiculously. Still the giant didn't understand. He muttered a few uncertain words to Jaro who replied firmly, in deep decisive tones. He accepted the biscuits and the tube of honey and stood awkwardly, holding one in each hand.

'*Danke!*' he said, '*Danke schön.*'

Daniel sat down by the stove and spooned coffee into the mugs.

'Where are you from?' he asked. 'What is your nationality?'

Then he remembered to put it into German.

'*Welche Staats an...*' he began to stumble.

No response.

He tried again, with different words.

'*Aus welchem Lande kommen Sie?*'

'*Welchem Lande?*' repeated Jaro – he didn't really understand.

'*Nationalität?*' said Daniel.

'Ah!' said Jaro, suddenly understanding. '*Wir sind Tschechen.*'

'Ah!' said Daniel. 'Prague! A beautiful city! *Praha – eine schöne Stadt.*'

Then he remembered he'd never been to Prague, never seen it, even in pictures. Feeling ridiculous he turned aside to see to the coffee. As they sat down together to drink it Raymond came over and sat beside them.

'They're Czechs,' said Daniel.

Raymond nodded. The giant produced a bar of chocolate from his pocket and broke it into four pieces.

'*Schweizer*,' he said. '*Sehr gut!*' He handed it round.

Raymond had not changed his mind. He regretted their coming. Nevertheless, he felt compelled to take a part in this exchange of courtesies. He sensed the tenuous alliance growing between the others, recognized the clumsy solicitude with which each man strove to sustain it as an attempt to establish life in one of the most inhuman places on earth. It was like carrying a stretcher, or pulling a rope, or shielding a flame that might otherwise go out. It called for one's support. So he supported it, in spite of himself. When the giant showed an interest in his helmet, he picked it up and held it out (the buckle, he saw, was really very loose: he'd noticed it the day before).

'Very strong,' he said.

He imitated the high-pitched whistle of falling stones, then, lifting his fist, crashed it down on top of the helmet. The giant understood. He pulled off his own scarlet woollen hat and shook it disparagingly.

'*Nicht sehr gut*,' he said.

But he, too, noticed the loose buckle. Tapped it with his finger.

'Needs fixing,' Raymond agreed, and thought to ask Daniel if he'd brought the needle (yes, he'd brought it – he always brought everything – it was in the little flat biscuit tin).

'Do you want to do it now?' Daniel asked, at the end of their meal. He was packing the last bits of equipment into the big sack.

But Raymond had gone off with the Czechs to the far end of the ledge and was now staring up at the rock. The upper face was hidden above the massive overhangs of the first roof. It thrust out from the steep slab on either side of him as far as he could see. In the centre it curved upwards like a Gothic arch. Here at the apex of the slab, seventy metres above the ledge, the great roof was split by a deep chimney. It offered a narrow passage to the central section of the face.

The first pitch was of the sixth, and hardest, grade. The slab was of light grey granite, very steep and smooth, and lacking any crack or groove that might offer a plain route to the roof. Three convex bands, one above the other, ran prominently across the rock. There was nothing else. Raymond looked at the slab for a long time. He recalled the terse phrases of the article in *Alpinismus*: a thirty metre run-out – one peg beneath each of the first two bands – nothing else. According to Schiavi there was no protection on the last band, the crux, at twenty-five metres. But the rock was dry. No ice (as far as he could see). No danger of stonefall. It was a pure rock pitch, harmless, though very severe. At last he found what he was looking for. He saw, six or seven metres up the slab, the rusty head of an old piton sticking out under the first band. He couldn't see anything under the second band. It was too far up. But he knew, now, where the line went.

'One might as well begin with a pitch of six,' he said.

'Can't get any harder,' said Daniel.

'Oh, yes!' said Raymond. 'It can always get harder.'

He fastened his helmet (it was still loose) while Daniel tied on to the double rope. He laid out the coils, loop by loop, and handed the free ends to the leader.

'*Viel Glück!*' the giant called out.

Raymond nodded. Turned to the slab.

He made two mantelshelves, one after the other, hoisting himself on small striations barely wide enough for the fingers of one hand. The second was particularly hard. There were no holds above the mantelshelf, and he inched his body up against the friction of the slab until he stood straight on the tiny ledge. Now the first band reared up from the rock no more than a metre above his head. He could see the peg plainly, lodged in a lateral crack on the underside of the bulge. He stretched his left arm as far as he dared without shifting the delicate balance of his body. He couldn't reach it. He tried again, this time with his right arm, searching the bottom of the band until his fingers came up against a narrow undercut. He pulled strongly against the sharp edge and brought both feet higher up the slab, leaning backwards on his right arm. He reached again for the peg and grasped it. It came out. Immediately he swung off balance, dropping the peg, pivoting out of control around the hold. Only a swift jab sideways with the right foot fended off the fall. The three men below watched in silence.

But if Raymond was startled by the incident he didn't show it. He leaned forward slightly, supporting himself against the rock with his forearm, and groped for the piton carrier. He chose a thin leaf-bladed peg, pulled out the big hammer (it was slung on a cord from his waist), and climbed up to the band. He slotted the peg into the crack and drove it home left-handed. Then he came down again to the ledge. His left leg was trembling, and he found it increasingly difficult to stand in balance on the tiny hold. He fastened two snaplinks on to the alloy karabiner, clipped one to the étrier, the other to the red rope and took hold once more of the undercut. The fingers of his right hand ached abominably. The pain seemed to run on wires along his forearm and up into the shoulder. He clipped the karabiner to the peg and grasped it.

'Red,' he shouted.

Daniel leant backwards, tightening the red rope with the full weight of his body, and Raymond stepped across into the étrier.

'*Schwer!*' said the giant.

Daniel grinned. Nodded.

But his eyes never left the figure flowing up the steep, smooth slab, pulling out over the bulge of the second band ('White rope!' it shouted), going up, it seemed, like the lark in the song. It reminded him. Something about a swimmer? Somebody's spirit like a swimmer? Yes! Furrowing happily across.

'*L'im-men-si-té pro-fon-de!*'

He remembered the heads turning towards him, monsieur's blunt finger stabbing out the syllables.

'What does it mean – *"L'immensité profonde"*?'

It means, monsieur, among other things, the north-east face of the Piz Molino. He would have liked to have said that.

'*Bitte?*'

It was Jaro. He'd gone along the ledge to his sack and come back with his camera.

Daniel grinned.

'They want to take a picture,' he shouted.

Raymond looked down from under the third band.

'Never mind the pictures,' he shouted. 'You watch the bloody rope.'

'Go on,' said Daniel to Jaro.

'How's it going?' he shouted.

But Raymond didn't answer. He had reached the crux. The third band was much more formidable than the first two. It stuck up from the rock like a chimney stack from a roof. Except that the slab was steeper than any roof. At its base it overhung slightly, offering a flat edge to the hand. This, and a small flake halfway up, was all that he could see. Beyond that, the rock curved back out of sight.

He remembered that Schiavi had found no protection here. But it was twelve years since the Italians had climbed this slab. He searched carefully but could find nothing that would take a peg. He noticed a small, round protuberance in the granite. Too far to one side to be of any use as a hold. There was a hairline crack on its upper slope. He leant into the slab slightly, resting on his forearm, took the hammer and chipped speculatively at the crack. It lengthened a little. He chipped at it again, gently, until he had picked out a narrow channel where it joined the rock. He took one of the thin wire slings from his shoulder and hung it over the bump, pushing it down into the crack and weighting it with two heavy karabiners. It wasn't much. But it would do for the move.

He clipped in the white rope and pulled out an arm's length of slack. Then he tried to work it out. Although he could reach it, the bottom edge of the band was still too far above him. He needed to get much closer. If he could get the upper half of his body above it, he could use the edge as a hold. He could push down against the slab with his feet and pull upwards against the edge as if he were lifting it. It would be very strenuous, but it would hold him in position long enough to go for the flake. It was really a simple mechanical problem.

But, as far as he could see, there were no holds that would get him up to the band. And even if he got there the convex curve would force him out beyond the vertical. He knew that if his body was pushed beyond a certain point the mechanics wouldn't work. He'd just fall backwards down the slab. And it was a blind move. Even if he got as far as the flake he didn't know what lay above it. There must be something there. Schiavi had climbed it (but that was twelve years ago, and he was not inclined to believe in the existence of holds he couldn't see and handle). But he was ten metres above the last peg. And the little wire 'runner' offered a very dubious protection. If he came off, and the 'runner' failed, he would fall almost twenty metres before he came to the peg.

But the real problem (he did not expect to come off) was to get up to the flake. If he got there – then found that the hold did not exist. . . . He thought his chances of reversing the move were probably sufficient. He was fairly confident of that. He decided on a swift advance up the slab, trusting his speed and the friction of the granite to get him up to the band.

He made three short strides and caught the flat edge sharply with both hands just below the level of his right knee. But the curve was steeper than he thought. He was forced backwards – felt his fingers slipping from the edge. Instantaneously he went for the flake – found it with his right hand – and swung out from under the bulge. For a fraction of a second he hung clear of the rock as he struggled to get his left hand up to the flake. He had misjudged the curve completely.

On the ledge, twenty-five metres below, the three men watched tensely as the leader committed himself to the critical move. Each of them, at some time, had suffered the same few seconds of extremity. Daniel took a firm stance and prepared himself for an upward strain as Raymond hauled head and shoulders up to the flake, turned one hand sideways on the hold, and began the desperate press downward to raise the lower half of his body. He heard a flat clattering noise (it was the karabiner hitting the slab below him) and he knew that the 'runner' had come off. But his arm straightened slowly – his waist came up to the flake – he reached for the top of the band. He found a shallow crack a full arm's length above his head. It was all he needed.

'He's there,' said Daniel loudly.

Raymond climbed swiftly up the last few metres of the pitch. Where the slab and roof met, almost at a right angle, there was a deep fracture, like a shelf, running the whole width of the slab. He placed two pegs, one above the other, at the back of the shelf and clipped in his belay sling, fastening his étriers to the lower peg. Then he sat quietly on the slab with his feet in the étriers and lit a cigarette. It was cold and dark under the roof. But all the country below was lit by sunlight. He could see the mountains gleaming grey and white across the valley, beyond the Zoccone spur. And the glacier, and the forest, and the meadows and even the river, and all of it still and shining.

Nothing moved. Even the noises were distant and muffled. Like the wind that brushed against his face. Sitting on the slab, over four hundred metres above the glacier, seeing everything spread out below him, he felt as if he were looking out from a secret place upon an unsuspecting world. The stillness and the great distance and the difficulties which now lay behind him contributed to his tranquility.

I have come from down there, he thought. After all these years, it still seemed remarkable.

He stubbed out the cigarette and took in both ropes until they were tight. He tied back the white rope to one of the karabiners. The red one he lifted over his shoulder.

'Come on!' he shouted. 'Use the white – leave the pegs for the others.'

The Czechs were sitting on the ledge, gazing out over the valley, talking quietly in their own language. They looked up when Daniel spoke to them. They didn't understand. He made a loop in his own rope and held it out to them.

'You want it?' he asked.

The giant smiled and shook his head.

'*Nein, danke*,' he said.

Daniel shrugged. It was their affair.

'Well!' he said, '*Auf Wiedersehen!*'

The giant raised a hand.

'*Auf Wiedersehen!*'

'*Viel Glück!*' called out Jaro.

Daniel made no attempt to climb the slab properly. It was his business to bring up the big sack as quickly as he could. He was carrying most of the leader's gear as well as his own and even with a fixed rope he found the pitch difficult. He pulled himself up the white rope gathering the étrier, the sling and the karabiners as he came up to them. It was simple, brutal climbing, which, normally, he loathed. It was not dignified. But for once he found the rough work exhilarating. They were going well, in good weather, and there were no more than four pitches of six on the entire route. He found it impossible to repeat Raymond's manoeuvre at the crux so he tied an overhand knot in the white rope, stepped into the loop and hauled himself up and over the band.

'All right?'

'Not too bad.'

He clipped his sling and his two étriers to the karabiner in the upper peg. Then he sat down on the slab and kicked his boots between the rungs.

'Smoke?'

The small man took the half-smoked Celtique and put it between his lips.

'Right then!' said Raymond.

'Right! Be careful.'

'Always,' said Raymond.

Daniel watched him go, stepping crab-wise across the slab, his hands criss-crossing in the deep crack. Every few metres he paused to test the old pegs, tapping them with the big hammer, clipping in the ropes, first the red, then the white. Daniel sat gathering in the slack which hung down over the slab in two great loops. He slid the ropes around his body and passed them out along the traverse. When the cigarette was finished he took it awkwardly in his gloved hand and crushed it against the rock. He was not impressed by the view. He scarcely noticed it. But he gazed steadily at the blue duvet receding in the general darkness of the roof, towards the dark corner almost a rope's length away. When the call came he unclipped his sling, cleared his gear from the stance and set off along the traverse.

It began gently. There were plenty of holds in the deep crack, and he climbed easily across the angle of the slab, following the upward curve of the roof. He heard his friend singing softly in the dark corner. Down below the Czechs were on the move. He wondered how the giant would fare on the hard moves. He caught fragments of laughter. Deep voices drifted up on the wind.

'Hallo, Tomas!' he called.

He waited for the answering shout, indistinct, unintelligible, but there somewhere below the long sweep of the slab. He moved on steadily, unclipping the ropes, collecting the karabiners. As he climbed further up into the recesses of the roof he passed small patches of ice. Pockets of earth scattered in the crack. Then a tiny plant with spiky, pink flowers growing precariously on the very lip of the shelf. Here, the roof tilted sharply. The crack narrowed to a few millimetres. He was almost at the centre of the lower face. At this point the slab immediately below him fell steeply into the great main wall which rose straight from the cave nearly four hundred and fifty metres below. At its top right-hand edge the slab was bounded by a short wall, like a vertical buttress supporting the roof. In the very corner of this junction the leader sat in étriers eating a bar of chocolate.

'You'll need étriers for the last few metres,' he said.

He wedged his chocolate in a small fissure and tightened the ropes as his second reached for the next peg.

'That plant,' he gasped, as he stepped up into the étrier, 'in the crack . . .'

'Houseleek,' said Raymond.

Daniel climbed up to the top rungs of the étriers. The big sack dragged awkwardly in the corner. It was hard work.

'How did it get there?'

'How did what get where?'

'That plant.'

'Bird. Or the wind.'

The pegs seemed a long way apart to Daniel. He had to climb to the top rung of each étrier, bend sideways to hold on to the karabiner, then stretch for the next peg.

'Do you think . . . it'll survive?'

'What?'

'That plant.'

'Who knows? It might.'

Only one peg between them now.

'You'd better belay me from there,' said Raymond.

He took the half-eaten bar of chocolate out of the fissure and tossed it down. Daniel caught it with one hand and put it between his teeth. He reached for the small hammer at his hip, drove a peg into the crack and secured himself to it with a short sling. He placed another peg beside the first and passed both ropes through the karabiner so that the pull, if it came at all, would fall directly upon the peg. Then he arranged himself in the étriers, tightened the sling securing him to the belay peg, turned sideways and took up both ropes at chest level. He ate the chocolate while Raymond prepared himself for the next pitch.

'Leave just the old pegs,' he said.

'Right. Where to now?'

'Okay,' said Raymond.

He crossed the short wall on one peg and passed out of sight.

It was an awkward stance for Daniel. Uncomfortable. He sat with his boots pressed against the wall leaning backwards against the tight sling, staring at the peg which held it. He'd no idea where Raymond was. Occasionally he felt a sharp pull on one of the ropes as it was tugged up through the karabiner. From time to time he eased his buttocks to relieve the pressure of the rungs. Each time he saw the sling move, and the karabiner twist slightly in the peg.

If you stared at it long enough you could convince yourself that the peg was coming out.

He remembered the old guardian at the Cabane des Planches who used to warn everyone of the dangers of roping down without protection. It was his obsession.

'*Tu sais, vieux, que tous les grands chefs se sont tués en rappel.*'

Gaston used to mumble that to everyone.

And everyone laughed.

'When you were young, Gaston,' they said, 'the mountains were much bigger.'

But it had happened to Daniel once. On the big limestone cliffs of Vercors. On a long rappel from a wooden wedge. He could have been killed. He remembered how the wedge jumped suddenly in the crack. At first he didn't believe it. Couldn't accept it was happening to him. He relaxed his grip on the ropes – stepped down again.

The wedge tilted sharply.

Christ! It's coming out!

He stopped dead against the rock and whipped the ropes around the descendeur to check the descent.

He hung there a long time. Didn't dare to move. Didn't know what to do. It began to hurt. First a dull ache spreading across his back. Then a sharpening pain as the thin harness cut into his thigh.

He shouted.

No one answered.

He heard the drone of cars passing on the road. Nothing else had changed. He thought of Gervasutti – '*le grand chef*' – climbing back to free a jammed rope. Suddenly the ropes collapsed on top of him. The white stone flashed past – then streaks of blue and vivid green across the valley – then the road – then the trees – then, as the limestone crag spun round again, he crashed backwards through branches and the spinning stopped.

Now, it amused him to think about it. The catastrophes one has survived become things to joke about. Sometimes he'd stare until he'd almost convinced himself that the peg was coming out. Then he would exert his will. Like a hammer. And drive it home.

Survival, he thought, is all that really matters.

CHAPTER FIVE

RAYMOND was in high spirits. It was still early, the weather fine. He perched like a bird on a narrow gutter above the chimney through which they'd climbed to reach the central section of the face. He had nailed everything to the rock. The ropes hung in neat loops over the rock. Now he sat eating rye bread and sausage, which he sliced against his thumb with a horn-handled knife, peering down into the depths of the chimney. He was much amused by what he saw between his boots.

'Hey, Tomas!' he shouted. 'No room here. You'll have to stay where you are till I've had my breakfast.'

The giant paused for a moment and looked up wearily at the pair of boots that blocked the exit above his head.

'Tell him!' said Raymond.

He looked expectantly at Daniel who shook his head. Raymond bent over the space between his feet.

'No room here,' he shouted. '*Oben alles voll!*'

He passed the coffee across the gap.

'Here!' he said.

Daniel shook his head. The exhilaration he had felt in the sheltered climbing below the overhang had evaporated, leaving a dry residue of fear. An hour earlier that fear stopped short at the first overhang. But now the real extent of their commitment climbed to its proper height upon the starkest wall he'd ever seen. It began here, at his left hip, and stopped at the great roof, three hundred metres vertically above his head. Between him and the roof lay the sestogrado crack, the pendule, the return traverse, and nothing (whatever he did, wherever he turned his mind) could relieve the staggering exposure.

At that moment a head in a red, woollen hat rose out of the rock beneath his feet.

'*Allez la France!*' it said.

Perhaps it was the only French that Tomas knew. Raymond burst out laughing at the beaming face between his boots. Then bent to hoist the giant to a seat on the edge of the chimney.

'Up you come!' he said. 'Have my place. See if you can cheer him up.'

He jerked his thumb towards his second.

'*Er ist sehr* . . .' He couldn't think of the words. 'He thinks we're all going to fall off.'

'*Bitte?*'

Raymond grinned and shook his head.

There were good reasons for his high spirits. The route now followed an unbroken line almost to the summit. Here, for the moment, the climbing was steep, but relatively easy. The rock was clean and free of ice at the surface. He thought of what it would be like with verglas in the crack, with real ice all the way up, and was grateful for the good weather. It was bound to hold long enough to get them over the roof. The fault was wide and jagged like the chimney below it. Narrower, but just as solid, with plenty of holds. Six to seven hours, he thought, depending on the pegs. That's all I need. After that there was only the corner.

He felt very confident. One more bivouac. The Masino hut tomorrow. Then it's over. Nothing but the most disastrous luck could stop him. Unless the weather broke a couple of hours before dawn. That would be bad. To be caught by storms on the upper face; to be up there, committed, in bad weather. But they were well equipped. The Czechs were evidently competent. His own second would do what had to be done. Then, for an instant, he remembered the terrible storm on the Plan. He shook his head. The storms here, he told himself, don't last as long as that.

Twenty metres up the dièdre he found the first piton. It almost fell out at the touch. He removed it. Italian. A thin-bladed Cassin, badly corroded. He noticed the initials stamped on the head. 'P.R.' It was Rinuccini's peg. It had been there for twelve years. He stared at the thing for a moment, wondering what to do with it. It didn't trouble him. He'd seen grimmer evidence on other mountains. But it was something they could do without.

'What's up?' shouted Daniel.

Raymond shook his head. He unbuttoned his thigh pocket and slipped the peg inside. Then he hammered in a new one, clipped in the red rope, and moved up. He climbed swiftly, pausing now and then to look up the long channel of the dièdre. He couldn't see much. The bulging walls on either side cut off most of the face. But he could see the roof, hanging like an enormous canopy. Still a long way off. He climbed with hands jammed in the crack, his feet straddling the gap from wall to wall, lifting his body steadily on small holds in the granite. It was called 'bridging', and he did it with great skill. He could climb even an overhanging dièdre with very little effort, as long as the walls were wide enough for him to stand vertically. He used to tell all the novices that.

'Attention!' he would say. 'Stand straight! Climb with the legs!'

He ran out almost a full rope's length until he had reached a point where the walls of the dièdre flattened suddenly. Here he rested. It wasn't possible to stand unaided. He placed the pegs and étriers and sat between the rungs with his boots on the sloping shoulder of rock. He could see much better now. Evidently he had reached the critical section. Above him the dièdre changed character. The rock rose almost vertically, protruding very slightly on either side of the crack which ran upwards, like a narrow gutter, for several hundred metres, then curved out of sight beneath the great roof.

He kept the rope tight while his second climbed and thought about the wall. He was impressed. Impressed, that is, as far as he would permit himself to be impressed by anything. Daniel imagined lightning striking the wall, or heard avalanches thundering down some terrifying couloir at the slightest provocation. But Raymond, who had endured these things, considered them as if they were no more than hazards in a textbook. If, as he always maintained, he had never climbed anything he could not reverse, it was because of this habitual assessment of possibilities. He took nothing for granted, invariably assumed the worst, and considered every means of avoiding its consequences.

Despite all opinions to the contrary he knew that in a crisis it was almost always better to retreat. On the upper face, above the roof, they would be exposed to the full force of any storm that struck the mountain. It was said that the route was irreversible. That above the pendule one was committed. He did not believe it. But a forced descent of the central wall would be a formidable task to which bad weather would bring immense difficulty and danger. The great roof – one of the biggest in the Alps – would have to be reversed. And below the roof, as far as he could see, there was nothing that could offer the smallest shelter on the long retreat. Each new descent would have to be made from étriers. Roping down was always hazardous. Many of the best men died that way. It was something he tried to impress upon the young men who came to him for instruction.

But he did not teach well. He had no talent for it. In the lecture room of the *École des Hautes Montagnes* he persistently reduced the experience of twenty years to a handful of propositions (for the most part commonplace paradoxes) which sounded trite in every ear but his own.

'All climbs end where they begin,' he would say. Or, 'The ascent is not concluded until one has descended safely.'

Whether such aphorisms were a crude simplification or the quintessence of his craft no one ever knew. But at night, in the Café des Nations, the novices mocked him, offering each other absurd advice across the wine-soaked tables.

'*Attention! Montez sur la tête*,' they said. '*Prenez conscience! Pensez, pensez avec les jambes!*'

And the older men would smile, remembering his formidable reputation.

He was not a popular man. After the Plan disaster, as the news swept through the bars and restaurants, they said of him 'Ah! He has a genius for survival, that one!'

He knew nothing of this. But had someone told him of it he would not have been surprised.

'In the valley,' he would have said, 'every man climbs well.'

But now, bridged across the dièdre for all the world like a man straddling the hearth in his own home, he kept the rope tight and pursued this hypothetical retreat with methodical thoroughness.

Above the pendule the fault closed for nearly seventy metres. That would be the critical passage. All the roping down would be hazardous. But a rappel of that length over blank rock would demand inexorable accuracy. In a blizzard there would be no room for error. A slow agonizing withdrawal; hours of waiting in the bitter weather: hunger, cold; they would have to endure all that. He knew how quickly determination dies in exhausted men. Civilized creatures (he knew it to his cost) were not good at surviving. And since experience had taught him never to expect too much from his companions, he thought it probable that he would have to provide the willpower for them all.

He considered all of this. He considered it, and he dismissed it. The sky was empty. The wind blew from the north-east. Beyond the shadow of the face the sun shone above the forest and in the meadow. There would be no disaster. But if it came he would know what to do.

But now his second had arrived at the stance. He paused just below the shoulder, took one hand from the crack, and passed his belay sling to the leader who clipped it into a karabiner. Then he surveyed the wastes of the great wall.

'Now it gets hard?' he asked.

'Yes,' said Raymond. 'Now it gets hard.'

All around them the wind stirred uneasily. Swaying the ropes and étriers. Ruffling their clothes. Daniel said nothing. But he sensed a rigour in this constant, restless movement. It disturbed him. He knew that they had reached a point of departure. Now, at last, the face fulfilled its reputation. Above them, in ever diminishing perspective, lay the dièdre. Like a stony track crossing a desert where nothing lived for long. The storms which swept the face killed everything. He turned his mind aside, thankful he was not required to lead what lay ahead, and worked silently, laying out the light rappel rope and securing the big sack which they would have to haul up the crucial pitches.

It was very cold. His fingers moved clumsily in the bitter air. It took him a long time to do what was necessary.

All this while Raymond crouched at the top of his étriers, cigarette in hand, waiting stolidly for everything to be prepared. But he was not unconcerned.

For him the next few hours would be critical. To stand here – not there. To act now – instead of then. Such things would determine whether he lived or died. Indeed, they were of the very nature of his life. He had endured stonefall, storm and avalanche. He had witnessed the pain of those he'd helped to carry down from the glaciers. He knew the good things which gave him joy, and the evil things which he fought against when he could and endured when he couldn't. And he sensed, in the bodies of the dead, in the canvas shrouds he'd helped to drag to the valley, the taste of tyranny at the heart of things. His life was so entirely circumscribed, so touched at every point by its presence, that he had come to see all living things in terms of mortality. And he suffered a profound sense of wrongness.

He had taken possession of his death. Now it occupied him like a disease. So he lived outside it, externally, stretched around a dark interior void. How to recover himself – that was his perpetual torment. But that moment of grace seemed granted only when conditions threatened survival. And after such effort that, extended to the limit of endurance, he could sustain it only if he must succeed or perish.

Yet at such moments on the great faces he seemed to enter the holy place. There he might ask 'I?' And somewhere among the silent walls and pitted icefields something seemed to answer '*Thou!*' Raymond was a sceptical man. He knew that confirmation was no more than an exalted extension of his own life. Yet it made no difference to his happiness. But he never spoke of that.

I cannot speak about that, he sometimes told himself: I cannot put that into words.

But he could feel it. He felt it now, through his hands shifting in the crack, in the pressure of granite varying against his knuckles, at sudden resistance to his toes twisted and pushed downwards. And more than anything did he feel it, now, with every movement of the wind. At this height it prowled constantly about the face. And he welcomed it, rejoiced at its noise all around him, enclosing his own harsh breathing, the scrape of his boots, the clinking of pegs and karabiners. He felt it pushing between his legs. It ruffled the sleeves of this cagoule, billowed the hood against the nape of his neck. Sometimes it struck so fiercely he was forced against the rock. Then he hung motionless, feeling the ropes plucking at his waist. Conscious of the mountain closed against him. When the wind dropped he climbed on.

The protrusion of the walls on either side of the crack was so slight as to be almost useless. Occasionally he saw tiny holds on the face, or chipped from the edge of the fault, but he chose not to use them. He climbed swiftly, with a rhythm that a practised man falls into unthinkingly, seeming to impose upon the crack's dimensions a regularity that wasn't really there. At every move his hands shaped to fit the configuration of the rock: sometimes clenched and twisted; sometimes open, with the fingers straight, or partly bent; sometimes with the thumb splayed across the index finger and the knuckles pressed hard against the granite. At every move he pulled against the jammed fist. Each time, he felt the coarse rock rasp across the backs of his hands. He felt it but it did not occur to him to think of it as painful. He could hang, if necessary, for five or six minutes from one jammed hand before the pain began to matter.

Daniel sat in étriers facing the rock. He heard the Czechs below him, their voices blown about by the wind which crashed now in waves against the face. With every shock he felt the doubled rope snatched violently, saw the man above him shrink against the rock. The wind poured over him. He could feel it streaming from his clothes.

'What about this wind?' he shouted.

'What?'

'This wind.'

'What about it?'

Daniel shook his head. The rope began to move again, and he guided it awkwardly through the karabiner with his gloved hand. He was cold. His neck ached from looking upwards. His knees were sore. Each thigh throbbed painfully. He peered down between his legs to where the Czechs were waiting thirty metres below, pressed against the wall. The red, woollen hat bobbed above an outflung arm as the giant pointed to something a long way off across the glacier.

'Hey! Tomas!' he shouted.

The giant looked up and waved, but whatever he shouted drowned in a great roar of wind. Daniel strained to look. He had to lean back against the pull of the sling at his chest. As he turned his head the wind struck his face so violently that he raised a shoulder to protect himself. He could see nothing. The sky was as vast and empty as the Russian steppes he'd read about in books. But then, behind the wind, he heard the sharp banging of a hammer. He felt the ropes pulled up urgently. He let them go until all the slack was taken up. Then he prepared the big sack for its ascent. It gave a lot of trouble. It flew across the face threatening to drag Raymond from the rungs of his étriers. Then he cursed, shouting angrily at Daniel, and leant far back on his belay, holding the sack's weight on one arm, gesticulating wildly with the other.

But when the sack had been hauled up to the stance, it was a great relief to Daniel. He was free of it for the first time that day. As he began the pitch he felt quite different. It wasn't as hard as he'd expected. The jams were very good. His boots wedged securely at each thrust of the foot. He looked across the face to the north-west and saw the great peaks of the Oberland, range upon range, receding in the blue haze. All the old delight flowed back again.

When he was very young, lying in the long dormitory just before he went to sleep, he used to imagine the acrobats. He was supposed to think about the Four Last Things. He tried to do so; he was an obedient child. But Death, the Judgement, Heaven and Hell were totally eclipsed by those marvellous bodies. They were not ordinary performers. They had no identity. No sex, no colour. Not even faces. They swept from bar to bar like birds. They flicked their bodies upwards in impossible somersaults, turned, dropped, twisted, fell in tumbling circles, stopped at the turn of a wrist, motionless, poised upon a rail. They never failed. They mastered nothing. They seemed happy simply to be there.

Below him the Czechs were on the move again. He caught snatches of deep voices drifting up on the wind. Whenever he looked up he saw the rope as solid as a hawser and beyond it squatted his companion, durable as ever, like an old boulder wedged across the crack. Only his hands moved, taking in the rope. At his lips a cigarette flickered. Daniel rejoiced. About him were men who worked, called to one another, drove out loneliness; and though they could not banish fear, they made it bearable. The wind battered him relentlessly. And he cursed it, as climbers do. But it no longer troubled him. He huddled against the face whenever it struck him, and when it dropped, he climbed on.

All this time Raymond was thinking of the pitch immediately above. He knew all the famous pitches on the classic routes: the Fissure de la Grand-mère on the Ryan arête of the Aiguille de Plan, the Lambert crack on the Dru, the Lépiney on the Peigne, the Fissure Fix and the Fissure Brown on the Blaitière. But no one had given a proper name to the sestogrado crack. Not even Schiavi. He'd spoken to him of it only the previous summer in Courmayeur. He spent a whole evening on the terrace of Schiavi's house in the Val di Ferret drinking bocca nera while the sun traversed the summits of the Grandes Jorasses. They sat together watching the last turrets washed with a light like cognac and the snowfields turning a ghostly blue beneath rich, black shadows which crept across the face.

The old Italian had a bald, curiously flattened skull. His skin was very brown and wrinkled. He looked out at the mountains of his valley from behind black, impenetrable glasses. Like an old lizard. Motionless, relaxing upon his terrace in the evening sun. He sat with one arm resting upon the table, his maimed hand crooked about the glass. He sipped his black, bitter drink and when he spoke it was in a low sibilant voice.

Yes! Up there was the Rifugio Gervasutti. Giusto's hut. Il grandissimo Giusto. Killed thirty years ago. Of Rinuccini and his brother he said nothing. But he spoke of Morra, his old companion. Old Morra! Still climbing as well as ever. And while he spoke Raymond was thinking of his first climb up there on the Grandes Jorasses by the Crête des Hirondelles many years ago. And of the swallows the Englishman wrote about so movingly. Dead swallows on the col. But there never were any swallows. It was all a joke. An English joke!

'The sestogrado crack? *Non, vieux!* I did not climb it. I survived it. *Jamais encore. C'est féroce, ca! C'est un passage d'une rigueur exceptionnelle.*'

The old guide shuddered. But whether it was the memory of the crack, or of poor Rinuccini, or simply a chill in the night air, Raymond never knew.

He watched impatiently as the small man struggled up the last few metres. Possessed now by a restless tension (*Nervenpfeffer*, the Munich men call it) he was anxious to begin. Yet he supervised the complicated changeover at the end of the pitch with customary caution. He checked the belays, ensured the solidity of the pegs (they were particularly secure) and seemed to Daniel to take an unconscionable time over the minutest details. But when, at last, he was satisfied he went swiftly.

For the first few metres there was no significant change. Except, perhaps, that the wall was flatter, more vertical. Then, gradually, the crack widened. He became aware that he was climbing an outer layer of rock which clung to the mountain's core like the split skin of an onion. The inner recess of the fissure was blocked, now, by some interior wall of a particularly coarse, crystalline granite. At each corner was a thin crack which might have taken a peg had it been possible to place one. He had pegs small enough. But he would have had to place them almost flat against the inner wall and it was quite impossible to strike them at such an angle. He worked with his left arm and leg wedged in the crack, gripping the sharp edge with his right hand high above his head, pulling strenuously to keep himself from toppling backwards. His right leg scuffled uselessly against the wall. The further he progressed the shallower the crack became. After fifteen metres' intense struggle there was room for no more than half a boot, and the width of a forearm. And he was still without protection. He felt the first flicker of alarm. He was not yet halfway up. He could not possibly climb such a pitch without a rest. In his forearm the great flexor muscle threatened to collapse at any moment. He needed desperately to relax. He looked down swiftly. His second seemed a very long way off. Raymond saw Daniel's face, bearded and dark under the red helmet, staring up at him intently, and he knew that if he couldn't place a peg within the next few metres he would have to go down.

He began the struggle again, knowing that every movement upward lessened his chances of a safe retreat. But at last he found a hair-line fracture at the back of the crack. It took him several minutes to get the piton in. He had to hammer it left-handed, and since this placed an intolerable strain upon his right arm, which alone held him upright, he was forced to work in stages, wedging his left arm back in the crack every few seconds. But the piton would go no more than a couple of centimetres into the rock and it cost him such an effort that there could be no question, any longer, of a retreat. He clipped the footsling into the tiny peg, and held his breath as he stepped into it. It jerked fractionally downward. He froze. The peg's bright eye stared back at him.

'Gently,' he shouted. 'Gently, for Christ's sake!'

But it held. He felt the rope tighten at his waist, drawing him up to the rock. He stood in the sling, his right arm hanging limply, his left still wedged, head bowed, resting against the crack. He stayed like that for a long time.

When he began again he had advanced no further than two metres before he heard the sharp, metallic note of the piton flying out.

He stopped. For a moment he considered whether he should replace it. A fall from this point would be very serious. On the other hand to replace it would make fresh demands upon his strength. He wasn't sure he could afford that. In any case he doubted whether the peg would hold even a slight fall. There would certainly be an opportunity for another, for he was quite sure nobody, neither Schiavi, nor anybody else, could have climbed this pitch without direct aid. Nevertheless he ran out twenty-five metres of rope before he was able to place the next peg, a small 'ace of spades' which went in no further than the last, and by the time he'd hammered home the third, five metres from the top of the passage, he was almost exhausted.

From time to time Daniel would call to him encouragingly, 'How's it going?'

Raymond did not reply.

He took a long rest at the third peg. The worst was still to come. He was well aware of that. But it was not until he raised his head to take stock of the situation that he realized how critical his position really was. Away to the right, perhaps eight metres and slightly lower down, was the flake, the sole link with the upper section of the central face. To reach it he would have to place a peg high in the crack, clip into it, and made a pendulum swing across the wall. This much he knew already. He knew, also, that to make the pendule successfully he would need to climb as high as possible above the level of the flake. But he was quite unprepared for the conditions in which the manoeuvre would have to be performed, for the crack closed abruptly just above his head. It simply ceased. It was as if a door had been slammed in his face. The rock above him was holdless and slightly overhanging. He could see the whole section, even Schiavi's pendule point, a rusted peg, well buried, perhaps five metres off. Between him and it there was nothing but a thin fracture a few centimetres long, scarred where a peg had formerly been placed. It was a full three metres away. The peg itself was missing.

It was then he realized, with horror, what the passage actually proposed. The next peg had to be placed by his second. He could see no alternative. He would have to bring up Daniel who might then climb over him to gain the necessary height.

The thought of it, of the whole manoeuvre resting on the security of one small 'ace of spades' (and that only half buried) appalled him. For a moment he considered the possibility of traversing directly to the flake. A glance at the wall dissuaded him. In any case he knew that Daniel could never climb the crack without direct aid from the rope. And to bring him up belayed from the flake, with the rope passing through the peg at a right angle, would throw all the load against its weakest point. The weight would force it sideways. It would fail.

Wearily he descended to the bottom rung of his étrier. He clipped another below it. Then he examined the peg. It seemed as frail as silver. But it was lodged sturdily in the horizontal crack and as long as the pull stayed vertical it would hold. He decided to put in another by its side. He did so, but he could force it in no further than the first. He clipped two karabiners to it. To one of these he tied back the white rope so that it hung vertically down the side of the crack. He unfastened the red rope from the first peg and passed it through the other karabiner. Then he belayed himself with a short sling. He arranged his étriers so that he could sit back with one leg in the first and his other leg bent behind him in the second. He turned his head and shoulders sideways and called down to Daniel.

'I shall have to bring you up,' he shouted.

He didn't say why.

'What about the sack?'

'Oh, Christ!'

There was no room for the sack. There was no room for another peg, either. He reached behind him, unclipped the light, 9 mm rappel rope from his back and re-fastened it at the front of his waist. Then he began another weary haul, fighting both the sack and the wind every centimetre of the way. When it arrived he simply clipped it to the last rung of the étrier on which he stood. Then he called to Daniel again.

'You'll have to stay there for a bit.'

Exhausted already, he thought, with the worst of it yet to come.

But it was a great relief to be doing nothing. He rested for a while, sitting idly in the étriers, and thought of that old Italian drinking bocca nera on his terrace, black glasses turned to the Grandes Jorasses. When the wind dropped he lit a cigarette, and with the charred match he sketched a slogan on the smooth granite wall: SCHIAVI – LUNATIC.

All the way up he kept his second on a tight rope. Daniel slipped continually. Had to grab again and again at the fixed rope. He was forced twice to tie a loop to rest in. At times he stopped altogether, considered, changed position, floundered, failed, changed again, while Raymond waited wearily, eyes fixed upon the pegs, wondering just how much longer it would be before they both fell.

He was bitterly cold. The wind enclosed him like a shroud. It blurred the sharp edges of things. Ropes, gloves, fingers blurred together. He ceased to feel the rung cutting his thigh. He had a sense of life retreating from the surface. He felt as if he were suspended in the act of falling backwards. Only the wind supported him, turning him to a stone fixed in the ice. But at intervals, like noises in a mist, he heard an erratic scuffling beneath him, the creak of ropes twisting under strain. They were courting disaster. He was sure of it. All his instincts urged him to move on. But the next move depended upon Daniel. So he held himself in check. He treated Daniel with great patience.

'OK,' he said. 'It doesn't matter. Take your time.'

But someone had to suffer for it, and since he would not permit himself to curse his second, he cursed Schiavi instead. He could not imagine how Schiavi had climbed this pitch. He wasn't big enough. He remembered now asking him about that – about the long reach at the top.

'How did you manage it?'

'I grew!' said the Italian, with a grin.

When Daniel arrived he was very subdued. He clipped his étriers to one of the karabiners that hung down beneath the white rope, climbed into them, and listened as Raymond told him, simply, what he wanted him to do. Daniel heard him in silence.

'I'll do my best,' he said.

He took the light hammer from his hip pocket and slung it from a short cord on his wrist. It was copied from a Stubai which he'd taken to the blacksmith at home.

'Can you make one like this,' he'd asked, 'but lighter?'

So the blacksmith made it and burnt his initials on the shaft. *Fabriqué par JN*. They had both been very proud of it. Daniel had used it in the Alps for nearly twelve years. It was the only piece of equipment he had never renewed. Now he turned sideways in the étrier to take a peg.

'It'll be an extra-flat,' said Raymond.

Daniel found one of medium length, unclipped it.

'You'd better take a short one, too.'

He did so. He put it between his teeth. It was hard. Icy cold. He gripped it tightly and climbed to the top of the étrier. Then, bent double, his right hand grasping the karabiner, he stepped across on to Raymond's shoulder and began the delicate manoeuvre to stand upright. For the first time he was in front of the rope. He heard, through the wind, the harsh gasping of his companion as he strove to bear on his body the great weight. His position was extremely precarious. Raymond's body sagged at each thrust and the wind veered so erratically that he had to fit every movement to the changing currents. But he moved so delicately, was so absorbed in the austere discipline of the moment, that he felt no anxiety at all. Bit by bit Daniel levered himself upright. At last he stood astride Raymond's head, with his arms resting on the wall. The rock swayed from side to side beneath his hands. He took the piton from his mouth.

'Hold on!' he said. 'Not long now.'

He reached for the thin crack. But Raymond's body dipped suddenly. Daniel was thrown off balance and had to grab for the wall. He rested there, head turned sideways, pressing against the rock. He could see the pegs under his feet and the taut ropes and, a long way down, the red flash of the giant's hat. Then he put the piton between his teeth and began again, this time sliding both arms up the wall until the fingers of his left hand locked in the crack.

It was a long time before the piton was finally placed. But it needed a great exertion of will to strike the peg gently. Not to hurry. To hold back from a full swing. All this while Raymond was thinking, not for the first time, that he was getting too old for this sort of thing. A shoulder on a safe stance was one thing. But in étriers, on one half-buried 'ace of spades', it was an extravagance that became less excusable as one got older. Yet it never occurred to him to complain. His second would do what had to be done as quickly as he could. His left leg was hurting acutely. It felt as if the blood hadn't flowed there for some time. But with Daniel trampling about on top of him, his whole body was so thrust down against the flexed limb that there was no possibility of relief. So the pain continued, sharpening all the time. Daniel seemed to have been banging for ages. You'll have to come down for a bit, he was about to say, when the banging stopped.

'How far . . .' he began.

'All the way,' shouted Daniel triumphantly. 'Shall I go on?'

'No! No! Come down.'

'As you wish.'

Daniel clipped an étrier to the new peg before he left it and then started to reverse the manoeuvre. As he did so Raymond looked at the comfortable flake away to his right and made up his mind to eat something, and rest when he got there. He really wanted to think about that now. But he kept the ropes tight instead and began unravelling the complexities of the pendule that lay ahead.

Traditionally, a pendule of this kind precluded retreat. After such a move, say, on the west face of the Grépon, or the south ridge of the Aiguille Noire de Peuterey, one was committed. The strategy, according to Schiavi, was self-evident: one left a rope in position. Either at the pendule, for a swing back across the wall, or at the top of the crack, for a hand traverse back from the flake. But it was not self-evident to the leader. He placed no confidence in fixed ropes. Anything could happen. One invariably wanted them when the weather was at its worst. He had no intention of leading a retreat through stonefall, storm and lightning to the security of a fixed rope that wasn't there. One might as well jump off.

'Where will you fix it?' asked Daniel.

'What?'

'The rope.'

'I shan't.'

He stood up in the étrier, but when he tried to move his left leg it hurt so much he could barely straighten it.

'If we have to, we rope straight down the wall.'

He unfastened the buckle below his knee and began to rub the leg vigorously.

But it was more than seventy metres down the wall. There were no stances anywhere. They would need to make three rappels to reach the ledge above the chimney. Each one from pegs.

Daniel looked at him doubtfully.

'Seventy metres?' he asked.

'Seventy metres!'

His leg felt a little easier. He pushed the red sock down to his ankle and let the buckle and strap hang loose about his calf. Then he began, stiffly, the climb up to the pendule point.

Unhappily Daniel watched him go. He would have preferred a fixed rope. He could not understand why Raymond had dismissed it. He was wrong. Despite his profound respect for Raymond he thought him wrong. And to be wrong here, in such a place. . . .

Then he remembered the guardian at the Cabane des Planches. An old man not right in the head, perhaps. But what he said was true. Nothing guarantees survival. ('It'll catch up with him one day,' he said, 'you'll see!') And when you thought about it you could see how it would happen. How could *he* marry – or keep a shop? Or serve tourists in a small hotel? The security of the valley, that ultimate comfort of the older guides – it meant nothing to him. He would go on until the end came. Like Lionel. A matter of luck. A jammed rope that suddenly gives way, a rappel sling that's rotten, the hidden crevasse. Gervasutti . . . Lehmann . . . Lachenal. . . . The best men did these things. It would begin on a day like any other day. High winds, perhaps, and bitter cold, like any other day. Hours of exposure on difficult rock, struggling to stay upright, striving to read the signs properly, to make the right choice. Exhaustion at noon, or nightfall. The last split second of collapse. . . .

'At . . . ten . . . tion!'

He looked up.

'*Vorsicht!*' he shouted. '*Seil!*'

Past him flashed the eighty metre rappel rope. It fell clear of Jaro, bounced in mid-air, and dropped its last coils a metre short of the giant's hat.

If the Czechs were startled they didn't show it. The giant made no move at all. Halfway up the crack, poised above the first peg, the Oberland cap opened suddenly like a lid for a dark face to peer upward, then dropped again as Jaro resumed the pitch. He climbed it like Raymond but with less apparent effort. He kept his body straight and despite the great strain on his right arm he never faltered. He looked very good.

They'll fix a rope to the flake, Daniel told himself. They're bound to.

As he made his preparations for the pendule Raymond felt a great emptiness. The crack had nearly finished him. A desperate man on critical rock, clutching and hoping. He had been reduced to that.

Among the best in Europe, he told himself. The Route Major, the Walker Spur, the north face of the Matterhorn, the Red Pillar of Brouillard, the Pear Buttress, the Peigne, the Verte, the Dru; a host of others. Names that were like decorations. Remembered without vanity, out of simple pride, so that he might recover what was lost.

Now they seemed like old battles that no longer mattered. (It was in the nature of old battles, he recognized, not to matter – except to old men.) Even the Plan, where his brother died (where everyone died except Varaud and himself), that disaster that had nothing to do with luck or anything less than sheer determination to survive. Even that was not enough. He had nothing left to hold back the weariness, to halt the conviction of strength fading, of the mind letting go. One day it would probably begin like this. He saw now how it might happen. A man might arrive exhausted at the top of the crack and fail at the pendule, keep missing it until he stopped trying.

Yet the crack, as least, was finished. It lay behind him. And he knew exactly what had to be done now. He must cross the wall at the first attempt. He could take a long rest at the flake. He could eat something. At the flake he could restore himself. One swing across the wall would put him right.

He threaded the doubled rappel rope through the descendeur (it was English, shaped in a figure-of-eight, the gift of an English climber who admired him). He clipped it to his waist and looked down. Daniel was back on the étriers five metres below. He was watching the Czechs. The flake seemed a very long way off. To gain enough momentum he would have to descend diagonally, away from it. On the wall below him, to the left, was a yellow patch shaped like a huge fist. Slowly he lowered himself, inching the rope through the descendeur, his feet pushing him far over to the left. Daniel was looking up now but the leader saw neither him nor the Czechs. He saw only the flake, and the grey rock passing beneath his boots. The further he descended the more difficult it became. The wind beat at him constantly. At last he could no longer hold himself. He let go. Then, when the rope swung, leaped, and as his body dropped, ran down across the wall. Almost immediately he saw that he was going to miss it. As the run carried him beneath its lower edge he grabbed with his right hand for a projection, swung for a moment, hauled himself up on to the flake and sank down beside it.

There he crouched, wedged in the narrow gap between the flake and the great wall, his body shaken by a violent spasm of weeping.

It was dark behind the flake. Still. All sounds muffled. Like a door closed against the wind. When he recovered, after a few seconds, he seemed to hear a ragged noise of cheering. He scrambled up a little in the flake and half turned to look down. They were all cheering. Daniel had released the climbing ropes and hung back on his sling, waving both arms. Jaro, who had no arms to wave with, gazed benevolently from his lodging in the crack, and many metres below the giant waved his red hat, while a far-off excited voice shouted '*Allez la France! Allez la France!*' over and over again.

They spent a long time at the flake. Daniel crossed easily on one fixed line of the rappel rope. Jaro followed him, singing exultantly. He left a short, ten-metre rope behind him just as Daniel had expected. When the giant crossed, all four of them were wedged together in the narrow gap like peas in a pod. The wind no longer troubled them. In this safe shelter the perils of the north wall (for a time, at least) might be forgotten.

Daniel scrambled deep into the recess and found a ledge for the stove to rest on. They passed mugs of coffee from hand to hand. They ate chocolate and biscuits. Jaro offered them the English cigarettes he'd bought at the Swiss border. Each man told of his fears at the pendule, crack or slab – and though they scarcely understood one another they laughed none the less. Raymond laughed with them. Jaro struck up his triumphant song again. He sang in German, in a fine deep voice, singing (so it seemed to Daniel) of joy and brotherhood and friendship, in that emphatic tongue. And Tomas joined in, too. Raymond sang with them. And the sound of their singing swelled in the narrow space behind the flake until the rock rang and the sound, redoubled, echoed across the face.

Daniel longed to join them. But he couldn't. He didn't know the words. In his excitement he longed to do something. He took a sharp flint from the debris behind the flake and scratched their names, and the initials of their countries, on the wall. None of them could remember the date so Daniel consulted his pocket diary (he took it with him everywhere). It was the fifteenth. The feast of the Assumption. He scraped it in white scratches on the dark rock. He produced a photograph from inside the diary and showed it to Tomas.

'*Mein Kind*,' he said. 'It's his birthday soon. *Sein Geburtstag.*'

'*Wie alt?*' asked Jaro.

'*Sechs!*' said Daniel. 'He'll be six.'

He explained that he'd be home for that. He wouldn't miss that. He spoke of the child with great joy. As he did so Raymond remembered that just two days would bring another anniversary. The seventeenth of August. The date which used to be dreaded by the old guides of Mont Blanc. *Le jour malheureux* – on which they would never climb. It was also the anniversary of his brother's death.

CHAPTER SIX

ALL THROUGH the long afternoon the ascent continued. They climbed the edge of the flake, crossed the return traverse and began once more up the dièdre. Hour after hour, pitch after pitch, on rock of the fifth grade they climbed for well over two hundred metres, with every stance in étriers, every belay hammered in the crack. They were still two separate ropes. Sometimes seventy or eighty metres separated the first man from the fourth. They were scarcely ever close enough to touch. But they climbed together now. Their voices echoed up and down the great wall as they called to one another. While the mountain slept, Daniel thought, like some gigantic beast – and they marching into its lair.

At last, in the evening, Raymond halted beneath the ten-metre roof. The wind had dropped a little but still came in from the north-west. There were no clouds. The sun was slipping down. To the north and west a hazy blue obscured the horizon.

It was cold and dark under the roof. He had expected to find ice, and he was not mistaken. The split rock looked as if it had been stuck together with a smooth cement. Pitons fixed in an ice-filled crack will not hold for long. So he attacked the ice with the north wall hammer, hitting upwards, chipping the long pick patiently into the crack (knocking his helmet several times against the roof.) Tiny particles of the fractured ice stung his face and pattered on top of the helmet. The larger lumps dropped past him straight to the glacier, eight hundred metres below. He crossed the roof an arm's length at a time, clearing the ice, driving pitons up into the crack, fixing the new tapes he'd brought specially for the roof (the new nylon webbing tapes with loops for the feet: once fixed they could be left in place).

As he swung from one tape to the next his helmet hit the roof again, hard this time, and was forced down sideways on to his cheek. He felt the buckle go. Now it kept slipping as he swayed about under the roof. He kept pushing it back, fuming, sweating with exertion. It was cold under the roof and the sweat felt cold and clammy on his back and shoulders. He was alarmed that he might lose it altogether. Eventually he had to take it off and fasten it to his waistloop.

But all this took a long time. And all the while the sun was dipping round and down.

Under the massive canopy of the roof Daniel (and Tomas, a few metres below) was cut off from the sight and sound of anything above. They could have heard nothing beyond the crash of Raymond's north wall hammer and the splintering of ice. But Jaro, a long way down the face, caught the first faint rumble. Like gunfire. At first he couldn't tell whether it was ice or stone that flashed past him, well out from the wall. Seconds later he was struck on the arm. He called out to warn them.

'*Vorsicht!*' he shouted. '*Steinschlag!*'

They looked down at him and waved.

But Raymond knew what would be happening above him. He felt the first flicker of alarm. It was the familiar warning. And the fact that he should feel it now made him more uneasy. He should have crossed the overhang at least an hour earlier. He even considered stopping under the roof till morning. But the thought of a bitter night in étriers, instead of in the sheltered cave beyond the glacis, only a few metres away, persuaded him. It wasn't far. Just a few more minutes. Then he could see to the helmet. So he worked on. At eight o'clock he passed uneasily beyond the lip of the roof.

Daniel felt the ropes taken up and tightened. He heard the leader's voice calling him to come on. He, too, thought of the cave, a meal, and a night's rest only a few minutes away.

As he unclipped his first étrier from the wall he heard a dry, distant clattering – then a drawn-out shout drowning in a rolling, thunderous roar. Oh, Christ! (he knew what it was) and then the most appalling explosion shook the roof and he clung in terror to his one remaining étrier, his face buried in his arms as lorry-loads of rubble poured from the rock. . . .

Oh my God, he began . . . *oh, my God* . . . mumbling the act of contrition, getting no further than the first few words as tons of rubble poured from the rock. Sun, air, everything was blotted out. Thick, choking dust filled everything. He could see nothing. As the dreadful noise receded down the face he heard, emerging from it, a voice shouting the same thing over and over again. The he realized he was still alive (was he hurt? he didn't feel hurt) and that Jaro, at least, was still alive because that was his voice shouting.

'*Der Führer ist gefallen! Der Führer ist gefallen!*' Over and over again. That's what it sounded like.

He was still too stunned to realize what had happened. Then there was another voice, closer this time, shouting in the strange language. He saw a murky shape flattened against the wall a few metres below. It was Tomas shouting at him. Calling out in German and saying, 'Get up to him! For God's sake get up to him!' Then, as the light came back, he saw two lines of climbing rope sliding gently down towards him over the lip of the roof.

He had a hand and foot in the first tape when he realized that Tomas was still shouting at him.

'*Ihr Seil! Geben Sie mir Ihr Seil!*'

But Daniel daren't untie the rope. Raymond might slide over the edge at any moment.

'What rope?' he shouted.

He didn't understand.

'I can't untie the rope.'

'*Ihr Seil! Geben Sie es mir!*'

The rappel rope! That was what he meant. He stepped back on to the étrier and clipped his sling to the peg. He took the coiled rope from the top of the sack, unfastened it, clipped one end to his waistloop and lowered the other end to Tomas. He didn't wait for the giant to tie on but set off immediately across the roof. He moved in panic, snatching at the nylon tapes, struggling to get his feet into the loops that swung aside as he lunged at them. Tomas watched him with alarm. After a couple of metres he gave a loud cry, twisted round in the tapes and blundered back towards the wall. He stepped on to the étrier and opened the sack that hung beside it. It was packed full. For almost a minute he groped inside the sack. He was on the verge of tears. At last he found the little first aid box, stowed it in his anorak and started back across the roof.

Now he moved more steadily. Whenever he glanced down he saw the giant looking up at him, and the tiny figure of Jaro, waiting patiently a long way down the wall. He asked himself if he had done everything. He was roped to Tomas. He had the first aid box. He could leave the sack to the Czechs. He pulled the doubled climbing rope back through the karabiners until it hung down in two great loops beside him. If the leader slid over the edge at least he would not fall on to a slack rope. And there were half a dozen pegs to hold him. The nearer he got to the lip of the overhang the more difficult it became to move freely. Each time he stretched for the next tape the weight of the three ropes held him back. At last he reached the tapes at the edge of the roof.

He hesitated. Then, fearfully, he stuck his head out from under the rock. He saw a short, steep wall, the ropes trailing down. He could hear nothing.

He shouted.

His voice echoed from the face. He shouted again.

Nothing.

So, filled with dread, he stepped up on to the short wall.

Oh, Christ! he thought. Don't let him be too badly hurt. Just below the top he paused again.

But nothing struck him. There was a smell of scorching. Fresh white scars pitted the glacis. Everything was still. The upper face dark and sombre. Like a gigantic monument against the sky. He saw the great walls of the dièdre towering. And Raymond's body, flung down before them.

He lay well back from the edge. So far back, Daniel thought, he should never have been struck. One arm flung out. The fair hair soaked with blood. A pool of blood still spreading under the head. It looked black in the failing light.

Must have been an odd stone, thought Daniel helplessly. When he reached Raymond, he had no idea what to do.

There was a dressing pad in the first aid tin. He remembered that. He took it out (Raymond, he saw, was breathing: was alive). Then, not knowing where to put it, he pressed the dressing where the blood seemed thickest and bandaged it (tightly? loosely? he didn't know) in place. Before he'd finished the black blood was welling up again. He covered Raymond with his anorak. There was nothing else he could do.

Tomas found him some minutes later, still crouched beside the body.

'I wanted to move him,' Daniel muttered.

He looked up at the giant.

'I thought his spine. . . .'

Tomas said nothing. He took off his duvet and began to slide it under Raymond. Daniel moved to help but the giant shook his head.

'Jaro,' he said. And pointed to the glacis.

Obediently Daniel went down the glacis and drove in a peg. First he had to haul the sacks. They were very heavy. He heard the sound of a heavy object dragging over the ledge, but he didn't look. He kept pulling in the sacks. When at last he turned around he saw that Raymond's body had gone. Only the pool of blood remained. He could still see it, even in the dark. He felt sick – was frightened he was going to be sick. He kept his eyes fixed on Jaro's rope moving spasmodically over the edge until at last the Czech came up.

'*Wie geht's?*' he asked.

Daniel shook his head.

They walked together to the cave at the foot of the dièdre. Dully Daniel saw that Raymond's gear – his hammer, his pegs and karabiners, his helmet – had been piled up at the entrance. A faint light gleamed on the helmet. It was dark in the cave. Tomas was working with the aid of a small torch. He had rebandaged Raymond's head, and now the bleeding seemed to have stopped. Raymond lay on the duvet with the torch on his chest, its beam directed at his arm. In the faint reflection from the walls of the cave his face was livid. Patches of black blood clotted his hair and beard. His eyes were closed. He looked at the point of death. Now Daniel saw for the first time that the arm was shattered, too. The sleeves of the anorak and the woollen shirt had been cut away at the shoulder. Tomas had dressed the arm and splinted it with half the demountable axe and three of the Charlet ice pitons. He was binding it to a small sling around Raymond's neck. Daniel looked at the little pile of blood-soaked cloth and shut his eyes.

'*Er müss ins Krankenhaus.*'

It was all Tomas could say. And it was right – stupid though it seemed to him to say it in such a place. This poor man needed attention in a hospital. Tomas wanted to explain that the bones of the forearm were broken and displaced. That they probably needed surgery. That the leader was suffering from shock. From concussion. Probably cerebral contusion. Possibly even more cerebral and cervical damage.

'*Er hat sich den Arm gebrochen*,' he said eventually.

He struggled vainly for more words. Then, in desperation, struck his head with his clenched fist.

Bewildered, Daniel turned to Jaro. The Czechs spoke together rapidly for several minutes. Then Jaro told him.

'*Ein Schädelbruch*,' he said.

A fractured skull! For a few moments there was silence. Tomas put his hand on the small man's shoulder.

'*Er ist ein sehr starker Mann*,' he said.

'How strong does he have to be?' asked Daniel bitterly.

Tomas fell silent. Then he reached out and took the helmet.

'I can mend that,' said Daniel.

Tomas looked blank.

'Mend it,' Daniel repeated. He didn't know the German.

He took the helmet and made the motion of sewing back the broken buckle.

Tomas smiled and nodded.

So he went out on the glacis. The moon was up. A few stars glittered in the frozen air. The ledge was like a landscape after a disaster. Sombre. Desolate. Littered with debris from the upper face. Nothing stirred.

He took his torch from the side pocket of the big sack and began to search for the flat tin which held the needles and the twine. Threading the needle was difficult with only the torch for light, but he got the twine through at last and began sewing back the buckle, running the needle through the holes in the leather strap. He had to peer at it closely in the torchlight. From time to time he looked back towards the tiny light moving eerily in the cave. If he stopped sewing he could hear the faint hiss of the stove, and voices talking quietly in a foreign tongue. For a moment he felt reassured. For a moment he closed his eyes and tried to pray, searching for the gentle images that made prayer feasible. But it was useless. Nothing came to him. Only the dull conviction that nothing – nothing at all – could change what had happened. It was all useless.

He heard the sound of a hammer. Jaro was breaking ice to melt on the stove.

Ice, and the thought of winter, evoked a memory of years ago. Fir trees. Oh, to grow . . . to grow . . . to get big and old. . . . It was the tale of the little fir tree. To get big and old. He'd thought so too. To go into the marvellous great world. He remembered it all clearly: the thick, soft pages, illustrations which he coloured with his crayons . . . and the dreadful end. Thrown out. Trampled beneath the children's boots. Cast into the fire. He'd cried at that. And he remembered how he'd torn out the last few pages to make the story stop on Christmas Eve. But that was useless too. He knew how it really ended. That it finished in the shocking fact of death. Death and dismembering. Nothing could alter that.

But the buckle was finished. Tight again. He put his things back in the sack and took the helmet back to the cave. Raymond hadn't changed. He was still unconscious. The same harsh, rasping breathing. Carefully Tomas fastened the helmet on the bandaged head.

The ice melted quickly. But it shrank so much there was hardly enough water to fill two mugs. Wearily Daniel began to get up, but Jaro waved him back and went out again with the hammer and the torch.

No one had anything to say. Daniel listened to the chip – chip – chip of the hammer, and lit one cigarette after another (he offered one to Tomas but the giant shook his head). A thin steam rose from the water in the pan. Daniel crouched beside it, eyes closed, his mind fixed dully on the steady hiss of the stove as if it were the only comfortable thing he had. He scarcely heard Jaro come back into the cave. The noise of the stove enveloped him. His head drooped. The acrobats were coming back. Cautious. Shadowy. Like wild animals at dusk. He woke with a start. The leader was stirring. Not much. No more than a slight movement. A faint, protesting noise. A groan. By nine o'clock he had recovered consciousness.

He was very confused. When Tomas spoke to him in German he didn't seem to understand. Daniel tried. He translated the questions. Put them again and again, but with no result. Raymond wouldn't answer. He seemed to have no idea of what had happened. Sometimes he muttered to himself.

The Aiguille du Plan seemed to be on his mind again. He groaned a good deal.

The questioning continued.

'Does it hurt here?'

'Does this hurt?'

'Can you move your toes?'

'Try to move your fingers.'

Jaro made a hot drink of concentrated milk and glucose. Raymond took it.

'What's the point of all this?' Daniel burst out despairingly. 'It's useless! Useless!'

But Tomas would not give up. He probed and manipulated, and laboured in broken German. So it went on. Step after step, by torchlight, in the frozen cave. When he was satisfied Tomas gave orders for the tent sack to be pegged to the wall of the cave. When this was done, and Raymond safely wrapped in his duvet and pied d'éléphant inside the tent, Tomas told them what had happened. A probable fracture of the skull; no injury to the spine; the possibility of damage to the brain. He couldn't tell for certain. He would have to wait.

Raymond lay quietly in the tent. He didn't move much. Only the occasional noise. Now and then his head turned from side to side. His face was ashy pale. He was evidently in considerable pain.

Tomas sat with him in the tent while Jaro and Daniel settled to endure the cold as best they could. The Czechs had very little bivouac equipment. Jaro produced two large polythene bags. He offered one but Daniel refused it. He fastened up the hood of his duvet and crouched down in the pied d'éléphant. Jaro squatted on his sack and gazed stolidly at the night. There was no wind. Nothing stirred. In the cave the air was solid. It bore down on everything. Breath vaporized and froze on the beard. The cold thrust between them. It severed all communication. After midnight there was silence. Each man withdrew into himself. As if life was only possible somewhere below the surface. In the darkness a match flared. A cigarette gleamed briefly beneath the hood, over lips fringed with ice. Daniel was facing the disaster. Bitterly he remembered the helmet. The ashen face fringed with blood. What a stupid thing to happen, he thought. Christ! what a bloody, silly stupid thing to happen.

CHAPTER SEVEN

JARO WAS THE FIRST to stir. He woke to the rank smell of sweat, to the stale remains of a weary day, and a night spent cramped in the plastic bag. His muscles ached. His hands shifting under the cagoule were damp and grimy. For some moments more he contrived to slip back from the grip of the new day. But his hands hurt. His bladder pressed him unremittingly. He struggled upright, stretching his stiff limbs, scratching his scalp with ragged fingernails. He lit the last of his English cigarettes. Then he went out on to the glacis.

It was the strangest dawn he had ever seen. Everything was flooded with green. It looked as if the earth was under water. Everything washed with the same green glow. Isolated clumps of fog clung to the land like pockets of green gas. As he watched, a flight of birds wheeled from the upper meadows, dropped over the great cliff of the moraine and settled down the valley.

Jaro shivered violently. He stood against the rock to urinate, and glanced around. He noted the condition of the face and the peculiar tint of green now diminishing in the eastern sky. His water froze over the rock in a thin, black glaze. Nothing had changed. He was reassured. He went back to the cave. Then he remembered the accident.

He paused, turned to the tent, hesitated, then knelt at the entrance. He listened intently. He could hear nothing. Daniel was still asleep, too. He lay huddled against the back wall, his knees drawn up to his chest. Jaro didn't wake him. He went to light the stove.

There was still some water frozen in the pan but the stove was empty. He opened his sack and shoved his hand down to the bottom. His fingers pushed through layers of clothing, encountered the shaft of an ice piton – then, impaled on its point, the small polythene bottle of cooking fuel. A sticky, glutinous mess covered the bottom of the sac. Miserably he removed the clothes and shook out the rest of the contents on to the floor of the glacis outside the cave. Bread, butter, cheese, sausage, even blocks of concentrated food: everything was saturated with the fuel. A tin of coffee, a small cylinder of glucose tablets and a tube of milk were all that remained. And he couldn't even light the stove.

He stood holding the empty sack in one hand, staring down at the little heap of spoilt food.

When Daniel woke it was to hear the Czechs talking quietly. He sat up.

'How is he?' he asked.

Tomas turned his head. He looked very low.

'*Er schläft*,' he said quietly.

Daniel dragged the stiffened bivouac sack from his legs. Across his back and breast, and down the length of his arms, his long-cramped muscles ached at the effort. The folds of the cagoule he wore over his duvet were seamed with frost that crackled as he went shivering to the bivouac tent. Gently, with a minimum of noise, he pulled the entrance open and pushed his head inside. But Raymond was not asleep. He was sitting up, his back propped on the climbing sack. He sat quite still. His eyes were open. His face, under four days' growth of beard, was grey and dirty, and gleamed with sweat. The eyes and mouth reflected nothing. It frightened Daniel.

'How is it?' he whispered.

'Is there anything to eat?'

His voice was just the same. Daniel was surprised.

'Right!' he said.

He withdrew from the tent. He felt relieved. The Czechs had turned away from the little pile of ruined food. On the glacis Jaro was laying out the pegs and wedges he would need in the hundred metre corner. At the mouth of the cave stood Tomas, watching him. It was a bright, cold morning. Seeing them both together like that, tired, dejected, in ill-fitting clothes (all the more vulnerable for the frail vanities of a red woollen hat, and a fine white cap from the Oberland) Daniel felt suddenly the great weight of the wall above them. It was far from over.

Then he saw the food, and the polythene container still pinned on the ice piton, and the cold stove.

'You're not eating?' he said to Tomas.

The giant shrugged and jerked his thumb at the ground.

'*Sie müssen essen!*' said Daniel.

He knelt down beside the big sack and fumbled with the cord.

'We have plenty,' he said.

It wasn't true. They had very little food.

He took a wrapped packet from the sack and held it out to Tomas who was about to take it when Jaro's voice cut fiercely between them.

'*Wir können nicht ihr Essen nehmen!*'

Daniel felt the harsh, emphatic collocation of *k*s and *n*s. Tomas hesitated, uncertainly.

'*Bitte!*' said Daniel mildly.

He tossed the packet back to Tomas who caught it automatically and then, to forestall all argument, he set their pan of frozen water on his own propane stove and (though he'd matches of his own) he asked Jaro to light the gas. Jaro got down on one knee beside the stove and felt for his pocket.

'*Hier!*' said the giant.

He held out his new Feudor. Jaro took it. He turned on the tap, flicked the little wheel of the Feudor and held out thc small flame to the burner. The gas ignited with a tiny plop, sputtered uncertainly for a moment, then settled to a steady roar.

'*Danke!*' said Daniel.

For a while the three of them watched the ice subsiding in the pan, and the vapour rising from it, crouched there around the stove, not speaking, as if the roar of gas, the little flame and the sight of ice melting were cheerful things for them to hear and look at.

'We'll need some more,' said Daniel.

He spoke in his own tongue but Jaro understood him.

'*Eis!*' he said.

He half rose.

'*Ich werde es holen*,' said Tomas.

He took Daniel's hammer and went out on to the glacis.

When the meal was cooked and the coffee brewed Daniel took a pan and a mug into the tent.

'How are things?' Raymond asked.

'Fine. Can you manage this?'

'I hope so.'

'All right?'

'Fine!'

Daniel went back to his own meal.

When they had finished they all went back to the tent. Tomas went in. Jaro stayed at the entrance, ready to translate. Daniel squatted at his side. He heard the rustle of clothing and the brief exchanges of the two men. The giant's voice stumbling in German, Raymond's terse replies. And long intervals of silence. He noticed that the wind had dropped almost to a whisper. He could see right down the glacier, right over the great cliff of the moraine and down the valley to Molino (smoke rising above the village, wood fires burning, children waking to the bright cold day: except that there it would not be cold at all, not really cold, just a sharpness that disappears as the sun climbs over the mountains). He shivered.

'*Sehr kalt!*' said Jaro.

Daniel nodded. If he stepped off the glacis, he mused, he would fall over eight hundred metres to the glacier: then to be able, like the acrobats, to stand up and walk away. . . . But it was all so far away. Again he felt the seriousness of his position. It was like waking to remember that nothing has changed. That yesterday's anxieties are not resolved by dreams. Nothing resolves itself.

At that moment Tomas crawled out of the tent. Now, with Jaro's help, he told Daniel what he must do. Several times in the night Raymond had passed out. He was sure the skull was fractured. The chance of further damage to the brain remained a possibility. They must remain here, on the glacis. The Czechs would go for the top. They were fit. It was a fine day. They would climb fast. By mid-afternoon they would reach the summit. They would get help, medical aid, equipment. Tomorrow, at first light, they would be back. All would be well. He was emphatic about that.

'*Alles wird in Ordnung sein!*' said Jaro firmly. '*Alles wird in Ordnung sein!*'

Had Raymond heard all this he would have smiled. He was not capable of such simple faith. They were still five hundred metres from the top. Much of the climbing was of the fifth grade, and the hundred metre corner still lay ahead. But Daniel listened gravely to Tomas's assurances that all would be well. He helped them make the last few preparations, and when all was ready he lifted the big sack on to the giant's back. Jaro was the first to go.

'*Viel Glück, Herr Führer!*' he shouted towards the tent. Then he turned to Daniel and held out his hand. He didn't say anything but took off his cap and, in an odd gesture of embarrassment, drew his wrist across his forehead as if he were mopping his brow. Daniel shook his hand.

Jaro climbed easily up the inner, overhanging wall of the cave, jammed a hand into the crack that split its apex, pulled on it tentatively, then, when it held, jammed the other hand in the crack and swung out from under the roof. There, for a moment, he paused, hands buried in the rock, feet bridged across the mouth of the cave, his fine white cap slanting down from the wall.

'*Viel Glück!*' he shouted again.

Then he pulled powerfully up and on to the face. He worked swiftly, with brisk, precise movements of hands and feet in the crack, his pegs and wedges jangling under his arm as he climbed steadily higher.

The sun's up there, thought Daniel. He's heading for the sun.

He watched as Jaro ran out a full length of rope in so short a time, and all performed so easily, done with such delight, that he felt again the old, hopeless envy of all men who seemed freer, happier, more accomplished than himself. He remembered the pigeons on the road from Metz. Scores of pigeons fluttering from baskets by the roadside. How they'd wheeled in a great curving circle above the poplars and swung off south over the low hills of Alsace.

'Where are they going?'

'They're going home,' he'd said.

'Are they going to the mountains?'

The little boy could imagine no journey beyond the great valley of the Rhine which had any other purpose.

'They're going wherever their home is.'

'They're going to the mountains,' the child decided.

'We saw some pigeons, maman,' he'd cried. 'Going home to the mountains.'

She'd looked at *him* then, and he remembered wearily how futile it had seemed to explain that he'd said nothing . . . meant nothing at all. I'll write that down, he told himself impulsively. It must be possible to explain these things. When I get back, he thought, it will be different.

When the giant's turn came, and the ropes were taken up, he turned to face the cave and put both hands into the crack above his head. He was so big he could reach it without stepping off the glacis. He pulled on the jams experimentally, then turned back to shake hands.

'*Auf Wiedersehen!*'

'*Viel Glück!*' said Daniel.

'You have been very good to us,' he added in his own language. He wanted to say it in German, but he couldn't think of the words. The giant seemed to understand.

'*Wir müssen einander helfen*,' he said.

He clapped Daniel on the shoulder and turned to the rock.

'Tomas!' said Daniel suddenly. 'Don't forget us.'

The giant nodded. He would soon be back. All would be well.

'*Alles wird in Ordnung sein*,' he said again.

As he turned to the rock a deep voice rang out above their heads.

'*Allez la France!*' it shouted.

Daniel looked up and waved.

'*Viel Glück!*' he shouted.

Then, as Tomas began the long climb up to the stance, he went to the tent. He pushed his head through the sleeve entrance. Raymond had passed out again. He looked very pale. Daniel left him and went back to the glacis to watch the Czechs.

The giant was now no more than a small blue figure crawling purposefully up the vast expanse of the wall, while Jaro had shrunk so far back into a deeper part of the crack that an occasional flash of red against the grey rock was all that could be seen of him. Above them, seemingly immediately above but still a good way off, were the huge hanging buttresses which formed the walls of the great chimneys that gave entrance to the upper face.

'God!' said Daniel. 'It goes on for ever.'

He stood there for almost an hour until his neck ached from looking upwards, staring after them as they receded between the buttresses which seemed blacker than ever to eyes screwed up against the light. He could hear Jaro's voice singing the great anthem he'd sung the day before. The words were indistinct and distorted between the narrow walls. But the tune was there. Clear. Unmistakable. It stayed in his mind long after the voice that sang had faded from the central face. He remembered what Tomas had said jokingly of Jaro, as they drank coffee on the first morning.

'*Er wird der Böhmer Troll gennant!*'

It heartened him now to think of the Bohemian dwarf advancing resolutely through those dark chimneys. Bellowing his defiant hymn. Shattering whatever ice remained with shrewd blows of his hammer. They would come back soon. He was sure of it.

He turned away from the face. There would be a long time to wait before the Czechs returned. What a tale it will make then, he thought. A tale to scandalize the ancients at the Café des Nations, who placed such a trust in the inevitability of misfortune. And, though he would not have admitted it to anyone, it was a relief to think that for Raymond and himself the climb was over. Yet, alone on the glacis, he felt a little flat now that the Czechs were gone.

He settled to pass the time as best he could. There was much that he could find to do. He unpacked the two sacks and laid out the contents in neat, separate piles on the rock before the mouth of the cave. He refolded the clothing and replaced it in the big sack. He counted all the pegs and wedges and clipped them on to the karabiners according to their different types and sizes. He re-coiled the ropes. He collected fresh ice from the glacis. He checked the food. Coffee, sugar, some tubes of milk, some cheese, a few biscuits and raisins, an end of sausage, and two bars of concentrated rations. It wasn't much. But it would be enough. The gas canister on the propane stove was empty. He took it off and screwed on a fresh one. It was the last canister they had.

I'll make some coffee, he thought, when I've cleaned the pans. He'll like a mug of coffee.

He began to clean the pans with grit from the glacis spread on a little cloth. As he started on the first one it occurred to him that he was on his own. The Czechs had gone. They had been there when they were needed. Now they were gone. The next act devolved on him. Slowly he rubbed the cloth round and round in the pan.

If it came to the worst, he thought, he would have to act alone. He felt isolated. But it was not unpleasant. Almost exhilarating. Like climbing a sensationally exposed pitch on good holds. Abstractedly his hand circled the pan as he imagined himself coping with the crisis, handling the worst that could happen (supposing he dies, he thought with sudden dread).

Then the first notes of thunder rolled through his fantasy with a long, sullen rumbling.

He put down the pan and went out on to the glacis. In the north-west a long black cloud, flat-topped like a wave, loomed over the Oberhalbstein. It was travelling east.

Daniel stared at it incredulously.

Only a few minutes earlier the sky was empty. Completely clear. He stared in astonishment at what seemed to him a shocking act of malice. Every few seconds the thunder rolled like gunfire. As he looked beyond the glacier he saw flights of birds rising and swooping down the valley towards the forest. The thunder grew more violent. Within seconds the echoes of one reverberation merged with the first rumblings of the next, while the cloud swept towards the north-east face. It moved with extraordinary speed. Daniel watched it coming as it poured unopposed over the low hills beyond Molino. He saw the lightning stab and flicker. In minutes the little Piz d'Averta, four kilometres away, was overwhelmed. He saw a gigantic, fiery lance punching into the summit cone.

It was like some dreadful apocalypse, full of horror and panic, in the beginning only partly known, now flowing back so wholly and terribly that he understood it for the first time. The rending noise in the yard. Aunt Catharine's white face. The cries of women as the labourers stove in the casks. Wine washing over the cobbles. The green and golden wine of Alsace. One old indomitable voice crying (against the crash of glass and splintering wood), '*Sois gentil! Sois fier! Sois sans peur!*' as the first tank nosed into the lane.

Then the light vanished in a whirling, smothering mist.

The storm came, not with the roll and crackle of thunder, but with the violent blast of the first shell. Then the staccato clatter of hail raking the face until the great walls of the dièdre were racing with a white cascade. He scrambled back from the glacis while enormous hailstones leapt and spattered in the aluminium pan. Thunder and lightning were simultaneous. A colossal crash exploded with a single flare at the mouth of the cave. Even through closed eyelids he was dazzled by the glare. For some moments he crouched against the back of the cave. Then, when awareness flickered back, he heard, as if through some appalling nightmare, a faint, familiar voice calling him to shelter. He crawled stiff-limbed into the tent.

The wind screamed after him. A sudden storm of hail spattered the tent, threatening to wrench it from the pegs. It was pitch dark. He could see nothing. His hand groped over a large boot.

'Fasten . . . the door!' yelled a voice.

Obediently he turned to do as he was told. Each time he gripped the thin fabric of the sleeve it whipped back out of his hand. The whole tent rocked. He had to roll into the doorway, pinning it under his body so that he could draw the tapes fast over the sleeve. The slight lull that followed was a blessed relief.

The voice came again. Muffled, but with an obstinate insistence.

'We'll . . . be . . . all right!' it shouted.

Instantly, another tremendous crash shook the glacis. A sheet of flame sprang up beyond the front of the tent as if the sky had caught alight. For a few seconds the livid glare banished the darkness. Daniel caught a glimpse of Raymond propped under the back wall. The corpse-like head helmeted. The good hand clutching a cigarette. Then the light collapsed in another monstrous explosion, echoed by a vast subterranean rumbling that seemed to come from the roots of the mountain.

Daniel sank back on to the folds of his duvet. Lightning! Lightning was capable of lopping off the glacis completely. The thought appalled him. He sat up suddenly and scrambled back to the door, groping through the darkness, his hands clutching at the wildly flapping walls.

'Where . . . you . . . going?'

'Axes,' he shouted. 'Must . . . move them.'

'No!'

The voice came back at him, muffled but with the same firm hold.

'Make . . . no . . . difference. If it strikes . . . come down . . . the dièdre.' Only then did Daniel realize that the fault must serve as lightning conductor to the upper face.

'Don't . . . worry!'

The voice found a faint way through the howling wind.

'We're . . . low down . . . we'll . . . get . . . through!'

The hail kept up a continual drumming against the walls. The wind struck blows from every angle, and the little tent ripped and wrenched at its anchorage.

'Must . . . unclip . . . front krabs!'

'What?'

'Get . . . the tent . . . down!' Raymond shouted. 'It'll . . . go . . . otherwise.'

Daniel fumbled for the door. As he did so one corner tore loose from the guy and half the tent collapsed on top of him. He struggled against the wrappings ferociously, terrified that the tent (and they inside it) might be bundled down and over the glacis. Then his hand groped across the tape. He pulled it loose and thrust his head and shoulders out throught the sleeve.

He was checked violently. He had to crawl through the entrance on his belly. The rock was soft and wet. He kept his legs inside the tent so that he could find his way back again, rolled over, and shone his torch at the front corner. The beam cut from the darkness a triangle of light through which the snow streamed in torrents. The corner of the tent was drawn taut and quivering against the wind. When he released the karabiner the fabric whipped suddenly from the beam of light. He heard a muffled shout. He swept the beam down and across the tent. It had been rolled up like a carpet. Then he began the struggle to get back inside. The tent resisted him ferociously. Eventually Raymond managed to separate the two front corners, thrusting at them with his feet, and Daniel wriggled back through the sleeve. He was exhausted.

'Hang . . . on . . . to the corner!'

They lay side by side, facing one another in the darkness with the loose cloth bundled up beneath their bodies, each gripping through the fabric the karabiner which held the back of the tent at his end, while the storm swept over them. How long they lay like that Daniel could not tell. He hung on grimly to the karabiner. At first his hand ached. Then it lost all sensation as the pain advanced along his forearm. When the cloth ripped loose from his fingers he realized that they were crooked in a kind of rigor, but gripped nothing. He changed hands.

From time to time a small voice shouted obstinately, as if through several layers of cloth.

'Hang . . . on! We'll . . . be . . . all right!'

The day wore on. Thunder crashed through the electric air. The shock of it left him quivering. In all his life he had never endured such a storm. But he hung on to the karabiner. In his terror of the lightning he tried to control it, telling himself that if he stuck to the karabiner, if he kept the tent from tearing, he would survive. He gave himself entirely to this delusion, praying for strength to cling to the karabiner. He couldn't speak to Raymond. But he listened to him. He clung to every word. He was grateful even for the craziest remarks. He was desperately afraid. But Raymond, as if deaf to all contrary opinion, with the storm at its height, maintained his obstinate judgement.

'It . . . can't . . . last,' he yelled. 'Can't . . . last!'

Another appalling crash shook the glacis, and another, and then a deafening whipcrack snapped through the air, followed by the most dreadful, ponderous crushing and splintering, and he was thinking, Christ! there goes the glacis, when he was struck massively on the back of the head. Vivid sparks of fire leaped from eye to eye. There was a tremendous roaring in his ears, the roaring of flames, and he reflected with queer, fascinated horror, that his brain was burning.

He must have lost consciousness for a few seconds, for he was next aware of a loud voice. It was shouting desperately, close to his ear.

'We . . . must . . . get . . . away!'

It was his own voice.

He felt sick and foolish. He was trembling violently. His body jerked and quivered. His legs shook so uncontrollably that he knew Raymond, lying at his side, must feel them shaking.

'Frightened!' he yelled.

'So . . . am . . . I,' Raymond shouted. 'Lightning . . . worst! Lino Casaletti . . . had a second . . . killed! On the Verte! Struck down . . . split second!'

'I think . . . I've . . . been struck!'

'Shock waves!' Raymond shouted.

Gradually Daniel's shaking subsided. His head ached. An occasional spasm shook his limbs. But he clung grimly to his karabiner. Outside the tent the wind raged on.

He stared blankly up into the darkness. A few centimetres above his nose the roof rattled incessantly. He became aware, gradually, of a discomfort in his left shoulder. Something pressing. It was Raymond's boot. That boot, planted solidly against his body, seemed the only durable, unyielding thing in the whole rattling, flapping, shifting universe. However slender Raymond's reserves of strength, however serious his injuries, they did not seem so now. That boot offered a resistance as concentrated and unmoved as the storm was wild and violent.

Then, quite suddenly, the wind backed. It was as if a great door had been closed against it. Occasional blasts still struck the tent. The terrifying noises persisted, but muffled, further off. They could hear frozen snow drumming on the fabric. The vivid shocks of light and the sharp crackle of thunder were still violent, but distinct now, no longer simultaneous. The centre of the storm had shifted.

'I hope ... the Czechs ... got off!'

Even as the words were yelled Daniel heard a low, distant rumble approaching through the wild noises of the storm. It was so far off that at first he thought it might be the St Moritz express crossing the valley, but it grew so swiftly, gathered with such a terrible vibration that the solid rock ...

He knew, then, what it was. He flung both arms up to protect his head and buried his face in his duvet.

The whole tent lifted. Daniel's hand was torn from the karabiner. He felt his body plunging through the fabric floor as the blast sucked out the thin sack like a paper bag. He heard a sharp cry of pain. Then he was struck violently himself in the mouth by some heavy solid object as they were tossed about in a terrifying panic of threshing arms and legs. He dug his fingers vainly through the tent floor, scrabbling for the solid rock, while Raymond clung desperately to the one remaining karabiner.

For hours the fresh snow had gathered on the icy slopes below the summit. Only a stroke of lightning, or a blast of the wind was needed to set it off. Now it had happened. The whole unstable mass was loosed, pouring off the ice like water, gathering between the funnelled walls above the hundred metre corner, bursting with a blast that could flatten a forest like a field of corn.

The whole face trembled as the great avalanche thundered down the dièdre. Daniel gave up the struggle with the rock and pressed the duvet against his head to stop his ears. Huddled on the floor of the cave with his eyes closed and his head buried in the down-filled jacket, all his senses straining to shut out the avalanche. He didn't move until its last echoes had died away down the face.

Then he felt Raymond's boot prodding his arm again.

'All ... right?'

The tent roof lay heavily over his head. As he pushed the cloth away from his face he felt the weight of fresh snow resisting his arm.

'All right?'

He thrust the cloth aside. There was a taste of blood in his mouth. He hadn't been aware of it before. He felt with his tongue. The lip was split. A tooth loose. Blood still seeping.

'Something ... hit me,' he mumbled.

He tried to speak without moving his lips.

'What?'

'Hit ... me ... in ... the face!' he shouted. This time it hurt.

'You'll ... be ... all right!' The last two syllables arrived together, as if pushed with immense effort through the almost solid air.

Now it was necessary to hang up the front guys again. Daniel undid the tapes around the entrance, but before he could get out he had to push the sleeve upward in front of him through a bank of snow. He crawled out. The darkness of the tent gave way to a grey murky light. It was bitterly cold. He stumbled, slipped through the thick powdery snow, his fingers fumbling for the front wall of the tent, feeling for the guys, clipping them back into the karabiners. It took a long time to repair the broken guy. All the while the snow piled up in wet, sticky clumps on the back and shoulders of his cagoule. It stuck fast to the tweed thighs of his breeches. It trickled between the thick fibres of his stockings. When the job was finished and he crawled back into the tent, he carried with him a large quantity of snow which oozed over his ankles between the rim of his boots and slithered down his neck to join the sweat drying coldly under the cagoule. He rolled miserably on to his pied d'éléphant and clutched the duvet with shrunken, saturated fingers.

'Christ!' he said.

'Never mind,' said Raymond. 'Warm and wet's better than cold and dry.'

'I'm bloody cold,' said Daniel viciously, 'and bloody wet as well.'

He knew it was far from over. Lightning and the terrible wind might strike as violently again. A blizzard might rage for days at a time on a north face such as this. If that happened, he thought, we're finished. We're as good as dead already.

He lay still on the soft folds of the pied d'éléphant, his head pillowed on the duvet, gazing sightlessly at the roof of the tent, sensing a vague wet warmth now rising from the down-filled cloth beneath his body. He thought of nothing. The long effort to hang on had exhausted him, left him with nothing in reserve to face the worst of all. We're going to die. It was as simple, as final, as that. And it was fixed in his mind. Locked there with such conviction that all his conscious efforts to take up his friend's confidence not only failed to overcome, but actually intensified his sense of death. And he had nothing left with which to ward it off. The Czechs were gone. Were dead, probably. And the storm would come again. Besides, in Raymond's confident assessments he saw a foolishness of such dimensions that it could come only from an insane determination not to recognize the facts.

He's mad, Daniel thought. Mad!

Outside, the wind howled unrelentingly.

Yet, gradually, his cold wet clothing warmed to the heat of his body. Beneath him the soft pressure of the duvet and the pied d'éléphant offered a damp, melancholy comfort, in which the harsh noise of the storm seemed strangely pacifying, like the crooning of a savage nurse. He lay in a kind of dream, brooding on Raymond's madness, remembering his brother André, first one, then the other; images shifting, converging, merging in one composite last scene fixed like a picture in the mind. Like a cartoon by Goya. Hooded figures in a blizzard. Tiny, before the Plan's gigantic bulk. All heads but one bent to a dark bundle in the snow. Close to the snow a lantern: light flashing under the outstretched arm: gleaming on an eye, the rim of a face in shadow, one half of a bearded mouth, parted, framing the words:'It's André – he's dying.'

Outside, the howling of the wind erupted from time to time in shrill flurries that drove fresh snow against the wall. The tent was stifling.

Tous les grands chefs se sont tués.

The words passed dreamily through Daniel's mind.

At the Cabane des Planches, in stained red slippers, Gaston shuffles between the tables. On the panelled walls he keeps a row of faded portraits. *Tous les grands chefs*. A long line of serious, bearded men – they began as crystal seekers, poor woodcarvers, hunters of chamois. Now they sit or stand, each in his own grave poise, like village elders, or prosperous, provincial public men: François Couttet, in middle age, descending a staircase; Old Melchior Anderegg, like Moses in a watch and chain, holding an ice axe; Jean-Antoine Carrel's remote face, turned back, perhaps to Chimborazo and Cotopaxi, years before.

Jean-Louis Belmonte calls it 'Gaston's graveyard'. They are very like the photographs the Italians put on tombstones. He takes great care of them. Often he'll pause in wiping the long wooden table by the wall and polish each glass front with the edge of a coat sleeve gripped between his fingers. Once a year, on their anniversaries, he fixes a black ribbon to each wooden frame. Oh, the young men don't care for it at all. Not at all. The guardian of the cemetery, they call him.

'*Tous les grands chefs*,' he says. '*Oui! Je les connaissais tout le monde!*'

'He couldn't have known them all,' said Belmonte, the young tiger. 'Some of that lot must have died almost a hundred years ago.'

That was true. But no one knows how old Gaston really is. You can't tell from his face. He's so old it doesn't matter. Like the survivor of an ancient race whose hold on life is to maintain this link with the famous dead. To preserve the memory of those English captains who dined off fresh trout and Château Lafite, carried up for them to the Refuge des Grands Mulets.

'There's Christian Almer,' he would say, 'the man who carried a fir tree to the summit of the Wetterhorn. And that great fellow there (pointing to Ulrich Lauener) on the Eiger glacier, when all the Chamonix men were terrified and said the séracs would crash down at the slightest sound, that fellow climbed the tallest pinnacle of ice and shrieked like the devil. Yes! Shrieked like the devil.'

Each aged countenance stares down indifferently from the wall. Only Maquignaz's hollowed, bandit's face gleams with amusement. He was killed too. *Tous les grands chefs*. Imseng, 'who had neither wife nor children and wanted none', who loved only the Macugnaga face of Monte Rosa, the great snow wall which made his name, then killed him. Johann-Josef Bennen, who trod the snow catenary on the Wetterhorn. Crossing that couloir on the Haut-de-Cry he saw the snow-field split above him, watched the crack widen, begin to slip, to slide . . .

'We are all lost,' he said. '*Wir sind alle verloren!*'

He might have spoken for them all.

Tous les grands chefs se sont tués. The snow closed in to fill the places they had left.

It was snowing now. Snow muffling, deadening, burying everything till not a trace was left.

CHAPTER EIGHT

THE COLD woke him. Bitter cold and cramp. A great weight of snow lay up against the tent. He put out his hand to touch the wall. It was stiff with ice. He had no idea how long he'd slept. The wind had dropped. It was pitch dark. It might be midnight, or the ıast hour before dawn for all he knew. Nothing moved. A profound stillness brooded over the mountain. He heard Raymond's low, deep breathing and guessed he was asleep. But his own sleep had brought him no relief from the hopelessness of their position. Except that now he felt a flicker of irritation, a faint desire to take a stand against the storm – a mood, perhaps, of the dream he'd woken from and still remembered.

Not a particularly narrow plank, he remembered. You could walk along it easily if it was just lying on the grass. Ten metres above the bottom step it was a different matter. Not many of the boys would even set foot on it. The few that dared did so as if they were treading a tightrope. Every precaution they took for their own safety seemed to increase the hazard. The outstretched arms plunged wildly, bodies dipped, swayed, as each boy lurched above the drop.

Raymond stirred in his sleep and muttered something that Daniel couldn't catch. He listened, but the disturbed moment seemed to have passed.

It was still the same plank you could walk along easily if it was lying on the grass. One knew that. That was a fact. Yet one little boy got halfway, then dropped astride the plank, clinging to it with his arms and legs. Nothing anybody said could make him move. A crowd of boys gathered in the court below. Some of them racing up the steps, scattering the little heaps of leaves that Brother Michael had swept down from the bank.

The boy was very frightened. He was crying.

'Come on! Crawl forward!' they shouted.

'No! Come back! This end's nearer.'

'Shut your eyes! said fat Martin.

'You fool!' they all shouted furiously. 'You'll make him fall.'

Then, quite suddenly, there was silence. You looked where everybody else was looking, to the top of the steps where Brother Jerome stood as still and as silent as a wraith. Not a sound. Only the boy's stifled little sobs.

Raymond stirred again, and called out in a sharp, protesting voice. 'No! No! Lionel!' he called.

It was strange how he always seemed to come at you silently and from above. Not like the other Brothers, who might have appeared among the boys at the bottom of the steps. Not like Brother Superior, whose kind, white head seemed to precede him like a light. A sort of *lumen Christi*. No. The face staring from the window, the dark shape moving in shadow on the landing, the tall figure at the foot of the bed – that was always Brother Jerome. He turned his pale, expressionless face on the crowd of boys. They drifted silently away. He strode softly to one end of the plank and took two firm paces forward, extending a long, black arm to the little boy, whose fear of a fall was lost in the far worse fear at his fingers' end.

'Take hold!' said Brother Jerome.

The boy was hauled to safety and the plank removed. And everyone was punished.

But the trick was not to think of falling off. Or learn to think of it so dispassionately that it no longer seemed very likely. Like the man who carried the bull on his shoulders. Learn to do it in stages. That night he and Denis slipped out from supper, took the plank from the shed, set it three times in position (first at the top – then there – then high above the bottom step) and marched across it. Then they went back to Benediction.

Daniel smiled to himself in the darkness. If only Brother Jerome's long black arm could reach up here.

It was a good memory. A good thing to hold on to. Suddenly he felt a surge of life inside him. An impulse to move – to feel the spring coming again – to climb in the sun on rough warm rock, with the hard move coming up.

But Raymond stirred again. Then, with a violent movement, he woke, crying aloud, struggling to sit up. Daniel leant forward and gripped his shoulder reassuringly.

'It's all right,' he said. 'Lie back!'

'What's the matter?'

'Nothing. It's all right.'

Raymond shuddered. His head ached. He felt cold. There was a bad taste in his mouth.

'What time is it?'

Daniel struck a match and looked at his watch.'Two o'clock,' he said.

'God, I'm thirsty!'

'I'll make a drink.'

He could hear the wind rising again. It seemed to creep into the silent space between them.

'How much fuel have we?'

'Not much'

'How much'

'About two hours. Perhaps more.'

'Yes – we should eat something,' said Raymond.

Daniel pushed his head and shoulders out through the entrance. The blizzard had stopped, but the snow had piled up deeply under a thick crust of frost. The little ventilation sleeve was almost buried. He pulled it out and cleaned the frozen snow from its mouth. The night was very cold and still, except for the wind. There were no stars. Only a blurred, wheyish moon that gave no light as he looked critically up at it. He scooped a panful of snow, slid back into the tent and closed the entrance. It was difficult to cook anything in the tent. He had to sit hunched forward balancing the pan precariously on the steel rods (burning his fingers in the process) while he gripped the stove between his knees. The flame curled like a luminous blue fringe around the bottom of the pan, its light glinting on the few hard, steel things that lay about. It lit nothing else. But its steady hissing filled the tent.

As the pan grew hotter, the snow shrank at the edges. The icy water crept higher, cutting hollows in the banks of snow. The flame attacked it from beneath. From time to time a hanging cornice collapsed into the water. Daniel watched as the snow sank in the pan. He saw how it was undermined, reduced, drowned. He thought of himself here in the hollow cave, generating heat at the very centre of the snow and ice. His heart beat steadily. The blood still kept its temperature. His restless desire to do something was taking shape, growing to a purpose. Be patient, it said. Wait here till the storm exhausts itself. Then strike. . . .

'Did I pass out again?' asked Raymond suddenly.

'What?'

'I think I fainted.'

'When?'

'Just now.'

'I don't know. You were restless. You called out Lionel's name. I thought you were dreaming about Gyalmo Chen again.'

It had been the first great post-war expedition. Something the press had taken up like a crusade, a quest for the Holy Grail of national pride. In Paris they built a monstrous wooden tower so that the more reckless citizens might imitate their heroes among the fixed ropes and pegs and wooden holds. Raymond had been profoundly shocked.

'What was it like?' asked Daniel. 'You never told me.'

Raymond made no reply. He kept silent for so long Daniel thought he wasn't going to answer.

'Gangtok!' he said suddenly. 'That's where it starts. That's where you meet the porters and the yaks.'

Then he began to speak.

'From there you go north-east to a place called Kupup – that means the summit of the saints. That's where the track divides. One path goes up to the Tang-la pass, then down into Tibet. That's the ancient road from India to Lhasa – the pilgrim's road to Chomolhari. You can see it a long way off, towering up beyond the pass. And Siniolchu, and Kabru, and even Kangchenjunga, a long way off to the north-west. The air's so clear.'

'All the great names,' said Daniel softly. 'Kangchenjunga . . . Chomolhari . . . Lhotse . . . Makalu . . . Everest. . . .'

'Chomo Lungma!'

'What?'

'Everest,' said Raymond. 'It's real name is Chomo Lungma. Goddess Mother of the world. That's what they call it.'

Raymond took a cigarette from the packet at his side, lit it, then lay back on the sack. The wind droned on outside the tent, but its noise was almost lost in the steady hiss of the stove. A steam was rising from the pan.

Daniel felt drowsy.

'At Kupup,' Raymond continued, 'above the road, there's a fortress carved from solid rock. Hundreds of years old. It faces north. Whatever comes from the north must pass beneath it. A great black shape against the snow. It's a grim place. The porters wouldn't camp there. A place of blood, they called it.'

He was silent for a while. The cigarette glowed in the darkness. He was a long way off. Daniel could sense that. And his voice seemed weary. But he carried on with his tale.

'We took the other path,' he said. 'North-west, to the Tum-la monastery. That's where you first see Gyalmo Chen. Set in a great chain of peaks, with the Rushung river hurtling through the greatest gorge in the world. You could put the Eiger in that gorge. . . .'

Daniel thought of that with awe.

'Gyalmo Chen is the holy mountain of the Lepchas. The Great Queen, they call it. They say that the Rushung river is her gift to them. And that every spring, when the snows uncover the fir tree forest, the rhododendrons burst into flower at the touch of her feet. That's what they say.'

Daniel forgot the pan of water steaming between his knees. He listened, spellbound.

'Every colour you can think of,' said Raymond softly. 'White, yellow, mauve, red, pink. All the colours.'

His cigarette glowed again in the darkness. He blew out the smoke, and went on more briskly.

'They have a ceremony called the *parikharma*,' he said. 'A kind of pilgrimage. They have to make a circuit of the mountain. Some of them *crawl* round the whole chain, over passes of five thousand metres or more. They have gloves tipped with metal. They lie face down, stretch out their arms and make a mark in the dust with the metal tips. Then they go to the mark, lie down, and mark the path again. And so on, right round the circuit. They eat and sleep where they lie. It takes many days. Some of them die. They acquire great merit by making that circuit. The *parikharma*, its called.'

He stubbed out the cigarette in the little tin at his side.

'That water's ready,' he said.

'They believe everything has a guardian spirit,' he went on.

'We believe that,' said Daniel.

He took the pan off the stove and set it carefully on the floor of the tent. Then he reached for the tube of milk.

'It can only protect you against yourself. It cannot guard against the man who wishes to do you harm. Only his spirit can do that. And there are evil spirits, too. The spirit of cold – the dysentery spirit – there's even a spirit of adultery. They are disembodied and they seek to enter men. The Lepchas do not say of someone – "he is an evil man". They say "he is possessed of an evil spirit". Sometimes men give themselves. Sometimes they are taken by force. But the gods are good as well as terrible. They can protect those who love them.'

'You admired the Lepchas,' said Daniel.

He handed a mug of hot sweet milk to Raymond who sat forward to take it.

'They are good,' he said. 'They are happy. They lead simple lives of work and prayer. Whatever its superstition a religion that can accomplish that. . . .'

He stopped again and was silent for a time, sipping meditatively at his drink. Now that the stove had stopped its hiss Daniel was conscious of the wind again, driving between them, separating them.

'We stayed three days at the monastery,' Raymond went on. 'We had to break down the loads. Everything had to be carried up the gorge. I used to talk to the Abbot. "'We do not ask what may exist after what exists,' he said. 'We follow the Way. We do it by our own strength alone."'

He paused, and drank again.

'Beyond the mountains you can see the Chinese guards patrolling the frontiers of Tibet. We saw them down in the Chumbi valley, a long way off. We saw the glint of their bayonets in the pass. If they cross the border the Lepchas will resist. No one will help them. Not us, not their gods, no one.'

'They will not blame their gods for that,' said Daniel.

'No!' said Raymond. 'I don't suppose they will.'

He finished his drink and handed the mug back to Daniel.

'"We are all bound upon the Wheel of things. Lives ascending . . . descending . . . far from deliverance." That is what they will say.'

Daniel did not understand about the wheel, and the lives. But he detected the note of bitterness and kept a sympathetic silence for a while, sipping at his lukewarm milk, until his child's desire to hear the story's end broke out again.

'Go on!' he said. 'You entered the gorge?'

'Oh, yes! We had to. There's no other way.'

Raymond was hesitant now, his voice faltering from time to time.

'It's the greatest gorge in the world,' he went on. 'Two thousand metres deep. You could put the Eiger in it – and at the bottom the Rushung river racing between the walls. Nothing can live in it. There's no path. Sometimes you're high up on the wall – sometimes stepping from boulder to boulder in the river bed. And there is something more. Something hard to describe. A kind of dread. The porters felt it more than us. We felt it perhaps because they did. Perhaps it had to do with the noise. Not just the usual river noise. But something behind it, like a much greater noise a long way off. Like,' he hesitated, 'say, an avalanche in the great central couloir. . . .'

In the dark Daniel nodded.

'It never stopped. The further we went the louder it grew. And we knew that if we lost a single porter the rest would turn back. We had to fix ropes for them. Three times we had to cross the river on bridges we made ourselves. After four days we came out of it, into a kind of basin filled with fir trees. Everything was soaking wet. And the noise – everyone shouting – the roar of water. . . .'

He paused, lit a cigarette, then he continued.

'Beyond the trees was a kind of inner amphitheatre. Great walls hundreds of metres high, with the Rushung river crashing down from a great slot in the rock.'

'You got through?' said Daniel.

'We got through. André found a way up the cliff to the upper gorge. We followed. We got the porters up somehow. Then we went on. For two more days. Sometimes by the water, sometimes high on the walls. Fixing ropes, crossing and re-crossing the river, the porters swaying under the loads and chanting prayers as they went. God knows what they thought of it all. Then, quite suddenly, round about noon on the sixth day, it was over. We passed beyond the walls.'

He stopped again.

'What we saw—' he began and hesitated.

'Yes?'

'So many things . . . I can't really describe. . . .'

Yet it poured out – as bewildering as it must have seemed to him all those years before.

'Beneath the snowline,' he said, 'a great meadow. Flowers – and butterflies, hundreds of butterflies. So many things, I cannot tell you. A great stillness. A softness of the air. Ferns – orchids – butterflies – so many things. Among the rocks there were sheep that had no fear of us at all. So tame you could touch them. You could stroke them with your hand. Greenness and colour everywhere. . . .'

Daniel was silent. He remembered a green valley near Allos, not far from Mont Pellat, in the little alps of Provence.

'And at the head of the valley – the holy mountain. Towers – great battlements of ice – glaciers like white channels against the grass. And so dazzling you couldn't bear to look. Surely the gods dwell here, the Lepchas said. Tsung-ling, they named it – the garden of the great lady. We must have been the first men ever to set foot in it.'

He drew for the last time on his cigarette, then stubbed it out.

'So we rested there for a while. Set up the base camp, prepared loads for the higher camps, and so on. Then we began. Up the main glacier, through the ice falls. Past séracs as big as churches, some of them. Day after day. And everything went like a dream. We pitched the last camp at seven thousand metres, in a small saddle on the arête. Lionel, André, Pasang Tendi and I. The wind was bad all night. Lionel was sick. He and Pasang should have gone for the top. He'd dreamed of it for years.'

Daniel nodded. He knew of Lionel's dream.

'We wanted it for him very much. But he was sick. He just wasn't up to it. So at dawn Pasang said, "I will care for him: the sahibs must finish it."'

He stopped. For some time now his voice had sounded faint and faltering. this time he was silent for so long that Daniel began to wonder uneasily if he had passed out again (it was so dark he could see nothing) and was about to enquire, when the tired voice began again.

'He gave me his khata – that's the white scarf they have (Daniel nodded) – to place close to the summit. I put it with the Abbot's prayer flag. Then we set off, André and I. It was snowing. Pasang watched us go. We turned round at the top of the slope. He was still standing there. Outside the tent. We waved. Then the mist swirled up.'

He paused. In the silence that fell between them Daniel caught a sense of all the lonely places of the earth – and of the courage that men bring there, like gifts for the gods.

'All the way up it snowed. We came to this big rock step in the ridge. I led it. Suddenly – I was in sunlight. We were there. Great peaks all around us. Kabru, Kangchenjunga, Chomolhari, Simvu, Siniolchu; they were all there. All glittering in the sun. I couldn't get over that. The sun! And we were there too. And there was the summit. Just a few more metres up the slope.'

'Yes!' Daniel said suddenly. 'I remember! You had to stop short of the summit.'

'It seemed so silly,' Raymond said, reflectively. 'So silly to stop like that. To have come all that way. Not to get up it properly.'

'You made a promise. It was right to respect it. To respect their gods.'

'Yes! We made a promise. We gave our word. I gave my word. I told them all that we stopped short of the last few metres.'

Raymond paused.

'That was a lie,' he said.

'It seemed so silly, then,' he went on. 'No harm could come of it. No one would ever know.'

But *you* would know, thought Daniel.

'Besides, it seemed wrong not to do it properly. Wrong to us. To ourselves. So we went on. We drove our axes into the summit. We took photographs. We even flew our flag from the top.'

At last he stopped.

Daniel floundered for words to fill the silence.

'Photographs?' he said. 'Surely. . . .'

'No!' said Raymond. 'We took those from below the summit. There were others that no one saw. Two. André had one. I have the other. I have it here.'

He reached behind him with his good hand. The movement must have hurt him for he gasped in pain. Yet he managed to unzip the little pocket in the top of his climbing sack, took out his wallet and tossed it across.

'It's in there,' he said.

It was too dark for Daniel to see. He had to switch on the torch. The photograph was in a little cellophane packet. He took it out. It felt cold and slippery between his fingers. He shone the torch and stared at it. He saw a black shape against a brilliant sky. A hooded, muffled figure. Ice axe held aloft in the familiar attitude. Teeth a white flash in the masked face. Under the padded boots steel teeth gripped the snow.

'It doesn't look like you,' he said.

'No,' said Raymond. 'It's the altitude. The ultra-violet light or something. The goggles don't help.'

Daniel held the photograph unhappily. He couldn't think of anything to say. Silently he tucked it back in its wrapper, replaced it in the wallet and handed it back.

'We'd brought some things to put in the snow,' Raymond went on. 'Some chocolate. Pasang's kharta. A crucifix. The Abbot's prayer flag. We buried them like thieves. . . .' The flat voice shook a little but kept its course. 'The gifts of simple men to the gods, and we buried them like thieves. Then we went down. And of course there was the blizzard. You know about that.'

The whole of France knew about it. Daniel kept a sympathetic silence.

'Snow avalanching all the time,' said Raymond softly. 'Goggles choked with snow. It took hours to get down. Hours. Looking for a tent that wasn't there any more. There was nothing. Only fresh snow. Oh, we looked for them. Christ knows we spent hours searching . . . shouting . . . probing in the snow. . . . But they were dead. They must have been swept straight down the south-east face. They were dead.'

He fell silent, and Daniel pondered on the agony of that night. Caught without shelter at seven thousand metres, with one's friends dead. At least he'd been spared that. He was thankful he'd not had to suffer that.

'You've never been back,' he said, 'have you?'

'We had come a long way,' said Raymond, after a pause, 'through difficult country. All that way, with so much effort, for' (he hesitated) 'a violation. That's what it was. For something that can never be put right.'

For the pride of a moment, Daniel thought.

'You didn't realize . . .' he began.

'No!' said the leader firmly. 'That's what it was. An outrage. And two men gave their lives for that.'

That's what shakes him so, thought Daniel. That Lionel would not have done a thing like that. Never. And yet who knows? Who can tell?

'It was a long time ago,' he said consolingly. 'It's all in the past now. What's done's done!'

'Men are defined by what they do.'

'Men are worth more than that,' said Daniel sharply. 'Besides, we have all done these things. I have done these things.'

'Then you will pay for them.'

Not for the first time Daniel felt a profound regret for all men who have no gods to pray to for forgiveness.

'You can go back,' he said impulsively. 'I'll go with you. Next year we'll go back. You and I together. . . .'

It was a foolish, desperate idea.

'No!' said Raymond. 'I shall never go back.'

Daniel's slim resources were exhausted. He could think of nothing else to say.

'There have been other things since then,' he said weakly.

'Yes! A brother left on the Plan. . . .'

'That was not your fault,' Daniel broke in harshly. He'd been through this before. 'André was strong. He was experienced. He was a professional. You couldn't have know what would happen. Besides, you had other duties. You had a client.'

'I had a brother, too.'

There was nothing left to be said.

Each man withdrew. It was like leaving the field of another indecisive battle. There was a space between them, a no-man's-land, dead ground filled by the wind which drove fresh snow against the tent.

There you have it, Daniel told himself. Bitterly, he remembered his foolish pride of the previous morning – that he could replace Tomas – that things would be all right after all. Recalling it now was painful and embarrassing. But perhaps a little of it did him credit. It was up to him. That bit was right, anyway. Except that the conditions were different now. They'd changed. And he did not really believe he was up to it. Even if the Czechs had reached the top, and the storm lifted, a rescue on the face would be difficult and dangerous. He couldn't be sure that the Czechs had got to the top. The chances were that they had not. He had to face that now.

Then he realized that he had been trying to face it all day. Ever since the lightning started. Not until now had he been able to do so. To go beyond the fact. To face its consequences.

'Some things' (put in a sombre voice) 'are forbidden, even here.'

'Forbidden?' Daniel wasn't really listening any more.

'Not by God,' said Raymond. 'I mean, simply, that we ought not to do them. It is as if they were forbidden.'

Daniel felt for a reply, hesitated, then let it drop. If the Czechs were dead it would be two more days before Lino raised the alarm at the Masino hut – that is, if Lino got there on time. He might not.

Suddenly, at the thought of Lino's homely face, his cheerful greeting, he was filled with anguish.

'What I mean,' said Raymond, 'is that there are some things that I cannot permit myself to do.'

'I don't see how you can say that,' Daniel said, suddenly irritated. 'I don't see how you can say that you do not permit yourself to do a thing when it is precisely that thing which you have done.'

'No – I make laws for myself,' Raymond insisted. 'I may do things which break them from time to time, but they are still things which I forbid myself.'

'Then you must forgive yourself,' Daniel said sharply.

'No one can do that.'

Daniel grunted. Food for one more day, he thought – if they were careful. And one cartridge of gas – already started.

'No one can do that.'

'What?'

'Forgive himself.'

'Then you must live with it.'

Immediately the words were out he was sorry. Shocked that his own hopelessness should come so easily between them. He didn't want that.

'Look,' he said consolingly. 'Forbidding – permitting – what does it all mean, really? Language is like a kind of searchlight. At a certain altitude it fails. It doesn't work any more. The light keeps travelling out but it's too weak to light up anything clearly any more. They trusted you. They asked you for a promise. Out of respect you gave it. And then broke it. That is what it amounts to. A betrayal, perhaps, but still a human act. Something we all do. Something I have done. None of us are guiltless.'

Raymond made no reply. In the silence and stillness the low murmur of the wind caught Daniel's ear, a confidential aide whispering discreetly, lest he forget the most important thing of all. The weather might lift. It might not. If it didn't, and they stayed where they were too long, they were as good as dead already. Nothing was certain, nothing was sure, but that. That if no one came to help them they would die. And since he could not be sure that anyone would come to help them, Daniel concluded bitterly that they must help themselves: bitterly, because he had never expected Raymond to be injured, or the storm to break so suddenly upon them, and because he wished things might be otherwise. But these things had happened. He had come on this adventure, and he must try to bear its consequences as best he could. He would do what he could. He did not really expect to succeed.

'Tomorrow,' he said, 'we must go for the top.'

Raymond made no reply.

'We can't stay here,' Daniel added. 'We have no food. We don't even know whether the Czechs. . . .'

'Look.' Painfully, Raymond raised a shoulder from the ground. 'If you fell . . .'

'I know that,' said Daniel. 'Do you think I don't know that?'

For some moments they were silent again. They heard the wind howling over the wastes of the north face. To Daniel it seemed an elemental voice confirming the decision.

'We have to go,' he said. 'Don't we?'

'Yes!' said Raymond.

Daniel realized that he had been wrong in thinking his life a preparation for something that never happened. It was happening now. For both of them this moment had always been out there ahead, awaiting their arrival. A destination to which they had to come.

Yes! Carried with us, thought Daniel. Like his photograph. Like the cheap toys in my sack. Like the letter I shall never finish now.

And he was not ready. He was not prepared at all. Oh, the good life wasted. Wasted! Years of dreadful waste!

Now the years behind seemed like a tragic misappropriation. Lies. Promises betrayed. A brother dead. A man reduced by years of argument. A woman's voice that spoke now only to itself . . . exhausted . . . at two o'clock in the morning ('and I thought I would get myself a little dog . . .').

'We must be mad!' Daniel said. 'You and I, we must be mad! All the lovely things in the world. All the lovely things, and we come to this God-forsaken place. We must be mad!'

He raised his left arm, the arm which bore on its underside his father's watch ticking against the pulse, and smashed it down against the rocky floor. The glass splintered. The little hands broke off.

For a moment he remained stock still, too stunned by his own impulse to realize what he'd done, or to feel the pain in his wrist.

Then he raised the watch to his head. In the silence its creaky ticking filled his ear.

PART TWO

CHAPTER NINE

AT NIGHT, at that altitude, nothing stirs. Nor can any sound carry.

The face lay under a bitter frost that always comes with the last hour before dawn. Only Raymond's breathing broke the silence. Harsh and rapid, it rose and fell . . . rose and fell.

He had passed out again. Perhaps he was just sleeping. Daniel didn't know. Too cold and wet to sleep for more than a few minutes at a time, he was wide awake now. His breath issued in puffs of watery vapour that turned to ice at the tent wall. His lips were cracked and sore. His loose tooth hurt. There was a bad taste in his mouth.

As he listened to his friend's breathing he wondered how *he* would face his fourth day on the wall. The man was crippled. How could he climb? Not without aid. He might not climb at all. Yet he'd survived half a dozen crises almost as desperate. But for him, six men instead of four would have died that day on the Plan. Perhaps he was still stunned. Still confused. But when – if – he recovered he would think of nothing but escape. That formidable will would not desert him.

For a moment Daniel felt the weight of that granite obduracy – that prodigious instinct for survival. And since Raymond was crippled, *his* arms would have to wield the axe and hammer, his fingers clutch at the ice, and there would be no relenting, no letting go until he'd suffered all the stations of collapse.

To rope straight down the wall was quite impossible. But time and time again during this last hour before dawn his mind slipped in imagination down the vast expanse of the central face: the grey rock slipping past, his body sliding nearer . . . nearer the ground, to the last bound out across the bergschrund, to the crunch of boots on the glacier, to the moment when he could pack up and go home. But each time he stopped short. If only there were three of them. It might be possible to lower an injured man – but he was checked again. Stopped. Forced back to the worn circle of doubts, hazards, fears, decisions made on insufficient information, equipment selected or abandoned, ropes and pegs to be fixed, trusted, and all of it now based on the bitter recognition that the Czechs were dead, that above him stood six hundred metres of vertical rock, verglassed, the cracks sealed with ice, the chimneys choked with rotten snow and rubble.

From time to time images of his wife and child slipped through his mind. And, momentarily, he held them there, considering the faces that stared remotely back at him. But they were too far off to matter any more. He had been three days and nights on the face. His friends were dead. His companion crippled. Filthy, wet, reduced to a physical squalor he could never tolerate at home, he had experienced a severing from all the objects of a clean, well-ordered life. Storm and avalanche had accustomed him to an icy world where nothing lived for long. And these privations weren't without effect: they attacked the comfortable casing of his mind, bared it to absence, darkness, death. Now, unprotected, it compacted to a single obdurate purpose. It was the only tenable purpose in a wilderness where men maintained themselves so brutishly and with such pitiful provision that the least chance could kill them. He was determined to get off. Cold, motionless, swaddled in the sodden clothing, he watched and waited for the dawn.

At first light he went out, floundering on hands and knees through the deep drifts until he could get out on to the glacis beyond the cave. The raw air stung his face. A bitter chill settled about his body. But after hours of crouching or lying in the muggy tent it was a relief to stand straight again. He was astonished at the great weight of snow which covered the rock. The rubble that had littered the surface two days before was blotted out. Here and there boulders or blocks of ice loomed up like shapes under a thick blanket, but the rest was obscured beneath a dense white sheet that slipped down to the mist. There was nothing to be seen. The village, the valley, the spires and turrets of the Zoccone spur, the glacier, even the upper lip of the great roof had vanished in the freezing fog.

It hovered like a ghostly wall around the face. Constantly it drifted in trailing strands wherever the eddies of the wind disturbed it, coating everything it brushed against with a thin film of frost. Ice materialized on Daniel's beard and eyebrows. His cagoule crackled as he walked.

Shivering, hunched in the soaking duvet, he trudged about the snow, peering up at the huge buttresses that hung like islands in the cloud. From time to time he stopped and looked to the north-west. There was Molino. It was strange to think that there were men asleep down there below the cloud. Families asleep, or waking, in houses whose roofs would shortly catch the first rays of the sun. He wondered if ever they looked up from their streets or pastures to see clouds trailing across the face, and if ever they thought what he always thought at such a sight – behind those clouds perhaps men are fighting for their lives. It was the same impulse that, at nightfall, made men like him pull on their boots again, take up ropes and axes and go out on to the glacier. He thought of the first rescue he'd ever been on. He could remember only bits of it. The speed of the guides; his fear of not being able to keep up; the white, frightened face turning and turning as the stretcher jolted over the snow. He did not doubt that beyond Molino, in the valleys, villages and little towns of half a dozen countries there were men who would do as much for him. But for all that mattered now he might have been standing on another planet. The sun which shone for other men did not shine here. Now it must not shine at all. If, at the next mid-day, the sun shone above the summit, the fresh show would avalanche. Darkness and cold were vital. If he prayed for anything he must pray for that.

At last he turned away from the fog and plodded up the glacis, stumbling as the snow crust broke and slid back under his boot. Once or twice he slipped and felt a clutch of panic lest he should not recover but slide on down over the edge of the great roof. When he got back Raymond was still asleep – or unconscious. Daniel tied up the sleeve to make a small, open circle in the tent wall. He crouched down on his haunches at the entrance. The flimsy roof, heavy with snow, pressed down on the back of his head, icy-cold at first, then wet with water drops that trickled down his neck. He rummaged in the big sack and produced a bulky canvas bag which he placed on the floor. He unfastened the draw-string and then drew out into the faint grey light the lobster-clawed, twelve-pointed Grivel crampons.

They were his own crampons. He removed the rubber cover that guarded the points and tested each one against his thumb. All sharp. He always kept them sharp. He lifted the first by its thin steel frame and placed it lightly on the snow. There is rested, poised on its points above the fragile crust: skeletal, motionless, its lobster claws held in a steely, warlike posture. He placed the other on the snow beside its mate.

There were only four cigarettes left in his packet. He lit one now, resolving to smoke no more than half of it. He took the north wall hammer, the climbing dagger, the top half of the demountable ice axe and his own small piton hammer and tossed them out on to the snow. He felt calm and empty. Many men had been in far worse situations and survived. Here on the glacis the snow was rotten. He thought it would be different higher up. Driven by the fierce wind, forced under pressure into the cracks and chimneys, it should compact into a thin, hard layer. The crystals would break down. Meltwater and the bitter frost would turn them into ice.

He picked up the ice axe and held it loosely in his right hand, flicking it from side to side with a practised movement of the wrist. It wasn't his. Even cut in half like this it didn't suit him. He put it back inside the tent. When he'd finished half his cigarette he squeezed out the end between his thumb and finger. He would have to smoke them all in halves. He would reward himself with one whenever he'd done something hard. Of course it would be patchy. There would be stretches that gave way. But in the cracks and chimneys, supported by the rock, it must surely hold.

Wherever there is snow, he remembered – it was a saying of the old guides – *there one can go*.

He clutched at this now.

The ice dagger and the two hammers lay there on the ground in front of him. His own hammer had dropped head first in the snow. The steel claw of the pick slanted up towards him, thick and rigid against the snow.

As he looked at them his mind turned back to Mont Blanc years before. To the great ice trinity of the Brenva Face. The Pear Buttress, the Sentinel, the Route Major. He thought of snow flashing past under the long glissade again. The Verte, the Blaitière, the Forbes Arête on the Chardonnet, the Innominate Ridge; one long glorious summer. . . .

At dusk, on the days he wasn't climbing, sometimes he used to stand within the little square of tents counting the dots that moved slowly over the Vallée

Blanche (four . . . five . . . six – black against the snow) then, happy his friends were safely home again, he knelt to light the stove.

He shook his head. A summer that had been a state of grace.

He put out his hand and took up the dagger in his fist. It was no more than a thin ice piton, bound at the head with tape. He made a few, swift stabbing passes, weighing the long, light peg against the solid curve of the pick. It seemed as flimsy as a paper knife. He put it back in the sack.

Snow changed, he thought. Temperature and stress were never constant. He had to climb straight up, on the four front points alone, belaying from whatever pegs the rock would take. For two days at least he would have to live and work beneath the vast unstable load of the summit snowfield – with no protection – upon a surface that might collapse at any second. And if he fell. . . .

'What time is it?'

Raymond's voice was weary but awake, as if he'd lain for a long time not sleeping but with eyes closed against the light.

'Time we made a move.'

Raymond hauled himself upright with his good hand and struggled clumsily to push the pied d'éléphant down over his hips.

'Here,' said Daniel. 'Let me do it.'

They cleared the tent as quickly as they could. Daniel passed things out. Raymond took them and tossed them onto the snow. When the tent was empty Daniel crawled out through the entrance. He surveyed the jumble of clothes, equipment and personal belongings strewn about the snow. The little chamois lay upside down, its carved white belly exposed between its stumpy legs. Anguish clutched at him again for a moment, but he shook it off. He had to shake off that. He picked up the wooden toy. One of the horns had broken off. He brushed the snow from its head and tossed it into the open sack.

'Can you manage to pack up?'

Raymond nodded.

They worked steadily without speaking. It was bitterly cold. The raw mist still hovered at the edge of the glacis. There was no sound except for the clink and thud of equipment, and the scuffle of boots in the snow. From time to time, scarcely distinguishable in the grey air, a few flakes drifted down. Eventually, when everything was done, Daniel looked around at the neat pile of equipment, and at the bare place in the snow where the little orange tent had stood. He gazed at the ice-fringed face of his gloved and hooded companion, dried blood clotting the beard and hair, and felt for a moment such an emptiness that he was overwhelmed.

He shuddered violently.

Raymond looked enquiringly at him but Daniel only shook his head.

'We'd better go now,' he said.

They tied on to one half of the doubled rope, leaving fifty metres free for Raymond who would climb it with the help of tapes and prussik clips. Daniel arranged a chest harness to keep him close to the rope as he climbed up it. That should keep him from falling backwards, Daniel thought. He should be all right with that.

'Can you manage these things with one hand?' he asked. He meant the prussik clips.

'I shall have to.'

Daniel knelt to strap the crampons to his boots. His fingers were cold and clumsy, and it took him a long time to thread the straps and fasten the buckles. He clipped the two hammers and one end of the rappel rope to his waistloop.

Raymond helped him on with the climbing sack, looped the slings and the piton carrier over his shoulder and handed him his helmet silently. Daniel put it on. He raised his hand to fasten the strap beneath his chin.

He could no longer see the great hanging buttresses that guarded the upper face. The main wall stood silently within its covering of cloud. From its centre the snow-filled crack of the direttissima rose and receded into the drifting mist. The wind was rising again. Flakes of snow which twenty minutes earlier had drifted singly and intermittently now drove down in short, spasmodic flurries. Daniel looked about the frozen desolation of the glacis, and at the bare spot in the cave and was prepared to take a long farewell of its pitiful security. But the soft pressure of ropes and straps, and the stealthy clink of steel whenever he moved, oppressed him. He was ready to go. Yet he hesitated and looked doubtfully at his companion.

'Do you think you'll be able to manage?' he asked again.

'I'll have to. Let's get on with it.'

The crack was fairly wide, and though he couldn't trust the thin layer of frozen snow which plastered the back wall (it broke away too frequently), he found sufficient holds among the small ledges and seams on either side. But it took a long time. Most of the crack was glazed with ice, and he was so aware of his profound responsibility, so certain of the consequences of a fall, that each placing of a single crampon point exacted the utmost caution.

So he went on. Working tightly, his instincts like voices in his ear: Take care. Don't fall. Do not exhaust yourself.

Yet there were other voices warning with equal force of the dangers of delay, of the effects of hunger and cold, of gradual exhaustion. And the urgency of all this was heightened now by the visible grimness of the face, isolated within its iron wall of cloud, cut off not only from the rich, warm colours of the forest and valley, but also from the comforting sight of life.

From time to time he came across new pegs driven into the crack. But they were no use to him. And the Czechs were gone. No voices broke the silence of the face. Only his own harsh breathing, the creaking of ropes, the chip – chip – chip of his own hammer pecking at the ice. His was the only human presence. His noise the only purposeful noise. This thought gripped him so powerfully that on one occasion he stopped still and listened. Nothing stirred except the wind. Behind him the ropes creaked softly. He thought of Sedlmayer and Mehringer creeping up the great icefields of the Eigerwand – slower and slower until storm and exhaustion stopped them altogether – of poor Longhi's cries: 'Fa – a – ame! Fr – e – ddo!' drawn out on the wind.

But the mild character of the crack persisted. After much patience and caution he ended a long run-out of almost fifty metres at a stance set like a saint's niche in the fault. It was snowing steadily now. He couldn't see Raymond. He could see nothing but the grey rock, curtailed by cloud, and the coloured ropes dropping down into the mist. He cleared the snow and ice from two new pegs driven into the top of the niche. They were Jaro's pegs. He clipped the rappel line to one of them, tied back the red rope to the other and leant out to shout instructions down through the cloud, straining to catch the indistinct replies that climbed back up to him. Then he began the arduous recovery of the sack, hauling it hand over hand through the karabiner above his head. The fingers he'd burnt on the stove the day before began to throb painfully as the thin line cut into his glove. When the sack was secured he removed the rappel rope. He tied back to the karabiner the white rope up which Raymond would climb on his tapes and prussik clips. He ran the red rope through a second karabiner clipped to the first, and when he was satisfied with his preparations he leant out again over the void.

'When you're ready,' he shouted.

He took up the red rope again. His hand was hurting badly, and it needed an effort of will for him to grip the rope firmly. But he'd begun to have doubts about the chest harness arrangement. The mechanics might not work. He thought of Raymond sliding the clips up with one hand, stepping into the swaying tapes, fighting to stay upright. He mustn't fall backwards. Each time the taut rope yielded he took in the slack swiftly and kept it tight. He leant far out over the drop, ignoring the pain in his hand and the numbness of his feet, straining his eyes to pick out the dark shape looming up through the cloud and falling snow. He was desperately concerned to bring him safely to the stance.

But this anxiety only sharpened his awareness of delay. It was all taking too long. Far too long. As the snow piled between his feet he felt the great weight of rock that separated them from the summit, the hundreds of metres still to be climbed. He lived through pitch after pitch of this slow, agonizing crawl up the rope.

Several times the movement stopped altogether. He assumed Raymond had passed out again, and gripped the rope grimly, determined to hang on to him, no matter how long it took.

But supposing he dies, he thought. Supposing he's dead now.

Gradually this anguish undermined his courage. As the slow minutes passed so the conviction grew in him that in a few hours' time they would simply peter out miserably somewhere on the upper face. When, at last, Raymond materialized through the shifting gloom Daniel brought him carefully up to the peg, but said nothing. Nothing sufficed to break the bitter silence in his mind.

Raymond spoke cheerfully.

'*Simple!*' he said. 'There's nothing to it.'

But his face was grey and exhausted. His clothes were plastered with snow. He sank into the crack below the stance while his companion unclipped the white rope.

'Here!' said Daniel. 'You forgot these.'

He handed down the prussik clips and tapes.

Then it began to snow in earnest. Daniel was determined to reach the shelter of the great overhanging buttresses in one long run-out if he could. The wind tore at the ropes ceaselessly. He could feel them snatching at his body. From time to time he shrank against the rock as little falls of fresh snow burst down the face. As the crack deepened, in its approach to the buttresses, he thrust himself further into it to escape the wind. Then he found it difficult to see the moves clearly. The falls of snow increased. He began to curse himself at his own rising panic. But he struggled on, and had just reached Jaro's peg at the mouth of the first chimney when he heard Raymond's voice shaken out in long syllables on the wind.'We . . . can't . . . go . . . on!'

Daniel knew it.

Bitterly he drew in the eighty-metre rappel rope, clipped it to the peg, and began the descent.

Just before mid-day they were back on the glacis.

Wearily they set about clearing the fresh snow from the cave. For Daniel especially it was a bitter setback. He felt himself the victim of a terrible unfairness at the heart of things. He had climbed well, with great determination. Now they were back again. They had achieved nothing. And their small store of energy had been reduced still further. It was as if the delicate structure of resistance that had begun to grow on the wall that morning had been summarily chopped down. And though he expected such a reaction in himself, although he knew that all men would suffer the same in such circumstances, this knowledge was powerless to hold back the dreadful sense of futility which crept through the mind like a paralysis. Deep down some instinct still flickered its desperate message to whatever pockets of resistance might remain. We must get off! We must get away! But there was no response.

All the while the wind drove fiercely at the glacis raising the fresh snow in great powdery clouds which fell on the floor of the cave. As they scraped the rock clear, so the snow drove in to cover it again. Daniel regarded its presence with a perverse satisfaction, as if it offered an ironic confirmation of his despair. But Raymond, despite his handicap, worked away grimly, shovelling the snow aside with clumsy, scythe-like sweeps of the axe.

'At least it keeps you warm,' he said, gasping, swaying in the snow.

Daniel made no reply.

Eventually they clipped the tent to the pegs. Daniel had to hold out the front wall like a canopy over the cave until Raymond had cleared as much snow as he could. Then he crawled inside, pulled the big sack to the entrance and struggled to get the stove, the food container and the down-filled bags in through the flapping folds of fabric. At last Daniel crawled in after him and tied up the sleeve. They huddled together, shivering and exhausted, while the storm drove once more over the face. For a long time they lay without speaking, hearing only the wind and the fresh snow drumming on the tent wall.

'We couldn't have gone on,' said Raymond, at last.

Daniel didn't answer.

'It would have been crazy.'

'I know!'

'In those chimneys. . . .'

'It's all right,' said Daniel. 'I'm not denying it. I'm not arguing.'

Raymond fell silent again. He thought of the blizzard at this moment sweeping the great slabs of the upper face, of fresh snow avalanching down the chimneys, of Daniel striving to find the right route, in failing light, with three hundred metres between them and the next bivouac at the foot of the corner. Here in the cave, at least for the time being, they were safe again.

He was very sorry this had happened. Not for himself. For him (sooner or later) it was almost inevitable. Not that he would ever yield willingly, not even to the inevitable. He would always fight for life. He would cower away in any hole or corner if it gave him a chance of life. But after the Plan disaster he had no illusions. For a few more years he had lived facing the mountains – had seen the snowfields sparkling high up the great faces, felt at his fingers' ends the rough warm rock. And he was grateful for that. But he knew how the circumstances that determined André's death could reduce the very best of men: strength, judgement, skill dwindling slowly, hour by hour, to the same dark bundle, crumpled in the snow.

But most of the men who came to climb with him had unfinished business to return to. Children to fear for. Wives to love. Parents to protect. They could not afford to die. None of them could live as free as he had lived since André's death. For his freedom seemed to flourish only in loneliness – at the far side of negation.

He wished very much he had not brought Daniel with him. He knew that he had suffered the same loneliness on the face that morning. He knew what he was suffering now, and thought, with pity, of what the next day must bring.

'I thought you were mad,' Daniel said suddenly. 'Last night I was quite sure you were mad.'

Raymond stared at him.

'I suppose I was very frightened. I didn't see how anyone in their right mind could not be as frightened as I was.'

'That's because you're only an amateur. If you were a professional it would have been different. You learn to accept these things. Oh, you might be frightened. But fear – lightning – stonefall – they're all a part of it. In the nature of things.'

They were silent for a while. Daniel listened to the wind's noise and the steady drumming of frozen snow on the fabric. He saw how blanched and bloodless Raymond's face looked in the dim, orange light.

'And death?'

'That too.'

'I couldn't look at things like that,' said Daniel. 'Not in a million years.'

'One has to. In the long run, anyway.'

'I don't!' said Daniel.

Raymond shook out the cigarettes in his last packet of Celtique.

'That's what I said,' he replied quietly. 'You're not a professional.'

He had eight left. It would not have occurred to him to save them, or smoke them in halves. He would smoke one whenever he wanted one. When they were gone he would do without.

'Well, whatever you think of amateurs,' said Daniel, 'if you're to get off this face you'll need me to lead it for you.'

'If you're to lead it,' replied Raymond, 'you'll need me to tell you how.'

He offered one of his cigarettes. Daniel took it silently and struck a match for them both.

Worlds apart, he thought.

It made him think of his marriage. Of their condition. That was the sacramental part of it, he supposed. Their dependency. Their need of one another. She, of him; he, of her. Yet it wasn't all. Each of them wanted something more. Something, he pondered, that in being beyond the other, was beyond them both. What it was he didn't know. He remembered her in the aftermath of some appalling scene. Sitting wretchedly together in the hours after midnight. Her voice. Her words, falling into the exhausted air.

'I only want to be happy. I can't help wanting that.'

And his own bitter response.

'I wanted to be a child for ever.'

For he'd believed he was right. Convinced that he'd acted as any man would act.

That was years ago. The rows were fiercer now. They went on longer, as if they'd both acquired stamina, as if time had made them tougher.

We are not fully human, he thought. Most of the time we live below the human level. And yet he knew that ultimately, when all savagery was spent (when neither had anything left to fight for) she could be reduced to the same, simple admission. And so could he.

'I only want to be happy. I can't help wanting that.'

So there are moments that restore us to humanity. Sometimes, in the aftermath of anger and violence he would feel a profound sorrow – a profound pity and love for things. That was a rescue, in its way. A moment of grace. Again he saw the red-rimmed eyes in rings of blurred mascara. Streaks of black staining the swollen cheeks. All those small vanities. They seemed infinitely pathetic now.

Suddenly, he was filled with an overflowing love and pity for her. For them both. For himself too. For all of them. He wanted to put right what had gone wrong. But there was nothing he could do. Nothing. And if he was useless in this respect, then everything was useless. It was all part of the great disaster.

'Sometimes,' he said, 'I think I would like simply to be. Not to be anything . . . or have to do anything . . . Simply to be. To be free.'

'That wouldn't do you any good,' said Raymond sombrely.

'No,' said Daniel. 'There's nothing remarkable about me. I'm not a Parisian – or a Marseillais – or a native of any famous, fashionable city. I'm not noted for wit or shrewdness or courage. I am not mean. I am not one of the persecuted. I am not any kind of refugee. I was born close to the border. Lived all my life there. Where the lines of demarcation have never been beyond dispute. Where even the language is unsettled. Not a good place to grow up. To learn what one's supposed to do.'

There was a silence between them. A strained silence. With Daniel's voice hanging at the edge of hysteria.

'I have never,' he declared emphatically, 'never stood a chance of doing anything as well as I would have liked.'

This time Raymond spoke.

'Perhaps tomorrow,' he said, 'you will have that opportunity.'

It was a chilling remark. And he knew it. He crushed out his cigarette in the little tin he used as an ashtray.

'Look!' he said gently. 'You rest. Sleep for a while if you can. I feel a lot better.'

It was true: he hadn't fainted for some time. 'I'll get us something to eat.'

He began his preparations for the meal with that phlegmatic indifference to both injury and the storm that was characteristic of his extraordinary adaptability. It would take a chain of quite extraordinary disasters ever to wear his life away. Yet he knew that it could happen. And this knowledge informed his capacity for endurance with great patience, and the cunning never to offer more resistance than was necessary to survive. He moved now, softly and deliberately, collecting neither more nor less snow than it required to yield just under half a litre, lighting the stove, setting the flame to the right height, laying out the tins and bar of concentrated food. He worked very quietly.

But Daniel could not sleep. He lay with open eyes, hard up against the back wall, his head turned towards the rock. The wet fabic of the tent lay across his face. It was like an icy skin. He listened to the steady hiss of the stove until its slender noise at last pierced like a needle through the great heaving of the storm. Then he closed his eyes.

For a long time he heard his friend's stealthy movements about the tent. He thought again of the snow subsiding in the pan, of the little flame maintaining its steady, insistent purpose right here at the heart of the storm. It was like a counter movement, taking shape in secret, behind closed doors. And he realized that Raymond was far from mad. He was a *grand chef* in a dreadful game. A grand master effecting expert nullifying moves. And the encounters endless. Endless. Daniel saw him squatting perpetually on some north wall, enduring the storms and terrors of the great faces, a contemptuous eye cocked at his malignant gods. You cannot starve me, he would say to them, more than I've always starved – nor cause me greater pain than I've always suffered – nor make me any lonelier. And there he would preside for ever.

Like an antique hero, thought Daniel. Chained to the rock. Waiting for the eagles to return.

Christ! Some of us are born in hell, he thought. In hell we live and move and have our being.

In his distress he cast about his mind for some other image – a consoling presence.

Hail holy queen, mother of mercy, he began silently, covering his face, pressing his fingers against his face, *hail, our life our sweetness and our hope.*

But the images that came were desolating. A child's face. Aunt Catharine's white face. Then the dead, dreadful countenance he'd seen as a child in pictures of the Holy Shroud. He remembered his grandmother dead – they tried to keep him out but he slipped in after they had gone – lying with the sheet drawn up to the neck, her face bound with a cloth. Implacable, that face. He bent and kissed its brow, but that was not what he'd come for. He had come to look at death. He came away, shuddering.

A blankness came over his mind. Empty. Like the sky he used to gaze at as a child. Vast over the flat brown fields.

Look to the south, Uncle Paul used to say. Look to the south – one day you'll see them. The long line of slender bodies. Slender necks and bills thrust forward to the north.

It was spring again. And they were flying home.

This memory, in the midst of despair and exhaustion, gave hope of better things. Next year, he told himself, I shan't climb. We'll go to Norway. Camp in the Opland. Fish for trout. Swim. Walk in the forests. Maybe we shall see the great cranes too.

Raymond bent over the precariously balanced stove and stirred with a cautious hand the disintegrating lumps of meat and vegetable. The pan slipped suddenly. He caught it with a spear-like thrust of the spoon and slid it back. A musty, disagreeable odour rose from the pan.

He sniffed, and thought, Christ! I hope it wasn't the snow we peed in.

He peered at it dubiously. It has a high calorific content, he told himself. It saves lives.

'OK,' he said. 'It's nearly ready. You can pour the wine.'

But Daniel was far away among the rocks and forests of the Jotunheim, dreaming of the fair, young son – of the blind, unwitting god who killed him – of Valhalla, in Gladsheim, where the heroes feasted – where all wounds were healed.

'I have a suspicion,' Raymond added, 'that we may have peed in this stew.'

But Daniel was dreaming of wolves at night in the forest – and of the great cranes dancing by the lake.

'Here you are then,' said Raymond finally. 'Whatever it tastes like remember it has a high calorific value. That might help to get it down.'

He passed a pan to Daniel who bent forward to take it. He was hungry. He ate swiftly, spooning the stew into his mouth, filled with a wild excitement. It was a revelation. It was an act of grace that would absolve him from the past. When I get back, he promised, things will be different.

'What's it taste like to you?' Raymond chewed doubtfully at his first mouthful, the spoon below his lips.

Daniel scraped the last stringy fragment of meat from the side of the pan, his mind filled with an eager, impatient joy to begin.

I'll write to her, he told himself. I'll do it now.

He cast the empty pan and spoon aside.

But he didn't write. It was still snowing fiercely. The wind kept driving fresh snow into the front wall until the fabric bulged under the great weight. The film of water vapour, which had clung in drops to the inner side above the rising heat of the stove, froze to a thick, uneven layer of ice. They seemed to be sinking into an icy gloom. It was too dark to write. And the batteries of the little lamp were almost drained.

For a long time they lay together side by side in the darkness. When they had to urinate they did so crouching uncomfortably above their parted knees, with a helmet gripped between the thighs – Daniel held it for his friend – praying it wouldn't overflow, cursing when it did, passing the slopping bowl awkwardly out through the entrance.

If this were a film, Daniel thought, we would die in the end. But we are real. We have responsibilities. Our friends are waiting. I do not intend to die. And since he couldn't write to his wife he tried to think of her as she had been in all the happy moments. . . .

He remembered her as she'd appeared one windy day, coming over a ridge in the Vosges, a long way off. A small figure under an enormous sky, in a blue anorak that was too big. He and the child set out to meet her at the head of the valley, and when they'd reached the place he'd sat on a boulder, his eyes fixed on the col, watching, hoping she'd had good weather, while the boy played among the rocks. He found a frog, Daniel remembered. She walked with her arms held by her sides, bowed under the unfamiliar sack. The scree clattered as she came down it, stumbling in the little boots she wore. Hand-made Italian boots he'd brought from Montebelluna. Her hair all blown back by the wind.

'Why do you have to climb?' she asked once. 'Why not be happy just to walk in the hills?'

But he had looked out from the doorway of his tent. He saw the black pine forests on the hillside across the valley, and above it the huge *ballon* of the summit dome, washed pink and a dark, misty blue. A late buzzard wheeled high up in the sky, gliding in slow, wide circles, hung almost still (hunting for rabbits, he thought: he heard its plaintive, mewing call, thin and urgent, like a kitten's).

He thought of her now. At home – waiting – not knowing from one day to the next – hoping, perhaps, he might turn in at any moment at the lane gate, dropping the big sack from his shoulder, tired, dirty, burnt dark by the sun.

Suddenly he was overwhelmed by an intense desire for his home. His eyes filled with tears.

Long after nightfall the storm raged on, until the tent was almost buried, and the atmosphere inside foul and stifling. They were so crushed together they could scarcely move. As the hours passed they suffered agonies of cramp. Daniel particularly suffered from the lack of air. It created a raging thirst which he tried to slake by gnawing pellets of frozen snow. But this only inflamed the sores on his cracked lips and made his mouth burn worse than ever. They finished the remaining biscuits and ate a handful each of raisins, but eating hurt Daniel's mouth and intensified his thirst. The air was so foul they dared not light the stove to melt water for a drink. And they'd need what was left of the fuel to cook the last bar of concentrated food. They spoke seldom. From time to time one of them muttered something – speaking offered some relief from the oppressive, stifling atmosphere – but for the most part they endured their ordeal in silence, as though each wished to conceal from the other his growing sense of hopelessness.

Time passed wearily. Raymond bore it dourly, scarcely moving, lying there as if he had put up the shutters and bars and was prepared to sit out the winter if necessary. But Daniel took it badly. He felt that he had been compelled to take part in a dreadful game, under terrifying rules, where the least infringement met with death. And then, when he was going well, he had been swept back to the start. Now he must begin again. Only this time it would be harder. There was no hope of moving before dawn. They had many hours to wait for that. Second by second, as each hour added fresh snow to the face their chances were slipping away. As he lay there listening to the storm he knew that he was present, watching and waiting, at the gradual extinguishing of life.

In all his life he'd never known anything like this. He had never even imagined anything like this.

Now he realized that the worst of life had always been like this. That always it must be like this for someone, somewhere. And perhaps the time had come for him to suffer what all men must have suffered since the beginning.

Imperceptibly in the darkness his lips moved through petitions he had used since childhood. But all the time he knew that if he opened his eyes he would see the tent looming in front of his face. That he had only to lift his fingers a few inches to feel the ice thickening on the fabric.

For the wind moved constantly. The little insistent sounds began again. The creak of frozen fabric, the soft scurrying patter of snow, like children late at night, demanding, demanding, until he came up wearily to the question they had both avoided.

'What sort of chance do we have?'

'Every chance,' said Raymond swiftly.

'I would prefer to know what you think.'

Raymond hesitated. He was no longer sure about himself. He'd fainted again, though he hadn't told Daniel. Another day and night at the glacis might very well finish them. Yet, even if they made a start at dawn the next day, they would have no chance of reaching the summit without another bivouac on the face. They had to survive at least another forty hours, if not more, with one meal left and perhaps just enough fuel to cook it. It wasn't enough. Above them were almost five hundred metres of rock and ice that would extend a strong man, climbing protected, in good weather. And Daniel had to face it alone, in appalling conditions, after four days' exposure on the face. Perhaps a man has a right to know where he stands, Raymond thought, so that he may do with dignity whatever has to be done.

But he could not bring himself to say it directly.

'Very well,' he said. 'I am not a religious man, like you. If I were I suppose I would pray.'

He paused. Daniel listened to the soft scurrying of the wind against the fabric. It reminded him of rats – rats in the barn at home.

'Though what you would expect to get from it,' Raymond added bitterly, 'I can't imagine. A fiery chariot would come in handy.'

'I have been praying,' Daniel said with dignity. 'Though I expect nothing. And I hope for no more than you. A change in the weather. Firm ice higher up. Enough strength.'

He thought of her coming over the ridge again alone, stumbling down the scree – the wind piling clouds above the col – yes, between the boulders the little boy had found a frog.

'You're a queer sort of Catholic,' said Raymond.

Daniel saw her coming out from the great boulders – beginning to run clumsily, her hair streaming out – and the child ran towards her – and he ran too, and so they were all running and laughing and calling to one another.

He smiled and shook his head. 'You do not understand,' he said.

'No,' agreed Raymond. 'I understand only the tangible things that happen. The rock I stand on. The things that threaten to dislodge me.'

All three of them had met with a stupendous collision of bodies – arms flung out, gasping for breath – and he fell backwards, laughing, and they all collapsed on the grass. . . .

'On the great faces,' Raymond added, 'that's all there is – men, and rock and ice.'

'Does nothing ever shake your certainty of that?' asked Daniel curiously.

'Nothing. Except,' he hesitated, 'oddly enough . . . perhaps . . . sometimes . . . music.'

Daniel was astonished. The idea was so extraordinary. He was astonished.

'Sometimes, I find myself supposing that the music is out there, in infinity, with no beginning and no end . . . as if,' he hesitated again, 'as if someone had brought back just a few moments of something that is going on for ever. It's my fancy, of course.'

That there should be these depths, Daniel thought. Even in the unlikeliest lives.

'It began with something I once heard a long time ago,' Raymond said. 'I've never heard it since. Perhaps I will, one day.'

For a long while Daniel was silent.

'That tune,' he asked eventually. 'How did it go?'

'There was a tune, I suppose,' replied Raymond. 'But nothing I could hum or whistle. It was so complex . . . so intricate. It seemed simply to exist. You know? It simply *was*.'

'Yes,' said Daniel doubtfully. 'I think so. I've heard tunes like that.'

He pulled the hood down over his eyes, drew in the sleeves of the duvet, and hugged his arms across his chest. He huddled close to his companion. The cold was venomous. But that night it had been so hot they made a bed upon the grass and made love there, and drank Calvados and watched the stars. He showed her the Plough and the Little Bear, and Scorpio, with its great red star.

An icy chill settled on his loins. It spread slowly across his back. The floor was hard, but he lay motionless. He was too miserable to move. But in the soft hollow of her belly that night the light had gathered like a luminious pool. Her skin gleaming like limestone in the darkness. He pressed his hand there, uncoiling his fingers in the moist hair, pushing them into the warm wet division of flesh until she reached out and drew him on to her. He felt her breast against his mouth – the salt, sour taste of her – and all night long the child had slept without stirring.

But Raymond did not sleep. He felt no pain, apart from the discomfort of cramp and the ache of stiffened limbs. He was tired, but he couldn't sleep. He lay awake hour after hour, silent and unmoving, lost in a fog of gloomy thoughts that thickened as the night wore on.

Men die every day, he told himself.

But not the men who occupied his mind: they died on the seventeenth of August. André, in silence, surrounded by comrades – poor Guérin, suffering agonies of fear – Maillot, alone, roped to the ledge where they'd been forced to leave him – René Lebadier – even Varaud was dead now: killed in the Pamirs. He alone survived.

He was not a superstitious man. But he had lived all his life in a valley where myths are precious, where old men's tales persist, and are remembered even by those who disbelieve in them. Now the familiar legend flooded back as potently as the names and faces of the men who perished. Alberico. Borgna. The great Ottoz and his companions, caught and swept away. Even Morra, Schiavi's old comrade. All killed on the seventeenth.

One day's as good as another, he thought. Dying or being born.

But this was still the one day above all. He said no prayers. He did not go to mass. But it was his own festival of the dead, and he kept it, just the same.

At length the wind dropped. If the snow still fell, it fell silently. No light of any kind penetrated the icy fabric of the tent. Through the close dark silence he heard the sound of steady breathing, regular and soft.

He's asleep, he thought. And he was glad. For the second time that day a generous pity welled within him. And a profound regret. He has no business here, he thought. A pious, domestic man who went to mass on Sundays with his family – he had no business here. Then he remembered that Daniel chose to climb – that he couldn't be entirely domestic, nor his piety sufficient – that he had *chosen* to put himself at risk in a place where all things were permitted.

We are alike in that, he thought. And yet he has no business here. He has better things to do.

For some time this phrase fixed itself painfully and accusingly in his mind. *He has better things to do.*

But suddenly a thought leaped within him like a revelation, and the phrase vanished, eclipsed in a flash.

He's good on ice!

It was true. Really good. Small . . . light . . . moved carefully. . . .

If the ice was hard, if he had enough strength. . . .

But these were questions that could not be answered now. The consequences of the weather, of the changes of temperature, the possible consolidation of snow and ice, these things marshalled themselves before him like factors in a complex intricate puzzle. And he was too tired to cope with it. His eyes closed. He was close to sleep. Yet his mind hung on to the persistent expectation (more belief than expectation – less belief than hope) that they might still get off.

He lay, quietly for a long time, emptied at last of despair and hope alike, waiting for sleep. And just before it came it seemed to him that he could hear Bach's discordant horns, the *corni di caccia*, blowing faintly through the darkness.

CHAPTER TEN

PAIN WOKE DANIEL. Like a tiny coal glowing and fading in his stomach.

For a few hours he had slept uneasily, twisting from side to side as the pain grew more insistent until a sharper spasm woke him. He groaned and opened his eyes. It was dawn again. The air was thick and foul.

He lay there drowsily for a long time, only half awake, bracing himself whenever the pain flared inside him, engulfed in the malodorous atmosphere. But it was dawn again, like a fact demanding his acknowledgement, and so at last he opened the sleeve and crawled out into the frosty air.

Thick fresh snow covered the glacis. There were no footprints, no marks of any kind. Not a trace of their activity remained. The wall of freezing fog stood exactly as it had twenty-four hours earlier. Nothing had changed.

He relieved himself sluggishly in the snow, shivering as the cold air struck his thighs.

She has always asked what happened, he thought. I do not know. In the beginning we understood nothing. We only wanted to be happy. We could not help wanting that. It was out there in front of us. Like a door on the horizon. Closed, but ours. It would open only to us. It seemed fixed there for ever, as if time had petrified, and we passed together along the road saying to ourselves, 'When we get there it will be grand! it will be marvellous!' But we never got there. Perhaps we never moved at all.

He fastened his climbing breeches and trudged back to the tent.

We felt things happening, he thought, but did not understand them. Growing older. Getting dressed each morning. Taking off our clothes at night. Trying to stay human. Failing mostly.

We have spent our lives, he thought, waiting for something that never happened.

But the pain, at last, was better now. He crouched at the entrance, reached inside and rummaged with one hand in the big sack.

Perhaps this was his disability. This radical dissatisfaction. An infirmity he was born with. To aspire continually. Always to fail.

His fingers groped over the edge of the little flat biscuit tin. He took it out. On the lid, once, had been a picture of a girl in peasant dress, smiling, offering a basket filled with honey cakes. At her ear a swarm of bees curled back to their row of hives in an orchard.

Yet there must be something else. An existence free from dread and self-disgust. Loving. Being loved. In a state of joy before all things. It could not be talked about. It could not be put into words. It was like a possibility that never chanced to happen. An alternative route that no one ever took.

The tin was scratched and battered now. The orchard and the bees were gone. And the girl's face was disfigured. No trace of a smile remained. Except in his memory, at the corner of the scratched mouth, in the mild eyes.

He opened the tin. On top lay a few postcards. Alpine views, of a kind sent home to friends by tourists. The top one caught his eye. He stared at it for a moment (a pretty meadow – soft grasses, larkspur, blue gentian; the great face of the Dru where two of his friends had died, serene as a cathedral) then put the cards aside. He took out his wallet, his passport, and the squirrel badge from Cortina he'd bought for the child. A notebook lay at the bottom of the tin. As he picked it up the empty, unused envelope dropped out from the leaves. He put the cards, his wallet, his passport and the badge back in the tin and laid the envelope on top. It was still clean and fresh, addressed in his small, neat hand, and stamped with a Swiss stamp. He took up the pen from the tin lid and opened the notebook. The blank, white page confronted him. He knew that he had to write something. But he didn't know what to say. For a long time he stared at the empty sheet of paper, nursing his need to write, striving to protect it from the hopelessness of saying anything that mattered any more.

He didn't know what time it was. His watch was broken. It ticked still but the hands were broken off.

So he wrote:

Dawn.
17 August.
N.F. Piz Molino.
In the cave above the great roof.

I cannot write much. It is almost time for us to go. We have been four nights on the face. There was an accident. Raymond is hurt. We met two friends but they are dead now. They died in the storm two days ago. The weather is still very bad. If we get off I shall not climb again. Not like this. Next year. . . .

He was about to tell her about Norway when it struck him. It no longer mattered. How was she to get this? If he got off the face the moment would have passed. His letter, its message of need, the explanations he had hoped to give, would slip into the debris of the past, would lie in the junkyard of events that could not be revoked, nor felt, even, exactly as they were. Not remembering, he would be ashamed.

And if he died. . . .

Either way it no longer mattered. He felt utterly impotent, gripped by events, crushed in the agonizing vice of things happening. He thought of the pitiful bundle of effects that they would send her. In his anguish he shook his head helplessly from side to side. Postcards . . . clothes . . . pegs . . . wedges . . . Strange bits of metal whose names she wouldn't even know. That she should look at them and think – he used these . . . cleaned them . . . kept them carefully. . . .

His heart burst at the thought.

Filled with terror at what was coming, agonized at the emptiness of what had been, he took up the envelope, turning it so that he should no longer see what he had written beneath the stamp, and tore it in pieces. He couldn't scatter them on the snow. At last he thrust them into his pocket and left them there.

But the letter remained. Unfinished. Spoilt. Done with. He could add nothing to it now. Gently he detached it from the book. Yet, as he read it through he realized that the words were too recent, too close to his own need, for him to stifle them completely. The desperate moment of loneliness was there on the page in front of him. He could not ignore it. He could not disown his own dependence.

At last, he thought, I know what it feels like to be myself.

He noticed, low down on the wall at his side, a horizontal flake overlapping the solid rock. He took his wallet out of the tin and removed the photograph and the few francs that remained of his money.

On a strip of cotton sewn into the leather hem she had stitched his name. He gripped it between his thumb and finger. His hand was so cold he couldn't feel it there, but he gripped it and tore it out. He put the photograph and the money back in the tin. Then he folded the letter carefully, slipped it inside the flap of the wallet, and thrust it down into the flake.

It's over, he thought. It's all over now.

He reached inside the sleeve and shook Raymond vigorously.

'Come on,' Daniel shouted. 'Let's get on with it!'

But he kept his face out of the tent so that Raymond should not see him crying.

The snow was very bad. The little cracks and seams he'd found the previous day had disappeared. Again and again, for metres at a time, the fault was choked with rotten snow. In such conditions the small hammers were useless and he had to use the ice axe, chopping with the adze held half an arm's length above his head. The snow collapsed on top of him like thick, wet flour. At first, at each of these obstructions, he was terrified lest he should chop down a solid block that might knock him from his steps. But he learnt quickly to carve the snow in pieces so that most of it passed between him and the rock. Behind the snow was hard ice and for a time he was almost happy, chipping expert nicks for his gloved hands and his crampon points. He worked hard.

Before long he was wet to the skin, yet he did not feel the cold. He kept moving. But it all took time. Almost an hour to reach the saint's niche. Almost as long again to bring up Raymond, who passed out again and had to be held for several minutes. Yet, when he began on the long run-out to the overhanging buttresses, the consequences of delay no longer troubled him. Time did not seem to matter any more.

It's all over now, anyway, he thought. We'll go on, he thought, until we can go no further and then we'll stop.

The past no longer mattered. He was not climbing for tomorrow, or the next day any more. Only for the present, for each move as he made it. And as he moved up the long approach to the buttresses he began an obscure, private celebration of his own technique. He took pains to do all things well. Every blow of the axe, each subtle, shifting pressure of hand or steel point done for its own sake.

Gradually he passed beyond sight of his companion. The mist closed in between them. He was alone. He stopped to listen, but the face was silent. There was no wind, no creak of ropes, nothing. He could see nothing but the mist and the snow-plastered rock.

He listened again. Absolute silence. He looked at the great, grey walls of granite that flanked him as far as he could see – at the little granite knobs, fixed in ice, beneath his fingers, at the cracks and wrinkles seamed with hard ice. He felt the solidity of all objects that offered him resistance, that shut him out from themselves. Nothing in the world would melt to receive him. He was alone.

He climbed on. He never thought how far he had to go to the buttresses. He made each move as it came. The axe swung into the snow, swung back, swung in again, swung back (reversed mechanically in the hand), chipped at the ice, swung back, chipped again. The splinters glowed like fire on his face.

If he fell, he died. He knew that. No one saw him. No one heard him. If he chose to stop now no one would know. But for the moment he chose to climb, climbing unaided, unprotected, climbing alone, climbing for himself, balanced on steel points and fingers, poised and alive because he willed it, and performed it.

At that moment, as he looked upward, he saw a dark mass take shape and thicken behind the mist above his head. Within minutes he had pulled himself up between the icy walls that split the great buttresses. When he was wedged there at the open mouth of the chimney, when he had fixed pegs and clipped in slings, and when he looked down at the two ropes dropping . . . disappearing below the vague grey mass that cut him off from the sight of his companion, from sight of the earth below, from any sight of life, he knew he wasn't ready.

He looked down at the steel points of his crampons gripping the icy walls, and the ropes dropping through the mist, dropping down to where Raymond waited for his call.

'Come on!' he shouted.

He took the red rope into his hands on each side of the karabiner and gripped it firmly.

'Come on! I've got you.'

But when he saw that powerful body dragging itself out of the mist – the grey, drawn face turned up towards him, he was profoundly shocked.

'I'm okay,' Raymond gasped.

He looked dreadful. His lips were colourless, his beard and eyebrows glazed with ice. Ice clung in fragments to the corners of his mouth. Only the eyes lived in a dead face fringed with ice.

'I feel better than I look,' he muttered.

He wedged himself into the chimney below Daniel and sank back against the wall. His head drooped momentarily over his broken arm, but he made an effort and kept it upright.

'Is it very bad? If so . . .' began Daniel.

'No! No! I'm okay. Let's get on with it.'

There was good hard ice in the chimneys and very little snow. They were set deep in the buttresses, one above the other, with a horizontal scoop and a wide platform like an eagle's nest separating them at twenty metres. He stopped there, brought up Raymond and then moved on into the second chimney.

The walls were narrow and enclosing, but he did not find the climbing difficult. He was small and the ice made his progress much less strenuous than it might have been had the rock been clean. He could climb here, as he had hoped, almost entirely on the crampon points, and he went fast. It was dark in the chimney. The walls enveloped him securely. He felt the solid pressure of his body, of his back and legs against the solid rock. He kicked the steel teeth of his boots backwards and forwards accurately, precisely. At every move the good, hard ice secured him.

But all the way he was uneasy. Time had begun again. Time, the nature of the face, Raymond's condition . . . they began to press heavily upon his mind. He became conscious of the dull pain in his hand and mouth. Pain gnawed intermittently inside his stomach. And now the mist was swirling in the upper reaches of the chimney. He raised his head to watch it pouring silently down between the walls. It thinned – hung – re-formed – thinned again, and through it he glimpsed the side walls opening, falling back. He lowered his head, pressed his hands against the wall behind him, raised his body and began again wearily kicking the points into the ice. In a few minutes he reached the top.

He wedged himself uncomfortably across the chimney. A rough projection of rock or ice dug into his back, but he disregarded it and looked out over the edge. As far as he could see, receding in the mist on either side, the great boiler plates of slab that formed the roof of the buttresses debouched into the upper face. Huge. Steep. Sheathed in ice. Broken only here, at the chimney mouth, where the shallow groove of the direttissima began. It was choked with snow.

And he thought, I'm not big enough, or strong enough, or good enough for this.

He knew that somehow or other he had to get out of the chimney and into some kind of stance in the groove above. But he couldn't see how to do it without aid. The pressure in his back began to hurt. He put both hands on the wall, raised his body slightly, and looked down.

It was Jaro's peg.

They had got this far, at least.

He thought of Jaro driving in that peg, and knew, instantaneously, that there must be another piton above him in the groove. It made all the difference. Unhurriedly now, he clipped an étrier to the peg, reversed his position cautiously, climbed up and, with one boot braced on the wall behind him, swung his axe into the snow.

He found the piton at the second blow.

Raymond arrived just as the first flakes of snow began to fall.

'We're going well,' he said.

He looked like death. Even in the chimney, with his body weight supported by the walls, he had taken almost an hour to make less than forty metres. Yet he fought to get into the étriers. Then he squatted, eyes closed, his head thrown back. One by one the snowflakes settled on his face. His sound arm hung down against the rock.

Daniel looked at him and thought of the hundred metre corner somewhere in the mist above their heads.

'If it's bad we could stop here – or go down to the ledge....'

'No!' said Raymond sharply.

His eyes opened. He shook the snow from his face. If they stopped now, they might stop for good. He knew that.

'No!' he repeated. 'We must go on.'

'But can you make it?'

'Yes!' said Raymond. 'I can make it. We must go on.'

As Daniel turned to begin the next pitch the mist swirled aside and for a few seconds over a hundred metres of the face was visible. Daniel saw great, grey walls curving backwards to infinity, and the direttissima like a long white ribbon, glittering with points of ice. But he could not see the corner. He did not know what time it was. He could not tell how many hours of daylight remained. There was no way of telling.

All that could be known for certain was revealed in these few seconds. The corner, and the bivouac at its foot, was hours away. The upper face began with a pitch of the sixth grade, and between this pitch and the corner there were no caves, or holes, or ledges, or any kind of shelter where they might spend the night. Then the mist rolled back again. But it was enough. In those few seconds Daniel finally understood the only terms on which he could expect to live.

Three metres up the pitch of six he fell for the first time. Jaro's peg, and what was left of Raymond's strength, held him. He had expected it. The whole section looked rotten.

'I don't like this,' he shouted. 'I'm putting on a runner.'

Even as he spoke the words he knew –

I'm going to fall – he won't hold me – he can't hold me –

'I've got you!' Raymond shouted.

At first he thought he'd broken his elbow. A most terrible pain flashed along his arm. Without thinking, without caring for the pain, he fought desperately to get back on the rock, fought to get up into the groove again, but when he reached the point from which he'd fallen he realized that the whole of his lower arm, from his elbow to his fingertips, was numb. He could feel nothing. His leg began to smart. He looked down. His red Cortina stocking was torn from the ankle to halfway up his calf. Blood oozed from the wound, mingling with scraps of wool. He looked up into the mist, staring up at the corner he couldn't see, and looked down again at Raymond.

'What's the point?' he said, simply.

'Look!' said Raymond. 'Just concentrate on this pitch. That's all.'

'That isn't all,' said Daniel.

'It is!' Raymond said, fiercely. 'Never mind what's up there. What you've got to think about is what's in front of you. Just the next few moves.'

Daniel saw the fierce, desperate intensity of the eyes that glared up at him from that grey, snow-plastered face. He turned back silently to the rock.

Ordinarily he might have climbed the groove by wedging or bridging, perhaps, with his hands jammed in the crack, or even by laying back against the sharp edge. But it was packed with blocks of half-consolidated, half-frozen snow, solid only in patches and held in place by weight alone like a wall of uncemented bricks. It was no more than a shaft of rubble. When he prodded it with his ice axe a strip two metres long collapsed in chunks the size of fishbowls and crashed down past the chimney.

'For Christ's sake,' yelled Raymond.

He climbed past the rotten section bridged on the icy, outer edges of the groove with his weight so badly distributed that at every move he thought he must come off. After a few metres he was so frightened that he made a desperate step across the groove and climbed up on to the slabs above the buttresses. He rested there, poised on the four front points, his hands on the hammer heads, each pick piercing the ice.

On rock as steep and featureless as this the sensation of exposure is fearful. The ice he stood on was little more than a thick verglas laid down on the smooth surface of the slab. He could see no chance of putting in a peg here, nor any likelihood of a peg until he reached the junction with the vertical face. He peered up into the mist. He tried despairingly to visualize what he'd seen during the few seconds when the mist had parted. He guessed that the slabs must go on for at least thirty metres. The thought of it appalled him. There was no alternative. He knew that if he stayed poised like this for much longer he'd start shaking. He'd come off.

The thing to do, he told himself, is to keep moving. But he couldn't bring himself to move.

Balance climbing, he told himself – three points of contact with ice, but moving all the time. Flow up it, he told himself.

'Keep moving!' Raymond shouted suddenly. 'If you keep moving you'll be all right.'

Silently, Daniel said a prayer. He disengaged his right boot, raised it, kicked the points into the ice, raised his left arm still clutching the hammer head, dug the pick into the ice and stepped up. He kept moving.

But the terrible exposure, the fearful insecurity of moving over such a surface at such an angle, was overpowering. After seven or eight metres his nerve had worn down to the point of failure.

He stopped.

He peered over his right shoulder, over the edge of the slab, into the groove at his side. It looked dreadful. But higher up, slightly above the level of his head and in the centre of the groove, he caught sight of a thin strip of red against the snow. And all around it there was a curious depression in the surface, like the hollow in the snow above a concealed crevasse.

He stared at it intently: thick as a cord – and bent – like a strip of perlon....

'Christ!' he said aloud. 'It's a sling!'

He jerked the pick out of the ice so suddenly he almost toppled backwards, recovered, grasped the north wall hammer by its spike, and slowly, without bending sideways, keeping all his weight above the crampon points, stretched it towards the sling.

It wouldn't reach.

He began to lean. His right boot clattered off the ice. He swung fractionally, checked himself with his left hand straining down on the other hammer, and drew back.

'Christ!' he muttered.

He bent his head forward against the ice. He was sweating.

'What the hell are you pissing about at?' yelled Raymond.

Sweat froze on Daniel's face. He knew he would begin to shake at any second. He was terrified.

For Christ's sake! he pleaded with himself. For Christ's sake!

But he didn't shake. Slowly, with extreme caution, he traversed upward to the very edge of the slab, paused, lowered his right leg, and with the ankle fully flexed drove all ten points into the ice that lined the side of the groove. He hooked the sling towards him with the tip of the hammer.

It jerked – and held. He put his weight, gently ... gently....

Still it held.

Cautiously he stepped across on to the hollow snow bed in the centre of the groove and, with one hammer hooked in the sling, chipped delicately at the snow around it with the other.

He took a full minute to uncover the wedge that Jaro had placed in the crack. And when he found it he knew there must be other wedges. He clipped into the sling.

'Look out for yourself,' he shouted. 'I'm going to clear this snow!'

Then, leaning back on the sling, with feet braced firmly against the unstable slope of the snow hollow, and fearful of the worst, he swung the adze up and attacked the snow. It splintered and crashed past him in frozen lumps. The splinters stung his face. Showers of snow filled his mouth and eyes, and he shouted exultantly, as he drove the axe: 'We're not bloody done for yet!'

There were wedges all the way up to the main wall.

But the wind rose again as he started on the wall, driving flurries against the face. And there were no more pegs or wedges. Only hard ice in the crack, ice coating the little holds at the edge of the wall. And he went more and more slowly, struggling against the ice, and the wind, and the cold, heavy weariness that was spreading along his arms and legs. And all the while the snow fell more heavily, whirling around him as the wind grew worse.

And he thought: we have climbed this far on Jaro's pegs – now he is dead – they must have died somewhere below me.

Now that he had passed the point of their deaths he didn't know how much further he could go on his own.

From time to time he slipped into fantasies of a rescue as he climbed, only to wake sharply and angrily, telling himself that this was all useless. Their friends were dead. No one could help them. They would die alone.

But when, a few minutes later, he found Tomas's red woollen hat he couldn't bring himself to face their deaths. It was caught fast in the crack, fixed on a rock splinter, and frozen in. He freed it with a few blows of the hammer and tried vainly to brush the particles of ice from off the wool.

We will meet at the Masino hut, he told himself. We will have a big party – old Lino, and perhaps Sepp, and maybe even Jean-Louis – and I will give this stupid hat back to him.

And he stowed it away carefully inside his duvet. It was frozen stiff. Its chill struck through him like a lump of ice upon his breast.

He kept going for a bit . . . for a few minutes longer . . . for a few more metres of rock . . . But the sight of that red hat had broken him. The spirit that had sprung up in the groove when he attacked the rotten snow and flickered intermittently for hours since, guttered and went out. At six o'clock, at a point seventy metres above the slabs and still more than a hundred metres from the foot of the corner, he turned and looked down at his companion, slumped in the slings below him.

'I can't go on,' he said.

For a moment Raymond made no reply. He knew that the makeshift bivouac at the foot of the corner was hours away. His face, now, was almost totally concealed behind a mask of snow and ice. As he raised it to study the wall a dozen different considerations passed through his mind. He was expert in extreme situations. He knew that Daniel was far from finished. Neither was *he* finished. Not yet, anyway. He'd passed out once or twice, but he was still going. Still going. On the other hand the light was bad. And it was snowing. And as far as he knew there was nothing that would pass for a bivouac between here and the corner. For a tired man struggling in failing light on steep, ice-covered rock a fall was always likely. And the thought of a fall, somewhere up there on the vertical face, was decisive. No. They could not expect to go much further.

But they could not stop here.

Above his head, and a stride or so away, a jutting lip of rock the width of a boot rose steeply, like a stair-rail, to the left in a diagonal line from the dièdre. It must be the false line taken by Schiavi. At about thirty metres it passed beneath a horizontal scoop and disappeared into the mist. Raymond looked at it. He thought of the Fissure Lépiney on the Aiguille du Peigne.

It was a natural ladder.

'I can't go on,' Daniel repeated. 'I'm sorry.'

'Can't means won't,' said Raymond automatically. He was still studying the fissure.

There was snow in the scoop. It was difficult to see it clearly. It kept shifting in the mist. He stared at it intently. Gradually it came to rest. A substantial patch of white against the grey rock, solid under the drifting mist.

'There's a ledge up there,' he said. 'Look! Up there to the left.'

Daniel bent backwards from the crack and peered up, craning his neck to see the fissure and the ledge. He studied them for a long time, in silence. And

Raymond waited patiently. He knew what had to be done. If they were lucky they might survive another night on that ledge. He would settle for that. And he knew Daniel would settle for it, too.

'Will it go?' asked Daniel suddenly.

'Yes!'

'If you come off you'll make a hell of a pendulum across the wall. . . .'

'I won't come off,' said Raymond.

Daniel shrugged. If he passed out again? Christ! What did it matter anyway?

'Okay,' he said.

At five minutes past six Daniel stepped on to the lip of the fissure, cleared the snow and cut his first step in the ice.

The snow layer wasn't very thick. Although the lip was steep he could have kicked his way straight up the ice, balanced, with his hands pushing sideways against the vertical wall. But Raymond had no crampons. So, at every move, Daniel cleared the snow and chipped a step into the ice. He was forced to cut left-handed, with his arm close to his body, chipping at the ice with cautious flicks of his wrist, terrified of swinging out of balance. Every few metres he stopped to drive a peg behind the lip of the fissure, and clipped in the red rope. He also had to drive the pegs left-handed. He hit at them ineptly, with clumsy lunges of the hammer. Sometimes he missed and struck the wall. All the while the snow fell steadily, filling the steps he'd cut.

It grew darker. The fissure seemed endless. His wrist ached from cutting. His right hand grew numb from contact with the icy wall. But he kept going – cutting – pegging – moving almost in a dream, remembering how he and Denis would climb the stairs at school on the steep smooth strip of wood that ran along the bottom of the banister outside the rail: there was a strip missing at the top – God, what a long step up it needed, and a tug on the rail that you thought might break just then – just at that point: and Denis had become a priest – oh, those depths again . . . those depths in people's lives. . . .

Just before seven o'clock he drew level with the scoop. It was perhaps an arm's length above his head. It had stopped snowing and the wind had almost dropped. From time to time it burst out in little icy gusts, flickering up the powder snow along the whole length of the upper lip. It was bitterly cold. A general gloom obscured the upper face. It was so dark Raymond could only just make out the figure of his companion poised there below the scoop, clipping into a peg, stepping up into a sling. He saw a head poke up, black against the grey snow, and an arm raised, and the axe descend. Then, a split second later, a long despairing cry echoed over the face.

He knew that what he feared most had happened. The ledge was not a ledge at all. It was useless. He saw that Daniel had slumped forward across the edge of the scoop, his head against the snow. He must have dropped his hammer. It was swinging at the end of its loop, knocking against the rock. Raymond heard it – tap – tap – tap. . . . Then it, too, stopped.

For a long time he looked up at the dark shape huddled against the face, willing it to come to life again. But Daniel never moved. And Raymond knew that there was nothing he could do. In different circumstances, with another man he might have raged – threatened – screamed obscenities – anything. . . . But these things were useless here. He knew what Daniel was suffering now: knew, too, that no one could help him.

And so he waited patiently, in silence, for the outcome of the struggle that Daniel had to fight with himself.

Minutes passed and there was no movement. No sign of life. At length he looked up past the dark figure against the patch of snow, up into the gloom where the face and the sky merged blankly into one grey bank of darkening mist. If there's anybody up there, he thought despairingly, for Christ's sake help.

'You must climb,' he called. 'If ever you want to see them again you must climb now. Do you understand? You must climb now!' He heard the sound of his own voice echoing forlornly over the expanse of rock. The phrases merging, fading, dying away across the void. But he went on calling: calling Daniel's name, again and again, sometimes angrily, sometimes with great gentleness, as if he were calling to a child, all the time bending his mind towards the dark, motionless figure, straining his eyes up into the mist, willing him to move again.

'There will be another ledge,' he shouted. 'A good one. I know it. But you must look for it. We're relying on you. We're all relying on you.'

So, at half-past seven, Daniel moved at last. He stood upright in the sling. Raymond watched him step down from the useless sloping shelf and start once more up the lip of the fissure. At length he disappeared into the mist.

There was another ledge. But it took Daniel almost an hour to reach it, and another hour to bring up Raymond, and it was so small and narrow they had to sit wedged together with their legs dangling over the face, and so shelving that only the pegs, planted in the rock behind them, held them and their gear from sliding off. They could not cook. They could not even use the bivouac sack. Instead, they draped it over their bodies to keep out the wind and the snow which drove in at them again. It settled on them like a shroud.

Daniel was near collapse. He seemed only half aware of what was happening, slumped against Raymond, complaining monotonously.

Eventually he stopped. He was silent for so long Raymond thought he was asleep. But suddenly he sat bolt upright. He put both hands on the ledge and made as if to step down into space.

Christ! Raymond flung out his good arm and hauled him back.

'It's the glacier,' said Daniel excitedly. 'It's come up to meet us. Look! There!'

He pointed into the mist and strained forward but was hauled back again.

'For Christ's sake!' cried Raymond.

Daniel stared fixedly into the darkness while Raymond held on to him grimly.

'No,' he said eventually. 'It's not there. I thought it was there.'

He closed his eyes and slumped back against the rock.

Got to get a grip, he told himself. Keep awake. Sing! We're here because we're here because we're here because we're here.

But he felt himself going again . . . slipping away. Trembling, he gripped the edge of rock. In the Albergo Montebello, he thought, the old men will abuse us. He felt Raymond fumbling for something at his side. He thought of the guides, their hard, emphatic voices: 'There is nothing we can do.'

Raymond had found the sling and was knotting it with one hand and his teeth.

CLIMBERS TRAPPED ON KILLER PEAK! That's how it will begin, he thought. Down there. That's how it starts. Reporters in the village. Camera crews. Technicians laying cable. Producers studying diagrams, cursing the weather.

Raymond slipped the knot into a karabiner and felt for the peg behind his back.

On the verandah of the small hotel – he thought of the boy's face at the window – maybe they will fix a telescope. Fifty centimes! Fifty centimes for a look. When the clouds lift all eyes turn to the face. *Viva! Viva la morte! Vive la mort!* Maybe in Münich, he thought, in Chamonix, a handful of men will hear the news. Will pack their gear and come south, remembering what it's like to die.

Raymond leaned across with a karabiner in his hand and groped for the peg at Daniel's side. Then he drew the sling tight through the karabiner, tight over his companion's chest, and back to his own peg.

'There!' he said, with satisfaction. 'That'll do it!'

He put his good arm across Daniel's shoulders and held him securely. *Tous les grands chefs*, thought Daniel sleepily, come quickly. Come for us soon ... for the north wall candidates ... for those swept by avalanche ... struck by lightning ... caught by stonefall in the unprotected couloir ... dying of exposure.... Holy Mary, Mother of God, pray for all that fall....

He was asleep. From time to time he groaned, shifting against Raymond's good arm.

He's dreaming, thought Raymond.

But not of the acrobats: no – he dreamed of a place he'd never seen before, where mountains towered over corries of broom and heather: there were foxes there, and trout under dark stones in the frothy stream; no snow ... no snow ... but soft rain falling in the night on granite ridges which he never climbed. He sat alone on a beach of silver sand ... he buried his legs in the sand ... covered his thighs with a mound of silver sand....

I shall lose this arm at least, thought Raymond.

But Daniel moved in a lane overhung with branches: the quiet trees spread over him on either side, between the shadows the sun glared back in patches from the road, and a small black and white bird darted ahead of him down the lane, swerving silently from side to side in front of him.

If I lose nothing else, Raymond concluded, I shall lose this arm.

But for the moment the only thing that mattered was the ordeal of the night ahead. Reluctantly he fixed his mind upon it: reluctantly, because he was exhausted – because he knew the effort it would cost him – because at this moment he was thinking, maybe this time it will be the end. He would not talk, or sing, or force his thoughts on happier memories. He would bend with the cold. He would let the snow pile up above him. He would shrink to a small hard centre of resistance. And when dawn came round he might still be there.

Hour after hour he sat like that, with his good arm around Daniel's shoulders, drawing his companion's body into his own bulk and strength, enduring the dreadful cold and the icy grip of the darkness. Whether he passed out or not, or slept, he didn't know. His mind wandered back through years of incident: of great faces he had climbed, or nearly died on, of men he'd known or known of – hard men like himself. All the north wall candidates.

All of them had come to this in the end.

Some wore the medal of St. Christopher. Some preferred a rabbit's foot, worn *pour la bonne chance*. Some carried transistor radios, to hear reports of the weather. Some studied the sky for a sign. Some put their trust in protective clothing, in fibre-glass helmets. Some tied intricate knots. Some fought the storm with hammers, with pegs driven deep. Some clung to the face in slings, sitting in étriers. Some sought to prolong life with screws, jammed nuts, expansion bolts, karabiners, channels, golos. Some punched holes in the ice, clawed pockets ringed with blood. Some fought with axes till the shafts snapped. They clutched at the rescue – that never came.

But some survived for a while. Grew middle-aged. Saw their children marry. Lived to take their grandsons up to the huts on Sunday afternoons in summer, to shake hands with the guardian, to point out the routes they'd climbed. Like veterans of the war. The lucky ones, for whom all wounds have healed. So the catastrophes one has survived become things to smile about. And the children never ask, '*Grandpère?* Who died there instead of you?'

But if they did, what would one say? That there, by the Plan there, the great guide Magaud watched his brother dying in the snow – saw three of his friends die, one by one, in the snow – and could do nothing.

It was his fifth night on the face. And he remembered how he'd spent his fifth night on the north face of the Plan, in the bitter knowledge that he'd delayed too long, that they should have descended many hours earlier, that the weather would not break and that now, whatever happened, at first light they must get away, they must get to the Requin. But while he waited on his own strength, they had already shrunk beneath the limit of resistance, had already passed the furthest point from which one can return. He could not have known how close they were to death. And so at dawn he'd led them out, weakened as they were, down through the most savage blizzard he had ever known, through snow waist-deep at times, driving them mercilessly because he still had strength and they had not. And four of them had died.

He heard again the voices calling faintly through the wild shrieking of the storm, felt his own despair and fury rising as he turned back into the wind, trudged back to the sérac, saw the torchlight, the little group of comrades, and Guérin plunging clumsily towards him – 'It's André – he's dying.'

The hours passed. But never for a moment did he loose his grip around Daniel's shoulders until the first, faint bars of light showed out from the face. Then he realized that it was the eighteenth of August at last, and somewhere out there, beyond the mist, the sun was coming up again.

And he relaxed, knowing they had survived, and he fell asleep.

CHAPTER ELEVEN

'LOOK!' said Raymond.

He tried again, patiently but emphatically.

'It's the obvious thing to do,' he said. 'It would save at least seventy metres.'

I'm freezing to death, thought Daniel. He sat in a stupor on the ledge. It was as if he'd sat all night on a block of ice. He had no feelings in his thighs or buttocks. He dug his nails hard into his fingertips and felt no pain. Both his feet seemed dead. When he kicked the toes of his boots together he felt nothing.

'Twenty metres at the most,' said Raymond persuasively. 'A traverse of twenty metres.'

Daniel stared mutely into space. For the first time in three days he could see the spires and turrets of the Zoccone spur across the glacier. He watched them coming and going eerily in the mist. Overhead the sky was leaden. The cloud boiled silently on the glacier a thousand metres down. It coiled like smoke among the rocks.

Les Merveilles du monde sauvage, he thought. Something like that. A thick brown book with a torn spine and heavy covers. And yet, a book of marvels. Marvellous names and pictures. Patagonia – range upon range of desolate spines and stacks. One like an arrowhead – or a spearblade in the cloud.

Must have been Cerro Torre, he thought. Hammered everlastingly. Perhaps the worst place in the world. I'll go there one day, he'd said. . . .

'We could reach the corner in a couple of hours,' Raymond urged. 'And then we're not much more than a hundred and fifty metres from the top.'

You're lying, thought Daniel, sourly.

He looked without enthusiasm at the crack. It began at the ledge on which he sat, and ran upwards across the wall. A thin crack marked by a flimsy line of snow that vanished at the dièdre. There was nothing else.

In childhood, he thought, everything is possible. Even at the other end of the world. Even Cerro Torre and the Towers of Paine. He'd never go there now. And it occurred to him that he'd never really accepted that idea before – that there were places in the world he'd never see. No one had ever asked him. And if they had he would have shrugged and said – Yes, there are places I shall never see – without any sense of being diminished. No one could name those places without, in a sense, making them available. To be born is to inherit any part of the world one chooses. But to realize one will never go there. . . .

Like making a will, he thought. That was something else he hadn't done.

'Twenty metres,' Raymond pleaded. 'Only twenty metres. And it could save us hours.'

He's right, thought Daniel. It was true. A twenty metre traverse into the dièdre (if it existed) would cut the distance to the corner by half. Seventy metres, certainly. And today every hour would count. And every metre. He looked again at the crack. It was perhaps twelve metres to the edge of the wall. Perhaps eight more into the dièdre itself (if Raymond had guessed right). If the crack went that far. . . .

He tried to work it out. Perhaps twelve metres to the edge of the wall. Maybe an hour's work. Ten or twelve pegs, he thought.

'It would do no harm to take a look,' said Raymond. 'It's not far. It wouldn't take much effort.'

But now a hushed, chilly breeze began to blow against them. The wind was rising again. And the mist rose with it, drawn in a sudden up-current of air, rushing against the Zoccone spur opposite, submerging all but the topmost ridge of rock that ran now like a parapet along the length of cloud.

'All right!' said Daniel eventually. 'I'll go.'

But it took an immense effort of will to reach for his equipment, to shift limbs stiffened after hours of cramped, frozen confinement on the tiny ledge – an immense effort even to bring himself to move at all. For some minutes he sat on in silence staring out towards the Zoccone spur. He saw the cloud massing behind the long parapet of rock; a long grey line of men, he thought, weary, frightened like himself, waiting to begin the dawn attack.

'What time is it?' he asked.

'Just before six o'clock.'

'I'll go at six.'

'At six, then.'

A few moments later, as if in answer to a score of whistles blown along the line, the grey regiment rose over the parapet and rolled slowly towards the face.

'It's six now,' said Raymond.

Daniel reached for his hammer. And though he'd grown accustomed to privations, though nothing came more readily now than this daily struggle for survival, for him to leave that tiny, icy ledge called for the utmost act of courage. It was like stepping off the edge of the word. Advancing into a swaying, tottering, lurching universe of creaking ropes, and icy metal things that clicked and clattered between frozen fingers, in which the last vestiges of sensitive touch were all but deadened by the gloves he wore. Movement was a frantic, hampered scuffle: fumbling to get boots into the nylon loops, treading the air like loose sand, hanging from stiffened limbs that ached under the load, clinging with one arm to the present, reaching for the next moment with the other, gasping the freezing air for breath under the strain.

And all the while the mist closed in around him. Gradually Raymond's figure diminished to a vague concentration of the cloud, and Daniel began to fear lest, when he reached the edge of the wall, he should not be able to see into the diédre. And then a new fear struck him. A short horizontal traverse on pegs was one thing. But suppose the crack took a steep upward climb to the dièdre? It might take fifty metres to get there, for all he knew. He stopped for a few moments and rested, his body swaying in the tapes. He pressed his head against the gloved hands clutching the karabiner.

'Oh, God!' he muttered. 'Please don't let it be like that.'

The thought of soloing a pitch like that without direct aid from the rope appalled him. Not because it was impossible. It could be done. The *grands chefs* could climb like that. He thought of Bonatti, alone on the south-west pillar: of Barbier – all three north faces of the Tre Cima. It called for strength, speed, precision – and a cold, clear knowledge of oneself.

But he was lucky. The crack led straight to the dièdre. As he moved round the edge of the rock he saw a thin seam bisecting the stone, and the snow-choked line of the fault lying like a shadow down the intersection of the grey, opposing walls.

Then a bird flew out from the face. A bird!

Still shaken he watched it go. Into the wind it flew, slower and slower . . . until it hung there, poised, the forward thrust of its wings matching the wind exactly – then it turned in a right, banking curve, and began to go up in the air, circling without effort on the updraught.

He clung with one hand to the karabiner and swung round to watch it climb. In summer larks went up like that at his feet – went up from little cups of grass. He bent all his heart and mind upon the climbing bird, followed it to where it hung for a moment – rolled sideways – then plunged down and disappeared.

The mist closed in behind it. But its passing seemed to leave a gap across the sky – an opening through which he saw dimensions of a larger world. It was a visionary moment. Something scarcely grasped. The acrobats of his childhood were still the same (secure, guiltless, they flew like birds between the bars). But his life lay in the encircling world beyond. It could not stop here, not at his fingertips, not at the boundaries of his nerves: it must flow as far as his eye could see, range as freely as his mind, rejoice in everything. . . .

Perhaps that is why we have been reduced like this, he thought. Deprived of those we love – stripped of all certainty – of grace – of God even – so that we may learn what it is to be ourselves. . . .

All this flashed upon him as the bird plunged out of sight. It lasted no more than moments. Then the hard, objective world came back at him through the mist. Rock, and ice, and snow.

For a moment everything had been revealed. Now it was gone. And what it was, he didn't know.

His thigh was hurting him. His wrist ached from gripping the karabiner. He became aware of a strange sound, thin and harsh, like the cry of an animal, dispersing over the huge expanse of rock. It was the sound of his own name.

He shuddered. It was bitterly cold.

'I'm here!' he shouted. 'It's all right. It'll go.'

He unclipped another peg with cold, reluctant fingers, stretched out, swaying in the loops, to place it and reached down for his hammer.

The traverse saved them over seventy metres. But it took them two hours to climb the remaining sixty metres to the corner.

A few metres above the traverse the angle of the fault fell back a little. It was still steep. But it sloped sufficiently for the falling snow to settle and offered an unstable lodging to whatever debris crashed down from the great corner. Ordinarily it would have been a difficult climb on good rock, with more or less ice according to conditions. But the huge avalanche three days earlier, and many hours of storm, had so affected the fault at this point that the whole character of the passage was transformed. The dièdre was no longer a roughly V-shaped corner, but a kind of gutter, like a steep scree gully, jammed with enormous blocks – whether of old snow, or ice, or rock, it was impossible to say since all were overlaid with fresh, or frozen, or partly frozen snow.

They kept close together, separated by no more than a few metres of rope at a time. Every three or four metres Daniel stopped, braced himself as best he could, and kept the rope tight enough to hold Raymond upright as he followed each step or handhold. For Daniel there could be no protection. The whole passage was unjustifiable. There was no technique to offer security in conditions such as these. The stability of the great blocks was always uncertain. The depth and texture of the snowcrust varied at each step. Each movement was hazardous and had to be rehearsed, its particular nature anticipated, probed with the axe – gently at first, then gingerly with the boot – while the steel pick or spike quivered as Daniel pressed it hard against the snow, held his breath and shifted his weight into the move.

There were terrifying moments when his foot dropped suddenly, only to be checked by something lower down beneath the snow. And in the split second of panic between anticipation and relief he felt such a clutch of terror that each new movement left him progressively less able to withstand the shock of fear, while each firm foothold became a little island of security that he could scarcely bring himself to relinquish. So he alternated continuously between terror and relief. It was like a strange pathological obsession, or a nightmare in which the solid ground gives way at every step. He was climbing at the extreme edge of self-control, continually, muttering piteous little prayers under his breath.

Eventually he stopped altogether. He turned to Raymond, grey and frozen-faced a few metres below.

'I think we should turn back,' he said gravely.

'We can't turn back,' said Raymond.

Daniel stared at him for a long moment. Then he raised his axe in an odd gesture of submission and turned back to the snow. Alarmed, Raymond watched him go. He won't get up, he thought.

But Daniel continued doggedly to hack a way up through the gully. Every few metres he stopped, made a stance and kept the rope tight for his companion. For a long time he said nothing. He seemed to have forgotten his anxiety over the condition of the snow. Then, suddenly, he began to complain of his feet. Each time Raymond came up to a stance, Daniel looked at him out of anxious eyes. His voice was frightened.

'I can't feel anything,' he said. 'I'm sure they're freezing. . . .'

It was possible, thought Raymond. A bivouac in the open, sitting on icy rock, knees bent. . . .

'Stamp them!' he said. 'Keep the blood moving!'

Whether or not Daniel's feet were frozen was of small importance beside his fear. That was what worried Raymond. Daniel was utterly convinced.

'I can feel them freezing,' he insisted.

'Wriggle your toes,' said Raymond.

He did so. But he kept forgetting. It was as if, in the grim concentration of the climb he could only think of one thing at a time, and he kept discovering that he was not wriggling his toes. Then it occurred to him that if they were frozen perhaps he wouldn't be able to tell whether he was wriggling them or not. This worried him more and more. Again he stopped and turned questioningly to Raymond.

'If I turned back,' he asked, 'what would you do?'

'I'd have to go on alone.' Raymond tried to keep the alarm out of his voice.

Daniel said nothing. He raised his axe once more in the gesture of acquiescence and began again up the gully. After a few minutes he stopped in a narrow place, between a huge block and the back of the dièdre, crouched, took off his outer windproof gloves and began to pull at the laces of his boot. Raymond thought he meant to slacken the straps of his crampons. But Daniel removed the crampon altogether and started to unlace his boot.

'No!' screamed Raymond. 'No! No!'

He scrambled frantically up the few metres of steep snow, stabbing desperate handholds with the pick of his hammer. When he came up just below the stance Daniel had removed one boot and was beginning on the other. His crampons, the boots and his gloves were piled precariously at the very edge of the snowslope.

'Got to rub them,' said Daniel calmly. 'They're freezing.'

Aghast at what he saw Raymond tried, none the less, to control his voice. 'No!' he said hurriedly. 'Not here!'

In his anxiety he made an involuntary movement of his broken arm to safeguard the equipment and cried aloud at the sudden pain. Daniel must have thought him about to fall for he made a quick grab at the arm which held the hammer. His hand struck against the discarded boot, dislodging the gloves, which toppled on to Raymond's shoulder, rested there for a moment while he stared at them despairingly, then slid off into space.

Daniel watched them tumbling down the snow.

'Christ!' he said. 'Oh, God!'

Ten minutes later they climbed out of the gully and stopped to rest in the little snow basin at the foot of the great corner. They were less than two hundred metres from the summit. Daniel peeled off his sodden, woollen gloves. He had to bite at the wool and drag them off between his teeth. His fingers were white and violet and numb. He raised them to his mouth. They had the touch of wax against his lips. He had forgotten about his feet. He sat miserably sucking his fingers one by one, too dazed to think of anything. But Raymond worked swiftly, rummaging in the big sack with one hand, pulling out the stove, the last bar of food, and all the spare socks he could find.

'Put these on,' he said.

Daniel stared uncomprehendingly at the red Cortina stockings.

'On your arms!' said Raymond.

He lit the stove and placed it between Daniel's knees, with a pan of snow on top.

'Look after this,' he said. 'Warm your hands. Make sure you don't burn them.'

Daniel did as he was told.

'You'll be all right,' said Raymond, thinking – he's *got* to get to the top – somehow he *must* get to the top.

And he sat wearily on the big sack and fumbled inside his duvet for the packet of Celtique.

Ultimately, he thought, it is the small disasters that destroy us.

He had one cigarette left. He lit it and surveyed the dièdre. It rose directly above a little ramp of frozen snow which inclined steeply from the basin where they were resting.

He looked up, and up ... had to bend his head right back to see the top. Mist hung at the far end of it, shifting continually between the steep, grim walls. Even in the dismal light he could see the pale glint of ice in the crack, and thin patches of verglas, like wet stains on the walls. The great corner. Most of it vertical, or overhanging. And a hundred metres high.

Forgetting the loss of Daniel's gloves, forgetting his own injuries, he smoked and gazed, totally absorbed, enacting in his mind the moves that must have carried the Italians so many years before. Each man silent, intimidated, and those tremendous walls streaming with water.... After three days on the face one would not be cheered by such a sight. He imagined Schiavi on the long overhanging layback at the top. Gripped, sweating, his strength going, praying for a place to rest, finding nothing, never stopping, feet pushing, hands crossing in the crack, hauling on the fingers, gasping 'fight it! fight it!' every overhanging metre of the way until the top. Now three of them were dead. And Schiavi finished. Only the corner remained – huge, empty, streaked with ice. Just as they had found it years earlier, offering now the same grim struggle it had offered then.

Raymond saw it all. He felt a profound respect for them, for the dead Italians. For all the north wall candidates he felt a profound respect. And he was glad he'd never married, or served tourists in a small hotel, or kept a shop. Despite all the deaths, despite everything, he was glad he was as he was. Grateful. He looked up in wonder at the great pitch, and wished desperately that he could lead it now.

Daniel sat with his back to the wind, his hands curled around the stove. If he raised his hand the flame wavered, its noise faltered. At school they had always been hungry. In the spring, sometimes, he used to go with Denis to the monks' garden after supper and eat the radishes which grew there. He'd never confessed it. He used to think that stealing was taking something to offend Our Lord, and he would never have done that deliberately. So no one had ever known. And that was strange because Brother Michael kept the garden. He must have known. He must have known and said nothing. He thought of Brother Michael leading the crocodile of little boys on Sunday afternoons in summer ... along the Rue Michelet ... the Jardin des Allées ... down the steep steps by the Church of the Sacred Heart, his soutane swishing over the cobbles of the Place Kléber, where the village boys ran alongside him shrieking '*Bonjour madame! Bonjour madame!*' – and Denis stepping out, fists clenched, threatening. . . .

Daniel rocked gently backwards and forwards over the stove. Ah, Denis, Denis. . . .

The stew stuck glutinously to the spoon. Raymond scraped it off against the side of the pan and offered it.

'Take it!' he said.

But Daniel seemed not to notice. He sat without moving, staring straight ahead at the rock.

It was beginning to snow again. Raymond withdrew the pan. It was cooling rapidly in the bitter air. A thin glaze had formed already over the brown surface of the stew. A few flakes of snow settled there. Raymond sheltered it against his body and looked down wearily.

'What's the matter?'

Daniel sat without any movement of the eyes, his face still rigidly to the rock.

'I do not understand you,' said Raymond. 'I don't know what's the matter with you. Whatever it is, you must put it out of your mind.'

He spoke simply, quietly, but with great earnestness.

'We have been lucky,' he said. 'Do you realize that? Very lucky. We are still alive. If we can climb this corner we may get off with our lives. Perhaps there will be amputations. Perhaps I shall lose this arm. Maybe you will lose toes and fingers, I don't know. But we shall have survived. We shall live!'

His voice rose emphatically with the last few words. Then he paused. He looked directly at Daniel.

'It is our duty at least to try to get away,' he said.

He hesitated. Then added, simply, 'I cannot do it without you.'

Daniel kept silent for so long that Raymond gave up hope of a reply. He looked away in despair – then turned, and gripped him with his good hand and shook him vigorously.

'You don't understand,' he said fiercely. 'We must *get away*. We *must* get away.'

But it took him almost half an hour to restore in Daniel the necessary sense of purpose, to induce him to eat, to make preparations, to study the corner. And even though he listened carefully to everything his companion said, he said nothing himself but stood nodding briefly – not looking at the corner but staring down at the snow, stroking the butt of his peg hammer with stiff fingers. Eventually, subdued and silent, his hands encased in the wet woollen gloves again, he kicked his way slowly up the steep ramp of frozen snow towards the towering line of the corner.

'Remember!' Raymond shouted anxiously. 'Think what you're going to do – then go fast!'

If you exist, he prayed, for Christ's sake look after him. Keep him safe.

Somewhere, somehow, there should be something that might offer Daniel the protection he could no longer give.

'Jam whenever you can!' he shouted. 'Keep going!'

Twice within the first few minutes Daniel fell. He fell twice from the same position, the awkward bulge on the short wall at the foot of the corner. He did not fall far. But the second time he landed badly and was so shaken that he slid almost the entire length of the ramp before he could get the long pick of his hammer into the snow. He came to rest at the bottom of the basin, almost at Raymond's feet, grey-faced and gasping. Raymond helped him up again. He was covered with snow. There was blood above the icy fringe of his beard.

'Verglas!' he gasped, '... can't get a grip ... skid straight off the wall.'

'Jam it!' said Raymond.

'Can't feel anything. I just can't feel anything.'

Nevertheless, at the next attempt, he tried to jam it, thrusting both hands deep into the fault, twisting and dragging them until they were wedged tight between the gritty walls of the crack. The jams held.

Slowly he climbed from under the bulge, up on to the slight shoulder above it, where he rested for a moment with his fists still wedged in the crack. There he rested, breathing heavily, conscious of his heart pounding after the strenuous effort, with trickles of fresh blood from the cuts and lacerations drying on his face. Just above him the corner sloped inward slightly for three or four metres, following the line of the shoulder on which he stood, then rose straight as the side of a house to the next stance almost twenty-five metres overhead.

He stared upwards. A long, long way above him the mist seemed to rise and fall constantly, an endless motion of vague comings and goings. He strained his eyes to follow each indefinite eddy, hoping to see the top of the corner. He felt the snow settling on his nose and cheeks, and heard the solemn, melancholy noise the wind makes between great walls – but he could see only an endlessly shifting and merging grey vista of rock and mist. He looked down. The doubled rope fell in twin curves to Raymond thirty metres below, and beyond him was the mist, and beneath the mist ... a thousand metres through the empty air ... the glacier, the valley and the world of men.

Lodged there, in a precarious stance on the sloping shoulder above the bulge, Daniel experienced a strange feeling that he had arrived at last at the crucial place.

As he began his preparations for bringing up Raymond he felt beyond any further doubt or hope that he was going to die. He had known it all his life. He had come face to face with it three days earlier at the very moment his eyes had lit on the line of that black cloud. The initial disbelief and the clutch of panic he had felt then was the shock of recognition. And for three days he had practised the gestures, rehearsed the attitudes and explored the various pretensions with which he might face the termination of a life as commonplace as anybody's life.

Now he knew that nothing was required. No gestures, no attitudes, no pretensions, nothing at all. yet it did not strike him as ironic that in the corner he would be called upon to make a desperate fight for life. It was simply something he had to do. Something that had to be concluded.

He had great difficulty in preparing the belay. He had to clear the crack of ice and place the piton with fingers that seemed to close on nothing. It was not until he saw strips of raw flesh between the tears in his gloves that he realized just how fiercely he had wedged them in the crack. Yet he felt only slight pain. The gloves were dirty and ragged now, and stained with fresh blood. He felt a distant, objective pity for his hands. More than anything he was immensely sorry. As he took in the ropes he felt immensely sorry. He thought of them, but they seemed to merge into one composite figure, child and woman, solid, like something carved in stone. He thought of them all the time, but he kept the ropes tight, and his eyes on Raymond. He felt no alarm. When Raymond arrived Daniel listened placidly to all he had to say, all the while studying the corner, wondering how far he would get before he fell.

Almost certainly he would have fallen had it not been for the pegs. At first he couldn't bring himself to trust them. When he saw the first, at thirty metres, just below the second stance, he didn't believe it was really there. Even when he'd clipped into it he couldn't bring himself to trust it and for several seconds he hesitated, bridging the crack with feet on either wall, before he moved his weight on to the sling. After that, at the worst places, whenever he was in trouble, almost at the point of failure, there was a peg. Below the swing under the overhang at forty metres, under the steep wall that led to the niche, at all the worst places there were pegs. There were four of them on the long overhanging layback at the top. Eventually he came to accept them, wondering neither who had placed them nor how long they had been there, simply clipping into each peg as it came towards him, resting, and leaving it behind him as he passed on his way.

But the condition of his hands worsened steadily. Familiar things he had handled half his life seemed to lose their shape, their hard identifying outlines melting the instant that he touched them. He had to push open the spring-loaded gates in the karabiners with the bottom joints of his fingers. He used his fists like wooden wedges on each jam, wrenching them into friction with the rock to make sure they held. Although they were badly mangled they didn't bleed much now, but the sight of them sickened him. He tried not to look at them. Yet he felt only a little pain.

Undoubtedly it was the pegs that kept him alive. And, as he climbed higher and higher up the great corner (and because he hadn't fallen yet), he began to think in terms of going further. Not of going home, or of getting to the hut. Not for a moment did he cease to feel that he was going to die. Yet he thought he might get further.

When I get to the top, he told himself (the top seemed an appropriate place), I'll sit down.

And so he concentrated all his energies on getting to the top. But it was the pegs that kept him alive. On the long, gruelling layback which concluded the dièdre, even with four pegs to rest at, he suffered a terrible diminution of his strength.

And so he came at last to the twin chimneys, the natural exit from the face. He was utterly exhausted – and so disorientated he was quite unable to choose which line to follow. When Raymond arrived he found Daniel gazing upward in bewilderment.

'I'm not at all sure about this,' he told Raymond. 'I don't like this at all.'

The twin chimneys were really one huge snow gully split through almost its entire length by a narrow projecting buttress. The gully was less than fifty metres long but very steep, much steeper than any roof, with a dangerous, heavily corniced exit. From below it looked vertical.

'We must keep going,' said Raymond.

Daniel remembered that he had to get to the top. Doubtfully, with much grumbling he began up the left-hand branch. For some metres he struggled upwards, slipping at almost every step in fresh powder snow a few centimetres thick that squeaked uneasily and slid down against the old, hardpacked névé underneath.

It's not on, he told himself.

It was hopeless. He came down.

'Try the other,' he muttered.

'The snow'll be just the same . . .' began Raymond.

'Try it anyway,' said Daniel.

It was just the same. He had to cut through the powder and chip steps in the névé. At every blow his face was sprayed with ice. It took a long time and much effort because he was forced to cut left-handed. The fingers of his right hand lacked all sensation. They were dead already. He was clumsy and wasted much of the little strength left to him with crude, inaccurate blows of the adze. He was well aware of it, knew his performance was falling short of what was required, and it worried him. He began to think he might not get to the summit. At every halt Raymond drove him on.

'We must keep going,' he said.

And Daniel knew he must keep going.

When I get to the summit, he told himself, I can let myself go. I can lie down. I can go to sleep.

But he had to get to the summit.

Cutting steps up the gully required an enormous effort. The steady, regular rise and fall of the adze gave way to a jerky, exhausted hacking at the ice. In the intervals between each spasmodic burst of activity he bent double over the axe, sometimes for minutes on end, gasping, so that it took longer and longer to cut each step. He was well aware of what was happening. He knew very well that his feet were freezing. But they were a long way off at the other end of his body. And though the fear of not getting to the top was a constant anxiety, since that was now the only aim he had, yet the malfunction of his body continually interposed itself between his mind and its objective. From time to time he stumbled across a consciousness that seemed not his own, as if it was someone else and not himself absorbed in the glint of the axehead as the yellow shaft flashed at the ice. And then he had to fetch the adze back from the line of little chips on which it had embarked. He was mesmerized by the sight of that jerky arm, no longer under his control, that rose and fell of its own accord. Spasmodically it hacked at the ice. It seemed to practise, in a crude beginner's way, its recent fresh-won separation from the body. Like the twitching limb of something killed. . . .

In his bewildered state he found himself driven back, protesting and frightened, back along the Rue de la Gare to that shop from which, as a child, he half-averted his eyes whenever he passed by. But now its window was alive with snapping, jerking, clicking horrors in glossy plastic and padded leather, rimmed with stainless steel, with steel buckles and bright yellow leather straps that clicked and creaked and wheezed merrily.

'Fight it!' shouted Raymond. 'Keep going!'

Whenever Daniel's progress seemed to falter Raymond drove him on. He, too, was near exhaustion. He had entered once again into the survival area – the territory of the desperate fight for life. But the summit was very close now. And the hut was only two hours beyond the summit. Once at the summit he could take control. He could lead them both down the Voie Normale. He could drag Daniel to the hut. But they must get to the summit. He kept close to Daniel, never more than a few metres behind, and drove him on relentlessly because he had to. Whatever happened they must not stop, they must not sit down. At all costs they must keep going.

Just after two o'clock they arrived at the head of the gully. Under the strong eddies and cross-currents at the top of the face the snow seemed to be cast in all directions, as the wind whirled in from every side, battering the two men with fierce flurries of hail. Daniel halted on the steep ice slope a few metres ahead of Raymond. Immediately above him the cornice jutted out into the gully. It hung in the air like an enormous wave, frozen, its underside jagged and grimy, pitted with craters and blackened by meltwater where it lay up against the rock. A small part of it had collapsed already, leaving a narrow vertical chimney between the frozen snow and the icy wall of the gully.

Raymond looked up at the tons of unsupported snow poised overhead and waited (he was feeling faint again . . . terrified of fainting now) while Daniel cut his way up the back of the gully, until he was directly underneath the cornice with the open mouth of the chimney no more than a metre above his head. There he paused and closed his eyes for a moment, and gathered himself for the final assault.

When his eyes opened again he experienced a moment of complete lucidity, of absolute detachment. Below him the icy slope of the gully fell away, dropped away to infinity. . . . He looked up. As if for the first time in six days he saw the sky, grey and implacable, like light at the end of a long tunnel, and walls of snow curving backwards towards the summit. Calmly he looked for a place to put the piton.

This, he told himself, will be the last . . . the last one.

He felt no pain from the various cuts and lacerations on his face. His hands no longer hurt at all. His right hand, up to the wrist, was like a block of wood. He could still move the fingers (but stiffly . . . very stiffly), and though they served to steady the peg in the crack he couldn't feel what they held. Twice he struck his hand. He saw the grey, swollen glove sink in under the hammer head. But he felt nothing. Several times he missed the peg altogether and struck the rock.

It took a long time to place the piton. At the last blow the haft of the hammer snapped clean across the line of the steel shank. The head dropped like a stone in the snow. He looked at the piece of wood he held in his hand. *Fabriqué par J.N.* – twelve years he'd carried it. He tossed it away down the gully. He saw it strike the steep slope many metres below and bounce out into the mist.

All around him the snow was falling straight down, softly, in big flakes. He saw the flakes falling but he couldn't feel them. They fell without a sound, straight down, as if the wind had stopped. He felt very tired. He looked down at Raymond and jerked his head towards the broken cornice.

'Almost there,' he said.

Wearily Raymond climbed the steps in the steep slope while Daniel did his best to keep the rope tight. His hands were almost useless. There was blood on the snow, and blood streaked along the rope. The glove that held it was black with blood. When Raymond saw Daniel's hands he opened his mouth to speak, but could say nothing. He only shook his head. Daniel turned in towards the chimney and tried to force his way up between the narrow, icy walls. But he was so weak, and his hands and feet were so crippled that he could make very little progress until Raymond got beneath, painfully, and heaved him up towards the snowfield. He disappeared over the lip of the cornice. Raymond sank back and watched the bloodied rope slithering up after him, sickened.

But Daniel felt no alarm at all. He was thinking of all the saints in coloured lights in the great east window. In red and blue, mostly. Some in a rich yellow. One in deep green. Here at the summit there was no colour other than the grey sky and the colour of the snow falling interminably, snow and sky together. *Tous les grands chefs*. Shepherds, poor woodcarvers, crystal gatherers, hunters of chamois. They were changed now. They wore their incorruptible garments now. Transfigured perpetually they lived in a state of grace before all things. But he knew them all the same. Those grave bearded faces. Melchior Anderegg (still with a coil of rope, he saw) huge and stern, like Moses before the tribes – and in the tree the little one they called *der Gletscherwolf* because of his long loping stride. He looked everywhere for Maquignaz's thin, bandit face. But he couldn't see him anywhere. He'll be there somewhere, he thought, he's bound to be there. . . .

The steep white slope flowed bumpily down towards him, and he floated over it in a dream. But there was still something that held him down, that stopped him veering off to the side. He was glad of that. He had to get to the summit. Yes . . . he'll be there somewhere, he thought; they were all there . . . in the great east window above the altar. And in their midst, enthroned in red and blue, *Notre Dame de la Belle Verrière*, her thin white arms folded around the child. The child wore a heavy head-dress that was familiar. He'd seen it before. He knew it! Was it the child's face staring from the window . . . or his child . . . or was it her face looking out at him? His grandmother's? And was he, then, the child. . . . He didn't know. It no longer mattered. For she sat not looking down at the child but outwards, at all who would look at her, the pale, kind face resolving all complexities. Above her head, with outstretched wings, rose the lark in the song his grandmother sang, going up . . . up . . . in the morning, with the dew all on its breast.

If this is the end of everything, he thought . . . if there is nothing more than this. . . .

He felt enormously relieved. To know, he thought, to *know*, after all that has happened to us. . . .

He was weightless now. He felt nothing. It was all so effortless. He seemed to stand aside from his body. His legs, below the knees, had disappeared altogether, but there was still something that held him down, that anchored him, that kept him at the level of the snow. And he was angry. He wanted to be off. He became aware of the ice axe rising and falling. He noticed the shaft of the ice axe just in front of him. It rose and fell jerkily at the end of his arm, driving into the snow, and he decided that it was the ice axe that kept him down. If he let go of it he would float away. But he couldn't release it. He couldn't open his fingers. His eyes filled with tears. He was overcome with desolation. Then he remembered that he had to get to the summit.

So he plunged on up the slope. The shaft of the axe rose and fell irregularly. He saw it driving into the snow, but he couldn't hear it. His ears seemed to be stuffed with cotton wool, behind which a ponderous, rapid thumping blotted out all other sounds. He couldn't even hear the song about the lark. But he could still see it, soaring up above familiar fields, hanging above the pine woods. . . . All at once he smelt the strong scent of resin from the deep bed of crushed cones and needles at his feet. And he felt an enormous happiness welling up . . . like the lark, singing like the lark; not the happiness of comradeship, but the astonishing happiness of entering a marvellous new land (oh, ferns . . . butterflies . . . so many things) with that image of the lark in the morning going up . . . up . . . before him into the clean air, leading him as he staggered knee-deep through the wet, sluggish snow, until he neared the crest of the slope where he was met by a fierce wind beating at his face, battering his chest and shoulders, tearing at his clothes, gathering him into it step by step until it embraced him wholly, and then he sighed and closed his eyes and sank down at last into the snow.

All the way up Raymond knew that the slope might avalanche at any second. It was bitterly cold. He heard the wind blowing above him with a harsh, dry sound but he couldn't feel it yet. He scarcely noticed the rope slanting down towards him through the falling snow, dark and solid, quivering like a hawser, drawing him up, safeguarding him at every step. He was exhausted, but his strange will (a kind of cold, controlling centre – and so indifferent it seemed a thing apart) drove him on. He knew he must keep going, and trudged on, thrusting the shaft of the north wall hammer before him like a blind man's staff. Before him was a clumsy stumbling track, as if a large wounded animal had trampled through the thick wet snow. It wound from side to side across the slope.

As he drew nearer the summit the sound of the wind grew louder and more harsh. And behind it he heard another sound, tuneless and spasmodic, rising and falling erratically, coming and going through the wind: it was Daniel singing.

There in the window was the mystery blazing in the midst, with faces of angels all around, and the *grands chefs* singing Jaro's hymn. . . .

Daniel's cracked voice pierced weirdly through the gusts of wind. He sat just below the summit, like a child sitting on a beach, with his legs and thighs buried in the snow. He was belayed to the ice axe and was taking in Raymond's rope. Most of the glove had gone from the right hand. Bits of it remained, scabs of blackened wool stuck to the flesh. The hand itself never left the rope. As he took it in he simply dragged the rope through the clenched, frozen fist, stripping away flesh and wool together at every pull. He lifted a frightful face towards Raymond, looked at him out of one eye – for the other was frozen shut – and grinned.

'We're there!' he said.

His beard and eyebrows were white with frost. Apart from the blackened areas of dried blood the rest of his face was bloodless. White dead skin peeled from his nose and lips. Only the one dark, hollow eye blinked in a dead face.

He should look after that hand, Raymond thought instinctively. He ought to save those bits of skin. Then he realized. It was as if he sensed the north wall candidates of twenty years gathering like ghosts around him in the snow. *C'est lui qui mourra!* they whispered, *c'est lui qui mourra!*

He knew. He knew for certain that, once again, he must suffer another survival, endure another death. He looked with awe and fear at the snow-shrouded figure grinning up at him from the snow.

'It's all over,' it said.

It smiled.

'It's finished!' it said.

'No!' said Raymond, gently. 'No, it's not finished. Not yet. We must get to the hut. We must keep going.'

'Going? I'm not going anywhere. You go!'

'No!' said Raymond. 'We've got to go together.'

'You will have it, won't you? You will have it so.'

Daniel paused. He looked away.

'You frighten me,' he said. 'You know? You and your go – you frighten me. You'd go on for ever if you could.'

He tried to get up but he couldn't. He tried and tried but he couldn't. His legs wouldn't move.

'It's no use,' he gasped. 'You go! I'll wait here. You go!'

Raymond put his good arm under Daniel's shoulders and tried to haul him to his feet. But it was useless. He kept falling down again.

'No use,' he gasped. 'You go!'

Raymond knelt beside him and began to massage his legs with one hand, rubbing and pummelling frantically, gasping for breath in his efforts to get the blood moving again. But it made no difference. After a while Daniel toppled sideways. But Raymond kept on trying. He wouldn't give up. 'Please,' he muttered between breaths, rubbing desperately, 'please – oh, please. . . .'

And he began to weep.

When they arrived they found him still on his knees, rubbing the frozen legs. Daniel's body was almost covered by the silent, still-falling snow. Raymond looked up as they approached.

'I didn't want this to happen,' he said to them. 'I didn't want it to be like this.'

He let them fasten him to the stretcher, but when he saw Jaro and Lino Casaletti unpacking the canvas shroud (kind Lino's face filled with distress – 'poor man,' he was saying, 'poor, poor man') he gave a terrible cry and started up against the straps. Weak though he was they had to hold him while Tomas prepared the hypodermic.

After that he quietened. He called once for Belmonte, the young tiger, but Jean-Louis was fighting his own battle on the Grandes Jorasses. There was no one there from his own country, no one who spoke his language, so he had to tell it in German, clutching at the arm of the man who stood above him (it was Sepp Böhlen, come from Münich) as they jolted over the snow.

'*Ich habe es nicht gewollt*,' he kept saying. '*Ich habe es nicht gewollt.*'

Until he fell asleep.

Throughout the Alps the snow was general. Already it had closed about three Austrians on the icefields of the Eiger. It was closing in for Belmonte (his second night, now, on the Shroud). In the high meadows above Molino it fell as rain, where Luc Couzy and Roland Guiccioli, from Grenoble, were camped close to the Zoccone glacier. For three days they had been hemmed in by the rain. From time to time each man went out, barefooted, standing alone in the wet meadow, wondering at the deserted orange tent across the grass, or staring up at the mist hiding the face. But they could see nothing (and were, perhaps, relieved). Mostly they slept, or talked, or ate a little (for they hadn't much) and waited for the weather to lift.

LIKE WATER AND LIKE WIND

LIKE WATER AND LIKE WIND

a novella by
David Roberts

Myself when young did eagerly frequent
Doctor and Saint, and heard great argument
   About it and about: but evermore
Came out by the same door where in I went

With them the seed of Wisdom did I sow,
And with mine own hand wrought to make it grow;
   And this was all the Harvest that I reaped –
'I came like Water, and like Wind I go.'

EDWARD FITZGERALD
The Rubáiyát of Omar Khayyám of Naisheápúr

Far north in Scythia, beyond the Arimaspians, we come to the 'Ripaean' Mountains and to the district which on account of the ever-falling snow, resembling feathers, is called Pterophorus. This part of the world is accursed by nature and shrouded in thick darkness; it produces nothing else but frost and is the chilly hiding-place of the north wind . . .

Pliny
Natural History, Book IV

Pterophorus, mtn., 9764′, 61°37′30″N.; 153°51′20″W.; at the head of unnamed glaciers feeding Desolation and Tired Pup Creeks. Name found on anonymous miner's 1917 ms. map.

Roth
Glossary of Alaska Place Names

PART ONE
August 1964

CHAPTER ONE

THEY WERE in their fortieth hour of bivouacking – afternoon of the second day – when Ed said, 'Let's go down.'

Victor shifted on the two-foot ledge and stared once more at the vertical ice-filled chimney that blocked out all speculation about the final thousand feet above. 'Now? But—?'

'It's not going to stop.' The snow, indeed, had picked up in the last hour.

'If we go down it's for good.'

'I'm too damned cold. This is getting scary.'

For the hundredth time Victor cursed himself for the decision they had made when they reached the ledge, forty hours before. He had wanted to attack the chimney – the apparent crux of the whole route – that evening. But it was late summer, with a solid six hours of darkness by now, and Ed's fussiness had won the day. Granted, it was a good thing they had spent that hour sorting and hanging the hardware, chipping the ice from their ledge, laying the rope to sit on; for neither of them had bargained for the storm that sneaked in that night from the south, behind the mountain. Yet with a rope fixed on the chimney, they could have prusiked up and bombed for the summit, storm or no storm. Victor was glad now that Ed had wavered first; but that minimal pleasure was dwarfed by the outrage of failure.

'We could come up again,' Ed was saying. 'The plane's not due for a week.'

'You know as well as I do. . . .'

After a while Ed answered. 'Yeah. But this is getting dangerous.'

'We're so close. Just to show those bastards down below—'

'We'd never get up the chimney now.' Ed waved his hand listlessly. 'Look at the rime.'

Three days before, as the week of rain and hurricane winds had at last ended, Victor had roused Ed at base camp for a six a.m. start. Only Arthur, loyal as always, had bothered to walk with them across the mile of frozen névé to the base of the route. Chalmers, still taking codeine for his 'broken' wrist, had not so much as offered a goodbye from his sleeping bag. Victor had heard the man moaning in the night, whether from pain or nightmare he was unsure.

Arthur had pounded them on the back and wished them luck. 'We'll give it a whack, anyway,' Victor promised, turning at once to the fixed ropes. Parting scenes embarrassed him.

By the end of the day, with the weather clearing steadily, they had reclaimed the tiny bivouac tent 2000 feet up, at the end of the highest fixed rope. The tent had been pitched there, on a down-sloping drift, seventeen days earlier by Victor and Arthur. Now it took Ed and himself an hour's digging to excavate the structure. Their sleep that night was cramped and fitful.

The next day had been the best of their climbing lives. On new ground the moment they scrambled above the tent, they were moving before the sun appeared in the cloudless northeast. Ed wanted to pack up the bivvy tent and take it with them, just as, in base camp, he had argued for six days' food rather than four. But Victor talked him into lightness and speed.

The climbing was intricate and devious; the granite seemed most rotten at this height, and every hold had to be cross-examined. The decent angle- and bong-cracks of the first 2000 feet were distant cousins to the bottoming runnels and grooves up here. On the rock they retained their crampons, skipping belays about half the time. The series of ceilings and featureless walls on which Ed had performed his weeks of binocular scholarship kept threatening now to funnel them into a dead-end. Yet the back alley of their route, full of traverses and zigzags, wended its possible way upward.

Down below they could watch the insect forms of their colleagues creep about on timid loops around the colony of tents. It was the finest day of the month, but the lethargy that had settled over base camp seemed to dictate to the others only domestic chores – drying out bags, perhaps, or repitching the tents, or patching the igloo. Victor knew that some of them – Chalmers not least – were waiting only for salvation by airplane, a week hence.

They snacked while belaying, drank but a few sips of lemonade the whole day. By seven p.m. they had found the two-foot ledge beneath the crux chimney, with its vertical snake of ice, a yard wide all the way up to the brow of the known universe. Ed estimated that the day's climbing had covered the equivalent of 25 ropelengths, gaining 1500 vertical feet. If so, they were a mere thousand feet below the top. They had done only one pitch of aid all day; the rest had demanded nerve as much as technique, trust in deceitful knobs and flakes, a crablike scuttling on crumbly slabs, crampon points hooked on crystals of quartz. More than once it had been Victor's drive that had taken them across the dubious patches.

The evening was happy and warm. Victor held the stove on his lap and brewed up tea and soup and more tea. They dissected the wonderful day – better even than Hungabee, Ed agreed. They analyzed the crump spirit that had seized upon the others. They spent an hour scheming against the chimney above them. Ed was for staying in the ice; but Victor thought it was too steep to chop steps in, and that the key would be stemming and bridging. He offered to lead the pitch, and Ed did not demur.

Shifting from one haunch to the other in the middle of the night, Victor opened his eyes; the stars seemed dimmer than before, the darkness murky. Only moments later the gusts of wind began, and then the flakes of snow. Within an hour, full storm.

They spent the whole day in the bivvy sack. 'It's just a flurry, or a series of flurries,' Victor said more than once. They nibbled at gorp and cheese and

Logan bread, and tried to stay warm. With a sinking heart Victor watched the rime ice form and build on the rounded edges of the chimney. The wind was the worst of it: it seemed to find all the apertures in their nylon cave, and sent draughts of chill into the clammy recesses inside their clothing.

They tried to kill the day with talk. Ed delivered soliloquies on gear. 'We should have brought one of those French butane stoves. No gas bottles, no priming. You just turn the thing on.' 'I really don't trust the manila ropes, even if they're five-sixteenths. I trust nylon. I trust the give.' Victor nodded, uninterested.

'Are you going to stay at Hopkins?' he asked, just to change the subject.

'I guess. For another year anyway. I can't hack the dorm-mother bit, though. How about you?'

'The fall?' Victor stretched his stiff limbs. 'I don't know. I haven't thought beyond the expedition. It's not real back there.'

'Working in a climbing store's not real. Not after a few years of it.'

'Spare me that shit,' Victor said, vexed. The hours of uncertainty were merging with his darker fear, of failure. Nothing had worked out since Hungabee.

'Sorry, Lionel.' Ed lapsed into silence.

The whimsical name jolted Victor out of his irritation. He looked over at his friend and felt a pang of nostalgia. But he saw in the blond patchy beard, the ascetic face, not the faint resemblance to Lachenal – it was the similarity of his own looks to Terray's, after all, that had spawned the whimsy of calling each other after the French mountaineering partners, that and, after Hungabee, the sense of a destiny together. Instead he saw Ed as Vera saw him, the shy, frail-looking aristocrat. He wanted to respond in kind, to voice the 'Louis' which would reassert that destiny. But all he said was, 'Let's cook dinner.'

'What do we have? The pork chops?'

The food warmed them slightly, but once he had turned off the stove the drifting flakes in the dusk seemed to victor all the more inescapable.

'Wind's down,' Ed said.

'Yeah. Tomorrow. Just wait.'

There was a long silence. 'Tell me about the trip with Vee last August.'

'I already have.'

'Not in detail.'

Victor sighed. 'What a wash-out. She was paranoid about bears from the first day, even though we never saw one. Then she got all psyched out about the plane not coming. Like our friend Chalmers.' He snorted. 'Here I thought the Brooks Range would be such a picnic after Foraker. I guess I was pretty hard to take, too. I kept going over everything that had screwed up on Foraker. Two fiascos in one summer, Jesus. If you'd been along it would have been different.'

'So why couldn't you just relax and enjoy the scenery?'

'With Vee? There was this range of unclimbed peaks, up the Nigu about twenty miles. Easy stuff, Colorado style, but I thought we could bag a few. Not Vee. "What if the airplane flies over to check while we're gone?" Christ.'

Ed had his wry smile. 'Always got to get somewhere else, don't you?'

'You know me.'

'How are things between you two?'

'I don't know.' Victor refastened his hood. 'I really don't know.'

He slept until the middle of the night when he woke suddenly from a bad dream. He found that he had started to slip off the ledge. His anchor rope had cut off the circulation in his left arm; he had dreamed it was frostbitten. Ed, evidently unable to sleep, was kicking his boots on the rock in a steady rhythm.

The morning was grey and windless. The snow showed no signs of stopping. Victor was alarmed that he could no longer see base camp in the white-out. He felt a surge of anger at Chalmers. He fumbled with the stove, noticing that his hands were clumsier than the day before. He was starting to shiver every now and then, and he could feel Ed shivering beside him.

They kept up the vigil with a minimum of conversation through lunch. Then, a few hours later Ed broke the silence: 'Let's go down.'

Victor kept up the objections, but his heart was not in it. He tried his last debating point. 'Look, Ed, there's no way we can get down to the bivvy tent before dark. One more night here.'

'I don't know if I can take one more night. I didn't sleep at all.'

'So where do we bivouac?'

'I don't know. We've got to move, I think. This is too much like that Frêney Pillar thing. The ones that didn't move died.'

Victor stared once more at the ice-filled chimney. 'I just can't stand the thought of giving up the summit. We're so close.'

'There's no chance now anyway,' Ed said wearily. 'You couldn't get five feet of this ledge in these conditions. Try it.'

'All right.' Victor started to get to his feet. 'We'll go down.'

CHAPTER TWO

IT TOOK THEM two hours to pack up. Except for the strands they had been sitting on, the ropes were frozen into grotesque tangles. Ed worked the goldline back to suppleness with patient strokes of his mittened hands. Victor tried to cram the frost-heavy bivouac sack into the bottom of his pack. A corner had frozen into the ice; when it didn't respond to his tugs, he gave an angry jerk, ripping the seam and leaving a piece of fabric in the ice. 'Take it easy,' Ed said sharply.

At least the hardware had been racked before the storm hit. The slings were stiff with ice, though. One of them had been tied in the middle to shorten it; Victor pried at the recalcitrant knot with his fingers, then with the pick of his axe, until, in disgust, he threw the thing into the void. 'Hey,' Ed said.

'We can't fart around with things that don't work.' But he felt ashamed of his petulance. As on Hungabee, in a situation like this it was he who stormed through difficulties with a Lachenal-like recklessness, Ed who grew methodical, double-checking everything like a man who couldn't see because he'd broken his glasses. At this very moment Ed was coaxing the dented pot inside its nesting lid. Through the heat of his impatience Victor felt a flicker of amusement.

The worst task was putting on their crampons. It was awkward standing on the small ledge to stamp their boots into the springy metal frames; their balance was bad, moreover, from two days of sitting. Victor's straps, too short to begin with, had to be stretched and clawed at to get the crampons on tight. He couldn't manage the job himself, so Ed knelt on the ledge and battled with the frozen leather.

In the first fifty yards Victor realized that the terrain beneath their bivouac ledge was in much worse shape than he had guessed. The rock was coated everywhere with frost feathers that had to be knocked loose before one could use a hold. There was no trace of their crampon marks from two days before, and a thin layer of rime disguised the patches of water-ice they had been able to circumvent on the way up. Once Victor, backing down without a belay, kicked a crampon through the rime and hit ice; his boot bounced off and he nearly fell.

It was alarming how little warmth he seemed to be gaining from the strenuous effort. The wind was up again, or perhaps their ledge had been sheltered from it. It seemed to be getting dark already. His watch was in his pocket – too much trouble to take off a mitten and fish it out.

The route had zigzagged so much that there were no possible rappels at first. Pitches they had moved together on two days before they had to belay carefully now. They leapfrogged downwards, traversing, climbing up short stretches, trying to stay on snow. The details began to confuse Victor. When Ed had joined him on a small platform he said, 'Where the hell are we?'

'We're on route.'

'You sure? It feels like we're too low. If we get into those vertical plates—'

'We're okay.' Ed pointed. 'Remember that prong?'

'No.'

'You used a sling on it on the way up.'

Good old Louis, Victor thought. What an eye for a route. He promised himself patience, but the dark weather in his mind was gathering. A sentence appeared behind his eyes, as if typed on a blank sheet: We could actually die on this thing. He passed an erasing wand over the sentence, but the black words were burnt into the paper.

They crept downwards, but with each pitch it seemed to Victor that they were moving more slowly. As he made his laborious way down the long tunnel of a couloir, hanging at times on the lodged pick of his axe, he cursed the dull, too-short front points of his crampons. The wind was gusting now – a possible sign, Victor thought, of the end of the storm. Meanwhile the sudden blasts of air threatened to wrench him loose from his awkward purchase on the world. Communication with Ed had dwindled to the briefest of belay signals.

He became aware that the grey sky full of storm had appreciably darkened. The watch in his pocket seemed as inaccessible as before. He hurried, nearly slipped again, forced himself to take his time.

Ed was wedged in a narrow fissure between a pillar of granite and a slab of ice. When Victor had joined him, he said, 'I've got two pins in. We can bivouac here.'

'Are you crazy? Standing up?'

'What's the choice?' Ed's voice sounded uncharacteristically listless. 'It's getting to be night.'

'There's hardly room for you here, let alone both of us.' In Victor's mind the phrase ran its repetitious loop: We could die on this thing, and not even have made the summit.

'No worse than that one on Hungabee.'

Victor looked hard at his friend's face. The complacency of the voice had alarmed him, and now he saw it mirrored in a strange sleepy calm about the eyes. Ice had caught in the straggly patches of Ed's beard. Victor tugged at his own with a mitten. 'All right,' he said finally. 'Maybe we can hang our packs and sit on them.'

An hour later it was dark. As he was trying to prop the stove on his pack and fill the reservoir with gas, Victor's feet slipped. His hand, swinging up to grab the anchor rope, knocked the stove off its perch. They heard it clank as it caromed off rock thirty feet below. Victor swore violently.

'It's all right,' Ed said groggily. 'I wasn't thirsty anyway.'

'Of course you are. We need water. Suck some snow. Goddamn it to hell.'

'I'm all right.'

We could die right here, Victor thought. We had it made, just a thousand feet to go, just the chimney and then clear sailing to the summit. We don't deserve this, not after a month full of storms. He cursed his clumsiness, and Chalmers, and the last two years of his life. He closed his eyes and picked at the ice in his hair. Suddenly a particular camp on the Nigu with Vera came to him whole, an image of paradise. Grayling cooking on a scrubwillow fire, Vee picking blueberries in the sunny meadow up the bank. He tried to picture her now jotting down notes in the safe, snug library where she spent each afternoon. If I get past this thing, he promised the djinn of his boyhood luckiness, I'll never take an easy day for granted again.

Ed was shivering. 'Just hang on,' Victor said. 'Get through the night.'

'Once we reach the fixed ropes we're all right.' The voice was slow, with a trace of slurring in it.

'We've got to be more than halfway down to the bivvy tent.'

'Less.'

'Are you sure?' Victor asked, disheartened, for he knew Ed's calculations would be accurate.

'They're probably giving us up for dead.'

'Arthur might come up.'

'Not in the storm. Chalmers will talk everybody out of it.'

'Fucking Chalmers,' Victor muttered. His feet seemed to have gone numb. He tried stepping in place, but it was too crowded. The thought of getting out the bivouac sack and trying to fit it around them was too complicated to take seriously. In his exhaustion he almost fell asleep. A thing like a dream flitted through his mind: he was being made to walk along a seacoast somewhere, but his legs sank into a marshy ooze, and then he was crawling on his knees, his arms buried in mud. . . .

The cold brought him back to reality. Ed was whispering to himself. 'What are you doing?' Victor asked.

'Counting things.'

'What?'

'Nights I've spent in the wilderness. Girls I've gone out with.'

'How many nights.'

'At least a hundred and thirty.'

'How many girls.'

Ed snickered. 'Not as many.'

A little later Victor was jolted out of a stupor by Ed's rummaging through his pack. 'Now what?'

'Getting my water bottle,' Ed said. 'We have to have water.' Victor moved to accommodate the fumbling. 'If we fill it with snow,' he said blandly, 'we can melt it with our body heat. I'll keep it inside my parka.'

Well, Victor thought, it's another way to fill up time. His own thirst was maddening.

Just before morning the snow stopped. 'Look,' said Victor.

'I know.' Ed shivered violently. 'Christ, I'm cold.'

'But it's over. The storm's over, at last.'

'Maybe.'

Because they had hardly unpacked the night before, it required little more than knocking out the anchor pitons to be off. The water bottle yielded only a sip or two apiece of slush. They did not bother to eat.

In the grey dawn light they could see out to the foothills in the northwest, bright with new snow, and even catch a glimpse of the tundra plain beyond, with its nameless braided river snaking westward. But base camp was eclipsed now by the series of sharp buttresses – the 'Dorsal Fins,' Ed had called them early in the expedition – which they found themselves among.

As the morning wore on, Ed's spirits rose steadily. Victor let his friend set up a series of rappel anchors, as he usually did, trusting in Ed's superior mechanical sense. And he gave himself over to the other man's routefinding, too. He felt that he was saving himself, coasting in Ed's wake, in case a new emergency should come. Gradually his own fear ebbed. We'll make it after all, he began to say to himself, just as we did on Hungabee. You can't stop Louis and Lionel.

Ed kept underlining the significance of the change in weather. 'It means they'll be out looking for us. They'll probably go up the fixed ropes and meet us at the bivvy tent, or even higher. If they have any brains, they'll be brewing up hot drinks.' Despite the compulsive talking, Ed's gear-handling remained methodical to an extreme.

Towards mid-afternoon they began to run short of hardware. Ed's over-caution with rappel anchors had depleted their supply almost without either man noticing. 'My brain's going about forty percent,' Ed joked. Victor nodded. The Dorsal Fins seemed more extensive than he had remembered. He was very, very tired, and a mood of vague apprehension was reclaiming his spirits.

Now Ed insisted on down-climbing three pitches it would have been easier to rappel. The afternoon hastened by; the sky kept its steely grey look, but there was no wind. Stopping on a belay ledge, Victor glanced across the glacier. It occurred to him that the rime-plastered pinnacles on the next ridge were beautiful, and with the perception came a stinging sense of loss. So damn close, he thought bitterly, just that chimney and then clear sailing.

'Almost there,' Ed shouted from the lower end of the rope. Victor summoned the energy to retrieve his watch. The hands had stopped at 10:15. He put the watch back in his pocket without winding it.

An hour later they traversed around the last of the Dorsal Fins. Victor's eyes picked out the bivvy tent, covered with snow. Ed said, 'Jesus Christ,' in a low numbed voice.

'What?'

'They haven't even left base camp.'

Victor stared at the distant squares of tent, the tiny lump of the igloo. There were a few short trails plowed out around camp, but none that headed toward the mountain. There were no figures visible. 'They think we're dead,' he said.

'Let's yell for help.'

'No,' Victor said vehemently. A ferocious anger had taken him over. 'Fuck the bastards. We'll do this all on our own.'

'I was counting on them. I was already tasting the soup.'

'Let's get over to the bivvy tent. We can sort it all out there. It's getting dark again.'

It took them more than an hour to get the tent swept off and themselves installed within. Victor spent fifteen minutes alone getting his crampons off. 'At least it's warm,' Ed said at last.

The fury in Victor had not ebbed. 'What are those bastards doing? Playing cards?'

'You know how it is. When you're cosy and it's storming out, you can't believe anybody could be climbing in it.'

'But this is life or death.' He shifted a leg; it seized up with cramp, making him howl as he tried to straighten it.

'How do you feel?' Ed said a little later.

'My throat's burning. I've never been so thirsty.'

'Shall we try the water bottle thing again?'

A couple of hours later they were able to drink about a third of a cup apiece. Victor's anger was unslaked. In a stupefied half-sleep he had visions of going at Chalmers with an ice axe.

The darkness made the bivvy tent claustrophobic. When either man moved, the other had to adjust his own position and remould a pocket of stale air in front of his nose and mouth. Slowly the warmth ebbed away. But in place of the darker, life-giving dread of the previous day. Victor felt, now that only a chain of fixed ropes separated them from the glacier, a petty irritability that magnified each discomfort into a real grievance. The sense of failure gnawed at him. For two years, he thought, everything has screwed up, Ed or no Ed.

Impulsively, he spoke. 'Let's get out of here.'

'Now?' Ed asked. 'In the dark?'

'Let's go on down. We can clip in to the fixed ropes. It's a cinch from here down.'

'What's the hurry?'

'I'm fed up with this mountain. We're not going to sleep tonight. Besides, the thirst is dangerous. The sooner we get water, the better.'

There was a long silence while Ed seemed to go over the logistics of retreat. 'What about all this gear?'

Victor was incredulous. 'Are you kidding? I'm not about to haul down the tent and stuff. Let the bastards come up for it. It's the least they can do.'

Another silence. Victor tried to get a distance on his own impatient rationalizing. But Ed's decision came as a surprise. 'All right.'

'No shit?'

'Yeah. I've had enough, too. We should be able to go down the fixed ropes in the dark.

'All right, Louis, let's move. By noon we'll be drinking the Courvoisier. If Chalmers hasn't finished it off.'

Packing was again a minimal chore. There was the faintest hint of light in the air – no stars in the sky, but a kind of afterglow radiating from the glacier below. It's funny, Victor thought, how it's never truly dark in the mountains. Not dark like in a cave. Once he had his crampons on, he clipped his waist loop into the manila line and started down, a hank of rope wrapped around his left forearm, his axe gripped in his right hand. 'It's easy,' he shouted up. Despite his utter tiredness, it felt good to be moving. At the anchor pin a hundred and twenty feet down he switched to the next rope, yelling up, 'I'm off!'

After three pitches he stopped to adjust a crampon strap. Within minutes he heard the clanking of hardware, but it was only in the last twenty feet above him that he saw Ed dimly outlined against the gloom. 'How's it seem?' he asked.

Ed's voice was neutral. 'It's all right. This is the top of that crack system. Where we decided not to go left.'

Victor laughed. 'If you say so. It could be the New York subway, as far as I'm concerned. Want to go ahead?'

'Sure.'

Victor watched his friend clip in to the rope then cautiously wrap two handfuls around his mitten. The hardware jangled. Ed moved downward into the darkness. Victor waited impatiently, thinking about all the things to drink at base camp. There was a sound of rocks being kicked off below. Vaguely he remembered leading these pitches with Arthur, three weeks before. There had been some scary run-outs on the crumbly rock. How full of hope they had all been then – how even the hardships had had the purposefulness of discovery.

Ed was taking a long time on the pitch. In Victor's head was a tune that had been running through his mind, he realized now, for the last three days. Hurry up, Ed, he said to himself. It was strange that he didn't feel colder. Only the parched burning in the back of his throat. . . . He scooped up a mittenful of snow and put it in his mouth. At last he called out, 'Are you off?' No answer. He yelled again, 'Ed! Are you off?'

He reached down and tugged at the rope: it was loose. So Ed had been off for a while; either Victor had not heard the call, or Ed had forgotten to give one. He gathered up the line in his hand. Something was wrong. The rope was too . . . what? Too *light*. With a growing panic he reeled the fixed rope in. After forty feet he came to the end. He took off his mitten and felt with his fingertips the ragged fibres where the rope had severed. 'Oh, no,' he said out loud. Then he shouted, first timidly, then at the top of his lungs: 'Ed! ED!' He listened. The answer he did not expect did not come.

In the darkness he leaned against the rock, hearing himself groan. 'All right,' he said softly, 'keep it together.' He had to figure out what to do for himself. He still had the climbing rope, coiled on the top of his pack. If only they had stayed roped. But no; likely as not he'd have been pulled off with Ed. That sound of rocks falling: it hadn't been rocks. Was there a chance that—? No, not after 2000 feet.

All the hardware was gone with Ed. So it's clear, he told himself. You sit here and wait till morning, then yell for help. He forced himself to sit down on the ledge. He scrounged an extra karabiner and reinforced his clip-in. But the silence and the solitude were intolerable. He heard the rapid pounding of his heart. I could rappel this pitch single-strand, he thought, leave the rope, and count on fixed ropes the rest of the way. But he couldn't count on them, that was obvious. All it would take was another sharp edge, somewhere below. From two days before, he heard Ed's prophetic words: 'I don't trust the manila . . . I trust nylon. I trust the give.

The urge to keep moving, to cope with the terror by forcing his way down, was powerful. But another part of Victor's mind kept warning, 'What if you go and get killed, too? Then nobody will know what you did.' He stood up. The blood rushed out of his head, dizzying him. All at once Ed's disappearance hit him, in a wave of grief that was like the longing of first-glimpsed love. The years of weekend climbs, the pilgrimage to the Rockies, the triumph of Hungabee, the two of them and his sense of luck – all negated now, made nothing in the arbitrary severing of a strand of five-sixteenth-inch rope.

I could shout now, in the middle of the night, shout for help. He opened his mouth, but no sound would come. An image of Chalmers' face arrived unbidden, deciding for him. With a grim attention to detail, Victor uncoiled the heavy goldline rope, moved along the ledge to the fixed-rope anchor, and tied a bowline through the eyes of both pitons. He flung the other end of the rope out into the darkness, wrapped the line in a Dülfersitz around his body, and started down.

It was morning by the time he unclipped himself from the lowest fixed line, just below the lip of the bergschrund. An hour before, they had seen him from base camp. Now all four of them were making a trail towards him; but they were still a quarter-mile away. Victor felt a ruthless pride that he had got off the mountain before they had been able to help him. He would have preferred to walk in to base camp unobserved; but at least now he could despise them without owing them any gratitude. The last few hours had been the worst. He had been plagued with aural hallucinations: of angelic choral voices tempting him to sleep, of car horns blatting and echoing from the granite walls. The swelling in his throat had given him the fear that he could not breathe freely. His toes were definitely numb. Overlying all had been the terror-filled anticipation of a sudden gift of slack each time he had hung on the fixed ropes.

He faced outward and staggered down the steep snowslope below the bergschrund. On the easy terrain he caught one calf with the crampon on the other foot and nearly fell. Panting, he stood still, then heel-kicked his way carefully downward.

Arthur was closest, a hundred yards away. Victor felt a sudden shyness. But there was Chalmers, just behind, his arm still ostentatious in its sling; and the anger washed away any self-consciousness. The other two were behind Chalmers. The gap closed.

Arthur held him under the shoulders. He shrugged himself loose. 'It's okay,' he said. His voice, scratchy and thin, sounded like another man's. 'We had it. I'm okay, I can stand up by myself.' There was fright in Arthur's eyes, a dull expectant look in Chalmers'. 'I got down by myself,' he lashed out. 'Where were you bastards all this time?'

'Where's Ed?' Arthur asked.

'He's gone. He's dead. The fixed rope broke. Where were you?'

Arthur took him under the shoulders again. 'Oh, Lord,' he said, his voice twisting. 'That's what I was afraid of. First that both of you, then when we saw just one this morning—'

'Do you have any water? I've got to have water.'

A bottle was produced. Victor chugged from it, feeling the pain in his throat surge back into being.

'On the way down?' Arthur persisted. 'How did it happen?'

'On the descent, yes. It just broke.'

'Did you make the top?'

As if hovering far above the glacier, a prehistoric bird observing an inconsequential scene, Victor saw himself nod. No, a closer voice shrilled in his ear: take it back now, while you can. But the anger in him gave his mouth words: 'We bagged it. It was beautiful up there. And we were almost down, and then the fucking rope broke. Last night in the middle of the night.'

There were tears in Arthur's eyes. In Chalmers', the dull look had a trace of pain. The others seemed almost sheepish. 'I can't feel my toes,' Victor said softly.

Chalmers spoke at last. 'Let's get back to camp. We can go out later and look for the body.'

Arthur's voice was charged with emotion. 'Poor Ed. I knew we should have gone out looking. What an incredible thing you guys did. This will be famous.'

CHAPTER THREE

VICTOR KOCH and Ed Briles had met four years before, at the University of Minnesota, only three months after Victor had come to Minneapolis. The drive east with Vera had marked the first time Victor had crossed the border of his home state, Montana, and so the unsettling voyage had been for him full of the unknown. But what was known, certifiable, in his universe was that he could not live without her. If she had to go to graduate school, he would follow. Asking her to marry him had been at first merely a means to an end; he was astonished that she had accepted.

They moved into a cramped apartment in student housing, surrounded by the wails of infants and the drone of TV soap operas through the walls. At the University Victor made a half-hearted start as a history major, getting just enough credits from Montana to put him in the sophomore class. He dropped out in late October to take a job painting the library. That ended in less than a month, with the first snows, and Victor found himself hanging around the apartment drinking beer, the unwatched TV on for 'company.' He fantasized about having a baby, not so much out of a desire for children as because he could think of nothing else that was supposed to happen after marriage. The boredom was like a quagmire. When Vera would come home from an evening class and choose a book about the Renaissance over going to bed early, he would sulk for hours. One day, exasperated, she said, 'Look, Victor, you used to love sports and being outdoors. Why don't you join the outing club?'

He signed up for a beginning-level snowshoe hike. The day began with a 4:00 a.m. departure from the city. The talk in the car, all about stoves and bindings and numbers of miles accomplished on other hikes, profoundly depressed him. There were two women along, both homely, both incessant talkers. On the trail it took Victor a while to get the hang of the bowlegged waddle, but once he had, he could not believe how slowly the group moved, how the people pampered their bodies, stopping to make major surgical operations on incipient blisters, fussing like mothers over liquid intake.

By mid-afternoon Victor was half a mile ahead of everyone else. He stopped at a trail junction and waited for the leader to catch up. The man, a tall, beefy sort, admonished him between panting breaths. 'Say, we'd appreciate it if you'd stick with the group. No chance of getting lost that way, right?'

'Sure.'

'Great stuff, isn't it?'

Victor nodded so as not to offend the man. 'Do you ever, you know, do anything different?'

'How do you mean different?'

'I mean do you just walk through the woods every time?'

The man laughed heartily. 'Too tamc for you? If you want some cheap thrills, we've got a sewering trip next Thursday night. Briles is leading it, and he's one crazy kid.'

The first sight of Ed did not impress him. The sharp-featured face was the type Victor considered 'Eastern,' and the body looked thin and unmuscular. But as they sneaked into the basement of the Neo-Gothic church in St. Paul, Ed spoke with an air of unmistakable authority. 'Okay, if you get scared, don't lose it, just talk to me. It's not really sewers, it's steam tunnels. Let's see if we can hit the garage near Macalester. I almost worked it out last time.'

Hours later, completely disoriented, Victor was astounded to hear Ed say, 'We're near Summit and Fairview right now.'

'How do you know?' he asked.

'You sort of keep making a map in your head. It takes practice.'

Later the group went out for pizza. Victor managed to sit next to Ed. After two beers he got up the nerve to say, 'That was fun. Do you ever go caving?'

'We've done spring-break trips to southern Ohio. It's not all that great unless you're really into it. Muddy and wet.' He tore off a wedge of pizza and gave Victor an appraising look. 'If you liked this, you ought to try climbing.'

Thus the long relationship was born. On his first day at Taylor's Falls, Victor displayed the aptitude that had made all sports easy for him. Thirty feet off the ground, he felt the playground blend of fear and exhilaration that had coursed through his veins in grade school every time he prepared to do his famous front flip off the top of the jungle gym. Driving back from their third outing, the car jammed with beginners, Ed said quietly, 'See? I told you.'

'What?'

'That you'd be a natural. Shit, there's dubs here that in three years haven't gotten to where you're at.'

Victor flushed with embarrassed pride.

'You use your arms too much,' Ed went on. 'And you're too impatient. Sometimes you don't stop and really look at the moves, and so you get hung up. But it'll come.'

On the weekend trips to Devil's Lake Victor encountered the first playground gang whose inner circle he could not crack. Ed, by virtue of some gutsy leads, had worked his way to the fringe of it. But the politics of the élite were defined by the late-afternoon adjournment to Mr Siffler's house, the ram-shackle farm building nearby that the old man – who had taken up climbing at 45 and who now, at 53, was still soloing 5.7's, despite his recent shoulder dislocation – had bought and renovated. As he stood with Ed, contaminated by the outing clubbers they had imported with them, watching the heroes tromp off to the ritual 'beer at Mr. Siffler's,' Victor burned with a passion to belong.

One night he brought Ed home for dinner. Afterwards, snuggled up beside Vera on the sofa, he asked, 'Well? What did you think?'

'He's good-looking, I'll have to admit.'

'I didn't mean that,' Victor said, both vexed and pleased. 'Isn't he an interesting guy?'

'It was a strange evening.'

'Why?' Victor moved a few inches away.

'I've never heard anybody talk so . . . so compulsively about something. Even you. All we talked about all evening was climbing.'

'It's not just climbing, Vee. It's people and getting up your nerve and stuff like that.'

Vera yawned. 'He's so critical.'

'You're not seeing him right.' Victor brooded. 'It's just that Ed's the kind of guy who doesn't take any shit.'

'What I do like is how much happier you seem. You're even drinking less.'

The next day, at lunch with Ed, he fished for the reverse appraisal. It seemed important to Victor that the two of them – his wife and, yes, his best friend – like each other.

'She seems like a good lady,' Ed offered. 'Damn good cook, too. She doesn't seem like the type who'll give you any crap about going climbing.'

'No,' said Victor, disappointed. 'She's too busy.'

'You should see Westerveldt. He has to call home collect the minute he's survived another weekend. Most good climbers aren't married. Or even really involved, as far as I can tell.' Ed smiled quickly. 'Look at me. How did you two meet, anyway?'

Victor launched into a half-hearted account of his past in Missoula, of meeting Vera at a dance, of how different she had seemed from the other women he had had, of her efforts to turn him into a plausible student, of following her career to Minnesota.

'She's older than you, then,' Ed said. Victor nodded. Though he seldom did so, now he allowed his thoughts to wander back to the past, even before Vera, while perfunctorily answering Ed's questions. Up to a certain age – as late as the eleventh grade, he realized – girls had meant nothing to him compared to sports. It was sports he had lived for, because he was good, yes, but mainly because of his mother's mysterious prohibition, when he was only seven, of all rough and boisterous fun. The five years he had disobeyed her had given him, he sensed now, his first firm knowledge of how things worked in the world. His skill at sports depended on the charm of secrecy.

Then, when he was twelve, his mother had finally explained the prohibition, had told him about the single working kidney he had been born with, and that if he ever suffered a sharp blow on the wrong part of the back, he might die. 'Why did you wait so long to tell me?' he had asked; his mother could not explain. From that moment Victor had learned two other basic facts about himself. The kidney was a thing to be ashamed of: his mother was ashamed of it. Like the surreptitious sports, it was a secret that had to be kept. Because it was clear that what he thought of as his 'luck' was somehow only a congenital charm that made him different from others. It explained his skill at sports.

Now, with Ed praising his climbing, he felt a confessional urge. He wanted to share the secret with Ed; it would forge a bond between him and this new friend he admired so much. But the older superstition – that to tell anyone about the kidney would be to dispel the charm of his luck – prevailed.

His mind continued to roam back over the past, while Ed rambled on with outing club gossip. His mother had explained the medical situation to the junior high tennis coach, and Victor had gone out for the team, though without much enthusiasm. But he lived for the illicit weekend games in the park, time she thought he was spending with friends listening to records or watching TV. Brutal games of tackle football on the dead, patchy grass, baseball on the makeshift diamond with the rock-hard infield, netless-hooped basketball on asphalt courts. Five more years of success that depended on secrecy – until, in the eleventh grade, his tennis coach, hearing from another student about one of Victor's spectacular diving catches in the outfield, had rechecked his medical records and, without even informing him, had phoned his mother.

Victor had taken up women as if they were an alternative sport. With his souped-up '49 Chevy, a pint of rum in the glove compartment, in the piney pullouts off the logging roads south of town he found it easy to manoeuver his dates into the back seat, to persuade them to do the things they weren't sure they should. It was his good looks, he thought, his football build, and the cocky air that went with them. But more than that, it was the plain fact that he had no fear of rejection.

Yet the sex itself, undeniably 'fun,' had been less important to him than the looks of envy on his friends' faces the next day in school. It occurred to him now, as he watched Ed talk, how to explain what he had felt then: that in fucking there was no 5.9. When the occasional girl told him that she loved him, his impulse was to say 'Thank you'; he had no idea what she really meant by the trite formula.

He had quit high school and moved out of his mother's house, ignoring her pleas, to seek the clean freedom he had felt only in the gliding flight after a potential triple in centre field, the tackle-shrugging run down the sidelines. Because there seemed more challenge in it, he had started hanging around the University, preying upon college women instead of the too-easy game his own age. It helped, he found, to eavesdrop in the student union, picking up the kind of small talk that allowed him to pass for a collegian. Within weeks he had perfected the disguise of a sophomore economics major. It bewildered him that no one saw through his web of lies. With a bed in an apartment – in lieu of the back seat of his car – he found as many college women succumbing to him as had high school girls.

Then he had met Vera at the dance, and when, after midnight, sitting on his sofa, she had pushed him away, laughing, 'But Victor, I don't even know you yet,' he had felt for the first time in his life the sting of rejection. He drove her back to campus in a tyre-squealing rage. A few days later he had run into her again. She had said, 'Let's go out again, Victor. You fascinate me.'

By the fourth date, with her teasing intelligence she had unravelled his recent imposture. She had had the look in her eyes of knowing so surely, that all his indignant fabrications had collapsed in a single spasm of confession. With his head in his hands, he said miserably, 'How can you even stand to be around me now?'

She took his hand and held it. 'Look, Victor, it's part of why you interest me. You have this intensity, and I know you're smart, and you have a funny kind of talent. Winning all those games and dares in grade school. Look at me.' Shyly Victor raised his head. 'So you've squandered the talent playing this silly game of pretend. But you could be something really good. An actor, maybe.' Victor shook his head. The talent was not really his; it was the old congenital thing, the kidney. 'You'll never know,' she continued, 'unless you go back to school.'

Over the next weeks, with a sense of dread, of watching a bank on which he was standing erode away as the stream cut beneath it, Victor discovered what the business about love meant. The urge for other women vanished. Meekly he underwent Vera's campaign of rehabilitation, acquiring through correspondence courses the high school diploma, starting his laborious voyage as a history major. When Vera got accepted at Minnesota, he knew that he had to hang on to her, and the only way he could think of was to ask her to marry him.

Now, in the warmth of his new friendship, he had a yearning to tell Ed all of this , even the secret life that up till now only Vera had penetrated. But an old caution put a finger to his lips. Drinking his third cup of coffee, he gave Ed only a skeletal version of that past, and indeed, Ed seemed interested in no more.

That summer the two of them spent three weeks in the Needles of South Dakota. By the following September they were climbing as well as all but a handful of the élite at Devil's lake. One day it happened. Digby, who had put up 'Avenger,' and whose 'Limelight' was still unrepeated, turned that Saturday afternoon to Ed and Victor and said casually, 'Why don't you guys pick up a couple of six-packs and come on over to Mr. Siffler's?'

The talk in the old farmhouse, for hours as the golden sunlight streaming through the windows dulled into dusk, rang in Victor's ears like ethereal music. Digby and Axelrod traded stories about rusty piton-eyes breaking off. Axelrod showed everybody how to reach for the hidden hold on 'Isotope.' McCarter bemoaned his difficulties getting the right party together for an expedition to Mount Foraker. Mr. Siffler took off his shirt and showed everyone his shoulder-operation scar.

Back at the University, the club held a special meeting to condemn Ed for his irresponsibility in leaving the beginners to fend for themselves all weekend. Ed listened for a while, then stood up and said, 'Fuck you all. Get somebody else to lead the chubbers. I quit.' Victor jumped up and added, 'Me too.' Outside, they headed straight for the pizza place where, laughing and whooping, they drank themselves into joyous incoherence.

The next July they drove out to the Canadian Rockies. Ed had climbed briefly in Colorado and the Wind Rivers; for Victor it was his first trip to real mountains. They started with guidebook routes around Lake Louise and found them remarkably easy. In a tavern in Banff they managed to join a table of aspirants circled in rapt attention around Jimmy Bryan, the emigré Welshman who had become the arbiter of standards in the Rockies. During a lull, Ed found the nerve to ask, 'What about that face on Hungabee? The one you see from Temple?'

Bryan squinted sharply through the cigarette smoke. 'It's totally daft. Loose as the bejeesus. It's a splendid-looking thing, but some lads from Edmonton went up on it and came back all whimpering and snivelling.' The man paused, scrutinizing Ed. 'You blokes wouldn't be from California?'

They were five days on the route. On the fourth, in marginal weather, a helicopter flew by. Ed and Victor waved; it was only later that they learned that the chopper had been searching for them, that the pilot had never spotted them, that they were subsequently given up for dead. That same day Victor pulled loose a block, fell twenty feet, and landed on his back. He got up and continued the lead, but the pain in his back was in exactly the wrong spot, the place he had been warned about. He pushed grimly through the rest of the day, as the clouds closed back over them, up to the horrible standing bivouac. He was thinking to himself, at last it's run out, all the luck. He decided that, as soon as the crippling pain started, no, as soon as the blood showed up in his urine, he would tell Ed the secret that he had shared with no one since his mother's death, and then insist that his friend try to solo on to save himself. He wondered how bad it was going to be to die that way.

All through the sleepless, dreadfully cold first half of the night he reviewed his childhood. The last clear memory of his father was of the beating that had led to the discovery, the blood for days in his urine, the doctor coming to talk to his mother, her tears and her hysterical screaming at his drunken father, just before he had left for good. Victor had linked the doctor with his father's disappearance; in adulthood he had never visited a doctor. The blood in his urine was logical – when you were hurt there was usually blood, and his father hurt him regularly. The misery of his early years had left him with no particular fear of dying, any more than he would later fear rejection from a woman.

But in the middle of the night, when he had to urinate, the flow was clear, without a trace of blood. At last the dawn came. He climbed in a stupor all day, his back stiff as an old man's; Ed took the hardest leads until, in total blizzard, they stood on the summit. The descent took another day and a half, during which they nearly got swept off a rappel by an avalanche. The weather cleared in the middle of the last night, and by noon the next day they were giggling and napping among the wildflowers in the impossibly green meadows.

In Banff, Bryan was speechless but magnanimous. He invited them up to Robson, but Victor and Ed were flat broke. They cadged contributions from hitchhikers and barely made it back to Minneapolis.

From Hungabee came a sense of shared destiny, bodied forth in plans for a dozen summers, in the private allusions to Terray and Lachenal. But the next June, Ed, who was graduating, was offered a job teaching maths at the

Hopkins school on the condition that he catch up with some education courses over the summer. Victor, deeply disappointed, accepted McCarter's invitation to the Foraker expedition the man had finally put together.

Everything went wrong. A scared pilot landed the men thirty miles from the base of their route. Then he airdropped from 150 feet; losses amounted to forty percent. To Victor's immense impatience, McCarter insisted on a tedious fixing of ropes on low-angled snowslopes. By the time they had run out of food the party had reached their so-called 'Camp V' at only 10,500 feet.

Victor met Vera at the Fairbanks airport. The three-week Brooks Range idyll he had planned went sour. The drab loneliness along the upper Nigu plunged him into an acute depression, while it terrified Vera. She resisted his efforts to clump off toward the unclimbed peaks, seeing no particular virtue in being *there* rather than *here*. She took a gardener's pleasure in the cinquefoil and fireweed and Arctic cotton, and spent hours gathering blueberries. Around the willow-twig campfires she would say, 'Let's really talk, Victor. About us. Something's changed.' But Victor's mind was on the Foraker fiasco. He missed Ed. It was during these weeks that he began, in the core of himself, to link the hunch of his lifelong luckiness with the presence of his friend; without Ed, the charm was broken. Back in Minneapolis Vera seemed to fade once more into her history books. Ed and Victor spent a restorative weekend at Devil's Lake and pledged the next summer to each other.

In February Victor gave Ed a call. 'The outing club's lined up a slide show. Rex Chalmers.'

'On Pterophorus?' Ed asked.

'Yes.'

'I'll be there. Think they'll let us inside the club room?'

Chalmers lived up to his reputation as a poor speaker. He also came across, it seemed to Victor, as cold and arrogant. He freely admitted that he was touring the country just to raise the cash to pay off his helicopter debt from the previous summer. In a bored tone he ticked off the mountain's history, from its 'discovery' by Blakey in 1959, the tracing down of the name to the miner's manuscript map, through the famous photo published in *Piton*, to the first expedition composed of Blakey protégés which, unable to cross Tired Pup Creek, never even saw the mountain. Despite the jaded narration, Ed and Victor sat breathless before the aerial views that flashed on the screen: the legendary upper plug of the mountain, like Devil's Tower in Wyoming but for the ice encrustations, looked as difficult as Blakey had prophesied. A little warmth crept into Chalmers' voice as he described his 1962 expedition, which had gotten nine hundred feet off the glacier on the southeast face; but it was mixed with obvious contempt for the weakness of his teammates.

It was then, Chalmers went on, that the mountain really acquired its status as a prize. When John Richards paired up with the Scot Ian McDougall, everyone guessed that the mountain had met its match; it seemed inconceivable that the pioneering Yosemite wall climber and the man reputed to be the best in the world on ice could fail. With gruff humour Chalmers recounted his bumping into Richards in a supermarket in Anchorage, where the Californian pumped him for information, his own sneaking over to Merrill Field where he called Talkeetna to cancel the pilot and immediately engaged a helicopter. It was Chalmers' hunch that a series of ramps, avoiding the prominent boiler plates, might afford a better route on the north face than the bottoming cracks of the southeast side. Camp was a gloomy, sunless niche on a strange, stagnant glacial tributary, actually depressed in altitude below the main ice stream it had once flowed into. By the end of July Chalmers and Arthur Bowen had reached a point 1500 feet up. The rest of the party, the man implied witheringly, were worthless. It was clear that he had spent the month animated by the fear of success on the opposite side of the mountain, and there was no concealing his glee when he mentioned that Richards and McDougall had turned back a pitch below Chalmers' own high point of the year before, or when he repeated the rumour (which Ed and Victor had already heard) that McDougall had been psyched out from the beginning.

Victor and Ed joined the gaggle of admirers after the show. Chalmers yawned ostentatiously, his eyes seldom fixed on his interrogator, as he answered questions. Victor's own pride kept him silent, but he heard Ed saying, 'Do you plan to go back?'

'Yeah. Maybe.' Chalmers cracked his knuckles.

'The north face again?'

'Probably. Not in July, though. Too icy still.'

'With the same group?'

Chalmers allowed himself a thin smile. 'Hell, no. Bunch of turkeys. Except Bowen, he's all right.'

Victor was surprised, even embarrassed, that Ed kept playing the sycophant. But now Ed said, 'That rime ice looked really shitty. We ran into the same-looking stuff on Hungabee.'

Chalmers' eyes instantly focused. 'You were on Hungabee? That face?'

Ed nodded. 'With Victor here.'

Chalmers picked up his slide trays, and in a way that clearly dismissed the others in the room said, 'Let's go out and get a beer.'

By the end of the evening Ed and Victor were part of the expedition. All spring they rock-climbed obsessively, so that by May they were putting in routes at Devil's Lake on a level with Digby's and Axelrod's best. A weekly correspondence with Chalmers in Denver kept them abreast of the filling out of the team; Bowen would go again, as well as some good young climbers from Salt Lake City. But there were clouds on the horizon. At least two other expeditions were headed for Pterophorus, one a group of relative unknowns from Oregon, the other led by Richards, who had talked some Yosemite Valley cronies into joining him. They were both slotted for early July, both for the southeast face. Chalmers considered jumping the gun on them again, but at last decided August was the only month for the north wall. He was going to head up to Anchorage in mid-July to handle the logistics himself.

Victor and Ed spent an anxious, newsless early summer, climbing every day and spending most of their free time together. It seemed to Victor that Vera had almost ceased to be part of his life, or to be no more than the familiar warmth beside him in bed each night. Yet he had never been happier, except for the gnawing of anticipation.

At last, on 25 July, the letter from Chalmers came:

They're out. Both parties. What stories they have. Richards has had enough, he says, never wants to go back. *Neither of them got more than 1500 feet up*. The Oregon party was established at base camp (our '62 camp) three days before Richards arrived. They had even fixed a few pitches. Get this. Richards ordered them off 'his' route! And the poor buggers obeyed him.

So the Oregon party tried a hopeless line around to the left, sort of the southwest buttress. Got 1000 feet up, but quit when one guy (I think his name was Gervin, or Garman, or something – nobody famous) fucked up a rappel and bought the farm.

Meanwhile Richards, Cowell, and the young hot-shot Richard Bakamjian went for it on the southeast face. You know how Cowell wrote up in his big-deal *AAJ* article how he'd never wear a hard hat? Well, on the first day he got plunked on the shoulder, so he borrowed Bakamjian's helmet and never took it off, day or night. They managed to get five pitches beyond our '62 high point, and then they said the rock got really terrible. Cowell kept saying, 'I don't like this, I don't like it at all.' Finally they bagged it and came down. Bakamjian had not said a word the whole time. They get off the last rappel and Cowell takes a deep breath and says, 'We're lucky to get off this thing alive.' Bakamjian says, 'You guys are chickenshit,' and walks off!

So you two get on up here pronto. We've got a mountain to climb.

CHAPTER FOUR

VICTOR SPRAWLED on the ice-bench that served as seating inside the igloo. Arthur was working at the clumps of ice on his gaiters, while one of the others had a stove going. 'There must be something else to drink,' Victor said. Chalmers picked up a water bottle with his good hand and shook it; a piece of ice rattled inside.

It was warm in the igloo, deliciously so. Not even on the descent from Hungabee had Victor felt so utterly exhausted. A few minutes before, Chalmers had asked for details about the climb, but Arthur, in his fussy, maternal way, had said, 'Later. Let's just get the man warm and comfortable, and look at his feet.'

Victor was grateful now for the chance to remain silent; for, stabbing its way through the fog of his tiredness, a wholly novel sense of alarm was spreading its branches. What have I gone and done? he thought. It's still not too late to change everything; I could pretend I misunderstood Arthur's question. But it was like hesitating to jump onto a train that was pulling out of the station; with each second the gap grew larger. His thoughts turned instead to a more practical realm: what would he have to seem to know, when he did tell the whole story? His mind felt fuzzy, as if he were slightly drunk.

A voice came from the door of the igloo: 'Guess what? Snowing again.'

'Shit,' Chalmers said. 'This place . . .'

'How's your wrist?' Victor asked. He had an instinct that it was Chalmers, if anyone, who could do him harm. Only Chalmers had seemed disappointed by the news of their success. 'Do you think it's broken?'

'I'm pretty sure,' the man said, averting his eyes. 'I tried shovelling with it the other day, and it really swelled up.'

Victor thought: it's not broken, you ass, you washed-up crump, it's just a convenient excuse to keep you out of action. Out loud he said, 'We just missed getting hit by some big chunks of ice up high. Just like the stuff that got you.' Chalmers nodded.

At last Arthur had removed the boots. He was holding Victor's bare feet in his hands. Victor watched himself wiggle his toes; there was still no feeling in them. 'Well?' he asked Arthur.

'There's some frostbite, I'd guess. I don't think it's too bad. You should stay off your feet for a few days. And get lots of liquid.' Arthur unbuttoned his own down jacket and pulled his sweater up, then placed Victor's feet against his stomach. 'See if this helps,' he said, shivering involuntarily.

'You don't have to do that,' Victor said.

'Be quiet.'

In the middle of the operation the nerve endings in his toes sprang all at once out of their slumber. The pain was sharp. Victor twisted on his ensolite seat, moaning. 'Rex,' Arthur said, 'get the codeine, will you?' Chalmers sullenly left the igloo and returned moments later with the medical kit. 'That's a good sign, that pain,' Arthur fussed. 'Here. Take one now and one later.'

Within minutes the codeine spread its dull euphoria through Victor's bloodstream. Arthur kept forcing hot fluids on him, but the pain of swallowing made him reluctant to drink. Chalmers fidgeted morosely on an opposite bench. At last he said, 'I suppose we should go look for the body before this snow covers everything.'

'Can I get you anything else?' Arthur asked.

'I just want to sleep.'

'I'll put you in my tent. Pete can move into the blue one.'

The blue one, Victor thought, with a numbed sense of irony. Not 'Ed's tent', anymore, but, superstitiously, 'the blue one.' For the same reason, no doubt, Arthur was oversensitively trying to relocate him. 'I'll stay where I was,' Victor said.

'You sure? You probably should have somebody with you to look after—'

'I'm OK. I just want to sleep. Thanks Arthur.'

At last in his sleeping bag, Victor wrapped himself in the warmth and horizontal comfort that he had been denied for so many days. His mind was blurry with codeine and fatigue. He heard the clanking of metal things as the others got packs together to go search for Ed's body. On the tent roof there was a steady ping of snowflakes. He was half into sleep when Arthur opened the sleeve door.

'I'd be glad to stay with you,' he offered. 'I'm not sure you should be alone.'

'I'm all right.' Victor laughed softly. 'What could happen to me here?'

Chalmers' head poked into view. 'You say it happened on the third pitch below the bivvy tent?'

'Third or fourth. I can't remember.'

'It could make a difference.' The characteristic irritation was in Chalmers' voice. 'We've got to figure out the fall line by sighting where the accident happened. Try to—'

'Leave the man alone, Rex,' Arthur ordered. 'Can't you see he's wiped out?'

Chalmers walked off. Arthur lingered for a moment. 'It's been hell down here,' he said conspiratorially. 'I know one fellow I'll never rope up with again, not if you paid me.' The genial face smiled ruefully.

'It's snowing like a mother, isn't it?'

'Yes, damn it. What a gloomy spot this is. See you in a few hours. Victor?'

'Hmm?'

'Suppose we do find Ed.' There was a pause. 'What should we do with him?'

'Throw him in a crevasse,' Victor said groggily. He meant to add something about that being what Ed would have wanted, but it came out: 'That's what I'd like, if it happened to me.'

At last he was alone. Sleep lapped at him like waves on a beach, but he could not get all the way under. The snowflakes pinged and slid on the blue nylon above his head. What have I done? he asked himself. The alarm was running through his veins. He thought for a long while about how he could back out of it. There had been no conversation about the summit since that first meeting. Except that Arthur had twice repeated his remark about how famous the ascent would become, and Victor had not mustered the effort to contradict him.

He rolled over and tried to sleep. His toes tingled with a dull pain. All the muscles in his body were sore, and his head felt the way it did when he was coming down with a fever. All at once it became obvious that he had only one choice. It would be manageable after all. A matter of consistency and plausibility, no more than that. It would be like the months on the Montana campus, convincing everyone – almost everyone – that he was a sophomore economics major. Because at the heart of his lie, thanks to Ed's death, was the safe secret privacy of it: no one else had been there. They might ask if he had left anything on the summit. Of course not, just as they hadn't on Hungabee.

He began to compose the details of his story. The first day above the bivvy tent – he could get the dates straight later – they had indeed climbed 1500 feet and bivouacked on the two-foot ledge. The next day, after the storm had begun, insteading of resting on the ledge, they had pushed on to the summit. The climbing had begun with Ed's brilliant lead, stemming and bridging up the vertical, ice-filled chimney. Above that, clear sailing to the summit. Only a few minutes on top, because of the storm. Then back down.

Back all the way to the two-foot ledge? No, that would be implausible.

Back half the way; an uncomfortable bivouac in a wedge segmented out of a steep snowslope some 500 feet below the summit. A bad night, then an early start; a long day down past the two-foot ledge, picking up the rest of their gear, down to the standing two-piton bivouac. The one that had really happened. The rest was real also. It would be simple.

Just before sleep he sensed that his secret would be like a criminal's – with him every day of his life, a homunculus buried within his flesh, threatening to be born.

When he awoke it was still snowing. He was not sure whether it was the same day or the next. He sat up; the stiffness all through his body convinced him that he had been unconscious for a long time. He listened and heard the faint mumble of voices inside the igloo, twenty feet away. The dryness in his throat felt like cotton stuffed inside his mouth. Stretching, he looked around the tent. Next to his own sleeping bag lay Ed's greasy old Bauer, just as he had left it the morning they had gone up on the mountain. For the first time the truth of Ed's disappearance fully came home to him, sending a constriction all through his neck and shoulders. The business of the summit was not so important after all. Arthur was exaggerating; not many people outside their own expedition would care all that much whether a certain mountain had been climbed or not. But without Ed there would be no more afternoons at Mr. Siffler's, no silent drives through the night towards the Rockies, no more of Louis and Lionel. And no sedentary later years, as he had unconsciously promised himself was their due, to sip their beers and reminisce about the exploits of youth.

He dressed slowly, grief making the motions laborious and formal. His feet protested as he forced them into his half-frozen boots. Outside, he noticed that a lot of new snow had accumulated. He shivered as a gust of cold wind caught him. Looking up, he could barely discern the outlines of the mountain in the storm.

As he entered the tunnel door of the igloo, a voice inside broke off. He crawled in and stood up; they were all staring at him. Arthur rose to offer him his seat on the ice bench. 'Morning,' he said heartily. 'Did you get some sleep?'

'I must have,' Victor said, testing his voice like a long-unplayed instrument, 'if it's morning.' He smiled. The faces were watching him intently. He took Arthur's seat. 'Do you have anything to drink?'

'Sure,' said Arthur. 'There's Wyler's in the bottle, and we're just brewing up another pot of tea. It's good you slept so long. You needed it.'

'Did you find—?'

'No,' Chalmers said with disgust. 'It's hopeless in this white-out. We couldn't orient on the mountain at all. And I'm afraid the goddam snow has already covered everything.'

'Maybe it doesn't matter. I don't believe in afterlife, and I don't think Ed did.'

Arthur went on, 'We're going to have another look when the snow stops. And Pete and I'll go up and get the bivvy tent.'

'Be careful when you do.' Victor was surprised at himself; he had never been one to worry about others' safety.

Almost shyly, Chalmers asked, 'Do you feel like telling us about the climb?'

'As soon as I get some tea.' He thought: Well, this is it. Whatever I say this time has to become truth. Someone handed him a cup of tea. He took a sip and looked up. The staring faces gave him a jolt; they had the look of *knowing*. There did not seem to be enough air in the igloo; perhaps the stove? He took a deep breath and spoke. 'The first day, whatever it was—'

'The fifteenth,' Chalmers said.

'I guess so. We got up to the bivvy tent.' It seemed to Victor that his voice was quavering. He forced on. 'We spent the night there. The next day was real long. We did all this zigzagging and traversing right. Ed kept track of the route. He figured out we gained 1500 feet. We stopped that night on a good ledge, right below this vertical ice chimney. We were really excited, knowing we were only a thousand feet below the top.'

'That's the night the storm began,' said Chalmers.

'Right. It wasn't too bad at first.' He was talking too fast. He stopped and took a gulp of tea, scalding his tongue. The faces watched and judged. He avoided looking at Chalmers. 'It was hard getting off in the morning, getting everything packed. We flipped for the lead and Ed got it. It was the most amazing lead I've even seen. This fucking chimney really was about vertical. Ed started up it, stemming and bridging, getting a couple of lousy Marwas in for protection, but staying off the ice itself. He could do this amazing kind of stemming, he was so loose and wiry. I don't know if any of you ever saw him—' Suddenly he was sobbing. His voice broke into high-pitched wails, and his eyes flooded with tears. He hid his face in his hands.

Arthur put his arm around Victor's shoulders. 'It's all right,' he said. 'Go ahead, get it out.'

Victor leaned against the other man's shoulder and wept. The treble voice he heard did not seem to be his own. After a minute or two he rubbed his eyes and peeked through his fingers, still sniffling. The others looked subdued, embarrassed, no longer distrustful. Chalmers was staring at the wet floor of the igloo. Victor closed his eyes and gave himself up to a new gust of sobbing. Arthur held him, murmuring, 'It's OK, it's all right,' rocking him slightly. At the hermetic core of his grief Victor recognized a curious liberation: he could cry as much for himself as for Ed, and no one else could tell the difference.

CHAPTER FIVE

ARTHUR WAS RIGHT after all. The news spread quickly through the climbing grapevine, and the October issue of *Piton* used tabloid-style headlines: 'Pterophorus climbed! Briles lost on descent, after summit dash with Koch.' In the same month came requests for articles from *Alpinismus* and *Mountain*, and a few weeks later a telegram from John Richards: 'Want you for featured speaker American Alpine Club Banquet Denver Dec. 4. Will cover air fare.' At the climbing store Victor found himself treated, even by his friends, with the careful awe normally reserved for celebrities. Digby called to offer congratulations and sympathy, and to invite him out to Devil's Lake. Victor made excuses. Climbing was not something he wanted to be doing right now.

Vera alone seemed unimpressed with the ascent. He had called her first thing from Talkeetna, only to have her burst into tears at the news of Ed's death. Although he thought it rightfully his own job, he accepted her offer to inform Ed's parents. Since then, Mr. Briles had adopted the practice of exchanging letters with Vera, not Victor, even though he had spent a whole Sunday composing a note of condolence.

One day in October Vera said, 'You're the one who really should be answering these, you know.'

'I'm no good at writing,' Victor said. 'I can't express myself on paper. I'm having a hard enough time writing this article for *Alpinismus*.' He snickered. 'Even though they're just going to translate it into German.' He went to the refrigerator and got a beer. 'Want one?'

Vera was in a bad mood. 'You take it all so lightly.'

'What? Their letters? Look, I only met them once.'

'But they really exist, Victor. Listen. "I don't know why they" – by "they" I suppose he means climbers – "I don't know why they keep talking about this great achievement. All me and my wife know is that our son is gone." What can I say to that, when I agree completely with him?'

'Say that it mattered to Ed.' Victor took a long drink of beer.

'Why don't you say it, dear? At least add a note to mine.'

'I've got to finish this article.'

The look on Vera's face was one of exasperation. 'All right, what should I say to this? "We also want to know if there is still any chance of finding our son's body. It would mean a lot to me and my wife to see him at least have a decent burial."'

'Tell him we looked for days. The blizzards covered everything.'

'What about next summer?'

'By then he'll be down in the ice. As good a burial as you could want.'

As December approached, Victor grew anxious about the Denver slide show. Arthur had sent him duplicates of all his best slides; but none of them covered terrain above the bivvy tent. The camera had been lost with Ed, which, Victor reflected, was a kind of blessing. But what would he show on the screen during all the climactic, crucial part of the telling? He had never in his life given a slide show.

Yet during these months the homunculus inside him seemed to settle into the dormancy of a dead organ, like his unused kidney. His luck had followed him beyond the obliteration of Ed.

One night in November he lay in bed beside Vera, sleepless as so often in recent weeks. 'What's the matter, Victor?' she said at last.

'Nothing. Just this insomnia.'

She put a hand on his chest. 'It's something about us, isn't it? I feel it, anyway.'

Victor had always feared her sensitivity. Now he countered, 'We hardly ever make love any more.'

'I know, dear. I'm sorry. When I work this hard, I get sort of asexual.'

Victor turned over, his back to her. She hesitated, then put her arms around him. 'I'm scared we're growing apart. It's been different ever since the climbing started.'

'Or since graduate school.'

'Both. But this fall you seem so unhappy. I know you're really upset about Ed. I can feel how much you miss him. You walk around the apartment all restless, the way you did that first year here. Last spring you'd have called Ed and gone bouldering on the bridges or something. But now it's all locked up inside you. You're like a little kid who can't show his feelings because he has to be brave.'

'I'm all right.'

'Another thing. I'm worried about your drinking.'

'Leave me alone.' Her probing threatened him: a single needle might find the homunculus. 'I'm handling it.'

'But it's way up from before. Not just beer any more. How often do you go through one of those fifths of bourbon?'

'I don't keep track.' But Vera had stirred up his old needful love for her. He *was* unhappy. He turned towards her, saying, 'Come to Denver with me.'

'Oh, hell, you know I can't. It's right before my orals.'

'But it's my big moment.'

'I'm sorry. Maybe next summer we can do something, when all this craziness is over.'

The AAC meeting was held in a posh downtown hotel. Lonely and nervous, feeling underdressed in his borrowed tweed jacket with the elbow patches, Victor wandered along the fake Gold Rush corridors from registration to business meeting to lunch. There was no one there that he knew. The afternoon slide shows intimidated him with their smooth deliveries and stunning photos. At the cocktail party, along with everyone else, he put on a name tag. Now total strangers came up to him, peered at the tag, and immediately acted like friends; but the allusions to his climb were oblique: 'I'm really looking forward to your show tonight.' Victor's anxiety mounted, and almost without noticing he had drunk three strong bourbons. He was surprised not to have run into Chalmers.

Now a face familiar from photographs was approaching him. It was John Richards, trailed by a retinue of younger athletes. There was an open smile on the uncomplicated face as Richards offered a hand. 'Congratulations, old man. Bitch of a climb. Sorry about your buddy, too.' The onlookers stared enviously as Richards steered Victor toward the bar. 'I'm supposed to introduce you. We have to sit up at the head table with the old farts. After the circus is over a bunch of us are going to hit Larimer Street. Come on out with us. I want to talk to you about something.' Victor nodded numbly.

He could eat only a few bites of the rubbery banquet chicken. Richards had obtained a bottle of wine, and kept filling Victor's glass. As each after-dinner honoree – men in their fifties and sixties – got up to utter a few words, Richards gave Victor a thumbnail sketch. 'This guy really is an old fart. So he raised a few bucks for the Research Fund. Big deal.' Or, 'This guy deserves it. We climbed his route on Keeler Needle, and it's still bitchin' hard.' As his own time drew near. Victor realized that he was fairly drunk. The alcohol had calmed him somewhat, but now he was scared that he would slur his words. The carefully prepared summit dash was a scramble of details in his mind.

Richards had left. From a great distance he heard Pterophorus being described as 'the toughest climb yet done in Alaska', heard himself being characterized and introduced. The applause prodded him toward the lectern. Victor fiddled with the microphone, coughed, and heard the explosion rattle through the huge hot room. He stood up. Hundreds of faces were fixed expectantly on his. There came a surge of pure panic. He opened his mouth and nothing came out. Finally a nervous whinny escaped, multiplied again through the room. He managed to blurt, 'I've never done this kind of thing before.' Currents of laughter lapped in the darkness, but he heard an edginess in them. 'Can we start the slides?' His's's sounded drunken to him. I can't go through with this, he thought, feeling his chest covered with sweat. When I get to the summit, they'll know.

He looked at the screen, away from the faces. There was the mountain. Somehow his voice began making words; when he could think of nothing else to say, he would plead, 'Next slide,' and an invisible hand would change the view. Then, all too soon, he was stuck on Arthur's single photo of the mountain from the glacier. He apologized, 'We don't have any pictures from above here, since Ed had the camera.' There was total silence in the room. He kept his eyes away from the people and recited. His voice was going too fast, running away from him, leaving him no air to breathe. But he was up the vertical, ice-filled chimney, onto the easier ground above, remembering details he had never known before – the bite that morning of his crampons into the rime ice, the taste of a lemon candy, the view from the summit. The descent went quickly, and as he approached Ed's accident, despite the deepening silence in the room, Victor heard his voice gain assurance. In a flat monotone he announced the death, and was aware of the sound of breaths drawn sharply in. Then it was over. To his surprise, the applause was thunderous; people were pushing back their chairs and standing up. In the triumph of the moment, Victor felt an aching sorrow, that neither Ed nor Vera could be here to share it.

An hour later Richards was buying the rounds, saying, 'To hell with the audio-visual aids. Just put a battered old sod up there in front of the mob and let him tell what it was like. Palm of your hand, old man.' Later, his head fuzzy from Jack Daniels, Victor was aware of Richards manoeuvering him away from the group, into a corner where the country-western band could be shouted over. 'Where?' Victor tried again.

'Kichatna Spires,' Richard shouted. 'Three-thousand, four-thousand-foot walls. Good granite. Nothing's been done yet, one party in there. What d'you say?'

Victor was smiling, drunk and happy. John Richards was asking him to go climbing. He heard himself say, 'Sounds good.' But beneath the flattered ebullience of the moment, he sensed a disturbance. He was not sure he wanted to go on another expedition next summer. It would be so hard to get in shape all over again, to get psyched up. And up high, above the gleaming glaciers, chopping the ice away, he might well feel, yes, *afraid*.

In February the issue of *Mountain* came out with his article in it. The climbing store gave Victor a party. Vera came to it, and though it was not the same as Denver might have been, when they got home that night Victor felt the old sense that their lives were interlocked for good, the snug closeness that he associated with Montana.

He started climbing again in April. The first afternoons at Taylor's Falls he was appalled at how clumsy and weak he felt on familiar climbs. The sedentary winter had put ten pounds on him; now he started running to trim down. The first time he climbed with Digby at Devil's Lake, he looked up at the forbidding line and said, 'I'm in shitty shape. You'll have to drag me up it.' Drag him up Digby did; but Victor hoped the man had not witnessed the thrashings of pure fear that drained all his energy on the lowest forty feet of the single pitch. Within days, however, his competence began to return.

Late in the month he got a call from Arthur. The man was out of breath. 'How are you?'

'Fine,' said Victor.

'No, I mean how are you handling it?'

'What?'

'That double-crossing skunk. I'm writing them a letter today. I can't believe it.'

'Slow down, Arthur. What is it?'

'You haven't seen *Piton* yet? Oh, no wonder.'

'For Christ's sake. What?' Victor sat down in a chair, suddenly weary.

'It's Chalmers. He says he doesn't believe you and Ed made it. He's going back.'

Victor felt he had to speak. 'That fucking bastard.'

'Nobody will credit him, Victor, I'm writing them a letter today. They didn't even call you to tell you this was coming out?'

'I have to get hold of the magazine. I'll call you back.'

'The May issue.'

It took Victor a full day – a day of dread so strong he found himself gagging every few hours – to locate a copy. When he did, he tore open the pages. The title read, 'Was Pterophorus Climbed After All?' Victor's eyes skimmed through Chalmers' pompous prefatory remarks and seized upon the 'evidence':

> The gist of my claim that Koch and Briles did not make the summit lies in the following facts:
>
> 1 Throughout the last days of the expedition, Koch was extremely vague about where the fatal accident happened.

2 His description of the last thousand feet – 'clear sailing' above a certain chimney – simply does not jibe with all the known photos of the mountain.
3 The time scale seems wrong. I don't think there was enough time for them to do what Koch claims they did.
4 It is hard to believe that anyone could have climbed at all on the 16th and 17th. At base camp we had difficulty even fighting through the storms to get to the base of the route.
5 At the Denver AAC show, Koch talked about the view from the summit. He told us they reached the summit in total white-out.
6 The thing that first aroused my suspicion was what Koch said the moment we met him, as he came off the mountain. First he said, in a sort of disappointed voice, 'We had it.' Then moments later he said, 'We bagged it.' I think the first remark was the spontaneous one, the true admission of defeat. I expected to hear, 'We had it, and then the storms ruined our chances,' or some such statement. But for some reason, Koch decided right then to claim the ascent.

The case seems strong and clear. I consider Pterophorus unclimbed and will be leading an expedition to the mountain this summer.

Victor's anger peaked in a spasm of pure rage. As it had on the descent, the image of attacking Chalmers with an ice axe flashed before his eyes. But in the same instant he began to check himself for wounds. How serious was the 'evidence'? Could he stuff the burgeoning homunculus back into its hiding place? So the bastard had been in Denver after all, lurking in the corners, hoping to pick up some silly little slip. The summit view had been careless, but he could cover it: a momentary break in the cloud cover. The vaguenesses about route meant little: he had always been poor at routefinding; Ed took care of that end of things. The time and the weather proved nothing. But what about that remark of his? Had he said, 'We had it'? Victor could not remember.

He tried to call Vera at the library, but could not locate her. As he walked back to the apartment, he forced himself to govern his rage and plan the dignified response. There was a note for him from Vera. 'Call Ron Winston at the *Mountain Journal* collect. Urgent.' Two numbers, business and home. So it was news everywhere. The thought of talking to Winston, the self-styled arbiter of American mountaineering, filled Victor with fresh terror. But as he sat there, staring at the note, it became clear that not to respond was to indicate weakness. He drank a large tumbler of whiskey very quickly and called the home number. Arthur, after all, had believed him, never doubted for a moment.

Winston was friendly, reassuring, talkative. He would be coming through Chicago in a week, on a trip West to gather material for a big summer issue. Could he meet Victor there for an interview? It would be the best way, Winston suggested, to clear his name once and for all, to relegate Chalmers to the oblivion he deserved.

By the time Vera got home Victor was dead drunk; but the call to Winston had given him new self-confidence. She read through the article in *Piton* with a frown on her face. 'What an unpleasant fellow,' she said. 'But you can easily prove he's wrong, can't you?'

'Of course.' Victor told her about the interview next week.

The frown was still on Vera's face. 'So it's really just his word against yours?'

'So what? I was there. He wasn't. It's as simple as that. Let's go to bed.' In the middle of the night Victor woke. He was shivering, covered with sweat; his arms were tight around Vera, the hands clutching at the bed sheets.

Victor met Winston in an austere, high-ceilinged hotel room. The man was ruggedly handsome, one of the smoothest conversationalists Victor had ever met. Although, to Victor's knowledge, Winston had ceased to climb about five years ago, he still spoke with a categorical air of authority about everything from bolting in Yosemite to the decimal ratings in the Shawangunks. An instinct of distrust crept over Victor; he would stick carefully to his version of the ascent.

For the next two hours he did just that, while the tape recorder spun away. Despite his encouraging nods, Winston seemed disappointed. At last he shut off the machine, stood up, and said, 'Well, I'm sure that does it. Come on downstairs, I'll buy you a drink.' Victor felt a surge of immense relief.

A couple of double bourbons later, Winston returned offhandedly to the subject. 'So how do you figure Chalmers? What's in it for him to spread all these aspersions?'

Warmed by the drinks and Winston's friendliness, Victor answered, 'Chalmers is through. He was psyched out from the beginning. He got a little bump on his wrist, so he walked around all month pretending it was broken.'

'He wants to go back.'

'He wants somebody to drag him up it. He couldn't stand that Ed and I did it without him. You should ask Arthur Bowen about Chalmers. He's like that German who keeps going back to Nanga Parbat.'

'Breitkopf?'

'Yes.'

'Have another.'

'One more, maybe.' The waitress went off.

'What about the weather business?' Winston went on.

'Sure it was bad weather. But Chalmers was so out of it, I'm not surprised he couldn't move his ass out of the igloo while we were climbing. They didn't even get up the fixed ropes to the bivvy tent to support us.'

'Chalmers—'

'Chalmers is a washed-out crump.'

'One last thing, Victor.' Winston pulled a photo out of his briefcase. 'I forgot this upstairs. How about marking in your route here? For the issue.'

Victor's spleen was up. 'See, that's the kind of bullshit Chalmers was pulling in *Piton*. And what the fuck does it prove? I could draw in a cute little dotted line here, or here, or here, and how the hell would you know which was right? Ed was the best damned routefinder you ever saw.'

Winston wrung his hand, thanking him effusively. On the train back to Minneapolis Victor got his first sound sleep in a week. The next day he sent Richards a note: 'Don't mind the bullshit in *Piton*. I've got an interview coming up in *MJ* that sets everything straight.' In the return mail was a postcard. 'No sweat. The guy's an asshole anyway. When we get together, remind me to tell you about Chalmers' first trip to the Valley. See you in July. I'm up for it. – JR.'

Over the next month Victor's life seemed to return to normal. His friends at Devil's Lake believed him, it was clear, and when they realized Victor was sick of talking about the controversy, they laid off. At last, in early June, the issue of *The Mountain Journal* came in the mail. Victor slid off the wrapper with a sense of pleasure and sat down to read the interview.

The heading came as a shock: 'Pterophorus Mystery Deepens. Gaps and Discrepancies in Victor Koch's Account. First Published Interview with Koch.' Stung and impatient, Victor read through the tape transcript. But for some stylistic editing, it seemed to be just what he had said. An italicized epilogue, in Winston's voice, followed:

> The above interview gives some idea of the difficulties of such an approach. Throughout our session, Koch seemed to stick doggedly to the same story. In recounting an incident a second or third time, he would repeat the identical phrasing, like a man grimly hanging on to a story others may not believe, in constant fear of contradicting himself.
>
> Personally, I found Koch to be defensive, distrustful, ill-at-ease. These qualities of course do not in themselves discredit his testimony. However, though initially sceptical of Chalmers' attack, I found myself wondering more and more whether there was any truth in it.
>
> One of the things that discomfited me was Koch's prolonged refusal to indicate on a photo exactly where his route had gone. He did not seem sure himself (and indeed, the reader will recall that a crucial vagueness about the route forms one of Chalmers' chief claims). I presented him with a good photo. After some uneasy parrying, he said, rather pathetically, to my mind, 'We might have gone here, or here, or here, I'm not sure. Briles would have known.'
>
> Koch seemed also to have an intense personal vendetta against Chalmers, implying that Chalmers had faked an injury to his wrist (is this idea of 'faking' something a projection on Koch's part?), and calling him such things as a 'washed-up crump' and a 'psych-out.'
>
> I came away from the interview very much uncertain whom to believe. If Chalmers' party climbs the mountain (they will apparently attempt the supposed Briles-Koch route) this summer, they may cast additional light on the controversy. (Rappel anchors on the upper part of the route, for instance, would certainly add credence to Koch's version. But Koch himself says the two men down-climbed nearly every pitch above the ice-filled chimney, in order to save hardware.) Probably we will never know the truth.

Rage filled Victor's afternoon; but late that night, with more than half a bottle of bourbon inside him, held tight in Vera's arms, he cried. He wept in delirious fits, recovered long enough to direct a stream of invective against Chalmers or Winston or nameless other 'betrayers', then gave in to the weeping again. Through it all Vera held him silently, stroking his head, supplying him with Kleenex. At last Victor fell asleep. Vera stayed up, holding his head in her lap, smoothing his matted hair.

He woke abruptly at 6:00 a.m. and sat up with a start. Pressing his eyelids with his thumbs, he groaned. 'God, I feel awful.'

'You drank a lot,' Vera said. 'Listen, Victor. I couldn't sleep all night, and I just sat here thinking.' She paused. 'I want you to be honest. You didn't get to the summit, did you?'

'What are you saying?' Victor gasped, his whole body rigid. 'Are you on their side?'

'Did you?'

She stared at him with her calm, knowing eyes, and at last he lowered his gaze and wept quietly. He held a hand out blindly and said, 'Vee, help me. You're the only one who knows. You won't leave me, will you? You didn't last time.' He sniffed and wiped his eyes. 'What in Christ am I going to do?'

After a pause Vera said, 'Tell them the truth. Come out with it and try to explain why it happened.'

Victor's voice was even and exhausted. 'No. I can't.'

'Why not? It's better than living with it all your life.'

'It's too late. You don't understand.'

Vera sidled up close and hugged him. 'I don't see why. It doesn't matter to me whether you made the summit or not. I love you for you, not for what you've done.'

Victor returned the embrace; but, dimly through the nausea of hangover, the possibility appeared that it had been a terrible mistake to confess, even to Vera. Anyone was capable of betraying him. 'No,' he said. 'It's not a matter of love. They eat you alive out there, once you've done something good. The fucking seventeen-year-olds sit there at Devil's Lake waiting for you to take too long on a 5.9 move, or grab a sling, and then they talk all afternoon about it.' Victor sighed. 'Oh God, what will I tell Richards?'

'Why do you need to tell him anything?'

'Vee, I don't want to go to Alaska. I don't want to climb this summer. Hold me again.'

'Then don't go. I'll get some time off, and we'll do something together. We'll drive up to Ontario.

Victor blew his nose. 'You don't understand. If I crapped out of the Spires, it would prove it to everybody. I have to go.'

CHAPTER SIX

On the sunny, windless sixth day of the expedition, Victor was pushing the route with Richards. They had left base camp early that morning, cramponed up the frozen snow of the steep, long couloir, and jumared up the fixed ropes. Sixteen hundred feet off the glacier, they were standing in T-shirts on a small ledge, sorting hardware. Richards had just nailed a vertical dihedral, effortlessly and fast. He wiped the sweat of his forehead now, saying, 'Bomber protection everywhere. Hard to believe we're up here in Seward's Folly, isn't it?'

Victor grunted. He was nervous about taking the lead which would be his first on the expedition. He wondered whether Richards was watching, criticizing already, as he racked his pitons.

'Hey, Victor, before you rush off, a couple of things. What are your thoughts about the other two?'

Victor scrutinized the horizon. He half wished for storm clouds. 'How do you mean?'

'I mean like they're young, and haven't done too much in the mountains. I'm worried that—'

'That they'll be too rash,' Victor finished for him. 'They do seem, you know, impetuous.'

Richards frowned. 'Actually, I was going to say the opposite. Too cautious, too conservative. Ah, never mind. Don't you love this granite?'

An hour later Victor was only sixty feet above his partner. He had dropped one piton and barely caught another. The silent impatience of the great Valley climber below him seemed to goad him not into speed so much as a fumbling inefficient haste. Some of the pitch felt as if it ought to go free, but each time he got more than a few feet above his last piece of protection, the stab of terror returned, and he had to climb back down and go on aid. Now he was close to weeping with futility. Why had he come at all on this expedition? It wasn't right, he wasn't ready, he was making a fool of himself. In front of Richards. Temporizing, he yelled down a question about their supply of pitons while he fussed with a balky étrier.

That night, mercifully, the storm came, in the middle of Richards' disquisition on the need to place a camp around the 1800-foot level and to use all four men simultaneously to make real progress. For the first time Victor had heard annoyance in the man's voice, and now, as their ears picked up the sound of the first flakes on the walls of the group tent, Richards cursed uncharacteristically. The two of them had added only four new pitches during the long day, and on the last Victor had surrendered the lead partway up.

He retired early to his solitary tent. As he pulled loose the string in the sleeve door, Victor thought it seemed to have been tied in a slip knot different from his own. Alarmed, he looked carefully at the battered day pack inside. Had one of the others been prowling around inside his tent? He listened for a moment for footsteps. Methodically, he undressed and arranged himself in his sleeping bag. Then he opened the pack, rummaged under the sweaters, took out the nearest quart water bottle, and held it up to the grey light. The dark liquid level was down to less than a third. And he had been so frugal so far! He recalculated: if the first bottle lasted only eight days, and the trip were a month long. . . . He poured a small tot into his plastic cup and sniffed the warm, pungent aroma, then licked the mouth of the bottle. Hearing a sound, he thrust the bottle hurriedly back into his day pack. Was one of the others spying on him? Had they smelled it on his breath? He was careful to drink only at night, only when he would not be in the others' company again for hours. But probably he should have brought vodka.

The storm lasted for ten days, with only two short let-ups. During each of them Richards irritably started getting gear and food ready for what he kept calling 'a big four-day push.' Victor counselled waiting and seeing, and then when in fact the weather closed back in, he sat in the group tent and soliloquized smugly about long-range cycles and the significance of storms from the southeast. He was developing a cough. More than once he said, 'I sure hope it isn't bronchitis.' The others kept a glum silence. In the group tent there was little recreation. There were binges of hearts, and poker for matches; but one of the men was plodding through *The Brothers Karamazov* at a rate of about forty pages a day and it was hard to talk him into playing. Richards went for long walks by himself, despite Victor's warnings about crevasses.

By the time the storm broke, Richards had decided on an all-out push, two men occupying the bivvy tent at the 2000-foot level while the other two fixed as many pitches above them as they could. Then the two in the tent would go for the summit. It was obvious that Richards would be one of them, but the other slot was open. Now the skies were gloriously clear, and at 5:00 a.m. Richards was bustling around getting ropes and hardware together. Victor came out of his tent and stood appraising the mountain. At last he said, 'I think we should give it a day.'

'What?' Richards stopped in his tracks. 'Look at the weather.'

'Look at the rime ice up high. It's going to be coming off when the sun hits it.'

Richards walked over. 'Man, we've just waited out ten frigging days of storm. We can't waste one like this.'

Victor coughed. 'It's probably a major break in the cycle. In which case a day or two either way—'

'Hey. I was thinking of you and me for the summit.'

Victor looked away, touching his throat. 'I don't know. I don't like this cough of mine. If it's bronchitis, I just don't know.'

Richards gave him a hard look. 'Maybe you should stay in camp then.'

'Maybe I should. We could wait a day.'

'Fuck it. We gotta move. I don't know how with three, though.'

The first day alone seemed a blessing to Victor. When the sun hit camp, he put his sleeping pad on the snow and sunbathed. He watched the others through binoculars until 4:00 p.m. when, on new ground, they rounded a corner and went out of sight. Until then he had been able to hear their belay signals. Now the sun went behind the peaks to the west, and the sudden chill, mixed with the silence, enfolded him in depression. He got out a new plastic bottle and started drinking. At last the fog of unhappiness lifted. He congratulated himself for not chancing complications with what were surely the first stages of bronchitis, and he felt that for the first time in months he was beginning truly to relax.

He woke suddenly in the middle of the night, cold sober. He had been dreaming about Chalmers. He stuck his head outside the tent; the morning sun was dazzling on the upper reaches of the mountain. Now the weather seemed doubly threatening, for, eighty miles to the south, Chalmers might well be taking advantage of the fine spell to push high on Pterophorus, up to the ice-filled chimney, beyond. He thought about Vera, and berated himself for confessing to her; for secrets never stayed kept, and she was bound to tell someone else, who would in turn. . . . He prayed to a private shade, the imp of his lost luckiness, against both Chalmers and his wife.

That day he held off drinking until 2:00 p.m. He scanned the mountain with the binoculars every hour and found himself listening for the stray sound; he would have liked at least to walk up the glacier to get a better look at the route, but alone, through the crevasses, it would have been foolhardy. At dinner he finished the bottle he had started the day before and opened another, the next-to-last. What a fool he had been not to bring more, for that spring he had come to know that nothing else could bring him calm quite so effectively, and now, in the potentially disastrous situation, he needed calm more than ever. The others had dashed up on the mountain all too impetuously; why, just this day he had seen a huge summit cornice break off on one of the other peaks and sweep its east face with avalanche.

A high layer of scud moved in during the night, and the following day was dull and steely, the classic harbinger of a big storm from the southeast. Victor waited anxiously, scouring the mountain with binoculars. The level in the water bottle crept imperceptibly down. By mid-afternoon he recognized that he was indeed in an emergency situation. He was by now fairly sure that he was the only one of the four left alive. They had no radio, and the pilot was not due for another two weeks. But there had been occasional planes in the sky, mail flights to Farewell, perhaps, or McGrath down on the Kuskokwim. He ought to make a signal. What was big enough? There was Richards' black tarp, the one they had futilely tried to concoct a sun still with; he could cut it into long strips and make a huge 'X' on the glacier.

The project was complete by early evening. There was no way for Victor to judge how visible the distress signal was from the air, but it was all he could manage with the materials at hand. It was not only the likelihood of tragedy on the mountain, it was the near certainty of his own bronchitis. He found that the whisky eased the soreness in his throat. Sitting inside the group tent, he caught himself listening as before, not for belay signals now, but for the blessed whine of a plane engine.

He was wakened in the wee hours by voices. They were nearby, and they were shouting for help. No, they were hooting and laughing and cheering. He jerked his clothes on and hurried out of the tent, knowing by his clumsiness that he was drunk. There in the ghostly light the three men were, arm in arm, stumbling across the last several hundred feet of glacier. Richards saw him and let out a loud whoop. Victor closed the distance, reminding himself not to breathe in the others' faces.

Richards blurted out, 'Oh, man, what a climb, what a gas. You should have been with us. You can't believe it up there.'

'You're all right, then?' Victor said, carefully forming the words.

'Happier'n a clam. Hey, what's with all this plastic all over the glacier?'

Victor turned to look at his 'X' as if he had never before seen it. 'It was, well, it was going to be a signal.'

The mirth had momentarily dissolved. The others looked at him and then at each other.

CHAPTER SEVEN

AS HE HAD the year before, Victor called Vera from Talkeetna. She seemed inordinately glad to hear from him. 'I was really worried about you, dear. This time was the worst.'

'I was fine,' Victor said gruffly.

'Did you mind not climbing the peak yourself?'

'Hell, no. It wasn't that great a climb. The younger guys didn't really know what they were in for. I didn't trust them in a pinch.'

'I'm just glad you're OK. I was having dreams—'

'Chalmers didn't make it, you know. He didn't even get to our bivouac ledge below the chimney.'

'That's too bad.'

'What do you mean?'

'I mean, I guess that's good.'

'Are you distracted, or something?'

'It's the connection, I think. Your voice is faint. Victor, when will you be here? We need to have a talk.'

'About what?'

'About us. About this coming year.'

'Go ahead.'

'Not on the phone. Hurry back here. I missed you.'

A week later, after dinner, Vera turned down the light and sat beside Victor on the sofa. 'Do you want another one?' she asked. He had been drinking only beer, a switch she seemed to support. Now, however, the odd mood she was in, as before a special occasion, made him uneasy. Through the ceiling he heard the muffled bass of a Kingston Trio record. They had been playing it up there for three years. Vera took his hand.

'I guess this is our talk,' Victor said, forcing a laugh.

'Well, I think we should.' He heard an equal nervousness in her voice.

'You start.'

She squeezed his hand. In the Brooks Range, that had become a ritual for them, the hand squeeze every morning, for good luck against the bears. It had seemed silly to him then. 'I have to decide about my professional future,' she began stiffly. 'My, um, the department has offered me a post-doctoral year.'

'Do you get paid?'

'Yes. Not much, of course. It's more of an honour.'

'Good. So take it.'

She looked at his eyes. He glanced quickly at her; there seemed to be pain in her face. 'Do you really want me to?' she asked.

'Of course. What's the alternative?'

'Looking for a job. Which might, which probably would mean moving away.'

'It sounds like the best—'

'Oh, Victor,' she broke in, 'I can't hide it. I'm having an affair.'

Victor let go of the hand in his. Nother could have prepared him for this. 'With who?'

'Keith.'

'Who the fuck is Keith?'

Vera looked on the verge of crying; but her voice was controlled. 'Keith, my professor. Dear, I hated you not knowing.'

He got up, went to the refrigerator, found a beer and levered the bottle cap violently off. 'How long has it been going on?'

'Since May.' Her voice was strangely flat. 'I didn't think it meant anything at first—'

'But now it does, is that it?'

'Yes, it does. I thought, if only you don't go to Alaska this summer, if we could go away together, we could work it out. But it's like we haven't communicated in years.' A deep sigh escaped her.

Victor paced, guzzling his beer. 'Did you tell him about me?'

'What about you?'

'You know, damn it. Quit pretending.'

'He knows about our marriage.'

'God damn it, cut it out. About the fucking mountain.'

Vera's eyes widened. 'Of course not. Why would I—?'

'You could betray me just like anybody.' The anger in him was gathering to a storm.

'Victor, come and hold me.'

'No.'

She ran her fingers through her hair. 'Oh, Victor, I just gave up when you insisted on Alaska. And then I was sure you'd get hurt, just to punish me.'

'You, you, you. What about me?' He found another beer. 'So you want to keep seeing this bastard.'

'I don't know. He means a lot. He's somebody to talk to.'

'And I'm not,' Victor said with intensity. 'And he's somebody to screw, and I'm not.' He stared with contempt at the cringing woman on the sofa, whose arms were hugging herself. 'You bitch! You fucking slut!' He ran out of the apartment, slamming the door.

A certain clarity of mind stayed with him through the evening, so that he had the foresight to visit a liquor store before ten, against the inevitability of the bars closing. Now it was 1:00 a.m. and he was walking through the streets. It was a crisp, clean evening, the kind when he and Ed would have stayed up talking and gone out to the pizza place. Ed was the only one, it was clear now, who had really been loyal to him. All the rest were betrayers. With Ed he could have done anything. They would have gone to the Andes, to the Karakoram, Patagonia. He shouted to the night, in what he thought was a French accent, 'Louis! Lionel!'

His steps were taking him to the bridges where he and Ed has used to boulder. He was not very drunk; if a policeman stopped him, he could walk a straight line with ease. When he got to the bridges he sat down in the darkness and opened the bottle of Old Grand Dad. The warm, familiar stinging soothed his throat, and within seconds he felt the glow bathing him with calmness. It was a good thing he had bought the bourbon. Whisky had the power to make the truth stand out all the more clearly, to tame the rage that was snarling inside him. Without it, he might have gone home and done something really violent. Something they could arrest you for.

A car went by; no one in it saw him. Victor placed the bottle carefully on the pavement and approached the nearest bridge pillar. His fingers itched with the familiar sequences hidden in the quarried stone. He looked down at his feet: tennis shoes – but when they were in shape they had climbed this route in sandals.

He was only six feet up when he fell off, but the slip was so unforeseen that he landed hard, bruising his tailbone. A memory of playground spills surged with the pain through his body; for a moment he wanted to cry like a child. Instead he spoke softly. 'Right on my ass. Right on my fucking ass.' He rolled on his side and rubbed his hip, kneading away the pain. Then the anger surged back, and he screamed, 'Ed! You bastard!'

He sat listening to his own voice as it seemed to echo through the streets. Would it bring the cops? But there was no one about; the world was empty. He crawled back to his bottle, the decisions suddenly clear in his head.

There was no one any more that he could trust. Fine. So he would go it alone. He had before; he could do it now. And he would quit climbing, quit it for good. That would show the bastards. None of it mattered, none of the Alaskan business, none of the fierce ego-building. He was beyond all that shit.

And tonight he would finish his bottle, and go to sleep right there, under the bridge. Bivouac. He giggled, and heard his own voice wail.

PART TWO

September 1978

CHAPTER SEVEN

THAT TUESDAY it was raining, which meant handball rather than tennis. After work Victor went home to his apartment, called his partner to confirm the time, called the 'Y' to recheck his court reservation, washed the breakfast dishes, took some meat out of the freezer to thaw, and changed into his athletic clothes. He was just leaving the apartment when the phone rang. It was one of those vexing choices, a question of minimizing disorder: the likelihood of being a few minutes late for handball against the uncertainty of not knowing who had made the call. It was an unusual hour for his phone to ring. He answered it. The voice was unfamiliar.

'This is he.'

'Victor? It's been a long time. This is Arthur Bowen.'

It took Victor a few seconds to place the name. When he had, the first reaction was dismay: now he would certainly be late for the handball. He said evenly, 'How are you?'

'Fine. How are you, Victor?'

'I'm fine. You sound long-distance.'

'I'm in White Plains. I'm in business for myself here. Things are going really well.'

There was an awkward silence. 'How did you get my phone number?'

Arthur laughed uneasily. 'It wasn't simple, my friend. You're not, you know, still climbing, are you?'

'No.' Victor looked at his watch. Three minutes had gone by. 'Are you?'

'Yes. Not like we used to. I go to the Gunks every weekend, though. I have a whole different attitude about it now. Listen.' The expectant edge in Arthur's voice was unmistakable. 'Since you're only about eighty miles from here, why don't we get together? I'm taking a trip to Boston next week, and it would be easy to stop in Hartford, either coming or going.'

One of the rules he had made years ago would have dictated a gentle 'no' at this point. But he was getting later and later for handball – the court cost $7.00 an hour – and besides, an old memory of Arthur's loyalty made the rule seem breakable. Brusquely he set a date and gave directions to his apartment.

His partner won three out of five games – the first time ever that Victor had dropped a match to that particular opponent. He went home blaming a new underspin slice that he had not yet mastered for the defeat; but that night he woke up at 4:00 a.m. and could not get back to sleep until 7:00. By the day

Arthur was due to arrive, Victor had resolved on a brief, friendly exchange of information, with no suggestion that they repeat the occasion.

Arthur's face was instantly recognizable, but his greying hair and genial wrinkles brought home to Victor the ages that had passed since they had climbed together. 'You're looking good,' he said, as he took Arthur's leather briefcase and put it in the front closet. 'Come in and see the apartment.'

'So are you,' Arthur said cheerfully, patting Victor's flat stomach with the knuckles of one hand. 'You must keep in shape.'

'I play a lot of handball, and I have a workout routine at the "Y." Make yourself comfortable. Can I get you a drink?'

Arthur was still standing, perusing the flower photographs on the walls. 'Whatever you're having.'

'I usually have tea this time of day. There's a bottle of scotch somewhere, though.' Victor smiled. 'I don't entertain much.'

'Tea's fine.'

The uneasiness persisted through the first cup. Victor fled to the kitchen and returned with crackers and cheese. Arthur kept looking around the neat apartment, as if in search of some misplaced object. 'So what does your business produce?' Victor asked.

'Oh, it's terribly boring to the layman. We supply the little doodads that make cable TV possible. That's the simplest explanation. This is good tea.'

'I'm trying a new Ceylonese brand. Another cup?'

Arthur held out his mug. Victor began to wonder how soon he could terminate the awkward visit. It was too bad Arthur had driven so far. What could he possibly want? 'How about you,' Arthur was saying. 'What exactly is SANOL?'

'It's a drug rehabilitation program.'

'Interesting. I wouldn't have thought—'

'I got involved because of my own addiction.' There was the usual startled look on Arthur's face. 'To the oldest drug of all. Alcohol. It's all right. I'm comfortable talking about it. If my life has any purpose these days, it's to get other people out of the gutter. Let's talk about you, though. You keep saying "we," so I assume you're married.'

Arthur smiled sheepishly. 'Yes. Very happily. Fran climbs with me a lot. We have two kids, Jonathan, seven, and Ruth, four. I'm very happy. Are you still—'

'Married? No.'

'I'm sorry.'

'There's no reason to be. I broke things off.'

'Are you still in touch with Vera?'

Victor was surprised that Arthur remembered his wife's name; the man had never met her. 'No. Not since the divorce was final, years ago. I think she's teaching somewhere on the West Coast.'

'Is there anyone then?'

'Not at the moment.' Victor scratched a mosquito bite on his forearm. 'Another cup?'

'No thanks. Too much caffeine, you know.' The awkwardness would not go away. Victor had the hunch that Arthur was looking for some cue. 'So you really don't climb at all?'

Victor shook his head. Arthur waited. 'I found in therapy that it wasn't right for me.'

'Do you want to explain?'

It was a little speech he had ready. 'I found that climbing was all tied up with this deep anger I had against the world. Which in turn derived ultimately from some bad early childhood experiences. I won't bore you with them. I'm happier now, without climbing. Sometimes the anger creeps back.' Victor smiled. 'Just the other day, in a handball game. But now I know how to govern it.'

Arthur stared into his empty mug while he fiddled with the handle. 'I wish I could drag you out to the Gunks, though, Victor. I've got a whole new attitude towards climbing that makes *me* much happier.' He looked up. 'I think we all used to be too serious about it. It shouldn't be a life-or-death sort of thing, and we shouldn't get our egos so involved. To me there's great pleasure in just climbing old classic routes, even 5.5's or 'sixes, at my own pace, my own way. And climbing with Fran is the best experience I've ever had. She can follow anything I can lead.' Arthur wiped his palms on his thighs. 'So couldn't I talk you into a weekend? Just for old times' sake? And to show you what I mean about climbing this new way?'

Victor smiled tolerantly. 'Thanks, Arthur, but no. I know my needs by now.'

'How old are you?'

'Thirty-eight.'

'I'm forty myself.'

'It's nothing to do with age.' Victor decided to force the awkwardness out in the open. 'Frankly, Arthur, why did you go to all this trouble to look me up?'

Arthur frowned, the way, Victor remembered, he always had when embarrassed. 'I guess it's that I always thought you got a raw deal. That Chalmers was at the root of it all.'

Victor sighed deeply. 'I've come to terms with even that. If I met the man on the street today, I could bring myself to speak civilly to him.'

'You hadn't heard then?'

'What?'

'Chalmers was killed on Manaslu. In an avalanche, along with three Sherpas. In 1972, I think.'

'Poor fellow.' Victor stared at the carpet. 'I don't think he was ever happy climbing. It must have really galled him that he didn't get up the route Ed and I had done.'

'Lord, it all comes back, doesn't it?'

'It does.' Victor closed his eyes. 'I can remember as if it were yesterday every step of the way above our bivouac ledge. I remember our conversation on the summit.' It was true; now, in his mind's eye, he saw Ed skilfully bridging his way up the atrocious chimney, saw himself take the lead on the mixed terrain above, saw the faint white outline of the summit against the blowing snow, saw himself turn in his joy to Ed. He opened his eyes. 'Sorry. I got carried away.' With the images had come an old pain in the throat, associated with his desperate thirst on the descent. Victor poured himself more tea.

'Before I go, I want to show you something. Where did you put my briefcase?'

'The front closet.'

Arthur returned with a magazine called *Climb*. 'Page thirty-four,' he said as he handed it over.

Victor looked at the impossible overhang being tackled on the cover. 'They didn't have this journal in our day, did they?' He turned to page thirty-four and was shocked by the title: 'The legacy of Victor Koch.' 'Who's Tom Kinney?' he asked.

'He's a young climber who's done some very hard things in Alaska. Read it.'

Victor read:

> Fourteen years have passed since the famous controversy over Pterophorus. The consensus of climbing opinion today is that Ed Briles and Victor Koch did not make the summit, and that Koch tried to fake the ascent on his return to base camp after Briles had been killed when a fixed rope broke. The consensus is based, of course, originally on Chalmers' article in *Piton* laying out the reasons why he thought Koch had faked it; secondarily, the interview with Koch in *The Mountain Journal* made his own case weaker, and the rumours of Koch's behaviour on Richards' expedition to the Kichatna Spires hurt his image all the more, along with his subsequent disappearing act from the climbing scene. Additional weight against the ascent came from Richards' two failures on the southeast face, and Chalmers' three failures, the last two on the north face (including, that is, the Koch-Briles expedition).
>
> In an absolute sense the truth will never be known. What interests me is that climbers have turned their backs so completely on Pterophorus and the unnamed peaks near it. The explosion of big-wall routes on the fine granite of the Spires and the peaks south of McKinley, along with Richards' and Chalmers' tales of the horrible decomposing rock on Pterophorus, have led to the neglect. But a very difficult mountain remains today with at most one, more likely no, ascent.
>
> If we can set aside the problem of whether Koch was telling the truth, it is worth noticing in how many ways his and Briles' attempt was years ahead of its time. In 1964 all hard climbs in Alaska were fixed to a point near the summit, with elaborate build-up of tent camps and supplies. In contrast, Koch and Briles 'went for it' from a bivouac tent only 2000 feet up; they were prepared to climb the last 2500 feet with only four days' food, no fixed ropes, and a bivvy sack. Today this would be regarded as admirable style. Second: climbers who knew Koch said that he was incomparable on the kind of dangerous mixed ground that mountains like Pterophorus are made of. He was supposed to have been very fast and very nervy on bad rock, loose and hollow snow, even on blue ice (taking into account the old step-chopping style). Technical and gear improvements have revolutionized big-wall routes of the kind found in the Spires. But there have been almost no improvements (except for bivouac gear) that would make a significant difference on a mountain like Pterophorus.
>
> Koch's legacy, then, is a call to all of us to turn our sights somewhat away from Yosemite-style routes on perfect granite in expeditionary ranges, in favour of a

> return to total mountaineering, to the acceptance of bad rock and devious routefinding and inaccessibility by airplane . . .

There followed a discussion of climbing possibilities in the unexplored parts of Alaska. Victor closed the magazine. The tight feeling in his throat had grown worse. 'Can I keep this?'

'Of course.'

'Thank you, Arthur.'

'How do you feel about it?'

It would, Victor knew, be a matter of days before he could sort out and subdue the feelings the article had provoked. But he said to Arthur, 'It's very nice. Do you suppose it will have any effect on the younger climbers?'

When Arthur left, the two men shook hands in the doorway. 'If you change your mind about an afternoon of climbing, let me know. And keep in touch, old man.'

During the next week Victor went about his business, and even his leisure, with an even more fastidious attention to routine than usual. He put the copy of *Climb* in a bottom drawer and refused to look at it again. On the days when his partners were occupied, he did a double workout at the 'Y.' One day he was walking past a downtown climbing store; for the first time in a decade he felt the urge to go in, and only avoided doing so with an effort of will. He concentrated on the reports and referrals he had to read at work, but the print kept blurring into phrases like, 'incomparable on dangerous mixed ground' and 'very fast and very nervy.' Several nights he woke in the small hours and lay in the darkness, feeling old, his life without purpose or promise. In the last few years, he would have said, he had not once been lonely; now he discovered a hunger for a confidant, someone to talk with the way he had done only with Vera.

At last he called Arthur. He had decided to go climbing once only, to prove to himself that he could do without it, in the same way that, if he really had to, he could drink a single glass of bourbon and yet never need a second. Obviously pleased, Arthur invited him for a weekend to meet his family. Victor pleaded a shortage of time, and arranged to meet Arthur at the Gunks.

It was a crisp, sunny Saturday when the two men met at the Uberfall. His initial excitement at the breathtaking sweep of the cliffs seemed dampened for Victor by the hordes assembled on the Carriage Road. 'This is incredible,' he said. 'I suppose we'll have to wait in line.'

'Not if we go down a ways. Glad you could make it. Shall we start with something 5.4-ish?'

As they walked down the road, Victor eyed Arthur's rack with suspicion. 'You don't even carry a hammer?'

'The resident pins are mostly solid. You'd get shamed out of the Gunks if somebody caught you pounding away.'

'But do you really trust those things?'

'You get used to them.'

Through Victor's head a number of thoughts were swarming. The cliffs looked alarmingly steep; he was afraid he might feel fear, even on an easy climb. He had only pretended to be interested in Arthur's notion of 'mellow' climbing; what he wanted was to see just how hard a 5.8 pitch seemed after all the years. Ideally, he would sense that, with practice, he could be at least as good as he had once been. Then, tested by temptation, he could go back to his normal life.

The first fifty feet were fine. Victor was beginning to feel smug about how easy the ladder-like steps in the rock were, when he found himself at grips with a small overhang. Arthur had hauled himself easily over the bulge, but Victor paused, hung on his arms, and tried to crane outward to look for the holds above. He felt his fingers cramping, and, shamefully, his calves were beginning to quiver. An angry burst of strength got him over, but he nearly slipped. Then he was seized with the idea that his tie-in knot was coming undone. The sense of open space about him was disturbing. He checked his knot and tried to breathe deeply. And that was only 5.4, he thought. I've lost it all; I never should have come.

On the belay ledge Arthur was beaming. 'What a day. How did it feel?'

Victor tried to catch his breath. 'I had a little trouble with that overhang. Wasted a lot of strength.'

'It takes getting back into. Want the next lead?'

'I don't think so.' There were scrapes on the backs of his hands already.

'It's only about 5.2.'

'You go ahead. I don't feel comfortable with those nuts yet.'

The whole day was upsetting. After another easy climb Victor felt tired and shaky. Arthur kept apologizing for him, repeating too earnestly that it took time to get the head for it again. In mid-afternoon he asked, 'Something a little harder?'

Victor wanted only to go home. But the test was incomplete. 'Sure,' he said. 'As long as you lead it.'

'5.7-ish?'

'Why not?' In his good years 5.7 had been child's play. Surely he could follow a climb of that rating now without making a fool of himself. Arthur led the way across the highway to an area he called the Near Trapps. Here the rock seemed even steeper, more angular, festooned with awesome ceilings. 'The crux is on the second pitch. Use your feet on the nubbins and it's not bad.'

But it was very bad. Some of the moves below gave Victor trouble, and by the time he had reached the crux he was feeling psyched out. The long step was across an empty void. Arthur, out of sight around a corner above and well to the right, had left a nut beyond the hard move. But, Victor thought, what if I fall and that nut comes out? I'll pendulum way out into space, maybe even be left hanging in the air. He tried to dry his palms on his pants. His throat was sticky, as if full of wax. At last he forced himself to go at the move. With one foot starting to shake itself off a nubbin, he yelled for tension. The pull came; Victor lunged for the sling dangling from the guardian nut and heard himself whimper with fear.

He had begun to recompose himself by the time he reached Arthur. The top of the cliff was only forty easy feet above.

'What do you think?' Arthur said, his voice that of a man whose party has not come off.

'I've had enough for today. It's, well, discouraging.'

'No reason for it to be. You haven't been out in years.'

'I thought I was in shape.'

'Gym shape's different. Look.' He pointed.

Across a featureless slab to their right, Victor saw a person climbing a dead-vertical layback. The head shook long blond hair out of the eyes, and he could see the face. It was a woman's. Victor looked below for a partner, and realized with a shock that there was no rope trailing. His breath caught in his throat. The woman moved, walking her feet up the opposing wall to just below her fingers, then making a quick, jerky series of hand-over-hand reaches to gain height. She paused, let go with one hand and dipped it hurriedly into a small bag of chalk hanging from her waist. There was a ten-foot section above her where the crack seemed to narrow almost to a seam. As the face turned again, Victor realized that he had seldom seen a woman so beautiful anywhere. It was excruciating to watch her, imagining the fall should she slip.

'Who is she?'

'Diana Volk.'

Victor had forgotten himself completely in the drama of watching. The woman's hesitation unnerved him; he wondered if she were in trouble. Then, with deliberation, but no false effort, she reached for and found the only places in the crack where her fingers would fit. Within seconds she had moved in her rough, efficient way up to the safety of a large ledge. She stood and shook out her arms, then, looking around, caught sight of the two of them. She waved and yelled exuberantly, 'Hello, Arthur.'

'You're looking great, Diana!'

'See you at Rudi's a little later?'

'Probably.'

The woman turned and climbed easily out of sight. Victor was still dumbfounded. 'How hard is that climb?'

'That's Head Trip. Hard 5.8' Arthur laughed. 'I can't get up it.'

'Does she solo a lot?'

'That was routine for her. She's easily the best woman climber in the East.'

'She's beautiful.'

Arthur frowned. 'Too many men think so.'

'What do you mean?'

'I'll explain later. Let's go on up.'

At the top of the cliff Victor stared out over the farms and trees while Arthur coiled the rope. His forearms were pumped up with blood, the muscles knotted, and his hands were covered with raw scrapes. He felt that he had let Arthur down. 'It's an amazing place,' he said, to fill the silence.

'You can see why some of the guys move to New Paltz. Sometime we should walk down to Mohonk, too. Even the hike there is lovely.' Arthur also sensed the letdown. 'How about stopping at Rudi's?'

'Somebody's house?' Victor asked, remembering Mr. Siffler's

'No, it's a tavern just down the road. A climbers' hangout.'

'I'd rather not.'

'The drinking?'

'It's not that. It's, well, the old business about—'

'Nobody will know about that.' Arthur cinched up the coil. 'It's all on a first-name basis. Come on, one beer for old times' sake.'

The feeling of paranoia that had struck Victor when they had walked into Rudi's – Arthur having been greeted with salvos of hellos – was ebbing now, as the two men sat in a corner and talked. Victor was nursing a Coke. 'That first beer after climbing,' Arthur said. 'I don't know anything better. Do you miss it at all?'

'No,' Victor lied. The smell of rock on his hands was bringing back all the old associations; he thought of that very first six-pack with Ed at Mr. Siffler's. His Coke was sweet and insipid. 'I'm surprised by something,' he went on.

'What?'

'You seem completely accepted here. I thought climbing had gotten really competitive.'

Arthur's eyes wrinkled. 'Oh, it's desperate. If I were a young prodigy trying to get Stanton or Welsch to recognize me, I'd be miserable. But everybody knows where I'm coming from. My friendships here mean a lot to me. And you know, when Fran comes up, she's included, too. It's not like the old 'oh, -that's-so-and-so's-chick thing.'

Victors eye wandered to the door, where he saw Diana Volk enter with a group of men. Arthur saw too. He continued, 'Diana's as much the reason as anything. People know they have to take women seriously as climbers now.' Arthur waved.

Victor looked at his watch. 'I should be getting back.'

'One more beer,' Arthur protested. 'I still want to check out how you feel about it all.'

'All right. A quick one.'

As Arthur was trying to catch the waitress's eye, Diana yelled across, 'Hey, Arthur. Let me buy you a beer. I owe you one.' The men around her had envious looks on their faces.

Arthur glanced at Victor. 'What do you say?'

Victor was torn. He hesitated, then said, 'Well, as long as you don't—'

'I know. Don't worry. Come on.'

The introductions were rapid and perfunctory. Arthur presented him, however, as 'Vic.' Through the first minutes of chat Victor sat burning with a private humiliation. He told himself, as he had countless times over the years, that the problem was all with the others – he could hold up his head out of simple pride in what he had done. If he had never actually climbed Pterophorus, that would be another matter. Slowly the preoccupation with himself wore away, and he drifted into the talk. A second Coke had arrived.

He watched the assembled faces, gradually discerning that all the power in the group lay centred in Diana. The seemingly nonchalant name-dropping and route-chatter was all aimed at winning her attention; and right now the frustration around the table was mounting, for she was showing interest only in Arthur. Behind his anonymity, he allowed himself to look at her. There was a tiny scar beside one very blue eye. She had a habit of wetting and licking her lips, and when she laughed her whole face was given over to it. The backs of her dirty hands were covered with tiny scabs. With alarm Victor realized that he was in the grip of a feeling he had not had, it seemed, for years and years.

It was hard for him to answer, then, when she suddenly turned the spotlight on him. 'How about you, Vic? Just started climbing?'

'No, I used to do it, years ago,' he managed.

'Around here?'

'In the Midwest.'

'Oh.' Her tongue teased at her lips. 'How did you like Slow Joe?'

'Is that what we were on?' Victor temporized. Arthur nodded. 'I had trouble with it. I'm pretty out of shape.' To divert the attention away from himself, he said, 'I was really impressed with your soloing that climb.'

'Did you do Head Trip, Diana?' one of the others intruded. She ignored him.

'That move across is hard,' Diana went on. 'It used to be done as aid.'

'Well, that's some comfort.' Abruptly Victor's defenses came to his rescue. Really, he told himself, this is banal, this empty chat. It was time he got on the road. The woman was being polite. He turned to Arthur. 'I should be going. Long drive.'

'Of course.' Arthur stood up. 'See you all next weekend?'

Victor allowed himself one last glance at Diana. In his infatuation he imagined a look of faint disappointment on her face.

In the car during the short drive back to the Uberfall, Victor asked Arthur, 'What did you mean before? About too many men—'

Arthur seemed deep in thought. 'Sometimes I think I'm too hard on her. She's in a tough position. All those guys are in love with her, as you could see. I suppose I'd act the same.'

'How does she act?'

'She lets them hang around, like puppy dogs. Then she'll turn all her charm on someone like me, because I'm safe, not after her. I get the feeling she does it just to torment them.'

'But you get along with her.'

'I love climbing with her. Here's your car. How about another weekend, sometime soon?'

'We'll see,' said Victor, reaching for the door handle. 'I'll call you.' He hesitated. 'So none of those guys was her—'

'Who knows? She goes through them the way other women go through boxes of Kleenex. That's I guess what bothers me. That, and the thing about Andy.'

'Who's Andy?'

'Was. One of the best young climbers here. Only eighteen. He was hopelessly in love with her. They were lovers for a month or two, then she dropped him. For someone who used to climb with Andy.'

'Go on.'

'He was found at the bottom of Birdline.'

'He was soloing?'

'Nobody was there to see. But everybody knows he must have jumped off.'

'Why?'

'Andy could have soloed Birdline in the dark. Also, they had a thing about it. It was "their" climb.'

Victor sucked air through his teeth. 'Can you really blame her for it, though?'

'I don't know. I suppose not.'

'She really is beautiful.'

'Oh, yes.'

CHAPTER EIGHT

DURING THE next two weeks Victor fell back on his methodical daily routines with a sober dedication. His handball game improved – simply, he thought, because he put a little more effort into winning each point. On his days alone at the 'Y' he kept up at first the double workout; but one afternoon in the middle of his third set of forearm curls the absurdity of the exercise came home to him. After that he found it onerous to complete a single workout, despite the habit of years' standing. At work, in the middle of precounseling interviews or over memos, he found his mind wandering as it had never used to.

The insomnia persisted. He would wake predictably around 5.00 a.m. and see in the neat, familiar furniture of his bedroom the accoutrements of a prison cell. Over the recent years he had convinced himself that saving others was noble and important work: he was careful not to sound Messianic about it, but the rare cases of true rehabilitation filled him with satisfaction. Now, however, at that predawn hour, the absence of any true quest of his own, for himself, glared him in the face. The rest of his life would be the same as it was now. Twenty years from now he would be coming home from the 'Y' to broil the thawing drumsticks.

For years he had dreamed very rarely, and remembered the odd exception only hazily. Now his short nights seemed to teem with exotic and disturbing visions. Several times he dreamed about Diana Volk, waking to find himself sexually aroused.

He reread Tom Kinney's article. It was disappointing that the man had not gone the small step further and asserted his faith in Victor's achievement: all the reasons for doing so were there, in his own argument. As he thought back over the day at the Gunks, the embarrassment and the fear tended to dwindle in memory. He began again to look at doorsills and building buttresses in terms of holds and routes. At last he called Arthur and arranged another weekend.

They made six climbs during a long Saturday, the weather as splendid as it had been before. Victor got up a pair of 5.7 routes without too much trouble, climbing in rock shoes Arthur had borrowed for him. He led a number of pitches up to 5.5. 'It's coming back,' he told Arthur happily, as they stood on top of the cliff.

'See? It doesn't have to be all guts-and-glory. It's a different thing, just climbing for the fun of it.'

On Sunday morning they were reading the bulletin board at the Uberfall when a young climber belaying his girlfriend up Horseman shouted down: 'Hey, Arthur, how you doing?'

'Good, Bernie. And you?'

'Hey, I hear Victor Koch is around here this weekend.'

Arthur turned a stunned face toward Victor, then answered, 'I don't know about that.'

'He'll probably wander in and tell everybody he's soloed Foops.'

Arthur shouted up, 'You just keep your mouth closed, Bernie, all right?'

Arthur caught up with him down on the highway, as Victor was getting into the front seat of his car. 'Wait a minute, Victor. It doesn't mean anything. He's just a young fool.'

Victor was beginning to control his emotions. After all the years, he knew how to do so deliberately. But the words that came out were bitter. 'See? I told you I couldn't be anonymous here. How did he know?'

'I don't have the faintest. I didn't tell anyone. Climbing gossip is incredible.'

Victor put the keys into the ignition. 'Thanks, Arthur. But it was stupid from the beginning. I should have known better.' Yet the sense of having been cheated prickled in his blood: he had just begun to climb well again.

Arthur said, 'Don't rush off. It doesn't matter what Bernie and the like—'

Anger broke through the control. 'Don't give me that bullshit, Arthur.' He was alarmed; it was the first time he had used a swear word in years. 'I'm going.' In the rearview mirror he saw Diana Volk approaching, a rope and a rack slung from her shoulders.

Arthur turned. 'Not, now, Diana. We're having a talk.'

She ignored him and poked her head close to the window. 'Hey, man, I just want to say I'm sorry. Bernie's a fucking asshole.'

The urge to flee was upon him. He started to turn the key. 'How did you—?'

'Oh, everybody's buzzing away about it up there. Listen.' She moved her head closer. Despite his anger and humiliation, the spell of her beauty kept him momentarily paralyzed. 'I don't give a shit what happened on some mountain way off somewhere back in the last ice age. You seem like an OK guy to me, and anybody Arthur hangs out with is stamped and certified. Let's go do a climb, the three of us.'

Arthur looked hopeful. 'No,' said Victor.

'I guess not, Diana.'

Clearly she was used to having her way. 'Nothing hard. A good long mellow climb.'

'No,' Victor repeated. 'Can't you see—?'

'It'll die down. Listen, we'll go way off to Millbrook. Nobody climbs there. Maybe we can put up something new.'

His own ambivalence kept him off balance, and the spell of her will and beauty, mingling with the traces of the dreams about her, pushed him over. 'All right,' he said. 'Just one climb.'

Diana and Arthur swung leads on the long meandering route she chose. While Victor belayed her he admired her economy of movement; during Arthur's leads, she forced an awkward trivial conversation on him. There was in fact no one else nearby; but Victor's thoughts were fixed on an image of a horde of detractors at the Uberfall. The afternoon sun on the yellowing treetops was achingly beautiful, a glimpse of a country from which he had been exiled. At the top he thanked Diana formally, his mind already dwelling on the drab but comfortable certainties of his future back in Hartford. She wormed his phone number out of him before he left.

The next evening she called. On Saturday, she said, she was going to be at a cliff called West Peak, not so far from Hartford. It was an undeveloped crag similar to Ragged. Nobody would be around. She wanted him to join her.

'But I can't climb at your level,' Victor said, feeling the flattery of her attention weaken him.

'There's just one hard thing I want to try, and it's only one pitch.' Victor supposed that Diana had planned to visit West Peak anyway. The alternative seemed unimaginable. 'You can clean it on jumars, or I'll rappel it. The rest of the day we can do moderate stuff. What do you say?'

Her spell was potent even over the telephone. Against the firm resolves of his dogged drive home from the Gunks, he heard himself say yes.

Every weekend for the next two months Victor climbed with Diana for at least one day. He could never fathom why she was eager to spend so much time with him, but he did not want to spoil anything by asking. With her leading above him, effortlessly dismissing the apparent difficulties, he began to feel the kind of confidence he had associated with Ed and with no one else. His own skill developed rapidly; soon he could follow most 5.9's and lead a well-protected 5.8. When Diana went off with someone else to try a really hard climb, he felt a vexation strangely like jealousy. When she soloed, he could not bring himself to watch, but waited anxiously for her to return.

His first time back at the Gunks – she had insisted on going there – Victor had an attack of nerves. After their first route she deliberately lingered at the Uberfall, hailing friends, trading gossip; initially irked with her, Victor slowly realized that to be seen with Diana was to be legitimized in the other climbers' eyes. That afternoon they drank at Rudi's and the celebrants crowding around the table included Victor in their questions and their laughter.

He climbed with Arthur a few times. On a high belay ledge, his friend complimented him. 'You're getting awfully good.'

'It's Diana. She's lucky for me.'

'Victor, it's none of my business, but—'

'But what?'

'Be careful.'

The relationship developed with its own odd logic. On any subject besides climbing, Diana seemed bored, her conversation automatic. She never asked him about Pterophorus, or his past, and he did not offer information about either. The weekends included Saturday nights drinking in New Paltz, after which she would throw down her sleeping bag next to his on the Carriage Road; yet he had never touched or kissed her, and so theirs did not seem like a real intimacy. It was in that very possibility, Victor knew, that the danger lay: the events of his past, Ed's death and Vera's betrayal, above all, had had the power to hurt him only because he had allowed himself intimacy. Yet his five-day week now dragged its way out against the anticipated weekend; each Saturday morning as he drove the highways towards his rendezvous, Victor fought down the dread that she might have forgotten, might not show up.

One night in October they were in a rowdy bar in New Paltz. The overzealous band prohibited conversation. Diana had been downing drafts steadily, and in fact everyone at the table seemed drunk except Victor. She had asked him to dance, but he had held up his palms, pleading incapability; instead she danced with a series of other partners, flinging herself expertly around the floor, tossing her blond hair, while Victor watched everyone in the bar watch her. The band took a break, but the juke box was almost as loud. A climber Victor vaguely recognized came up to Diana and shouted in her ear. She waved him away, but he kept yelling; Victor saw by the muscles in the face that the man was furious. Finally he heard Diana shout, 'Hey, fuck off!' Victor started to get to his feet, as the climber was clutching a beer bottle with dangerous intensity. But instead of violence, abruptly the man spun away, choosing retreat.

After the bar closed, Victor drove Diana back to the cliffs. There was a gibbous moon, and the trees were swaying in a warm wind. Sleeping bag in hand, Victor started up to the Carriage Road. Diana clasped his arm, saying, 'Let's go up on top. Across the road. It's such a night.' The touch of her hand on his arm – the first such contact – sent Victor's blood racing.

They found a clearing at cliff-edge, with barely enough room for their bags on a bed of pine needles. The sense of a drop just beyond reminded Victor of mountain bivouacs. He got into his sleeping bag. Diana paused halfway inside her own, her hands starting to unbutton her shirt. 'Victor, can I ask you something?'

'Certainly.' He sat up to look at her. Her hair was gleaming with the moonlight behind her.

'Do you find me unattractive, or something?'

Victor's pulse quickened. Was she drunk, after all those beers? But no one held liquor better than Diana. He said, 'Of course not.'

'Well, what is it then? You haven't showed, you know, the slightest interest.'

Impulsively, Victor blurted out the truth. 'I don't want to ruin anything. I'm half in love with you, and it scares me.'

Diana laughed gaily. 'Well, for Christ's sake. Let's make love, then.' She undid the rest of her buttons and threw off her shirt; she wore nothing underneath. 'I'll get in your bag. Unzip it all the way.'

Long after the sex was over and Diana lay on her back, asleep, Victor leaned on one elbow, feasting his eyes on her. His rapture had a streak of pure greed in it. This is all mine, he said to himself, mine to have and touch and hold. The years of sterile caution stretched like a wasteland behind him.

The working week began to seem to Victor nothing more than an ordeal of patience. About the rest of Diana's life, which she was so bored when describing, he remained largely ignorant. She lived for climbing, as she put it. He was not really sure what her occupation was – something to do with a dance company in New York City. She never invited him to her apartment in Manhattan; instead, it was assumed that they would meet every weekend at the Gunks. Through Diana he gradually joined the circle of top climbers at the tables in Rudi's and the diner in New Paltz; gradually they seemed to accept him, or at least to cease regarding him as a curiosity of nature.

On a Thursday in early November Victor stared at the newspaper in dismay. The forecast was unequivocally for freezing rain all weekend. He had never phoned Diana before, so that now it took a long while to get up the nerve. She did not answer all that afternoon or evening. He finally reached her Friday morning.

'Did I wake you up?'

'No,' she said sluggishly. 'Yes, I guess you did. Ugh. Wait a minute while I put the coffee water on.'

When she had returned, he said, 'Diana, it's supposed to rain all weekend.'

'I know.'

'I thought maybe I could come see you in New York. We could spend the weekend there.'

There was a long silence. Thursday's premonition of trouble seemed to Victor to be assuming material form. 'Diana?' he asked.

'I'm thinking. There must be someplace in the East where it won't rain. What about Seneca?'

'It's awfully far for a weekend.'

'Take Monday off.'

'I can't. Wait. The paper says even West Virginia.' He paused. 'Would you like me to come down?'

'Damn it. I want to climb. I'll tell you what. I'll come up there.'

'Great. Friday night?'

'Saturday. There's this performance Friday. What will we do?'

'I'll think of things.'

As it turned out, they spent most of the weekend in Victor's apartment. Diana seemed restless, pacing the floor as she peered at the flower photographs or examined the spartan furniture; but when Victor suggested entertainments – a movie, a flute recital – she seemed uninterested. They spent much of the time making love. As always, Victor's sense of luxury and privilege manifested itself in his urge to pore over every square centimetre of her body. Diana accepted the homage as if it were naturally her due; in sex she drove confidently toward her own orgasm, reaching it often before he had his.

On Sunday afternoon the subject of Pterophorus at last came up. Uncharacteristically shy, she asked him if he wanted to tell her about it, adding, 'If it's too painful, forget it.'

'Not at all. I haven't talked about it in years. Did you see Tom Kinney's article in *Climb*?'

'No. Some of the guys were talking about it, though.'

Victor resisted the vanity of ferreting the copy from his bureau drawer. He launched into a long resumé of the expedition. When he spoke of Chalmers, it was not in heat, but with philosophical pity. He described the summit dash with an abundance of detail.

Diana seemed contemplative. She tossed her hair out of her eyes and said, 'So you really did it. I didn't tell you this before, but the guys talking about it . . . well, all but one or two of them were positive you hadn't.'

'I know.'

'Damn it, there must be some way even now you could prove you did it. Did you leave anything on the summit?'

'No. We were too tired.' Victor had a dim memory of suggesting to Ed that they deposit some object there, in the snow; but he could not be sure it hadn't been Ed's idea. 'I don't care about proving it any more. I've come to terms with the whole thing.'

Later, in bed again, Diana asked, 'Do you really love me?'

'Of course.' He wanted to ask if she loved him. But he said, 'Why do you like me?'

She kissed his ear teasingly. 'I don't know. You're so different from the others. You've been through a lot, that makes you interesting. Maybe it's just that you didn't go after me. I'm not used to that.'

Victor puzzled over his disappointment. Diana yawned, stretching, while he gazed at her breasts. 'Why did you get divorced?' she asked.

'We were on different tracks. She was headed for her history career, and I was a college dropout. But the thing I couldn't forgive, the thing I'm still angry about, is that she sided with the others, the ones who claimed we hadn't made it.'

'That's incredible.'

'I know. I was pretty mixed up by then. I was drinking a lot. I had these rages.'

'You're so, you know, even-tempered now.' She rubbed her hand across his chest. 'Want to make love again? Can you?'

'Let's try.' As he took her in his arms, the sense of wealth flooded through him again.

Afterwards she resumed the discussion. 'So you really went off the deep end with the booze? I suppose I could myself. What's it like?'

'The scary thing is that you're not really aware what's happening. There are so many defences, so many rationalizations for having a drink. Even when I was having serious memory blankouts, waking up and not knowing where I was, I didn't know what trouble I was in.'

'What did you do all those years? Stanton says nobody in climbing knew what had happened to you.'

The only person Victor had ever told about the bad years was his therapist, when he had finally gotten to SANOL and begun to want to save his life. Now he started to brush aside Diana's curiosity, as he had Arthur's. But the prospect of a lifetime of secrecy struck him all at once as empty and depressing. And she lay there beside him, her warm skin against his, the hand circling on his chest.

'If I tell you this, will you promise you'll never tell anyone else?'

'I promise,' she said easily.

He closed his eyes, as he always had with his therapist. 'When I left Vera in, let's see, 1966, I was at loose ends. I got a job painting houses that spring. It was what my father had done, and it was the only thing besides climbing I knew how to do. My god, it was boring, though. I fell in with a card shark who taught me poker scams. We went to Reno and cruised for tourists looking for what they thought was a friendly game upstairs in somebody's room. He'd use me to bump the pots in seven-card hi-lo, or vice versa.'

'What's that?'

'It doesn't matter. We made some big killings, but I blew a few pots, too. I was drinking all the time, and it got hard to keep track of the signals.'

He opened his eyes briefly to look at Diana. Her gaze was calm but attentive. He went on, 'A guy caught on to my partner dealing seconds and nearly beat the life out of him. I got out of town. I went to Las Vegas, got a job taking the change out of slot machines. I tried out for blackjack dealer, but my hands weren't good by then. I got into a strange line instead. It was a male escort service. Getting paid by lonely ladies to accompany them to parties and things. Diana, there are more lonely women in Las Vegas than anywhere on earth. Sometimes they wanted sex, too, and it would mean extra money. But they weren't young. I would drink so I could go through with it, but then I'd have trouble. I think I lost all interest in sex for a few years because of it. And when you're drinking as much as I was, you lose interest anyway.' He opened his eyes again. 'Does this shock you?'

'Not at all,' she said, kissing the back of his hand. 'I'm fascinated.'

Victor pressed his fingers against her mouth. 'I got into drugs – not taking them, just dealing. It was 1969, and there was a big demand for mescalin and LSD and peyote. I got into a really bad thing in Mexico.' Should he tell her everything? Something about her nonchalance bothered him. He chose to summarize. 'The upshot was that I had to get as far away from there as possible. Which is why I ended up in New England.

'I spent two years really scraping along. I'd get bartending jobs but always lose them for drinking. I sort of let myself go about then, not changing clothes for weeks at a time, living in the cheapest rooming houses and not paying rent, getting evicted or just clearing out. I don't even remember large parts of those years. The one thing I learned really well from that time is what it's like to be alone. Finally I passed out drunk on a bad cold night in New Haven. The police got me to a hospital, but I came close to dying even so.' Victor surveyed his fingers. 'I don't know why I didn't get frostbite. Especially since I'd had some on Pterophorus.' He closed his eyes once more. 'I was in and out of hospitals. I tried A.A. but it didn't stick. I know now that I just wanted to die, to get down under and forget how everybody I cared about had betrayed me.' Victor paused. The angry feeling was coming back. His habitual cautionary mechanism went into play. 'To make a long story short, I finally happened upon a rehabilitation programme that worked. And I've been with SANOL since.'

'Why are they so good?' Diana asked, stretching.

'It's too long to tell. They remake you from scratch, essentially. For instance, I didn't used to talk this way.'

'You mean sort of formal?'

Victor smiled. 'SANOL believes that language embodies one's pathology. When I was down and out, all I talked was slang and profanity. I've learned to speak all over again. I learned to read, to like good music, to think for myself. The most important thing I learned was how to be alone and feel OK about it. And how to govern the anger. It's the key to all the rest. My father beat me when I was a child—' The uneasiness bloomed in Victor's brain. Something to do with Diana's languid acceptance of everything that he was saying. If nothing could shock her, nothing could be that important, either. 'I'll go into it all some time. I don't want to bore you.' He turned and nuzzled her bare shoulder. 'Does this change how you feel about me?'

'Silly, of course not. I'm glad you told me. It makes us closer.' She smiled her all-embracing smile.

'It felt good to tell somebody. To tell you.' But that was not exactly true; the disturbance lingered. 'I love you, Diana.'

She kissed him for answer. 'Hey, what'll we do next weekend?'

It was almost December. The crowds at the Gunks had dwindled; the gatherings at Rudi's had become cosier but less animated. One afternoon the talk wandered to Alaska. Brewer and Stanton were discussing the unclimbed walls in the Ruth Gorge. Brewer seemed half-serious about going there. Stanton was dubious because of rumours of lousy rock. Victor felt the stirrings of the old infectious expedition urge. The wind was gusting bitterly outside. Stanton abruptly asked Victor, 'You've been up there. Ever see the Ruth Gorge?'

Caught off balance, Victor cleared his throat. 'Actually I have. On the flight in to Foraker. It's impressive.'

'I didn't know you'd done Foraker.'

'We didn't do it. It was a fiasco. We only got to ten-five. We were too slow.'

The change in atmosphere around the table was unmistakable. There was a tension waiting to be discharged, and the faces fixed on his were hungry with curiosity. Victor pressed his knee against Diana's under the table. Stanton, sensing the discomfort, said, 'Well, summer's a long way off, anyway.'

When they parted that Sunday afternoon, Diana said, 'Let's give it one more weekend. Did that bother you, in the bar?'

'No,' Victor said. 'Let's make it Friday night, too.'

'I don't know. I hate these cold nights. I wish our bags zipped together.'

'Let's stay in a motel.'

The moment at Rudi's, however, stuck with Victor through the week like a speck of dust in the eye. His apartment became claustrophobic, and even the pattern which the fall had begun to assume – the work week as a rite of preparation for Diana – left him edgy now and morose. They had not discussed how – or even whether – to see each other after the climbing was done for the year. December, January and February seemed to represent a gulf that gaped before him, a reminder of the absence of any quest in his future. He had followed a few 5.10's, and was solid now on 5.9: among the Gunks regulars, only Jacobs was climbing so well at his age. But what would the climbing with Diana ever become, but more of itself? And would she eventually grow tired of it?

He had an upsetting dream involving both Ed and Vera. He tried in the morning to banish the lingering overtones with coffee and the paper. As he stared at the meaningless newsprint, all at once there came creeping among the alien letters the micro-organism of an idea.

He spent Friday night with Diana in a motel near the Thruway. They took a bubble bath together and Diana drank champagne, and they made love all through the night. In the morning she rose, naked, and pulled open the curtains. 'It's snowing,' she said. 'Damn it.'

'Let's go on up for a walk anyway. Around by the Outback Slabs. I want to talk about something.'

Well bundled, they strolled hand-in-hand down the Carriage Road. There had been not even another parked car on the highway. Diana said, 'What is this thing you want to talk about?'

Victor held out a palm and caught a snowflake. 'This may sound crazy, but listen. I want to go back. With you.' He squeezed her hand.

'Back where?'

'To Alaska. To Pterophorus.'

She stopped walking. 'Are you serious?'

'Yes. I've been thinking hard about it. If I climb it again, nobody can ever doubt me. It's the answer. And with you – well, I know we could do it together.'

'I haven't done any mountaineering to speak of.'

'We'll train. We'll go ice climbing all winter. We can train in June in the Wind Rivers, say.'

'I was planning on the Valley in June.'

'It doesn't matter. You'll pick up things really fast. It would be us, Diana, against everybody. We'll keep it a secret until July.'

'I can't afford to go to both the Valley and Alaska.'

'I'll pay your way.'

She took a long deep breath, then shook the snow out of her hair. 'Let's go get a cup of coffee somewhere and talk this over.'

CHAPTER NINE

VICTOR TAUGHT himself modern ice climbing by consulting Chavois' book, which had just been published. To have showed up at Chapel Pond and begged a lesson from Stanton or Brewer would have been too obsequious, and might have dropped the hint that something was up for Alaska. Diana had trouble getting away from the city and did not take to ice climbing very well: she hated the cold, especially when they camped out, and seemed unsure of herself on ice the way she never had on rock. Distrustful as ever of the complexities of gear, Victor at first made hesitant progress with the various tools he swung at the gullies and slabs. Everything was simplified, he found, if one soloed; and Diana's absence dictated that choice often enough anyway. As the ice he assaulted on his solitary weekends grew steeper and longer, the phrase 'very nervy and very fast' rang in his head, a talisman of success.

At home Victor spent the evening hours making lists, poring over the maps, jotting down from memory notes about the route. After weeks of pondering approaches, he decided on a flight in to Desolation Creek. Ferrying loads for thirty miles to base camp would be slow and discouraging, but it was surer and cheaper than an airdrop – and in better style, too, as Tom Kinney would appreciate. Under the glare of his desk lamp, he slaved over poundage and hardware and food, the kind of obsessive fussing Ed had once been far fonder of than he. When he talked to Diana over the phone about details, she seemed bored, parrying his questions with the formula, 'Whatever you think's best.'

For the first time in ages his life seemed to concentrate on a meaningful, specific event in the future. More than once he caught himself marvelling, 'This is why it was always so good, why we used to do it year after year; this is what gave the twelve months shape and sense.' He dug out the few letters he had received from Ed and reread them, sniffing for the elixir of their former quest. Two qualms only troubled him during the early winter: the problem of precisely when and how to announce his plan to the world, and the possibility, ineradicable no matter how he scribbled and charted into the night, of failure on Pterophorus.

In March he resumed meeting Diana at the Gunks. Brewer invited them to sleep on the floor of his apartment in New Paltz, which solved the cold-camping problem. In the snug silence of the living room, however, Diana seemed squeamish about making love, for fear Brewer would overhear. Except for that aspect, their weekends together seemed at first to afford Victor all the gratification the fall had. Diana was climbing well, having no trouble with 5.8's even when there was still snow on the ledges.

He invited her to share his week off at spring vacation with a trip to Seneca. Work in the city, however, prevented her. He spent half the week in Boston shopping for gear and half the week at the Gunks. Diana joined him on

Thursday but had to leave Saturday afternoon, a pattern, she told him that the dance group would force upon her for the rest of the spring. Thus in April Victor had to resign himself each weekend to only one day of climbing with her, one night of drinking in New Paltz and sleeping together. To keep up his shape, he climbed Sundays with Stanton and Jacobs, and occasionally with Arthur. He seemed stuck at a level of difficulty, however, unable to lead the harder 5.9's, or to follow more than a few 5.10's that happened to be 'made' for him. After a particularly galling back-off, Jacobs joked, 'What the hell do you want? We're old men, Victor.' He throttled a petulant response.

One afternoon in April he was sitting on the Grand Traverse Ledge with Diana. Only an easy pitch remained above. She said, 'Before you dash off, I want to talk about something.'

Victor fiddled with a sticky karabiner gate. 'What is it?'

'I was talking with Brewer the other day, and I asked him how many people you ought to have for a big route in Canada or Alaska.'

'Diana, you didn't—'

'Relax. I didn't breathe a word about our plans. It was purely, you know, theoretical.' Victor sat down beside her. She was wearing knickers and a bright blue tank top that emphasized her breasts. Despite his irritation he felt the tug of desire. 'Anyway,' she went on, 'he thought two was iffy. Three or even four would be better.'

'What does Brewer know?'

'He knows a lot. He did all those—'

'I know what he's done,' Victor snapped. In the silence that followed they could hear the clanking of hardware on a nearby route.

Diana persisted. 'He said the problem with two is you've got too much weight per person. He said the two girls who did the Nose almost couldn't haul their own gear.' She looked at him coolly. 'And we're talking about ferrying loads thirty miles in?'

'You don't understand. I wanted this to be just us, just you and me. We have this destiny together, Diana.' He hated himself for saying the word out loud.

'Yeah, but.'

Victor sighed. For weeks he had been going over weights, juggling the figures to come up with manageable loads. Diana had never carried a heavy pack, and she weighed only 120 pounds. 'Brewer's right,' he said at last.

'Who, then?'

'I don't know.' He had been thinking long and hard about Arthur; but that was the wrong choice, even if the man could be persuaded to go.

'Let's keep our eyes out.'

Everything seemed so simple to her. 'But not a word about—'

She waved an impatient hand. 'I know, I know.'

In May began a pattern of quarrels, the first they had had. They occurred regularly on Friday night, after an evening of drinking and dancing. Diana would pick the quarrel, teasing or nagging at Victor until he was goaded to respond. Sometimes she would simply leave him at the table drinking his Coke while she danced all night with others, or traded gossip promiscuously. Late in the night, after he had sulked for hours, he would turn to her with words of apology. 'That's OK,' she would say. 'I got pretty loaded.' It disturbed him that she could not bring herself to apologize, not once, but he attributed her inability to do so to her youth. She would give him her body instead, and always Victor would slip back into the dark pool of his incredulity at having her, and he would lie awake for hours after she was asleep, running his fingertips over her thighs and stomach and breasts.

He got through the weekends on the strength of the four or five climbs they would do each Saturday. Diana was climbing brilliantly, leading 5.10's with confidence. He never tired of watching her move with that strange nervous efficiency up the thinnest of sequences, or pass an overhang that was already making his palms sweat as he sat below. But back in Hartford the disturbances in their relationship nudged him out of the comfort of his charts; his eyes would leave the figures and maps to stare at the walls of his study while he tried to pin down what was wrong. His thoughts traversed the years back to the planning months with Ed: how mutual the obsession had been in those days! In a bad moment he let himself wonder if the main reason Diana was willing to go to Alaska was that he was paying for it.

One night in May, as they were lying in their sleeping bags on the Carriage Road, Victor kissed Diana and said, 'There's something I want to tell you that I've never told anybody.'

'Go ahead.'

It was not something he could deliver over as easily as she seemed to think. He wavered. All through his adolescence and early childhood he had been sure that to share his secret would be to lose his luck. But a few nights before, lying sleepless in his apartment, he had decided that the malaise between them needed some counter-magic, a charm to reinforce the climbing bond that was stronger than luck. Hesitantly he started, 'After my mother died, there was no one who knew about this.' The telling became easier, as soon as he had spoken the plain fact about his kidney. He told her about his playground prowess, about starting climbing, then about his fall on Hungabee, and how close he had come to telling Ed. In the dark with his arms around her shoulders, he felt very close to crying; but it was a warm purgative feeling. At last he was done. 'So now you know, too.'

She hugged him. 'But why was it a secret?'

'Don't you see? I thought I explained it all.' The malaise perched on his shoulder. The scarecrow of his tale had failed to chase it away.

'It's nothing to be ashamed of, having one kidney.'

'It's not that. It's the whole thing.'

'Do you really believe it caused you luck?'

'I don't know,' Victor said dispirited. 'Maybe I don't have the luck any more. Maybe it went away when they started listening to Chalmers.' He turned over. To himself he said, And maybe it left tonight, when you blabbed it away to her. He struggled against tears, until the habit of control regained its power.

In mid-May Diana announced that she had found a likely third. His name was Derek Hudson. 'You've seen him at Rudi's,' she said. 'I know you have.'

'His name's familiar.'

'He's real strong. He's pushing Stanton these days. I've been climbing a lot with him on Fridays.'

'Does he have any mountaineering experience?'

'Yeah. He's ice climbed in the Palisades, and I know he's done stuff in the Cascades.'

'He's pretty young, isn't he?'

'He's my age. For Christ's sake, Victor, time's getting short.'

Diana arranged a sequestered meeting in a New Paltz cafe. Derek's tall, wiry, dark good looks were indeed familiar to Victor. A competitive instinct put him on guard, but as they talked, Derek's shy politeness won him over. At last Victor unfolded the plan. The young man did not seem as surprised as Victor might have expected. Nor did he have any difficulty deciding. He seemed flattered to be invited to Alaska, glad for a chance to go on an expedition – as simple as that. The three of them climbed together that afternoon and the next Saturday. Derek was a powerful leader, not so much graceful as immensely strong, with a prodigious reach. Victor warmed to the man's quiet poise, and August took on in his mind the promise of success.

In late June Diana and Derek drove out to Yosemite. A postcard informed Victor that they had done the Salathé in three days, despite intense heat. In Hartford he threw himself feverishly into the last weeks of planning, exhausting himself to the point where even his work at SANOL began to suffer – something he had never previously allowed to happen. He ran five miles a day to get in shape, but found less and less time for climbing. His last act before leaving was to mail a long letter to Arthur, explaining the expedition and asking him to spread the news of it through the climbing world.

He took a bus to Edmonton, where he waited a day for Derek and Diana. With minor breakdowns they continued up the gravel highway to Anchorage in Derek's old Volvo, taking four days for the passage. Exhausted, Victor slept most of the hours he wasn't driving. There was only desultory conversation, mostly about the month in the Valley. They arrived at midnight on a clear day. Victor pointed jubilantly to the hulking outlines of the three great volcanoes across Cook Inlet to the west. 'It's back there a ways, behind Gerdine. We'll be there in no time.'

But it took two days of frantic shopping in Anchorage, and another two days of waiting in Talkeetna, before their pilot was able to deposit them on the gravel bar where Desolation Creek exited westward from the mountains. Neither Diana nor Derek was much help with the last-minute logistics. On the flight in the pilot told Victor that the summer had been the driest in years. As they flew past the numberless unclimbed peaks, Victor saw that the snow cover was down to a minimum: blue ice gleamed everywhere. Then came the first glimpse of Pterophorus. Victor grabbed Derek's arm and pointed, shouting over the engine noise. Derek gave voice to a whoop. Diana, in the back seat, smiled.

The first stages of the hike in, however, had a demoralizing effect. The loads were heavier than Victor had calculated, and for the first two days they were reduced to triple-packing, until, at Diana's insistence, they cached ten days' food and some of the hardware and went ahead with double loads. A drizzly overcast set in on the third day, and the debris of the lower moraines gave only the most illusory relief to their treadmill progress. The marches were exhausting, six miles' effort yielding a gain of only two miles in their advance. They took lunch breaks in a glum silence, batting away the mosquitoes. The two small tents made for unsociable camping, with dinner passed from one door to the other.

Diana's mood grew progressively more irritable. She was developing blisters, and neither she nor Derek was in the kind of hiking shape to keep up the pace Victor set. Every afternoon it was Diana who pleaded for the halt. In the tent she fell asleep early, too tired to make love. Derek was willing to talk for hours, however, and several evenings Victor kept up long dialogues with him, their voices raised to pass from tent to tent over the patter of rain on the fly. He began to appreciate the younger man's deference and politeness. Always during the planning months his private image had been of Diana and himself going for the summit. Now he began to wonder whether, should they fail to go as a rope of three, Derek was not the more likely companion.

After six days they had covered only nineteen miles. That evening, as they sat crowded into Derek's tent for dinner, Diana demanded a rest day.

'But we've only got fourteen days' food left,' Victor protested.

'I don't care. My blisters are killing me. Besides, listen to the rain.'

'You've got to move in bad weather up here. You can't pamper yourself. What do you think, Derek?'

The dark eyes met his own, then glanced away. 'I'd like to get there, but I'm pretty beat myself.'

'We're only five miles from the junction. You can see the mountain from there.'

Diana spoke. 'Look, I need a rest day, OK? You're driving us like a goddamned slave master.' In a softer voice she added, 'I didn't think it was all going to be like this.'

He kneaded the muscles in her neck. 'All right Diana. I'm sorry. I'm just so hyped for getting there.' Derek looked relieved. 'What do you want to do with the day?'

'We can play poker,' Diana said. 'I brought a deck.'

'Not for money,' said Derek, exchanging a look with Diana.

Hours later, when they were alone in their tent, Victor confronted Diana. 'What was that about?'

'What?' She yawned as she got into her sleeping bag.

'That remark about the poker. "Not for money," he said.'

'How do I know?'

'Diana, have you told him about everything? About what I did during those years?'

'Goddamn it, leave me alone.'

'Keep your voice down.'

'Fuck you.'

Victor brooded. He could feel the magnetic pull of the mountain, as if it were right outside the door of the tent. And now they had to waste the whole next day on account of blisters. Perhaps he could gain something by ferrying loads all day by himself. Had he been reading too much into Derek's remark? But the glance between the two had seemed full of irony. He could not leave it alone. 'Why would Derek say "not for money" unless he knew I'd been a card player?'

'Fuck it all,' said Diana. Suddenly she was getting out of her sleeping bag and putting on her clothes.

'What are you doing?' Victor asked in alarm.

'Victor, you schmuck. You're so nearsighted. Yeah, Derek knows all about you. I told him. So he let it slip.' She was throwing her belongings into a stuff sack. 'I'm going to sleep in his tent the rest of this trip. I've been fucking him for months. I don't want to sleep with you any more. You're so goddamn demanding. And I'm not sure I want to go on with this expedition. I think I want to go back and wait for the plane.'

Through the ringing in his ears Victor managed to say, 'Diana. Please. Wait.'

'You're so pathetic, Victor. I can't believe you didn't catch on. Why do you think I started coming to the Gunks on Thursdays? And all last fall, I used the dancing stuff just to keep you away from the city. There was even a guy back there I was getting it on with. I suppose it was good for a while, you and me, but I'm sorry now we ever got started. And I don't know why I let myself get talked into this trip.' Her eyes blazed. 'You think you can own me. Nobody owns me.' Then she was gone.

Victor sat unmoving in his tent for an hour, listening to his heart pound. It was almost beyond the power of his long-practiced control to quell the impulses that were coursing through his veins. At last he heard a succession of noises, all too familiar. Unbelievably, Diana was making love with Derek, was broadcasting to him the sounds of her own orgasm.

He put on his cagoule and went out into the drizzly night. When he had walked a mile up the glacier, he sat down on a moraine boulder. It was almost dark, and the drizzle had a nasty chill to it. He looked at his hands. They were shaking. But the dim outlines of a course of action were forming in his mind.

CHAPTER TEN

AS HE HOPED, the other two were sound asleep when he returned to camp. With care to make no noise, Victor packed up in the heavy drizzle. The note he left in the now-empty tent read:

> You're right. There's no point going on with the trip, given what's happened. I have been very upset and so I am starting the hike-out alone. Take your time returning to the Creek, as the plane, you remember, isn't due for the aerial check for another nine days. I've taken the hardware as it's the heaviest and most

> valuable. Leaving my tent – will camp light, using a bivvy sac. Throw away all expendables and you can make it in one heavy load. If you get to the gravel bar and I'm not there, it's because I've decided to hike on out to Lime Village to get word out we want to be picked up. Don't worry about me – faster if one man goes, and I'm in shape. Just wait at Desolation Creek for the plane.

The note had neither salutation nor signature. At the last minute Victor pondered adding a few regretful words to Diana, but his rage vetoed the impulse.

With the heavy pack on his back, he hiked down-glacier until the pair of tents was out of sight. Then he made a sharp turn, headed for the edge of the glacier, turned again and, having effectively circled camp, settled into a steady upward trudge. His legs were sore from the previous day's effort, but he seemed to float along. The grey gloom of 5:00 a.m. combined with the rain to shrink his sphere of being around him.

The realization was growing on him that he had always misunderstood his own luck, the thing that he called his destiny. The kidney had nothing to do with it: the worm in the apple was trust. He had always been too trusting, had given himself over whole to others. For with trust came the opportunity for betrayal. It was clear now, as he strode along the mottled ice, that all the difficulties in his life had been occasioned by betrayal – first by Chalmers, then by Vera, now by Diana. Only Ed, among those he had deeply trusted, had justified the loyalty.

So the answer was the simple one he had resolved on now – the same choice, really, that he had made that night under the bridge in Minneapolis so long ago: to go it alone. When they woke and found the note, Diana and Derek might be puzzled, but it would never cross their minds that he was in fact still heading for the mountain. And even if they did think, days from now, to search up-glacier, they had shown so little interest in the maps that he doubted whether they would even recognize the junction with the stagnant glacial arm when they stumbled upon it. He was alone in the universe.

As for the climb itself, Victor had to recognize the odds against him. And there was, he admitted, a significant chance of getting killed. But did it matter? Did anything in the world matter more than Pterophorus? How fast he would be able to travel, unencumbered with Diana's blisters, with the fears or hesitations of weaklings. He was pretty sure that he could do the climbing solo, if he self-belayed the harder spots. In his notes back in Hartford, he had indicated that he thought no single pitch had been more difficult than 5.9. There was so little aid, too, and the pitons they had left in 1964 should still be in. The spectre that gave him pause was his memory of the vertical ice-filled chimney a thousand feet below the top. His recollection of Ed's lead had him bridging strenuously near the rounded lips of the chimney, using ice screws for protection. Perhaps this time he could attack the ice directly. All that ice work that he had done alone last winter was vital now. True, no single pitch in Vermont or New Hampshire had been quite vertical. But he would see when he would see.

The plan was brilliantly simple. As long as he had the energy, he would force the march right to the base of the mountain. He felt capable of twelve miles in a single push – already he must have covered two. He would find a spot to bivouac below the route, try to get a good night's sleep, then go for it the next morning. Three days' food on the climb – soloing, he was bound to be fast. He could wear a pack on the mixed ground, haul it on the steeper pitches. In leaving his tent behind, he had eschewed the single most conspicuous sign of his presence. No airplane, even, would be able to spot him on the mountain. This time he would be sure to take photos all the way, and to leave some piece of gear on the summit. He would return to civilization, seemingly from the grave, and at last there would be no sceptics and belittlers.

The plodding effort lulled him gradually into a numbness, almost a euphoria. He had been forcing himself not to think about Diana, not to remember the sounds from the other tent. Something – adrenalin, he supposed – seemed to be doing the work of movement for him. But he knew that he would need rest and food, to be ready for the climb the next day. He forced himself to make a lunch stop at 8:00 a.m.

Halfway through his second candy bar, his feelings crashed in upon him. A wild pang of loss surged through his limbs as he pictured Diana. With her image came a throng of memories from the fall, when he had been so vain as to believe that she could love him. She was right: he had been a nearsighted fool; for now a dozen details that had puzzled him in May – absences, discrepancies, looks of preoccupation on her face – made perfect sense in terms of her taking up with Derek. He remembered Arthur's prescient warning way back in October, and the story about the climber found dead at the bottom of Birdline, which, out of consideration, he had never quizzed her about.

He did not think he was angry with Derek. The man would discover in his turn what Diana was like. Only Derek's extreme passivity rankled, as did the fact that they had exchanged not a word after Diana's outrageous flaunting of her sex with him. Victor was sad about the destruction of what had begun to seem like a good friendship. But he had placed no blind hopes in Derek, had invested no love.

Shortly after lunch he came to the junction. The mist had been rising from the bottom all morning, and now as he stared up the stagnant arm, he could see grey rock far in the distance that might well be the lower reaches of the north face of Pterophorus. Only seven more miles, he told himself, as he made the tricky traverse through the séracs and left the main ice flow for good. He thought he recognized a particular sérac: was it possible it had stood for fourteen years? He picked his way through the ubiquitous rock debris, around dank potholes in the ice, slipping on rubbly slopes, clawing here and there with his axe for purchase. The going was much slower than on the main glacier, but he was animated now by the wall at the head of the gloomy canyon that gradually took on detail as he approached.

His tiredness was catching up with him. He took another rest stop, and resolved to go only two more hours. The drizzle had not let up, despite the rising clouds; the temperature seemed to have dropped a few degrees. He was soaked with sweat inside his cagoule.

At last he made a camp, pitching the nylon fly like a lean-to from a large rock, scraping a level site for his bivvy sack on the ice underneath. He guessed he was only two miles from the base of the mountain. He crawled into his jacket and half bag and fell asleep.

Within the hour he awoke, shivering. Everything was too wet for comfortable sleep. A wind had come up, and the rain seemed half snow. He needed sleep desperately. He thought about taking a sleeping pill, but decided against it on the grounds that he needed alertness as much as sleep. After turning over a dozen times, he sat up and cooked himself a cup of tomato soup. It was 5:00 p.m. The soup restored his confidence. He decided to go on up and begin the climb. By the time it grew dark he might be five hundred feet off the glacier. There were good bivouac sites down below, he remembered. It might actually be warmer and drier on the mountain.

As he trudged toward the head of the glacier, Diana's betrayal weighed on his spirit like extra pounds in his pack. The damnable thing, he made himself acknowledge, was that he was still in love with her. It would take days, weeks – the climb itself – to cure him of the folly of caring about her. Now he hated her, too, as he had hated no one since Chalmers.

At last he came to the névé line. It was a good mile further-up-glacier than it had been in 1964. The summer had indeed been incredibly dry. Above the Dorsal Fins, especially, there would be an abundance of bare ice. The grey-black wall ahead of him was taking on hints of familiar features; he could not be sure, but he thought he recognized the dihedrals that marked the start of the route. Snow was falling lightly, and the wind was up. He turned at one point and saw with satisfaction that his shallow footprints were starting to drift full only moments after he had passed. There would not be even that ephemeral trace of his passage.

The sky seemed all at once to grow brighter. He looked up. The mist was beginning to coalesce into distinct clouds; he could follow their movement as the strong south wind blew them down the glacier. Suddenly a patch of summit ridge flashed into view through a hole in the clouds. Amber sunlight fell on half a dozen castellated promontories, which were gleaming with fresh rime. The sight filled Victor with fear and joy. The mountain belonged to him.

The glacier was sloping upwards towards its termination in abrupt slabs of granite. Victor appraised the features before him and decided he was too far to the right for the beginning dihedrals. If only he had paid better attention to such things in the old years. He began traversing to his left, kicking four-inch-deep steps in the hard snow.

There were clean-cut pieces of rock scattered along his path, the relatively recent debris from collapsing fins and towers above. A series of crevasses narrowed his route to a transverse lane. He had been going for about ten minutes when an odd detail caught the corner of his eye and slowed him. The apparent piece of rock fifty yards up the slope seemed to have a faded orange hue. He stared at it for a moment. There was a crevasse between him and the object. He retraced his steps to make an end run of the crevasse.

As he approached the vaguely coloured thing, he saw that it was some kind of gear. A small *mélange* of gear, in fact: a pack, the torn remnants of some garment, and, remarkably, a boot, sole up. He bent over and grasped the boot; it was half frozen into the snow. He dug around the boot with his axe. The axe uncovered something sticking out from the snow. It was a bone. Victor recoiled in horror.

'It's Ed,' he said softly, out loud. He recognized the Löwa boot. The details of debris took on a sudden gestalt: he could see the position of the body. 'The dry summer,' Victor murmured. 'He's come out of the glacier, after all these years.' He knelt and tugged at the orange cagoule. The rotten fabric tore easily in his fingers, uncovering sodden wool and more bone – the back of the skull, Victor saw. Again he recoiled. There was a nylon loop of hardware still associated with the body: he could see a broken karabiner and a rusty soft-iron piton. He put his hand out and touched the skull, then sniffed at his fingertips.

Standing up again, he looked from the debris upwards along the line of clean granite that had been Ed's fall. The clouds were blowing off the summit ridge, and there were sparkles of light in the ice crystals up high. Victor thought he could see the ledge below which the fixed rope had broken. With the clarity of a revelation their last days together sprang into his mind: the horrible storm, the forty hours of waiting, the anguish of the decision to go down. A chill settled behind his shoulders, at the top of his neck. He said out loud, 'We didn't climb it, then.'

He looked around. It was as if someone had been there, just behind him. Were those dots down the glacier Diana and Derek? No, they were just rocks. A rage seized him. He screamed into the wind, 'Yes I did! I did climb it! I did!'

He looked down again. The pieces of Ed's body seemed to say, 'No, we didn't. Don't you remember?' Once more Victor was possessed by the conviction that there were people coming up the glacier. He whirled around and stared at the distant rocks sitting on the ice. He was sure one of them had just moved. Perhaps they knew he was looking, and had frozen in place, imitating inanimate objects. He held his breath, listening, but heard only the whistle of the wind.

In a frenzy he seized the boot and yanked on it. The leg bone came loose with it. He scuttled downhill fifty feet to the middle of the crevasse, approached the edge, and threw boot and bone in. A dull thud of impact was succeeded by a fainter one. Hurriedly he returned to the body. When he grasped the cagoule, it ripped into shreds in his hands. He gathered up all the loose gear and clothing that was not frozen into the ice and made a second trip to the crevasse. On his third effort he started excavating with his axe around the back of the skull and the other bone – a hip apparently – that protruded from the glacier. When he had got enough of the hip exposed to get a good hold, he yanked furiously on it. The bones broke and an asymmetrical piece of pelvis was left in his hands. He hacked at the ice around the skull. Down a few inches, muddy in the ice, there seemed to be something like flesh – the front of Ed's face? He got the pick of his axe under it and pried. The skull came loose, minus the jawbone. He returned to the crevasse. The pelvis was clotted with a heavy mass of ice and wool. Victor lugged his burden to the lip of the crevasse and pushed it in. Again the inconclusive thudding sounds. On his hands and knees he leaned over the edge to look in. It was very dark inside.

He leaned a little further, and heard a sudden soughing sound, deep but close. The world gave way beneath him. He was falling. In a flash of awareness he knew that the overhanging snow must have broken beneath his weight. He seemed to be upside down. His head hit something hard.

When he came back to consciousness, he had no idea how much later it was. He felt his forehead and looked at his hand in the murky darkness. His fingers were wet. He tasted the wetness, but could not tell if the flavour were blood. There was pain all through his body, and he was cold. He looked up at the tiny gap in the ceiling through which he had fallen. On the Lacuna Glacier below Foraker he had fallen twenty feet into a crevasse. This time, he guessed he was about forty feet in. His eyes seemed relatively accustomed to the darkness. He looked around.

The first hope, of walking out one end of the crevasse, was dashed: he had come to rest on a jammed platform of ice, beyond which on either end the gulf opened as the crevasse widened and deepened. So he would have to climb up one wall and tunnel through the overhanging lip. He still had his pack on, with the crampons attached. But where was his axe?

With a sting of dismay he pictured the axe left in place beside his excavation site. Well, he said to himself, you've got an ice hammer. It should be tough, but not impossible. He rolled up on one knee and screamed with pain.

Pulling his pants leg up, he looked at the damage. There was a bone protruding through the skin, shattered splinters of it covered with blood. He reached down and felt a greasy smear of blood. Whimpering, he felt his head go black again. He came back in a matter of moments.

Somewhere in the pack, he thought grimly, is the first-aid kit. But when he came to the small box of pills and tape and band-aids, the full hopelessness of his situation came home to him. He groaned out loud. The pain was getting worse. He fished a couple of codeine tablets out of the bottle and chewed them down.

Next to him on the platform were pieces of Ed's cagoule, along with the partial skull and the boot and bone. The pelvis seemed to have vanished further down the crevasse. He tore loose a strip of cagoule and tied a tourniquet around his lower thigh. But he was too weak to tighten it sufficiently to make the blood stop spreading. There was a dank, putrid odour in the air.

I can't make it myself, Victor thought. The only hope in the world is if Diana and Derek come up the glacier. Then he remembered the careful strategem of his note, the twelve miles between him and them, the wind drifting full his footsteps. He groaned again. He was starting to shiver. He managed to find his dacron jacket and fit it over his shoulders.

The sense of despair lightened. It was clear what he could do. He opened the medical kit and shook out all the codeine. There were about fifteen tablets. One by one he chewed them. Then he found the sleeping pills and managed to swallow all of them.

Within moments the pain had been reduced to an ache so remote it seemed to be happening to someone else. His brain was fogging over. He reached out and grasped Ed's skull, then propped it up beside himself, the empty eye sockets facing towards him.

'So this is what it all comes to, Louis,' he said out loud. 'This is all we ever did, is go and get ourselves killed. This is that wonderful destiny I thought we had. But at least we ended up in it together, and at least we managed to vanish. They'll never find us down here, those bastards, so they'll never know what happened to us.' He yawned mightily. The skull stared back at him. 'All for a mountain. All just to be able to say we were first. But what else would have been any better. Not a person, not a job – we knew that. It's as good a way to die as any – you must have known that, just in the second that the rope broke.' It was hard to keep his eyes open. His lips felt fuzzy. 'Louis, goddamn it, we were good on a rope together. They didn't come any better than we were. I'm sorry, old man, I wanted to end up on the summit, I wouldn't have minded dying there. But this is okay, too. It's quiet and cosy, and we don't have to go out in the cold ever again. . . .'

SOLO FACES

SOLO FACES

a novel by
James Salter

CHAPTER ONE

THEY WERE AT WORK on the roof of the church. All day from above, from a sea of light where two white crosses crowned twin domes, voices came floating down as well as occasional pieces of wood, nails, and once in the dreamlike air a coin that seemed to flash, disappear and then shine again for an endless time before it met the ground. Beneath the eucalyptus branches a signboard covered with glass announced the Sunday sermon: Sexuality and God.

The sun was straight overhead, pouring down on palm trees, cheap apartments and boulevards along the sea. Sparrows hopped aimlessly between the bumpers of cars. Inland, dazzling and white, Los Angeles lay in haze.

The workmen were naked to the waist and flecked with black. One of them was wearing a handkerchief, its corners knotted, on his head. He was dipping his broom in tar and coating the shingles. He talked continuously.

'All religion has something to do with the heat,' he said. 'They all started in the desert.' He had the kind of immature beard that seems like dark splinters beneath the skin. 'On the other hand, if you examine it, philosophy comes from temperate regions. Intellect from the north, emotion from the south . . .'

'You're splashing that stuff, Gary.'

'In California there are no ideas. On the other hand, we may see God. This is madness, working up here. I'm dying of thirst,' he said. 'Did you ever see *Four Feathers*? The original one – Ralph Richardson loses his helmet and it's like he's been hit with a sledgehammer. Bang! he goes blind.' He held out his hands for a moment, as if searching, and then lapsed into the climax from something else, 'Shoot-a me! Keel-a me!' In his blackened face, teeth appeared like a sandwich unwrapped from dirty paper.

He stood and watched his companion work, steady, unhurried. The roof was shimmering, hidden in light. Far below were the doors through which women, spied on from above, had gone in and out all day. A sale was being held in the basement. On the next level, aisles and benches – he had never actually been in a church, he tried to imagine what was said there, how one behaved. Above it, he and Rand. It was all one great angelic order. Flesh, spirit, gods. Wages, three dollars an hour.

The steepness slowly reached up to him as he stood, his feet sideways on the narrow cleats. It rose in waves, he could feel it begin to enfold him. The scaffolding seemed a long way down, the ground farther. He thought of falling, not from here – he pressed with his feet, the cleats were firm – but from some unknown spire, suddenly borne by nothing, free, drifting past windows in one long instant, the shadow glimpsed incredibly from within. He stood there, staring down.

He wanted to be talked to. The work was numbing. He was bored.

'Hey, Rand.'

'What?'

'I'm tired.'

'Take a break,' Rand said.

A breed of aimless wanderers can be found in California, working as mason's helpers, carpenters, parking cars. They somehow keep a certain dignity, they are surprisingly unashamed. It's one thing to know their faces will become lined, their plain talk stupid, that they will be crushed in the end by those who stayed in school, bought land, practised law. Still, they have an infuriating power, that of condemned men. They can talk to anybody, they can speak the truth.

Rand was twenty-five or -six. He lived with a Mexican girl, or so they said, a tall girl whose arms were covered with fine black hair. Where had he met her, Gary wondered, what had he said to her at first? It was a summer job, Gary was merely gliding through it, he would never know. For a long time afterward, though, whenever he was in the valley and saw the dust following a lone pickup on a road through the fields, the memory would come to him, an image of a yellow Mustang, the top half-gone, the driver familiar, shirtless, wind blowing in his hair.

It was a world he scorned and at the same time envied, men whose friend he would like to be, stories he would like to know.

One thing he imagined again and again was meeting ten years from now – where, he was not sure, in the northern part of the state perhaps, up in the grasslands, the bypassed towns. He could see Rand clearly, faded, older. What he could not see was whether he had changed.

'How've you been?'

'Hi, Gary.' A shrug. 'Not bad. How about you? You look like you're doing all right.'

'Ever get down to L.A.?'

'Oh, once in a while.'

'Look me up,' Gary said. 'I'm just off Wilshire, here's my card . . .' And he began to describe his life, not the way he wanted to but foolishly, disliking himself as he did, talking faster, throwing one thing on top of another, like giving money to someone who stood there saying nothing, merely waiting for more. There was no way to turn from him, there must be some amount that would put gratitude in his face, that would make him murmur, thanks. Here, Gary was saying, take this and this, this, too, all of it. He was disgracing himself. He could not stop. The day was hot there in Ceres or Modesto. The rivers were stagnant, the creeks dry. Beyond the town in open meadows sheep were bleating. Rand had turned and was walking off. Despite himself, he called,

'Hey, Rand!'

What he wanted to say was, Look at me, don't you think I'm different? Can you believe I'm the same guy?

All this in the glittering light above the church, marooned like sailors on its black dorsal. He began to work again, balancing himself between the highest cleat and a gutter at the base of the dome. From there he reached up. His broom nearly touched the peak but not quite.

'You'd better put in another cleat.'

'I'm all right,' he said.

He stretched a little more. Holding the tip of the handle, balancing it, he could barely reach the top. He felt a sudden triumph. He was weightless, a lizard. He existed in a kind of joy. At that moment his whole life gave way – his foot slipped off the cleat. Instantly he was falling. He tried to hold on to the shingles. The broom clattered down the roof. He could not even cry out.

Something hit his arm. A hand. It slid to his wrist.

'Hold on!'

He would have clutched anything, a leaf, a branch, the handle of a pail. He held tightly to Rand's hand, his feet still kicking at the air.

'Don't pull,' he heard. 'Don't pull, I won't be able to hold you.' An inch at first and then an inch more, the pact they had managed to make was breaking. 'Try not to slip!'

'I can't!' Terror was choking him.

'Get your fingers under a shingle.' Rand was beginning to be pulled off himself. He dared not say this.

'I'm slipping!'

'Get hold of something.'

At last he was able to. Almost by his nails he held to a shingle.

'Can you stay there?'

Gary did not answer. He was clinging to a monster by a single scale. Rand had already started to descend. He ran along the scaffold beneath, and hurriedly began to hammer in a cleat. A final cry came down,

'My hands are slipping!'

'It's all right. You've got a cleat. Turn face up, so you can see where you're going.'

Beneath them the minister, staring upward, was holding the fallen broom.

'Is everything all right?' he called. He was a modern figure who disdained holy appearance; he drove a Porsche and mingled passages from various best-sellers with prayers for the dead. 'You must have dropped this.'

Gary stood on the scaffolding. He was shaking, he felt helpless.

'Thanks,' was all he could say. Even later, having coffee at the food truck near the yard, he could not speak of it. He was still in a kind of daze.

'That was a close one,' Rand said.

Girls from the laundry were wandering across the street in white smocks, laughing, talking. Gary felt weak, ashamed. 'The scaffolding would have stopped me,' he said.

'You'd have shot right past it.'

'I don't think so.'

'Like a bird,' Rand said.

CHAPTER TWO

ABOVE LOS ANGELES the faint sound of traffic hung like haze. The air had a coolness, an early clarity. The wind was coming from the sea which as much as anything gives the city its aura. A benign light flooded down, onto the shops, the awnings, the leaves of every tree. It fell on lavish homes and driveways and into the faded back streets where houses with five-digit numbers languished beneath great names: Harlow Avenue, Ince Way. There are two Los Angeleses, they like to say, sometimes more, but in fact there is only one, six lanes wide with distant palms and one end vanishing in the sea. There are mythic island names of small apartments – Nalani, Kona Kai – dentists, Mexican restaurants, and women sitting on benches with undertaker's advertisements on the back. The cars shoot past like projectiles. Against the mountains tall buildings mirror the sun.

There are certain sections, out of the way, neglected, like bits of debris in the wave. One of these is Palms. Backyards with wire fences. *For Rent* signs. Dusty screens.

Beneath a jacaranda tree shedding its leaves on the roof stood an unpainted house such as one might find in the country. There were four white posts along the porch. The yard was overgrown and filled with junk. In the back, a weedy garden. In one window, a decal of the flag. Above, an empty sky of precipitous blue. A grey cat, tail pointing straight up, was carefully making its way through the grass. Two doves clattered upward. The cat, one paw raised, watched them. In the driveway, chalky from exposure, a Mustang was parked.

The house belonged to a young woman from Santa Barbara. She was tall, white-skinned. It was difficult to imagine anyone describing her as Mexican. Her hair was black. Her mother was a socialite who shot herself in the leg attempting suicide. Her father taught modern languages. Her name was Louise Rate, 'R-A-T-E,' she added, especially on the phone.

Rand had been living there for a year, not really in the house since his room, which he rented, was the toolshed, but he was not a tenant either. At their first interview a nervous silence fell between them, a silence during which, he later found out, she was telling herself not to speak. She opened the door to the shed and preceded him in. It was a long, narrow structure built on the back of the house. There was a bed, a dresser, shelves of old books.

'You can move these around if you like.'

He gazed about. The ceiling was painted alternately white and the green of boat hulls. There were boxes of empty bottles. In the house the radio was playing; the sound came through the wall. She seemed abrupt, uninterested. That night she wrote about him in her diary.

She was a moon-child with small teeth, pale gums, awkward polished limbs.

She called him by his last name. At first it seemed with scorn. It was her style.

She was working in a urologist's office. The hours suited her and also the pleasure of reading the files. She was living in exile, she liked to say.

'It's sort of a mess. I haven't had time to straighten it up. It's a nice street, though. It's very quiet. What sort of work do you do?'

He told her.

'I see,' she said. She folded and unfolded her arms. She couldn't decide what to say. The sun was pouring down in the warm afternoon, traffic was going everywhere. Through the windows could be seen neighbouring houses where the shades were always drawn as if for an illness within. And there was an illness, of lives that were spent.

'Well . . .,' she said helplessly. The stirrings of a well-being close at hand, even of a possible happiness, were confusing her. 'I suppose you can have it. What's your name?'

He hardly saw her the first few days. Then, briefly, appearing in the doorway, she invited him to dinner.

'It's not a party or anything,' she explained.

The candles were dripping on the tablecloth. The cat walked among dishes on the sink. Louise drank wine and stole glances at him. She had never really seen his face. He was from Indianapolis, he told her. His family had moved to California when he was twelve. He had quit college after a year.

'I didn't like the cafeteria,' he said. 'I couldn't stand the food or the people who ate there.'

He had been in the army.

'The army?' she said. 'What were you doing in the army?'

'I was drafted.'

'Didn't you hate it?'

He didn't reply. He was sitting with his arm curved around the plate, eating slowly, like a prisoner or a man who has been in mission houses. Suddenly she understood. 'Oh!' she almost said. She could see it: he was a deserter. At that moment he looked up. Don't worry, she tried to tell him silently. She admired him, she trusted him completely. He had hair that had gone too long without being cut, fine nostrils, long legs. He was filled with a kind of freedom that was almost visible. She saw where he had been. He had crossed the country, slept in barns and fields, dry riverbeds.

'I know . . .,' she said.

'You know what?'

'The army.'

'You wouldn't have recognized me,' he said. 'I was so gung ho, you wouldn't believe it. We had a captain, Mills was his name. He was from Arkansas, a terrific guy. He used to tell about the chorus of soldiers that gathered outside when General Marshall was dying. They stood in the dusk and sang his favourite songs. It was just the idea of it. The other guys, what did they care? But I wasn't like them. I believed. I was really a soldier, I was going to officer candidate school and become a lieutenant. I was going to be the best lieutenant in the whole damned army. It was all because of that captain. Wherever he went, I wanted to go. If he died, I wanted to die.'

'Is this true?'

'I used to copy the way he dressed, the way he walked. The army is like a reform school. Everyone lies, fakes. I hated that. I didn't talk to anyone, I didn't have any friends. I didn't want to be soiled. You're probably not interested in this. I don't know why I'm telling you.'

'I am interested.'

He paused, thinking back to a period of faith.

'We had a first sergeant, an old-timer, he could hardly write his name. We called him Bobo. I knew he liked me, I didn't know how much. One night at a beer party I went up to him to ask about my chances for promotion. I'll never forget it. He looked at me, he kind of nodded. He said, "Rand, I been in the army a long time, you know?" In "knee arm forces," is what he actually said. "My old man was a marine, I tell you that? A China Marine. You probably never heard of the China Marines. They were the worst soldiers in the world. They had houseboys cleaned their rifles for them and shined their shoes. They had White Russian girl friends. Why, they didn't even know how to roll a pack. I was a kid there; I remember all that. Tell you something, I was in Korea – a long time ago – that was rough. I was in Saigon. I've soldiered everywhere, you name it. I've jumped in snowstorms, we couldn't even get a squad assembled till two days later. I've jumped at night. I've jumped into rivers – by mistake, that was. I've known guys from all over, and let me tell you something: you are going to go a long way in this army, you are prob'ly going to be one of the best soldiers I ever seen!"'

'Did he mean it?'

'He was drunk.'

'What happened?'

'I never even made corporal.'

The immense southern night had fallen. It glittered everywhere, in houses along the beach, supermarkets open late, the white marquees of theatres.

'Here,' she said, 'have some wine.'

'I could have been a captain. I could have worn bars.'

His blue shirt was faded, his face strangely calm. He looked like a cashiered officer, like a man whose destiny has been denied him.

'I thought you were a deserter,' she confessed.

'An apostate,' she heard him say. 'I was all army. We're tenting tonight . . . I was a believer, can you imagine that?'

That night he slept in her bed. They would have been enemies otherwise. She knew she was hasty and nervous. Perhaps he wouldn't notice. The bed was very wide, her marriage bed. The sheets had scalloped edges. It was the first time since her divorce, she confided.

'My God,' she moaned, 'can you believe that?' And a while later, 'Was that story you told me true?'

'What story?'

'About the marines?'

'What marines?'

In the morning she followed him to work.

Women look like one thing when you don't know them and another when you do. It was not that he didn't like her. He would watch as she sat, dressing for the evening, before a folding mirror. In the circle of light her mysterious reflection did not even acknowledge him but watched self-absorbed as she applied the black around her eyes. Her necklaces hung from a deer antler. There were pictures cut from magazines tacked to the wall.

'Who is this?' he said. 'Is this your father?'

A brief glance.

'That's D. H. Lawrence,' she murmured.

A young man with a moustache and fine brown hair.

'You know who that looks like?' he said, amazed. He could hardly believe it. He turned toward her to let her guess, herself. 'Hey . . .' he said, 'look.'

She was staring at her reflection.

'Can you believe these thin lips?' she wailed.

Yes, then he liked her. She was sardonic, pale. She wanted to be happy, but could not be, it deprived her of her persona, of what would remain when he, like the rest of them, was gone. Something was always withheld, guarded, mocked. She was impatient with her son, who bore it stoically. His name was Lane, he was twelve. His room was down the hall.

'Poor Lane,' she would often say, 'he's not going to amount to much.'

He was failing at school. The teachers liked him, he had lots of friends, but he was slow, vague, as if living in a dream.

There were nights they returned from somewhere in the city, weary from dancing, and weaved down the hallway past his door. She was making an attempt to be quiet, talking in whispers.

Her shoe dropped with the sharpness of a shot onto the floor.

'Oh, Christ,' she said.

She was too tired to make love. It had been left on the dance floor. Or else she did, halfheartedly, and like two bodies from an undiscovered crime they lay, half-covered in the early light, in absolute silence except for the first, scattered sound of birds.

On Sundays they drove to the sea. In the whiteness of spring the sky was a gentle blue, a blue that has not yet felt the furnace. Small houses, lumber-yards, flyblown markets. The final desolation of the coast. The streets of Los Angeles were behind them, the silver automobiles, men in expensive suits.

Seen picking their way down the slope from the highway to the beach, half-naked, towels in their hands, they seemed to be a family. As they drew closer it was even more interesting. She already had a stiffness and hesitation that are part of middle age. Her attention was entirely on her feet. Only the humorous, graceful movements of her hands and the kerchief around her head made her seem youthful. Behind her was someone tall and resigned. He hadn't yet learned that something always comes to save you.

She was a woman who would one day turn to drink or probably cocaine. She was high-strung, uncertain. She often talked about how she looked or what she would wear. She brushed the sand from her face, 'What do you think of white? Pure white, the way they dress at Theodore's?'

'For what?'

'White pants with nothing underneath,' she said, 'white T-shirts.' She was imagining herself at parties. 'Just the red of lipstick and some blue around the eyes. Everything else is white. Some guy comes up to me, some smart guy, and says, "You know, I like the colour of your nipples. You here with anyone?" I just look at him very calmly and say, "Get lost."'

She invented these fantasies and acted them out. One minute she would accept kisses, the next her mind would be elsewhere. And she was never really sure of him. She never dared commit herself to the idea that he would stay. Afraid of what might happen, she was frivolous, oblique, chattering to herself like a bird in a forest so as not to be aware of the approach of danger.

Early one morning he rose before five. It was barely light. The floor was cool beneath his feet. Louise was sleeping. He picked up his clothes and went down the hall. On top of rumpled sheets Lane was sleeping in his underwear. His arms were like his mother's, tubular and smooth. Rand shook him lightly. The eyes glinted open.

'You awake?' Rand asked.

There was no reply.

'Come on,' he said.

CHAPTER THREE

ON THE car windows, mist had formed. Newspapers lay on the lawns. The streets were empty. Buses were driving with their lights.

The freeways were already full, a ghostly procession. Over the city lay a layer of clouds. To the east the sky was brighter, almost yellow. The bottom was spilling light. Then suddenly, breaking free from earth came the molten sun.

The buildings of downtown appeared, tall and featureless. They seemed to turn slowly and reveal an unknown face of greater detail, a planetlike face lit by the sun.

A river of cars was pouring inward out of a brilliance that obscured the road signs. Some twenty miles farther, among the last apartment buildings and motels, were the first open hills. There was less traffic now, nurses driving homeward, Japanese, bearded blacks, their faces bathed by dawn like true believers. It was seven o'clock.

Near Pomona the land began to open. There were orchards, farms, vacant fields, the fields that once made up the country. A landscape more calm and pure lay all about, covered by soothing clouds. The blue air of rain hung beneath. A group of white objects tilted like gravestones drifted by on the right.

'What are those?'

Rand looked out at them.

'Beehives,' he said.

The sky was breaking into bright fragments.

At Banning they turned off. They were far from the city now, a generation away at least. The houses were ordinary. There were trailers, limping dogs. The road had begun to climb into barren hills. At each curve was a view of wide, patterned farmland falling away below. Ahead was emptiness, land that had no owner.

'It's nice from here on,' Rand said.

The mountains were the colour of slate, the sun behind them. The valley, with its highway like a silver vein, was seen for the last time. Beyond it a great range of mountains had appeared, peaks still white with snow. The road was silent, smooth.

'How high are we?'

'Two, three thousand feet.'

The scrub trees vanished. They were speeding through forests of pine. Along the roadside lay banks of snow.

'Look, a dog.'

'That's a coyote.'

It turned before they reached it and disappeared into the trees.

They dropped down into a valley and small town. Gas stations, a triangular park. It was all familiar. He knew the way as if it had been yesterday. A wooded road past houses with names like Nirvana and Last Mile, then some green water tanks, and there it was, a great dome of rock, its shoulders gleaming in the sun. A tremor of excitement went through him. The sky was clear. It was nearly nine o'clock.

They parked, the doors on both sides open, and changed their shoes. Rand got a small rucksac and coil of rope, red as flannel, from the trunk. He led the way, down off the road to a half-hidden path. They followed this for a while and then turned upward and began to climb. The pines were tall and silent. The sun trickled through them to the forest floor. Rand moved steadily, unhurriedly, almost with a pause between his steps. There was no point in wasting strength here. Even so, it burned the legs; sweat began to glisten on their faces. Once or twice they paused to rest.

'This is the hardest part. It's not much farther,' Rand said.

'I'm okay.'

A large boulder which only an ice age could have borne was up ahead, close to the base of the main rock which seemed to have lost its size. The great slabs that almost plunged into the forest had vanished. Only a few of them, the lowest, could be seen.

Rand uncoiled the rope. He wrapped it twice around the boy's waist and watched as the knot was tied. The other end he tied to himself.

'You want to go first?' he said.

It was easy at the start. With the unschooled agility of a squirrel, Lane moved upward. After a while he heard a call,

'That's a good place to stop.'

Rand began to climb. The rock felt warm, unfamiliar, not yet giving itself over. Lane was waiting in a niche forty feet above the ground.

'I'll just go on,' Rand said.

Now he went first, the boy belaying. As he climbed he put in an occasional piton. He hammered them into cracks. A metal link, a karabiner, was snapped to the piton and the rope run through it.

Far below was a small upturned face. Rand climbed easily, assured in his movements. He looked, felt, tried, then without effort, moved up.

The rock is like the surface of the sea, constant yet never the same. Two climbers going over the identical route will each manage a different way. Their reach is not the same, their confidence, their desire. Sometimes the way narrows, the holds are few, there are no choices – the mountain is inflexible in its demands – but usually one is free to climb at will. There are principles, of course. The first concerns the rope – it is for safety but one should always climb as if the rope were not there.

'Off belay!' Rand called. He had reached a good stance, the top of an upright slab. There was a well-defined outcrop behind him. He placed a loop of nylon webbing over it and clipped to that. He pulled up what free rope there was, passing it around his waist to provide friction if necessary.

'On belay!' he called.

'Climbing,' came the reply.

Lane had watched him carefully, but from below he could not tell much after a while. It seemed, in places, there must have been some trick – there was no way to climb – but with the rope tugging gently at him, he managed. It was steeper than it looked. He was slight, flylike. He should have been able to cling to the merest flaws. His foot slipped off a tiny hold. He somehow caught himself. He put his toe back where it had been, with less confidence. This part was very hard. He stared up, his legs trembling. The slabs above were sheer, gleaming like the side of a ship. Beyond them, a burning blue.

He was forgetting what he should do, struggling blindly, in desperation. His fingers ached. There was resignation heavy in his chest.

'Put your right foot where your left is!'

'What?' he cried miserably.

'Put your right foot where your left is and reach out with your left.'

His fingers were losing their grip.

'I can't!'

'Try.'

He did as he was told, clumsy, despairing. His foot found a hold, his hand another. Suddenly he was saved. He began to move again and in a few minutes had forgotten his fear. Reaching Rand, he grinned. He had made mistakes. He'd been leaning too close to the rock, reaching too far. His moves had not been planned. Still, he was there. A feeling of pride filled him. The ground was far below.

To the left, on a more difficult route, smooth, exposed, were two other climbers. Rand was watching them as he straightened out the rope. They were on an almost blank wall. The leader, hair pale in the sunlight, was flat against it, arms to either side, legs apart. Even in extremity he emitted a kind of power, as if he were supporting the rock. There was no one else on all of Tahquitz.

Rand turned from watching them. With a movement of his arm, he commented, 'There it is.'

The forest was falling beneath them, the valley. Though still far from the top, they had entered a realm of silence. There was a different kind of light, a different air.

'The next part is easier,' Rand said.

The mountain had accepted them; it was prepared to reveal its secrets. The uncertainty was gone, fear of poor holds, of places where a toe stays only because of the angle at which it is placed, indecision – one move achieves nothing, there must immediately be another, perhaps a third. Hesitate and the holds vanish, draw back.

The top was level and dusty, like the forgotten corner of a park. Sitting on a rock in the sun were the two other climbers. They were in worn shirts and climbing pants, their rope and equipment lay near their feet. The leader, who was wearing tennis shoes, glanced up as Rand approached.

'I thought that was you,' Rand said. 'How've you been, Jack?'

Cabot merely extended a leisurely hand. He had a broad smile and teeth with faintly jagged edges, of a lustreless white. His hair was rumpled, soiled, as if he had slept all night on a porch. He was amiable, assured. His voice had a certain warmth.

'The lost brother,' he said. 'Sit down. Want a sandwich?' He held one out, a graceful lack of deliberation in his movement. The sun glinted on his hair. His shoulders were strong beneath the faded shirt.

'I saw you struggling down there.'

'Have you ever been on that?' Cabot asked.

'The Step?'

'You own it, right? You bastard.'

'I wouldn't say that.'

'Where've you been? I've been looking for you.' There followed some scraps of song, Cabot singing as if to himself. 'Some say that he is sinking down to mediocrity. He even climbs with useless types like Daddy Craig and me . . . Hey,' he called to Lane who was ten feet off, not daring to join them, 'how did he do? Did he manage all right?'

Rand was dividing the flattened sandwich.

'I asked everyone about you,' Cabot said. 'Jesus. Not a clue. You know, I thought of you so many times. Really.'

He had been in Europe, in villages where the only telephone was in a bar and the walls of the houses were two feet thick. He'd spent the summer and fall there. The names of mountains every climber knows were now his own, the Cima Grande, the Blaitière, the Walker Spur.

'The Walker?'

'Well, we didn't make it to the top,' Cabot admitted. He was hunched forward a bit as if in thought. 'Next time. Of course, it only comes in shape every two years, if that. You want to do it?'

'Me?'

'You've been to France, haven't you?'

'Sure. Who hasn't?' Rand said.

'You have to go. You've got to get to Chamonix. It's more than you even dreamed. You go up the glaciers for five or six hours, you can hear the water running underneath. And the climbs!'

Rand felt his heart beating slowly, enviously. He felt unhappy, weighed down with regret. He turned to the other man.

'Did you go?' he asked.

'No,' Banning said, 'I'm not that lucky.' He was in medical school, his climbing days were numbered.

Lane could not hear what they said, their voices were carried away by the wind. He could see them sprawled at their ease, the blond man leaning back and smiling, a piece of waxed paper fluttering near his foot. He was reminded of his mother and father talking when he had been younger, discussing things he was not meant to hear. There are conversations we are barred from, not one word of which can be imagined. He sat quietly, content to be near them, to have come this far.

Banning would become a doctor and disappear from climbing before he'd had his fill of it. Jack Cabot, it was hard to say. He was the kind of man who mapped out continents – climbing might not release him, might make him one of its myths. As for Rand, he had had a brilliant start and then defected. Something had weakened in him. That was when he was twenty, long ago. He was like an animal that has wintered somewhere, in the shadow of a hedgerow or barn, and one morning mud-stained and dazed, shakes itself and comes to life. Sitting there, he remembered past days, their glory. He remembered the thrill of height.

'Who was that?' Lane asked.

'Back there? Oh, a friend of mine.'

They made their way in silence.

'Did you used to climb with him?'

Rand nodded.

'Is he good?'

'Yeah, he's good.'

'He looked terrific.'

'Watch your step here,' Rand warned. He was moving more slowly. The slope of the rock had steepened. Towards the edge it dropped away. 'I knew someone who fell right here.'

'Here? It's easy,' Lane protested. 'How could he fall?'

'He was running and he slipped.'

There were boulders far below.

'That's the hard way down,' Rand said.

In Chamonix the *aiguilles,* the tall pinnacles, were covered with snow. There were peaks on all sides, silent, bare. The glaciers descended slowly, half an inch an hour, centuries deep.

CHAPTER FOUR

BEHIND THE house were sections of piñon that had lain there so long the earth had taken their shape. The wood had hardened, fragments of a column shielding a world of ants.

Swinging the hammer in heavy, rhythmic blows, Rand was splitting logs. A forgelike ringing echoed as the wedge went deep and a clear, final sound as the wood came apart. The morning surrounded him, the sun spilled down. He was shirtless. He looked like a figure in medieval battle, lost in the metal din, in glinting planes of sunshine, in dust that rose like smoke.

From the house, Louise was watching. Occasional glances, impatient, half-resigned, like a woman whose husband is intent on some ruinous, quixotic labour. Lane was in his room. He could hear the blows.

The car was gone, sold that morning. The sound of the wedge being driven was steady and unvarying. She went to the door.

'Hey, Rand.'

His head came up.

'Don't you think you've done enough?'

'I'll be finished in a while,' he said.

At last it stopped. She heard the logs being piled against the house. He came in and began to wash his hands.

'Well, I always said I'd do that. You've got enough for the winter, anyway.'

'Wonderful,' she commented.

'You might need it.'

'I can't even make a fire,' she said. He was drying his hands, brushing bits of bark from his waist. Suddenly she realized she had no way to remember this image. He was going to put on a shirt, button the buttons. All this simply would disappear. She felt a shameful urge to reach out, put her arms around him, fall to her knees.

They had been in a bar the night before. It was noisy, crowded. There was something he had to tell her. He was leaving, he said. She could hardly hear him.

'What?'

He repeated it. He was going away.

'When?' she asked foolishly. It was all she could manage to say.

'Tomorrow.'

'Tomorrow,' she said. 'Going where?' She wanted to think of something incisive that would hurt him, make him stay. Instead she murmured, 'You know, I really liked you.'

'I'll be back.'

'You mean it?'

'Sure.'

'When?'

'I don't know. In a year. Maybe two.'

'What are you going to do, go back to climbing? Lane told me you met your old friends.'

'Friend.'

'Is he going with you?'

'No.'

'Well . . .' She was looking at her glass. She tried to force a smile and suddenly turned away.

'Are you all right?'

She didn't answer.

'Louise . . .'

She was weeping.

'Come on . . .'

'Oh, forget it,' she said. Her nose was running.

'. . . I'll take you home.'

'I don't want to go home.'

Someone at the next table asked, 'Is anything wrong?'

'Mind your own business,' Rand said.

'Yes,' she agreed. She had already risen and was gathering her things.

They drove home in silence. She sat against the door, her narrow shoulders hunched. She was folded like an insect, legs drawn up beside her, arms crossed.

In the morning her face was swollen as if she were ill. He could hear her breathing. Somehow, it seemed conscious, sorrowful, close to a sigh. As he listened it seemed to grow louder to become, he suddenly realized, the sound of a jet crossing the city at dawn.

He left behind some cardboard boxes filled with letters, shoes, fishing equipment. The letters were from an old girl friend, born in Kauai, who had cut his palm one night and, to seal their love, raised it to her mouth and drunk the welt of blood.

CHAPTER FIVE

IN GENEVA it was raining. The bus station was behind a church. There were only a few passengers when the driver appeared, climbed into his seat, started the engine, and steered his way into traffic to the ceaseless beat of the windshield wiper and the voice of a comedian on a radio beneath the wheel.

Soon they were roaring along streets of small towns, barely skimming the sides of buildings. Pharmacies, green trees, supermarkets sailing past. In a front seat Rand sat high above it all. They were crossing railroad tracks, he was looking down into gardens, lumberyards, at girls running in the rain with wet hair.

The sky went pale. A few seconds later, ominous and near, like artillery, came the thunder. He felt he was being rushed to battle across borders, through wet fields covered with mist that stretched out on either side. It was summer. The rivers were milky green. There were bridges, barns, cases of empty bottles stacked in yards, and sometimes through the clouds, a glimpse of mountains. He knew no French. The cluttered towns with their shops and curious signs – he did not take them seriously. At the same time, he longed to know them.

The lights of oncoming cars began to appear, a sulphur yellow. The rain had ceased. The mountains lay hidden in a kind of smoke. It seemed as if the stage were being set and then suddenly, at Sallanches, the valley opened. There, at its end, unexpected, bathed in light, was the great peak of Europe, Mont Blanc. It was larger than one could imagine, and closer, covered in snow. That first immense image changed his life. It seemed to drown him, to rise with an infinite slowness like a wave above his head. There was nothing that could stand against it, nothing that could survive. Through crowded terminals, cities, rain, he had carried certain hopes and expectations, vague but thrilling. He was dozing on them like baggage, numbed by the journey, and then, at a certain moment, the clouds had parted to reveal in brilliant light the symbol of it all. His heart was beating in a strange, insistent way, as if he were fleeing, as if he had committed a crime.

They arrived in Chamonix in the evening. The square in front of the station was quiet. The sky was still light. He stepped down. Though mid-June, the air was chill. A taxi took two other passengers off to some hotel. He was left alone. The town to all appearances was empty. He had a strange impression, almost a warning, that he knew this place. He looked about him as if to confirm some detail. The hotels that fronted the station seemed closed; there was light in the entrance of one. A dog trotted up to the edge of a low roof and stared at him. Above, in the trees, were the last rays of sun. He picked up his bedroll and pack and began to walk.

There was a bridge across the tracks. He went in that direction, away from town, and soon was on a dirt road. The pines had begun to darken. He came to a large villa in a garden overgrown with weeds. All sorts of junk was piled along the side, a rusted stove, flowerpots, broken chairs. Above the door was a metal sign: Chalet something-or-other; the letters had faded away. The window casements were deep, the shutters closed. He went around to the back, where there was a light, and knocked.

A woman came to the door.

'Is there a place to sleep?' he asked.

She did not answer. She called into the darkness of the house and another woman, her mother, appeared and led him up some flights of stairs into a room where he could stay for ten francs – she made it clear by holding up two hands with outstretched fingers. There were bunks with bare mattresses. Someone's belongings were already there, shoes and equipment strewn beside the wall and on the single shelf a loaf of bread and an alarm clock.

'I'll take it,' he said.

There was a washroom with one bulb. Everything was bare, unpainted, dark with years. He went to bed without dinner that night. It had begun to rain again. He heard it first, then saw it on the window. Like a beast that knows things by scent, he was untroubled, even at peace. The odour of the blankets, the trees, the earth, the odour of France seemed known to him. He lay there feeling not so much a physical calm as something even deeper, the throb of life itself. A decisive joy filled him, warmth and well-being. Nothing could buy these things – he was breathing quietly, the rain was falling – nothing could take their place.

CHAPTER SIX

CHAMONIX WAS at one time an unspoiled town. Though crowded and overbuilt there are aspects which remain – the narrow curving streets, the sturdy barns, the walls built thick and left to crumble – that reveal its former character and vanished appearance. It lies in a deep V in the mountains, in the valley of the Arve, a river white with rock dust that rushes in a frenzy beside the streets. Overshadowing the town are the lower slopes of Mont Blanc with the snouts of glaciers alongside.

The Alps are new mountains, forced up from the crust of the earth, folded and refolded in comparatively recent times, four or five epochs ago. Mont Blanc itself is older. It is a block mountain, formed by a vast cleaving before even the time of the dinosaurs and drowned in seas that covered Europe after they disappeared. This ancient granite rose again when the Alps were born, higher than all that surrounded and clung to it, the highest point in Europe.

Adjoining is an army of pyramids and pinnacles, the *aiguilles,* which have drawn climbers – the English to begin with and then others – for more than a hundred years. At first sight they seem to be numberless. They lie in ranks and rough arcs to the south and east, some of the largest, like the Grandes Jorasses, almost hidden by those that are closer.

The north faces are the coldest and usually the most difficult. They receive less sun, sometimes only an hour or two a day, and are often covered in snow throughout the year. The winters are cold, the summers brief and often cloudy. The people are mountain people, hard and self-reliant – for years the Chamonix guides accepted in their ranks only those born in the valley. At the same time new roads opened the town to the world. In July and August huge crowds arrive. The restaurants, hotels, even the mountains themselves are filled. In September, as if by decree, everyone vanishes and there remains nothing but the blue letters that spell CARLTON shining mournfully at night above empty streets.

It rained for days, clouds covering the mountains, a cold steady rain. The dampness crept indoors. He sat by the stove in a plaid shirt and boots. Two young Germans who had come back soaked the first afternoon occasionally uttered a phrase or two. Bad weather, they would say. South wind is always bad. Where was he from? Ah, California! They nodded that was all.

Then one day it was clear. The mountains appeared. There was activity everywhere, one could feel it. Chamonix with its tin roofs and small shops came forth into sunlight.

In the post office the doors to the telephone booths were constantly opening and closing, the high, impatient voices of the clerks filled the air. He stood in line. In front of him was a Japanese with a two-day growth of beard – to pay for stamps he searched a small, canvas bag. In it he found a purse. He opened it. There was another, smaller purse within.

'Can you believe this?' Rand said. There was a bearded face behind him, an American face.

'Now he's going to find out he doesn't have enough money.'

The Japanese had shaken some coins onto the counter; he evidently thought he had more. He shook the purse again. A single coin dropped out. Not enough.

'I'll lend it to him,' Rand said. 'What, do they weigh every letter?'

'Sometimes they weigh it again after you put the stamps on.'

'What's the reason for that?'

'Please. It has nothing to do with reason. You've never been to France?'

His name was Neil Love. He was easy to talk to, a travel agent, in Chamonix for his third season. Wryly, he described the local scene which included bone-poor English stealing fruit and sitting for hours over a single bottle of beer. The Japanese were different. They came in vast numbers, armies of them, and could be found in the mountains everywhere, sleeping in cracks and upside down, frequently falling off – it was not unusual to see one in mid-air.

'They only buy round-trip tickets for half of them,' he said. 'Where are you staying?' Now was the time to get a camping site, before the crowds showed up, he advised.

'Where do you camp?'

'Come on.'

He led the way. They walked up past the cemetery where Whymper, who was the first to climb the Matterhorn, lay buried. Beyond were woods. Ferns and dense greenery were everywhere. The town was not visible from here, only the sky and, opposite, the steep face of the Brévent.

'Where are we?'

'The Biolay,' Love said. 'Later in the year it doesn't smell too good.'

He had already made up his mind about Rand judging from his clothes, the veins in his forearms, the cared-for equipment, but above all from a certain spot of coldness somewhere in him. He did not know him by reputation or name, but that meant nothing. He was absolutely sure of his sizing-up.

'What have you been climbing?' he asked.

'Nothing yet.'

'You're not one of those maniacs who start out by doing the Bonatti Pillar?'

'No, I'm just getting into shape.'

'It takes me all summer. Would you like to do something?'

'Whatever you like,' Rand said amiably.

They decided on Pointe Lachenal. Conditions on it weren't bad, Love had heard. And the approach, in his words, was conceivable.

'What's the climb like?'

'It's rated T.D. *Très difficile*. I'm not really the world's champion climber,' Love admitted.

'Is that right?'

'But I know how to climb.'

What was almost a friendship sprang up between them in the green of the woods, the earth fragrant from the rain, the air pure and still. There were the blackened stones of old campfires on the ground. Love's eyeglasses glinted. 'Love and Rand, that's like blood and sand . . .'

'Glove and hand.'

'Much better!'

They made some tea. The pleasant hours of afternoon passed.

Early in the morning they were making their way toward the *Col de Rognon*, a low ridge on the side of Mont Blanc. The snow was firm underfoot, not yet softened by the sun. Great peaks and pinnacles, all of them strange and unknown, were everywhere.

They were walking unroped. Love moved awkwardly. The terrain was steep.

'Good snow,' Love said.

When they paused for a moment, Rand asked offhandedly, 'Anyone ever show you how to self-arrest?'

'Not really,' Love said.

'Let me show you. If you're falling down a slope, first try the pick' – he demonstrated with his ice axe – 'then the edge, and if neither works, drive in the shaft.'

The explanation seemed to open the door to certain vague dangers. Love considered they might do well to rope up but decided to say nothing. He started off again. After a while he pointed.

'There it is.'

They had crossed the ridge and off to the right, the early sun on its face, was a wall like a lump of anthracite. There were greater peaks behind but this one seemed to stand out despite its smaller size, like a menacing face in a crowd upon which one's gaze happens to fall.

At its foot Rand stared up. It was at least seven or eight hundred feet high. He reached out with his hand. The surface was chill, as if asleep. There was a vertical crack, the start of the route. He felt a sudden uncertainty as if here, for some reason, in this remote place, his ability to climb might be lost. His confidence had vanished. He put his hands on the rock, found the first foothold, and began to climb. Slowly, metre by metre, the uneasiness left him. He made his way upward.

At the first belaying stance he took off his sweater and stuffed it in his pack. The sun was warm. Love was coming up beneath, his beard already dishevelled. When he raised his face he looked like a young Karl Marx.

Rand was at home. It seemed he knew instinctively where holds would be. The route was not hard to find, marked in many places by pitons which he removed as he went, clipping them into his own supply.

'We really shouldn't be taking them out,' Love said. 'They leave them there to save time.'

'Never trust a piton you don't put in yourself.'

'Isn't that a little strict?'

Rand shrugged. 'On belay?'

'On belay,' Love said.

'Here's a traverse. You're going to like this.'

Love was beginning, psychologically, to lose ground. In places that Rand passed without comment, he found himself struggling. He knew he must climb at his own pace, but he was conscious of being slower, that someone was waiting. He flexed his fingers, his eyes on the rock in front of him, trying not to think of anything except the next hold.

The sun lay on them now with all its weight. A kind of dizziness, a sense of abandonment came over Love. The white of the glacier and the snowfields far below seemed to shimmer and rise. The sky was a flawless blue.

Thirty minutes later they heard something above them. Voices. They searched the face.

'Over there.'

Off to the right, near a ridge toward which they were heading, were two figures. For Rand a certain pleasure he had felt was now gone; they were not alone, they were following another pair. Love listened.

'French,' he said.

The leader was wearing a red sweater, talking to his second, then turning to hammer in a piton. He struck it a glancing blow – out it came. The steel rang as it hit the rock far down and shot straight out, glinting for a moment as it disappeared against the flatness of the glacier.

'*Merde*.' They were laughing and shouting at one another, their voices floating down. The leader was trying to put in another piton. It came out, too, but he caught it. Suddenly he went limp in a parody of helplessness and frustration.

Before long, they had caught up to them. Rand was fifteen feet or so below the second man. There he had to wait, interminably, unable to move. He became impatient. He looked up:

'Hello,' he called.

There was a brief downward glance.

'Can we go ahead?'

They had resumed their shouts in French, they didn't answer.

Suddenly from near the leader's foot something sprang loose, gathering speed.

'Rock!' Rand hugged the wall. Leaping, arcing, the rock went by. It was the size of a shoebox. He heard it explode against the wall below.

'You son of a bitch.' He shouted, 'You shouldn't be climbing! You should be playing golf!'

Love came up beside him.

'That nearly hit me,' he said, concerned.

'Next time he'll kick down something bigger.'

'Try and call out earlier.' He leaned there resignedly, his beard awry. 'My reflexes have always been a little slow. Anyway, I hope you don't mean bigger. The whole face of the Blaitière broke loose one time.'

'One of these guys must have been climbing it.'

'Actually, the French are very good climbers. As good as any. The Italians, too. I'm not very fond of Germans. I suppose they'd have to be included,' he decided. He glanced down. They were about halfway. The glacier had become very small. It seemed he was somewhere – he had felt this many times before – where a terrible event, some suspension of physical law, might take place and everything he knew, was sure of, hoped to be, in one anarchic moment would dissolve. He saw himself falling.

This feeling alternated with one of confidence. A layer of frailty had been stripped away and a stronger, more spiritual being remained. He almost forgot where he was or what he had given himself to. His eye wandered over the silent peaks. He was awed by their immensity and stillness. He was, in a sense, part of them. Whatever happened, their majesty would enhance, even justify it. He felt equal to the climb, immeasurably close to his companion whose character he admired more and more.

'There's the Aiguille du Géant,' he pointed out. 'And there are the Grandes Jorasses.'

Rand was looking upward.

'We're going to be here all night,' he said.

Finally the way was clear. The French were far ahead. Love had begun to tire, he could feel it, he was losing his strength. The rock became implacable. He could feel its malevolence.

He watched Rand above him, still in harmony with it, still undismayed. A movement one way, no good, another slightly different, this one successful. There were times when he seemed to be doing nothing, not even exploring the surface, and then would reach out, pull, try to get his foot on some flaw. He moved in smooth advances and pauses, even retreats, like a snake swallowing a frog, motionless, then a slight flurry, then a pause. If a thing did not work he would withdraw, change position, flex his fingers to loosen them and try again. The physical acts are not hard to imagine but the endless succession of them, far up on a wall – that is another thing. And the distance beneath.

Gathering himself, Love followed. There were moments when he nearly gave up, his legs began to shake. If he fell, the rope would hold him but more than anything, more than life itself, he did not want to, he dared not fail.

Section by section, some easier, some not, they went on to the top. The others were not in sight. It was over. As they unroped, the anguish Love had felt, the shame at his weakness and lapses of will, all vanished. He knew an exultation beyond words. In his whole life, it seemed, he had never felt more worthy.

'Not a bad climb,' Rand said.

'As the woman on the bus said when she saw the Pacific for the first time . . .'

'Yeah?'

'I imagined it would be bigger.'

They descended to the north on a slope covered with snow. It was steep, they had to stamp out steps. Suddenly Love, who had lost all thought of danger, slipped. His feet went out from under him. He began to accelerate.

'Self-arrest! Self-arrest!'

He did not make the slightest attempt to help himself but slid like a rag doll, faster, bumping, bouncing as if he would come apart. Far down, luckily, the snow was soft. He came to a stop and lay still. There were clots of ice in his beard. His knuckles were raw.

'Didn't you hear me?' Rand cried, hurrying to him.

'Oh, yes, I heard you,' he said, gazing up. 'I heard you. I said, he is my friend.'

'What?'

'My very good friend,' Love said.

The public baths were in the basement of a building called La Residence, led to by a weedy path and entered through some flimsy doors. Inside was a booth where soap and towels were dispensed. It was crowded there. The doors to the showers opened and closed. There was the sound of cascading water and strange languages, the odour of steam. A woman in carpet slippers collected a franc apiece.

The woman knew Love. Where had he been climbing, she asked?

'Pointe Lachenal,' he said casually.

'*Très bien*,' she said. She had black hair and gold teeth. She glanced at the figure sitting next to him.

'*Avec ce monsieur?*'

Yes, Love confirmed.

'What do you suppose takes them so long?' Rand said. He was watching the shower doors.

'They're in there washing their clothes. It's forbidden of course.'

More people were coming to the entrance. Some, seeing the line, turned away. Suddenly Rand sat up.

'Hey!' he cried.

It was the red sweater, the one that had been above them. He jumped to his feet.

'Hey, you!' He bumped into people in the doorway. 'You!'

Down the corridor he ran. Near the door he grabbed the sweater. He held it tightly.

'Hey listen. The next time,' he said it slowly to have it comprehended, 'I'm going to throw you right off the goddamned mountain.'

There was a look of utter bewilderment.

'You understand?'

A flat English voice responded, 'No. Not at all. What's the trouble?'

'Weren't you climbing on Pointe Lachenal?'

'Sorry.'

As Rand released him, the Englishman straightened his clothes. He looked even smaller and more wary, like a turtle about to pull in its head.

'Sorry. There was someone on the mountain with a sweater like yours.'

'So I gather,' he said.

CHAPTER SEVEN

JOHN BRAY had, besides his red sweater, a dirty suede jacket and the face of a thief. He smoked French cigarettes. There was a fever blister on his lip. He was twenty-two.

'The guides are looking for the bastard who's pulling all their pins,' he said. It was raining. They were sitting inside the National, the floor filthy from wet boots. 'They don't think it's so funny.'

'Too bad.'

'You're screwing up their act.'

'Come on. I was a guide,' Rand said.

'Is that right? Where?'

'In the Tetons.'

'Never heard of them. They must be new.'

'Have you heard of the Himalayas?'

'The Hima-what?' Bray said. Then, in a low voice, 'Look out, here they come.'

A group of Japanese was entering, looking around to find an empty table.

'Hello,' Bray said with a wave of his hand as they squeezed past. 'Nice weather, isn't it?'

They were nodding and acknowledging in some confusion. Humour does not readily translate.

'Having some good climbing?' he asked.

Finally they understood.

'Oh, yes. Crime,' they said.

'Where have you gone? The Triolet? Grépon?'

'Yes, yes,' they agreed.

'Good luck.' He waved after them, smiling. 'Nice little fellows,' he said in an aside to Rand. 'They come here by the thousands.'

'I've already heard the story.'

'Which one?'

'About a bit of a nip in the air.'

Bray had a wry, grudging laugh.

'What's that? I don't know that,' he said.

Outside the rain came in gusts. The campgrounds were drenched, the paths slick with mud. The National, which was known as the English bar, was cheap and unadorned. There is a strain of English whose faces are somehow crude as if they were not worth finishing or touching with colour. It was these sullen faces that filled the room.

'Never stops raining here,' Bray said. 'You have to wait for what they call a *beau fixe,* stretch of good weather. Then it's all right.'

'Where are you going then?'

'You mean climb? I hadn't decided.'

'Want to do one?'

'What are you thinking of?'

'You know the Frêney?'

Bray glanced at him. 'You mean that?'

'Are you interested?'

'I might be, yes.'

'Why not, then?'

'Um ... be a couple of days on it, wouldn't we?'

'I would think so,' Rand said. In fact he had no clear idea.

The Frêney was a buttress, inaccessible and huge, on the side of Mont Blanc. There had been famous tragedies on it.

'That's where Bonatti got in all the trouble, isn't it?'

'Was it Bonatti?'

'Yeah, sure, I'd be interested,' Bray said.

He had a thick cigarette in his small fingers and his head bent forward as if in suspicion. He was a plasterer. British climbing had changed since the war. Once the province of university men, it had been invaded by the working class who cut their teeth on the rock of Scotland and Wales and then travelled everywhere, suspicious and unfriendly. They came from the blackened cities of England – Manchester, Leeds. To the mountains they brought the same qualities – toughness and cynicism – that let them survive in the slums. They had no credo, no code. They had bad teeth, bad manners and one ambition: to conquer.

CHAPTER EIGHT

DOWN A CURVING, dawn street in the stillness, at the hour when shutters are still closed and all that distinguishes this century from the last are empty cars ranked along the gutters, Rand walked. He was carrying a large pack and a rope. He passed almost no one – a lone woman going in the other direction and a white cat without a tail hunting in a garden. As he came close the cat stepped into some bushes. It had a tail, almost invisible, perfectly black.

At the cable car station there were people already waiting. They stood silently, some chewing bits of bread, and watched him approach. Bray had not arrived. Several guides wearing the blue enamelled badge were with their clients. He slipped off his pack. Two or three stragglers came down the street. It was a few minutes before six. He felt a certain detachment. It seemed he was made of cardboard and was waiting among other cardboard figures, some of whom occasionally murmured a word or two.

There was a stirring – the ticket seller had entered the booth inside. The crowd, like animals knowing they are about to be fed, began to press closer to the doors.

At the last moment a figure came hurrying toward him. It was one of the English climbers in a thick sweater and corduroy pants.

'John can't come,' he said. 'He caught some bug.'

'When did that happen?'

'This morning. He has a bad throat.'

The doors had been unlocked. The crowd was moving forward. It was a long walk back to camp. He had packed the night before, carefully putting everything in a certain order.

'Do you want to meet him here tomorrow?'

'No,' Rand said.

'You're not going, anyway?'

'Tell him I hope it's not serious.'

He was among the last to get a ticket. The cable car lurched slightly as he stepped aboard. For a moment he felt nervous, as if he had made a fatal mistake, but then they were gliding up, over the pines, ascending at a steep angle. The town began to shrink, to draw together and move off. Noiselessly they swept upward.

Bray was in a sleeping bag, his clothing scattered about. He raised himself on one elbow.

'Did you find him?' he asked.

'Yeah, he was there. I told him you were sick.'

'What did he say?'

'He went up anyway.'

'Went up?' Bray said.

The sun had risen. It was filling the trees with light. Bray had a moment of remorse. The day was clear, the mountains beckoned.

'He wouldn't go alone,' Bray said.

'Perhaps he'll meet someone up above.'

'Yeah, they're standing in line.'

'Is he the one who said he'd throw you off the mountain?'

'You've got it backwards.'

'You were going to throw him off?'

'No.' Bray cut him short. 'Did you tell him I'd go tomorrow?'

'I don't think you're going to see that much more of him.'

The sky was absolutely clear and of a perfect colour. It was ideal for climbing. Late in the day it became calm. The wind began to shift. Suddenly, from nowhere, there were grey streamers in the air and, as if to announce them, thunder. Climbers hurried down. Rain, which might be snow at higher altitudes, started.

The sound of it woke Bray who had been sleeping fitfully. He was startled. He was able to see a little in the dark. It had gotten very cold. The grass of the meadow below was jerking in the rain. His thoughts, somewhat confused, went quickly to the Frêney. Like a great ship, at that moment, it was sailing through clouds and darkness. There was a sudden bolt of lightning, very close, an ear-splitting clap. The silence swam back quickly and in it, like a kind of infinite debris, the snow was pouring down.

The next morning he got up early and went into town. The rescue service was in an old building next door to a garage. It was still raining. There were bicycles inside the entrance; upstairs a door slammed. Two men came down the stairs in hats and blue sweaters. They passed him and went out.

On the second floor was a bulletin board and the office. A short-wave radio was going. No one spoke English. Finally someone came to the counter who did.

'Yes?'

'I want to report someone missing.'

'Where?'

'On the Frêney Pillar.'

'How do you know? Were you with him?' the guide asked.

'No, he's alone,' Bray said.

'Alone?' The guide was half-listening to something on the radio at which he and the others suddenly laughed. Bray waited. 'Why is he alone? You know, we can't do anything until the storm has passed.'

'How long is it supposed to last?'

The French were always the same. They never answered a question, pretended they didn't understand. He waited until the guide, who had nothing else to do, finally noticed him again.

'Come back tomorrow.'

'Thank you so much,' he said.

They hadn't made a note, they hadn't asked for a name. He went downstairs. There were two police vans parked across the street. It was raining like winters in England, days of going to work while cars, their windows up, dry and warm inside, splashed past. He was used to working in the cold, in unheated houses, and going off on weekends to climb in the cold as well, not a meteor figure like Haston or Brown – it took big climbs to do that, incredible climbs – but somewhere close behind. He was lingering near the edge of things awaiting his chance. He could climb as well as any of them. The confidence on absolutely impossible routes, the spirit to dare them, that was perhaps what he lacked. It might come. In any case, he was waiting.

He walked back in the rain. The longer the storm lasted, the less were the chances. Up there it was cold, ice forming in great, invincible sheets. All the features of the rock would be covered, whole routes obliterated. He was lucky, he could have been up there. Diarrhoea had saved him.

'I couldn't go,' he would often say later. 'I was too busy.'

It was one of those ironies that mark risky lives.

CHAPTER NINE

IN THE SILENCE of the peaks and valleys, fading and then drifting forth came the dull, unmistakable beat of rotors. From a distance the helicopter resembled an insect slanting across the snowfields, lingering, then moving on.

The rain had stopped. There was blue sky visible behind the clouds. Snow covered everything in the upper regions, every horizontal, every ledge. The summits were still shrouded, the cold clinging.

A climber was caught on the Central Pillar of Frêney, that was what they were saying. The sound of the rescue helicopter going back and forth became more and more ominous, like one of those disasters where nothing is announced but the silence tells all. Accidents were common. Occasionally there was one that stood out because of its inevitability or horror. Really cruel instances never vanished; they became part of climbing, as famous crimes became part of an era.

The search stopped in the late afternoon. A lone figure had been seen on the glacier. At noon the next day, dirty and exhausted, the pack hanging from one shoulder, Rand came walking up the path to the campground. He looked neither to the right nor left, as if there were not another soul on earth.

Love was sitting outside his tent and called to him. Rand walked on. From inside his parka he took out a bottle of wine. The cork had been pulled. Still walking, he began to drink.

On reaching the tent he simply dropped to his knees and disappeared by falling forward, his feet outside. After a moment they were drawn in behind him.

Bray found him lying there, eyes open.

'What happened?' he asked.

Rand's gaze drifted over slowly.

'I thought they were going to bring down a frozen body.' Bray said. He waited – there was no reply. Then;

'That was some *beau fixe*.'

'How far up did you get? Where were you?'

Rand had closed his eyes when he lay down, but only for a minute. They had opened again by themselves. He lay there teeming with words, like a dying man who could not confess, who would take them with him to the grave.

'It caught me by surprise,' he finally said, 'it came in so fast. I didn't have time to do anything. I got to a small ledge. At first it was just rain . . .'

'And then?'

'I stayed there. That night and the next day.'

'You weren't frightened?'

'Frightened? I was paralyzed,' he said. 'I thought how stupid I'd been. I went up for the wrong reason, I didn't know anything. No wonder it happened.'

There were other faces attempting to see in. Rand's voice was too low to be heard.

'Finally I decided I had to try and get down,' he said. 'I made some rappels. The rope was frozen. Hands were numb. I chopped holds. I was afraid I'd drop the axe, it would come out of my hand and that would be the end.'

'Did they find you? I alerted the mountain rescue.'

'They flew by. I don't know if they saw me.'

Bray nodded. He was ashamed of what he had earlier felt, of having so easily given up someone for dead. The drained, low voice seemed to come from uncalculated depths, from an inner man. The weary face touched him deeply. He recognized the defeat in it, the renunciation. At that moment something bound him to Rand, he would have liked to acknowledge it but he remained silent. Instead he picked up the bottle.

'Want some?' he asked.

Rand shook his head.

'Not bad,' Bray said, drinking. 'Where'd you get it?'

'Don't remember.'

He fell asleep. His boots were on. He was lying in the disorder of retreat, his fingernails black with dirt. He slept for eighteen hours, people walking up and down the path. In town they were already telling his story.

CHAPTER TEN

IN THE FALL he found a room behind the *papeterie,* along the Impasse des Moulins, in a house by the river. The campground was empty, the town had become still. September light fell on everything. A lazy, burning sun filled the days.

Cowbells ringing mournfully in the high meadows, the closed lives of local people, the cool green forests – these seemed to spell out the season. The peaks were turning darker, abandoning their life. The Blaitière, the Verte, the Grandes Jorasses far up the glacier, he began to look at them in another way, without eagerness or confusion. There was a different sky above them, a sky that was calm, mysterious, its colour the blue of last voyages.

His hair was long, he was growing a beard – it was already fanning out, filling with wildness like a prophet from the Old Testament. They knew him in the shops where he had begun to speak a halting French. He was clean, he was dry. He walked to his room in the evening with the end of a long, narrow loaf of bread sticking out of his pack.

Later he lived in a room behind a small museum, the Musée Loppe, which was at the end of a passageway, and then in the attic of a house near the station, a large house with green shutters and faded walls. It was entered by a garden gate in the shade of an alley. Two café tables were rusting near the door. Inside was an odour of cooking and tobacco, warm, oppressive. His room had a small skylight and balcony with a set of double doors hung with curtains that once were white. Across the way was a garage and the rear of the Hôtel des Étrangers. Rain fell on the metal roof. Occasionally there was the soft clatter of a train.

He stood outside Sport Giro, looking at boots in the window. Someone motioned him to come in – it was the owner at the door.

'You don't need to stand in the rain,' he said.

'*Merci.*'

'You speak French?'

'Not really.'

'I think you do,' Giro said.

The salesgirl barely glanced up. 'If you look like that, you don't have to speak,' she remarked in French. 'Eventually you have to say something besides "thank you,"' Giro replied. 'Such as?' she said.

Giro's homely face made an expression of resignation.

'I didn't quite understand that,' Rand said.

'It's nothing.'

The girl had turned away. She had a certain disinterest, even insolence, that annoyed him. Ordinarily he would have known how to respond but here the language baffled him.

He thought of her the next day at the baths. The water poured over him, gleaming on his limbs. Here he was more confident, unrestrained. He dreamed of possessing her, gratifying dreams. Her hands were banging on the wall, he was wading in cries . . .

The woman in her flowered wrap asked, '*Vous êtes anglais, monsieur*?'

When she found he was not, she confided in him. The English were very dirty, she said. Even the Arabs were cleaner. Had he been to England?

'England? No,' he said.

Unexpectedly she smiled.

This woman at the Douches Municipales, Remy Giro, an infrequent stranger – there were not many he talked to. There was a teller at the Banque Payot who glanced at him in a certain way. She was about thirty, with a narrow face that had something hidden in it, like a woman who has ruined herself for love. He watched her boredom and absence of expression as she counted thickets of hundred-franc notes for a young businessman. When Rand stepped forward she raised her eyes for a moment. He was prepared for it. It was as if he had caught her by the arm. Sometimes he saw her from the street through the iron-barred window. She was married, he knew. He had seen the gold band on her finger.

The days grew colder, the first snows fell. It was beautiful, even glamorous, with the darkness settling and snow drifting down. He felt he would journey through winter easily, but as weeks passed he began to see how much he had been mistaken. He had ventured too far. It was like a drive across desolate country in a tiny car. The ice was on the windshield, the horizon white. If the engine failed, if he somehow happened to run off the road . . .

He had not counted on the loneliness, the terrible cold. He felt he had made a desperate error. He was stranded. The shutters of the houses were closed at night. The room was unheated, he was never really warm. Over the radio came announcements of girls who had disappeared from home – these were among the first things he was able to understand . . . *Seize ans, mince, longeur un metre quatre-vingt, yeux verts, cheveux long, châtains. Téléphonez 53.36.39,* etc. Sometimes he caught a few words of the news.

It was as if the battle had moved on and he had somehow been left behind in a foreign town. Everyone had gone, the camp was abandoned, he was wintering alone.

He found some illegal work – he had no permit – sweeping up in a machine shop on the road toward Geneva. It was behind the Hôtel Roma; the lighted windows and parked cars taunted him as he passed in the evening on the way home.

He thought almost every day of Louise. *Yes, come, come at once,* he wrote sitting in a bare café filling sheet after sheet of paper. He read them over slowly and sent a postcard instead. On and on came tremendous snowfalls, mountains gleaming above the town and ragged ten-franc notes received on Saturdays as pay. There was no easy way into this world.

One night on a corner he saw the teller from the bank reading the movie posters. She was alone. His heart jumped. He stood beside her.

'*Bonsoir.*'

She did not answer. She turned and looked at him as if judging him coldly.

The first time she had seen him she felt herself tremble. She was susceptible to certain men, she handed her life over to them. His eyes, his burnished face – he was the type she threw everything away for, she had already done it twice.

He did not know this. He could hardly speak to her because of the language, and she seemed reluctant to talk. She had a bare, defiant face. Her husband was away somewhere visiting his parents. She had a child.

They walked by the river, the water was rattling past. He felt an almost physical pain being near her, the desire was so great. He wanted to look at her, regard her openly, see her smoke a cigarette, remove her clothes. Her name was Nicole Vix.

He managed to kiss her in a doorway. She would not tell him where she lived. She stood as if she had taken her last step on crippling heels. She put her face against his chest and allowed him to touch her breasts.

He saw her in the bank the next morning. She was not the sort of woman to smile. He didn't know how to proceed – he couldn't come in every day. Also her husband was coming back. They had exchanged a passionate signal, but as it turned out he was not able to meet her again.

The winter passed. It was difficult to remember what became of the days, they faded like those of school, the first year, the hardest. You could not tell from looking at him that he had been lonely, that he had stood at society's edge envying its light and warmth, wanting to be part of it, determined not to be; none of this was in his face.

Above, the *aiguilles* glittered. The mountains were asleep, the glaciers hidden in snow.

CHAPTER ELEVEN

THERE WAS a single tent in the meadow. From far off it looked like the first arrival, from closer, the last survivor. Within, it had been made comfortable, some books arranged on a flat stone, an alcohol lamp, a few curled photos taped to the pole.

The grass was already knee-high, the early flowers scattered about. It was May. Huge slugs the size of fingers drifted slowly across the stones. Below was the narrow road that became the path to Montenvers, although no one took it at this time of year. Above, the blue sky of France. A van had stopped on the road, tilted slightly as if in a rut.

A lone figure came up through the grass walking purposelessly, sometimes turning completely around. Rand was watching. The winter was over but he was strangely inanimate, tired of himself and the solitude that had been pressing down on him. There seemed nothing that could end it. He was lying alone among his few possessions as if wounded when suddenly he felt an overwhelming joy, like a castaway seeing a naval lieutenant in whites step onto the beach. The blond hair was shining in the sun.

'My God,' he said.

'Hello, buddy.' It was Cabot.

'I can't believe it. What are you doing here?'

'Looking for you.'

'Stop lying. How'd you find me?'

'It wasn't hard.' He looked for a place to sit. 'Everybody in town seemed to know where you were.'

'I've made a lot of friends,' Rand said.

'I bet you have.' He looked at him closely. 'So, how've you been?'

'Well, it seems to snow a lot here. A lot of people come. French mostly. Italians. I don't know who they are. Am I glad to see you. Are you here alone?'

'No. Come on down to the van.'

Rand stood up. He still could not believe it. 'Tell me, are you going to stay around for a while?' he said.

From the road, Carol Cabot saw them start down, her husband's arm around the other's shoulder, walking and suddenly running, not in a straight line but in great, drunken circles. She could hear shouting – it was Rand, he was making huge leaps and his arms flew about wildly. They came running up to her.

'What's happened?' she asked.

'Here he is,' her husband said.

She knew Rand slightly but hardly recognized him. She tried to remember what he looked like. She had seen him only a few times and retained the image of someone tall, confident, someone with dirty hair and a kind of secret energy. Now he looked like an outlaw. He smelled of tree bark and smoke.

'Hello,' she said. 'When Jack said you were over here somewhere I thought we were going to have trouble finding you.'

She was an Arizona girl, easy and optimistic, finer than her husband in certain ways. When they walked along the streets of town, she was stylish, dreaming. Her bare arms were crossed, a hand clasped on each shoulder. She would stop to look in store windows while her husband and Rand walked on and then stroll unhurriedly after them. Cabot never turned to see where she had gone. He sometimes put his arm around her, continuing to talk, when she was near. She would stay then. Often it seemed she wasn't listening.

Cabot had become stronger. He'd been working as a carpenter, framing with a heavy hammer. His forearms bulged.

'How's your French?' he asked Rand.

'Not too good.'

'What? Didn't you have a French girl friend?'

'I didn't have any kind.'

Cabot suddenly admired him.

'I don't believe it,' Carol said calmly.

'It wasn't that I didn't give it any thought.'

He seemed to them despite his appearance – as if wearing the clothes of two or three vanished companions – to be particularly well. His eyes were shining. He was filled with life. They talked about it afterwards.

'He looks like some kind of holy man,' Carol said.

'More like Natty Bumppo.'

'Who?'

'The Deerslayer,' Cabot said.

'You know I'm stupid. Who is that?'

They took him to dinner at Le Choucas – perhaps it was her face or the well-being they represented, but the heads of passers-by in the street turned. The next day they drove to Saint-Gervais and the valley beyond. Old farms with stones on the roof stood among the newer chalets. The mountains were huge and white.

'What sort of conditions do they have up there?'

'The snow's still heavy,' Rand said, 'but they say it's firm. I heard them talking about it a few days ago. It isn't how much snow they have but the state it's in.'

'There must be some climbs we can do. I'd like to start getting in shape.'

'You look all right.'

'I got very nervous being away from here. I began thinking about you, for instance. There are certain climbs I wouldn't want you to do without me.'

'I think you're safe.'

'Maybe for the moment, but I worry. There are climbs you just can't stop thinking about. You can't get your mind off them. Do you ever have that feeling?' He paused. 'The problem is, there are other people who could do them. Keeps you awake at night.'

'So, tell me, what are you thinking of?'

'We'd have to be ready.'

'Come on,' Rand said.

Cabot was still evasive. 'We'd have to be in very good shape.'

'For what?'

Cabot waited.

'The Dru,' he said.

'Are you kidding? Something easy, you mean.'

'Right up the middle.'

A single granite face, grey and isolated, seemed to shift forward in Rand's mind, detach itself from the landscape and become even more distinct. Dark, with black lines weeping down it, a Babylonian temple smashed by centuries, its pillars and passages sheared away, the huge fragments floating through thousands of feet of air to explode on the lower slabs, legendary, unclimbable for decades: the Dru.

Rand looked at the ground. 'The Dru . . .' He had a shy, almost embarrassed smile.

'What do you think?'

'Jack, I've been waiting for you,' he said.

The mountain is like an immense obelisk. It was first climbed by the easiest routes. The North Face, after years of attempts, was only conquered in 1935. The West, most difficult of all, survived until after the war. It was finally climbed in 1952.

This West Face seems pointed, towering. It is like a spire. It does not reveal, from in front, its full depth and power. From the valley – Les Tines – one sees it is not a mere finger but a powerful head, the head of a god.

The regular route begins to the right, up a steep couloir that is a channel for rockfall and where a number of climbers have died. From the top of the couloir a series of terraces brings one toward the centre and from there the way goes up through more than fifteen hundred feet of implacable wall.

This route was of little interest to them.

There is climbing that is tedious and requires brutal effort; it is almost a kind of destruction. To climb without holds, without natural lines, to work against the inclination of the rock, as it were, is ugly though sometimes essential. The more elegant way is rarer, like a kind of love. Here, the most hazardous attempt is made beautiful by its rightness, even if it means falling to one's death. There are weaknesses in the rock, flaws by which its smoothness can be overcome. The discovery of these and linking of them is the way to the summit.

There are routes the boldness and logic of which are overwhelming. The purely vertical is, of course, the ideal. If one could follow, or nearly, the path that a pebble takes falling from the top and climb scarcely deviating to right or left, impossible as it may seem, one would leave behind something inextirpable, a line that led past a mere summit.

The name of that line is the direct.

In June, after three weeks of lesser climbs, they walked up to Montenvers on the steep path through the forest. From here the classic outline of the Dru was visible, somewhat shadowed by the mountains behind it, distant, remote. They descended to the glacier which lay like a winter river below the station and hotel.

The glacier is dangerous only when covered with snow. That year it had melted early. The surface was grey with pulverized rock and carried granite blocks of all sizes. They passed two other people, a man and woman, both deaf – they were signing to each other as they moved in silence. From the blue of crevasses came a chill breath and the sound of trickling water. On the far side they climbed the steep bank and started along the faint track that winds up through scrub and small pines. It was warm. They walked without speaking. The Dru, visible from the glacier, had vanished behind intervening ridges. Looking up now, they saw it again, only the tip like the highest mast of a ship, then gradually the rest. They continued the long, uphill walk. It had already been three hours. The trees and undergrowth ended, there were patches of snow. At last they reached the outcrop that stood like an island in the snowfields at the foot of the Dru, the *rognon* it was called.

It was noon. The sky was clear, the air seemed still. Above them the mythic face soared as if leaning slightly backward. The light was streaming across the top. There was snow in the great couloir, snow on the high ledges. The rock was pale in places, almost rusted. There were huge sheets like this, gilded with age. From somewhere came a faint whispering and then a roar. It was off to the right. They watched a graceful flow of rock come down the face, the snow streaming ahead of it and bursting like the sea. The sound slowly died. There was silence. The air was cold. Rand took off his pack. He stared upward.

'That is some piece of rock.'

Cabot nodded. In the dank shadow it was somehow as if they had swum to this place and surfaced. The chill in the air was like spray, their faces dim.

They sat down to examine it closely. They rejected the couloir. It was off to the side as well as being the start of the normal route, but the rest was one vast apron filled with overhangs and downward-facing slabs. Almost in front of them, however, there seemed to be a slanting fault that led to a group of arches. They would come out on a sort of ledge five hundred feet up.

'Then there's a series of cracks,' Cabot remarked. They were faint, vertical lines; in places they almost disappeared. It was difficult to tell if they really faded to nothing. There might be a way to link them.

Cabot was looking through binoculars – their field was small, the image unsteady and jerking. On up to an overhanging wall above which was wedged an enormous block, a well-known feature, the *bloc coincé*. Past that and up. They would be joining the end of the regular route which would take them the rest of the way.

For hours they examined it, noting every detail. Rand was writing it down with the stub of a pencil. The sun, coming over the left side, hit the face as they finished, flooding it with a vast, supernal light.

'That's about it,' said Cabot finally.

Rand took the glasses for a while before they started down. He was silent. He was touched by a certain solemnity.

A great mountain is serious. It demands everything of a climber, absolutely all. It must be difficult and also beautiful, it must lie in the memory like the image of an unforgettable woman. It must be unsoiled.

'How long do you think it's going to take?'

'Two days, maybe three,' Cabot said.

'How many pitons?'

'I think everything we've got.'

'Weight's going to be a problem.'

Cabot didn't answer. 'That's a terrific line,' he said, his eye ascending one last time. 'It could take us right to the top, you know?'

'Or farther.'

CHAPTER TWELVE

HE WAS SWIMMING, far out to sea. Something was out there, a person, the air was ringing with faint, fading cries. His arms were heavy, the swells were becoming deeper. He tried to call out himself, his cries were borne away. Someone was drowning, he hadn't the courage to reach them. He was giving up. His heart was leaden. Suddenly he woke. He had been dreaming. It was two in the morning.

There followed hours of the same thoughts repeated again and again. The dark face of the mountain filled not only sleeplessness but the entire world. Its coldness, its malice would be revealed only at certain times. Long before dawn he lay, victim to these fears. The iron hours before the assault. His eyes were already wearied by images of what was to come, the miraculous had drained from his palms.

The weather had not been good. The delay was eating at his nerves. Each morning they woke to overcast skies or the sound of rain. Everything was ready, ropes, pitons, supplies. Every day they sat in idleness.

Weather is critical in the Alps. The sudden storms are the cause of most disasters. The casual arrival of clouds, a shifting of wind, things which might seem of little consequence can be dangerous. The sun, moreover, melts the ice and snow at higher altitudes, and rocks, sometimes of unbelievable size, break loose and fall. This happens usually in the afternoon.

One must know the mountains. Speed and judgment are essential. The classic decision is always the same, whether to retreat or go on. There comes a time when it is easier to continue upward, when the summit, in fact, is the only way out. At such a moment one must still have strength.

It cleared at last. They walked to the station. Their packs were huge, they weighed at least fifty pounds. Ropes slung over their shoulders, when they moved there was a muted clanking like the sound of armour.

His chest felt empty, his hands weightless. He felt a lack of density, the strength to cling to existence, to remain on earth, as if he were already a kind of husk that could blow away.

This great morning, this morning he would never forget. Carol was standing among the tourists. A group of schoolchildren had arrived with their teachers for an excursion to the Mer de Glace. Rand stood near a pillar that supported the roof. The sun was warm on his legs. His clothing, different from theirs, the loaves of bread sticking out of his pack, the equipment, set him apart. A kind of distinction surrounded him, of being marked for a different life. That distinction meant everything.

They boarded the train. The seats around them were empty. Amid the shouts of children and the low, murmured talk of couples, young men with cashmere sweaters around their necks, a shrill whistle blew. The train began to move. Carol walked along beside it as far as the platform's end.

The valley fell away. On the opposite side the Brévent reared like a wall, a faint path zigzagging up it. An elderly Englishman and his wife sat nearby. He had a turned-down hat. There were blotches on his face.

'Very beautiful, isn't it?' he said.

'I prefer the Cervin. The Cervin is much nicer,' his wife replied.

'Do you think so?' he said.

'It's majestic.'

'Well, here you have majesty.'

'Where?'

'There.'

She looked for a moment.

'No,' she said. 'It's not the same.'

The train rocked gently. The conversation seemed like scraps of paper floating from the window as they went upward. At Montenvers a crowd was waiting to go back down.

By three that afternoon they were camped beneath the Dru. That evening they had a good meal, soup, thick pieces of bread, dried fruit, tea. Afterward a bar of chocolate. They planned to start at dawn. Above them the face was silent. The slanting rays of sun fell on their shoulders, on the warm, lichened rock and dry grass. They watched the sun go down in splendour behind the shoulder of the Charmoz. Cabot was smoking. He held out the thin cigarette as he exhaled. Rand took it from between his fingers.

'Where'd you get this?'

'Brought it with me.' He leaned back, his thoughts drifting off. 'And so,' he said, 'they waited for morning. I love this time. I like it best.'

'Here . . .'

Cabot reached for it. He inhaled deeply, smiled. It seemed he was a different man here, calmer; the strength remained but not the vainglory that clung to him below. The well-to-do family, school, athletic teams, what these had done for him the mountains had done for Rand. A deep companionship and understanding joined them. They were equals. Without a word, it seemed, they had made a solemn pact. It would never be broken.

The light had faded. It was growing cold. By nine-thirty they were asleep. An hour later there was thunder, distant but unmistakable. By midnight it began to rain. In a torrential downpour they went down the next day, soaked and miserable. They slept in the back of the van, the three of them, piled together like dogs while chill rain beat on the roof.

Three times they were to walk to the foot of the Dru. The weather was against them. It had pinned down everyone else as well. Bray was in town. He had talked to one of the guides, a man from the villages who knew the lore.

'There's something they call the wind for the year,' he explained. 'It comes on the twenty-third of January. This year it was from the west.'

'What does that mean?'

'A good day, then two or three of rain, and so forth. Variable.'

'I could have told you that,' Cabot said.

In the second week of July they started up again. The weather had cleared, climbers were swarming into the mountains. Two were near them on the glacier, one a girl carrying a big pack. Her boy-friend was far in front.

'What's he bringing her up for?'

'To milk her,' Cabot said.

She wore glasses. Her face was damp. Later, having fallen two or three times on the ice, she cried out in frustration and sat there. The boy went on without looking back.

On the *rognon* another party was already camped – two Austrians; they looked like brothers. Cabot was immediately alarmed.

'Let's go over on the far side,' he said.

That evening they could hear, from across the valley, the whistle of the last train going down. Later there was singing. It was the Austrians.

'What do you suppose they're doing? Do you think they're doing the same thing we are?'

'I don't know,' Rand said. 'Where were they when it was raining?'

'We'd better start early,' Cabot decided.

At five in the morning, they broke camp silently and went down onto the glacier that lay between them and the base. It was already light. Their hands were cold. Their footsteps seemed to bark on the frozen surface.

'If they're not up yet, this will wake them,' Rand said.

'They're doing the regular route anyway.'

'How do you know?'

'There they are.'

There were two small figures far off on the right, making for the couloir.

'Nothing to worry about now,' Rand said.

'Right.'

Between the glacier and the rock there is a deep crevasse, the bergschrund; they crossed it without difficulty. The granite was dark and icy cold. Rand put his hand on it. It seemed he was touching not a face but something in the order of a planet, too vast to be imagined and at the same time, somehow, aware of his presence.

It was just before six when they began to climb.

'I'll take the first pitch, all right?' Cabot said.

He took hold of the rock, found a foothold and started up.

CHAPTER THIRTEEN

'OFF BELAY!'

After a bit, a rope came curling down. He tied Cabot's pack to it with stiffened fingers and watched as it was hauled up, brushing against the rock. The rope came down again. He fastened his own pack to it. A few minutes later he was climbing.

At first there is anxiety, the initial twenty feet or so especially, but soon it vanishes. The rock was cold, it seemed to bite his hands. Pausing for a moment he could hear behind him the faint sound of trucks in the distant valley.

He reached the place where Cabot was belaying. They exchanged a few words. Rand went ahead. He climbed confidently, the distance beneath him deepened. The body is like a machine that is slow to start but once running smoothly seems it can go forever. He searched for holds, jamming himself in the crack, touching, rejecting, working himself higher.

By noon they were far up – they had reached a snow-covered ledge that formed the top of the apron. From here the main wall began. Rays of sun, far above, were pouring past the invisible summit. Sitting on a narrow outcrop they had something to eat.

'Not too bad, so far. Can I have some water?' Cabot said.

Somehow in taking it there was a slip – the plastic bottle dropped from his hand. He tried to catch it, but it was gone, glancing off the rock below once, twice, three times and dwindling into the white of the glacier, which after a long pause it hit.

'Shit,' he said calmly.

Rand did not comment. There was another bottle but now only half the supply remained. The mountain magnifies. The smallest event is irreversible, the slightest word.

A sequence of vertical cracks began. Rand was moving upward. At the top of the first one it was necessary to go to another off to the left. Between, it was nearly blank. The holds sloped downward. He tried, retreated, tried again. He had to reach a nub eight inches farther out. The smoothness threatened him, the lure of a last half foot. His face was wet. His leg began to tremble. Ready, he told himself. He leaned out. Reached. His fingers touched it. He moved across. From beneath, it seemed effortless, as if he were skimming the rock and barely needed holds. Cabot merely saw him put in a piton and go on. Just then the sun passed from behind the face and blinded him. He shielded his eyes. He could not be sure but he thought he saw the *bloc coincé* far above.

From Montenvers that afternoon they were visible by telescope. Large sections of the mountain were pale in the sun. Some distance beneath the great, overhanging block, two specks could be made out, motionless. A white helmet glinted.

The afternoon had passed, they were still in sunshine. The warmth was pleasant. There is always endless waiting, looking up, neck stiff, while the leader finds the way. The silence of the face surrounded them, the greatness of the scale.

Suddenly, from nowhere, a frightening sound. The whine of a projectile; Rand hugged the wall. Something unseen came down, thudded, careened and was gone. He looked up. Above him, an awesome sight. The brush of a great wing seemed to have passed over Cabot. As if in obedience, slowly, he was bowing. His legs went slack, his arms slipped away. Without a sound he performed a sacred act – he began to fall.

'Jack!'

The rope went taut. Cabot was hanging above him and off to one side.

'Jack! Are you all right?'

Cabot's head had fallen forward, his legs dangled. There was no reply.

One man cannot lift another with the rope, he can only hold him. Rand had a good stance but consequences were already seeping into his mind. He let some rope pass through his hands. Cabot's foot was moving slightly. It touched a hold, perhaps to use it for support, but slipped off. His head hit the wall.

'Jack! Are you okay?'

Silence.

'Jack, below you,' he called.

There was a better place farther down. Talking to him as he did so, Rand let out more rope. As a piece of clothing can catch on a sliver, something seemed to snag Cabot and he stayed, unseeing, clinging to the rock.

Rand finally worked his way up to him. At that moment Cabot's head turned slightly. His chin, the whole side of his face, was bathed in blood. His eyes were closed like someone fighting drunkenness. Blood drenched his shirt. Rand felt suddenly sick.

'How bad is it? Let me see.'

He half expected the wet gleam of brains as he removed the helmet. The blood rushed forth. It was dripping from the jaw.

'Do you have a bandage?'

'No,' Cabot barely muttered.

He made one with a handkerchief that darkened as he tied it. He wiped the jaw to see if the flow was stopping. His heart pounded. He tried to see if blood was coming from the ear, which meant serious concussion or a fractured skull.

One thing seemed certain even at that moment: Cabot was going to die.

'Does it hurt?'

A slow nod. The blood would not stop. Rand wiped his fingers on the rock and tried to collect fleeing thoughts. He hammered in a piton and clipped them both to it. Cabot's head had fallen forward as if he were asleep. A thousand feet lay below them. There were two or three hours of daylight left. In any case they could not stay here.

Some distance above was an overhang that might conceal a ledge. That was the best hope. Perhaps he could reach it.

'I'm going up to see if there's a ledge,' he announced.

Cabot was ominously silent.

'If there is, I'll get you up. Will you be all right? I'll bring you up afterwards.'

Cabot raised his head slightly, as if in farewell. His eyes were dim, he managed to part his lips in a faint, terrifying smile, the smile of a corpse. His teeth were outlined in blood.

'Hang on,' Rand said.

A sickening fear spilled through him as he started, nor did it lessen. He was alone, climbing unprotected. He was worse than alone. He made his way upward, chilled by the malevolence of the wall, imagining it might shed him completely by merely cutting loose the entire slab he held to.

The last train had long since gone down from Montenvers. The only eyes at the telescope were those of curious guests of the hotel out for a stroll before dinner. What they saw were details of a magnificent landscape, roseate and still. The light was pure, the sky clear. They, as well as all of creation, were unaware of the chill shadow beneath the overhang and the single figure, heart-empty, hidden in it.

He worked slowly outward, hammering pitons into a narrowing crack and standing in his *étriers* – slings which bore his entire weight. The crack stopped. He searched desperately; there was no place for a piton. Leaning out, he reached around the lip and felt for holds. His hand found one. He might be able to pull himself up, brace one foot against the last piton, and somewhere farther on find another. His fingers felt and refelt the unseen rock. He still had the strength for one big effort. He took a breath and swung out, bent backward, his free hand searching. Nothing. He managed to get a little higher. Nothing. A rush of panic. He was feeling about frantically. At the very top of his reach he found a hold. In tribute to his struggle the rock had relented. He pulled himself up and lay panting. The ledge was a foot wide, uneven, but it was a ledge. He set about bringing up Cabot.

CHAPTER FOURTEEN

THE SUN HAD gone down behind Mont Blanc. It was colder. The sky was still light, the small Bleuet stove making tea.

Cabot sat slumped and motionless. The blood had dried on his head and face but his eyes, staring down, were vacant.

The cup was passed between battered hands.

'How's your head? It seems to have stopped bleeding.'

Cabot bared his black-edged teeth. He nodded slightly.

'I think we're all right for now,' Rand told him.

Cabot was silent. After a moment, he murmured, 'How's the weather?'

The sky was clear. The first pale star had made an appearance.

'We don't want to fool with the weather,' he mumbled. This seemed to exhaust him. He sank into meditation. Rand took the cup from his hand.

In the distance the lights of Chamonix were visible. As it grew darker they became more numerous, distinct. They meant warm meals, conversation, comfortable rooms, all of it unattainable as the stars. It was colder now, it had come quickly, covering the peaks. The long vigil of night began.

Cabot was covered, hands in his pockets, bootlaces loosened. The wall was in shadow, the brown of ancient monuments. A feeling of intense isolation, a kind of claustrophobia came over Rand. It was as if he could not breathe, as if space were crushing him. He fought against it. He thought of where he was and of what might happen. The three cold stars in the belt of Orion shone above. His mind wandered. He thought of condemned men waiting out their last hours, days in California, his youth. His feet were cold, he tried to move his toes. Hours passed, periods of oblivion, of staring at the stars. There were more than he had ever seen. The coldness of the night increased them. They quivered in the thin air. On the dark horizon was the glow of Geneva, constant through the night. A meteor came down like a clot of white fire. An airplane passed to the north. He felt resentment, despair. His eye went down the wall, a thousand feet. He was falling, falling. Cabot never moved; from time to time he moaned.

At first with only the slightest changing of the sky's tone, dawn came. The blue became paler. The stars began to fade. Rand was stiff, exhausted. The huge dome of Mont Blanc soared into light.

'Jack. Wake up.' He had to shake him. Cabot's eyes flickered. They were the eyes of a man who could do nothing, who was dissolute, spent. 'It's daylight.'

'What time is it?'

'Five-thirty. Beautiful morning in France.' His fingers numb, he somehow lit the stove and got out food. Without seeming to, he tried to examine the inert figure.

'I feel better,' Cabot unexpectedly said.

Rand looked at him,

'Do you think you can make it down?'

'What?' There was a pause. 'No.' He was like a powerful beast that has fought and is bloody and torn, seems killed but somehow comes to its feet. 'Not down,' he said. 'I'm all right. I can make it.'

'I don't think so.'

'I can make it,' Cabot insisted.

'The hardest part's ahead.'

'I know.'

Rand said no more. As he was putting things away and sorting out gear, he tried to think. Cabot was strong, no doubt of it. He seemed in control of himself for the moment. They had come a long way.

'You're sure?' he finally said.

'Yes. Let's go on.'

At first he could not tell, the start was slow. They were stiff from long hours and the cold. Rand was leading. Soon he saw that Cabot could barely climb. He would stay in one spot as if asleep.

'Are you all right?'

'I'm just taking a little rest.'

They proceeded with frightening slowness, as one does with a novice. From time to time Cabot would make a gesture: it's all right, I'll just be a minute, but it was nearly always five or ten. Rand had to pull him up with the rope.

They had passed the *bloc coincé* and begun an inside corner where two great slabs of rock met like an opened book. It seemed they were not really here, they were part of some sort of game. They were going through the motions of climbing, that was all. But they could not go down. The time to have done that was earlier, not after they had struggled up an additional five hundred feet. They were near the place where the first party to climb the face had retreated, going around to the north side and descending. Exactly where that was, Rand did not know. He looked for the bolts that had been placed years before but never found them.

They came to a wide slab, chillingly exposed. The holds were slight, hardly more than scribed lines. There was no place to put in a piton. As he went out on it, Rand could feel a premonition, a kind of despair becoming greater, flooding him. It is belief as much as anything that allows one to cling to a wall. He was thirty minutes crossing as many feet, certain as he did that it was in vain.

'It's not as bad as it looks,' he called.

Cabot started. He moved very slowly, he was moving by inches. A third of the way across, he said simply,

'I can't make it.'

'Yes, you can,' Rand said.

'Maybe there's another way.'

'You can do it.'

Cabot paused, then tried again. Almost immediately, his foot slipped. He managed to hold on.

'I can't,' he said. He was done for. 'You'll have to leave me here.'

Silence.

'No, come on,' Rand told him.

'I'm going back. You go on. Come back for me.'

'I can't,' Rand said. 'Look, come on,' he said casually. He was afraid of panic in his voice. He did not look down, he did not want to see anything. There is a crux pitch, not always the most technically difficult, where the mountain concedes nothing, not the tiniest movement, not the barest hope. There is only a line, finer than a hair, that must somehow be crossed.

The emptiness of space was draining his strength from him, preparing him for the end. He was nothing in the immensity of it, without emotion, without fear and yet possessing an anguish, an overwhelming hatred for Cabot who hung there, unwilling to move. Don't give up here, he was thinking. He was willing it, don't give up!

When he looked, Cabot had taken another step.

That evening they were on a ledge far up the face. The overhangs barring the top were above. They had not noticed, until late, the arrival of clouds.

The first gusts blew almost gently but with a chill, a warning of what was to come. In the distance, the crackling of thunder. Rand waited. He tried to disregard it, hoping it would fade. It came again. It was like an air raid heading closer but still it might pass them by. The clouds were more dense. The Charmoz was disappearing, going dark. Lightning, brilliant in the dusk, was hitting the Brévent. The face of the Dru was still clear, softened by the late hour. The thunder crackled on.

Rand felt helpless. He saw the storm approaching, coming up the valley like a blue wave with scud running before it. He sat watching it fearfully as if it might notice him, veer his way.

Then he heard it, a strange, airy sound all around them. He recognized it immediately, like the humming of bees.

'What's that?' Cabot said.

'I'm not sure.'

They were in clouds. In a matter of seconds the Dru had gone. They could see nothing. The sound seemed to come from directly overhead and then from closer, almost inside their ears.

'It's getting louder.'

Rand did not reply. He was waiting, barely breathing. The mist, the coldness, were like a blindfold. He listened to the eerie, growing hum.

Suddenly the dusk went white with a deafening explosion. Blue-white snakes of voltage came writhing down the cracks.

Lightning struck again. This time his arms and legs shot out from a jolt that reached the ledge. There was a smell of burning rock, brimstone. Hail began to fall. He was clinging to his courage though it meant nothing. He could taste death in his mouth.

Cabot was huddled at his side; he had ended the day moving even more slowly than before. Corpselike in darkness he sat, the earsplitting claps of thunder like the end of the earth itself not even stirring him, a dead weight that was dragging Rand down. There was another flash of lightning. The pathetic figure was clearly visible. Rand stared at it. What he saw he never forgot. It reached across ghosted days to haunt him forever. Half-hidden beneath the bandage, open and gazing directly at him was an eye, a calm, constant, almost a woman's eye that was filled with patience, that understood his despair. Is he alive, Rand wondered? The eye shifted, gazing slightly downward.

An immense explosion. He trembled. There were nine hours until dawn.

CHAPTER FIFTEEN

THE STORM STOPPED at midnight. Afterward it froze. Their clothes were wet; the hail had turned into snow. From time to time there came breaks in the cloud when it was possible to see a little, even in darkness, and then the thick wave returned, in absolute silence, sweeping in as if to bury, to obliterate them. Rand was shivering. It was an act of weakness he told himself, but he could not stop.

Finally the sky grew light. There were storms still hanging in the air. Their gear was frozen, the ropes stiff as wire.

They managed to make some tea. In the distance, like hostile armies, an endless line of black clouds was moving. If the weather held, they might try to reach the top. Rand sipped the tepid, metallic-tasting liquid. He had no resolution, no plan.

For an hour they moved dazedly among the heaps of gear. To straighten it out required the greatest effort. The temptation to sit down and rest was overwhelming. There was snow on every bit of rock, in every crack. The sun was hitting the ridges to the west. Rand was still shivering. It seemed to him to have gotten even colder.

The rock, when he touched it, was like the sides of a deep, sunken wreck. He blew on his fingertips to warm them. His arms and legs felt weary. He heard the sound of birds darting near. For a moment, in fantasy, he dreamed of soaring, arms outspread, skimming, as they did, the face.

Cabot seemed stronger, he moved more easily. Above them the mountain had massed its final obstacles. Everything was leaning outward: walls, fragments, dark broken roofs.

'We've got to get above this while the weather is good.'

'Tell me,' Rand muttered. He felt a strange reversing of things. Instead of being encouraged, he felt drained, as in the final laps when, having given all, one is passed. A single thing sustained him: the summit was near.

'We're going to make it,' Cabot said later. He was like a captain coming back to the bridge, a bloody figure borne forward to make himself seen.

A final overhang, the last rope-lengths, and they were there. It was nearly noon. Green valleys, glaciers shone below. They were above all but the highest peaks. They stood in silence, too deeply moved to speak. The bivouac spot at the base seemed weeks, even years behind. They still had to descend into a notch and climb some more to go down, but that was not important. The West Face was below them.

Cabot surged ahead. He led the way. He was moving quickly, almost with too much haste, espcially on rappels – descent by means of the rope. Descending is always dangerous, the worst seems over.

'What's the rush?' Rand reached out to hold him back.

'Let go.'

'You're kicking stuff down.'

'Stop worrying,' was all he said.

That night they stumbled into the Charpoua hut and slept for eighteen hours. When they reached Montenvers a large man came out of the hotel. He was a reporter from a Geneva paper.

'What happened?' he asked. Cabot looked like the victim of a fight. 'Were you hit by rockfall? When? How high up were you?'

He spoke calmly, intimately. He wrote down nothing. He knew the mountains well, having climbed himself. There was an ease about him, that of an aristocrat who has been out in the garden and is wearing old clothes. He knew the entire history of the Dru and how it had been climbed. His eye was sharp, his nose even more so.

Ils livraient leurs vies à la montagne – they bared their lives to the mountain, he would write, *les étalant à son pied.* They laid them at its feet.

The climb was one thing, its confirmation by such a man was another.

That night at dinner in Chamonix, Cabot sat in a sport shirt open at the neck. The bandage was white on his darkened face. He had asked for a table in the back. He had a slight headache, he admitted, but he was elated.

'The best climbing writer in Europe,' he said. 'I never thought he'd be up there.'

'How did that happen?' Rand asked.

Cabot shrugged, 'They hear about these things.' He was pouring out wine. 'He knows the Dru. If he writes about you, that's all you can ask.' He was interrupted by the handshake of a noted guide who had made many first ascents. Rand's hand was grasped as well. 'Thank you. *Merci.*'

'Who was that?' Carol asked.

Glory fell on them lightly like the cool of the evening itself.

Glancing at her husband, Carol commented, 'I did expect you to take better care of him.'

'I never thought we'd make it,' Rand confessed.

'You must have.'

'It was foolish.'

'No, it wasn't,' Cabot said. His face was discoloured and blue on one side, handsome on the other, like halves of a personality. 'It would have been foolish if we died.'

'Yeah, I know. It was superb,' Rand murmured.

'Wait and see.'

'He was lucky it hit him in the head,' Carol remarked. 'It could have hurt him otherwise.'

They had a big dinner, over which they lingered. Cabot was telling all he remembered: nothing from the time he was hit until he said, go on, come back for me, and Rand had told him simply, I can't. Then came the storm. Carol was listening vaguely – there is a drunkenness that seems like wisdom.

'What're you talking about?' she said.

'I'm telling about the storm.'

'The same one?'

'Don't interrupt,' he said.

Disconsolately she leaned her head on Rand. He could smell her hair, feel her warmth; it was calm, unending, like fields which stretched out of sight. She'd been waiting for her husband for four nights and days.

'The storm,' she muttered. 'Isn't it over yet?'

'Oh, what's the use?' he said.

'How's your head? Looks awful.'

He seemed not to hear.

'Did you see Noyer come over and shake our hands?'

'Is that who it was?'

'Was, is, and will be.' Noyer was famous, like Lachenal and Terray.

'Let's go home,' she said. 'I'm sleepy.'

'Let's go,' Rand agreed. His happiness had passed its limit. He was tired. He wanted to lie beneath the stars, look up at them, no nearer or farther away than they had been two nights before. As he stood, the chair fell over. The waiter who was a climber himself hurried to pick it up.

'Good night,' he said to them in English.

Rand turned at the door. He was tall, eccentric, haggard. At that moment, though he did not realize it, he was launched on a performance which would become irreversible as time went by. On his face were weariness and the haze of ordeal. He raised an arm.

'Yeah, good night,' he said. 'Keep the change.'

CHAPTER SIXTEEN

HE WAS FAMOUS, or nearly. There was a tent, people knew, somewhere back in the trees, where like a fugitive he had a few possessions, those he needed: rope strewn in dense coils at his feet, heaps of pitons, boots. Almost less than ever was known about him now. There were stories that missed him completely, like confused shots fired in the dark.

He became even more elusive, at least for a time. It only fed the rumours. Every tall, dirt-glazed American was thought to be him. He was seen and talked to in places where he'd never so much as set foot.

A passion for climbing had come over him. As soon as he finished one, he was ready to start another. He climbed the Blaitière with Cabot and then went back with Bray to the Dru and did the regular route. He was either insatiate or absolutely exhausted but then would rise fresh the next day. He was swept up in it entirely as if for the very first time. When he climbed, life welled up, overflowed in him. His ambitions had been ordinary, but after the Dru it was different. A great, an indestructible happiness filled him. He had found his life.

The back streets of town were his, the upper meadows, the airy peaks. It was the year when everything beckons, when one is finally loved. The newspaper clippings were folded and put away. He pretended to scorn them. He kept them despite himself. The true form of legend, he believed, was spoken. He did not want to be catalogued, he said, read and discarded like sports scores and crimes.

'Everyone's written about their climbs,' Cabot argued, 'Whymper, Hillary, Terray. How else would you know about them?'

'What about the ones we don't know?'

'For instance?'

'Have you ever heard the way they climbed the Walker? Three of them came over from Italy, they didn't even know where it was. They asked the guardian at one of the huts, where are the Grandes Jorasses? Up there, he said. That's how they found it. I don't know if it's true; it's what they say.'

'It's only in about ten books. It was Riccardo Cassin,' Cabot said.

'I can't explain it. It wouldn't mean as much if I'd read it.'

'How do you know?'

It was morning, the light still new. Unknown sentinels stood distant, pale. He could have them, he had only to go forth. He was like the sun, touching remote peaks, they awoke to his presence. The thought of it made him reckless. He felt an immense strength. He saw an immortal image of himself high among the ridges – he was willing to die to achieve it.

'I don't want anybody to know how we climbed the Dru, only that we did it. Let them imagine the rest.'

'That's nice, but there are a thousand climbers out there,' Cabot gestured, vaguely.

'So?'

'Only the names of a handful are going to last.'

'That's too much like everything else,' Rand said. The strength of what he was feeling kept him from speaking. What he had done, what he would do, he did not want explained. Something was lost that way. The things that were of greatest value, that he had paid so much for were his alone.

He felt solitary, deep, like a fish in a river, mouth closed, uncaught, glistening against the flow. He saw himself at forty, working for wages, walking home in the dusk. The windows of restaurants, the headlights of cars, shops just being closed, all of it part of a world he had never surrendered to, that he would defy to the end.

Late in the season Remy Giro took him to the home of a man named Vigan. It was in an old, established section overlooking the town. Henri Vigan was past forty, familiar in mountaineering circles although only a passable climber himself. He had inherited some factories from his father; they were near Grenoble. He greeted Rand warmly.

'I'm so pleased to meet you,' he said. He was open in manner, generous, a man one likes on sight. 'You're a native of Chamonix, I think, more than I am. *Vous parlez français?*'

'He doesn't speak. He's a wolf,' Remy said. 'He lives a secret life, he travels alone.'

'All the better,' Vigan remarked.

'An Alpha wolf. The leader.'

'That's what I imagined. What can I get you to drink?' Vigan asked.

The edge of Rand's beard had turned gold with the summer. His lips shone in its halo. He accepted a glass of wine.

'Let me introduce you to some of my friends,' Vigan said.

Confident faces, unrecallable names. The guests were scattered in groups throughout the house. Some seemed to know him, at least who he was, others not to care. They were talking, laughing, at ease. All this had existed when he was sweeping floors up behind the Hôtel Roma, when he fell into bed at Christmas drunk from a bottle of wine. He wanted to avenge himself. He could not be had so cheaply. He was not theirs for a handshake and a compliment. Then he heard,

'Catherin, I think you know . . .'

'Yes,' she said, 'thank you.' She shook hands. She apologized for it with a helpless gesture. 'So frog,' she explained.

Languid, graceful, she was the salesgirl from Remy's shop. He was unnerved without knowing why.

'I didn't know you spoke English,' was all he could say.

'Yes. A little. Some.' Her teeth were narrow and white. Her shyness, which he had not noticed before, which had not existed, was extreme. 'That was quite an adventure you had on the Dru. Your friend was very lucky.'

'Oh, you heard about that?'

She didn't reply. It was as if she disapproved of the inanity of his answer. 'Is he still here?' she finally said. 'I haven't seen him.'

'He went to Zermatt. He's doing the Matterhorn.'

'And you?'

'Me?'

'You didn't go?'

'I decided to stay here.'

They were interrupted by Vigan who returned with someone he wanted to introduce. There was some conversation, mostly about the excellence of the season and certain routes climbed so often that excrement was a problem on them, a new objective danger, they lightly agreed.

Catherin, he saw, had wandered into the garden. It was the hour of evening when, viewed from Les Tines, the Dru is bathed in a vast, almost rose-coloured light. The swallows were circling. The last, melancholy sounds of a tennis match drifted up through the pines from the Mont Blanc Hotel. The unhurried way she had left, the possibility of its meaning, that there was someone with her, someone she had to return to, filled Rand with bewilderment, almost sorrow.

In the garden he was relieved to find her alone. She was gazing out over the town, the lights of which were just beginning to appear.

'Tell me something,' he said. 'Why did you pretend you didn't speak English?'

'I didn't pretend,' she said. She was reserved, polite. She was interested in certain things and those things only. 'Why did you decide to stay here instead of going with your friend?'

'I had no plans.'

'That's it, you see. Neither did I.' She had a slow smile, one reluctantly given. He had no idea what she thought of him or what she was thinking at all.

CHAPTER SEVENTEEN

SHE LIVED NEAR the cable car station in a house with stone gateposts and an iron fence. It had been a large villa but there had been a decline in its status, like the palaces taken over by troops in a revolution. It contained a number of ill-defined apartments. The walls were bare, the plaster faded.

They drove back from an evening in Argentière; it was their first. He knew much more about her. Her father was English. She liked to joke. At the same time she kept a certain distance – it was like a dance. He might touch her, she would not protest, but she would do no more than patiently submit.

'You're very strange,' he told her.

'No, I'm not strange,' she said. 'I'm quite ordinary.'

'I don't believe it.'

'Too ordinary.'

'Then what am I?'

'I don't know.'

'You must have an opinion.'

'Not yet,' she said simply.

'Have you always lived in Chamonix?'

'Oh, no. I just came here for fun. I liked it, I liked the people.' She had stopped the car. 'This is where I live,' she commented.

He turned his head. There was a ghostly building set back from the street.

'It's a big house.'

'There are three families in it.'

'It must be big. Can I come in?'

'Oh . . . I don't think so.'

'Why not?'

'Really, it's not that interesting.'

'The house?'

'Me,' she said.

'Just for a few minutes.'

They walked to the door. It was heavy, the top was glass with iron bars. She fumbled with some keys.

'Let me go in first.'

The door closed behind them. She went up the stairs. In the room she turned on a light.

'There. You see. That's all there is.'

He attempted to embrace her but she turned away.

'What is it?' he asked.

'Do you really want to?'

'No, I'm just kidding.'

'I'm very flat up here,' she said simply. 'Practically a man.'

'I don't care.'

After a moment or two she began to remove her shirt. There was resignation in her movements. She turned off the light and stepped from the last of her clothes. On the main highway beyond the window traffic flowed past. They lay in her narrow bed.

He seemed urgent, overpowering to her. She had no desires of her own. She had abandoned them, she accepted his. His intensity almost frightened her, his abruptness. As soon as it was over he fell asleep.

In the morning a sun like searchlights was pouring into the room. She returned from somewhere with a small white cup in each hand. Naked down to the sheet that crossed his waist, he was sitting up in bed. His torso seemed to haunt her. It was almost as smooth as hers.

Familiar sounds of morning, cups and indolent spoons. He was less interested in her this morning, she saw. Her heart was beating sadly. Around his neck was a pale green string of narrow beads; she saw them in the mirror as she dressed.

'You can stay if you like,' she said.

He watched her silently.

'I have to go to work,' she said. She gave a fleeting smile as if required.

He lay in bed. A womanly smell still clung to it. He could hear footsteps elsewhere in the house, they seemed aimless. Opening and closing of doors. The empty cups were on the floor. As if it had suddenly started, he noticed the ticking of her clock. He felt luxurious. He took himself for granted, his legs, his sexual power, his fate. A consciousness that had faded came to life. It was like a film when the focus is blurred and shifting and all at once resolves; there leaps forth a hidden image, incorruptible, bright.

When he went by the shop he said a few whispered words to her. Her expression softened, she did not reply. The thing that betrayed her was an unexpected childish gesture. After he had gone, elated by his visit, she took hold of the end of the counter, leaned back and pulled herself dreamily forward, leaned back and did it again.

'*Vous êtes bien?*' Remy inquired.

'*Très bien.*'

CHAPTER EIGHTEEN

THE CURTAIN had fallen. September was a month of good weather and beautiful light, but the town was nearly empty, everyone had gone.

'I wouldn't mind staying around,' Bray lamented, 'but Audrey's coming to Geneva. I said I'd meet her.' She was his girl friend. 'This is the only time she could get away. Besides, my money's gone. I'm not like you, I can't live off women.'

He'd been driving Catherin's little car around town.

'So, I'm afraid that's it,' Bray said. He could have been a small-time crook with nerve and a taste for cheap display. He liked to smoke big cigars after dinner, drink Martell. The mountains had saved him.

He hadn't the imagination which is indispensable to greatness. Supreme climbs need more than courage, they need inspiration. He was a sergeant in the ranks – perhaps, in tumultuous times, he might be a colonel, one who wears his blouse unbuttoned and gets drunk with the men.

Audrey was a nurse. She had the characteristics of her class, she was scornful, outspoken. She hated foul language and foreign cooking and was indifferent to sports. Her youth, in part, softened these things. In many English women there is, despite reputation, a strong sensuality, even if denied. Her face was unfriendly, but it was the extraordinary skin which made her body luminous that Bray dreamed of. His letters were filled with an erotic imagery one would never expect.

'Why don't you come to England? Tear yourself away. There's work. You could work with me.'

'Doing what?' Rand said.

'Plastering. It has a tradition. O'Casey was a plasterer.'

'Who?'

'O'Casey. He wrote plays. You've heard of him. It doesn't matter. We'll throw in a little culture, too.'

'Maybe I'll come.'

'We'll be back here in December, anyway,' Bray said.

'What for?'

'The Eiger. Cabot asked me to come.' He was obviously pleased. 'He didn't tell you?'

'No.' After a pause, he added, 'What about the Eiger?'

Suddenly Bray was embarrassed. He realized something was wrong.

'Ah, well, I thought . . . I thought you knew. He's going to do a winter ascent.'

'Oh, yeah?' Rand managed to say.

'I thought you knew all about it.'

Rand felt as if he had been slapped in the face.

'No,' he said.

'Sorry.'

'That's all right,' Rand said.

He hardly heard the words, they were slipping by. It was going to be like Scott . . . his push to the pole . . . bivouacs prepared in advance, bunkers, with two or three weeks of food so that they could ride out any storm. The BBC would be filming.

'I see.' He suddenly hated Bray. The feeling that something had been stolen from him was crushing his heart.

'I suppose everybody wants to climb it,' Bray said lamely.

'They don't want to climb it, they want to *have* climbed it.' He was searching his pockets for money. 'Here,' he said, putting some on the table, 'pay for mine.'

He walked out into the empty afternoon. The sun threw light against the buildings. He felt utterly abandoned, ill.

'What's wrong?' Catherin cried.

Desperation glittered from him. He slumped on the bed.

'Don't you feel well?' she said.

'I'm all right.' He lay back.

'What is it?' she said.

'It's nothing. Cabot is going to do a climb, that's all.'

'He can climb. Is that bad?'

'He's going to do the Eiger.'

Please, what is it? You look as if you were going to die.'

That night he lay awake while over and over in his mind turned the same bitter thoughts. The room seemed small. He longed to be up in the woods, alone. The sky would calm him, the icy galaxies. He felt he'd been caught away from home. He wanted to go to ground.

He remembered the girl from Kauai who had cut his hand. She believed in the occult. She was humourless, intense. Write down the names, she had said, of your three closest friends and I will circle the name of your deadliest enemy.

CHAPTER NINETEEN

THE AUTUMN DAYS have a fever. The sun is departing, it gives forth all that remains. The warmth is mysterious, it carries a message: farewell.

Catherin saved him. In her small car they drove off on weekends, Aix-les-Bains, Chambéry. In the countryside they pulled off the road and descended, feet slipping, a steep embankment. The hillside was facing the sun, not a house, not a person to be seen. The fallen leaves had drifted deep, they came to the knee. They ate from a basket she had prepared and lay sprawled afterwards, bees feeding on the remnants of the meal.

An hour went by, an hour and a half. Slowly Rand sat up. Catherin's eyes swam open for a moment.

'Oh, God,' she breathed.

'What is it?'

'I'm still asleep.'

'Wake up.'

'It's so hard,' she said weakly. 'When I die, I hope I don't have to wake afterwards. It would be so difficult.'

He knelt beside her. She leaned against him. There was a faint plop – two moths, grey as wood with one spot of dazzling blue, had fallen, attached to one another. They did not move.

'You see?' she said.

There was a stream below. They walked down through blue and violet flowers, scattered, abandoned by summer. Then through a dry orchard. At the far end a goat, all white, was staggering about on its hind legs to eat from the branches. It would be cold that winter. The mice had left the pastures. The leaves were already down.

They looked back. Half-hidden in the earth were long, stone walls built to retain the hillside. The sun was facing. The white of the car glinted far above.

The last rites of autumn. They walked up slowly. She was out of breath; she had to stop. He carried her the rest of the way, not in his arms but over his shoulder, cheek against her haunch. She didn't struggle. She hung quietly, touching him as if he were a horse.

In Annecy they walked by the lake. An empty dock stretched out into the water. The varnished boats creaked. He lived an entire life in Annecy, in a hotel with an iron balcony and the letters H-O-T-E-L fixed to it. The television cost a franc. A bottle of Perrier was outside the window. They went to bed at midnight. Her bracelets crashed on the table glass.

'Too much to drink,' she managed to announce. The windows were open. An occasional car, driving too fast, zoomed along the street.

Dawn turned the mountains dark. The sky was pale, the hour unknown. He went out on the balcony. Annecy was blue. The buildings had a phantom form, they were rising as if from the sea. A single eye looked up at him from among the bedclothes, an eye still stained with makeup. A drugged voice said, 'What are you doing up in the middle of the night?'

A lifetime and more. He began to actually see France, not just a mountain village filled with tourists, but the deep, invisible centre which, if entered at all, becomes part of the blood. Of course, he did not know the meaning of the many avenues Carnot or boulevards Jean Jaurès, the streets named Gambetta, Hugo, even Pasteur. The pageant of kings and republics was nothing to him, but the way in which a great civilization preserves itself, this was what he unknowingly saw. For France is conscious of its brilliance. To grasp it means to sit at its table, sleep beneath its roofs, marry its children.

Immortal mornings. His genitals were heavy, like the dark, smooth stone carved by the Eskimos. They had a gravity, a denseness he could not believe. He drew aside the sheet. She was naked. Her hair was strewn across the pillow. She was like a drowned woman, she was sunk in bed like a burial at sea. He placed a hand on her, proprietary, calm. The first cars were driving past. Someone's footsteps echoed in the street.

This love was the act of one person, it was not shared. He was like a man in a boat on a wide lake, a perfectly still lake at dawn. There was no sound except that of oars in the oarlocks, creaking, creaking, a man alone in a boat that slowly begins to shudder, to cry. Afterwards they lay close, like comrades.

His hair was like hers. His arm lay near her side, the muscle, sleeping, the light barely tracing it.

'Are we going back to Chamonix?' she asked.

'Let's keep moving. Let's stay ahead of them.'

'I'd like to take you to Paris.' She was stroking the arm with her finger. 'I want to show you off.'

'Where would we stay?' He was filled with a sublime weariness, as if he had just fallen into bed after an unforgettable party. 'What about your job?'

'Oh, Remy won't care. It's very slow now, anyway.' She seemed to drop off to sleep. 'I have some money,' she said. 'We'll have a nice time.'

They rose at noon to look for a restaurant. They were famished.

The apartment was on a small street off the Avenue du Maine. They arrived in the evening, a blue evening the colour of storms, and drove along the river in streams of traffic, then through dense neighbourhoods. The early darkness was lit by storefronts. The buses were roaring by. There is an electric thrill to the city seen at this hour and for the first time. He was dazzled. The trees still held their enormous leaves. Outside restaurants there were stands selling oysters, the baskets tilted forward for customers to see. The streets were crowded. The city was singing to him, flowing like a great, unimagined dream.

There were only two rooms, strangely empty of furniture as if someone had just moved out. A kitchen, a long, narrow bath with red walls. The water limped into the tub, a gas heater roared to life when the hot was turned on. There were photographs and invitations stuck in the mirror. The refrigerator, there being no space elsewhere, was in the front room.

The woman who owned it, Madame Roberts, came around the next day.

She had a long mane of hair and shapely legs. She admitted to being forty-five. It was her daughter who lived here normally and who was away.

'In Rome,' she explained. 'She's decided to go to school. She took a lot of things. I hope you can be comfortable.' She had a very frank gaze. 'But you're used to sleeping in worse places, aren't you?' she said to Rand. 'Catherin has told me about you, your fantastic life. You're not an intellectual, are you?'

'An intellectual?' he said.

'Good, I'm sick of them.' She had strong, white teeth; she brushed them with salt. She owned a shop across the river: imported clothing, accessories, things like that – she'd started it herself.

'It's very nice. I have a certain clientele. Catherin knows. I treat them very well. I have good things.' Her presence was rich, full of life. She rummaged in her handbag for a cigarette. Her legs, in stockings that had a metallic sheen, were crossed above the knee. She'd been a mannequin, that was how she started.

'The first time I had absolutely no confidence. There was a woman in the dressing room who had experience. She saw how frightened I was. She took me aside. "Just remember," she said, "when you go out there – you are young and beautiful and they are shit". Everything I did, I did for myself,' she said. 'No one gave me anything. My husband gave me half the apartment when we were divorced. He put up a brick wall. He kept the living room and kitchen and I got the bedroom and bath.'

Her business she conducted like the famous courtesans. The men who came to her she classified as *payeurs, martyrs* or *favoris*. 'As long as they don't compare notes. Being a mannequin was a help; I developed a taste for luxury.' Her voice was powerful and flowing. She used it like a stream of water. Her laugh was hoarse, the laugh of a free woman. 'I developed a taste for it, but I didn't let it ruin me,' she said.

Paris was filled with such women, he saw them on the streets, in buses, everywhere. Students, married women, extravagant faces in bars and cafés. In the windows of *parfumeries* gleamed seductive advertisements for the care of breasts and skin. His eye lingered on them like a young husband looking at whores.

In a bar off Boulevard St Michel there was a girl with her eyes outlined in black and a bright silk scarf wrapped around and around her swanlike neck.

'Who is it, someone you know?' Catherin asked – it took him by surprise – she was leafing through a magazine. He began to read over her shoulder. It was November. Nights were cold, but days still fair. Paris was opening itself to him, he thought.

There were friends of Catherin's. '*Bonsoir*,' one said, extending her hand. Her name was Françoise. A dark-haired man was behind her; he shook hands disinterestedly.

'This is Michel,' she said as they sat down. 'Michel has lived in England. You're English?' she asked Rand.

'No,' he said.

'*Americain,*' Michel commented wearily. '*C'est vrai?*'

'That's right.'

Michel nodded. It was too simple. *'Vous êtes grimpeur?'* he said offhandedly. Françoise had told him.

'Speak English,' she said.

'Je ne parle pas anglais.'

'Yes, you do.'

'It's too difficult,' he said. He then told a story in French about a party he had gone to in London. A girl had come over and asked why he was off by himself. He told her he was French, he didn't speak English. Oh, she said, in two months he would speak it fluently. He'd been there two years, he told her. She didn't talk to him again.

'Oh, tu m'énerves,' Françoise said.

They sat in silence.

'What have you climbed?' he asked in French. 'I had a good friend who was a climber.'

'Who?' said Françoise.

Michel said, 'You don't know him. He was in the army. He liked the army, he was one of those, but he got in some trouble and had to leave. Afterwards, he began to climb seriously. First not far from Paris, then down at Marseilles, and in the Alps. He was very strong, very pure. In some ways he was like a child.'

Rand was watching him suspiciously. Michel was aware of it. He spoke more slowly, unaffectedly, as if to them all.

'He began to climb the most difficult peaks in Europe. Climbing is more than a sport. That's true. *Ça dure toujour* – it lasts forever.'

They were sitting in silence, listening. A sensation of panic had come over Rand. He could not believe these sentences were following one upon the other. Michel's eyes were looking directly into his.

Rand smiled. He wanted to break this spell, to show that he was not subject to it.

'Who's this friend?'

'I can only tell you,' Michel went on, 'that his dream was to become one of the greatest climbers of all time.'

'Is that right?' A confusion was seizing him. He had a sudden, strange sense of isolation, as if all the people surrounding him, sitting at nearby tables, talking, laughing, were part of what was being enacted, were even aware of it.

'I don't know anything about climbing,' Michel went on. He was confiding, he wanted to become a friend. 'I saw him not long ago. I hadn't seen him for almost a year. Something had happened to him. I don't know. He had left his wife, he wasn't working. Still he felt if he climbed one more mountain, the most difficult, everything would somehow fall into place. It was like a drug. He constantly had to have more and more, and the doses had to be bigger.'

Rand said nothing. He stared coldly.

'He was always an idealist. He had great inner strength, more than you've ever seen. But something had changed in him, I could see it in his face. He had done everything and he was still unhappy. Two weeks ago . . .'

Rand's heart was pounding. The panes of illusion were slipping from his life. He felt himself disappearing.

'I don't like this story,' Catherin interrupted.

'I don't like it, either. Furthermore, I don't believe it,' Françoise said.

'But it's true,' Michel said.

'I don't think so.'

'Then I don't tell it.'

'Go ahead, finish it,' Rand said.

Michel smiled.

'Go ahead.'

'Two weeks ago, on an easy climb, he fell to his death.'

'Why don't you talk about something you know?' Françoise complained.

'I said I knew nothing. That's what makes it fascinating. I'm interested in the psychology of it. It's a story of someone completely unlike me. I don't have courage. I don't have the slightest bit. Intelligence, that's all.'

'Too much intelligence and not enough of something else,' she said.

'Here is a man with courage.' He indicated Rand. 'He doesn't like me. Look.'

'Oh, you are boring!' Françoise said.

'Look, he wants to fight. He wants to take his fists and smash what he doesn't like. That's the American spirit.'

'Will you shut up?'

'Why don't you hit me?' he challenged.

Rand stared at him.

'What's wrong? Can't you speak?'

'I'm leaving. Come on,' Françoise said.

'But the story was true!' he called out as they left. 'You know that, don't you? You see? He knows.'

CHAPTER TWENTY

'MICHEL! MICHEL is a *pede* and a drunk. You should have thrown him into the street,' Colette Roberts said. She was having a hurried coffee before opening her shop. In the morning her face had a visible weariness like the city itself. The flat, winter light, the drabness.

'Michel is not even French,' she said. 'He's a Polish Jew. Your hair, you know, looks like the rumpled tail of a big rooster.'

He felt handsome in her presence, alive. She was like a mirror in which he saw himself perfectly. She knew how to manage things; she was not an amateur in life.

'Where is Catherin?' she asked.

'She had to go to the bank.'

'Come by and have a drink this evening. I have a friend coming from Nice.' Someone entering the bar greeted her. She turned to them, smiled. 'I'm late,' she suddenly realized. 'Come at six.' She dropped some coins on the counter. She was a woman who would never be down for long.

In the mornings he read, sitting near the window, a copy of the *Tribune* a day or two old. In the afternoon they would go out.

The tunnels of the Métro were filled with slogans. The talk in the cafés was always political, fierce. On the kiosks were posters of scandal, exposé. France was like a great, quarrelling family, the Algerians, the old women with their dogs, the people in restaurants, the police – a huge, bickering family bound eternally by hatred and blood.

There were afternoons of emerging soft-eyed from movies and walking past the grey vaults of the Montparnasse Cemetery, feet cold, to reach home. Afternoons when light snow was falling from nowhere and the city was blue as ice, the sound of traffic far off. Or in cafés, talking and watching the crowd. A woman in a green silk shirt sat alone at a nearby table. She was reading something taken from her handbag. A timetable. Suddenly her eyes opened wide. She was talking to herself, astonished. She rose, put on her coat, and ran out.

Secret afternoons, undisclosed. Silence sealing the windows. In the filtered light she seemed mythic, gleaming, as if for the first time the marvel of a body was revealed. She was wearing only her underpants. The blood was beating slowly in his neck. Samurai hours. The shutter of a camera clicked.

'Will they develop these?'

'Of course,' she said.

'I doubt it. They'll steal them.'

She was sitting cross-legged on the bed when he came out of the bath, lazily playing solitaire. The kings and queens had names, the jacks were Hector, Lahire. He lay beside her, watching.

'Is this what they mean by wasting your life?'

'You're joking,' she said.

Great as it was, the city could not sustain him. Faint in its streets, its chill, winter passages, came a lonely sound, small, incessant, something being chipped away bit by bit. The pale sky only made it louder. It was the sound of an ice axe, Cabot's. It would not stop.

At four in the morning he woke. The sky, the streets were absolutely silent. Somewhere, half in dream, the dark wedge of the Eiger loomed in an empty sky. It had snowed in the mountains. The roads were white, the valleys blanketed. A strong wind was blowing. Snow poured down the face in streams.

He had entered a room where Cabot lay dying. He could not believe it, he was numb, but when he saw the coffin and the face within it, the sealed eyes, the fine hair, suddenly he was felled by grief, knocked to his knees. He was weeping unashamedly.

Catherin was trying to wake him.

'What is it?' she said. He could not answer. 'What happened? You were crying out.'

He lay there with his arms around her. Neither of them could sleep.

CHAPTER TWENTY-ONE

THE EIGER is the great wall of Europe. It exists in a class by itself. Six thousand feet high, twice the height of the Dru, and more treacherous. It is black except for the snow which in winter clings everywhere, hiding the fields of ice. The climbing is difficult, the danger from storm and falling rock extreme.

The first attempts were all fatal though they forged the way. Men fell or froze to death, their bodies remaining on the face grotesquely, for long periods of time. In 1938 it was finally climbed.

There is an old hotel, the Kleine Scheidegg, not far from the base. The rooms are comfortable, the downstairs is filled with photographs of those who have made the climb. Above, so immense that it cannot be seen, the mountain soars.

They were all staying at the hotel – Cabot had gotten five climbers, he was trying to find a sixth. Early in the morning, before dawn, they would leave for the foot of the wall, trudging across frozen fields. At night they returned exhausted.

'You know anyone else we could get?' he asked Bray.

'I know someone in Paris.'

Cabot glanced at him. 'Is there anyone you know in England?'

Bray said, 'Not for this.'

It was like a war in a city besieged. All day they fought furiously. At night they slept in their beds.

Carol was there; she was the leading woman. Audrey, who came in January, was pale beside her. In the evening, if no one was back, they ate together, sometimes with the television crew. A chain-smoking man named Peter Barrington was the producer.

'Huh! Damned cold today,' he said, batting together his mittened hands. 'Glad I'm not up there. Where's our pilot this morning?'

He'd made films on architecture and English poets. Then he'd gone to Nepal, which made him the expert on mountaineering, he said with a captious air. He knew all the jargon, however. He used it freely. Cabot, he secretly called 'The Strangler.' Much of his time was spent in the bar at a table with an overflowing ashtray – he was waiting for certain equipment, for the weather to improve, for a call from London.

'Good morning, Peter,' they would say.

'Beautiful morning, isn't it? What do you suppose we should do today? Take a few more pictures of the mountain?'

'We could do that.'

'What are they up to today?'

It had been slow going. Cabot had broken his thumb in a twenty-foot fall. It hadn't stopped him; he kept at it, doing as much as anyone, even more. He was the only one who believed they would reach the top. The others were mere soldiers, automatons.

The face was completely frozen. That prevented any rockfall to speak of but the cold was intense. Avalanches of snow were frequent. Slowly, with unwavering determination, a route, completely new, was being pushed up. Fixed ropes were left in place so that going up and down could be managed quickly. The focus of effort was always the highest point.

By mid-January they were halfway up the wall. Two well-stocked bivouacs dug out of snow had been established, bunkers Cabot called them. They had to make a third. The fixed ropes would then be taken down and, starting from the bottom, one man would attempt the climb. That had not been the original idea – it had come to him as time went on. From the third bunker it would be one sustained push, carrying food and equipment with him. He would climb to the summit alone.

But the third bunker defied them. They were on a very steep part of the face. There was no snow, only solid ice that had to be chipped away inch by inch. Their hands were frozen, their feet. Three hundred feet above was a place where it looked slightly better.

There's going to be no third bloody bivouac, Bray was thinking. There's going to be nothing. He was exhausted, his fingers were burning with cold. He could feel nothing in his feet. He was afraid of losing his toes, having them freeze, but it did no good to think of it. He hated the clear, cold weather that had come two days before. He hated Cabot. Ten more, he muttered to himself as he chopped at the ice. Small slivers shot off like spray. Every other blow did nothing. All right, then, another ten, he vowed.

'How are you doing up there?'

Cabot was almost directly below. Bray could see the top of his head. He didn't answer.

'How's it going?' Cabot called.

'I can't do it,' Bray muttered.

'What?'

'My hands are freezing.'

After a while he came down.

'How far did you get?'

'Not very far. It's like cutting steel.'

'Let me try.'

Cabot went up using the jumars – devices with one-way ratchets in them. Pushed up alternately, they had long, nylon loops to stand in. He went up smoothly, spinning around slowly on the taut rope. Soon there was the distant, rhythmic sound of his axe. It was ten in the morning. They'd been at work since dawn.

'They're predicting good weather. They expect it to last through the week,' Barrington said. 'It's coming from the east.'

They had come back to the hotel. It was too cold to stay on the face and not that much time was lost in going up the ropes. It could be done in darkness.

'Incredible cold. I don't know how you do it,' Barrington said. 'Can you see a place for the last bunker?'

'Not yet,' Cabot said. 'We'll find one.'

Carol had gone to Munich to talk to some television people. The curtain had not risen for the final act but it would not be long. Something had been sacrificed in the way it was all arranged. The climb was not classic – it was, in a sense, corrupt. The conquest of heights by any means and for whatever purpose is questionable. Of course, this was never brought up. The involvement was too great and Cabot was too compelling a figure. He was the kind of man who did not conform to standards, he created them.

'It's just that if we could take advantage of the good weather . . .' Barrington said.

'We're trying.'

'Because, afterwards, it could be . . . difficult.'

'Look, would you like to go up there yourself?' Cabot said.

Barrington reddened. 'I'm afraid that wouldn't accomplish much.'

'No.' Cabot suddenly changed his tone – the soup was being served, he drew the plate toward him. 'Don't worry,' he said. 'We'll get it. It's just a little farther.'

Bray was two chairs away, hunched over, eating in silence.

'There's the man who's going to do it.'

It fell on the ears of a sullen acolyte with blistered lips, weary of it all.

'He'll do it. And gentlemen in England now a-bed will think themselves accurs'd they were not here, right?'

Bray continued eating as if he hadn't heard. Later Audrey came down. They'd been married in the fall. They hadn't taken a honeymoon, two days in Brighton, that was all.

'You've eaten,' she complained. 'I thought you were going to wait for me.' She sat down. 'What did you have?'

'I think it was a cutlet.'

'God, your face. Look at it.'

'What, this?' He touched his lip.

'Are you going up again tomorrow?'

'I suppose so. Ask him.'

She turned to Cabot.

'Are you?' She wasn't sure why she disliked him – his arrogance they all had some of that.

Cabot was tired, too. His face was scalded from the cold. His eyes were red. In the corridor, afterward, he stopped her.

'Don't discourage him,' he said. 'It's hard up there.'

There was music coming from the bar. Along the corridor over their heads passed the sound of someone running. Then laughter, again from the bar. White-aproned cooks were at work in the warmth of the kitchen. Guests sat in front of the television. In the office someone was totalling bills. On the face of the Eiger even the ropes were frozen. They dangled in the darkness like strips of wood.

'Is John really tired?' Cabot said.

'Well, you know he's a fool. He doesn't complain,' she said.

'I know.'

They sat for a while in the bar. Cabot's blond, scattered hair seemed dull in the subdued light. He was like a derelict seen in the shadows, indistinct, something helpless about him. Perhaps he was asleep.

The next morning they went again. They had decided to stay on the face until they reached the snowfield that seemed to lie above. Bray went first. They had left the hotel in darkness and all the way across the icy fields, a way they had travelled many times, not a word was said. Once Cabot slipped and fell. Bray hadn't turned.

All day he bore the brunt. They were making their way up an ice-filled crack. It was twenty minutes' work to move a foot. The crack slowly widened, he was braced against its sides. Bray felt he was there alone. A strong feeling came over him, a detachment, almost euphoria as if he were nothing more than a photograph. The silence beneath him vanished, fear fell away. He kept on working upward. He was clinging to nothing, balanced there somehow. He felt his foot begin to slip. He tried to hold on.

'Tension!' he cried.

The rope tightened off. It wasn't enough.

'I'm coming off!' Three thousand feet above the valley he began to fall. He saw it all clearly, he deplored it, he hardly cared.

The rope caught him abruptly. Somehow his leg was entangled in it. He was hanging upside down, ten feet from Cabot.

'Are you all right?'

'I've lost my glove,' he said.

Cabot lowered him.

'What happened?'

'Couldn't do it.' He was breathing hard, his bare hand thrust inside his jacket. 'I couldn't hold on.' It was far into the afternoon. The sun had passed its zenith. The sky seemed white. 'Next year I'm going back to plastering,' he said.

'You sure you're all right?'

Bray nodded. He looked down. Suddenly he felt frightened. His courage had gone. After a while, he asked. 'Are you going up to try?'

'You only have one glove.'

'Anyway, look at the weather,' Bray said. Clouds had appeared in the distance.

He was spent, that much is certain. Late in the day the two figures which had been motionless for hours began to descend. Perhaps the rope had been worn against the ice. Perhaps a rock had cut it. No one would ever know. To those who were watching, a speck of colour seemed to free itself and move very slowly, almost to float, down the face. And with it, the cry, 'Someone's fallen!'

Audrey often passed her time in a sitting room where the guests had tea. She would talk to people, write postcards and read. It was warm there and comfortable, sitting, drinking tea, receiving the curious glances of tourists and their identical questions. Where are they? they asked and she would point them out as well as she could.

'Oh my.'

'How far up are they?'

'A long way.'

'Doesn't it make you nervous?'

'I don't think about it,' she said.

She had heard nothing. She saw something that frightened her, people were suddenly rising all along the veranda. There was a crowd at the telescope.

'What is it? What's happened?' she asked. She'd been reading. The book lay face down beside her. As she stood up, she felt unsteady. She could not hear what they were saying, she could not hear anything. It was like a vacuum. In a moment the eyes of the crowd would turn toward her. She was certain of it. 'Please. What's happened?' she said.

CHAPTER TWENTY-TWO

THAT NIGHT IT began to snow. In the dusk it fell softly. People were talking at dinner. Waiters glided across the room. Some time after seven, Cabot, who had been out for hours at the foot of the wall, knocked on the partly open door.

'Come in.' It was Barrington's voice. Audrey was sitting in a chair, a cardigan around her shoulders.

'Hello, Jack,' Barrington said. 'Are they all back?'

Pieces of Bray's equipment were scattered around, boots behind the door, socks drying on the radiator. Cabot sat down. He found it hard to speak.

'We got back a little while ago,' he said.

'Is it snowing hard?'

'Pretty hard. One thing that's almost sure,' he said, not looking at Audrey, 'he was unconscious the whole time.'

'How do you know?'

'I was there. I saw it. I saw him hit his head, right at the start.'

'You saw that?'

'Yes, that's probably so,' Barrington confirmed. 'It's very jagged there.'

The word was disturbing. 'Jagged . . .'

'Lots of outcrops.'

'I hope you're right,' she said.

They were silent. The immense length of the fall and the helplessness of the climber, falling, filled the room. After a while Barrington rose and left. He would look in later, he said.

'I don't know what to tell you,' Cabot finally broke the silence – the shock had been great for him. 'The rope . . . it must have caught on something. I can't imagine. It's . . . it could have happened to anyone.'

'Don't be silly,' she said.

'It was just one of those impossible accidents.'

'No, it wasn't. It wasn't an accident. I knew you would kill him,' she said. 'I knew it the first time I laid eyes on you.'

'What do you mean?'

'Oh, yes.'

'It's not true.'

'Isn't it?' she said. 'Oh, yes. He was only a little man, I mean compared to you, but he was loyal, he had a good heart. You could make him do anything. All you had to say was you didn't think he could do it and he would go and try. Well, you know that. I've seen you make him. So the rope broke and now he's gone. Last night he was here. He stood right in front of that mirror. He was dead tired, but you'd never get him to stop because he was tired. Now, where is he? I don't even know where he is.' She had begun to cry. 'You'll go on,' she said. 'You'll get to the top. You won't even remember him.'

'That's not true.'

'Oh, yes it is,' she said bitterly.

'Listen, Audrey, it's hard to explain.' He paused for a moment. 'I didn't make him do anything, he did it for the same reason I did. Nothing can make you do it. You do it because of yourself.'

She stood by the window staring out at the snow. She was hugging herself, her arms clasped beneath her breasts.

'I'm afraid I don't understand,' she said wearily. The way she was holding herself, as if she could expect nothing more from life, the clothes and cosmetics on the dresser, the pale square of bed reflecting light, these seemed to be speaking for her. The room was warm. The silence was mounting, like a bill that would have to be paid.

'Come and have dinner. You don't want to be alone tonight,' he said. 'If you like, we'll eat in the bar. I'll ask them to serve us there.'

'I don't want to go to the bar.'

'It'll do you some good.'

'Leave me alone.'

He put his arm around her.

'Audrey . . .' He tried to say something else, but said nothing.

She nodded, she didn't know why. She'd begun to cry again, the tears running down her cheeks.

'What's going to happen to me?' she said.

'You'll go back to England.'

She looked at him.

'Is that all?' she said.

He made a vague gesture.

'Is that all?'

'I'll meet you in five minutes,' he said.

She did not answer.

'Are you coming downstairs?'

'Yes,' she finally said.

'In a few minutes?'

'Yes.'

He did not move. He saw there was no need to. Instead he put his hand on her breast; he had been looking at it for weeks.

'Don't,' she said. He felt her shudder but she did not move. 'Don't.'

He turned her towards him.

It was as if they had spoken, as if it had always been agreed. Carol was still in Münich. The snow fell through the night.

There was a small item at the bottom of the page, CLIMBER KILLED IN FALL. His eye was skipping the words. The blood left his face, he tried to read calmly:

Wengen, Jan. 24. Authorities identified today a 23-year old English climber who fell 3,000 feet to his death on the Eiger yesterday . . .

It was Sunday in Paris and cold. Around him people were talking, the television was on. He felt as drained and colourless as the day. Suddenly everything was dreary. He was irritated by French being spoken, by the strangers around him, by the ignorance of the world. He thought of Bray, a little grinning man in a dirty jacket, small hands. Are you coming to England? We'll work together, he said. The two of us. Side by side.

CHAPTER TWENTY-THREE

CATHERIN CAME down the stairway buttoning her coat. He had been waiting for her outside.

They walked toward the centre of town. There were people everywhere; Chamonix was filled with the last crowds of winter. Cars passed, spattered with mud.

'Well, what did he say?'

'It's definite,' she said.

'Definite?'

'The test is positive.'

'I don't understand it. How could that be?'

'It just is,' she said.

He was silent. He stared numbly into shop windows as they walked.

'Would you like a coffee?' she asked.

They sat near the back, Rand slumped in his chair.

'Well, I see the news has thrilled you,' she remarked.

'It's not that. It's just . . .'

'What?'

'It's just a surprise.'

'Well, I'm surprised too.'

'It's not exactly what I was planning on.'

'I see that.'

The waitress returned with the coffee.

'What *are* you planning on?' Catherin asked. She took three cubes of sugar and dropped them in the tiny cup.

'Not family life.'

She said nothing.

'I wouldn't be a good father.'

'How do you know?' She was slowly stirring her coffee. 'You'd be a very good father.'

'Don't have it,' he finally said.

'It's too late.'

'What do you mean, too late?'

'It's sixteen weeks.'

The number meant nothing to him. He was sure she was lying. 'I'd like to know how it happened,' he insisted. 'How could it?'

'I don't know. Something went wrong.'

'What?'

'Is this the investigation? Why didn't you investigate before we started?'

'I can't be a father,' he said.

She was silent.

'Perhaps you don't want to marry. That's what you mean.'

'Perhaps.'

'Yes. I understand.'

A terrible heaviness hung on him. He gazed around the room vaguely, as if for a different idea.

'Well, I don't know what to do *Merde*,' she said.

'Catherin, you know what my life is like.'

'*Ça veut dire quoi?*' After a while she added, 'What do you want? Do you want to go on like you are?'

'You don't go on like you are. A year from now, two years, I won't be the same.'

'What will you be?'

'How should I know? I don't want to be tied down.'

'You won't be,' she said. 'I promise. You can always do anything you like.'

The words thrilled him. He might have accepted them on the spot if she had not been so abject. Besides, she would forget what she was saying now, her instincts as a woman would come out. That was what always happened.

'You want me to get rid of it,' she said finally.

Yes, he thought, but for some reason said nothing. There is a moment when the knife must be pushed in coldly, otherwise the victim triumphs. He looked at her, aware that the moment was passing.

'Oh, hell,' he muttered.

She knew that she had failed him. She felt helpless, in despair. They sat in silence.

'Talk to me,' she pleaded.

He said nothing.

That spring he was seldom in Chamonix. He was up in one refuge hut or another, sometimes for days. It was early in the season. The sleeping rooms were empty, the mattresses side by side. *After 9.00 p.m. Silence,* commanded the signs.

Occasionally other climbers appeared. They rarely spoke. The huts were still cold from winter, with outdated tariffs pinned on the wall. It was difficult when he came back down. He came less often and stopped at the shop.

'*Ça va*?' he murmured awkwardly. Her shape did not seem to have changed.

'How was it up there?'

'Still a lot of snow.'

'So that's where it is,' she said.

He failed to smile. As soon as he could, he left, somewhat sensitive to what she might say. He hated parting comments. There was a kind of agreement that they were still somehow together, at least the appearance was maintained. In a town as small as Chamonix things are found out quickly although, in the strictest sense, they were outsiders.

'I'm going up to Argentière,' he said one day. 'If conditions aren't too good, I might wait around for a while up there, you know?'

'You don't have to hurry back,' she said. 'I'm not going to be here.'

It was like a sudden blow.

'Oh? Where are you going?'

There is a time when one says, I love you more than life itself. I will give you anything. Somehow the memory of that flickered before her – she was leaving, she had already decided – it was like a last glance back.

'I'm going to Paris,' she said.

'Well, I'll see you when you come back.'

She did not answer. She was remembering his face for the last time. Her silence frightened him.

'Or will I?' he said.

'No, I don't think so.'

Suddenly he was desperate. He was tormented by her. He loved her and this love was choking him. He wanted her and she was leaving.

'What are you going to do in Paris?'

'I'm going to stay with a friend,' she told him.

'Who?'

'What difference does it make?'

What difference? It was maddening. All the difference in the world, suddenly. He tried to make her tell him but she would not.

The friend was Henri Vigan. Catherin had once been his mistress – for two years – and left because he would not marry her. She went back to him. He accepted her willingly. If she wished, he said, he would consider the child as his own.

She settled in Izeaux – Vigan had his box factories near there – in an old house right on the street, built in the days when only an occasional carriage or cart passed by. The outside walls were plain, even drab, but the interior was warm and comfortable as only French country houses can be, with many doors giving onto the garden. There she was happy or at least freed from the difficulty of loving the wrong person. It would be wrong to say she did not think of him, but she did so with less and less frequency.

Vigan was kind and understanding. He was also flattered to have her back, doubly so since she had come from the arms of a younger, daring man. When she wanted to return to Chamonix to get her clothes, he forbade her.

'I'll have someone collect them and take them up to my house. You can't wear them now, anyway.'

He found her more beautiful, as pregnant woman often are. Her appetite, her need for rest, and the return of her good humour filled him with a deep satisfaction. She was luminous with a contentment that is only hinted at in the wake of the sexual act. This was the fullest aspect of it and it was he who luxuriated in its warmth. The days before she came to Izeaux faded and were forgotten.

'I was really miserable,' she confessed. 'I had the most depressing thoughts. I wanted to kill myself and have a gravestone like Dumas' mistress with nothing but four dates, one in each corner: the date I met him, the date we first made love . . .'

It was early summer. The doors to the garden were open.

'As I remember, those were the same dates.'

'No.'

'I thought it was that memorable night you left the party together.'

'Was it that obvious?'

'It was absolutely plain.'

'Please,' she said.

'I envied you.'

He was filled with a sense of well-being. In the light from the windows, late in the day, he looked no more than thirty-five. The clothes in his closet and bureau drawers were always neatly arranged, even the small shining scissors and various bottles on the bathroom shelf. *Le Monde* was on the entrance table, with the letters, the bedclothes were fresh, the cook, a woman from the village, was good-natured and calm. His views on politics Catherin disagreed with, he was secretive about money, she would have preferred a younger man, but all in all she felt very disposed toward him, she felt they were bound together in a way that would not be undone. She liked the well-worn surfaces, the comfort of the house. She admired the details of his life.

Of Rand she thought only rarely. She received no letters from him, not even as the birth of her child drew near, but then, of course he did not know where to write.

CHAPTER TWENTY-FOUR

HE DID THE North Face of the Triolet and the *éperon* ridge of the Droites, alone. He could have found a companion, almost anyone would have jumped at the chance, but he left Chamonix by himself and for one reason or another he began climbing that way.

The Triolet is steep, the ice that covers it never melts. It is always climbed with crampons.

He started early. The face was like a huge, descending river, steepening all the way. Its breath was cold. The sound of his crampons Rand kicked into the ice was crisp in the silence. He worked methodically, an ice axe in each hand. He became lost in the rhythm. The thought of slipping – he would have shot down the incline as if it were glass – first came to him only when he was far up, and it came in a strange way. He had paused for a moment to rest. The tips of his crampons were driven in a fraction, barely half an inch – that half-inch would not fail. A kind of bliss came over him as he realized this, a feeling of invulnerability unlike anything he had known. It was as if the mountain had ordained him; he did not refuse it.

He was happy, held there by the merest point of steel above all difficulties somehow, above all fears. This is how one must feel at the end, he thought uneasily, a surge of joy before the final moment. He looked past his feet. The steepness was dazzling. Far above him was a great bulge of ice. There were two ways past it, two ways only.

Each step, each kick into the rime, methodical, sure, took him farther and farther up. He thought of Bray. For a moment it was as if he were there. These lonely faces, these days, were still his, he existed in them. Broken and dead, he was not gone. He had not disappeared only stepped offstage. The day brought back thoughts of him together with the feeling of triumph as he passed the overhang, the view that awaited at the top.

He was often seen, rope over one shoulder, a pack on his back, headed out. He was off for a stroll, he would say. In the morning he woke among peaks incredibly white against the muted sky. There is something greater than the life of the cities, greater than money and possessions; here is a manhood that can never be taken away. For this one gives everything.

A strange thing's happened to me, he wrote to Cabot. *I've lost all fear of death. I'm only climbing solo these days. I did the N. Face of the Triolet and the Couturier on the Verte. Fantastic. I can't explain it. What's happening in the States? Where have you been?*

It was not only solitude that had changed him but a different understanding. What mattered was to be a part of existence, not to possess it. He still knew the anguish of perilous climbs, but he knew it in another way. It was a tribute; he was willing to pay it. A secret pleasure filled him. He was envious of no one. He was neither arrogant nor shy.

Early in August he arrived at the small refuge hut on the Fourche. It was evening. On the long trek across the glacier he had passed Pointe Lachenal, the Grand Capucin. The sun had passed behind Mont Blanc. He made his way in twilight.

The hut was nearly full. The vast face of Mont Blanc, directly opposite, had sunk into darkness. Voices, when they spoke, were low. Most of the climbers had gone to sleep.

'*Bonsoir*,' someone whispered. It was a guide, one of the younger ones. Rand knew him by sight.

'*Bonsoir.*'

'*Beau temps, eh?*'

'Incomparable.'

The guide moved his hand one way and the other – who knew how long it would last – and glanced at the entry Rand had made in the book. 'Brenva, eh?'

Rand did not reply.

He made some soup and found a place on the wooden sleeping shelf. As he drew the blanket around him there was a cough in the darkness, the cough of a woman. He turned his head slightly. He could not see her. A sudden loneliness swept over him. He was frightened by its strength. Lying there he fell into dreams. Catherin came to him, just as she was when they first had met. The newness of her dazed him, exactly as then. The little Renault parked behind the shop, the smell of her breath, her sudden smile. How impossible ever to tire of her, her scent, the white of her underclothes, her hair. Her face among the pillows, her naked back, the watery light of mornings in which she gleamed. Her slender hand touching him – he could feel these things, images collapsed in his head. She became a harem, a herd, his mind was wandering, multiplying her as she cried, as she yelped like a cur. The memory overwhelmed him. In the darkness he lay like a stone.

At dawn the sky was overcast. It had begun to snow. No one would climb that day. A few parties had already started down. He noticed the woman who had coughed, he heard her complaining, in fact. She was English, wearing a thick sweater and climbing pants unfastened at the knee. He watched her comb her hair. She turned to him to ask:

'What do you think?' 'Will it clear?'

'Hard to say.'

'I can't decide whether or not to go down.' Her voice seemed amiable. 'How do you manage to stay so calm?'

Rand was boiling water.

'Could I have some tea?' she asked. She watched as he poured it. 'Are you really doing the Brenva?'

'Depends.'

'And you're going alone.' She put in three spoonfuls of sugar. 'Isn't that asking for trouble?'

'Not really,' he said.

Her eyes were direct and grey. She was English but not like Audrey. She was a different breed.

'But one mistake and it's all over, isn't it?' A pause. 'My guide seems to think you're some sort of outlaw,' she said.

'Well, guides sleep in warm beds.'

'And you?'

'Occasionally,' he said.

'I would imagine.'

'Are you here for the season?'

'Just a fortnight. I'm with my husband, he's a very good climber, he's been doing it for years. I'm afraid he's a bit irritated at the moment. He's hurt his leg. He fell on the Blaitière, so I came with a guide but I think I'm a bit over my head. You're the American who does everything by himself, aren't you? I don't think I know your name.'

'Rand.'

'Yes, that's it. Rand . . .?'

'Vernon Rand.'

'I saw you come in last night. To be truthful, it frightened me. I wasn't sure I should even be up here. When I saw you, I knew I shouldn't be.'

'Well, you have a guide.'

He was watching from across the room.

'Even if I had three of them,' she said.

Her name was Kay Hammet, she was staying at the Hôtel des Alpes. She left at noon. By then it was snowing harder than before. That night there were only four of them and two went down the next day.

There were plenty of blankets then. He lay bundled up, asleep much of the time, waking to see the snow still falling. The wind made the metal walls creak. There was one other person in the hut. Not a word passed between them.

The storm lasted three days. Afterward, the clouds stayed low, covering the peaks.

On the sixth day, at noon, the door opened and a man walked in, stamping the snow from his feet. It was Remy Giro.

'*Salut,*' he said.

'You're the first person to walk through that door in a week.'

'I believe it. It's terrible out there. Do you have any soup?'

'No, do you want tea?'

'Anything,' Giro said. He watched the stove being lit. 'What have you been doing up here?'

'Not much.'

Giro glanced up at the young man sitting at the far end of the hut.

'It was full up when I got here,' Rand explained. 'It's interesting how they leave, first the guides and clients, then the ones who really didn't want to climb anyway. Then the English, out of food. Finally there's no one left but me and' – he gestured toward the back – 'the Phantom.'

'Don't you think it would be more comfortable in town?'

'I have my legend to think of,' Rand said offhandedly.

'Have you heard what's happened?'

'No, what?'

'You haven't heard the helicopters?'

'What is it, an accident?'

'Two Italians are trapped on the Dru.'

'Where?'

'One is badly hurt.'

'That's no surprise. Where on the Dru?'

'The West Face, far up. Above the ninety-metre dihedral. The whole face is solid ice.'

They had done two-thirds of the climb and been caught by the storm. They tried everything possible to come down; the ice was too severe. On the second day, realizing they had to do something, they decided to go up again and force the summit. That was when one had fallen. They were somewhere beneath the overhangs.

'They've been there for a week.'

'They're still alive?'

'They were this morning. They've tried everything to reach them. They even lowered a cable from the top but it was too far out. Now they're trying to go up the North Face and cross over.'

'Who?'

'Everyone. The gendarmes, the mountain troops.'

'What about the guides?'

'Of course. The guides.'

'They're giving advice.'

'No, no. They're trying too. There are two hundred people involved.'

'Why don't they go up the West Face?'

'Ahh,' he said.

'Have they tried?'

'I don't think so,' Remy said.

'Even the guides?'

'The guides are trying to go up the North Face.'

'Maybe they'll find somebody trapped there,' Rand suggested.

'They're trying,' Remy defended them.

Rand nodded. He began putting things in his pack. 'Five days they've been trying?'

'It won't last much longer,' Remy said calmly.

'Who's this over there? Do you know him?' Rand asked.

'I've seen him in town.'

'Can he climb?'

'Probably. Why else would he be there?'

Rand called to him. The young man looked over, unhurriedly.

'Do you want to climb?' Rand asked. In response there was a slight, almost indifferent gesture. 'Come on,' he said.

CHAPTER TWENTY-FIVE

IN CHAMONIX the effort had reached its final stage. There was little hope. The many attempts of the rescuers only made it more painful, more clear. Calmly, knowingly – for Chamonix knew its mountains – people watched the inevitable. The two Italians still somehow alive on the highest part of the Dru were lost.

It was true they had tried to lower a cable from the top. It had hung far out from the face. The conditions were unimaginable. One rescuer had already been killed.

In the streets, looking for anyone he knew, Rand found a friend of Bray's.

'Do you want to take a crack at it?'

'Don't they have hundreds of people up there?'

'Not where we're going,' Rand said.

'I've never been on the Dru.' He was a schoolteacher, earnest, somewhat shy. He had very red, almost feverish lips and coarse hair. His name was Dennis Hart. 'All right,' he said.

From the army they managed to borrow extra equipment, a radio, even some food. On the way back into town they enlisted another climber, a Frenchman, Paul Cuver.

'We'll be there by seven tonight,' Rand told him. 'They're giving us a helicopter to the foot of the Dru.'

'A helicopter?'

'That's right.'

His plan was simple. All other attempts had rejected it out of hand. Rather than seek the most practicable, he would try the most direct way. He didn't know how bad the conditions would be, but he knew the route. They would leave fixed ropes behind to aid in the descent. If they were at the base of the Dru that evening, with luck they might reach the Italians on the second day.

They waited until eight o'clock. The helicopter never appeared. Instead they took the train to Montenvers, a special trip was made just before dark. A girl from the hotel kitchen gave them coffee. They sat on the ground by the doorway. The dining room windows were alight and people were having dinner.

It was after ten when they started down the steel ladders that led to the glacier. The sky was black. They could see nothing above or below. The cold breath of the ice age rose to meet them. By the jerky light of headlamps they began to make their way. Even at night, in the most dismal hours, the glacier creaked slowly. The sound of hidden water came from beneath.

On the far side the uphill path began. The packs were heavy. From time to time someone slipped and fell in the dark. It became colder, whether from the late hour or altitude one could not tell.

At two in the morning they reached the *rognon*. They crawled into their sleeping bags and lay down wherever they could. The young climber who had come with him from the hut, Hilm, did not have one. He slept leaning against his pack, a worn jacket pulled up over his head.

Daylight awakened them. It was after six. There were patches of blue in the sky. The clouds looked thin. The Dru was dark, ominous, dusted with snow. Like a huge organ in a cathedral it seemed capable of deep, chilling tones.

On the lower portion there seemed to be little ice. Higher, it was difficult to tell. The very top, where the roofs were clustered, was hidden by cloud.

'See anything up there?'

Rand had the binoculars.

'No,' he said.

'Where are they, exactly?'

'I'm not sure,' Rand said.

'There's an awful lot of snow on it.'

'Let's have some tea.' He was already unpacking the things to prepare it. His eyes burned from lack of sleep. His limbs felt stale. 'It doesn't look bad. It looks like it's clearing.'

Not long after came the faint, wavering sound of a helicopter. It was far off. Finally they saw it, coming up the valley. It turned toward the Dru.

'Why don't you call them and see what's going on? Something may have happened,' Dennis said.

'What do you mean?'

'I don't know. They may have died.'

An impenetrable static came over the radio as soon as it was turned on. It was difficult to hear anything. *'Allô, allô,'* Rand called. The helicopter was nearly overhead. *'Les Italiens,'* he was repeating, *'comment vont-ils?'*

The helicopter was banking, close to the face. He had the radio to his ear. There was chatter he could not understand. Then, faintly, *'Ils agitent leurs mains . . .'*

'What did he say?'

'They're waving. They're alive.'

'Oh. Good,' Dennis muttered.

They were eating bread and jam with dirty fingers, sorting out the gear. Rand and Dennis would lead, the other two were to follow. The couloir looked safe. They'd try it. They descended to the snowfield.

At the base of the mountain, Rand looked up. From here it had lost its shape. Cold as steel, it seemed to rise on and on. Had he really climbed it? Had he climbed it twice?

'Hello, you son of a bitch,' he murmured.

It was 7:00 a.m. There were at least twelve remaining hours of daylight. He stood there, taller than the others, almost ungainly, storklike. He was wearing a knit cap under his helmet. Cuver crossed himself with a barely visible gesture. Not bothering to rope up they began to climb.

CHAPTER TWENTY-SIX

DENNIS HAD BEEN in Chamonix three weeks. It was his first visit. He had never made, here or in England, he had never imagined a climb like this. He could not believe he was doing it. At any moment he expected to be unable to go on. He dared not think about it. Late in the morning as pitch after awesome pitch unrolled, hardly aware of how it was happening he found himself on the most terrifying face.

The climbing was harder than he'd dreamed. The snow had to be cleared from holds. Higher up there was ice, a slick, unyielding ice that could not be completely chopped away. His hands were cold. He was breathing on his fingers, clenching and unclenching, trying to warm them.

In more than one place he called for the rope; he could not have gotten up otherwise. His helmet was crooked, his gear in disarray. He was on a small cliff, close to the ground, he told himself, it was delicate but there was no risk. If necessary he could jump down, he pretended. He must not let the vastness affect him, if he did he was lost.

Whatever the others felt, he knew they would never reach the stranded climbers. What might happen apart from that, he would not guess. All that allowed him to go on, all that preserved him from panic was a kind of numbness, an absolute concentration on every hold and a faith, complete, unthinking, in the tall figure above.

The clouds were lower. By two in the afternoon it began once more to snow.

'The weather's coming in,' was all Rand said.

Dennis waited for something more.

'Shouldn't we go down?' he asked.

'It doesn't look that bad. You've climbed in worse than this.'

'Actually, I haven't.'

Dennis clung beside him, waiting. The snow was coming in sideways, stinging their eyes.

'We can't stay here,' Rand said. He looked up to find the way. In his worn clothes and gauntness he appeared to be a secondary figure, someone in the wake of failed campaigns. It did not matter. He would do it. He was not merely making an ascent. He was clinging to the side of this monster. He had his teeth in the great beast.

That evening they bivouacked in the storm. The wind was blowing their matches out. The smallest act took on immense dimensions. They were wet and cold. Cuver sat huddled next to Rand. On the far side of him, half-hidden, was Hilm, the fragment of his profile as impassive, withdrawn, as if they were still on the Fourche. What his thoughts were, Rand could not tell. His own, obsessive, slow, stretched like an ocean current for endless miles. He was thinking of Cabot and the nights they had spent like this.

He was remembering Cabot. There are men who seemed destined to always go first, to lead the way. They are confident in life, they are the first to go beyond it. Whatever there is to know, they learn before others. Their very existence gives strength and drives one onward. Love and jealousy were mingled there in the darkness, envy and despair.

From above the snow slid down in airy sheets. None of them slept. They sat silent and close together till dawn, on the the narrow ledge, tied to the rock.

The sky grew clearer. In the early morning the snow stopped. They climbed all that day, slowly at first and then more quickly, bodies warming, the icy ledge of the night left far behind. In the afternoon the sun came through the clouds. It raised their spirits. They heard the helicopter but did not see it.

Dennis had outclimbed his fear. An exhilaration that was almost dizzying came over him. He was one of them, he was holding his own.

Far above a length of rope was hanging by itself. Rand pointed.

'There they are,' he said.

'Where?'

'See it?'

'No, where are you looking?'

'Beneath the overhangs. There. Paul!' he called down. A face looked up. He pointed again.

'I see it,' Dennis cried. 'Way up.'

'We're not going to reach them today.' He cupped his hands to his mouth. 'Hello!' he shouted. The sound dissolved in space. There was no answer. 'We're coming!' he called. '*Veniamo!*' He paused. 'Do you hear them?' he asked.

'No.'

'Hello!' he shouted again. 'Hell-o!' He waited. The vastness of the face was the only reply. As loudly as he could he cried, 'We're coming!'

In response, as slow as a dream, something white, a bit of cloth, a handkerchief came floating clear. They had heard him. They were alive.

The clouds were in a layer smooth as water. They had lost their darkness, their density. Beneath them was a band of open sky, a narrow horizon crushed by light.

They called to the Italians from their second bivouac. A head appeared, cautious, almost disinterested. Rand waved. In the morning they would reach them.

CHAPTER TWENTY-SEVEN

TALL, UNSHAVEN, a childish grin on his face – such was the image that incredibly rose from the void. The two Italians had been hunched on the narrow ledge for nine days. Nine days of exhaustion, of cold, expecting they would die.

It was the man who was injured, he had broken his shoulder. The girl, who was as ragged as he, had astonishing white teeth. She said something in Italian. Rand couldn't understand it.

'*Parl' italiano?*' she asked.

A little, he indicated.

'*È spaccato,*' she said.

'Ah, *spaccato,*' Rand repeated uncomprehendingly. Dennis was just below the ledge.

'Come up,' Rand told him. 'Can you understand Italian?'

'We have company,' Dennis said as he reached them.

'What do you mean?'

'Down there. Look.'

It was another party, made up of guides. They had crossed over from the North Face and were now just below. They were calling to him.

Two rescue parties arriving at the same time or nearly – the story reached

Chamonix that afternoon. What made it more extraordinary was the discussion that had taken place between them. The guides had come up an easier route and there were seven of them. They wanted to bring the Italians down. No, Rand told them. The helicopter was flying past, there were crowds at Montenvers.

'No,' he said. 'We got here first. They're ours.'

Against the vertical rock in sunlight, motley and at ease, were the amateurs who had made the rescue – photographs would be in every European paper – and the reply to the guides, *'Ils sont à nous.'* In Chamonix nevertheless was a wonderful mood of satisfaction, as if the reputation of the town had been saved.

That evening they reached a ledge halfway down. The weather had been mild all day. The small stove was burning in the dusk. The worst seemed behind them. A cup half-filled with bouillon passed from hand to hand until it reached the injured man.

'Molto grazie,' he murmured. He would never forget the courage of his rescuers, he said later, in the hospital. His cheeks were black with a two-week beard. His fiancée was beside him.

'We could not move,' she said in Italian. 'The ice was everywhere. After Sergio fell, he could not use his arm. We had very little food. The storm went on. We were finished. Then came this beautiful American.'

She was broad-faced, like an Oriental, and had a silky, dark moustache. She was full of passion and life. *Questo bel' Americano* . . . he'd had his picture taken with the others, lounging like fishermen, when they got down to the *rognon*. Then, returning to town, he somehow disappeared. He sneaked in the back door of Sport Giro and into a small office where Remy found him, eating a tangerine. He did not want to talk to any reporters. He wanted the pleasure of being notorious, unknown.

It was not to be so simple. They were looking for him everywhere, the town could not hide him. Remy came back to tell him they were in the front of the shop.

'Look, they're not going to leave you alone.'

'Do they know I'm here?'

'The reporters? No, of course not. They came to buy equipment, what do you think?' he said.

Someone was already at the door.

Rand attempted to slip past them, refusing to talk.

They would not let him leave, he was too singular, too bizarre.

'No,' he told them. 'No.'

'Oh, be decent. It's not we who want to see you,' one of them said.

He had always been an actor, the call had never come. Now, in the parking lot in front of the Hôtel des Alpes across the way, he was given his role. He was weary but full of grace. Listening patiently to the questions, he tried to respond. He wore a shy smile, it sometimes grew broader, a smile on top of a smile. His long face loomed on the screens of France, gaunt, natural, the wind blowing his dirty hair. Did he feel himself a hero, they immediately asked?

'A hero,' he said, 'no, no. It wasn't an act of heroism. It was more a debt I owed the mountain. Anyway, it wasn't me. Four of us did it. I was one of them.'

That night they would see him from their dinner tables, mixed in with cabinet ministers and accidents at sea. Women would watch from kitchen doorways as he looked shyly down at the ground.

This was the mountain he had climbed with Cabot and again with Bray. Bray was dead.

'Yes.'

'The great faces exact their price.'

'No, not that way,' he said. 'You pay, yes. You have to give everything, but you don't have to die.'

They were watching in old people's homes, in cafés. In the large house in Izeaux, Catherin in her last weeks of waiting saw it. Vigan was at her side. She could feel the child move within her as she watched. She sat quietly. She did not want to reveal the intensity of her interest or the stab of emotion that went with it. She felt faint.

'But John Bray, killed on the Eiger . . .'

Rand was silent. 'Yes,' he admitted. 'I mourn for Bray. Not really for him, for myself.'

'By that, you mean . . . ?'

Ah, well, he couldn't answer. 'He died, but that's not the end of it,' was all he could say.

'When you think that the guides of Chamonix,' Vigan said, 'the gendarmes, the army, all of them . . .' He did not finish the sentence. He rose and stood watching the end.

'You love the mountains . . .' they said.

'Not the mountains,' he replied. 'No, not the mountains. I love life.'

Whoever did not believe him did not have eyes to see. People remembered. It gave him a name. *'Bonjour, monsieur,'* the woman greeted him at the *douches*. His honesty had touched them. That worn, angelic face, filled with happiness, stayed in one's thoughts.

That night he had no worries, no concerns. He let his glass be filled and relived the climb. Afterward he slept at Remy's. He slept as he had the first time, long ago, as if all the earth were his own chamber. He slept untroubled, with swollen hands.

When he woke he was famous. His face poured off the presses of France. It was repeated on every kiosk, in the pages of magazines, his interview read on buses by working girls on their way home. Suddenly, into the small rooms and houses, the ordinary streets, he brought a glimpse of something unspoiled. For two hundred years France had held the idea of the noble savage, simple, true. Unexpectedly he had appeared. His image cleansed the air like rain. He was the envoy of a breed one had forgotten, generous, unafraid, with a saintly smile and the vascular system of a marathon runner.

CHAPTER TWENTY-EIGHT

IN THE STREETS of Paris drivers lowered their windows and called to him. It was phenomenal. His face alone made people turn. Someone would come up to him and in a few minutes there was a crowd. They took him as their own.

'Mon légionnaire,' Colette mocked. 'How do you like having Paris as your garden?' she said. She was pleased by his fame. She took it as a matter of course. About Catherin she did not inquire. Most likely she knew.

Her apartment was on a top floor near the Place des Vosges. People had been invited for drinks – everyone was eager to meet him. Bottles and glasses on the table, the balcony doors open – how beautiful the city seemed, the elegant, worn buildings, the trees, taxis queueing up at the corner, the traffic, the evening light. Her friends were journalists, women, businessmen. They were talkative, well dressed. They had carved out lives.

'How does one climb alone?'

'Alone!' a woman cried. 'Is that true?'

'Tell me, what protects you?' someone said –

He saw himself reflected in a mirror on the opposite wall among women's bare arms, the backs of men's heads. The smoke and murmur of conversation rose.

'Nothing actually protects you', he said. The murmur of conversation quieted around him. 'It comes from within,' he explained. 'It's not like gambling. It's not a matter of taking chances.' They assumed that a climber is courageous, that like a boxer there is latent in him the strength to kill. 'You're prepared for everything,' he told them. 'If your foot slips you have your hand. You never try something unless you're sure you can do it. It's a question of spirit. You have to feel you'll never come off.'

'Ne pas monter bien haut, peur-être,' a woman recited, *'mais tout seul.'*

'What's that?'

'Rostand,' she said. She was wearing a silk shirt and ivory necklaces. There was something about these women, poised, calmly wise.

Later, an almost oceanic blue had covered the sky. The television was on. He sat drunkenly on a couch. People were still talking animatedly. Colette was running her finger along one of his.

'Am I going to spend the night alone?' she asked. She was looking at his hand. Her face was astonishingly young.

Paris and triumph. In his pocket were two thousand francs for the rights to photographs of the rescue. How easily it had come. He remembered music playing, the soft air of night. Her bedroom had thick curtains, chairs, fish barely moving in a greenish, square tank. Her robe was half open. She took his hands.

'You're not too tired?' she asked.

She had a clever face, a face that knew him. Her hair was rich, disorderly, it smelled like almonds. He fell asleep almost immediately, like a vagabond in a barn.

In the morning she picked up a bottle of Evian water from beside the bed and drank. She offered it to him. The bed was large. She slept, smoked, ate apples in it. Her face was naked, her breath a little stale. Her arms were faintly yellow near the armpits, otherwise she might have been thirty.

'You were quite a success last night,' she said.

'Was I?'

'Though you wouldn't go to dinner.'

'No,' he said. 'I'm like an animal. I eat when I feel like it, I sleep when I feel like it.'

'Yes, I noticed.' A stumpy-legged cat with bitten ears was stepping back and forth across them. *'Bonjour, Pilou.'*

So, she would have two animals, she said genially. Despite the disappointment of the first night she was ready to accept him. This was morning; she sat up and combed her hair. The curtains remained closed, the maid opened them at noon.

Colette looked after him, she advised him, sorted out his clothes. He was lazy, basking in the warmth of self-approval without the ability to judge things for himself. An article he had written appeared in the paper. It was absolutely foolish, she said, it was affected, it didn't sound like him.

'What do you mean?'

'You have to be more or less intelligent if you want to give opinions,' she said.

'Is that so?'

'Yes it is.'

There were offers to do advertising. He turned them down.

'Now that, you see, is definitely not intelligent,' she said. 'After all, there's nothing wrong in it. People like your face, why not let them see it?'

'It was against his principles,' he said quietly. 'It was not only against his principles but more, it was something he despised.'

'Ah, that.' She merely shrugged. 'They know you're accepting a little money, they don't care. Nothing could pay you for what you did. The Romans rewarded their heroes,' she said. 'In Genoa, they were given houses.'

'It still doesn't make it right.'

'You sold the photos to *Paris Match,*' she reminded him.

'They would have been published anyway.'

'Perhaps. Look, my darling, in ten years, who will know the difference?'

'And if it's only me?'

She admired him. It was a question he was asking, he wanted her approval. 'Yes,' she agreed, 'that's something. The only trouble, with your habits, you may not be here.'

She was the world, he realized, and he an outsider. Moreover, through a friend she even arranged it so he would be paid more. On the rue de Rivoli she bought him a beautiful jacket of soft leather. She had no particular reason – she felt like it, she said.

He tried it on in front of the mirror.

'Well?' she asked.

The illusion of distant traveller was vanishing. Concession was on his shoulders. 'I look like one of your friends.'

'Is that bad?'

That night they dined at Lipp. A film star was across the room, annoyed by this boyish rival. At the end of the meal he unexpectedly came to the table and shook hands. His instinct was infallible – every eye in the restaurant was on him. He was making a film at Billancourt.

'Come out and visit me,' he said.

September passed. October. The splendour of fall. There is a season of life that lasts forever. Her taste, her telephone, her friends – he adopted all of these. There were nights he felt he'd been dancing too long, he yearned for a simpler life. But it was brief. It went away. The big dishevelled bed was his and none other's, the maid who came four times a week, the jacket of glove leather, the kisses on his hands as if he were a priest. He could do anything, he could have anything.

'Would you like to go to Belle-Ile?'

'Where's that?'

'It's an island. You take the train from Paris. In the morning you're at the sea.'

'It's fabulous,' Simone agreed. She was the woman who had quoted Rostand. 'The ocean, the rocks, the air. It's a paradise.'

'In November?' he said.

'It's the best time!' they cried.

'Let me go with you,' Simone said. 'I'll find a place to stay.'

Colette made a slight, parental sound with her tongue. 'Another time,' she commented.

As a friend, Simone accepted this faint cautioning. She understood. They were talking about the beautiful solitude, the sea, when there was a crash from below. Two cars had collided in the street. Colette went out on the balcony.

'My God!' she cried. Someone had hit her car which was parked in front. 'Look at this! Can you believe it?'

She ran downstairs. They watched from above.

'That's so awful,' Simone said, staring down. 'Is that hers? That one? How could someone do it?' She felt a hand placed near the small of her back. She remained looking down. 'I can't understand it,' she continued.

Her profile revealed nothing, but the flesh beneath the fabric of her dress had changed: it was unknown but no longer forbidden. Her shoes, her stockings, the weight of her breasts, they were silently being collected. Colette was looking up with a shrug of annoyance, of pleading. She called out something.

'Quoi?'

'On ne peut pas imaginer!' she cried.

His hand moved slightly, possessively. She seemed unaware. She stood motionless, like a bird in cover. Not a word had passed between them, not a glance.

'A thousand francs, at least,' Colette said angrily as she returned, 'and the colour will never be right. Can you imagine? While we were sitting here!'

Her complaints, her misfortune seemed to isolate her. She didn't want to go to dinner. She was too upset.

'You have to eat. Please, come,' Simone said.

'No, that's all right.'

'Please.'

She failed to notice anything. They went down the stairs. They had barely turned the corner before they embraced.

One woman is like another. Two are like another two. Once you begin there is no end.

CHAPTER TWENTY-NINE

WOMEN ARE sensitive, they are shrewd. In the morning there was something strange, perhaps it was a slight sense of distance or even a faint, undetected scent to his skin. Colette watched him sleep. She woke him as she left.

'What time is it?' he murmured.

'Nine o'clock.'

He turned over. She was looking at his bare shoulder, the side of his head, in calm appraisal.

'Where did you go last night?'

'Hmm?' He was suddenly wide awake but did not show it.

'Where did you eat?' she said.

'Daru,' he yawned. It was a lie.

'Was it pleasant?'

'It was all right,' he said.

'I'll call you later.'

It seemed somehow threatening. When the front door closed he jumped up and went quickly to the phone. Simone's number was in the address book. He dialled but there was no answer, she had already gone out. He paced around the apartment, a kind of panic hovering over him. It was a cloudy morning. Traffic sounds rose from the street.

That night they stayed at home. He was uneasy, he tried to seem calm. Whatever she said alarmed him. He knew she was patient, astute. He found himself somehow apprehensive of all that represented her, the apartment, the shop, the comfort surrounding her, the friends with the house on Belle-Ile.

Her face looked suddenly older. He could see it clearly, the dryness, the lines around the mouth. He resented her knowledge, her assurance. At the same time, he didn't want to give her up. The evening news was on. The room was filled with a flow of soft French he was barely listening to and the crackle of wood in the fireplace. He must have yawned.

'Tired?'

'A little.'

'You can go to bed early tonight,' she said.

'I probably will.'

'I'm going to Geneva this weekend. Would you like to go?'

'Geneva?'

'You've heard of it?'

'How long will you be gone?'

'Just until Monday.'

'I don't think so,' he said. 'I'll probably stay here.'

'You won't be bored?'

'No.'

'You're sure?' She was regarding him.

'Yes, I'm sure.'

'Um.'

'Look,' he said unconcernedly, 'I think you know this already. I went home with Simone last night.'

She admired the coolness of his confession, the brevity. She could not have improved on it herself. 'Yes, I know,' she said, matching it.

He was slightly thrown off. 'I don't believe in hiding things.'

She did not reply.

'You're not angry?'

'I'm just curious why you did it.'

'I don't know,' he admitted.

'You're tired of me already,' she said somewhat wistfully.

'No, that's not it,' he said.

'It didn't bother you that it might hurt me?'

'Annoy you.'

She gave a brief, mirthless smile, 'But what is the philosophy behind it?'

'Philosophy?' The word surprised him.

'What is the reason?' she asked. 'When someone trusts you, you mean you don't feel any regret if you betray them? Going from woman to woman, from place to place like a dog in the street, that fulfils you? The hero with gorgeous ideals, beautiful ideals, you turn your back for a minute and he sleeps with your friend. It's disgusting.'

He was silent.

'Say something.'

'What?'

'I don't know. Say: Colette, forgive me, you gave me too much, somehow I resented it, I had to do something. Or, Colette, this woman was helpless, foolish, I wanted to find out if she was even the same kind of creature as you, is she really a woman, I thought? Or you could say, Colette, I forgot who I was. I forgot I am really an American, the kind one detests, stupid, ungrateful.'

'It's that bad?'

'It's ugly,' she said somewhat wearily. 'I'm going to bed.'

On Friday she went to Geneva, to a comfortable hotel on Place Longmalle where she usually stayed. The city seemed fresh, the weather clear. She attended to her business, had dinner and settled down with new magazines in a smooth, white bed. Unhappy, yes, but she was familiar with it. She knew the medicine for it, she knew it would pass. Further, she knew she would forgive him and they would begin again, much as it was before.

She was wrong.

He had left the apartment and gone to Simone's. He was there only a short time. Simone was nervous, high-strung, she ground her teeth in her sleep. Her pubic hair was harsh.

'You're grinding your teeth.' He shook her.

'What?' she said, dazed.

He told her again.

'Why did you wake me up?' she complained. Now she would not be able to go to sleep again.

After Colette, she seemed careful, dull. The sexual attraction did not disappear – she carried that with her despite herself – but it was too much trouble to isolate among all the medicines, real and figurative, that cluttered her life. She was a drama critic for small, Catholic journals. The shelves were piled with books leaning against one another, her table was covered with papers. There was none of the casual comfort of Colette's. These were three rooms where the mind was at work. The only thing she said that made him like her was once, in exhaustion, 'You make love like someone in a novel.'

After three days he left.

'Where is he?' Colette asked calmly as they were having a conciliatory lunch. She had already forgiven Simone. They were like two patients who have had the same illness.

'I found him extraordinary,' Simone admitted. 'But he also made me nervous. I never really knew what to talk about with him. He's not exactly a polymath. He knows nothing about politics, art, and yet I found myself perfectly willing to believe in him. Whatever it is, he has it despite himself.'

'I think it's mainly an ability to look good in old clothes.'

'I don't know where he's gone,' Simone said. 'He was very unsettled. Actually I felt sorry for him. I knew he would leave, it was only a matter of time. His ambition, as far as I can see, is very unclear.

'His ambition?'

'You know him better. Don't you agree?'

'I'm not sure what his ambition is. There's no question, though, where he's going. He knows exactly.'

'Where is that?'

'Oblivion,' she said. It was not so much a prophecy as a dismissal. She was casting him out of their lives. He would wander elsewhere exiled, a vanishing figure. 'You know, he has a child in Grenoble, a son.'

'He's married?'

'No, no. She's one of his many wives. He has greater and lesser wives.'

'Original,' Simone said dryly though the idea intrigued her.

They were not wives, they were not meant to be wives. They were witnesses. For some reason he trusted only women and for each of them he assumed a somewhat different pose. They were the bearers of his story, scattered throughout the world.

CHAPTER THIRTY

HE WAS DRIFTING downward, from the world of cafés and lights to another of dismal streets and long walks home after midnight when the Métro had closed, a city of chance encounters in the company of a strange girl he first saw outside American Express who also had no place of her own. She was blond, clean-faced, an heiress.

'I think I read about you somewhere,' she said.

It was at a party in someone's apartment. A thin-legged dog with a coat of beautiful brown ran ceaselessly from window to window looking out. There was endless striking of matches to light a small pipe.

'Aren't you famous?' she asked. Her name was Susan de Camp. She was sitting across from him. Very matter-of-factly she pulled up her skirt as she spoke and crossed her legs. The pure, narrow white of her underpants was directed straight at him.

In spite of the off-handedness of her life she had a healthy appearance. She was tanned from being in Sicily. Her arms had a golden down. She was scrubbed, alert, casual.

'Where are you staying?' she asked. He was her friend, she'd made up her mind. 'Can I trust you?' She had gone to good schools, a brilliant student, in fact. She'd been married to a man in Kenya. 'He was fabulous, but he was a drunk. He'd been married at least three times I found out later. You want to go in here?' she asked him. 'This isn't a bad place.'

It was on the corner of rue Verlon. The windows were glazed from the cold. Inside were a number of women, waiting.

'They're always here,' she said. 'I like to come and watch them. Can you imagine the stories they could tell? I always say hello.'

'Bonsoir,' he greeted them with a sweep of his arm. Several of them replied.

'I told you,' she said. 'They're my friends. Probably they know Gordon.' Her ex-husband – he had been a publisher, a pilot, he owned a coffee plantation. He was still madly in love with her.

'Where is he now?'

She gave a slight shrug as if bored by the conversation.

'I have some friends near here,' she said. 'You want to go there?'

That night he lay beside her brooding, more and more discontent, for half an hour, trying to make pleasure finally open its wings.

'That's all right,' she said. 'Really, I'm used to it.'

A sense of disgust and uselessness filled him. The act of love, even disinterestedly or in degradation, is still the most serious act of all. Rather than disappoint her, the failure seemed to bring her closer to him. Perhaps, in fact, she was used to it. Perhaps she even preferred it.

'Really,' she confided. 'I'm fine.'

During January they wandered together. In the stuffiness of endless bars they sat waiting to meet someone or merely waiting. The afternoons were sombre. Often it rained. Paris is like a window. On one side there is comfort and well-being, on the other everything is cold and bare, the streets, the cafés, the cheap, ascending smoke. He thought of Chamonix and the clear morning air, standing in the station, the weight of a pack upon him and the solemn, reassuring clank of metal from the bandolier of it hung on his shoulder. Here, hardship was misfortune; there, it was the flavour of life.

Susan sat bundled up in a scarf and a camel's hair coat. She was an outcast. She had tried everything, gone beyond all possible forgiveness of her family, she loved to joke about it, sending them telegrams saying she was so cold she couldn't get out of bed, she was hungry, she was sick.

'Let's go over to the American Library,' she suggested, 'maybe somebody's there. There's a guy named Eddie who's writing a book on the Middle Ages. Maybe he'll buy us dinner,' she said. 'I went home with him once.'

They walked along the river. There were small fires burning on the *quai*, men sitting beside them. He felt a sense of camaraderie towards them, they were poor, free. He grinned at them, he was at ease.

One of them held out his palm.

'J'ai rien,' Rand said, almost proudly. He turned his pockets inside out to show them. *'Rien.'*

'La veste,' the man said hoarsely.

'Oui, la veste,' the others cried.

'They don't believe you. What about your jacket?'

'This? Someone gave me this.'

The scornful cries followed them from a distance.

'I don't think you convinced them.' Her face was hidden in her collar.

'You don't believe I've lived like that?'

'Oh, I believe it.'

'They've been drinking,' he said.

That night he looked at himself in the mirror. His face seemed uninteresting. The longer he stared at it, the duller it became.

'What's wrong?'

'Nothing. I'm out of shape.'

'You look terrific.'

'Do I?' he said. He didn't hate her, she was decent, friendly, it was himself he was tired of. He was tired of following her around, of having her pay for things. He had passed forgiveness also. He could not imagine what he was doing here, what he was waiting for, what he expected to find.

Paris – it was like a great terminal he was already leaving, with a multitude of signs, neon and enamel, repeated again and again as if announcing a performance. The people of Paris with their cigarettes and dogs, the stone roofs and restaurants, green buses, grey walls, he had held their attention for a moment. The *affiches* with his face on them were vanished but he had stayed on. He saw it clearly as, at a certain place in life, one sees both the beginning and end: Paris had forgotten him.

CHAPTER THIRTY-ONE

THE SKY WAS flat, the sun a flaw in it. A layer of silence lay above everything. Beneath it, in the streets, sounds were hollow as if in a tin. A winter day in Chamonix, a day when the whiteness eats one's bones.

The Carlton had the look of a building that has been bombed out and only one wing remains. The balconies had iron railings, the windows were faced in stone. The mansard roof was covered with snow which a man was shovelling. There was something attached to his boots. It was crampons, the points of which, it later turned out, were punching holes in the roof. A voice called up from below,

'Hey, Vern! Vern!'

The shovelling continued. The snow fell in wavering sheets through the air.

'Hey, Rand!'

Hat pulled over his ears and parka patched with tape, he went over to the edge. Someone was waving from the street.

'Who's that?' he called.

'Nick! Nick Banning!'

'Who?'

Banning was a doctor, in his first year of residency, but he looked the same. He looked young.

'What are you doing up there?' he asked when Rand came down.

'What am I doing? Christ.' He was unshaven, his eyes red-rimmed. 'What are you doing in Chamonix?'

'I came to see the sights.'

'Well, there's Mont Blanc,' Rand said.

Banning ignored it. 'I read all about you,' he said. 'I was telling everyone: I know him! It was sensational.'

'It was all right, I guess.'

'All right?'

'If you want the truth, it damn near ruined me.'

'You look great.'

'I know,' Rand said caustically.

'It couldn't have ruined you.'

Rand took off his hat and rubbed his face with it.

'Believe me,' he said.

'You were a hero!'

'I just talked a lot. The French have an expression' – he remembered Colette – *'il faut payer,* you have to pay.'

'You're going to have to explain that to me.'

'Yeah, well, it would take a while.'

Banning had driven from Geneva in a rented car. His pack and sleeping bag were in the back seat. He'd planned to find a place to camp, even in the middle of winter. He had longed to climb these legendary peaks.

'I don't know how much longer I'll be able to do something like this,' he confessed.

'With me it's the opposite problem,' Rand said.

'Do you know anywhere I could sleep?'

'You can stay with me. There's always room for a friend. Speaking of friends, what do you hear from Cabot?'

'You should have been there when he heard about it. He tried to call you, but you'd gone to Paris.'

'Really? Is that true?'

'I haven't seem him for a while,' Banning said. 'I just haven't had the time. I hear a lot about him.'

'Where is he?'

'California.'

'I've written to him a few times,' Rand admitted. 'Not lately.'

'He's a strange guy. He's like a searchlight. When he turns your way, he just dazzles you. Afterward, you're left in darkness, you might as well not be alive. Don't misunderstand, I like him. He's in a class by himself. I think he'd do anything for you, but he's absolutely driven. He wants to be first. He wants to be number one. You know that.'

'Maybe he will be. Who's he climbing with these days?'

'Various people.'

Rand nodded. The conversation was depressing him. The street seemed empty, sound had drained away.

'One thing I'd really like to do,' Banning said. 'I'd like to take a look at the Dru. Can I get up there this time of year?'

'Not in the snow,' Rand said. 'It wouldn't be too easy.'

'Where is it?'

'Oh, it's up there. I'll take you to a place where you can see it later.' He seemed vague, uninterested in the idea.

Toward evening he was livelier. They went to the Choucas where a photograph of him hung on the wall. He began to tell stories of Paris, sleeping in various beds, being hailed on the boulevards.

'They don't expect me to do anything ordinary any more, that's the trouble.'

'So, anyway, what are your plans?'

Rand was silent for a moment.

'Well, don't say anything about this, but there's something I've been thinking about for a long time. In fact, we even talked about it once. The Walker.'

'I remember.'

'That was before I ever came over here. I'd never even heard of the Dru. The Walker, that was always the big one.'

As he was talking, his mind went back to the days when he had first climbed. He was fifteen. He remembered seeing another climber, older, in his twenties, rolled-up sleeves, worn shoes, an image of strength and experience. Now, with absolute clarity, he saw that climber again, his face, his gestures, even the very light. It seemed that in spite of all that had happened in between, the essence, an essence he had seen so vividly in that unknown face still somehow eluded him and he was struggling again, still, to capture it.

'I'm going to do the Walker,' he said. He had barely spoken the words before adding, 'I'm also going to do the Peuterey.' He felt no pride, no pleasure in announcing it. It was somehow flat. 'I don't know what I'm going to do.'

Banning was listening politely.

'Can you imagine what it would be like to solo the Walker? What kills them is, I'm not really a great climber. I'm not that talented.'

'Come on.'

'There are lots of guys with more talent.'

'Not really.'

'Lots of them,' Rand insisted. The wine had been vanishing, glass after glass. The noise of other conversations rose around their own.

They drove on a snow-covered road. The night was clear. A cold moon illuminated everything, the sky was white around it. Shreds of cloud blew across like smoke. They passed the empty fields of the Biolay. The pines were dark. There was not a house or light. Banning slowed down.

'Are you sure this is the road?' he said.

Rand merely motioned onward. A kilometre farther on they came to a barn that was standing by itself. In front of it was a stone trough. Rand broke the crust of ice.

'You want some water?' He was drinking from cupped hands. 'Cow water,' he added.

He led the way inside into a room meant for storage. It was clean, the floor was of heavy boards. By the light of a lamp, Banning looked around – some clothes, equipment, a shelf of books, a radio.

'The batteries are dead,' Rand said. He was lighting the stove. Soon there was a fierce crackling of wood, loud as shots. 'It warms up pretty fast,' he said.

'How'd you find this place?'

'Oh . . .' Rand shrugged.

'Do you have to pay much?'

'Nothing. Of course, it isn't worth anything.'

'Anyway, you're by yourself.'

'Yeah, this is the lowest refuge. Capacity: one.'

'That's all?'

'At the moment. You want to dry your boots?' He began unlacing his. He sighed. 'It's a long struggle.'

'In Chamonix?'

'There are times you even think you're ahead. You know, there was always one thing about Cabot: you're up there together, nothing, just space under both of you, but somehow you're a little farther out than he is, you're risking more.'

'How?'

'I don't know. That's just the way it is. You know what I liked about him, the thing I envy most? Carol, his wife.'

'I'm getting married next month myself. Hey, what's this?' He had picked up a book.

Rand looked up. He reached for it. 'Let me have that,' he said. 'Do you know anything at all about this guy?'

'Who is it?'

'Mayakovsky. I have to find out more about him.' He was flipping through the pages.

'Never heard of him.'

'And you're a doctor. Here. Have you ever read his last letter? He wrote it to a girl friend. You know, he shot himself. *The small boat of love is shattered against the flow of life. I'm through with it. Useless to dredge up the sorrow, the sadness, the . . .*' Here he faltered, 'I don't know how to say it, *les torts réciproques . . . Be happy. V.M.*'

Banning had not been impressed with Rand when he first met him. He hadn't known that much about him, he'd even thought him ordinary.

'I didn't know you were interested in poetry.'

'Actually I'm interested in very few things, that's the problem,' he muttered. 'Do you want to know what I'm really interested in? It's disgusting. Making people envious – that's it. That's all it is. I wasn't always that way. There may have been a tendency but not much. I was stronger.'

'I envy you,' Banning said.

'Don't.'

That was what he would remember, those words casually uttered and Rand lying asleep, as if dead, the snow unmelted on the floor near his boots. In the morning there was light through the ice-glazed windows and the sudden rumble of something outside – Banning jumped up to see what it was. The train to Montenvers was passing not far off. In the daylight the room was even barer, an inventory of its contents would not fill a dozen lines. Above the shelf there was a postcard pinned. The handwriting was a woman's. The final line he remembered also. *I know you have glory waiting for you,* it read. It was signed with an initial C.

CHAPTER THIRTY-TWO

THERE WERE TWO reporters waiting by the bridge over the tracks. They followed him across.

What could he tell them? he asked disarmingly – he was taking the train, that was all. One of them snapped pictures as they stood on the platform. There was a crowd. People were turning their heads to look.

Was he going up to the Walker? Was he going to climb it alone?

'You've got all these people wondering what's going on,' he said.

'You're carrying a lot of equipment,' they noted.

'It's not as heavy as it looks.'

'How many kilos?'

'Oh, maybe ten.'

'You mean twenty-five,' one said.

They talked in a bantering fashion; Rand denied nothing, but admitted very little. Meanwhile a strange metallic pounding hung in the air. He turned to look – it was a workman repairing the rails.

'What are conditions like on the Walker?'

'I'm not really sure. Have you heard?' he asked.

'Ice,' one of them said.

'I wouldn't be surprised'. He looked again toward the workman. The hammering had a solid quality, unhurried, clear. Iron singing as it entered granite – the thought crossed all three minds.

'Perhaps you should take him with you,' they joked.

A light turned red. In the distance, a somewhat ominous rumble. The train was coming.

From Montenvers he descended to the glacier, a lone figure with a pack. There were groups of inexperienced climbers learning to walk on the ice, others heading up in various directions or coming back. Gradually he passed them, passed the Charpoua and the iron ladders fixed to the rock at Les Egralets. By noon he had started up the Leschaux Glacier itself. He was moving steadily, stopping only occasionally to rest.

Afterward they said he had seemed different, it was hard to describe. He was a bit dishevelled, perhaps, as if a measure of caring had lessened. His ardour had lost its edge. They expected him to appear at the Leschaux hut, but he didn't go up to the Leschaux. He went on alone up the glacier.

He'd been paying no attention to what was ahead, but more and more he could feel it there, a presence in the sky. He could sense it as, from miles away, one feels the sea. He was carrying too much, ice axe, crampons, a sleeping bag, food for five days. Every pound was crucial. Still, he needed it all. He had a sketch of the route with every scrap of information he could find, where it crossed the ridge line, where the rock was no good. Finally he stopped and raised his head.

Dark, flanked by snowfields, the greatest pillar of the Grandes Jorasses soared four thousand feet in an almost unbroken line. The bottom was in sunlight. Farther up, it was nearly black.

A human face is always changing but there is a moment when it seems perfect, complete. It has earned its appearance. It is unalterable. So it was with him, that day, as he gazed up. He was thirty – thirty-one if the truth be known – his courage was unbroken. Above him lay the Walker.

There had been good weather, a spell of it, perhaps enough to clear the ridge of ice. From the base he could not tell, the scale was too vast. He might be early, but the weather would not hold indefinitely. The snowfields didn't seem too large. The rocks at the base looked clean.

He had planned for two nights on the face. About halfway up lay the Grey

Tower, the most difficult part. From there, retreat was said to be impossible, the only way off was to continue to the top. He could see no other parties; he was alone. For a moment he felt the chill of desolation but gradually took heart. He began to scramble over easy rocks, not thinking far ahead, emptied soon of everything except the warmth of movement.

It was cold by the time he reached the first ice which was harder than he expected, even with crampons. He had an intimation that worse was ahead. Carefully he worked his way upward.

In the late afternoon he had reached a vertical wall. The holds were not good. He had climbed only a short distance when he decided he could not do it carrying his pack and climbed down and took it off. He tied one end of the rope to it, then started again with the other end fastened to his waist. The rock was slick in places, he didn't trust it. He was climbing poorly, making mistakes. A wind was blowing. It made the face seem even more ominous and bare.

Suddenly his foot slipped off. He caught himself.

'Now, don't get stupid,' he muttered. 'You can do this. You could do this blindfolded.' He looked up. There was a piton. Just get to that. It had been climbed before, he told himself, it had been climbed many times.

'A little farther . . . There.'

He clipped a karabiner in and tied to it. He was breathing hard. More than that, he was chastened. He pulled up his pack.

On top, finally, was a ledge, a good one. He paused to calm himself. It was late. If he went on, he might be caught by darkness. It was better, he decided, to bivouac here.

The stars that night were brilliant. From the ledge he gazed up at them. They were very bright – their brightness might be a warning. It could mean a change of weather. It was cold, but was it that cold? He could not be sure. He felt secure but utterly alone. Within himself, over and over again, he was turning the vow to climb this pillar. The higher he went, the icier it would become.

The difficult part lay ahead. In a corner of his mind he was already abandoning the attempt. He could not allow that corner to spread. He tried to stop thinking. He could not.

In the morning it took him nearly an hour to sort out his things. It was very cold. There is a way of climbing dangerous pitches with the rope tied in a large loop and clipped to pitons along the way, but it means going back down to unclip and takes time. He tried this once or twice but found it clumsy and abandoned it.

The rock was now glazed with ice. He had to clear the holds; even then a thin covering sometimes remained. This part of the Walker the sun did not reach. Several times he slipped. Talking to himself, reciting, cursing, he kept on, stopping to read the route description whenever he could . . . *65 ft with overhang.* The folds had begun to tear.

He began the overhang. The pack was pulling him backward, off the face. He was afraid, but the mountain does not recognize fear. He hammered in a piton and clipped an *étrier* to it. He waited, letting the venom drain from his blood, and blew on his fingertips stinging from the cold. The Grey Tower was still ahead.

The ice became worse. Things he could have done with ease were dangerous, even paralyzing. Off to the west there were clouds. He was nervous, frightened. He had begun to lose belief in the possibility of going on. The long, vertical reaches beneath him were pulling at his feet. Suddenly he saw that he could be killed, that he was only a speck. His chest was empty, he kept swallowing. He was ready to turn back. The rock was implacable; if he lost his concentration, his will, it would not allow him to remain. The wind from yesterday was blowing. He said to himself, come on, Cabot would do this. The kid at the Choucas.

At the foot of the Tower was a difficult traverse. Slight holds, icy footing, the exposure severe. There are times when height isn't bad, when it exhilarates. If you are frightened it is another story.

He was standing with one foot on a small knob. Above was a steep slab with a crack running up it. He began chopping it clean with his axe. He started up. The footholds were off to the side, no more than the rims of faint scars, sometimes only a fraction of an inch deep. He had to clear these, too. His toe kept slipping. The crack had begun to slant, forcing him out on the slab.

There was nothing to hold to. He tried to put in a piton, bits of ice hitting him in the face. There were only ten feet more, but the rock was slick and mercilessly smooth. Beneath, steeply tilted, the slab shot out into space.

His hand searched up and down. Everything was happening too fast, nothing was happening. The ice had weaknesses but he could not find them. His legs began to tremble. The secret one must keep despite everything had begun to spill, he could not prevent it. He was not going to be able to do this. He knew it. The will was draining from him.

He had the resignation of one condemned. He knew the outcome, he no longer cared, he merely wanted it to end. The wind had killed his fingers.

'You can do it,' he told himself, 'you can do it.'

He was clinging to the face. Slowly his head bent forward to rest against it like a child resting against its mother. His eyes closed. 'You can do it,' he said.

They came up the meadow to find him. He was sitting in the sunlight in a long-sleeved undershirt and faded pants like a convalescent.

'What turned you back? Was it the weather?'

'No,' he answered slowly, as if he might have forgotten. There was nothing to withhold. He waited silently.

'Technical problems . . .' someone suggested.

He could hear the faint whirring of a camera. The microphone was being held near.

'There was ice up there, but it wasn't that.' He looked at one or another of them. A summer breeze was moving the meadow grass. 'I didn't prepare,' he said, 'that was the trouble. I wasn't ready. I lacked the courage.'

It was true. Something had gone out of him.

'But turning back takes courage.'

He nodded. 'Not as much as going on.'

'What will you do now? What plans do you have?'

'I don't know, really.'

'Will you stay in Chamonix?'

'I'd like to get away for a little rest, I think.'

'To the States?'

'Perhaps,' he said.

As they were packing to leave, one of the journalists came over to him. 'I don't know if you heard the news. It just came this morning.'

'What news?'

'Your friend, Cabot . . .'

'What about him?'

The air itself seemed to empty.

'He fell.'

'Fell? Where?'

'In Wyoming, I think.' He turned to someone else. 'Wyoming, *n'est-ce pas? Où Cabot est tombé'*.

It was Wyoming.

'The Tetons,' Rand said.

'Perhaps. I don't know.'

'Yes, sure it was the Tetons. Was he hurt?'

'Yes.'

'How bad?'

'I think very.'

The blood was slipping from his face. 'But he's alive.'

A faint shrug.

'You don't know?'

They spoke quickly to one another in French.

'Yes, he's alive.'

'How far did he fall?' Rand cried.

'It's not certain. A long way.'

CHAPTER THIRTY-THREE

HE HAD SLEPT all afternoon, or nearly. He was listless, exhausted. The days seemed long.

Toward evening he wrote some letters. He stood on the steps of the post office after it had closed. Faces he recognized passed. He was not sure what he felt, if he was merely nervous and depressed or if the curve of life itself had turned downward. From the outside he seemed unchanged, his face, his clothes, more – his rank. He remained, in the eyes of some, a legend. *Il faut payer.*

Later that night, in a café near the centre of town, he saw a familiar face. It was Nicole Vix, alone. She looked older. There were circles beneath her eyes. For a moment she glanced in his direction, their eyes met. It was a shock, like one of those relentless stories where as she goes down in the world he rises and years later they see one another again. He could hardly believe this was the woman for whom he was racked with longing that first, hard winter. She was worn, dispirited. Her moment had passed. He had an impulse to go over to her – she was someone who had been important to him in a way, someone he remembered.

'Hello.' She looked up. 'Are you still working at the bank?' he asked her.

'Pardon?'

'Do you still work at the bank?'

'No,' she said, as if she had never seen him before.

'Where are you now?'

'I'm sorry,' she said.

'Don't you remember me?' It was about three years ago, the winter.

'I'm sorry,' she shrugged.

In that instant he tasted a bitterness that was intense.

If he could have left that night, he would have. He had finally turned toward home, his thoughts were all there. Still, they nodded to him as he came along the path from the Biolay in the morning, raised their hands in greeting behind shop windows. He felt like someone who had retired. A strange music – final chords – hung over the town.

On a Sunday he came down the road carrying his things. The lowest field was filled with buses, they were parked in ranks. The people who had come on them had not even wandered off. They were having picnics on card tables. Men in undershirts were lying in the grass, their wives or girl friends minding children.

At the hotel across from the station were two busloads of Japanese. They were getting out to have lunch at long tables set beneath the trees. All of them were neatly dressed, polite. The women wore sweaters. Many were young.

He stopped among them as if they were children. He was a head taller. He spoke to them in French. At first they did not answer, they were too shy, but his voice and manner were so friendly that soon they began to respond. Would they like a souvenir of Chamonix, he asked? He unfastened his pack and took out his pitons – they were used for climbing, up there, in the mountains, he explained. They were put in the rock.

'Ahh,' they said, uncomprehending.

'Here. Like this.'

'Ah!' They were giggling, talking. 'Weight heavy.'

'Very heavy. Take it, it's for you.' He was handing them out.

'Oh, thank you. Thank you.'

'Where are you from?'

'Kyoto.'

'Here, take it. You, too.' He was giving it away, the worn steel he had driven into granite that faces blue air. 'This one,' he said, 'was used on the Dru.'

They tried to understand him. Ah, yes. The Dru.

CHAPTER THIRTY-FOUR

CATHERIN STEPPED from the doorway and into the sunlight. Her car was across the way near a small park surrounded by trees – really not much more than a place where three streets came together. The grass was always tall and untended. Though it faced Vigan's house, was only a few feet away, she had never entered it. She was searching for her keys when she noticed someone sitting in the shade. From the first moment she recognized him. She waited there, her heart racing nervously, as he rose and came toward her.

'Hello, Catherin,' he said.

He had changed from the last time she had seen him, even from the interviews on television. She could not tell what it was. She greeted him more or less calmly, hardly conscious of what she was saying.

'You look surprised to see me,' he said.

'Not really.'

'Didn't you get my letter?'

'What letter?'

'I wrote to you, it was at least a week ago.'

'I never received it,' she said simply.

'That's strange.' He waited. 'Well, I said I might be coming, that's all.'

She began to look for her keys again. He stood there. His letter had not reached her, nor in a sense had he. There was a distance between them, the invisible distance between what we possess and what we will never possess. She was even dressed differently. She was wearing clothes he had never seen before.

'How long have you been here?' she asked, not looking up from her handbag. Vigan had left the house only an hour earlier. The cook had then come. 'Did you just arrive?'

'I got here at about eight this morning.'

'I see.'

'I walked around the town for a while . . .'

'I see.'

'Not really. What are you looking for?'

'I have them,' she announced, holding them up. 'How did you find the house? Well, you had the address, I suppose.'

'It's no secret, is it?'

'No.'

'How have you been?' he said.

'Very well. And you? You look a little tired.'

'I've been travelling.'

'From where?'

'Chamonix.'

'Yes, of course.'

'How's your baby?' he asked.

'He's fine.'

'What did you name him?'

'Jean,' she said, the way the French say it.

'Jean.' He repeated it once or twice. 'How did you pick Jean?'

'It goes with Vigan,' she said.

'Ah. What . . .' He found himself hesitating. 'What does he look like?'

'He looks a bit like you.'

'Is that right?'

'Yes.'

She had nothing for him, he could see that. Nothing remained. She was cool, uninterested. She had already assumed the beauty that belongs to strangers.

'Do you think I could see him?'

She did not reply. Within her was confusion. Further, she was nervous – someone coming along the street might see them standing here. Vigan himself might return. Ever since the baby had come he was more affectionate and unpredictable. He might turn the corner at any moment with a huge bunch of flowers on the seat beside him. And yet, here before her was the lost, unforgotten face of the man who was the father, who would always be.

'Well?'

'I don't think you should have come,' was all she could say.

'I had to.'

'No, you didn't.'

'It was now or never,' he said simply.

'What do you mean?'

'I'm going home.'

She felt a shock go through her. Even though he had abandoned her, he was now doing more, he was vanishing forever from her world.

'When are you going?'

'Tomorrow. I just came to say good-bye.'

'Ah, well. He's asleep,' she said. 'He's taking his morning nap. Besides the cook is there.'

'I don't want to see the cook.'

'Look, it's very difficult.'

He said nothing. He had only a mild desire to see his child, it was merely curiosity, but the brevity, the calmness of her refusal was annoying him.

'You know, I'm getting married,' she said. 'Henri is going to adopt him.'

'When?'

'In the fall.'

'So I may never see him again. This could be the last time.'

It was everything, his worn clothes, the faint lines in his forehead, the innocence that clung to him no matter what. He was not weak, he was not begging, he stood there patiently.

'You must promise to go,' she said. 'You must give me your word.'

'Don't worry.'

'You promise?'

'You seem nervous about something. What is it? What do you think I'm going to do, steal him? I want to look at him, that's all. Is that so much?'

'Wait here,' she said and went inside.

He closed his eyes. When he opened them again, the street was empty. It was not hard to imagine he was elsewhere, in any provincial town, even Chamonix. Behind the walls and fences were small gardens, rows of green laid out in careful mounds. These houses, these villages, except for the antennae on the roofs, were unchanged from a century before. He had grown to know this country which was not his own. He felt a sudden overwhelming grief at the thought of leaving it. Something swept over him like a wave. He felt himself – his chest – beginning to crack, to fall apart. He could not help it. He loved her and this love had betrayed him. He stood there trying to withstand things: the houses, people passing, his own worthlessness. He wanted to run, to come back another time with his strength renewed, when he could hurt her somehow instead of suffering this useless longing, this regret.

Above him he heard a sound. He looked up.

The shutters of a window on the second floor had opened and after a moment Catherin appeared. In her arms she held her child. She stood as if alone, calm, unobserved. She was silent, focusing on it all her attention and love. From that distance Rand could barely discern its face. He could see the small hands, the pale hair. After a while Catherin looked down. The infant was moving its arms.

'What?'

She had said something, a silent word Rand could not make out. But she did not repeat it. Instead she drew the child closely to her, hesitated, and stepped back into the room. After a minute her hands reached out to close the shutters.

'Catherin!'

It seemed as if all that had gone before was a journey, that the road had brought him here and ended. He did not know what to do. He stood there. Above him the leaves were sighing faintly, the weight of languorous hours upon them, of endless summer days.

It was in Grenoble on the way north that what she had said finally came to him, like a piece of a puzzle that is turned over and over and suddenly falls into place. He saw it plainly, the long blank wall of the house, the window, the small arms moving aimlessly, one simple word: good-bye.

CHAPTER THIRTY-FIVE

A PALE AFTERNOON hung over the sea. It seemed that California was even more crowded, there were more people, more cars. The string of houses stretched farther up the coast. New businesses, signs. At the same time, he recognized it all. It was unchanged. Near Trancas a car slowed down to pick him up. The driver was a heavyset man in a rumpled suit. He'd come straight from Mexico City, he said, heading for Seattle. He'd only stopped for gas.

'Where are you heading for?' he asked.

'Up to Santa Barbara.'

'You should have caught the local. What's your name?'

'Rand.'

'Call me Tiger,' he said. He was balding, hair combed long across his scalp. He hadn't shaved. 'Ever been to Mexico?'

'Yeah.'

'I go there all the time. You can have a fabulous time in Mexico. It used to be you could see championship fights for five dollars. That was twenty years ago. Things have changed. When's the last time you were there?'

'Not for a while. I've been in France.'

'Is that right?' he said. 'Where were you, in Paris? I've been to Paris. I used to go there a lot. Are you going back?'

'Maybe. I don't know.'

'You want a good address?'

'Okay.'

He glanced over, 'I mean, really good.'

'Sure,' Rand said.

'The Louvre!' he burst out laughing and reached into his pocket. 'You smoke cigars? Here. Hey, why don't you drive with me to Seattle? Ever been there? I bet you haven't. Great place. That's where I live.' Come on. My wife will cook us a tremendous dinner. Her name's Galena, how do you like that? She's Russian. She's a goddess, a real goddess. They have an expression for women like her. You know what it is?'

'No.'

'Heavy hitter. You like that? That's what she is.'

He dropped Rand off on the highway at Santa Barbara.

'See you around,' he said. He sped off.

The day was warm. The sea horizon shimmered. Birds were singing as he walked uphill.

The house was a white Victorian or at least influenced by the period. It was low, only one storey high, and set back from the street.

He rang the bell. There was a sound of footsteps, a pause, and Carol opened the door. She was in a shirt and pants. Her face was bare as if she had just gotten up or washed.

'Rand!' she cried. She embraced him. 'I'm so glad to see you. You look wonderful. Did you just get in?'

'This morning,' he said. 'How are you?'

'Not bad. Really not bad. We've had wonderful weather. Come on in.'

He followed her into the hall.

'Nice house.'

'It's very nice. Wait till you see the garden. Just leave your things there. Let's go in back.'

She led the way through the kitchen and opened the screen door. There was a porch and two wooden steps.

'Darling,' she said, 'look who's here.'

A man was seated by a glass table in the shade of the trees. He turned his head. He was wearing a blue sport shirt with a bamboo pattern. His arms were powerful. He raised one.

'Hello, you bastard.' It was Cabot. He was sitting in a wheelchair. He turned himself around and extended his hand. 'I thought it was time you appeared.'

'Same old Jack. How've you been?' Rand asked.

'What a question.'

'You look fine.'

'Oh, don't mind all this,' Cabot indicated. 'You'll get used to it. When did you get in? How long can you stay? We've got a room for you, did Carol show it to you?'

'Not yet,' she said.

'It's the best room in the house. It's the room I'm going to die in. Come on', – he started off in his wheelchair – 'follow me, as they say.'

He was paralyzed from the waist down, his legs in the limp cloth of a cripple's pants. The fall had almost killed him; he had been in a coma for a week. At first they thought he would never come out of it and only half of him did. For days he lay while they conducted tests and treated him. Meanwhile he was engaged in a secret, crucial effort of his own; he was trying by any means, even by force of will alone, to make some movement with his toes. He could almost see them do it but they never did. He would start again and continue until he was exhausted, lie quietly for a while and begin once more. He had no pain, no feeling, nothing at all. His legs might have belonged to someone else.

'His spine was broken,' Carol explained when they were alone. 'The nerves don't regenerate, I guess you know that. Almost any other nerve they can patch together, but this one they can't.'

'Why is that?'

'The doctor explains it by saying it's like a Transatlantic cable that's been cut. Those thousands of tiny strands, it's impossible to match them up again.'

'And that's it?'

'I'm afraid. He'll never get out of his chair.'

'What else does it affect? Any inner organs?'

'Everything below the waist,' she said.

Outside birds were singing in the full heat of afternoon. The sound seemed to cover the house. Rand felt drowsy. Looking out at the haze-covered hills, he felt he had come to a kind of hospital himself, that he had an illness they would not yet divulge.

That evening Cabot's lawyer dropped by. She was a woman, no older than Rand, aggressive, confident. Her name was Evelyn Kern.

'Glad to meet you,' she said. 'I've heard so much about you.'

They were filing a suit against the insurance company. The settlement after the accident had been small.

'We have to get him some money to live on,' she explained, 'not to mention medical expenses.'

It was very easygoing and casual. They sat and drank. They talked about the past.

'I hear you tried the Walker,' Cabot said.

'That's about all you can say – I tried.'

'What happened?'

Rand shrugged.

'Your glass is empty. Carol, get him a drink, will you? How high did you get?'

'I could have gone higher.'

'A lot higher, as they used to say.'

'What is the Walker?' Evelyn asked.

'It's part of the Grandes Jorasses, a ridge that goes straight up.'

'It sounds terrifying.'

'It's a classic. I always wanted to do the Walker,' Cabot remarked.

'Maybe you will,' Rand said.

There was an awkward silence.

'You going to carry me up that, too?'

'Who knows?'

So began his visit. The garden was filled with pines and a pair of huge palms. Past the back fence was cane grass, tall and rustling. Carol often worked outside, weeding and watering the plants. She knelt on the ground, the nape of her neck bent forward, bare. Her legs were lean and tanned. She sat back, aware of Rand's presence.

'This is my green tent,' she explained. The branches met over her head. Sunlight filtered through.

On the other side of the hedge a neighbour, Mrs. Dabney, was watering. She was in her sixties. She had a kerchief over her head and wore a halter which gave glimpses of ruined flesh. Her husband had had two heart attacks.

Rand sat sunning himself on the steps, shirtless.

'You're going to frighten her,' Carol warned.

'Frighten her?' Mrs Dabney was keeping up a spray of water on her jade trees to show she was occupied. 'She comes a little closer every day.' He raised his voice. 'Those are beautiful hibiscus, Mrs Dabney,' he called.

'They're the state tree of Hawaii,' she answered, 'did you know that?'

'No, I didn't.'

'We were just there for a two-week visit,' she said. 'My husband and I.'

'Is that right?'

'We went to all the islands,' she said with a friendly smile.

Blue Pacific days. In the morning mist, the sound of birds. The dark, shadowy fronds plunged down from the heights of the palms. Carol's footsteps in the hallway. Sometimes, lying in his room, Rand imagined they were lingering.

He knew she was watching him. He could feel her glance in the kitchen or at the table. At times, without deliberation, their eyes would meet – she would not look away. He had always admired her. She was returning this admiration.

Cabot drank. He had two or three before dinner and then wine; he couldn't sleep otherwise. If he came to the surface in the predawn hours the same thoughts kept passing through his mind. The wheelchair with its chrome glinted in the moonlight near his bed.

He had never slept well, even before the accident. In those days when he woke he would dress in the darkness and go out and walk. Sometimes he was gone for hours. When dawn came he would be on the highest point around, watching the sky lighten and then turning homeward.

That had been taken from him. He lay now staring into the dark. He'd prayed to God, he'd read poetry, philosophy, trying to force his life into a new shape. During the day it seemed to work but at night it was different, it all leaked away and he was a boy again imagining the world and what he would do in it, except that his legs lay soft as rags.

He raised himself on his elbow. One at a time, he lifted his legs to the floor. He pulled his wheelchair close and lowered himself into it. Silently he went down the hall.

'Vern.' He pushed open the door. 'Are you awake?'

'No.'

'Talk to me.'

'What's wrong?'

'I can't sleep.'

Rand fumbled with the light.

'If I have a couple of drinks I'm usually all right, but tonight I just couldn't sleep. It's funny, I used to watch my father pouring it down. I had nothing but contempt for him in those days. Some nights he couldn't even talk.'

'What time is it?' Rand asked.

'About three.'

'Come on in.'

'You don't mind?'

'No.' He sat up. 'No, I've been wanting to talk.'

Cabot grinned. 'You? Talk?'

'I'd like to find out what really is wrong,' Rand said.

'What's wrong? I'm a lousy cripple.'

'Is that true?'

Cabot stared at him.

'I've been watching you. You're sitting there reading. Evelyn comes by, you have a few drinks. You're taking it very calmly.'

'That's what you think.'

'Carol is, too.'

'You just don't know,' Cabot said.

'What do you mean?'

'You don't have any idea. I'm not calm. I'm just waiting.'

'Waiting for what?'

'The truth is, I was planning to shoot myself. I told that to someone at the hospital, another paraplegic. I thought I was going to show him how a man behaves or some damn thing. All he said was, make sure you don't miss and paralyze your arms.'

'How is it you still have strength in your arms?'

'Didn't Carol explain it to you?'

'She tried to.'

'My arms . . .' He reached over for Rand's hand. He began to press it to one side, his other hand holding a wheel of the chair. They struggled against one another. The sinews of his neck stood out; slowly he was forcing Rand's arm down. Finally, he released it. He was breathing hard. 'It's down here I'm a little weak,' he said.

'I was going to ask about that.'

Cabot said nothing. He seemed almost disinterested.

'What exactly do you have left?'

'Below the waist, nothing.'

'Nothing?'

'Absolutely zero,' Cabot said amiably.

'I was right. You're taking it calmly.'

'Well, you try it.'

'And your wife is, too.'

'She hasn't got much choice.'

'There's always a choice.'

'She hasn't left yet, if that's what you mean.'

'Oh, she's not going to leave . . .'

'I'm glad to hear that.'

'. . . not as long as you're in a wheelchair.'

'What makes you so sure?'

Rand shrugged.

'Because I'm not,' Cabot said.

'She wouldn't leave a cripple.'

'You think that's what's keeping her here?'

'Ah, Jack, I don't care about that. I'm thinking about something else. You know the first thing I heard was that you were probably going to die. But you didn't, you fought your way back. Then I hear that you're crippled . . .'

'Go on.'

'Do I believe that?'

'That's not really the question,' Cabot said quietly. 'The question is: can *I* somehow believe it?'

Until morning, when the pale green tendrils of Mrs Dabney's star pine waved dreamily as if beneath the sea, they talked, their voices sometimes raised in argument but more often quiet, confiding. There was an understanding between them, the kind that has its roots at the very source of life. There were days they would always remember: immense, heartbreaking effort and at the top, what rapture, they had shaken each other's hand with glowing faces, their very being confirmed.

CHAPTER THIRTY-SIX

CAROL HAD GONE for the evening. The house was still, it was the chance Rand had been waiting for. He sauntered into the room and sat down.

'Evelyn was here earlier. You missed her,' Cabot said. He was watching the evening news as usual, a glass in his hand.

'What did she have to say?'

'Oh, legal stuff. She wanted to talk about you. She's very interested in you.'

Rand had gotten up and was pouring a drink.

'It probably doesn't surprise you,' Cabot said.

'No.'

'I don't know what you said to her. You told her something about climbing ...'

'Too much,' Rand commented.

'Anyway, it floored her.'

The hour was tranquil. In the dusk a bat flew recklessly above the dark pines, changing direction like a bird that has just been hit.

'I decided to see if I could shock her,' Rand admitted. 'So I told her the truth.'

'Such as?'

'I told her I'd been climbing for fifteen years. For most of that, ten years anyway, it was the most important thing in my life. It was the only thing. I sacrificed everything to it. Do you know the one thing I learned about climbing? The one single thing?'

'What?'

'It is of no importance whatsoever.'

'Is that what you told her?'

'Whatsoever,' he said.

'What is?'

'I don't have to tell you: the real struggle comes afterwards.'

Sometimes when they talked it seemed as if they had arranged themselves casually – Cabot had merely sat down in a wheelchair that happened to be there. It was as if he might stand up at any moment, discarding his incapacity like throwing off a blanket. Sometimes he actually seemed on the very point of rising and then, as if warned, he relented. Rand had noticed this. It's difficult to know what convinced him, perhaps something hidden. Truth lay beneath the surface.

The California night was falling, the ocean darkness. Another day had passed. He sipped his drink and reflected quietly.

'Something's happened to us, Jack.'

'Has it? I hadn't noticed.'

'It's happened to me, too. I'll tell you something I bet you're going to try and deny.'

'What?'

'You're being betrayed.'

'Ah, that.'

'I mean it.'

'We never are but by ourselves betrayed ...', Cabot recited.

'That's only half of it. Do you want to know the rest?'

There was a silence. Cabot waited.

'The people who claim to be helping you, Carol, Evelyn, the doctors, they want to keep you in that chair.'

'Oh, have another drink.'

'I mean it.' He was silent for a moment. 'You know, I always believed in you, I did from the first.'

'So?'

'In your strength, desire. Your will to succeed.'

Cabot made some vague reply.

'I still believe in you.'

'What are you getting at?'

'You've surrendered. I've seen you though, when you weren't aware of it, start to stand up.'

'It's a reflex.'

'I know you can do it,' Rand said.

Cabot wheeled himself to the table near the door to turn on the lights.

'I know you can do it, but you're not going to. You've given up.' He was speaking to Cabot's back. 'And if you've given up, where does that leave me?'

'You?'

Rand waited.

'I don't know,' Cabot admitted. He was filling his glass. 'I know where it leaves me. I'm not a victim of hysteria or some destructive urge. I know you think that, but there are such things as physical problems. No amount of belief can overcome them. I mean, death is an example. Do you believe in death?'

'I don't know.'

'Well, I do.'

'But you're not dead.'

'No.'

There was a dedication in Rand's voice, a seriousness that would not be put aside by indifference or drink. He was trying to force out the truth or some form of it, difficult because truth was reluctant and could alter its appearance. It was one thing in the high reaches of the Alps. It was another in a house in Montecito lighted against the darkness where Cabot was sitting on a rubber cushion in a gleaming chromium chair with something twisted in him, some crucial part that could not be touched.

'You were always ahead of me,' Rand said. 'I'd never have gone to Europe except for you.'

'You might have.'

'Do you remember the nights we camped at the foot of the Dru?'

'. . . unfailingly bringing rain.'

'You gave me all that. You made me do the greatest things of my life.'

Cabot didn't know what to reply. 'It's funny, isn't it?' was all he could say.

'Now you just have to do one more thing . . .'

'You know, you're like my aunt. She says if I only pray, if I pray hard enough, then who knows what will happen? She won't stop telling me that, she'll never stop believing in it. She's a nice woman, I've always liked her, but she's not a doctor. God's a doctor, I know, but Auntie, listen to me, even God can't make me walk. I've tried. I really have tried.' He looked at Rand openly. He was too proud to beg but he was asking for understanding. 'Believe me,' he said.

'I've talked to your doctor.'

'Oh, yeah?'

'He told me something I can't understand: there's nothing physically wrong with you. Something is keeping you in that chair.'

Cabot in the confusion of drunkenness was hearing things he knew were untrue. They seemed to swim crazily, daring him to refute them.

'All right, something's keeping me in this chair,' he said wearily.

'What is it?'

'I don't know.'

'Have you lost your courage? Like me?' Rand said.

'I don't think so.'

'Can you prove it?' Rand said. He poured his glass half full like an adversary prepared to spend the night and at the same time raised his hand from between his legs. In it, cool and heavy, was a pistol.

Cabot stared at it. 'That's mine,' he remarked.

'There's a bullet in it. You don't have to do anything I don't do.'

A car turning up the driveway, Mrs Dabney at the back door, the telephone ringing, Cabot was waiting for a summons back to reality.

'If you've lost your courage, you've lost everything. It doesn't matter after that.' Rand drank. 'I'll go first.'

Cabot suddenly reached for the gun.

'Don't,' Rand said, holding it away from him. He cocked it and spun the cylinder. 'The leader never falls.'

Cabot watched him put the muzzle almost carelessly next to his temple and pull the trigger. There was an empty click.

'Your turn.'

'No.'

Rand said nothing.

'I can't,' Cabot said.

'Have a drink.'

'I've had enough.'

'You've already died,' Rand said.

'Not quite.'

'I was with you. We were caught up there. Lightning was hitting the peak. You're not going to back down now?'

'I'm not drunk enough.'

'Go ahead,' Rand commanded.

Cabot stared at the gun. Its darkness was intense. It was radiating power. He picked it up. He put it to his head. Slowly he pulled the trigger. *Click*. The hammer fell on an empty chamber. A sudden rush of happiness, almost bliss, swept over him. Rand reached for the gun.

'Climbing,' he said. He raised it to his head once more. Another click. 'Come on up.'

The bullet was in one of the remaining chambers. The gun came to his hand like a card in a poker game. Cabot barely looked at it. He was staring at Rand. He had a sense of dizziness as the blunt, heavy muzzle touched his eye, an eye that would not even, he thought clumsily, have time to blink. It was going to end like this. He resisted it, he tried not to believe it even as he knew it was true. The end, which was impossible, which was never going to come. His face was wet. His heart was beating wildly. His face showed utter calm. He squeezed the trigger.

Click.

'Now we're getting somewhere,' Rand said.

'That's enough.'

Rand had hold of the barrel,

'We've come this far.' His eyes were burning, his concentration was intense. 'One more.'

He raised the gun. Cabot reached forward to stop him. A glass went over and crashed to the floor. Almost in the wake of it, concealed, the hammer fell.

Silence. Cabot took the gun.

'That's it,' he said.

'No.'

They stared at one another.

'I can't.'

'One more.'

He closed his eyes. The room was spinning.

'You have to,' he heard.

The lights of the world would go out, the night devour him, he would be at peace. He was this close to it. His thoughts were tumbling, pouring past. He was clinging to the final moments.

'Pull.'

He could not.

'Pull!'

His finger tightened.

'Pull!' Rand urged.

The hammer fell. A click.

He hardly knew what was happening. Rand had leaped to his feet.

'You did it!' he was shouting. 'You did it! Now get up! Get up! Suddenly he grew calmer. 'You can do it,' he pledged. 'You can! Get up!'

He began to shake the wheelchair. Cabot's head was bobbing. They were like drunken students breaking furniture. Belief was flooding the room.

'You can! You can!'

Across the narrow path between the houses, Mrs Dabney sitting with her bathrobe-clad husband could hear the shouting.

A violent force was pulling at the wheelchair, tilting it, spilling Cabot to the floor where he sat in a heap, legs bent curiously, and began to laugh.

'Walk to me!'

Cabot was laughing.

'Walk to me! Jack, you did it. You can walk!'

Cabot tried to catch his breath. The room was spinning around. 'Oh, God,' he was pleading helplessly, 'please.' It took him a moment to realize he was alone.

'Vern?'

He heard nothing. He called, dragging himself toward the door, 'Vern.'

The hallway was empty. There was a faint sound from the back room. Even if he had never heard it before, it was unmistakable, the sound of cartridges being inserted.

'Vern!' he called.

Rand came out, his hand at his side. He seemed strangely calm. 'This works now,' he said.

Cabot's glance fell for a second to the gun.

'Look at you. Your chair's on its side, you're sitting there. You can't even get up.'

'I can get up,' Cabot said.

'You're useless. We're both useless,' he said. 'The only question is, who should shoot who?'

He seemed completely dispirited. Cabot felt a sudden, deep sympathy toward him – he did not know why it was so overwhelming.

'Jack . . .', he heard.

'Yes?'

He looked up. The gun was raised.

'I'm going to count to ten. If you don't get up and walk toward me, I'm going to pull the trigger, I swear that before God. Because you're not a cripple. I know that.'

'I know what you're trying to do.'

'One.'

'I didn't know there was no bullet in it,' he said. 'You weren't risking anything, but I was.'

'Two.'

'Oh, hell,' Cabot said, abandoning the struggle. He turned his head, not even looking up. He'd had enough of it.

'Three.'

Cabot waited stoically.

'Four.' Rand was holding the gun in both hands, steadying it.

'I can't walk,' Cabot said impatiently.

'Five.'

'Jesus Christ, I can't even piss.'

'Six.'

'Go ahead, shoot,' he said.

'Seven. Get up, Jack. Please.'

Cabot raised his eyes. As if the idea were his own, he put his palms on the floor. He began to try and stand.

'Eight. Get up.'

With the strength of his upper body which was considerable, he was trying – like an animal in the road dragging its hindquarters – he was struggling to somehow get to his feet. His face was wet. The veins stood out in his forehead.

'Nine.'

He did not hear it. Everything in him was concentrated on the effort.

'Ten,' Rand said.

A deafening explosion. Cabot fell. Another, the sound was immense in the closeness of the hall. The second shot, like the first, made a hole in the wall behind Cabot's head. He was lying, cheek pressed to the floor. Rand fired again. Once more.

Carol came home toward midnight. She'd been at a friend's. She found her husband on the couch, his shirt dirty, hair dishevelled. The wheelchair sat empty.

'What is it. What happened?'

He was watching the television. The room was a mess.

'Nothing,' he said. 'It's all over. I thought you were coming home at eleven.'

'I lost track of the time. What have you been doing?'

'Nothing, really. Rand fired some shots.'

'Shots?'

'Mrs Dabney got excited and called the police.'

'He fired shots at what? Where is he?'

'He's gone,' Cabot said. 'I guess he'll be back. He borrowed the car.'

Just then she noticed the bullet strikes.

'My God,' she said. 'What are those?'

'Holes,' he said.

CHAPTER THIRTY-SEVEN

'LOUISE?'

'Yes,' a sleepy voice said, 'who's this?'

'You don't know?'

There was a pause.

'Rand? Is that you?' she said. 'Where are you?'

'I see you haven't forgotten my voice anyway.'

'What time is it?'

'It's about seven-thirty.'

'You always did get up early. Where are you? Are you in town?'

'No.'

'Where?'

'Oh, I'm up north here. How've you been?'

'Pretty good. And you?'

'How's Lane?'

'I'll tell you when I see you. He's been in trouble.'

'What kind of trouble?'

'I'd rather not talk about it on the phone.'

'That's too bad. Is he there?'

'He spent the night at a friend's. Where, up north?'

He looked around.

'Oh, I don't know,' he said. 'I'm in some gas station.'

'When did you get back?'

'A few days ago.'

'Well, come on down.'

'I will,' he said. 'I wish I were there right now.'

'Well, why aren't you?'

'I had some things to do.' He'd wanted to talk to her, but now he did not feel like it. There was really nothing to say. 'You know those boxes of mine?

'Yes. What about them?'

'There's a good fishing rod in one of them.'

'A fishing rod?'

'Lane might like it.'

'Are you all right?' she asked. 'You sound a little strange.'

'Do I? No, I'm all right.'

'I got your letter,' she said.

Farther down the road there was a bridge beneath which a small stream was flowing. He walked down the embankment and washed his face. The sun was coming up behind the hills. There were empty beer cans in the water.

He drove with a lazy contentment, his thoughts drifting. The invincible country floated past. He was seeing things with a fantastic slowness, faces in windshields, names of towns. He was thinking of his father and going hunting as a boy. They had an old 20-gauge and a handful of shells. The wind was blowing across the fields. Far off they could see the huge, wavering flocks heading south. They had no decoys. A man came along and told them they'd never get any geese that way. They had no licence either.

A whole life seems to pass on the road. The sun shifts from one window to another, houses, cities, farms rise and disappear. In a field near Shandon he saw a dead colt, the mare standing alongside it, motionless, leaning slightly. The colt seemed shrunken as if melting into the earth.

He remembered the year they drove from Indiana with a bag of hard-boiled eggs and nothing else. His dog wouldn't eat eggs, they had no extra money for food. They parked by a river in Utah in the evening. Clouds of insects rose. The current slid by, green and silver. In Elko they drove up a bumpy road to a kennel next to – he would never forget – the Marvin Motel.

'We'll be back for him in a couple of days,' his father told the man.

The dog was sitting behind the wire fence, his white chest showing, watching them drive away.

He thought of Cabot. The mountain had been covered with snow when they were coming down. They had abseiled down the ridge. It was cold, especially lower down when they passed through waterfalls. Cabot was strong, stronger than he was by then. They came down as fast as they could, it was riskier than the climb.

He turned east near Volta and crossed the valley. By then it was afternoon. He was not, he said to himself, a short-term soldier. The hands on the wheel were veteran's hands. His heart was a loyal heart. There is a length to things determined by hidden law. To understand this, to accept it, is to acquire the wisdom of beasts. He was a veteran, a leader, but his pack was scattered, gone. Behind him was a California where wave after wave of migrants had come to rest. They had bought houses, worked, run stores. Behind were refineries, suburbs, empty bottles in the streets. Ahead was the final refuge.

The road was empty, it seemed to drink him, to lead him forth. The late sun was flooding the land. In the rearview mirror it was brilliant, like a shot. One white horse was standing alone, no sky, no earth, like a print.

He saw himself in the mirror, past the life of which he was the purest exemplar, which he thought would never spoil. He was suddenly too old. His face was one he once would have scorned. He was facing winter now, without a coat, without a place to rest.

That evening he came to a town, Lakeville. Dirt sidewalks, frame houses, yards stacked with firewood. The supermarket had its lights on. On a hill was an abandoned church. Enormous trees. Quiet, cool air. Near the outskirts was a corrugated iron warehouse. Kids were playing softball near the trailer park. He sat on an old engine block. The evening was silver and calm. He had meant to drive farther but he could not. Something had gone wrong. He was almost in tears.

He had gone as far as he could, had climbed as high. He could go no farther. He knew what was happening, his knees were beginning to tremble, he was coming off. At that moment he did not want to slip, still grasping desperately for a hold, but instead to suddenly jump clear, to fall like a saint, arms outstretched, face to the sky.

He thought of dying. He longed for it. His world had come apart. He wanted to have everything, every animal, insect, the snails on the garden path, girls with their sunburned shoulders, airliners glinting in air, all, to cease their clamour and resume at last the harmony he had the right to expect. He had no fear of dying, there was no such thing, there was only changing form, entering the legend he was already part of.

He lay all night on the ground, face down, exhausted. Early in the morning he headed north. He was going up into the mountains, the Sierras.

There were many stories. A climber was seen alone, high up on Half Dome or camping by himself in the silent meadows above Yosemite. He was seen one summer in Baja California and again at Tahquitz. For several years there was someone resembling him in Morrison, Colorado – tall, elusive, living in a cabin a few miles outside of town. But after a while he, too, moved on.

Cabot always expected a card or letter. It would be slow in coming, he knew, but eventually he would hear something. For a long time he believed that one way or another Rand would reappear. As the years passed, it became less and less sure.

They talked of him, however, which was what he had always wanted. The acts themselves are surpassed but the singular figure lives on. The day finally came when they realized they would never know for certain. Rand had somehow succeeded. He had found the great river. He was gone.

CHAPTER THIRTY-EIGHT

IT WAS A GREY day. The clouds were low and level as the land. The gulf was flat. Birds were sitting on it. From time to time the surface of the water broke and scattered – jack were feeding beneath. The sign was unlit at Ruth's. Outside a few cars were parked.

'Watch it! Watch the run!' Bonney cried. 'Ah, hell.'

'Right up the middle,' the bartender said.

'They're killing us. All right, give 'em the field goal.'

'What is it, thirty yards?'

They were silent, watching the preparations.

'Now block it!' Bonney called.

'The kick is up . . . it's . . . no good! No good, off to the right!' the announcer said. The crowd was roaring.

'All right!' Bonney cried.

Ruth's was on the highway just at the edge of town. It was a Mexican restaurant at night.

The screen door slammed. Bonney's brother came in. 'Hey, where've you been?' Bonney said. 'I thought you were going to watch the game.'

'I fell asleep. You know what happened? Some woman woke me up at eight this morning.'

'Some woman?'

'Yeah, she was real sorry, she said. She could tell I was asleep. I said, who is this? You know what she said? It's your mother, she said. I said, lady, my mother's been dead for three years.'

'Who was it?'

'How should I know? What's the score?'

'Twenty to three.'

'Favour who?'

'Dallas.'

'I'm dead! What period?'

'Third quarter,' Bonney lied. 'You already missed most of the game.'

'The third quarter? Already?' Dale Bonney pulled up a stool and sat down. He was younger than his brother, not yet thirty. He didn't look like him, he was shorter and his hair was nearly gone. The brothers were inseparable. 'Give us a beer,' he said. 'You make any bets?'

'Did you?'

Dale nodded.

'How many points did you get?'

'Six.'

'Six? Forget it,' Ken Bonney said.

The blue team was moving now. One of their backs had gone thirteen yards.

'Who was that? Was that Hearn?' Ken said. 'Is that who it was?'

'I think so,' the bartender said. 'No, Brockman.'

'Brocklin.'

'Is this really the third quarter?'

There was another run and a fumble.

'Oh, for God's sake!' Ken cried. The runner was hurt, he was lying on his back. '*That's* Hearn!' he said as if he'd suspected it. 'Get him out of there! Hearn, you're through! Put in somebody younger!' The player was being led slowly off the field. Ken turned away from the bar. He made a helpless gesture to the only other customer sitting at one of the tables. 'Would you bet on a team like this?' he asked.

The man looked up. 'Which one?' he said.

'Hearn – what are they thinking of? They *want* to lose.'

There was a pause.

'Go on,' the man said.

'I give up, that's what.'

'You know a lot about it, eh?' There was something too calm, almost indifferent in the voice.

A faint warning, the glint of danger, reached Bonney. He turned away. The door banged. A woman came in wearing soft crepe slacks and high heels. 'Hi, Paula,' he said.

'Hi, Ken.' She sat down with the man at the table. 'Sorry I'm late,' she said.

'How's Fraser?' Ken called from the bar.

'He's fine. He's in Atlanta.'

'What's he doing there?'

'He's living there,' she said. Then, across the table, 'Have you been here long?'

'Forty-two minutes.'

'God, can't you be exact? Who's playing?' she asked.

'I don't know. Dallas and somebody,' he said.

Paula Gerard was a teacher. She was divorced. Actually, she admitted, she'd never been married, she just took his name. She had dark hair and a quick, carefree smile. She always seemed a little untidy, perhaps it was her clothes. She told outrageous stories, especially when she was drinking. She swore they were true.

She'd been divorced for almost a year. Fraser was a businessman. He never really worked. He played tennis, drank, and spent his family's money. He was really very funny, she said. Once they flew to London and on the immigration card under 'Sex' he wrote, yes, a lot. But he was spoiled and weak. She'd put up with him for years. She'd done things she never thought she'd do, she said.

Bonney watched them drive away. 'Who was that?'

'Some guy, I don't know his name. She's been going with him for a while.'

'What is he, a little crazy?'

'Could be,' the bartender replied.

The afternoon was fading. Throughout the east, in the ominous quiet that surrounds stadia, the final quarter was being played.

They drove along the sea which was metallic, smooth. The neon of motels and roadside restaurants was on. He seemed moody – that was often so. She used to blame it on his working alone; he ran a wrecking yard for a man in Pensacola, it was over toward the bay. A car would be brought in crushed almost double, doors jammed, the seats glittering with broken glass. 'Have to be some drunk to live through that,' the tow-truck driver would say.

He liked it, the solitude, the sun. From beyond the fence the faint sound of traffic came. Within, in dust and silence, the battered front ends were set in rows, headlights missing, wheels gone. There was rust everywhere, spiders spinning beneath the dash. To one side, like a fated Panzer unit, were lines of Volkswagens, square-backs, sedans, most of them down on their rear axles, their noses raised like dying beasts. There were stickers on the windows from Texas, Georgia, *Turista* Mexico.

He had a small apartment, two rooms and a kitchen, neat and somewhat bare. There was a wooden table with books above it on a shelf, a hammock, a wicker couch. The sun came through the windows in the morning and poured on the empty floor. He had few friends. On weekends he slept late. There was never a newspaper, not even a magazine. He was recovering from something, an illness, a wound. He had no plans. Occasionally he talked of buying a boat and one night, unexpectedly, about France.

'You've been to France?'

'I used to live there,' he said.

'I didn't know that. When was that?'

'Oh, a while ago,' he said. That was all.

Sometimes she found him lying in the hammock late at night, barefoot, the television on, arms folded over his head as if to keep out the light.

She began preparing dinner. It was almost evening, it had started to rain. She appeared from time to time in the doorway of the kitchen, passing back and forth. She was somewhat lanky, all arms and legs. The room grew slowly darker, the doorway more and more bright. There was the sound of her mixing things, running water. The refrigerator door opened and closed. She came into the room with a piece of buttered bread and a can of beer. She sat down beside him. The wind was blowing now, the window spattered with rain.

'Are you hungry?'

'Not very.'

'Why don't we wait then?' she said. She looked at her knees. Her hair was unfastened and hanging down. She gathered it idly in her hand. 'I had a letter from Fraser,' she said.

'Oh, yeah?'

'From Atlanta. He's quit drinking, he says. Even has a job.' The gusts of rain were sweeping against the house. 'He wants me to come back,' she said.

There was silence.

'I thought that was all finished.'

She shrugged.

'Do you want to go?'

She didn't answer. After a moment he turned away. It was as if he'd forgotten her, as if he was thinking about something else. There were always long waits with him, like descents.

'Why are you telling me?' he said finally.

'Don't you want to know?'

He didn't say anything. It was too much trouble to explain. He didn't want to live again anything he had already lived. He did not want it all repeated.

'It's really raining. It looks like a storm,' he said. The words, the sentences were jammed and awkward. He could not seem to work them free. 'You want me to tell you what to do? Don't go back,' he said.

'Why not?'

'It's finished. Once it's over, it's over.'

'Not always,' she said.

'Well, maybe you're right,' he said. 'I guess there are no rules.'

'I really don't know what you want,' she said. 'That's the thing.'

'I don't think that's the thing.'

'I don't really know you.'

'You say you don't, but you do. You know, all right. I'm a fake,' he said calmly, 'just like the rest of them.'

There was silence. He sat with his thoughts.

'You know, I'm thirty-four,' she said.

'Is that right?'

'Yes.'

'I thought you were thirty-two.'

'No, I'm thirty-four. I just thought you should know.'

'That's not so bad.'

'I want to trust someone,' she said. She was not looking at him but at the floor. 'I want to feel something. With you, though, it's like somehow it goes into empty air.'

'Empty air . . .'

'Yes.'

'Well, what you have to do is hold on,' he said. 'Don't get scared.'

'I am scared.'

'Hold on.'

'That's it?'

'I can't tell you any more than that. It wouldn't be the truth.'

'Hold on . . .' she said.

'That's right.'

He sees it there in the darkness, not a vision, not a sign, but a genuine shelter if he can only reach it. In the lighted room are figures, he sees them clearly, sometimes seated together, sometimes moving, a man and a woman visible through the window, in the dusk, the Florida rain.

VORTEX

VORTEX

a novel by
David Harris

BOOK ONE

GORDON

CHAPTER ONE

McChord Air Force Base, South of Seattle

THE ROOM was small and felt too tight. It was in the middle of the building and didn't have any windows and the jerks they had assigned to him both smoked. Holley hated cigarette smoke. It nauseated him and made him sweat, but every time he tried to go out for some air the thought that he might miss something reeled him back like a fish on a line.

Matheson had taken off from Prince Rupert, in B.C., at 9:00 a.m. that morning and headed west and then southwest. Around noon he had thrown Holley into a panic by landing at some town called Williams Lake, but the RCMP said that they had got a man to the airstrip before anyone left the plane. They said that both the pilot and the passenger used the washroom and then walked up and down the strip for a few minutes while the plane was being refuelled.

Just a pit stop, thought Holley. Just a chance to have a leak and stretch the legs. But he told them to search the washroom anyway.

Then the little Cessna was up again and pointed south and Holley forgot the cigarette smoke, forgot his nausea, and began pacing the room in excited anticipation.

Just one more hour, he thought, just one more hour. As soon as Matheson crossed the forty-ninth parallel the aerial surveillance would be taken over by the U.S. Air Force, and wherever Matheson landed, Holley would be about thirty seconds behind him.

He rolled a couple of quick fantasies of that scene, and the one he liked best was the one in which Matheson tried to resist arrest so that Holley could beat the shit out of him with his bare hands.

This time, thought Holley, nothing can go wrong. There was a storm building over the North Cascades and the little aircraft would have to go around it to the east or west, but either way, it had to come down somewhere, and when it did . . . Holley replayed the scene again in his mind.

The jerk with the headphones interrupted his thoughts. 'He's starting to turn east.'

They had gone over all the possibilities as soon as the clouds started to build, and the Air Force guys he'd talked to all figured that if a real storm developed the pilot would probably turn east as far as the edge of the weather, coming into the U.S. somewhere over Okanagan county in north central Washington.

Holley said nothing, and the radio operator lit another cigarette and made notes in his logbook. Half a cigarette later he said, 'It's definite, he's heading east. Sounds like the weather is really turning rotten over the Cascades.'

Holley didn't care about the weather. All that mattered was getting his hands on that bastard Matheson and if he was heading east then Holley had to get moving now.

'Okay, I'm going to round up my team and get your chopper pilot moving. You keep those phones glued to your head and I'll be back here in about five minutes, just before I take off. You got that?'

The radio operator stubbed out his cigarette and said, 'That's what they're paying me for.'

Holley fought down an urge to punch his lights out right there, and headed for the door. He was halfway down the long hall when the other operator started yelling after him. 'Hey, come back. Come back. They've turned around.' Then he was running, all thought of being cool in front of the jerks gone. He charged into the room shouting, 'What the fuck are you talking about?'

The chain smoker gave the headphones to the other operator and said, 'They were headed east, just like I said, and then suddenly they turned real hard south and headed straight for the big clouds, and the RCMP pilot says he can't follow them and we can't get any radar on them from here because of the mountains.'

'You listen to me,' screamed Holley. 'You tell those assholes in the spotter to follow them. I don't care if they fly down a volcano, I want that spotter right behind them.'

He was yelling, but neither of them seemed to care. The chain smoker lit another cigarette and was almost smirking when he told Holley, 'You better see the Colonel about that. I don't give orders to no one around here, not even to Canadian cops.'

Holley slammed the door behind him in blind rage. Those bastards! Stinking useless coward bastards! Seven months setting this up just so some god damned chickenshit Mountie pilot could blow it for him.

And those half-wit fuckups in the radio room. He could hear them laughing through the door. They were probably both hypes themselves and had been secretly hoping Matheson would pull it off the whole time. What he wouldn't give for about five minutes in private with both of them.

He slammed out of the building into the grey Seattle drizzle, the heat of his anger boiling the raindrops off his black skin.

CHAPTER TWO

North Cascade Mountains

MT. REDOUBT (8956 ft.), N.E. Face. 1st. ascent F. Beckey and J. Rupley, 1971: '... around rock divide between branches of the Redoubt Glacier, then work west through crevasses to ascend glacier arm close to face on Redoubt. Above this, climb over schrund and up 600 ft. ice apron. Continue on steep snow and ice crest to final couloir leading to notch in summit ridge. Couloir itself or loose rock to right may be used. An exposed alpine climb; be prepared to bivouac.'

Alpine Guide to Southwestern British Columbia, by Dick Culbert.

Alex Townsend reached carefully upwards until he could grasp the karabiner with his left hand and unclipped it from the rope. He raised his right foot and kicked it into the loose snow a little higher up. Gradually he stood up on it until his weight was spread as evenly as possible between his feet, and waited to see if this new step would crumble out from under him.

When it seemed that it would hold for a while he began pawing at the snow around the karabiner with his mittened left hand, exposing a two and a half foot length of sling and an aluminium deadman. He was sure he could have had the deadman out with one sharp tug, but that would probably have been enough to collapse the snow under his feet.

This is insane, he thought. If I slip I'll pull Gord off and we'll both die.

He looked up the rope to where his partner was trying to plant another deadman a hundred and fifty feet above.

'Hey Gord.' The figure above, clad shoulder to ankle in blue nylon, stopped burrowing and looked down. 'This is crazy. These deadmen aren't worth a damn. I'm going to untie.'

Somewhere beneath all this rotten garbage he knew there was a sheet of solid ice. Ice into which they could sink bombproof ice screws, but the act of digging down to find it would probably be more dangerous than continuing without protection. He looked up. About four hundred feet above them the face necked down into a short couloir and then opened again, hourglassing into another, smaller snow face. As far as he could remember from the guidebook description the original route went that way and then up a bit of rock to the right.

All in all, there must be over a thousand feet still to go to the summit, and if it was like this most of the way it wasn't going to be any fun at all. Looking down didn't help. If either of them came off while they were tied together, they'd both go for a last wild ride into the jumbled seracs of the big glacier below. The deadmen were just tokens.

Still, it was quite a view. Twenty-five hundred feet down to the hanging valley where they had bivouacked last night, and nothing but mountains in all directions.

A shout from above interrupted his wandering thoughts.

'Are you ready?'

'Yeah, I'm ready, I've untied.'

Slowly, patiently they began again, each feeling both more and less comfortable without the rope, and gradually the distance between them diminished as Alex was able to make use of the steps that his partner was so laboriously kicking, and with about three hundred feet to go to the bottleneck above, Alex was only twenty feet behind.

'Hey, Gord, what do you think about the ice bulge over there to the right? I really wouldn't mind getting off this junk.'

'I don't blame you.'

'It's not much steeper, and at least it'll be solid. I'm going to traverse over and have a look.'

Slowly Alex Townsend began to ease rightwards toward a blue-grey bulge in the face, ice too steep for the snow to cling.

As he got closer, the face began to steepen and soon he realized that he wasn't going to be able to make it with just his ice axe for help. But, he reasoned, if the angle was increasing the snow should be getting shallower.

He transferred the axe to his left hand and started excavating with his right, all the movements small and controlled. He only had to go about eight inches. He cleared an area about one foot in diameter and then transferred the axe back to his right hand.

He brought the axe back about a foot and then swung it lightly forward. The pick embedded in the ice about one third of an inch and nothing cracked or shattered.

Reassured, he brought the axe back slowly to a point well behind his shoulder and then arced it forward and down in a smooth blur. The curved pick penetrated the ice over an inch and a half and there was very little cratering and cracking.

Perfect.

He clipped the axe sling to his harness, and with one hand on the axe head for balance, began kicking away at the snow with first his left, and then his right foot until he had the front points of both crampons securely into good ice.

Feeling comfortable for the first time in over an hour, Alex undid the chest and waist straps of his pack, eased his right arm out from the shoulder strap and brought the pack around to where he could reach his ice hammer, strapped along one side. It was awkward trying to stand in balance and untie the hammer. The axe looked good, would probably hold a fall, but he didn't want to find out for sure.

Finally the hammer was free. He slipped the pack back on, and began to clear the snow as high as he could above his head. As soon as a bit of ice showed through he planted the pick of his hammer with a single hard swing.

Fifteen minutes of careful clearing and climbing later he had completed his rising traverse to the foot of the ice bulge, with his partner Gordon Wilson only a few feet behind him. The face had steepened to just over seventy degrees and the ice was a fine condition, firm and dry, but not brittle.

'Shall we just keep going?' said Alex 'Or do you want the rope?'

'No, let's do it. I'll just keep on trailing the rope behind me – there's nothing for it to hang up on and it'll be handy if we want it. Do you want a couple of screws?'

Gordon Wilson was still carrying all the ice and snow hardware except for the one deadman Alex had removed earlier. Now he took two slings from his shoulder and handed them across, followed by two ice screws passed carefully, one at a time.

'How do you feel about taking a break here first? Maybe have a drink and a chocolate bar?' Asked Gordon.

'Sounds good to me. We've made good time so far so we might as well take a break.' Alex looked up at the clouds towering above the top of the face, 'Best not hang around too long though; it looks like the weather might not hold much longer.'

So they set about turning a few square feet of ice on this remote north face into a temporary rest stop. Two ice screws in right to the eye and joined by a long sling, ice hammers thunked in as deeply as possible, small steps chopped to take the strain off calf muscles, and finally their axes sunk into the ice overhead.

Each of them clipped in to three anchors; their packs hanging from the screws, they relaxed into their sit harnesses. Toes against the face, asses hanging out over empty air, they passed a water bottle back and forth and let their minds drift a little as they talked the lazy talk of men who have known each other for a long time.

Ten minutes and two Mars bars later Gordon Wilson began coiling the rope that was still hanging free from his harness. 'Might as well pack this rope away for now. If you carry it, I'll carry all the hardware.'

'I thought you were just going to trail it.'

'I was, but it'll be easier this way. I won't have to be careful about catching it in my crampons. Besides, you being so skinny and light, you'll be ahead of me and you can drop me a top rope if I need it.'

'Okay,' said Alex, 'but don't expect me to haul your two hundred pounds of lard up this thing by myself.'

'Not likely. And anyway I'm down to almost one ninety-nine. Here take this.' He handed Alex the rope and then continued. 'You know, it's a good thing I'm a climber, otherwise I bet I'd weigh three hundred pounds when I got old.'

Alex shrugged into his pack and began removing the ice screw he had been hanging from. 'You think climbing is going to keep you from getting a beer belly?'

'No, but I figure it'll keep me from getting old. Especially if I climb shit like that,' he pointed to the snow they had been on, 'in weather like this.'

Both men looked up. The grey sky had darkened and thickened and was beginning to descend.

'I hope the ceiling doesn't drop too low or we'll be finding our way back to the campsite by touch.'

'I think it'll hold off for a while, but we'd better get moving.'

They began the vertical ballet, the ice dance that combines cold precision with total freedom. Axe in. Hammer in. Kick in the right frontpoints and stand up on them. Kick in the left points. Then repeat the whole sequence again and again and again. Creativity in repetition. Climbing as the ultimate contradiction. Dance with death and learn to live.

As they gained height the distance between them grew, Alex pulling further and further ahead as Gordon had predicted. The weight difference had something to do with it; but Gordon Wilson knew that there was more to it than that.

He had been climbing as long as he could remember, since his parents had first taken him into the hills as a young boy almost thirty years ago, and he knew that Alex had less than five years' experience. But he also knew that Alex was a far better climber. A natural climber – fast, safe and smooth.

He looked up and thought to himself that if he tried to climb that fast it wouldn't be ten minutes before he missed a placement and fell to his death.

Gordon Wilson was a human fire plug. His body was thick and strong and his movements were easy and relaxed but not very graceful. He had a dense blond beard and moustache, and heavy blond hair hung to his shoulders.

He worked part time for a Vancouver printer, an arrangement which suited both himself and the printer. This left him time to do a lot of climbing and skiing, and provided about half the money he needed to live the way he wanted to. To make up the difference he grew and sold a little dope.

After several hundred feet of steep-and-easy the angle eased off a little and they were forced once again to kick into a layer of rotten snow. Swirling mist now hung heavily around the summit and the sky was black above them. They looked with distaste at the upper snowfield.

Alex waited until Gordon had caught up. 'We could,' he said, 'try the rock.'

The snowfield was bordered on the right by a rib of slabby rock. 'It doesn't look too hard, and it should be faster than this snow.'

'I hope so, 'cause I think we're going to get dumped on pretty soon.'

They climbed carefully right and soon found a way across the moat between snow and rock. Standing on a small ledge they surveyed the rock above them.

'This doesn't look too bad at all. Let's just leave the rope in your pack and go for it.'

'Okay with me.' Alex nodded in agreement. 'The rope would slow us down and I think I'd like to get a look at the descent route before we get socked in completely.'

'Me too. Still, it didn't sound that difficult,' said Gordon, sitting down on the ledge and undoing his crampon straps. 'But you never know – Alan was pretty drunk when he described it to me and you know what he's like when he's drunk.'

'Yeah, all the climbing he's ever done gets homogenized by the beer and pretty soon you can't tell whether he's talking about a snow plod or a death route.' Alex had his crampons off and was lashing them to the top of his pack. 'But I have to admit that he was right about this being a worthwhile route. And it would be even better after a dry winter. It would . . . what?'

'Be quiet for a minute, I think I hear something.'

Then Alex heard it too. The sound of a small airplane approaching from the east. They looked at one another and Gordon spoke. 'I sure hope he knows what he's doing. He sounds awfully low.'

'He must be . . .' Alex's reply and the sound of the engine were lost in a blast of thunder.

'Jesus Christ! That wasn't very far away. We'd better haul ass if we don't want to get fried.'

The rock was perfect – Mountain granite shattered in big blocks, rough to the touch and solid underfoot – but on this day there was no joy in climbing it. Their minds were filled with the falling sky and falling temperature and they both knew that there was no retreat. To get down they must first get up the last few hundred feet and find a descent route on the south side.

As they moved upward the sound of the aircraft engine increased, blotted out occasionally by rolling blasts of thunder.

'He must be just on the other side of this ridge.'

'It almost sounds like he's below us. He must be trying to fly down the valley below the cloud, he . . .'

The engine went berserk. From a few thousand rpm it screamed up almost to the limit of hearing. Then nothing. Silence.

The two men stared at each other. Alex struggled for words. 'Jesus, I . . .'

Gordon Wilson said, 'It doesn't matter, Alex. Either he made it or he didn't. It's not our problem yet. When we get up this hill, then it can be our problem. Right now we've just got to think about the next hundred feet. Okay?'

'Okay. Sure. You're right, you're right. But I think he must have crashed, and we'll have to go looking. But you're right, let's get up first.'

With that he was away, and once again Gordon was left behind to marvel at the speed and grace with which Alex could move.

When he reached the ridge crest he could see Alex about twenty-five feet away at the top of a steep gully, uncoiling the rope. Fifteen hundred feet below on the broad south face of the mountain, a small yellow aircraft lay silent and broken in the snow, visible and then invisible through the ragged mist that blew around the peak.

'D'you think anybody's alive?'

'I don't know. It looks pretty bashed up to me, but I guess we better go and check.' Gordon shrugged out of his pack and began digging through it. 'I've got the second rope in here, I think we're going to need it – it looks like two long raps.' He got the rope out and started to uncoil it.

Alex took an end and tied the two ropes together. 'I guess we should figure out how to get from the plane over to the descent route. I think we can do it even if we get whited out, if we just make a slightly rising traverse east from the plane and above the rock bands there, and then contour straight across the face until we hit the east ridge.'

Gordon checked the anchors and was passing one of the ropes through the rappel slings. 'Looks about right to me. This is probably the descent Alan was talking about, and the summit's just up there, another hundred feet or so.'

'Guess we're not going to see it this time.'

They each picked up a rope and threw the coils as far out as they could. Alex leaned out and looked down. 'Looks like they're okay.' He threaded the ropes through his karabiner brake and backed toward the edge.

'Alex.'

'Yeah?'

'Go slow. Alan said the gully was really loose, so find a sheltered spot for the next station and try not to kick too much debris down onto the ropes.'

'Okay, see you later.'

Two long rappels brought them to the top of the snowfield. They were out of the summit mists and had a clear view of the scene below.

'Look at that! You can see skid marks halfway across the face; and it looks like it's only got one wing.'

'Jeeees-us. It looks like he flipped into the air when he hit those rocks.'

'Poor bastard. I hope he bought it on the first hit.'

They stared downhill for a few moments more, then silently coiled and packed the ropes and unstrapped their axes.

Alex went first. Leaping the moat he landed on the snow and began a long swooping glissade toward the wreckage. Feet together, upper body facing the fall line and angulating from the hips he was a skier without skis, linking turns and taking advantage of every irregularity of the terrain to control his wild descent.

Then, at last, when it seemed that he must overshoot his target or else crash into it, he rocked back hard on his heels, sending up a spray of snow and skidding to a stop ten feet from where the wreckage lay in a slight hollow, one of the few low-angle areas on the face.

He looked up to see Gordon Wilson in full flight several hundred feet above, body upright and loose, knees taking the bumps. Three hundred feet . . . two hundred . . . long blond hair streaming behind, expressionless face belying intense concentration . . . one hundred feet . . . fifty feet, then back on his heels and a snowy halt two feet away.

Together they stared at what had once been a Cessna 185 four-seat airplane, now a crumpled monument to the force of inevitable gravity; and together they walked toward it and peered in through the hole where the pilot's door had torn away.

'Oh my God.'

Both the wing and the door on the pilot's side had been torn off along with half the pilot. There was blood everywhere. The interior of the little aircraft and the clothing of the pilot and passenger were sodden. The two climbers stood staring, frozen in morbid fascination. Then:

'Jesus Christ, Alex, that other guy is still alive!'

They charged to the other side of the wreck, but could not force the door and in the end they had to move the body of the pilot out onto the snow before they could free the passenger from his seat belt and haul him, bloody and unconscious, back out the way they had entered.

'Do you think there's any chance that this thing might blow up Gord?'

'No, I don't think so,' said Gordon. 'If it was going to burn it probably would have started already, or blown up when it landed.' He knelt beside the unconscious survivor and began wiping the blood from what had once been a handsome, middle aged face.

Ten minutes later they had done all that they could. The man they had pulled from the wreckage seemed to have no broken bones – his only visible injury a ragged gash across his forehead. His clothes were bloodsoaked, but there was no way to tell how much had been his own and how much had come from the pilot.

When Alex had unbuttoned the bloodstained shirt to check for wounds on the chest and abdomen the cold air had woken the man briefly. His eyes opened and he groaned and mumbled incoherently for a few seconds before falling back into unconsciousness.

Gordon put what was left of the first aid kit back into his pack and stood up to gaze toward the summit they had almost reached, but it was now obscured by cloud and even this far down in the valley the wind was beginning to blow.

'I guess we have to drag this guy out.' He looked down at the still form. 'That's just going to be a real bitch.'

'I know, but with a storm coming on there's no way we can leave him here. It might be a week before anyone could get in with a chopper. We'll just have to wrap him up in our extra clothing and hope we can get him out.' Alex paused for a moment and then continued. 'What about the valley below us? Do you know where it comes out? Maybe we could take him out that way.'

Gordon looked west, the way Alex was pointing. 'I know that it eventually joins up with a trail system that leads to the highway that goes to the Mt. Baker ski area, but we'd probably be bushwhacking for about two days just to get to the trail.' He turned and pointed back to the east ridge. 'I think our best bet is to go over the ridge and down the glacier, just like we would have done if this hadn't happened.'

He stripped off the thick pile jacket he was wearing and began to put it on the man they had pulled from the wreck. 'I'm not looking forward to getting him down the Depot creek headwall, but I guess our first job is to get him over the ridge.'

'I've got my bivvy sack with me; maybe if we put him in that he'll slide easier on the snow.' Alex took a small stuff sac from his pack and pulled a bright yellow Gore-tex bivouac sack out of it.

'Here, lift his legs and I'll slide it up. Good. Now if you can lift his hips, I'll pull it right over him.'

They stood up and looked at each other. Both were covered in blood, and there were red patches in the snow and red smears on everything they had touched.

The nylon cocoon on the snow stirred and moaned, and a gust of wind whistled a response across the gaping hole in the wreck. The two men stared down at the sac, again still and silent, as a light rain began to fall.

'I wonder who he is. You didn't find a wallet or card case did you?'

'Huh? A wallet? No, I didn't even look.' Alex knelt once more and reached into the bivvy sack, groping for hip pockets.

'Here we go, it looks like he . . . Holy shit! Has he ever got a stack of money here. There must be fifteen or twenty hundred dollar bills.'

Oblivious to the increasing rainfall Gordon Wilson reached out a hand. 'Thanks.' He too looked at the pack of hundreds, his forehead creasing in concentration above thick eyebrows as he counted. '. . . twenty-two, twenty-three hundreds and one ten. Now let's see who he is . . . uhn . . . here we are: his name is Walter F. Matheson, and he seems to be from San Francisco.

'Here, put this into one of the packs.' He handed the wallet back to Alex and started toward the gaping doorway. 'I think I'll have a look inside the plane.'

As Gordon clambered once again into the flightless bird, Alex Townsend pulled a 9mm. rope from his pack and began uncoiling it. When it lay in a loose heap on the snow beside him, he pulled four slings from his pack and began untying them, cursing softly when he had to use his teeth on knots jammed too tight for his numb fingers.

Methodically, ignoring the rain, he began retying the slings in the form of a crude harness around the unresisting Walter Matheson.

'Alex.'

Gordon's voice was hoarse and soft and Alex did not hear it over the rising wind.

'Alex.' Still soft, but harsh and insistent this time. Alex turned to see Gordon crouched in the ruined aircraft kneeling on the seat with his head and shoulders sticking through the gaping wound in its side.

'Alex, I think you better come and look at this.' He lifted a small aluminium suitcase, obviously heavy, out of the plane and dropped it at his companion's feet.

It was not locked, and Alex lifted the lid and stared at the contents. Slowly he bent down and picked up a sealed plastic bag – one of over a dozen in the case. It weighed a little over two pounds and was full of lumpy, flaky powder, as white as the snow around them.

'Aaghh, fuck. What are we going to do now?'

CHAPTER THREE

North Cascade Mountains

HE AWOKE DRIFTING, flloating on a tide of pain, but soon slipped away again to nowhere.

And awoke again. And more pain, to send him back.

And again.

And again.

Afterward he would forget most of the pain and remember other things.

Things hazy and unclear – images unfocused by the pain through which he had observed them; but a few memories were etched sharp and permanent: cold hands on his chest and gut; much rain; fragments of conversation;

'. . . fucking hill go on forever?

'. . . turning to snow . . .'

'. . . easy Alex, a few more minutes and it's all downhill . . .'

But clearest of all were the faces. Two faces which seemed to be peering at him whenever he awoke.

Long blonde hair. Blonde moustache flowing into long blonde beard. All so yellow that everything else looked red. Red cheeks, red forehead, broad red nose and thick red lips. Warm concern in the blue eyes. Think of Santa Claus at thirty. Before the white hair, before the belly.

And the other face dark and saturnine. The short hair dark and curly, nose narrow and hooked. Thin lips and white teeth. And the eyes. No comfort or concern in those eyes. They were dark and still and every time he thought of them he remembered the pain.

CHAPTER FOUR

North Cascade Mountains

IN SOUTHWESTERN British Columbia, as in most mountainous regions, roads tend to follow river valleys. One such parallel road and river system starts in the remote North Cascade range, just north of the Canada-U.S.A. border where tiny Depot Creek runs beside a rutted dirt track. Growing water volume is matched by wider and smoother road surfaces. The dirt becomes gravel where Depot Creek enters Chilliwack Lake, and widens considerably where the lake is drained by the Chilliwack River.

As the river is swollen by its tributaries the road widens again and the gravel is replaced by good pavement until finally, not far from the spot where the Chilliwack joins the mighty Fraser River for the last sixty miles of its journey to the Pacific, the two lane blacktop joins the trans-Canada highway for the last sixty miles of *its* journey to Vancouver.

At 5:30 a.m. on that late August morning there was not much traffic on any of these roads, but along the shore of the Chilliwack River, about half way between its headwaters and its confluence with the Fraser, an old and road-weary Volkswagen van chugged its way slowly into the breaking day. At the wheel, Alex Townsend fought off sleep and thought about the other occupants of the van.

He thought of Gord Wilson, his friend and regular climbing partner for over three years, now sleeping hunched against the passenger door. In the city Gordon was unremarkable. His powerful body did not show through the nondescript clothes that he wore, and the only thing that set him apart from the rest of Vancouver was his profusion of blond hair. But in the mountains he stood apart. His great physical strength and many years of experience made him a fine climber.

Somehow though, Alex mused, there was more to it than that. There were many good climbers, and technically, Alex himself was better than Gordon. But in the high mountains, where thin air and insidious cold sap the strength and numb the will, success and survival do not depend on technique alone, but on strength of character, intelligence and an ability to get along with others – qualities that ran deep in the man sleeping beside him.

But even more than, that thought Alex, Gord had a sense of humour, and that was something that was becoming increasingly rare these days. Many of the climbers that he met now didn't seem to be having much fun, and it reminded him of all the serious-faced young giants who had turned football from a good time into a heavy business.

At least Gord didn't make climbing into some kind of religion.

On that thought Alex fell asleep. He woke up when his head hit the steering wheel, and found that he had almost drifted off the left hand side of the road.

'Time for a break, Alex,' he said aloud.

He stopped the van and climbed wearily out the door. Leaning back against the van he fumbled with his fly and then arched a golden stream onto the road. The morning was pleasantly cold, and as Alex idly watched the steam rising from his warm urine, he thought of the other passenger, Mr. Walter Matheson.

It had taken almost eighteen hours to haul him and his shiny aluminium suitcase out to the road. When they had stopped for a snack at the foot of the ice bulge on the ascent, they had argued about the time it would take them to return to the van once they reached the summit. Alex had thought six hours, but Gordon had said they could do it in five if they pushed a bit.

Five hours! What a joke. It had taken them all of that just to pull the deadweight of Matheson and his suitcase over the east ridge and down to the hanging valley below the glacier. And the weather. Christ, what a storm. The temperature had fallen rapidly and the rain soon turned to sleet. The only good thing about the whole episode was that they had been working so hard that they hadn't noticed the cold. Not at first anyway.

Once they reached the ridge things had become easier for a bit; the glacier hadn't been too badly crevassed and it was all downhill until they reached the valley. But by then it was dark and they were both beginning to feel the cold, and there was no more snow on which to slide their unconscious burden. Nothing for it but to take turns carrying him through the bush. A horror show from beginning to end.

They had tried everything from slinging him over their shoulders like a sack of flour to making complicated harnesses of rope and slings and strapping him on like a great floppy one hundred and fifty pound pack.

They had no sure knowledge of the man's injuries and they doubted that he would survive the rough journey out. But they had left their sleeping bags in the van and they knew that he would surely die if they left him behind while they went for help. At least this way they would not have to come back for the body.

When they finally reached the top of the Depot Creek headwall they had again debated whether to leave him and go for help or try to carry him out themselves.

'What do you think?'

'I don't know, how does he look?'

'Just a second, let me get my headlamp, it's too dark to see much.'

'Well, he's still alive anyway. At least dragging him over the snow wasn't too bumpy.'

'His head seems to have stopped bleeding, and he's breathing okay.'

'How's his heartbeat?'

'It's still beating.'

In the end they had decided to carry on. They felt that if he had sustained any severe internal injuries he would be dead already, and that the most important thing now was warmth. He had lost a lot of blood, and the sooner they got him into the van, with its powerful gasoline heater, the better. He would probably die on the way out, but he would certainly die if they left him.

Finally, just as the sky was beginning to lighten in the east, they had reached the road and the parked van. They stripped off his soggy clothes, wrapped him in a sleeping bag and laid him on a foam pad in the back of the van, beside his suitcase.

His wound was bleeding again, and Gordon rummaged through the van until he found a clean shirt which he tied around the bloody head.

'He's still breathing. I thought for sure he was going to die.' said Alex.

'Yeah, he sure lost enough blood. Did you see the inside of the bivvy sack when we took him out of it?'

'Where's the nearest hospital?'

'Probably in Chilliwack. You know that little city just where we turned off the freeway?'

'Right. Okay, I'll drive for a while if you want, and you can get some sleep.'

'You sure you're okay to drive?'

'Of course I'm not okay. I'm totally thrashed. But so are you, so you sleep for a bit, and then we can trade off.'

'Thanks.'

Now, an hour later, Alex was wondering if he should wake his friend and let Gordon drive. But the cool morning air felt good, and he decided to keep going. Besides, it was less than an hour to Chilliwack.

He climbed back into the van, checked on the man in the back, who actually seemed to be sleeping rather than unconscious now, and headed west.

He tried to think about this man named Walter Matheson and his fifteen kilos of white powder, and about a dead pilot lying in the bloody snow beside a crumpled airplane. He knew it was important to think but he just couldn't focus his mind for more than a few seconds at a time. All he could think of was how nice it would be to sleep. To be wrapped in a big warm down-filled bag in a tent somewhere high in the mountains, drifting cosily away. . . .

His face hit the steering wheel again, and this time his nose began to bleed. 'No problem,' he thought to himself, 'I'm already covered in other people's blood. Maybe the pain will keep me awake for a while.'

As he drove into the gradually brightening day his mind drifted back in time almost four years. He hadn't been living in Seattle for long and it had been less than a year since the divorce. Somebody – he didn't remember who – had told him of a two thousand foot granite wall just north of Vancouver.

It supposedly had some incredible routes and was only two minutes walk from the road. It had sounded too good to be true, but he had gone up to see for himself.

The rock, which was called the Chief, turned out to be even better than that. It was on the coast overlooking a beautiful inlet and a logging/mining town with the odd name of Squamish. It was on that trip that he first met Gordon Wilson.

This chance encounter had begun a climbing partnership still going strong after four years. They had climbed together up and down western North America. Weekends rockclimbing at Squamish in British Columbia and at Index and Leavenworth in Washington, or mountaineering and skiing in the North Cascades and in B.C.'s Coast range. Two nine day weeks in Yosemite. And three memorable expeditions to the big mountains of Alaska and the Yukon.

And through it all they had even managed to remain friends. Or maybe friends was the wrong word. Alex often wished that there was someone with whom he could be completely open, someone to go to when he felt small and alone; but after four years he was fairly sure that Gordon would never be that person.

Gord was strong and self-assured, and he maintained a closely guarded personal space which nothing penetrated. In either direction.

None the less, Gordon Wilson was the closest thing to a friend that he had. Alex had never made friends easily, and starting life all over at the age of twenty-six had made it even harder. Now, at thirty-one, it still wasn't easy.

But it was getting better. The view from the top of Mt. Logan was a lot better than anything he had seen out the window of his office; and although he didn't make even a third as much money working at the garage as he had writing programmes in Silicon Valley, at least he didn't have to drink himself to sleep any more.

As the pendulum of his thoughts swung back into the present he tried again to think about the man lying behind.

What was in the suitcase?

Heroin?

Cocaine?

It had to be some drug. Slowly, into his fatigue-dulled mind came the realization that he had stumbled into the world of large scale crime. The suitcase must be worth a fortune.

He thought of all the newspaper stories he had read, all the dozens of newscasts....

'... *today announced the breakup of a major heroin trafficking ring* ...'

'... *in a shootout when they tried to intercept a shipment of three kilograms of cocaine* ...'

'... *believed to have been killed to prevent him from giving evidence* ...'

Christ! There must be thirty or thirty-five pounds in the suitcase. Fifteen kilos. Fifteen kilos! How much was that worth in dollars? In human lives?

And then he thought of the bloody, dismembered corpse they had left by the airplane, and his whole body began to shake and he had to stop the van because he could hardly hold on to the steering wheel.

'Gord. C'mon Gord, wake up.'

'Hnnn?'

'Wake up!'

'Uhn, okay, I'm awake. What's happening?'

'I'm wasted, Gordie.'

CHAPTER FIVE

San Francisco

LIKE SOME malevolent black spider in its lair, William Holley sat in his office and brooded. Nobody disturbed him. His temper was legendary; everyone on the San Francisco Police Department had heard about it, and nobody, from the Chief to the greenest rookie, wanted any part of it.

He brooded that way for two days after his return from Seattle. On the third day he didn't show up until almost eleven, and went straight to the office of the Chief of Detectives. He didn't fool around with any bullshit about Hello, or How are you, he just walked in and said 'I want off it.'

He pulled a file folder from his briefcase and said, 'Everything I know or suspect is in there. Give it to someone else.' He tossed the folder on the Chief's desk. 'Or better still, drop the whole thing entirely.'

The Chief looked at Holley and sighed inwardly. How do you supervise a volcano? 'Okay Lieutenant, tell me about it. I take it that last weekend's operation was a failure?'

'It wasn't a failure, it was a fuckup. The RCMP fucked up and now we're back to where we were a year ago, which is exactly nowhere. You can read it all in there,' Holley pointed to the file, 'but the bottom line is that Tomlinson is going to go on supplying heroin to half of California and we are going to have to go on watching him do it.'

He stood up. 'The only hope we had was to nail this Matheson with a bagful and put the screws on him, but now that the Mounties have taken that away from us we're shit out of luck. Period. End of story.'

Holley was as black and hard as a piece of obsidian and the Chief of Detectives was a little afraid of him. He chose his words carefully. 'You've got other things to do Lieutenant, so go ahead and do them. I'll read your report and think about the whole business and let you know what I've decided in a day or so, okay?'

'There's nothing to decide. The only way to stop him is to have him hit. Until we're prepared to do that we're wasting our time. He doesn't go anywhere near the shit personally, the money he makes is getting laundered somewhere else, and nothing anybody says about him is going to be worth a shit in court. We've been up one side of this and down the other a hundred times.' He started for the door but stopped and turned around just before he went through it. 'The one chance we had was with this Matheson and now he's probably dead. If you can't drop it then give it to somebody else.'

CHAPTER SIX

Vancouver

SLOWLY, AN INCH at a time, Alex surfaced from the depths of a bleak and empty sleep. He was being shaken and someone was calling his name.

'Wake up Alex.'

'Wake up.'

'WAKE UP!!!'

'Oohhnnn?'

'Come on, we're home. Wake up. We've got work to do.'

'Huh? Where are we?'

'Alex, for Christ's sake wake up. Here, drink this.'

Obediently Alex took the offered bottle and came partially awake when warm beer foamed in his mouth and throat.

'Gah. That's awful.'

Still holding the bottle, he stumbled from the van and looked around him. Summer sunlight filtered through leaves still wet from the storm of the day before and illuminated the garbage cans of a residential alley.

'Where are we?'

'In the lane behind my house.' Gordon was opening the big side door of the van. 'Give me a hand and we'll get this guy inside. I don't think any of the neighbours are watching.'

Alex was confused. 'I thought . . . What happened at the hospital?'

'Alex, I don't think a hospital would be a very good idea.'

'But we don't know what's wrong with him. He could have all sorts of internal injuries. He could die if we don't take him to a hospital.'

'Yeah, I suppose he could, but I think we're just going to have to take that chance. Look, help me get him inside, and we can talk about it, okay?'

Vague fear shook him again, but he was too tired and confused to argue, and he nodded and said 'Okay.'

They manoeuvred Walter Matheson out of the van. He was semi-conscious and they managed to stand him up between them, one of his arms across each of their backs, and half walk, half carry him into the yard and up a short flight of steps to the back door.

'I don't have the key for this door with me,' said Gordon. 'Watch him for a minute while I go around to the front and open it from the inside.'

Alex stood silently, scowling at the inert form on the small porch until he heard the click of the lock being unset.

The house was dim after the bright sun and at first Alex could not see much. Gordon led the way into the bathroom, where they laid the injured man on the floor. Turning to Alex he asked, 'Are you awake now?'

'I think so, I'm pretty tired, but I'm awake.'

'That's good, 'cause we've got some heavy deciding to do.' Gordon plugged the bath and started filling it with warm water. 'But first let's get him cleaned up.'

'Why don't you want to take him to a hospital?' Gordon started to answer, then stopped and looked down at Walter Matheson on the floor. 'Come into the hall for a minute.' He led Alex out of the bathroom. 'I don't know how unconscious he really is.'

When they were well away from the bathroom door he stopped and faced Alex. 'Just how badly do you want your name connected to fifteen keys of cocaine?'

'What are you talking about?'

'If we take him to a hospital what are you going to tell them? Are you going to tell them about the drugs?'

Alex started to speak but Gordon cut him off. 'No, don't answer, just think about it. As soon as we mention that he had a suitcase full of coke we are suddenly going to be the only witnesses in a multi-million dollar narcotics case. *The only witnesses*.'

Alex felt the muscles clenching along his spine and a sour taste rose in the back of his throat as his friend continued.

'And if we don't tell them, if we just take him in and say we found him in the plane, what do you think he's going to do when they let him out? He's going to come looking for his suitcase is what he's going to do.'

'But there must be some way we can do it. Drop him somewhere and then phone an ambulance without giving our names. Something like that.'

Gordon shrugged his thick shoulders. 'Maybe so. But we'd better think it over pretty carefully first. Anyway, he's lasted this long, so another hour or two won't make any difference. Let's give him a bath and put him to bed and then we can figure out what to do.'

He started toward the bathroom, but then turned and Alex could see a smile behind the bushy beard. 'Besides, there's God knows how many million dollars in that suitcase and the one thing I do know for sure is that if we give it to the police or flush it down the toilet not one cent of it is going to rub off on me.'

They put Walter Matheson in the tub and he seemed to wake up.

'Aaahh.' Eyes unfocused, leaning slightly forward, he brought his hands slowly up and cradled his face in them. He remained in that position for a long time, not speaking, the warm water lapping around him.

Gordon left to find some towels and Alex sat on the rim of the old tub and said nothing.

The voice, when it finally came, was weak and scratchy. 'It was raining.'

Alex could think of no response, so he continued to sit silent.

'Raining.' Walter Matheson raised bloodshot, gummy eyes and said quite distinctly, 'I think that it was raining.'

'That's right, it was raining, but you're alright now, we've brought you home.'

How inane, thought Alex; but what else was there to say? A thousand questions whirled and burned in his mind. He wanted to grab this man by his bloody hair and shake him and demand answers and explanations. . . .

'Why couldn't you have crashed your fucking airplane somewhere else?'

'Why couldn't you have died in the crash?'

'Why don't you just die right now?'

But instead, he picked up a cloth and began gently wiping away the blood.

Gordon returned and they finished the bath. Walter Matheson did not seem to mind. Whenever they asked him to move, to learn forward or back, to turn his head or lift an arm, he responded like a slightly retarded child who is anxious to please. He often seemed confused and moved the wrong way, but he was generally cooperative and relaxed. He did not speak again.

Gordon pulled the plug and together they lifted him to his feet. What was left, with all the filth gone, was a medium-sized, fit looking man of about fifty. Loss of so much blood had given a pale, almost translucent quality to his skin, and blood again welled from the large wound on his forehead and dripped slowly down his right cheek.

The vertical position was too much for him and his knees slowly bent until the two younger men were supporting his full weight. Their blood-stained and dirty clothes made a strange contrast to his clean and still-wet body.

They sat him down on the toilet and began towelling him dry.

'That's good enough Alex, let's get a bandage on his head and get him into my bed.'

CHAPTER SEVEN

Vancouver

HIS THROAT was on fire.

For some unknown time that was all he knew. He had no conscious thought, no subconscious impulse, no sense of personal identity; only burning thirst.

Then his universe expanded and to the thirst was added pain. Starting at the back of his skull and spreading down his spine into every muscle and bone, dull throbbing pain accompanied him on his journey to consciousness.

First came the realization of identity: once again there was an I. Where there is pain there is life. He knew he was Walter Matheson, and he was alive.

For a time that was enough, but eventually his universe expanded again. Faces and places floating randomly across his mind's eye added the flesh of personality to the skeleton of identity until eventually full consciousness returned.

What happened?

Where am I?

Shoving aside his thirst and ignoring the pain he struggled to a sitting position.

Dizziness and nausea.

Try again.

And again.

Finally, compromising, he got two pillows behind him and managed to maintain a semi-sitting position.

A brass bed. He could feel the cold metal against his shoulder. Curtain-filtered daylight in a small room. Sun outside and warm air fluttering the curtain. Hardwood floor, heavy oak dresser, open clothes closet and one closed door.

He wondered what was on the other side of that door?

Maybe he could get a drink.

Then voices. Two voices. He could hear them faintly through the door. One voice just ordinary, just like any other voice; the other somehow odd. Harsh consonants and shortened vowels. A Canadian.

And with the thought of Canada the gates of memory fell open, and once more he knew the insanity of thunder and lightning, and the terror and agony of the crash.

CHAPTER EIGHT

Vancouver

'ARE YOU SAYING that if we take him to a hospital we're eventually going to get killed?' asked Alex.

They were in the living room of Gordon Wilson's small house, weighing the consequences of samaritanism. They were both clean and dressed in fresh clothing, each according to his custom. Gordon Wilson in blue jeans, a green T-shirt advertising Heineken beer, and leather sandals over thick grey socks; and Alex, who had shaved as well as showered, wore slacks of light grey wool, a slightly darker grey cotton shirt with very fine white pinstriping, grey socks and black moccasins.

'Yeah, probably.' Gordon was deep in an overstuffed armchair, a mug of tea balanced on one of the broad arms.

'So what do you suggest we do?' Alex was sitting on a straight-backed wooden chair that he had carried in from the kitchen. He was tense and unhappy.

'Well to start with I think we should go over all the alternatives we can think of and try to figure out what's likely to happen in each case. You used to write some pretty complex programmes so this should be a piece of cake. If *a*, then *b*, *c* and *q*; if *not a*, then either *x* or *y* but not both. That kind of thing.'

Alex was angry. How could Gord sit there complacently drinking tea and trying to be funny? He wanted to strike out with words, to lash his friend with abuse. He could feel increasing blood pressure, feel his skin begin to sweat and crawl. He fought for control and finally stood up and said 'Give me a couple of minutes.'

He went out the front door and sat at the top of the steps, and stared at the trees and lawns of the quiet old neighbourhood.

Gordon was not surprised. He had seen this happen before, though always when they were climbing. In the face of something difficult or dangerous, or after a near accident; whenever Alex felt emotion overriding self-control he would excuse himself with the same words, 'Give me a couple of minutes', walk a few feet away, sit down, and go into a trance.

It wasn't yoga, or T.M., or self-hypnosis, or bio-feedback or any other pop/psych technique, it was just Alex's way of dealing with emotional overload.

'Sorry Gordie.' Alex returned and sat down again. 'Got a bit out of control there.' He was calmer now and he knew that Gordon was probably right. As usual. 'Let's go over it one thing at a time and see where we stand.'

'Okay, first things first. I checked the suitcase while you were in the shower, and I'm pretty sure it's coke. The only way to tell for sure would be to snort some but I'm not going to do that until I know for a fact that it's not some kind of experimental rat poison.'

'Could it be heroin?' Alex asked.

'I don't think so. I've only seen heroin a couple of times, and it was more powdery. But I've seen lots of coke and this sure looks like cocaine.' He paused, lost in thought. 'Fifteen kilos of cocaine. That's about . . .' His voice trailed off and his eyes lost their focus. 'I can't even count that high. Shit. Two million maybe. Dollars.'

He paused again and scratched through his beard along the line of his lower jaw. 'You know, I've never had two million dollars worth of cocaine in my house before.'

They were both tired. The climb the day before had been demanding, and hauling Walter Matheson and his suitcase out to the road had been worse. Gordon had had one hour's sleep and Alex just over two in the last thirty; but they were used to going short of sleep and working hard on long climbs, and they were familiar with the dangers of mental fatigue.

Slowly and carefully Gordon led Alex down the path he had been exploring almost from the instant he had discovered the suitcase in the blood spattered aircraft.

If they took the injured man to a hospital they must decide whether to report the suitcase. If they did, then Matheson would eventually come to trial and as Gordon put it, 'Sooner or later the word is going to get out that the only thing connecting him to all that shit,' he pointed toward the suitcase which lay on the floor beside his chair, 'is our testimony.'

If they kept the suitcase and said nothing then Matheson would undoubtedly come looking for them as soon as he was out. Even if they could convince him that they were in fact holding the suitcase for him until he recovered there was a good chance that he (or someone) would have them killed just for insurance.

'He would probably feel real bad about it; after all we did save his life, but he might still do it.'

So, taking him to a hospital was out. Short of murdering him and flushing his cocaine down the toilet the only safe course was to do as Alex had suggested – dump him out on a street corner somewhere and call an ambulance anonymously.

'But that would still leave us with the problem of the suitcase. We can flush the coke, or mail it to the police, but Alex, I don't think I want to do that. That cocaine is going to change hands four or five times, and generate God knows how many million dollars before it disappears up somebody's nose. If we're careful, and if we don't get greedy, we can get some of those dollars for ourselves.'

For a while, maybe twenty seconds, Alex was silent. Then he found his tongue. 'You mean steal it from him and sell it ourselves?'

'NO, NO, NO! That is the one thing that would absolutely, one hundred percent for sure get us killed. There is no way you want to get involved in selling this much cocaine. That is a whole other world and you don't even want to *know* about it, let alone get involved in it.'

Alex started to speak but Gordon cut him off. 'You know that I sell a little dope now and then, right? Well I've been doing that for about ten years now, and if there's one thing I've learned about the drug business it's that I'm happy to stay small time.'

He stopped for a moment and then went on quietly. 'Alex, the people who deal at this level are different from you and me. It's not that they're not nice people, although I guess some of them aren't, it's just that they're different. They play in a different league and by a whole different set of rules. You or me getting involved with them would be like a caterpillar trying to cross a freeway.'

'Well how can you make money out of it without getting involved?' asked Alex. 'If it's that dangerous why don't we just drop him somewhere near a hospital and flush everything down the toilet. I don't want to get killed.'

In a surprising gesture of warmth Gordon reached out and rested his hand on Alex's shoulder. 'Neither do I, believe me.' He withdrew his hand. 'But I've got an idea, and I think that there's a way in which we can do this guy Matheson a favour – something he'll appreciate a lot more than being taken to a hospital – with no danger to ourselves.'

Alex began to speak but once again he was cut off.

'Look, I know that you probably don't want to get involved in anything too illegal. That's fine, you don't have to if you don't want to, but listen to what I'm going to say and then after you've slept on it and thought about it for a while you can decide. Okay?'

Outside the house leaves and flowers bobbled in a light breeze and the noon sun warmed the city of Vancouver on a fine summer day. The air had been washed by the storm of the night before and the weather was perfect; clear and hot without being oppressive. Inside the house Alex Townsend grew cold and felt a droplet of nervous sweat run down his ribcage as Gordon continued.

'This guy Matheson was smuggling a shipment of cocaine into the U.S. At first I couldn't figure out what he was doing there, but the more I thought about it, the more sense it made. These mountains are by far the least guarded way into the States, and getting drugs into Canada is child's play. So even though it's a roundabout route – South America to Canada to the U.S. – it's a lot safer than going through Miami or San Diego.'

He stood up out of the armchair, stretching and yawning, then walked to the kitchen, speaking over his shoulder as he went. 'And he's not some flunky courier. Do you want some tea?'

'Tea? How do you know he's not? No, I don't want any tea.'

'I looked in his wallet again. I spent some time in the Bay Area in the late sixties and I know San Francisco a bit. You don't get an address in Pacific Heights by being somebody's errand boy. And he's got business cards for something called Matheson Hydraulics with offices in San Francisco and Portland.'

Gordon returned to the front room and sat down with a fresh cup of tea.

'Anyway, just for the time being, let's say that he *is* bringing cocaine into the U.S., and that he's more than just somebody's pack mule.

'Now, try to look at this situation from his point of view. What is he going to be thinking when he wakes up? He doesn't know where he is, or how he got there. He hasn't really seen us and he won't have any idea where his suitcase is. He's going to be more than just a little bit freaked, especially when he finds out that he's still in Canada and has to find another way of getting across the border.

'So, I'm going to make him an offer he can't refuse. I'm going to tell him to fly back to San Francisco and leave the suitcase with me. I'll deliver it to him in a few days . . . no, no, wait a minute, let me finish. There's a way that we can do this that gives absolute protection to both of us, so that we can't get caught and he can't touch us afterward. When he's gone back to California we'll just take the coke and hike back up to Mt. Redoubt and then thrash our way down that valley we looked at – the one you asked about, but I said was too bushy to drag him out. It'll be a bit of a grunt, but we won't have too much trouble if we keep our packs small, and after a day or so of bushwhacking we'll connect with the Mt. Baker trail system. From there we just drive down the highway to San Francisco and deliver it to him.

'There's no way it can go wrong. There's nothing, not one thing in the universe to connect us to this stuff. It was just blind cosmic chance that we were there when he came down, and we'd be crazy not to take advantage of it.'

Alex said nothing, but his mind was in a turmoil. Blind chance? Life as a cosmic crap shoot? Was God out there somewhere with His jacket over the back of His chair and His cuffs rolled up, hunched over His cupped hands crooning, 'Come on Little Joe, come on Little Joe'?

There had to be more to it than that. And yet Gordon was right, there *was* no chance of getting caught. They could haul *ten* suitcases full of cocaine across the border and never have to worry about trying to act nonchalant and honest in front of Customs, never feel the trickle of fearsweat in the hollow of the spine, never hear that voice behind the dark lenses asking, 'Anything to declare?'

Gordon was still speaking. '. . . and to protect ourselves from any sort of danger from Matheson we just have to make sure that he never sees you or your van. I'll be the only one he sees at either end, and I'll make sure he knows that I've got a partner who's been in from the beginning and will give his name to the police, the IRS, and every newspaper in the country if anything happens to me. Especially the IRS. He just *can't* want them checking his books.

Alex didn't know what to say. He was being forced toward a decision he was unprepared to make, and fragmented thoughts ricocheted through his tired mind. '. . . absolutely foolproof plan . . . Mafia . . . smuggling is glamorous . . . drugs kill . . . things go better with coke . . . how many years in jail . . . how much money . . .' Madness.

Gradually his mind cleared and he was able to isolate the essence of his problem from the crazy swirl. Gordon's plan might not be perfect at it stood, but Alex was sure that they could make it perfect; and there was no question that he could use some extra money – who couldn't?

No, the basic question was very simple. Do you or do you not want to be instrumental in introducing fifteen kilograms of cocaine to the people of America?

So simple and yet so complex. He had once snorted a couple of lines of cocaine at a party in L.A. and experienced nothing more than a numb nose. As far as he knew it wasn't addictive the way heroin was, or Valium or alcohol, and he wasn't entirely sure what people saw in it.

But if the inherent rightness or wrongness of cocaine traffic was open to debate, its legal status certainly wasn't. Alex was happy to be a citizen of the United States of America. He enjoyed living there and he mostly agreed with what he thought America had done and stood for over the years. He had no desire to break the law of his country, but at the same time it was obvious that not all laws were just. Any country that could make conscription legal and cannabis illegal. . . .

If only it had been something other than cocaine. It would have been so easy to flush away bags of heroin. So easy to help out if it had been hash, or diamonds.

'I don't know Gord. I just don't know. I could use some extra money but I don't want to wind up bringing fifteen kilos of misery into the world. Do you understand what I'm saying?'

Gordon rose and walked to the front window. He stood looking out, silhouetted against the summer sun. When he spoke he didn't turn around and his voice was soft and his words hard to catch.

'To the best of my knowledge, there's nothing evil about cocaine, and I don't think that there are hundreds of thousands of slavering coke-heads out there who are ready to kill for their next fix. Shit, they used to put the stuff in soft drinks.'

He turned around and the light rimmed his blond hair, almost like a halo. 'Most of the misery that this will cause will come from its money value. The same misery that you'd cause by smuggling gold or diamonds or rare stamps. And don't kid yourself, anything that's worth over two million dollars and can fit into a small suitcase is going to cause some misery. The only difference is that this stuff probably wasn't stolen from anybody the way gold or stamps would have been.'

'But the cocaine itself isn't addictive?'

'There are probably people who get addicted, but it's not like heroin or booze.' He paused, and then said 'Look, the clearest way I can put it is to say that if I thought I was going to be spreading a lot of misery among innocent people I wouldn't get involved. You know me well enough to realize that.'

He walked back across the room and sat down on the arm of the big chair, facing Alex directly, and said, 'I don't have the wisdom of the Universe at my disposal, so I just go along and try to enjoy my life as much as I can without hurting anyone else. I sell a little pot to help with the mortgage. Does that make me a monster? You know it doesn't. There are people who howl about marijuana corrupting kids and leading to God-knows-what, but you've smoked enough dope to know that that's bullshit. The same people make a lot of noise about cocaine, but that's all it is, noise.

'I've done enough coke to be able to say that I'm never going to get addicted to it, and I believe that any harm that comes out of it comes from human greed, not from the cocaine itself. That's the best answer I can give you.'

Alex bent in the chair and worked his face with the heels of his hands. He needed sleep. He didn't want to think anymore, to answer this terrible question. Then, unexpectedly, he once again felt his friend's hand on his shoulder, and heard Gordon speaking.

'Do you remember when you were a kid Alex? Thinking about what it was going to be like when you grew up? You never knew just how it was going to happen but you knew that someday you'd be grown up, and you'd know all the answers.'

He stood up once again and Alex, still hunched, heard him continue.

'You're grown up now Alex, and so am I; but I never did find any of those answers. I always thought that one morning I'd wake up and find myself an adult, but it never happened, and now I realize that I've been "grown up" for a long time and just never knew it.'

'It's probably the same with getting old. You expect that some day you'll wake up old, but it isn't going to happen that way. What'll happen is that one day you'll realize that you've been old for the last five years; and then, if cancer doesn't get you first, you're eventually just going to dry up and die.'

The words seemed to Alex as if they were coming from the far end of a long tunnel; reverberant and charged with hidden meaning.

'But what's going to happen to us? You and I aren't going to get any pension or monthly visit from our grandchildren. What's going to happen is that one of these days an avalanche is going to get you, or a belay is going to pull, or you'll break a leg someplace where you need two legs to get out.

'Maybe that's part of what keeps us climbing and keeps us digging being alive but there are still a few things left that I want to do and I think that it's going to be easier to do them if I can make twenty-five thousand dollars next week by delivering a suitcase full of cocaine to San Francisco.'

He stopped speaking and silence grew in the room. Alex rose and went to the window. He stood looking out, but his vision was turned inward and he saw nothing. After a long time he turned and said simply,

'Okay.'

Gordon heated a can of soup and took that, a pitcher of water, and a bowl, spoon and drinking glass in to the bedroom. He was out again very quickly and said to Alex, 'He's awake and eating the soup. I think he's going to be alright.'

He disappeared down the basement stairs and returned a minute later with two foam pads.

'I think we should get some sleep now, before he's up and about. Go ahead and crash right there on the couch, I'll sleep in front of the bedroom door. He won't be able to get out without waking me and I'll make sure he doesn't see you. We can talk about how to make the delivery foolproof later.'

Alex lay down on the couch, exhausted and ready for sleep, relieved that he did not have to think any more. But doubt and fear nagged him, and sleep was slow in coming. He rose and walked down the hallway to where Gordon was lying in front of the bedroom door.

'Gord.' He nudged at the body on the floor with his foot, then bent down to whisper when the eyes opened.

'Gord, what makes you so sure that he's going to go for your plan. Everything depends on him accepting your idea. What if he doesn't?'

Gordon slowly sat up and yawned, then said 'He already did. I talked to him while you were in the shower this morning. He's only too pleased to have us carrying for him, going to pay us fifty thousand dollars. American dollars. Now go back to bed and get some sleep.'

CHAPTER NINE

U.S./Canada Border

THERE IS a certain inevitability about the speeches made when politicians from America and Canada gather, and the phrase 'the longest undefended border in the world' usually figures prominently. But while this border makes great fodder for speeches, it is an unending nightmare for the DEA. Policing the approximately five thousand miles which separate America from its northern neighbour is impossible. Given sufficient men and equipment the waterways of the east and the open farmland of the prairies could be covered, but how do you control five hundred miles of uninhabited mountains?

There is no way. The only thing which keeps down the volume of drugs crossing these mountains is the same thing which makes them hard to police. The terrain is steep and travel is difficult and dangerous and most importers are content to accept the stricter control of the Mexican border and the major American sea- and airports in return for the relative physical ease of travel through them.

But for those willing to make the effort, the mountains remain the surest way of bringing illegal drugs into the United States of America. It is true that this means that the shipment must first be brought into Canada, but this is laughably simple, and both the net cost and the net risk can be reduced even though two borders must be crossed instead of one.

If there is no rush, if a little extra time is no problem, then the cheapest, most secure way is the oldest way of all: hire someone to carry the goods through the mountains on his back. Still, this is no easy task. The wide valleys of the Rocky Mountains are policed and supervised, and the more westerly ranges have a way of policing themselves. They are steeper and more forbidding, glaciated and avalanche prone, dangerous, even to an experienced climber.

But climbers are natural smugglers. Many of them are outsiders by nature and tend to think of the law as something that applies to other people. They are used to taking risks: and most important, they are used to careful planning.

For Alex Townsend and Gordon Wilson, carrying fifteen kilograms of cocaine through the mountains was a relatively simple and straightforward task; less dangerous, less strenuous and less complicated than their climb of the week before.

And yet, simple as it was, they spent the two days after Walter Matheson's departure scrutinizing every aspect of their plans, making certain that absolutely nothing would go wrong.

– What if we run out of gas? Or something equally stupid?

Buy extra jerry cans. Check the tool kits in each vehicle. Oil. Water. Battery. Spare tyre.

– What if the weather turns bad?

Take your Gore-tex and pile, we're not waiting for the weather on this one. Don't forget your bivvy sack.

Food. Maps. Compass. Headlamps, matches, stove, first aid.

Take a rope. Just a short one though, we don't need extra weight. Don't forget your prussiks.

Sunscreen. Insect repellent. Sunglasses, ice axe, water bottle.

And on. And on.

It was just a two day hike. No technical climbing, just a walk in the mountains and a bit of glacier-bashing, but for twenty-five thousand dollars each they were willing to double-check the details.

The only hitch in their otherwise smooth preparation came when Alex phoned his employer to say that he would be a few days late getting back to Seattle.

As he said later to Gordon, 'I guess he just got tired of my three and four day weekends, and this was the overload that blew his fuse.'

'I never understood why you wanted to work in that garage anyway.'

'It wasn't that bad.'

'Good, bad or indifferent, you're going to make enough in the next few days to take the sting out of getting fired, so I wouldn't worry about it too much.'

'I guess. And things are starting to pick up now so I'll probably be able to find something else.'

It had been a strange two days. Walter Matheson stayed in the bedroom where Gordon brought him his meals. Alex parked his van several blocks away, and he and Gordon spent their time planning and bullshitting in a nervous and preoccupied way. Gordon took Matheson out on the second day to a clothing store to get something to wear and Alex went shopping to replace the sleeping bag that had been bloodied beyond salvation.

On the third morning Gordon drove Walter Matheson to the airport, and they realized that their preparations were complete. They had gone over everything many times, looked for anything that might go wrong, planned for every eventuality. Now it was time to act.

They put the suitcase in Gordon's closet and left Vancouver at midmorning the next day in separate vehicles and drove southeast along the TransCanada highway for about 45 miles. Here, where the highway is almost tangent to the forty-ninth parallel, they turned south and crossed the border at the tiny town of Sumas, Washington.

Alex went through customs first, with no problem. Gordon was right behind in his little brown Datsun, but customs wanted to talk. Alex waited about a mile down the road, until Gordon caught up about fifteen minutes later.

'What happened?'

'Ahh, that stupid fucker didn't like the colour of my car or something. Maybe he hates longhairs, I don't know. Maybe he was pissed that I could take the day off and he couldn't. Who knows. Anybody that works for customs has got to be a bit of an asshole to start with. They searched the car and gave me the red ass.' Then he grinned a huge grin and said, 'Good thing I changed my mind about bringing Walter's little bundles of joy along for the ride.'

'You're joking.'

'I thought about it for a while. They hardly ever check anybody at this crossing, and it would have saved two or three days of hard work, but in the end . . . well, who needs twenty years in jail.' He laughed. 'Anyway, I didn't do it and there was nothing for them to find.'

The road wound southeast through a few miles of farmland and then climbed up for three quarters of an hour into the Mt. Baker National Forest. At the Nooksak river, just past the Department of Highways maintenance yard, they turned left onto a gravel road marked 'Hannegan Campground'. A little less than five miles later this road ended at a parking area and campground where there were signs pointing to the beginning of a trail and a large covered notice board carrying a map of the North Cascades trail system and a list of rules and the penalties for their infraction.

The map did not show any trail leading into Canada, nor was there any indication of the penalty for smuggling narcotics through the area.

They left some canned food, a six-pack of Labatt's Blue, and some clean clothes in Alex's van, locked it up and left it there, parked beside three other dusty cars whose owners were hiking somewhere nearby. Presumably being careful to camp and move their bowels only in approved locations.

Their return to Vancouver in Gordon's Datsun was uneventful, Canadian customs merely asking if they had anything to declare and waving them through when they said they hadn't.

Alex was silent for most of the drive. The border crossings had shaken him and the sharp corners of reality were intruding into his acceptance of Gordon's plan. He had a sudden urge to bail out right then, while he still could.

Just like a big alpine climb, he thought. You make plans, go over all the details of the route, select your equipment and make the approach. Then, at the base of the climb, you get your last chance to back off, for you know that somewhere on the climb you are going to cross the line of retreat.

He tried to analyze the source of his discomfort. What could possibly go wrong? Nothing. He knew that. They could not be caught and as long as they were careful about avalanche slopes and crevasses they couldn't get hurt. Nor could anything go wrong at the other end. Gordon's delivery arrangement was fireproof.

He finally identified his unease as a barely conscious revulsion at the idea of being associated with criminals. He didn't mind the thought of actually *being* a criminal – in fact there was something almost glamorous about smuggling cocaine – but to associate with criminals. . . .

'Sometimes I'm so middle class it's frightening.'

'What?'

'Nothing, just thinking out loud.'

It was late afternoon when they reached Vancouver. Gordon took the Grandview exit and soon they were westbound on East 12th Avenue where the rush hour traffic was going mostly the other way, hardly slowing them at all.

Even here, in a lower class residential area, the city was attractive and Alex suddenly realized that although he had visited Vancouver dozens of times he had never seen a slum or any kind of ghetto. Even the so called Skid Road area around lower Main St. was clean and spacious compared to some of the districts he had seen in the large cities of California and the Northwest.

'Gord.'

'Yeah?'

'Let's eat somewhere really good tonight.'

'Sure. Why? You feeling rich already?'

'No, it's just that I've had a lot of good times around Vancouver and I don't know when I'm going to be here again.'

'What are you talking about? You can be back next week if you feel like it. This is only going to take us a few days – it's not as if you were off to Afghanistan or something.'

'I know, I know. But somehow I feel that . . . that . . .' Alex paused and watched the city rolling by outside the window. 'I don't know exactly how I feel. Sort of strange, like I'm saying goodbye to something.'

He looked across at Gordon and said, 'I guess I sound like an idiot. But I'd still like to eat somewhere nice. Do you know someplace quiet, with good food and maybe a view of the city?'

Gordon thought for a short time. 'View of the city? Yeah I suppose so. There's a place on top of Grouse Mountain – you have to take a cable car to get there, and you look down on the city from about four thousand feet up. And there's the Salmon House in West Van. It's got a pretty good view and the food's okay but I've never liked it very much.'

He drove in silence for a while, then said, 'Wait a minute, wait a minute, I've got a much better idea. You want a real view of this place? Of what Vancouver is really about?'

The main dining room at the Cannery overhangs the water and from a window table Alex and Gordon watched the lowering sun expand and redden, dominating the harbour as it sank into the Pacific. Along the waterfront, monster loading cranes stood in sharp silhouette until the sun was gone and a million watts of artificial light outlined them in a new and even starker geometry.

The meal was as good as the view, and somewhere between the second bottle of wine and the café royales they decided to go to Yosemite when they finished their business in San Francisco.

'It's only two hundred miles, and it would be a shame to pass so close and not stop for a while.'

'And I guess that I don't have to worry about getting back to work on time.'

At ten-thirty the next morning, the thirtieth of August, Alex Townsend walked across the border slash with eight kilograms of cocaine in his pack. No bells rang and the Lord did not strike him dead. He continued down the trail wondering what he had expected to happen and wondering if it was disappointment he felt when nothing did.

He finally decided that this kind of crime, like the border he had just crossed, was a matter of political definition, and that perhaps he had worried too much about it. The forest didn't change at the forty-ninth parallel, the big old firs were the same on one side of the border as the other. If they didn't care, why should he?

The trail they were following was the same one they had taken a week before when they had come to climb the north-east face of Mt. Redoubt. There are vague references to it in one or two climbers' guidebooks, but it appears on no map in either Canada or America and is not known to the government of either country. To reach it they had dodged potholes and logging trucks all the way up the Chilliwack River valley, turned south on rapidly deteriorating roads to the end of Chilliwack Lake, and then bumped along for a mile or two in the ruts above the marsh at the end of the lake until the Datsun would go no further. From there, a few hundred yards of walking had taken them into a jumble of old logging slash and the unmarked start of the trail less than a quarter mile north of the border.

The trail rambled several miles southwest through the ancient forest of the Depot Creek valley and then came to an apparent end at the base of the waterfall which sprawls in little leaps and jumps down the thousand foot headwall at the end of the valley. But the two men had been this way before; they walked through the spray at the base of the falls and climbed very carefully up twenty feet of slimy, mossy rock until they reached dry ground and the continuation of the trail.

'It must have been a pretty dry year when they cut this trail.'

'I guess so, but it sure feels good to cool off in the spray.' Gordon took off his pack and squatted down to drink from the creek. 'Do you want to stop here for some lunch?'

Alex considered the headwall above them and replied, 'No, if I stop to eat now I'll never force myself up that. Let's just have some gorp and a drink and then get it over with. We can stop and eat at the top.'

The Depot Creek headwall is not a technical climbing challenge. Rather, it is a quadricep-pumping, lung-bursting grunt up through steep forest and ankle-turning talus that suddenly ends in a hanging valley below the magnificent north face of Mount Redoubt. When they reached the top of the headwall they both collapsed. Alex was panting, guzzling from his water bottle and trying to talk, all at the same time. 'How did we ever manage to carry Matheson down that?'

'Yeah, and in the dark!'

After a lunch of peanut butter and honey sandwiches and gatorade they crossed the valley and unpacked their crampons, rope and ice axes and ascended the small glacier that drops from Redoubt's west ridge. From the ridgecrest they looked down into Bear Creek valley, a tangle of green with Bear Creek glinting silver and white at the bottom, and the North Face of Bear Mountain rising dark and ominous on the other side. Below and to their left, bright yellow against Redoubt's snowy white skirt, was the broken aircraft lying exactly as they had left it.

They looked at it and then at each other, but neither spoke.

They stayed high as long as they could, but eventually had to drop down and the heat of the late afternoon found them in hand to hand combat with the bush of the valley bottom. Devil's club tore at their clothes and skin and the slide alder was so thick and tangled that in places they could not keep their feet on the ground as they struggled through it.

'Can you imagine,' asked Alex, wiping salty sweat from his eyes, 'what it would have been like trying to carry him out this way?'

'I don't even want to think about it. It would have taken days.'

They camped that evening in a small clearing beside the creek. Supper was more sandwiches, a can of salmon, and tea.

'It ain't haute cuisine, but it's a lot better than that freeze-dried shit,' was Gordon's verdict.

They were tired, but neither was quite ready for sleep so they built a small fire to keep the mosquitoes at bay and sat, watching the flames. Alex finally broke the silence.

'What happened with you and Louise? I didn't see any sign of her at your place and you haven't mentioned her all week?'

'I guess we sort of split up.'

'She catch you in bed with the milkmaid?'

'No, nothing like that this time. In fact, that's the funny thing about it. I haven't even looked at anyone else in over a year, and let me tell you that has sure as hell never happened before. And I think it was the same with her.'

Gordon threw more wood on the fire. When he resumed speaking there was something almost wistful in his voice, a trace of confusion. 'I liked her a lot, it was a real comfortable thing we had going, but she got an offer from an agency in Toronto. They liked her work and she said that she would have a lot more opportunities there than in Vancouver . . .

'She wanted me to come with her.' His voice tailed off and he stared at the fire. 'Have you ever been in Toronto Alex?'

'No.'

'It's the ass end of nowhere. I couldn't live there – it would be like you moving to Cleveland or some place like that.'

'I was in Cleveland once,' said Alex.

'Well Toronto's like that, only even more boring. There's about three million people there and most of them actually like it. In fact they're smug about it. But you know something? I even thought about doing it. I liked her that much. And I still miss her.'

Then he laughed. 'But I finally decided that I'm only going to have this one life, and I'll be damned if I'm going to spend it in Toronto.'

He had been leaning back against his pack, and now he turned around and reached down into it.

'Here, try this.' He handed Alex a fifth of Armagnac, the misshapen bottle looking strangely natural in this wild place.

They passed the bottle back and forth a few times in silence, then Gordon asked, 'What about you? Still waiting for Miss Wonderful to walk into your life?'

'I guess so. I don't know.' Alex could feel the brandy starting to work on him, a gentle amber fog billowing through his mind. 'Sometimes I wonder if I'll ever find anyone. It's so easy to get laid, and so hard to find someone to love. I get pretty frustrated sometimes.'

'Maybe you should just relax and enjoy getting laid now and again, and stop worrying about True Love.'

Alex could hear the capitals. 'I can't Gord. I've been married once and I know how good it can be. Maybe I'm too much of a romantic, but I'm willing to wait as long as I have to.'

'It's your life, I suppose, but just be careful you don't run out of patience and start building dream castles around someone. I've seen that happen to a few people and boy, can it ever get messy.' Gordon capped the bottle and put it back in his pack. 'Anyway, we've got a long day in front of us, so I'm going to crash.'

They woke just after sunrise and breakfasted on granola with powdered milk and several cups of tea. Two hours later they broke out of the bush onto the North Cascades trail system which they followed for four sweaty hours up and over Hannegan pass and down to Alex's van.

They drank warm beer and ate smoked oysters out of the can with their fingers, and Gordon talked and sang nonstop all the way to Seattle.

'Just as ugly as ever.' Gordon was admiring the non-view from Alex's living room window. He turned and looked around the room. 'But at least it isn't so bad inside now. Goddamned if I know how you stood it here at first. It was about as homey as the men's room in a bus station.'

Alex lived in a decaying apartment in a small building on East Fir. It was the first vacancy he had looked at when he arrived in Seattle, and he had taken it without any thought. He furnished it with what was on sale in the bargain basement of the nearest department store and had lived in it that way for two years before he first imprinted it with something of his slowly developing personality. Then, gradually, he began to replace the instant furniture with solid, comfortable pieces until, in its present state, it was a pleasant enough residence for a single man.

It did not have the solidity and warmth of a real home, and there was still a temporary feeling in it. But Alex was not yet a solid person, and there was still something temporary about him too.

But he was working on it. He had arrived in Seattle empty, held together only by negatives; running from, rather than coming to. Now, four and a half years later, he was almost a whole man and had even begun to dream; not exactly about his future, but about the possibility that he might have a future worth dreaming about.

They both showered and changed. Alex put on light wool pants in medium brown, a white shirt with brown pinstripes, a coffee coloured pullover wool vest and brown socks and mocassins. Gordon wore his usual T-shirt and jeans. He asked, 'You hungry?'

'Yes, but I don't think there's much in the kitchen.'

'Good, you're a terrible cook anyway. Let's grab a beer and a sandwich somewhere and head straight back to pick up my car. We can camp right there if we're tired or drive back to Vancouver and stay at my place. Then in the morning we can pack up all my rock climbing gear, come back here to get your gear and the coke, and then head for California.'

'Okay, but give me a few minutes. I'll postdate a couple of cheques for my slumlord, and I should probably phone Eleanor . . .'

'You deceitful swine!' shouted Gordon. 'You told me you didn't have anything going for you here. I can't trust anybody anymore. Does she have a sister?'

'She's *my* sister you horny clown. She came up here a few months ago to do a Masters in some kind of esoteric biology. I don't see her much but I always let her know when I'm going to be out of town for a while. If I don't keep in touch then my whole family gets worried and they come up here to make sure I'm okay.

'She's a genuine, right out of the mould, Townsend. You wouldn't like her, and even if you did she sure as hell wouldn't like you.'

CHAPTER TEN

San Francisco

WALTER MATHESON had a slight headache. He had debated seeing his doctor about it, but then decided that a mild headache wasn't unreasonable considering that it was only a week since the crash. He would give it another week before he called the doctor. In the meantime, aspirins seemed to help, and a tumbler or two of whiskey in the evening didn't hurt either.

And when he thought about it, a sore head was a small price to pay for his freedom.

He poured a drink and made a silent toast to the memory of the pilot, Kiniski. If he hadn't spotted the other aircraft. . . . But he had, and although it was too bad about the crash, at least Walter had been prepared for the police when they arrived.

Ever since he returned from Vancouver he'd been expecting to be questioned. Good luck to them. With the pilot dead and that climber, Wilson, carrying for him there was no way he could be connected to anything. The plane crash was turning out to be an unbelievable piece of luck.

He was almost caught up at the office, and Marion accepted his story about a fall down a rocky hillside near the fishing lake and was taking 'extra special care of my poor husband'; and even that snotty black bastard from the Police Department hadn't been able to put a dent in his good humour.

He finished his whiskey and laughed out loud. Let them try to charge him with anything. Let them tap his phone, audit his books, anything they wanted. He was so clean he squeaked, and after maybe two more shipments he would kiss the whole lot of them goodbye. Goodbye to stupid, fat Marion, goodbye to snotty suspicious cops, goodbye to the whole city and country. And he didn't even have to worry about the pilot anymore.

Now, if only that Wilson would phone, and his head would stop hurting. . . .

CHAPTER ELEVEN

San Francisco

ALEX TOWNSEND was nervous. He sat on the bed in his hotel room and looked at the entertainment guide on the bedside table. He turned the pages absently for half a minute then stood up and dropped the magazine on the bed behind him. He walked to the television and turned it on. He stood in front of it and changed slowly through about half the channels then angrily slapped the off switch. He looked at his watch, then crossed the room, opened the big sliding window and stepped out onto the balcony.

It was a warm summer morning and the city of San Francisco was spread out above, below and around him, but he didn't really see it. He looked at his watch again and then turned back into the room and stood staring at the telephone, willing it to ring.

Gordon had said he would call every half hour and now twenty-five minutes had passed since the last call. That call had been short and to the point. Alex had answered on the first ring and Gordon had simply said, 'It's all set. I'm meeting the man in a restaurant called the Bayview in a couple of minutes.

It's right downtown, not that far from your hotel. There's plenty of people around and I can't see any way anything can go wrong. It's quarter to eleven now so I'll call you by eleven-fifteen. Okay?'

'Okay, just be careful.'

'Yeah.'

Alex paced the room and looked at his watch again. Twelve past. He wondered what to do if the telephone didn't ring. Leave immediately? Wait an extra few minutes? Their emergency plan was for Alex to leave immediately if Gord didn't call on time, and then to call Gordon's hotel every hour or so from a pay phone.

He had just decided that he would give Gordon five minutes' grace when the shrilling telephone startled him so badly that he dropped a magazine that he didn't remember picking up.

'Hello?'

'Everything's okay Alex. I'm downstairs in the lobby, so pack up your pyjamas and toothbrush and meet me down here. I'll buy you lunch.' He giggled. 'I think I can afford it.'

They ate in the hotel dining room and Gordon described what had happened.

'I called Matheson this morning at his office. He said I should call another number and ask for Carl. So I did that, and this guy Carl said that I should meet him at the Bayview Restaurant. It's one of those plastic twenty-four hour places, but it had a parking lot for customers only, which is probably why he picked it.'

'So what happened?' Alex was like a schoolboy trying to pry information from a friend who had just done something exciting and forbidden. He tried to sound casual, but he was burning with curiosity, and more admiration than he wanted to admit.

'Nothing much. Carl, if that's really his name, met me there right on time and we made the swap in the parking lot. He gave me this . . .' Gordon pointed to a cheap-looking vinyl attaché case on the chair to his left, '. . . and I gave him the big suitcase. The whole thing took about three minutes.'

'But how did he know who you were? How did you know that there was the right amount of money in the case? How did he know that you weren't ripping him off?'

Gordon looked at his friend with amused curiosity. 'You've been watching too much television Alex. He knew what I looked like because I had told him on the telephone, and we each knew what was in the other guy's case because we opened them up and looked.'

'In the parking lot?' Alex's voice rose an octave and cracked on the last two words.

'Relax, relax. We sat in the car I rented and he looked in my suitcase and I looked in his. I didn't count the money down to the last dollar and he didn't weigh the coke, but we both checked that each case looked about right.' Gordon took a spoonful of soup, then said, 'And what the hell, Matheson knows where I live, and I know where he lives, so nobody is going to be ripping anybody off. What would be the point? Anyway, the whole deal took about three minutes and nobody paid the least bit of attention to us, so relax and enjoy your lunch.'

Alex took a bite of his club sandwich then asked with his mouth full, 'What about this guy Carl?'

'What about him? He's a sort of medium sized black guy who's had his face kicked in a few times. I don't even know if his name is really Carl. He's Matheson's bag man, that's all I know about him. That's all I *want* to know about him. He didn't talk much except to say that Matheson wants me to give him a call sometime in January or February if I want to do another carry.'

'Another?'

'Yeah, I guess he likes me.'

CHAPTER TWELVE

San Francisco

LIEUTENANT WILLIAM HOLLEY was furious. His anger simmered just below the surface and some of the guys in the drug squad had started a pool based on the hour and day that he would finally explode. Even the secretaries and the com-ops were getting their money down.

The last time he had been this way was when Judge Partington had given a suspended sentence to a kid that Holley had caught with almost half a kilo of smack. He had sat at his desk brooding, not talking to anyone for three days after that. On the fourth morning he had shown up with a split lip, a badly puffed eye, and two fingers in splints. But cheerful and ready to go back to work. When somebody asked him, 'What does the other guy look like?' he had just smiled and said, 'Which one?'

This time it was worse. He had taken Matheson's escape from the RCMP as a personal insult and when he heard that Matheson had appeared back in the city he had hurled a telephone book across the room and stamped out of his office.

Three days later he was still boiling. The pilot and the airplane were gone – disappeared as though they had never existed. And yet they couldn't have crashed because here was Matheson alive and well in San Francisco with a bullshit story about being marooned at some lake and cutting his head on the way out. Did he expect Holley to *believe* that?

Holley knew exactly what had happened. The airplane had come through the storm and landed at some private field in eastern Washington or Oregon. The airplane, and the body of the pilot were in a deserted barn or garage and probably wouldn't be found for ten years. It looked like the pilot had got in one good lick before Matheson murdered him, but that was the only satisfaction he could find.

Then came the last straw. A strictly from hunger check of incoming passenger lists showed that Matheson had flown into San Francisco on a Canadian Pacific Airlines 737 from Vancouver. *Vancouver*! It didn't make any sense at all. What the fuck was he doing in Vancouver?

The RCMP pilots might be idiots, but there was good civilian and military radar all along the Fraser valley and everybody agreed that the little Cessna hadn't come back over the border.

Holley gave up trying to think. He went home, drank most of a bottle of vodka and passed out before supper.

He awoke a little after midnight and made the first of many trips to the bathroom. After a while he stopped going back to bed between spasms and just lay on the cold tiles where he eventually fell asleep just before dawn.

He got to his office in the middle of the next afternoon, a little shaky but calmed right down, and started asking around to see who knew anybody in the Vancouver Police Department.

CHAPTER THIRTEEN

Vancouver

POLICE DETECTIVES almost always work in pairs. There are a lot of good reasons for this, but when one partner gets sick, the other is often unable to carry on alone with the job they were working on.

Andy Cutler and Doug Popov had been working a trio of real nasties. Dirtballs with a maim-for-money service and a seemingly inexhaustible supply of acid and speed. When Popov came down with a cold bad enough to keep him in bed, Cutler decided to give himself some time off from the case.

As he explained to his Sergeant: 'Rico, these guys are not only stupid, they're mean. They're also bigger than me and I am not going anywhere near them alone. I'll shuffle paper and answer the telephone for a day or two until Doug is healthy again.'

The day passed uneventfully. Cutler caught up on his paperwork and spent a lot of time on the telephone. Most of the calls originated within the Department and were simply requests for information or requests to speak to a particular member of the drug squad. The few calls from the outside were equally dull. Complaints about kids smoking pot in a parking lot; or offers of information, like:

'Uh, listen, I know where these guys are going to be doing a deal on some hash, right? And I was thinking that it'd probably be worth something for me to tell you, right?'

The usual.

Then, late in the afternoon, just as he was about to call it a day, he caught one from the switchboard.

'Sir, San Francisco P.D. is on the line. It's a Lieutenant Holley, and he wants to talk to someone in Drugs.'

'Okay Ellen, put him through.'

'Yes sir. Hello sir, you're connected to Detective Cutler, go ahead please.'

'Detective Cutler? I am Lieutenant William Holley of the Narcotics Investigation Section of the San Francisco Police Department. I am investigating the actions of a man whom I suspect to be bringing large amounts of cocaine into this country through the Canadian province of British Columbia, and I believe that he may have spent some time in Vancouver in the last two weeks. I would like to ask for some help from your department, but before I do I would like you to verify that I am who I say I am.'

Cutler always felt uneasy with people who spoke formal English, and this guy was a positive steamroller. At least his meaning was clear. 'Okay. Hang up and I'll call you back.'

'Fine.'

Cutler broke the connection and rang the switchboard again. He got the same operator. 'Ellen, it's Andy Cutler in Drugs. Will you call San Francisco P.D. and see if they'll connect me to a Lieutenant William Holley in the Narcotics Investigation Section? Thanks.'

He hung up and lit a cigarette. This sounded more interesting than kids smoking pot in the parking lot.

Andy Cutler was a quiet man in his late thirties. He had a long body and a long, lined face under curly blond hair; and blue eyes that were still full of excitement even after eleven years of police work. He smoked too many cigarettes and felt guilty enough about it to run two or three miles every other day, but not guilty enough to quit smoking.

Most of the time he enjoyed police work and felt it important. He was not a redneck or a law 'n order fanatic, just a man who believed that a policeman who did his job with intelligence and compassion was making an important contribution to the society in which he lived.

He had done well since joining the Vancouver force, making Detective after only seven years, and he knew that he would get Sergeant in the spring. And through it all he had even managed to keep his sense of humour.

Now, as he went back to the last of his paperwork he wondered just what Lieutenant Holley wanted, and why anyone would be smuggling 'large amounts of cocaine' to the States via B.C. Why bother? It must be somebody doing it privately, an amateur who thought that getting fancy was the way to fool Customs and the police.

The telephone rang on his desk. 'Hello sir, I've got Lieutenant Holley on the line from San Francisco, shall I connect you?'

'Yes, please.'

'Alright sir. Hello sir, I have Detective Cutler on the line, go ahead please.'

'Thank you. Detective Cutler?'

'Hello Lieutenant, how can I help you?'

'You can help by telling me what a man named Matheson was doing before he flew out of Vancouver on twenty-ninth August. I've written up a full report on this and I'll telex it up to you, but here's the general picture.' Holley's voice was still crisp and intense, but the formality was gone.

'I was working a guy named Carl Adams a couple of years ago. We knew he was riding shotgun on heroin deals for one of the big importers here, a concert promoter named Tomlinson, and we were pretty sure he had pulled the trigger a couple of times. One day we got a tip that there was a big deal going down and we staked him out. It turned out that there was no deal, he just had a meet with a guy and nothing changed hands. We had them covered with a blanket, I mean we had five guys watching and I *know* nothing changed hands. We followed them both away from the meet and got nothing except that this other guy went home to a very nice piece of real estate in Pacific Heights, which is not exactly the low rent district.'

Cutler was taking notes and wondering where this was going.

'We checked him out. His name is Walter Frederick Matheson and he's an engineer. He runs his own company and he's completely legit. He really is a full time engineer – well thought of, very successful, no record, no extravagant lifestyle, nothing. So what the hell is he doing meeting with a piece of human trash like Carl Adams? I mean Adams really is the quintessential ratbag, and anybody he talks to has just *got* to be dirty.'

Cutler wrote 'quintessential ratbag' on the margin of his notepad and drew a circle around it.

'So I dug a little deeper on this Matheson, figuring that it was probably blackmail, but guess what I found?' Holley's voice sharpened, became even more intense. 'I found two things. One, he's got a brother in Peru; and two, he takes a week or two off every year, sometimes twice a year, and goes fishing in Canada. More specifically he goes salmon fishing out of a town called Prince Rupert, which is an isolated little place right on the coast and he . . .'

'Smack city,' interrupted Cutler.

'What?'

'Prince Rupert. We used to call it smack city. It's actually a fairly busy seaport with a really big fishing fleet. A lot of heroin comes in through there.'

There was silence at the other end while Holley thought about this new piece of information. Cutler didn't say anything more, just stubbed out his cigarette and waited. Finally Holley said 'Hm. I didn't know that. But I don't think there's any real connection between that and this Matheson business. I think he's strictly on his own. Let me explain. After I found out about the brother in Peru I leaned on a couple of people I know and they told me that the people that Carl Adams works for are in the coke business in a minor way. We thought they were strictly into heroin, but it seems that they also get a bit of cocaine now and then, maybe ten or fifteen keys, maybe twice a year. It gets stepped on of course, but the word is that it's pure as can be when they get it.

'So,' Holley's voice bored on, 'it looks to me that the brothers Matheson have an import-export business going. The one in Peru either sends it or takes it up to Canada on a boat and Walter meets the boat and brings the shipment back into America from there. He then sells it to Adams' people and sends the money down to Peru. Does that scan okay for you?'

Cutler had been trying to think of a way to work the phrase 'quintessential ratbag' into his next conversation with Rico and the question caught him off guard. He reviewed the conversation quickly and then said, 'That seems reasonable to me, have you managed any hard evidence? Can you talk to Peru about the money end of it?'

Holley just snorted. 'Not fucking likely. What government wants to talk about drugs going out and money coming in? But I do have a certain amount of evidence.' He explained how he had set up a cooperative deal with the DEA and the RCMP and how everything had gone perfectly until somehow Matheson had discovered the RCMP surveillance and disappeared into the storm over the North Cascades.

'What does the pilot have to say?' asked Cutler.

'Well, that's where the evidence starts to get less hard. You see the pilot isn't anywhere to be found. Matheson flew into that storm in the afternoon of twenty-third August and showed up at the Vancouver airport to board Canadian Pacific Airlines flight 117 to San Francisco on the twenty-seventh. The pilot and the plane are still missing. The RCMP say he didn't come back to Canada, and he hasn't shown up anywhere here. What I think is that they got through the storm okay and landed at some private field in Washington, and that Matheson offed the pilot right there and hid the plane, probably in an old barn or garage. But what I *can't* figure out is what the hell is going on with this flight out of Vancouver. It just doesn't make any sense at all.'

'And I suppose you don't want to talk directly to Matheson until you've got something hard enough to pull him in with?'

'No, there's no problem there, the fact that the plane went missing on a flight he chartered gave us all the excuse we needed to talk to him, but he had a bullshit story all ready for us, and even though I know he's lying, I don't see what I can do about it. I mean we can prove that he crossed the border in an airplane, but we can't prove that he brought in any coke.'

Cutler asked, 'Just what is his story?'

'He says he chartered the plane to take him fishing at some little lake the pilot knew about. He says the pilot put him down at the lake and never came back. He says that the lake is pretty remote, quite a few miles from the road and that after waiting for a couple of days with no food or camping equipment he thrashed his way out through the bush and hitchhiked to civilization. He's got a pretty good head wound which he says he got when he took a bad fall in some rocks on the way out from the lake, and things aren't too clear to him after that. He says he thinks he must have hitchhiked to Vancouver, or maybe taken a bus. He says he really doesn't remember much until he got back to San Francisco.

'Anyway, that's the problem: we know he's lying about being stranded at the lake, I mean there were two RCMP guys in the plane behind him all the way to the border. And I'm dead sure that he's bringing in regular shipments of cocaine; but there's not much we can do about it with what we've got. So, what I'd like to know is why he went back to Canada and what he did there until the twenty-seventh. Maybe I'm grabbing at nothing, but if there's any way you can help me on this I'd sure appreciate it.'

Cutler stretched and yawned, holding the receiver away from his head, then said, 'Okay, let's see if I've got this right? You suspect that a San Francisco engineer named Walter Matheson has an arrangement with his brother in Peru whereby the brother brings or sends ten to fifteen kilos of cocaine to Prince Rupert once or twice a year and that this Walter Matheson picks it up there and smuggles it into the U.S. by light plane. He then sells it to a big heroin dealer, named Tomlinson – who is the one you're really after – and then sends the profits back to Peru. On his last trip you had the RCMP follow him. They saw him take off from Prince Rupert and followed him non-stop to the Canada–U.S.A. border where he apparently became suspicious and flew into a storm. This was on twenty-third August. He showed up four days later on a flight from Vancouver to San Francisco, but the light plane and its pilot are still missing. Is that right?'

'That's right. I've been looking for a way to nail Tomlinson for about three years now but he keeps his hands completely clean. At least as far as his heroin business is concerned. Maybe he hasn't been so careful with this little side deal. Maybe Matheson knows something, and if I can give him the choice of talking to me or doing twenty years of hard time maybe he'll tell me something.

'Like I said, I may be grabbing at nothing, but I want Tomlinson pretty bad, and this is the only way I can think of to get at him. I've tried everything else. About ten times.' He sounded angry and disgusted.

'Okay.' Cutler made a quick note and then said, 'I've got a couple of questions.'

'Shoot.'

He looked down at his notepad, then asked, 'First, had the plane actually crossed the border, or was it just heading that way when the RCMP lost contact?'

'Very definitely across the border. They had good visibility on the Canadian side and they say he didn't come back out.'

'Okay, next question is whether the RCMP are working on this from the Prince Rupert end?'

'Yeah, they are, but . . .' Holley paused '. . . but mostly from the point of view of the missing airplane. I had a few harsh words for them after they blew the aerial surveillance and I don't think they're going to be putting a lot of energy into this on my behalf.'

'I see.' Cutler made an aimless doodle on his pad and then asked, 'Do you have any theory yourself about why he came back to Canada?'

'Mister Cutler, I don't have even the vaguest beginning of a theory as to why he would do a thing like that. It doesn't make any sense to me at all. As long as he's claiming that he spent the twenty-fourth and twenty-fifth at this lake, which, by the way, he claims not to know the name of, and that he hitchhiked or took a bus from there to Vancouver then he doesn't need any kind of alibi and there's no need for him to go back. So *anything* you can turn up for me might help.'

'What about this wound on his head: how bad was it, and how recent, and how do you figure it?'

'Pretty bad. He even took the bandages off to show me. It was at least four inches long, big enough to take maybe twenty-five stitches, but it hadn't been stitched. It was a kind of ragged cut that ran most of the way across his forehead just above the eyebrows. It still hadn't healed up when I saw it, but it must have been about a week old judging from the state of the scab and the shiners it had given him. My guess is that the pilot got in a good shot with a wrench or something before he was killed.'

Cutler thought for a long time and finally said, 'If the cut on his head was gory enough, I might be able to find someone at the airport who remembers him, but all that would prove is that he was at the airport, and you already know that. There's a chance that he might have given the airline a Vancouver address or telephone number, and I'll check that out; but what we really need is to find out if he did anything with his credit cards while he was here. If he was here a week ago the companies should be starting to get their copies about now. Can you check that out for me?'

'I've already started work on that, but the companies don't like to give that sort of information away.'

'Well, keep on it, because it's likely to be the only way I'll be able to find anything for you . . . excuse me a minute, I'll be right back.'

A dark, heavy-set man in a brown three piece had left an office at the far end of the room and was walking toward the elevators. Cutler put his hand over the mouthpiece and stood up and called after him. 'Hey, Rico.' The man turned and Cutler said, 'Can you hang on here for a minute while I finish this call?'

The man said 'Sure.' and walked back toward Cutler's desk.

Cutler spoke into the telephone again. 'Sorry about that, but I wanted to catch my Sergeant before he left for the day. Now, where was I? Oh yeah, I'll check on the airport and the airline for you, and anything else I can think of, and you work on the credit card thing. And you'll send up a telex on all this? And photos of Matheson? . . . Good, and in the meantime, can you give me a quick description?'

He wrote quickly as Holley described Matheson and then said, 'Okay, I've got it, but will you wire up some photos anyway?' He listened for a minute more and then said, 'Sure, no problem. Glad to help,' and hung up.

The afternoon shift was coming on and throughout the big room there was an exchange of How ya doin's and See you tomorrow. Cutler filed the notes he had made into his desk and stood up. He was only two inches taller than the Sergeant's five feet ten, but it looked like more, the difference exaggerated by their bodyshapes; he thin and the shorter man thick-shouldered and bearlike.

'Got time for a beer?' asked Cutler.

'Sure. As long as I'm home by six, Angie'll let me live. What's on your mind?'

'I just got a strange phone call. Let's go over to the club and I'll tell you about it.'

They left the station and crossed the street to the Union building, a six storey structure of concrete and glass with a restaurant on the first floor, a credit union on the second, traffic courtrooms on the fourth, and mostly lawyers and accountants on three and five. It is owned by the Vancouver City Policeman's Union and the top floor is occupied by the Police Athletic Club, a members-only bar and nightclub where the athletic events are dancing and elbow bending.

The bar was beginning to fill as the two men ordered beer and found a small table by a window.

'I caught a funny one on the telephone this afternoon Rico.' The Sergeant's name was Richard Hofstadter. He had the well-dressed, jowly appearance of an old style hood and Cutler called him Don Rico. 'A guy from the San Francisco P.D., a drug squad Lieutenant named Holley, wants some information about . . .'

They drank their beer and Cutler repeated Holley's conversation. '. . . and he really sounded intense. He could have put the whole thing on the telex in about two paragraphs, but he seems to be taking this one personally.

'Anyway I'll see if anyone at the airport remembers this Matheson, or if there's anything still in the C.P Air computers. I don't expect much, but I can see why Holley's interested. What would bring this guy back to Canada?'

'What about the obvious thing?' Hofstadter had a low coarse voice that matched his appearance.

'What obvious thing?'

'He flew up here as a tourist, went through customs, everything official and clean and okay, now he's back in the States but he hasn't officially crossed the border, so he sneaks back up and flies home. Maybe he just wants the cancelled airplane tickets as proof that he went and returned like five thousand other tourists.'

'I suppose that's possible,' Cutler didn't sound convinced. 'But Customs doesn't keep any records of who crosses that border and when they return. If anyone ever asks, all he needs to say is that he took a bus.' He finished his beer and asked, 'Another?'

'Sure, why not?'

Returning with two more bottles Cutler sat down and said, 'You're probably right, and the guy did get quite a crack on the head somewhere along the line, so maybe he wasn't thinking too carefully. Still, there's something that bothers me about all this, something in the back of my mind that I can't get at.'

'Hmph.' Hofstadter grunted and drank. 'You're probably not going to find out a damned thing, so it's all academic anyway. But you'll enjoy it more than actually doing useful work for this department, and it'll get you out of my hair for the day, so why not dig around and see what you come up with.'

They drank their beer slowly, talking idly and listening to the babble of conversation at the next table as a group of young patrolmen relaxed after a day on the streets.

'. . . weaving in and out of traffic all across the viaduct, and when we finally get him pulled over he turns out to be the world's biggest asshole. He's *not* drunk, and he's not going *anywhere* with any fucking cops. Not drunk! You should have seen him. He could hardly walk, and when we get him to the basement he's not going to take any breath test, and then he tries to pick a fight with Willy, and then, get this, he shits himself. Right there in his pants, deliberately. So we say fuck this, and book him, and the first thing he does when we get him upstairs is to pick a fight with the jail staff. They broke one of his teeth putting him away so you know what's going to happen.'

'Don't I just. He's going to scream assault, and everybody's going to forget that he was drunk out of his mind and driving through the city at a hundred kilometers an hour, and he'll get off.'

'Hah, you think that's bad. One night last week I was on with Duffy and we saw a guy who . . .'

Cutler and Hofstadter finished their drinks and got up. As they walked to the elevator Hofstadter said, 'Do you have anything planned for this Saturday?'

'I don't think so, what's up?'

'Nothing too much. Angie and I were wondering if you'd like to come over for the afternoon and join us for a couple of beers and then steaks on the barbecue. Interested?'

The elevator opened and when it had purged itself of a load of eager athletes the two men got in and started down.

'Who is she?' asked Cutler.

'Who?'

'Whoever it is that Angie has lined up for me.'

'What a suspicious mind you have.'

They left the building and walked toward the police garage. Cutler said, 'C'mon Rico, you know that Angie's goal in life is to see me married to someone she's picked. I can't even remember the last time I went to your place for dinner and didn't find some friend of Angie's there for me.'

'You complaining?'

'Complaining? Are you crazy? Your wife has got some raunchy friends. I'm just curious is all.'

'Well, drop by on Saturday afternoon and you'll be able to satisfy your curiosity.'

'Okay. See you tomorrow morning.'

They were walking toward their separate cars when suddenly Cutler stopped and turned around.

'Rico. Hey Rico.'

Hofstadter waited by his car as Cutler jogged over. 'Listen Rico, I just figured out what's been bugging me about this San Francisco thing.'

'So?'

'It's the wound on the guy's forehead. Straight across above the eyebrows and kind of ragged he said. You know what that sounds like to me? It sounds like dashboard is what it sounds like.' Cutler was excited. 'You remember what we used to pull out of MVA's, on the passenger side, before people started wearing chest straps?'

Hofstadter scratched his cheek and thought about it. Then he said 'Yeah, a lot of people with horizontal gashes on their foreheads. The lap straps would hold them to the seat but they'd fold forward and prang their foreheads against the dash.' He continued scratching his cheek absently. He needed a shave. At five-thirty in the afternoon he would always need a shave. 'You don't see much of that anymore, with padded dashboards and full chest straps, so what do you think happened?'

'I think that a lot of small airplanes still have lapstraps and hard dashboards. I'll bet they crashed in that storm and Matheson walked away from it.'

'What about the plane and the pilot?'

'If they crashed in the mountains or in a forest the plane may never be found; and the pilot, well who knows. He could have been killed in the crash, or killed after the crash, or he could be lying on the beach at Puerta Vallarta with his share of the profits. No way to tell yet.'

'Sounds reasonable enough to me.'

'It sounds a lot more reasonable than the pilot giving him one in the head with a wrench,' said Cutler, 'but it still doesn't explain why Matheson came back here.'

CHAPTER FOURTEEN

Yosemite Valley

THE MOON was still three days away from full but it was bright enough to paint the dry hills pale silver and glint on the two lane blacktop. Inside the van Alex leaned against the passenger door and watched the dark shapes of trees and occasional small buildings appear in the distance and then quickly rush by. The noise of the motor and the vibration of the van soothed him and settled him into a warm trance, suspending time as they rattled through the night.

The yellow light from the dashboard faintly outlined Gordon's features behind the wheel, a half smile just visible through his beard. He spoke.

'What did they pay you at that garage?'

'Ten-forty an hour, why?'

'No, I mean take home, per month.'

'A little over eleven hundred if I worked the whole month, but I usually took a few extra days off so it was under a thousand most months.'

'So in a year you were taking home about twelve thousand?'

'I guess so. About that.'

'This week you took home twenty-five thousand. That's more than you would have made in the next two years at the garage. Have you thought about that?'

'Yeah, a little bit.'

'So why aren't you smiling?'

Alex sat silent for a bit, watching the reflections of the white lines flash by on the inside curve of the windshield. Then he said, 'I'm glad to have the money, don't think I'm not. One day I want a little house in a small town in the mountains somewhere, maybe in Alaska, and this money puts me a lot nearer to that. And if we do more jobs for him that'll help too, but I'm not smiling for two reasons:

'The first is that something left over from my middle class childhood keeps whispering to me that I've done something I shouldn't have . . . I know, I know, that's a silly attitude and I'll probably get over it, but right now it still bothers me.

'The second reason is that I just can't believe that there are no strings attached to this, that we're safe now. You have no idea how nervous I was waiting at the hotel. I really didn't expect to see you again. I was sure they'd kill you.'

It was Gordon's turn to be silent before answering. He thought about Alex's response for a minute or so and then said, 'The last thing in the world that Matheson wants is for something to happen to me. Even assuming that he could find out who you were he'd have to be completely crazy to have us killed. He was taking a big risk bringing the stuff in by plane, and he knows it. We're his guaranteed ticket to everything money can buy, there's just no way he wants anything bad to happen to us.

'As for you worrying about the morality of the whole thing, well in a sense that's a problem you're going to have to handle yourself, but I really think that you're making too much out of it. Cocaine just isn't that kind of problem.'

Alex was still watching the flashing reflections of the white line in the window, and didn't turn as he spoke. 'I'm sure you're right, and I know I'll be okay in a while, but I can't smile about it just yet. Give me a few more days and I'll be fine.'

But he was smiling even as he said the words and they both started to laugh. Then they turned the last corner into the valley and the south face of El Cap was blazing in the moonlight above them and they fell silent, staring up in awe.

CHAPTER FIFTEEN

Yosemite Valley

ALEX AND GORDON slept in the van that night and the next morning set up their tent in Sunnyside Campground, a walk-in tenting area on the north side of Yosemite Valley known to climbers as 'Camp Four'.

Once the tent was up Gordon unzipped the semicircular cookhole in the floor near the door and gave a ceremonial burial to the fifty-thousand dollars.

'We won't be needing them until we head back into the real world, and they'll be safer under here than anywhere else.' He tamped the dirt back into place and zipped the cookhole shut. 'Now, let's go climbing.'

Millions of people pass through Yosemite National Park every summer. For many of them it is an opportunity to say 'Ooohh! Wouldja lookit that' as they crane their necks to look up out of the windows of their cars and tour buses; for some it is an opportunity to do a bit of hiking and photography in one of the most beautiful places in the world, and for some it is a summer job selling food in a supermarket. But for the rockclimber, Yosemite Valley is as close to heaven as he will ever get. The quiet forests of the valley floor are walled for seven miles by huge monoliths of beautiful tan granite. Food is cheap, beer and dope are plentiful, and the sun almost always shines.

After a week of rock climbing in this granitic never-never land, Alex no longer thought much about what he had done to earn his twenty-five thousand. He hadn't forgotten, but it didn't seem to matter. All that mattered was the climbing.

And therein lies part of the magical attraction of this ridiculous activity. When a climber is stretched to his limit, high above his last protection, when all that separates him from a long fall to injury or death is the absolute concentration of his entire mental and physical power, then everything outside the immediate present disappears completely. It doesn't matter what political party is in power, or how many children are starving in Ethiopia. To the climber *in extremis*, politicians and starving children do not even exist. *Nothing* exists except the few square feet of rock immediately in front of his eyes. And if the climb has been hard enough, then the external world reasserts itself only slowly.

The post-climb mental state is a painless floating, dreamy and timeless like a post-coital trance, but better because it lasts longer and has no overtone of emptiness. Stripped of all the romance, climbing is just another mindwipe, another kind of junk.

Alex was climbing well. He climbed steadily through the first week, mostly with Gordon Wilson, but occasionally with others; climbers met in Camp Four or in the bar in the evening, or old acquaintances from the Vancouver and Seattle scenes. He started with some familiar classics: the east buttress of

Middle, Nutcracker with the 5.9 start, the first five pitches of the Central Pillar of Frenzy. Nothing of more than moderate difficulty, but all good routes and all long enough to give a feeling of having done a climb rather than an exercise routine.

Then he began working on shorter routes of increasing difficulty, sharpening his technique and striving for the mind control needed on the long hard route that embody the spirit of Yosemite climbing.

After a few days of this he felt ready to push it a little and talked Gordon into an attempt on Serenity crack.

'I've heard that the bottom of the first pitch is pretty gross, but it's supposed to be nice above that, and I want to see if I can lead the thin crack at the top of the last pitch.'

Gordon wasn't particularly interested. He had climbed the first two pitches three years earlier, and hadn't enjoyed it a lot. His heavy body and large hands made thin cracks too much work for too little reward.

'Well it's not my favourite kind of climb, but I'll be happy to come along and belay as long as you don't mind leading the whole thing.'

'No, that's okay with me, but if you'd rather not do it I'll try to round up someone else.'

'Don't worry about it. Anything you can lead, I can jumar. I'll just take a six pack and my walkman and turn my mind off for the day, get a suntan.'

They started early the next morning, because Serenity crack lies on a concave face that becomes almost intolerably hot by midday. But early as they were they could hear voices above them as they scrambled up to the base of the climb. Female voices, and the metallic snapping of karabiners.

'Sounds like we've got a couple of ladies ahead of us.'

'I hope they're planning to do Maxine's Wall, not Serenity. I don't want to get stuck below them.'

'Alex, you're getting entirely too serious about this. Relax. If they're on Serenity then you can do Maxine's Wall, it's a good climb. Or we can sit on the ledge and watch them climb. There's worse things in the world than watching women climb.'

The women were getting ready to start Maxine's Wall. Gordon was quick to start a conversation, and Alex envied the affability that led so quickly to ease with strangers.

Anne-Marie was a knockout. She was French but looked like every-man's image of California. Blonde hair and blue eyes. Movie starlet body tanned golden brown and bursting out of bright yellow shorts and snug T-shirt. Lots of smiles and Gordon was doing his schoolboy French act for her.

'Ah. Tu es Française. Je suis Canadien.' And then having to switch back to English when he couldn't follow her response. Which was fine, because she spoke English as well as he did, if with an accent. She wanted to know about Quebec and the strength of the separatist movement, but Gordon could only shrug and say that he really didn't know much about it, but that he'd heard that there was some good climbing there, especially in the winter.

The other one seemed a few years older – maybe twenty-seven or twenty-eight. She had long, almost blonde hair tied low at the back so that it covered her ears, and slate grey eyes that took in a lot more than they gave out. Her body seemed lean and strong, but not much figure showed through the sweat pants and loose T-shirt that she wore. Her name was Linda and aside from the fact that she had a smooth alto voice, that was all that Alex found out about her.

Anne-Marie said that she was going to try the first pitch of Maxine's Wall, which started just to the right. It would be very hard for her but there were lots of bolts and a fall wouldn't be serious, and if she could manage the first pitch then she would rappel back down and spend the rest of the day swimming. Alex watched her trying first moves and decided that she would be lucky to get off the ground, let alone succeed on the harder section above.

He wanted to stay and talk to Linda who he found more attractive than her golden, jiggly companion, but he was unsure of what to say, so he just finished tying in and shouldered his rack.

'You ready, Gord?'

'All set.'

He turned to the woman. She was intent on watching her partner but she seemed to sense him looking at her and turned so that their eyes met briefly before she gave her attention back to Anne-Marie. Over her shoulder she said, 'Have a good climb.'

'Thanks. Same to you.'

She didn't reply and Alex turned to the rock cursing his ineptitude. But that was soon forgotten as he came to grips with the bombed out pinscars that make up the first forty feet of Serenity Crack. The most secure technique seemed to be to curl his first two fingers behind his thumb and insert them, with the thumb up, into the square holes that were sometimes over an inch and a half on a side. Incredible to think that this had once been a rurp and knifeblade crack! Then he was twenty-five feet up and trying to decide whether to try for some protection. There was no way to get any kind of nut into these scars, but maybe a No. 1½ Friend would go. He finally decided to forego any protection and just go for the bolt fifteen feet above. People had climbed this forty feet unprotected for years before the advent of Friends, and after all, it was only 5.9.

He clamped the lid down on his mind and concentrated on his fingers and toes. Thirty feet. Chalk up again. Thirty-five. Too far to fall, but the bolt only a few moves away now. Careful, careful. There, it's within reach. But no fast moves, no grabbing. Clip a karabiner to the bolt. Now clip in the rope. There. Take a deep breath. Look up. The crack above widening, looking better. Not easier, but protectable.

Look down. Gord leaning against an old stump, talking to the thin blonde and watching voluptuous Anne-Marie who had finally made it to the first bolt on her route, about fifteen feet off the ground.

'I've got a runner on, Gord, so you can think about giving me a belay.'

'You're on.'

He moved on. The crack was a real crack now and he could get solid fingerlocks. He put a nut in as soon as he could, to back up the bolt, and then moved up smoothly and was at the belay bolts in less than three minutes. Clip. Clip. Tie the rope off. Get in a nut to back up the bolts.

'Okay Gord, I'm off. Come on up.'

'Alright. I'll be up in a few minutes.'

The stance was much too steep to sit so he leaned back into his harness and let the morning sun work on him as he looked around. Even though he was only one pitch up the view was great. Especially over toward Sentinel and the Cathedrals. Down below Gordon was just about ready to jug up and the French girl had managed about five more feet.

The rope went tight below the belay bolts as Gordon started up on his jumars. He had made about six feet and Alex had leaned back out and was staring up at the intersection of sky and valley-rim when there was a high pitched shriek from below. He twisted around in time to see the last of Anne-Marie's short fall. She was hanging about five feet below the bolt and Alex's first thought was that the way she was climbing this would be just the first of many falls for her. Then he saw blood running down her leg, and she was yelling, and Gordon was back down on the ground and helping Linda lower her.

Alex began sorting out a rappel. He kept looking down and was suddenly amazed to see Gord yanking down the girl' yellow shorts and the white panties under them to reveal a small but bloody gash on her left buttock.

The scene below quickly resolved into the administration of minor first aid from Gordon's pack. Anne-Marie was laughing through her tears and patted Gordon's head as he knelt beside her, applying gauze and then taping it down with adhesive tape. Alex decided that the three of them had the situation under control and stayed where he was.

Gordon used his T-shirt to wipe most of the blood from her leg and then stepped back. She attempted to pull up her panties, but it apparently hurt her to bend and she asked Gordon to help. Alex wondered why she hadn't asked her friend Linda.

The three below had a brief conference and then Gordon called up. 'I'm going to help Anne-Marie down to the hospital. Can you manage to sort things out yourself? I'll leave the jumars and my rope here for you, okay?'

'Yeah, I'll manage.'

There was another conference below and Gordon's arm was around the injured girl's waist. Then: 'Alex, Linda says she'll come up if that's okay with you. I can get Anne-Marie down myself.'

I'll just bet you can, thought Alex. 'Sure, that's fine with me, and you can take your rope and jumars down with you then – we'll use their rope for the rappel. Just don't forget about the hospital, if she cut herself on the bolt she might need a tetanus shot.'

'Yes Doctor. See you later.' And he was on his way, giving Anne-Marie more help than she appeared to need. But she didn't seem to mind. Then there was only the thin woman with the enigmatic eyes tying in to the end of his rope and getting ready to climb.

She clipped one end of the other rope to the back of her waist belt, then tucked the first aid kit back into the pack, shrugged into the shoulder straps and snugged them down. She looked up and shouted, 'Okay?'

Alex clipped the rope into one of the bolts above, pulled it up until it was tight between them, and slipped it round his back.

'Okay, you're on belay.'

She had some difficulty with the first section and her weight came on to the rope once, but when she reached the point at which the crack widened enough to admit her fingers she was fine. She was slower following it than Alex had been leading, but her movements were smooth and she didn't flail or thrash.

As she approached the belay Alex was able to take a more careful inventory of her features. Her face was slightly tanned and the skin was still tight over good bones. There were creases of course, no one in real life survives almost thirty years without some of those, but no sag. Her eyebrows were several shades darker than her hair and her nose had a definite, but not prominent bridge. As she got closer Alex could see that her eyes were not grey, but actually a pale, washed out blue, and they glittered with concentration as she worked her way upward.

Her lips were a thin straight line, but when she reached the belay her concentration relaxed and she broke into a smile that showed a wide mouth and a very crooked lateral incisor on the upper left.

She tied herself in, clipped the pack and the second rope to one of the bolts and smiled again. 'Thanks for the belay. I hope you didn't mind.'

'No, not at all. In fact I'm glad you came up, it'll save me a lot of hassle getting down. How's your friend? Was she cut badly? I couldn't tell from up here.' Did he sound as stilted to her as he did to himself?

'Oh, I don't think you have to worry about her. She's not badly cut at all – she just scraped the bolt as she slid past. I don't even know if all that gauze and tape was necessary, a bandaid would probably have been fine, but they seemed to be enjoying themselves so I didn't want to say anything.'

They both laughed and Alex began to relax. 'Did you want to get back down right away? I was planning to do the whole climb, but if you want to check up on your friend we can rap out from here.'

'I'd really like to go on, if it's alright with you. Anne-Marie isn't my friend . . . that is, I only met her two days ago. And I doubt if she wants checking up on right now anyway.' She looked up at the crack above then said, 'Does it get a lot harder? I don't think I can climb anything too much harder than what we just did.'

'I've never done it before, but only the last twenty feet of the last pitch is supposed to be really hard. There's some 10a on the next pitch and then some easier climbing, around 5.7 I think.' Alex thought over everything he had heard about the climb and then said 'I don't think there'll be any problem. You didn't have any trouble with the crack below once you got past those weird pinscars, so you should be okay.'

He began reracking the pieces she had cleaned out of the first pitch, but stopped when he noticed her fidgeting beside him. She was using a wide, padded waist belt rather than a sit harness, and couldn't get comfortable on the steeply sloping stance.

'There's a set of aiders in the pack, why don't you use them. It'll take the strain off your waist.'

He helped her to rearrange herself in the aiders and she said 'I never would have thought of that. I've never stood in aiders before.'

'Never?'

'No, I've done all my climbing in the east, it's been all free climbing.'

'Where?'

'Mostly in the Shawangunks. Have you been there? Just outside of New York?'

'No I never have. I've talked to a few people who climb there, and it sounds like everything is either vertical or overhanging.'

She laughed. 'Everything *is* pretty much vertical or overhanging, but there are so many holds that there are routes every few feet all along the cliff.'

Alex was almost ready to go. 'Well, who knows, maybe I'll get there one day. Are you all set?'

She took up the slack and flipped the rope around her back giving him a belay as he unclipped himself from the bolts. Then he remembered the second rope. 'Why don't you clip the other rope to the back of my harness. You've got enough to carry with that pack.'

Then he was away and all thoughts of his new partner vanished from his mind as he worked carefully up the second pitch. It was just a little harder than the first and he had no real trouble. He climbed a little less quickly, but still smoothly and under control, placing protection whenever he came to a decent rest spot, and was soon at the next belay.

Linda found it difficult, and it was obvious that she was at the limit of what she could climb with no falls. When she was secure, and had wiped the sweat from her eyes, she gave Alex another crooked-tooth smile and said, 'That was something else. Christ. I thought I was going to come off about six times. This is infinitely better than the Gunks. Why didn't I come here years ago?'

She was smiling and laughing, and talked enthusiastically while they made ready for the last pitch. Alex laid back and enjoyed her enthusiasm, let it recharge his emotional batteries. When he had reracked all the gear and was ready to start the last lead he said, 'I think this last pitch isn't as long as the others. It'll be pretty easy at first, but then it'll get quite hard, 10c I think, and I don't know if I'm going to be able to do it. I *should* be able to, I've done things that hard on short routes, and it's only really hard for about twenty feet; but it's hot, and I've already done two pitches.' He looked down. 'And I'll have a few hundred feet of air below me.'

'What you're trying to tell me,' she interrupted, 'is that you might fall off, and that you want me to be paying close attention to my belaying. Right?'

'Right.'

'Don't worry. I might not know anything about aid climbing, but I've caught lots of falls.'

'Okay, see you later.'

And up he went, climbing quickly through the first fifty feet, and then coming to a complete stop. He got in a solid nut and took stock of the final section above him, trying to sort out in his mind the sequence of moves needed to get him up it.

It was a thin crack, barely big enough for fingertips, and there didn't seem to be any footholds at all. He was hot and tired and thirsty and wondered if he would be able to do it at all. He stretched a tentative left hand high above and felt the first hold with his outstretched fingers. Not much there. Not much at all.

He backed down and thought about it a little more, scanning the rock above for anything that might work as a toehold until finally he thought he had it. Up with the right hand, not the left, and left foot way out there. Then left hand, right hand, and finally a foot just barely into the crack to take a little of the strain off his arms and give him a chance to fumble a number one friend off the rack and ram it home above.

He was in the groove then, and the climbing became what climbing should be as instinct and intellect went into overdrive and he powered up the remaining ten feet until with one last careful pull he was on the ledge.

He set up a belay, pulled up the second rope and then took up the slack in the lead rope. 'Okay, you're on belay, come on up.'

Twenty-five minutes later she collapsed on the ledge beside him. For several minutes she just lay there staring at the sky and saying nothing, clenching and unclenching her hands in a slow rhythm. Then she sat up and looked down at what she had just climbed.

'I've never done anything that hard in my life. Look at my hands!' She offered them for Alex's inspection. They were dirty and covered with small cuts and tears, some of which oozed a little blood.

'How did you lead that? I must have fallen off fifteen times. I'm exhausted. And what's in this pack? It felt like somebody was putting another rock into it every five feet on this last part.'

Alex lifted the pack from her shoulders and loosened the top. He reached in and pulled out a large bundle wrapped in Gordon's pile jacket. 'What we have here,' he said as he pulled the jacket open, 'is the secret piece of equipment that enables the famous Yosemite climbers to cling to smooth vertical walls, defying gravity and amazing the tourists below.' The jacket fell away to reveal six cans of Budweiser.

He separated one can and pulled off the tab. 'Would you care for a beer?'

'I don't believe it! Would I care for a beer?'

She took the can and tipped it up, draining almost half of it before putting it down again.

'Oh God, does that ever taste good!'

They sat looking around the valley and sipping beer in the hot sun.

'How is it that you've done all your climbing in the Gunks? You don't sound like you're from New York.'

'I'm not. I grew up in South Dakota, but I escaped to California as soon as I could. I think I was sixteen, and it was like being let out of prison. People talk about rednecks in Alabama and Mississippi; they should spend some time in South Dakota. Anyway I lived in California, and Oregon for a little while, until three years ago when I went to New York for a photo workshop. I somehow just wound up staying there. This is the first time I've been back. I guess it's kind of weird for a Californian to start her climbing in New York, but that's what I did.'

Then she asked, 'What about you? Have you been doing this all your life?'

He finished his beer and began sorting the gear and putting it away in the pack. 'No, only for about five years. Looking back on it now it seems funny that I could grow up in California and not start enjoying the outdoors until I was almost twenty-five; but my family lived in the Los Angeles area and for most of my life I didn't even know that there *was* an outdoors.'

He began setting up a rappel. 'Are you ready to go down?'

'Sure, if you want to. I could sit up here forever, it's just so beautiful.'

Alex thought that *she* was beautiful. She had a crooked tooth, her hands were torn and dirty, and after the hard climb she needed a bath and a change of clothes. Her eyebrows were too dark, she was too thin and wiry, and from where he stood he could see, down the neck of her loose T-shirt, that she had hardly any breasts at all. But he could not deny her beauty. It shone from her eyes and radiated from her smile. It vibrated from her healthy body and filled him with wonder.

Did he dare say anything? What *could* he say? And what would be the point? She probably had a husband and three children waiting at the campground. Still, nothing venture, nothing win.

'Have you seen the view from any of the lookouts on the valley rim?'

'No, I only arrived here three days ago and this is the best view I've had. And anyway, I don't think that I could do any of the climbs that lead to the top.'

'You don't have to climb at all. There are roads up there.' He pointed to the southern rim. 'And I was thinking . . .' he braced himself '. . . that if you're interested, I could drive you up there tomorrow. That is, I don't know if you're here with anybody, or what your plans are, but . . .' He let the sentence hang, and felt adolescent.

'Oh Alex, I'd love to.'

He floated down the rappel to the descent ledges, wondering why he bothered with the ropes at all. When they were back on the valley floor he said, 'Do you want to do another climb this afternoon?'

'I'd like to, but I don't think my hands could stand it. I think that I'll spend the afternoon walking, and try to get oriented. This place is so huge, and I almost feel lost in it. I don't even know where the roads go, let alone the trails.' She stopped and looked up at him and he realized that she was less than five and a half feet tall. Her slim body and erect posture had made her seem much taller. She carried on, almost shyly, 'If your friend is still occupied with Anne-Marie, and you can't find another partner . . . I could fix up some lunch for us . . . that is, you could be a tour guide for the afternoon. If you didn't mind?'

If he didn't mind.

They ate their lunch in El Cap meadows and between bites of avocado and tomato sandwich Alex tried to point out some of the big El Cap routes. 'There's over twenty separate routes from bottom to top now, and at least half a dozen major variations. And that's just the ones I've heard about; there may be four or five more in the last year or so.'

'Have you climbed any of them?'

'Not a one. Gordon and I are planning to do the Salathé in a couple of weeks.'

She wanted to know where the route lay and how hard it was and who had climbed it first, and when. He did his best to show her, but the southwest face is three thousand feet high and at least as broad and she couldn't follow his pointing arm at all.

He told her what he could remember about the first ascent in 1961 by Frost, Pratt and Robbins, and how Frost and Robbins had come back a year later to make the second ascent in only five days, and with no fixed rope.

'. . . and as to how hard, that's difficult to say. I think you can keep the free climbing down to 5.9, with maybe just a bit of 5.10, and the hardest aid is A3, but most of it has gone free now so you can make it just as hard as you want – right up to 5.12.

'We'll just do as much as we can free and aid the rest. Neither of us is out to prove anything, we just want to enjoy the route as much as possible.'

They left the meadows and walked up to the foot of the Nose, the great south buttress of El Capitan, then uphill to the right along the base of the southeast face as far as the cavernous overhanging wall that marks the start of the Pacific Ocean Route, in its time the hardest aid climb in the world.

Then back down and across the meadows to the other side of the valley and up to the base of Middle Cathedral Rock.

Where El Cap had been monolithic, hot and intimidating, Middle seemed friendly and attractive. A place to climb just for the sheer kinetic joy of it.

'What brought you here? This is a long way from New York?'

She thought about the question for a long time before answering and Alex began to wonder if he should have asked. Then she said, 'I'm not sure I can pin it down exactly. It was a combination of things.' She was speaking quietly, testing her words before giving them away.

'I guess everyone who climbs dreams about a trip to Yosemite some day, but for me that was still a long way in the future. Then there's the fact that I hadn't been back to the west for three years. There were a lot of things that I liked about California, and I left some friends there when I moved to New York. But I probably wouldn't have come back for that just yet either.'

She stopped and thought carefully about what she would say next. 'But in the last few months I've had some major problems with the work I've been doing, and I finally decided to pull the plug.' She looked up at the two thousand feet of rock above her then sat down with her back to a tree. 'It just happened that my . . ., that a friend of mine was headed west on a combined holiday and business trip, so I tagged along for the ride, sort of on impulse.'

She suddenly smiled. 'And I thought, "What the hell, why not bring along my rope and EB's and hurl myself at the sheer walls of Yosemite."'

'And here you are.'

'That's right, here I am.'

In the late afternoon they stopped for a drink in the cool of the Mountain Room bar. There were a few tourists, and one table of British climbers celebrating their return from something that grew more difficult and dangerous with every round they ordered. Alex and Linda bought beer and retreated to the furthest corner.

'What made you stay in New York? You said you went out there for a photo workshop, but it sounded like you had planned on coming right back.'

'I *had* intended to come back. All I took with me was one change of clothes; but one of the other people at the workshop had a line on a job that was too big for him and asked if I would help.'

The beer left a line of foam across her upper lip. She wiped it off with the back of her hand and suddenly Alex had a vision of Karen Allen as Marion in Raiders of the Lost Ark. They could be sisters. Linda's hair was blonde, but she had the same kind of angular beauty, the same slim figure and the same go-to-hell attitude.

When he returned to reality, Linda was saying '. . . just perfect. After so many years of useless, nowhere jobs, it was like, like . . . I don't know how to describe it. It was like a fairy had waved a magic wand just for me. To transform me from junior assistant nobody on the dullest paper in California to what seemed like a big glamour job as a New York City photographer.'

She drank some more, then laughed. 'There were a few worms in the big apple though. The guy who waved the wand actually *was* a fairy. Can you imagine how I felt? Spending most of my waking hours with the most exciting man I'd ever met and finding out that he was a committed gay?

'And then after we finished that job we pretty much starved for the next year, which wasn't very magical at all, but we stuck it out and by the beginning of this year we were doing pretty well. We had good jobs and they were getting better; but somehow the whole thing was beginning to lose its appeal. We'd been working really hard for almost three years and I finally realized that I just wasn't that dedicated. I love photography, I really do, but not with the absolute blind dedication that it would have taken to make it in any sort of major way.'

They finished their beer and went back out into the light and heat. 'Michael, my partner, had it. He lived for photography. And he's good enough to make it as big as he wants. But there were days when I just wanted to walk in the park, or take off to the Gunks to climb, or even just lie around my apartment and read, and I couldn't do that and still carry my share of the load.

'So I made myself a deal. I would work my ass off for three more months. Commit myself entirely, and see how I felt at the end of the time. If it felt alright, then fine, I'd go on with it and become rich and famous with Michael; if I was still unhappy with it then I'd take the next three months off completely. Not go anywhere near the studio.'

They began walking again and he asked, 'So what happened with the three months at hard labour?'

'It didn't work very well. I knew it wouldn't work, but I had promised myself three months so I stuck it out. Besides, it wouldn't have been fair to Michael to just walk away, so I told him what was happening and he had two and a half months to decide what to do.'

'So now you're on the second three-month plan? The three months where you don't go near the studio?'

'Not exactly. By then I knew for sure that I didn't have what it takes to be successful in New York, and I'd seen enough in three years to know that New York is definitely not the place in which to be unsuccessful, so I just sold Michael my share of the business and closed the door behind me.'

They walked until the sun went down and Sentinel Rock was lit with a rich purple alpenglow.

'Do you still want to go up on the rim tomorrow?' he asked.

'Yes, do you?'

'Yes, and I think we should go early. I haven't been up before eight since I got here, but it might be nice to be up there in the early morning.'

'Whatever time you think is fine with me.'

'Okay, I'll pick you up at your campsite at six-thirty. It'll be cold and dark and horrible, but that way we'll have as much of the day as we want.'

'Shall I pack some lunch?'

'That would be nice.' Then, while he stood, feeling awkward, trying desperately to force himself to touch her, to say goodnight without appearing foolish, she put her hands on his shoulders and stood on her toes to kiss him quickly on the lips.

'Thanks for the day Alex.'

Then she was gone, melted away in the dusk, and Alex was left transfixed, with the smell of her lingering sharp around him and the cold burn of her lips on his.

The next morning found them looking down on the valley from Sentinel Dome and Glacier Point, then walking the trail to Nevada Falls. As they walked they spoke of the pasts which had led them to this place. So very different, yet so much the same. She, running from her middle American family, through poverty and life on the streets of Los Angeles, to the long dreamed of success in New York; and he running from the desolating boredom of middle class professional and family life to the crystalline reality of the mountains and the dirt-under-the-nails reality of the garage.

'... and you're not the only one who's abandoned a job. I quit mine just before I came here.' They stepped aside to let a group of camera-slung Japanese go by and then Alex continued, 'I probably should have quit sooner, it was a hassle every time I wanted an extra day off, but for some reason I just hung on and hung on ... partly I guess because I really do like working on engines, and partly because it was easier to go on than to quit, in some ways.'

That evening their kiss was longer and Alex held her close before saying goodnight. When she had gone he went to the meadow where he sat by himself and stared up at the huge granite walls around him. They shone cold in the pale starlight, but all he could see was the image of her, luminous in his mind, until finally the cold drove him shivering to his tent where he lay down and could not answer when Gordon asked what sort of day he'd had.

He climbed with her all the following day, and did not return to his own tent, but stayed the night in hers, where the heat of their passion pushed back the dark and consumed the world, leaving only two bodies writhing slowly in the light of a single candle; and two minds, locked more tightly than the bodies until climax sent them spinning to the far ends of the universe.

CHAPTER SIXTEEN

Vancouver

ANDY CUTLER'S partner was over his cold and back on the job. They were sitting in Sergeant Hofstadter's office drinking coffee and discussing the case they were working. Cutler was speaking.

'We've already got good film of two of them selling about eight hundred dollars worth of speed to Doug here. It's enough for a conviction, but we want all three, and we want them put away for a while and selling a bit of speed isn't going to do that, so we'd like to set up an assault.'

Doug Popov was thirty and had only made Detective five months earlier. He took over the story. 'I know that they're doing that kind of thing on a semi-regular basis. The word's out that if the pay is right they'll do just about anything short of murder. Broken legs, disfigurement, rape, whatever you want; and I'd guess that it won't be long before they get to murder too.'

He was short and swarthy, a natural actor who could fit comfortably into any social dynamic. He had let his hair go greasy and his hands go dirty. The three suspects had accepted him without question.

'I've been complaining to them about the asshole foreman on the jobsite where I'm working. That he has it in for me, that he's trying to get me fired, and that I'd really like to beat the shit out of him but I can't because I need the job.'

Cutler broke in, 'They've already said that they'll do beaters on this foreman if Doug's willing to pay them for it, so there's no question of entrapment, and we want to set up a scene with me as the foreman; but it's kind of risky and I'm not going to do it without pretty substantial backup.'

'Hah!' snorted Hofstadter. 'I should fucking well hope not. Just what have you got in mind?'

'We've found a construction site that looks ideal. It's part of the new stadium that the city is building, and the area is deserted at night. Once they agree to work me over Doug will tell them that I work late sometimes and then give them a tip one night when I'm supposedly there alone. The site is perfect. There's only one way to get to the foreman's office and we can seal the place behind them, and there are rooms on either side with connecting doors where we can hide as many of our guys as we want. We can wire it for sound, no problem, and the light's good enough that we can get video too.'

'So how many men are you going to need?'

'Rico, these guys are animals. I think we're going to want at least five in addition to Doug and myself. Doug?'

'For surc, at least five. In fact maybe six or seven.'

Hofstadter thought for a bit and then said, 'Maybe I can set something up with ERT. If we can get half a dozen of the biggest guys on the Tac squad into the connecting rooms we might be able to pull if off with some degree of safety for you.'

He scratched his cheek and looked at Cutler. 'But under no circumstances are you guys going to proceed with this until I've personally seen your 'ideal' setup, and checked the entrapment angle with the legal department. Right?'

'Right,' said Popov.

'Don't worry, Rico. If anything goes wrong I'm going to be hamburger. I'm not going off half-cocked on this one.' Cutler looked at his watch. 'I'm expecting a call from San Francisco in about ten minutes; maybe when I'm done with that we can all go down for a look at the construction site, maybe even take someone from the E.R.T. if they're interested.'

'Suits me,' said Hofstadter. 'I think I saw Tom Forbes about twenty minutes ago. I'll see what he has to say about using his E.R.T. guys on this.'

The two detectives started to leave and stopped when Hofstadter spoke again. 'And Andy, about going off half-cocked. Angie was talking to her friend Margaret yesterday – the one you met at our barbecue the other night – and from what she tells me I don't think we have to worry about you going off *half*-cocked.'

Cutler coloured and left the office. He sat down at his desk in the Detectives' room, lit a cigarette and went to work on the endless stack of paper that is such a big part of every policeman's life. At 9:02 the phone on his desk rang and the switchboard connected him to Lieutenant Holley in San Francisco. They went right to business.

'I'm afraid I haven't got much for you, Lieutenant. I found a stewardess that remembered him on the flight. She says he slept most of the way and the only reason she remembers him at all is because of the bandages on his head. Canadian Pacific Airlines has him reserving the tickets in San Francisco two months ago, on the eighteenth of June, which means he may have come back here simply to use the tickets, to add weight to his story about the fishing trip. Did you get anywhere with the credit cards?'

'As a matter of fact, I did. I've got two purchases on American Express. One is from a men's clothing store and one from a restaurant. They're both dated twenty-sixth August, so he was in Vancouver at least one day before he flew out.'

'I probably won't get anything,' said Cutler 'but if you give me the addresses I'll check them out for you.'

'I'd sure appreciate that. The restaurant is called The Butcher, at twenty-six seventy-six West Broadway, and the clothing store is Mark James Ltd, at twenty-nine forty-one West Broadway. At least I assume it's a clothing store, because the receipt is for a suit, a shirt, some shoes, and underwear and socks.'

Cutler noted the names and addresses and then sat silent, staring at the tip of his pen.

'Are you still there Mister Cutler?'

'Andy. Call me Andy. Yeah, I'm here. I was just thinking that the restaurant and the clothing store are only a couple of blocks apart, but that neither of them is anywhere near a hotel. I wonder what he was doing out there.'

'Is that area pretty far off the beaten track?' asked Holley.

'Not really that far, and in fact those are pretty decent places to get a suit and a meal; they're just not the places you'd expect a stranger to show up.'

'Remember that he's probably been going through Vancouver for several years now on his fishing trips. He may have learned about them on a previous trip, or maybe a hackie took him there.'

'Well I'll check them out and let you know, but before you hang up I want to ask you something.'

'What?'

'Has there been any search made for the airplane, the one that flew into the storm?'

'Not really.' Holley sounded surprized. 'I mean where would we start looking? I sent a request to the State Police in Washington and Oregon to contact me if they get any reports of a Cessna 182, with or without those Canadian ID numbers, turning up in strange circumstances, but they're not going to be able to do much about searching for it.'

'No, no, that's not what I meant.' interrupted Cutler. He explained his feelings about the head wound. '. . . and I think it's possible that the plane, and maybe the pilot, are still up in the mountains somewhere. I don't know if you can persuade your search and rescue people, or the Airforce, or whoever, to have a look, but it can't hurt to fly over the area where it disappeared.'

Holley wasn't impressed. 'You mean you think Matheson walked away from an air crash?'

'It's just an idea.' said Cutler. 'People walk away from forced landings and minor crackups in small aircraft all the time, and it could certainly give him the head wound you saw.'

Holley still wasn't impressed. 'I suppose it's possible, but it doesn't seem too likely.' He stopped for a moment then said 'But, I suppose it fits the facts as well as my theory, so I'll see what I can do. And you'll check out the restaurant and the store?'

'No problem. In fact I think I can do it this afternoon and I'll let you know tomorrow what I find out.'

'Okay Mister Cutler, thanks a lot.'

CHAPTER SEVENTEEN

Vancouver

THE RINGING TELEPHONE woke him from deep sleep. He rose from bed and stumbled through the familiar darkness to the living room and picked up the receiver.

'Uhn?'

'Mister Cutler?'

'Uhuh.'

'Mister Cutler, this is Lieutenant Holley in San Francisco. Sorry to bother you in the middle of the night like this, but something has come up that you might be interested in.'

'No?'

'Mister Cutler, are you awake?'

'Uh, I don't think so. Can you hang on a minute?'

'Yes, of course.'

He put the telephone down and switched on the lights. The room was identical to ten million others in highrise North America. Department store furniture, console TV, 'component' stereo with dozens of controls and adjustments sitting in a book shelf with about twenty-five records, a collection of Book of the Month Club main selections and a dozen or so paperback best sellers.

Cutler yawned, scratched himself absently and tried to remember why he was up.

'Oh, yeah,' he said half aloud. He walked to the bedroom, found his bathrobe, went to the kitchen and pulled a large bottle of Canada Dry from the refrigerator. Standing in the spill of light from the open refrigerator he unscrewed the cap and took a long drink straight from the bottle then went to the living room and picked up the telephone, a pad and pen, and returned to the kitchen.

He spoke as he walked. 'Hello Lieutenant, what can I do for you?'

'Not a thing, Mister Cutler. This time I might be able to do something for you.'

Cutler hit the kitchen light switch and sat down at the table. He took another drink from the bottle and said, 'What do you have in mind?'

'A little sightseeing tour.' Holley's voice was as crisp and efficient at 1:30 a.m. as it had been for their other conversations, and Cutler wondered if he was talking to a man or a machine. 'I'm sorry that I had to call at this time of night, but I've been out on a job and just found out about this myself.' He paused, but before Cutler could say anything he continued. 'They found the plane. Right where you said it would be, and I think they found the pilot too.'

Cutler smiled to the emply kitchen. 'How did they find it?'

'Exactly the way you said they could. By flying a search in the mountains. I didn't think there was a chance in hell that you were right about Matheson walking out of a crash, but it looks like you were. One of the search and rescue pilots spotted it late in the afternoon. The ID numbers on the wing match up and he said he thought there was a body lying beside it, but he couldn't tell for sure.

'Anyway, there wasn't enough light left for them to do anything so the site is still undisturbed and I talked them into letting me go in first, before the FCC get there and mess everything up, and I thought you might like to come along for the ride.'

'Come along for the ride?'

'Sure, we'll be flying out of Seattle and we can pick you up in Bellingham, which looks on the map to be only an hour or so from Vancouver. But it's all going to happen in about five hours, so that's why I'm calling now.'

Cutler said, 'Uh?'

'Look, I know this isn't actually your case, or even really a Vancouver case, but shit, it's a free ride in a helicopter, and the wreck is way the hell back in the Cascade Mountains and apparently the scenery is really something else. Snow, glaciers, the works. So I thought you might just like to tag along if you could take the time off.'

Cutler thought about it. Why not? I've got nothing on my plate that can't be put back another day, and God knows I've got lots of overtime banked. Where and when do we meet?'

The noise was overwhelming and Cutler had to lean forward to hear the conversation in the front seats.

'I can't put it down anywhere near here Lieutenant. The best I can do is hold it over those boulders long enough for you to jump out.'

'Alright, let us out and come back in an hour to pick us up.'

'Okay, one hour it is.'

The small chopper banked and dropped toward a group of large rocks sticking up out of the snow. The pilot said, 'I shouldn't be doing this. I want you guys ready to bail out the second I give the word. Get your belts off now and unlatch your doors.' He turned his head part way round and yelled to Cutler, 'Did you hear that?'

'Yeah, I'm set.'

The chopper settled slowly above the rocks. Down. Back up. Down again and back up. Finally the pilot said, 'Okay, I think I can manage. This time you go when I shout.'

Down again and 'GO!!'

The two men scrambled out and crouched as the blast from the rotors tore at their clothing and hair and the little helicopter with Washington State Police markings leaped back into the sky.

They were on a small rocky outcrop in the middle of the broad south face of Mt. Redoubt, about forty feet away from the wreckage of Kiniski's Cessna. High above them the morning sun lit the summit ramparts, and the glare from the snow was harsh even through their sunglasses. Several hundred feet below them the snow gave way to bouldery rubble, with the green tangle of the valley bottom another thousand feet below that. On the other side of the valley, dark and forbidding, was the two and a half thousand foot north face of Bear Mountain.

Cutler looked at Holley and decided that he looked almost as dark and forbidding as the mountain across the valley. He was the same height as Cutler, a little over six feet, but had broader shoulders and a leaner waist. He wore a beautifully tailored dark blue three-piece with a pale blue shirt and a dark blue tie. The clothes suited the man so well that they seemed designed for wear in just this place, and made Cutler feel inadequate in his old jeans and wool shirt.

But it was the face that held his attention. It was the handsomest face Cutler had ever seen. Holley was black, but his features were sharp and Cutler thought that some of his forebears must have been Arabic or Ethiopian.

He was about forty-five. His short hair was going grey and there were deep trenches running down from beside his nose past the corners of his mouth, but he had the timeless look of volcanic strength barely under control. He had introduced himself as William Holley, but Cutler, who wasn't normally much impressed with rank or procedure, could not call him by name.

'Well Lieutenant, shall we go and have a look?'

'Might as well.'

The snow had softened enough in the sun to provide secure footing and by mountaineering standards the slope was not steep, but neither man felt secure and the forty feet to the airplane took almost two minutes. They stopped about five feet from the nose and Cutler said, 'Shall we circle it?'

'Yes. But we might as well have a look at the body first.'

They had seen the body from the air, lying on the snow below the wreck. It had appeared to be lying half on its side with one arm outflung, the other hidden underneath. Now they descended fifteen feet and traversed toward it for a closer look.

'Jesus.'

They saw that the body was lying face down, not on its side, and that the left arm wasn't tucked underneath, wasn't anywhere. The snow was red under the shoulder.

The helicopter was gone and their breathing was the only sound on the mountain. Cutler looked up at the wreck and down at the body. Without its wing the plane looked strange, not like an aircraft at all; but even without its arm the body was just a body. He bent down and carefully eased a wallet from the back pocket, then stood up and moved to where Holley could see as he went through its contents. He fanned out a thick stack of brown banknotes. Canadian hundreds. 'Whoever he is, he didn't die broke.'

He put the money back and flipped through the plastic windows of the card section, then handed the wallet to Holley and said, 'Gerald Kiniski. It looks like we've found the pilot, but I don't think he's going to answer any of the questions you wanted to ask him.'

Holley slipped the wallet into one of his own pockets and said, 'Let's finish our walk-around and then come back for a thorough look at this,' he pointed to the corpse with his toe, 'and then start on the plane.'

'Okay, but what about that big bloody patch by the tail?'

'One time around and then we check it out, okay?'

'Sure, okay.'

They were becoming used to the angle of the slope and made their circuit of the wrecked aircraft without too much trouble. There was a long shallow skid mark stretching away to the east, and nothing else.

'I suppose that if we followed the skid mark we'd eventually find that guy's arm and shoulder,' said Holley.

'I suppose. I wonder where the wing is. Funny we didn't see it from the air.'

'It could be a long way down the hill. As soon as we're through there'll be an inspection team from the FCC in for a look. They'll find it somewhere.'

They completed their circuit and stood by the body. Cutler said, 'Too bad we didn't find this sooner, before whatever tracks there were got melted away.'

Holley began stamping out a flat area in the snow. 'Don't worry too much about it. It's only thanks to you that we found it at all, and anyway, it crashed in a storm so the tracks probably got filled in right away. Look at the skid mark, it should be at least three feet deep, and it's barely visible at all.' He continued flattening the snow. 'Give me a hand rolling the body onto this flat area.'

The corpse gave them nothing more than the wallet they had already taken, and they were both thankful that the overnight weather had been cold at this altitude.

The bloody patch by the tail was slightly lower than the surrounding snow and there was a faint path between it and the hole where the pilot's door had been.

'What's this?'

Holley picked up a white loop that had been invisible on the white snow from farther away.

'Let me have a look.'

'It's some kind of webbing tied in a loop, but I've never seen anything exactly like it before. It feels like its woven of nylon or some synthetic.'

'Whatever it is, it's probably Matheson's, it's got a big black M written on this end.'

Neither man could identify it and Holley tossed it over beside the body.

'I guess it's time to check the plane.'

Inside the aircraft they found a lot of dried blood, a large leather suitcase, and a small plastic case full of folded maps. The interior was cramped and Cutler smudged his clothing reddish brown in several places. Holley emerged unmarked.

The suitcase had been embossed with the initials WFM. Inside it were clothes, toothbrush and paste, razor and shaving cream, cologne, towel, a paperback novel, and a plastic trash bag containing clothes that had very obviously been worn by a fisherman.

Holley repacked the suitcase, throwing in the loop they had found. 'What I would really like to know is how in hell Matheson got from here to Vancouver. Did you see the blood on the passenger side window and dashboard? How in hell could anyone live through a crash like that, let alone walk out of here? I mean, look at that wreck! How could anyone live through that?'

'I don't know. But then look at the automobile accidents that people walk away from.'

'I know, I know.' Holley closed and latched the suitcase and stood up. 'Anything else you can think of?'

'Not really. You've got the wallet?'

'In my pocket.'

'Who's going to bring the body out?'

'Probably the FCC.'

'We should make sure it gets printed and that we all; you, us, and the RCMP get a set of prints.'

Holley pulled a small leather bound notebook from inside his jacket pocket and made a note with what looked like a gold pencil. 'Okay, I'll take care of that, and as soon as everyone here is satisfied I'll see that it gets shipped back to Prince Rupert.' He put the notebook away and said, 'Maybe you can notify the RCMP. Let them handle the family, if there is any.'

Cutler said, 'Okay, and I'll . . .' He stopped and cocked his head, listening. 'Sounds like our taxi is on his way.' He picked up the suitcase and started toward the rock outcrop where they had been dropped off, but then stopped and turned when Holley said:

'Let's get the pilot to fly us around the general area for a while. We probably won't see anything much, but I'd like to find out just where we are in relation to Vancouver, and where the nearest roads and towns are.'

Two hours later they walked into the Trawler, a seafood place on Bellingham's small waterfront. Cutler had changed into clean clothes: light grey pants, white shirt and light grey jacket, and a blue tie with red stripes. The clothes were fresh but Cutler, as always, looked rumpled. As they sat down he wondered how Holley had avoided smudging his suit in the airplane, and how it could still look like he had put it on just five minutes ago.

Their young waitress was looking at Holley with obvious lust and ignored Cutler. Holley ignored *her* and said to him, 'Order whatever you want, the city of San Francisco is paying for it.'

Cutler asked the waitress, 'What do you recommend?'

'Beg your pardon?' She dragged her eyes away from Holley.

Cutler gave up. 'I'll take steamed clams and a dark Heineken if you've got it.'

Holley ordered the same and the waitress pulled herself reluctantly away.

'So, Mister Cutler, what do you think?'

'I think that after we review everything we know about this we're going to be more confused than ever.' Cutler ran a hand through his curly hair. 'But first of all tell me how you see it now.'

Holley leaned back in his chair and stretched his long legs out in front of him. 'Okay. To start with, there's something you may not know, I can't remember if I put it in the report I sent you or not. Before Matheson took off from Prince Rupert he put two suitcases in the plane; a leather one, which we just found, and an aluminium one, the kind photographers use, which we didn't find. I think they're called Halliburtons.'

The waitress brought their beer, simpered at Holley, and left.

'Yes, I remember that. It was in your original telex.'

'Okay, then this is how it looks to me.' Holley drank some of his beer and paused to order his thoughts. 'Matheson picks up the coke in Prince Rupert, charters Kiniski to fly him across the border, and takes off. They approach the storm that's building over the Cascades and turn east to go around it, but somehow twig to the surveillence – maybe the RCMP pilot got careless with his radio, or came too close – so they decide to risk flying through the storm. But it's worse than they expect and they crash on Mt. Redoubt. The pilot buys it in the crash but Matheson is lucky and gets out of it with just the cut on his head.' He closed his eyes briefly and then continued. 'His door is stuck so he turfs out the body of the pilot, grabs the aluminium suitcase full of coke and staggers off down the mountain into the valley. He probably follows the stream until he gets to that trail that the chopper pilot pointed out to us and then follows that until he reaches the road. After that, nothing makes sense.'

Anger and frustration edged Holley's voice and he raised a fist, then let it fall softly onto the table. 'I talked to our pilot while you were changing, and from what he says it would be quite a feat to get from the crash site to the trail system. He says that the bush in these valleys is worse than jungle, that in places it's so thick that you can't get through at all, and that it would take a full day for a healthy man who knew what he was doing to get from the plane to the nearest road. And that's in *good* weather.

'That means that Matheson couldn't have reached the road any earlier than late on the twenty-fifth, and probably not until some time on the twenty-sixth.' He rapped his knuckles sharply on the table top. 'That road is here in America. Yet we know he was in Vancouver on the twenty-sixth.

'All I can think of is that he hitched a ride with someone to Bellingham or Seattle – and God knows what kind of story he told them to account for the way he must have looked – then cleaned himself up and stashed the case somewhere and went to Vancouver so that he could catch the flight to San Francisco to make his fishing story look reasonable. Maybe a taxi driver turned him on to the restaurant and he just noticed the men's wear store in the next block and bought the clothes on impulse. Is clothing cheaper in Vancouver than here?'

'I don't think so. I think that it's still cheaper down here even with the devaluation of the Canadian dollar. But that's not why he bought them anyway.'

'What? How do you know that?'

Cutler looked up to see the waitress approaching with their meal. 'Just a minute. Here comes lunch.'

This time the waitress made a point of ignoring Holley completely. He didn't seem to notice that either. The clams were good and both men ate in silence for a few minutes. Then Cutler said, 'About the clothing. Did you get the message I left for you last Wednesday?'

'That you had checked out the restaurant and the store and that they remembered him and you'd send the details in a telex?'

'That's right, did you get the telex?'

'Nope. But I haven't checked my box since Thursday so it's probably there waiting for me.' Holley ate a clam and continued. 'It's been kind of busy these last few days.'

'Well you probably aren't going to like this, 'cause it pretty much blows the last part of your theory. I went to the restaurant and got nothing. Nobody remembers him, but at the men's wear store they remember him real well. He arrived there wearing an old denim shirt and a pair of blue jeans both of which were about two sizes too big for him. He had a big bandage on his head and a story about being in an accident in which he lost his luggage and ruined the clothes he was wearing. He said that a good Samaritan had loaned him the jeans and shirt until he could buy some new clothes.

'Several people on the staff there noticed him and they all identified him from the picture you sent up. They also said that he was quite pale and seemed pretty weak. But his credit card checked out okay and they had no reason to believe that he was anything but an unfortunate tourist. I think it's a pretty safe bet that if he'd gone to someplace like Seattle or Bellingham he would have bought the good clothes there so that he wouldn't have to cross the border in bloody rags.'

'Shit!'

'Yeah. And there's something else that's pretty strange too.'

'Do I want to hear it?'

'Probably not, but it's not in my telex so I might as well tell you.' Cutler drained his beer and caught the attention of the waitress. He ordered another beer and Holley asked for some tea.

'I had some slack time on Friday,' said Cutler, 'so I ran a check on all the hotels I could think of where a guy like that might stay, and turned up nothing at all. Not a trace. That doesn't rule out the possibility that he used a phoney name, or that he stayed in some cheapo hotel, but that doesn't seem likely to me.'

He ate the last clam on his plate. 'No, if he's the kind of guy who spends almost eight hundred dollars just to get something to wear on the flight home, then he probably would have stayed in a decent hotel. If he stayed in a hotel at all.'

Holley was about to speak but Cutler cut him off. 'There's one other thing, although this isn't for sure. If he spent a day and a half fighting his way through bush that's worse than jungle he probably would have been pretty torn up. Scratches all over his face and hands. But nobody at the clothing store said anything about that. They all commented about the bandage on his head, and they didn't say he *wasn't* scratched up, but I've got the feeling that they would have mentioned it if he had been. I'll check that out for you, but I'm pretty sure of what I'll find.'

The tea and beer arrived. The waitress had apparently given up on Holley, treating him like any other customer, and was startled when he thanked her for the tea.

Holley gently tapped one long black forefinger against the table top and looked around the restaurant. His eyes slid over the room vacantly and Cutler wondered if he was really seeing anything. Probably not. Then he spoke. 'Mister Cutler, it seems that I've got a problem.' His voice was soft, but Cutler could sense a strong undercurrent of anger. 'I had a perfect chance to put that bastard up against the wall with the choice of talking to me or doing twenty years, but it got blown and now that he knows we're on to him I'll never get another chance.'

He looked out the window at the ocean, flat and grey in the noon sun. 'I suppose that I'll keep digging away and hope that something new turns up, because I sure as hell can't make any sense of what we've got so far. I mean, the most reasonable explanation now is that he found Aladdin's lost lamp on that mountain and flew back to Vancouver on a rug.'

He took a sip of the tea and brought out his notebook and pencil. He spoke as he made notes to himself.

'I'll tell the Prince Rupert RCMP what we found and ask them to check Kiniski's background. Matheson probably used him before, and he may have talked to somebody.'

He scratched his upper lip with the pencil. 'What else? I suppose I should ask the FCC to be looking for a Halliburton suitcase full of cocaine, in case it got thrown out in the crash, and I'll have a look at the maps we found in the wreck, but they looked like standard aviation maps and they probably won't tell me anything new.'

He finished his tea and asked, 'Is there anything you can think of that I've missed? Any ideas at all?'

'Not really,' replied Cutler. 'There's that loop of whatever it was that we found by the bloody area. You might see if anybody can tell you what it is. I can't think of anything else.' He finished his second beer and stood up. 'I'll ask around, see if anybody in our drug squad knows anything about Matheson. I don't think they will but who knows? Maybe he has some connection in Vancouver. After all, if he didn't stay in a hotel that night, where did he stay?'

Holley was about to put his notebook away but suddenly reopened it and made another note. 'I'll see if I can dig up any business connection for him in Vancouver. If he found himself stranded there he might have called up some business acquaintance and asked if he could stay overnight.'

He stood, and after tucking two dollars under his plate he walked to the cashier.

The sun dazzled them when they stepped from the dark of the restaurant. They stopped by Cutler's car, a twelve year old Chevy Bel Air that might once have been blue.

'Can I drive you back to the Police station, Lieutenant?'

'No, I don't think so thanks. I'll have to go there eventually to pick up the suitcase and my pilot, but right now I'm going to take a walk and think this whole business over.'

'Good luck. If anything turns up in Vancouver I'll let you know, and I'd sure appreciate it if you'd let me know how it all turns out.'

'I'll do that Mister Cutler, although it may turn out that I just decide to drop the whole thing. In any case thanks for all your help, you've gone out of your way for me and I appreciate that.'

'No problem, Lieutenant. Thanks for the invitation today.'

They shook hands and Holley walked slowly away with his hands clasped behind his back and no particular expression on his face.

CHAPTER EIGHTEEN

Yosemite Valley

THE DAYS grew to weeks and September turned to October. As if by unspoken agreement Alex and Linda did not analyze their affair or talk of the future. Each seemed to find in the other the piece that had been missing from his or her life, and each was content to enjoy the magic while it lasted.

For Alex it was as if windows had been thrown open on a musty corner of his mind, to let sunlight and seabreeze in to clean away the cobwebby dark. He had never met anyone like her. She was friendly without being pushy, honest without being offensive, beautiful (to his eyes), and her take it or leave it attitude forced him to be more open and honest with himself.

She saw in Alex everything that had been missing in the men she had met in New York. There, it had seemed that no matter how deeply she probed she encountered only guile and subterfuge, costume and design; whereas Alex was Alex all the way through. Solid without being dull, dependable yet somehow still mysterious, and (in her eyes) darkly handsome.

Gordon took the whole thing philosophically. During the first two weeks, while Alex and Linda were oblivious to the world around them, he climbed with others, enjoyed the multi-national kinetic frenzy of Camp Four, and finally borrowed Alex's van for a trip to Los Angeles, returning four days later with a dozen new tapes, two ounces of sinsemilla and a medium-sized stuffed bear which he said he had picked up hitchhiking just south of Fresno.

He gave the bear to Linda, saying, 'I'm sure Alex is great in bed, but I thought you might like someone intelligent to talk to every once in a while.'

She took the bear and hugged Gordon. Then she started to cry. 'I'm going to go back to my tent and talk to my bear. Do you mind staying with Gordon tonight, Alex?'

'No, I don't mind.' He put an arm around her shoulders and asked, 'Is something wrong?'

More tears came, but she said, 'No, I'm okay. Honest. But I think I want to talk to this bear for a while.'

When she had gone Alex turned to Gordon and said, 'I wonder what that was all about?'

'Well Alex, you've been living with her, and you know her better than I do, or at least you should, but from what I gather she's had a fairly tough life, and I kind of doubt that very many people have given anything to her that didn't have a hook hidden in it somewhere.'

'But a teddy bear? I don't understand.'

Gordon sat down at the big picnic table that was kitchen and dining room for the nine who shared the tentsite. It was late afternoon and the denizens of Camp 4 were beginning to drift home after another day of climbing and climb-watching.

'I think it's time that I had a little father-to-son talk with you.' He stood up again. 'But not here. I see some of our sitemates returning from another day in the mines.'

Three young grimies were approaching, slung about with ropes and hardware and talking happily in German. They dropped their gear in front of their tent and came to the table. Two stood back slightly, but the third spoke in very slow English. 'Hello Gordon. It is good you are back again here.'

'I don't think I could have taken much more of L.A.'

'Yes? Is it not very good, the large city?'

'No, the city is very good. But I'm not so good as I used to be. Here, I brought you guys some presents.' He pulled six carefully rolled joints from his shirt pocket and passed them two each.

'Oh, thank you. Very nice.'

'Danke.'

'Danke.'

'Be careful with this stuff Walter, it's pretty potent.

'Po-tent?'

'Yeah, potent. Strong. Powerful.'

'Oh yes, strong. We are smoking hashish in Germany. That is very stronger.'

'No Walter, this shit is very stronger than your hashish.'

Walter translated to his companions who looked at Gordon curiously.

'Well don't say I didn't warn you. Oh, thanks.' One of the Germans had gone to his tent and returned with a six pack.

'So what did you guys climb today?'

'Today we are climbing on the Cookie cliff. It is very difficult and we are falling off, but after perhaps many attempts we are all climbing Outer Limits. It is very good now. After.'

'It's always very good after.'

Walter lit one of the joints, took a big hit and passed it around the table. As it started a second round Gordon turned to Alex and said, 'No more for you and me – we've still got to have that father-to-son chat.'

The German boys were on their third hit and one of them was getting out another joint. Gordon took it from him and put it back in the young man's pocket. 'Nein, nein.' He held up a hand with fingers spread, 'Fünf minuten, okay?' Then he turned to Walter and said, 'You tell Kurt that he should wait five minutes before he smokes any more.'

He took Alex's arm and said, 'Untrance yourself and come for a walk with me. See you guys later.'

Afterward Alex couldn't remember where they had walked but all of Gordon's words stayed with him.

'You really didn't understand what I was saying, did you?'

'No, not really.'

'Think about it. She ran away from some town on the prairie and went to Los Angeles when she was fifteen or sixteen, right?'

'Yes.'

'Do you have any idea what life is like for a sixteen year old runaway in that city? When you're sixteen you don't stay at the Holiday Inn until you find the right suburb to move into. You live on the street and take your comfort wherever you can find it; and you learn that the more suspicious you are and the less you trust anyone, the safer you're going to be.

'It's not an easy world to escape from, and even if you do get out you can never get rid of the scars.'

'Yes but . . .'

'And the only difference between the New York advertising world and the streets of L.A. is that the damage you get when you let your guard down is financial instead of physical.'

Gordon stopped walking and looked straight into his friend's eyes. 'So now do you understand why she's crying? She's crying because she's starting to realize that you're not just using her as a convenient fuck, or as a stepping stone to something else; that you like being with her because just being with her lights up your life a little bit.'

Alex moved in with Linda in the Upper Pines campground. She had a large, old fashioned canvas tent with a lot of floor area and enough room to stand up in. It became unbearably hot in the afternoon sun but was otherwise very comfortable.

They climbed together about a third of the time. Alex wanted to continue climbing with Gordon in preparation for their attempt on the Salathé wall, and Linda enjoyed climbing with some of the other women and girls she had met. She also learned how to use jumars and after that spent many days hanging beside hard climbs with a battered old Nikon F photographing the new gladiators in their vertical arena.

They were sell suited to one another. Their backgrounds were just similar enough to give them some common ground but different enough to prevent the insipidity which so pervades most man/woman relationships.

They made love often and in a few weeks taught each other more about giving and receiving pleasure than either had learned in a lifetime.

Finally the day came when Alex realized that he could not imagine any future for himself that did not include her. It went far beyond *we*. Certainly that was part of it – their closeness was generating that third, joint personality that so many people mistake for the manifestation of love – but more than that, Alex found that her presence changed his concept of *I*.

She had caused in him the emergence of a whole new level of self-awareness and self-respect. And with the self-awareness came a new awareness of others. An appreciation of them in their own right rather than as walk-ons in the drama of his own life.

He tried to explain it to her. 'It was as though other people existed only relative to me. As though when they disappeared from my sight they simply ceased to be, coming back into existence only when I next saw them. Their lives, that is their personal lives, were about as real to me as the lives of the characters in a soap opera.'

They were sitting in the shade of a big pine beside Tenaya Lake, several hours walk from the noise and crowds of the valley centre, and had only seen three other people all morning.

'But now it's different. Somehow being with you has opened my eyes to other people. I can see everyone around me caught up in life just like I am. It's really frightening to look back and realize that I could see other people in such inhuman terms, like cardboard cutouts floating in and out of my life.'

'I can't imagine you ever mistreating anyone.' Linda stretched out so that her head was on his lap and her long legs, bare below ragged cutoffs, were in the sun. Alex stroked her hair and replied, 'I don't suppose I ever did mistreat anyone in any overt way. But I didn't treat them as real people either. Think of going to a restaurant and having a meal. Does the waiter exist solely to bring food to you? No way. He works there the same as I worked in my garage or you worked in your studio. He's got friends and a life of his own. Maybe his kid is sick. Maybe his girlfriend is leaving him. Maybe anything. And yet for all these years I never saw that. He was just a human-shaped food-serving machine that ceased to exist as soon as I left the restaurant.'

'What about me?' asked Linda. 'Am I just a human-shaped orgasm-serving machine programmed to thrash and moan artistically underneath you every night?'

'Sure, and everytime I close my eyes afterwards you wink out of existence.' He ran a thumbnail along the line of her jaw and said, 'Actually it's just the opposite. Every time I close my eyes, night *or*, day, you're there waiting for me. Not just an image, but an essence; as if your personality was imprinted in my mind.' He looked down at her. 'Can you understand what I'm trying to say?'

She lay still, with her eyes closed, for over a minute, then she looked at him and said, 'I think so. Because the same thing happens to me. The instant I stop concentrating on something else, there's old Alex, dominating my thoughts and making me feel warm and tingly all over. It's spooky. Spooky but nice.'

For a long time they sat in silence, thinking their separate thoughts. The sun gradually enveloped them completely and they were both content to let it work its lazy magic.

'Linda.'

'Mmmm.'

'Can we talk about what comes next?'

'Mmmm?'

'Are you awake?'

She put up a hand to shield her eyes from the sun and looked at him. 'I'm awake.'

'What I was talking about earlier, about coming to accept other people on their own terms. That's important to me, and somehow you made it possible. And this business of you being inside my mind and me in yours; I don't understand it, all I know is that I like it and I don't want it to stop.' His voice was quiet and very serious. 'Before long I'm going to want to leave the valley, I know that, but every time I try to think about it I come face to face with a big nothing, a blank. I can't imagine life without you now; and yet I can't quite imagine life with you either. We're living in a sort of time warp here, as if reality had been suspended for us.'

She took one of his hands and placed it so that it rested partly on her breast and partly on her ribcage. He could feel simultaneously the softness and the hardness of her, and underneath, the slow steady rhythm of her heart.

'Am I so unreal?' she asked.

'You're more than real. You've turned my life upside down and opened a hundred new doors for me. Being with you is a foretaste of paradise, and I can't imagine what it would be like to have to go back to a life without you.'

She sat up and faced him. 'Most of those things are true for me too, Alex. You've shown me that there are people in the world that I can like and trust. I feel that the world has become a better place since I met you, and I can't imagine what it would be like without *you*. But I'm not ready to talk about it yet.' She stood up and brushed herself off. 'Let's walk a bit.'

They walked slowly, hand in hand, along the lake shore. She spoke again. 'There are things that I still have to settle for myself, questions hanging on from what I left behind in New York.'

They walked on and she continued, 'I'm not trying to avoid your question. It's important to me too, and I know that we're going to have to talk about it soon.' She stopped and turned to face him. 'You and Gordon are planning to do the Salathé pretty soon aren't you?'

'We're going to start the day after tomorrow. We just decided yesterday.'

'How long do you think it will take you?'

'I imagine about four days. We're going to take food for three and water for four.'

'When you come down we'll talk. Okay?'

'Okay.'

CHAPTER NINETEEN

Scenes on a Wall

Day 1, 7:00 a.m.

Alex stood with his hands deep in the pockets of his pile jacket and shifted from one foot to the other, wishing that there was some way up the first pitch that didn't involve cold and pain and fear.

He checked his tie-in one last time, clipped the haul line to the back of his harness and began jogging on the spot, trying to generate some warmth and enthusiasm.

It was always like this. All worthwhile climbs seemed to start in the cold and dark, and for the thousandth time in five years he asked himself why he didn't take up some other, saner, recreation. But then he looked up at the colossal wall above him, dark and heavy at the bottom, lightening gradually as dawn worked its way down from the summit headwall three thousand feet above, and he knew that in an hour the morning light and warmth would have reached down to where he was testing himself in ways that no golfer ever could, catching the start of a four day wave that no bowler would ever ride.

He put on a small day pack containing a waterbottle, a pair of jumars and a set of aiders; shouldered the rack and turned to Linda who had driven them to the start of the El Cap trail and walked in to the base of the route with them.

'See you in a few days.'

'Have fun.'

He put his arms around her and pulled her in close.

'You'll think about what we were talking about?'

'Of course. Don't worry about it Alex, just have a good climb. I'll be watching you every day from the meadows, and I'll be waiting for you when you come down.'

'I'll miss you while I'm up there.'

'No you won't. Now get going. The sooner you go, the sooner you'll be back.'

She broke free of his hardware encumbered embrace and turned to Gordon.

'Take care of him for me, okay?'

'Don't worry, I need him to tow me up all the hard bits, so I'll be real careful with him.'

They kissed and Linda turned away and walked down the trail.

7:40 a.m.

'What's in this haul bag? It must weigh sixty pounds.'

'Just wait until the end of the day, it'll feel like a hundred and sixty.'

'I can hardly wait.'

They rearranged themselves, and Gordon prepared to lead the second pitch, a relatively short 5.8 crack.

'This looks more my style. It would have been aid for sure if I'd tried to lead the first pitch.'

'Your time's coming,' Alex replied.

They had planned the route for maximum enjoyment, each of them to lead those pitches best suited to his own capabilities; and with no preconceptions about acceptable 'style'. They would free climb what they felt like free climbing and aid what they felt like aiding.

11:30 a.m.

'Hungry?'

Gordon had taken a small food bag from the haul bag.

'A little. Mostly I'm thirsty.'

They were sitting on a ledge at the top of pitch six and Alex was feeling good. The sun was on them but there was enough of a breeze to keep it from being oppressive; and the ground was satisfactorily far below.

'We could split a can of salmon.'

'Sure.'

The can opener was on a string tied to the food bag and Gordon set to work with it. Soon they were passing the can back and forth, digging out bites of salmon and spooning up the salty broth.

'Not a bad start,' said Alex.

'At this rate we'll be on Hollow Flake by mid-afternoon.' Gordon finished the salmon and licked as much of the juice out of the can as he could. 'This is a hell of a climb, Alex, I'm glad I let you talk me into it.'

'Say that in four days and I'll believe it.'

Gordon had had some second thoughts about the climb and had even suggested giving it up and making a run for the Bugaboos, but Alex had argued that they were there, they were in shape, and that if they didn't do it now they'd regret it forever.

'Come on Gord,' he had said, 'we've been climbing here for a month and a half. There isn't a pitch on the Salathé that we can't crank off with no sweat. Let's just go up and have a few days of vertical fun. Everybody I've ever talked to about it says that it's *the* classic pure rock climb in the whole world. We can go to Alaska or the Bugaboos and do some real climbing next spring, but as long as we're here . . .'

3:40 p.m.

This is bizarre, thought Alex. Gord was running, flat out, back and forth across the face above. The rope ran from his harness to a point about forty feet above him and he was galloping, body parallel to the ground eleven hundred feet below, straining at the end of each swing to reach the Hollow Flake crack, far out to the left. Finally, concentrating all his effort, crossing the face in great bounds, he lunged and sank first one precarious hand and then a foot and another hand into the wide crack.

'YEEEEEE HAH!'

4:20 p.m.

'Welcome to the Hollow Flake Hilton.'

Gordon was holding out an open water bottle as Alex pulled over the lip and surveyed the ledge.

'Thanks.' He took the bottle and tilted it up, leaning back on his jumars and gulping until it was empty. 'So this is home, huh?' He handed the bottle back, clipped himself in to the belay anchors, and sat down with his back to the wall and his feet stretched out in front of him.

They were on a broad, boulder strewn ledge with plenty of room for a comfortable night. 'Not a bad spot.' Alex stood up again and lengthened his tie-in, giving himself a twenty foot leash. 'I'm going to the men's room. If the waitress comes by while I'm in there, order me a beer will you?'

He checked his pocket for toilet paper and walked to the far end of the ledge where he arranged himself as comfortably as possible.

'Pretty airy shitter,' he said when he returned to the belay. 'Must be a three or four hundred foot free fall off the end of the ledge. Anybody climbing the wide cracks on Excalibur would be exposed to some unusual hazards.' He scrunched around, trying to find the best compromise between maximum comfort and maximum exposure to the sun.

'The waitress came by with your beer,' said Gordon, producing a sixteen ounce can of Budweiser from behind the haul bag.

'What!'

He popped the top and handed it to Alex.

'Is this for real?' Alex held the can at arm's length. 'Is this a beer I see before me, the open top toward my mouth? Come, let me drink thee.'

He swallowed once, twice, three times and passed the half empty can back to Gordon. 'Did you sneak that into the haul bag when my back was turned?'

'This one and three others, one per day.' Gordon drained the can. 'I thought we might appreciate them.' He smashed the can to a disk and put it on the ledge beside him and looked up at the wall above. 'How are you feeling?'

'Not bad at all. About twice as good as I was before you gave me the beer.'

'Good. Let's fix a couple of pitches before supper then.'

'Are you serious?'

'Sure, why not? We've got over three hours of light left, we might as well do something with it.'

Alex was amazed. 'And you're the guy who wasn't even sure he wanted to do this climb . . .'

Day 2, 7:15 a.m.

'What's for breakfast?' Alex peered out of his bivvy sac to see Gordon rummaging in the haul bag.

'Same thing as was for supper last night. Same thing as we'll be having for supper and breakfast for the next three days. Salmon, gorp, dates, dried fruit and cheese.'

'Mmmmm, good.' He sat up and looked at his watch. 'What are you doing up so early? We don't need to be up before noon today.'

Gordon brought out the food bag and began mixing gatorade powder into a water bottle. 'I've been up for half an hour.' He passed the bottle and a bag of mixed dried fruit to Alex. 'I've been looking at the topo and I think we should make a change in our plans. Look . . .' He squatted beside Alex and produced the topographic line diagram that was their route map on this vertical journey.

'First of all, how do you feel?'

Alex stretched and let his mind wander through his body. 'Pretty good actually.' He looked at his hands. 'Didn't even tear up my hands too badly.' The hands were curiously pink where he had taped them against the abrasion of the rock, and filthy elsewhere. Small tears and cuts had scabbed over during the night. He flexed his fingers one at a time and asked, 'So what's this new plan?'

'Well, look, I feel as good as you do, and the way we're going, with three pitches fixed, we'll be on El Cap Spire in less than four hours. If we started now, we could easily be there by noon, and if we push on instead of staying there, we'll be able to make it to the Block for tonight's bivvy.' He traced the line of the route with his finger. 'It's only four more pitches, and even if there is a lot of aid we should be able to do it in six hours or so – shit, it's all 5.9 and A1 except for one short section of A2 here, on pitch 23.'

Alex crawled out of his sleeping bag and bivvy sac and walked to the front of the ledge to relieve himself. He was wearing all his clothes as well as his harness, and like Gordon, he had slept tied to the belay anchors.

'I thought you wanted to bivvy on top of the spire.'

'I did. I still do in a way, but if we do that, then tomorrow night we'll have that shitty bivvy on Sous le Toit ledge and a hell of a long day the day after that. But look at the topo, if we make it to the Block tonight, then we can have a reasonable day tomorrow and make it to Long ledge without killing ourselves tomorrow night. And the day after will be easy. We can sleep in all we want and still get over the top and down to the valley in good time.'

Alex took the topo and stared at it for a while, then said, 'Sure, what the hell, let's go for it. We'll be on El Cap spire for lunch anyway, and we can decide what to do then.'

9:00 a.m.

'Holy shit!' They were below the Ear and Gordon was staring up at what he had to lead.

Alex said nothing, just looked into the great open mouth that yawned down at them and was silently thankful that it was not his lead.

Slowly and carefully Gordon worked his way across, chimneying horizontally, nothing but air for fifteen hundred feet between him and the ground. Then, ten feet out, he said, 'Hey Alex, this thing really *is* only 5.7.'

His voice was distorted by the rock and his words almost indistinguishable. At first Alex couldn't believe what he had heard. This was supposed to be the most frightening lead on the climb and Gordon sounded like he was enjoying it.

Fifteen minutes later Alex was following it and even with the top rope he was shitting bricks. Was Gord crazy?

'Are you crazy?' He had reached the belay, where Gordon was leaning back in his belay seat smiling gently and looking as if he'd just returned from a morning stroll. 'How could you possibly have enjoyed that? I was freaked out following it.'

Gordon's blue eyes shone in the morning sun. He said, 'I wouldn't say I enjoyed it. In fact I'd say I was scared shitless half the time, but I sure am pleased with myself now. Now that it's done that is; while I was doing it I just kept saying "two hundred people have done this before, and they all say it's only 5.7." I just said that over and over, and after the first couple of moves I pretended that I was only five feet off the ground, doing some real easy boulder problem. And it worked.'

'Five feet off the ground?' Alex looked down from where they hung, at the sloping granite wall dropping down, down, down to the valley floor so far away that individual trees were hardly distinguishable in the forest. 'Man, you *are* crazy.'

11:45 a.m.

Lunch time on El Cap spire. The heat of the sun poured down on them and they soaked it up gratefully. After six weeks in the valley they were both tanned and used to the heat, glad to have it in mid-October.

Gordon sat, legs dangling over the edge of their island in the sky, slicing salami and cheese with a little red Swiss army knife.

'I can see why they say this is the finest bivvy in the valley,' said Alex. He was lying on his back with his forearm shading his eyes.

'It's not bad,' responded Gordon. 'Here, take this.' He passed several slices of meat and cheese. 'It's not like a real summit bivvy, but it's definitely the class of *this* place.'

Alex sat up and began eating. 'I can't believe how well you're climbing. It's almost as if you've learned something in the past six weeks.'

'Yeah, well you haven't been too aware of what's going on around you lately.'

The thought of Linda suddenly filled his mind and Alex said, 'No I suppose not.'

'In fact, I'm surprised you didn't give up the idea of this climb yourself,' said Gordon.

'It's kind of strange I guess, but somehow with Linda it's not like that. In fact it's sort of the opposite. Being around her makes me want to do other things, do good climbs, meet other people.'

He checked his tie-in and then came and sat by his friend, legs hanging over the edge. 'I mean, I know I spend a lot of time with her, it's still pretty new and exciting, but even so I feel a whole lot more open to the world than I used to. It probably doesn't show too much yet, but I really do feel that way inside.'

Gordon's smile flashed through his tangled beard. '*I* can see it. Somebody who didn't know you very well would probably think that you were completely wrapped up in her, but I can see the difference clearly enough.' He cleaned the blade of the knife on the thigh of his sweatpants and folded it up and put it away in the food bag. 'Ever since I met you I've figured that you would be a pretty nice guy if you ever came out of your shell, and I can see now that I was right.

'She's the best thing that could have happened to you. Shit, if she wasn't so skinny I'd push you off here and go down and let her be the best thing that ever happened to me.'

He scratched himself through his beard and went on, 'If you stay with her another couple of months you might even be human enough to take out in public.'

'Gee, thanks.'

'*Are* you going to stay with her for another couple of months?'

'I don't know for sure. She's thinking that over while we're up here. I'll find out when we get down.'

'Ahah! She loves me, she loves me not.' Gordon stood up and adjusted his harness. 'I wouldn't worry about it if I were you. I can see the whole thing pretty clearly from the outside, and she's just as bent out of shape over you as you are over her.'

He closed the food bag. 'Do you want to top up your water bottle?'

'Might as well, it'll be that much less weight in the haul bag.' Alex got up. 'I can't believe this place.' He looked around at the absolutely flat ten by fifteen foot top of the spire. 'I wonder why it's flat like this?'

Gordon didn't answer. He poured the last drops from a one gallon plastic jug into Alex's water bottle and put the empty jug back into the haul bag; then began sorting the gear he needed for the next pitch.

Day 3, 11:30 a.m.

'Are you telling me that they *freed* this?'

They were hanging in belay seats, tucked in the corner under the big roof. Gordon was looking down at the pitch he had just led. 'I don't believe it. How could anybody free that?'

'I don't know, Gord, but they did. I think in '79 or '80. Maybe '81. I'm not sure exactly when, but two guys did this whole route with only about two hundred feet of aid.'

'That's depressing. Maybe I should give this up and get into bowling or something.'

'If you think it's depressing that they did the last pitch free wait'll we get over this roof. They did most of the roof free and some of the headwall above.'

'That's not humanly possible.'

'I saw pictures of it in *Mountain* a while back.'

'Shit.'

'Think about it the other way round,' said Alex.

'What do you mean?'

'Instead of thinking about how much we had to aid compared to them, think about it compared to the first ascents. Robbins and Pratt and Frost were the best rock climbers around then and they could only free about 30% of it.' Alex had racked up and was ready to start leading the roof. 'Even though we're probably going to have to aid everything from here to the top except for the last pitch and a half, we'll still have freed about 70% of it.'

He clipped his aiders into the first of many fixed pieces leading to the lip of the roof. 'Am I on belay?'

'You bet.'

He moved out right, hanging awkwardly in his aiders, and looked back. 'Anyway who cares? Are we having a good time, or are we having a good time?'

Gordon looked down twenty-five hundred feet and then shook his head slowly. 'We may be crazy, but we are definitely having a good time.'

11:45 a.m.

'Oh God Gordie, it's beautiful up here. Wait until you get over the roof.'

2:30 p.m.

'One more pitch and we've got it in the bag Alex.'

Gordon was hanging free, toes against the wall, leaning back in his belay seat, watching Alex clean the last placements from the pitch he had just led. Their ropes dangled below, well out from the overhanging wall.

'Aren't you glad we made it to the Block yesterday?'

Alex, still ten feet below, took time off from his cleaning and leaned back, suspended on his jumars.

'Yes,' he answered, 'you're ever so clever; but I want you to know that I've figured out *why* you wanted to do it this way.'

'Yeah?'

'Sure. You said you brought along four cans of beer, right?'

'Right.'

'We were going to be on the wall four full days and have one can per day, but this way, by getting to Long ledge today, we don't have to worry about the fourth day, and we can have a whole beer each tonight.'

He heaved up on his top jumar and made another foot of progress. 'If we get to Long ledge tonight we only have three pitches left for tomorrow, which means that we'll be back in the valley by late afternoon, well before the bar closes. Right?'

He made another foot and unclipped the rope from the piece above, swinging out into space when he let go. Another three heaves up on his jumars and the piece, a number one friend, was at chest level and he freed it from the crack and hung it with about twenty-five other pieces on his rack.

'But I don't mind, cause the sooner we're down, the sooner I'll see Linda again.'

CHAPTER TWENTY

Yosemite Valley

'DINNER AT THE Four Seasons?'

'Sounds good to me.' They reached the road, and after a last look up at the monolith they had climbed, began trudging east. Alex continued. 'If we can make it that far. Carrying all this junk back is worse than anything on the climb. Too bad we haven't got keys to my van. That would make ev . . . What are you doing?'

Gordon had shrugged out of the haul bag and was dumping it out on the ground. 'We *have* got keys. I always keep mine in my first aid kit.' He snapped the top off a small tupperware box and pulled out a single key. 'Here we go. Shall we flip to see who goes to get it?'

Alex took the key and said, 'It's okay. I'll go. You've carried down the heaviest load. Watch the gear, I'll be back in about twenty minutes.'

He walked and jogged alternately and in fifteen minutes reached the Camp Four parking lot. He thought about going to the tent for a clean T-shirt but decided that until he washed his body there wasn't much point in putting on clean clothes. Besides, his clothes were all in Linda's tent in the Upper Pines campground anyway.

Five minutes later he was helping Gordon throw their gear into the back of the van.

'Do you mind if I drive over to Linda's campsite before we go back to Camp Four?' asked Alex. 'I'll just let her know that we're back and see if she wants to come to supper with us.'

'Sure, fine by me.'

They drove in silence for a few minutes and then Alex said, 'I'm starting to float.'

'I've had a buzz on since half way down,' said Gordon, 'and it just keeps getting better.'

'Yeah, what a route. What a far out climb.' Alex was rolling. 'What did you think of the Ear? I'm sure glad that was your lead and not mine.'

'Hah. I was trying to figure out some way to get you to lead it. That's the most ridiculous thing I've ever done.'

They babbled on as they drove the one-way loop that led to the Upper Pines campground, the big-wall buzz getting them higher and higher. Then they were at the campground and Alex drove slowly toward Linda's campsite.

'What's going on?' asked Gordon.

'Huh? What do you mean?'

'You must be really flying, you've driven us to the wrong campsite.'

'You're right. I must have turned down the wrong row. I thought that was our site there, the one with that camper trailer on it.'

He stopped and began to turn the van around. 'Hey. Wait a minute. This is the right row. Look, seventy-seven, seventy-nine . . . We're in eighty-three, where that trailer is. What's going on? Where's the tent?' Alex jumped out of the van, leaving it blocking the road, and ran to site eighty-three.

A middle aged couple with matching blue track suits looked up in shock from their picnic table as Alex raced up to them and shouted, 'Have you seen Linda . . . How long have you been here?'

The man stood up and said 'Who are you? What do you want here?'

Alex fought for control. 'Four days ago, there was a woman named Linda Cunningham staying on this site. Do you know where she is?'

'We arrived yesterday and I haven't any idea where any woman you're looking for might be.' The man clamped his jaw shut and tried to pull in his stomach. 'And I think you should leave or I'll report you to the Ranger.'

'Ranger? What are you talking about?' Alex didn't understand. 'I'm looking for someone who was staying here. Did she leave a message for me?'

The older man backed up a step and said, 'I don't know what you're talking about. Leave us alone.'

Alex's whole body slumped in defeat. She was gone. He turned and stumbled blindly toward the van. The couple watched him in fearful curiosity. 'I've never seen anything so disgusting. What kind of clothes was he wearing? He was filthy. Filthy!'

'Maybe he was a punk rocker.'

'Well whatever he was, he'd better not come back here.'

Alex reached the van, but did not get in. He stood by the passenger door saying nothing until Gordon got out and helped him in.

'Just sit down Alex. I'll drive us back to Camp Four.'

Alex sat with his face in his hands as Gordon pulled the van away. Then he looked up and said, 'I wanted her to come back to Seattle with me. Or maybe the two of us to go to Alaska. She said she'd have to think about it, but that she'd give me an answer when we got back from the climb.'

Gordon made no reply and Alex buried his face in his hands again. When they arrived at the Camp Four parking lot Alex said, 'I think I'm going to get drunk tonight, Gordie. Can you kind of make sure that I don't do anything too stupid?'

'Sure, don't worry. Here, carry this pack back to the tent.' He handed Alex the small pack and shouldered the haul bag himself. 'C'mon, lets get this stuff dumped off and then we can grab a shower and get some food. If I'm going to be up all night taking care of you I'm going to need some calories.'

'Okay.' Alex walked down the familiar path to Gordon's tent. He stared at the ground and saw nothing around him. His feeling of loss was so strong that it was actually physical. It twisted his stomach and knotted all the muscles in his forearms. He tried to blank his mind, but the thought of her was overpowering. 'Don't think,' he said to himself. 'Just keep putting one foot down, and then the other. A month from now it will be alright. Concentrate on that and it won't be so bad now.' But he couldn't do it. Couldn't keep her out of his mind. Desolation overwhelmed him and he could feel tears burning on his face.

And then she was calling his name, walking toward him. He stopped, understanding nothing as her arms went around him. He let himself go and cried openly, tears of joy and grief mixing on his cheeks.

She stepped back from him. 'Alex. What's wrong?'

But he couldn't speak. Could only reach out and pull her back to him, oblivious to the stares of the people around them. Finally he said, 'We went to your campsite. And I thought that . . . I thought . . .'

She began crying too. 'Alex, you idiot. How could you think that?'

She saw Gordon and broke away from Alex to give him a hug and a kiss. 'I thought I told you to take care of him.'

'Yeah, well I thought I *had* taken care of him. I got him up and down again in one piece, but then I let my guard down, and zingo, look what happened.'

She grabbed Alex by the hand again and hugged them both. Then she stepped back and said, 'You guys smell awful. I'm going to take you both to supper, but first you shower, right?'

Alex was still not sure what was happening. 'But what about your tent. Did you find a spot here in Camp 4? And what happened to your face? You've got a big bruise on your cheek. Did you fall?'

'Not exactly. Look, sit down for a minute and I'll try to explain. And you sit down too,' she said to Gordon, who had started to walk tactfully away. 'You'll hear about it all eventually anyway.' Then she turned to Alex and said 'Do you remember that I told you about a friend who was coming out here on business and who gave me a ride? Well it wasn't exactly just a friend. It was a guy that I've been seeing a lot for the past year or so. He had about a month's worth of work to do in the west, and he dropped me here and was going to pick me up when he was done. He wasn't interested in climbing and when he was finished with his business we were going to take the scenic route home. Reno, Vegas, New Orleans.'

The sound of her voice receded and his vision began to tunnel. She was setting him up for a goodbye. He knew it.

'He came to pick me up last night and . . .' It *was* going to be goodbye. Alex dropped his head into his hands. '. . . and I told him I wasn't going.'

She put her hands on Alex's shoulders and he looked up at her. She said, 'And here I am.'

Alex put his arms around her waist and hid his face against her stomach. His voice was muffled. 'Where's your tent and all your stuff?'

'It was all his. Tent, sleeping bag, stove, everything except my climbing equipment. He took it all away with him.'

Alex stood and took her chin in his hand and tilted her face so that the left cheek was toward the light. The bruise on her cheekbone had begun to colour. 'He hit you didn't he?'

'Yes, he hit me, but I think I probably had it coming.' She gave them a big crooked smile and said, 'Besides, I gave him a pretty good kick in the balls. He'll be feeling that longer than I feel this.'

'Anyway, that's the whole soap opera, and here I am if you want me.'

'If I want you?' Alex was stunned. He wanted her more than anything else. More than *everything* else. He tried to speak, but could find no words.

Gordon spoke for him. 'The man's in shellshock Linda. He's had too many ups and downs for one day.' He turned to Alex. 'Listen. She just told you that she wants to stay with you. She's given up home and hearth for you. What she really wants to say, but is too much of a coward to admit even to herself, is that she's fallen in love with you.' Then he said to Linda. 'And as for him, he's pretty strung out from the climb and from finding you gone, but when he gets himself under control he'll tell you that he loves you too.'

He ducked into his tent and came out with clean clothes, a towel, soap and shampoo; and said to them 'Once you've both done that we can get down to the important thing, which is supper. I'm going to have a shower.' He turned to Linda, 'When the boy wonder comes back to earth send him for one too. I'll meet you back here in about half an hour.'

Supper was an exuberant celebration. Alex got back on his high and was soon reliving the climb with Gordon. They each ate two orders of spaghetti with meatsauce and drank gallons of beer to wash it down. Linda ordered a small steak and let the two men do most of the talking, knowing that they had shared something important, but not minding.

Around them was the swirl of humanity on holiday. Quiet, well dressed tourists from Japan and the midwest. Noisy, carelessly dressed tourists from everywhere else. Hikers, nature lovers, photographers, climbers. The usual mixture of people enjoying autumn in the park, all contributing to the cheerful, slightly drunken ambience of the restaurant.

They finished eating just after nine and ordered coffee. Linda asked for a Remy Martin, but their young waiter didn't know what that was.

'It's Cognac,' she said. 'If you haven't got any, just ask the barman for three snifters of the best brandy he has, okay?'

'Okay.'

She was wearing a loose weave-white wool sweater with a high roll collar. The light of the candle on the table gleamed on her tanned skin and Alex was torn between his conversation with Gordon, and the need to stare at her in awe and wonder.

The restaurant was beginning to empty and the atmosphere was changing from noisy cheerfulness to relaxed intimacy as the remaining diners lingered over last drinks. Alex and Gordon were still high from the climb. Linda sipped her brandy and listened to them talk. She was tired and happy and riding a high of her own. She had never felt for anyone what she felt for Alex. No one had ever affected her this way. She eased her chair back from the table and pulled her feet up onto it so that she was sitting with her chin resting on her knees and her hands clasped round her ankles. The brandy was beginning to take her and she let herself drift while the two men talked.

Alex dominated her thoughts and she tried to analyze his effect on her. He gave her a feeling of emotional security. Not physical or financial security, but emotional. With Alex she felt no need to keep her guard up, no need to analyze his every word and action looking for hidden meanings and motives. Around him she felt free. She loved him, and she needed his love, but there was not pressure to try to please him for fear of losing it.

She took a small sip of her brandy and kept the liquid in her mouth, letting it run only slowly down her throat. Alex and Gordon were still a million miles away and she went back to her own thoughts. Any love affair she had seen or been a part of had been based on some form of emotional blackmail and she wondered now if she had simply been living among unhappy, insecure people, or whether what she and Alex had was something unique.

She looked at him. He was turned toward Gordon and in full right profile to her. The four days on the wall had burned away all traces of subcutaneous fat and now, in the candlelight, he was piratically handsome. His dark, slightly curly hair, aquiline nose and darkly tanned skin gave him a Levantine appearance, and the physical effect on her was strong. Watching him gave her a shivery sensation like she used to get on the first days of spring when, as a child in South Dakota, she would find a spot out of the wind and let the sun wash the winter from her body. She could never quite escape the wind though, and its occasional cool touch would raise goosebumps on her skin. But the sun would be warm enough that it didn't matter and the sensation had been strongly erotic.

Now, as she looked at Alex, the same shivery contractions rippled the surface of her skin and she realized that she was massaging herself through the fabric of her pants. She put her feet down and reached for her brandy glass to distract herself.

Alex and Gordon were in high gear. Talking fast, interrupting each other, and using a lot of arm and body motion as they relived moves from the climb.

'... and what about the middle of that pitch above the spire. You know, where you stem off those tiny little edges and then make that long reach to ...'

'Yeah, yeah. That was great. I thought for sure you were going to fall off.'

'*You* thought I was going to fall? How do you think I felt?'

Linda listened for a few more minutes and then interrupted. 'Has anybody given any thought to tonight's sleeping arrangements? I don't have a tent anymore, remember?'

'Uh, no, not really' said Gordon. 'We can all fit into my tent, but it will be a pretty tight squeeze.' He looked at Linda and then at Alex. 'I suppose since you've been separated for so long you'll want some privacy though, so why don't I just crash in the van and you two can have the tent to yourselves. I've got a two inch foam pad on the floor which you may appreciate.'

'Well ...' said Alex.

'I suppose we might.' Linda was smiling. 'On the other hand it looks like you two are going to be up all night with this post game analysis.' She turned to Alex and continued, 'I'm going to call it a night. It's been a pretty wild day for me, and I think I'll just crawl off to the tent. When your libido gets down off the wall come and wake me up. If you're sober enough to do anything, that is.'

'I ...' Alex was obviously torn.

'Oh, don't worry. I'll survive another few hours without you. I know you're still two thousand feet high so just stay here. I'll settle the bill and ...'

The two men began to protest but she cut them short and said, '... I will so. This is on me and I'm not going to listen to any more bullshit from either of you.'

She signalled the waiter for the bill and stood up when he arrived with it.

'I'm going to get some sleep.' She stood behind Alex with her hands on his shoulders, preventing him from getting up. She leaned over and nibbled the lobe of his right ear. Gordon smiled and the young waiter blushed. 'You stay up as long as you want. We've got lots of nights together to look forward to, but you two are never going to have the night after this climb again, so enjoy it while you can.'

Gordon had risen and she hugged him, kissed him once, hard, and said, 'This time, take better care of him, okay?'

And she was gone.

For a minute neither of them spoke. Then Gordon, still standing, picked up his brandy, raised it to the door through which she had gone, and drank it down. 'Do you have any idea how lucky you are?'

'Yes.'

'I hope so.' He sat down and said, 'If only she had a sister. With maybe a little more meat on her.'

The waiter, who seemed almost too young to be serving drinks, returned to the table with two more snifters. 'The lady asked me to bring these for you.'

When he had gone, Alex said, 'I do know how lucky I am. This is the best thing that ever happened to me.' He tasted the drink, and when he spoke again it was as much to himself as to his friend. 'You know, when I was first married I was only twenty and it was all kind of unreal, but after a while I started to realize that I was into something good.

'Even when we split up we didn't quarrel or argue and I think our feeling for one another was as strong as ever; we just realized that we had some completely incompatible needs and would be better off apart.

'It took me a long time to get over that. I knew that I'd eventually find someone else, but I never expected or hoped for anything very much different.'

His eyes refocused on the present and he looked directly at Gordon. 'But this, what I've got with Linda, goes so far beyond that, so far beyond anything I've ever experienced before, that I sometimes wonder whether I was even alive for the last thirty years.'

'So what are you going to do?'

'Do?'

'I mean what are your plans? Honeymoon on Mars? Whitehouse in '96? You seem to have found the key to universal happiness, and I'm just curious to know what you're going to do with it.'

'I really haven't any idea. Maybe open a combination garage and photo studio in Talkeetna.'

'Will it have a guest bedroom?'

'You bet.' Alex held his snifter so that the brandy was lit by the candle on the table. He stared into it for a few moments then said, 'I really don't know what we'll do. Probably go back to Seattle for a while and see how it works out, living together in the real world. We haven't talked about that yet, so I don't really know.

'But no matter where we wind up, I think that we'll probably want to leave here quite soon. Within a few days.'

'I've been thinking pretty much the same thing myself,' said Gordon. 'I've enjoyed the last month, but I think I've had about enough. The Salathé . . . well there's nothing like it I guess, but still, it's time to get back to the mountains to do some real climbing. So if you two go to Seattle in the next few days I'll catch a ride with you and then spend a couple of months in Vancouver working. Maybe after Christmas I'll go to the Rockies for a month or so and then sometime in February we can get in touch with Matheson and see if he's ready for another shipment. Taking it across in the middle of winter should be interesting.

They sat silent for a while, and then Alex said, 'I guess I'm going to have to figure out how to tell Linda about that. Do you want me to keep you out of it?'

'No, I don't care. I don't think she'll mind.' He laughed. 'But that's enough talking about the future. Let's adjourn this meeting to the bar and . . . uh oh.' He was looking over Alex's shoulder and his smile was gone. Alex turned to see a thin black man approaching the table. He was of middle age and middle height and wore the kind of clothes that used to be called casual. Dark slacks, open necked blue and white print shirt and a light jacket with both buttons done up. As he got closer Alex saw that his face was badly scarred and that his nose was bent to the right.

Gordon's description of Carl, the bag man, came back to him: '. . . a sort of medium sized black guy who's had his face kicked in a few times . . .' The fearsweat began to trickle down his sides.

The man sat down in the chair that Linda had used and said, 'I've got a message for you.' His voice was high and coarse and his brown eyes seemed empty as they flicked back and forth between the two younger men.

Gordon said to Alex, 'Look, I've got some business to talk over here, would you mind if I asked you to leave? I'll get in touch with you tomorrow.' But Alex knew that Carl, if that really was his name, had been addressing them both. He started to speak, but Carl cut him off.

'Forget it. Mr. Matheson wants to see you both. He said I should tell you he's got a job for you.' He turned to Alex and stuck out his hand. I'm Carl. You're Alex Townsend.'

Alex took the hand automatically. It was bony and thin, like the rest of the man.

'Mr. Matheson is waiting, so if you're finished supper I'll take you to him right now.'

Alex couldn't speak. How had they found out about him? How had Carl known they were in this restaurant? He couldn't think, could only grip the arms of his chair and hold on tightly.

But then he calmed down. There was no danger. He repeated that to himself. Carl seemed friendly enough, and he was just passing a message. He was too small and too old to be any kind of threat.

Gordon said, 'Where is he staying? It would probably be better for us to see him tomorrow morning.'

'Nah. You hafta do it tonight.' Flick, flick, flick. The brown eyes danced back and forth. 'He just drove out here this afternoon and he's gotta go back tonight. We been looking all over to find you.' Flick. Flick. 'Mr. Matheson isn't gonna be here tomorrow morning.'

Silence. Alex and Gordon looked at one another and then at the little bag man. Gordon spoke. 'Do you mind if we talk in private for a minute here?'

'Sure. You go ahead. I'll just go get myself some cigarettes.' He stood up and walked toward the cashier's counter.

'How did they find out about us? How'd they know we were here? What d'you think he wants?' Alex's questions tumbled out in a mad confused torrent, but Gordon cut him off sharply.

'Shut up. None of that matters. We've got about one minute before Carl comes back so just listen to me and do exactly what I say.'

Alex fell silent and grabbed a long breath. 'Give me just a few seconds.' He turned his chair around and sat with his elbows on his knees and his chin resting on his closed hands. He shut his eyes and drew two more slow breaths then turned around again.

'Okay.'

'Alright, I'll go to this meeting, but you're not going to. As soon as we leave here, you go to the van and drive away. Don't go home to Seattle, and don't go to any place you've stayed before. Just take Linda and camp somewhere, or go to a motel for a couple of days. Then rent a car and come back here. If everything is alright, which it probably will be, I'll be waiting in Camp 4, but don't come walking in there to find me. Just find somebody we both know and ask him to take a message to me. Okay?'

Alex ran it through his mind again and said, 'Okay.'

'Good, now Carl's coming back, so let's just take it easy.'

Carl sat down and peeled the cellophane from a package of cigarettes and lit up, then stowed the package inside his jacket. He blew smoke and said, 'So?'

'So we're ready to go, but there's one thing,' said Gordon.

'What's that?'

'Only one of us is going.'

'Whacha mean only one?'

'Come on, you know what I mean. You take me to see Matheson. No problem there, I *want* to see him. But Alex stays away. That way we all know that everything is going to be smooth and easy, right?'

'Hey, nothin' heavy's going down here. The only thing heavy is what happens to me if I don't bring you both back. Mr. Matheson told me he wants to see you both. You wanna get me in trouble?'

'Come on Carl, there's nothing you can do about it right? So let's you and me get going and leave Alex to finish his drink.'

Carl sucked on his cigarette and blew more smoke. He looked at it and said 'Fuckin' low-tars. No satisfaction. I should stick to Luckies. Yeah, sure, I know whacha mean. So let's go.' He stood up, leaving his cigarette burning in the ashtray.

Gordon stood up with him. Standing beside the small black man he looked like a muscular Viking, and Alex felt some comfort coming back. Gord could take care of himself.

'Okay, see you later.'

He watched them leave and then signalled the waiter.

'Do we still owe anything?'

'No sir, the lady paid for everything.'

Alex handed him a five and said, 'Well, take this anyway.'

The young man took the money. 'Thanks.' Then he said, 'Uh, I hope you don't mind, but I heard you and your friend talking about the climb you just did. It sounded like it was the Salathe.'

'That's right.'

'I thought so. I started climbing this year and I'm planning to do it some day too. What did you think of it. I've heard that it goes almost all free now.'

Alex did not want to talk. He felt as though he had been wrung out and left in the wind to dry. 'Well, it might if you can climb overhanging 5.12, but for us there was still a fair bit of aid.'

He wanted desperately to get away, to be with Linda, to touch her and know that the universe was still unfolding as it should. He said, 'Look, I really can't talk about it now, I've got to get going. My ladyfriend and I are leaving the valley as soon as I get out of here, but you can talk to Gord – the guy with the long hair that we had supper with. He's in Camp 4 and he'll be around for a few more days.'

'Oh. Okay. Thanks anyway.'

Relief. Now he could go. 'No problem. I wish I could stay and talk with you.' He stood up from the table. 'His name is Gord Wilson and he's on site fourteen.'

He went to the coat rack by the entrance, put on the sweater and parka that he had left there, and then walked slowly toward the door. He felt drained. Physically and emotionally. He had never had a day anything like this and he wanted only to lie down and let the heat from Linda's body ease him into deep dreamless sleep. But he knew Gord was right and that he should get away. He would let Linda drive and find somewhere out of the park to pull the van off the road for the night. Or better still they could go to Modesto and get a hotel room. It was only a couple of hours drive, and then he could spend a day or two there, sitting in the sun, with no more excitement, no surprises and no ups or downs.

He pushed through the inner doors, into the dark foyer and was suddenly looking into a scarred black face. 'Wha . . . gghhh!' Something slammed into his stomach and he doubled over in pain unable to speak or breathe. He could see dark slacks and small black loafers. The feet walked out of his vision and he knew that they had moved behind him. He tried to straighten up, tried to turn around but something struck the back of his head and the whole universe imploded softly inside him.

Blackness and blinding flashes of light chased around his mind. Vertigo and nausea seized him and all sense of time and space vanished. All that remained was a voice, barely understandable.

'Okay Alex baby, let's walk. C'mon now, walk, let's go.'

Part of his mind came back. He was staggering across dark pavement. A parking lot. He stumbled and something held him up. Somebody. Someone was helping him walk across a parking lot. Then he was beside a car, a big dark car, maybe green, or blue; and whoever was helping him walk opened the door and helped him get in. He clung to the steering wheel as the door closed. He was dimly aware that there were other people in the car, in the back seat, and then the passenger door opened and a man got in and looked at him out of empty brown eyes in a scarred face, and everything came back.

Carl was pointing a gun at him and saying in his high, rough voice, 'Look in the back Alex baby.'

Alex turned. Gordon was slumped in the corner behind him, eyes open but unmoving, breathing loudly through his mouth. On the other side was a big man with another gun. Alex couldn't see him very well but he seemed to have dark hair cut short and spiky, and looked quite young. He was wearing black clothes.

'Okay Alex baby, start her up, but don't put her in gear.'

Alex did as he was told. The car was an old Chev but the engine caught immediately. He released the key and once more clutched the steering wheel with both hands. He was shaking with fear and nausea and knew that if he looked at Carl he would lose control completely.

'Awright pal, I'm gonna tell you some things and you listen to me, cause they're real important.' The voice was like a rusty nail being driven into his mind. 'The first thing is that you keep your hands on the wheel and do exactly what you're told. No stupid tricks with jamming on the brakes or blinking the lights or any of that kind of shit, cause the first thing you do, Big Robbie breaks both your arms and I do the driving. D'you understand?'

Alex was paralysed. Mindless. But he understood. Finally he looked up and said, 'I understand.'

'That's good. Now the next thing is that as long as you do what you're told, there's no more rough stuff. You got that? You just cooperate and nothin's gonna happen to you. I hadda teach you a lesson, show you who's in charge, but now you just do what I tell you and everything's copesettic.' He took out a cigarette with one hand and lit it with a Bic lighter. 'Now, back out of here, and when you get to the road, turn left.'

As he drove the nausea left him and his mind began to clear, but the fear remained and he could think of nothing to do.

'Hey Carl.' The big youth in the back seat had a quiet voice. 'I think the hippy is waking up.'

'Okay Alex baby, pull the car off to the side. Slow and easy.' When the car was almost stopped Carl said, 'Just a little further ahead, so the moon gives us a little light.'

Alex let the car slide forward out of the shadow of a big pine and into the pale light of the waning moon.

As the car stopped Gordon hunched forward and mumbled, 'Going to be sick.'

Carl said to his partner, 'Round the other side and take care of him Robbie.' Then to Alex, 'Hands through the wheel and on the dashboard. *Right now*.' Alex did as he was told.

It was awkward and he knew he could never untangle himself in time to do anything. Carl's gun was halfway between him and Gordon and his eyes were flick, flick, flicking from one to the other. Then Big Robbie was opening Gordon's door from the outside and holding the back of his coat as he leaned out and threw up loudly.

When he was done he sat up by himself and stared stupidly around the car, wiping his mouth and chin on the sleeve of his jacket. The door slammed shut beside him and seconds later Robbie was back in the other side and had his gun out again.

Carl said, 'Can you hear me hippy?'

'Yeah.' Gordon's voice was thick.

'Good. Listen real close while I tell you what's happening. We're gonna drive down the road and meet the man. You do what I say and nothing happens. You fuck up and we blow you apart. You got that?'

'I said you got that?'

'Yeah, I unnerstand.' Gordon's words were slurred. 'Jus don' drive fast or I get sick.'

Carl laughed and said to Alex, 'You heard your buddy. No fast driving or he's gonna barf, so just put your hands back on the wheel and take us out of here, nice and easy.'

Alex drove. And tried desperately to think of some way out, but all that came to him was jamming on the brake. That might bounce Carl into the windshield, but the big man in the back would probably kill them both. He did not believe that Matheson was waiting for them. Matheson had somehow found out who Gordon was using as a backup and had simply ordered their execution. Carl was just saying that Matheson was waiting and that nothing was going to happen to them to keep them quiet until he got to some deserted spot where he could kill them. Alex felt lonely and helpless and the weight of his mortality began to crush him.

Headlights came at him out of the darkness and flew by, but they only reinforced his loneliness.

'Okay slow down, we're almost there. Carl's voice was showing excitement and Alex decided that as soon as he was out of the car he would run. He would not stand and let this man slaughter him like a helpless steer.

'See that road on the right? Turn in there and drive along it slowly.'

Alex turned onto a narrow paved road and drove up it about a quarter mile until it ended at a concrete building with a small floodlit parking area.

'Drive into the parking lot and turn the car around.'

He did as he was told. Gordon groaned as the car went through the one hundred and eighty degrees.

'Now drive back out onto the road and park on the shoulder.'

When that was done Carl said, 'Now, keep your left hand on the wheel and put her in park with your right, but don't shut her off . . . now turn off the lights and put your arms back through the wheel with your hands on the dash.'

Alex hunched forward and put his hands on the dash. He knew nothing about guns, but the ones these men were holding seemed enormous and the fear of death was blotting out all thought.

'Where is Matheson?' he heard himself saying.

Carl giggled. 'Well I guess I must have forgotten to tell him about our little party tonight, Alex, 'cause I don't see him at all.' The brown eyes no longer seemed empty, but glittered with a kind of excitement that was more frightening than the guns.

'Now listen to me and I'll tell you what's gonna happen here. I gave your pal in the back seat a briefcase full of money a while back. I counted it and I know there was fifty big ones in it. Big Robbie followed him back to the hotel where you were staying and then followed you almost all the way out here. But he ran out of gas just near the park entrance. We know you didn't put the money into any bank before you came here and we did some checking around and we know you been here ever since, so you still have that case full of money somewhere.

'So, what's gonna happen now is that you are gonna tell me where it is and then the two of us are gonna go and get it while Big Robbie waits here with your hippy pal.' Carl's eyes were practically jumping out of his head. His face was not clearly visible in the dark car, but Alex could see the whites of his eyes dancing crazily.

'Now Alex sweetheart, where is it?'

Alex's mouth worked spastically as the overwhelming desire to speak, to do as he was told, crashed head on against the almost sure knowledge that by speaking he would sentence himself to death. And Linda. Oh God. Linda was asleep in the tent, right on top of the money. The thought of bringing this animal to where she lay was more than he could stand, and he clamped his mouth shut.

Carl's voice stabbed into him again. 'Don't want to tell me? Well then let me tell you something. You *better* tell me, cause if you don't then we haul you both out of the car and Big Robbie goes to work. We'll see if watching your friend get his knees smashed makes you talk better.'

Alex was physically shaking, his arms knocking against the inside of the steering wheel. He was balanced on the very edge of sanity. If he told Carl what he wanted to know, then they would all be killed. First Linda, then him, and then Gordon. There was no way that Carl was going to let them live. But if he didn't tell, then Gordon would be tortured and killed and then the same thing would happen to him.

He tried to speak. He tried to keep himself from speaking.

'Okay Alex baby, I warned you.' The eyes flicked to the back. 'I'll cover them, you go round to the other side and haul the hippy out of the car and then I'll bring this one out. And Robbie . . .'

'Yeah.'

'Don't hurt him yet. Let's get them over into the light where Alex here can get a real good view of what happens to his friend.' The high pitched voice was full of excited anticipation.

He must escape. He must.

Big Robbie was dragging Gordon out and he and Carl were alone in the car. He reached a decision. If Carl ordered him out the driver's door he would make a run for it. Big Robbie would be watching Gordon and he might be able to reach the forest. If Carl got out first and ordered him to come out the passenger door then as soon as his hands were out of the steering wheel he would throw the car into gear and floor it.

He knew he probably wouldn't make it, but at least it was better than letting them lead him to his death like a helpless cow in a slaughterhouse.

'Okay pal, the emergency brake is by your left foot. Step on it good and hard and then we're going to get out my side.'

All hope left him. He could not hope to get the brake off before Carl shot him. He did as he was told, stamping down on the brake and then coming out the passenger side.

'Okay sweety, around the car and watch your friend go for his last walk.'

He saw Gord sagged against the car, right hand clutched to his abdomen, left hand hanging onto the door post, obviously still groggy and in pain from the beating he had received while Alex sat in the restaurant telling himself that everything was alright.

Big Robbie, in his new wave clothes and haircut, was standing beside him, waiting patiently, looking bored. In the light from the parking lot Alex could see that he was hardly more than a boy, no more than eighteen or nineteen. But enormous.

'You know Robbie, I think there's enough light here, so why don't you just go ahead.'

'Okay.'

The big youth put his gun away and Carl said to Alex, 'Too bad your friend is only half awake, he'll miss the best part of the show.'

As Big Robbie stepped toward him Gordon slowly lifted his head. It was the first movement he had made and the others all looked at his face as it came into the light and no one saw his right arm fly up until it was too late.

Big Robbie screamed in agony and fell to his knees clutching spasmodically at the red plastic handle of the pocket knife protruding from his chest and Gordon was already in the air as Carl brought his gun around. He crashed into the smaller man as the sound of a shot exploded in the night. They fell heavily to the ground and the gun bounced under the car.

Big Robbie had let go of the knife handle and was trying awkwardly to pull his gun from its holster as Alex began to react to what was happening around him. He leaped at the youth and tackled him clumsily, knocking him from his kneeling position. Alex had not been in a fight since his childhood and had no idea what to do. He scrambled to his knees and swung his fist blindly. He felt it hit something and then his breath was choked off as huge hands clamped down on this throat. He tried to pry at the fingers as black spots began to dance in his vision.

The hands were like steel clamps and he could not move them, but suddenly the pressure relaxed and Big Robbie was clutching at the knife again. Alex saw the handle of the gun and grabbed it from the holster as Robbie's body convulsed and he was thrown to one side.

He looked up to see Carl scrambling for the car. He pointed the gun and pulled the trigger. The explosion jarred his arm all the way to the shoulder and the rear window shattered as Carl let off the emergency brake and slammed the transmission into drive. He fired and missed again as the car rocketed away with tyres screaming, out of sight around a bend in the road.

'Are you okay, Gord?'

'Gord?'

He went down on one knee and touched Gordon's shoulder. 'Are you hurt Gordie?'

But there was no response, and when Alex finally took his eyes from Big Robbie and looked down he saw the large bloodstain that had spread across his friend's back. He pulled up the bloody jacket and shirt to find the middle part of the left side a mass of blood, bone, and strange pieces of flesh and tissue.

'*Gordie*!' he screamed.

Alex sat on the ground with Gordon's head in his lap. He made small unintelligible sounds and several times ran the tips of his fingers through the long blond hair. Otherwise he was motionless, staring into the forest across the road, seeing nothing, tears seeping slowly out of the inside corners of his eyes and running down his face onto his shirtfront.

After a time he stood up and walked dazedly to the other body. The big youth lay on his back, eyes open to the night sky, his chest soaked with blood that looked almost black in the dim light. He too was dead.

Alex put the pistol he was holding into one of the pockets of his jacket and bent down to pick up Gordon's little Swiss Army pocket knife from where it lay beside Big Robbie's right hand. As he folded it closed he could see Gordon, sitting on El Cap spire with his legs dangling over two thousand feet of air, smiling as he served up pieces of cheese and salami cut with this same knife.

He tried to close his mind to the image, but he could not, and once again tears filled his eyes.

Still in a daze he picked up Carl's gun from where it had fallen and then started back toward the body of his friend, but before he had taken two steps he was stabbed by the sudden thought of Carl taking a last desperate gamble and searching the tent. Finding Linda there, asleep.

'*NO*.'

He was running down the dark road toward the highway, unmindful of the heavy pistol in his pocket slapping against him as he ran; unaware of the other pistol still in his hand, or of his voice yelling madly, 'NO, NO, NO!'

Gradually the madness receded and he realized that he had two or three miles to go. He desperately wanted to run, to race to Linda as fast as he could, but he knew that it was too far and that full speed running would just exhaust him.

So he jogged, and the rhythm of his pounding feet held back the huge wave of fear and shock that he knew would inundate him as soon as he let his guard down. He concentrated on one thing, and repeated over and over to himself, in time with his strides, 'She's alright, she's alright, she's alright . . .'

As he reached the main road, headlights lit the trees ahead and without thinking he dived into the forest and lay panting with the gun pointed out in front of him, but the car was a white Volvo which whipped by without slowing down. He stood up slowly and put the gun into the remaining empty pocket of his jacket and began jogging again.

A few more cars passed him each way, but he could see their headlights coming and took shelter in the forest while they passed. None of them was an old blue Chev.

Twenty minutes of steady jogging and he reached El Cap meadows. The traffic was heavier and there were people out walking. He was close to Linda and more than ever he wanted to break into an all out run, but he held himself back, forced himself to slow to a walk, to be just one more tourist out for an evening stroll before bed.

His mind was racing out of control again and furiously he clamped a lid on it. Carl was probably half way to San Francisco. He would not risk coming here. Linda was alright. Asleep in the tent.

As he approached Camp 4 his terror alternately waxed and waned. What if Carl *had* taken a last chance and tried to search the tent? Surely he would have killed Linda. But if he had done that, the whole place would be in an uproar now and since all was quiet then she was surely alright.

But what if . . .

He was among the tents now. A few people sat around scattered campfires, but most of the camp was asleep and no one took any notice of him. He reached his own site and knelt in front of the door of Gordon's tent. His pulse hammered in his ears as he unzipped the door and crawled in. He could feel her legs through her sleeping bag. He reached for her shoulder and shook her lightly.

She moved.

BOOK TWO

ALEX

CHAPTER TWENTY-ONE

Yosemite Valley

SHE HALF WOKE to the touch of his hand on her shoulder. 'Mmmm?'

She levered herself up onto one elbow and opened her eyes. The tent was dark and she could see nothing. 'Alex?'

'Linda, I . . . I . . .' His voice was choked and he was having trouble speaking.

She sat up. The door was open and through it she could see the campsite in the moonlight. She was wearing only a T-shirt and it was cold outside the sleeping bag. She threw her arms around his neck and tried to pull him over on top of her but he resisted and she could feel his body tremble.

Fully awake now, she said, 'Alex, what's the matter? You're shaking all over.'

'I . . . It's Gordie. They've killed Gordie.'

'WHAT??!'

'They killed him and . . . and . . . oh God, I was afraid that they'd killed you.' He collapsed against her, sobbing.

She wanted to hold him, to hold his head against her breasts and comfort him, and at the same time she was shocked and wanted to cry out 'Who killed him? What happened? WHAT IS HAPPENING?' But everything she had learned on the street came back as if the last five years had never been. She scrambled out of her sleeping bag and, shoving Alex to one side, she ran out the door. The moonlight gleamed on her bare legs and buttocks as she scanned the area for any sign of danger.

The scene was peaceful. Quiet conversations around distant campfires. No menace. Inside the tent Alex was as she had left him, kneeling in the dark, saying nothing. She found her pants by touch and as she struggled into them she demanded, 'What happened?'

Alex drew a great ragged breath and let it out slowly, then, speaking in a dead, emotionless voice said, 'Before we came to the valley, Gord and I smuggled fifteen kilos of cocaine into the country. It wasn't ours, we just carried it for a guy and he paid us fifty thousand dollars. Two other guys from

San Francisco found out we had the money. They found us in the restaurant after you left. They beat us up and said they'd kill us if we didn't give it to them. We fought them and they killed Gordie. I've got their guns but one of them got away.'

He didn't move as he spoke, but knelt in one position and let the words roll tonelessly into the darkness.

'The money is under the tent. They would have killed you. They were going to torture Gord to make us tell. The one that drove away is called Carl. He's a snake. He *wanted* to kill us. I think at the end he didn't even care about the money anymore.'

She had finished dressing, and ran outside again. Nothing. Back in. Alex had bunched the foamy into the rear of the tent and unzipped the cookhole by the door and was digging at the earth with his fingers. Before she could speak he said, 'Linda, listen to me.' His voice had regained some life but it was still full of strain. 'Right now I'm barely under control. I just saw my best friend get killed and . . . and . . .' He fought for control. 'And I feel like I'm coming apart inside. We've got to get away from here, and I don't know if I can drive. You might not want anything more to do with me after this, but . . .' his voice broke and he shuddered once, '. . . but can you drive me to San Francisco? Please?'

In the dim light coming through the open front of the tent she could just see his face and the shining tears that ran slowly down it. She put her hands on his shoulders and bent forward to kiss him gently.

'No more foolish talk, Alex. I love you, and I'll do whatever I can to help you . . . to help us.' She let him go and pulled her sleeping bag and a small pack from the end of the tent where Alex had pushed them. 'Everything else of ours is in your van and we can go anytime, but first you'd better tell me a little more. Even if it hurts you to talk about it, you've got to tell me so that we don't do anything stupid. Where did this happen? In the restaurant?'

'They caught us in the parking lot and took us to a place in the forest, past El Cap. Nobody saw any of it.'

He dug again and then with both hands pulled the vinyl briefcase out of its hole. 'Take this and wait outside.' He handed her the case and hastily scooped as much dirt as he could back into the hole and zipped it up. He pulled the foamy back into place and shook Gordon's sleeping bag out on top of it and crawled out of the tent, zipping it shut behind him.

'The man who shot Gord is named Carl. He's black, with a scarred up face, maybe forty-five or fifty with real short hair. I've got his gun so he probably won't be back, but he knows my van, and if he's got another gun . . .'

Linda finished stuffing her sleeping bag into her pack and walked to where he was standing. She looked up at him and he could see the half-moon reflected in the pupils of her eyes. 'Do you have the gun?'

'I've got both their guns.' But he made no move to produce them, as if somehow by not bringing them out he could erase what they had done.

'Do you know anything about guns, Alex?'

'No.'

She took his hand and said, 'Give them to me.'

One at a time, reluctantly, he took the two weapons from his pockets and gave them to her. He was starting to tremble again and he sat down at the picnic table and gripped its rough edge as tightly as he could. Linda checked the loads in the two pieces, then tucked one into the pocket of her own jacket and put the other on the table in front of him.

'Alex, this one is ready to fire. All you have to do is pull the trigger. You're probably not going to hit anything, but you'll scare the shit out of anyone who attacks you.'

'How do you know about guns?' He hadn't touched the weapon on the table and his voice was a dull monotone.

'I grew up in South Dakota. Now put it in your pocket and let's go.'

But his muscles were full of sand and he could not move. He sat staring at the pistol on the table, the weight of what had happened pressing him further and further down.

'Alex.' He barely heard her.

'Alex!' He looked up slowly and caught the palm of her right hand across his face. All of her strength had gone into the blow and it staggered him off the bench and sent a shockwave of pain and surprise surging through him.

Her voice came at him in a harsh whisper, and her words shocked him even more than the blow. 'Wake up you stupid son of a bitch.' She had grabbed the front of his jacket in both hands and was shaking him as hard as she could, her voice hissing at him from only inches away. 'Gordon's been killed? Well get fucking mad about it! If the bastards that did it are still around here then you had goddam well better be ready for them. You can cry about it later. Right now you've got to get mad, you've got to hate, Alex, hate. Do you understand?'

His strength returned under her onslaught. He took her wrists and broke her grip on his jacket.

'Linda, I need about a minute to myself. I'm okay, I'll be alright, but I just need a minute.' He let go of her and sat down on the bench with his back to her. He blanked his mind and concentrated on his breathing until some calmness came back to him.

While he sat Linda slipped the pack onto her back and then moved into the shadow of the big pine that grew at the edge of their site. She stood silently, looking slowly around into the night.

It was about a minute and a half before Alex stirred. He stood up, slipped the gun into his pocket, picked up the case full of money and walked to where Linda stood under the tree. His step was purposeful and when he spoke there was some strength in his voice. 'I'll be okay.'

He cupped the back of her head with his hand, his fingers through her hair, and kissed her. 'When we get to San Francisco I'll try to explain everything and you can decide what you want to do then, but what happened tonight is this: the two guys from San Francisco took us to a deserted parking lot at some kind of power substation just a couple of miles from here. They were going to break Gord's legs but he got his knife out somehow and managed to stab one of them and then jumped on the other one, the little black guy called Carl. I don't know just what happened because I was fighting with the one Gord had stabbed but there was a shot and then Carl was running for the car.

I managed to get the first guy's gun and shot at Carl, but I missed and he drove away.

'Gordon was dead. Carl had shot him. And the other guy was dead too, from the knife wound. I found Carl's gun on the ground. Gord must have knocked it away from him somehow, so I took the knife and both guns and then came here.'

He thought back over what had happened.'Nobody saw it happen and I would guess that Carl is on his way back to San Francisco; or maybe he'll try to hide out somewhere, because he was working for the guy we carried the cocaine for. A guy named Walter Matheson. He's the reason that I've got to go to San Francisco.'

'He set this up?'

'No. I think Carl was doing this on his own, screwing his boss around. I don't want to see Matheson, but it's the only way I can think of to protect myself.'

'I guess maybe I got the wrong impression, Alex. I'm sorry I hit you.'

'It's okay. You got me back under control and I *am* mad. But I'm also frightened half out of my mind, and upset about Gordie. I'm not in complete control of myself, I can tell, but I'll be okay for a while.'

He pulled her close to him and held her tightly. 'Now let's go to San Francisco and get a hotel for the night.'

There were few people still up in Camp 4 and they met no one they knew. They approached the van from opposite sides, but saw no sign of Carl, and soon they were on the road.

The van was the old style, with a full bench seat in the front and once they were clear of the park gate Linda pulled Alex down so that he was lying stretched out across the seat with his head in her lap. He fell immediately into a deep and dreamless sleep and woke only briefly when she stopped to stretch her legs and empty her bladder just west of Modesto.

He slept all the way to the coast and woke again only when she parked the van and shook him.

'Uhnn?'

'Wake up Alex, we've arrived.' She shifted him into a sitting position.

'Uhn, where are we?'

'We're in the underground parking lot of the Hyatt Regency Hotel and I need to turn on the interior light but I can't figure out how.'

'The switch is kind of hidden. Just a minute.' Still half asleep, Alex reached under the dash for the switch he had installed there. The interior light came on, and dim as it was, the mess on his clothes was obvious.

'Do you have any clean clothes?' asked Linda.

'In the back somewhere, what about you?' Some of the bloodstains on his jacket had smeared onto her.

'I've got a suitcase back there too.'

The back of the van was cluttered and messy but they both found clean clothes and changed into them. He had never seen her in anything but jeans and T-shirt or plain blouse and sweater, and when she stepped out of the Van into the light of the parking lot he was stunned. She was wearing a matching skirt and jacket in rough wool, mostly grey-green, but with hints of brown and rusty orange; and a blouse of heavy apricot silk with a loose scarf-style collar. Her hair, which she normally tied back in a simple pony tail was coiled behind her head and pinned with a small leather and wood barrette.

'I wish this were some other time.'

She understood, and said, 'Thank you Alex.'

She pulled a small suitcase from the van, locked the doors, and took his arm. 'I wish it was some other time myself,' she said, and led him toward the entrance.

When they were secure in their room, she took him to bed and made slow, gentle love to him, and afterward held him till he was once again asleep.

CHAPTER TWENTY-TWO

San Francisco

'GOOD AFTERNOON, Matheson Hydraulics.'

'Hello, I'd like to speak to Walter Matheson please.'

'Who's calling please?'

'Uhn, tell him it's Gordon Wilson.'

'Thank you Mr. Wilson, hang on please.'

There was about a minute of silence, then,

'Mr. Wilson?'

'Yes?'

'Mr. Matheson is busy at the moment. If you leave your number he will call you back in a short time.'

'Uhn, no, I . . . I'm afraid I can't do that. Look, this is extremely important to Mr. Matheson personally, and it'll only take a couple of minutes. Could you please check with him one more time?'

'Alright. Hang on please.'

Another minute of silence, then a male voice,

'Wilson? I don't think that this is appropriate.'

'Uhn, I'm not actually Wilson. You may not remember me very well, but we did meet when you first met him, and I've got to talk to you.'

'I see . . . I'm not sure that there's anything useful for us to talk about at the moment. Perhaps I'll get in touch with Wilson in the spring.'

'Mr. Matheson, your man Carl found us last night, and Gord isn't going to be dealing with you anymore. Or with anyone. I think we should talk.'

'Where is Carl?'

'I don't know. He left in a hurry and he might be looking for you.'

'When and where can we meet?'

'Anywhere, as long as it's soon.'

'Alright, how about the bar in the St. Francis Hotel at three. That's about half an hour.'

'Is that near your office?'

'It's not far, why?'

'I'm not far from there, but I don't know the city, so let's make it quarter past three okay?'

'Alright. How will I recognize you?'

'Believe me Mr. Matheson, *I* will recognize *you*.'

Walter Matheson hung up the phone and reached for the bottle of Anacin that he kept in the top right hand drawer of his desk. What was going on? Was this some kind of trick? He spilled two tablets into his hand and walked to the small bathroom adjoining his office.

What kind of trick could it be? The only thing he could think of was blackmail, Wilson or his partner saying 'Give me money or I'll tell the world.' Well he could handle that. He only had to buy himself a few more months, and he didn't really believe that it was blackmail anyway. No, it was probably exactly what his caller had said; that bastard Carl trying to work some deal of his own.

And who was the caller? Alex something. He remembered dark features in a lean face. And dark eyes.

He swallowed the tablets with a glass of water and wondered for the thousandth time what to do about the headaches. Any sort of crisis and *wham*, someone started working on his skull with a jackhammer. Maybe he should see a different doctor. He returned to his office and put on his jacket.

If it was true that Carl had somehow gone into business for himself then this could be Carl trying to lure him into a trap. But that was stupid. If Carl wanted to kill him, he'd come for him at home, not in the middle of the day in the city.

He looked in on his secretary. 'Dianna, something's come up and I'm going to have to go to a meeting. I don't know if I'll be back today or not. If anything comes up for me just take messages and I'll deal with it tomorrow.'

'Okay Mr. Matheson.'

He left by his private door and was soon riding the elevator down the seventeen floors to ground level. He was going to phone John Tomlinson, and he wanted to make the call from some place where he could see who went into the St. Francis.

But first he needed a drink.

CHAPTER TWENTY-THREE

San Francisco

When Alex left the St. Francis he did what Linda had told him to do. He walked into the nearest department store and mised with the crowd of shoppers as best he could. He left by a different entrance and caught the first bus that came by, rode it for a few blocks and then got off and walked until he found a taxi. He had the driver let him off two blocks from the Hyatt Regency.

Five minutes later he let himself into their room. It was empty, as he had known it would be, but there was a bottle of Remy Martin on the table by the window and he knew it was Linda's way of saying 'Everything is going to be fine. Sit down and have a drink and just relax until I call'. Beside the bottle was a single glass. Not a hotel glass but a real snifter of good crystal. He wondered how she had managed that.

However she had done it, he felt better. Less alone. And there were flowers. He walked to the low table and bent to pick up a small pewter vase in the shape of a pitcher with two roses in it. One red and one white.

As he replaced the vase on the table the telephone rang on its stand by the bed.

'Hello.'

'Alex? Is everything alright?'

'Everything is fine. Where are you?'

'Downstairs.'

'Okay, come on up.'

'No, not yet. You wait there for a few more minutes. Have a drink or something and then come down and go to the Wicker Works. It's a bar just across the street from the hotel. Just wait there for a few minutes and I'll come in as soon as I'm sure no one is watching you.'

He felt panic starting to lap again at the edges of his reason. 'What's going on? Did you see someone follow me here?'

'No, I didn't see anything, but let's give it a few more minutes just to be sure. Let's not take any chances. Now have that drink and relax. Think about how much I love you.'

Her voice, and the thought of her love, calmed him and he said. 'You're right. I guess I'm a bit edgy, but you're right about not taking any chances. I'll see you in ten or fifteen minutes. And thanks for the flowers . . . they help.'

'You're welcome. See you soon.'

He didn't want to stay in the room by himself. He wanted to go downstairs as fast as he could, forget the elevator, race down the five flights of stairs and find her, hold her. But she was right, it was better to wait just a little longer.

He poured a drink and took it out onto the balcony. The room was not high enough to give any view and the traffic noise from the streets below soon drove him back inside. He turned on the television and went slowly around the dial, but nothing he saw made any sense to him. His reality had been reduced to gunfire in the night, irrevocable death, and burning love. What he saw on the screen offered him neither consolation nor escape.

He shut it off and drained his glass. Surely more than five minutes had passed? He rinsed the glass in the bathroom, dried it on one of the hotel towels and put it back on the table.

Out the door. Wait for the elevator as forty-five seconds pass like forty-five minutes. Down and into the lobby. Don't look around. Hands in pockets. Be nonchalant. Out into the street where sunlight and traffic were both starting to wane. Down to the corner and wait for the light with everybody else, then across the street and back up to the Wicker Works.

Inside, it was all ferns and rattan and well dressed secretaries washing away the nothingness of another day in their office towers.

He ordered rye and water out of habit and then wished he hadn't, for the thought of drinking rye whiskey made him think of the parties that Gordon held every November. Although parties was not quite the right word. Gatherings. Evenings when a large but loosely knit group of friends consolidated the memory of another year in the mountains with stories, slides and films. An evening of beer and smoke and rye whiskey. Good food and good friends and a technicolour tour of the high places of the world. The Rockies, Yosemite, the Canadian Coast Range, Alaska, the Eastern Arctic, the Alps, the Andean Ranges and the high Himalaya.

But Gordon would host no more such evenings. Alex finished his drink and ordered another. Maybe if he got drunk he would be able to keep the nostalgia flowing, to think of Gordon as he had been, to accept the fact of his death slowly, a little at a time.

Linda arrived before the second drink. Alex, lost in his thought, was not aware of her until she sat down opposite him and said, 'So?'

He lurched back to the present and was once again riveted by the sight of her. She was wearing the same suit she had put on in the van the night before, her hair again coiled behind her head. Her beauty was the beauty of intelligence and strength, the crooked tooth in her wide smile adding warmth and humanity but no softness.

He told her of his meeting with Walter Matheson '... and I think we don't have to worry any more. I told him what had happened and I think he believed me. And I told him that I didn't want anything more to do with this business.'

The waitress brought his drink and took Linda's order for a brandy and soda.

'Anyway, I didn't tell him my name and he seemed to accept that I wanted out, but it was really weird ...' He tasted the new drink '... it was like he wasn't all there. Or that he wasn't there all the time.'

'What do you mean?'

'Well it just seemed that every once in a while he'd space out, get lost in the ozone for a few seconds and then make a real effort to snap back to what was going on. And once he even started mumbling to himself about headaches, almost as if I wasn't there.'

'What about that animal Carl, the one that killed Gordon?'

'Yeah, well, I think they're going to kill him.'

Alex shivered and finished his drink in a gulp. 'Gord once told me that the people involved in this kind of thing were different from ordinary people. I didn't really believe him then, but now I think he was right. This guy Matheson talked about Carl as if he were already dead.'

He put his empty glass back on the table and said, 'That was the most frightening thing I've done. Walking in to meet him, and wondering if he would decide to have me killed. Or if he had already decided.'

'Did you tell him that you'd arranged protection for yourself? That if he tried for you he'd get burned?'

'No, I didn't have to. He just seemed to be totally unconcerned about me. He wanted to know what had happened and then he asked if I was interested in taking over for Gord. When I said I wasn't, that was it, he just seemed to lose interest. It was strange, he sort of retreated into himself – like his mind had suddenly teleported to Venus or something.'

Alex sat and thought about it, replaying the scene in his mind. 'I wonder if he got his brain a bit scrambled in the plane crash. He sure as hell cut his head open . . . anyway, whatever his problem is, it's his problem and the only thing left for me to do is to go back to the valley tomorrow and pretend that I don't know anything.'

The muscles along his spine contracted slowly at the thought of going back, and unconsciously he gripped the table edge.

'Alex, your knuckles are white.'

'Sorry, I was just thinking about going back. I'm probably going to have to talk to the police, maybe identify Gord's body . . . I don't know how I'm going to handle that . . .' He looked across the table at her. 'I think I'm probably going to drink too much tonight. I hope you don't mind.'

'No it's alright. I'll do my best to take care of you.' She looked around the room. 'But not here, okay?' If you want to get numb that's fine with me, but let's do it somewhere less trendy.'

Alex had had a drink in the hotel and two drinks in the bar all in less than an hour and he was starting to float.

'What about the bottle in our room? Let's go there and if I get stupid, or maudlin, it won't matter. And anyway I don't feel like meeting the public tonight.'

They stood up just as the waitress arrived with Linda's drink. 'Excuse me, did you forget about your drink?'

Linda took a five from her purse and laid it on the waitress' tray and said, 'Have it yourself or give it to someone else, we're leaving.' She took Alex's arm and led him to the street.

'I really dislike places like that.' She still had her arm through Alex's and now she pulled him along. 'C'mon, let's walk for a while. I need to burn off some energy.'

Alex hung back and she stopped and faced him. 'Alex, I'm not asking you to be happy. I know that you're sad about Gordon, and frightened about what might happen, and that you need support; but you're forgetting that Gordon was *my* friend too, that *I'm* sad about his death, that *I'm* frightened about the future, that *I* need support too. Now walk with me up and down these streets and hold my hand so tight that it hurts me.'

CHAPTER TWENTY-FOUR

Yosemite Valley

GORDON HAD DIED on Thursday night, and now, Saturday afternoon, Alex and Linda were rolling through the dry hills and forests on their way back to Yosemite Valley to confront that death again.

They had discussed it over and over until Alex felt that he could face whatever questions the police might have for him. He still felt only partially under control but the knowledge that Linda needed his support as much as he needed hers had strengthened him and he knew that somehow he would be able to get through the next few days.

When they reached Camp 4 they found Gordon's tent gone and the ground underneath it dug up in a circle of almost six foot radius. Groups of climbers milled around the site and Walter, the young German, saw them before anyone else. He stepped away from the group and took them aside.

'Walter, what's going on? Where's the tent? Where's Gord?'

'Alex, you must listen. There is much sadness about Gordon. He is found yesterday killed from the pistol, and the police have take the tent and equipments.' He put his hand on Alex's arm and said, 'I know he is your friend. I sorry to tell you.'

'What are you talking about? Where is he?' Alex's knees were shaking and the muscles of his abdomen contracted spasmodically. He did not have to fake anything. Linda took his other arm and she and Walter guided him to a bench.

'Yesterday they are finding the body and the Ranger is seeing the wounds of climbing on the hands and is coming here to ask for informations. It is your friend Gordon, but he not killed by the falling, he is killed by the pistol, by the gun.'

'Where is he?'

'Maybe I think in the hospital. Or they are taking him away. I do not know.'

Alex stood and looked at Linda, and the tears in his eyes were real. 'Take me to the hospital. Please.'

CHAPTER TWENTY-FIVE

Vancouver

ANDY CUTLER hung up his telephone and lit a cigarette. He wanted to stand by the window and look out at the city, which he knew would be all sharp edges and clean black shadows in the October light; but until he made Sergeant he wouldn't have an office with a window, so he left his desk and walked across the big detectives' room to visit Rick Hofstadter who was a Sergeant and had one of the best windows in the building.

He entered without knocking and said, 'Got the coffee on Rico?'

Hofstadter wouldn't drink the coffee in the cafeteria and kept a kettle and filters in his office. 'Sure, pour yourself a cup. I'll trade you for a smoke.'

They made the exchange and Hofstadter lit up. 'So what's happening?'

'You remember I told you about William Holley? That Lieutenant on the San Francisco force that phoned me about the coke importer – the one that was flying the stuff in from Prince Rupert?'

'Yeah, I remember. His airplane flew into a storm and then he turned up in

San Francisco a week later with a story about being stranded on a fishing trip. You went for a look at the wreck a couple of months ago. Guy's name was Mathews or something like that.'

'Matheson. That was back in August. Apparently this guy Matheson is pretty smooth. We found his suitcase in the wreck in the mountains just over the border south of Chilliwack Lake, and Holley was going to spring that on him, but Matheson beat him to it – phoned him up and said he'd been trying to get in touch with the pilot because he'd left his suitcase aboard, and asked if Holley knew whether it had been found.'

Cutler walked to the window with his coffee. The midmorning sun played in his blond hair and threw the bags under his eyes into sharp relief.

'Any chance of checking his bank accounts? Maybe getting some cooperation from the tax people?' Hofstadter asked. 'If this guy is actually smuggling in planeloads of cocaine it's gotta show up on his balance sheet somewhere. Unless he's giving the stuff away.'

'Not likely. He's got a brother who's a mining engineer in Peru, which is probably where he gets the stuff, and the two of them have quite a few legitimate businesses down there. That's probably where the money goes. It probably gets laundered through about six different companies and stays in Peru.'

'And your friend Holley hasn't got a chance of finding anything out down there, right?'

'Right.' Cutler tried to scrunch himself up onto the window sill, his back against one side of the frame and his feet against the other, but the sill wasn't quite wide enough and he almost fell off. 'I wouldn't exactly call Holley my friend either. He's too intense for me. In fact I wouldn't be surprised if he wears his badge to bed. But he's interesting – sort of a study in applied fanaticism. And I think he's pretty good. He sure hasn't missed much on the Matheson thing. He put it all together by himself from just a few bits of information, and if that RCMP spotter hadn't screwed up he probably would have put Matheson into the bag with a plane load of coke.'

Hofstadter scratched his nose and said, 'The RCMP actually saw this guy get into the plane and followed it down to the border? No chance he's telling the truth about the fishing lake and hitchhiking down here?'

'I wondered about that, so I looked into it myself. I know a few guys with the RCMP and I asked them to check it out. They said that it was solid. Matheson got on the plane with two suitcases in Prince Rupert, a regular one and one of the shiny aluminium cases photographers use, and they followed him right to the storm.'

Cutler returned to the desk. 'So it sounds to me as though Holley's right, but for the time being there's not much he can do about it except eat his liver.' He took a cigarette and threw the pack back at the desktop. 'But that's not what I wanted to see you about.'

'No?'

He walked to the window again and smoked in silence, ordering his mind and going over the telephone call he had just received. Then he asked, 'Does the name Gordon Wilson mean anything to you?'

Hofstadter thought for a short time and then replied 'No, I don't think so. Should it?'

'I don't know.' Cutler had his back to the room, holding his coffee cup with both hands, the cigarette dangling from his lips. 'I got a call a few minutes ago from Holley in San Francisco. Apparently two bodies were found on Saturday in the forest in Yosemite National Park in California, about two hundred miles east of San Francisco. One shot, one stabbed, both male.

'Holley found out about it because one of the dead guys was from the Bay area. It was some low grade thug who worked for another guy named Carl . . . Carl . . .' Cutler put his coffee down on the windowsill, pulled out his notebook and flipped through the notes he had made during the telephone call. '. . . named Carl Adams who does a lot of odd jobs for one of the big importers down there.'

Cutler looked up from his notes and added, 'Adams was once seen meeting with this Matheson, which is what got Holley going on this whole thing in the first place.'

Hofstadter thought about this for a minute and then said, 'Okay, I get it. I imagine you're going to tell me that the other corpse was Gordon Wilson, and since Holley called you about it, and since you're asking me about it, he must be from around here somewhere. Right?'

Cutler was amazed. How could anybody who looked and dressed like an extra in an old gangster film be as good as Hofstadter? 'Rico, when they make you Superintendent of Detectives you won't forget who gave you all those cigarettes will you?'

Hofstadter laughed. 'You'll owe me so much for coffee by then that I'll have to promote you just so you can afford to pay me.' Then, seriously, 'But unfortunately I don't think I know anything about Gordon Wilson. Do they know anything down there?'

'Not a damn thing. They didn't even know his name until some acquaintances of his identified the body. It seems that he was a mountain climber and he and a friend were in this Yosemite Park because there are some big rock walls there.

'But you're right about him being from Vancouver. This friend, who's an American by the way, doesn't seem to know too much. Apparently he was having dinner in a restaurant with Wilson and then Wilson went away somewhere with a middle aged black guy he called Carl. There's a waiter in the restaurant who confirms all this and the descriptions of this Carl match up with Carl Adams, the one that led Holley into all this in the first place.

'Now this Carl has disappeared, and the Sheriff's people in Modesto, who've got jurisdiction in this, haven't got any ideas at all. Holley says he's going to go and talk to them and he asked if I could look at it from this end.

'The dead guy's friend gave the Sheriff's man an address and said that this Wilson was single and worked part time for a printing company called Ambledon printing.'

Cutler looked at his notes again and read aloud. 'The body was a white male, about thirty years of age. Shoulder length blond hair, thick blond beard and moustache. Five feet eleven inches, one hundred and ninety-five pounds. No needle marks or signs of regular drug use. He was muscular and seemed to be in excellent health except that both hands as far up as the wrists were covered in very fresh scabs, some quite large.'

He looked up again. 'The park Rangers say that the scabs are very common with rock climbers. They get them from jamming their hands into cracks in the rock faces when they climb, and the friend confirms that he and Wilson had just done a very hard climb the day before the killing.'

'What's this friend's name?' interrupted Hofstadter.

Cutler checked his notes. 'Alexander Townsend. Lives in Seattle.'

'And Wilson, what's his address?'

'Thirty-two sixty West Fourteenth. I checked with the city, it's a private home and Wilson was the sole owner.'

Hofstadter snorted. 'A thirty year old long hair with a part time job and he owns a house in Kitsilano?'

'Yeah, that's what I thought, but it seems he bought it about ten years ago. It's a small place and he got a good mortgage.'

'It'd have to be pretty good if he could afford it when he was twenty and only has to work part time to pay it off.'

'Well, who knows? Maybe he inherited. On the other hand maybe he's involved in this cocaine thing in a major way.'

Cutler emptied his coffee cup. 'Anyway, whatever the story is on this guy, I figure it's worth having a look at the house. So if it's okay with you I'll go and do that now.'

Hofstadter snorted again. 'If it's okay with me! What a crock. Since when has me being your Sergeant made the slightest bit of difference to what you do? Here, don't forget these.' He tossed the cigarette pack across the room. 'Let me know what you find out, and make me a copy of the description of this Wilson. I'll see if anyone around here knows anything about him.'

Cutler was almost out the door when Hofstadter called after him, 'What were you pretending to be at work on when you got that telephone call?'

'Nothing that can't wait. It was those bikers out in district three, the ones with the laboratory in the basement. Their court date was postponed again, so this'll give me something to do to keep me from drinking up the rest of your coffee.'

'Okay, have fun. And if I'm around when you get back let me know what you found.'

The thirty-two hundred block on West Fourteenth Avenue is quietly residential. Huge old poplars shade the street, small and medium sized houses sit well back on neatly clipped lawns. Small orderly hedges and large disorderly flowers are everywhere.

Most of the houses were built in the thirties and forties and many are still occupied by their original owners. 3260 was small and well kept. With stucco walls and green asphalt shingles it looked like almost all the other houses on the block.

A large pear tree dominated the front yard and Cutler thought he could see a weeping willow behind the house. He didn't stop in front of it but drove on and parked at a corner two blocks away.

'Two-two.'

'Go ahead two-two.'

'I'm in the thirty-two hundred block on West Fourteenth. Have you got a patrol car nearby?'

'I've got several units within a few minutes of that area, shall I send one to meet you?'

'I'd prefer a one-man unit if that's possible.'

'Um, just a minute two-two.'

Cutler leaned back against the headrest and smoked patiently. He let his mind ramble unchecked, facts, fantasies and images tumbling over one another like water rushing down a stream.

Every detective has a different method of working. Some jot ideas down on paper, some bounce ideas off other detectives, or off their wives; Cutler liked to stack up all the information and all the facts at his disposal, shuffle them thoroughly and then toss them randomly through his mind.

It didn't always help, but it never hurt and he knew from long experience that it had a calming effect on him and made him more alert in the following hours. Even a minute or two helped.

'Two-two?'

'Two-two.'

'I've only got one one-man unit in a marked vehicle in your district. That unit is ten-sixty-two right now, how urgent is this?'

'No rush, just tell me where he's eating and I'll meet him there.'

'It's the White Spot, Broadway and Vine.'

'Thanks.' Cutler stubbed out his cigarette and was about to sign off, then he added 'Who is it? I mean which P.C. is in that unit?'

'Two-eight-two, two-two.'

Fucking numbers. The badge number meant nothing to him. He had wanted a name and suspected that the dispatcher knew it. Patience.

'Can you give me a name to go with that number please?'

'That's constable MacGregor, two-two.'

'Thank you, ten-four.'

Cutler didn't know MacGregor. In fact he'd never heard of MacGregor. Sometimes he toyed with the idea of transferring to the police force in a small city or town. Somewhere he could get to know everyone on the force and a good percentage of the citizens. But he knew it was something he could never really do. He needed the city. Needed to walk its streets and feel the ever accelerating pulse of its life. Andrew Cutler was a quiet man, but he drew his sustenance, spiritual, emotional and intellectual, from the current of anonymous human electricity that flows so strongly in a big city.

Pushing open the heavy double doors of the White Spot he looked around and soon spotted the only police uniform in the restaurant. Constable MacGregor was short for a police officer, had medium length brown hair, brown eyes, and a clean, tanned complexion carefully set off with just a hint of green eyeliner and a rich burgundy lipstick.

There are some things, thought Cutler, that aren't that bad about a big city police force.

She looked up from the newspaper she was reading and gave him an efficient once-over. He could see the card file flipping over behind her eyes, see her fast glance past him and to both sides, analyzing the geometry of confrontation as he approached. Then he saw her relax a bit and knew that she had tagged him as a fellow cop.

'I'm Detective Cutler. Andy Cutler. May I join you while you finish lunch?'

She looked at him absently for a few seconds, her face and eyes giving nothing away, and then said, 'Please do.'

Her voice was pleasant but emotionally neutral. Cutler sat down opposite her and said, 'Sorry to interrupt your break. I wanted a one-man unit and the dispatcher said that the only one-man unit was having lunch here so I thought I'd just drop in and order a coffee and brief you while you ate. If that was alright with you.'

Her face and eyes relaxed as he spoke and her response was warmer. 'Yes, that's alright with me. Actually I'm finished anyway,' she gestured at the debris on the table in front of her, 'and I was just about to go back to work.'

'Did you have anything coming up this afternoon?'

'No, I'm just on patrol.'

'Well, I'm afraid this isn't likely to prove too exciting.' Cutler remembered how he, like all constables, had been excited whenever he got a chance to work with the detectives. 'I'm going to search a house in the thirty-two hundred block on West Fourteenth. Do you know that area?'

'It's mostly residential isn't it?' She thought a bit and then said, 'You know, I've been in district four for three years now, and I can't remember a thing about that block, so it must be pretty quiet.'

She swallowed the last of her coffee and grimaced. 'God. I don't know why I drink this slop. So you want a uniformed officer and a blue and white along so that the neighbours don't call the police when you enter the house?'

She's just like Rico, thought Cutler, knows what I'm going to say before I can say it.

'That's right. The house belongs, or belonged, to a guy named Gordon Wilson who was killed in the States over the weekend, and who *may* be involved in a big drug deal . . .'

As he spoke he puzzled over her reaction to him. Why had she been so remote at first and then only partially thawed out? The timing was all wrong. Her first reaction had been understandable, it was the reaction of any policeman when approached by a stranger, but when she tagged him as another cop she only relaxed part way. It wasn't until he started explaining why he wanted her that she dropped the pose of cool politeness.

'. . . so anyway when I drove through the neighbourhood I realized that I was going to need uniformed backup to keep the 911 phone from ringing off the wall, and since there was no need to take two guys off patrol I asked for a one-man unit. You're the only single on this shift so here I am.'

He stopped speaking for a moment and then added, 'By the way, what's your first name?'

She had been listening carefully to his story and answered the question before she was aware of it.

'Valerie.'

But even as she spoke the impersonal mask came back into place and the brown eyes hardened.

He had it now. He held up both hands, palms toward her, and said, 'Easy, easy, I've been on this police force for eleven years. In all that time I haven't made a single pass at a policewoman. Not one. This is business and I'll call you Constable MacGregor if that makes you happier.'

She looked at him for a little longer. She could see nothing but honest good humour in the drooping lids and light blue eyes. She relaxed again.

'No, please, call me Valerie. It's just that half the guys on the force seem to think that the PW's are there for their own personal amusement. It gets pretty tiring.'

'I suppose it must.' Cutler stood up. 'If you're finished lunch we might as well get moving.'

Constable Valerie MacGregor rose from behind her side of the table. She may have been short for a police officer but she was tall for a woman. Slim without being thin, and her arms were as tanned as her face. Her uniform didn't give much away about her figure except that she had a small waist.

Cutler said, 'Will you phone in and tell your Corporal that you'll be working with me for a few hours? Don't use that thing.' He pointed to the tranceiver she had just picked up from the table. 'We don't need any spectators or helpers. I'll head over there now and wait for you. It's a small stucco house on the south side of Fourteenth between Blenheim and Trutch. About the fourth one from the corner of Trutch.'

As he drove Cutler thought about the policewoman he had just met. She reminded him of Hofstadter. Which was pretty funny considering the physical differences, but she had the same quick mind and the same straightforward nature.

He turned on to Fourteenth and parked in front of the little house and pretended not to watch the elderly neighbour pretending not to watch him. After two or three minutes the patrol car pulled in behind him and the neighbours stopped pretending.

They locked their cars and stood together on the sidewalk, she looking at the house and he looking at her. The autumn sunlight threw her features into topographic relief without being harsh. She had a strong face with high cheekbones. A straight nose fell from real eyebrows to a real mouth. No cuteness or artifice. It was, Cutler thought, a face made for expressing real emotion. Her eyes had looked brown in the artificial light of the restaurant but here in the sun he could see that they were a mixture of browns and greens. Hazel.

He brought himself back to reality and hoped she hadn't minded him staring. 'We might as well knock on the door before we do too much skulking around.'

The front door was in a small covered porch six steps up. Their knocking was answered only by empty silence and the door was securely locked.

They walked around the house clockwise. The lot was a standard city lot, thirty-three feet by one fifty, but it seemed large because the house was small. The front yard was grassed and continuous with the lawns of the houses on either side, the rear was enclosed on one side and the back by a low wooden fence and on the other side by a tall, dense hedge. A back gate opened to a wooden stand with two empty garbage cans in a gravelled lane.

An old weeping willow dominated the backyard and beneath it was a heavy picnic table with attached benches. Six steps led up to a small deck and the back door. Under the steps were dozens of cases of empty beer bottles.

They continued round the house until they were back at the front door. The house appeared empty – there were curtains drawn across the basement windows and the main floor windows were too high to let them see in.

'Do you know anything about picking locks?'

'Just the kind where you can work on the tongue with a knifeblade.' she replied. 'The front door looked like a good quality deadbolt to me.'

'Well maybe the back door won't be as tough. You walk around that way and check all the windows you can reach, and I'll go this way.'

Just over a minute later they met in the back yard.

'Nothing?'

'Nothing.'

'Okay, let's have a look at this door.'

The back door lock was as good as the front, and the door itself didn't budge or rattle when Cutler threw a tentative hip into it.

He sighed. 'Oh well. Now you get to watch how a shit-hot Detective finesses his way past a locked door.'

He looked into the one neighbouring back yard that he could see to make sure no one was watching then drew his revolver and smashed the small pane of glass set into the centre of the door near the top. He knocked out as many of the fragments as he could and then reached up and through the broken window. But it was too high and even on tiptoe he couldn't reach down to the lock.

He sighed again, took off his jacket and handed it to the policewoman. 'I'll kneel down so you can stand on my back. Put my jacket on so you don't cut yourself on the glass.'

He knelt down on all fours so that his back offered a level platform about two and a half feet above the deck. Craning his neck to look up at her he added, 'And you might take off your shoes.'

She stepped up on his back, one foot on his shoulders, one foot over his hips. He tried to hold steady as he felt her lean and stretch. There were metal on metal noises and a muffled 'Damn.' More noises and then she stepped lightly down.

As he rose she wiped her forehead with her left hand and said, 'I think I got it.'

She had been bracing her left hand high above the door, just under the eaves, and now there was a smear of dirt where she had touched herself. His coat hung halfway to her knees and the sleeves were well past her fingertips. With her shoeless feet and smudged face she looked like a Gasoline Alley urchin. And very desirable.

He took the coat from her and removed a handkerchief from one of its inside pockets.

'Hold still.' He cupped the back of her head in one hand and cleaned the grime from her forehead. Looking into her eyes he knew that she would accept when he asked her to dinner – and that she knew he would ask.

But duty first.

'Wipe your hand on this.' He gave her the handkerchief and turned the doorknob.

She slipped on her shoes and stepped in behind him.

They were in a small hallway looking into a pleasant sunlit kitchen/breakfast nook.

'What are you looking for?'

'Nothing.'

'Nothing?'

'Nothing specific. Nothing and everything. The guy who lived here was found dead in California, in some national park. Apparently he was a mountain climber and there are some rock faces in that park. He'd been shot in the chest and there was another body beside him that had been stabbed. The other body was some no-mind heavy on the San Francisco drug scene. Dumb. Just a kid, but lots of arrests – assaults, B and E's, possession, that kind of thing. The guy I've been working with on this says that the stab victim usually worked for another guy named Carl Adams who was seen with Wilson shortly before the killings, and who had been seen with a man named Walter Matheson who is suspected of smuggling cocaine into the States from up here.'

He paused and then went on. 'So it's all pretty tenuous, it could be anything. Wilson, the guy who lived here, might have been an innocent bystander or he might have been masterminding a huge coke operation.' He paused again. 'He only worked part time and he had to make his house payments somehow.

'So I don't really know what I'm looking for. Fifty kilos of cocaine in the cupboard under the sink? Dead bodies in the basement?'

'A huge collection of Old Masters in the attic?' said Valerie, getting into the spirit of the conversation. 'A secret transmitter under the floorboards with a codebook in Albanian?'

'That's right, subtle clues which might lead us to believe that the deceased had fallen in with evil men.'

Valerie drew herself up to full height and adopted the pinched, nasal voice and clenched cheeks walk of one of Vancouver's more obnoxious trial lawyers. 'So as you can see Your Honour, my client is essentially an honest young man, and only ran this multinational narcotics cartel to support his widowed mother.'

She turned her back for a second and then turned once more to face Cutler from behind an imaginary judge's bench. She peered nearsightedly out over imaginary reading glasses and in a deep, pompous voice said, 'Uh, no shit, eh?'

Cutler had recognized the caricatures and they were both laughing. Gradually the laughter stopped and they simply looked at one another. Finally he said, 'First things first, okay?'

'Okay.'

They moved into the kitchen. 'I really *don't* know what I'm looking for. Right now I'm just looking. For anything. Let's just wander around separately and see what we see. Touch all the doorknobs and light switches you want, but be careful of everything else.'

Andy Cutler was a good cop. He put Constable MacGregor out of his mind and began working. He hung up his coat and walked slowly through the house. It was a small house and he didn't open any cupboards or check the basement, so his tour only took a few minutes. He stood in the middle of each room and looked slowly around three hundred and sixty degrees, then went on to the next.

When he had seen each room he walked to the living room and sat down in a large overstuffed armchair and closed his eyes.

Valerie MacGregor had watched and taken part in several house searches in her four years on the force but she had never seen one like this. For almost a minute she stood watching Cutler in the chair, then she shrugged her shoulders and started for the top of the stairs leading to the basement but stopped again when Cutler stood up.

He turned to her and said, 'Tell me about the guy who lived here.'

The question took her completely by surprise. Everything this man did surprized her. 'I . . . I can't really say . . . I mean we haven't really had a good look at anything. I . . .'

'I know all that. Try anyway.'

'Okay, if you want me to. But just let me think for a minute.' She looked slowly around the room. Fireplace with three quarter full wood box. Solid wooden bookshelves jammed with books. Hardwood floor with a good rug. Two armchairs and a couch all in the overstuffed style of the forties. Old but solid, with good upholstery. Low coffee table – solid, like the bookshelves. Fairly new console television.

What else? A couple of old-fashioned upright lamps with heavy cloth shades. Large window area looking over the front yard. A fairly large room. Light and spacious enough that the heavy furniture was not oppressive.

What else? A pair of framed prints on one wall, colour photographs, one of a mountain with snow blowing off the top and the other of somebody climbing steep ice. And a framed reproduction of Breughel's 'Peasant's Wedding' over the mantlepiece.

What else? Complex and expensive looking audio components and what looked to be several hundred records shelved with the books. Two very large speakers near the front of the room. The sound system bothered her, but she wasn't sure why.

She sat down in one of the chairs and asked herself Who lived here?

'You said that he was a climber, but if you hadn't told me that I would have said that he was pretty much like most of the other people on the block. A sort of quiet old man who took good care of his house. He probably wasn't rich, but he made enough to buy this little house and some solid furniture – maybe twenty-five years ago.

'He was probably retired, maybe a widower or a bachelor since there doesn't seem to be any feminine feel to the place.'

She had been speaking quietly, thoughtfully; now she stood up and in a more normal voice said, 'Something about the stereo bothers me though. But I'm not sure what it is.'

'Probably the fact that not many "retired widowers" have multi-thousand dollar component stereos,' said Cutler. 'This is a funny kind of job. A man was murdered in California. He might or might not be involved in heavy crime. There might or might not be something here that's significant. We might or might not recognize it.

'The guy has no record, not even a parking ticket, and neither Rick Hofstadter nor I have ever heard of him. We'll ask around, check with the neighbours, find out what we can; but this part, this house search, is different. We're probably not going to find any stash of cocaine in the basement, or any hidden code books; whatever clues there are are probably small and easy to miss. That's why I gave the place a quick walk-through, just to form a general impression so that anything unusual will have a chance of standing out a little more clearly.'

He stood up. 'Now, let's shake the place down.'

For a while there was nothing much. Cutlery and utensils and some canned food in the kitchen drawers and cupboards, but nothing perishable. The refrigerator was unplugged and the garbage container was empty. The sugar, salt, flour and baking powder containers contained sugar, salt, flour and baking powder.

The bedroom was clean and tidy. Large brass bed nicely made with a thick down comforter folded at the foot. Department store clothing in the closet. Blue jeans and Levi shirts mostly, no suits and no ties. Nondescript collection of T-shirts, socks and underwear in the dresser along with several well made but not stylish wool sweaters. No jewellry anywhere and nothing under the bed.

Cutler removed the comforter and peeled the bed one layer at a time. Near the foot of the bottom sheet were several large reddish-brown stains, faint but quite noticeable.

'What the hell?'

'Maybe he has hairy feet and cut himself shaving,' said Valerie, then giggled.

He peeled the last sheet and looked at the mattress. Clean.

'Help me turn this over.'

On the other side of the mattress were more stains, near the head of the bed. Together they shook out the bottom sheet and put it back on, reversed top to bottom. The stains on the sheet matched those on the mattress. The pillowcase was clean, but the pillow itself was prominently stained.

The living room yielded nothing of interest except a carved wooden box with a tight fitting lid sitting on the bookshelves. In it was one plastic bag containing about half an ounce of marijuana and another containing a few grams of black hash. Lying loose in the box were a small wooden hash pipe, three boxes of wooden matches, a half empty package of pipe cleaners and two spare screens for the pipe.

The bathroom was just a bathroom. Drano and cleansers under the sink along with spare toilet paper and a large plastic basin. Aspirin, bandaids and scissors in the medicine cabinet. Soap and shampoo on the ledge of the tub.

Valerie MacGregor turned back to the sink and medicine cabinet. 'It's strange, there's no toothbrush or toothpaste, no shaving equipment, no deodorants . . .'

Cutler said, 'Yeah, but not that strange. He probably took the toothbrush and paste with him, the description I got said he had a thick beard so he probably didn't shave, and there are a lot of people who don't use deodorants or aftershaves.' He paused. 'In a way it goes with the clothes and the dope and the long hair. He probably bathed regularly and figured he didn't need any chemicals on his skin.'

The basement was unfinished except for a small room, about eight by twelve, that had been built in one corner. There was a furnace in the opposite corner, a freezer along one wall, a lawn mower and a rake and a workbench with a moderate collection of tools along another; but what first caught their interest was a large three-level industrial shelving unit against the remaining wall. It was stacked with multicoloured equipment and clothing, both loose and in boxes.

Cutler walked closer and stared. 'What *is* all this shit?' He picked up a smooth rope of blue and gold threads. It was coiled neatly in two and a half foot loops. 'This is some kind of rope, but what is all this other stuff? Did you ever see anything like *this*? It looks like something out of a medieval war.'

'It's an ice hammer.'

He stared at her.

'All this stuff is for climbing.' She began pointing at things. 'That one in your hand is an ice hammer, these are crampons, these are karabiners, here are some pitons, these loops of flat material are slings, these are . . . '

'Do you actually climb mountains?' He sounded horrified.

'No, but I had a friend who did. I tried it a few times and didn't like it much, but I learned a bit about it.'

Cutler picked up a white sling from the pile on the shelf and said, 'Tell me more about this.'

'What do you mean?'

'What is it made of? What is it used for?' He peered at the tag ends of nylon protruding from the knot. 'And what am I going to order when Holley buys me the best dinner in San Francisco?'

'What are you talking about?'

'See this?' He showed her the black ink on one end. 'It's a W isn't it? Wilson just marked it with his initial. Holley and I found one by a plane wreck which I'll tell you about in a few minutes and we assumed that it was an M, for Matheson. Hah! I knew that nobody walked out of there alone, I just knew it. Now, what is this thing.'

'It's called a sling. It's just a piece of one inch nylon webbing about five feet long. The two ends are tied together with a special knot that won't slip. Climbers use them for all kinds of things. Hanging things on, connecting ropes to pitons; they're just sort of general purpose things that people carry with them when they go climbing.'

'I see.' He told her how they had found the other sling and not known what it was. 'Now let's have a look at the rest of this stuff while I think about that dinner Holley is going to buy me.'

One by one they emptied and repacked the boxes. They contained clothing, sleeping bags, tents and camping equipment, ice climbing equipment and odds and ends of rock climbing gear.

'Nothing for us there. I wonder what's in that room?' Cutler walked across the basement and tried the door. It opened and he peered into the darkness, groped inside and found a light switch.

'Well, well, well. Now we know how he paid the rent.'

It was a growing room. Wire mesh, pumps, plastic plumbing, gravel beds, rows of lamps that could be raised or lowered and a shelf at the far end that held jars of fertilizers, jars of seeds, and a large germinating tray.

Behind him Valerie said, 'I don't understand.'

'It's a growing room with all the latest equipment for the grow-your-own pot gardener.'

'He grew his own pot in here?'

Cutler snorted. 'His own? Do you know anything about wet gravel hydroponics?'

'No.'

'Well if you know what you're doing you can get half a pound from each plant. At least half a pound. And if you know what you're doing you can duplicate just anything – Columbian, Hawaiian, Californian Sinsemilla, anything at all. If this guy was even moderately successful he could have pulled five pounds out of here three or four or even five times a year. That's as much as twenty-five pounds a year and even if it wasn't great he'd be getting a minimum of a thousand a pound for it. That's twenty-five grand a year and no taxes. Minimum. And possibly over a hundred thou if it was really first class.'

Ffifteen minutes later he was on the telephone, holding it carefully by the earpiece.

'Hi Rico, it's Andy. I'm at Wilson's house on West Fourteenth. We need Ident down here . . . No, no jackpot, but plenty just the same – bloodstains in the bedroom, a pot farm in the basement . . . Yeah, that's right, and about five pounds of pot in the deep freeze . . . No they're not fresh, but Holley told me that Matheson had a bad cut on his head and most of the stains are on the pillow and around the head area; *and* I've got something that puts this guy Wilson at the site of the plane wreck . . . Right, if he wasn't dead Holley would want to talk to him real bad . . . Yeah, I'll be here . . . Okay thanks, see you tomorrow.'

He hung up the telephone and sat in the big armchair hunched forward with his elbows on his knees and his face in his hands. After almost a minute he looked up and said, 'What shift are you on?'

'Six to four.' She looked at her watch. 'In fact I'm due off in about half an hour.'

'Christ, I don't know how you can handle those ten hour days.'

'Three day weekends help a lot.'

'I suppose so.' He paused then said, 'I was going to suggest supper, but if you've got to be at work by six in the morning . . .' He let the question hang.

She looked down at him. 'My next three day weekend starts in twenty-five minutes.' There was heat in her eyes and in her voice. 'What do you like to eat?'

CHAPTER TWENTY-SIX

San Francisco

HIS HEAD HURT. The headaches had almost disappeared when Wilson's friend dropped the roof in on him. Now they were back and getting worse. Maybe it was just the tension getting to him, and when he resolved this immediate problem the headaches would go away. He decided to give it one more week and then see about getting some serious medical attention.

At least Carl wouldn't bother him again. It had been a distinct pleasure to arrange that. Walter Matheson was not an exceptionally violent man, but the thought of Carl's corpse floating in the bay gave him more relief from the pain in his head than aspirin, and a pleasant sensation – kind of tingly – all over.

He didn't even need to justify it to himself. Carl was treacherous scum and had gotten exactly what he deserved.

He poured himself another drink and looked around the room. It was the only room in the house that was really his and his alone; and he had decorated it to his own taste. He liked everything about it from the rough cedar panelling on the walls to the view out the window, but nonetheless he was looking forward to the day when he could leave it, and the house, and the whole life he lived here, for the last time.

Two more shipments . . . maybe even one really big one. . . . If only Wilson hadn't gotten himself killed. . . . Maybe Wilson's friend would change his mind if Walter explained how important this was . . .

CHAPTER TWENTY-SEVEN

Vancouver

WHEN ANDY CUTLER got to work the next morning he found a large scrap of white paper on his desk with the words 'SEE ME' scrawled on it in bold black felt pen. The note was unsigned but he knew where it had come from.

'You wanted to see me Rico?'

'Uhuh. Pour yourself a coffee and sit down, I've got big news for you. But first you tell me whether this Gordon Wilson business is something we're going to have to deal with here; and if it is, can you handle it yourself or will you need Popov?'

Cutler tasted his coffee and then sat down and lit a cigarette. 'I think we're probably going to have to do something about it. I'm not sure that it's going to get us much, but we should do *some* work; and no, I won't need Doug. Why? Is he sick?'

Hofstadter plundered Cutler's cigarette pack. 'No, he's fine, it's you that's sick.'

'Me?'

'Yup. You're about to come down with the same disease I've got.'

'Cerebral flatulence? Terminal insipidity? Middle age spread?'

'Nah, those are just the symptoms. The disease is responsibility.'

'Responsibility?'

'Yeah. They're going to give you Sergeant in a couple of weeks. I'm not supposed to tell you about it, but since it's obviously going to affect assignments for you and Popov you might as well know now. Just try to look surprised when you get the official word.'

'Will that mean I won't have to call you Sir and salute you anymore?'

'Hah!' Hofstadter snorted and lit his cigarette. 'What it means is that you'll have to start working for your paycheques again. However, the next two weeks will be something of a holiday – even by your standards – because I can't assign you to anything new, so you'll get to answer the telephone and sort a lot of paper.'

He dragged on the cigarette and continued, 'Now tell me about yesterday.'

'Wait a minute,' said Cutler. 'What's the story on this Sergeant thing? Why now? I wasn't supposed to get bumped until sometime next year.' He had forgotten his coffee and smoke. '*I* know how good I am, and what a valuable contribution I make, but what woke them up upstairs? Why the sudden rush?'

'Because Al Ericson is resigning effective Christmas, and Stumpf, in Fraud, was in a bad MVA last week and is going to be off duty for at least six months, and we were already short two Sergeants anyway, and the Board, with its limited vision, has decided that you are the one to take up the slack. Now tell me about yesterday. What did you find in that house and what do we have to do about it?'

They were well into their second cup of coffee when Cutler finished, '. . . so what I think is that Wilson probably helped Matheson out of the mountains and let him stay in the house on West Fourteenth – which,.by the way, is only a couple of blocks from where Matheson did a lot of shopping on his credit cards. Anyway, Wilson may or may not have helped get the coke to San Francisco, I don't know about that, and then he went off on his holiday. Maybe he tried to blackmail Matheson, or maybe Matheson just decided to have him hit for insurance, but the main thing, from our point of view anyway, is that prior to all this he probably wasn't involved in anything more serious than growing and selling a little pot.'

Cutler finished the coffee and leaned back in his chair. 'But that's only probably, so we'll have to do a bit of work on this – talk to the neighbours, his employer, maybe track down some of his friends and see if anybody has any idea why he was in the area where the plane went down.'

'Any chance he could have been there to meet the plane?'

'Rico, you didn't see where that plane went down. No way an airplane could land anywhere near there. Even the helicopter couldn't land. We had to jump out while he hovered.'

Hofstadter pulled fresh cigarettes for both of them, but then put them back in the pack and rooted around in his desk. He produced a package of cigars and said, 'If you're going to get promoted we might as well celebrate.'

Once the cigars were drawing well Hofstadter said, 'So you think that this Wilson's being at the wreck was just coincidence?'

'I think so, but I'm not sure. He was a mountain climber and there are lots of mountains there, but on the other hand they may have been planning to drop the stuff to him and then fly back to Prince Rupert,' said Cutler. He drew on the cigar and exhaled a cloud of blue smoke. 'You know, I think I might even enjoy being a Sergeant.' He puffed contentedly for a while and then said, 'I don't know much about mountain climbing, but I've heard that mountain climbers always go in pairs. If that's true then there may have been someone else there. If we can find out who it was then we may find the answers to all of these questions.'

'If whoever it was hasn't already been killed too.'

'Yes, there's that.'

'So what are you going to do about it?'

'Right now? Right now I'm going to go and talk to old Fred in Personnel to see if there's anyone on this Police Force who knows enough about mountain climbing to point me to someone who might know something about Wilson.'

Cutler stood up. 'So I'll get to work on that. Thanks for the cigar, and thanks for telling me about the promotion. If I'm finished at a reasonable hour I'll buy you a drink.'

'You mean you'll buy me a *couple* of drinks and try to pump me about your new assignment.'

'Yes,' said Cutler, and started for the door.

'And one other thing, Andy.'

'Yes?'

'This could be the last of the good weather and Angie and I will probably try and get one more barbecue in before the monsoons. Do you want to come over Saturday?'

'That would be nice.'

'Okay. Now, do I tell Angie to find a friend for you or will you bring Constable MacGregor?'

Andy Cutler blushed bright red and almost dropped his cigar. 'How did you know about that?'

'Sergeants know everything. You'll find out for yourself in two weeks. Now go and find a mountain climber who knows all about drug smuggling and murder.'

Constable Jamie Barr, when Cutler finally reached him on the telephone, said that he was strictly an amateur who liked to get out into the mountains whenever he could.

'Nothing too technical, just a snow plod now and then.'

'So you don't know anything about this Gordon Wilson?'

'No. If he's climbing in Yosemite valley then he's way out of my league, but I know someone who can probably help you. Got a pen handy?'

'Shoot.'

'Okay, the name is Goossens. G-O-O-S-S-E-N-S. Paul Goossens. He lives at three twenty-five East Twenty-third Avenue, and his number is 873-2509. He rents the top floor of a house there. He's a really good climber and he seems to know everybody in the climbing scene around here.'

'He's a friend of yours?'

'Yes, he is. He's too good for me to climb with, but we ski a lot together in the winter.'

'Do you know where he works? Or where I can reach him during the day?'

'As a matter of fact you can probably get him at home. I was talking to him last night and he said he was going to spend the day working on his house. I think he's trying to build a balcony outside his bedroom window.'

'He doesn't work?'

'Oh, now and again. He's a carpenter and general construction labourer when he feels like it. A lot of climbers are like that.'

'Well thanks for the information. I'll give him a call and see if I can drop over for a visit.'

'Okay, see you around.'

Cutler hung up and dialled Goossens' number. He let it ring a dozen times and then dialled again. Still no answer. He decided to go anyway. If this Goossens really was working on a balcony he might be outside, or off picking up some nails or whatever. Besides, he didn't have any other ideas and if Goossens wasn't there he could leave a message for him taped to the door.

Three twenty-five East Twenty-third was a big old three storey frame house and Cutler could see someone on a ladder working outside a third floor window as he drove up. As he got closer he could see that it was a young man with a droopy moustache and brown hair flowing halfway down his back.

He parked the car and got out. Goossens, if that was who it was, paid no attention, did not seem to have noticed his arrival, and carried on hammering.

'Hello.'

No answer.

'Hello!' Louder. 'Paul Goossens?'

Still no answer. Was he deaf? Cutler put a tentative hand on the ladder. He hated ladders, but the young man seemed unable to hear, so . . .

As soon as he put his weight on the bottom rung the hammering stopped and curious eyes were staring down at him from behind medium thick lenses.

'Mr. Goossens?'

The young man removed a set of headphones that had been hidden in the long hair and said, 'Sorry, don't hear much of anything with these on. What did you say?'

'I'm looking for Paul Goossens.'

'Why?'

'I need some information about mountain climbing, and Jamie Barr said you might be able to help me.'

The morning sun glinted off the lenses of Goossens' wire frame glasses as he thought about what Cutler had said. 'You a friend of Jamie's?'

'Not really. I'm a co-worker.'

'You're with the police?'

'That's right.'

'And you want to get into climbing?'

'Not a chance. I don't even like stairs. But I want to talk about it if you can spare me a little time.'

'Okay. Just hang on a minute.' He disappeared through the window and a minute later emerged through the front door of the house, closing it behind him. He walked down the steps and offered Cutler a hand. 'I'm Paul Goossens.'

'Andy Cutler.' Goossens was just below middle height and dressed in faded, patched jeans and a faded blue T-shirt. The brown eyes behind the wire frames were openly curious as they looked Cutler over carefully. Goossens was in his mid-twenties and looked to Cutler as if he had just materialized from 1967 – a thin, muscular hippy.

'So you want to talk about climbing?'

'Mostly I want to find out about a man named Gordon Wilson. I understand that he was a mountain climber, and Jamie Barr said that you knew most of the mountain climbers around here.'

'Hmmmm. Have you got some ID?'

Cutler showed him his badge.

'You mind telling me what this is about?'

Cutler thought about that. Goossens had likely been a friend of Wilson's and probably knew all about the basement room. He would want to be protective and give as little to the police as possible. So . . .

'I want to find out why he was murdered.'

'WHAT??'

'He was found dead, shot in the chest, on Saturday morning. I want to find out who killed him.'

Goossens was stunned. The spring had gone out of his posture and he stood slumped, a beanbag man about to submit to gravity.

Cutler bored on. 'His murder is related to the fact that he's a mountain climber, and if I don't get some help from you there's a good chance that another mountain climber will be murdered.'

Goossens sat down on the front steps and said nothing. Cutler looked down at him for a while, then knelt so that their eyes were on the same level. 'Look at me Paul.'

Goossens looked up and Cutler said, 'I'm a cop. I know all about the pot farm in your friend's basement, but I don't give a shit about that. For all I know you've got a pot farm in *your* basement, but I don't give a shit about that either. What I care about is that there may be somebody, maybe another friend of yours, who is going to be murdered very soon unless I get some help and information.'

The eyes behind the glasses were far away. 'I thought he was in the Valley.'

'Where?'

'Yosemite. In California.'

'That's where he was found, in a deserted parking lot by a power substation.'

'Oh Christ.' Paul Goossens stood up. 'How can I help?'

'The Lancelot?'

'C'mon Rico, if I'm buying, then I get to pick the bar.'

'But why a cesspool like the Lancelot?'

'Because I've got some business to do there later tonight and I want to check the place out.'

'Oh, alright, alright.'

The Hotel Lancelot is on Main Street, just north of the Canadian National Railway station and on the fringes of Vancouver's skid row. It is small and poorly cared for. End of the line shelter for end of the line people.

'The mountain climbing club meets here? In this dump?'

'It's not really a club and they don't actually call themselves *mountain* climbers, just climbers.'

'Fascinating.'

'Now Rico, relax. We don't have to stay here, I just wanted to get a look at the place.'

'Great. So now you've seen it and we can go somewhere civilized.' Hofstadter looked around. 'Unless you want to check around a bit more and make sure that this is really the bar – that we haven't wandered in to the men's room by mistake.'

They left, but Cutler was back at 8:30 p.m. that evening. He was dressed in jeans and a loose wool sweater over an old work shirt. Goossens had told him that there were half a dozen regulars, climbers who showed up virtually every Wednesday, and another dozen or so irregulars, any of whom might show up on a given night. 'Most of them know Gord, and somebody's bound to know who he was down there with. Just don't expect to see anyone much before 9:30 p.m.'

He took a table near the corner where Goossens told him they usually sat, and stretched a glass of beer and a newspaper over half an hour. The bar was quiet. A few old men nursing beer and memories, and four greasy pool players shooting hi-low for drinks. Not a woman in the place and ninety percent of the tables vacant.

The climbers began drifting in just after 9:00 p.m. and by 9:45 p.m. there were eight of them around three small tables pulled together. They ranged in age from just over twenty to just over forty and most of them wore blue jeans and old shirts with either wool sweaters or zip-front jackets in some kind of furry pile. They laughed a lot without seeming to drink very much, and they all looked healthy and fit.

Their conversations were fast and lively and, aside from a bit of talk about the economy, not much of it made sense to Cutler, eavesdropping from behind his newspaper.

'... crampons? No we didn't have any, just EBs and one tool each and it had hardened up pretty good overnight, but it was suncupped so we managed okay till we got to the foot of the buttress ... What? No, mine is the Molson's, I wouldn't drink what they've got on tap here. Anyway, we soloed up a few hundred feet of easy fifth and then it got steep so we got out the rope and after that it was great; mostly five-eight, five-nine with a bit of ten and a *great* bivvy ledge half way up ...'

Or:

'... but it's all psychological – no one really needs it up here.'

'Oh yeah? Go and hang out on Crime of the Century on a hot day. See if your hands don't sweat.'

'Maybe, but it's still psychological. I mean maybe it's true that there are some routes that won't go on some days without chalk, but the people who use it use it all the time. Look at John there. He even chalks up to belay. He probably chalks up to piss ...'

Or:

'... so what's left for us? The frontier, the cutting edge, is over in the fuckin' Himalaya, and who can afford to go there? Sure there's lots of new routes to do here, but they're just more of the same. What can we do here that wasn't done in Europe twenty years ago?'

'Waterfalls. We've got waterfalls here like nowhere else. Nobody in Europe or the States is doing anything like Polar Circus. Not unless they come here that is. And what about Slipstream and Aggressive Treatment? Or what about anything in Alaska in the winter?'

'Yeah, I suppose. Paul was up there last winter. He didn't climb anything technical, just skied for three weeks and checked out a lot of possibilities. He said he was going to go back this winter in February to try something, but I'm not sure exactly what.'

'Hey, speak of the Devil. There's Paul now.'

'So it is. Doesn't look too stable though, does he.'

Paul Goossens was walking slowly toward the group at the tables. He was unsteady on his feet and Cutler thought he had probably hit the bottle fairly hard that afternoon. He stopped beside Cutler's table and said 'Guess I might as well introduce you, huh?'

Cutler stood up and followed the younger man.

'This is Andy.' Everyone was looking up at them. Goossens was obviously drunk. 'This is Eric, Bernie, John, Doug, other John, Al and Peter.' His arm waved vaguely around the circle as he gave the names. Then he pointed to a skinny youth of about twenty-one on the far side of the table. 'And I don't know who that is.' He fell into an empty chair and said to no one in particular, 'Andy wants to talk to us.'

'Hello?'

'Hello Lieutenant, it's Andy Cutler calling from Vancouver.'

'Ah, Mister Cutler. Nice to hear from you.'

'Yeah, well, I'm sorry to bother you at this time of night but I've got something that you're probably going to want to move on right away.'

'And what might that be?'

'You got a pen and paper handy?'

'Yes.'

'Okay. You remember the name Alex Townsend?'

There was silence for a few seconds, then Holley said, 'He was the friend of Wilson's who had been climbing with him before he was killed.'

'That's right. You want him real bad.'

'Why is that?'

'Because he either killed Wilson, or he's about to be killed himself.' Cutler paused for a moment as a new thought struck him. 'Or possibly both. In any case I think he knows all about Walter Matheson.'

'That would be nice.'

'But he also seems to have been Wilson's closest friend and the two of them may have carried the cocaine across for Matheson, so he may not be cooperative.'

'Perhaps not at first.'

There was silence on the wire after that, then Holley spoke again. 'What exactly have you got?'

'I'll tell you in a minute, but first have you still got that white loop that we found in the snow by the wreck?'

'Not here in my bedroom, but yes, I've got it downtown.'

'Well you hang on to it Lieutenant, because it's the sling in which you are going to hang Matheson's ass.'

'Mister Cutler, are you sober?'

'No Lieutenant, I'm not. I just made Sergeant today, and I think I'm falling in love, so no, I'm not sober.'

'Congratulations.'

'Thanks. Actually, I've been in love before, in fact I fall in love pretty often, but I've never been promoted to Sergeant before, so I thought I might celebrate. Anyway, you'll only have to listen to me babble for a couple of minutes. I'll telex all this stuff down to you in the morning, but here's what I've got . . .'

Later that night, as he was on the edge of sleep, he suddenly remembered that Hofstadter had evaded his question.

'Val.'

'Mmmm.'

'How did Rico know about us?'

'Who?'

'Us. You and me.'

'No, who knew?'

'Rico. He invited us to a barbecue this weekend. I only met you yesterday and he knew about it this morning.'

'Who's Rico.'

'Hofstadter. Rick Hofstadter. My Sergeant.'

'Oh, him. Isn't he nice? He's so cute sometimes.'

'No. No he isn't. But even if he is, how did he know?'

'He talked to me on the phone this morning.'

'He phoned you? How did he know you were here?'

'He didn't. Actually he wanted to talk to you but you were already gone. He just recognized my voice.'

'He just recognized your voice?'

'Sure. I worked for him for a couple of months about two years ago.'

'In Drugs?'

'Sure. I mostly just hung around in bars and listened to people talk. It wasn't as exciting as it is on TV.'

'So why didn't I meet you?'

'Were you hanging around in bars a lot?'

'No. Well sometimes. Are you sure it wasn't just over three years ago?'

'No.'

'No it wasn't; or no, you're not sure?'

'No, I don't want to talk about it any more.'

'It's just that if it was three years ago I did a six month shift in Major Crimes, so that would mmmmm. Ah. Yes. I think I rrrghhhh ...'

CHAPTER TWENTY-EIGHT

Interstate-5

LINDA WAS DRIVING – had been driving all day as they cruised steadily north on I-5. Alex had bought a bottle of Christian Brothers brandy in some town they passed through before noon and now it was two thirds gone.

'Where'r we?'

'About thirty or forty miles from Eugene.'

''S'great town. Ec'logical cap'tal 'f the world.'

'What?'

'Great town. Compulsory gelding f'r cars 'n trucks, 'n everybody runs five miles 'fore breakfas'.'

'Alex, what are you talking about?'

'Eu-gene Ore. Kids grow up big 'n strong 'cause they all get four ounces 'f milk 'n a bowl of sugar-free eco-pops f'r breakfast.' He stopped talking and held the brandy bottle up so that he could look through it at the road ahead, but he didn't drink.

'Wanna see some llamas?'

'What?'

'Llamas. Beautiful animals. Turn right at Eugene 'n drive over the mountains. 'S about, a hunnerd miles.'

'Alex the only llamas round here are in that bottle.'

'Nope. Whole herd of llamas. Whole fuckin' llama ranch jus' over the mountains. At Sisters.'

'Sisters?'

'Town call Sisters. Stupid name. We c'n camp at the pass. Nice campsite there, 'n you can take llama pictures.'

By the time they reached Eugene Alex had fallen asleep. Linda looked at the map, and found that there was a town called Sisters just over a hundred miles east. Did she really want to photograph llamas? *Were* there any llamas? Then something on the map caught her attention. Lava beds. The llamas probably existed only in Alex's mind, but the McKenzie lava beds sounded interesting, and if it took them out of their way, well, what difference?

God knew she could use a day or two in limbo, and it wouldn't hurt Alex to spend a day or two drying out and getting his mind clear before they reached Seattle. She knew that eventually the police were going to want to talk to them again, and that they had better have their story straight when the man came knocking at their door.

CHAPTER TWENTY-NINE

Vancouver

WHEN THE SWITCHBOARD told him that Lieutenant Holley was calling from San Francisco P.D. Cutler thought about answering the phone with, 'I thought I told you never to call me at work', but decided Holley wouldn't be amused; so he settled for 'Hello Lieutenant.'

Holley didn't even say hello, just went straight to it. 'Mr. Cutler, I'm going to see Alex Townsend in Seattle tomorrow and I'd like you to be there.'

Cutler was glad that he hadn't tried to be funny. He said, 'What have you got?'

'Right now I've got the square root of sweet fuck all, and I'm not very pleased about it. I talked to the trooper who ran the investigation in Yosemite and do you know what he told me?' Holley's voice was rising. 'He told me there was "No way this Townsend could be involved." Not only was he on the way to San Francisco when it happened, he actually cried about his buddy's death – "Saw it with my own eyes, he was really broken up" – what a bunch of shit. If that moron was on this force I'd see that he got traffic control and rock concerts for the rest of his life.'

'You check any of this for yourself?' asked Cutler.

'Of course I did. Wilson, Townsend and some woman had supper in a restaurant in the park. The waiter is some kind of climbing groupie and he remembers them very clearly. The woman, who seems to be Townsend's girlfriend, left about 9 o'clock and Carl Adams – the short prick that I saw meeting Matheson last spring – came in a little while later.

'He talked to Wilson and Townsend for a few minutes and then he and Wilson left. Townsend left a couple of minutes later. This waiter wanted to talk to him, but Townsend said he and his girlfriend were leaving the park right away.

'They showed up at a hotel here in San Francisco about 4:30 a.m. the next morning; and that, and some tears, is why Townsend couldn't *possibly* have been involved. Jesus.' Holley's voice was filled with disgust.

'Where did the killings take place, and how long does it take to drive from this park to San Francisco?'

'The bodies were found about three and a half miles from the restaurant and the drive only takes five hours. Less if you push it a bit.'

Cutler did a bit of arithmetic and then asked 'Do you have any idea of the time of the deaths?'

'Sure. Sometime between the last time they were seen alive and the first time they were seen dead.'

'One of those, eh?'

'One of those.' Holley answered, and then said, 'And if I didn't get much there, I got even less when I went out to the park and tried to talk to some of the climbers there. Nobody knows anything.'

'Nobody *knows* anything, or nobody's *saying* anything?'

'Nobody knows.'

'You're sure of that?'

Holley's reply was angry and loud. 'Nobody lies to me. Nobody.' Then he calmed down and said, 'I mean, everybody lies, but nobody fools me about it.' He stopped again, then continued, 'I don't think anybody did know anything. Wilson and Townsend and Townsend's woman were there for a little over a month. Quite a few people knew them, but the problem is that these climbers have a pretty transient, day-to-day life there, and nobody seems to have known them very *well* . . .'

'What's the story on this girlfriend?' interrupted Cutler.

'Her name is Linda Cunningham, she's white, in her late twenties, is kind of thin, and has blondish hair. In other words, I don't know anything more about her than I do about anything else, so I'm just going to have to have a little face to face chat with Alex Townsend.'

Cutler reached for a cigarette but found his pack empty. He tucked the telephone against his shoulder and began searching his desktop and then all the drawers. He spoke as he hunted. 'You've had him picked up in Seattle?'

'Not picked up, no,' replied Holley 'I got on to Seattle this morning and I've just heard back from them now. Townsend is at his home address and the Seattle Police are willing to watch him until we get there. They'll haul him in if he tries to leave town but otherwise just watch him. I want to come on to him cold so he doesn't have any time to set up.'

Cutler's search was unproductive and he said, 'Can you hang on Lieutenant? I'll be back in a minute or so.'

'Sure. Or do you want me to call back?'

'No, this'll only take a minute.' He had seen a cigarette pack on a vacant desk nearby and he walked over and looked into it. There were three left and he took them all, lighting one on the way back to his own desk.

'So, you want me in on this?'

'If you can make it.' Holley paused, and Cutler was about to ask why when Holley spoke again. 'There are several reasons for that. One is that you people are working on this anyway and you may have some questions you'd like to ask him yourself; the second is that I'll want somebody along both as a witness and as a backup. I could probably get a Seattle uniform for that, but I'd rather have someone who knows something about this business and you're the only one who does; and third, well, the third thing is that you may be able to get something out of him that I can't.'

Cutler couldn't imagine anyone withholding something that Holley really wanted. 'I doubt that, Lieutenant.'

'No, I'm serious. I had our people do some checking on this Townsend. Before he moved to Seattle he was pulling over a hundred thousand a year as a consulting systems analyst *and* he had family connections good enough that he could pretty well have written his own ticket. Then one day he divorced his wife and gave her every cent he had, and a month later he was working in a garage in Seattle. I don't know the story behind all this, but the bottom line is that he's probably smart enough to yell for a lawyer the minute I lean on him, and with the family he's got that would likely be the last time I see him. Sure, sure, if he's involved we'll get to him eventually, but not until long after the people I really want have had time to either cover themselves or disappear.'

Cutler didn't understand. 'And you think I'd do any better than you? I've got zero authority in Seattle. He doesn't even need a lawyer to tell *me* to get stuffed; and as for backing you up, I don't have the right to carry a gun outside the city of Vancouver, let alone in another country.'

'Don't worry about that, I'll get that fixed; but that's not too important anyway, the important thing is that you are a sympathetic and reasonable sort of person and I'm not. I've got a temper you wouldn't believe and I can't afford to screw this one up. Townsend is just about the only lead I've got left and if it turns out that sympathy and understanding is the way to get him talking . . . well, I'm not very good at that.'

Cutler put his cigarette down and said, 'And you think I am?'

'Yes. And you're also a whole lot brighter than you appear, which may be an advantage here; and you're white, which may also be important. Now, will you do it?'

CHAPTER THIRTY

San Francisco

WERE THE HEADACHES getting worse? Sometimes he thought they were, and sometimes he wasn't sure; but he was sure now that he wasn't going to go to any more doctors about it. The last one had wanted to do a CAT scan. To hell with that. Nobody was going to look inside *his* head. Besides, the headaches would stop as soon as he was out of the country. That was obvious, but he couldn't tell them that.

He poured another glass of Scotch and leaned back in his chair. Damn that Wilson for dying. Damn, damn, damnation. One more big shipment would do it. Just one more, and now Wilson was dead.

Kiniski dead, Wilson dead, Carl dead. The world around him was full of dead people who would have helped him if they were alive. Except Carl. Good riddance to Carl.

But at least they couldn't get him into trouble if they were dead. That was one good thing. But it would have been better if Wilson could have made one more carry before getting himself shot. Instead of leaving him with the biggest shipment of his life all ready to go and no way to bring it in.

Shit.

He would have brought it in himself if that black bastard policeman hadn't caught on. That would have been the best way to end it, bringing in the last lot himself. Look the border guard straight in the eye and just *will* him to pass the car unchecked. It was just a matter of having the right kind of dominant personality. But not with them watching his every move.

He drank off the whisky and poured a refill.

Sometimes he thought he knew who was watching him but it was hard to be sure. There were a lot of blacks in the Bay Area and he couldn't always tell which of them was working for that arrogant bastard that had been so snotty with him. Right in his own house.

He drank some more and stared angrily around the room. It was his favourite place, this room, but he didn't like it any more. The sooner he was in Lima the better.

Why couldn't it have been that cop instead of Wilson? For that matter why couldn't Wilson's friend have been shot instead of Wilson? Wilson would have helped, but he had been shot; his friend wouldn't help and he got away. Where was the justice in that?

Still, the friend hadn't seemed too bad a fellow. Maybe if it was explained to him just how important this shipment was he would realize that he should do his share of the work.

Walter Matheson finished his drink and smiled slowly at the panelled walls of his study. That's what he would do. The friend's name was Alex something, and he lived in Seattle – he had overheard that much when they thought he was unconscious. It shouldn't be too hard to find him. His name might even be in the newspaper coverage of the murders in Yosemite. And once he knew where to find friend Alex he would just have to slip away from all the blacks who were watching him and take a quick flight to Seattle.

CHAPTER THIRTY-ONE

Seattle

THEY AWOKE SLOWLY, a little at a time, snuggling into each other's arms and in no hurry to leave the warmth of the bed. After a while Linda spoke.

'You're a nice man, Alex, but you've got shitty taste in housing.'

'It is pretty ugly isn't it?'

'It's worse than ugly. How did you manage to live here so long?'

'I don't know.' Linda rolled onto her side, facing away and Alex nestled behind her, spoon fashion. 'I guess I never noticed how bad it was.' His hand was on her breast and he could feel her nipple stiffening as he rolled it between thumb and forefinger. 'I'm glad we're moving,' he said. 'It's actually kind of exciting – the thought of going house hunting with you.'

'Exciting is it? Is that why you're poking into me?' She reached back between them to where Alex's erection was fighting for room to grow. 'I was hoping that it was just me that was exciting you.'

Alex let his hand slide down over her abdomen and onto her pubic mound, tangling his fingers in the coarse hair. She pushed against his hand and parted her legs slightly, letting first one and then two fingers slip into her vagina, and then back out to massage her gently. He nibbled at her earlobe and whispered 'The spirit is more than willing, but the flesh has to pee.'

He disentangled himself from her and from the bedding and as he left the room he heard her mutter, 'Men!'

As he stood in front of the toilet waiting to detumesce he thought of one of Gordon's favourite jokes: 'The epitome of torque is waking up with an erection so intense that when you push it down to piss, your heels lift.'

The thought of Gordon had come unbidden into his mind and he was surprized to realize that while he was still sad about his friend's death, and frightened by the memory of that night, that at least he was able to maintain control, to think of the now and the future, as well as the then. Perhaps time *would* heal his wounds.

If he was given any time.

Later, as he and Linda floated in post-coital trance she said, 'Alex, I think we should look for a new place this morning.'

'Mmm?'

'The sooner we're out of here the safer we'll be.'

'I suppose so, but I really don't think anyone's going to come looking for us. Matheson just didn't seem interested in me at all. And besides, he doesn't even know my name; how would he find me?'

'How did that Carl person find you?' Linda rolled him off and sat up, letting the covers fall to her waist. 'If he wants to find you he'll find you. Enough people know your name and know that you're from Seattle that it wouldn't take that much work for him to track you down; but if we get a new place in my name, and not in Seattle, or at least not in Seattle proper, then we'll be a lot safer.'

She looked down at him lying on his back with his eyes half shut. 'Are you listening?'

'Yes.' His eyes opened and he stared at the ceiling. The plaster was cracked and stained and needed painting. 'Yes, I'm listening. You don't have to convince me again, I'm just as interested in being safe as you are. And this place is such a dump that I'd want to move anyway.' The whole apartment was cracked and stained and in need of paint. How *could* he have lived here? 'But we don't have to go looking for a few minutes yet.' He reached up for her.

'Nope.' She threw the covers off and jumped around so that she was straddling him; half kneeling, half sitting on his stomach. 'Up and at 'em soldier. We've got a lot to do today.' A cascade of blonde hair engulfed him as she leaned down for a kiss. 'Why don't you start some coffee while I go to the bathroom and then we . . .'

Four sharp knocks resounded from the door. 'Who can that be? It's not even 9 o'clock.'

Alex lifted her off and rolled out of bed. 'I don't know. There's a guy downstairs who sometimes comes up for coffee in the morning, it's probably him.' He was pulling on sweatpants and T-shirt. 'Get dressed as fast as you can . . .' He threw yesterday's clothes from the dresser where she had left them '. . . then open the windown and get ready to jump. It's only about eight feet to the ground.' There was more knocking at the door. 'I'll look through the peephole and if it's anybody I don't know I think we should run for it.'

He walked as softly as he could across the living room and put an eye to the spyglass, then straightened up and unlocked the door and opened it to the two inches that the safety chain allowed. 'Yes?'

When he returned to the bedroom Linda was standing to one side of the open window. He said to her, 'It's alright, it's the police. They say they want to talk about Gordon's murder.'

He stripped off his sweatsuit and put on grey wool pants, a white shirt with a very faint pattern of small blue squares, grey socks and black slip-ons. As he buckled a narrow black belt Linda whispered, 'What kind of police are they?'

'What do you mean?'

'Are they wearing uniforms? Are they detectives? Are they Seattle police?'

'There's one in a Seattle uniform and two in suits. One of them is from San Francisco and the other from Vancouver. I guess they're detectives.'

'Well, we knew this was going to happen.' Linda began undressing. I'm going to put on clean clothes and go to the bathroom and then I'll join you.' She kissed him and then turned to her suitcase.

CHAPTER THIRTY-TWO

Seattle

IT STARTED OFF in a very low key. The uniformed Seattle Patrolman accepted Linda's offer of coffee and sat quietly by himself in the living room. The other two both said 'No thank you' and sat at the table in the kitchen/dining room which was really the only place in the apartment that four people could sit in face to face conversation. The big black in the three-piece suit started off by introducing the other man, 'This is Sergeant Cutler of the Vancouver Police.'

The rumpled blond man with an engaging smile nodded to Linda and offered a hand to Alex across the table, but didn't say anything. Alex thought he looked tired, as if the trip to Seattle had taken him three days rather than three hours.

Holley turned to Linda and continued, 'And I am Lieutenant Holley from the San Francisco police. As I explained to Mister Townsend, Sergeant Cutler and I are both working on the murder of Gordon Wilson in Yosemite Park last week and we'd like to ask you a few questions.'

Linda looked at Alex, then back at the policeman and said, 'Yes of course, anything we can do to help.'

'Good,' said Holley. 'Now as I understand it you people knew Wilson for about four or five years, is that correct?'

Alex answered, 'I've known him for that long, but Linda only met him this summer, just before he was ... before the murder.' He could feel his heartbeat starting to pick up and the first drops of sweat forming in his armpits, but his voice sounded steady.

Holley pulled out a leatherbound notebook and a gold pen and made a quick note, then said to Alex, 'How well did you know him?'

'Pretty well I guess. He lived in Vancouver and I didn't see him every day or anything like that, but I knew him fairly well.'

'About how often *did* you see him?'

Alex thought about that. 'It varied. I'd go climbing with him for two or three days and then maybe not see him for a month. I suppose that on average I saw him for maybe three days a month – more often in the summer but less in the winter.' He thought about it. How often *had* he seen Gordon? He'd never kept track. Looking back over the last few years it seemed that they had spent a lot of time together, but it was almost always climbing and that magnified it out of proportion.

'But this summer you spent two months with him in California?'

'Sorry?' Alex had been lost in the past and didn't catch the question.

'You said that you would spend two or three days together once in a while, but the officer who interviewed you in Yosemite Park says that you told him that you had both been there for two months. Had you ever spent a long period with him before?'

'Oh, I see. Sure. We went to Alaska a couple of times, and to the Yukon Territory in Canada once – those were all for over a month. And we went to the valley, to Yosemite that is, last year and the year before for about ten days each time.'

Holley digested this information and then said, 'These trips were what? Holidays? Business?'

'They were climbing trips. We climbed mountains together.'

'Just the two of you?'

'Sometimes we'd go by ourselves but a lot of times we'd go with a few other people.'

Nobody spoke for a while, then Holley said, 'Tell me about Wilson.'

'What about him?'

'What was he like? You probably knew him as well as anyone.'

'He was really nice. A nice guy, everybody who knew him liked him. He wasn't anything special, I mean he wasn't ever going to be Mayor of Vancouver, or a TV star or anything, he just worked and lived like everybody else; but he was . . . he was . . .'

Alex was starting to lose control. He had never realized what Gordon meant to him until after his death. He squeezed his hands into fists beneath the table and tried to carry on '. . . He was just a good person. He was pleasant, bright, good to talk to . . . you know what I mean.'

Holley looked at him coldly. 'I know what you're trying to say, and Sergeant Cutler has talked to a few people who knew him in Vancouver and they all say the same thing – that Wilson was just an ordinary guy, that everybody liked him, that he was a really fine fellow. But . . .' He tapped the table with his forefinger for emphasis and repeated, 'BUT, either they're all wrong or I'm misunderstanding something.'

He tapped the table again. 'You see, from where I stand, this Wilson doesn't look anything like ordinary. Ordinary guys have jobs that they go to every day, and Wilson seems to have spent most of his time climbing mountains, and yet he could somehow afford the mortgage on a nice little house. Ordinary guys don't look like leftover hippies. Ordinary guys don't spend four days hanging on rockfaces. Ordinary guys don't have pot farms in their basements. Ordinary guys don't have business arrangements with criminal scum like Carl Adams; and finally, ordinary guys aren't found dead alongside sadistic young trash like Robbie Hepburn.'

Holley's voice was rising and the words stung like whips. Alex could feel the sweat soaking his shirt. He didn't know what to do or say. Holley stared at him and said very quietly, 'Let's get something straight here. Gordon Wilson was no ordinary guy. He was involved with some really ugly people, doing ugly things, and he paid for it with his life. Now, tell me about him.'

Alex couldn't speak. He was wringing his hands together under the table and his heart was hammering in his chest. Hammering so hard it hurt him. He brought his arms up and rested his elbows on the table, but couldn't stay still, and had to put them down in his lap again. Holley's eyes burned into him and he felt an overwhelming desire to either run away from the house or tell everything he knew.

'I think you *are* misunderstanding something, Lieutenant.' All their heads turned in surprise when Linda spoke. 'I don't know anything about these criminals you say Gordon was dealing with. I'm sure that that's some kind of horrible mistake – they must have thought he was someone else – I just don't believe that he would be involved with people like that, he was too nice a person.'

'But all those other things, the things you were talking about, that no ordinary person would be like that; well that's just because you probably don't know anything about climbers. I didn't either until a couple of years ago, but a lot of them are like that. They work part time and they go off for weeks or months on their climbs. I've come to know some fairly well and they aren't *really* very different. It just seems that way if you aren't involved in climbing yourself. I mean, look at Alex here – he's been working full time at the same place for several years and when he wants to go on a long climbing trip he just arranges to take some time off without pay.'

She put her hand over Alex's and said, 'I went to Yosemite more as a tourist than anything else and met Alex and Gordon there. They took me climbing and introduced me to some of their climbing friends and, well it *is* a different kind of life, but they're not criminals just because they don't have a nine-to-five job like you do.'

She sounded sincere and slightly angry and Alex was thankful for her interruption. He cleared his throat and brought Holley's attention back to him. He spoke, and hoped that his voice would not give him away. 'Gordon told me that he sold some marijuana that he grew. I don't know if that makes him a criminal in Canada or not, but I just don't believe that any of the other things you're implying are true. The only thing I can think of is that maybe the man who came to the restaurant wanted to buy some marijuana from him, or sell some to him, but why would they kill him for that?'

'You'd never seen him before?'

'No, never.' That, at least, was the truth.

'And you don't know where they were going?'

'No.'

'Okay, let's just go through it one step at a time. You first met Wilson when?' Holley and the detective from Vancouver both had their notebooks on the table and their pens poised.

'About five years ago.'

'How did you meet him?'

Alex was back on comfortable ground and he answered without hesitation. 'I had been climbing for a couple of years and I heard that there was a good place to climb just north of Vancouver, so I went up there for a look and just ran into him.'

'Okay, and after that you started to go mountain climbing with him at irregular intervals. Sometimes just for a day or two and sometimes for more than a month, is that right?'

'Yes.'

'And when did you find out he was a drug dealer?'

'I didn't . . . That is I . . . He . . .'

Alex was starting to come apart again when Linda interrupted, 'Just what are you trying to do here?' Holley swung around to her and opened his mouth to reply but she cut him off, 'Are you looking for whoever killed Gordon or are you just here to badger us about not reporting something that for all we know isn't even a crime in Canada?'

Holley looked like he was going to explode, but the Canadian detective spoke first. 'We're looking for whoever killed your friend, but we've got a problem.' His tone was mild. 'You see almost all murders are committed by family or friends. But Wilson didn't seem to have any close family, or none that we could find, he didn't have any current lover or girlfriend, and everyone who knew him says he was the world's nicest guy, and that he never quarrelled with anyone.'

He looked from Alex to Linda and back again. 'So if it wasn't family or friends, what was it? Virtually all other murders are either holdups, kidnappings or rapes that get out of hand; or just random psychotic violence. That doesn't seem to be the case here either, though, and that leaves only one possibility. The few murders that don't fit either of those categories almost all involve people in highly organized crime, and on the evidence we have it's fairly clear that your friend's death falls into that category.'

He sounded sincere and almost sympathetic, with none of the primitive animal power that radiated from Holley. 'Alex, you yourself told the officer who interviewed you in the park that Wilson recognized Carl Adams, the man who came into the restaurant. You said something to the effect that Wilson told you that he had some business to talk over with Adams, and believe me, Adams is a well known part of the criminal underworld in San Francisco; and the man whose body was found with Wilson's was also a known criminal and an associate of Adams. They both dealt in drugs and so did your friend . . .'

Cutler spread his hands and shrugged, as if to say, 'what else *can* we think?'

Lieutenant Holley had calmed down enough to speak in a normal tone and he took up his interrogation once again.

'Let's just talk about what happened before the murder then.' He looked at Alex. 'You and Wilson had been in Yosemite how long?'

'Uh, about a month and a half I think, maybe two months.' Alex had calmed down too and he felt some of his self-control returning.

'You arrived there when?'

'I don't know the exact day. It was at the end of August. There was a full moon that night so you could look at a calendar and find out for sure, but it was sometime around the twenty-ninth or thirtieth.'

Both officers made a note and Holley continued. 'And between then and the night of the killings you didn't see Carl Adams at all?'

'The only time I *ever* saw him was in the restaurant. He came in and sat down, and Gord said that they should go somewhere else. I never saw him before that.'

'Wilson didn't introduce you? Didn't say where they were going? Or why?'

'No.' Alex was sweating again.

'Don't you think that's strange? If you're having dinner with a friend and someone you know comes to the table do you just walk away with no explanations at all?' Holley was relentless.

'No. I mean . . .' Alex was in trouble. 'I mean no I wouldn't do that, but I just assumed Gord was going to buy some pot from him.'

They had known that question would be asked and they had agreed that a minor dope deal was the best answer. 'I don't *know* that that's what it was, it just seemed . . . well, what else could it be?'

The two policemen looked at each other and then back at Alex. Holley spoke. 'That's what we'd like you to tell us.'

They waited. Implacable, patient, exuding inevitability. Alex was helpless. Squirming.

'Is there anything else you'd like to ask us?' Linda came to his rescue. 'We were planning to go out for breakfast this morning and . . .' She let that statement dangle and Holley looked at her with some irritation.

'Okay, let me ask *you* a couple of things. How did you meet Wilson?'

'I already told you that. I came to California on a holiday. I met Alex,' she nodded toward him, 'by chance. He was rock climbing, I was rock climbing, and we just ran into one another. We spent a lot of time together after that and I met Gordon through Alex.'

'And you never had any idea that he might have been involved in anything more serious than selling the odd bag of dope, right?' The sarcasm was heavy and obvious.

'Lieutenant, I didn't even know he did *that*, and I don't like the tone of your questions. If you can't conduct yourself any better than you have so far . . .' she was looking straight at him and she stood up from the table as she spoke, '. . . then I think you'd better leave.'

Her face had darkened and her voice was rising. Holley started to reply but she shouted him down. 'Our friend was killed and all you've done so far is sit there and accuse him of being some kind of criminal.' Her voice came back down. 'Well that's a bunch of shit. If you want to ask questions that are going to help find whoever killed him, fine; but we've already told you about three times that we don't believe he was doing anything wrong.'

She stood with her fists on her hips, glaring at him.

Holley put his hands up in surrender and said, 'Okay, okay, I'm sorry if I offended you. Just simmer down and I'll try again. Okay?'

For a moment she said nothing, just kept on staring at him, and Alex thought that she was going to lose her temper completely.

'Miss Cunningham?' It was Cutler, his voice calm and quiet. 'I know this isn't easy for you, for either of you, but we'd like to ask just a few more questions. It won't take long, and then you can go and get some breakfast.'

He looked at her enquiringly, and finally she sat down and said 'Alright, but if there's any more of that "How long did you know he was a drug dealer" bullshit then you can ask the rest of your questions to our lawyer.'

They were all silent for a time, then Cutler turned to Alex and said, 'According to the trooper who talked to you in Yosemite, you and your friend had been on a long rockclimb for a couple of days, is that right?'

'Yes. For about four days.'

'And when you finished that you met Miss Cunningham and the three of you went for supper at the restaurant. Why don't you just tell us about that evening in your own words. If we have any questions, we can ask them when you're done, alright?'

Sergeant Cutler seemed friendly and relaxed and Alex felt much more comfortable talking to him than to Lieutenant Holley. 'There's really nothing to tell you. We climbed a route on El Capitan. It took us about three and a half days and when we got down we met Linda at our campsite. Gord and I had a shower and then we all went to the Four Seasons for supper.'

'What time would that have been?' asked Cutler.

'I don't know exactly, probably around seven or so.' Alex looked to Linda, 'About seven?'

'Something like that.'

'Anyway, it was sometime around seven. We had supper, and sometime around eight-thirty or nine Linda said that she was going to go back to the tent. We had decided to go to San Francisco for a few days and she was going to get everything packed.'

Alex looked quickly at Holley to see how this lie was being received, but Holley just looked back at him expressionlessly.

'I stayed in the restaurant with Gord for another drink and to talk some more about the climb, and about twenty minutes or half an hour later – just as we were about to leave – the man you call Carl Adams came in.'

He was trying to stay calm, and he found that as long as he didn't look at Holley he felt much better. He shifted in his chair so that he was facing more toward the Sergeant from Vancouver and carried on with his lie.

'I really don't remember what he said. We'd had quite a lot to drink and I was still really high from the climb. All I remember is that he was a sort of middle size, middle age black man with a scarred up face; and that Gord said that they had some business to do.'

He looked at Holley and said, 'We were about to leave anyway, so it didn't seem very strange that Gord would go somewhere with somebody else.' He turned back to Cutler. 'They left, and I sat there for another couple of minutes. I would have left right away except that the waiter wanted to talk to me about climbing. But I was only in the restaurant for a few minutes and then I went back to the tent and Linda and I left for San Francisco.'

Silence. Broken finally by Linda who said, 'I drove. Alex slept most of the way. In fact somewhere along the way I pulled off the road, I think somewhere near Modesto, and slept for a couple of hours too, so we didn't get to San Francisco until about three or four in the morning.'

She reached out and took Alex's hand. 'We went back to Yosemite a couple of days later to pick Gordon up and come back here, but someone had killed him.'

More silence.

Finally Holley said, 'Okay, there's just one more thing we want to ask you about.'

Alex wished he didn't have to look into those hard brown eyes, but as long as Holley was speaking, he couldn't help himself. He gripped Linda's hand tightly and tried to stay calm.

'Just before you and Wilson went to Yosemite Park you climbed a mountain here in Washington called Mt. Redoubt, is that right?'

'No.' How had they known about that? 'We were planning to, but Gord decided that he wanted to do it solo.' Thank God he and Linda had had time to plan this.

He continued to lie. 'We were all set to do it, packed up and ready to go, but then Gord changed his mind. He said he had had some problems with his girlfriend – she had moved to the east – and he wanted to be alone to think about it for a few days. So I came back here and waited for him. He took three or four days to climb it and then we went to Yosemite.'

Holley's black skin had become a mottled purple as he listened to Alex's answer and when he spoke he was obviously angry. 'And of course you don't know anything about who he met up there in the mountains, do you? Or anything about smuggling cocaine, do you? And you don't know anything about your friend's murder either do you?'

He rose up out of his chair and leaned over the table, keeping both hands pressed down on it as though in an effort to keep himself from doing violence. 'Do you think I believe one word you've said here? Do you think that? Do you think I'm stupid? Do you?'

He was almost roaring. Alex was terrified and began to answer, involuntarily, unable to stop himself. But before he had said more than two words Linda rose and leaned over the table until her face was only inches away from Holley's.

'Get out of here!' Her voice was low and full of power. It stopped Holley cold, as if she had slapped him, and it seemed to wake something in Alex, for he sat upright and looked at Holley without flinching.

For a few seconds no one moved or spoke as each of the four searched for the word or action that would end the impasse in his or her favour. In the end it was Alex who spoke. He stood up and put a hand on Linda's shoulder, easing her back gently from her confrontation with Holley, and said, 'I think you'd better leave now Lieutenant.'

All the insecurity that he had felt while answering the questions was gone. He had lied to the police and he knew he had lied badly, but it was done and now he was in control again.

Holley looked from Alex to Linda and back to Alex. Without a word he picked up his pen and notebook, turned from the table and walked out.

Sergeant Cutler, who was still sitting, started to speak but changed his mind. He put his notebook and pen into the inside breast pocket of his jacket and stood up slowly, as if he were tired, and standing took most of his energy.

'I'm sorry . . .' He shrugged his shoulders and left the kitchen. He spoke briefly to the uniformed patrolman and followed Holley out the door.

'Thanks for the coffee, Miss Cunningham.' The patrolman put his empty cup on the kitchen table. 'Lieutenant Holley asked me to ask both of you to please notify him if you change your address or if you plan to leave Seattle for more than two or three days.'

They both just looked at him.

'You can tell Lieutenant Holley to shove it up his ass.' Linda's eyes were bright and her face was still flushed. She stood with her fists on her hips, glaring, until the young cop backed down and turned and left the apartment.

CHAPTER THIRTY-THREE

Seattle

FOR A TIME, over a minute, they just sat on the couch in the living room. Alex felt the used-up and thrown away emptiness that too much adrenalin leaves behind as it ebbs from blood and brain. But there was relief too. Relief that he had come safely through a difficult ordeal.

Gordon was dead and nothing that he did or said now would bring him back to life. That was true and absolute and final, and the lies he had just told were the first step toward acceptance of that finality, and toward the carrying on of his own life.

As that realization, and the thought that the interview with the police, a thing he had been dreading, was now over began to penetrate his consciousness the feelings of relief became a flood that washed through him with orgasmic intensity; and he sank back into the cushions of the old sofa limp and exhausted.

When he opened his eyes half a minute later it was as though the millenium had come and gone. The room was still the same shabby amalgam of cracked plaster and dusty furniture, and the view out the window was as dismal as it had been for the last four years, but Linda's radiant beauty illuminated the room and filled the future with golden promise.

He reached out and took her hand. 'Let's go out and get some breakfast. We can buy a paper and look through the rental listings while we eat.'

'Okay.' She stood up without releasing his hand and then pulled him to his feet. 'But if you're going to wear nice clothes like these you'll have to get rid of this.' She scraped the back of her free hand against the grain of his beard.

'Yes boss.' He kissed her and began walking toward the bathroom, but stopped halfway there when someone knocked at the door.

Directing Linda toward the bedroom with a gesture he walked quickly into the entranceway and looked through the spyglass to see the detective from Vancouver standing in the hall. He looked weary, as though he had had to carry a heavy load on his trip back up the stairs.

Alex opened the door and said, 'Did you forget something?'

'No, not really.' The detective took a small leather case from his jacket pocket and removed a business card from it, then replaced the case and took a pen from the same pocket and wrote briefly on the card before handing it to Alex.

'I want you to take this and hang on to it. It's got my home number as well as the number of my office at the Vancouver Police Department.'

In the dim light of the hallway he looked somehow both old and young at once.

'I know you were with your friend when he found the wreck and that you helped him get Matheson back to Vancouver . . .'

Alex was stunned. He slumped against the doorframe.

'. . . Somehow you've managed to convince yourself that lying to us is the right thing to do, and, for the moment at least, there's not much we can do about it . . .'

The tired eyes looked right into his soul and Alex had to fight to keep from telling everything.

'. . . but I want to give you a piece of advice. You've stumbled into something that's a hundred times more evil and dangerous than you think. It's killed your friend . . .'

The words were like knives, flaying him alive.

'. . . and eventually it's going to kill you . . .'

He felt exposed and helpless and it took all of his will to remain silent.

'. . . If you want to talk to me before that happens, you can get me at either of those numbers. I've got no authority down here and you can talk to me without compromising yourself or the lady. It won't bring your friend back but it might stop the same thing from happening to you or to someone else.'

And then he was gone and Alex had barely enough strength to close the door and stumble back to the couch.

CHAPTER THIRTY-FOUR

Seattle

HOLLEY AND CUTLER rode in silence, staring out into the cold rain as Quinn, the Patrolman, drove. The Sundance Tavern, which Quinn said was the best place he knew of for lunch, was not far away. It was on the corner of Eleventh and Pike in an area of discount stores and low income housing, and from the outside it looked as shabby as the rest of the neighbourhood. Inside there were three pool tables, a lot of very old wood, some old photographs and beer advertisements, and a sound system good enough to pump muscular rock into two rooms without making conversation difficult.

Quinn said he wasn't hungry and sat down with the sports section of the Post-Intelligencer. Cutler and Holley walked to the bar and studied the menu chalked overhead. Holley looked dark and forbidding, with thunderclouds gathered over him, and no one made any jokes when he ordered the quiche of the day and a cup of tea. Cutler decided on the barbecued beef in a bun and a bottle of Budweiser. He waited for the beer and then sat down with Holley, who looked at him stonily and said, 'So?'

Cutler took a tentative drink from his beer glass. 'Waste of time, Lieutenant. I told him that we knew he was lying, that sooner or later he was going to be killed, but he didn't buy it.'

Cutler took another sip and wished that he had ordered something other than beer. 'He halfway wanted to tell me, I know that, but something was holding him back and the only thing I can think of is that he believes he's in more danger if he talks to us than if he doesn't.'

Holley's fist hit the table.

'GOD DAMN IT!'

Heads turned, but Holley didn't care.

'If that God damned woman hadn't been there I would have wrung him dry. He would have talked to me until there weren't any more words left in him.' With visible effort he calmed himself and carried on. 'Alright Mister Cutler, let's walk through this one more time. Listen to me and tell me if you spot anything we might have missed.

'Matheson picked up a suitcase full of blow in Prince Rupert and flew south to the Canadian-American border. We know that because the RCMP followed him all the way. We can't prove it was cocaine, but I've talked to Matheson and I *know* it was. Right?'

'Right.' said Cutler.

'Okay. Then the pilot twigs to the surveillance and flies into the storm but he crashes on the south side of Mt. Redoubt and buys it in the crash. We know that because we saw the wreck and found his body, and we know that it happened during the storm because the skid marks and all the tracks had filled in, and that was the only storm between the time he flew into the cloud and the time we found him. Right?'

'Right.'

'Wilson and Townsend found the wreckage and helped Matheson, who had survived the crash, back to Vancouver. We know that Wilson was there because we found his climbing sling by the wreck and we know that . . .'

Holley stopped talking as the bartender came to the table with their food. Cutler's barbecued beef came in a huge bun dripping with sauce along with a green salad and a big side of home fries. He picked up the bun and bit into it, leaning over the plate to keep the sauce off his clothing. The meat was tender and delicious and the sauce was the best he had ever tasted. Slightly hot, with a piquancy that awoke his smoke-abused taste buds and let the flavour of the meat come through unmasked.

Holley ignored his food and continued from where he had left off.

'So we know Wilson was there because we found his sling and we know Townsend was there because he can't lie worth shit.'

'True enough,' said Cutler around a mouthful of fries, 'but I don't see any way we can knock his story apart as long as he sticks to it.'

Holley lifted a spoonful of soup but stopped halfway to his mouth. 'Unless we can show that it wouldn't be possible to climb that mountain alone.' He put the spoon back in the bowl. 'Did any of the climbers you talked to say anything about that?'

Cutler shook his head and said, 'No. Nobody said anything about that one way or another, but I'll ask around when I get back.'

Neither man spoke for a few moments. Holley tried his soup, then said, 'Assuming we don't get anywhere with that, and we probably won't, that leaves us knowing that Wilson and Townsend helped Matheson back to Vancouver but unable to prove it. We also know that they helped smuggle the shit across the line, again because Townsend is such a poor liar. Two months later Wilson is murdered by people who work with Matheson and talking about that makes Townsend *really* sweat. He's obviously lying about what happened that night, but once again there's not a single fucking thing we can do about it as long as he sticks to his story and his girlfriend backs him up.'

Cutler drained his beer and signalled the bartender for another. He was glad now that he had ordered beer after all.

'So,' Holley bored on, 'we know that he's involved in this right up to his neck, we know that he's going to get offed unless he comes to us – and no matter how much trouble we can cause for him it's got to be better than being shot, so why isn't he talking to us?' Holley's voice was full of anger. 'What does he know that makes him think he's safe? What could possibly make him believe that?'

'I've been asking myself that question for the last half hour,' said Cutler, 'and the only thing I can think of is that he's got something on these people that he thinks will keep them off his back. You know, something like "If anything happens to me, a letter will be sent to . . .". But I just don't believe he's that stupid.' He drank some of his second beer and looked around the tavern, then wiped his lips with a napkin and pushed his plate toward the end of the table. 'Other than that, I'm afraid I don't have any ideas at all.'

Holley was silent for a long time. He too looked round the tavern without really seeing anything. Finally, with difficulty, he clamped the lid down on his anger and frustration and said, 'I was hoping to be able to go back to San Francisco with everything I needed to offer Matheson the choice of co-operating with me or going to jail, but I blew it, and now I'm back at square one.'

He stood up. 'Mister Cutler there's two things I'd like to ask you to do for me . . .'

Cutler rose and said, 'Sure, anything I can do to help.'

'Thank you. The first is to talk to your climbers again and find out if it's possible that Wilson could have climbed Mt. Redoubt by himself, and the second is to run Townsend's girlfriend, Cunningham, through your computers and let me know what turns up.'

'You think she's got a record?'

'I don't know what I think about her.' Holley put some money on the table. 'Did you get the feeling that she was lying to us at all?'

Cutler thought back over the interview. 'No, I don't think so. She got fairly pissed off with you, and she was certainly doing her best to keep you off Townsend, but I didn't feel that she was actually lying about anything.'

Holley looked at him for a while. 'Think about it. She verified his story about that night; so either she's lying too and neither of us picked it up, or else Townsend was telling the truth, which he most definitely fucking wasn't.'

'I'll be damned.'

'Exactly. Nobody gets that good at lying to the Police without a fair amount of practice, so let's check her out.'

CHAPTER THIRTY-FIVE

CONTENTS OF A TELEX from Andy Cutler to William Holley

1: A solo climb of Mt. Redoubt would have been dangerous but possible for a climber of Gordon Wilson's ability and experience.

2: Linda Cunningham does not appear in any file to which I have access.

3: Good luck.

CHAPTER THIRTY-SIX

Tacoma

FOR ALEX the following days were a slow climb from Hell. The interview with the police, and especially the encore with Sergeant Cutler, had almost broken his resolve. He walked mechanically through the remainder of the day contributing nothing to Linda's search for a new house, and slept badly that night. The next day started similarly with Alex, morose and unhelpful, letting Linda drag him along on her search for a new home.

The second place they looked at was the top floor of an old three storey house in Tacoma, about twenty-five minutes south of Seattle on I-5. It was taller than any of the nearby houses, the rooms were large, the ceilings high, and there were just enough windows to provide a feeling of space and light without being cold or glassy.

Without furniture it was bare and lifeless, but even through his neurotic lethargy Alex began to feel the potential of the place; and, if he didn't pirouette through the arch between kitchen and dining area, or waltz with an imaginary lover in front of the fireplace as Linda did, he at least felt a lightening of his load and a desire to join her in turning these empty rooms into a home.

By midafternoon the next day they had moved everything they wanted from Alex's old apartment – mostly his tools and climbing equipment – and four days later the new place was decorated and furnished to their, or at least to Linda's, satisfaction.

At ten-thirty on that grey Wednesday morning they carried the last chair up the two steep flights of stairs and dropped it in the middle of the living room.

'That's it. I resign.' Alex wiped the sweat out of his eyes. 'If you want any more furniture moved you'll have to find a new man.'

Linda dragged the heavy chair into the corner below a standing lamp. 'That's okay. I don't think we need anything more until we decide what to do about all my stuff in New York.'

'You mean we're finished? You're not going to drag me to any more junk stores and pawn shops?'

'That's right.'

'No more antique stores? No more garage sales?'

'None.'

'All-right!' Alex whooped and tried to turn a cartwheel, but the room wasn't big enough and he finished up sprawled half on a large couch and half on the floor. 'Let's celebrate,' he said from this position.

'You need a bath. And anyway, where were you planning to celebrate at 10:30 a.m.?'

He stood up and said, 'The bedroom will do just fine for a start.'

'After you have a bath, big boy. I'm not . . . Alex, what are . . . ALEX! . . . Put me down you animal . . .'

But even upside down over his shoulder she still had most of his shirt buttons undone by the time they reached the bed.

All things pass. Alex Townsend and Linda Cunningham soon found the immediacy of their fear receding and the poignancy of their loss blunted. They were still afraid, and they still missed Gordon, but their lives went on. Moving to the new house helped.

They began to see some of Alex's old friends and acquaintances and two weeks after the move Alex found work.

'Trucks?'

'Not just.'

'What do you mean "Not just"?' She had been on the floor of the spare bedroom with a tape measure and pen and paper, trying to decide how to arrange her darkroom when Alex walked in with the news.

'I mean not just trucks. Cascade Timber is huge. They've got company cars and all kinds of heavy machinery. Skidders, graders, cats, spar trees; and they're always breaking down.'

'But why you? What do you know about that kind of machinery? I thought you just worked on cars?' She recorded the measurements and pocketed the tape.

'Well, yeah, mostly. I've done *some* heavy duty work, but the main thing was that I just happened to show up at the right time.'

Linda stood, then bent slowly from the waist until her palms were flat on the floor, and her hamstrings fully stretched. She looked up and said 'You just happened to show up at the right time?' She stood upright again and arched the other way, stretching quadriceps and abdominals.

'Yeah, I had coffee this morning with a couple of guys I know, mechanics that I used to work with, and one of them said that he knew that a couple of guys had just quit at Cascade; so I thought what the hell, why not give it a try? I've got enough saved that I don't really *have* to go back to work for a while yet, but this sounded like the sort of job I'd like; and I'd have had to start looking eventually, so I just went out to see what I could see; and they offered me a job.'

He had wandered into the kitchen, and now called back 'How come there's no coffee waiting for me? If I'm going to be a proper heavy duty mechanic, you'll have to learn to have coffee ready when I get home. And bring me supper in front of the football game, right?'

'Piss off.'

'Oh. Well in that case, why don't I make you a cup of coffee.'

'That's more like it. And you might as well learn to bring me brandy in the darkroom.' She came into the kitchen and clasped her arms around him from behind. 'Will you have grease under your fingernails all the time?'

He measured coffee into the filter as best he could with her hanging on to him. 'Under my fingernails, over my fingernails, up my arms to the elbow, all over my face and thoroughly matted into my hair.'

'I'm sure I'll love it.'

'Especially when you see my coarse, grease blackened, workman's hands sliding down the satiny white skin of your loins.'

'My loins is okay. You can have your coarse, animal way with my body, but if you ever get grease on any of my lenses I'll castrate you on the spot.' She let him go and hit him lightly on the shoulder. 'Capische, Townsend?'

Alex sprinkled a few grains of salt onto the coffee and then poured boiling water over it. 'Speaking of your lenses, it looks like I'm not going to start his job until next week so why don't you pack up your camera and your long underwear and come skiing with me for a few days?'

'Skiing? I've only skied about three times in my life. I don't have any skis, I don't even have any long underwear.'

She pulled him over to the window and pointed out into the drizzle. 'And besides, that doesn't look like snow to me.'

He poured coffee for both of them. 'Don't worry about any of that. It's not even noon yet. We can get you skis and boots and all the winter clothing and equipment you need this afternoon and leave tomorrow. There'll be tons of snow in the mountains and we might as well put it to some use.'

It wasn't until two hours later when Alex was actually pulling a pair of metal-edged cross-country skis off the rack that she realized he wasn't talking about any kind of skiing that she had ever heard of.

CHAPTER THIRTY-SEVEN

Coast Range Mountains

THEY ROSE EARLY and were northbound on I-5 by 6:00 a.m., across the border without incident before 8:00 a.m. and passing through Vancouver at 8:30 a.m. Light rain was falling from low cloud, and the population was on its way to work.

'Not much to see now, but if there's time on the way back we should spend a day here. It's quite a beautiful city,' said Alex.

'Looks like any other city to me.'

'If the sun's out when we get back here you'll see what I mean.'

Linda twisted on the seat so that she was facing him. 'Maybe it would look better right now if I weren't so hungry. We didn't really have much of a breakfast . . .'

'Okay, let's find a restaurant and get something to eat. I'm hungry too.'

After breakfast they drove north, first along a fjord, and then through a range of mountains of which Linda caught only the vaguest glimpses through the heavy dull cloud. The surface of the fjord was the same shiny grey as the surface of the wet road, the only colour relief coming from the slightly lighter grey of the rock by the roadside and the greenish grey of the forest.

After two hours Alex pulled into a small parking lot below the Blackcomb Mountain Ski area. The sky was still low and grey and light rain was still falling on the sodden rocks and trees around them.

'Alex?'

'Mmm?' He was in the back of the van putting food, clothing and equipment into their packs.

'Is this it?'

'This is it.'

'Alex, there's no snow. How do we ski without snow? And the lifts aren't even running. I don't think this place is open.'

He came to the front and pointed out the window. 'If it weren't clouded up like this you would see a vista of snowy peaks gleaming white in the sunshine, their every summit beckoning, and your heart would gladden with thoughts of floating down through clouds of fluffy white powder, your skis flashing in the crisp morning light as you . . .'

'Horseshit.' She punched him in the shoulder.

'Well, the diction maybe; but we really are surrounded by big mountains, and higher up they really are covered with snow on which we will be skiing for the next few days.' He grinned. 'Actually, for the first day or so I'll be skiing and you'll be falling over a lot, but you'll get it under control before long.'

He passed her an armful of clothing. 'But we've got a bit of a walk in the rain first, so let's get dressed and get going.'

With skis strapped to their packs they hiked steadily upwards for almost two hours, first on an abandoned mining road and then on a well maintained trail in a misty pine hemlock forest. As they walked Alex described their route and destination. 'We're travelling up the south side of Fitzsimmons Creek valley. There are two big commercial ski areas, with all the hotels, restaurants, bars and nightclubs anyone could ever want, on Whistler Mountain and Blackcomb Mountain at the mouth of the valley.

'There are ridges of mountains running east from both Whistler and Blackcomb, and this valley lies between them. We go up to the end of the valley, cross a pass to the north called Singing Pass, and drop down just a short way on the other side to a hut beside a little lake called Russet Lake. The mountains above the hut are the eastern end of the chain that starts with Blackcomb. They're high enough to keep snow all year round and I'm not going to tell you how beautiful they are because you'd just think I was exaggerating.'

They climbed gradually and soon patches of snow began to appear. By the time they left the mining road for the trail the drizzle had turned to snow and snow completely covered the ground. Not enough to ski on, but a sign of what was to come. Half an hour later Alex stopped and said 'The snow's getting deep enough that it'll be just as easy to ski as walk, so let's have a bit of lunch and then start doing what we came to do.'

Skiing uphill on gentle trails is easy and Linda managed the next two and a half hours without much difficulty. The snow deepened and the forest thinned out as they gained altitude and the trail became less and less distinct until Linda could no longer see it at all. In the cloudy, snowy weather all directions were the same, each cluster of small trees indistinguishable from the next.

'You realize Alex, that if anything happens to you, I'll never find my way back.'

'As far as we're going to get today you could just turn around and follow our tracks, and tonight I'll show you how to use a map and compass, so don't worry about that.'

The snow was soft and fresh and for Alex, in front, breaking trail became increasingly laborious. Finally he stopped and dropped his pack in a clearing in the centre of a clump of stunted trees.

'Let's stop here. It'll take a while to set up camp but there should be enough light to get in an hour or so of skiing on the slopes above us.'

For Linda it was like learning life's basic skills all over again. Winter changed everything. Setting up a tent, cooking, eating and drinking, even something as ordinary as sitting down to rest – all seemed infinitely more complicated and difficult in the bottomless, soft snow. But the new clothing Alex had chosen for her kept her warm and dry and she soon began to enjoy herself.

And the skiing. On the trail up it had seemed easy, not very different from walking, but downhill . . .

At first it was impossible. She could not turn the long narrow skis, and could not go further than a few yards without falling over. But the falls were painless in the deep soft snow and gradually some of the things Alex showed her began to make sense. By the end of an hour she was tired and sore, but she could do a reasonable facsimile of a telemark turn as long as the slope was gentle, and she was looking forward to the days to come.

After supper they crawled into zipped-together sleeping bags and Linda surprized herself by sleeping through eleven hours in complete warmth and comfort.

It wasn't actually snowing when they woke at seven, but it had snowed heavily overnight and the trees around their tent wore huge white mantles which collapsed at the slightest touch.

They spent most of the morning skiing the perfect powdery snow on the gentle slopes above the camp. Linda learned quickly and by the time they stopped for lunch she was even able to put together an occasional set of two or three linked turns.

Lunch was cheese, sausage, crackers and lots of soup. They ate sitting on their packs in front of the tent and Linda stared up at the slope they had been skiing and the cloud that hid its top.

'Alex, why is nobody else here?'

'What do you mean?'

'This is absolutely incredible. Even with all the cloud it's beautiful, and the skiing is fantastic. I don't understand why there aren't hordes of people here.'

Alex munched a salami covered cracker and thought about it. 'I don't know. There's a hut just a couple of hours further on and later in the winter it gets crowded on weekends, and there's sometimes a few people there during the week, but as long as you stay clear of the hut you'll hardly ever see anyone. And at this time of year, November, even the hut is empty most of the time.' He ate another cracker. 'I guess the weather is just so dismal in Vancouver and Seattle that nobody's willing to get out in it. Nobody believes that there's good skiing until sometime in mid-December.'

He laughed, then said, 'And this is one of the most popular arcas. If you go to any one of a thousand other places you won't see another person, even during the Christmas holiday.'

'But it's so beautiful . . .'

They took the tent down after lunch and loaded their packs for the ski to the hut. The crest of the pass, where they stopped two hours later to remove the climbing skins from their skis, was above tree line, but with the heavy snowfall of the night before it appeared soft and round, rather than rocky and harsh. The cloud cover was beginning to thin but was still low enough to hide all but the bases of the mountains around them. Down below, about a third of a mile ahead, the hut was a strange orange and blue shape against the snow.

The slope down was gentle but Alex warned Linda that 'skiing downhill with a pack on is not the same thing as skiing without a pack. You're going to fall over about fifty times in the next fifteen minutes. Try to keep your sense of humour.'

The hut, when they reached it, turned out to be a steeply curved A-frame about twenty feet long and twelve feet from floor to roof peak. Inside were wooden sleeping platforms on two levels and two long tables against opposite walls with two benches between them.

Linda found it charmless and felt colder inside than out.

'Alex?'

'Yes.'

'Were you planning to stay here?'

'That's up to you. I don't particularly like these huts myself, but I thought you might prefer it to the tent.'

'Prefer it to the tent?' She looked around at the bare walls, the dirty tables and floor. 'The tent is warm and cheerful. This place is like . . .' She searched for words '. . . is like some proto-gothic outhouse.' She stepped back outside and spoke through the doorway. 'And just when it's starting to clear up, I'm not going to close myself off inside there.'

Alex joined her outside and looked at the sky. It *was* starting to clear. The ceiling had lifted noticeably since they left the summit of the pass and the cloud layer seemed to be thinning to the south west. He couldn't actually see blue sky, but he could sense hints of blue through the grey veil.

He looked at his watch.

'How do you feel?'

'Fine. Why?'

'No, I mean physically. Are you tired or do you still have some energy left?'

She looked at him questioningly. 'I feel pretty good. I'll probably sleep like a baby tonight, but I've got lots of strength left for the rest of the day. What are you planning?'

'A little surprize. Bring your pack inside.' He picked up his own pack from where he had dropped it by the door and carried it into the hut.

Inside, she found him emptying his pack onto the main sleeping platform. When she put her pack on the floor beside him, he picked it up and began emptying that as well.

'So?' she asked.

'So this may be hard to believe, but we are in the middle of a spectacular mountain range.' He began sorting the contents of the packs into two piles. 'Right above this hut is a mountain called Mt. Whirlwind. You and I are going to climb it and bivouac on the summit tonight. Tomorrow morning, if the weather has cleared, you'll have the view of your life. You'll begin to understand why Gord was always talking about getting into the mountains to do some real climbing, and you'll want to shoot every roll of film that you have.'

He finished his sorting and began to put the contents of one of the piles back into their packs. 'I'm going to leave behind everything that isn't absolutely necessary so that our packs are as light as possible. I'll just leave the extra stuff here until we . . .'

'You *do* realize . . .' she interrupted him '. . . that I've never climbed a mountain before?'

'No problem. A summit bivvy in the winter is the perfect way to start.' He cinched the lid of her pack and handed it to her. 'This won't be a technical climb. It looks impressive as hell but in fact we can ski right to the summit, so don't worry about anything.'

Outside the hut, as they were sticking skins back on to their skis, Alex pointed to the east and said, 'The mountain that's just starting to loom out of the cloud right above us is Mt. Fissile. It's the ugliest pile of dirt and loose rock you ever saw, but it looks pretty good in winter.'

To Linda it looked huge and forbidding, a monstrous white pyramid whose base dominated the scene round them and whose apex was lost in the cloud.

'We're going to climb that?' She was incredulous.

'No, it's hardly worth climbing. We're going to climb Mt. Whirlwind which is just visible to the right.' He pointed, and Linda could distinguish, barely, a ghostly shape in the clouds behind Fissile.

Twenty minutes later they were well on their way, traversing the broad base of Mt. Fissile as the dissipating clouds alternately veiled and unveiled their goal. Where Fissile was broadbased and squat, Mt. Whirlwind appeared tall and slender; a perfectly proportioned and beautiful lady beside a grotesque, misshapen hulk.

Slowly they gained altitude, zigzagging up the lady's skirts and then on to her shoulder where they stopped to look up at her crown, now crystalline, sparkling white against a cobalt blue sky.

Finally, two and a half hours after leaving the hut, they reached the summit. Around them, in the clear light of the late afternoon sun, was a new world; a trichrome world of blue, white and grey. Intense blue for the now cloudless sky: shining, radiant white for the snow covered mountains that jutted and strutted in proud disarray from horizon to horizon; and here and there a streak or patch of brownish grey for the walls and rockfaces too steep for the snow to cling.

Linda could not speak. She stepped her skis slowly around through a full circle on the small flat space that was the summit of Mt. Whirlwind.

Below her, somewhere, roads ran through forested valleys, became highways that were the arteries of a civilization filling towns and cities; but the roads, and the cities, and the sweating scheming millions that filled them were invisible, the fact of their existence tenuous and insubstantial in this much vaster world of rock and snow and sky.

'Alex.'

'Yes.'

'We could be the only people in the universe.'

He stood beside her, put his arm around her waist and said, 'When we're up here like this, we *are* the only people in the universe.'

Alex cooked a thick bouillabaisse of canned fish and rice in the one pot he had brought up with him, and as they ate they watched the sun go down and the mountains around them change from white through orangey-pink to magenta, and finally darken to silhouettes against a clear, star-filled sky.

The temperature fell rapidly, but covered in layers of pile and goretex Linda was snug and warm. She was awed by the scale of the alpine world around her, and by the number and intensity of the stars; and later, as she lay in the double cocoon of her sleeping bag and bivouac sac, with the glory of the universe blazing in the sky above her and the warmth of Alex's body along her left side where their bivvy sacs nestled together, she felt, for the first time in her life, complete and at absolute peace.

They breakfasted on tea and a mixture of nuts, raisins and chocolate that Alex called gorp, and then made the two thousand foot run down to the hut in perfect powder. Linda fell what seemed like hundreds of times, but the snow was soft and forgiving and the day was beautiful and she did not mind. She marvelled at the grace with which Alex carved turn after turn, seemingly without effort, and laughed with pleasure the few times that he ploughed the snow with his face.

It was still early when they reached the hut, and Alex began preparing a second breakfast for them.

'Today is Saturday,' he said as he ate his porridge, 'and with weather like this there will be people coming up here for sure, and I'd just rather not see anybody else. How do you feel about that?'

'I think I'd like another day of being the only people in the universe.'

'Okay, let's go back to where we camped the first night and then up the other side of that valley a bit. We can camp in the trees and no one will see us and we won't see them.' He put down his empty bowl. 'We can head back out on Sunday morning and be back in Seattle by mid afternoon.'

'And you can start your new job Monday morning and come home with greasy hands Monday night.' She put her empty bowl beside his. 'Maybe I should just stay up here and you can visit me on weekends.'

That night they used the tent again, and made long, slow love in their zipped together bags. Afterwards as they lay, still entwined, Linda said 'You know Alex, you really don't have to go back to work if you don't want to. We must have almost a hundred thousand dollars between us . . .' She rolled over so that she could look at him in the light of the little candle lantern that hung from the dome of the tent. 'I've got well over thirty, and you said you had about ten thousand that you had saved, plus the fifty that you and Gordon made. It won't last forever, but you certainly don't have to take a job right away.'

At first Alex said nothing, didn't move or give any sign that he had heard. When he finally spoke he kept his eyes shut.

'I don't know what to do about the money. Maybe I should just give it all to the Salvation Army.'

He lay silent again and Linda didn't disturb him. Eventually he spoke again. 'All the money that Gord and I got paid was in the package you sent to your friend in New York. Neither of us had actually used any of it before Gord was killed, and now I'm not sure that I should spend it.'

He snuggled closer against her.

'But I think that the reason I feel that way is because Gord was killed, not because of what we did to earn it.'

He opened his eyes and turned his head so that he could see her. 'Do you understand what I'm saying?'

'I think so. If nothing had happened, if you and Gordon had had fun in the valley and then come home for the winter that you would have spent it and enjoyed it; but now after what happened to Gordon, you can't bring yourself to touch it.'

'That's right.' He closed his eyes and let his head roll back. 'But that's really a hypocritical attitude isn't it?'

'Yes.'

'But you know,' he opened his eyes again 'even if I decided to keep it and spend it, I'd still go back to work.'

He raised himself up on one elbow and looked down at her. 'Do you think that's silly?'

'No, it's probably something you can't help. I know that even if I had more money that I could ever spend I'd still be trying to sell pictures one way or another.'

'That's how I feel. I like working on engines and the money doesn't really matter that much.' He paused. 'There's only two things I really like, climbing and engines.'

He tangled his fingers in her hair and kissed her gently. 'Or, there *were* only two things. Now there's three.'

She ran a fingertip down his chest and trailed it over his thigh. 'There's no engines or rockfaces here, but we can practice number three again if you like.'

She lay on her back with one leg bent and he entered her lying on his side with his top leg across her bottom one. They didn't move much, just lay like that, rocking a little from time to time until sleep claimed them.

CHAPTER THIRTY-EIGHT

Tacoma

'DO YOU KNOW anything about cocaine?'

They were on their way south, about halfway to Vancouver. Alex was driving and Linda was nodding, half asleep, on the seat beside him. 'What?'

'I asked if you knew anything about cocaine.' He looked across the seat at her and then quickly back to the twisting road.

'Your conscience eating at you?'

'Yeah, kind of.'

She sat up straighter and stared out the window. The good weather had ended sometime during the previous night and on the highway it was as grey and wet as it had been on the way up.

'For a while, about a year after Michael and I set up our studio and the work was starting to come in, we did a lot of it. He hung out with a bunch of rich gays and there was never any problem getting it, and then we started to make good money and I could afford a fair bit myself.'

She turned so that she was sitting sideways on the seat, leaning against his right shoulder with her knees drawn up in front of her.

'I did enough of it to realize that if I did any more I'd be locked into it, so I quit entirely. I'm not strong enough to mess with anything that good.'

'That's strange. Gord said just the opposite. He said he'd done enough to know he'd never get hooked. He said it was okay, that he liked to treat himself to a toot now and then, but that it wasn't addictive like booze or heroin.'

'And you?' She asked 'You never tried it yourself?'

'Once. I didn't get anything out of it, though.'

'Nothing?'

'Not really. It made my nose itch, and I sneezed a lot, but that's all.'

'You probably had something that was about one percent cocaine and ninety-nine percent god knows what. Same with Gordon. Vancouver's hardly the cocaine capital of the world and what Gordon was buying was probably cut pretty much to nothing. You could snort that kind of stuff forever and all you'd get is poor.'

She wriggled against him, trying for a more comfortable position.

'In New York we could get anything from street sweepings to nearly pure cocaine, and anyone who's freebased really good coke knows how fast the hook can go in. There may not be a physiological dependence the way there is with pills or booze or junk, but that doesn't mean you don't need it. But Alex . . .' She turned so that she could see him and her voice was serious '. . . giving the money to the Sally Ann or throwing it away isn't going to bring Gordon back to life and it isn't going to take that cocaine out of circulation. If you don't want to keep it, that's fine with me, I've got lots of money right now and you said you had over ten thousand yourself, not to mention a pretty good job coming up, so we can live without the money; just remember that everything that happened will still have happened after you give the money away.'

She fell silent and several miles of wet highway unwound beneath the van before she spoke again.

'Just do one thing for me though.'

'What?' he asked.

'Wait for a month or so. Let's leave the money wherever Michael's hidden it for a few weeks, and then if you still feel like giving it away, fine, you can give it away.'

She turned away from him again, and rested her back against his right side. 'Christmas is only a few weeks away. Let's think about that, and get you settled in your new job, and then sometime in January you can decide what to do with the money, okay?'

'Okay.'

CHAPTER THIRTY-NINE

Vancouver

ANDY CUTLER had never hosted a real Christmas party before, and he was smart enough not to try anything fancy himself. He simply laid in half a dozen bottles of rye whiskey, two bottles each of white rum, gin and vodka, gallons of mix, a few cases of beer, and hired a caterer to do several hundred dollars worth of turkey and hot and cold snacks.

Only about twenty people had been invited but word of his promotion had spread and considerably more than twenty showed up to offer congratulations and press the flesh. Nobody got sick or obnoxious and there were enough civilians to keep it from degenerating into a police bull session.

By 2:00 a.m. only the Hofstadters and Valerie MacGregor were left. All the windows were open and the polluted air of the apartment was gradually being exchanged for fresh. The caterer had removed all of her equipment and taken away a glad bag full of disposable plates, glasses and cutlery. Cutler and his three remaining guests put the empty bottles out of sight in the kitchen and then sat in the living room with their shoes off to share a final Christmas drink.

Angela Hofstadter was taller than her husband and as fair as he was dark. Her feet were up on the coffee table and from where Cutler sat, directly opposite, her legs seemed to go on forever. She looked at him over nylon shrouded toes and said 'Are you pretty happy to be out of Drugs?'

He thought about it for a while and finally answered, 'Yes and no. Mostly yes I think. I'm going to miss working with your old man, and with a couple of the other guys, but I sure won't miss the kind of people we had to deal with. I'll definitely be dealing with a better class of scum in Major Crimes than I dealt with in Drugs.'

He finished his drink and chewed the ice cube, then went on. 'Her job . . .' he nodded toward Valerie, returning from the kitchen with a tray of coffee, '. . . is a lot better in that respect than mine was. At least the cop on patrol meets a cross section of society. It's maybe not the same cross section that most people meet – it's definitely weighted toward the asshole end of the population curve – but it's not too bad. But a detective, and especially a detective in Drugs, spends most of his time with people who . . . Well, you've been married to a cop long enough that I don't have to tell you stories about that.'

They all took coffee and after her first sip Angela said, 'But surely you must meet *some* nice people. Even the drug world can't be totally populated with anii can it?'

'Anii?' asked Cutler.

'Plural of anus.'

'Oh. I see.' Cutler drank some coffee and thought about his reply. 'On the whole I'd have to disagree. I think the world would be a better place if ninety-nine percent of the people I've had to deal with over the past few years had never been born.'

'I've never heard you talk that way.'

'I hardly ever do talk this way, Angie, but I've been thinking back over the four years I spent in Drugs and the only people I've met that I'd spend time with by choice have either been victims of, or witnesses to, drug related crimes.' He took some more coffee and continued. 'And even most of those have been pretty sleazy; so yes, I guess I am pretty happy about leaving Drugs.'

Valerie MacGregor, sitting sideways in a big armchair with her legs over one of the arms, said, 'Oh come on Andy, it can't have been that bad. Somewhere amongst all those jerks there must be a few nice ones. Surely you don't believe that everyone who uses drugs is an asshole?'

'That's true, lots of decent people use all kinds of drugs, but they aren't the people we were dealing with. We got the dealers, the fixers, the organization guys, and the hard guys, guys who would break your arm if they thought you were standing between them and a ten dollar bill.' He paused for a moment and then said, 'Although, to be fair, I did meet one guy who wasn't too bad.'

He turned back to Angela Hofstadter. 'I don't know if Rick ever mentioned this to you or not, but over the last few months I've been peripherally involved in a case where a couple of guys, basically really nice people, helped smuggle a bunch of cocaine from Peru into the San Francisco area. I think they got involved more or less by chance and I don't even know if they got paid, maybe they just did it for the excitement. But the one I've talked to was as pleasant a guy as you could hope to meet. Good looking, lives with a nice woman, educated, good family background, the whole thing; just like the movies.'

'So there you are,' said Angela. 'It really isn't as bad as you made it sound. You *do* meet some nice people.'

'Yeah. Except that the other guy, the one who helped him with the smuggling, has already been murdered, and this guy is going to be killed soon himself. He thinks he won't be, but he's wrong.'

Angela looked at him in surprise. 'That's horrible. Can't you do something to warn him?'

'I did warn him, but he thinks he's bulletproof. And anyway, now that I'm finished in Drugs it's not my case anymore.' Cutler finished his coffee and stood up. He walked to the open window and looked at the lights of the city spread out below him and said over his shoulder, 'It never really was my case, Angie, and the last I heard it was soon going to be nobody's case at all. As long as the people involved, the two that are still alive that is, keep their mouths shut there's nothing anyone can do except stand out of the way and let them die.'

Angela Hofstadter shuddered. 'Ugh. This is too depressing for a Christmas party. Who started this talk anyway?'

CHAPTER FORTY

Tacoma

'MERRY CHRISTMAS TOWNSEND.'

'Nnn?' Alex woke slowly to a vision of beauty. Weak winter sunlight filled the bedroom and as his eyes cleared he saw Linda standing by the bed. She was wearing a lounge robe he had not seen before, a high collared robe of raw apricot silk. Delicate apricot, the colour of sunrise over a misty lake.

He sat up. 'Merry Christmas to you too.' He rubbed his eyes and then stretched, twisting first one way and then the other with his hands clasped behind his head.

She had been carrying a tray and now she bent and placed it on the night table. On it was a Christmas package, medium large and soft looking. She leaned over and kissed him. 'Open this package now and then go and shave. I'll go to the kitchen and start a proper Christmas breakfast, but you don't get any until you've shaved and washed.' She slapped his wandering hand from the fold of her robe, 'Or any of that either.'

In the package was a pair of leather slippers, pyjama style shirt and pants in rich burgundy silk, and a dressing gown, also silk, but of a green so deep as to be almost black.

Her 'proper Christmas breakfast' was fresh grapefruits, freshly ground coffee and a lot of Remy Martin. It was the start of the best Christmas he had ever had.

They spent the day drinking brandy and making love. And once in a while opening presents in front of the fire, which they both felt was better than a tree. The presents were small things mostly – books, records, a bit of climbing gear, odds and ends for the kitchen and house, and some clothing.

At the end of the day, after a supper of cold meats and homemade buns and a selection of pickles and chutneys, they went to bed early and recaptured, for the half hour that they stayed awake, the feeling of being the only two people in the universe.

CHAPTER FORTY-ONE

Tacoma

HE CRUISED past the house in the early afternoon but there were two black women standing on the sidewalk about half a block away and he decided against stopping. Were they police spies? He didn't know, but he knew that if a private individual with a few hundred dollars to spend could trace Townsend to his new home, then so could the police.

Why take chances?

He drove on several blocks and then parked and tried to decide what to do. He didn't want to spend more than the weekend away from San Francisco, and he obviously couldn't park in front of Townsend's place in broad daylight.

What to do? Rent a hotel room? Not in a grotty town like this. And besides, with the number of blacks that worked in hotels word would spread on their grapevine in no time. He had taken a big enough chance with the flight up here and the car rental; no sense in taking any more chances.

Same for the telephone. Talking on the telephone would be crazy.

He couldn't think. There was danger everywhere and the pounding in his head was like a sledgehammer. He took two Tylenols from the bottle in his pocket and washed them down with a long pull from the fifth of scotch on the seat beside him. The whiskey burned its way down into his stomach and almost immediately he felt better. Everything snapped into focus and he felt clearheaded and decisive.

He looked at his watch. 2:30 p.m. No problem. He would go back to Seattle and catch a movie somewhere, or maybe find a woman. Then have a quiet supper and come back to Tacoma in the evening. He'd park a few blocks away and in the dark he'd be able to walk up to Townsend's house just like somebody from the neighbourhood.

He took another hit on the scotchman and pulled back out onto the road.

CHAPTER FORTY-TWO

Tacoma

'LOOK, I really don't care if you impress them or not.' Alex was exasperated. 'It would be great if you liked them and they liked you, but it really doesn't matter that much. I don't even know how much *I* like them; if they weren't my parents I probably wouldn't cross the street to see them.'

'That's easy for you to say, but they *are* your parents, and what do I know about rich lawyers?'

They were in their bedroom, packing clothes into a small suitcase. Linda continued, 'What if I do something really dumb?'

'You mean like fart at the dinner table? Or say shit in front of my mother? Come on Linda, they're human too. And anyway it's only for tomorrow and Monday, it's not as if we were going to be moving in with them.'

He closed the suitcase and said, 'There. We can throw our toothbrushes in when we're finished with them tomorrow morning and we'll be ready to go.'

'Have you got the tickets?'

'I put them in the front pocket of your camera bag along with a couple of magazines to take on the plane with us.'

'Some money?'

'Yes, I went to the bank this morning and . . .'

The doorbell rang and Linda said, 'I'll get it. It's probably Mr. Olsen coming up from downstairs. I told him that I wanted to put a darkroom in the spare room and he said he'd have to see exactly what I was going to do before he'd okay it. He said he might come up and check tonight.'

But it was not Olsen who walked into the living room with her, it was Walter Matheson, and Alex felt the world that he had built in the last two months begin to slide out from underneath him. He looked desperately round the room for some weapon, for an escape, but there was nothing; only Linda, still behind Matheson, offered any chance. He cleared his throat loudly and spoke, hoping that his voice would not crack.

'Mister Matheson.' Pause. Surely Linda would realize. 'I didn't expect to see you again.'

Walter Matheson was dressed in a brown suit and wore a three quarter length cashmere overcoat over that. The coat glistened with water droplets and Alex briefly wondered when the rain had started.

'Yes. But things have changed and I decided I'd better look you up.'

He took off his coat and handed it to Linda as though to a servant and turned back to Alex. 'I've got a business proposition to discuss with you, but I think we should do it in private . . .' he hooked a surreptitious thumb at Linda, who had not moved, '. . . don't you?'

What was going on? How had he found them? Alex could smell the alcohol on the man's breath from where he stood eight feet away, but he wasn't acting drunk or aggressive and with sudden relief Alex realized that he was not about to be killed.

He looked to Linda, still holding the wet coat. 'Mister Matheson and I have some business to discuss. Would you mind leaving for a while? Maybe go to your studio or something?'

He walked to her and took the coat from her hand and guided her toward the front door. He hung the coat in the closet and removed a coat and sweater for Linda. As he helped her on with the sweater he whispered, 'That's Walter Matheson, the guy we carried the cocaine for. He probably wants to get me to carry some more. I don't think he's got a gun or anything, and I'll just try to convince him that I'm out of it for good. Okay?'

She let him help her with the coat and whispered back fiercely. 'I'm not going anywhere. Just because you didn't see a gun doesn't mean he doesn't have one, do you understand?' Her voice was harsh, commanding.

'Yes, I understand, but I really think he just wants to talk.'

'Maybe so, but I'm going to be right outside this door. If he does anything you don't like, you just yell and I'll come through the doorway with as much noise as I can, and maybe we can jump him. Okay?'

'Alright.'

He closed the door behind her and returned to the living room where Walter Matheson was standing, looking around at the furniture and the prints that Linda had framed and hung on the walls. Alex expected him to say something like 'Nice place you've got here' or, 'Nice to see you again' but instead Matheson just planted both hands deeply into his pant pockets as if to keep them under control, and said:

'Have you got any whiskey?'

Alex looked at the man closely, then said, 'Just a minute.'

He went to a glass fronted cabinet that Linda had found in a second-hand shop and removed two shot glasses and a bottle of Seagram's V.O. rye. He poured the two drinks on a side table by the cabinet and carried them to the low coffee table in front of the fireplace and said, 'Why don't you sit down?'

But Matheson didn't sit down immediately. He brought a bottle of Extra Strength Tylenol from his pocket and shook two tablets from it, chewed them hard and then picked up the whiskey and chased them down, killing the drink in one long swallow.

He didn't look good. When Alex had last seen him in the bar in San Francisco he had been surprised at how well he had recovered from the crash, but now, two months later, he looked far worse. His face had lost its firmness and was beginning to sag. There were dark bags under his eyes and the spring had gone from his spine. Two months ago he had looked healthy, successful, and in control. Now he looked thin and pale and nervous. Alex wondered what had happened.

'Is it safe to talk here?'

What did that mean? 'Do you mean is the house bugged?'

'Exactly. Do the police know you're here? Have they talked to you?'

'No.' Lie. 'I moved here after I saw you in San Francisco and the police don't know where I am.'

'Good, good.' Matheson walked to the sideboard and poured himself another drink, then returned to the coffee table bringing the bottle with him. He sat down in one of the chairs flanking the fireplace. Alex sat across from him and took a small sip from his glass.

'How did you find me?' He was feeling much more confident. Matheson had obviously been drinking earlier, and with a couple of stiff ones here he was not going to be able to do anything fast enough to take Alex by surprize.

'Easy. Same way the police will find you if they bother looking. Your name and your girlfriend's name were in the paper with that business in Yosemite. You didn't change your names or leave the Seattle area so it wasn't hard to find you. And there's something else . . .' his voice dropped and he leaned forward, '. . . I noticed a lot of blacks around this area.'

'It's a mostly black district. Our landlord is black.' Was Matheson all there?

'That's not good. There's a cop in San Francisco who wants to get me. He's black, and you know about blacks.'

He *isn't* all there, Alex thought. 'What about them?'

'Just think about it. That cop can put his ear to the ground and pick up all kinds of things. Bellhops, cab drivers, musicians, they're everywhere. You don't notice them, but they see everything we do, and they can pass information about us back and forth across the country as fast as we could by using a telephone.'

Matheson was cruising in the Asteroid belt and Alex was not sure what to say. He settled for, 'Okay, I'll be real careful.'

He tasted his drink again and the taste of the rye brought with it thoughts of Gordon. He put the glass down and asked, 'Just what was it you wanted to see me about.'

'Things have changed in the last little while and I need you to bring in another load for me. I know you said you weren't interested but when you hear what I have to say that's going to change.'

Off the subject of blacks and police Matheson seemed rational. The drink had steadied him and he appeared to be gaining some control over his mind.

'I know you're probably worried that what happened to your friend could happen to you, but you can forget about that. Carl Adams is dead, so you can stop worrying about him.'

Walter Matheson stopped talking and looked at his second drink as if noticing it for the first time. He picked it up, sniffed at it and then threw it back just as he had the first one.

'That's nice whiskey.' He poured himself a third glass, about half the size of the first two, and said 'You also don't have to worry about anyone else doing the same thing, because this time there isn't going to be anyone else.'

Alex just wanted out. Wanted to tell Matheson to find somebody else, or bring in his own cocaine, but he was afraid to say anything. If Matheson was as crazy as he seemed then best to tell him whatever he wanted to hear, whatever would make him leave happy; and then figure out what to do about it after he'd gone.

'This time I'm going to handle it myself. You can bring it in from Canada through the mountains just like you did last time and I'll take delivery personally. No one but you and me will know about it, and you can walk away in complete safety. How does that suit you?'

'I don't know. I'm not sure that this is a good time. Going through the mountains at this time of year wouldn't be very easy.' But even as he said the words Alex realized that it *would* be easy. As easy as doing it in the summer, and a lot safer.

'I understand what you're saying, but don't worry, this is going to be worth your while.' He reached into his breast pocket and brought out a very fat envelope. 'Here's your down payment.' He handed it across the table. 'Count that.'

The envelope was about two inches thick, and inside were hundred dollar bills in three separate packets, each held together with elastic bands. Two of the packets were of similar size and the other was smaller. Alex picked one of the large bundles and began counting. Matheson sat and watched, saying nothing until he finished.

'Ten thousand, right?' He pointed to the other two packets. 'And another ten thousand there and five thousand in that one.' He drank his third drink. 'That's twenty-five thousand. And you get another seventy-five when you deliver. One-hundred-thousand-dollars.' Matheson enunciated each word carefully. 'That should go a long way toward making it seem easier. *And* . . .' he tapped the table for emphasis, '. . . And, you'll be absolutely safe. You see, this is going to be my last operation and I'm going for the fence on this one. It's going to be big, and I'm going to handle it all myself and then get out of the country. I'm the only one who'll see you, and I'm the only one who'll know you're coming.'

He stopped speaking suddenly and looked at Alex as though waiting for an answer, but all Alex could think of to say was 'I see.'

That seemed to be satisfactory, for Matheson went on, 'Good. I'm glad you agree. Now, here's what will happen . . .'

Alex wondered what Matheson would have done if he'd said 'I don't see' or 'That's crazy' or 'Peter Piper picked a peck of pickled peppers'. Probably nothing. He seemed to be conducting both sides of the conversation himself.

Alex tuned back in '. . . on the west coast of Vancouver Island at a small fishing village called Tofino. There's one hotel there and one motel. You go to the *motel* on the 17 February, that's a Friday, and stay there until someone contacts you. It will probably be that night, but it might be the next night or the night after. Anyway, stay in your room after seven o'clock every night until someone brings you thirty kilos of cocaine. After that you bring it across the mountains and deliver it to me in San Francisco and pick up your seventy-five thousand. Okay? You know where Vancouver Island is?'

Thirty kilos. That was sixty-six pounds of cocaine. *Sixty-six pounds*!

'Yes, I know where it is.'

'Good. To get to Tofino all you have to do is take the ferry from Vancouver to the town of Nanaimo, and then it's a couple of hours' drive from there to Tofino. How long is it going to take you to get it across the border and down to San Francisco?'

'It depends on the weather. If the weather's good, it'll take about two or three days to cross the border and then another day at least to get to San Francisco. Say five days. Maybe seven or eight if I run into bad weather.'

Alex couldn't believe what was happening. How could he be sitting here talking calmly about the effect of the weather on the delivery of thirty kilos of cocaine. This was what had killed Gordon.

'Alright. I'll expect to hear from you by the twenty-second or twenty-third. Or a few days later if the weather is bad up here.' Matheson poured a fourth drink and took it all at one swallow, as he had the first three. 'When you get to San Francisco take a room in one of the downtown hotels and call me at my office any time betwen 8:30 a.m. and 3:00 p.m. Just tell the receptionist that you're . . .' He thought for a few seconds, '. . . what was your friend's name again? Wilson? Right, just tell her that your name is Wilson and I'll make sure she puts you through to me, and we can arrange someplace to meet.'

'On the telephone?'

'Sure. All you're going to say is "Hello, this is Bill, or Fred or whatever his name was, Wilson, and I'd like to see you"; and I'll say "fine, let's have a drink at Joe's Bar'. No problem. We go to the bar and make our arrangements there.'

Matheson picked up the whiskey bottle and studied the label. 'Seagram's V.O., huh? I'll have to remember that.' He put the bottle back on the table and stood up. 'I'm glad you're cooperating on this. It saves me a lot of trouble and as you can see . . .' he pointed to the money on the table, '. . . you're going to do pretty well for yourself. A potful of money for not much work and no risk. Not a bad deal at all.'

He started for the front door. He was unsteady after the four drinks, and his speech was beginning to slur. 'You remember everything I said? Go to the motel, not the hotel, on the 17 February. Stay in your room in the evenings and someone will get in touch with you.'

Alex handed him his overcoat.

'When you get to San Francisco call me and say that your name is Wilson and we'll arrange things from there.'

He opened the door and started down the stairs, hanging on to the handrail, then stopped and said, 'If anything changes I'll get in touch with you, otherwise I'll expect to hear from you around the twenty-second or third.' He carried on down the stairs and out the front door.

Alex was in a trance. He walked slowly back to his chair and sat down again. He picked up his whiskey but didn't drink, just held it in his hand and stared at the money on the table. He heard the door open and looked up as Linda crossed the room and took the chair opposite.

'So what happened? What's this all about?' She stirred the pile of hundreds with a finger, knocking several of them onto the floor.

'I think he's crazy.' Alex's voice was flat and emotionless. 'I didn't say ten words the whole time he was here. It was like I'd already agreed to do it for him and he was just giving me a briefing on the when and how.'

He put his glass back on the table and continued in the same toneless voice. 'He wants me to go up to Canada and pick up thirty kilos of cocaine, carry it across the border and deliver it to him in San Francisco. This . . .' he pointed to the money '. . . is his down payment. It's twenty-five thousand dollars. I get another seventy-five thousand when I make the delivery.'

'And you agreed to all this? Are you fucking crazy?'

'I didn't agree or disagree. I didn't say one word. *He's* crazy. What was I supposed to do? Tell him to get lost? What if he has a car full of heavies downstairs? What if he comes down on you? No thank you.'

Alex was coming out of his trance. He stood up and said, 'I think I'd like to be out of his reach when I tell him I'm not going to do it.'

He stared agitatedly around the room. 'I've got to get out of here. Let's drive in to Seattle and walk around downtown or something.'

CHAPTER FORTY-THREE

Seattle

IT WAS SATURDAY NIGHT in Seattle. Cold rain was falling and people were scurrying from car to restaurant, from restaurant to theatre, from bar to bar. Lights reflected in the wet streets and buses and cars hurtled by, their occupants cocooned from the evil weather and barely visible behind misted windows and flashing wipers.

Alex and Linda were oblivious to it all. They walked up one street and down the next, turning left or right without conscious thought, staying in the approximately ten by ten block area that constitutes downtown in a city that isn't quite big enough to have an uptown. They had been walking for an hour, but were no nearer to a solution to their problem than they had been at the start of their walk when Linda had said, 'If he really is leaving the country after this shipment, then it probably doesn't make any difference to him what the police find out. The sensible thing for him to do is to kill you when you make the delivery. That saves him seventy-five thousand and leaves one less person behind who knows anything.'

'But what about the money he gave me? Why would he give me that much if he was just going to shoot me?'

'Twenty-five thousand? That's nothing. If twenty-five thousand will keep you happy until you make the delivery then he's made a hell of a bargain.' She stopped and looked up at him, oblivious to the rain hitting her face. 'Do you have any idea how much he can make with thirty keys of coke?'

'No.'

'Do you know anything about cocaine at all?'

'Just what Gord told me, and what you've told me. Other than what I've read in magazines and newspapers that is.'

They turned a corner and walked on through the rain and Linda said, 'Basically he's got two choices. Depending on how greedy he is, how much risk he's willing to take and how much time he's willing to put into it; he can either sell the whole lot of it at once to someone who's into full time dealing, or he can try to sell it off in smaller amounts, a kilo or a pound at a time, to smaller dealers. But if he's really leaving the country right away then he's probably got someone lined up to take the whole thirty kilos.'

'I think that's what he does, because he said that Carl, the one who shot Gord, worked for somebody else, and it was Carl that took the whole shipment last time.'

'So what's happening ...' said Linda '... is that Matheson has some connection in South America, in Bolivia, or Peru or Columbia, where he can buy cocaine. He has it brought up here and sells it to somebody and never actually gets involved in the distribution business at all.'

'So how much can he sell it for?'

'If it's any good he'll probably be selling it for something like fifty thousand a kilo, whatever that works out to.'

Alex did the multiplication in his head. 'One and a half million.' He stopped walking and said, 'But Gordon said he thought that the load we brought in, which was only fifteen kilos, would be worth about two million.'

'It would have been worth a lot more than that eventually, but Matheson would only be getting somewhere around fifty a key for it unless he was distributing as well as importing.' She took Alex's arm and walked on. 'It gets more and more profitable at each step. Matheson sells it for fifty thousand dollars a kilo, but whoever buys it is going to cut each kilo half and half with something else and then resell the sixty new kilos for about fifty thousand each, which means about three million. If he paid Matheson one and a half that gives him a profit of one and a half million, but he has to make a lot of one and two kilo sales, which ups the risk by quite a bit.'

'And then?'

'And then,' she continued, 'whoever bought a kilo will cut it again – at least half and half – and sell it in ounces or grams, for as much as a hundred and fifty a gram; and if you try and figure the profit there you'll run right off your calculator.' She looked up at him. 'Go ahead, work it out. Just say the average price will be one hundred a gram. That's a hundred thousand a kilo, but for each kilo that he bought he gets two kilos after it's been cut, so that's two hundred thousand dollars for each fifty thousand dollar kilo, and there were sixty of those.'

'*That's twelve million dollars*.' Alex was stunned.

'Plus one and a half million at the first sale and three million at the second sale. Don't forget those.'

'Fifteen, sixteen and a half million.'

'It's hard to say exactly, but it'll be something like that. Somewhere around fifteen million by the time it's all over, but Matheson's share is only one and a half million.' She paused. 'So even if it's costing him a few hundred thousand to buy it and have it shipped up here he can still afford to lay twenty-five thousand on you to keep you happy for a while.'

Alex did not want to be involved. He wanted only to return the twenty-five thousand and tell Walter Matheson to find somebody else, to leave him to live his life in peace. But what could he do? If he refused to help, there was a chance that both he and Linda would be killed immediately. If he went through with it then he might well be killed on delivery. If he went to the police he would probably be killed before he could testify at any trial.

They walked and talked, but they could think of no safe way to make the delivery or to protect themselves afterward, and finally they gave up trying.

It almost seemed the best chance they had was to go through with the smuggling and hope that Matheson was telling the truth. That he *would* pay the seventy-five thousand and leave the country, leave them in peace.

Cold, wet and depressed they returned to the van and drove home. They shared a long hot shower and went to bed, wondering if a normal life would ever be possible for them; wondering how long life could last for two caterpillars in the middle of a freeway.

Linda half-woke and rolled over to snuggle against Alex, but he wasn't there. She sat up. It was dark and felt like the middle of the night. Where was he? Still not fully awake she stood and stumbled out of the bedroom to find him in the living room. There were maps spread out all over the floor and Alex was kneeling in the middle, measuring distances and making notes on a sheet of paper.

'What are you doing?'

He stood up and stretched. 'I couldn't sleep.' He said. 'I kept thinking about a way out of all this, and I think I've found it.'

They had turned the heat down in the house when they went to bed and Linda was hugging herself against the cold. 'How?'

'Put some clothes on and I'll show you.'

Soon they were both kneeling in front of three small maps. 'These things show the area along the border where Gord and I came across last time. That's Mt. Redoubt on the far right and you can see all the trails marked in green. Now, what we do, you and I, is to pick up the cocaine in Canada and bring it across here . . .' he pointed to a bright green line just to the west of Mt. Redoubt. 'We can drive to within half a mile or so of this trail on the Canadian side and then just ski the length of the trail till it ends here at the Hannegan Campground where we'll have a car stashed.'

His finger traced the route across two of the maps. 'That's what Gord and I did, except that we went up and over the west ridge of Mt. Redoubt and missed a section of the trail. Now,' he pointed to the third, westernmost map

'. . . the road from Hannegan Campground joins the main road not far from a little town called Glacier. And here . . .' he pointed to a spot halfway between Glacier and Hannegan Campground '. . . there's a trail that comes right down to the main road, called the Excelsior Pass Trail.'

'That green line with all the zigzags?'

'That's right. The zigzags mean that the trail climbs very steeply – see how close together the contour lines are?'

'Yes. So?'

'So what we can do is this: We tell Matheson that we are going to meet him in the town of Glacier and that he should take a room in the motel there. Then, when we've brought the load across we take it to the Excelsior Pass Trail and stash it just a little way off the road, and I'll wait there. You go to a telephone – there's a couple of bars and gas stations along the road that you could call from – and call Matheson and tell him where the cocaine is and that he should go there and pick it up and leave the money.'

Linda was not impressed. 'So how does that protect you? If anything, he can shoot you more easily there than in San Francisco.'

'No, that's the beauty of it. He's never going to see me. He can bring along ten carloads of goons and it won't make any difference. The *only* thing we need to make this work perfectly is a pair of portable transceivers.'

Alex stood up and went to the liquor cupboard and returned with a bottle of Remy and two snifters. 'Here's how it works.' He poured them each a drink. 'You call him from the gas station or wherever and then drive back and hide the car somewhere near this Excelsior trail. Then you pick a spot nearby, on the other side of the highway where you can hide in the trees and wait. When he arrives you call me on the transceiver and I go up the trail a bit until I'm out of sight. You can tell me if there's anybody with him and you can tell me when they've gone that it's safe for me to come down.

He drank half his cognac and continued. 'If he's left the money for us, then fine, I'll pick it up and come down to the road and we can drive away. If he hasn't left the money, if he decides to rip us off, well there's nothing we can do about it, but at least he won't have been able to kill me. If he brings people like Carl and his friend you'll be able to see how many go up the trail and how many come back out, and even if they know I'm hiding up the trail they won't be able to catch me. I can get up a steep trail a lot faster than any of them are going to be able to, and there's a good chance that there'll be enough snow that they won't be able to chase me without skis anyway.'

Linda sipped her drink and studied the map, but said nothing. Finally she spoke. 'Assuming that Matheson will come up to this Glacier place, it would probably work, in fact it's probably a good idea; but what I don't understand is why you want to do it up there in the first place. Why make things complicated with a bunch of screwing around in the snow with walky-talkies when we could do the same thing in San Francisco? We could stash the coke someplace, tell him where it is and then watch while he picks it up.'

'I thought of that. In fact I'd rather do it in San Francisco if we could because I don't think he's going to be very happy about coming up here, but there are two problems that I just can't see any way around.'

He finished his drink and started to pour another, but changed his mind and put the bottle down. 'The first is that anyplace we leave a suitcase in San Francisco, it could be stolen before Matheson gets to it; and the other thing is, even if we could find a safe spot to leave it, how are we going to know it's safe to pick up the money? All he has to do, if he wants to kill me, is to leave somebody watching the place he's put the money and whenever I come to pick it up, bang.'

He picked the bottle up again and poured them each a second drink. 'No, if we do it up in the mountains then I can sit on top of the cocaine until you radio me that he's on his way up the trail, and we'll know with absolute certainty whether or not it's safe to pick up the money.'

'If he pays.'

'Yeah, if.'

They both sat silent after that. Finally Alex said, 'I'm not suggesting this because I want to do it. If there is some way to get out of the whole business then I'll take it, but the only way I can think of is to mail the twenty-five thousand back to Matheson and then disappear. Move to New York or someplace like that.' He sounded desperately unhappy. 'And if we have to do that anyway, I'd rather do it with an extra hundred thousand dollars.'

CHAPTER FORTY-FOUR

Vancouver

ANDY CUTLER left the elevator and walked gingerly across the room where he had spent so much of the last four years.

'Hey, look who's here.'

'Howyadoon Andy?'

''Samatter Andy, can't stay away from Drugs?'

'He's hooked. He's a Drugs addict.'

Cutler fended of the humour and limped into Sergeant Hofstadter's office. 'Got a coffee for me Rico?'

'Sure, help yourself. How's it going upstairs?'

Cutler poured a cup and settled very carefully into a chair. 'Upstairs is fine, but I think my body's been run over by a truck.'

Hofstadter shoved aside the report he had been reading and picked up his cigarettes. 'Smoke?'

'Thanks.'

They lit up and Hofstadter asked, 'So what happened to your body?'

'You know how Val's into fitness – all those dance classes and racquetball? Well I decided I should maybe try to get into a little better shape myself, but I think I overdid it.'

Hofstadter laughed, then said, 'But you've always run haven't you?'

'Yeah, but not very hard. Couple of miles every other day.' He shifted in his chair and grimaced with pain. 'What actually happened was that Val came out with me for a run on Friday and cleaned my clock.' He sounded bitter. 'She doesn't even run, right? Just plays racquetball and does those stupid aerobics, and I couldn't come close to keeping up to her; so I figured I'd better shape up.'

Hofstadter was laughing again. 'So what did you do? Try to do it all in one day? Try to run a marathon or something?'

'Kind of. I came down to the club on Saturday and got Willy, the trainer, to show me around the weights. It felt okay, so yesterday I came down again, went for a run and then gave myself a real workout in the weight room.'

'Found out you're not seventeen anymore huh?'

'Seventeen? Christ! I feel like a hundred and seventeen. There isn't one part of my body that doesn't hurt. Not one! And that's not the worst of it either.' Cutler lowered his voice and leaned across the desk. 'She stayed at my place last night, and this morning we woke up and we're both feeling a little horny, so we start playing around a bit and pretty soon I roll over on top of her but my stomach muscles were so sore from the situps yesterday that I couldn't get up on my elbows and knees. It hurt so much I couldn't keep a hardon.'

He sounded disgusted. 'And she laughed at me. Laughed! As soon as I stop hurting I'll teach her something.'

'Poor Andy. Poor pussy-whipped Andy. Wait till I tell Angie. She'll never let you hear the end of this one. She'll . . .' The telephone rang and he picked it up. 'Hofstadter . . . Sure, just a minute.' He pushed the phone across the desk. 'It's for you. You want to take it here or in your office?'

Cutler stubbed out his cigarette and said, 'Here's fine if I can borrow some paper.' He took the receiver. 'Cutler . . . Fine, put him through.'

Five minutes later he hung up the phone. Hofstadter looked up from his paperwork and raised thick eyebrows inquiringly.

'That was Holley,' said Cutler. 'Lieutenant Holley, the narcotics guy in San Francisco. You remember I was telling Angie the other night that everyone involved was either dead or sitting tight and that Holley was pretty much back at square zero?'

'And now?'

'Now he's finally had a bit of luck. Someone that he caught with his pants down is trying to talk his way out of ten years in the pen with news about a big shipment of coke that's going to be handled by the people that Holley's been after for so long.'

Hofstadter stood up and walked over to his coffee pot and poured himself a cup, then said, 'From what I remember, he had his share of bad luck on this, so I guess he was about due for a break. But how does it affect you?'

'Actually Rico, now that I'm out of Drugs it probably affects you more than me, but I wouldn't mind handling it if it's okay with you.'

'What is it?'

'Nothing much. It's just that this guy, the promoter that Holley's fixated on, doesn't normally deal in cocaine, so he figures that there's a reasonable chance that Matheson is involved again. He's got him under loose surveillance and he's asked all the airlines and car rental people, and the U.S. Customs to put a flag in their computers for the name Matheson, and he's asking if we'll do the same up here.

'It would probably take me longer to explain it to one of your people than it would to do it myself.'

Hofstadter scratched his chin with his thumb and said, 'Sure, go ahead, just file a copy of your report with me and if anything comes of it let me know.'

'Not likely that much will come of it. Matheson's been burned pretty good up here, so he's probably bringing this one in through Miami or Portland. If it is Matheson. Still, we can but try.'

He stood up slowly and carefully. 'Thanks for the tea and sympathy Rico. If I survive this fitness thing I'll give you a call in a couple of days to see if you and Angie want to come over for supper on the weekend.'

CHAPTER FORTY-FIVE

San Francisco

HOLLEY DRUMMED his long fingers slowly on his desk and wondered why, if Matheson was bringing in another load, he wasn't moving. All he had done for the last week was to go to his office in the morning and come home at night. Big deal. Big dealer.

Still, there was no choice. It fit the pattern of Matheson's previous shipments, so he had to be watched. But it was so fucking frustrating. The tempo of his fingers on the desk slowed even further. Half an hour in private with Walter Frederick Matheson and Holley would know everything there was to know about the man, and there would be no more guessing games about who was supplying what, and for how much, to whom.

He sighed. Money. It all came down to money. He could walk into any of fifty nearby bars, pick virtually anyone there, take him into the washroom and slap him senseless in his search for information. It didn't matter whether the man knew anything at all as long as he was poor. Nobody gave a shit one way or the other what Holley, or any cop, did to a nameless junkie, but let him so much as raise his voice to someone with money and he could kiss the case right off.

His fist crashed on his desk. Fuck it. He could play the game as well as anyone, and if Tomlinson was dealing massive amounts of smack, then he, William Holley, would deal with him massively.

He leaned back in his chair and rolled a few fantasies through his mind, and soon felt much better. The frustration was gone, his head was clear and he saw what he had been missing. If Matheson wasn't moving that didn't have to mean he wasn't involved. Maybe he had just been scared enough by the close call last time to run this one by remote control.

Five minutes later he was on the telephone explaining what he wanted to a Sergeant Hemslo in Seattle P.D. Narcotics.

'What I want is for you people to wire this Townsend down so tight that he can't scratch his ass without me knowing about it before he's finished doing it; but since you probably have a few other things going, and since this is kind of a long shot anyway, I'll take whatever you can give me and be happy with it.'

'Well sir, I'll tell you, normally what you would have got would have been the next thing to nothing at all, but as it happens I just might be able to help you.'

Hemslo was a slow talker and Holley gussed that he had come from somewhere a long way south and east of Seattle.

'We have some of our people doing a course at the academy right now. Some of our officers that is, not recruits. They're doing a course on surveillance technique and I don't see why they should be given an artificial problem if we can give them a real one and help you folks out at the same time. So why don't you just give me all the names and addresses again to make sure I copied it all, and we'll get on it for you.'

CHAPTER FORTY-SIX

Tofino (Canada)

7:30. He turned on the TV. There were only two channels and after an hour he had no idea what he had watched.

9:30. He had read every piece of printed material in the room but couldn't remember one word. He tried the crossword puzzle in the newspaper he had bought in the lobby but couldn't focus on it. He poured a drink. And another.

10:30. He finished his fourth drink and turned off the lights. He lay on the bed, fully clothed, and soon fell into unhappy, restless sleep.

At 11:15 he woke to the ringing telephone.

'Hello.'

'Mister Townsend?' A man's voice – nothing special about it.

'Yes. Who is this?'

'I want to meet you Mister Townsend. I'm at the hotel, just down the road. I want you to wait for ten minutes then get in your van and drive down there. I'll be waiting in the bar.'

'Who are you?'

'Don't worry about that, I'll recognize you, just don't leave your room for ten minutes and don't forget to bring your van.'

'Are you . . .' But the line was dead. Alex hung up the phone and looked around the room. Nothing. A nothing motel room in a nothing town. He wished Linda was here with him instead of in a hotel in Vancouver. He picked up the brandy and walked to the bathroom where he took a hit straight from the bottle and rinsed it round his mouth then spat it into the sink.

He left the bottle uncapped on the counter top, put on his jacket and, in a state of equal parts fear and anticipation, left the room and walked to his van.

He started it up and was about to release the handbrake when a voice from behind froze him solid.

'Don't move.'

The muscles of his back and abdomen went rigid and his sphincter clamped down hard. He was paralyzed with fear and couldn't have moved if he'd wanted to.

'Okay, now listen.' A man's voice, the same one he had heard on the telephone, 'I want you to drive out of town on the main road. There'll be a turn off, a dirt road on the right, in about three miles. I'll let you know in plenty of time. Just drive normally and don't try to turn around and look at me.'

Alex tried to relax, tried to tell himself that he was in no danger, that these people *needed* him; but the terrible ride on the night Gordon was killed came back and shook him and he could barely keep his hands on the wheel.

He drove, and gradually gained control. The fear was still there, the memory of the drive with Carl would not go away, but there had been no particular menace in the voice behind him, and they really did need him alive to make the delivery. Some of the adrenalin drained away and he began to feel better.

'Alright, slow down. In a minute or so you'll come to the turn off . . . Okay, there it is. Slow down and turn in . . . Now just a couple of hundred yards down this road you'll come to a spot where you can turn around.'

Branches slapped the windshield and scraped the side of the van, then came the wide spot and Alex made a three point turn and stopped.

'Kill the lights.'

He did as he was told.

'Okay pal, this is where I get off. The shit's here in the back in a suitcase, just give me a couple of minutes to get clear and then go back to the motel and get some sleep.'

Whoever it was opened the side door and stepped out into the darkness. The door slammed shut and Alex was left alone with the clatter of the engine.

He was on the first ferry the next morning and parking the car in the lot beside Linda's hotel at 10:20 a.m. Ten minutes later he was in the shower in her room washing away the sweat and smell and memory of the night. He called out to her to join him and they made soapy, slippery love, sitting in the bottom of the shower stall with the hot spray beating down on them.

When they were dried and dressed Alex said, 'It's going to take at least four hours to drive to the trailhead, so I guess we better get going. I'd rather stay here in Vancouver for a day or two, but I don't know how long this good weather will last, so . . .'

'I understand.'

CHAPTER FORTY-SEVEN

San Francisco

HE WOKE UP feeling better than he had in weeks. He took only one Extra Strength Tylenol before breakfast instead of the usual three, and was almost cheerful as he sat at the table and listened to his wife chatter.

As he sipped his coffee he wondered idly what she would do if he interrupted her and said, 'Marion, you old gasbag you, do you realize that this is the last time I'll ever have to look at your bloated body across the breakfast table?' On reflection he decided that she probably wouldn't do anything; just say 'That's nice dear' and carry on telling him what Sue Ann somebody-or-other had said yesterday.

Thank God for prostitution.

And he wondered what she would do when he didn't come home from the 'meetings in Atlanta' next week. Call the police? That would be pretty funny, and he smiled at the thought. Then, suddenly, it wasn't funny anymore. He didn't care what she did or didn't do. He just wanted to be finished with her. He stood up, said goodbye, got through her fat embrace by thinking about what he would be looking at across the breakfast table in Lima next week, picked up his coat, attaché case and suitcase, and left the house forever.

As he drove toward the centre of the city his mood lightened. Walter Matheson had left his house at 7:30 a.m., as usual, and would leave his office at 9:00 a.m. to attend a meeting on the other side of the country. And that is the last that would be known of him. Somewhere between his office and the airport Walter Matheson would drop from the sight of the world.

He smiled. No matter how deep you probed he was solid gold all the way through. He was tough – he had shown that in Korea. He was smart – he had shown that at M.I.T.. He was successful – he had shown that every day since he opened his office. His studies were the ones they based their forecasts on, built their hydroelectric megaprojects on. His house showed how successful he was. His cars, his clothes, his holidays. Everything about him showed that. He was what all the little people in the world wanted to be.

He laughed out loud. Stupid bastards. Anybody who would work his ass off for forty-five years just to be able to afford to play golf in Hawaii for two weeks every winter until his heart exploded had to be an idiot.

Not him. He had seen the maggots in that chocolate bar a long time ago, and he had other plans. He was retiring *now*, in the prime of his life, and not with the kind of bank account that would limit him to some condo full of geriatrics in Florida or Hawaii or Puerto Rico either.

He would spend his retirement fucking the most beautiful women in South America in his own villas in cities like Lima and Buenos Aires, and he had more money waiting for him down there than any doctor or engineer or corporation man could get if he lived to be a thousand. He had more money *in cash* in the attaché case on the seat beside him than most so called successful people had in total when they retired.

He reached out and patted the case, and felt a thrill go through him at the touch.

Inside the case was everything he needed to get out of the country. There was cash: a chamois leather money belt with compartments all the way round holding 250 one thousand dollar bills, 50 one hundred dollar bills, and three small vials of baguette-cut emeralds – worth as much as the cash in any large city in North America or Europe. Twice as much if he wasn't in a hurry.

And there was a complete new identity: passport, credit cards and driver's licence in the name of Leonard Charles Findlay. All current and all indistinguishable from the real thing. The very best Japanese forgeries, arranged by his brother and shipped up only weeks ago.

And finally there was his protection and insurance: A Smith and Wesson .38 Police Special and a box of shells. He knew he couldn't risk trying to take it onto the airplane with him, but that didn't matter, there were plenty more like it in Lima.

As he got closer to his office his head started to hurt again and he took two more Tylenols from the bottle in his pocket. The headaches had been worse than ever lately, but the knowledge that they would be stopping within a week made it a little easier to take. That, and the decision he had made to leave no one behind who could connect him to anything illegal. After all, he might want to come back some day. He doubted it, but there was no sense in burning bridges if he didn't have to.

Tomlinson, the dealer, and whatever partners he might have were one thing; none of them had actually seen him with the cocaine in his hands, and they weren't going to be talking about it anyway; but this mountain climber was another matter. He had seemed nice enough, and he had saved Walter's life, but ever since he had phoned with his crazy plan about making the exchange up in the mountains Walter had been suspicious.

He would go up there and make the exchange all right, but what Townsend got in exchange for the cocaine was going to be half an ounce of lead.

CHAPTER FORTY-EIGHT

Vancouver

EVER SINCE his promotion and transfer, Andy Cutler's eating habits had gone downhill. For the two months he had either grabbed something from the cafeteria and brought it back upstairs to eat at his desk, or skipped lunch entirely. But sitting in his kitchen with coffee and the morning paper he decided that today, finally, he felt on top of the new job. Today he would only work till eleven-thirty or twelve and then take the rest of the day off. Start the weekend early with a good lunch at a good restaurant, maybe at one of the big hotels; and then maybe just walk around downtown a bit and do some window shopping. He needed a new suit and had noticed in the paper that some of the department stores still had sales on.

Driving to work he decided that some new shirts and pants wouldn't be a bad idea either, and that ten or ten-thirty would be a better time to knock off. There was nothing that needed his immediate attention, and he had worked most of the last three weekends so he was due for some extra time. Ten o'clock it would be.

When he reached his office there was a message on his desk from the switchboard requesting that he call Lieutenant Holley of the San Francisco P.D. as soon as possible. It was marked only ten minutes ago.

He cleared some space on his desk, emptied his ashtrays, made sure that pen and paper were handy, lit a cigarette and picked up the phone.

'Lieutenant, it's Andy Cutler in Vancouver, I've got a message here that you wanted me to call you.'

'I think Matheson is making his move and I wanted to let you know and to ask you to do a couple of things for me.'

No hello, no how are you doing, just straight to it. Well, that was Holley.

'Sure, whatever I can.'

'Good. Here's what's happened. I've had teams of three guys on Matheson for the last week and yesterday morning he just walked away from them. He went to his office in the morning and that was the last they saw of him. His car's still in his parking lot and his office says that he's gone to Atlanta for a series of meetings and won't be back for a week.'

'You must be a bit unhappy about that.'

'I am, Mister Cutler, but nowhere near as unhappy as the guys who said they were watching him. If they'd lost him in heavy traffic, or walking in a crowded shopping area I could understand it, but that building he's in is square, and if he slipped out of it while three of my detectives were watching then either he's Houdini, or two of them were having coffee somewhere.' He paused, then said, 'but it happened and there's nothing I can do about it now.'

'You don't think he went to Atlanta?'

'I've checked every airline that flies out of the entire Bay Area. Walter Matheson didn't fly to Atlanta or anyplace else. No one of that name flew anywhere or has a reservation to fly anywhere in the next two months.' He snorted. 'Not that that means dick-all. He could have flown anywhere he wanted using another name. I've got people checking out lists of all airline passengers who bought tickets for cash, but that's going to take too long to be of much use, so what I'd like to ask you to do is to notify the RCMP in Prince Rupert that he might be showing up again and ask them to watch for him, and for anything on the docks that might be there to meet him.'

Cutler made a note and said, 'Sure, no problem there. And I'll remind Customs and the airlines as well. Anything else?'

'There's one other thing. I'm not sure what it means, but it could be important. You remember Townsend in Seattle?'

'Yes, why? Has he vanished too?'

'You got it, Pontiac. I asked Seattle P.D. to put a watch on him. They called early this morning and told me a couple of things. The first is that he's moved. He and that Cunningham woman have rented a place in Tacoma, just south of Seattle. It was lucky I told them about her because the new place is rented in her name, and so is the telephone.'

Cutler dragged on the cigarette and said, 'I thought Townsend was supposed to notify you of any change of address.'

'I guess he forgot. Anyway Tacoma police found the place and talked to the owner and found out where Townsend is working, which is as a mechanic for some lumber company. They talked to his boss this morning and it turns out he's taken a couple of extra days off, starting yesterday, and has gone skiing, but they don't know where.'

Cutler said 'Hmmmm,' and Holley continued:

'Now let me put all this in perspective for you. You remember that I told you that I heard that there was some coke on the way?'

'Yes.'

'Well I've had that confirmed by a couple of other people. It's still a bit vague, and I haven't got any names or exact dates, but it looks like a fairly big shipment of coke is expected to hit town sometime in the next week or so. Word hasn't reached the street, so I'm pretty sure it hasn't actually arrived yet, but if the middle level dealers know about it, it can't be far off, so what I suspect is that Matheson is on his way to pick it up, and that maybe Townsend is going to help him again.'

'You could be right, Lieutenant.'

'I could be wrong, too, but what the fuck else have I got to work on? Which brings me to the other thing I need your help on . . .'

'What's that?'

'Assuming that they are bringing it into Canada first, and I've got people working on the other assumption, how are they going to get it down here from there?'

Where was Holley headed? 'I'm not sure I know what you mean. They could take it any number of ways. Car, bus, boat, airplane . . .'

Holley cut him off: 'The problem, Mister Cutler, is that they know that they're under suspicion. I just can't see either of them throwing a suitcase full of blow into the back seat and driving across the border with his fingers crossed. The same goes for flying. They've got to believe that wherever they clear Customs they're going to get the deluxe treatment – fluouroscopes, x-rays, ultrasound, the works – and it's still the middle of winter so I don't see them hiking through the mountains, so what are they going to do?'

The tone of the question was rhetorical and Cutler waited for the answer.

'The only thing I can think off' said Holley, 'is to hire a small plane again. That wouldn't be very smart either, because we've got to be looking for it, but . . .'

'But you'd like to ask me to keep an eye on the charter services anyway, right?'

'If you would. I don't think it's necessary, but I wouldn't be doing my job if I didn't ask. Can you do that?'

Cutler thought about it for a few seconds. 'What I'll do is give the names and descriptions of Matheson, Townsend and the woman to the RCMP and ask them to circulate them to every charter service they can in B.C. and Alberta. It's not going to be anywhere near one hundred percent effective, there's a lot of hungry pilots around, and the RCMP aren't going to be giving it top priority, but it's something. And I'll do the same with all the city police forces I can think of.'

He stubbed out his cigarette and wished he had some coffee. 'Like you say, it's probably not necessary, but it won't hurt.'

Holley said, 'Thanks a lot. I imagine that Matheson is bringing this one in through Miami or Mexico, or even through Atlanta, where he said he was going. But I know he's used the Canadian route before, so I've got to go through the motions.'

Cutler sympathized. Car chases and gunfights might sell movie tickets, but going through the motions was what ninety-nine percent of police work was about.

'You're right, Lieutenant. Matheson is probably in Miami or San Diego and Townsend is probably skiing with his girlfriend at Aspen, but I guess we have to go through the motions and . . .' He broke of in mid sentence and groaned aloud, then said, 'Oh shit!'

'What?'

'So much for my weekend.'

'What are you talking about?'

'Lieutenant, I was planning to take most of today off, start the weekend early. Spend some time with my girlfriend, maybe do some shopping today and then head out of the city for a day or two. It would have been my first time off in twenty-six days.'

'But?'

'But I just remembered something.' Cutler was weary. Sometimes he wished that he could turn his mind off, stop it from applying itself to problems that weren't really his. 'I spent some time with some climbers a few months ago, when we were looking into the Wilson murder, and one of the things they talked about all the time was skiing in places like Alaska and the Yukon. I'd never heard of any ski resorts up there so I asked one of them about it and he told me that what they all do is something called ski-mountaineering. It's sort of a cross between cross-country and downhill and apparently they can ski just about anywhere. Uphill, downhill, even right up to the tops of mountains . . .'

Holley said 'And so?'

'So what this guy said was that anywhere you could go in the summer, you could go in the winter if you knew what you were doing . . .'

'Yeah, so?' Holley still didn't see.

'So one thing they all agreed on was that Wilson and Townsend knew what they were doing.'

'Shit.'

'That's right, Lieutenant. I don't know what you're planning for your weekend, but it looks like I'll be spending mine talking to climbers and helicopter pilots.' He lit another cigarette and continued, 'I'll do some checking and try to find out whether it's possible for someone to hike or ski across the border at this time of year, and if it is I'll get back to you and we can start talking about organizing air searches.'

Holley didn't reply immediately. Then he said, 'Mister Cutler, don't think that I don't appreciate what you're doing for me. If it turns out that it would be possible for Townsend to bring the shit in on skis and you wind up spending your weekend in a radio room somewhere, I'll personally guarantee that there will be two tickets to San Francisco on your desk on Monday morning. You bring your ladyfriend down here next Friday and I'll treat you to the best weekend this city can offer.'

CHAPTER FORTY-NINE

North Cascade Mountains

HIS LOAD was uncomfortably heavy. Thirty kilos of cocaine was sixty-six pounds, the tent and their sleeping bags and underpads added just under eighteen more; stove, food, fuel, pots and eating utensils was about ten; extra clothing maybe eight or nine; maps, compass, first aid, toilet paper, etcetera, came to another four or five; and the skis and poles which were strapped to their packs added about fifteen.

He tried to add it all up in his head as he walked but he kept losing track. Finally he got it right. Sixty-six plus eighteen plus ten plus nine plus five plus fifteen. One hundred and twenty-three pounds. And then the packs themselves were another four or five each, so that meant a total of a little over one hundred and thirty, and he was carrying a good bit more than half. He did some more arithmetic and finally decided that he must have about eighty pounds on his back. No fun at all. Especially not the first hour.

They left the van at 8:00 and crossed the border slash fifteen minutes later, but they couldn't find the start of the trail, and wasted a lot of time crashing around in spooky forest looking for it. Long beards of spanish moss hung from the trees and it was easy to imagine trolls and goblins behind the huge trunks in the dim light.

Once they found the trail though it hadn't been too bad. The track was in decent shape and none of the creeks they had to cross presented any serious problem.

About an hour and a half after picking up the trail they stopped for a break beside the largest stream they had seen so far. Alex dropped his pack and collapsed on top of it.

'Thank God this trail isn't steep.' He sat for a few minutes, breathing heavily, then dug his waterbottle out of his pack and went down to the stream and filled it. 'Here, have some water.'

Linda took the bottle and drank slowly, passing it back when it was half gone. Alex took it and drank, then refilled it and drank some more.

'This is Bear Creek. This is where Gord and I joined the trail when we carried the last lot over.'

Linda was puzzled. 'But we've only just started. I thought you went over Mt. Redoubt so that you could avoid this trail. Why did you go a whole day out of the way just to miss three miles, when there's twenty more miles to go?'

'It was summer then. The three miles we missed were the three miles leading from the Canadian border. These trails are crawling with hikers in the summer and there are quite a few Rangers around to make sure that everybody camps in the designated places and carries out their garbage. We thought that there would probably be a couple of them watching the area right around the border, and we just didn't want to take any chances.'

Linda thought about that and then said, 'So why didn't *we* go that way?'

'No need to at this time of year. There won't be anybody on these trails, campers or rangers. We won't see a soul until we get to the other end where we left the rental car. Besides, I don't even know if we *could* have gone that way. At this time of year it would probably have taken two or three extra days, and exposed us to some severe avalanche danger.

They rested a few minutes longer, neither saying much until Alex stood and said, 'Better get going.'

They struggled into their packs and began the slow march along the valley bottom. The sun came and went with the vagaries of the cloud cover, and the temperature in the dripping, silent forest hovered just around freezing.

'How's your load?' he asked.

'Heavy. Not as bad as yours must be though. How are you doing?'

'The load's heavy, but I'll manage. The load in my head is heavier. I wish we didn't have to do this.'

He walked a few steps in silence then said, 'We *could* still back out you know.'

'What do you mean?'

'We could drop the loads right here and just not go through with it. Go back to the van and drive to Seattle to pick up what we need and then go to New York or wherever.'

Linda stopped and turned to face him. 'Alex, if we had just disappeared with the twenty-five thousand dollars we might have pulled it off, they might have figured it wasn't worth the effort to find us. But if we disappear while we've got thirty kilograms of their coke . . . Well, they'd never stop looking. All the money in the world wouldn't be enough to keep us hidden if we did that.'

She stood, hands on hips, staring up at him until he said, 'You're right. I know you're right. I just wish there was some way out of this, some way we could just go back to Seattle and live like normal people.'

'Well, there isn't. But we're safe as long as we stick to your plan and as long as we disappear afterward. If we deliver on schedule, and with no hassles, then nobody is going to go to a lot of trouble about us. If we sit still and make it easy, then sure, someone might decide to kill us; but if we disappear, then nobody is going to work up a big sweat looking for us. And probably . . .' she relaxed a little, '. . . probably they will pay us, to keep *us* from coming after *them*.'

'Us go after them? Are you crazy?'

'Nope.' She smiled, but there was no humour in her voice. 'You went up against two guys with guns and killed one, got both their guns and chased the other one away.' She reached up and touched his cheek. 'You and I know that you're just a frightened little mouse, playing in a game with a bunch of big, hungry cats; but to this Matheson, and to whoever sent those creeps after you, you must look pretty deadly. They probably feel like pussycats playing with a panther.'

They hit skiable snow in the early afternoon at about thirty-two hundred feet. They had already eaten lunch but they were still hungry, so they snacked while they stopped to put on skis and skins.

'We're almost there. Only four miles to go, but the pass is near five thousand feet and I think we're just over three thousand here so it's going to be a real grunt,' said Alex. 'It'll take two hours anyway with these loads. How are you doing?'

'I'll be fine. I'm not saying that it's fun, but I'm doing okay, you're the one with the big load.'

'At least getting the skis off our backs and onto our feet will help.' He shrugged into his pack and said 'Ready?'

'Lead on Bwana.'

The last half mile up to the pass was the worst. They were tired, the snow was soft, and the hill seemed to go on endlessly. It was a broad open slope with high avalanche danger; but there was no other way and by four o'clock they were just below the saddle. Alex dropped back slightly and let Linda go ahead, breaking trail; and waited for the words he knew she would say when she reached the crest and saw the magnificent crags and spires of Mt. Shuksan silhouetted across the valley against the afternoon sky.

'Oh God, Alex, hurry up and look at this, it's beautiful!'

He came up beside her and dropped his pack. 'Quite a sight isn't it?'

'Let's camp right here.'

Alex looked around. They were in an exaggerated saddle with open slopes dropping away in front and behind and sketchily forested hills rising to the left and right.

Immediately on their right was a clump of knarled old spruce, big around at the base but kept disproportionately short by the altitude. There was a nice flat spot behind them and he was tempted to say yes.

'No. Not quite right here.' He struggled to pick up his pack one last time. 'I think we'd better climb up to the left there, just a couple of hundred feet, so that we're well off the trail.' He pointed. 'See, just below the skyline there's two groups of trees. If we camp behind them we'll be out of sight of anyone who happens by, and we'll still have a view.'

He looked up thoughtfully, as if trying to see through the hill. 'In fact, we'll have a view out over the whole of the North Cascades. C'mon, it'll only take another twenty minutes or so, and the view will be worth it.'

CHAPTER FIFTY

North Cascade Mountains

FOR THE FIRST TIME in seven months Walter Matheson woke without any trace of a headache. The alarm in his watch chirped at 4:30 and he was up and out of bed almost before he realized he was awake. He put on the outdoor-type clothing he had bought in Seattle, strapped the revolver in its shoulder harness over the checked wool shirt and put some water on to boil in the kitchenette.

God Damn, but he felt good. He hadn't felt this good since Korea. In fact he felt even better than he had in Korea. Korea had been pretty good, but here *he* was in charge. There was nobody to give him any orders, nobody to yessir, nossir. He was it. He had planned this whole operation, he had pulled it off, and in about seventy-two hours he would begin twenty or thirty years of enjoying the rewards.

He checked the mirror in the bathroom. It was a three-way and came right down to the counter top. He could see himself from the waist up and from all sides. He looked good. The day-old beard, the lumberjack shirt and the gun under his arm gave him a real don't mess with me look that he knew would cool out anybody who got in his way. And underneath the shirt, invisible to the world, was a quarter of a million in cash and that much again in beautiful green stones. Enough to buy his way into or out of anything he wanted.

He returned to the kitchenette and made coffee. As he drank it he recalled last night when he had first looked carefully at the maps he had bought, trying to decide what route Townsend would use. There was a road across the border that led to this area and it was possible that Townsend would try that. The crossing was at a town called Sumas and from the look of the road map it would be a fairly popular crossing for any Canadian coming to the Mt. Baker ski area. Townsend could just throw a ski rack onto any car with Canadian plates and come across like a hundred other people for a day's skiing.

But that meant telling the U.S. Customs that he was a Canadian, and risking them tearing the car apart if they found out he wasn't.

A look at the topographical maps showed that east of the Sumas crossing the border went through a range of steep, glaciated mountains, with several passes crossing north to south and a few trails marked on the map that went almost to the border. To Walter Matheson it didn't look very promising, but to a mountain climber like this Townsend it would probably be a piece of cake.

He knew that Townsend would have some complicated plan for the delivery – why else would he have insisted on meeting in this stupid motel – so he would just have to figure that plan out and get to Townsend before Townsend could put it into operation. It was Korea all over again. 'If they think we're going to move through *here*, then they'll probably try to ambush us *there*, so we have to figure out how they'll get to there and set up an ambush of our own.'

But there were so many possibilities, and his head was hurting worse than it ever had. He looked at one route after another, but he just couldn't concentrate. It was like someone was inside his skull trying to bore his way out with a red hot poker.

And then he had seen it. He had been looking at a pass about twenty miles east when the words 'Mt. Redoubt' came blazing up off the page. The memory of the plane crash exploded in his mind and the man with the poker finally broke through his skull to the outside.

He had passed out at that point and awoken half an hour later sprawled on the floor beside the kitchenette table. As he clawed himself upright he realized that the pain was gone. Completely and utterly. Gone as if it had never been. And at the same time he knew with absolute certainty that Townsend would be coming up the valley below Mt. Redoubt. It was no longer a matter of weighing possibilities, of one route being more probable than another. There was now *only* one route. His life had changed when Townsend found him on Mt. Redoubt and now it would change again when he found Townsend there.

Fate? Karma? Kismet? Whatever, the game would be played to its end on the same ground where it had started.

He finished his coffee, and was soon driving through the predawn darkness, humming tunelessly and smiling the secret smile of a man who knows all the answers.

It was really all so obvious and so easy. He would walk in to a good ambush point, kill Townsend as he came by, carry the cocaine out himself and be in San Francisco again tomorrow. He would make the sale tomorrow night and fly to wherever his fancy took him. Maybe a few days in Rome would be a good way to start his new life. He liked that. San Francisco to Lima. Via Rome.

There was one other car in the parking lot at the trailhead, a newish Citation that would be Townsend's getaway car. He laughed out loud, then grabbed his rented snowshoes from the back seat and set off up the trail.

He was wearing streetshoes and no jacket, but he didn't feel uncomfortable or cold. He was surrounded by some of the finest mountain scenery in the forty-eight states, but he didn't see it. His intention was to carry thirty kilograms of cocaine back down this trail and he didn't have a backpack; but he had tapped into the energy source of the universe and he knew that he could carry twice that, ten times that, if he wanted to.

By 7:40, when he reached the crest of Hannegan pass and hid himself behind some big trees all of his toes had frozen and his left foot was solid almost to the proximal end of the metatarsals, but he didn't know or care. He was in the pilot seat where he belonged. He could see forever. He was Superman. He was God.

He was Walter Matheson and seven months after his accident an intracranial aneurism was spiralling him ever more swiftly into madness and inevitable death.

BOOK THREE

LINDA

CHAPTER FIFTY-ONE

North Cascade Mountains

THEY WERE ALREADY awake when the sun turned the top of their small tent into a translucent golden dome. Carrying the heavy loads had left them both exhausted at the end of the day and they had slept from sunset almost to sunrise, over twelve hours. But neither felt rested or refreshed and neither had much to say as they wriggled into their clothes.

Alex unzipped the door and stepped out, saying that he would get the stove going for tea, then poked his head back through the door and said, 'The food bag is tucked between the sleeping bags. I think there's a couple of cans of salmon in it for breakfast.'

She cringed. Canned salmon for breakfast? Then she realized with surprize that the thought of oily, salty salmon had her salivating in a way that bacon and eggs or granola could never have.

Fifteen minutes later breakfast was finished and they were on their second mug of tea. Alex looked at his watch.

'Ten to eight. Hmm.'

He stretched as best he could in the small tent then said 'It's about an hour to the car and then maybe another hour to get set up on the Excelscior Pass Trail; even if it takes Matheson a couple of hours to get there, that's still only four hours.'

He drank off the last of his tea and began pulling on his boots. 'So I'll have five or six hours of daylight to get back down to the car and even if Matheson has some heavies along and I have to screw around in the bush for a while to get away from them I'll still make it back before dark.'

Linda said nothing. She was lacing her boots and trying to think of some way their plan could go wrong, but she could see nothing worse than inconvenience. Matheson might not come until later in the day, in which case Alex might spend a few chilly hours waiting; or Matheson might have been delayed and not show up until tomorrow, in which case they would simply return the whole show tomorrow. But in any case they would be safe, and no matter what Matheson tried in the way of a double cross, the worst that could happen was that she and Alex would have to move east with a hundred thousand instead of a hundred and seventy-five thousand.

No, this time they were covered. There would be no careless slip-ups and no one catching up with them a month from now. She finished tying her bootlaces and followed Alex out the door, zipping it shut behind her.

The sun was well up and the whole world sparkled. To the south and east the glaciated spires of the North Cascades stood on proud parade, and to the west, shining in the morning sun, were the jagged rock towers and tumbling icefalls of Mt. Shuksan. The air had the clarity that comes only with icy, bone chilling cold, but it was beautiful, and for a minute Linda gave herself a holiday to a world in which Walter Matheson did not exist and she and Alex were here in the mountains to enjoy a few days of skiing and sunshine.

When she came back to reality Alex had struck the tent and was putting the last of their loads into the packs.

'Alex.'

'Uhuh?'

'We don't have to move to the east you know.'

'What?'

'Afterward, after today, we could move somewhere that would be far enough away to be safe without leaving the mountains couldn't we? Like Colorado? Or Alaska?'

'We can move anywhere we want to.' He stood up and looked around him. 'I don't want to leave the Seattle area. I like my job, and I like this part of the world; but I don't want to be killed, and there'll be good jobs in other places.' He clamped on his skis. 'But we don't have to decide now. When we're finished here we can go to New York and stay with your friend Michael for a little while. Maybe I'll like it there.' He shouldered his pack and picked up his poles. 'Or we can go skiing or climbing somewhere for a while and think it all over. Don't worry. We may have problems, but we've also got a fair bit of money stashed away, and we've got each other.'

That thought comforted her. They would be able to take a room in a quiet hotel somewhere at the end of the day, probably seventy-five thousand dollars richer, and plan the rest of their lives.

She started to put on her skis but suddenly felt the familiar early morning message from her lower intestine, more urgent than usual after two huge mugs of tea.

'Can you wait a few minutes Alex? I've got to go the the bathroom.'

'Sure.' He said. 'Or better still, I'll take off now and check out the trail down from the pass.'

'Whatever you like.' She kissed him on the tip of his nose and hugged him clumsily through all the layers of clothing they were wearing, and then stood back as he kick-turned a hundred and eighty degrees and shuffled through the trees to the edge of the hill. She plodded through the deep snow behind him and watched as he flew down the slope below, cranking smooth turns despite the heavy pack on his back, heading toward the pass and then banking right and going further down the slope the way they had come up yesterday, finally coming to a stop about two hundred and fifty feet below the pass.

She smiled to herself. He hadn't been the least bit interested in 'checking out the trail', he had just wanted to get in a few extra turns.

Which was fine. It would take him ten or fifteen minutes to climb back up to the saddle so she could have a leisurely shit and get a few pictures of Mt. Shuksan, and maybe a few of the campsite, before the sun got too high.

'First things first though,' she said aloud, and went looking for the toilet paper.

She was on her knees in the snow trying to sort out the best shot of a section of a wind-gnarled pine. The tree was in the right of the frame, her pack and skis in the centre but further back and slightly out of focus, and the blurred mass of Mt. Shuksan was in the background just as she wanted it. But something was bothering her and she wouldn't make the exposure until she found out what it was.

She checked the frame from left to right. Mountain, sky, pack and skis, tree. Nothing lying around on the snow to distract the eye, light at the right angle, aperture set for just the right blur – mountain out of focus completely and pack and skis out of focus just enough to leave the tree as the main attraction. What was wrong?

Angrily, she lifted her head, hoping to see bare-eye what she was missing through the finder.

Then she knew. Voices. The picture was fine but she could hear voices where there should only be silence. She couldn't hear the words, but she could hear the anger and all thought of photography vanished as she ran frantically toward her skis.

ALEX! Someone had found Alex!

She clamped her mouth shut and screamed soundlessly as she floundered through the snow, each step taking forever while her mind raced at lightspeed through a hundred nightmares. She pulled her skis from where they were standing and threw them flat on the snow, then fumbled with desperate, clumsy hands to clamp the bindings down on the toes of her boots. But her fingers belonged to somebody else and her feet wouldn't obey her mind.

Finally both skis were on and she stood up and grabbed for her poles, but haste tangled her feet and she collapsed face first in the snow.

On the verge of hysteria she rolled over and levered herself back upright, spitting snow and swearing and crying incoherently. She grabbed the poles and raced clumsily to the brow of the hill and without stopping to think, beyond being *able* to think, she planted both poles and shoved off with fear-amplified strength.

Below her, hobbled by his skis and pack, Alex was struggling desperately with a man in a red shirt. She locked into the sight and pointed her skis downhill. She had never gone this fast before, but in her tormented mind she seemed to be making no progress at all, skiing in snow that was glue and in air so thick she could feel it holding her, pushing back against her.

Then the man in red broke free and smashed Alex across the face with something in his hand. A gun! Fear lashed her and she bit down hard to remain silent while in her mind she was screaming 'No, don't do it you bastard, don't shoot him or I'll kill you. I'LL KILL YOU. I'LL KILL YOUI'LLKILLYOUKILLYOU.'

Alex swayed, blood streaming from his face and the man stepped back and raised the gun.

She wasn't close enough. She would never get there in time.

'Aaaiiieeeee . . .'

Her scream was louder than a thousand sirens. The man jerked as the gun fired, and tried to turn, tried to bring his weapon to bear on her, and died in instant pain as the tip of her ski pole came through his left eye and into his brain with her full weight behind it.

CHAPTER FIFTY-TWO

Vancouver

THERE WERE TOO many people. To get the job done really only required the pilots and a couple of climbers who were familiar with the mountains along the border. Everybody else could be briefed later and it wouldn't make the slightest difference to the operation, in fact everything would run more quickly and smoothly that way. But since this involved several different agencies from two countries the name of the game had become protocol, and Andy Cutler was rapidly losing interest.

The RCMP would be doing the flying on the Canadian side and in addition to their pilots they had sent along Inspector Mandell to oversee their interest in the case. Mandell had jughandle ears, a bald head and no sense of humour at all. He didn't like the idea of using his people on an American operation that was unlikely to produce any result, he didn't seem to like Cutler, and he definitely didn't like the longhaired climber in the corner.

The American DEA would be making the arrest and had sent two field agents up from Portland. One of them was a woman and Inspector Mandell didn't like that very much either.

The U.S. Air Force, which was going to handle the flying on the American side, had sent two pilots and an observer, a Colonel who wasn't too happy about the idea of having the RCMP involved at all. He remembered what had happened the last time RCMP pilots had tried to help on this particular case, and had made it clear to Mandell that the success probability of the mission would go up sharply if USAF did the flying on both sides of the border.

And the Vancouver Police Department had decided to send one of its own brass along. To do what, wondered Cutler. Observe all the other observers? It turned out to be a tall, impressive looking Captain named Sutherland who took one fast glance around the room and called Cutler aside.

'Sergeant, who really matters here?'

Cutler wasn't sure what that meant until Sutherland added, 'In terms of the air search that is.'

'Only the pilots sir, and those two guys in the corner with the maps.'

'Okay Sergeant, watch this.'

Captain Sutherland moved to the front of the room, and without seeming to raise his voice, caught everyone's attention with his first word.

'Gentlemen, Madam, as you all know we're here to finish a job that should have been finished almost a year ago . . .' Cutler could see Mandell glaring, and the Air Force Colonel smiling, '. . . I believe that the reason for the failure on that occasion was inadequate preparation and inadcquate communication and coordination between the various agencies involved . . .' Mandell lightened up a bit and the DEA types keyed in on 'communication and coordination' '. . . so I'm pleased to see this many senior people here today . . .' Sutherland looked like the kind of lawyer who sat on a lot of boards and all the 'senior people' were quite happy to suck up to him. 'Now, since there isn't much time I suggest that we get started right away. I've reserved a more comfortable conference room for us upstairs and lunch will be available for anyone who wants it.'

Cutler doubted that he had reserved any room or ordered any lunches. But there would be plenty of empty rooms upstairs at noon on a Saturday, and a call to the cafeteria would have lunch available quickly enough.

'Sergeant Cutler,' Sutherland made it sound like an afterthought, 'if you could see to the others, we should be done in an hour or so . . .'

He opened the door and somehow, without seeming to do anything, separated Mandell, the DEA agents and the Air Force Colonel from the group and led them out of the room. Less than a minute later he was back, and in a voice just loud enough for everyone still in the room to hear, he spoke to Cutler.

'Okay Sergeant, I've cleared the deadwood out of the way for you. I'll keep them amused upstairs until you're finished here and then try to get them to buy whatever you've planned. How long is it going to take you?'

'Probably about an hour sir.'

'Fine. We'll be in Room 502, just call me there when you're done.' And he was gone, leaving Cutler feeling awed, and everyone else feeling important and ready to work.

Soon there were maps spread everywhere and the two climbers, Paul Goossens and a friend of his named Henderson, were going over all the routes they felt possible for a man on foot or on skis at this time of year, and the pilots were making notes and putting marks on their own maps.

Cutler didn't contribute much himself, except to make sure that there was plenty of coffee and sandwiches.

CHAPTER FIFTY-THREE

North Cascade Mountains

SHE WAS FACE DOWN in the snow and her legs and skis were tangled beneath the corpse of Walter Matheson. She made no move to extricate herself or to clear the snow away from her nose and mouth. Her mind was numb and she floated in a timeless trance, drifting slowly over the glowing red embers of hell.

But when her first inhalation brought a lungful of snow, her body jerked into action without guidance, and as she twisted onto her side her mind returned.

ALEX! Oh God . . . *He had shot Alex*. Frantically she tried to pull free, to run to where Alex lay only a dozen feet away, but her legs were trapped and she couldn't move.

She grabbed Matheson's body and rolled it off her legs. She stared for one brief instant of madness into the bloody eye socket and then drew her knees up so that she could reach her feet and unlatch her bindings. It was then, lying in the snow on her side, groping for her feet, that she heard the sweetest sound of her life.

'Linda?'

The last binding came free and she rolled onto her feet and ran to him.

'Alex, oh Jesus, Alex, are you alright?'

Sobbing with joy and sorrow she fell to her knees in the snow beside him. He was lying on his back, still strapped into his pack, pressing his right shoulder with his left hand and staring at her in pain and bewilderment.

'What happened? How did you get here?'

She said nothing, just took his face between her two hands and kissed him as gently as she could, then began unfastening his pack straps.

'What happened? Matheson was here and he shot me . . . Has he gone? . . . Where is he? . . . I think he's crazy . . .'

He lay still, speaking slowly, confused.

'Shut up. He's not coming back. He's dead so don't worry about him.'

The straps were all loose but she left him lying against the pack and moved to undo his ski bindings.

'Can you move your right arm?'

He lifted the arm an inch or two and gasped with pain. 'It hurts, God how it hurts.'

She finished with the skis and then said, 'I'm going to have to take your jacket and shirt off. Even if it does hurt, I've got to do it Alex, okay?'

'Okay.'

Alex was able to sit up, and the jacket and zip-front pile shirt came off easily, but underneath he was wearing a body-hugging long sleeve undershirt and he groaned with pain and almost passed out when she raised his arm to get it off over his head.

The shoulder was a mess, especially at the back where the bullet had exited, but there was no arterial blood spurting out and he had been able to move the arm, so she hoped that the damage was less serious than it appeared. At least the front, the part Alex could see, didn't look too bad.

He sounded fairly calm and rational and she wondered if she would have been able to hold herself together as well if it had been her who had been shot.

She took off her own jacket and light pile sweater. The sweater was made of a fleecy material called bunting and was the softest garment available. She draped it over his shoulder and tied it in place as well as she could with his undershirt, then helped him into his pile shirt and outer jacket. She could feel the cold through her own underwear and was glad for Alex's sake that there was no wind.

She looked at him. He seemed alright, didn't appear to be going into shock. 'Do you think you can ski, or should I set up the tent so you can wait while I go for help?'

'I don't know. Help me up.'

She put her jacket back on and then, as gently as she could, she helped him stand and watched as he took a tentative step, watched him stare in fascination when he saw Matheson's strangely mutilated face.

'What happened to him?'

Alex stepped slowly through the snow until he was looking straight down at the dead man.

'Did someone shoot him too? I don't remember anything after he shot me.'

'We were lucky Alex, that's all,' she said quietly. 'He didn't hear me coming and I just managed a lucky stab with my pole.' She came to stand beside him. 'I wonder how he knew to come here?'

Alex put his uninjured arm around her and leaned on her for support.

'He said that he knew everything, that he could figure out my route because he had unlocked the secret power of his mind. He was crazy Linda, completely insane.'

They stood like that, she supporting him, and neither able to look away from the strange face for almost a full minute. Finally Alex said, 'If you can help me put on his snowshoes and rig some kind of sling for my arm I'll try to make it down to the car.

He shuffled back along his own footsteps and sat on the pack while she untied the snowshoes from Matheson's frozen feet, and transferred them to his. When she finished that she took off her jacket again and then her undershirt. Despite the sunshine it was cold, and gooseflesh rose on her skin and her nipples puckered before she could get the jacket back on. Her undershirt was the same stretchy, long sleeved kind that Alex had been wearing and using the two of them she was able to fashion a fairly comfortable sling for him.

'Just sit there for a minute Alex.' She walked toward the body. 'I'm going to drag him behind those trees, and the pack too.'

She took a strong grip on the collar of the red shirt and began to pull. It was hard work, made harder by the deep snow, and it took several minutes to make the fifteen feet to the shelter of the trees. She was sweating hard when she finally got there and she squatted down beside the corpse to catch her breath. She wiped her forehead and was about to stand up and return for the pack when she saw the light tan of some kind of leather belt or pouch where Matheson's wool shirt had pulled clear of his pants.

At first with idle curiosity and some revulsion, but then with growing excitement she pulled the shirt out all the way around and unbuckled the belt, knowing by its weight and feel what she would find inside . . .

CHAPTER FIFTY-FOUR

Vancouver

THE MEETING was going well enough, but Cutler was unhappy. He liked Paul Goossens and truly regretted having had to lie to him, but he was sure that the young climber would not have agreed to help otherwise.

On the other hand, Cutler thought, maybe I told him the truth. For all I know Townsend *is* being forced to do this against his will. But he doubted it. If Townsend was carrying another shipment across for Matheson it was probably for one of the usual reasons. Money or adventure. Probably both.

It was too bad. Townsend had seemed like a nice guy and Cutler almost felt sorry for him. He had fallen into this by accident, but soon, if the pilots got lucky, he would be in the slammer.

Fuck it. Cutler stubbed out a cigarette with more force than he needed. Just fuck it. If Townsend got sent up it would serve him right. He had had every chance. Holley had bent over backward to treat him well but he had lied from start to finish and refused every offer of help.

Cutler lit another cigarette and calmed down. Townsend was probably skiing at Lake Tahoe or Aspen, and Matheson was probably having the shipment brought in through Miami, and the whole thing would go the same route that ninety percent of all drug cases went. Down the fucking tube.

He poured a cup of coffee and leaned back against the wall and tuned out the talk of passes and trails and altitudes and search quadrants; thought of Valerie, and what they should do next weekend.

'Sergeant Cutler?'

Someone was calling his name and he snapped back out of dreamland.

'Sergeant Cutler?'

It was a very young constable looking at him from the doorway.

'Yes?'

'Sorry to interrupt sir, but there's no telephone in this room and there's a call for you. A long distance call. You can take it in 213 if you like. I'll have them switch it through.'

Cutler was grumpy and unhappy and didn't want to talk to anybody on the telephone. But he didn't want to hang around this room either, and it was probably Holley so he could hardly refuse to answer.

'Sure, lead on.'

He was gone for more than fifteen minutes and when he returned he walked into the room and said nothing for another minute. He just stood and listened to the talk at the table, watched fingers pointing to maps and pencils making notes.

Finally he spoke.

'Party's over folks.'

They all looked up at him.

'It looks like we're not going to need an air search after all.' He looked at the two RCMP pilots. 'You guys can go home, and you guys . . .' he turned to the USAF pilots, '. . . are to wait here. It looks like one of you is going to get to take the DEA people into the hills. The bigshots are on their way downstairs and they'll tell you all about it.'

He turned to the two climbers and said, 'You guys come with me.'

He took them to the next room. 'Paul, your friend Alex Townsend is on his way to a hospital in Seattle. I've just spoken to his girlfriend on the telephone. She says he's been shot, but it looks like he's going to be okay. I'm sorry I can't tell you anything more than that right now, except that it looks like I was right, that he was doing this under threat and I doubt that he'll be charged with anything.'

He looked at them in silence for a few seconds then said, 'Do you know where Hannegan Pass is?'

They both nodded.

'And you can get around on skis okay?'

They nodded again.

'Well, if you go back to the other room and make those two facts known you'll probably be asked to shepherd a couple of American narcs on an investigation. You'll get to see a fairly fresh corpse and sixty-six pounds of cocaine.'

The two climbers started for the door but Goossens stopped halfway there and said, 'Do you want me to call you when we get back to let you know what happened?'

Cutler took a deep drag on his cigarette and spoke through the smoke as he exhaled. 'You can call if you want to,' he walked past them and out of the room, 'but nobody's going to be answering my telephone this weekend.'

CHAPTER FIFTY-FIVE

Seattle

THE SUN WAS STREAMING in through the window and the room looked as cheerful as a hospital room ever can. Linda had bought the biggest, most colourful Fuschia she could find and put it on a table by the window, and brought a stack of books and magazines, which now lay in disarray on the floor beside Alex's bed.

They had told the same story over and over. On Saturday night to the Seattle Police and on Sunday morning first to the DEA and then to Lieutenant Holley who had flown up from San Francisco. The story hadn't varied, and it had been easy to tell because it was almost true.

Almost. There had been one addition and one omission. The addition was death threats from Walter Matheson: Alex and Gordon had saved his life after the crash and he had responded by threatening to end theirs if they did not carry his cocaine. The omission was the matter of money: they said nothing of the fifty thousand dollars.

The same for Gordon's death. They told it almost as it had happened, adding only that Matheson had ordered the deaths.

And finally they told of trying to disappear by moving to a house under Linda's name, and of Matheson finding them and once more ordering them to carry for him or die. And again they failed to mention money. Or rather, Alex failed to mention the twenty-five thousand he knew about, and Linda failed to mention the vastly larger sum he didn't know about. She had put the money belt on under her jacket when she was out of Alex's sight and had not mentioned it to him on the walk out or the drive to Seattle. She had known that he would be hospitalized and probably heavily drugged, that there was a risk that he might be unable to maintain the lie under police interrogation. If that happened . . . well, what he didn't know he couldn't talk about, and the contents of that belt would be waiting at the end of whatever the courts did to them.

But it hadn't happened. The cathartic effect of being able to tell most of the truth for the first time in six months, and the emotion blunting effect of the demerol, had made it easier; letting him tell his small lies without guilt, letting him face Lieutenant Holley without fear.

A week after Alex had been carried into the emergency ward of Harborview hospital the attending physician in charge of his case told him that he was going to heal just as well at home as at the hospital.

'Stay in tonight, and I'll have another look at you in the morning, but I don't think that there's anything that we can do for you here that can't be done at home. You may or may not regain 100% of the motion in your shoulder joint, but it'll be close. You'll lose some of your strength, but all things considered you're lucky to be alive at all.' He started for the door. 'Have your ladyfriend change the dressings twice a day and come and see me in my office in a week.'

When the doctor was gone Linda said, 'Do you feel up to a short walk?'

'Sure, there's nothing wrong with my legs.'

Alex struggled into jeans and a sweatshirt and Linda helped him with his socks and shoes.

'There's a park just a block from the hospital, let's go and get some fresh air while the sun is still shining.'

The day was warm for the first of March and they sat together on a bench in the little park letting the afternoon sun melt the winter from their bodies.

'How do you feel?'

'My shoulder hurts like hell every time I move, and I'm worried about whether I'll get my strength back, but I just feel so good about being clear of Walter Matheson that I think you could cut off my other arm and I wouldn't mind.' He dropped his good hand into her lap and she took it in both of hers. 'You have no idea how good it felt to be able finally to tell the truth, and to be able to lie down at night without worrying about who might be knocking on the door in the morning.'

He stood up and stretched in the sun, rotating his upper body one way and then the other. 'Just to be standing here in the sunshine with you seems to be almost a miracle.' He looked down at her. 'Do you understand what I'm saying? For the first time in six months we can make plans for tomorrow without having to wonder if we'll still be alive tomorrow.'

She tugged him gently back onto the bench. 'I've got something for you.' She reached into her purse. 'If you're making plans for tomorrow you might like to have a look at this.'

It was an envelope addressed to Linda. Inside was a brief handwritten note on a single sheet of paper:

'Thanks for your letter. Why don't you drag your new man out here for a visit sometime soon? Everybody misses you. Especially me.'

It was signed 'Love, Michael'.

'Michael?' said Alex. 'Oh, the photographer. Your partner.'

'Ex-partner.'

'You want to take a holiday in New York?'

'Someday. The important thing is that he says he got my letter.'

'Your letter?'

'Actually, it wasn't a letter, it was a package with a letter inside.' She turned on the bench so that she was facing him. 'I didn't know how it would go at the hospital Alex. You aren't much of a liar, and if the police got rough with you, especially if you were groggy and weak, I thought that there was a chance you might not be able to hold it all together.'

Alex started to interrupt, hesitated, then said, 'I understand.'

'Anyway, it looks like it's all over and the police are finished with us, so . . .'

She told him of finding the money belt on Walter Matheson's corpse, and of her decision not to tell him. 'There was two hundred and fifty-five thousand dollars in there Alex. And three little bottles full of what are probably emeralds. So I just put it all in a package and sent it off to Michael for safekeeping. This letter is just him telling me that he received it and that everything's okay.'

'Two hundred and fifty thousand dollars?'

'Two hundred and fifty-five. Plus a bunch of emeralds. Plus the fifty thousand from last summer, plus the twenty-five thousand from this winter. All together Michael has Three hundred and thirty thousand dollars and three bottles of emeralds hidden away for us somewhere in New York.'

'Three hundred and thirty thousand dollars?'

'Plus a bunch of emeralds.' She stood up. 'If you're coming home tomorrow I'm going to have to get going. If I don't clean up the house and do some grocery shopping tonight you're going to take one look at the place and go straight back to the hospital.'

She helped Alex to his feet and continued, 'Anyway, I hope that two hundred and fifty-five thousand dollars and three jars of emeralds makes your last night in hospital a little more tolerable.'

Money had never been important to Alex. He had grown up in a family that had had enough never to worry about it, and as a young graduate he had landed a job which allowed him to carry on not worrying. When he quit that job and began to live on the wages of a junior mechanic he had had no trouble adjusting – he had been unhappy with money and he was now happy without, *ergo* money was not relevant. But that evening, lying on his hospital bed in the spring twilight, he began to realize something that anyone who grows up poor knows almost from birth: money that you have suffered for is always important.

Three hundred and thirty thousand dollars. And the emeralds. Four hundred thousand? Half a million? A million? What would they do with it?

The last thought in his mind as he fell asleep was that it really didn't matter what they did with it. They had each other and they had their freedom. No amount of money was as important as that.

CHAPTER FIFTY-SIX

Seattle

SHE SAW HIM sitting on the front steps as she pulled Alex's van in to the kerb and almost drove away again, but decided that it would be pointless. There was something inevitable about the man and she felt that wherever she might drive away to, he would be waiting for her when she arrived, so she shut off the engine and stepped out.

He stood up and approached the van. 'Miss Cunningham, I'd like to talk to you for a few minutes.'

'Does it matter if I want to talk to you, Lieutenant?'

'Not particularly. I'd rather we sat down with a drink somewhere and talked peaceably, but I can probably get the Tacoma Police to book you for something and we can go down to the station and do it the hard way if you'd rather. It's really up to you.'

For a moment she debated telling him to fuck himself, then shrugged her shoulders and said, 'Come on upstairs. You can help me carry the groceries.'

'Miss Cunningham,' Holley was sitting in the living room in a chair to the right of the fireplace, 'before I say anything else there's two things I want to make clear. The first is that as long as you and your friend Townsend stick to your stories there's not a court in the country that would convict you of anything. In fact, if I were stupid enough to charge either of you with anything I'd probably get reprimanded.'

Linda didn't say anything. She was half standing, half sitting on the edge of the sideboard on the other side of the room.

'That's the first thing. The second is that I personally don't think that you've been telling the truth.' He paused for her reaction, but she continued to lean against the sideboard saying nothing, so he continued. 'Alex may be a pretty nice guy, but he's not much of a liar and it's pretty clear that he wasn't pushed into this business by any threats from Walter Matheson. He *chose* to get involved. I don't know why, maybe money, maybe for the adventure, maybe because his friend was involved, but it was his choice.'

He paused again but Linda remained silent.

'What do you know about Walter Matheson?'

'Just what I said I knew about him in the statements I made to you, to the Seattle Police and to the DEA.' She walked across the room and sat down in a chair facing him. 'Look, you're here because you want something, so why don't you stop screwing around and just tell me what it is, okay?'

He kept himself under tight control. 'Very well, what I want is to put a man named John Tomlinson in prison for the rest of his life, and in order for me to do that, now that Walter Matheson is dead, Alex is going to have to go back into the cocaine business.'

She looked at him without saying anything for almost thirty seconds, long enough for him to decide that she was not going to say anything at all. Then she spoke quietly: 'Tiger bait doesn't have a very high survival potential Lieutenant, and Alex has already paid a pretty high price. What makes you think that he'll be willing to get involved again? And why are you telling me about this? If you want Alex to help you why don't you go to the hospital and ask him?'

'I don't think Alex likes me very much.'

'And you think *I* do?'

'No, but you're a little more sensible than he is. You're not going to fall apart or run for a lawyer if I say something that upsets you. And as to the price he's paid, let's not get the violins out yet. He's still alive, which is maybe more than he deserves, and I get the feeling that he didn't come out of this broke either.

'I'm not an idiot Linda.' It was the first time he had used her name and it startled her. 'And I've spent more than twenty years dealing with every kind of lie that can be told. When he made that first carry with Wilson, money changed hands. So let's not cry too much about poor Alex.'

Linda stood up. 'I think this meeting is over, Mr. Holley. You've read all the statements, and you just said yourself that there's nothing anyone can do to us, so why don't you leave. If you want to talk to Alex I can't stop you, but if you push him you *will* be talking to his lawyer.'

Holley made no move to go, just smiled and said, 'Sit down, sit down. I have absolutely no intention of talking to Alex. If I can't convince you then I'll walk out the door and you'll never see or hear from me again.'

Linda sat down. 'So what are you going to do, tell me that this guy you want to put in prison is some kind of monster, that it's our moral duty to help you?'

Holley replied with quiet intensity, 'I happen to think that he is a monster. Personally I'd like to see him in the gas chamber and not in jail, but I also think that one of the things that makes this country a good place to live is that cops like me don't get to make those decisions. And I think it's the moral duty of every decent human being to help put a stop to people like him.

'If I were talking to Alex that's exactly what I'd say, and he would probably buy it, because I think he is a pretty decent guy. But I also know that you'd be the one who made the decision, and I'm pretty sure that you'd let half the human race go down the drain before you let him get involved in this again. You may have a soft spot for Alex Townsend, but it's the only soft spot you've got.'

She started to speak, but he cut her off. 'John Tomlinson is one of the biggest smackmen on the west coast, and I think that you lived in the gutter long enough – yes, I do my homework – long enough to know what that means in terms of human misery. Matheson was selling coke to him, and he's waiting for the thirty kilos you were carrying.'

'So?'

'Have you read any newspapers this week? Watched any news?'

'Why?'

'You haven't seen your name have you?'

'What are you trying to say?'

'The body of an unidentified white male was found in the North Cascades last weekend. He had obviously been murdered but that was all that anyone knew. There was nothing about thirty kilos of cocaine, and no mention of you or Alex, just one unidentified body. Page one for a day and then page nineteen and then nothing. Sometime soon we'll identify the body from its fingerprints and that'll make headlines for another day or so and that's going to be it, no one will ever know what happened and in two weeks the whole thing will be forgotten. But Tomlinson will know what happened, and he'll probably be just as happy to buy from Alex as from Matheson.'

'And you'll be there when he does. Right?'

'That's right.'

Linda didn't buy it. 'And while you're shooting the tiger who's looking after the bait? No thanks Lieutenant; get some undercover hotshot from the DEA to do it for you, or do it yourself, but leave us out of it.'

She stood up again. 'You said that if I said no, you'd never bother us again. Well I'm saying no. Do you understand?' She crossed the room and waited by the door of the entryway.

Holley followed her across the room, walked through the entryway and stopped at the top of the stairs. 'The reason I want Alex is that Tomlinson may already know about him.' The sympathy had gone out of his voice, and he looked down at Linda with no apparent emotion. 'I won't be calling you again. If you won't cooperate, you won't cooperate, and I'm going to have to try something else. It probably won't work but it's the only thing I can think of.'

He stepped down one step, but was still far taller than Linda. 'When I get back to California tomorrow I'm going to get the word out that you and Alex hijacked that coke.' He was implacable, immutable, a black stone-man, and as he spoke Linda could feel herself growing old. 'Nobody is likely to care much about Matheson, but like I said, Tomlinson is expecting his thirty kilos.'

He started down the stairs, but stopped halfway and turned to face her one last time. 'That shipment is worth a few million to him. I expect that he'll take time out of his busy schedule to come and pick it up.' He turned and descended the remaining stairs, speaking over his shoulder as he went. 'Nothing's free Linda, nothing at all.'

APPENDIX

A Bibliography of Mountain Fiction

Short Stories, Novels, Drama, Films

The following list includes books specifically about climbing, adventure stories set in wild or mountainous country, stories about skiing, and tales about everyday life in mountains. It is a bibliography for those interested in the spirit and influence of mountains in fiction. It has been organized with the minimum of technical jargon and abbreviations, in the hope that it will be more illuminating and entertaining for the general reader.

Authors are listed alphabetically, followed by a chronological list of their work. The country and date of first publication is noted, followed by a list of the main publishers. Where a book has been published simultaneously or with a just a short delay in the UK then the US, or vice versa, only one date is given. Subheadings are included before the compiler's summary and assessment. This is sometimes followed by publisher's jacket comments where they add some extra information. Contemporary review comments (undated if in a journal following the year of publication) and other expert comment (usually taken from well-known retrospective articles) are also added. All regular journals and magazines that review books, the main retrospective articles and anthologies are noted in a preliminary list and thereafter noted in shortened form to save space.

A star system to indicate merit has been incorporated with the obvious proviso that this is highly subjective. Comparisons are invidious – how can one piece of literature be measured against another if the intent and content are poles apart? Thus the absence of stars does not necessarily mean that the story lacks merit. However those with stars come with our wholehearted recommendation! Other works of merit can be identified by contemporary review comment, though it is well to remember that tastes change with the passage of time.

An invaluable starting point for this bibliography was the list compiled by Jill Neate and contained in her *Mountaineering Literature* (Cicerone Press, 1986) which is often referred to as 'Neate'. This is laid out in a conventional manner for library reference and should be consulted if fuller publication details are required.

No summary of this nature can ever be complete; few weeks go by without the discovery of more titles that could be incorporated. We very much hope people will write and advise us of items we have missed, of unrecognised classics and to tell us of new material as it appears. Such correspondence should be sent to: Audrey Salkeld, 7 Linden Road, Clevedon, Avon BS21 7SL.

Magazines: Climber and Hillwalker (Glasgow); *Climbing* (Aspen); *High* (Sheffield); *Mountain* (Sheffield); *Mountain Gazette** (Denver); *Mountain Life** (London); *Off Belay** (Seattle); *On the Edge* (Oldham); *Rock and Ice* (Denver); *Strand Magazine** (London); *Summit* (Fleetwood, Pennsylvania). **indicates magazines now defunct*

Journals: The Alpine Journal (London); *American Alpine Journal* (New York); *Appalachia* (Boston); *Climbers' Club Journal* (London and Sheffield); *The Fell and Rock Climbing Club Journal* – abbreviated to *Fell and Rock Journal* (Lancaster); *Himalayan Journal* (Bombay);

Anthologies: A Treasury of Mountaineering Stories, edited by Daniel Talbot (Putnam, New York) 1954 – sometimes referred to as *Talbot's Treasury*; *The Games Climbers Play* (Diadem, London) 1979.

Critical essays (in date order):

Alps across the Footlights by J. Monroe Thorington (*American Alpine Journal*, 1940).

Stranger than Fact: The Climber in Fiction by E. Cushing and J. Monroe Thorington (*American Alpine Journal*, 1942).

The Writer in Snowdonia by Wilfrid Noyce (*Snowdon Biography*, Dent, London, 1957).

Mountaineering Fiction by Leroy D. Cross (*Appalachia* 135, 1962).

Mountains and Literature by Claire Engel (*Mountaineering in the Alps*, Allen and Unwin, London, 1971).

Literature and Art by Hugh Merrick (*Companion to the Alps*, Batsford, London, 1974).

Mountains in the Strand by Kevin Fitzgerald (*The Alpine Journal*, 1979).

Fiction in Mountaineering Literature by George Pokorny (*Climbing* 52, 1979; *The Alpine Journal*, 1980).

Mountaineering Fiction by W.R. Neate. A paper presented to the Sports Fiction Seminar, University of Birmingham, 1981.

Solo Faces: American Tradition and the Individual Talent by William Dowie (*Essays on the Literature of Mountaineering* edited by Armand E. Singer, West Virginia University Press, 1982). A critical discussion on *Solo Faces* (James Salter) and *Dangler* (Charles Gaines).

Spinning the Great Climbing Yarn by Jim Vermeulen (*Climbing* 110, 1988).

SHORT STORIES

TIM AHERN

Headwall *
US 1989
Ascent

Gay dancer gets into climbing, performs well, and captures first ascent local experts can't manage. Homo-phobic prejudices displayed by some, but the narrator at least is inspired to review his whole attitude to climbing.

GRANT ALLEN

The Adventure of the Impromptu Mountaineer *
UK 1898
Miss Cayley's Adventures – Part 5, Strand Magazine Vol.XVI

Humorous piece in which the intrepid Miss Cayley rescues the man she refuses to marry.

AL ALVAREZ

Summertime **
UK 1971
Daily Telegraph Magazine (London) and collected in *One Step in the Clouds.*

An accident on British rock. Powerfully captures the sick feeling of shock.

Night Out **
US 1971
New Yorker (New York) also *High* 27 and collected in *One Step in the Clouds.*

Young man/older man epic on Dolomite climb. (Inspired by the author's ascent of the Comici Route on the Cima Grande with Mo Anthoine.)

ANON

The Lost Chamois Hunter – A Tale of the Matterhorn
UK 1869
Every Boy's Annual (Routledge, London).

High Quest
UK 1967
Adventure Stories for Boys (Hamlyn, London)

Two young men re-enact their grandfather's climb to find out what happened.

PAT AMENT

A Moment of Personal Peril
US 1986
Rock and Ice 15

Another young man/older man story, where the latter suffers a chronic short-term memory loss; how will this affect him when they climb together? (May or may not be fiction – but told as a short story.)

BERNARD AMY

The Greatest Climber in the World *
UK 1978
Mountain 24 and collected in *The Games Climbers Play.* Translated from the French by Beverley Davitt.

'A modern Zen classic (of sorts)… Detailing the adventures of various Chinese mountaineering masters, the story culminates with an artistic prescription lodged in an innocent, virile, no-mind.' Michael Tobias, *Climbing* 48

Transgression *
UK 1985
Mountain 103. Translated from the French by Tim Lewis.

White foreigner wants to climb forbidden rock towers in Indian Territory. Initiation into night-time 'mushroom' ceremony helps him understand: 'Climbing is worth nothing unless it is a form of disobedience by gesture.' Not-climbing can also be an act of disobedience.

NICK ARNETT

A Climbing Classic (by Bob Bigrocks)
US 1983
Climbing 79

A small voyage into description of the bizarre Mungashungagong, as he is known to his Nepalese friends (translates roughly into 'Robert who has large stones').

MEL BANKS

Future Chock
US 1978
Climbing 48

Yosemite Valley, sometime in the future: features The Cruddy Co.; tourcard-holding, shaven-chested niceness; and The Pits.

Mechanical Advantage
US 1979
Climbing 53

Garvey and the climbots – last rock climber in the world versus the robots.

Rock of Ages
UK 1981
Mountain 81

Set many years into the future, with the Climbist Order of Monks.

First Person Approximal
US 1986
Climbing 96

Set in the future where the Privileged (or Privvies as they are amusingly known) experience climbing through the mode of 'vicarions' on the rock, whilst they themselves remain safe in a 'telepresence chamber.'

NICK BARRETT

Heaven Can Wait *
UK 1981
Oxford University M.C. Journal also *Crags* 29

Amusing, very short story of the climber-on-trial-for-his-ethics-and-abilities genre. But this climber is dead, so he gets to be judged by The Greats. Packed with good lines.

Rescue at Stoney *
UK 1983
Oxford University M.C. Journal

Runyon pastiche. Guy rescues wimp from first pitch of Alcasan hoping to win affections of said wimp's luscious doll. Grateful though she is, however, she fails to fall for his macho display, still having eyes only for the wimp.

RALPH BATES

Sirocco and Other Stories
US 1939
Random House (New York)

Wailing Precipice
UK c1939
First publication unclear: possibly from *The Miraculous Horde* (Cape, London) or maybe from his book *43rd Division*, a story of patrol actions in the Pyrenees during the Spanish Civil War. Collected in *A Treasury of Mountaineering Stories.*

Warfare in the mountains: lone rifleman has a good climb and rounds it off with an orgy of shooting.

PHIL BERGGREN

Shangri-La *
US 1988
Climbing 107

The leader of a trekking party stumbles upon a remote village, before being drawn to climb the mountain beyond. From village to his experience on the mountain is from Heaven to Hell, and there is a raven circling overhead....

MARTYN BERRY

Last Climb *
UK 1964
The Climber's Fireside Book (Heinemann, London)

Two men do their first and last climb on Cloggy as an atomic 'rocket' lands on Liverpool. (Naïvely dated in light of subsequent nuclear development.)

TALBOT BIELEFELDT

A Matter of Character
US 1984
Ascent

...and Ferndecker's character isn't all his mutterings would have you think. Nor his profession.

GEOFF BIRTLES

A Very Remarkable Man: The Climber
UK 1982
High 4 and 5

Spoof autobiography of big-name climber.

ALAN BLACK

The Shape of Things to Come
UK c1975
Scouting (London) also *Mountain Life* 18

If the Wardens take over... Cautionary tale set in North Wales.

ALGERNON BLACKWOOD

Pan's Garden
UK 1912
Macmillan (London)

Subtitled: A Volume of Nature Stories. Tales illustrating the powers of nature over man's mind, such as the old myth of the lady of the snows.

PHYLLIS BOTTOME

A Splendid Fellow *
UK 1946
Masks and Faces (Faber, London) and collected in *A Treasury of Mountaineering Stories.*

Alan Hamilton sets off to climb Kinchinjunga with Nancy Loring, daughter of a former president of the Alpine Club. If she performs well and proves herself 'submissive and faithful to the core', he will afterwards offer her his hand. She does, and he does... but her eyes have been opened.

W.E. BOWMAN

Binder Remembered (by O. Totter) *
UK 1985
High 28

More Rum-Doodling (see under novels). Binder's and Totter's early holidays together.

KAY BOYLE

Maiden, Maiden *
UK 1946
Thirty Stories (Simon and Schuster, New York) and collected in *A Treasury of Mountaineering Stories.*

Young woman goes to Alps with her (older, married) lover, and is attracted to their young guide. The two men set out on a climb together, but only one returns. Formed the basis for the film *Five Days One Summer* starring Sean Connery, Betsy Brantley and Lambert Wilson.

'D.H. Lawrence-like love affair between an English woman of sophistication and a primitive Swiss mountain guide.' Daniel Talbot

E.F. BOZMAN

The Princess and the Glass Mountain
UK 1930
Climbers' Club Journal and collected in *TheMountaineer's Weekend Book* Seeley Service (London) 1950.

Mock fairy tale: booted young man from the Alpine Club wins the young (and of course exquisitely beautiful) princess in face of rivals clad only in 'rubbers'. A snub to the modernists.

ELAINE BROOK

Rites of Passage *
UK 1990
One Step in the Clouds

Those with experience of Tibetan mysticism will understand the deeper journey hidden within this story.

ETIENNE BRUHL

The Great Match **
France 1930
Origin unknown. Published in English in *Appalachia* 1932 and collected in *A Treasury of Mountaineering Stories* and in *Ascent* (1980).

Competing French and Italian teams attempt route on Frêney Face of Mont Blanc. The place of voyeurism in modern mountaineering.

'Some of Bruhl's ideas are remarkably prescient... he believed that the 'spiritual factor' in climbing would vanish in the future and that few mountaineers would still attempt serious climbs solely from 'love of the sport'.' Allen Steck and Steve Roper, *Ascent*

JOHN BUCHAN

The Knees of the Gods *
UK 1907
Scottish Mountaineering Club Journal and collected in *The Mountaineer's Week-end Book* Seeley Service (London) 1950.

Dreaming mountaineer foresees a socialist future in which no less than five ex-presidents of the Alpine Club serve on the British Cabinet. Physical training and the reform of diet have produced national good health, so that the Cuillin Ridge may now be traversed overnight in winter and a succession of Aiguilles run up in a day! (Buchan may have predicted speed-climbing, but he sure as hell had no inkling of any end to Empire.)

HOWARD BUSSEY

Upper Crust
US 1970
Ascent

An extrapolation of an embryonic trend in climbing: the professional guiding service

A.E.C.

A Day's Play, A Climbing Story
UK 1912
In *Tales True and Otherwise* (Jones and Evans, London).

ROBIN CAMPBELL

The Adventure of the Misplaced Eyeglasses *
UK 1979
Scottish Mountaineering Club Journal

A further adventure for Sherlock Holmes and Dr. Watson in Scotland with Raeburn and Collie. Very successful parody.

The Case of the Great Grey Man **
UK 1986
Scottish Mountaineering Club Journal and collected in *One Step in the Clouds.*

Sherlock Holmes on Ben Macdhui, this time with Munro (he of the tables).

ANNIE N. CARRERA (pseudonym for Sue Kemp)

Showdown at Long Canyon *
US 1987
Rock and Ice 21

Entertaining tale of young Californian hotshot and famous German climber competing to make first free ascent of big desert route. But who better to perform this task than the man who put up the climb with aid ten years before?

GREG CHILD

The View from Credibility Gap *
US 1986
Rock and Ice 13 (titled *Credibility Gap*)

All the characters in this story display gaps in their personal credibilities. Wilson and Bernice, married for two years, thrive on continual argument. Follett is caught between the two. Deposited on a glacier in the Kichatnas, they have to contend with the boredom forced upon them by storms and their own company. A game of musical tents ensues until the weather clears and the two men set off for their summit. Attempt is abandoned when they believe they see wild beast near base camp and decide they must 'save' Bernice.

No Gentlemen in the Himalaya **
US 1985
Climbing 89 and collected in *One Step in the Clouds.*

Catholic priest leads Himalayan expedition to investigate strange new religion. Amusing twist.

In Another Tongue **
US 1988
Climbing 110 and collected in *One Step in the Clouds.*

Young and older porter discuss the inexplicable ways of foreign climbers on K2.

GEOF CHILDS (Geoffrey Childs)

The Flesheaters
US 1975
Climbing Nov/Dec and collected in *Mirrors in the Cliffs*

Explores how opportunists build their reputations on the fatal accidents of others.

Bah *
US 1985
Rock and Ice 10

Strange aftermath of Karakoram expedition – (how some cultures just don't mix!). A charming portrayal of bestiality.

Leviathan **
US 1984
Ascent and collected in *One Step in the Clouds.*

Powerful expedition story.

Poontanga *
US 1975-6
Ascent

Spoof. Tragic expedition recreated from letters of lost leader.

M. AMOS CLIFFORD

The Ghost of Don Gregorio
US 1987
Rock and Ice 18

A story of ignorance and violation of long-established cultures. Two climbers bag first ascent. In so doing they destroy, and the destruction is fuel for their further successes.

LARRY COATS

Ice Cold
US 1986
Rock and Ice 15

Beware of visiting your friends in hospital after a climbing accident, lest their problem becomes yours. (Interestingly, has character called Irvine, dressed in shabby tweed knickers.)

JAMES COLLINS

The Only Way is Up
US 1975
Climbing Nov/Dec

In which a 16 year-old learns that the substance of climbing is doing, not talking about it.

JEFF CONNOR

My Uncle George
UK 1974
Mountain Life 13

Story of small boy discovering mountains and the surprising world of mountaineers on a weekend trip to North Wales.

The Hardest Climb of his Life *
UK 1974
Mountain Life 14

Terminally ill man settles for one last climb that is just beyond his abilities: better to die thus than waste away. Successfully past the crux, however, he changes his mind and makes it to the top. Thought provoking miniature with ironic final knife-twist.

'COPPERHEAD'

The Hulking Brute
US 1981
Climbing 66

Perspiring Hulking Brute fails yet again on *Nemesis* but mysterious stranger experiences no such problems.

RICHARD COUCHON

A Wall of Eternity
UK 1979
Off Belay 45

Paul becomes entranced with climbing on a mausoleum built into a hillside, and climbs there once too often.

DAVID CRAIG

The Escapist **
UK 1988
One Step in the Clouds

Climb stimulates man to ponder problems of his jaded marriage.

WILLIAM CRAIG

The Lost Arrow
US 1978
Climbing March/April

The fastest ever descent from Lost Arrow – when it falls down.

KEN CROCKET

October Day **
UK 1988
Scottish Mountaineering Club Journal as *Raeburn's First Climb* and collected in *One Step in the Clouds.*

Young boy's escapism leads to exciting new pastime – and hope.

JOHN DANIEL

The Fall
US 1977
Climbing Nov/Dec

After falling for the first time in eight years, a climber is alone while his friend goes for help. He ponders retrospectively the lost innocence of youth in both climbing and love.

The Way of the White Serpent **
US 1980
Ascent and collected in *One Step in the Clouds*

A shortage of women causes chosen young males of tribe to undergo rigorous test. Winner gets the woman – but losing has its consolations, too.

PETER DEBENHAM

Mountain Brothers
UK 1970
Evening News – 24 June (London)

An old man lies to save his friend's feelings.

ED DOUGLAS

The Sacred Well
UK 1989
On the Edge 15

A man's conscience prevents him from facing dead climbing partner's wife.

Nothing but the Devil
UK 1990
Climbers' Club Journal

The meeting of ethics, old and new; spotty, lycra-clad youth is confronted by the ghost of Mallory and fails to fully exploit a unique opportunity.

J.H. DOUGHTY

Dream Rocks
UK 1939
Hill-writings of J.H. Doughty, collected by H.M. Kelly, (Rucksack Club, Manchester).

SIR ARTHUR CONAN DOYLE

The Final Problem ***
UK 1893
First published in *Strand Magazine* Vol.6 and collected in *Memoirs of Sherlock Holmes* (Newnes, London 1984).

Describes the disappearance of Holmes and Moriarty, locked in deadly embrace, above the Reichenbach Falls. (The whole story has an alpine setting, Holmes and Watson crossing the Gemmi Pass.)

BIL DUNAWAY

The Suspended Idol
US 1972
Climbing July/Aug

An interesting assignment for a skier/climber: to bring a 30lb box over the Austrian/Swiss border – until the box gets stuck.

G.J.F. DUTTON

The Ridiculous Mountains **
UK 1984
Diadem (London) also in paperback reprint 1990 with illustrations by Albert Rusling.

The escapades of The Doctor and his two friends in the Scottish Highlands, a collection of 20 humorous stories which lovingly distil the Scottish experience like fine malt whisky. The individual stories were first published as follows:

The Loosening Up (1968)
A Good Clean Break (1974)
Finishing off a Top (1974)
The Craggie (1975)
Once in a While (1976)
Flies (1977)
A Yacht Meet (1978)
A Cave Meet (1981)
An Occasion (1982)
Man's Faithful Friend (1983)
UK 1968-1983
Scottish Mountaineering Club Journals

Chalking it Up
UK 1982
Climber and Rambler May

Fixing Us Up (originally titled *The Dreepie*)
A Stiff Upper Lip
UK 1983
Cold Climbs (Diadem, London)

Sportsmanship
A Wet Day
One of the Least Frequented Parts of Scotland
A Daughter of the Revolution
Winter Homes for All
Old Man Ahoy
UK 1984
The Ridiculous Mountains (Diadem, London)

'Every story is different… and full of a rich, pungent and almost stinging flavour, of which one never tires.' Jo Light, ***Fell and Rock Journal***

'…it is best to dip into them [the collection] occasionally rather than go through at one sitting, as in this way they preserve their freshness.' Geoffrey Templeman, ***Alpine Journal***

'Quiet sense of humour, bordering on restraint.' Muslim H. Contractor, ***Himalayan Journal*** **42**

Midges **
UK 1990
One Step in the Clouds. Originally read at the Mountain Literature Conference, Bretton Hall, 1989.

The Doctor's wiles defeat Wee Dander and his gang.

J. MENLOVE EDWARDS

End of a Climb **
UK 1937
Climbers' Club Journal and collected in several anthologies, also in *Menlove* (Gollancz, London) 1985.

Dreams and thought-flows of man relaxing after a climb.

Letter from a Man **
UK 1937
The Mountaineering Journal (Birkenhead) and collected in *The Games Climbers Play* also in *Menlove* (Gollancz, London) 1985.

Scenery For a Murder ***
UK 1939
Climbers' Club Journal and collected in *The Games Climbers Play* and also in *Menlove* (Gollancz, London) 1985.

A murder may or may not have happened, but the murderer undoubtedly exists – the siren song of the mountains.

A Great Effort **
UK 1941
Climbers' Club Journal and also in *Menlove* (Gollancz, London) 1985.

The narrator has recently been asked how he climbs, and pondering here cites an example of a route on which he made Great Efforts, but from which he had eventually to descend. His mental attitude is, however, undefeated.

NICK ELLENA

The Ledge
US 1973
Climbing Jan/Feb

Return to the scene of the climb causes man to relive previous accident.

H. F. ELLIS

Himalayan Adventure
UK 1977
Climbers' Club Journal

Another tall tale of derring-do (well in this case derring-didn't).

LES ELLISON

Doubt
US 1983
Climbing 79

Canyon expert sets out to tackle hard wall with ageing pioneer but dreams and realities merge as the climb begins.

ST. JOHN GREER ERVINE

The Mountain *
UK Date unknown
From *The Mountain and Other Stories* (Allen and Unwin, London) and collected in *A Treasury of Mountaineering Stories*.

Naive untravelled bachelor with lifelong desire to see mountains goes to Switzerland, where he is lured to his death by a terrible 'Young Woman'.

PHYLLIS R. FENNER (compiler)

Perilous Ascent
US 1970
Morrow (New York)

Subtitled: Stories of Mountain Climbing. An anthology. Authors include Don Knowlton, David Lavender, Edwin Muller, Robert Murphy and James Ramsey Ullman.

D.K. FINDLEY

Man in the Sky
US 1937
Colliers Magazine March (New York)

KEVIN FITZGERALD

Your Lovely Hills are Very Dangerous
UK 1974
Mountain Life May

Set in 1951. Dipsomaniac hallucinates his way from Llanberis Pass to Beddgelert before metamorphosis into sober climber. Other published stories exist, as well as fragments of autobiography written as short stories.

ROGER FRISON-ROCHE

Their Kingdom
France 1948
Extracted from *The Grand Crevasse* (see novels) and collected in *A Treasury of Mountaineering Stories*.

A short love story in the Alps.

DAVID GANCHER

The Ascent of Typewriter Face
US 1984
Ascent

Let your fingers do the climbing.

TERRY GIFFORD

The Downfall of St. Valentine's Day
UK 1987
Climbers' Club Journal

An ice climb on Kinder on St. Valentine's Day, which is also the Celtic feast of Imboc.

The Lady and the Raven
UK 1988
Climbers' Club Journal

A climb in Borrowdale where Lady meets the Raven at the turning of the year.

STEVEN GOULD

Peaches for Mad Molly **
UK 1989
The Best of New SF3 edited by Gardner Dozois (Robinson Publishing, London)

A *Mad Max*-style future: climbers live outside 750-floor tower block menaced by 'Howlers' and corruptible security men. Even the best of them need speed, cunning and gadgetry to survive. Exhilarating imagery.

MAXWELL GRAY (pseudonym of Miss Mary G. Tuttiett)

The Mysterious Guide
UK 1908
An Innocent Imposter (Longmans, London)

Subtitled: an Alpine Adventure

DAVE GREGORY

The Old Man's Pigeon Loft **
UK 1984
High 25 and collected in *One Step in the Clouds.*

The old man helps the climbers to help him.

The Horoscope *
UK 1984
Climbers' Club Journal

Beware the self-fulfilling prophecy! (More a skiing than climbing story.)

The Black Hollow
UK 1986
Climbers' Club Journal

Jealousy leads to murder on the crag (but poetic justice is done).

The Club
UK 1987
Climbers' Club Journal

Conversation overheard from behind two newspapers.

The Avon Party **
UK 1988
Climber and Hillwalker September

The world's first 'Climberware Party'.

New Year's Eve
UK 1988
Climbers' Club Journal

Skiing short story.

GREG GRIFFITH

The Red Sea
UK 1988
On the Edge 5

It's the 21st century (again) and rock climbing is big money for the manufacturing corporations. Red Luther is the best climber in the world: what is his secret?

M. JOHN HARRISON

The Ice Monkey
Running Down
UK 1988
The Ice Monkey and Other Stories (Unwin Paperbacks, London).

Potent, gritty stories. The first telling how climbing can foul up relationships; the second how self-absorbed malevolence can bring down mountains – in this case Pavey Ark. Original and most beautifully written.

MARC HELPERIN

The Schreuderspitze
US 1977
New Yorker 42 (New York), also in *The Best American Short Stories: 1978* (Houghton Mifflin, Boston) and *Prize Stories of the Seventies* from O. Henry Awards (Garden City, New York, 1981)

ERNEST HEMINGWAY

An Alpine Idyll **
US 1930s
First publication unknown, probably Scribners (New York) but collected in *Collected Short Stories* (Cape, London 1939) and *The First 49 Stories* (Cape, London 1944).

Very short, very macabre tale bringing new meaning to the term lantern-jawed. Two skiers who come into remote alpine village hear how a farmer, whose wife died when the village was snowbound, had to prop her frozen corpse in the coalshed till spring. At least it gave him somewhere to hang his lamp.

TOM HIGGINS

In Due Time
US 1972
Ascent

Contemporary satire written as A Play in Three Acts.

The Fiend
US 1969
Ascent

Being the world's best rock climber isn't enough for John: but at the age of twenty his fingers break off and he is burnt out. Such a disappointment to his mother.

BERNARD HOLLOWOOD

Pens Over Everest
UK 1952
Punch – 20 August (London). Reprinted in *Ascent* 1967.

Spoof expedition piece.

STAN HOLMES

The Adventures of Pinky Peterson and Arnie Offwidth
US 1982
Climbing 75

Yosemite in the future where Peterson and Offwidth discover joys of climbing for survival the old-fashioned way (as so many climbers in futuristic stories seem to!).

CHARLES HOOD

Bright Fire, Bright Ice **
US 1983
Climbing 77 and collected in *One Step in the Clouds*.

Sci-fi climbing. Rich eccentric pays his own fare for a one-way trip to Europa, one of Jupiter's moons. There are a lot of Crag X's Out There waiting to be explored.

Twelve Scenes from the Life of Crow
US 1984
Ascent

Crow is a solitary climber: he ice climbs; skis; goes mad in Antarctica; imitates lizards; climbs in the Himalaya and paints murals on crags and boulders; he can't get one-inch webbing to match his pants. He talks to an Inca mummy and finally to a real woman and they live together. An incident-packed mini-yarn.

The Climbing Wars
US 1989
Ascent

'Whimsical whodunit... Charles Hood is a unique manipulator of words and ideas, and we see him chuckling as he wove his reverse alphabetical tale of Alpine intrigue... Hood got his inspiration from *The Ski Murders* by George MacBeth.' Allen Steck and Steve Roper, *Ascent*

TOM HOPKINSON

Mountain Madness
UK 1935
Chambers Magazine (Edinburgh) and collected in *The Transitory Venus, Horizon* magazine (London) and in a *Treasury of Mountaineering Stories*

A group of climbers at a mountain inn discuss who is the greatest climber they have ever known. The proprietor believes he knows who – paradoxically a non-climber.

W.D. HORTON

The Swallow
UK 1985
Rock and Ice 11

Man climbing, partner below, and a swallow. Man falls, swallow dives, and in the confusion the one becomes the other.

WILLIAM HOWARTH

Wildmen
US 1974
Climbing July/Aug

Subtitled: from a tale by Ivan Lindgren. Climbers stripped of their clothing by dense undergrowth and vicious rock of a mountain, drape themselves in foliage to preserve decency, thus fuelling tourists' rumours of Sasquatch and Wildman sightings.

The Curmudgeon
US 1974
Climbing Sept/Oct

First of tales in which The Curmudgeon and friends feature. They encounter a freshly-returned-from-India Philadelphian hippy who proceeds to outclimb them in a very competitive and unenlightened-consciousness manner.

Volcanoes
US 1974/75
Climbing Dec/Jan

The Curmudgeon and friends are distressed to find sixty-three members of the walking, jogging, hiking and filing-up-mountains club 'The Volcanoes' camped below their climb.

Getaway
US 1975
Climbing Sept/Oct

The Curmudgeon and friends encounter Rangers' bureaucracy.

A Little Guiding Philosophy
US 1977
Climbing Jan/Feb

A light-hearted warning on the dangers of sponsorship in mountaineering.

A Solitary Bird
UK 1979
Off Belay 46

Three climbers have survived an avalanche – or so one of them thinks.

DAVE HUMBERSTONE

Bolt to the Future – 1998
UK 1988
High 73

Futurist forebodings with sport-climbing on Kilnsey, Malham and Gordale cocooned in bureaucracy, rules and red tape.

C.L. INKER

The Ascent of F Sharp
UK 1946
Journal of Midland Association of Mountaineers (Birmingham)

PAUL INSKIP

A Painful Mistake
UK 1982
Clevedon Mercury 5 February

Paul (16) resents returning to school while his companions stay to have fun hiking up an Andean peak. Nevertheless it's not always so lucky to be able to do what you want. (Written when the author was fourteen.)

STEVEN JERVIS

For the Record
US 1989
Ascent

Two men involved in fatal accident in the Cascades come back with separate versions of what happened.

JOE KELSEY

The Man Who Climbed Too Well
US 1984
Ascent

Further variation on Faust/Mephisto theme, though in this story there's no dramatic pact.

SCOTT KIMBALL

Free Motion
US 1984
Climbing 74

Subtitled: A Game of Amusement. Somewhere in America,sometime in the future, climbing is to be reduced to little more than a glorified arcade game. A very basic narrative.

KURT KRUEGER

Old Number 5
US 1982
Climbing 74

Subtitled: A Love Story. The 'narrator' is a number five Chouinard Stopper (all the stoppers and hexes and karabiners have characters, but they're very cutesy). Opportunity to view the climbing world through the senses of a different medium flawed by sentimentality.

LARRY KUZNIAR

It's a 5.10 Mantel into Heaven, Brother
UK 1976
Mountain 51 and collected in *The Games Climbers Play.*

Brave new world of regulated and monitored climbing in Yosemite.

MIKE LEAVER

Death of a Climber
UK 1987
High 61

Male climber's libido kindled as he introduces two female associates to the rocks, caves and mountains of Wales. Overambitious and inept erotica that might have improved with editing. 'The wind caught hold of their short night-dresses, as they stood like sirens against the barren landscape.'

STANISLAW LEM

Aniel's Accident *
Poland 1970s
Publisher unknown. From *More Tales of Pirx the Pilot* (Harcourt Brace, New York) 1982, translated from the Polish *Opowiescl o pilocie Pirxie* by Louis Iribarne. Collected in *Ascent* 1989.

Sci-fi. Search for missing quarter-ton robot on earthlike planet reveals it has inexplicably started climbing – because it malfunctioned, or because it was there?

RANDOLPH LICHFIELD

One Shall be Taken
US 1900
New Magazine.

VLADIMIR LIDIN

Glaciers
Soviet Union 1920s
From *Short Stories out of Soviet Russia* compiled and translated by John Cournos (Dent, London) 1929. Collected in *A Treasury of Mountaineering Stories.*

The other-worldliness of the mountains lulls Russian geologist into making a terrible confession to his friend. At high altitude, the friend seems to understand and to forgive, but as they return to more mundane reality, it becomes apparent that this is not so.

JEFF LONG

Female
US 1978
Mountain Gazette 72

On an all-male Himalayan expedition Matthew suffers retinal haemorrhages. As his sight recovers, he takes to wandering away from Base Camp, where one day he encounters ... a female.But she is not human. Only Matthew ever 'meets' her, and that by presence and feelings, not by sight. Does she exist, or is she mere fantasy?

The Soloist's Diary
US 1974
Ascent also collected in *Mirrors in the Cliffs.*

Rumours of an impossible wall have attracted many climbers: the summit seems unattainable – you are condemned to climb forever, or die in the attempt.

Cannon Mountain Breakdown
US 1975
Mountain Gazette 33

Public voyeurism of mountaineering accident, as seen by group of climbing bums.

Resurrection *
US 1976
Ascent

Grisly, nausea-invoking piece. Kurtz awakes on the mountain: he is dead – and alive. He moves around in the crevasses and ice caverns, his flesh rotting, his mind only half-knowing, noting but not understanding. Is this a tale of the living dead? The movements of dead bodies through glaciers? Or the way in which the living keep alive memories of their dead heroes? Described by the author as a satire on *The Soloist's Diary*.

The Ice Climber *
US 1976
Climbing March, and collected in *The Games Climbers Play.*

In the aftermath of shock following fatal accident on an ice route, the survivor is unable to recapture the reality of his friend and the fact of their accident. Already time is moving him on, away from both. Penetrating vignette of grief and bewilderment.

In Gentle Combat with the Cold Wind **
UK 1977
Mountain 56 and collected in *One Step in the Clouds.*

Ghost story. Climber gives lift to elderly hitch-hiker who turns out to be...

The Dead Peacock **
UK 1980
Mountain 76

Odd fact/fiction story of Chinese ascent of... Everest, was it?

Feathers
US 1981
Climbing 64

Subtitled: a United States of America Fairytale. Two climbers making a winter ascent of The Diamond (inexplicably) come under fire from Special Forces. One is killed and the other is left to fend off attacks from abseiling soldiers toting machine guns and grenades. Militaristic fantasy redolent of post Vietnam preoccupations.

Cannibals **
UK 1983
Mountain 89 and collected in *One Step in the Clouds.*

Chilling Himalayan expedition story. Two men are snowbound in a tent. When rescuers arrive, they find one only still alive and the partially-eaten remains of the other.

Angels of Light **
US 1984
Ascent

Amended and expanded later into novel of same name (see novels).

The Virgins of Imst **
UK 1990
One Step in the Clouds

Outsider beats villagers to high mountain cave housing their sacred 'virgin' and discovers her true identity.

JOHN LONG

The Devil's Wardrobe
UK 1980
Mountain 75

Fear of big wall exposure leads narrator to quit Yosemite and repair to Berkeley. There he stumbles on ancient man of mid-Eastern extract, who directs him to pass forty-five nights in a room full of coats. A tale of forbidden fruit.

Becoming Nothing *
US 1984
Climbing 84

Frostbite-maimed climber interviewed by psychiatrist remembers a non-existent partner. But the big question is – does the interviewee himself exist?

Willard the Gringo
US 1987
Rock and Ice 19.

Subtitled: Adapted from 'Ali the Persian' *Arabian Nights*. The story uses a classic format to poke fun at the Park Service with the poser – just how much can you fit into a threadbare daypack?

A Fool and his Money
US 1988
Climbing 110

Penniless student climber on a scholarship at expensive college falls for beautiful Latin American aristocrat who plays hard to get.

'I was appalled at your publication of John Long's story.... a banal repetition of the worst cliches in literature, climbing and woman-hating.' Jean Ella – writing to *Climbing* 112

For Everything its Season **
US 1989
Rock and Ice 31 and collected in *One Step in the Clouds.*

Steve Alexander is finally persuaded to talk of his first ascent of The Citadel with Russ Owens. Russ used to partner Steve's brother Vic until Vic was mysteriously killed on one of their climbs. Psychological thriller that keeps you guessing.

GEORGE MACBETH

The Ski Murders
UK 1964
First published in *Ambit Magazine* (London) then collected in the *Domesday Book* Scorpion Press (London) 1965.

A parody of the typical 'James Bond-type' thriller, written as a long poem.

WARD MARDEN

Rope's End
US 1982
Essays on the Literature of Mountaineering, edited by Armand E. Singer (West Virginia University) 1982.

Climber Vane plans revenge on old rival, ex war-hero Grant Messner.

A.E.W. MASON

The Guide
UK 1908
The Odd Volume (Simpkin Marshall, London) and reprintedin *The Sunday Express* (June 10, 1928)

The sadness of a Chamonix guide who finds the idea of an early death more appealing than the old age which now confronts him.

GUY DE MAUPASSANT

Ulrich the Guide **
France 1880s
Publisher unknown. *The Strand Magazine* Vol.XI 1896, and collected as *The Inn* in *The Mountain Inn and Other Stories* (Penguin, Harmondsworth) and in *A Treasury of Mountaineering Stories.*

Being snowed in for the winter, alone apart from a dog, can fire a man's imagination and turn his mind.

DAVID MAZEL

Future Chalk *
US 1987
Rock and Ice 17

Subtitled: Free Climbing with 'Conviction' in the 1990s. Humorous court case in which defendant is brought to book for violation of purist principles. Wonderful punchline.

C.E. MONTAGUE

In Hanging Garden Gully ***
UK 1923
From *Fiery Particles* (Chatto and Windus, London) and frequently collected, including in *One Step in the Clouds.*

Humorous tale illustrating how ignorance can breed confidence. One to delight the epicure – elegant and witty.

Action **
UK 1928
Action and Other Stories (Chatto and Windus, London) and collected in *A Treasury of Mountaineering Stories.*

At fifty-two, lonely widower, Christopher Bell suffers minor stroke leaving him numb down one side of the body. After reading the works of a great mountaineer, he ponders the problem of margin for error: just how finely can you pare it and still be safe? With little to lose apart from invalid old age, he decides to put it to the test.

SALLY MOSER

Confessions of an Ex-Valley Girl
US 1986
Rock and Ice 13

A window on a way of life with more 'memories' than 'confessions'.

VLADIMIR NABOKOV

Lance
US 1952
New Yorker – 2 February and collected in *Stories from the New Yorker* and *Nabokov's Dozen.*

Somewhat inscrutable story set in the future and using narrator's imagined descendant as the main subject. At a guess, Lance (this descendant) sets off to climb on another planet and sees there something the President doesn't wish to be known to the public. Hard to say for sure, though.

BARRY NELSON

The Climbing Mogul
US 1979
Off Belay 44

Head of equipment empire lacking climbing experience organizes expedition to much-tried Greenland 'big-wall'. Will he realize his ambition?

CHRIS NOBLE

Slater's Tale
US 1984
Ascent

Slater is dead, but a strange story he once told of his experiences on a mountain lives on in the narrator's memory. When he meets the doctor who tended Slater he learns a key fact that lends credibility to the tale.

SYBILLE NOEL

The Magic Bird of Chomo-Lung-Ma
US 1931
From *Tales of Mount Everest, The Turquoise Peak* (Doubleday, New York)

Collected Tibetan legends of demons and snowmen, by wife of early Everester.

M.O.

The Madness of the Mountains
UK 1902
Macmillan's Magazine August

Negative and unconvincing tale of woman who is both wife and mother of climbers. She so dreads mountain accidents that it ruins her life and eventually kills her – not the others.

BOB PARKER

Sequel to Victory
US 1972
Climbing May/June

A ski-mountaineering ghosty on the Marmolada.

JIM PERRIN

Fictive Heroes *
UK 1980
Crags 27 and collected in *On and Off the Rocks* (Gollancz, London).

A story with two endings, though the second end is another beginning.

On the Rocks with Cathy Powell *
UK 1988
Climber and Hillwalker December

Fictional climb and interview with the heroine of *One Green Bottle* (see novels, under Coxhead) where the end of the book is retold leaving Cathy climbing on Tryfan, an ageing ghost.

GREG PRITCHARD

Sid Lives
UK 1990
On the Edge 17

Sid Vicious didn't die. Malcolm McLaren helped him fake his death and exported him to 'Oz' where he became a hard rock climber. But no one can live for ever, even if they've already lived twice.

C.L. RAWLINS

Touch
US 1984
Climbing 83

A seconder's angry thoughts about the leader as he first belays and then follows a hard rock pitch.

Gloria in Excelsis *
US 1985
Climbing 88

More thought-wracked seconding, this time on an ice pitch, with the climber agonizing over his lost love and his dead friend as he hammers up the face.

The Soloist
US 1985
Climbing 90

Poignant love letter from talented woman climber struggling to equate being both feminine and physically good to her upstaged and embittered ex-boyfriend.

ROBERT L. REID

The Jam Jam Man
US 1973
Mountain Gazette 12

Cheerful vulgarity. Thrutch gets a queer notion, inspired by the words of Chouinard: 'Make a member of your body small. Place it in a crack. Then make it large, thereby lodging it.' It is to be part of the mountain, to think like it, become one with it. But high on his big climb, he forgets to think like the mountain and is in trouble. Time to go for the ultimate jam!

ANNE MARIE RIZZI

Conjugations
US 1975
Climbing May/June

Futuristic commercialization of climbing. Young boy watches TV climbing celebrity talk show with Grandpa, and infers that said Grandpa has principles.

DAVID ROBERTS

Backing Off *
US 1976
Climbing Jan/Feb

Climber confronts the diminishing ambition of approaching middle-age.

A Storm from the East **
US 1976
Mountain Gazette 49

The End of the Affair. Climbing in Wind Rivers: *he* gets burnt by lightning, *she* has to get them up the route.

Burnout in the Maze *
US 1984
Outside May, and also in *Moments of Doubt* (The Mountaineers, Seattle) 1986.

Years of guiding students will eventually wear you down – the repetition of deeds, words and attitudes, the inevitability of characters and events. It only takes one thing or one person to precipitate the final burnout.

KIM STANLEY ROBINSON

Ridge Running
US 1984
The Magazine of Fantasy and Science Fiction January, and collected in *Planet on the Table* (Tor Books, New York 1986 / Futura, London 1987).

Three old friends go hiking and camping in the mountains. Such trips used to be a regular feature, but in recent years the men have grown apart, and one – Joe – after a car accident the year before, has been left with his mind inclined to wander in very bizarre ways. (Set, by the way, in the 21st century, but not at all futuristic.)

STEVE ROGERS

The Disastrous Climb
UK 1970
Sports Stories for Boys (Hamlyn, London)

Improbable 'Boys Own' twaddle with obligatory ingredients: manly punch up, crime, even the mystery map. Very jolly.

IAN ROWE

Icarus
US 1972
Ascent

A lot is packed into this very short story: a variety of nationalities and clothing; thinking and reacting at cross-purposes; the best and second best climbers in the world; slag heap climbing, Superman and sexism. It culminates in an arcing, burning body, as the title hints. Bizarre indeed, with strange asides: 'Next day he was out trapping hedgehogs which he gave to Tinkers in exchange for underarm skin-grafts at the University of St. Giles, but his nose was not in it.'

PETER LARS SANDBERG

Gabe's Fall, and other Climbing Stories ***
US 1988
Birchfield Books (North Conway), Diadem Books (London) 1990

Contains the following stories, all except the title story having been published earlier:

Hawsmoot
US 1963
Phoenix Point West March, *Literary Cavalcade* (Scholastic Magazines) March, 1967), *The Personal Response to Literature* (Houghton and Mifflin, Boston) 1972, *Outsiders: American Short Stories for Students of ESL* (Prentice Hall) 1984 and recorded for blind listening in *Choice Magazine Listening* January 1967.

Cocksure young German invites other climbers to follow him unroped up a hard climb. Only one takes up the challenge – an unlikely fifty-five year old who walks with a cane...

The Devil's Thumb
US 1965
Phoenix Point West October, and collected in *Literary Cavalcade* (Scholastic Magazines) 1970; *Order and Diversity, The Craft of Prose* (John Wiley) 1973; *Traits and Topics* (Scott, Foresman) 1976.

Spectators gather to watch a climber attempt first ascent of a desert tower. His younger partner (Meyer) would desperately like to lead himself, but when the leader falls several times, Meyer in fact does all he can to ensure the older man's successful ascent. Youth comprehends age.

The Rhyme of Lancelot
UK 1968
South Dakota Review Autumn, and *Best Little Magazine Fiction* (New York University Press) 1970.

Michael (60) and Jame (female, 55) have been friends for four years and lovers for three months. Is their love going stale, or will a pleasant walk to the mountain summit prove the catalyst needed to revive the relationship?

The Old Bull Moose of the Woods
US 1972
Playboy (Chicago) and collected in *Playboy's Laughing Lovers* (Playboy Press, Chicago) 1975.

Chauvinist male vies with Equalist woman for remote pinnacle climb. They both achieve the route – and a climax after Equalist inexplicably seduces Chauvinist on the summit!

Calloway's Climb
US 1973
Playboy (Chicago). Winner of a 'Martha Foley Award', *Best American Short Stories: 1974* (Houghton Mifflin, Boston). Dramatized as TV movie in 1978, starring Mariette Hartley and Patrick O'Neal, with Mike Hoover as Calloway.

Couple, trying to rejuvenate their marriage, go camping in the mountains and witness a climbing accident. With help from a younger and better climber (Calloway), they go to the assistance of the cragfast survivor, cutting him loose from dead climber's body. But husband feels jealous when wife and Calloway rope together for the rest of the climb.

B-Tower West Wall
US 1975
Playboy (Chicago)

Big wall expert is forced to do night burglary of Boston skyscraper for criminals who have his child.

Gabe's Fall
US 1988 (written 1977)
Birchfield Books (North Conway)

Climber falls and is seriously injured leaving his less experienced fiancee to finish the climb and arrange rescue. Will this change their relationship?

BEN SANTER

In the Crevasse *
UK 1990
One Step in the Clouds

Young climber's first alpine season coincides with family crisis.

ANNE SAUVY

Les Flammes de Pierre
France 1982
Montalba (Paris)
Le Jeu de la Montagne et du Hasard
France 1985
Montalba (Paris)

Two collections of short stories, several of which were subsequently translated into English including:

La Fourche ***
UK 1985
The Alpine Journal and collected in *One Step in the Clouds*. Translated from the French by Jane Taylor.

Jaded mountaineer revives his career after signing a pact. Silly old Faustin.

Time Reversal **
US 1986
Climbing 95 and collected in *One Step in the Clouds*. Translated from the French by Jeremy Bernstein.

Old man relives his past only to realize it is part of the present, too.

The Collector ***
US 1989
Ascent. Translated from the French by Franco Gaudiano.

Scarred by First World War, protagonist devotes life to secretly 'collecting' prize summits in Alps, intending to make his obsession public when he retires.
'... full of suspense and pathos, ends with a twist worthy of Guy de Maupassant.' Allen Steck and Steve Roper, *Ascent*

2084 ***
UK 1990
One Step in the Clouds. Translated from the French by Jane Taylor.

The future climbing world gone mad in an Orwellian stranglehold of rules and regulations.

FRANK SAVILE

The Suffragette *
UK 1908
Strand Magazine Vol.36

Headstrong girl attempts local hard climb to prove anything man can do, woman can do better.

MICHAEL SAWICKY

Mark on the Wall
US 1987
Climbing 104

Climbing in the future, where the aim is to do first descents, leaving a smooth unclimbable line above – one's 'mark on the wall'. Very short and mildly amusing.

F.H. SHAW

The King's Move
UK 1920
Christmas Story-teller (Cassell, London).

JOHN SHERMAN

Satisfaction Guaranteed
US 1988
Climbing 107

The narrator loses his soul through a Faustian encounter or two in the Mens' Room at Yosemite Lodge.
'not funny... he degrades himself as well as the thousands of gay men and lesbians who read Climbing..' Richard Devitt – writing to *Climbing*

DON SHOEMAN

The Education of a Mountaineer
US 1981
Climbing 65

A fictional memoir. Driven by guilt that his advice had sent his hero-worshipping friend Julien to his death, Hem solos an unclimbed peak in India.

The Zealot
US 1982
Climbing 71

A mountain fable. From drink and drugs to love of God in five short pages.

JOE SIMPSON

Meltwater **
UK 1990
One Step in the Clouds

The horror of losing a close friend on a Karakoram peak.

DERMOT SOMERS

Cliff Hanger
Eire 1984
The Irish Press 12 July

In anger, Vincent takes up Mick's teasing suggestion that he climb two routes in half the time of Mick's and Janette's ascents.

Mountains and Other Ghosts
UK 1990
Diadem (London)

A collection of short stories including the following mountain pieces (some previously unpublished).

Nightfall ***
Eire 1983
The Irish Climber (Dublin)

Holocaust of WW3 bursts as two men climb Eiger. Powerful and well-written story which conveys sense of climbing history.

The Lug Walk **
Eire 1984
The Irish Press March

John Paul and Maria are ridiculous characters who set out to complete the thirty-three-mile Lug Walk. No pound of old chestnuts reworked into a story here, but good, inventive,comic narrative that keeps you laughing to the end.

The Old Story
Eire 1984
The Irish Climber (Dublin)

During a retreat from the Wicklow Hills in evil weather, climbers glimpse vision of three ascending figures – fugitives from an Elizabethan terror – which echoes outrage down the centuries.

Face Lift *
UK 1986
High 44

Willard, ex-SAS and mean with it, can't find a new route within his capabilites. Never mind: the army has taught him a trick or two – and soon it's goodbye to some well-loved favourites.

Whom the Gods Love *
UK 1989
Climber and Hillwalker April

Chilling story of excess: excess of beauty, talent, of parental love and vicarious ambition. Lonely, gifted youngster is pushed into climbing by his fey and green-eyed mother.

The White Graph **
UK 1990
One Step in the Clouds

Older climber, recovering from breakup (marital, financial, emotional) sucks wisdom and the power of survival from his alpine climbing – but this has to be at the expense of another's ego.

Dark Mourne **

Scalp-prickling cross-border tale of three Irish teenagers staying in an old climbing hut, whose creaks and shadows seem to echo past horrors. Fears are laid to rest by the arrival of friendly climber. All should be well now.

The Climber and Walker

Two climbers complete the Walker Spur: Cathy through desire and enthusiasm, Peter through a need to conquer rather than to win. Cathy leads most of the route but fears her achievement will be belittled by Peter relating an ego-saving version of it to his pals.

The Island

Frightening tensions erupt when hardened group of delinquents are taken on experimental outdoor programme.

The Climber Who Courted Death

With ambiguous affection a friend remembers the thwarted career of dead climber, whose ambitions always ranged ahead of the way things turned out.

Pure Natural Honey

Folksy design student meets modernist sculptor (she in love with textures; he turned on by space); they both see beauty in mountains, but will they appreciate each other's art?

The Priest's Breakfast

Fell-runner is accosted by man on Connemara summit and obliged to hear uncomfortable legend of an ungodly local priest, his fallen niece and her only friend, the crippled shoemaker.

A. CORALIE STANTON

The Conversion of Mr. Bertie Vallance *
UK 1901
Strand Magazine Vol.2 (London).

Another turn-of-the-century tale of assertive and achieving females encountering pomposity from not-so-achieving men who think a woman's duty is to look attractive for them.

ADALBERT STIFTER

Rock Crystal
Origin and date unknown
Published in English by Collins (London) and collected in *A Treasury of Mountaineering Stories.*

A Christmas fairy-tale in the mountains, in which xenophobia and interfamilial dislike are conquered through temporary misfortune. Sickly-sweet children – with more than a touch of 'Rapture of the Heights'.

F.J. STIMSON

Mrs Knollys and Other Stories
US 1897
Scribners (New York).

TERRY STORRY

Sean's Story
UK 1990
High 87 (Winner of 1989 *High* Writing Competition).

An accident (or accidents) and a court case – stories within stories. Enigmatic piece which takes a few readings to understand.

ANNE W. STRAWBRIDGE

Shadows of the Matterhorn
US 1931
Publisher unknown. Re-published in Zurich 1950s as a 19 page booklet (copy in A.C. Library).

GEOFFREY SUTTON

The Man Who Broke the Needle
UK 1948
The Fell Days (Museum Press, London)

In a collection of essays and fictional stories, mostly set in the Lake District.

JOHN SVENSON

Tension
US 1974
Climbing Sept/Oct

Group spot other climbers in distance just before turning in for the night. One member has paranoid dreams of who they are and how good they might be on the mountain.

The Victory Party
US 1975
Climbing March/April

Two guys on six-day El Cap climb. Their friends go up to meet them and get paralytic before the climbers even top out.

DANIEL TALBOT (editor)

A Treasury of Mountaineering Stories ***
US 1954
Putnam (New York), Peter Davies (London)

Volume of chiefly fictional short stories (all listed here under authors).

'Some of the stories are better than others. In what respect? I have endeavoured to answer this question… the ratings expressed in the following table are impressions, on the basis of 10 for the best in this particular collection.' Francis Farquhar *American Alpine Journal*

The gradings are for firstly 'Literary Quality' and secondly 'Mountaineering Interest'.

Maiden, Maiden *Kay Boyle* 10/10
Action *C. E. Montague* 10/10
Little Mother up the Mörderberg *H.G. Wells* 10/9
The Great Match *Etienne Bruhl* 8/10
Rock Crystal *Adelbert Stifter* 10/7
A Splendid Fellow *Phyllis Bottome* 9/8
Climbing for Goats *Stewart Edward White* 10/7
Mountain Madness *Tom Hopkinson* 8/8
Top Man *James Ramsey Ullman* 8/8
Their Kingdom *Roger Frison-Roche* 8/8
The Ascent *Ray B. West Jnr* 8/7
The Mountain *St. John Greer Ervine* 8/7
Wailing Precipice *Ralph Bates* 8/6
Glaciers *Vladimir Lidin* 7/5
The Inn *Guy de Maupassant* 9/2
Over the Mountain *Ruthven Todd* 6/4
The Stream *Emily Hilda Young* 5/1

H.F.W. TATHAM

The Footprints in the Snow
UK 1910
The Footprints in the Snow and Other Tales (Methuen, London).

JOHN THACKRAY

Bivouac
US 1988
Climbing 108

Two climbers pinned down by storms in tent on mountain discuss the intense emotions of climbing and former rock-climbing glories. A strange noise in background eventually comes to get them… (Written as dialogue, which is not always convincing.)

PETER THOMAS

The Old Man and the Crag
UK 1982
Cambridge University M.C. Journal and *New Zealand Alpine Bulletin* 70.

Year 2032. After climbing

SCOTT THOMPSON

Ai Viene la Tormenta
US 1989
Rock and Ice 35

Accident relived in the victim's dreams, taking him to his acceptance of death.

GORDON THOMSON

Children Like Climbers Often Fall **
US 1983
Climbing 78 and *One Step in the Clouds.*

Moving tale of brain-damaged climber.

M. TINDEL

The Champion Lady Mountaineer
US 1899
Pearson's Magazine April

RUTHVEN TODD

Over the Mountain
UK 1939
Harrap (London)

Hallucinations on a mountain that no-one has managed to cross. Ghoulish ending.

JAMES RAMSEY ULLMAN

Top Man
US 1950s
Curtis Publishing Co (New York?) and collected in *A Treasury of Mountaineering Stories*

Expedition tale in which moral justice is done.

WALT UNSWORTH

'Me and the Lads' stories: amusing in the one-upmanship 'toughs *v* toffs' way:

Gone to Earth
UK 1978
Climber and Rambler May

A Big Effort
UK 1978
Climber and Rambler June, and in *This Climbing Game* (Viking, London).

Rough Shoot
UK 1978
Climber and Rambler November, and also in *The Winding Trail* (Diadem, London).

Limestone Lil
UK 1979
Climber & Rambler July

A Rustle in the Snow
UK 1982
The Great Outdoors December

PAUL A.W. WALLACE

The Twist and Other Stories
US 1923
Reference: AAC Library List

IRA WALLACH

The Conquest of Tillie's Lookout
US 1960s
Mad magazine as gathered from the notes of Mitchel Hackney, and in *Ascent* 1969.

As can be expected from *Mad*-originated material, a joke article in which the climb of a small bump is described in major-expedition terms. Contains a glossary of its parodied mountaineering terminology.

ROBERT WALTON

El Peligroso *
US 1989
Ascent

Science fiction: ascents of amazing routes on different planets, culminating in El Peligroso, the biggest alpine wall in the solar system – on Uranus's moon, Miranda, where someone (or rather, something) has already attempted a first ascent.

MICHAEL WARD

The Forgotten Afternoon
UK 1990
On the Edge 16

Song reminds man of the afternoon when a two-man, one-woman climbing triangle finally split. (He climbed for the woman, but lost. She'd 'got Bette Davis eyes'.)

GUY WATERMAN

The Bronx Plumber **
US 1976
Off Belay October and collected in *One Step in the Clouds*.

Quixotic 'ghost' story. Visionary plumber gets Mallory-moments when mending blocked toilet.

The Gearfreak Caper **
US 1976
(by Rex Slim) from *Off Belay* and in *Climber and Rambler* and collected in *This Climbing Game* (edited by Walt Unsworth, Viking, London)

The hard-bitten, all-American, so-many-fingers-of-rye detective, already a creature of parody, parodied yet further here. Steaming, voluptuous women offer everything a man could want, for a price: tents for titillation, stoves for seduction, rucksack for readies and ice screws. Naturally this nice little vice ring gets its come-uppance from Claudius Fox, Private Dick.

The First Ascent **
US 1980
Off Belay April

Paradise Lost-inspired alabaster cliff guarded by angels – superb tongue-in-cheek portrayal of the irresistibility of a route crying out to be climbed.

H.G. WELLS

Little Mother up the Mörderberg ***
UK 1910
Strand Magazine Vol.39 (London) and collected in *A Treasury of Mountaineering Stories* and *Ascent* 1971.

Humorous tale in which flamboyant bighead (with a dislike for stick-in-the-mud school of climbing) takes his mother on an improbable alpine climb. The descent proves every bit as exciting as the ascent.

RAY B. WEST JNR.

The Ascent
US Date unknown
Epoch Magazine (Epoch Associates) and collected in *A Treasury of Mountaineering Stories*.

Young woman fails to have the amazing experience she expects on reaching the summit of a mountain – but finds all the thrills when she attempts a more complicated descent.

STEWART EDWARD WHITE

Climbing for Goats
US/UK 1920
From *The Killer* (Doubleday, New York / Hodder and Stoughton, London) and collected in *A Treasury of Mountaineering Stories*.

Senseless murder of animals in a mountain environment.

DAVE WILCOCK

Fallen Angel
UK 1990
Mountain 133

Another Faustian pact which demands too high a price for winning a competition.

BRIAN WILKINSON

Cul-de-Sac
UK 1981
Mountain 81

John and Ray, on a hitch-hiking, plum-route-picking tour of the English Southwest, tackle Heroica. Defeated, Ray abseils from rotten tape, and John is left stranded and benighted to ponder his situation and Ray's fate.

EMILY HILDA YOUNG

The Stream *
UK Date unknown
Publisher unknown. Collected in *A Treasury of Mountaineering Stories*.

What appears at first to be a tale of jovial dislike turns into one of cruel deeds, done in mistaken appeasement to Nature. A man from the city is unhinged by the mountain environment.

COLIN ZACHARIAS

Steppin' in the Slide Zone
US 1986
Rock and Ice 16

Set in the future, with the Sixth Rockarama Fest in Kansas.

NOVELS

JACOB ABOTT

Rollo in Switzerland
Origin and date unknown (possibly Switzerland)
Darton (Rahway, New Jersey) 1854

One of a series of children's stories by this author.

MARTHA ALBRAND

None Shall Know
US 1945
Little Brown (New York), Chatto and Windus (London)

A Call from Austria
US 1963
Random House (New York), Hodder and Stoughton (London)

ALLAN ALDOUS

McGowan Climbs a Mountain
UK 1945
Oxford University Press

Young adult adventure story set in the Himalaya.

Mrs ALEXANDER (pseudonym of Annie French Hector)

A Second Life
UK 1885
R. Bentley and Son (London) – in three volumes

Heroine fakes death in a crevasse on the Mer de Glace to escape from her husband.

MABEL ESTHER ALLAN

Shadow over the Alps
UK 1960
Hutchinson (London)

Climbing to Danger
UK 1969
Heinemann (London)

Teenage romantic fiction set in North Wales.

AL ALVAREZ

Hers
UK 1974
Weidenfeld and Nicholson (London), Random House (New York)

Short chapter on climbing in eternal triangle story.

JIM ANDREW

Bar-room Mountaineers
UK 1965
Cassell (London)

Passing references to climbing in story of juvenile delinquency.

LUCILLA ANDREWS

The Crystal Gull
UK 1978
Harrap (London)

ANON

An Alpine Tale
UK 1823
Westley (London)

By the author of *Tales from Switzerland*.

Captain of the Cumberland
UK 1873
Publisher unknown

Subtitled: Ready, O Ready, or These Forty Years. A naval story with two chapters on Alpine climbing – Monte Rosa and Mont Blanc.

Chateau of Leaspach
UK 1827
Newman (London)

Subtitled: or, The Stranger in Switzerland.

Continental Adventures
UK 1826
Hurst Robinson (London) – in three volumes

The Lost Chamois Hunter
UK 1869
Routledge (London)

Subtitled: A tale of the Matterhorn.

MATTHEW ARNOLD

Empedocoles on Etna
UK 1896
Publisher unknown

ELIZABETH ARTHUR

Beyond the Mountain *
US 1983
Harper Row (New York).

A women's Himalayan expedition provides the opportunity for the heroine to examine her obsessive relationships with her husband and brother, and atone for the guilt she bears after their deaths.

'Naomi [one of the expedition members] says.... "this is the first expedition I've ever been on where I won't sleep with one of the other climbers," and then brags of the current standing of her love-making record, which is 18,000 feet on Pumori. But it is not entirely true that she will remain celibate on this trip. The Sherpas become notches in her belt, and driven by a seemingly unsuppressible lust, she orders two of them (two, mind you!) up to a high camp to serve as field husbands. Justifiably outraged, her team mates chide her for moral and logistical reasons. After all, what expedition has ever built a contingency plan to include a couple of high altitude studs, let alone one based upon an admirable feminist ideal of wanting to climb their peak "without sherpa support"? ...[the book does] a disservice to women mountaineers.' Greg Child, *Climbing*

'Climbing fiction this good is a rarity.' Steven Jervis, *American Alpine Journal*

'a work of high literary art that probes male-female relationships to an expressionist depth more akin to August Strindberg than to any contemporary novelist.' David Bentley, *Climbing* 82

MONTGOMERY ATWATER

Ski Patrol
US 1943
Random House (New York), Faber (London)

Rocky Mountain background.

Ski Lodge Mystery
US 1940s
Publisher unknown

Story climaxes on mountain peak.

Snow Rangers of the Andes
US 1967
Random House (New York)

Young adult story of espionage and romance.

MARGARET ATWOOD

The Journals of Susanna Moodie
Canada 1970
Oxford University Press (Toronto)

Surfacing
Canada 1972
McClelland and Stewart (Toronto)

This celebrated novelist, raised in the Canadian backwoods, draws repeatedly on the Wilderness experience and myth in her work. *Journals* tells of a nineteenth century Ontario pioneer; the narrator of *Surfacing* is woman on remote North Quebec island, haunted by a 'wendigo' (creature of wilderness myth who has crossed over from human to natural universes).

DESMOND BAGLEY

High Citadel
UK 1965
Collins (London), Doubleday (New York)

Thriller. Two men escape over a high pass in the Andes.

Running Blind
UK 1970
Collins (London), Doubleday (New York)

Manhunt through wilds of Iceland (made into television series).

The Snow Tiger
UK 1975
Collins (London), Doubleday (New York)

Avalanche devastates New Zealand mining township. Subsequent enquiry reveals intrigue and ruthless exploitation.

OLAF BAKER

Shasta of the Wolves
US 1919
Dodd, Mead and Co. (New York), Harrap (London)

A children's fiction book. Located in the Rocky Mountains.

ROBERT MICHAEL BALLANTYNE

Freaks on the Fells
UK 1865
Routledge and Co (London), Crosby and Ainsworth (Boston).Nelson (London) 1913.

Rivers of Ice
UK 1875
Nisbet (London)

A tale of alpine adventure and glacier action.

The Rover of the Andes
UK 1885
Nisbet (London)

Subtitled: a tale of adventure in South America.

World of Ice
UK 1880s
Publisher unknown

JACK BANNATYNE (pseudonym of William J. Gaston)

The Mountain Eagles
UK 1983
Hale (London)

Sopwith Camels of the Royal Flying Corps in Italian Dolomites during First World War – hero discovers enemy squadron is led by old climbing partner. Frequent climbing references, but little description.

PHYLLIDA BARSTOW

Glacier Run
UK 1983
Century (London)

JOHN BARTROPP

Barbarian
UK 1933
Chambers (London)

Subtitled: a tale of the Roman Wall. Contains nocturnal cliff-climbing episode.

ROBERT BATEMAN

Young Climber
UK 1959
Constable (London)

Five boys on an adventure course in North Wales. (One of a series on various adventurous activities.)

PETER BATES

The Red Mountain
UK 1966
Hale (London)

Thriller. Prisoner of war escaping over the Alps to Switzerland.

VICKI BAUM

Marion Alive
UK 1943
Michael Joseph (London)

At one point the heroine falls into a crevasse, loses her ice axe and breaks her ankle.

SAMUEL BECKETT

The Lost Ones
France 1971
Les Editions de Minuit (Paris). Calder and Boyars (London) and Grove Press (New York) 1972. Translated from the French *Le Dpupleur* by the author.

'Little known to either the climbing community or Beckett's own literary following, *The Lost Ones* imparts a moving, existentialist profile of humanity condemned to futile ascension. A society of "climbers" is followed as it suffers the statistical incompatibilities and limited terrain of its environs. Most traumatizing, however, is the height and subsequent inaccessibility of the top, that summit to which Beckett's parable society is relentlessly striving.' Michael Tobias, *Climbing* 48

MARGARET E. BELL

Danger on Old Baldy
US 1944
Morrow (New York)

ROBERT AMES BENNETT

Avalanche Gulch
UK 1933
Collins (London) 1937

IRENE ELLIOTT BENSON

Campfire Girls Mountaineering
US 1918
Doubleday (New York)

Subtitled: or Overcoming All Obstacles

MONSIGNOR ROBERT HUGH BENSON

The Coward
UK 1912
Hutchinson (London)

Features a vivid Alpine passage, the author having climbed with his celebrated literary brothers (A.C. and E.F. Benson).

KENNETH BENTON

Craig and the Jaguar
US/UK 1973
Walker (New York), Macmillan (London)

Cordillera Blanca thriller involving a climb on the Jaguar.

JOHN BLACKBURN

Bound to Kill / Blue Octavo
US/UK 1963
M.S. Mill (New York) / Cape (London)

NORMAN BOGNER

Snowman
UK 1977
New English Library (London)

The abominable Snowman, now twenty five feet high and eating human flesh, terrorizes new ski complex in western USA. Humans win in the end, of course.

'Hardly worth the reading time.' Edward Pyatt, *The Alpine Journal*

KATHLEEN BOOTHROYD

Dixons of Ellerthwaite
UK 1932
Hurst and Blackett (London)

Rustic romance – intellectual's daughter marries Lakeland fell farmer.

'Should obviously make a fine novel... but when she begins to fill in the details her touch is apt to become disappointingly uncertain... The book has a special value for all who love Lakeland Fell Country.' (Unattributed – probably Katherine Chorley) *Fell and Rock Journal*

HENRY BORDEAUX

Footprints in the Snow
UK 1913
Fisher Unwin (London)

The House of the Dead / The House that Died
UK 1913/1923
Fisher Unwin (London)

Gloomy tale set in the Maritime Alps with chamois hunting but no real climbing.

W.E. BOWMAN

The Ascent of Rum Doodle **
UK/US 1956
Parrish (London) / Vanguard (New York) and periodically since in paperback reprints: Dark Peak (Sheffield) 1979; Arrow/Arena (London) 1983 and 1989.

Satirizes the classic 'gritted teeth' type of Himalayan expedition account exemplified by Tilman's *Ascent of Nanda Devi*.

'The rummiest climbing book.' Unattributed *Scottish Mountaineering Club Journal*

'Minor classic of English whimsy.' Sean French

'Does for mountaineering what *Catch 22* did for the Second World War...should be stocked in every home.' Miles Kington, *Sunday Times*

'A rather laboured skit.' T.S. Blakeney, *The Alpine Journal*

'For a real belly laugh, one has to return to *Rum Doodle*' Geoffrey Templeman, *The Alpine Journal* (after the book's republication in paperback).

KAY BOYLE

Avalanche
US 1944
Simon and Schuster (New York), Faber (London)

World War II story involving espionage, romance and adventure in the French Alps with some climbing.

'Richly emotional.' George Pokorny

His Human Majesty
US 1949
McGraw Hill (New York)

E.F. BOZMAN (Ernest Franklin Bozman)

X Plus Y
UK 1936
Dent (London)

Subtitled: the Story of Two Unknown Quantities. Includes climbing episodes, that of a 4000-metre Graian peak at the end of the story being the most descriptive.

'... nor does the author lose sight of the fact that when X is added to Y and the sum squared... a new compound possessing the characteristics of each of the unknowns has come into being. This idea is cleverly worked out in an English setting which shifts finally to the Alps; the characterization is vivid and sympathetic; there is a lot in this novel to think about and enjoy.' Karl Brunning, *The Mountaineering Journal*

MELVYN BRAGG

A Time to Dance
UK 1990
Hodder and Stoughton (London)

Relishers of fellside romances will remark on the modern spice injected into the genre by this well-known Lakelander. His latest novel has jaded and very married ex-bank manager falling for eighteen year-old Mensa virgin.

'...the ultimate male menopausal bimbo fantasy' Victoria Glendenning, *The Times*

Others of his novels with a Lake District setting include:

A Place in England (c1970);
Josh Lawton (1972);
The Maid of Buttermere (1987).

'His Cumbria is as potent a literary region as Hardy's Wessex, Lawrence's Midlands and Housman's Shropshire.' *New Statesman*

MADELEINE BRANDIES

The Little Swiss Wood Carver
US c1929
Grosset and Dunlap (New York)

Minor climbing incident in this Alpine story.

CLAUDE BRAY

Ivanda
UK 1894
Warne (London)

Subtitled: or, The Pilgrim's Quest: a tale of Tibet.

VIVIAN BRECK (pseudonym of Vivian Gurney Breckenfield)

High Trail
US 1948
Garden City (New York)

CONSTANCE BRIDGES

Thin Air
US 1930
Brewer and Warren (New York)

WOODROW BRIDGES (pseudonym of William Woodbridge)

Shooting Skyward
US 1912
Smith-Kinney (Tacoma)

Includes satirical account of an ascent of Mt. Rainier.

EMMA BROCK

High in the Mountains
US 1938
Whitman (Chicago)

Subtitled: Robi and Hanni in the Swiss Alps. Climbing scenes in children's story set in the Alps.

E. BROWN

Dark Rainbow
Origin and date unknown
Publisher unknown

JOHN BUCHAN (Lord Tweedsmuir)

John MacNab
UK 1925
Hodder and Stoughton (London) several subsequent editions, including Penguin paperback.

Set in the Scottish Highlands: three public figures go poaching, for excitement – by sportsmanlike means, of course.
Several of this famous author's books have climbing scenes or are set in a mountain background including:

Prester John (1910)
The Thirty-Nine Steps (1915)
Mr Standfast (1919)
The Three Hostages (1924)
Mountain Meadow (1940)

PEARL S. BUCK

Other Gods
US 1938
P.F. Collier (New York). Macmillan (London) 1940. Later published by John Day and Co (New York) and Methuen (London) c1949. Also appeared in *Good Housekeeping* magazine under the title 'An American Legend'.

Subtitled: an American legend. Mountaineering background.

NELL BUCKLEY

Stuart in Tibet
UK 1948
George Newnes (London)

A children's book.

KURT BURGBACHER

White Hell
Germany 1961
Franz Schneider (Munich). Methuen (London) 1963. Translated from the German *Pilot in der Weissen Hölle* by Stella Humphries.

Subtitled: a story of the search and rescue service in the Alps.

CHRISTOPHER BURNS

The Condition of Ice
UK 1990
Secker and Warburg (London)

Climb of Eiger-like north face (the Versücherin or Temptress) by London night-school teacher and adulterer' (Tinnion) and his Swiss childhood friend (Hansi), set against growing threat of Nazism and war.

'Chill, frosty book... For all their battles of survival instincts, clanging choices, and amputated extremities, Tinnion, his suburban lover, the aloof Hansi, the sinister Max remain peripheral to the book. It is the Versücherin, streaked with snow, fear and death, that stands at the heart, awesome, immutable, indecipherable.' Sabine Durrant, *The Times*

SAMUEL BUTLER

Erewhon
UK 1872
Trubner and Co (London)

Opening chapters accurately portray Butler's mountain exploration in New Zealand. The descent into Erewhon is based on the Val Ticino.

MARTIN CAIDIN

High Crystal
US 1975
Arbor House (New York), W.H.Allen (London)

JOANNA CANNAN (Joanna Pullein-Thompson)

Prolific author, active from the 1920s to the 1960s writing some books under her married name. Selected titles concern mountaineering:

Ithuriel's Hour / The Hour of the Angel *
UK 1931
Hodder and Stoughton (London) / Doubleday (New York). Pan Books (London) 1949, renamed as *The Hour of the Angel.*

Old-school sportsman, Sir Clement Vyse, recruits the experienced John Ullathorne to help him tackle unclimbed Tibetan peak. But Ullathorne resents Vyse's flirtation with his young wife and, perched precariously atop the glittering peak, the two climbers confront each other. A life is lost. But is it murder?

'Astonishing book for a woman to have written.' *The Sunday Times*

The Lady of the Heights
UK 1926
Fisher and Unwin (London). Hodder and Stoughton (London) 1931.

Under Proof
UK 1934
Hodder and Stoughton (London)

The Hills Sleep On
UK 1935
Hodder and Stoughton (London)

Thriller that starts in the Alpine Club and reaches a climax in Tibet.

A Hand to Burn
UK 1936
Hodder and Stoughton (London)

Sequel to *The Hills Sleep On* but with little actual climbing.

The Body in the Beck
UK 1952
Gollancz (London)

A whodunit involving Oxford University climbers in the Lake District.

LEGRAND CANNON Jnr

Look to the Mountain
US/UK 1942
Henry Holt (New York) / Cassell (London) 1944

New Hampshire setting.

GLYN CARR (pseudonym of Showell Styles)

Death on Milestone Buttress
UK 1951
Geoffrey Bles (London)

This and the following books are all period 'detective' stories with amusing moments, mostly involving a fair amount of climbing. The principal character is Shakespearean actor/manager and amateur sleuth, Sir Abercrombie Lewker, known to his intimates as 'Filthy'. Three earlier thrillers written by Showell Styles: *Traitor's Mountains* (1946);*Kidnapped Castle* (1947) and *Hammer Island* (1948) also feature Sir Abercrombie Lewker.

Other titles include:
Murder on the Matterhorn (1951)#
Corpse in the Crevasse (1952)
Youth Hostel Murders (1952)#
Death Under Snowdon (1954)
A Corpse at Camp Two (1955)
Murder of an Owl (1956)
The Ice-Axe Murders (1958)
Swing Away Climber (1959)#
Holiday with Murder (1960)#
Death Finds a Foothold (1961)
Death of a Weirdy (1961)
Lewker in Norway (1963)
Lewker in Tirol (1967)
Fat Man's Agony (1969)
UK 1951-69
Geoffrey Bles (London) # denotes titles also published in the US by Dutton (New York) and (for *Swing Away Climber*) Washburn (New York).

'A good puzzling story on the classic crag' Wilfred Noyce (re. *Death on the Milestone Buttress*)

'Unpleasantly kinky writer with no head for heights is found dead, apparently after climbing accident, above a North Wales valley upon whose village community has descended another of those arty-nasties. Sir Abercrombie Lewker... smells murder and though nearly swamped by sheer weight of suspects gets his man. Quietly enjoyable.' John Clarke, *Evening Standard* (re. *Death of a Weirdy*)

'Lewker, professing age and decay but not actually exhibiting them much, examines the matter of an Austrian politicaster found shot dead on a mountain-side, and himself only narrowly escapes murder by freezing. Recommended reading even for types who feel compulsion to stay at sea-level' *Sunday Times* (re. *Lewker in Tirol*)

DANIEL CASOLORO

The Ice King
US 1981
Whitemore Publishing Co. (Ardmore, Penn)

ROBERT CHARLES (pseudonym of Robert Charles Smith, who also used the pseudonym Charles Leader)

Sun Virgin
UK 1974
Hale (London)

Setting is Sangay in Ecuadorian Andes.

WINDSOR CHORLTON

Rites of Sacrifice
UK 1989
W.H. Allen (London)

Another trans-Himalayan spy thriller. American anthropologist is enlisted by Tibetan freedom fighters to smuggle out defecting Chinese general during Cultural Revolution.

ISOBEL CONSTANCE CLARKE

In an Alpine Valley
UK 1937
Longmans (London)

JON CLEARY

Pulse of Danger
US / UK 1966
Morrow (New York) / Collins (London)

Members of botanical expedition flee from Chinese soldiers, escaping over the Bhutan Himalaya.

ROGER CLEEVE

The Toad Beneath the Harrow
UK 1969
Allen and Unwin (London)

E.H. CLEMENTS (pseudonym of Eileen Hunter)

High Tension
UK 1959
Hodder and Stoughton (London)

Thriller.

CLIFT AND JOHNSON

High Valley
US 1950
Publisher unknown

Novel of Tibet.

'CLIMBER & CLUTCH'

Hobbs and Larkins in North Wales
UK c1880
Publisher unknown

Amusing sketches and writings about "amateur" climbing in North Wales.

WILLIAM E. COCHRANE

Class Six Climb
US 1979
Ace Books. Combining three serialized episodes from *Analog* magazine.

Routine sci-fi. Team of foreign climbers apply big-wall tactics to ultimate challenge – a very large tree venerated by locals as a god. Lots of symbolism, revolution, passion.

W.G. COLLINGWOOD

Thorstein of the Mere
UK 1895
Edward Arnold (London). Titus Wilson (Kendal) 1905, and Heinemann (London) 1929.

Romance of Norse Lakeland; written for a child, but good reading for all ages.

'Certain of his images almost hurt by their sharp beauty and every paragraph is drenched in noble feeling for the fells and the dales...' *Fell and Rock Journal* 1930 (Unattributed – probably the Journal editor, Katherine Chorley.)

The Bondwoman
UK 1899
Edward Arnold (London). Heinemann (London) 1932.

A saga of Langdale.

Dutch Agnes: Her Valentine
UK 1910
Edward Arnold (London). Heinemann (London) 1931.

Imaginary diary of the Curate of Coniston from 1616 to 1623 – set against the religious and political climate of the day.

'The entries are as spontaneous and real as if they had appeared on the Curate's parchment page direct in the wake of his scratching quill... The pictures of the Coniston country and the Coniston folk are perfect. Collingwood's touch is exquisite... a book to dip into again and again.' *Fell and Rock Journal* 1932 (Unattributed – probably Katherine Chorley.)

VICTOR COOK

Anton of the Alps
UK 1912
Methuen (London)

Story reaches climax atop Alpine peak.

EDWARD H. COOPER

The Monk Wins Out
UK 1900
Duckworth (London)

A mixture of mountaineering and horseracing.

NELLIE CORNWALL

Hallvard Halvorsen
UK 1888
Partridge (London)

Subtitled: or, The Avalanche: a story of the Fjeld fjord and Fos.

STATA A. COUCH

In the Shadow of the Peaks
UK 1909
Greening (London)

Set in Mexico and including a description of an ascent of Popacatepetl.

LYNN COVINGTON

A Mountain Tale
US 1963
Carlton Press (New York)

ELIZABETH COXHEAD

June in Skye
UK 1938
Cassell (London)

One Green Bottle **
UK 1951
Faber (London), Lippincott (Philadelphia), in various paperback editions since and collected in *One Step in the Clouds.*

A stimulating climbers' romance, based in Snowdonia and Birkenhead. Condemned by the then Bishop of Chester for its explicitness, *One Green Bottle* was immediately recognized among mountaineers as an important work.

'May have started a new direction in mountain writing… From the moment when she [Cathy Canning] consents to sleep with Leonard Head, whom she dislikes and despises, in order to be given a pair of climbing boots, we know what we are in for… Certainly I have never observed at youth hostels or on the hills some of the happenings that seem to be commonplace here; nor a university lecturer (from Oxford, be it said) so despicable as Michael Derwent… the important theme is the slow winning of a personality through the variety of this experience:..' Wilfrid Noyce, *Snowdon Biography*

'Still a leading contender as the finest climbing novel ever written,' Jill Neate

Figure in the Mist
UK 1955
Collins (London)

SAMUEL RUTHERFORD CROCKETT

Lone March
UK 1899
Hodder and Stoughton (London). Originally published in magazine form as *A Woman of Fortune.*

Includes an unconvincing climbing description in the vicinity of the Eiger.

RUPERT CROFT-COOKE

The White Mountain
US 1933
Cosmopolis, Falcon (London)

Escape to the Andes
US 1938
Messner (New York)

A.J. CRONIN

Enchanted Snow
Origin and date unknown
Publisher unknown

Ski-thriller.

STELLA MARTIN CURREY

To the Mountain
UK 1949
Selwyn and Blount (London)

MONICA CURTIS

Landslide
UK 1934
Gollancz (London)

Story of imaginary European Fascist State, with some climbing.

ALPHONSE DAUDET

Tartarin on the Alps ***
France 1885
Calmann-Levy (Paris)
Editions du Figaro (Paris), Routledge (London/New York) 1887. Translated from the French by Henry Frith. Reissued periodically by Everymans Library (Dent, London / Dutton, New York).

In this story (a follow-up to *Tartarin of Tarascon*) the grandiloquent hero (an unlikely mountaineer) attempts to save face by climbing the major summits of Switzerland. A classic.

'On the whole, Tartarin keeps within credible limits and the satire is both amusing and fair. It came as a revelation to the greater part of the French public.' Claire Eliane Engel, *Mountaineering in the Alps*

RENÉ DAUMAL

Mount Analogue ***
France 1952
Librarie Gallimard (France). Vincent Stuart (London) 1959. Translated from the French *Mont Analogue* by Roger Shattuck. Now published by Shambhala (Boston) and Penguin Books (Harmonswoth)

Subtitled: a novel of symbolically authentic non-Euclidean adventure in mountain climbing. Unfinished surreal allegory by late avant garde poet, writer-philosopher and student of G.I. Gurdjieff.

'…has touches of both physics and metaphysics, yet is neither science fiction nor mystic, although an appreciation of all these elements will enhance the reader's understanding.' George Pokorny

'An arguable work of art, Daumal's classic is, inviolably, a delightful reading experience. The background to Alexandros Jodorawsky's surrealistic film *The Holy Mountain*, Daumal's unfinished novel… has long been bought up for film rights by a Gurdjieff sect in Paris with whom he was associated.' Michael Tobias, *Climbing* 48

LIONEL DAVIDSON

The Rose of Tibet
UK 1962
Gollancz (London)

Gripping thriller about clandestine mission into Chinese-occupied Tibet.

J.V. DIBBEN

Mountain Adventure
UK 1947
Epworth (London)

Junior fiction. Thrills and adventure among the peaks of the lower Himalaya.

AUBREY DIEM

First Rains of Autumn
Canada 1985
Kitchener (Ontario) Aljon Print-Craft

Wartime resistance in the Valle d'Aosta involving a baled-out US airman, a beautiful innkeeper, sabotage and a night chase over the mountains.

WALT DISNEY

Mountaineering Mickey
US/UK 1937
Publisher unknown Collins (London)

Walt Disney Productions presents Donald Duck, Mountain Climber
US 1978
Random House (New York)

MANI DIXIT

The Red Temple
Nepal 1977
Sharda Prakashan Griha (Kathmandu)

Set in Pokhara: action packed story of Khampa rebellion – hippies, drugs and associated killings.

JIM DODGE

FUP
US 1983
City Miner Books (Berkeley)

A zany novella about a hundred-year old card sharp living in a ranch with his grandson and a magic hen…

'… may not be great literature, but it's never boring… it's hard to disagree with Gary Snyder's final assessment that "there's a ninety-nine per cent purity in this nutty novel".' Charles Hood, *Climbing*

MAURICE DOLBIER

Nowhere Near Everest?
US 1955
Knopf (New York) with illustrations by Virgil F Partch.

Almost a satire on Bowman's *Rum Doodle*!

CHARLES DORIE

Beyond the Sunset
UK 1935
John Murray (London)

JUNE DRUMMOND

Cable Car
UK 1965
Gollancz (London), Reinhart (New York)

A thriller staged in an imaginary European state.

F.R.G. DUCKWORTH

Swiss Fantasy
UK 1948
Benn (London)

OWEN FRANCE DUDLEY

Only Masterful Monk
UK 1940
Macmillan (London)

DOUGLAS V. DUFF

On the World's Roof
UK 1949
Blackie (London/Glasgow). Peal Press (London) without original illustrations.

Thriller for young adults. Nazis, hiding in Tibet, develop secret weapon for world conquest.

ANNE DUFFIELD

Glittering Heights
UK 1937
Cassell (London)

LAWRENCE DUNDAS

He liked them Murderous
UK 1963
Hammond (London)

Thriller set in the Andes.

MARY DUNSTAN

Jagged Skyline
UK 1935
Constable (London)

Superstition and ski mountaineering.

He Climbed Alone
UK 1948
Heinemann (London)

Alpine climbing and romance. Others of this author's novels may well have a mountain background: *Live On; Banners in Bavaria; The Driving Fear; Winter Rhapsody.*

R.B. EKVALL

Tents Against the Sky
US 1954
Farrar Strauss Young (New York)

A Tibet-based novel.

BARRY ENGLAND

Figures in a Landscape **
UK 1968
Jonathan Cape (London)

Two captured soldiers make their escape across an alien landscape but are relentlessly pursued. Story reaches a climax on drenched mountainside. (Filmed, starring Robert Shaw and Malcolm McDowell.)

GEORGIA ENGLEHARD

Peterli and the Mountain
US 1954
Lippincott (Philadelphia)

The cat that climbed the Matterhorn – based on true story of a kitten that followed climbers up the Hörnli Ridge and was carried down from the summit into Italy by another climbing group.

HAL G. EVARTS

The Secret of the Himalayas
US 1962
Scribner's (New York)

HARRIET EVATT

The Mystery of the Alpine Castle
UK 1950s
Publisher unknown – probably Bobbs-Merrill (New York)

DONALD C. EYRE

John Sikander
UK 1954
Hale (London)

'..novel much after the style of Ganpat, based on a quest in the Karakorum for a lost heir to a title... readable thriller...' H.W. Tobin, *The Alpine Journal*

RON FAUST

Snowkill
US 1974
Nordon (New York)

Journalist becomes involved in deadly Alpine man-hunt for Nazi fugitive.

Tombs of Blue Ice
US 1974
Bobbs-Merrill (New York). Robert Hale (London) 1976

Wolf in the Clouds
US 1977
Bobbs-Merrill (New York)

GEORGE MANVILLE FENN

The Crystal Hunters
UK 1890
S.W. Partridge (London)

Subtitled: a boy's adventure in the higher Alps. A celebrated writer of boys' stories turns his pen to mountaineering and Alpine adventure.

In an Alpine Valley
UK 1894
Hurst and Blackett (London)

WINIFRED FINLAY

Peril in Lakeland
UK 1953
Harrap (London)

THOMAS FIRBANK

Bride to the Mountain
UK 1940
Harrap (London)

The author of *I Bought a Mountain* turns to fiction in this story of sheep-stealing, murder, climbing and romance in the Welsh hills.

KEVIN FITZGERALD

Throne of Bayonets
UK 1952
Heinemann (London)

Subtitled: a story for a journey. Fitzgerald, whose satirical articles have entertained readers of the Climbers' Club Journal for many years, created a Bulldog Drummond-like character called Commander Feston whose adventures are recounted in eight entertaining books. This one, set in North Wales, gallops along at a Buchanesque pace with a gunfight in the bar of the Pen Gwynant Hotel and final shoot-out on top of Lliwedd. The other books in the series, some of which have short mountain or climbing scenes are as follows:

Not So Quickly (1943)
It's Safe in England (1949)
Quiet Under the Sun (1950)#
Trouble in W2 (1951)
It's Different in July (1955)
It's Dangerous to Lean Out (c1958)
Kill Him Gently Nurse (1960)
UK 1943-60
Heinemann (London) # indicates title also published in US by Little Brown (Boston)

IAN FLEMING

On Her Majesty's Secret Service
UK 1963
Cape (London)

Eleventh James Bond adventure, set amid Alpine snows.

COLIN FORBES

Heights of Zervos
UK 1970
Collins (London)

A war adventure – battling to capture a monastery atop a mountain in Greece.

D.K. FORSTER (Daphne Kathleen Forster)

Twin Giants
UK 1952
Hammond (London)

A Himalayan story.

ROGER FRISON-ROCHE

First on the Rope
France 1941
Arthaud (Grenoble and Paris). Methuen (London) 1949, Prentice-Hall (New York) 1950. Translated from the French *Premier de Cordée* by Janet Adam Smith.

Chamonix guide story set in interwar years. '... far too much crammed into far too small a space... But it is the behaviour of the characters, and not the action, which will make the climber's hair stand on end. Is a leading guide's decision to retreat so easily reversed by taunts as to his courage from his American client... (inexcusably named Bradford Warfield, Jr.)? ...Would good guides bicker so woefully? Tom Brocklebank, *Alpine Annual* 1950

'Novelettish' Hugh Merrick *Companion to the Alps* 1974

Grand Crevasse / Last Crevasse
France 1948
Editions Arthaud (Grenoble and Paris). Prentice-Hall (Garden City, New Jersey) 1951 / Methuen (London) 1952. Translated from the French *La Grande Crevasse* by Janet Adam Smith and Nea Morin.

Another everyday story of Chamoniard folk.

'Frankly ridiculous in the impossibilities it demanded of one's belief.' Hugh Merrick *Companion to the Alps* 1974

Return to the Mountains
France 1957
Arthaud (Paris). Methuen (London) 1961. Translated from the French *Retour a la Montagne* by Hugo Charteris.

A sequel to *The Grand Crevasse*.

CHARLES GAINE

Dangler
US 1980
Simon and Schuster (New York)

New Hampshire adventure school seen by its founder as way forward for mankind.

MALCOLM GAIR

Snowjob
US 1962
Doubleday (New York), Collins (London)

Skiing thriller; Swiss Alps.

GANPAT (pseudonym of Maj. M.L.A. Gompertz)

Snow Rubies
UK 1925
Blackwood (Edinburgh), Houghton Mifflin (Boston)

Adventure story in the Kashmir mountains. Weird cave dwellers capture heroes.

The Voice of Dashin
UK 1926
Hodder and Stoughton (London), George H. Doran Co (New York)

Subtitled: a romance of wild mountains.

High Snow
US 1927
Doubleday (New York), Hodder and Stoughton (London)

'Romance' in which hero is based on the character of Professor Kenneth Mason. Plot incorporates a crossing of the Khardung Pass above Leh.

Mirror of Dreams
US 1928
Doubleday (New York), Hodder and Stoughton (London)

ANDREW GARVE (pseudonym of Paul Winterton)

Ascent of D.13
US 1968
Harper Row (New York)

Race to find secret weapon in crashed aeroplane in this tale of espionage and climbing on Turko-Russian border.

BILL GASTON

Death Crag
UK 1965
Hammond (London)

NEWTON GAYLE (pseudonym of Maurice Guinness)

Sinister Crag
UK 1938
Gollancz (London), Scribner's (New York)

Lakeland thriller involving a gang and murder.

JOHN GEDDIE

Beyond the Himalayas
UK 1882
Nelson (London)

Subtitled: a story of travel and adventure in the wilds of Tibet.

STELLA GIBBONS

The Swiss Summer **
UK 1950
Longmans, Green (London)

Mannered novel (dedicated to Elizabeth Coxhead and Kathleen Goddard) set in idyllic chalet above Grindelwald. Its main character – gentle, refined and fortyish – is a childless lady enjoying summer away from home with oddly-assorted houseparty. Much talk of climbing but none in the action; alpine descriptions, however, are fresh and frequently surprising.

GEOFFREY GILBEY

She's and Skis
UK c1937
Hutchinson (London)

Ski story, romantic and humorous.

SUSAN GILLESPIE (pseudonym of Elizabeth Constance Turton-Jones)

Himalayan View
UK 1947
Geoffrey Bles (London)

F.R. GILLMAN (Frederick Russell Gillman)

Max of the Mountains
UK 1937
University of London Press

A story of a journey to Switzerland

ANTHONY GLYN

Kick Turn
UK 1963
Hutchinson (London)

RUMER GODDEN (pseudonym of Margaret Haynes Dixon/Margaret Rumer)

Black Narcissus
US 1939
Little Brown (Boston) and Penguin Books (Harmondsworth/London)

Anglo-Catholic nun in a Himalayan convent falls in love with an Indian prince. (Made into highly-rated film starring Deborah Kerr, David Farrar, Sabu and Jean Simmons.)

CHARLES GOS

Song of the High Hills
Switzerland 1940s
Victor Attinger (Neuchatel). Allen and Unwin (London) 1949

Wistful Alpine romance with convincing climbing passages. This author wrote a number of novels in French.

JANET GOWER

Snow in Austria
UK 1935
Centaur Press (London)

DAWSON GRATRIX

He and Ski
UK 1929
Jenkins (London)

BERKELEY GRAY (pseudonym of Edwy Searles Brooks)

Lost World of Everest
UK 1941
Collins (London)

A shock awaits intrepid young Everester, Lord Gresham, when he and his team fall into weird world of caverns beneath the mountain.

ROWLAND GREY

In Sunny Switzerland
UK 1884
Kegan Paul (London)

Subtitled: a story of six weeks.

PAULA GROGGER

The Door in the Grimming
US 1936
Putnam (New York)

PAUL GROVES

The Climber
UK 1977
Hutchinson (London)

MARTIN HALE

Empire in Arumac
UK 1966
Cape (London)

Andean thriller.

L. HALLIDAY (Leonard Robson Halliday)

Top Secret
UK 1957
Hammond (London)

MARC HAMMOND

Killer Mountain
UK 1980
Futura (London)

Yugoslav adventure with fugitives and a crashed aeroplane.

HAN SUYIN (see under Suyin)

GEORGE HARDING (pseudonym of G.H. Raubenheimer)

The Sky Trap
UK 1972
Macmillan (London)

Thriller set in the Drakensburg

RONALD HARDY

The Face of Jalanath
UK 1973
Cassell (London), Putnam (New York)

High altitude action. Seven hand-picked mountaineers (each with a murky past) on a mission from Kashmir to destroy Chinese nuclear city. They must plant H-bomb on Jalanath's sheer face.

'The moral quality of the book is deeply disturbing... the 'heroes'... are red-hating, masculine archtypes who gain tacit approval by their vengefulness, remorse, resourcefulness or death... Political actions shoud be discussed in moral terms, not in terms of sensation and entertainment.' Jim Perrin, *Mountain* 28

'Knowledgeable mountaineerese.' Athan Pantseas, *Chicago Mountaineering Club*

FRANK HARPER

Night Climb
US/UK 1946
Longmans, Green (New York / London)

Subtitled: the story of the Skiing 10th. Fictional account (based on fact) of US mountain troops, fighting in Europe during the Second World War.

BEATRICE HARRADEN

Out of the Wreck I Rise
UK 1912
Nelson (London), Stokes (US)

A swindler dies in an avalanche.

AL HARRIS (See entry under Lucy Rees.)

DAVID HARRIS

Vortex ***
UK 1990
Diadem (London) as part of *One Step in the Clouds.*

Climbers in North Cascades stumble across crashed airplane and get sucked into deadly drug-running organization. Tension and menace maintained to last page, an impressive first novel.

M. JOHN HARRISON

Climbers ***
UK 1989
Gollancz (London)

Anecdotal episodes introduce reader to a molecular attachment of climbers while following the central character (seeking solace after a failed marriage) through a year on the crags. Action moves between London and the Peak District. Includes the story 'Gaz and Sankey' collected in *One Step in the Clouds*.

'not so much about climbing as the strategies of escape we all devise to make the world bearable' *Jacket notes*

'...a single provocative and abrasive pinnacle standing above a hitherto largely featureless wasteland. We all have ghastly memories of some climbing novels. Ambitions, rivalries, beautiful girls, dastardly guides and heroic clients (or heroic guides and dastardly clients) impossible precipices and avalanches... writing down at the same base-camp level of tabloid imagination... [we found] in this book fiction used to extend realism... writing lean, clear and compelling... biting and unforgettable descriptions, echoing with unstated overtones; and ever in the background a tightly zipped-up compassion... Because of this control we find ourselves accepting the tiresome contemporary litter of expletives... [we all] agreed this broke new ground in climbing literature,' G.J.F.Dutton (on behalf of colleagues, Robin Hodgkin and Tom Price) judging the Boardman/Tasker award. The book won (on a majority vote) but proved very controversial, triggering a plethora of strongly divergent opinions:

'Gloomy atmosphere infects the whole book... characters unlikeable and unhappy.' Ian Smith, *High*

'Not a novel! Blatant journalism!' Geoff Birtles

'...most depressing look at the whole business ever written... vague, sprawling, aimless...' David Rose and Steve Dodd, *Climber and Hillwalker*

'...most accomplished novel ever to be written around the subject of climbing... There is a good deal which is depressing or even shocking, but there is also an undercurrent, a bursting, good-day sunshine harmony, which expresses all our best hopes in a bad time.' Jim Perrin, in the same issue of *Climber and Hillwalker*

DUFF HART-DAVIS

The Heights of Rimring
UK 1980
Cape (London), Atheneum (New York)

International intrigue and mayhem. Spy thriller set in Nepal, involving Tibetan exiles and the Dalai Lama's treasure.

NORMAN HARTLEY

The Viking Process
UK 1976
Collins (London)

Thriller. Some climbing.

SIMON HARVESTER (pseudonym of Henry St. John C. Rumbold-Gibbs)

Forgotten Road
US 1974
Walker (New York)

Spy thriller set in the Hindu Kush.

DOUGAL HASTON

Calculated Risk *
UK 1979
Diadem (London)

Full-blooded Scottish/Alpine climbing adventure. The central characters, John Dunlop and Jack McDonald (macho Haston/Harlin composites) have little time for lesser mortals – and one use only for women.

The novel was finished (but uncorrected) and published posthumously and Haston might well have improved it in later drafts; much has been made of the ironic similarity between Haston's own death while skiing off piste in the Riondaz couloir above Leysin and an incident described in the book – was he test-running a plot idea?

'The hero has no time for most of the human race... The descriptions of climbing will never be bettered.' Michael Craig, *The Alpine Journal*

'...the reader is able to grasp the feeling of extreme commitment ...McDonald, much like the author, can hardly accept the world as it is. He drives every aspect as he explores himself and others, and in the process he changes everything he comes into contact with.' Mike Covington, *American Alpine Journal*

'A humourless story of two condescending and uninteresting supermen who battle against adversity as lesser mortals fall weakly by the wayside... The odd divorcee, homosexual or liberated American woman may conjure up ultimate depravity for an ageing Aunt but your Padarn-hardened climber is not going to be impressed.' John Sheard, *Mountain* 74

'Surely more than the extrinsic motives of money and fame or the tawdry intrinsic one of personal ambition were involved in Haston's pursuit of High Places. At least we must hope so, for otherwise mountaineering has lost its way. ...the book reads quite well, given the appalling content.' Robin Campbell, *Scottish Mountaineering Club Journal*

EDWARD H. HAWKINS

Wellspring
US 1969
Echo House (New York). McGraw Hill (New York) 1978.

Racy spy thriller set high in Colorado mountains. Poisoned headwaters – FBI, CIA and sinister foreign powers all seem to be involved. (Name of modern-day 'mountain man': John Parlin!)

LARRY HEALEY

The Hoard of the Himalayas
US 1981
Dodd Mead (New York)

Murder and suspense on expedition to highest unclimbed peak in Himalaya (by this American mystery writer).

BEN HEALY

The Millstone Men
UK 1966
Hale (London)

HERGÉ (pseudonym of George Rémi)

Tintin in Tibet
France/Belgium 1960
Editions Casterman (Paris and Tournai). Methuen (London) / Atlantic/Little Brown (Boston) 1962.

GERARD HERZOG

Jackson's Way / The Jackson Route
France 1976
Publisher unknown. Farrar Strauss and Giroux (New York) / Collins (London) 1978. Translated from the French *La Voie Jackson* by Hilary Davis.

Alpine climbing story clearly inspired by the Frêney Pillar tragedy of 1961.

DOUGLAS HEWITT

Mountain Rescue *
UK 1950
Eyre and Spottiswoode (London)

Escaped German prisoner of war on the run in North Wales is helped by a climber in 3-day manhunt.

'True... the crag of Craig Du is a synthetic creation. But there is a breath of reality about every touch of the descriptions given... prose throughout is tense yet sparing, a fit robe to a remarkable study.' Wilfrid Noyce *Snowdon Biography*

JACK HIGGINS (pseudonym of Harry Patterson)

The Iron Tiger
UK 1966
John Long (London). Fawcett Books (New York) 1975. Pan Books (London) 1989.

Gun-running across the Himalaya.

PETER HILL

The Enthusiast
UK 1978
Peter Davies (London), Houghton Mifflin (Boston)

Set in Snowdonia. Climber murdered *en route*.

JAMES HILTON

Lost Horizon **
UK 1933
Macmillan (London)

Genre-setting Himalayan adventure story: strange events follow arrival of kidnapped party of Westerners at the secluded Tibetan monastery of Shangri-La. Filmed in 1937, starring Ronald Coleman and again in 1972 with all-star cast headed by Peter Finch.

WILLIAM HJORTSBERG

Alp
US 1969
Simon and Schuster (New York), Barry and Jenkins (London)

Black comedy. First ascent of the north face of 'Juggernaut.'

'Humorous and mildly pornographic... very appealing to climbers conversant with mountaineering literature.' Jill Neate

'Characters include the fashionable number of perverts; none is the least sympathetic, so that their large-scale destruction leaves us unmoved... The author is a complete cynic, sneering at everyone; unfortunately his readers only discover this after they have paid for the privilege.' Edward Pyatt, *The Alpine Journal* (1975)

SILAS KITTO HOCKING

The Great Hazard
UK 1915
Fisher Unwin (London)

Some alpine climbing.

GARRY HOGG

Climber's Glory
UK 1961
Bodley Head (London)

North Wales setting. Romance and climbing.

DARYL HOLME

The Young Mountaineer
UK 1874
Nimmo (London)

Subtitled: or, Frank Miller's lot in life – the story of a Swiss boy.

KARE HOLT

The Race
Norway 1974
Glydendal Norsk Forlag (Norway), Michael Joseph (London) 1976. Translated from the Norwegian *Kapplopet* by Joan Tate.

A 'documentary' novel of the Scott/Amundsen race to the Pole.

A.R. HOPE (pseudonym of Ascott Robert Hope Moncrieff)

Seeing the World
UK 1909
Wells Gardner (London)

Subtitled: The Adventures of a Young Mountaineer.

JOHN HOPKINS

The Attempt
UK 1968
Secker and Warburg (London)

Haunting novel of quest and adventure in mountains and deserts of Peru.

TIMOTHY HOUGHTON

The First Season
UK 1967
Robert Hale (London)

Alpine ski adventure.

ROGER HUBANK

North Wall **
UK 1977
Hutchinson (London), Viking (New York)

Young man and older man on Dolomite big wall.

'Read at a deeper level, the author has postulated a conflict between two types of 'desire' and assigns them, respectively, to the two main characters… Daniel, seeks the challenge and the thrill and strength that a constant reaffirmation of danger creates. Raymond, is depicted more dispassionately and climbs (we are led to believe) for the same reason that he breathes, because there is no other choice possible for him: 'What you call 'victory' or 'defeat' is meaningless. That we have survived again is the only victory. It is significant to us alone. There is nothing else.

'The author… gives his descriptions of danger and the technical problems involved with a big climb a realism and tautness rarely found.' Eric Davis, *Climbing* 52

ALAN HUNTER

Gently to the Summit
UK 1961
Cassell (London)

Thriller based on Snowdon where Superintendent Gently solves a mysterious death.

ZORA NEALE HURSTON

The Man of the Mountain
UK 1941
Dent (London)

FREDRICK R. HYDE-CHAMBERS

Lama – A Novel of Tibet
UK 1984
Souvenir Press (London)

Historical, not climbing.

HAMMOND INNES (Ralph Hammond Innes)

The Lonely Skier
UK 1947
Collins (London)

Thriller featuring isolated Dolomite chalet and Nazi gold.

This popular author makes frequent use of mountain and wilderness settings for his adventure novels. Others include: *The Blue Ice* (1948), *The White South* (1949), *Campbell's Kingdom* (1952), *The Land God Gave to Cain* (1958).

MARJORIE SCOTT JOHNSTON

The Mountain Speaks
UK 1938
Cassell (London)

Mountain setting an integral part of the characters' lives in this romance. Climbing features and a rescue.

Pilgrim and the Phoenix
UK 1940
Hamilton (London)

An Alpine border village just before the outbreak of war with fugitives from Nazi persecution seeking asylum.

'…hardly a mountaineering novel, but it is true to say that it could never have been written except by a mountaineer… All of us today are questioning the basic tenure on which we hold our civilization… are traditional values of that civilization itself adequate foundations on which to build a solution to our problems? … [the author's] answer may not seem enough for everyone, but it is gallant and honourable… We as mountaineers will understand the book all the better because our minds are attuned for the setting… emphatically a novel for us to read.' Katherine Chorley, *Fell and Rock Journal*

W. JUDSON

Winter Kill
US 1970
Publisher unknown

Adirondacks setting.

ROBERT KATZ

The Spoils of Ararat
UK 1978
Houghton Mifflin (Boston)

FANNY KEMBLE

The Adventures of John Timothy Homespun in Switzerland
UK 1889
Richard Bentley (London)

THOMAS KENEALLY

A Victim of the Aurora
UK 1977
Collins (London and Glasgow)

Story of an Edwardian South Polar expedition by one of Australia's most distinguished novelists. Team is one of hand-picked heroes, yet each conceals a secret guilt. In the claustrophobic isolation of polar camp truths begin to emerge.

NORA KENT

Summer Pilgrimage
UK 1963
Macdonald (London)

Lakeland walking party complicated by romantic entanglements.

Twilight of Hester Lorimer
UK 1965
Macdonald (London)

'Murderous passions and climbing around Zermatt.' Jill Neate

JACK KEROUAC

The Dharma Bums
US 1959
New American Library (New York), Andre Deutsch (London)

Young men on Zen-trail find solitude in the High Sierra. (They are thinly-fictionalised versions of Kerouac and his long-time friend, the poet Gary Snyder.)

HENRY KLIER

A Summer Gone
UK 1959
Geoffrey Bles (London)

Climbing in Austria and on the Matterhorn.

JOHN KNITTEL

Via Mala
UK 1934
Hutchinson (London), Stokes (US)

MATTHEW KOSTKA

Climb to the Top
US 1960
Doubleday (New York)

MARC LAIDLAW

Neon Lotus
Canada/US/UK 1988
Bantam (Toronto / New York / London)

Sci-fi roof-of-the-world fantasy: reincarnate Tibetan scientist has mission to recover sacred relics and free the Land of Snows from the Chinese yoke.

DEREK LAMBERT

Kites of War
UK 1969
Michael Joseph (London)

P.S. LANG

Where the Soldanella Grows
UK 1915
Heath, Cranton and Ouseley (London)

STEWART LANG

The Iron Tooth/Claw
UK c1906
Henderson (London)

Subtitled: a thrilling story of mystery and adventure in the Alps.

'Curious "penny dreadful" describing the mountaineering exploits of two Messenger boys in pursuit of criminals.' Jill Neate

BOB LANGLEY

Traverse of the Gods *
UK 1980
Michael Joseph (London)

Wartime thriller set on the Jungfrau and the north face of the Eiger.

'Characters are striking, the tension unrelenting, and the climbing scenes emotionally shattering.' Tom Waghorn, *Manchester Evening News*

'really captures the feel of mountaineering.' Chris Bonington

East of Everest
UK 1984
Michael Joseph (London)

Himalayan spy thriller. Tracey Morrill believes her husband to have been killed in a mountaineering accident until the day a CIA man walks in and tells her he is waging guerrilla warfare in Tibet. Her job: to get him out.

EMMA LATHEN (pseudonym of Mary J. Latis and Martha Hannissart)

Pick up Sticks
US 1970
Simon and Schuster (New York), Gollancz (London)

Murder thriller which starts out on the Appalachian trail.

D.H. LAWRENCE

Women in Love
UK 1921
Martin Secker (London)

In final pages Gerald staggers to his death in the snow of a Tyrolean mountainside. (Filmed, starring Oliver Reed, Alan Bates, Glenda Jackson and Jennie Linden.)

CHARLES LEADER (pseudonym of Robert Charles Smith. See also entry under Robert Charles)

Frontier of Violence
UK 1976
Robert Hale (London)

Himalayan setting.

MRS AUBREY LE BLOND

The Story of an Alpine Winter
UK 1907
Bell (London)

Romance and winter sports set in St Moritz and Davos.

MOLLY LEFEBURE

Scratch and Co
UK 1968
Gollancz (London)

Subtitled: the Great Cat Expedition. A children's story about an ascent of Scafell Pike, told in the style of an expedition book.

M.Y. LERMONTOV (Mikhail Yurievich Lermontov)

A Hero of our Time
Russia 1840
Publisher unknown. Penguin Books (Harmondsworth) 1974. Translated from the Russian *Geroi nashego vremeni* and with an introduction by Paul Foot.

Lermontov (1814-1841) was Russia's 'Shelley' and his inspiration the Caucasus Mountains. In this, his one novel, the melancholic hero, Pechorin, eventually shoots a man on a cliff. Lermontov himself died in a duel in the Caucasus, aged 27 (stage-managed, it is said, by the Russian Secret Police).

L.D. LERNER (Lawrence David Lerner)

A Free Man
UK 1968
Chatto and Windus (London)

Set in Iceland.

CHARLES LEVER

The Dodd Family Abroad
UK 1859
Chapman and Hall (London)

MARJORIE LLOYD

Fell Farm Campers
Fell Farm for Christmas
Fell Farm Holiday
UK 1940s/1951
Puffin Books (Harmondsworth)

Fell Trek
UK 1950s
Hutchinson (London)

Stories of the 'Browne Family' for young readers. Set in Lakeland.

ANGELA LOCKE

Search Dog
UK 1987
Souvenir Press (London)

Fictionalized account of Cumbrian rescue dog.

ANN RUTGERS van der LOFF

Avalanche!
Netherlands 1954
Publisher unknown. University of London Press, 1956 and Puffin Books (Harmondsworth) 1959. Translated from the Dutch by Dora Round.

Children's story including many avalanches and the evacuation of Swiss alpine villages. Promotes the Pestalozzi Children's Village for War Orphans. Awarded the 'Best Children's Book of the Year' when first published in the Netherlands.

JEFF LONG

Angels of Light ***
US 1987
Beech Tree Books / William Morrow (New York)

Yosemite: Camp Four bums discover two tons of drugs and a smuggler's corpse in frozen High Sierra lake. But profits are short term. Soon they are enmeshed in web of violence and revenge. Inspired by a real incident when a plane crashed in the Sierras in 1977 (see report in *Mountain* 56).

'... a story of double jeopardy – the world's most dangerous sport wedded to the world's most desperate business.' Jacket Notes

'Top grade climbing fiction... The author pays especially close attention to shaping the characters into believable people. This book isn't for the non-climber ... (your mother would be shocked.)' Bill Hatcher, *Mountain* 119

'...A climbing western, with [philosophical] overtones. [the characters] are compared to mythical heros. There are deliberate overtones of Greek mythology, Arthurian legend and the Bible. Long's surest touch is with the climbing scenes...which maintain vividness while conveying a sense of both anxiety and of exhilaration.' Steven Jervis *American Alpine Journal*

'Long's finger is on the pulse of the climbing scene and his understanding of climbing's emotional aspects taps into the collective unconscious of the mountaineering world... he has given birth to the Great American Climbing Novel... perhaps it could be made into a TV mini-series thus allowing locals to ride the wave of free flowing cash once again.' Sally Moser, *Rock and Ice* 20

'Few [of the Yosemite climbers] could be as nasty, self-centred or weird as some of Long's characters... the value of these personnel, as repulsive or exasperating as they might seem, is in how each highlights traits we all share to some degree.' Jim Vermeulen *Climbing* 104

'Climbers will relish this rapturous and penetrating paean to their passion.' *Publishers Weekly*

'A celebration of word-music entirely appropriate to the mytho-poetic setting of mountain climbing in Yosemite... a great yarn.' *Rocky Mountain News*

HENRY WADSWORTH LONGFELLOW

Hyperion: a romance
US 1839
Publisher unknown. Scott (London) 1857, Bennett (London) 1865.

A romance with an Alpine background.

ARNOLD LUNN

Family Name
UK 1931
Methuen (London)

Though Claude loves Pamela, he must 'marry money' to recoup the family fortunes and he becomes engaged to a lady with the necessary financial qualifications. The future looks bleak as she dislikes mountaineering, but his problems are solved when in an unguarded moment he slips off the Lauteraarhorn.

'Climbing episodes are as well done as any in the range of fiction, but the book is equally interesting for its exposition of the author's original views of society and the world.' E. Cushing and J. Monroe Thorington

'If a novel is meant to divert rather than to edify then *Family Name* should be enjoyed by all mountaineers.' *Cambridge Mountaineering* 1932

'The mountaineering scenes are excellent, although the author cannot always resist the opportunity they afford for a maxim or a moral... he introduces incidents in it as pegs on which to hang his views of contemporary social and ethical problems!! (which includes an intense debate about the relationship between jew and gentile).' Unattributed – possibly Edward Strutt, *The Alpine Journal*

The novel is valuable for the new perspective it provides on Lunn – who was something of a *bête noir* to the Alpine Club. This review was a good deal kinder than those he received for many of his books in *The Alpine Journal*.

PETER LUNN

Evil in High Places
UK 1947
Methuen (London)

Thriller with some skiing.

'Only towards the denouement does one tend to feel that the psychology is manipulated... none the less this is an ingeniously-contrived affair with a credible Swiss detective.' Graham Sutton, *Fell and Rock Journal*

ELIZABETH LYNN

Sardonyx Net
US 1981
Berkeley Books (Berkeley)

Science fiction. Small but excellent section on ice climbing with 'advanced' tools. Generally well written, and dealing amongst other things with slavery, drugs, starship technology. Female protagonist.

ALEXANDER MACDONALD

Through the Heart of Tibet
UK 1910
Blackie (London)

Story for boys describing difficulties of reaching Lhasa.

O.S. MACDONELL (Oliver Stephen Macdonell)

George Ashbury
UK 1933
Selwyn and Blount (London)

Smuggling and whisky distilling in Lake District. The scene is laid... 'between Borrowdale, Ennerdale and Buttermere... with narrow escape of a supposed murderer from the myrmidons of the law. He [the author] handles his material well with a good narrative style.' W.P. Haskett Smith, *Fell and Rock Journal*

CHARLES MACHARDY

The Ice Mirror
UK 1971
Collins (London)

Climber loses his nerve after leading two companions to disaster on the Eiger North Wall. Fear and the wall – both – have to be conquered if he is to survive to win the girl he loves.

'Has you hanging on by your finger tips,' *Daily Express*

HAMISH MACINNES

Death Reel
UK 1976
Hodder and Stoughton (London)

James-Bondish adventure – much oil, blood and water – set on West Coast of Scotland and climaxing on phallic sea stack.

HELEN MACINNES

Horizon
UK 1945
Harrap (London)

'Thriller set in wartime Austrian Tyrol.' Jill Neate

NIGEL MACKENZIE

Seven Days to Death
UK 1959
Wright and Brown (London)

Thriller with a Himalayan setting.

AMY MCLAREN

From a Davos Balcony
UK 1903
Duckworth (London)

ALISTAIR MACLEAN

The Guns of Navarone
UK 1957
Collins (London), Doubleday (New York)

Group of wartime saboteurs gain a mediterranean island by cliff climbing techniques. (Filmed, with all-star cast headed by Gregory Peck.)

ROBERT MACLEOD (pseudonym of Bill Knox)

Path of Ghosts
UK 1971
John Long (London)

Thriller with some climbing.

DUNCAN MACNEIL

Sadhu on the Mountain Peak
UK 1971
Hodder and Stoughton (London)

A 'James Ogilvie' story: frontier days on the Khyber Pass.

ANGUS MACVICAR

The Atom Chasers in Tibet
UK 1957
Burke (London)

Jolly spiffing children's adventure. Little proper climbing but lashings of mountain environment and fair sprinklings of 'om mani padme hum'.

JANET MCNEIL (Janet Alexander)

Search Party
UK 1959
Hodder and Stoughton (London)

Search and rescue in Mourne Mountains provides soul-searching opportunity.

G.R. MAIR

Goddesses Never Die
Origin and date unknown
Publisher unknown

Thriller, set in Himalaya.

K.M. MANFRED

Peelah
UK 1904
Swan Sonnenschein (London)

Subtitled: or, The Bewitched Maiden of Nepal. Anglo-Nepalese girl is mesmerized and abducted from England to Nepal.

ETHEL MANNIN

Ragged Banners
UK 1931
Jarrolds (London), Knopf (New York)

Men are Unwise
UK 1934
Jarrolds (London)

The terrible consequences of one man's desire to climb.

Late Have I Loved Thee
UK 1948
Jarrolds (London)

A Catholic novel with lengthy climbing section set in Austrian Alps.

ANNE MANNING

An Idyl of the Alps
UK 1876
Hall (London)

The Year Nine
UK 1858
Hall (London)

Subtitled: a Tale of the Tirol

ERNEST MANSFIELD

Astria, The Ice Maiden
UK 1910
Lonsdale Press (London)

A romance based on Spitzbergen.

MARION MANVILLE

Up the Matterhorn in a Boat
US 1897
Century (New York) and serialised in *Century Magazine*

Ballooning story.

ANDY MARSHALL (female author)

Climb Every Mountain
UK 1982
A.H. Stockwell (Ilfracombe)

Includes a little Alpine climbing.

JOHN MASEFIELD

Sard Harker
UK 1924
Heinemann (London)

Hallucinatory climbing episode, crossing imaginary range in central America.

A.E.W. MASON (Alfred Edward Woodley Mason)

A Romance of Wastdale
UK 1895
Elkin Matthews (London). Hodder and Stoughton (London) 1914

Jealousy and murder in the Lake District. Subsequently filmed with a scene showing dummy being hurled from Kern Knotts (ref. *The Alpine Journal* 278).

The Broken Road
UK 1907
Smith Elder (London)

Mainly Indian setting, but passing references to climbing in the Dauphiné.

Running Water **
UK/US 1907
Hodder and Stoughton (London) / Century (New York). First published in serial form in *Century Magazine* 1906-1907.

Acknowledged masterpiece of mountain fiction by author of *The Four Feathers*. Includes a murder attempt on the Brenva Ridge.

'Mr Mason knows something of the business, and writes as we should expect of peaks and passes, of rock-faces and ice-slopes... as a true lover of the glories of the heights, and his vivid descriptions will attract many readers who do not care for the nefarious schemes of the low society from which he draws his heroine, only in order to place her on an Alpine pedestal. Her father is described as a climber... We confess since he turns out to be also an ex-convict and a would-be murderer – to some feeling of relief on finding that in other respects he is distinguishable from an ex-president of the Alpine Club...' Unattributed – possibly George Yeld, *Alpine Journal*

This review was noteworthy being the first occasion the AJ dealt with fiction. The ex-president referred to is Coolidge, who made the Brenva ascent fictionally given to the rogueish father; Coolidge threatened legal action, claiming to have been maligned. The intense speculation among alpinists of the day about the characters in the book is described in detail in Mason's obituary notice:

'...Mason had in fact used much unwritten

Alpine lore in the drawing of his characters, and especially in that of his villain, 'Garratt Skinner'....the photograph in which the villain was identified was suggested by Whymper's engraving in *Scrambles* of the 'The Club Room of Zermatt in 1864'; and what we may call the 'superficial' characteristics of 'Garratt Skinner' were derived from various different individuals – whilst the darker side of the villain was his alone, as also was his unfortunate criminal record. But the mosaic of this character offered good opportunity of speculation, and Montenvers was lively with various identifications ...' Tom Brocklebank, *Alpine Journal* 278

F. Van Wyck MASON

Himalayan Assignment
US 1952
Doubleday (New York)

Subtitled: a Colonel North novel. Feminine wiles, and a desperate chase in Himalayan blizzard.

RICHARD LAKIN MASON

The Fever Tree
UK 1962
Collins (London)

Set in the Himalaya.

JOHN MASTERS

Far, Far the Mountain Peak
UK 1957
Michael Joseph (London), Viking (New York)

Peter Savage, civil servant and mountaineer, a man of ruthless ambition, is forced to confront his false values on Himalayan peak. Includes an account of an ascent of the Zmutt Ridge of the Matterhorn.

The Himalayan Concerto / Himalayan Orchestra
UK 1976
Michael Joseph (London) / Doubleday (New York)

Himalayan spy thriller. Composer is asked to investigate troop movements on Sino-Indian border under guise of collecting folk music.

WHIT MASTERSON (pseudonym of Robert Wade and William Miller)

Man on a Nylon String
UK 1963
W. H. Allen (London), Dodd Mead (New York)

Yet another Eigerwand thriller. Famous mountaineer hangs frozen on a rope to be gawped at daily by ghoulish trippers. Playboy climber is hired to cut down body and retrieve its sinister secret. Murder and a seductive widow come into it, too.

BERKELEY MATHER

The Pass Beyond Kashmir
UK 1969
Collins (London), Scribner's (New York)

The Break in the Line / The Break
UK 1970
Collins (London) / Scribner's (New York)

Thriller culminating in the Himalaya.

ERIC MATHIESON

Mountain Month
UK 1965
Hamilton (London)

HUGH MERRICK (pseudonym of Harold Albert Meyer)

Pillar of the Sky
UK 1941
Eyre and Spottiswoode (London)

The reputed discovery of a mountain higher than Everest in Central Tibet leaves Alpine Club sceptical; it refuses assistance to the hero who, like Maurice Wilson, plans to fly a light aeroplane to his objective.

'...[The hero's mentor] can easily be identified to members of the FRCC... Mr Merrick brings so much imaginative power, allied to a real understanding of the mountains and a sensitive story, that the reader follows him willingly... The story is laced by romance and personal tragedy, indispensable to a novel concerned as much with spiritual development and character as with exploration and adventure.

'The chief flaw is the inordinate length of the introduction...' Marjorie Scott Johnston, *Fell and Rock Journal*

Andreas at Sundown
UK 1944
Hale (London)

Old alpine guide reflects on his loves and climbs.

Out of the Night
UK 1957
Hale (London)

Ageing climber embarks on last fateful climb.

The Breaking Strain
UK 1960
Constable (London)

Incompetent climber leads his party to disaster on alpine peak.

HENRY SEATON MERRIMAN (pseudonym of Hugh Stowell Scott)

The Slave of the Lamp
UK 1892
Murray (London)

A sea-cliff climb features in this semi-thriller.

GWEN MOFFAT

Lady with a Cool Eye
UK 1973
Gollancz (London)

Set in North Wales, this was the first of a series of crime thrillers, many featuring the adventures of amateur detective, Miss Melinda Pink, a kindly, middle-aged, semi-retired climber and writer. Others are as follows:

Deviant Death (1973)
The Corpse Road (1974)
Miss Pink at the Edge of the World (1975)#
Over the Sea to Death (1976)#
Short Time to Live (1977)
Persons Unknown (1978)
Die Like a Dog (1982)
Grizzly Trail (1984)
UK 1973-84
Gollancz (London) # denotes titles also published in the US by Scribners (New York)

'Gripping... I was sorry when I had finished it... and look forward to another good piece of escapism.' Tony Moulam, *Mountain Life* (re. *Miss Pink at the Edge of the World*).

Hard Option *
UK 1975
Gollancz (London)

Owen Parry, ageing leader of Welsh mountain rescue team basks in the publicity of each successful rescue. Though he finds it increasingly hard to keep up with younger team members, he is unwilling to relinquish to them any of the responsibility or glory. It is an unbelievably cool young woman climber who effects his eventual emasculation. (Gwen Moffat was, for many years, closely involved with the mountain rescue in North Wales.)

'Whether the reader considers modern rescuers to be over-organised vultures waiting to strike or heroes who risk life and limb to provide a splendid service to help fools who should be stopped, *Hard Option* should make compelling reading.' Barbara James, *Mountain Life* Oct/Nov 1975

'a compelling story... with moments of near cosmic illumination.' Audrey Salkeld, *Mountain* 46

The Buckskin Girl
UK 1982
Gollancz (London)

Resourceful heroine is the central figure of historical novel of the Old West of America.

MAX MOHR

Philip Glenn
Germany 1930s
Publisher unknown. Sidgwick and Jackson (London) 1932. Translated from the German *'Die Freundschaft von Ladiz'* by Countess Nora Purtscher-Wydenbruck.

'A novel about Alpine climbing and skiing dedicated to the memory of D.H.Lawrence. ...hence there is too much sex and too little climbing. After death of a female friend, Glenn starts up a friendship with Xavier Ragaz. They go up to a hut, where they spend several days getting fit, and incidentally indulge in discreditable pursuits. Ragaz is a married man with a family... Otherwise, if in execrable taste, the tale is well told.' Sydney Spencer, *The Alpine Journal*

A.R. HOPE MONCRIEFF (see also A.R. Hope)

Seeing the World
UK 1909
Wells Gardner Darton (London)

Subtitled: adventures of a young mountaineer.

C.E. MONTAGUE

The Morning's War
UK 1913
Methuen (London)

Believed to have two good chapters on Alpine climbing.

Right off the Map
UK 1927
Publisher unknown

Political and social fantasy.

ELIZABETH RIDER MONTGOMERY

Three Miles an Hour
US 1952
Dodd Mead (New York)

Story for young adults. The scene is the Olympic Mountains in the north-western United States.

BARONESS ISABELLE DE MONTOLIEU

The Avalanche
France 1820s
Publisher unknown. H.N. Batten (London) 1929.

Subtitled: or, The Old Man of the Alps.

LAURENCE MOODY

The Young Kings
UK 1960
Rupert Hart-Davies (London)

JOAN MORGAN

He Lives Amid Clouds
UK 1947
Chapman and Hall (London)

WARD MUIR

The Amazing Mutes
UK 1910
Stanley Paul (London)

Subtitled: their week in lovely Lucerne

TALBOT MUNDY

Ramsden
UK 1926
Hutchinson (London)

Climbing, etc. in the Himalaya.

KIRK MUNROE

Rick Dale
US 1896
Harpers (New York), Edward Arnold (London)

TOM MURPHY

Aspen Incident
US 1978
St. Martin's (New York)

JANE W. MURRAY

Walk the High Horizon
US 1979
Westminster (Philadelphia)

W.H. MURRAY (William Hutchinson Murray)

Five Frontiers / Appointment in Tibet
UK 1959
Dent (London) / Putnams (New York)

Spy thriller. Located variously in the Hebrides, Maritime Alps and Nepal.

Spurs of Troodos
UK 1960
Dent (London)

A sequel to *Five Frontiers* set mostly in Cyprus.

Maelstrom
UK 1962
Secker and Warburg (London)

Set in the Western Highlands.

Dark Rose the Phoenix
UK 1965
Secker and Warburg (London), Mackay (New York)

A. Van der NAILLEN

On the Heights of the Himalaya
US 1900
Fenno (New York)

JANET NEEL

Death on Site
UK 1989
Constable (London)

On holiday near Inverness, spunky Francesca Wilson and her (incognito) Police Inspector-lover, witness climbing fall. The victim, a 'professional' climber, survives that one, but it's only the start of a suspenseful web of intrigue.

'Ms. Neel writes with sprightly humour, a genuine talent to bemuse, and a forthright heroine in Francesca.' Unattributed*Sunday Times*

TERRY NEWMAN

No More a Brother
UK 1958
Cassell (London)

In the Alps a climbing accident involves the hero's brother.

BRUCE NICOLAYSEN

Perilous Passage
US 1976
Playboy Press (Chicago)

WILFRID NOYCE

The Gods are Angry
UK 1957
Heinemann (London), World Publications (Cleveland and New York)

Deals with a Himalayan ascent.

'A story portraying varying reactions of the climbers – to the mountain, their families, to work and the Sherpas.' Jill Neate

EDWIN CAMILLO OPPENHEIM

Some Peaks
UK 1898
Fisher Unwin (London)

OUIDA (pseudonym of Marie Louise de la Ramée)

Moths
UK 1880
Chatto and Windus (London)

RICHARD OWEN

Eye of the Gods
US 1978
Dutton (New York)

JOHN OXENHAM

Their High Adventure
UK 1911
Hodder and Stoughton (London)

Quest for the Golden Rose
UK 1912
Methuen (London)

J. MACDONALD OXLEY

On the World's Roof
Origin and date unknown
Publisher unknown

TSEWANG YISHEY PEMBA

Idols on the Path
UK 1966
Cape (London)

Novel set in Tibet, written by a Tibetan.

M. PEMBERTON (Sir Max Pemberton)

White Motley
UK 1913
Cassell (London)

Story of crime and romance involving flights over the Alps.

ELLIS PETERS (pseudonym of Edith Mary Pargeter)

Piper on the Mountains
UK 1966
Collins (London and Glasgow)

A thriller. In the Tatras a daughter attempts to discover how and why her father died.

GILBERT HENRY PHELPS

Winter People
UK 1963
Bodley Head (London)

Set in the Andes.

C. PHILLIPPS-WOLLEY

Snap
UK/US 1889
Longmans, Green (London/New York)

Subtitled: a Legend of the Lone Mountain. Contains an outstanding collection of climbing illustrations by H.G. Willink.

SUSAN PLEYDELL

Brighouse Hotel
UK 1977
Collins (London)

Story of mountain rescue, romance and climbing in Scotland.

NOEL POCOCK

Below Zero
UK 1911
Hodder and Stoughton (London)

A travesty of winter sport, with verses adapted to the occasion by A.E. Johnson.

HUGH POPHAM

Beyond the Eagle's Rage
UK 1951
The Bodley Head (London)

ELIZABETH PRITCHARD

The School in the Himalayas
UK 1961
Pickering and Inglis (London)

For juveniles.

RICHARD PURSLOW

Sleep Till Noonday
UK 1963
Heinemann (London)

Rock climbing in North Wales with a climax on Cloggy.

'Not a book to be recommended. It is deplorable that the literature of our sport should be debased by sexual adventures.' R.G. Inglis, *Scottish Mountaineering Club Journal*. (And not as you might think 'Disgusted of Tunbridge Wells' – others approached to review the book had declined.)

CHARLES-FERDINAND RAMUZ

Terror on the Mountain
France 1925
Grasset (Paris). Harcourt Brace (New York) 1967. Translated from the French *La Grande Peur dans la Montagne.*

When the Mountain Fell
France 1936
Grasset (Paris). Pantheon (New York) and Eyre and Spottiswoode (London) 1949. Translated from the French *Derborence* by Surah Fisher Scott.

Two men buried alive under landslide.

ARTHUR RANSOME

Swallows and Amazons
UK 1932
Cape (London)

This children's adventure and some of its sequels are set among the Lakeland Fells.

DIANA RAYMOND

The Five Days
UK 1959
Cassell (London)

Man on the run among the hills of Northern England.

The Climb *
UK 1962
Cassell (London)

Three men come to climb deadly North Face of the Heide (obviously the Eiger), each for personal reasons. That said, surprisingly little of the action centres on the climb itself – it is more about its effect on the people directly and peripherally involved. One is reminded of the other 'lady' novelists – Coxhead, Gibbons, Renault.

The Dark Journey
UK 1978
Cassell (London)

Has some climbing.

Mountains, in a more general way, feature in other Diana Raymond books: *Joanna Linden* (Cumberland), *Between the Stirrup and the Ground* (Skye).

ERNEST RAYMOND

The Mountain Farm
UK 1966
Cassell (London)

Romance and climbing in the Lake District.

Two other novels by this author are set in the Lake District but with little climbing interest: *The Five Sons of Le Faber* (1948) and *Nameless Places* (1954)

ROBERT RECHER

Rudi of the Mountains
UK 1964
Oliver and Boyd (Edinburgh)

A story about children and a young alpine guide. For young adults.

LUCY REES and AL HARRIS

Take it to the Limit **
UK 1981
Diadem (London)

Back home on the raunch. The torrid North Wales scene of the late sixties, with precious little flower power, but plenty of boozing, brawling and dedicated hedonism. Hard days on the crags, hard nights in cottages and the chilly backs of vans. Tragic love triangle provides break-neck action: Luke (driven, neurotic), his steady climbing partner Bob, and Kate who loves them both. Climax reached on Yosemite big wall climb.

'does not overplay the decadent section of the climbing scene in the sixties (which certainly carried on well into the seventies)... characters seem believable too.' Rosie Smith

'Oh dear! Another exposé of what things are like at the high sharp end of the climbing scene, where the main stimulus comes apparently from non-conformity, alcohol and sex... Climbing was never like this before.' Peter Hillman, *Alpine Journal*

'It is impossible now to separate in the mind this Harris-inspired book from the recent death of Harris himself. It will inevitably be read with an eye for clues to his complex nature. Harris was a professional climber in that climbing fitted as a risk sport into life-as-a-whole, which he also treated as a risk sport. (He died not on a climb but while pushing his limits as a fast driver.) It was his expertise in 'the gambling life' that provided the incident and characterisation which Lucy Rees scripted. The book... is tragic but with elements of black farce. Luke, the pivotal figure of a triangular relationship,...relentlessly piles sensation upon sensation without being able to derive satisfaction from any of them. It is achingly sad. Even the authors could see no living solution to the predicament.' Tim Lewis and Audrey Salkeld, *Mountain* 82

'Raised as I was in a diluted non-conformist background, deeply indoctrinated by the supposed Protestant work ethic, the antics of Harris and his drop-out circle both fascinated and appalled me. So might a teetotal, hardworking dormouse have gazed upon an alcoholic, sunbathing cobra. There is enough material in the book for several novels... but perhaps Harris knew better than we how short a span was left to him and used his material as profligately as his life-style used his energy.' Dave Gregory, *Climbers' Club Journal*

MAYNE REID

The Plant Hunters
UK 1858
J and C Brown (London). Routledge (London and New York) 1890.

Subtitled: or, Adventures among the Himalayas.

The Cliff-Climbers
US 1865
Tichnor Fields (Boston)

Subtitled: or, The Lone Home in the Himalayas. Sequel to *The Plant Hunters*.

MARY RENAULT (pseudonym of Mary Challans)

North Face *
UK 1949
Longmans (London), Morrow (New York)

Little climbing takes place in the action, but it is used throughout as a metaphor with which to chart the delicate, developing romance between two climbing enthusiasts, bruised by earlier experiences. Set immediately after the war. Interesting period piece.

HETTIE RICHIE

Death Runs on Skis
UK 1935
Methuen (London)

Above average adventure of the 'treasure hunt' type, with vivid characterizations.

WILLIAM H. RIDEING

Boys in the Mountains and on the Plains
US 1882
Appleton (New York)

ANNE RIDER

A Light Affliction
UK 1967
Bodley Head (London)

Himalayan setting.

RITA (pseudonym of Eliza Margaret Humphreys)

Edelweiss, A Romance
UK 1890
Spencer Blackett (London)

DAVID ROBERTS

Like Water and Like Wind ***
US 1980
Ascent (San Francisco) and collected in *One Step in the Clouds*

Climber claims an Alaskan ascent to which he feels morally entitled, with terrible consequences. Clearly inspired by the Maestri/Cerro Torre mystery, and drawing on his own experiences on Mt Huntingdon and Mt Dickey, Roberts produces one of the most inspired pieces of mountain fiction yet written.

'Craftsmanship of a very high standard is evident in every paragraph. Skill as a stylist is undeniably there.' Andy Harvard, *American Alpine Journal*.

'A damned good yarn.' Bill Peascod, *Fell and Rock Journal*

KIM STANLEY ROBINSON

Green Mars **
US 1988
Tor Books (New York) in *Tor Double* paired with Arthur C. Clarkes's *A Meeting with Medusa*

Climbing the highest mountain on Mars (many explicit and hidden references to British climbers of the seventies).

Mother Goddess of the World **
UK 1988
Robinson Publishing (London) in *Best New SF2* edited by Gardner Dozois, and also collected in *One Step in the Clouds.*

To Everest, with mysticism, Mallory, and ambition.

Escape from Kathmandu **
US 1989
Tor Books (New York), Unwin Hyman (London)

Four interlinked Nepalese stories (including *Mother Goddess*). Others involve rescuing a captured yeti; a brush with ex-president Jimmy Carter (and entourage of Secret Servicemen); halting the construction of a new road through the mystical city of Shangri-La... and more. Entertaining fantasy which publishers claim belongs 'somewhere between *Raiders of the Lost Ark* and the adventure tales of H. Rider Haggard.'

'A delightful romp.' *Publishers Weekly*

DAPHNE ROOKE

Boy on the Mountain
UK 1969
Gollancz (London)

Group of young people growing up in Westland, New Zealand. Some climbing.

A. WREN RUMNEY

The Dalesman
UK 1911
Titus Wilson (Kendal)

MARION RUMSEY

Danger on Shadow Mountain
US 1970
Morrow (New York)

SALMAN RUSHDIE

The Satanic Verses
UK 1988
Viking (London)

Characters include Alleluia Cone, who climbed Everest without oxygen – and met the ghost of Maurice Wilson.

JOHN RUSKIN

The King of the Golden River
UK 1851 (2nd edition)
Publisher unknown. Later paperback edition Dover Publications (London).

Subtitled: Or The Black Brothers, a legend of Stiria. A children's book.

JAMES SALTER

Solo Faces ***
US 1979
Little Brown (Boston), Collins (London) and collected in *One Step in the Clouds.*

Vernon Rand, the central figure, falls victim to the bleak rootlessness that can follow in the wake of a hard climbing career. He is a man of sexual attractiveness, but unable to settle for the limitations love would bring; he has an instinctive distrust of security, yet is being destroyed by insecurity. Rand comes to the Alps from his native California, where his exploits soon make him a living legend. When two Italians are trapped on the Dru, he leads a daring rescue, which serves to confirm his celebrity. But what can a legend do when friends are gone and powers fade? It is no secret that the character of Rand was inspired by Gary Hemming ('Le Beatnik' as he was known in France), who sparked and drifted his way through the alpine scene of the mid-sixties before putting a bullet through his head at the age of thirty-five.

'Captures the genuine feel of climbing – not its melodrama but the skill and concentration, rigour and elation. What is rarer is the fact that Salter has done all this in a complex and sophisticated novel.' Al Alvarez

'inconsequential, open-ended and utterly purposeless.' Edward Pyatt, *The Alpine Journal*

'A fine, exciting and sensitive novel.' Norman Mailer

'Strange and interesting book.' Graham Greene

'The book is so convincingly written that one might assume that this was in fact an autobiography. It is the events in between [the climbing] which are filled with detail and which give such realism... the streets and bars of Paris... or the Gauloise smell of cafes in rural French towns and the summer heat of rundown Californian back streets.' John Sheard, *Mountain* 74

'Juxtaposes egos and dreams that come forward, meteorlike, then vanish... Rand and Cabot live out their powerful destinies with noble clarity. Salter has achieved a realism here that is not likely to be forgotten.' Michael Tobias, *Climbing* 57

'Rand pursues his quest, that elusive inner peace with himself that so many look for but few find. James Salter has skilfully blended fact and fiction to create a gripping story.

'Solo Faces is very fine fiction, well crafted and intelligent. Far from the regular works of mountaineering fiction this book deserves to be read.' Geordie Howe, *Canadian Alpine Journal* 1984

PETER LARS SANDBERG

Wolf Mountain *
US 1975
Playboy Press (Chicago)

Psychopath-on-run stalks mountaineering party in remote mountains of Colorado. He guns down one of two adults supervising group of teenage girls and imprisons rest of party to rape and murder at leisure. Vietnam war vet happening on scene also gets trapped, but leads escape bid. Gripping manhunt through blizzard-swept mountains. Plot has lot to do with male/female attitudes and tensions.

'Tingling he-man adventure... keeps reader tied to the page as if he were roped to a climbing party,' *Victoria, Texas Advocate*

'Something to read on an evening after a hard day, when the mind cannot quite grasp Dostoyevsky but refuses to resort to Readers Digest... Rape and murder are included as violent elements, a requisite of modern tales. They are not shocking except as an indication of what a 'wilderness experience' might entail..' Anne Marie Rizzi, *Mountain Gazette*

LAWRENCE SANDERS

The First Deadly Sin
US 1973
Putnam (New York)

'Starts and ends with rock climbing sequences. Murder, sex and perversion in the life of a New York City climber.' Jill Neate

MALCOLM SAVILLE

The Sign of the Alpine Rose
UK 1950
Lutterworth Press (London)

For juveniles.

DOROTHY L. SAYERS

Five Red Herrings
UK 1931
Gollancz (London)

A 'Lord Peter Wimsey' story about crime and climbing in Scotland.

WALDEMAR SCHMIDTMAN

Devil
Origin and date unknown
Century (New York) / Appleton (London) 1936. Translated by the author.

Subtitled: the life story of a chamois in the Austrian Alps.

B. SCHULTZE-SMIDT

A Madonna of the Alps
US 1895
Little Brown (Boston)

RICHARD SCHWEIZER

The Last Chance
Origin and date unknown
Publisher unknown. Secker and Warburg / Lindsay Drummond (London) 1947. Translated by Lord Sudley.

J.M. SCOTT (James Maurice Scott)

The Silver Land
UK 1937
Hodder and Stoughton (London)

The Other Side of the Moon
UK 1946
Hodder and Stoughton (London)

The Will and the Way
UK 1949
Hodder and Stoughton (London), Dutton (New York)

Cheerful tale of a treasure hunt involving the beneficiaries of a will, set on and around Monte Rosa.

'If Dornford Yates had been a member of this Club he would probably have written a novel like this.' Francis Keenlyside, *Climbers' Club Journal*

Touch of the Nettle
UK 1951
Hodder and Stoughton (London)

Thriller set in the Italian Alps, with a man-hunt on storm-swept summits as its climax.

Other Half of the Orange
UK 1955
Heinemann (London), Dutton (New York)

Mystery and romance. Searching for a man believed dead, with climbing around Mont Blanc.
Titles of other works by this author suggest they too may have mountain or polar backgrounds (*The Pole of Inaccessibility; Snowstone*)

MARJORIE SCOTT JOHNSTON (see under Johnston)

'EDWARD SCRAMBLE'

Whimpers Amongst the Alps
UK 1923
Publisher unknown

An ill-fated attempt on the 'Maulwurfshaufen' (Molehill).

ROBIN SHAW

Running
UK 1974
Gollancz (London)

A poetry professor and an ex-convict climb together and plan the perfect crime.

NICHOLAS SIZE

The Secret Valley
UK c1928
Titus Wilson (Kendal)

Guerilla warfare waged by fellside Norsemen against the Norman invader. 'Romantic' treatment of mainly historical data.

ALBERT RICHARD SMITH

Struggles and Adventures of Christopher Tadpole at Home and Abroad
UK 1848
Willoughby (London)

Climbing Mont Blanc in Chapter 30.

FRANK SMYTHE

Secret Mission
UK 1942
Hodder and Stoughton (London)

British inventor of secret weapon and his beautiful daughter seek sanctuary from Nazi thugs in the Nepal Himalaya.

'F.S. Smythe, making his first fictional march, has outflanked or bridged the crevasses. His attack, though a trifle stereotyped, is competent and concise; he diverts us plausibly with false clues then on sure ground – a mission to unknown Nepal is the theme – commands our interest by the picturesqueness and the authenticity of his detail, and the speed at which his plot moves... Tension increases towards the climax; and a love interest (neat but not gaudy, as befits such a tale) is used with unexpectedly dramatic effect to conclude the adventure.' Graham Sutton, *Fell and Rock Journal* 1944

E.M. SNEYD-KYNNERSLEY

A Snail's Wooing **
UK 1910
Macmillan (London)

Subtitled: story of an Alpine courtship. Life and climbing around Zermatt before the Great War. Written in an appealling contemporary style and 'very funny'.

'An utter hoot... the only book that has distracted us in bed.' Geoff Milburn (when asked to comment on this list).

CHARLES H. SNOW

The Seven Peaks
UK 1936
Wright and Brown (London)

ARON and O'LEARY SPILKEN Ed.

Burning Moon
US 1979
Playboy Press (Chicago)

Adventure, with inevitable chase, in Grand Tetons. Light summer reading:

'Two women – white, suburban, politically aware – become weary of the endless grind of pointless work. They decide to take a chance and strike out for the big pay-off. In this case that means robbing a resort in the Tetons. They enlist the aid of a joke-cracking San Francisco queen.' Eric Davis, *Climbing* 53

JOHANNA SPYRI

Heidi
Switzerland 1880
Publisher unknown. Dent (London) 1906, Dutton and Co (New York) 1909. Numerous editions since.

Growing up with Grandpa on lonely Alp. Children's classic.

WILLIAM GORDON STABLES

In Regions of Perpetual Snow
UK 1904
Ward Lock (London)

High adventure on Himalayan glaciers (by this well-known Scottish writer of boys' books).

ARTHUR D. STAPP

Mountain Tamer
US 1948
Morrow (New York)

AARON MARC STEIN

Alp Murder
US 1970
Doubleday (New York)

COCHRANE STEWART

Windslab
UK 1952
Hodder and Stoughton (London)

Set in Austria in 1945: five men, two women stranded in a climbing hut carelessly sited beneath windslab slope overhung by large cornice. Clearly a disaster is waiting to happen...

'Unfortunately 244 pages elapse before it does [and] in the meantime we get some sloppy writing and much superficial characterisation:
"Roger, I know, has gone up to see Monique... he has never told her that he killed her husband. Life is too short."
'... the reader will not be unduly surprised a few pages later when the guide attempts to rape both women in turn. Recommended if hut-bound ...with nothing else to read.' Robin Plackett, *Climbers' Club Journal*

MARY STEWART

Wildfire at Midnight
UK 1956
Hodder and Stoughton (London)

Thriller set on Skye and with some climbing scenes.

RUDOLPH STRATZ

Where Snow is Sovereign
Germany 1900s
Publisher unknown. Dodd Mead (New York) 1909. Translated from the German by Mary Stafford.

Subtitled: a Romance of the Glaciers. Focuses on women climbing with guides.

ANNE W. STRAWBRIDGE

Dawn After Danger
US 1934
Coward-McCann (New York)

Some mountaineering episodes.

Above the Rainbow
US 1938
Stackpole Books (Harrisburg)

Some mountaineering scenes in this psychological tale.

TERENCE STRONG

That Last Mountain
UK 1989
Hodder and Stoughton (London)

SAS and Soviet teams clash in Arctic mountains of Sweden.

SHOWELL STYLES

This prolific author (who also uses the pseudonym Glyn Carr – see separate entry) has written many adult, young adult and children's books, usually with a mountaineering background. They include:

Traitor's Mountain
UK 1946
Selwyn and Blount (London), Macmillan (New York)

Fast-moving spy thriller (the first of a series of eighteenbooks featuring his portly theatrical detective, Sir Abercrombie 'Filthy' Lewker. The first three were thrillers by Showell Styles, the rest 'detective' stories by Glyn Carr.

Kidnapped Castle
UK 1947
Selwyn and Blount (London)

Dark Hazard
UK 1947
Selwyn and Blount (London)

Finishes with an ascent of Pillar Rock.

Hammer Island
UK 1948
Selwyn and Blount (London)

The Lost Glacier
UK 1955
Hart-Davis (London), Vanguard (New York)

Thriller: climbing in the Himalaya.

Kami the Sherpa / Sherpa Adventure
UK 1957
Brockhampton Press (Leicester) / Vanguard (New York) 1960.

Teenage English boy and young Sherpa attempt to rescue members of Himalayan climbing party.

Shadow Buttress
UK 1959
Faber (London)

Scottish guide loses his sight, but wins his way back to the mountains.

The Flying Ensign
UK 1960
Faber (London)

Naval historical novel with some climbing.

Tiger Patrol
UK 1957
Collins (London)

Boy Scout story with a little climbing.

Tiger Patrol Presses On
UK 1961
Collins (London)

The Lost Pothole
UK 1961
Brockhampton Press (Leicester)

Two boys hunt for an ancient pothole containing treasure.

The Shop in the Mountains
UK 1961
Gollancz (London)

First story about Simon and Mag Hughes; climbing in North Wales.

The Ladder in the Snow
UK 1962
Gollancz (London), Vanguard (New York)

Second 'Hughes' story, this time climbing in the Swiss Alps.

Necklace of Glaciers
UK 1963
Gollancz (London)

Third 'Hughes' story – thriller involving climbing in Austrian Tyrol.

The Camp in the Hills
UK 1964
Benn (London)

The Pass of Morning
UK 1966
Gollancz (London)

Fourth 'Hughes' story. Norway this time.

Journey with a Secret / Mystery of the Fleeing Girl
UK / US 1970
Gollancz (London) / Scholastic Book Services (New York)

'Foreign agents, murder, dangerous mist-enshrouded moors, the vivid background of the Welsh countryside, and a chilling run-for-your-life chase.' Jacket notes

The Snowdon Rangers
UK 1970
Faber (London)

Young adult story of rock-climbing in Wales.

A Tent on Top
UK 1971
Gollancz (London)

CONSTANCE SUTCLIFFE

Our Lady of the Ice
UK 1909
Greening (London)

Subtitled: a story of the Alps. Alpine guide, after losing his client, dies trying to save the brother.

GRAHAM SUTTON

Damnation of Mr. Zinkler **
UK 1935
Cape (London)

Zesty black parable. 'Rock' Grenfell, famous mountaineer, arrives in Hades after bad fall; there he meets a film tycoon and an idealistic young woman. Rebelling against a totalitarian regime that will countenance no risk-taking, he eventually climbs back to the Overworld.

Shepherd's Warning
UK 1946
Collins (London)

Historical novel based around the sheep-farming Fleming family of West Cumberland with scene on Pillar Rock. Action, suspense and

'...usual quota of fugitive rebels and lovely maidens [but] could only have been written by one deeply familiar with the touch and individuality of the Rock itself. ...a story pervaded by a profound sense of the value of human integrity.' Kathleen Howard, *Fell and Rock Journal*

Smoke Across the Fell
UK 1947
Collins (London)

Stirring historical romance set in West Cumbria.

North Star
UK 1949
Collins (London)

Young son of the Fleming family seeks a career on the stage.

Fleming of Honister
UK 1953
Hodder and Stoughton (London)

Another Fleming historical novel. In this the hero (in 1873) is a geological expert during the construction of the Settle to Carlisle railway.

The Rowan Tree
UK 1955
Hodder and Stoughton (London)

Historical novel, set in the Lake District.

'Not a book for those who insist on a happy ending, but as an absorbing tale of intrigue and adventure against the unchanging background of farm, fell and sea. It can be warmly recommended.' W.G. Stevens, *Fell and Rock Journal*

HAN SUYIN (Elizabeth Comber)

The Mountain is Young
UK 1958
Cape (London)

Nepalese politics and chit-chat. Damning portrayal of Western ex-pats. Philosophies of love, and dangers of road engineering in big mountains also feature.

MARGARET SYMONDS

A Child of the Alps
UK 1920
Fisher Unwin (London)

Story of girl's mingled artistic and peasant nature.

GORDON TAYLOR

Place of the Dawn
US 1975
Original publisher unknown. Hamlyn paperbacks (London) 1979.

How the innocent love affair of liberated American girl and Turkish archaeologist unleashes the powerful forces of an ancient taboo, turning a climbing expedition into a 14,000 foot death trap.

'A novel of cold terror.' Jacket notes

'Harrowing.' *Publishers Weekly*

'Emotional and violent.' *Pittsburgh Press*

ROB TAYLOR

The Breach
US 1981
Coward, McCann and Geoghegan (New York)

Thinly-veiled 'fictional' account of actual accident on Kilimanjaro. Rob is a serious-minded alpinist, Harley Warner, the most famous rock-climber of his day; their two styles compensate each other admirably, but their disparate personalites doom the enterprise from the start.

'... surfaces beyond the controversy to tell a powerful story of man's will to survive the ignominy of misplaced confidences as much as the will to survive the mountain's elements. At the story's core is Taylor's account of enduring a gruelling rescue and recuperation in a strange world short of compassion,' *Summit* July-August 1982.

'It is the tone of bitterness, self-pity and to a great degree, self-aggrandizement, that I find so objectionable... the story does have great potential which is wasted byTaylor's wallowing in an emotional morass of his own making.' Mike Kennedy, *Climbing* 70

'The story is not merely arresting but shocking... Warner is drawn as unremittingly vain, shallow and even duplicitous... [The Breach] for all its flaws, gives its own account commendably.' Steven Jervis, *American Alpine Journal*

D.M. THOMAS

Lying Together
US 1990
Gollancz (London)

Among other fantasies are encounters with Eiger martyrs... Sedlmayr, Mehringer, Harlin...

GUY THORNE

The Greater Power
UK 1915
Gale and Polden (London)

Subtitled: a story of the present campaign in Italy. World War I – hauling big guns up precipices.

MICHAEL TOBIAS

Déva **
US 1982
Avant Books (San Diego)

Erotic Himalayan fantasy. In 1976 two lovers, Ghisela (strong, sensitive, somehow naïve) and Michael (passionate, but a sceptic) are summoned by Allain (anthropologist and mystic) to meet Central Asian ancient (100 years old yet still climbing like a goat). In the Ladak Himal, sexual energy reveals its hidden essence, nature and the spiritual converge to transcend human ecstasy, and the experience of ascension assumes a single-pointed concentration, an encounter with unfathomable wisdom. Well – something like that!

'...reads a little like Kerouac, a little like Gilbrahn and a little like the Dr. Bronner's soap label.' Stuart Pregnall, *Summit* Sept/Oct 1988

'.. a 21st century novel about our own times... *Déva* is the work of an obviously – here and there too obviously – encyclopaedic mind. Esoteric references are as hazardous to the book's flow as the polysyllables that lie stitched into the text. These obstacles mar, but do not ruin what is in the end a highly intelligent, and often times brilliantly told tale.' Jeff Long, *Mountain* 89

'The images are rich, abundant and insistent. The plot and characters... are fresh. A provocative metaphor of ascent, attractive to those who have a passion for the obsure, or, more likely just looking for an unusual read.' Charles Hood, *Climbing*

RUTHVEN TODD

Over the Mountain
UK 1939
Harrap (London)

Mountaineering allegory about democracy and fascism.

PAUL TOWNEND

Died O'Wednesday
UK 1959
Collins (London), Walker (New York) 1962.

Thriller, set in Switzerland.

Man on the End of the Rope
UK 1960
Collins (London), Dutton (New York)

Another gruesome Eiger yarn – entertainingly dreadful. Could the mystery climber dangling on the Mördwand be playboy baron, Wendelin Mendoza? In a run-down Alpiglen hotel, the world's pressmen gather, watching, waiting and running up their expense accounts.

LOUIS TRACY

The Silent Barrier
UK 1910
Ward Lock (London)

Set in the Engadine. A tale of love, climbing and attempted crime.

NIGEL TRANTER

Cable from Kabul
UK 1968
Hodder and Stoughton (London)

A thriller with Hindu Kush and Karakoram locations.

Rio d'Oro
UK 1974
White Lion Publishers (London)

Andean setting.

'TREVANIAN' (believed to be pseudonym of a US academic, Professor Whittaker)

The Eiger Sanction
US 1972
Crown (New York), Heinemann (London)

Stylish cliff-hanger. Curiously dated now. Art professor/collector Jonathan Hemlock is a hit man on the side (well he has to pay for his Van Goghs somehow – and he only eliminates opposition agents). His latest contract must be fulfilled on the Eiger North Face. (Filmed, starring Clint Eastwood and George Kennedy.) 'a put-on, a witty 007-type fable of danger, mayhem and treachery.' *Boston Globe*

'... writer may well be trying to send up mountaineering.' Edward Pyatt, *The Alpine Journal*

'plenty of action, plenty of sex.' *New York Times*

'skilful writing keeps the book exciting to the end, but the real mystery is not who did the murder, but who did the book!' Galen Rowell

HENRI TROYAT

The Mountain
France 1952
Flammarion (Paris), Simon and Schuster (New York), British publisher unknown. Translated from the French *'La Neige en deuil'* by Constantine Fitzgibbon.

Two alpine guides, brothers, set out for scene of aeroplane crash – their motives however are worlds apart. (Filmed, starring Spencer Tracy and Robert Wagner.)

GEORGE TUGWELL

On the Mountain
UK 1862
R. Bentley (London)

Based in Wales.

GEORGI TUSHKAN

The Hunter of the Pamirs
Soviet Union 1930s
Publisher unknown. Hutchinson (London) c1944. Translated from the Russian by Gerard Shelley.

Subtitled: a novel of adventure in Soviet Central Asia.

MARK TWAIN (pseudonym of Samuel Langhorne Clemens)

A Tramp Abroad
US 1879
American Publishing Co (Hartford, Connecticut). Chatto and Windus (London) 1880. Also in volumes 3, 4 of *The Writing of Mark Twain* (1899).

Travels in Europe written in a semi-fictional style with several mountaineering episodes. A humorous classic.

JAMES RAMSAY ULLMAN

The White Tower
US 1945
Lippincott (Philadelphia), Collins (London)

Five men and one woman of different nationalities take up the challenge – an ill-assorted xenophobic bunch that no sane person would dream of tying together on a mountain. Unpalatable now, but well enough written in a purplish way. (Filmed, starring Glenn Ford, Lloyd Bridges.)

'Beyond reach of the hatred and bloodshed that was tearing Europe, the White Tower stood sublime... an eternal challenge to mankind.' Jacket notes

'The existence of any peak in the Alps requiring several bivouacs on the normal route, is too laughable almost to mention.' Claire Eliane Engel

'Ullman... fell into an avalanche of error.' Hugh Merrick

'A tale so authentic and complete as to hold the expert enthralled; yet so explicitly and vividly told, that the man who has never set foot on a climb can appreciate every movement. There are few classic mountaineering tales; this is going to be one of them.' Graham Sutton, *Fell and Rock Journal*

'Most mountaineering fiction is a enjoyable as being force-fed on stale chocolate eclairs, but for me the genre achieves diarrhoeal depths with the buttock-clenchingly bad *White Tower*.' Steve Ashton, *Climber and Hillwalker*.

The Sands of Karakorum
US 1953
Lippincott (Philadelphia), Collins (London)

A search set to the north of the Altai Mountains and north-west of the Gobi.

'...vivid account of life and travel in modern Red China and Mongolia.' *Time and Tide*

Banner in the Sky
US 1954
Lippincott (Philadephia), Collins (London)

Swiss dishwasher joins English climber for ascent of the fabled 'Citadel'. Young adult story, drawing loosely on the first Matterhorn climb. (Filmed by Walt Disney as *Third Man on the Mountain*, starring Michael Rennie and James MacArthur.)

'saccharine concoction.' Athan A Pantsios

'"There are many ways," Mr Ullman writes, "in which this story resembles the true story of the first climbing of the Matterhorn." We found no resemblances except the date... The author has absolutely no sense of period and very little idea of procedure normal on mountains. ...notwithstanding these irritations, [he] invents quite an exciting story which will no doubt give great pleasure, but not to the readers of this Journal.' D.F.O. Dangar, *The Alpine Journal*

And Not to Yield
US 1970
Doubleday (New York), Collins (London)

Long and discursive novel in which American climber, Rick Venn, doesn't climb the Himalayan mountain of his dreams (Dera Zor), but gains personal illumination.

'... the book has neither hero nor romance, humour nor beauty; the dialogue is appalling. In places it aspires to the sentimental... The climbing is accurately described.' Mike Baker, *The Alpine Journal*

SURESH VAIDYA

Kailas
Origin and date unknown
Publisher unknown. Queensway Press (London) 1937

OWEN VAUGHAN (pseudonym of Owen Rhoscomyl)

Vronina
UK 1900s
Publisher unknown. Duckworth (London) 1907

Subtitled: a tale of the Welsh Mountains. Good description of mountain scenery and the enjoyment of it; a little climbing.

JAN-FRANCOIS VIGNANT

The Alpine Affair
US 1970
Chelsea House (New York)

HUBERT WALES

The Thirty Days
UK 1915
Cassell (London) – published in serial form in America under the title of *The Brockbank Riddle*.

A spiritual thriller that begins with an ascent of Mont Blanc.

DAVID RAINS WALLACE

The Turquoise Dragon
US 1985
Sierra Club (San Francisco)

'Who killed salamander expert Tom Blackwell? ...Snappy whodunit serving up requisite sex, violence and car chases – but interleaved with an environmental message. Definitely the butler didn't do it!' Charles Hood, *Climbing*

HUGH WALPOLE

Prolific novelist (1884-1941) whose boldest and strongest work is contained in the *Herries Chronicle*, a historical sequence set in Cumberland and incorporating: *Rogue Herries* (1920); *Judith Paris* (1931); *The Fortress* (1932); *Vanessa* (1933).

MAURICE WALSH

The Key Above the Door
UK 1923
Chambers (London)

Based in Scotland with some references to Skye.

The Hill is Mine
UK 1940
Chambers (London)

Subtitled: a tale of the Cairngorms.

E.M. WARD (Edith Marjorie Ward)

Mountain Water
Alpine Rose
Dancing Ghyll
UK 1935/1937/1937
Methuen (London)

All with a mountain background.

GERTRUDE WARDEN (pseudonym of Mrs. Wilton Jones)

The Crime in the Alps
UK 1908
White (London)

Thriller. A bomb in a pocket barometer will explode at a certain altitude.

FORREST WEBB

The Snowboys
UK 1973
Hodder and Stoughton (London)

Tabloid-adventure thriller set on Arctic expedition.

H.G. WELLS

Ann Veronica
UK 1909
T. Fisher Unwin (London)

One chapter on climbing in Switzerland.

WILLIAM WESTALL

Her Two Millions
US 1887
Harpers (New York) in three volumes.

'Story set mainly in Switzerland, but partly around Mont Blanc. Husband pushes his wife into a crevasse.' Jill Neate

ROBERT WEVERKA

Avalanche
US 1978
Bantam (New York)

Based on the screenplay by Claude Pola of a feature film starring Rock Hudson and Mia Farrow.

JON MANCHIP WHITE

Nightclimber
UK 1968
Chatto and Windus (London), Morrow (New York)

Readable thriller. Forty-one year old, who in his student days had repeated all the original Cambridge nightclimbing routes besides adding more of his own, is enveigled by millionaire into performing a giant leap for avarice. Storyline, flimsy in places, maintains pace towards explosive finish.

PHYLLIS WHITNEY

Snowfire
UK 1973
Heinemann (London)

Romantic fiction with ski background: Linda visits Julian's brooding mansion to clear her brother of the murder of Julian's wife, but is soon enmeshed in a storm of conflicting emotions, dark secrets and strange forebodings....

Two other novels, *Spindrift* and *Silverhill*, by this author may be of the same ilk.

C.N. and A.M. WILLIAMSON (Charles Norris and Alice Muriel Williamson)

The Princess Virginia
UK/US 1907
McClure Phillips (London and New York).
Methuen (London) 1913.

Begins with a climbing adventure.

H. SCHUTZ WILSON

Philip Mannington
UK 1874
Publisher unknown.

Subtitled: A novel and Eisleben. In two volumes.

LEIGH WILSON

Do You Go Back Dismayed?
UK 1949
Methuen (London)

A climber masters his fear to return to the Himalaya in search of a friend held prisoner by savage tribesmen.

RICHARD WINCOR

Sherlock Holmes in Tibet
US 1966
Wesbright and Talley (New York)

An astonishing account of Holmes' hitherto unknown years, now revealed in a most extraordinary narrative from his own notebook.

JOHN WINGATE

Avalanche
UK 1977
Weidenfeld and Nicolson (London)

Based in the Tirol, but with little climbing content.

HAROLD WISE

Mountain Man
UK 1934
Skeffington (London)

STANLEY WOLPERT

The Expedition
UK 1967
Cassell (London)

International team on yeti-quest, and all on the run from life. As if members weren't in enough danger from the abominable beast and each other, there is political skullduggery afoot too.

ELIZABETH YATES

High Holiday
UK 1938
Black (London)

Subtitled: a story of the Swiss Alps. Agreeable Alpine climbing story for young adults.

Climbing Higher
UK 1939
Black (London)

CHARLOTTE M. YONGE

The Dove in the Eagle's Nest
UK 1866
Macmillan (London) in two volumes.

Historical tale about mediaeval Germany (with some mountain references).

DRAMA & FILMS

For want of space we cannot, as we had hoped, list here all the stage plays, films, and radio and television dramatizations that have centred on mountains or incorporated mountain climbing. Many, however, have been adapted from short stories and novels and will already have been noted briefly in this bibliography.

Of the rest, special mention should be made of the German mountain films of the nineteen twenties and thirties by Arnold Fanck and his protégés Luis Trenker and Leni Riefenstahl. Among these were *Der Berg des Schicksals* (Peak of Destiny – Fanck, 1924); *Der Heilige Berg* (The Holy Mountain – Fanck, 1926); *Die Weisse Hölle vom Piz Palü* (The White Hell of Piz Palü – Fanck, 1929); *Das Blaue Licht* (The Blue Light – Riefenstahl, 1932); *SOS Eisberg* (SOS Iceberg – Fanck, 1933); *Der Verlorene Sohn* (The Prodigal Son – Trenker, 1934). All are visual classics, whose artistry is too often dismissed under the slur of 'Nazi cinema'.

The satirical verse drama *The Ascent of F6* by W.H. Auden and Christopher Isherwood (first performed in London in 1937), although still widely acclaimed, is often regarded these days as 'political camp', over-laden with jingoism and moral superiority ('unnervingly close to Mrs Thatcher's Britain and the Falklands spirit 1982' – Nicholas De Jongh in *The Guardian*, 1983.) Recently it spawned a musical successor: *The Ascent of Wilberforce III*, an extravaganza by Chris Judge Smith and J. Maxwell Hutchinson (1982).

In *Coming Down*, a radio play by Dave Sheasby (BBC Manchester, 1988), friends of a dead Himalayan climber gather for his wake. Although 'not based on any known incident' – according to the author – it is easy to see the inspiration of Rouse and Diemberger among the characters. And for those who enjoy picking up such inspirational character clues, Christopher Green's 6-part television series *Fell Tiger* (BBC1, 1985) must have offered a field-day – with his brooding northern climber-hero, outdoor centre staff and a Volvo-driving expedition-leader.

Barry Collins' powerful stage and radio play *The Ice Chimney*, imagining the last hours of Maurice Wilson on Everest, is included in this collection; *K2* by Patrick Meyers, originally a Broadway production, is currently being re-shaped for the Big Screen; and a cinema film dramatizing Joe Simpson's epic *Touching the Void* is also expected. Several screenplays have been written around the Mallory and Irvine story. Triumphs and tragedies have been 'recreated' with more or less authentic liberty, and there have been 'biopics' of (among others) Lucy Walker and Hermann Buhl. The award-winning *Mort d'un Guide* (1974. Subtitled version: Death of a guide, BBC2 1976) has been seen as 'transparently based on René Desmaison ... a scarcely-veiled critique of the whole gamut of ploys used by a commercially-orientated climber' – Ken Wilson, *Mountain 45*.

E5,6b is a musical comedy, written and directed by Mark Greenop, and performed on a specially-constructed climbing wall by teenage drama students; a sequel *E5 6c* is to be previewed at the 1990 Edinburgh Festival.

There are more…

Introducing our Contributors

AL ALVAREZ Born in London, 1929. Poet, novelist, literary critic and author of books on suicide, divorce, gambling, North Sea oil, as well as the acclaimed *Feeding the Rat*, a profile of Mo Anthoine.

ELAINE BROOK Elaine Brook has climbed around the world: she went to Baffin Island with an expedition organized by Doug Scott, and with Peter Hackett to Mt. McKinley. In Nepal she has been to Makalu with Reinhold Messner and spent seven months on a traverse of the Himalaya from Gangtok to Leh. Her first book *The Windhorse*, written with her blind friend Julie Donnelly, tells of a trek they made to Everest; *The Snow Lion* relates her lone journey from Shishapangma through Tibet to Lhasa. She and her husband Lakpa Sherpa run trekking holidays, dividing their time between Nepal and the U.K.

ROBIN CAMPBELL Became the editor of *The Scottish Mountaineering Club Journal* after Dutton, and developed and enhanced its acerbic style. As a lecturer of psychology at Stirling University he did research in the language communication of young children. Fascinated with Victoriana (particularly in climbing matters) he is also a dedicated student of Sherlock Holmes and his stories faithfully develop the 'Holmes' tradition linking it to Scottish climbing history.

GREG CHILD Australian, now living in Seattle with his wife Sally Oberlin. Began rock climbing at the age of 12 and pioneered many hard free climbs at Mount Arapiles during the mid-seventies. In 1978 he visited Yosemite where he made the second ascent of El Cap's Pacific Ocean Wall; other visits yielded two 9-day first ascents, Aurora and Lost in America. His first Himalayan trip was to Shivling in 1981, since when he has been on several major Himalayan expeditions. Child received the American Alpine Club's Literary Award in 1987 and in 1988 his first book, *Thin Air* was published in the UK.

GEOF CHILDS 43 years old, married, and currently employed as the Director of a large recreation facility in upstate New York. In 1979 he made the first ascent of Paiju North as a member of a four-man Anglo-American Karakoram expedition. During the past couple of years he has been working on a novel, and in deference to what he sees as encroaching physical decrepitude, has added sea kayaking and small boat expeditioning to his avocations. When he needs lessons in humility he plays squash or reads his rejection slips. Many people think he is Greg Child.

BARRY COLLINS Yorkshire playwright, born 1941 in Halifax where he still lives. His plays have included *The Lonely Man's Lover* (1974), *The Witches of Pendle* (1976), *The Strongest Man in the World* (1980) and *Atonement* (1987). He has also written two drama documentaries for the BBC, *Nada* (1985) and *Land* (1987), and is currently working on two feature films.

ELIZABETH COXHEAD Elizabeth Coxhead who died in 1979 at the age of 70 was a writer of vigour and elegance. As a journalist she worked on the staff of *The Lady*, *Liverpool Daily Post* and *The Guardian* and was always interested in social issues. She wrote eight novels, of which *One Green Bottle* is perhaps the best remembered today; in 1958 her *The Friend in Need* (about deprived children in a large city) was filmed as *A Cry from the Streets*, starring Max Bygraves.

DAVID CRAIG Born in Aberdeen in 1932; lives now with the writer Anne Spillard in Cumbria, where he does most of his climbing. His book of essays *Native Stones* was runner-up for the Boardman-Tasker Award for Mountain Literature in 1987 and his stories have appeared in (among others) *New Writing*, *Writers 16*, *The Literary Review* and *The Scotsman*. *On the Crofters' Trail* is due from Cape in 1990 and a novel from Carcanet the following year. David Craig teaches Creative Writing at Lancaster University.

KEN CROCKET Editor of *The Scottish Mountaineering Club Journal*. Ken Crocket's first essay into writing was a short story on rock-climbing for his school magazine. This was doubly fictional, since at that time no rock climbing had actually been done by the author! He has made up for that since, and is the editor of a number of Scottish guidebooks. He works as a cell biologist in Glasgow.

JOHN DANIEL Since writing *The Way of the White Serpent*, John Daniel has turned to non-fiction and poetry, his poems appearing in various American literary magazines and environmental journals. *Common Ground*, his first collection, was published in 1988. He teaches Creative

Writing at the Northwest Writing Institute in Portland, Oregon, and is currently at work on a book of essays and a second volume of poetry.

G.J.F. DUTTON Has suffered, he says, from a wide variety of interests and publications. G.J.F. Dutton will long be remembered as the energetic editor of *The Scottish Mountaineering Club Journal* at a time when Smith, Haston and Patey were in their prime. Author of the preposterous 'Doctor' stories, twenty of which have been collected as *The Ridiculous Mountains* (recently reissued in paperback), Dutton has also published two volumes of poetry *Camp One* (1978) and *Squaring the Waves* (1986).

JOHN MENLOVE EDWARDS Born 1910. Outstanding British rock climber responsible for many Welsh routes that are still among the most popular today. His writing was of no less a pioneering nature than his climbing, though he wrote with effort and sadly left but a small body of work. Edwards was a psychiatrist; he was also homosexual and a conscientious objector, and lived an increasingly tortured existence, racked by feelings of guilt, failure and self-doubt before finally committing suicide in 1958.

DAVE GREGORY Sheffield born, bread-and-buttered. Dave Gregory can surely lay claim to being the founder member of that tightly-packed climbing community based around the Hunter's Bar area of the city. He started climbing, on Stanage, in his teens and for thirty-five years has been actively concerned in the production of Peak District guidebooks. Teaches Physics, and is married with two children, one of whom has also developed the climbing bug. The other, he says with some relief, is fairly normal.

DAVID HARRIS Editor of *The Canadian Alpine Journal*, is a graphic designer and a publisher of climbing-related material. David Harris lives in Vancouver with his wife and young family. *Vortex*, which he wrote in 1983, is his first novel, but he is currently at work on a second, another thriller. This will again feature a climber as one of the protagonists, but set this time against a background of political intrigue.

M. JOHN HARRISON Since 1966 'Mike' Harrison has published six novels and three collections of short stories. *In Viriconium* was runner-up for the Guardian Fiction Prize in 1982; and *Climbers*, from which the piece in this collection is an extract, won the 1989 Boardman-Tasker Award for Mountain Literature – besides exciting unprecedented passion in the climbing press. After ten years in Yorkshire and the Peak District, Harrison now lives in Southeast London, where he is working on a metaphysical thriller.

CHARLES HOOD Teaches English at Antelope Valley College in California. Has one wife, Bonnie, and one daughter, Amber Willow, 'who can howl louder than any siren'. They live in their truck or travel abroad for part of the year, working the rest of the time. As they are now based in the desert town of Quartz Hill, Hood no longer goes sea kayaking but instead has become a hard-core bird twitcher. Recently changed his middle name to Wulfgar in order to evade arrest warrants out on a Californian who shares his original identity.

ROGER HUBANK Teaches in the English Department at Loughborough University. Described by Al Alvarez as 'utterly authentic ... a genuine and moving work of imagination', *North Wall* was his first novel. Is currently at work on a fictional explanation of the Scafell tragedy of 1903, in a novel which moves between the Boer War and Wasdale Head and features some of the notable pioneers of the period.

JEFF LONG Has spent the past five years writing a history of the Texas Revolution – not a romantic Alamo story but an examination of the first bleak expression of US/Central American relations. His first climbing novel *Angels of Light* (1987) was set in Yosemite and is widely regarded as one of the best pieces of mountain fiction ever written. His second will be based in the Himalaya and involve issues of human rights. Jeff Long lives in Boulder, Colorado.

JOHN LONG Big John Long – 'Largo' as he is known – is the archetypal action man, a real-life rock-climbing, jungle-exploring Indiana Jones. He also kayaks, makes films, and 'shoots tubes' (rides the piped watercourses that re-route rivers for hydro-electric schemes). Above all, he tells stories. For years his gutsy tales, true and tall, have delighted readers of outdoor magazines, and a collection *Gorilla Monsoon* was published in 1989. As a free-lance scriptwriter, Largo divides his time between Hollywood and Venezuela, where he lives with his wife and young daughter.

GUY DE MAUPASSANT 1850-1893. French novelist of the Naturalist school and master of the short story, usually characterized by having a twist in the tail. He was encouraged to write by his godfather, Gustave Flaubert. His output was phenomenal; in the 13 years before his early death of general paralysis in an asylum for the insane, he produced (besides poetry) 6 novels, 3 books of travel sketches, four plays and 300 stories.

C.E. MONTAGUE 1867-1928. Author and essayist. Montague joined the staff of the *Manchester Guardian* in 1890, where he rose to become assistant editor and chief leader writer. Of his novels, *Right Off the Map* (1927) is probably the best remembered. *Disenchantment* (1922) is an account of the First World War, written with bitterness and restraint. Montague's style belongs more appropriately to the last century than this: his elegant *In Hanging Garden Gully* shows a facility for quiet wit. Mountaineering has featured in others of his works, notably the short story *Action*.

DAVID ROBERTS Began his climbing and mountain writing as a Harvard undergraduate in the nineteen-sixties. His books have included *The Mountain of My Fear* (1968), *Deborah: A Wilderness Narrative* (1970), *Like Water and Like Wind* (in *Ascent* 1980) and *Great Exploration Hoaxes* (1982). He writes regularly for more than twenty-five national periodicals, from which a selection of articles was collected in 1986 under the title *Moments of Doubt*.

KIM STANLEY ROBINSON A native of Southern California, Kim Stanley Robinson lives currently near Washington with his wife Lisa Nowell and son David. His science-fiction novels *The Wild Shore, Icehenge, The Memory of Whiteness* and *The Gold Coast*, and a short story collection *The Planet on the Table* have all been critically acclaimed. *Mother Goddess of the World* is one of four interlinked Nepalese fantasies included in *Escape from Kathmandu*, published recently.

JAMES SALTER The author of several novels including *Light Years* and *A Sport and a Pastime*, as well as the short story collection *Dusk*. He lives in Sagaponack, New York.

PETER LARS SANDBERG No doubt because many of his short stories first appeared in *Playboy* magazine, Sandberg has frequently been accused of sexism. Certainly, he explores themes of male dominance and the exploitation of women in these and in his climbing novel, *Wolf Mountain*, but rather with the effect of demonstrating a vulnerability behind the presented façades of his characters. Men and women alike in his stories tend to be victims rather than ultimate wielders of power. A collection *Gabe's Fall and Other Climbing Stories* appeared in the US in 1988 and in the UK in 1990.

BEN SANTER American climatologist currently working on modelling on the greenhouse effect at the Max-Planck-Institute in Hamburg. He enjoys creative writing as a contrast to the very precise style demanded for the scientific record. *In the Crevasse* is his first non-scientific piece to be published.

ANNE SAUVY French *alpiniste* married to an Oxford don. She is a writer of extraordinary range and elegance ('*une raconteuse formidable*') and has published two volumes of short stories, all having a mountain background. Sadly, too few of these have been translated into English, but sufficient to attract high praise and draw comparison with her celebrated compatriot, de Maupassant.

JOE SIMPSON After completing an MA in English and Philosophy at Edinburgh University, Joe Simpson chose to devote himself full-time to climbing. In 1985, with his partner Simon Yates, he went to the Andes, where he was badly injured high on Siula Grande. His epic retreat after Yates was obliged to cut the rope that joined them, has become one of the world's great survival stories. Simpson's *Touching the Void* has won him the Boardman/Tasker Award for Mountain Literature as well as the National Cash Register Award for Non-Fiction and is shortly to be made into a feature film. *Meltwater* is his first foray into fiction; a novel follows.

DERMOT SOMERS Born 1947 in County Roscommon in the Irish Midlands, Dermot Somers lives now in the Wicklow Mountains, south of Dublin. He took up climbing at the age of 27 and has made successful ascents of the six great Alpine north faces. He first began publishing short stories in the early eighties, and writes in both Irish and English. A collection *Mountains and Other Ghosts* will appear later this year.

GUY WATERMAN Guy Waterman and his wife Laura are Vermont homesteaders, avid hikers, trail workers and outdoor writers, living – by choice – without such amenities as electricity, plumbing, telephone, motor access. Waterman worked first as a jazz pianist in the nightclubs of Washington, DC, then as an aide and speechwriter for political figures (writing speeches for three US presidents, among others). Later he was speechwriter for the president of the General Electric company. He contributes to *Baseball Digest*, is a member of the Milton Society (able to recite 8 hours' worth of *Paradise Lost* from memory), and is a published authority on Ragtime.